Dawn Halliburton

The Velvet Quartet

JUDE DEVERAUX

The Velvet Quartet

The Velvet Promise

Highland Velvet

Velvet Song

Velvet Angel

Rhapsody
Garden City, New York

The Velvet Quartet

This edition was especially created in 2003 for Rhapsody by arrangement with Pocket Books.

Published by Rhapsody, 401 Franklin Avenue, Garden City, New York 11530.

ISBN: 0-7394-3766-6

Printed in the United States of America

The Velvet Quartet

The Velvet Promise

To Jennifer
for melting wax and double Fridays

Prologue

JUDITH REVEDOUNE looked across the ledger at her father. Her mother, Helen, was beside her. Judith felt no fear of the man in spite of all he'd done over the years to make her fear him. His eyes were red with deep circles beneath them. She knew his ravaged face was due to his grief at the loss of his beloved sons; two ignorant, cruel men who were exact replicas of their father.

Judith studied Robert Revedoune with a vague sense of curiosity. He didn't usually bother with his only daughter. He had no use for women since his first wife died and his second, a frightened woman, had merely given him a girl. "What do you want?" Judith asked calmly.

Robert looked at his daughter as if seeing her for the first time. Actually, the girl had been kept hidden most of her life, buried with her mother in their own apartments amid their books and ledgers. He noticed with satisfaction that she looked like Helen had at that age. Judith had those odd golden eyes that some men raved about, but which he found unsettling. Her hair was a rich auburn. Her forehead broad and strong, as was her chin, her nose straight, her mouth generous. Yes, she would do, he thought. He could use her beauty to his advantage.

"You're the only one I have left," Robert said, his voice heavy with disgust. "You will marry and give me grandsons."

Judith stared at him in shock. All her life she had been

trained by Helen for life in a nunnery. Not a pious education of prayers and chanting, but one of high practicality, leading to the only career open to a noblewoman. She could become a prioress before she turned thirty. A prioress was as different from the average woman as a king from a serf. A prioress ruled lands, estates, villages, knights; she bought and sold according to her own judgment; she was sought by men and women alike for her wisdom. A prioress ruled and was ruled by no one.

Judith could keep books for a large estate, could make fair judgments in disputes, and knew how much wheat to grow to feed how many people. She could read and write, manage a reception for a king, run a hospital; everything she would need to know had been taught her.

And now she was expected to throw all of this away and become the servant of some man?

"I will not." The voice was quiet, but the few words could not have been louder if they'd been shouted from the slate rooftop.

For a moment, Robert Revedoune was bewildered. No female had ever defied him with such a firm look before. In fact, if he didn't know she was a woman, her expression would have been that of a man. When he recovered from his shock, he hit Judith, knocking her halfway across the little room. Even as she lay there, a trickle of blood running from the corner of her mouth, she stared up at him with absolutely no fear in her eyes, merely disgust and a touch of hatred. His breath caught for a moment at what he saw. In a way, the girl almost frightened him.

Helen was over her daughter in minutes and, as she crouched there, she drew her eating dagger from her side.

Looking at the primitive scene, Robert's momentary nervousness left him. His wife was a woman he could understand. For all her outward look of an angry animal, he saw weakness deep in her eyes. In seconds he grabbed her arm, the knife flying across the room. He smiled at his daughter as he held his wife's forearm in his powerful hands and snapped the bones as one would break a twig.

Helen never said a word, only crumpled at his feet.

Robert looked back at his daughter where she still lay, not yet able to comprehend his brutality. "Now what is your answer, girl? Do you marry or not?"

Judith nodded briefly before she turned to aid her unconscious mother.

Chapter 1

THE MOON cast long shadows over the old stone tower which rose three stories high and seemed to scowl down, in a tired way, at the broken and crumbling wall that surrounded it. The tower had been built two hundred years before this wet April night in 1501. Now was a time of peace, a time when stone fortresses were no longer needed; but this was not the home of an industrious man. His great-grandfather had lived in the tower when such fortifications were needed, and Nicolas Valence thought, if he sobered long enough to think, that the tower was good enough for him and future generations.

A massive gatehouse looked over the disintegrating walls and the old tower. Here one lone guard slept, his arm curled around a half-empty skin of wine. Inside the tower, the ground floor was littered with sleeping dogs and knights. Their armor was piled against the walls in a jumbled, rusty heap, tangled with the dirty rushes that covered the oak plank floor.

This was the Valence estate; a poor, disreputable, old-fashioned castle that was the butt of jokes throughout England. It was said that if the fortifications were as strong as the wine, Nicolas Valence could hold off all of England. But no one attacked. There was no reason to attack. Many years ago, most of Nicolas's land had been taken from him by young, eager, penniless knights who had just earned their spurs. All that remained was the ancient tower, which everyone agreed should have been torn down, and a few outlying farms that supported the Valence family.

There was a light in the window of the top floor. Inside, the room was cold and damp—a dampness that never left the walls even in the driest summer weather. Moss grew between the cracks of the stone, and little crawling things constantly scurried across the floor. But in this room, all the wealth of the castle sat before a mirror.

Alice Valence leaned toward the mirror and applied a darkener to her short, pale lashes. The cosmetic was imported from France. Alice leaned back and studied herself critically. She was objective about her looks and knew what she had and how to use it to its best advantage.

She saw a small oval face with delicate features, a little rosebud mouth, a slim, straight nose. Her long almond eyes of a brilliant blue were her best feature. Her hair was blonde, which she constantly rinsed in lemon juice and vinegar. Her maid, Ela, pulled a pale yellow strand across her mistress's forehead then set a French hood on Alice's head. The hood was of a heavy brocade, trimmed in a wide cuff of orange velvet.

Alice opened her little mouth to once again look at her teeth. They were her worst feature, crooked and a bit protruding. Over the years she had learned to keep them hidden, to smile with her lips closed, to speak softly, her head slightly lowered. This mannerism was an advantage, for it intrigued men. It gave them the idea that she did not know how beautiful she was. They imagined awakening this shy flower to all the delights of the world.

Alice stood and smoothed her gown over her slim body. There were few curves to it. Her small breasts rested on a straight frame with no hips, no indentation to her waist. She liked her body. It seemed clean and neat compared to other women's.

Her clothes were lush, seeming out of place in the dingy room. Close to her body she wore a linen chemise, so fine it was almost gauze. Over this was a luscious gown of the same heavy brocade as the hood. It had a deep, square neck, the bodice fitting very tightly to her thin frame. The skirt was a gentle, graceful bell. The blue brocade was trimmed with white rabbit fur; a deep border along the hem, and wide cuffs around the hanging sleeves. About her waist was a belt of blue leather set with large garnets, emeralds and rubies.

Alice continued studying herself as Ela slipped a rabbit-lined brocade cloak about her mistress's shoulders.

"My lady, you cannot go to him. Not when you are—"

"To marry another?" Alice asked as she fastened the heavy cloak about her shoulders. She turned to gaze at herself, pleased with the result. The orange and blue was striking. She would not go unnoticed in such an outfit. "And what has my marriage to do with what I do now?"

"You know it's a sin. You cannot meet a man who isn't your husband."

Alice gave a short laugh as she adjusted the folds of the heavy mantle. "Do you want me to ride out to meet my intended? Dear Edmund?" she asked with great sarcasm. Before Ela could reply she continued. "You needn't go with me. I know the way and, for what Gavin and I do, we need no one else."

Ela had been with Alice for too long to be shocked. Alice did what she wanted when she wanted. "No, I will go. But only to see that you come to no harm."

Alice ignored the elderly woman as she had all her life. She took a candle from the heavy metal holder by her bed and went to the iron-banded oak door. "Quiet, then," she said over her shoulder as she eased the door back on its well-oiled hinges. She gathered the brocade gown in her hand and threw it over her arm. She couldn't help but think that in a few short weeks she would leave this decrepit keep and live in a house— the Chatworth manor house, a building of stone and wood surrounded by high, protective walls.

"Quiet!" she commanded Ela as she threw an arm across the woman's soft stomach and pressed them both against the damp wall of the dark stairwell. One of her father's guards walked clumsily past the foot of the stairs, retied his hose, and made his way back to his straw pallet. Alice hastily snuffed the candle and hoped the man did not hear Ela's gasp as the pure black stillness of the old castle surrounded them.

"Come," Alice whispered, having neither the time nor the inclination to listen to Ela's protestations.

The night was clear and cool, and, as Alice knew they would be, two horses waited for her and her maid. Alice smiled as she threw herself into the saddle on the dark stallion. Later, she would reward the stableboy who took such good and proper care of his lady.

"My lady!" Ela whined in desperation.

But Alice did not turn because she knew that Ela was too fat to mount the horse by herself. Alice would not waste even one of her precious minutes on an aged and useless woman— not when Gavin waited for her.

The river door in the wall had been left open for her. It had rained earlier and the ground was wet, yet there was a touch of spring in the air. And with it came a sense of promise—and passion.

When she was sure the horse's hooves would not be heard, she leaned forward and whispered to him. "Go, my black devil. Take me to my lover." The stallion pranced to show he understood, then stretched his front legs long and straight. It knew the way and ate up ground at a tremendous rate.

Alice shook her head, letting the air blow against her face as she gave herself over to the power and strength of the magnificent animal. Gavin. Gavin. Gavin, the hooves seemed to say as they thundered on the hard-packed road. There were many ways that the muscle of a horse between her thighs reminded her of Gavin. His strong hands on her body, the strength of him that made her weak with desire. His face, the moonlight glinting on his cheekbones, his eyes bright even on the darkest night.

"Ah, my sweet, careful now," Alice said lightly as she pulled back on the reins. Now that she was nearing the trysting place, she began to remember what she had so carefully tried to forget. This time Gavin would have heard of her impending marriage, and he would be angry with her.

She turned her face to catch the wind directly. She blinked rapidly until the tears began to form. Tears would help. Gavin always hated tears, so she had used them carefully during the last two years. Only when she desperately wanted something did she resort to the trick; thus it did not grow thin from overuse.

Alice sighed. Why couldn't she speak honestly to Gavin? Why must men always be treated so gently? He loved her, therefore he should love what she did, however disagreeable to him. It was a useless hope and she knew it. If she told Gavin the truth, she would lose him. Then where would she find another lover?

The memory of his body, hard and demanding, made Alice push the heels of her soft shoes into the horse's side. Oh yes, she would use tears or whatever else was needed to keep Gavin Montgomery, a knight of renown, a fighter without equal . . . and hers, all hers!

Suddenly, she could almost hear Ela's needling questions. If Alice wanted Gavin, why then was she promising herself to Edmund Chatworth, a man with skin the color of a fish's belly, with fat, soft hands and an ugly little mouth that formed a perfect circle?

Because Edmund was an earl. He owned land from one end of England to the other, estates in Ireland, Wales, Scotland, and, it was rumored, in France as well. Of course Alice could not know exactly the extent of his wealth, but she would. Oh yes, when she was his wife, she would know. Edmund's mind was as weak as his body, and it would not be long before she controlled him as well as his property. She would keep him happy with a few whores and tend to the estates herself, unhampered by any man's interfering demands and commands.

Alice had a passion for the handsome Gavin but that did not cloud her judgment. Who was Gavin Montgomery? A minor baron—not rich, but poor. A brilliant fighter, a strong, handsome man, but he had no wealth—not compared to Edmund. And what would life with Gavin be? The nights would be nights of passion and ecstasy, but Alice knew well that no woman would ever control Gavin. If she married Gavin, he would expect her to stay home and do women's work. No, no woman would ever control Gavin Montgomery. He would be as demanding a husband as he was a lover.

She pushed the horse forward. She wanted it all—Edmund's fortune and position and Gavin's passion. She smiled as she straightened the gold brooches, one on either shoulder, that held the flamboyant mantle in place. He loved her—Alice was confident he did—and she would not lose his love. How could she? What woman came close to her in beauty?

Alice began blinking rapidly. A few tears and he would understand that she was being *forced* to marry Edmund. Gavin was a man of honor. He would understand that she must uphold her father's agreement with Edmund. Yes, if she were cautious, she would have them both; Gavin for the nights, Edmund's wealth for the day.

Gavin stood silently—waiting. The only part of him that moved was a muscle in his jaw, flexing and unflexing. The silver moonlight glinted off his cheekbones until they looked like knife blades. His straight, firm mouth was drawn into a severe line above a cleft chin. His gray eyes were black with anger, almost as black as the hair that curled about the neck of the wool jacket.

Only long years of strenuous training as a knight allowed him such rigid outward control. Inside, he was seething. This morning he'd heard that the woman he loved was to marry another; to bed with another man, her children belonging to him. His first impulse had been to ride straight to the Valence keep and demand that she deny what he'd heard. But his pride held him back. This meeting with her had been arranged weeks ago, so he forced himself to wait until he could see her again, hold her again and hear her tell him, from her own sweet lips, what he wanted to hear. She would marry no one but him. Of that he was sure.

He stared across the emptiness of the night, listening for the sound of hoofbeats; but the countryside was silent, a mass of darkness broken only by the darker shadows. A dog skulked from one tree to the next, eyeing Gavin, wary of the silent, still man. The night brought back memories of the first time he and Alice had met in this clearing, a wind-sheltered place open to the sky. In the day a man could ride past it and not notice it, but at night the shadows transformed it into a black velvet box, only big enough to hold a jewel.

Gavin had met Alice at the wedding of one of her sisters. Althought the Montgomeries and the Valences were neighbors, they rarely saw each other. Alice's father was a drunkard. He cared little for his estates; he lived—and forced his wife and five daughters to live—as poorly as some serfs. It was out of a sense of duty that Gavin attended a wedding there, as a representative of his family actually, his three brothers having refused to go.

Out of the dung heap of filth and neglect, Gavin saw Alice—his beautiful, innocent Alice. He could not at first believe she was one of the family of fat, plain daughters. Her clothes were of the richest materials, her manners delicate and refined, and her beauty . . .

He'd sat and stared at her, as several of the other young men did. She was perfect; blonde hair, blue eyes, a little mouth that he ached to make smile. Right then, before he'd even spoken to her, he'd become infatuated with her. Later, he had to plow his way through men to get to her side. His violence seemed to shock Alice and her lowered eyes, her soft voice had mesmerized him further. She was so shy, so reticent that she could hardly answer his questions. Alice was all and more than he could hope for—virginal yet womanly.

That night, he asked her to marry him. She gave him a startled look, her eyes like sapphires for a moment. Then she lowered her head and murmured something about needing to ask her father.

The next day Gavin went to the drunkard and asked for Alice, but the man gave him some nonsense about the girl's mother needing her. His words were strangely halting, as if he'd been coached and spoke a memorized speech. Nothing Gavin said could make Valence change his mind.

Gavin left in disgust, furious at being thwarted from

having the woman he wanted. He had not ridden far when he saw her. Her hair was uncovered, the setting sun making it glow, the rich blue velvet of her gown reflecting her eyes. She was anxious to hear what her father's answer was. Gavin told her, angrily, and then he'd seen her tears. Alice tried to hide them, but he could feel them as well as see them. In minutes, he was off his horse, pulling her from hers. He didn't remember how it happened. One minute he was comforting her. The next, they were here, in this secret place, their clothes removed and in the throes of passion. He did not know whether to apologize or rejoice. Sweet Alice was no serf to tumble in the hay; she was a lady, someday to be his lady. And she was a virgin. Of that he was sure when he saw the two drops of blood on her slim thighs.

Two years! Two years ago that had been. If he had not spent most of the time in Scotland, patrolling the borders, he would have demanded her father give Alice to him. Now that he'd returned, he planned to do just that. In fact, if need be, he would go to the king with his plea. Valence was unreasonable. Alice told Gavin of her talks with her father, of her begging and pleading with him, but to no avail. Once she showed him a bruise she received for pressing Gavin's suit. Gavin had been insane then. He'd grabbed his sword and would have gone after the man if Alice hadn't clung to him, tears in her eyes, and begged him please not to harm her father. He could refuse her tears nothing, so he sheathed his sword and promised her he would wait. Alice reassured him that her father would eventually see reason.

So they had continued to meet secretly, like wayward children—a situation that disgusted Gavin. Yet Alice begged him not to see her father, to allow her to persuade him.

Gavin shifted his stance now and listened again. Still there was only silence. This morning he'd heard Alice was to marry that piece of water-slime, Edmund Chatworth. Chatworth paid the king an enormous fee so that he would not be called upon to fight in any wars. He was not a man, Gavin thought. Chatworth did not deserve the title of earl. To think of Alice married to such as that was beyond imagination.

Suddenly all Gavin's senses came alert as he heard the muffled sounds of the horse's hooves on the damp ground. He was beside Alice instantly and she fell into his arms.

"Gavin," she whispered, "my sweet Gavin." She clung to him, almost as if in terror.

He tried to pull her away so he could see her face but she held him with such desperation that he dared not to. He felt the wetness of her tears on his neck and all the rage he'd felt during the day left him. He held her close to him, murmuring endearments in her little ear, stroking her hair. "Tell me, what is it? What has hurt you so?"

She moved away so she could look at him, secure in the knowledge that the night could not betray the lack of redness in her eyes. "It's too awful," Alice whispered hoarsely. "It is too much to bear."

Gavin stiffened somewhat as he remembered what he'd heard about her marriage. "Is it true then?"

She sniffed delicately, touched a finger to the corner of her eye and looked up at him through her lashes. "My father cannot be persuaded. I even refused food to make him change his mind, but he had one of the women . . . No, I won't tell you what they did to me. He said he would—Oh, Gavin, I cannot say the things he said to me." She felt Gavin stiffen.

"I will go to him and—"

"No!" Alice said almost frantically, her hands clasping his muscular arms. "You cannot! I mean . . ." She lowered her arms and her lashes. "I mean, it's already done. The betrothal has been signed and witnessed. There is nothing anyone can do now. If my father withdrew me from the bargain, he would still have to pay my dowry to Chatworth."

"I will pay it," Gavin said stonily.

Alice gave him a look of surprise; then more tears gathered in her eyes. "It wouldn't matter. My father will not allow me to marry you. You know that. Oh, Gavin, what am I to do? I will be forced to marry a man I do not love." She looked up at him with such a look of desperation that Gavin pulled her close to him. "How could I bear to lose you, my love?"

she whispered against his neck. "You are meat and drink to me, sun and night. I . . . I will die if I lose you."

"Don't say that! How can you lose me? You know I feel the same about you."

She pulled away to look at him, suddenly happier. "Then you do love me? Truly love me, so that if our love is tested, I will still be sure of you?"

Gavin frowned. "Tested?"

Alice smiled through her tears. "Even if I marry Edmund, you will still love me?"

"Marry!" He nearly shouted as he pushed her from him. "You plan to *marry* this man?"

"Have I a choice?" They stood in silence, Gavin glaring at her, Alice with eyes demurely lowered. "I will go then. I will go from your sight. You needn't look at me again."

She was almost to her horse before he reacted. He grabbed her roughly, pulling her mouth to his until he bruised her. There were no words then; none were needed. Their bodies understood each other even if they couldn't agree. Gone was the shy young lady. In her place was the Alice of passion that Gavin had come to know so well. Her hands tore frantically at his clothes until they quickly lay in a heap.

She laughed throatily when he stood nude before her. His body was hard-muscled from many years of training. He was a good head taller than Alice, who often towered over men. His shoulders were broad, his chest powerfully thick. Yet his hips were slim, his stomach flat, the muscles divided into ridges. His thighs and calves bulged muscle, strong from years of wearing heavy armor.

Alice stepped away from him and sucked her breath in through her teeth as she devoured the sight of him. Her hands reached for him as if they were claws.

Gavin pulled her to him, kissed the little mouth that opened widely under his as her tongue plunged into his mouth. He pulled her close, the feel of her gown exciting against his bare skin. His lips moved to her cheek, to her neck. They had all night, and he meant to spend his time making love to her.

"No!" Alice said impatiently as she drew away sharply. She flung her mantle from her shoulders, careless of the expensive fabric. She pushed Gavin's hands away from the buckle of her belt. "You are too slow," she stated flatly.

Gavin frowned for a moment, but as layer after layer of Alice's clothes were flung to the ground, his senses took over. She was eager for him as he was for her. What if she did not want to take too long before their bodies were skin to skin?

Gavin would have liked to savor Alice's slender body for a while, but she pulled him quickly to the ground, her hand guiding him immediately inside her. He did not think then of leisurely loveplay or kisses. Alice was beneath him, urging him on. Her voice was harsh as she directed his body, her hands firm on his hips as she pushed him, harder and harder. Gavin at one time worried that he would hurt her, but she seemed to glory in the strength of him.

"Now! Now!" she demanded beneath him and gave a low, throaty sound of triumph when he obeyed her.

Immediately afterward she moved from beneath him, away from him. She had told him repeatedly this was because of her warring thoughts as she reconciled her unmarried state with her passion. Yet he would have liked to have held her longer, enjoyed her body more, even perhaps made love to her again. It would be a slow lovemaking this time, now that their first passion was spent. Gavin tried to ignore the hollow feeling he had, as if he had just tasted something but was still not sated.

"I must leave," she said as she sat up and began the intricate process of dressing.

He liked to watch her slim legs as she slipped on the light linen stockings. At least watching her helped some of the emptiness dissipate. Unexpectedly, he remembered that soon another man would have the right to touch her. Suddenly he wanted to hurt her as she was hurting him. "I too have an offer of marriage."

Alice stopped instantly, her hand on her stocking and watched him, waiting for more.

"Robert Revedoune's daughter."

"He has no daughter—only sons, both of them married," Alice said instantly. Revedoune was one of the king's earls, a man whose estates made Edmund's look like a serf's farm. It had taken Alice a while, those years while Gavin was in Scotland, but she'd found out the history of all of the earls—of all of the richest men in England—before deciding that Edmund was the most likely catch.

"Didn't you hear that both sons died two months ago of wasting sickness?"

She stared at him. "But I've never heard a daughter mentioned."

"A young girl named Judith, younger than her brothers. I heard she had been prepared by her mother for the church. The girl is kept cloistered in her father's house."

"And you have been offered this Judith to marry? But she would be her father's heiress, a wealthy woman. Why would he offer to—?" She stopped, remembering to conceal her thoughts from Gavin.

He turned his face from her, and she could see the muscles in his jaw working, the moonlight glinting on his bare chest, still lightly covered in sweat from their lovemaking.

"Why would he offer such a prize to a Montgomery?" Gavin finished for her, his voice cold. Once the Montgomery family had been wealthy enough to stir the envy of King Henry IV. Henry had declared the entire family traitorous and then set about breaking up the powerful family. He had done so well that only now, one hundred years later, was the family beginning to regain some of what it had lost. But the memories of the Montgomery family were long, and none of them cared to be reminded of what they had once been.

"For the right arms of my brothers and myself," Gavin said after a while. "The Revedoune lands border ours on the north, and he fears the Scots. He realizes that his lands will be protected if he allies himself to my family. One of the court singers heard him say that the Montgomeries, if they produced nothing else, made sons who lived. So it seems I am made an offer of his daughter if only I will give her sons."

Alice was nearly dressed now. She stared at him. "The

title will pass through the daughter, won't it? Your eldest son would be an earl, and you when her father dies."

Gavin turned abruptly. He hadn't thought of that, nor did he care about it. It was strange that Alice, who cared so little for worldly goods, should think of it first.

"Then you will marry her?" Alice asked as she stood over him and watched as he hastily began to put on his clothes.

"I've not made a decision. The offer only came two days ago, and then I thought—"

"Have you seen her?" Alice interrupted.

"Seen her? You mean the heiress?"

Alice clamped her teeth together. Men could be so dense at times. She recovered herself. "She is beautiful, I know," Alice said tearfully. "And once you are wed to her, you will never remember me."

Gavin stood quickly. He didn't know whether to be angry or not. The woman talked of their marriages to other people as if they made no difference to their relationship. "I have not seen her," he said quietly.

Suddenly the night seemed to be closing in on him. He'd wanted to hear Alice deny the talk of her marriage, but instead he found himself talking of the possibility of his own marriage. He wanted to get away—away from the complexities of women and back to the soundness and logic of his brothers. "I don't know what will happen."

Alice frowned as he took her arm and led her to her horse. "I love you, Gavin," she said quickly. "Whatever happens, I will always love you, always want you."

He quickly lifted her into the saddle. "You must return before someone discovers you're gone. We wouldn't like such a story to get to the brave and noble Chatworth, would we?"

"You are cruel, Gavin," she said, but there was no sound of tears in her voice. "Am I to be punished for what is out of my hands, for what I cannot control?"

He had no answer for her.

Alice bent forward and kissed him, but she knew his mind was elsewhere and this frightened her. She pulled sharply on the reins and galloped away.

Chapter 2

IT WAS very late when Gavin rode into sight of the Montgomery castle. For all that their property had been stolen from them by a greedy king, these walls remained theirs. A Montgomery had lived here for over four hundred years—since William conquered England and brought with him the already rich and powerful Norman family.

Over the centuries the castle had been added to, reinforced and remodeled until the fourteen-foot-thick walls enclosed over three acres. Inside, the land was divided into two parts; the outer and the inner bailey. The outer bailey housed the servants, the garrison knights and all the hundreds of people and animals it took to run the castle. The outer bailey also sheltered and protected the inner bailey, where the houses of the four Montgomery brothers and their private retainers stood. The entire complex set atop a hill, backed against a river. No trees were allowed to grow within half a mile of the castle: any enemy would have to approach in the open.

For four centuries the Montgomeries had held this fortress against an avaricious king and private wars. It was with pride that Gavin looked at the looming walls that were his home. He walked his horse toward the river then dismounted and led it through the narrow river passage. Apart from the massive front gate, this was the only entrance. The main gate was covered by a portcullis: a spiked fence that could be lowered with ropes. Now, at night, the guards would have had to wake five men to raise it. So, Gavin went to the narrow private entrance, a quarter mile of eight-foot-tall walls that led to the back entrance, the top of the walls guarded by men who walked back and forth on them all night. Gavin nodded to each guard as he was challenged. No man who valued his life ever slept while on duty.

During the reign of King Henry VII, the present king, most castles had fallen into decline. When he had taken the throne, sixteen years ago in 1485, he decided to break the power of the great barons. He banned private armies and he put gunpowder under the control of the government. Since the barons could no longer wage private wars for profit, their fortunes suffered. The castles were expensive to maintain, and one after another the thick walls were abandoned for the comfort of a manor house.

But there were those who through good management and hard work still retained the use of the powerful old structures. The Montgomeries were such a family, and they were respected throughout England. Gavin's father had built a strong, comfortable manor house for his five children, but he'd built it inside the castle walls.

Once inside the bailey, Gavin saw that there was much activity. "What has happened?" he asked the stableboy who took his horse.

"The masters have just returned from a fire in the village."

"Bad?"

"No, sire, only some of the merchants' houses. The masters needn't have gone." The boy shrugged, as if to say that there was no understanding nobles.

Gavin left him and entered the manor house, built against the ancient stone tower that was used now for little except storage. The brothers preferred the comfort of the big house. Several of the knights were settling down to sleep, and Gavin greeted a few of them as he hurried up the broad oak stairs to his own quarters on the third floor.

"Here is our wayward brother," Raine called to him cheerfully. "Miles, do you think he rides about the countryside at night and neglects his responsibilities? Half the village could have burned to the ground if we acted as he does."

Raine was the third Montgomery brother, the shortest and stockiest of the four. He was a powerful, thick man. He would have been formidable looking, and on a battlefield he was; but most of the time, as now, his blue eyes danced and deep, long dimples pierced his cheeks.

Gavin looked at his younger brothers, but he did not smile.

Miles, his clothes blackened with soot, poured a flagon of wine and offered it to Gavin. "You have had some bad news?" Miles was the youngest brother, a serious man with piercing gray eyes that missed nothing. His smile was rarely seen.

Raine was immediately contrite, "Is something wrong?"

Gavin took the wine and sank heavily onto a carved walnut chair, facing the fire. It was a large room with an oak floor, covered in places by carpets from the Orient. On the walls were heavy wool tapestries of hunting scenes and the Crusades. The ceiling was of heavy, arched timbers, both decorative and functional. White plaster filled the gap between the beams. It was a man's room and the large, dark furniture in it was carved intricately. At the southern end was a deep bay window with seats covered in red sendal. The glass in the mullioned windows was from France.

All three of the brothers were dressed in simple, dark clothes. Linen shirts, loosely gathered at the neck, fit close to their bodies. Over these were wool doublets, long vestlike garments that reached to the top of their thighs. A heavy, short, long-sleeved jacket went over the doublet. The men's legs, exposed from the top of the thigh, were encased in dark wool hose, tightly fitting the massive bulges of muscle. Gavin wore heavy boots to his knees. At his hip was slung a sword in a jeweled scabbard.

Gavin drank deeply of the wine, then watched silently as Miles refilled it. He could not share his unhappiness about Alice—even with his brothers.

When Gavin did not speak, Miles and Raine exchanged

glances. They knew where Gavin had been and could guess what news had given him an air of doom. Raine had met Alice once, at Gavin's discreet urging, and found in her a coldness he did not like. But to the besotted Gavin, Alice was perfection in a woman. Whatever he thought of her, Raine had sympathy for Gavin.

Not so Miles. He was untouched by even the hint of love for a woman. To him, one woman was the same as another; one served the same purpose as well as any. "Robert Revedoune sent another messenger today," Miles interrupted the silence. "I think he is worried that if his daughter isn't delivered of a son soon, she might die and leave him no one to inherit."

"Is she sickly?" Raine asked. He was the humanitarian of the brothers, concerned for a hurt mare, a sick serf.

"I've not heard so," Miles answered. "The man is mad with grief that his sons are gone and that he has merely one puny daughter left. I've heard he beats his wife regularly to repay her for so few sons."

Raine frowned into his wine cup. He did not believe in beating women.

"Will you give him his answer?" Miles pressed as Gavin still did not answer.

"One of you take her," Gavin said. "Bring Stephen from Scotland or you, Raine, you need a wife."

"Revedoune wants only the eldest son for his daughter," Raine grinned. "Otherwise I would be more than willing."

"Why this haggling?" Miles said angrily. "You are twenty-seven years old, and you need a wife. This Judith Revedoune is rich—she brings an earldom with her. Perhaps through her the Montgomeries can begin to regain what we once had."

Alice was lost to him and the sooner he faced that the sooner he could begin to heal, Gavin decided. "All right. I agree to the marriage."

Immediately, Raine and Miles let out the breath they had not realized they'd been holding.

Miles set his wine down. "I asked the messenger to stay. I'd hoped to tell him your answer."

As Miles left the room, Raine's sense of humor took over. "I have heard she is only this tall," he held his hand near his waist, "and she has teeth the size of a horse's. Besides that . . ."

The old tower was drafty; the wind whistled through the cracks. The oiled paper over the windows did little to keep out the cold.

Alice slept comfortably, nude beneath a linen coverlet, filled with goose down.

"My lady," Ela whispered to her mistress. "He is here."

Drowsy, Alice rolled over. "How dare you wake me!" she said in a fierce whisper. "Who is here?"

"The man from the Revedoune household. He—"

"Revedoune!" Alice said as she sat up, fully awake now. "Bring me my robe and fetch the man to me."

"Here?" Ela was aghast. "No, my lady, you cannot. Someone could hear you."

"Yes," Alice said absently. "It is too great a risk. Let me dress. I'll meet him under that elm tree by the kitchen garden."

"At night? But—"

"Go now! Tell him I will be there soon." Alice quickly threw her arms into her bedrobe, a gown of thick crimson velvet lined with gray squirrel fur. She wrapped a wide belt about her waist and slipped her feet into soft leather slippers dyed gold.

It had been nearly a month since she'd seen Gavin, and in all that time she'd had no word from him. But only days after their night in the forest, she had heard that he was to marry the Revedoune heiress. And now a tourney to celebrate the match was being cried from one end of England to the other. Every man of importance was being invited; every knight with any skill was asked to participate. At every word she heard, Alice grew more jealous. How she'd like to sit beside a husband such as Gavin and watch a tourney fought to celebrate *her* marriage. No such plans were being made for her wedding.

Yet, for all she heard of the plans, nowhere could she hear a word about Judith Revedoune herself. The girl was a name with no face or figure to it. Two weeks ago, Alice had come upon the idea of purchasing a spy to find out about this elusive Judith, to find what she looked like, what Alice must compete with. She gave Ela orders that she was to be told when the man arrived, no matter what time.

Alice's heart was beating quickly as she ran through the path of the weed-choked garden. This Judith was an absolute toad, Alice told herself. She *had* to be.

"Ah, my lady," the spy said when Alice was near. "Your beauty outshines the moon in radiance." He grabbed her hand and kissed it.

He disgusted her, yet he was the only man she could find who had access to the Revedoune family. The price she'd had to pay him was outrageous! He was a slimy, oily man, but at least his lovemaking had not been so. Was any man's, she wondered. "What news?" Alice asked impatiently as she hurriedly pulled her hand away. "Did you see her?"

"Not . . . closely—"

"Closely? Did you see her or not?" Alice demanded, looking straight into his eyes.

"Yes, I saw her," he answered firmly. "But she is heavily guarded." He wanted to please this blonde beauty, so he knew he must conceal the truth. He had seen Judith Revedoune, but only from a distance, as she was riding away from the manor with her women. He wasn't even sure which bundled figure was the heiress.

"Why is she kept guarded? Is her mind not sound that she cannot be trusted to be free?"

Suddenly he was afraid of this woman who questioned him so sharply. There was power in those cold blue eyes. "There are rumors, of course. She is seen by no one except her women and her mother. She has lived her life among them, and always she has prepared for the church."

"The church?" Alice began to feel some of the tension

leave her. It was common knowledge that whenever a deformed or retarded daughter was born, if the family were rich enough, the creature would be pensioned and given to the nuns to care for. "Then you think she could have a weak mind or be malformed in some way?"

"Why else, my lady, would she be kept hidden all her life? Robert Revedoune is a hard man. His wife limps from a time when he threw her down the stairs. He wouldn't want the world to see that he has a monster for a daughter."

"But you aren't sure this is the reason she is hidden?"

He smiled, feeling safer. "What other reason could there be? If she were sane and whole, wouldn't he bring her out for the world to see? Wouldn't he have offered her in marriage before his sons' deaths forced him to do so? What man would allow his only daughter to enter the church? Only when a man has many daughters does he allow that."

Alice was staring quietly ahead into the night. Her silence made the man grow bolder. He leaned closer to her, put his hand over hers and whispered into her ear. "You have no reason to fear, my lady. There will be no beautiful bride to turn the Lord Gavin's head from you."

Only Alice's sharply drawn breath gave any indication she had heard. Did even the most common of men know about her and Gavin? With the skill of a great actress, she turned and smiled at the man. "You have done well and you shall be . . . suitably rewarded." She left no doubt as to the meaning of her words.

He bent and kissed her neck.

Alice moved away, hiding her revulsion. "No, not tonight," she whispered intimately. "Tomorrow. Arrangements must be made so we can spend more time together." She ran her hand under the loose tabard, along his upper thigh, and smiled seductively when his breath caught. "I must go," she said with seeming reluctance.

There was no hint of a smile on her face when her back was to him. She had one more stop to make before she returned to bed. The stableboy would be glad to help her. She would not allow any man to speak freely of Gavin and her . . . and this one would pay for his words.

"Good morning, Father," Alice said cheerfully as she bent to brush her lips against the cheek of the gnarled and filthy old man. They were on the second floor of the tower, a floor left open as one enormous room. This was the great hall: a room used for eating, sleeping for the castle retainers, and all the daily activities.

She looked into her father's empty cup. "Here, you!" she said sharply to a passing servant. "Bring my father more ale."

Nicolas Valence took his daughter's hand in both of his and looked up at her in gratitude. "You are the only one who cares, my lovely Alice. All the others—your mother and sisters—try to keep me from my drink. But you understand how it comforts me."

She pulled away from him, hiding her feelings at his touch. "But of course, dear Father. That is because I alone love you." She smiled sweetly at him.

After all these years Nicolas still marveled that he and his ugly little wife could have created such a lovely girl. Alice's pale beauty was a sharp contrast to his own darkness. And when the others raged at him and hid his liquor, Alice sneaked bottles to him. It was true—she did love him. And he loved her, too. What little coin there was, didn't he give it to her for her clothes? His lovely Alice wore silk while her sisters wore homespun. He'd do anything for her. Hadn't he told that Gavin Montgomery that she couldn't marry him, just as Alice had told him to? Of course Nicolas didn't understand why a young girl wouldn't want to marry such a strong and rich man like Gavin. But Alice had been right. He picked up his refilled cup and drained it. She'd been right—now she was to marry an earl. Of course Edmund Chatworth was nothing like one of those handsome Montgomeries, but Alice aways knew what was best.

"Father," Alice said smiling, "I would like a favor from you."

He drank yet a third cup of ale. Sometimes Alice's favors

were not easy to grant. He changed the subject. "Did you know that a man fell off the wall last night? A stranger. No one seems to know where he came from."

Alice's expression changed. Now the spy would tell no one of Gavin or that she asked about the Revedoune heiress. Quickly, she dismissed the thought. The man's death meant nothing to her. "I want to go to the wedding of the Revedoune woman to Gavin."

"You want an invitation to the wedding of an earl's daughter?" Nicolas was incredulous.

"Yes."

"But I cannot. How could I?"

This time, Alice waved the servant away and refilled her father's cup herself. "I have a plan," she said quickly and smiled her sweetest smile.

Chapter 3

THE FIRE raged up the side of the stone and hungrily devoured the wooden second story of the merchant's shop. The air was thick with smoke and the men and women who formed a line to pass the buckets of water were blackened. Only their eyes and teeth remained white.

Gavin, his body bare from the waist up, used the long-handled ax viciously as he chopped away the building next to the blazing shop. The vigor with which he worked did not betray the fact that he had been working like this for a full two days.

The town where the building burned, where three others stood in ashes, was his. Twelve-foot walls enclosed the town, running down the hill from the great Montgomery castle. This town's taxes supported the Montgomery brothers; in return, the knights protected and defended the inhabitants.

"Gavin!" Raine bellowed over the roar of the flames. He too was filthy from smoke and sweat. "Come away from there! The fire is too close to you!"

Gavin ignored his brother's warning. He did not look up at the burning wall that threatened to fall on him. His chopping became more vigorous as he fought to knock the seasoned timbers inside the lower stone walls, where the man on the ground could soak them with water.

Raine knew it was no use to yell at Gavin anymore. He tiredly signaled the exhausted men behind him to continue pulling the timbers off the wall. Raine was past exhaustion, yet he had had four hours of sleep—four more than Gavin. Raine knew from experience that if one square inch of what Gavin considered his was endangered, the man would neither sleep nor rest until it was safe.

Raine stood on the ground, his breath held as Gavin worked beside and under the burning wall. It would collapse at any moment and Raine could only hope that Gavin would soon finish hacking away the timbers and climb down the ladder to the safety of the ground. Raine murmured every oath he knew as Gavin flirted with death. The merchants and serfs gasped as the wall of fire teetered back and forth. Raine thought he would like to forcibly bring Gavin down the ladder, but Raine knew his strength was no greater than his older brother's.

Suddenly the timbers fell inside the stone walls, and Gavin was immediately on the ladder. He had no more than touched the ground when Raine made a flying leap and knocked his brother out of the path of the sheet of fire.

"Damn you, Raine!" Gavin bellowed in his brother's ear as Raine's heavy body lay on top of him. "You're crushing me. Get off!"

Raine was too used to Gavin to take offense. He stood up slowly, his muscles aching from the work of the last few days. "That's the thanks I get for saving your life! Why the hell did you stay up there so long? Another few seconds, and you would have been roasted."

Gavin stood up quickly, his soot-blackened face turned toward the building he had just left. The fire was contained inside the stone walls now and would not be leaping to the next building. When he was satisfied that the buildings were safe, he turned to his brother. "How could I have let the building burn?" he asked as he flexed his shoulder. It was scraped and bleeding where Raine had skidded him across the gravel and debris. "If the fire had not been stopped, I might not have had a town left."

Raine's eyes blazed. "I would rather have lost a hundred buildings than you."

Gavin grinned. His even white teeth shone against the blackness of his dirty face. "Thank you," he said quietly. "But I think I'd rather lose a little flesh than another building." He turned away and went to direct the men in the dousing of the structure that was next to the one he had hacked to pieces.

Raine shrugged and walked away. Gavin had been master of the Montgomery estate since he was sixteen years old, and he took his responsibility very seriously. What was his was his, and he would fight to the death to keep it. Yet the lowest serf, the worst thief, if they were residents of the Montgomery holdings, would get the fairest treatment from Gavin.

Late at night, Gavin returned to the manor house. He went to the winter parlor, a room off the great hall that served as a family dining room. The floors were covered with thick carpets from Antioch. The room was a recent addition and was paneled with the new linenfold paneling, the walnut carved to look like the draping of fabric. One end of the room was dominated by an enormous fireplace. The stone mantel above was sculpted with the Montgomery leopards.

Raine was already there, clean and dressed in black wool, an enormous silver tray in front of him heaped high with roast pork, chunks of warm bread, dried apples and peaches. He fully planned to eat every pound of the food. He grunted and pointed toward a large wooden tub filled with steaming hot water set before a roaring fire.

Gavin's fatigue was catching up with him. He slipped off his braies—a tight garment of hose and underpants—and his boots, then slipped into the water. It stung his recently blistered and cut body. A young servant girl appeared out of the shadows and began to wash Gavin's back.

"Where is Miles?" Raine said between mouthfuls.

"I sent him to Revedoune's. He reminded me that the engagement was to take place today. He went as my proxy." Gavin leaned forward, letting the girl wash him. He did not look at his brother.

Raine nearly choked on a piece of pork. "You what!"

Gavin looked up in surprise. "I said I sent Miles as my proxy for the engagement to the Revedoune heiress."

"Good God, haven't you any sense at all? You can't send someone else as if you were purchasing a prize mare. She's a woman!"

Gavin stared at his brother. The firelight showed the deep hollow in Gavin's cheek as his jaw muscles began to flex. "I am well aware that she is a woman. If she weren't, I wouldn't be forced to marry her."

"Forced!" Raine leaned back against the chair, incredulous. It was true that while Gavin's three younger brothers were traveling freely about the country, visiting castles and manors in France and even the Holy Land, Gavin had been chained to a ledger. He was twenty-seven and in eleven years, except for the recent uprising in Scotland, he had hardly left his own home. Gavin did not know that his brothers often made allowances for what they considered his ignorance of women other than the daughters of the lower classes.

"Gavin," Raine began patiently, "Judith Revedoune is a lady—an earl's daughter. She has been taught to expect certain things from you, such as courtesy and respect. You should have gone in person to tell her that you wish to marry her."

Gavin held out his arm as the servant girl ran a soapy cloth over it. The front of her coarse woolen dress was wet, and it clung to her full breasts. He looked into her eyes and smiled at her, beginning to feel the first risings of desire. He glanced back at Raine. "But I don't want to marry her. Certainly she cannot be so ignorant to think I'm marrying her for any reason besides her lands."

"You cannot tell her that! You must court her and—"

Gavin rose out of the tub and stood while the girl climbed on a stool and poured warm water over him to rinse him. "She will be *mine*," he said flatly. "She will do as I tell her to. I have seen enough highborn ladies to know what they are like. They sit in their upstairs solars and sew and gossip while they eat honeyed fruit and grow fat. They are lazy and stupid; they have had everything they ever wanted. I know how to treat those women. I sent to London a week ago and ordered some new tapestries from Flanders—something silly like a nymphet cavorting about a woods so she won't be frightened by scenes of war. I'll hang them in the solar and give her access to all the silk threads and silver needles she can use, and she will be content."

Raine sat quietly and thought of the women he had met in his journeys about the country. Most of them were like Gavin's description, but then there were women of intelligence and fire who were more like companions to their husbands. "What if she wishes to have a hand in the estate affairs?"

Gavin stepped out of the tub and took the soft cotton towel the girl handed him. "She will not interfere in what is mine. She will tend to what I tell her, or she will repent it."

Chapter 4

SUNLIGHT STREAMED through the open windows, slanting across the rush-covered floor, playing with little dust motes that glittered like specks of gold. It was a perfect spring day, the first of May, the sun shining, the air filled with the sweetness that only spring can bring.

It was a large, open room, half of the entire fourth floor of the half-timbered house. The windows facing south admitted enough light to warm the room. It was a plain room, for Robert Revedoune would not part with money for what he considered frivolous, such as carpets and tapestries.

This morning, though, the room did not look so sparse. Every chair was covered with a splash of color. There were garments everywhere; beautiful, lush, brilliant garments, all new, all part of the dowry of Judith Revedoune. There were silks from Italy, velvets from the Orient, cashmeres from Venice, cottons from Tripoli. Jewels winked everywhere: on shoes, belts, circlets. There were emeralds, pearls, rubies, enamels. And all of it was laid upon a background of fur: sable, ermine, beaver, squirrel, curly black lamb, lynx.

Judith sat alone amid this splendor, so quietly that someone entering the room might not have seen her except that Judith's person outshone any fabric or jewel. Her little feet were encased in soft green leather, lined and bordered with white ermine, spots of black dotting the fur. Her dress fitted her body tightly about the bodice, the long sleeves draping from wrist to past her waist. The waist was snug, revealing its tininess. The square neckline was low; above it, Judith's full breasts showed to advantage. The skirt was a soft bell that swayed gently when she walked. The cloth was of gold tissue, fragile and heavy, iridescent and shimmering in the sun. Her waist was encircled with a narrow belt of gold leather set with emeralds. On her brow was a thin cord of gold, a large emerald suspended in the middle. A mantle of emerald-green taffeta hugged her shoulders, fully lined with ermine.

On another woman the sheer brilliance of her green and gold gown might have been overwhelming. But Judith was more beautiful than any gown. She was a small woman with curves to make a man gasp. Her auburn hair hung down her back to her waist, ending in heavy curls. Her strong jaw was set and she held her chin high. Even now as she thought of the dreadful events to come, her lips were full and soft. But her eyes were what riveted attention. They were a rich, deep gold that grabbed the sunlight and reflected it off the gold of her gown.

She turned her head slightly and looked outside at the beautiful day. At any other time she would have been pleased by the weather, wanting to ride across the fields of fragrant flowers. But today she sat very still, careful not to move and crease the gown. It was not the dress that kept her so still, but the heaviness of her thoughts. For today was her wedding day—a day she had long dreaded. This day would end her freedom and all happiness as she knew it.

Suddenly the door burst open and her two maids entered the large room. Their faces were pink from just having raced back from the church where they had gone to get an early look at the groom.

"Oh, my lady," Maud said. "He is so handsome! He is tall with dark hair, dark eyes and shoulders . . . !" She held her arms out to their fullest extent. She sighed dramatically. "I don't see how he managed the doorways. He must turn to the side." Her eyes danced as she watched her mistress. She did not like to see Judith so unhappy.

"And he walks like this," Joan said as she threw back her

shoulders until the blades nearly touched and took several long, firm strides across the room.

"Yes," Maud said. "He is a proud one. As proud as all those Montgomery men. They act as if they own the world."

"I wish they did," Joan giggled, then rolled her eyes at Maud, who tried hard not to laugh with her.

But Maud was more interested in her mistress, and for all their teasing, Judith had not given even a hint of a smile. Maud held her hand, signaling Joan to be silent. "My lady," she said quietly, "is there anything you wish? There is time before you leave for the church. Perhaps—"

Judith shook her head. "I am past help now. Is my mother well?"

"Yes, she is resting before she must ride to the church. It is a long distance and her arm—" Maud stopped, sensitive to her mistress's look of pain. Judith blamed herself for Helen's broken arm. Her own conscience was enough without Maud's clumsy reminders. Maud could have kicked herself. "You are ready, then?" she asked gently.

"My body is ready. It's just my thoughts that need more time. Would you and Joan see to my mother?"

"But my lady—"

"No," Judith interrupted. "I would like to be alone. It may be my last moment of privacy for some time. Who knows what tomorrow will bring?" She looked back toward the window.

Joan started to reply to her melancholy mistress's words, but Maud stopped her. Joan could not understand Judith. She was rich, this was her wedding day and, best of all, her husband was a young and handsome knight. Why was she not happy? Joan shrugged her shoulders in dismissal as Maud pushed her through the doorway.

For weeks the preparations for Judith's wedding had been taking place. It was to be a sumptuous and elaborate affair, and would cost her father a year's rents. She had kept the books for every purchase, noting the thousands of ells of cloth to be used for the massive canopies to shelter the guests, totaling the food to be served; a thousand pigs, three hundred calves, a hundred oxen, four thousand venison pasties, three hundred tuns of ale. On and on the lists went.

And all for something she desperately did not want.

Most girls were reared to think of marriage as part of their future, but not Judith. From the day of her birth, Judith had been treated differently. Her mother had been worn out from miscarriages and years spent with a husband who beat her at every opportunity when finally her daughter was born. Helen looked at the tiny bit of red-haired life and lost her heart to it. Whereas she never fought her husband, for this child she would risk hell. She wanted two things for her little Judith: protection for her against a brutal and violent father, and guaranteed protection from all such men for all Judith's life.

For the first time in her many years of marriage, Helen stood up to the husband she feared so much. She demanded of him that her daughter be given to the church. Robert couldn't have cared less what was done with the girl or her mother. What did a daughter matter to him? He had his sons from his first wife, and all this groveling, mewling creature could produce were dead babies and one worthless daughter. He laughed and agreed to allow the girl to go to the nuns when she was of age. But to show that sniveling creature who was his wife what he thought of her demands, he tossed her down the stone stairs. Helen still limped from where her leg had been broken in two places from that fall, but it had all been worth it. She kept her daughter to her in complete privacy. There were times when Helen might not have remembered she was married. She liked to think of herself as a widow, living alone with her lovely daughter.

They were happy years. She trained her daughter for the demanding career of a nun.

And now it was all to be thrown away. Judith was to become a wife: a woman who had no power other than what was given to her by her husband and ruler. Judith knew nothing about being a wife. She sewed poorly and knit not at all. She did not know how to sit quietly for hours, allowing her servants to work for her. But worst of all, Judith did not even know the meaning of subservience. A wife must keep her eyes lowered to her husband, must take his advice in all things; but Judith had been taught that she would one day be a prioress, the only woman considered to be an equal by men. Judith had looked at her father and brothers with level eyes, never flinching even when her father raised his fist at her, and for some reason this seemed to amuse Robert. She had a pride that was uncommon in women—or even in most men, for that matter. She walked with her shoulders back, her spine straight.

No man would tolerate her quiet, even voice which discussed the relationship of the king to the French or talked of her own radical views as to the treatment of the serfs. Women were supposed to talk of jewels and adornments. Judith was often content to let her maids choose her clothing; but let two bushels of lentils be missing from the storehouses, and Judith's wrath was formidable.

Helen had gone to great pains to keep her daughter hidden from the outside world. She was afraid that some man might see her and want her and Robert would agree to the match. Then her daughter would be taken from her. Judith should have entered the convent when she was twelve, but Helen could not bear to part with her. Year after year she'd selfishly kept her daughter near her, only to have all the time and training come to nothing.

Judith had had months to prepare herself for marriage with a stranger. She had not seen him, nor did she care to. She knew she'd see enough of him in the future. She had known no men besides her father and brothers and therefore anticipated a life spent with a man who hated women, who beat them, who was uneducated and unable to learn anything except how to use his strength. Always she'd planned to escape such an existence, now she knew it was not to be. In ten years' time would she be like her mother: shaking, eyes shifting from side to side, always afraid?

Judith stood, the heavy gold gown falling to the floor, rustling prettily. She would not! Never would she show her fear to him; no matter what she felt, she would hold her head high and look him straight in the eye.

For a moment, she felt her shoulders droop. She was frightened of this stranger who was to be her lord and master. Her maids laughed and talked of their lovers with joy. Could the marriage of a nobleman be like that? Was a man capable of love and tenderness, just as a woman was? She would know in a short while. She straightened her shoulders again. She would give him a chance, Judith vowed silently. She would be a mirror of him. If he were kind, she would be kind. But if he were like her father, then she would give as good as she got. No man had ever ruled her and none ever would. Judith made that a vow also.

"My lady!" Joan called excitedly as she burst into the room. "Sir Raine and his brother Sir Miles are outside. They've come to see you." Joan gave her mistress a look of exasperation when Judith stared at her maid blankly. "They are your husband's brothers. Sir Raine wants to meet you before the wedding."

Judith nodded and stood to greet the visitors. The man she was to marry showed no interest in her; even the betrothal was done by proxy, and now it was not him but his brothers who came to greet her. She took a deep breath and forced herself to stop trembling. She was more scared than she realized.

Raine and Miles walked down the broad spiral stairs of the Revedoune house side by side. They had arrived only last night; Gavin had postponed facing his forthcoming marriage for as long as possible. Raine tried to get his older brother to meet his bride, but he refused. He said he would see her for years to come—why start the curse early?

When Miles had returned from his duty of proxy at the engagement, Raine had been the one to question him about the heiress. As usual, Miles said little, but Raine knew he was hiding something. Now that Raine had seen Judith, he knew what it was.

"Why didn't you tell Gavin?" Raine asked. "You know he's dreaded what he calls his ugly heiress."

Miles did not smile, but his eyes glowed in memory of the

vision of his sister-in-law. "I thought perhaps it would do him some good to be wrong for once."

Raine smothered his laughter. Gavin sometimes treated his youngest brother as if he were a boy instead of a twenty-year-old man. Miles's silence in not telling Gavin of his fiancée's beauty was one small punishment for all the times Gavin had ordered his little brother about. Raine gave a short laugh. "To think Gavin offered her to me and I didn't even try! If I had seen her, I would have fought him for her. Do you think it's too late?"

If Miles answered, Raine didn't hear him. His thoughts were elsewhere as he remembered his first sight of his little sister-in-law, whose head hardly reached his shoulder. He saw that only before he was close enough to see her face. After one look at her eyes, as pure and rich a gold as any from the Holy Land, he saw nothing else. Judith Revedoune had looked up at him with intelligence, evenly, as if she were assessing him. Raine had merely stared, unable to speak as he felt himself being pulled under by the current of those eyes. She did not simper or giggle like most young maidens, she met him as an equal. He found the sensation heady. Miles had to nudge Raine to make him speak to her. Raine never heard a word anyone said, but merely stood and stared. He had a vision of carrying her away from this house and these people, of making her his. He knew he must leave before he had other such indecent thoughts of his brother's wife.

"Miles," he said now, his dimples cutting deeply into his cheeks, as they always did when he tried not to laugh aloud, "perhaps we can both repay our elder brother for demanding too many hours on the training field."

"What do you plan?" Miles's eyes burned with interest.

"If I remember correctly, I just saw a hideous dwarf of a woman with rotted teeth and an incredibly fat backside."

Miles began to smile. Truthfully, they had seen just such a hag on the staircase. "I see what you mean. We must not lie, but neither need we tell all the truth."

"My idea exactly."

*   *   *

It was still early morning when Judith followed her maids down the wooden stairs to the great hall on the second floor. There were fresh rushes on the floor, the tapestries had been taken from storage and hung, and running from the door to the far side of the room was a thick path of rose petals and lilies. These she would walk on when she returned from the church—a married woman.

Maud walked behind her mistress, holding aloft the long train of the fragile gold dress and the ermine-lined mantle. Judith paused just before she left the house, taking a deep breath to steel herself.

It took her eyes a moment to adjust to the bright sunlight and see the long line of people who had come to attend the celebration of the marriage of an earl's daughter. She was unprepared for the cheer that greeted her; a cheer of welcome and of pleasure at the sight of the splendid young woman.

Judith smiled in return, nodding her head toward the mounted guests and at the serfs and merchants who also had come to the festivities.

The procession to the church would be like a parade, meant to show the wealth and importance of the king's earl, Robert Revedoune. Later he could claim so many earls, so many barons, came to honor his daughter's wedding. The jongleurs headed the procession, heralding the way enthusiastically for the beautiful bride. Judith was lifted onto a white horse by her father, who nodded approval at her dress and bearing. She rode sidesaddle for this auspicious occasion; the unaccustomed position felt awkward, but she did not show it. Her mother rode behind her, flanked by Miles and Raine. The multitude of guests followed in order of importance.

With a great clash of cymbals, the jongleurs began singing and the procession started. They progressed slowly, following the music makers and Robert Revedoune who walked, leading the reins of his daughter's horse.

In spite of all her vows and promises, Judith found herself growing more nervous with each step. Now her curiosity about her new husband began to eat at her. She sat erect, but her eyes strained toward the church door where two figures stood; the priest and the stranger who was to be her husband.

Gavin was not so curious. His stomach was still uneasy after the description that Raine had given him. It seemed the girl was simpleminded as well as ugly. He tried not to look at the rapidly approaching procession but the noise of the jongleurs and the deafening cheers of the thousands of serfs and merchants who lined the way to watch, kept him from hearing his own thoughts. In spite of himself, his eyes were drawn to the procession. He had not realized they were so close! When Gavin looked up and saw the auburn-haired girl on the white horse, he had no idea who she was. It was a full minute before he realized that she was his bride. The sun flashed off her as if she were a pagan goddess come to life. He stared, his mouth slightly open. Then he broke into a grin. Raine! Of course Raine would lie. Gavin was so relieved, so happy, that he did not notice that he was leaving the church portal, taking the steps two and three at a time. Custom dictated that the groom wait for the bride's father to lift her from her horse, escort her up the steps, then present her to her new master. But Gavin wanted to get a better look at her. He did not hear the laughter and cheers of the onlookers as he shouldered his father-in-law aside and put his hands on his bride's waist to swing her off her mount.

At close view, she was even more striking. His eyes feasted on her lips, soft, full and inviting. Her skin was creamy and pure, smoother than the finest satin. He nearly gasped when he finally gazed into her eyes.

Gavin smiled at her in pure pleasure, and she smiled back at him, exposing white, even teeth. The roar of the crowd brought him back to reality. Reluctantly, Gavin set her on the ground and offered his arm to her, clasping his hand over hers as if she might try to flee. He had every intention of keeping this new possession.

The onlookers were thoroughly pleased by Gavin Montgomery's impetuous behavior, and they gave voice to their approval. Robert scowled at being pushed aside then saw that each of the guests was laughing.

The marriage ceremony was performed outside the church so all could witness the joining, rather than the few who could squeeze inside the church. The priest asked Gavin if he would take Judith Revedoune for his wife. Gavin stared at the woman beside him, her hair unbound, flowing in thick, soft waves to her waist where it curled under perfectly. "I will," he replied.

Then the priest asked Judith as she stared just as openly at Gavin. He wore gray from head to foot. The doublet and the broad-shouldered jacket were of soft Italian velvet. The jacket was fully lined with a dark mink that formed a wide collar, the fur narrowly edging the front of the garment. His only ornament was the sword slung low about his hips, its hilt embedded with a large diamond that flashed in the sunlight.

Her maids had said Gavin was handsome, but Judith had no idea that she would see a man with such an air of strength about him. She had expected some blond and delicate young man. Instead, she looked at his thick black hair curling along his neck, saw the lips that smiled at her and then the eyes that suddenly made chills run along her spine.

To the joy of the crowd, the priest had to repeat his question. Judith felt her cheeks burning as she said, "Yes." Most definitely, she would take Gavin Montgomery.

They gave promises to love, honor and obey, and when the rings were exchanged, the temporarily silent crowd let out another roar that threatened the church roof. As Judith's dowry was read to the guests and onlookers, it could hardly be heard. Judith and Gavin, a beautiful young woman and handsome young man, were a great favorite with them. The bride and groom were handed baskets of silver coins which they tossed to the people at the foot of the steps. Then the couple followed the priest into a quiet and relatively dark cathedral.

Gavin and Judith were given places of honor in the choir, above the press of the guests below. The two were like children, stealing glances at one another throughout the long, solemn mass. The guests watched adoringly, enchanted by this marriage with its fairytale beginning. The jongleurs were already composing songs to be sung at the banquet later. The serfs and middle class were outside the church, comparing observations on the exquisite clothes of the guests and most of all on the beauty of the bride.

But there was one person who was not happy. Alice Valence sat beside the fat, dozing figure of her husband-to-be, Edmund Chatworth, and stared at the bride with all the hatred in her soul. Gavin had made a fool of himself! Even the serfs had laughed at him when he bounded down the stairs after that woman like a boy running toward his first horse.

How could anyone think that red-haired bitch was beautiful? Alice knew that freckles always accompanied red hair.

She looked away from Judith to Gavin. Gavin was the one who made her angry. Alice knew him better than he knew himself. For all that a pretty face could send him somersaulting like a clown, she knew that his emotions ran deep. When he said he loved her, he did. And she would remind him of that as soon as possible. She would not allow him to forget her when he was bedded with that red-haired devil.

Alice looked at her hands and smiled. There was a ring . . . Yes, she had it with her. She felt a little more secure as she looked back at the bride and groom, a plan forming in her mind.

She saw Gavin take Judith's hand and kiss it, ignoring Raine who reminded him that they were in church. Alice shook her head. The silly woman didn't even know how to react. She should have lowered her lashes and blushed; Alice's blush was quite becoming. But Judith Revedoune merely stared at her husband, watching his every move as he pressed his lips to the back of her hand. Most unfeminine, Alice thought.

At that moment Alice was not unobserved. Raine glanced down from the choir loft at Alice and saw the scowl that creased her perfect brow. He was sure she had no idea she was doing so; Alice was so careful to show only what she wanted to be seen.

Fire and ice, he thought. Judith's beauty was like fire to

Alice's icy blondeness. He smiled as he thought how easily fire melted ice, but then remembered that it all depended on the heat of the fire and the greatness of the block of ice. His brother was a sane and sensible man, rational in every aspect except one—Alice Valence. Gavin adored her; he was insane when anyone even hinted at her flaws. His new wife held an attraction for him, but for how long? Could she overcome the fact that Alice held his heart? Raine hoped so. As he looked from one woman to the other, he realized that Alice might be a woman to worship, but Judith was a woman to *love*.

Chapter 5

AT THE end of the long wedding mass, Gavin took Judith's hand and led her down the steps to the altar where they knelt before the priest as he blessed them. The holy man gave Gavin the kiss of peace, which he then transmitted to his wife. It should have been a kiss of duty; but though it was over quickly, Gavin's lips were lingering, causing Judith to gaze at him, her golden eyes mirroring her pleasure as well as surprise.

Gavin grinned widely with pure joy, took her hand in his and led her at a half-run from the church. Once outside, the crowd threw a shower of grains that by sheer volume was almost lethal. He lifted Judith onto her horse, her waist tiny even when swathed in layers of fabric. He would have liked to put her onto his mount with him, but he'd committed enough of a *faux pas* when he'd first seen her. He started to take the reins of her horse, but Judith led her own animal and he was pleased; his wife would need to be a good horsewoman.

The bride and groom led the procession back to the Revedoune manor house, Gavin holding her hand tightly as they entered the freshly cleaned great hall. Judith looked at the rose petals and lilies spread on the floor. Only a few hours ago, these flowers had seemed an omen of the dreadful thing that was about to happen to her. Now, looking at Gavin, his gray eyes smiling into hers, the idea of being his wife did not seem so dreadful at all.

"I would give a great deal to know your thoughts," Gavin said, his lips close to her ear.

"I was thinking that this marriage does not seem nearly as bad as I once thought."

Gavin was stunned for a moment then he threw back his head and bellowed with laughter. Judith had no idea that she had insulted him and complimented him in one sentence. A well-trained young lady should never have admitted to disliking the idea of marriage to any man chosen for her. "Well, my wife," Gavin said, his eyes sparkling, "I am more than pleased."

Their first words to each other had been spoken—and then there was time for no more. The bride and groom must stand in line and greet the hundreds of guests who congratulated them.

Judith stood quietly beside her husband and smiled at one guest after another. She knew very few of them since her life had been so secluded. Robert Revedoune stood to one side, watching his daughter, making sure that she did nothing wrong. He would not be certain he had her off his hands until the marriage was consummated.

Judith had been concerned that her clothes would be overly rich but as she watched the guests, murmuring "thank yous," she knew her attire was conservative. The guests were dressed in peacock colors; several of them, all on one body. The women wore reds, purples and greens. There were checks, stripes, brocades, appliqués, and lush embroidery. Judith's gold and green stood out through its understatement.

Raine suddenly grabbed Judith's waist, lifted her high above his head, then planted a sound kiss on each cheek.

"Welcome to the Montgomery clan, little sister," he said sweetly, deep dimples in his cheeks.

Judith liked his honesty and openness. Miles came next. She had met him when he came as proxy for Gavin. He had stared at her like one of the hawks in the mews.

Miles still stared at her in that odd, piercing way, and she stole a glance at her husband, who seemed to be badgering Raine about some jest about an ugly woman. Raine, shorter than Gavin, wore a black velvet jacket trimmed with silver. He was a handsome man with his deep dimples and his laughing blue eyes. Miles was as tall as Gavin, but of slighter build. Of the three brothers, Miles's clothes were the brightest. He wore a dark green wool doublet and a brilliant green jacket, lined with dark sable. About his slim hips was a wide leather belt set with emeralds.

They were all strong, handsome men; but as she saw them together, Gavin seemed to outshine the others. At least, it seemed so to Judith. Gavin felt her eyes on him and turned toward her. He took her hand from her side and kissed her fingers. Judith felt her heart race as he put the tip of one finger in his mouth, touching it to his tongue.

"I think you should wait a while, brother, although I can see the reason for your impatience," Raine laughed. "Tell me again about fat, overbred heiresses."

Gavin released his wife's hand reluctantly. "You can laugh at me all you like—but it is I who has her, so I have the last laugh. Or maybe 'laugh' is not the right word."

Raine gave a throaty sound and nudged Miles. "Come on, let's see if we can find any more golden-eyed goddesses in this place. Give your new sister-in-law a kiss of welcome and let's go."

Miles lifted Judith's hand and kissed it lingeringly, his eyes on hers all the while. "I think I shall save the kiss for a more private time," he said before following his brother.

Gavin put his arm around Judith's shoulders possessively. "Don't let them upset you. They're only teasing."

"I rather like their teasing."

Gavin smiled down at her, then abruptly released her. Touching her had nearly set him on fire. The bedding was many hours away. If he was to live through the day, he knew he must keep his hands off her.

Later, as Judith accepted a kiss from a withered woman, countess of someplace, wearing a shimmering gown of purple satin, she felt Gavin stiffen beside her. She followed his eyes down the line to a woman so exquisite that several men did little but gape at her. When she came to stand before the bride, Judith was taken aback at the hatred that smoldered in those blue eyes. She was almost tempted to cross herself in protection. Titters drew Judith's attention and she saw that several people were greatly enjoying the sight of the two women, both beautiful, but so different, face to face.

The blonde woman moved quickly past Gavin, refusing to meet his eyes and Judith noticed an expression of pain on her husband's face. It was a puzzling and disconcerting encounter which she did not understand.

Finally the reception was over. All the guests had spoken to the newly wedded couple, Judith's father had given each person a gift, according to his or her importance and at long last the trumpets sounded for the feasting to begin.

While the guests had greeted the bride and groom, the tables had been set about the great hall. Now they were being covered with food: chicken, duck, quail, crane, pheasant, partridge, as well as pork and beef. There were meat pies and twelve kinds of fish. Vegetables, seasoned with spices from the Orient, were abundant. The first strawberries of the season would be served, as well as a few of the rare and expensive pomegranates.

The estate's portable wealth was seen in the gold and silver dishes used by the most important guests who sat at the head table on a slightly elevated platform. Judith and Gavin had matching glasses—tall, slender, made of silver, the bases of finely worked gold.

In the center of the grouping of tables was an open area. Here jongleurs played and sang, Eastern dancers moved enticingly, acrobats cavorted and one traveling troupe put on a play. The noise was tremendous, filling the two-story-high room.

"You do not eat much," Gavin said, trying not to shout, but it was difficult to be heard over the din.

"No." She looked at him and smiled. The idea that this stranger was her husband kept running through her mind. She would like to touch the cleft in his chin.

"Come," he said and took her hand, helping her rise. There were catcalls and jeers, obscenities by the dozen when

Gavin led his bride out of the great hall, but neither looked back. They strolled outside. The fields were full of spring flowers, which swept along the skirt of Judith's long gown. To their right were the tents of tomorrow's tourney participants. From each tent crown flew a pennant which identified its occupant, and everywhere was the Montgomery leopard. The banner held three leopards, placed vertically, worked in glittering gold thread, set on a ground of emerald-green.

"They are all your relatives?" Judith asked and Gavin looked over her head.

"Cousins and uncles. When Raine called us a clan, he meant it as such."

"And are you happy with them?"

"Happy?" He shrugged. "They are Montgomeries," he said, and that seemed to answer the question for him.

They stopped on a little hillside, from where they could see the tents below. He held her hand as she spread her skirts and sat down. He stretched out beside her, full length, his hands behind his head.

Judith sat with her back to his face. His legs stretched before her. She could see the way the muscle curved out above his knee then rounded toward his thighs. Judith knew without a doubt that each of his thighs were bigger than her waist. Unexpectedly, she shivered.

"Are you cold?" Gavin asked, at once sensitive. He raised himself on his elbows and watched as she shook her head. "I hope you didn't mind leaving for a while. You will think I have no manners—first at the church and now this. But it was too noisy, and I wanted to be alone with you."

"I too," she said honestly as she turned to face him.

He lifted one hand and took a curl of her hair, watching it wrap itself about his wrist. "I was surprised when I saw you. I had heard you were ugly." His eyes sparkled as he rubbed the curl between his fingers.

"Where did you hear that?"

"It was common talk that that was the reason Revedoune kept his daughter hidden."

"It was more that I was hidden from *him*." She would say

no more, but Gavin understood. There was little he liked about the bully of a man who beat anything smaller than himself and groveled before anything larger.

Gavin grinned at her. "I am quite pleased with you. You are more than a man could hope for."

Suddenly Judith remembered the sweet kiss in church. What would it be like to kiss again, at leisure? She had so little experience with the ways of men and women.

Gavin's breath stopped as he saw her gazing at his mouth. A quick glance at the sun told him it was still many hours before he could have her all to himself. He would not start what he could not finish. "We must return," he said abruptly. "Our behavior will set tongues wagging for years as it is." He helped her stand then, as she stood so close to him, he looked down at her hair, inhaling the spicy fragrance of it. He knew it was warm from the sun, and he meant only to place a chaste kiss on the part of it; but Judith lifted her face to smile at him. In moments, his arms were around her, his lips on hers.

Judith's small education about men and women had come from her maids, who giggled and compared the lovemaking of one man to another. So Judith reacted to Gavin's kiss, not with the reticence of a proper lady, but with all the enthusiasm she felt.

His hand went behind her neck, and her lips opened under his. She pressed her body close to his. How large he was! The muscles of his chest were hard against her softness, his thighs like iron. She liked the feel of him, the smell of him. Her arms tightened about him.

Suddenly Gavin drew back, his breath coming in short, shallow gasps. "You seem to know too much of kissing," he said angrily. "Have you had much?"

Her mind and body were too full of the newness of tingling sensations to be aware of his tone. "I have kissed no man before. My maids told me it was pleasant, but it is more than pleasant."

He stared, knowing an honest answer when he heard one. "Let's return now and pray for an early sunset."

Judith turned her reddened cheeks away from him and followed his lead.

They walked back toward the castle slowly, neither of them speaking. Gavin seemed to be absorbed in the erecting of yet another tent. If he had not held his wife's hand so tightly, she would have thought he'd forgotten her.

With his head turned away, he did not see Robert Revedoune waiting for them. But Judith did. And she recognized the rage in his eyes and braced herself.

"You little slut!" Robert hissed. "You are panting after him like a bitch in heat. I'll not have all of England laughing at me!" He raised his hand and brought the back of it across Judith's face.

It took Gavin a moment to react. He would not have imagined a father striking his daughter. When he did react, he plunged his fist into his father-in-law's face until the older man sprawled on the ground in a complete daze.

Judith glanced at her husband. His eyes were black, his jaw flexed to granite.

"Don't you dare touch her again," Gavin ordered in a low, deadly voice. "What is mine I keep—and care for." He stepped toward Revedoune again.

"Please, no," Judith said and grabbed her husband's arm. "I am unhurt, and you have repaid him for what was only a little slap."

Gavin did not move. Robert Revedoune's eyes went from his daughter to his son-in-law. He knew better than to speak. Slowly he got up and walked away.

Judith pulled on her husband's sleeve. "Don't let him ruin the day. He knows nothing except his fists." Her mind was whirling. The few men she had known would have thought it a father's right to strike his daughter. Maybe Gavin thought only of her as property, but something in the way he had spoken made Judith feel protected, loved almost.

"Here, let me look at you," Gavin said, his voice showing that he was working hard at controlling his temper.

He ran his fingertips over her lips as he felt for any bruised places or broken skin. She studied the darkness of his jaw where his whiskers lay just below the cleanly shaven skin. His touch made her knees weak. She lifted her hand and placed one fingertip on the cleft in his chin. He stopped his exploration and looked into her eyes. They stared at each other silently for a long moment.

"We must return," he said very sadly. He took her arm and led her back to the castle.

They had been gone longer than they realized. The food had been cleared away, the trestle tables dismantled and stacked against the wall. The musicians were tuning their instruments as they got ready to play for the dancing.

"Gavin," someone called, "you'll have her all your life. You shouldn't hoard her now."

Judith clung to Gavin's arm, but she was quickly pulled away into a circle of energetic dancers. As she was pushed and pulled through the quick, vigorous steps, she tried to keep her eyes on her husband. She did not want to let him out of her sight.

A man's chuckle made her look up. "Little sister," Raine said, "you should give the rest of us a glance once in a while."

Judith smiled at him just before a strong arm whirled her about, feet off the floor. When she returned to Raine's side, she said, "How can I ignore such handsome men as my brothers-in-law?"

"Well said, but if your eyes don't lie, my brother is the only one to put the light of the stars in those bits of gold."

Again someone whirled Judith away, and as she was lifted in the man's arm, she saw Gavin as he grinned down at a pretty little woman in a purple and green taffeta gown. Judith watched as the woman touched the velvet across Gavin's chest.

"Where's your smile?" Raine asked when she came back to him. He turned and looked at his brother.

"Do you think she's pretty?" Judith asked.

Raine controlled himself from laughing aloud. "Ugly! She is a little brown mouse of a woman, and Gavin would not have her." Since everyone else already has, he thought to himself. "Ah," he sighed. "Let's leave here and get some cider."

He grabbed her arm and led her to the opposite side of the room from Gavin.

Judith stood quietly in Raine's shadow and watched as Gavin led the brown-haired woman onto the dance floor. Each time he touched the woman, a swift feeling of pain shot through Judith's breast. Raine was absorbed in some talk with another man. She put her cup down and walked slowly through the shadows at the edges of the hall and made her way outside.

Behind the manor house lay a small walled garden. All her life, when she needed to be alone, Judith had gone to this garden. The image of Gavin holding the woman in his arms was branded in fire before her eyes. Yet why should she care? She had known him not even a full day. Why should it matter if he touched someone else?

She sat down on a stone bench, hidden from the rest of the garden. Could she be jealous? She had never experienced the emotion in her life but all she knew was that she did not want her husband either looking at or touching other women.

"I thought I would find you here."

Judith glanced up at her mother, then down again.

Helen quickly sat beside her daughter. "Is something wrong? Has he been unkind to you?"

"Gavin?" Judith asked slowly, liking the sound of the name. "No. He is more than kind."

Helen did not like what she saw on Judith's face. Her own had once been like that. She grabbed her daughter's shoulders although the movement hurt her half-healed arm. "You must listen to me! I have put off talking to you for too long. Each day I hoped something would happen to prevent this marriage, but nothing did. I will tell you something that you must hear. Never, *never* must you trust a man."

Judith wanted to defend her husband. "But Gavin is an honorable man," she said stubbornly.

Helen dropped her hands to her lap. "Ah yes, they are honorable to each other—to their men, to their horses, even; but to a man a woman means less than his horse. A woman is more easily replaced, less valuable. A man who would not lie to the lowliest serf would think nothing of creating the biggest tales to his wife. What does he lose? What is a woman?"

"No," Judith said. "I cannot believe all men are like that."

"Then you will have a long and unhappy life as I have had. If I had learned this at your age, my life would have been different. I believed myself to be in love with your father. I even told him so. He laughed at me. Do you know what it does to a woman to give her heart to a man and have him laugh at it?"

"But men do love women—" Judith began. She could not believe what her mother said.

"They love women, but only the one whose bed they occupy—and when they tire of her, they love another. There is only one time when a wife has any control over her husband, and that is when she is new to him and the bed magic is upon him. Then he will 'love' you and you can control him."

Judith stood, her back to her mother. "All men cannot be as you say. Gavin is . . ." She could not finish.

Helen, alarmed, went to her daughter and stood before her. "Don't tell me you think you are in love with him. Oh Judith, my sweet Judith, have you lived in this house for seventeen years and learned nothing, seen nothing? Your father was the same way once. Although you may not believe it, I was once beautiful and he was pleased with me. This is why I say these things to you. Do you think I want to tell my only child this? I prepared you for the church, to spare you. Please listen to my words. You must establish yourself with him from the first; then he will listen to you. Never show him your fear. When a woman reveals that, it makes the man feel strong. If you make demands from the first, he may listen to you—but soon it will be too late. There will be other women and—"

"No!" Judith shouted.

Helen gave her a look of great sadness. She could not save her daughter from the hurt that awaited her. "I must return to the guests. You will come?"

"No," Judith said softly. "I will follow in a moment. I must think for a while."

Helen shrugged and left by the side gate. There was no more she could do.

Judith sat quietly on the stone bench, her knees tucked under her chin. She defended her husband against what her mother said. Over and over she thought of hundreds of ways to show that Gavin was so very unlike her father, most of them created from her imagination.

Her thoughts were interrupted by the sound of the gate opening. A thin woman entered the garden. Judith recognized her immediately. She dressed to have people notice her. The left side of her bodice was green taffeta; the right was red. The colors were reversed on her skirt. She moved with an air of purpose. From her hidden bench behind the honeysuckle, Judith watched. Her first impression in the receiving line had been that Alice Valence was beautiful, but now she did not seem so. Her chin appeared weak, her little mouth stingy, as if it would give as little as possible. Her eyes glittered like ice. Judith heard a heavy, male footstep outside the wall, and she moved toward the smaller gate her mother had used. She wanted to give the woman and her lover privacy, but the first words stopped her. It was a voice she had come to recognize.

"Why did you ask me to meet you here?" Gavin asked stiffly.

"Oh, Gavin," Alice said, her hands going to his arms. "You are so cold to me. Can you have forgotten me? Is your love for this new wife so strong?"

Gavin frowned at her, not touching her, but not moving away either. "You can talk to me of love? I begged you to marry me. I offered to take you without a dowry. I offered to repay your father what he gave to Chatworth, yet still you would not marry me."

"You hold this against me?" she demanded. "Didn't I show you the bruises from my father? Didn't I tell you of the times he locked me away without food or water? What was I to do? I met you when I could. I gave you all I had to give a man, yet this is how I am repaid. Already you love another. Tell me, Gavin, did you ever love me?"

"Why do you talk of my loving another? I haven't said I

love her." His annoyance remained unabated. "I married because the offer was good. The woman brings riches, lands and a title also, as you yourself pointed out to me."

"But when you saw her—" Alice said quickly.

"I am a man and she is beautiful. Of course I was pleased."

Judith meant to leave the garden. Even when she saw her husband with the blonde woman, Judith meant to leave, but it was as if her body turned to stone and she could not move. Each word she heard Gavin speak thrust a knife through her heart. He had begged this woman to marry him and taken Judith, because of her wealth, as a second choice. She was a fool! She had been seeing their touches, their caresses as a spark of love, but it was not so.

"Then you don't love her?" Alice persisted.

"How could I? I have spent less than a day with her."

"But you *could* love her," Alice said flatly and turned her head to one side. When she looked back at him, there were tears in her eyes—great, lovely, shining tears. "Can you say you will never love her?"

Gavin was silent.

Alice sighed heavily, then smiled through her tears. "I had hoped we could meet here. I had some wine sent."

"I must return."

"It won't take long," she said sweetly as she led him to a bench against the stone wall.

Judith watched Alice, fascinated. She was watching a great actress. She'd seen the way Alice turned her head and deftly stuck her fingernail in the corner of her eye to produce the needed tears. Alice's words were melodramatic. Judith watched as Alice seated herself carefully on the bench, avoiding crushing the stiff taffeta of her dress, then poured two goblets of wine. In a slow, elaborate production, she slipped a large ring from her finger, opened the hinged lid and slowly poured a white powder into her drink.

As she began to sip the wine, Gavin knocked the goblet from her hand, sending it flying across the garden. "What are you doing?" he demanded.

Alice leaned languidly against the wall. "I would end it all, my love. I can withstand anything, if it is for us. I can bear my marriage to another, yours to another, but I must have your love. Without it I am nothing." Her lids dropped slowly and she had a look of such peace, as if she were already one of God's angels.

"Alice," Gavin said as he gathered her in his arms, "you cannot mean to take your own life."

"My sweet Gavin, you don't understand what love is to a woman. Without it I am already dead. Why prolong my agony?"

"How can you say you have no love?"

"You do love me, Gavin? Me and me alone?"

"Of course." He bent and kissed her mouth, the wine still on her lips. The setting sun deepened the applied color on her cheeks. Her dark eyelashes cast a mysterious shadow across her cheeks.

"Swear it!" she said firmly. "You must swear to me that you will love only me—no one else."

It seemed a small price to pay to keep her from killing herself. "I swear it."

Alice rose quickly. "I must return now, before I am missed." She seemed completely recovered. "You won't forget me? Even tonight?" she whispered against his lips, her hands searching inside his clothes. She didn't wait for his answer, but slipped from his grasp and through the gate.

The sound of clapping made Gavin turn. Judith stood there, her dress and eyes ablaze in a reflection of the setting sun.

"That was an excellent performance," she said as she lowered her hands. "I haven't been so entertained in years. That woman should try the stage in London. I hear there is need for good mummers."

Gavin advanced toward her, his face mirroring his rage. "You lying little sneak! You have no right to spy on me!"

"Spy!" she snarled. "I left the hall for some air after my *husband*"—she sneered the word—"left me to do for myself. And here in the garden I am a witness to that same husband groveling at the feet of a pasty-faced woman who twists him about her fingers like a bit of yarn."

Gavin drew back his arm and slapped her. An hour before he would have sworn that nothing could have made him harm a woman.

Judith slammed against the ground, landing in a mass of swirling hair and gold silk. The sun seemed to set a torch to her.

Gavin was instantly contrite. He was sick at himself and what he had done. He knelt to help her stand.

She retreated from him and her eyes glinted hatred. Her voice was so quiet, so flat, that he could hardly hear her. "You say you did not want to marry me, that you did so only for the wealth I bring you. Neither did I want to marry you. I refused until my father held my mother before me and snapped her arm like a splinter of wood. I have no love for that man—but for you I have even less. He is an honest man. He does not one hour stand before a priest and hundreds of witnesses and swear undying love—then in another hour pledge that same love to someone else. You are no man, Gavin Montgomery. You are lower than the serpent in the Garden of Eden, and always I will curse the day I was joined to you. You made that woman a vow and now I make you one. As God is my witness, you will rue this day. You may get the wealth you hunger for, but I will never give myself to you freely."

Gavin moved away from Judith as if she'd turned to poison. His experience with women was limited to whores and friendships with a few of the court ladies. They were demure, like Alice. What right did Judith have to make demands of him, to curse him, to make vows before God? A husband was a woman's god, and the sooner this one learned that the better.

Gavin grabbed a handful of Judith's hair and jerked her to him. "I will take whatever I want whenever I want, and if I take it from you, you will be grateful." He released her and pushed her back to the ground. "Now get up and prepare yourself to become my wife."

"I hate you," she said under her breath.

"What does that matter to me? I bear you no love either."

Their eyes locked—steel gray against gold. Neither moved until the women came to prepare Judith for her wedding night.

Chapter 6

A SPECIAL room had been readied for the bride and groom. A large corner of the solar had been partitioned off around one of the fireplaces. An enormous bed had been set up in the room and sheets of the softest linen were spread across it. A coverlet of gray squirrel, lined with crimson silk fell across the sheets. Rose petals littered the bed.

Judith's maids and several of the women guests helped undress the bride. When she was nude, they pulled the covers back, and Judith entered the bed. Her mind was not on what was taking place around her. She kept calling herself a fool. In just a few hours, she had forgotten seventeen years of what she had learned was true about men. For a few hours she had believed a man could be kind and good, capable even of love. But Gavin was the same—perhaps even worse than the others.

The women laughed riotously at Judith's silence. But Helen knew there was more than just nervousness involved with her daughter's behavior. She whispered a silent prayer, asking God to help her daughter.

"You are a fortunate woman," an older woman murmured in Judith's ear. "My first marriage found me wedded with a man five years older than my father. I wonder now that no one helped him perform his duties."

Maud giggled, "Lord Gavin will need no help—I'll wager that."

"Perhaps the Lady Judith will need help, and I would offer my . . . ah . . . services," laughed someone else.

Judith barely heard them. All she remembered hearing was her husband pledging his love to another woman, the way he held Alice and kissed her. The women drew the sheet just over Judith's breasts. Someone combed her hair so that it cascaded softly over her bare shoulders to rest in thick auburn curls around her hips.

Through the oak door the women heard the noise of the men arriving with Gavin carried aloft on their shoulders. He entered feet first, already half-undressed, the men yelling their offers of assistance, their wagers as to the competence of his performance of the task ahead. They were silent as they stood him on his feet and stared at the bride who waited in the bed. The sheet accented her creamy shoulders and the full swelling of her breasts. The candlelight deepened the shadow above the sheet. Her bare throat pulsed with life. Her face was set in a firm, serious expression that caused her eyes to darken, as if they smoked. Her lips were hard, as if carved of some warm vermilion marble.

"Get it done with!" someone shouted. "Do you torture him or me?"

The silence was broken. Gavin was quickly undressed and pushed to the bed. The men watched avidly as Maud drew the covers aside, giving them a glance of bare hips and thigh.

"Now out!" a tall woman ordered. "Leave them be."

Helen gave her daughter one last look, but Judith gazed down at her hands in her lap and saw no one.

When the heavy door slammed shut, the room suddenly seemed unnaturally quiet and Judith was achingly aware of the man beside her. Gavin sat looking at her. The only light in the room was from the flames in the fireplace across from the foot of the bed. The light danced on her hair, played with the shadows of her delicate collarbones. At this moment, he remembered nothing of a quarrel. Nor had he any thoughts of love. He knew only that he was in bed with a desirable woman. He moved his hand to touch her shoulder to see if the skin was as smooth as it looked.

Judith drew sharply away from him. "Don't touch me!" she said through clenched teeth.

He looked at her in surprise. There was hatred in her golden eyes, her cheeks flushed red. If possible, her anger made her even more beautiful. Never had he felt such a raging desire. His hand went about her neck, his thumb digging into the soft flesh. "You are my wife," he said in a low voice. "You are mine!"

She resisted him with all her strength, but it was nothing compared to his. Easily, he pulled Judith's face to his. "Never will I belong to you!" she spat at him before his lips closed on hers.

Gavin meant to be gentle with her, but she enraged him. This woman made him want to curse her, to strike her again. But most of all he wanted to possess her. His mouth came down brutally hard on hers.

Judith tried to move away from him; he hurt her. This was no sweet kiss of the afternoon, but more of a punishment to discipline her. She tried to kick at him, but the sheet that separated them entangled her feet and she could hardly move.

"I will help you," Gavin said and tore the sheet away, pulling it from under the mattress. His hand still held Judith's neck, and when the sheet was gone and she lay nude before him, he relaxed his grip as he gazed upon her. He stared at her in wonder; her full breasts, small waist, round hips. Then he looked back at her face, her eyes blazing. Her lips were reddened from his kiss, and suddenly there was no power on earth that could have stopped him from taking her. He acted as a starving man—one desperate for food—who would kill or maim to get what he must have.

He pushed her to the mattress and Judith saw the look in his eyes. She did not understand it, but she was afraid of it. He planned more than a cuff of his fist now. Of that she was sure.

"No!" she whispered and struggled against him.

Gavin was a seasoned knight. Judith had no more strength to him than a gnat to a piece of granite. And he paid her as much attention. He did not make love to her, but used her body. He was beyond thinking of her as anything but what he desired and so desperately needed. He moved on top of her, one thigh forcing hers apart. He kissed her again, hard.

When Gavin felt the tiny membrane that stopped him, for a moment he was bewildered. But he plunged on, oblivious to the pain he caused Judith. When she cried out, he stopped her lips with his and continued.

After he finished, he rolled from her, one heavy arm across her breasts. It had been a release for him, but for Judith there had been nothing resembling pleasure.

In minutes, she heard his slow breathing and she knew he was asleep. Silently, she slipped from under his arm and left the bed. The coverlet of squirrel pelts had been knocked to the floor. She picked it up and encircled her body with it. She stared at the fire, telling herself she would not cry. Why should she cry? Married against her will to a man who vowed, on her wedding day, that he would never love her, could never love her. A man who told her she was nothing to him. What reason had she to cry when the life before her appeared to be so pleasant? Could she look forward to years of doing little else but bearing his children, sitting at home while he roamed the countryside with his beautiful Alice?

She would not! She would find her own life and, if possible, her own love. Her husband would come to mean as little as possible to her.

She stood silently, controlling her tears, and all she could seem to remember was the sweetness of Gavin's kiss that afternoon, so different from his attack of tonight.

Gavin stirred in the bed and opened his eyes. At first he did not recall where he was. He turned his head, saw the emptiness beside him. She had gone! Every inch of his skin tightened until he noticed Judith in front of the fireplace. He did not think of his sudden fear, but was relieved that she was still with him. She seemed to be in another world and did not hear him turn onto his back. The sheets were liberally sprinkled with blood and Gavin frowned at them. He knew he'd hurt her, but he didn't understand why. Alice had been a virgin when he took her, but she had shown no pain.

He looked back at his wife, so small, so alone. It was true

he had no love for her but he had used her harshly. A maiden did not deserve rape.

"Come back to bed," he said softly, smiling a bit. He would make love to her slowly, by way of apology.

Judith straightened her shoulders. "No, I will not," she said firmly. She must begin by not letting him control her.

Gavin stared at her back, aghast. The woman was impossible! She made every sentence a contest of wills. His jaw set, he rose from the bed to stand before her.

Judith had not really seen him nude before and his bare chest, covered with dark hair over sun-bronzed skin, drew her eyes. He looked formidable.

"Have you not learned that you will come to me when I call?"

She lifted her chin and met his eyes. "Have you not learned that I will give nothing to you freely?" she countered.

Gavin stretched out his hand and took a curl from her hip, winding it about his wrist, again and again, pulling Judith nearer as she shrank from the pain. The coverlet fell away and he pulled her bare skin against his.

"Now you use pain to take what you want," she whispered, "but in the end I will win because you will grow tired of fighting."

"And what will you have won?" he asked, lips close to her.

"Freedom from a man I hate, a brutal, lying, dishonorable—" She stopped when he kissed her. It was not the kiss of an hour before, but one of gentleness.

At first, Judith refused to react to him but her hands went to his arms. They were hard, the muscles prominent, and his skin was so very warm. She became aware of the hair on his chest against her breasts.

As his kiss deepened, he loosened his hand from her hair, his arms encircling her shoulders. He moved her so her head tucked into the curve of his shoulder.

Judith gave up thinking. She was a mass of sensation— every feeling new and undreamed of. She pressed closer, running her hands over his back, feeling the way the muscles moved, so different from the smoothness of her own back. He began to kiss her ears, little nibbles on the lobes. Gavin gave a low, throaty chuckle when Judith's knees turned to water and she collapsed against the strength of his arm behind her back. He bent, put his other arm beneath her knees, his mouth never leaving her neck, and carried her to the bed. He kissed her body from her forehead to her toes and Judith lay silent, only her senses alive.

Before long she could bear no more kissing. She ached all over, and she pulled his hair to better meet his mouth. She fastened on his lips hungrily, with greed.

Gavin's senses, too, were reeling. Never had he had the leisure to make love to a woman as he did tonight, and never had he imagined the pleasure of it. Judith's passion was as fierce as his own, yet neither rushed their lovemaking. When he moved atop her, her arms held him tightly, pulling him nearer. There was no pain for Judith this time; she was ready. She moved with him, slowly at first, until they exploded together joyously.

Eventually Judith fell into a deep, exhausted sleep, her leg thrown over Gavin's, her hair twisted round and round his arm.

But Gavin did not fall asleep immediately. He knew that this was the first time for this soft woman he held, but in a way he felt as if he had just lost his virginity, too. And that was certainly an absurd idea. He could not possibly remember all the women he'd taken to his bed. But tonight was infinitely different. Never had he experienced such passion. With other women, when he felt his arousal at its height, they drew back. But not Judith. She had given as much as he gave.

He picked up a lock of her hair from across his neck and held it up, letting the firelight play though the strands. He held it to his nose, then to his lips. She moved against him and he snuggled closer. Even in sleep she wanted him nearby.

Gavin's eyes grew heavy. For the first time he could ever remember, he was sated and content. Ah, but there was the morning. He smiled before he drifted asleep.

* * *

Jocelin Laing returned his lute to its leather case and gave a barely perceptible nod to the blonde lady before she left the room. There had been several offers that night from women to share their beds. The excitement of the wedding and especially of seeing the handsome couple undressed and put to bed had sent many people off to find pleasure of their own.

The singer was an especially handsome young man; hot, dark eyes under long, thick lashes; dark hair that waved away from perfect skin that stretched over high cheekbones.

"Busy tonight?" one of the other singers called, laughing.

Jocelin smiled as he fastened his lute case but did not answer.

"I envy a man with a bride such as that." The other man nodded toward the stairs.

"Yes, she is beautiful," Jocelin agreed. "But there are others."

"Not like that one." The man moved closer to his friend. "There are some of us meeting with a few of the brides' women. You are welcome to come."

"No," Jocelin said quietly. "I cannot."

The singer gave Jocelin a sly look, gathered his psaltery and left the great hall.

When the enormous room was quiet, the floor spread with hundreds of straw mats for the sleeping retainers and guests of lesser importance, Jocelin made his way upstairs. He wondered how the woman he went to meet could have arranged a private room. Alice Valence was not rich, and though her beauty had won her an earl's ring, she was not one of the higher-born guests. On this night, when the castle was overflowing, only the bride and groom had a room alone. The other guests shared beds set out in the ladies' solar or in the master bedroom. The beds were large—often eight-foot squares—and with the heavy curtains surrounding them, they seemed like individual chambers.

Jocelin had no trouble entering the room set aside for the unmarried women; several men had slipped through the door already. It was easy to see the bed curtains slip aside and glimpse the blonde. He went to her quickly. The sight of her filled him with desire. Alice held out her arms, hungry for him, almost violent in her passion and any attempt Jocelin made to prolong their pleasures met with resistance. She was like a storm, full of lightning and thunder.

When it was over, she did not want Jocelin to touch her. Always alert to a woman's moods, he obeyed her unspoken wish. Never had he seen a woman who did not want to be held after lovemaking. He started to don his hastily discarded clothes.

"I will be married in a month," she said quietly. "You will come to my husband's castle then."

He did not comment. They both knew he would be there; he just wondered how many other men she asked.

A single ray of sunshine came through the window, its heat tickling Judith's nose. Sleepily, she brushed at it then tried to turn away but something held her by the hair. She lazily opened her eyes and saw the strange bed canopy overhead. When she remembered where she was, she felt her face grow hot. Even her body seemed to blush.

She moved her head toward the other side of the bed and looked at her sleeping husband. His lashes were short, thick and dark, a new growth of beard starting on his cheeks. Asleep, his cheekbones were not as sharp. Even the deep cleft in his chin seemed relaxed.

Gavin lay on his side, facing her and Judith let her eyes roam over him. His broad chest was liberally covered with dark, curling hair. The muscles made large, shapely mounds. His arms were capped by round, firm muscles. Her eyes drew down to his hard, flat stomach. It was only after a moment that her eyes went lower. What she saw did not seem so powerful but as she watched, his manhood began to grow.

She gasped and her eyes flew back to his. He was awake, watching her, his eyes growing darker by the moment. No longer was he the relaxed boy-man she had awakened to, but a man of passion. Judith tried to move away but Gavin still held her trapped by her hair. What was worse, she did not truly *want* to resist. She remembered that she hated him; but

69

more than that, she remembered her pleasure when he made love to her.

"Judith," he whispered and the tone of his voice made chills run along her arms.

He kissed the corner of her mouth. Her hands pushed weakly against his shoulders but even at his slight touch, her eyes closed in surrender. He kissed her cheek, her earlobe. Then, as she gasped for breath, his mouth came down on hers. His tongue sweetly touched the tip of hers. She drew back, startled. He smiled at her as if he understood. Last night Judith thought she'd learned all there was to know about love between a man and a woman, but now she thought, perhaps she knew very, very little.

His eyes were smoky-gray as he pulled her to him again. He ran his tongue along her lips, touching the inner corners especially. She parted her teeth for him and tasted of him. He was better than the richest honey; hot and cold, soft and firm. She explored his mouth as he had explored hers. She had no idea of shyness. In truth, she had no ideas at all.

She ran her hands over him as he lowered his head to her neck, running his tongue along the pulse beat there. Instinctively she leaned her head back, her breathing deeper, quicker.

When his lips and tongue touched her breasts, she nearly cried out. She thought perhaps she might die under such torture. She tried to pull his head back to her mouth but he gave a deep, guttural laugh that made her shiver. Maybe he did own her.

When she thought that she would lose her mind, he moved on top of her, his hand caressing the inside of her thighs until she was shaking with desire. When he entered her, she cried out; there was no relief to her torment. She clutched at him, her legs about his waist as she rose to meet each thrust. Finally, when she was sure she would explode, she felt the pulsing throbs that released her. Gavin collapsed on top of her, holding her so close that she could hardly breathe. But at the moment she didn't really care if she ever did breathe again.

An hour later the maids came to dress Judith, waking the bridal couple. Suddenly she was very aware of her hair and her body wrapped around Gavin's. Maud and Joan had several things to say about Judith's abandonment. The sheets were stained, and there were more linens on the floor than on the bed. The squirrel coverlet was on the other side of the room by the fireplace.

The maids pulled Judith up and helped her to wash. Gavin lazily lolled on the bed and watched every movement.

Judith would not look at him; she could not. She was embarrassed to the very depths of her soul. She detested the man. He was everything she hated; dishonorable, a liar, greedy, yet she had acted with no pride when he touched her. She'd made a vow to him—and to God—that he would get nothing from her, but he took more from her than she'd wanted to give.

She hardly noticed as her maids slipped a thin linen chemise over her head, then a gown of deep green velvet. The dress had been embroidered with intricate gold designs. The front of the skirt was divided, revealing a wide stripe of the silk underskirt. The sleeves were full and gathered at the wrists. They were cut in places, and the lighter green silk underdress was pulled through the slashes.

"And now, my lady," Maud said as she handed Judith a large, flat ivory box.

Judith stared at her maid in surprise as she held the box open. On a black velvet bed lay a wide collar of gold filagree, the tiny wire in places as thin as hair. Along the bottom of the necklace was a row of emeralds, many of them perfectly matched in size, none of them bigger than a raindrop. "It is . . . beautiful," Judith whispered. "How did my mother—"

"It is your bride's gift from your husband," Maud said, her eyes sparkling.

Judith could feel Gavin's eyes on her back. She whirled and faced him. The sight of him in bed, his skin so dark against the whiteness of the sheets, made her knees weak. It took great will, but she bent one knee and curtsied. "Thank you, my lord."

Gavin's jaw clenched at her coldness. He would have liked

the gift to thaw her somewhat. How could she be so hot in bed, so cold and haughty out of it?

Judith turned back to her maids and Maud finished fastening the buttons of the gown. Joan plaited the top layer of her mistress's hair, and intertwined the braids with gold ribbons. Before they finished, Gavin commanded them to leave the room. Judith did not look at him as he hurriedly shaved and dressed in a dark brown doublet and hose, a tawny wool jacket over it, the lining of golden lynx.

When he stepped toward her, she had to forcibly calm her hammering heart. He held his arm out for her and led her to the waiting guests below.

They attended mass together, but for this mass there was no hand kissing or staring at each other. They were solemn and sober throughout the service.

Chapter 7

THE GROUNDS outside the Revedoune manor rang with noise, the air charged with excitement. Brilliantly colored pennants were everywhere, fluttering from the stands and from the tents that covered the field. The clothing flashed in the sunlight like jewels. Children dashed in and out of knots of people. Vendors, with large boxes hanging about their necks, hawked their wares, selling anything from fruit and pies to holy relics.

The lists itself was a sand-covered field a hundred yards long with two rows of wooden fences along both sides. The inner fence was short—only three feet high—but the outer one was eight feet. The space inside was for the squires and horses of the participating knights. Outside the tall fence, the merchant class and the serfs pressed for a view of the games and jousts.

The ladies and the knights who did not participate sat on terraced benches high enough above the lists to see everything. The benches were canopied and marked with sendal banners displaying the colors of each family. Several areas bore the Montgomery leopards.

Before the joust began, the knights walked about in their armor. Depending on the wealth of the knight, the quality and modernity of the armor varied greatly. There could be seen the old-fashioned chain mail or the newer plates sewn onto leather. The richest knights wore the new Maxmilian armor from Germany. It covered a man from head to foot in fine steel. There was not an inch that went unprotected. It was a heavy protection, weighing well over a hundred pounds. On top of the helmets were plumes showing the colors of the knight.

As Judith and Gavin walked toward the tourney grounds, Judith was bewildered by all the noise and smells surrounding them. It was new and exciting to her, but Gavin had his own contradictory thoughts. The night had been a revelation. Never had he come near enjoying a woman as much as he had Judith. Too often his couplings had been hurried or secret meetings with Alice. Gavin did not love the woman who was his wife—in fact, he found talking to her infuriating—but never had he known such uninhibited passion.

Judith saw Raine coming toward them. He was dressed in full armor for the joust. The steel was etched with tiny gold fleurs-de-lis. He carried his helmet under his arm, and he walked as if he were used to the enormous weight of the armor. And he was.

Judith did not realize she dropped her hand from Gavin's arm when she recognized her brother-in-law. Raine came toward her quickly, a dimpled smile on his face, a smile that had turned many feminine knees to water.

"Hello, my little sister," he grinned down at her. "This morning I thought I had dreamed such beauty, but I see you are more than I remembered."

She was delighted. "And you make the day brighter. Will you enter the events?" She nodded toward the sand-covered field.

"Both Miles and I will take part in the joust."

Neither of them seemed to be aware of Gavin as he scowled at them.

"And these ribbons I see the men wearing," Judith said. "What do they mean?"

"A lady may choose a knight of her favor and give him a token."

"Then I may give you a ribbon?" She smiled at him.

Raine was immediately on one knee before her, the hinges

of the armor creaking, steel against steel clanging. "I would be honored."

Judith lifted the transparent veil that covered her hair and took one of the gold ribbons from a braid. It was obvious that her maids had known about the giving of favors to a knight.

Raine smiled at her as he put his hand on his hip and she tied the ribbon around his upper arm. Before she finished, Miles walked to the other side of her and knelt also. "You would not favor one brother over the other, would you?"

Today, when she looked at Miles, she understood what other women had understood about him since he had his first beard. Yesterday she had been a virgin and had not known the meaning of his intense gaze. She blushed prettily and bent her head to slip another ribbon around her other brother's arm.

Raine saw the blush and began to laugh. "Don't start on her, Miles," he laughed, for Miles's women were a common joke about the Montgomery castle. Stephen, the second brother, once complained that Miles had impregnated half the serf girls by the time he was seventeen, the other half by eighteen. "Don't you see Gavin glaring at us?"

"I see both of you making fools of yourselves," Gavin said with a snarl. "There are other women here. Go find one of them to parade yourselves before like braying jackasses."

Judith had barely finished tying the knot of the ribbon on Miles before Gavin's fingers bit into her arm and he forced her away. "You're hurting me!" she said, trying to pry his fingers loose but making no progress.

"I will more than hurt you if you flaunt yourself before other men again."

"Flaunt!" she jerked her arm but only succeeded in tightening Gavin's grip. All around her were knights kneeling to ladies, receiving ribbons, belts, sleeves of gowns, even jewels, and yet he accused her of flaunting herself. "A dishonest person always believes dishonesty of others. Maybe you seek to accuse me of your own faults."

He stopped and stared at her, his eyes dark. "I accuse you

only of what I know to be true. You're hot for a man, and I will not have you playing the whore for my brothers. Now sit here and cause no more strife among us." He turned on his heel and stalked away, leaving Judith alone in the stands garlanded with the Montgomery crest.

For a moment, Judith's senses did not function; she could neither see nor hear. What Gavin said was unjust and she could have dismissed it as such, except that he'd thrown in her face what they did in private—that she could not forgive. Had she done wrong in responding to his touch? If so, how did one stop? She could barely remember the events of the night. It was all one delicious red-velvet blur to her. His hands on her body had sent waves of delight through her; after that, she recalled little. Yet he threw it at her as if she were unclean. She blinked back tears of frustration. She was right to hate him.

She mounted the steps to enter the Montgomery seats. Her husband had left her alone to meet his relatives. Judith held her head high and refused to let anyone see that tears were beginning to well.

"Lady Judith."

A soft voice finally penetrated her senses, and she turned to see an older woman dressed in the somber habit of a nun.

"I would like to introduce myself. I met you yesterday, but I am not sure you will remember. I am Gavin's sister, Mary." Mary was staring at her brother's back. It was not like Gavin to walk away and leave a woman unattended. All four of her brothers—Gavin, Stephen, Raine and Miles—were extremely courteous. Yet Gavin had not smiled once at his bride, and although he did not participate in the games, he went to the tents. Mary could not understand him at all.

Gavin walked through the crowds to the tents at the end of the lists. Many people slapped him on the back and gave him knowing winks. The closer he got to the tents, the louder came the familiar clang of iron and steel. He hoped that the sanity of mock war would calm him.

He held his shoulders back, kept his eyes straight ahead.

No one would have guessed the blind rage that filled him. She was a bitch! A conniving, masterful bitch! All he could think was that he wanted to beat her and make love to her at the same time. He had stood there and watched as she smiled so sweetly at his brothers; yet when she looked at him, it was as if he were something detestable.

And all he could think of was the way she'd been with him during the night. She had kissed him greedily, held him to her hungrily, but only after he had forced her to come to him. He'd raped her once, used the pain of her hair twisted around his arm to command her to him the second time. Even the third time, he had had to act against her initial protest. Yet she laughed and gave his brothers gold ribbons—gold like her eyes. If she gave such passion to him whom she freely admitted she hated, what would she be like with a man she liked? He had watched her with Raine and Miles, imagined them touching her, kissing her. Suddenly it was all Gavin could do to keep from knocking her to the ground. He wanted to hurt her, and he had. At least there was some satisfaction in that, except that he got no pleasure from it. In truth, the expression on her face only made him more furious. The damn woman had no right to look at him so coldly.

Angrily, he threw back the flap of Miles's tent. Since Miles was on the field, it should have been empty, but it wasn't. Alice stood there, her eyes sedately lowered, her little mouth submissive. She was a welcome relief to Gavin, who'd had too much in the last day of a woman who snarled at him then drove him insane with her body. Alice was what a woman should be—calm, a subordinate to a man. Without thought, he grabbed her, kissing her violently. He enjoyed it when she melted in his arms. She offered no resistance, and he was glad of that.

Alice had never seen Gavin in such a mood, and she silently thanked whoever was responsible. Yet, for all her desire, she was no fool. A tournament was too public, especially when so many of Gavin's relatives camped nearby. "Gavin," she whispered against his lips, "this is neither the place nor the time."

He pulled away from her immediately, feeling that at that moment he could not stand another reluctant female. "Go then!" he stormed as he left the tent.

Alice looked after him, a frown creasing her smooth brow. Obviously, the pleasure of bedding his new wife had not turned him from herself, as she feared it might. But still he was not the Gavin she knew.

Walter Demari could not take his eyes off Judith. She sat quietly in the Montgomery pavilion, listening attentively to her new relatives as they welcomed her to the family. Every minute since he'd first seen her, when she left the castle to ride to the church, he had watched her. He'd seen Judith slip away to the walled garden behind the tower, seen the look on her face when she returned. He felt as if he knew her, and more than that . . . he loved her. He loved the way she walked, with her head up, her chin firm, as if she were ready to face the world no matter what lay ahead. He loved her eyes, her little nose.

He'd spent the night alone, thinking of her, imagining her as his.

Now, after a sleepless night, he began to wonder why she was not his. His family was as rich as that of the Montgomeries and more. He'd been a frequent visitor to the Revedoune manor, a friend to Judith's brothers.

Robert Revedoune had just purchased a lapful of fried wafers from one of the vendors and was holding a mug of verjuice.

Walter did not hesitate or take time to explain what had become a burning issue to him. "Why didn't you offer the girl to me?" he demanded, towering over the seated man.

Robert looked up in surprise. "What ails you, boy? You should be on the field with the other men."

Walter sat down and ran his hand through his hair. He was not an unattractive man, but neither was he handsome. He had eyes of a nondescript blue and a too-prominent nose. His lips were thin, shapeless, and could easily be cruel. His sandy hair was carefully curled into a tight little roll about his neck. "The girl, your daughter," he repeated. "Why didn't you offer her to me? I spent enough time with your sons. I'm not rich, but my estates rival those of Gavin Montgomery."

Robert shrugged, eating a wafer, the jelly oozing out between the crisp layers, and drinking deeply of the sour verjuice. "There are other rich women for you," he observed noncommittally.

"But not like her!" Walter responded vehemently.

Robert looked at him in surprise.

"Can't you see she is beautiful?" Walter asked.

Robert looked across the pavilions that separated him from his daughter. "Yes, I see she is beautiful," he said with disgust. "But what is beauty? It fades in no time. Her mother once looked like that, and you see her now."

Walter did not have to look back at the nervous, emaciated woman who sat on the edge of her seat, ready to spring should her husband decide to cuff her. He ignored Robert's remark. "Why did you keep her hidden? What need was there to keep her from the world?"

"It was her mother's idea." Robert smiled slightly. "She paid for the keeping of the girl, and it made no difference to me. Why do you ask me these things now? Can't you see the joust is about to begin?"

Walter grabbed Robert by the arm. He knew the man well, knew him for the cowardice of his actions. "Because I want her. Never have I seen a woman more desirable. She should have been mine! My lands ajoin yours. I am a fit match for her, yet you did not even show her to me."

Robert pulled his arm away from the young man. "You! A fit match?" he sneered. "Look at the Montgomeries that surround the girl. There is Thomas, nearly sixty years old. He has six sons, all living, and all producing more sons. Next to him sits Ralph, his cousin, with five sons. Then Hugh with—"

"What has this to do with your daughter?" Walter interrupted angrily.

"Sons!" Robert bellowed in the man's ear. "The Montgomeries produce more sons that any other family in England. And what sons! Look at the family the girl married into. The youngest, Miles, won his spurs on the field of battle before he was eighteen, and already he has fathered three sons of the serf girls. Raine spent three years touring the country from one tournament to the next. He was undefeated and won a fortune of his own. Stephen serves now in Scotland with the king, and already he leads armies though he is only twenty-five. And last comes the eldest. At sixteen he was left alone with estates to run, brothers to care for. He had no guardian to help him learn the work of a man. What other sixteen-year-olds could do as he did? Most of them whine when they are not given their way."

He looked back at Walter. "And now you ask why I give Judith to such a man? If I cannot produce sons that are strong enough to live, perhaps I can get grandsons from her."

Walter was furious. He'd lost Judith merely because the old man dreamed of grandsons. "I could give her sons!" Walter said through clenched teeth.

"You!" Robert began to laugh. "How many sisters do you have? Five? Six? I lose count of them. And what have you done? Your father runs your estates. You do little, except hunt and tickle the serf girls. Now leave me and don't cry to me again. If I have a mare I want bred, I give her to the best stallion. It will be left at that." He turned back to look at the joust, dismissing Walter from his mind.

But Demari was not a man to be dismissed so easily. Everything Robert said was true. Walter had done little of merit in his short life, but that was only because he had not been forced to as the Montgomery men had been. Walter had no doubt that had he been forced, by the early death of his father, into a position of responsibility, he would have done as well or better than any other man.

He left the stands a changed man. A seed had been planted in his mind and that seed began to grow. He watched the games begin, the gold Montgomery leopard everywhere, and as he saw it glitter in the sun, he began to think of it as an enemy. He wanted to prove to Robert and to the Montgomeries, but mostly to himself, that he was everything they were. The longer he stared at the green and gold pennants, the more he was sure he hated the Montgomeries. What had they done to deserve the rich Revedoune lands? Why should they have what should have been his? For years he'd suffered the company of Judith's brothers, yet had never taken anything in return. Now, when there was something he wanted and should have had, he was denied it because of the Montgomeries.

Walter left the fence and started walking toward the Montgomery pavilion. The growing anger at the injustice he felt gave him courage. He would talk to this Judith, spend time with her. After all, by rights, she was his, wasn't she?

Chapter 8

JUDITH SLAMMED shut her chamber door so hard that even the stone walls seemed to shake. It was the end of the first day of her marriage, and it could easily qualify as the most horrible day of her life. It should have been happy, a day full of love and laughter—but not with the husband she had! There had not been an opportunity missed by Gavin to humiliate her.

In the morning he accused her of being a whore for his brothers. When he stalked away and left her to herself, she talked to other people. One man, Walter Demari, was kind enough to sit by her and explain the workings of the tourney. For the first time that day, she began to enjoy herself. Walter had a knack for seeking the ridiculous, and she greatly enjoyed his humor.

Gavin suddenly reappeared and commanded her to follow him. Judith didn't want to cause a scene in public, but in the privacy of Raine's tent, she told Gavin what she thought of his behavior. He left her alone to take care of herself, but when she showed any enjoyment, he took it away from her. He was like a small boy with a toy he didn't want but made sure no one else could have it. He'd sneered at Judith then, but she saw with satisfaction that he had no answer for her.

When Raine and Miles came in she and Gavin stopped their quarrel. Later, she walked with Miles back to the tourney. It was then that Gavin truly demeaned her. As soon as

Alice Valence appeared, he practically ran forward. Gavin looked as if he could eat her, devour her, yet at the same time he looked at her with reverence, as if she were saintly. Judith had not missed the sidelong look of triumph Alice gave her. Judith pulled her eyes away, straightened her back and took Miles's arm. She would let no one see how she'd been publicly embarrassed.

Later, at dinner, Gavin ignored Judith, even though they were seated side by side at the high table. She laughed at the jester, pretended to be pleased when an extremely handsome jongleur composed and sang a song to her beauty. Truthfully, she hardly heard him. Gavin's nearness had an unsettling effect on her, and she could enjoy nothing.

After the meal, the trestle tables were dismantled and pushed against the wall to make room for dancing. After one dance together, for the sake of propriety, Gavin had proceeded to whirl one woman after another in his arms. Judith had more invitations to dance than she could accept, but soon she pleaded fatigue and ran up the stairs to the privacy of her room.

"A bath," she demanded of Joan, whom she'd dragged from a corner of the stairwell where she was intertwined with a young man. "Bring a tub and hot water. Maybe I can wash away some of today's stench."

Contrary to what Judith believed, Gavin had been very aware of his wife's presence. There had not been a moment when he had not known where she was or whom she was with. It seemed she had talked for hours to some man at the tourney. She laughed at his every word, smiling up at him until the man was obviously besotted.

Gavin had pulled her away for her own good. He knew Judith had no idea how she affected a man. She was like a child. Everything was new to her. She looked up at the man with nothing hidden, nothing held in reserve. She laughed openly at what he said, and Gavin could see the man took her friendliness for more than she meant it to be.

Gavin meant to explain this to her, but when she attacked him, accusing him of all manner of insulting things, he would have died rather than explain his actions. He'd feared that he might wrap his hands about her lovely throat. At least Alice's brief appearance had calmed him. Alice was like a cool drink for a man just stepped from the rages of hell.

Now as he held his hands on the fat hips of an unattractive young woman, he watched Judith mount the steps. He did not dance with her, afraid he might apologize. For what? he wondered. He'd been kind to Judith until that time in the garden when she'd started acting insane, making vows she had no right to make. He was right in taking her away from the man who obviously thought her smiles meant more than they did, but she made Gavin feel as if he were wrong.

He waited a while, danced with two more women, but Judith did not return to the great hall. Impatiently, he climbed the stairs. In those brief seconds, he imagined all sorts of things she could be doing.

When he opened the door to the chamber Judith lay up to her neck in a tub of steamy water. Her auburn hair was piled atop her head in a soft mass of curls. Her eyes were closed, her head resting on the rim of the tub. The water must have been very hot because her face was lightly dampened with sweat. All his muscles froze at the sight of her. She had frowned at him, raged at him and even then she was magnificent, but now she was innocence personified. Suddenly he knew that this was what he wanted from her, this was all he needed. What did it matter that she despised him? She was his and his alone. His heart was pounding as he closed the door behind him.

"Joan?" Judith said languidly. Receiving no answer, her eyes flew open. She saw the look on Gavin's face and knew his thoughts. In spite of herself, her heart began beating quickly. "Leave me to my privacy," she managed to whisper.

He ignored her as he advanced, his dark eyes grown darker. He bent over her, took her chin in his hand. She tried to pull away but he held her fast. He kissed her, roughly at first but then his grip and kiss became gentle, deep.

Judith felt herself drifting. The pleasure of the hot water, his hand on her cheek, his kiss, weakened her. He pulled away from her and looked into her eyes, the gold warm and glowing. All thoughts of hatred were gone from them. There was only the nearness of their bodies. Their hunger for each other overcame any hostility or even thoughts of who loved whom.

Gavin knelt by the tub, his hand moving to the back of Judith's neck. He kissed her again, ran his mouth along the curve of her neck. She was moist and warm and the rising steam was like his growing passion. He was ready, but he wanted to prolong his pleasure, drag it out to the height of near-pain. Her ears were sweet and smelled of the rose-scented soap she used.

Suddenly he wanted to see her—all of her. Gavin put his hands under Judith's arms and lifted her. She gasped at the unexpected movement, at the coolness of the air after the heat of the water. A soft, warm towel hung within arm's reach, which Gavin wrapped her in. Judith did not speak. Somewhere, buried in her mind, was the knowledge that words would break the spell. He touched her tenderly—no harsh demands, no bruising. He sat on a bench before the fire and stood her between his legs as if she were a child.

Had someone spoken of such a scene, Judith would have denied that it could happen, that Gavin was an insensitive brute. She felt no embarrassment by her nudity while he remained fully clothed, only wonder at the magic of the moment. Gavid dried her carefully. He was a bit clumsy, too rough at times, too gentle at others.

"Turn," he commanded and she obeyed as he dried her back. He tossed the towel to the floor and Judith held her breath. But he did not speak. Then he ran his fingers down the deep indentation of her spine. She could feel the chills his touch brought. His one finger said more than a hundred caresses.

"You are beautiful," he whispered throatily as he placed his palms on the curve of her hips. "So very beautiful."

She did not breathe, even when she felt his lips on the side of her neck. His hands moved so torturously slow to her stomach, across her ribs and up to her breasts, which waited for him, begged for him. She released her pent-up breath and leaned back against him, her head resting against his shoulder, his mouth still on her neck. He ran his hands over her, touching her skin, exploring her body.

When Judith was nearly insane with desire, he carried her to the bed. In seconds, his clothes were on the floor and he was beside her. She pulled him to her, sought his mouth. He laughed at her grasping hands, teasing her, but there was no ridicule in his gray eyes. There was only the wish for prolonging their pleasure. A sparkle came to her eyes, and she knew she would have the last laugh. Her hands moved downward. When she found what she sought, there was no more laughter in his eyes. They were black with passion as he pushed her down beside him.

It was only moments before they cried out together, both released from their sweet torment. Judith felt drained, her bones weak as Gavin moved partially away, though his leg was still across hers, his arm across her breasts. She sighed deeply just before falling asleep.

Judith woke the next morning, stretching like a cat after a nap. Her arm slid across the sheet only to meet emptiness. Her eyes flew open. Gavin was gone and by the sun streaming through the window, it was late morning. Her first thought was to hurry outside, but the warm bed and the memory of last night kept her where she was. Judith turned to her side, ran her hand over the indented place beside her, buried her face in his pillow. It still smelled of Gavin. How quickly she'd come to know his scent.

She smiled dreamily. Last night had been heaven. She remembered Gavin's eyes, his mouth—he filled her every vision.

A soft knock on the door sent her heart beating, then calmed abruptly when Joan opened it.

"You were awake?" Joan asked, a knowing smile on her face.

Judith felt too good to take offense.

"Lord Gavin rose early. He arms himself."

"Arms himself!" Judith sat bolt upright in the bed.

"He only wishes to join the games. I don't understand why; as the bridegroom, he doesn't have to."

Judith lay back against the pillow. She understood. This morning she could have soared from the top of the keep and come only lightly to earth. She knew Gavin must feel the same. The joust was a way to expend his energy.

She threw back the covers and jumped from the bed. "I must dress. It is late. You don't think we could have missed him?"

"No," Joan laughed. "We won't miss him."

Judith dressed quickly in a gown of indigo blue velvet with an underskirt of light blue silk. About her waist was a thin belt of soft blue leather studded with pearls.

Joan merely combed her mistress's hair and put a transparent blue gauze veil edged in seed pearls on it. It was held in place by a braided circlet of pearls.

"I'm ready," Judith said impatiently.

Judith walked rapidly to the tourney grounds and took her place in the Montgomery pavilion. Judith's thoughts were at war with each other. Had she imagined last night? Had it been a dream? Gavin had made love to her. There was no other word for it. Of course she was very inexperienced, but could a man touch a woman as he touched her and not feel something for her? The day seemed brighter suddenly. Maybe she was a fool, but she was willing to try to make something of this marriage.

Judith craned her neck to see the end of the tourney field, to catch a glimpse of her husband, but there were too many people and horses in the way.

Quietly, Judith left the stands and walked toward the tents. She stopped along the outer fence, oblivious to the serfs and merchants who crowded about her. It was some minutes before she saw him. Gavin in normal attire was a powerful man, but Gavin in full armor was formidable. He mounted an enormous war-horse of dark gray, its trappings of green serge, green leather stamped and painted with golden leopards. He swung easily into the saddle, as if the hundred pounds of armor weighed nothing. She watched as his squire handed him his helmet, his shield, and finally his lance.

Judith's heart leaped to her throat and nearly choked her. There was danger in this game. She watched breathlessly as Gavin charged forward on his great horse, his head lowered, his arm braced against the lance. His lance struck the opponent's shield squarely just as his own shield was hit. The lances broke and the men rode to opposite ends of the field to obtain new ones. Fortunately, the lances used in battle were stronger than the wooden ones used in games. The object was to break three lances without losing the stirrups. If a man was unseated before three runs were made, he had to pay the worth of his horse and armor to his adversary—no trifling sum. Thus had Raine made a fortune on the tournament circuit.

But men did get hurt. Accidents happened constantly. Judith knew this and she watched fearfully as Gavin rode again, and again neither man lost his stirrups.

A woman near Judith giggled, but she paid no attention until words reached her. "Her husband is the only man who carries no favor—yet she gives gold ribbons to his brothers. What do you think of such a hoyden?"

The words were malicious and meant for Judith's ears; yet, when she turned, no one showed any interest in her. She looked back at the knights who walked among the horses or stood at the end of the field near her. What the woman said was true. All the knights had ribbons or sleeves waving from their lances or helmets. Raine and Miles had several, and on one arm they each wore a frayed gold ribbon.

Judith only meant to run across the edge of the field and catch Gavin before he charged his opponent for the third time. She was new to the joust and had no idea that what she did was dangerous. The war-horses, bred for strength, size and endurance, were trained to help a man in times of war. They could use their great hooves to kill as easily as a man used a sword.

She did not hear the gasps as man after man pulled his horse back from her racing figure. Neither was she aware that several of the people in the stands had seen her and now stood, their breaths held.

Gavin looked up from his squire as he was handed a new lance. He could feel the gradual hush come over the crowd. He saw Judith immediately and realized there was nothing he could do. By the time he dismounted, she would have reached him. He stared, every muscle rigid.

Judith had no ribbon to give him but she knew he must have a favor from her. He was *hers!* She pulled off her gossamer veil as she ran across the sand, slipping the braid of pearls back over her hair.

When she reached Gavin she held up the veil for him. "A favor," she smiled tentatively.

He did not move for a moment then lifted his lance and held it down beside her. Quickly, Judith knotted a corner of the veil securely above the shaft. When she looked up at him and smiled, he leaned forward, put his hand behind her head and nearly lifted her from the ground as he kissed her. The nosepiece of the helmet was cold against her cheek and his kiss was hard. When he released her to sink back on her heels in the sand, she was dazed.

Judith was unaware of the suddenly quiet crowd, but not so Gavin. His bride had risked her life to give him a favor, and now he held his lance high—in triumph. His grin seemed to reach from one side of the helmet to the other.

The crowd's roar of approval was deafening.

Judith whirled, saw that every eye was upon her. Her cheeks flamed and her hands covered her face. Miles and Raine ran from the sidelines, threw their arms protectively around her and half-carried her to safety.

"If you hadn't pleased Gavin so much, I would turn you over my knee for that," Raine said.

Another cheer went up as Gavin unhorsed his opponent. Judith did not enjoy being the center of so much laughing. She picked up her skirts and made her way as quickly as possible back to the castle. Perhaps a few minutes alone in the garden would help her cheeks return to their normal color.

* * *

Alice slammed into the tent of the Earl of Bayham, a rich place of silk walls and Byzantine carpets erected for the comfort of Edmund Chatworth.

"Something is wrong?" a deep voice behind her asked.

Alice whirled to glare at Roger, Edmund's younger brother. He sat on a low bench, his shirt removed as he carefully ran the edge of his sword along a whetstone he turned with his foot. He was a handsome man, blond hair streaked by the sun, a straight aquiline nose, a firm mouth. There was a curved scar by his left eye that in no way detracted from his good looks.

Many times Alice wished Roger were the earl instead of Edmund. She started to answer his question, then stopped. She could not tell him of her anger as she saw Gavin's wife making a spectacle of herself in front of several hundred people. Alice had offered him a favor, but he would not take it. Gavin said there was too much talk of them already, and he would not cause more.

"You play with fire, you know," Roger said as he ran his thumb along the edge of the sword. When Alice made no comment, he continued. "The Montgomery men do not see things as we do. To them right is right and wrong is wrong. There is nothing in between."

"I have no idea what you mean," Alice responded haughtily.

"Gavin will not be pleased when he finds you have lied to him."

"I have not lied!"

Roger raised one eyebrow. "And what reason did you give him for marrying my brother the earl?"

Alice sat down heavily on a bench opposite Roger.

"You didn't think the heiress would be so beautiful, did you?"

Alice's eyes blazed as she looked up at him. "She is not beautiful! Her hair is red and she is sure to be covered with freckles." She smiled snidely. "I must ask what cream she uses to cover them on her face. Gavin will not think her so desirable when he sees—"

Roger cut her off. "I was at the bedding ceremony and saw a great deal of her body. There were no freckles. Don't delude yourself. Do you think you can hold him when he is alone with her?"

Alice stood and walked to the tent flap. She would not let Roger see how the words upset her. She *must* keep Gavin. At all costs, she must keep him. He loved her, deeply and sincerely, as no one had ever loved her. She needed that as much as she needed Edmund's wealth. She did not let people see inside her; she hid her hurt well. As a child she'd been a beautiful daughter born among a gaggle of ugly, sickly sisters. Her mother gave all her love to the others, feeling Alice had enough attention from her nurses and the castle visitors. Scorned by her mother, Alice turned to her father for love. But the only thing Nicolas Valence cared for came from a bottle. So Alice learned to take what was not given to her. She manipulated her father into buying rich clothes for her, and her enhanced beauty made her sisters' hate for her stronger. Besides her elderly maid, Ela, no one loved her, until Gavin. Yet all the years of struggling, trying to obtain even a few pennies, made her desire financial security as much as love. Gavin was not wealthy enough to give her that security, but Edmund was.

Now, one-half of what she needed was being taken from her by a red-haired witch. Alice was not one to sit back and let the future take care of itself. She would fight for what she wanted . . .

"Where is Edmund?" she asked Roger.

He nodded his head to the linen partition across the back of the tent. "Asleep. Too much wine and too much food," he said in disgust. "Go to him. He will need someone to hold his sick head."

"Easy, brother!" Raine commanded Miles. "His head is sore enough without banging it against a tent pole."

They carried Gavin on his shield, his legs hanging off the edge, his feet dragging in the dirt. He had just finished un-horsing his second opponent when the man's lance slipped upward, just before he fell. The blow caught Gavin just above his ear. It was a hard blow which dented his helmet. Gavin saw only blackness and heard a ringing in his head that drowned all other noise. He managed to stay in his saddle, more from training than strength, as his horse turned and went back to the end of the field. Gavin looked down at his brothers and his squire, gave a sickly smile, then slowly fell into their uplifted arms.

Now Raine and Miles transferred their brother to a cot inside their tent. They removed the damaged helmet and put a pillow beneath his head.

"I will fetch a leech," Raine said to his brother. "And you find his wife. There is nothing a woman likes more than a helpless man."

Several minutes later, Gavin began to regain consciousness. Cool water was being pressed on his hot face. Cool hands touched his cheek. He was dazed when he opened his eyes. His head roared. At first he couldn't remember whom he saw.

"It is I, Alice," she whispered. He was glad there were no loud noises. "I have come to care for you."

He smiled a bit and closed his eyes again. There was something he should remember, but couldn't.

Alice saw that in his right hand he still clutched the veil Judith had given him. Even as he fell from his horse, he'd managed to loosen it from his lance. She didn't like what that seemed to signify.

"Is he badly hurt?" a woman asked anxiously outside the tent.

Alice leaned forward and pressed her lips to Gavin's unresponsive ones, guiding his arm till it went about her waist.

The light from the opened tent on his face and the pressure on his lips made Gavin open his eyes. His senses came back to him then. He saw his wife, flanked by the scowling figures of his brothers, staring at him as he embraced Alice. He pushed her away and tried to sit up. "Judith," he whispered.

All the color drained from her face. Her eyes were dark

and enormous. And the look she gave him was again of hatred. Then, suddenly, it changed to one of coldness.

The quick change of pressure in his injured skull as he tried to sit up was too much for Gavin. The pain was unbearable. Gratefully, everything went black. He fell heavily back onto the pillow.

Judith turned quickly on her heel and left the tent, Miles close beside her, as if she needed protection from some evilness.

Raine's face was dark when he looked back at his brother. "You bastard—" he began, then stopped when he saw Gavin was again unconscious. Raine turned to Alice, who looked up at him triumphantly. He grabbed her upper arm and pulled her to her feet. "You planned this!" he sneered. "God! How can I have such a fool for a brother? You're not worth one of Judith's tears, yet I think you have already caused her many."

Raine was further enraged when he saw a slight smile at the corner of her mouth. Without thought, he drew back his arm and slapped Alice with the back of his hand. He did not release her arm. When she looked back at him, Raine drew his breath in sharply at what he saw. Alice was not angry. Instead, she stared at his mouth. There was the unmistakable fire of passion in her eyes.

He was shocked and disgusted as he'd never been in his life. He threw her against a tent pole so hard she could scarcely draw her breath. "Get away from me!" he said quietly. "And fear for your life if our paths ever cross again."

When she was gone, Raine turned back to his brother, who was beginning to move again. A leech who came to attend to Gavin's sore head, stood shaking in the corner of the tent. The anger of one of the Montgomeries was no pretty sight.

Raine spoke to the man over his shoulder. "See to him—and if you have any treatment that will cause him more pain, use it." He turned and left the tent.

It was night when Gavin woke from a deep, drugged sleep, induced by something the leech made him drink. The tent was dark and he was alone. Gingerly, he swung his legs over the edge of the cot and sat up. His head felt as if someone had made a deep cut from one corner of his eye, across the back of his head to the other eye, and now the two halves were being pulled apart. He propped his head in his hands, closing his eyes against the awful ache.

Gradually, Gavin was able to open them. His first thought was that it was odd that he was alone. He would have thought either his squire or his brothers would be with him. He straightened his back and was aware of a new pain. He had slept several hours in his armor, and every hinge, every ridge had imprinted itself, through leather and felt, into his skin. Why had his squire not undressed him? Usually the boy was very conscientious.

Something on the floor caught his eye and he bent and lifted Judith's blue veil. He smiled as he touched it, remembering clearly how she'd run toward him, smiling, her hair flowing behind her. He'd never been so proud in his life as when she handed him the favor, although he'd held his breath when she came so near the war-horses. He ran his fingers across the border of seed pearls, held the gauze against his cheek. He could almost smell the scent of her hair, but of course that was impossible after the veil had been next to his sweaty horse. He thought of her face when he looked down at her. Now, that was a face worth fighting for!

Then Gavin seemed to remember it changing. He dropped his head back in his hands. There were pieces of the puzzle missing. His head hurt so much that it was difficult to remember. He could see a different Judith—not smiling, not snarling as she had the first night of their marriage, but a Judith who looked at him as if he no longer existed. It was a struggle to fit all the pieces together. Gradually, he remembered the lance hitting his head, then someone speaking to him.

Suddenly it was all clear. Judith had seen him holding Alice. It was strange that he could not remember wanting Alice's comforting.

It took all Gavin's effort to stand. He had to remove his armor. He was too tired and weak to walk while weighed down so heavily. No matter how much his head hurt, he had to find Judith and talk to her.

Two hours later, Gavin stood inside the great hall. He'd looked everywhere for his wife but could not find her. Every step caused him more pain until now he was nearly blind with the constant ache and the weariness of fighting it.

Through a haze, he saw Helen as she carried a tray of drinks to some guests. When she returned, he pulled her to a darkened corner of the hall. "Where is she?" he asked in a hoarse whisper.

Helen's eyes blazed at him. "You ask me now where she is?" she sneered at him. "You have hurt her, as all men hurt women. I tried to save her from this. I told her all men were vile, evil creatures not to be trusted—but she wouldn't listen. No, she defended you and what did it earn her? I saw her lip on her wedding night. You beat her before you even bedded her. And this morning many people saw your brother throw that Valence whore—your whore—from your tent. I would die before I told you! Better I had killed us both before I gave Judith to such as you."

If his mother-in-law said any more, Gavin did not hear her. He was already walking away.

He found Judith, minutes later, sitting beside Miles on a bench in the garden. Gavin ignored his younger brother's malevolent scowl. He didn't want to argue. All he wanted was to be alone with Judith, to hold her as he had last night. Perhaps then his head would stop throbbing.

"Come inside," he said quietly, each word difficult.

She rose immediately. "Yes, my lord."

He frowned slightly and held his arm out for her but she did not seem to see it. He slowed for her to walk beside him but she still walked a bit behind him and to one side. He led them into the manor and up to their room.

After the noise of the great hall, the chamber was a haven, and he sank onto a cushioned bench to take off his boots. He looked up to see Judith standing at the foot of the bed, unmoving. "Why do you stare at me so?"

"I am waiting for your command, my lord."

"My command?" he frowned, for all the movement hurt his pounding head. "Then undress yourself for bed." He was puzzled by her. Why didn't she rage at him? He could have handled her anger.

"Yes, my lord," Judith answered. Her voice was a monotone.

When he was undressed, Gavin went slowly to the bed. Judith was already there, the covers to her neck, her eyes staring up at the canopy. He climbed under the covers and moved close to her. Her skin against his was soothing. He ran his hand down her arm but Judith did not react. He leaned over, began to kiss her but her eyes did not close and her lips were unresponsive.

"What ails you?" Gavin demanded.

"Ails me, my lord?" she said evenly, looking steadily into his eyes. "I don't know what you mean. I am yours to command, as you have told me often enough. Tell me your wish and I will obey. Do you wish to mate with me? Then I will obey." She moved her thigh against his and it took Gavin a few minutes to realize that she had spread her legs for him.

He stared at her, aghast. He knew crudity was not natural to her. "Judith," he began, "I wanted to explain about this morning. I—"

"Explain, my lord? What must you explain to me? Do you explain your actions to the serfs? I am yours no less than they are. Just tell me how I may obey you and I will."

Gavin began to move away from her. He did not like the way Judith looked at him. At least, when she hated him, there had been life in her eyes. Now there was none. He left the bed. Before he knew what he did, he pulled on doublet and boots, his other clothes thrown over his arm, and left the cold chamber.

Chapter 9

THE MONTGOMERY castle was silent as Judith left the big, empty bed and slipped her arms into a mink-lined, emerald-green velvet bedrobe. It was very early morning, and the castlefolk were not awake yet. Since Gavin had dumped her on the doorstep of his family estate, Judith had hardly been able to sleep. The bed seemed too large and too empty to give her much peace.

The morning after Judith refused to respond to his love-making, Gavin had demanded they depart for his home. Judith had obeyed, speaking to him only when necessary. They traveled for two days before reaching the Montgomery gates.

Upon entering the castle, she had been impressed. The guards on top of the two massive towers that flanked the gate had challenged them even though they could see the Montgomery leopards flying. The draw-bridge was lowered over the wide, deep moat and the heavy spiked portcullis was raised. The outer bailey was lined with modest, neat houses, stables, the armorer, the mews, and storage sheds. Another gate had to be unlocked before they entered the inner bailey where Gavin and his brothers lived. The house was four stories with mullioned glass windows in the top floor. A bricked courtyard was in the center, and Judith could see a garden with fruit trees just blooming behind a low wall.

She wanted to tell Gavin what she thought of his stewardship, but he had not given her a chance. He had done little more than give a few orders then abandoned her amid the baggage. It was up to Judith to introduce herself to the retainers.

During the past week, Judith had become very familiar with the Montgomery castle, and had found it a joyful place to work. The servants had no objections to a woman's direction. She buried herself in tasks and tried hard not to think of her husband's affair with Alice Valence. Most of the time Judith was successful. Only at night did her loneliness haunt her.

A noise in the courtyard made her run to the window. It was too early for the servants to be about, and only a Montgomery would be allowed through the smaller back gate. The light was too dim to tell who was dismounting the horses below.

She flew down the stairs to the great hall.

"Be careful, man," Raine bellowed. "Do you think I am made of iron that I can stand so much banging about?"

Judith stopped at the foot of the stairs. Her brother-in-law was being carried into the room, feet first, one leg heavily bandaged. "Raine, whatever has happened to you?"

"Cursed horse!" he said through clenched teeth. "It can't see where it is going even on the brightest of days."

She went to him as his men set him down in a chair by the empty fireplace. "Am I to understand that your horse caused this?" she smiled.

Raine stopped frowning, his cheeks beginning to dimple. "Well, maybe it was partly my own fault. He stepped into a hole and threw me. I came down on my leg and it snapped under me."

Judith immediately knelt and began to unwrap his foot which was propped on a stool.

"What are you doing?" he asked sharply. "The leech has already set it."

"I don't trust him and will see for myself. If it isn't set straight, it could leave you lame."

Raine stared at the top of her head then called to his man. "Fetch me a glass of wine. I'm sure she won't be satisfied until she causes me more agony. And fetch my brother. Why should he sleep when we are awake?"

"He isn't here," Judith said quietly.

"Who isn't here?"

"Your brother. My husband," Judith said flatly.

"Where did he go? What business called him away?"

"I am afraid I don't know. He set me on the doorstep and left. He didn't speak to me of any matter that needed his attention."

Raine took the cup of wine his vassal held for him and watched his sister-in-law as she probed the bone of his leg. At least the pain kept him from giving full vent to the anger he felt for his brother. He had no doubt that Gavin had left his beautiful bride to go to that whore, Alice. His teeth clamped down on the rim of the cup as Judith touched the break.

"It is only a little out of line," she observed. "You hold his shoulders," she said to one of the men behind Raine, "and I will pull the leg."

The heavy sendal of the tent was coated with water. Fat droplets collected on the ceiling and as the rain outside jarred the tent, the water dripped down.

Gavin swore loudly as more water hit his face. Since he'd left Judith, it had done little but rain. There was nothing that was not wet. And worse than the water was the tempers of his men—blacker even than the sky. They had been roaming the countryside for well over a week, camping in a different place each night. Their food was hastily prepared in between cloudbursts and consequently was usually half raw. When John Bassett, Gavin's chief vassal, had asked his master the reason for the meandering journey, Gavin had exploded. John's level look of sarcasm made Gavin avoid his men.

He knew his men were miserable; he was himself. But at least he knew the reason for the seemingly pointless trip. Or did he? That night at Judith's father's house, when she'd been so cold to him, he decided to teach her a lesson. She felt secure in a place where she'd spent her life, surrounded by friends and family. But would she dare to act so disagreeably when she was alone in a strange household?

It worked out well when his brothers decided to leave the newly wedded couple alone. In spite of the rain dripping through the sendal of the tent, he began to smile at an imagined scene. He could see her facing some crisis—perhaps something cataclysmic, such as the cook burning a pot of beans. She would be frantic with worry, would send a messenger for him, to beg him to return and save her from disaster. The messenger would not be able to find his master since Gavin was not at any of his estates. More calamities would occur. When Gavin returned, he would find a tearful, repentant Judith who would fall into his arms, grateful to see him again, relieved that he'd come to save her from a fate worse than death.

"Oh yes," he said, smiling. All the rain and discomfort would be worth it. He would talk sternly to her and when she was completely contrite, he would kiss away her tears and carry her to their bed.

"My lord?"

"What is it?" Gavin snapped as the delicious vision was interrupted, just when he was about to imagine what he'd allow Judith to do in the bedroom, in order to obtain his forgiveness.

"We were wondering, sir, when we were to go home and get out of this cursed rain."

Gavin started to growl that it was not the man's business, then closed his mouth. He began to smile. "We will return tomorrow." Judith had been alone for eight days. That was time enough for her to learn some gratitude . . . and humility.

"Please, Judith," Raine pleaded as he grabbed her forearm. "I have been here two days, yet you have not given me a moment of your time."

"That isn't true," she laughed. "Only last evening I spent an hour with you at the chessboard, and you showed me some chords on the lute."

"I know," he said, still pleading, but dimples appearing

on his cheeks, although he didn't smile. "It's just so awful here alone. I can't move for this cursed leg, and there is no one to keep me company."

"No one! There are over three hundred people here. Surely one of them—" She broke off as Raine looked at her with such sad eyes that she laughed. "All right, but only one game. I have work to do."

Raine gave her a dazzling smile as she went to the other side of the chessboard. "You are the best at the game. None of my men can beat me as you did last night. Besides, you need a rest. What do you do all day?"

"Put the castle to rights," Judith responded simply.

"It always seemed to me to be in order," he said as he moved a pawn forward. "The stewards—"

"The stewards!" she said sharply as she maneuvered her bishop to attack. "They don't care as does one who owns an estate. They must be watched, their figures checked, their journals read and—"

"Read? Do you read, Judith?"

She looked up in surprise, her hand on her queen. "But of course. Don't you?"

Raine shrugged. "I never learned. My brothers did, but it didn't interest me. I have never known a woman who could read. My father said women couldn't learn to read."

Judith looked at him in disgust as her queen put his king in mortal danger. "I think you should learn that a woman can often best a man, even a king. I believe I have won the game." She stood.

Raine stared at the board in wonder. "You can't have won so soon! I didn't even see it. You kept me talking so that I couldn't concentrate." He gave her a look from the corner of his eye. "And my leg pains me so that it's hard for me to think."

Judith looked at him with concern for a moment, then began to laugh. "Raine, you are a liar of the first water. Now I must go."

"No, Judith," he said as he lunged and grabbed her hand and began to kiss it. "Judith, don't leave me," he begged. "In truth, I am so bored I may go mad. Please stay with me. Just one more game."

Judith was laughing very hard at him. She placed her other hand on his hair as he began making outrageous promises of undying love and gratitude if she would only stay with him an hour longer.

And that was how Gavin found them. He had forgotten his wife's beauty by half. She was not dressed in the velvets and sables she had worn at their marriage, but in a simple, clinging gown of soft blue wool. Her hair was pulled back into one long, thick auburn braid. If anything, the plain garment made her even more lovely than before. She was innocence, yet the lush curves of her body showed her to be all woman.

Judith became aware of her husband's presence first. The smile on her face died immediately and her entire body stiffened.

Raine felt the tension in her hand and looked up at her questioningly. He followed the direction of her eyes and saw his scowling brother. There was no doubt as to what Gavin thought of the scene. Judith started to pull her hand away from Raine's grasp, but he held it firmly. He would not give the impression of a guilty man to his angry brother. "I have been trying to persuade Judith to spend the morning with me," Raine said lightly. "I have been confined to this room for two days with nothing to do, but I can't persuade her to give me more of her time."

"And no doubt you have tried every persuasion," Gavin sneered, his look directed at his wife who stared at him coldly.

Judith jerked her hand away from Raine. "I must return to my work," she said stiffly, as she left the room.

Raine attacked first before Gavin had a chance to do so. "Where have you been?" he demanded. "Only three days married, and you drop her on the doorstep like so much baggage."

"She seems to have handled the situation well," Gavin said as he sank heavily into a chair.

"If you hint at something dishonorable—"

"No, I don't," Gavin said honestly. He knew his brothers well, and Raine would not dishonor his sister-in-law. It was just a shock after what he had expected . . . and hoped . . . to find awaiting him. "What happened to your leg?"

Raine was embarrassed to confess falling from his horse, but Gavin didn't laugh as he usually would have. Wearily, Gavin lifted himself from the chair. "I must see to my castle. I have been away a long time and I'm sure it's close to falling down about my ears."

"I wouldn't count on that," Raine said as he studied the chessboard, going over each of Judith's moves in his head. "I've never seen a woman work as Judith does."

"Bah!" Gavin said condescendingly. "How much woman's work can one do in a week? Embroider five ells of cloth?"

Raine looked up at his brother in surprise. "I didn't say she did woman's work, I said I haven't seen a woman work as she does."

Gavin didn't understand, but neither did he press Raine for an explanation. As the lord, Gavin had too much to do. The castle always seemed to flounder mightily after he'd been away for a while.

Raine knew his brother's thoughts and called after him. "I hope you find something that needs doing," he laughed.

Gavin had no idea what his brother was talking about and dismissed the words as he left the manor house. He was still angry that the scene he'd dreamed had been destroyed. But at least, there was hope. Judith would be glad he had returned to solve all the problems that had developed in his absence.

When Gavin rode through the baileys that morning, he had been so anxious to get to his weeping wife that he hadn't noticed any changes. Now he observed subtle alterations. The half-timbered buildings in the outer bailey looked cleaner— almost new, in fact, as if they'd been recently chinked and whitewashed. The gutters that ran along the back of the buildings looked as if they'd been emptied recently.

He stopped in front of the mews. Here the falcons were kept—merlins, peregrines, sparrow hawks, tiercels. His falconer stood in front of the building, a hawk tied by the leg to a post, while the man slowly swung a lure about the bird.

"Is that a new lure, Simon?" Gavin asked.

"Yes, my lord. It's a bit smaller and can be swung faster. The bird is forced to fly faster, and its aim must be truer."

"Good idea," Gavin agreed.

"It's not mine, sir, but the Lady Judith's. She made the suggestion."

Gavin stared. "The Lady Judith told you, a master falconer, of a better lure?"

"Yes, my lord," Simon grinned, revealing two missing teeth. "I'm not so old as I don't know a good idea when I hear one. The lady's as smart as she is lovely. Came down here first morning she was here and watched me for a long time. Then, just sweet as can be, she made a few suggestions. Come inside, my lord, and see the new perches I made. Lady Judith said the old ones was the cause of the birds' sore feet. She said tiny mites get in them and hurt the birds."

Simon started to lead the way into the building, but Gavin didn't follow. "Don't you want to see?" Simon asked sadly.

Gavin hadn't recovered from the fact that his grizzled falconer had taken advice from a woman. Gavin had tried to make hundreds of recommendations to Simon, as his father had, but to their knowledge, Simon had never done what either man wanted. "No," Gavin said, "I'll see later what changes my wife has made." He could not keep the sarcasm from his voice as he turned on his heel. What right did the woman have to interfere with his mews? Certainly women liked hawking as well as men, and certainly Judith would have her own hawk—but the care of the mews was a man's work.

"My lord!" a serf girl called, then blushed when Gavin looked at her so fiercely.

She curtsied and held out a mug to him. "I thought perhaps you'd like some refreshment."

Gavin smiled at the girl. Here at least was a woman who knew how to act properly. He looked into her eyes as he sipped; then his attention was drawn to the drink. It was delicious! "What is this?"

"It's the spring's strawberries and the juice of last year's apples after they are boiled, then a bit of cinnamon."

"Cinnamon?"

"Yes, my lord. The Lady Judith brought it with her from her home."

Gavin abruptly thrust the empty mug back at the girl and turned away. Now he was truly starting to get annoyed. Had everyone gone mad? Quickly, he made his way to the far end of the bailey, to his armorer's. At least in that hot place of forged iron he would be safe from a woman's interference.

The sight that greeted him was shocking. His armorer, an enormous man, naked from the waist up, muscles bulging from his arms, sat quietly by a window—sewing. "What is this?" Gavin demanded angrily, suspicious already.

The man smiled and held up two small pieces of leather. It was a design for a new hinge that could be used on a knight's armor. "See, the way this is made, the hinge is much more flexible. Clever, isn't it?"

Gavin clenched his jaw tightly. "And where did you get this new idea?"

"Why, from the Lady Judith," the armorer answered, then shrugged when Gavin stormed from the shed.

How dare she! he thought. Who was she to interfere in what was his, to make change after change without so much as asking his approval? These estates were *his!* If any changes were to be made, they were to be made by him.

He found Judith in the pantry, a vast room attached to the kitchen, kept separate from the house for fear of fire. She was buried, head and shoulders, inside an enormous bin of flour. Her auburn hair was unmistakable. He stood close to her, taking full advantage of his height.

"What have you done to my home?" he bellowed.

Instantly, Judith came out of the bin, narrowly missing banging her head on the cover. In spite of Gavin's height and his loud voice, she was not afraid of him. Until her wedding less than two weeks ago, she had never been near a man who wasn't angry. "Your home?" she answered in a deadly voice.

"And pray, what am I? The kitchen maid?" she asked as she held out her arms, covered in flour to her elbows.

They were surrounded by castle servants who backed against the walls in fear, but who would not have missed such a fascinating scene for anything.

"You know damn well who you are, but I will not have you interfering in my business. You have altered too many things—my falconer, even my armorer. You are to tend to your own business and not to *mine!*"

Judith glared up at him. "Then pray tell me what I'm to do if I'm not to speak to the falconer or whoever else needs advisement."

Gavin was puzzled for a moment. "Why, women's things. You are to see to women's things. Sew. See that the maids cook and clean and . . . make face creams." He felt the last suggestion was inspired.

Judith's cheeks blazed, her eyes glittering with little splinters of golden glass. "Face creams!" she snarled. "So now I am ugly and need face creams! Perhaps I should also make lash darkeners and rouges for my pale cheeks."

Gavin was bewildered. "I didn't say you were ugly, just that you are not to set my armorer to sewing."

Judith's jaw was set firmly. "Then I will not do so again. I will let your armor stay stiff and cumbersome before I talk to the man again. What else may I do to please you?"

Gavin stared at her. The argument was not going his way at all. "The mews," he said weakly.

"Then I will let your birds die of soft feet. Is there anything else?"

He stood there dumbly with no answer for her.

"Now I assume we understand each other, my lord," Judith continued. "I am not to protect your hands, I am to let your birds die, and I am to spend my days concocting face creams to cover my ugliness."

Gavin grabbed her by the upper arm and lifted her from the floor so that they faced each other. "Damn you, Judith, you are not ugly! You are the most beautiful woman I have ever seen." He stared at her mouth, so close to his.

Her eyes softened and her voice was sweeter than honey. "Then I may set my poor brain to something besides beauty enhancers?"

"Yes," he whispered, weakened by the nearness of her.

"Good," she said firmly. "Then there is a new arrowhead I should like to talk with the armorer about."

Gavin blinked in astonishment, then set her on the floor so hard her teeth jarred together. "You will not—" He broke off as he stared at her defiant eyes:

"Yes, my lord?"

He stormed from the kitchen.

Raine sat in the shade of the castle wall, his bandaged leg thrust before him, sipping Judith's new cinnamon drink and eating rolls still warm from the oven. Every now and then he tried to suppress a chuckle as he watched his brother. Gavin's wrath was apparent in his every move. He rode his horse as if a demon chased him and thrust his lance viciously through the stuffed quintain that represented his foe.

Already the fight in the pantry was being told and retold. In another day it would reach the king in London. In spite of his mirth, Raine felt sorry for his brother. He'd been bested publicly by a bit of a girl.

"Gavin," he called. "Give the animal a rest and come sit awhile."

Reluctantly, Gavin did as his brother bid when he realized that his horse was covered with foam. He threw the reins to his waiting squire and walked tiredly to sit beside his brother.

"Have a drink," Raine offered.

Gavin started to take the mug then stopped. "Her new drink?"

Raine shook his head at his brother's tone. "Yes, Judith made it."

Gavin turned to his squire. "Fetch me some beer from the cellar," he commanded.

Raine started to speak then saw his brother's eyes strain across the courtyard. Judith walked from the manor house, across the sand-covered training field toward the line of war-horses tethered at the edge. Gavin's eyes watched her hotly; then, as she stopped by the horses, he started to rise.

Raine grabbed his brother's arm and pulled him down to the seat again. "Let her alone. You'll only start another quarrel which you will no doubt lose again."

Gavin started to speak, then stopped when his squire handed him a mug of beer.

When the boy was gone, Raine spoke again. "Don't you do anything except bellow at the woman?"

"I don't—" Gavin began, then stopped and gulped more beer.

"Look at her and tell me one thing that is wrong with her. She is beautiful enough to rival the sun. She works all day to set your home to rights. She has every man, woman and child, including Simon, eating from her hand. Even the war-horses dantily take apples from her palm. She is a woman of humor, and she plays the best damn game of chess in England. What more could you want?"

Gavin had not taken his eyes from her. "What do I know of her humor?" he said bleakly. "She has never even called me by my name."

"And why should she?" Raine demanded. "When have you ever so much as said a kind word to her? I don't understand you. I have seen you woo serf girls with more ardor. Doesn't a beauty like Judith deserve sweet words?"

Gavin turned on him. "I am not a simpleton to be told by a younger brother how to pleasure a woman. I was in women's beds when you were with your wet nurse."

Raine did not reply but his eyes were dancing. He refrained from mentioning that there were only four years' difference in their ages.

Gavin left his brother and went to the manor house where he called for a bath to be prepared. As he sat in the hot water, he had time to think. As much as he hated to admit it, Raine was right. Perhaps Judith did have a reason to be cool to him. Their marriage had started on the wrong foot. It was too bad he had had to strike her on their first night, too bad she had entered his tent at the wrong time.

But that was over now. Gavin remembered how she said he would get nothing from her but what he took. He smiled as he lathered his arms. He'd spent two nights with her and knew she was a woman of great passion. How long could she keep from his bed? Raine was right, too, when he mentioned his brother's ability to woo a woman. Two years ago, he'd made a wager with Raine about a certain icy countess. In a surprisingly short time Gavin had climbed into her bed. Was there a woman he could not win when he set his mind to it? It would be a pleasure to bring his haughty wife to heel. He would be sweet to her, court her until she begged him to come to her bed.

Then, he thought, nearly laughing aloud, she would be his. He would own her and she would never again interfere in his life. He would have everything he wanted—Alice to love and Judith to warm his bed.

Clean and dressed in fresh clothes, Gavin felt as if he were a new man. He was elated at the idea of trying to seduce his lovely wife. He found her in the stables, precariously suspended from a high rail of a stall gate, talking soothingly to one of the war-horses as the farrier cleaned and trimmed an overgrown hoof. Gavin's first thought was to tell her to go away from the beast before she was hurt. Then he relaxed. She was very good with horses.

"He's not an animal that is easily tamed," he said quietly as he went to stand beside her. "You have a way with horses, Judith."

She turned to him with a suspicious look.

The horse felt her tension and jumped, the farrier barely able to move before the hoof struck him. "Hold him still, my lady," the man ordered without looking back. "I have more to do and I can't get it done if he prances about."

Gavin started to open his mouth to ask the man what right he had to speak to his mistress in such a tone, but Judith didn't seem to take offense at the man's words.

"I will, William," she said as she held the horse's bridle

firmly and stroked the soft nose. "You weren't hurt were you?"

"No," the farrier answered gruffly. "There! It's done now." He turned to Gavin. "My lord! Were you about to say something?"

"Yes. Do you always order your mistress about as you did just now?"

William turned red.

"Only when I need to be ordered about," Judith snapped. "Please go, William, and see to the other animals."

He obeyed instantly. Judith looked defiantly at Gavin. Instead of the anger she expected, he smiled.

"No, Judith," he said. "I didn't come to quarrel with you."

"I didn't know there was anything else between us."

He winced, then reached out and caught her hand, pulling her reluctantly after him. "I came to ask if I could present you with a gift. See the stallion in the far stall?" he asked and pointed as he dropped her hand.

"The dark one? I know him well."

"When you came from your father's house, you brought no horse of your own."

"My father would rather part with all the gold he owned than one of his horses," she said, referring to the wagonloads of portable wealth that had accompanied her to the Montgomery estate.

Gavin leaned against the gate of an empty stall. "That stallion has produced some beautiful mares. They are kept on a demesne farm some distance away. I thought perhaps tomorrow you would go with me and choose one for your own."

Judith didn't understand his sudden kindness, nor did she like it. "There are palfreys here that are sufficient for my needs," she said evenly.

Gavin was quiet for a moment, watching her. "Do you hate me so much, or do you fear me?"

"I do not fear you!" Judith said, her back as straight as an iron rod.

"Then you will go with me?"

She stared into his eyes then nodded curtly.

He smiled at her—a genuine smile—and Judith unexpectedly remembered what seemed a long time ago; their wedding day, when he had smiled at her often.

"Then I will look forward to tomorrow," he said before leaving the stables.

Judith stared after him, frowning. What did he want from her now? What reason did he have for giving her a gift? She did not puzzle over the matter for long, for there was too much work to be done. The fishpond was a place she had neglected, and it desperately needed cleaning.

Chapter 10

THE GREAT hall of the manor house was alive with the flickering light from the fireplaces. Some of the more favored of the Montgomery men were playing cards, dice, chess, cleaning weapons or simply lounging. Judith and Raine sat alone at the opposite end of the room.

"Please play the song, Raine," Judith begged. "You know I am no good at music. Didn't I say so this morning, and that I would play a game of chess with you?"

"And would you like for me to play a song the length of your game?" He strummed two chords on the fat-bellied lute. "There, I'm sure I've played as long as you did," he teased.

"It's not my fault you were beaten so quickly. You use your men only to attack and don't protect yourself from the attack of others."

Raine stared, his mouth open, then began to laugh. "Is this a bit of wisdom I hear, or an unadorned insult?"

"Raine," Judith began, "you know exactly what I mean. I would like for you to play for me."

Raine smiled down at her, the firelight gleaming on her auburn hair, the wool dress showing off her tantalizing body. But her beauty wasn't what threatened to drive him insane. Beauty was sometimes found even in the serfs. No, it was Judith herself. He had never met a woman with her honesty, her logic, her intelligence. If she were a man . . . He smiled. If she were a man, he wouldn't be in such danger of falling hopelessly in love with her. He knew he had to get away from Judith soon even though his leg was only half-healed.

Raine glanced over her head and saw Gavin leaning against the door frame, watching his wife's profile illuminated by the flames. "Here, Gavin," he called. "Come and play for your wife. I find this leg pains me too much to enjoy anything. I have been giving Judith lessons, but she is no good at all." His eyes twinkled as he looked down at his sister-in-law, but she merely stared at her hands which were clasped in her lap.

Gavin strode forward. "I'm glad to hear there is something that my wife doesn't do to perfection," he laughed. "Do you know that today she had the fishpond cleaned? I hear the men found a Norman castle at the bottom of it." He stopped when Judith stood.

"You must pardon me," she said quietly. "I find I am more tired than I knew, and I wish to retire." Without another word, she left the hall.

Gavin, the smile gone from his face, sank into a cushioned chair.

Raine looked at his brother with sympathy. "Tomorrow I must return to my own estates."

If Gavin heard, he made no acknowledgment.

Raine signaled to one of the servants to help him to his chamber.

Judith glanced about the bedchamber with new eyes. No longer was it hers alone. Now her husband had come home, and he had the right to share it with her. Share the room, share the bed, share her body. She undressed hastily and climbed beneath the sheets. She'd dismissed her maids earlier, wanting some solitude. Although Judith was tired after the day's activities, she stared at the linen canopy with open eyes. After a long while, she heard footsteps outside the door. She held her breath for a long moment then hesitantly the footsteps retreated. She was glad, of course, Judith told herself, but that didn't warm the cold bed. Why should Gavin want her, she thought as quick tears came to her eyes. No doubt he'd spent the last week with his beloved Alice. No doubt his passion was completely spent and he wanted no more from his wife.

In spite of her thoughts, her fatigue from the long day eventually conspired to make her sleep.

She awoke very early. It was still dark in the room; only the faintest light came through the shutters. The entire castle was still asleep, and Judith found the silence pleasant. She knew she could not sleep longer, nor did she want to. This still-dark time of the morning was her favorite.

She quickly dressed in a simple gown of finely woven dark blue wool called perse. Her soft leather slippers made no sound on the wooden steps or as she walked through the sleeping men in the great hall. Outside, the light was dark gray but her eyes quickly adjusted. Beside the manor house was a little walled garden. It had been one of the first things Judith had seen at her new home and one of the last she felt she could give her attention to. There were rows of roses, a great variety of color, their blooms almost hidden beneath dead stems on the long-neglected bushes.

The fragrance in the cool early morning air was heady. Judith smiled as she bent over one of the bushes. The other work had been necessary, but the pruning of the roses was a labor of love.

"They belonged to my mother."

Judith gasped at the voice so near her. She had heard no one approach.

"Everywhere she went, she collected slips of other people's roses," Gavin continued as he knelt beside Judith, touching one of the blooms.

The time and the place seemed otherworldly. She could almost forget that she hated him. She turned back to her pruning. "Your mother died when you were small?" she asked quietly.

"Yes. Too small. Miles hardly knew her."

"And your father didn't remarry?"

"He spent the rest of his life mourning her, what little time was left to him. He died only three years after her. I was only sixteen."

Judith had never heard him sound so sad before. Truthfully, she had heard little in Gavin's voice except anger. "You were very young to have been left with the running of your father's estates."

"A year younger than you, yet you seem to run this property well. Far better than I did, or have done since." There was admiration in his voice, yet a bit of hurt also.

"But I was trained for this work," she said quickly. "You were trained only as a knight. It would have been harder for you to learn what to do."

"I was told you were trained for the church." He was surprised.

"Yes," Judith said as she moved to another bush. "My mother wished for me to escape a life such as she has known. She spent her girlhood in a nunnery and was very happy there. It was only when she married that—" Judith stopped, not wanting to finish the sentence.

"I don't understand how life in a nunnery could prepare you for what you've done here. I would have thought you spent your days in prayer."

She smiled down at him as he sat in the gravel path beside her. It was getting lighter now, the sky beginning to turn a rosy pink. She could hear the clatter of the servants in the distance. "Most men feel that the worst thing that could happen to a woman would be to deprive them of a man's company. I assure you that a nun's life is far from empty. Look at St. Anne's. Who do you think runs those estates?"

"I never thought about it."

"The prioress manages estates that make the king's look poor. Yours and mine together could fit into a corner of St. Anne's. My mother took me to meet the prioress last year. I spent a week at her side. She is a constantly busy woman ordering the work of thousands of men and acres of land. She does not"—Judith's eyes sparkled—"have time for woman's work."

Gavin was startled for a moment then he began to laugh. "A thrust well delivered." What had Raine said about her sense of humor? "I stand corrected."

"I'd think you'd know more about a nunnery since your sister lives there."

A special glow came over Gavin's face when his sister was mentioned. He smiled. "I cannot imagine Mary running anyone's estates. Even as a child, she was so sweet and shy that she seemed of another world."

"And so you let her enter a convent."

"It was her wish, and when I inherited from my father, she left us. I wanted her to remain here and not marry if she didn't want to, but she wanted to be near the sisters."

Gavin stared at his wife, thinking that she had come very close to spending her life in a convent. The sunlight caught fire in her auburn hair; the way she looked at him, without anger or hatred, made his breath catch.

"Ow!" Judith broke the spell as she looked down at her finger, nicked on a rose thorn.

"Let me see," Gavin said as he took her small hand in his larger one. He brushed away a drop of blood from her fingertip then raised it to his lips, as he looked into her eyes.

"Good morning!"

Both of them looked up at the window above the garden.

"I hate to disturb your lovemaking," Raine called down from the manor house, "but my men seem to have forgotten me. And with this damned leg, I am little more than a prisoner."

Judith pulled her hand from Gavin's and looked away, her cheeks, for some reason, flushing.

"I will go and help him," Gavin said as he stood. "Raine says he is leaving today. Maybe I can hurry him along. Will you ride with me this morning to choose a mare?"

She nodded her head but didn't look at him before he left the garden.

"I see you're making some progress with your wife," Raine said as Gavin roughly helped him down the stairs.

"It would have been more if someone hadn't started bellowing out the window," Gavin remarked bitterly.

Raine snorted with laughter. His leg hurt and he didn't

look forward to the long journey to another estate, so he was in a bad mood. "You didn't even spend the night with her."

"Of what concern is that to you? Since when do you notice where I sleep?"

"Since I met Judith."

"Raine, if you—"

"Don't even say it. Why do you think I am going when my leg hasn't even begun to heal?"

Gavin smiled. "She is lovely, isn't she? In a few days I will have her eating out of my hand; then you'll see where I sleep. A woman is like a hawk. You must starve it until it is eager for food; then it will be easily tamed."

Raine stopped on the stairs, his arm about Gavin's shoulder. "You are a fool, brother. You may be the biggest fool ever created. Don't you know that the master is often the servant of his hawk? How many times have you seen men carry their favorite hawk about on their wrists, even in church?"

"You talk nonsense," Gavin said, "and I don't like being called a fool."

Raine set his teeth together as Gavin jerked his leg. "Judith is worth two of you and a hundred of that icy bitch you think you love."

Gavin stopped at the foot of the steps, gave his brother a malevolent look and moved away so quickly Raine had to grab the wall to keep from falling. "Don't you speak of Alice again!" Gavin said in a deadly voice.

"I damned well will speak of her! Someone needs to. She is ruining your life and Judith's happiness. And Alice isn't worth a strand of Judith's hair."

Gavin raised his fist then dropped it. "It's good that you're leaving today. I won't listen to anymore about my women from you." He turned on his heel and stalked away.

"Your women!" Raine called after him. "One owns your soul and the other you treat with contempt. How can you call them *yours?*"

Chapter 11

THERE WERE ten horses inside the fenced area. Each one was sleek and strong with long legs that inspired visions of the animals running across flowery fields.

"I am to choose one, my lord?" Judith asked as she leaned across the fence rail. She looked up at Gavin beside her, watching him suspiciously. All morning he had been exceptionally pleasant; first in the garden, and now as he gave her a gift. He'd helped her on the mount, taken her arm when she, in an unladylike gesture, climbed atop the rails. She could understand his irritation, his scowls, but she was quite leery of this new kindness.

"Any one that you want," Gavin answered, smiling at her. "They have all been gentled and are ready for a bridle and saddle. Do you see one you like?"

She looked back at the horses. "There isn't one I don't like. It's not easy to choose. I think that one, the black one."

Gavin smiled at her choice, a mare with a high-stepping, dainty gait. "She is yours," he said. Then, before he could help her down, Judith was on the ground and through the gate. Within minutes, Gavin's man had the mare saddled and Judith swung onto her animal's back.

It felt wonderful to ride a good horse again. To Judith's right lay the road to the castle; to her left, the dense forest, a hunting ground for the Montgomeries. Without thought, she took the road to the forest. For too long she had been confined inside walls and jammed between people. The great oaks and beeches looked inviting, their branches connecting overhead to form a private shelter. Judith did not look back to see if she was being followed, but only plunged ahead toward the waiting freedom.

She rode hard, testing the mare and herself. They were compatible, as she knew they would be. The horse enjoyed the run as much as Judith.

"Quiet now, sweet one," Judith whispered when they were well inside the forest. The mare obeyed, daintily picking her way between the trees and bushes. The ground was covered by ferns and hundreds of years of accumulated foliage. It was a soft carpet and a silent one. Judith breathed deeply of the clean, cool air and let her mount decide the way.

The sound of running water caught Judith's attention, as well as her mare's. A stream, deep and cool, ran swiftly between the trees, sunlight playing through the overhanging branches. She dismounted and led her horse to the water. As the mare quietly drank, Judith pulled handfuls of sweet grass and began to rub the sides of the horse. They had galloped hard for several minutes before reaching the forest, and the mare was sweaty.

Judith was engrossed in her pleasant task, glorying in her horse, the day, the roaring water. The mare perked up her ears and listened, then backed away nervously.

"Quiet, girl," Judith said, stroking the soft neck. The horse took another, sharper step backward, threw her head back and neighed. Judith whirled, grabbing at the reins of the frightened animal and missed.

A wild boar approached, sniffing the air. It was wounded, its tiny eyes glassy with pain. Judith tried again to get the reins of her horse but the boar began its charge and the mare, wild with fear, took off. She grabbed her skirts and began to run. But the charging pig was faster than she. Judith made a running leap at a low-hanging tree branch, caught it and began to pull herself up. Strong from a lifetime of work and exercise, she swung her legs to another branch just as the boar reached her. It was no easy task to keep herself on the tree as the crazed boar charged and recharged the trunk at her feet.

Finally, Judith was able to stand on the lowest branch while holding onto another one above her head. As she looked down at the boar, she realized she was very high off the ground. She stared with sightless fear, her knuckles turning white as she grasped the overhead branch with all her strength.

"We must spread out," Gavin ordered his man, John Bassett. "There's not enough of us to go in pairs, and she couldn't have gone far." Gavin tried to keep his voice level. He was angry at his wife for galloping away on a strange horse into a forest unknown to her. He'd stood with the horses and his men, watching her ride away. He expected that as soon as she reached the edge of the woods, she would return. It took him a moment to realize that Judith was going into the forest.

Now he could not find her. It was as if she'd vanished, swallowed by the trees. "John, you go north, around the edge of the trees. Odo, take the south. I'll try the center."

Inside, the forest was quiet. Gavin listened carefully for any sign of her. He'd spent a great deal of his life here and knew every inch of the woods. He knew the mare would probably head for the stream that ran through its center. He called Judith several times, but there was no answer.

Then his stallion pricked up his ears. "What is it, boy?" Gavin questioned, listening hard. The horse took a step backward, his nostrils flaring. The animal was trained in hunting, and Gavin recognized the signals. "Not now," he said. "Later we'll look for game."

The horse didn't seem to understand, but pulled his head down against the reins. Gavin frowned then let him have his head. He heard the sound of the boar rooting at the base of the tree before he saw it. He would have led his mount around the beast had his eye not caught sight of a bit of blue in the tree above.

"God's teeth!" he whispered as he realized Judith was

pinned in the tree. "Judith!" he called but got no answer. "You'll be safe in a moment."

His horse put its head down in anticipation of the charge, while Gavin drew his longsword from the scabbard on the side of the saddle. The stallion, well trained, ran very close to the boar and Gavin leaned half out of the saddle, his powerful thighs gripping hard as he bent and sent the sword through the animal's spine. It squealed once and kicked before it died.

Gavin jumped quickly from the saddle and retrieved the weapon. He looked up at Judith and was astonished at the sheer terror on her face. "Judith, it's all right now. The boar is dead. He can't hurt you." Her terror seemed out of reason with the danger. She had been safe enough in the tree.

She didn't answer but kept staring at the ground, her body as rigid as his iron lance.

"Judith!" he said sharply. "Are you hurt?"

Still she neither answered nor acknowledged his presence.

"It's only a short jump," he said as he held his arms up for her. "Let go of the branch above and I'll catch you."

She didn't move.

Gavin was puzzled as he looked again at the dead boar, then up at his terrified wife. Something besides the pig frightened her. "Judith," he said quietly and moved so he was in the line of her vacant stare. "Is it the high place that frightens you?" He wasn't sure, but she seemed to move her head in a tiny nod. Gavin grabbed the lowest branch near her feet and easily swung himself up beside her. He put his arm about her waist, but she gave no hint that she was aware of him.

"Judith, listen to me," he said calmly and quietly. "I'm going to take your hands and lower you to the ground. You must trust me. Don't be *afraid*." He had to pry her hands loose and she grabbed onto both of his hands in panic. Gavin braced himself against a branch, and lowered Judith to the ground.

Her feet had no sooner touched the earth than he jumped down beside her. She was trembling as he pulled her into his arms. She clutched at him fiercely, desperately. "Hush, now," he whispered as he stroked her head. "You're safe now." Judith's trembling didn't stop, and Gavin felt her knees give way. He lifted her into his arms, and carried her to a tree stump, where he sat and held her as if she were a child. He'd had little experience with women outside of bed and none with children, but he knew her fear was extraordinary.

He held Judith tightly, as tightly as he could without crushing her. He smoothed her hair away from her cheek where she'd begun to perspire, her face hot. He rocked her and held her even closer. Had someone told him that being only a few feet off the ground could cause such terror, he would have laughed, but now he didn't find it amusing. Judith's fear was very real and his heart went out to her, that she should suffer so. Her small body was shaking, her heart beating as wildly as a bird's and he knew he must make her feel safe again. Gavin began to sing, quietly at first, not really paying attention to the words. His voice was rich and soothing. He sang a love song, of a man returning from the Crusades to find his true love waiting for him.

Gradually, he felt Judith begin to relax against him, the awful trembling subsiding. Her hold on him loosened, but Gavin didn't release her. He smiled and kissed her temple as he hummed the tune. Her breathing became more even until she lifted her head from his shoulder. She pushed away, but he held her firmly, not wanting to release her. Judith's need of him was oddly reassuring, although Gavin would have said he didn't like clinging women.

"You will think that I'm a fool," she said softly.

He didn't answer.

"I don't like high places," Judith continued.

He smiled and hugged her to him. "I guessed that," he laughed. "Though I would say that 'like' was a mild word. Why are you so afraid of high places?" He was laughing now, glad that she had recovered. Gavin was startled when she stiffened. "What have I said? Don't be angry."

"I'm not," she said sadly, relaxing again, comfortable in his arms. "I don't like to think of my father—that's all."

Gavin pushed her head back to his shoulder. "Tell me about it," he said seriously.

Judith was quiet for a moment, then when she did speak, he could hardly hear her. "Actually, I remember little of it— only the fear remains with me. My maids told me of it many years later. I was three years old and something disturbed my sleep. I left the room and went to the great hall, which was alive with light and music. My father was there with his friends and all of them were drunk." Her voice was cold, as if she told a story about someone else.

"When my father saw me, he seemed to think it a great joke. He called for a ladder and carried me, under his arm, to the top of it and set me on a high windowsill, well above the hall. As I said, I remember none of this. My father and his friends fell asleep, and in the morning the maids searched for me. It was a long time before they found me, though I must have heard them call. It seems I was too frightened to speak."

Gavin stroked her hair and began to rock her again. The thought of a man setting a three-year-old child twenty feet above the floor, then leaving her all night, made his stomach turn over. He grabbed her shoulders and held Judith away from him. "But you are safe now. See, the ground is quite near."

She gave him a tentative smile. "You have been good to me. Thank you."

Her thanks did not please him. It saddened Gavin that she had been so harshly used in her short life that she felt her husband's comforting was a gift. "You have not seen my woods. What do you say we stay here awhile?"

"But there is work—"

"You are a demon for work. Don't you ever play?"

"I'm not sure I know how," she responded honestly.

"Well, today you will learn. Today shall be for picking wildflowers and watching the birds mate." He wiggled his eyebrows at her and Judith gave a very un-Judith-like giggle. Gavin was enchanted. Her eyes were warm, her lips sweetly curved, and her beauty was an intoxicating sight. "Then come," he said as he lifted her to set her on her feet. "There is a hillside nearby that is covered with flowers and some rather extraordinary birds."

When Judith's feet touched the ground, her left ankle buckled beneath her. She grabbed Gavin's arm for support.

"You're hurt," he said as he knelt to look at her ankle. He turned and saw Judith bite her lip. "We'll put it in the cold stream water. That should keep it from swelling." He swept her into his arms.

"I can walk if you'll help me a bit."

"And have my knighthood taken from me? We are taught, you know, in the ways of courtly love. The rules are quite firm about beautiful ladies in distress. They must be carried whenever possible."

"Then I am only a means to further your knightly status?" Judith asked seriously.

"Of course, since you are a great burden to tote about. You must weigh as much as my horse."

"I do not!" she protested vehemently then saw his eyes were sparkling. "You're teasing me!"

"Didn't I say the day was for merriment?"

She smiled and leaned against his shoulder. It was pleasant to be held so close.

Gavin set her at the edge of the stream, then carefully removed her shoe. "The hose must go," he smirked. He watched with delight as Judith raised the skirt of her long gown to reveal the top of her hose, tied with a garter just above the knee. "If you need assistance . . ." he leered as she rolled the silk tube off her leg.

Judith watched Gavin as he gently bathed her foot in the cold water. Who was this man who touched her so gently? He could not be the man who had slapped her, who had flaunted his mistress before her, who had raped her on their marriage night.

"It doesn't seem to be hurt badly," he said as he looked back at her.

"No, it doesn't," she said quietly.

A sudden breeze blew a lock of hair across her eyes. Gently, Gavin brushed it away. "What do you say I build a fire and we roast that hideous pig?"

She smiled at him. "That would be pleasant."

He scooped her from the bank, then tossed her playfully in the air. She grabbed his neck in fright. "I could grow to like this fear of yours," he laughed, as he pressed her to him. He carried her across the stream to a hill which was indeed covered with wildflowers, and built a fire under an overhanging rock ledge. In minutes he returned with a dressed haunch of the boar and set it to roasting over the fire. He wouldn't let Judith move or help in any way. When the meat was cooking and there was a plentiful supply of firewood, Gavin left her again and returned in moments with his tabard raised about his hips, as if he carried something.

"Close your eyes," he said, and when she obeyed, he showered her with flowers. "You can't go to them, so they must come to you."

She looked at him, her lap and the ground around her covered in a riot of sweet-smelling blossoms. "Thank you, my lord," she said, smiling brilliantly.

He sat down beside her, one hand behind his back, leaning close to her. "I have another gift," he said as he held out three fragile columbines to her.

They were beautiful, delicate things of light violet and white. She reached to take them but he moved them from her grasp. She looked at him in surprise.

"They're not free." He was teasing her again, but the expression on her face showed him she didn't know it. He felt a pang of remorse that he had hurt her so badly that she should look at him so. Suddenly Gavin wondered if he were any better than her father. He ran a finger lightly down her cheek. "It's a small price to pay," he said gently. "I would like to hear you call me by my name."

Her eyes cleared and were warm again. "Gavin," she said quietly as he handed her the flowers. "Thank you, my . . . Gavin for the flowers."

He sighed lazily and leaned back on the grass, his hands behind his head. "My Gavin!" he repeated. "It has a nice sound to it." He moved one hand and idly twisted a curl of her hair about his palm. Her back was to him as she gathered the flowers around and put them into a bouquet. Ever orderly, he thought.

Unexpectedly, it occurred to him that it had been years since he'd had a peaceful day on his own lands. Always the responsibility of the castle had nagged at him, but in a few days his wife had so ordered matters that he could lie about in the grass and think of little but the sound of honeybees and the silky texture of a beautiful woman's hair.

"Were you really angry about Simon?" Judith asked.

Gavin could barely remember who Simon was. "No," he smiled. "I just didn't like a woman to accomplish what I couldn't. And I'm not so sure that this new lure is better."

She whirled to face him. "It is! Simon agreed instantly. I'm sure the hawks will catch more game now and—" She stopped when she saw him laughing at her. "You are a vain man."

"I?" Gavin asked, bracing himself upon his elbows. "I am the least vain of men."

"Haven't you just said you were angry because a woman did what you couldn't?"

"Oh," Gavin said as he relaxed back on the grass, his eyes shut. "That's not the same. A man is always surprised when a woman does anything but sew and manage children."

"You!" Judith said in disgust then grabbed a handful of grass with a clod of dirt attached to it and threw it in his face.

He opened his eyes in surprise then pulled the grime from his mouth. His eyes narrowed. "You will pay for that," he said as he stealthily moved toward her.

Judith backed away, fearful of the pain she knew he would cause her. She started to rise but he grabbed her bare ankle and held it fast. "No," she began before he descended on her . . . and began to tickle her. Judith was surprised as much as anything, then she began to giggle. She drew her knees to her chest to try to keep his hands from her sides, but he was merciless.

"Do you take it back?"

"No," she gasped. "You are vain—a thousand times more vain than a woman."

His fingers ran up and down her ribs until she thrashed about under him.

"Please stop," she cried, "I can't stand any more!"

Gavin's hands stilled and he leaned close to her face. "Are you beaten?"

"No," she said, but added quickly, "though you may not be as vain as I thought."

"That is a sorry apology."

"It was made under torture."

He smiled down at her, the setting sun making her skin golden, her hair spread about her like a fiery sunset. "Who are you, my wife?" he whispered, devouring her with his eyes. "You curse me one moment, enchant me the next. You defy me until I could take the life from you; then you smile at me, and I am dazed at your loveliness. You are like no other woman I have ever known. I have yet to see you put needle to thread, but I have seen you up to your knees in the muck of the fishpond. You ride a horse as well as a man, yet I find you in a tree shivering like a child in a mortal fear. Are you ever the same from one moment to the next? Do two days ever find you the same?"

"I am Judith. I am no one else, nor do I know how to be anyone else."

His hand caressed her temple; then he bent and touched his lips to hers. They were sunwarmed and sweet. He had barely tasted of her when the heavens suddenly opened with an enormous blast of thunder and began to empty a heavy torrent of rain on them.

Gavin uttered a very foul word Judith had never heard before. "To the overhang!" he said, then remembered her ankle. He picked her up and raced with her to the deep shelter, where the fire sputtered and crackled, the meat fat dripping into it. Gavin's temper was not helped by the abrupt shower. Angrily, he went to the fire. One side of the meat was burned black, the other raw. Neither of them had thought to turn it.

"You're a poor cook," he said. He was annoyed at having a perfect moment destroyed.

She gave him a blank look. "I sew better than I cook."

He stared at her, then began to laugh. "Well met." He looked out at the rain. "I must see to my stallion. He won't like standing in this with his saddle on."

Always concerned for the welfare of animals, Judith turned on him. "You've left your poor horse unattended all this time?"

He did not like her tone of command. "And where, pray tell, is your mare? Do you care so lightly for her that you don't care what has become of her?"

"I—" she began. She had been so enthralled with Gavin that she had given her horse no thought at all.

"Then set yourself to rights before you order me about."

"I wasn't ordering you."

"And pray, what else then?"

Judith turned away from him. "Go then. Your horse waits in the rain."

Gavin started to speak then changed his mind as he went into the rain.

Judith sat rubbing her ankle, scolding herself. She seemed to make him angry at every turn. Then she stopped. What did it matter if she made him angry? She hated him, didn't she? He was a vile, dishonorable man and one day of kindness wouldn't change her feelings of hatred for him. Or could it?

"My lord."

She heard the voice as if from far away.

"My Lord Gavin. Lady Judith." The voices came closer.

Gavin swore under his breath as he tightened the cinch he had just loosened. He'd forgotten all about his men. What spell had that little witch cast on him that he forgot his horse and even worse, forgot his men who diligently searched for them? Now they rode about in the rain, wet, cold and no doubt hungry. For all he would have liked to go back to Judith, perhaps spend the night with her, his men must come first.

He walked his horse across the stream and up the hill. They would have seen the fire by now.

"You are unharmed, my lord?" John Bassett asked when they met, water dripping off his nose.

"Yes," Gavin said flatly, not looking at his wife who leaned against the rock ledge. "We were caught in the storm and Judith hurt her ankle," he began, then stopped when John looked pointedly at the sky. A spring cloudburst was hardly a storm, and both Gavin and his wife could have ridden the one horse.

John was an older man, a knight of Gavin's father, and he was experienced in dealing with young men. "I see, my lord. We have brought the lady's mare."

"Damn, damn, damn!" Gavin muttered. Now she'd made him lie to his men. He went to her mare and savagely tightened the cinch.

For all the pain in her injured ankle, Judith hobbled quickly toward him. "Don't be so rough with my horse," she said possessively.

He turned on her. "Don't be so rough with *me*, Judith!"

Judith silently stared through the half-open shutter at the starlit night. She wore a bedrobe of indigo blue damask lined with light blue silk, trimmed around the neck, down the front and around the hem with white ermine. The rain had cleared and the night air was fresh. Reluctantly, she turned away from the window to her empty bed. Judith knew what was wrong with her, though she hated to admit it. What sort of woman was she that she pined for the caresses of a man she despised? She closed her eyes and could almost feel his hands and his lips on her body. Had she no pride that her body betrayed her mind? She slipped off the robe and slid, nude, into the chilly bed.

Her heart nearly stopped when she heard heavy footsteps pause outside the room. She waited, breathlessly, for a long while before the steps receded down the hall. She banged her fist into the feather pillow and it was a long, long time before she slept.

Gavin stood outside her door for several minutes before going to the room he now used. What was wrong with him? he demanded of himself. Where did this new timidity with women come from? She was ready for him; he'd seen it in her eyes. Today, for the first time in many weeks, she'd smiled at him and for the first time ever, she'd called him by his first name. Could he risk losing that little gain by forcing his way into her chamber and again risk causing new hate?

What did it matter if he raped Judith again? Hadn't he enjoyed it the first night? He undressed quickly and slid into the empty bed. He didn't want to rape her again. No, he wanted her to smile at him, to call his name and hold her arms out to him. Gone from his mind were all thoughts of triumph. He fell asleep remembering the way she'd clung to him when she'd been frightened.

Chapter 12

GAVIN WOKE very early after a fretful night's sleep. The castlefolk were beginning to stir, but the sound was still subdued. His first thought was of Judith. He wanted to see her. Had she really smiled at him yesterday?

He dressed quickly in a linen shirt and a coarse woolen doublet, secured with a wide leather belt. He pulled linen hose over his muscular calves and thighs, tieing them to the linen braies that he wore as a loincloth. Afterward, he hurried down the stairs to the garden and there cut a fragrant red rose, its petals kissed by pearly drops of dew.

The door to Judith's chamber was closed. Silently, Gavin opened it. She was asleep, one hand tangled in her hair which was spread across her bare shoulders and the pillow beside her. He placed the rose on the pillow and gently removed a curl from her cheek.

Judith opened her eyes slowly. It seemed a part of her dreams to see Gavin so near. She touched his face gently, her thumb on his chin, feeling the unshaved bristles, her fingers on his cheeks. He looked younger than usual, the lines of care and worry gone from his eyes. "I didn't think you were real," she whispered, watching his eyes as they softened.

He moved his head slightly and bit the tip of her finger. "I am very real. It's you who seem to be a dream."

She smiled wickedly at him. "Then we are well pleased with our dreams, aren't we?"

He laughed as he put his arms around her roughly and rubbed his cheek on the tender flesh of her neck, delighting in her squeals of protest as his whiskers threatened to remove her skin. "Judith, sweet Judith," he whispered as he nibbled her earlobe. "You are always a wonder to me. I don't know if I please you or not."

"And would it matter so much if you did not?"

He drew back from her and touched her temple. "Yes, I think it would matter."

"My lady!"

They both looked up as Joan burst into the room.

"A thousand pardons, my lady," Joan said, sniggering. "I didn't know you were so well occupied, but the hour grows late and there are many who call for you."

"Tell them to wait," Gavin said heatedly as he held Judith tightly as she tried to push him away.

"No!" Judith said. "Joan, who summons me?"

"The priest asks if you wish to begin the day without mass. Lord Gavin's man, John Bassett, says some horses from Chestershire have arrived. And there are three cloth merchants who want to have their wares inspected."

Gavin stiffened and released his wife. "Tell the priest we will be there and I will see the horses after mass. And tell the merchants—" he stopped, disgusted. Am I master of this house or not? he demanded of himself.

Judith put her hand on his arm. "Tell the merchants to store their wares and attend mass with us. I will see them after mass."

"Well?" Gavin asked the skinny maid. "You've been told what to do. Now go."

Joan hugged the door to her back. "I must help my lady dress."

Gavin began to smile. "I will do that. Perhaps I'll find some pleasure in this day besides duty."

Joan smirked at her mistress before she slinked around the door and closed it.

"Now, my lady," Gavin said as he turned back to his wife. "I am yours to command."

Judith's eyes sparkled. "Even if it concerns the matter of your horses?"

He groaned in mock agony. "It was a silly quarrel, wasn't it? I was angry at the rain more than at you."

"And why should the rain have made you angry?" she teased.

He leaned back over her. "It kept me from a sport I much desired."

She put her hand on his chest, felt his heart hammering. "Do you forget the priest waits?"

He leaned back. "Come, then, up with you and let's see to your dressing. If I can't taste, I may at least look my fill."

Judith gazed into his eyes for a moment. It had been nearly two weeks since he'd made love to her. Maybe he had left her right after their marriage to go to his mistress. But Judith realized that Gavin was hers right now, and she would make the most of that possession. Many people told her she was beautiful, but she usually dismissed them as flatterers. She knew her curved body was quite different from the thin one of Alice Valence. But once Gavin had desired her body. She wondered if she could make those eyes darken from gray to black.

She slowly pulled an edge of the coverlet back and stuck out one bare foot, then drew the coverlet to mid-thigh. She flexed both feet. "I think my ankle has quite recovered, don't you?" She smiled up at him innocently, but he wasn't looking at her face.

Very slowly, she moved the coverlet away from her firm, round hip, then exposed her navel, her flat stomach. She slipped slowly out of the bed and stood before him in the early morning light.

Gavin stared at her. He hadn't seen her nude in weeks. She had long, slim legs, round hips, a tiny waist and full rosy-tipped breasts.

"Damn the priest!" Gavin muttered as he held out a hand to touch the curve of her hip.

"Do not blaspheme, my lord," Judith said seriously. Gavin looked up at her in surprise.

"It's always a wonder to me that you wished to hide all that under the guise of a nun." Gavin sighed heavily as he looked at her, his palms aching with the desire to touch her. "Be a good girl and fetch your clothes. I cannot bear this sweet torture any longer. Another moment, and I would rape you before the priest's very eyes."

Judith turned to her clothes chest and hid her smile. Would it be rape, she wondered.

She took her time dressing, enjoying his eyes upon her and his strained silence. She slipped on a thin cotton chemise embroidered with tiny blue unicorns. It barely reached to midthigh. Matching drawers came next. Then she put her leg up on the edge of the bench where Gavin sat stonily, and carefully pulled the silk stockings over her legs, held in place by garters.

She reached across him for her dress of rich, brown cashmere from Venice. Silver lions were embroidered down the front and along the hem. Gavin's hands trembled as he fastened the buttons down the back. A silver filigree belt completed the costume, but Judith could not seem to manage the simple buckle by herself.

"Done," she said after a long time of struggling with the uncooperative garments.

Gavin let out his long-held breath.

"You make an excellent maid," she laughed, whirling about in a sea of brown and silver.

"No," Gavin said honestly. "I would die in less than a week. Now come below with me and don't tease me anymore."

"Yes, my lord," Judith said obediently, her eyes twinkling.

Within the inner bailey was a long field with a heavy carpet of sand. Here the Montgomery men and their chief vassals trained. A straw dummy swung from a gibbet which the men made sword passes at as they rode their war horses. A ring attached between two poles was the object of more passes with both sword and lance. There was also a man who was slashing at a four-inch post buried deeply in the ground by using a two-handed grip on his sword.

Gavin sat down heavily on a bench at the edge of the training ground. He took off his helmet and ran his hand through his sweat-dampened hair. His eyes were sunken into dark pits, his cheeks drawn, his shoulders aching with weariness. It had been four days since that morning he'd helped Judith dress. During that time he'd slept very little, ate even less, so that now his senses were taut.

He leaned his head back against the stone wall and thought that there was little more that could have happened. Several serfs' cottages had caught fire, and the wind had sent sparks into the dairy. He and his men had fought the fire for two days, sleeping on the ground where they fell. One night he'd spent in the stables with a mare that delivered a colt by breech birth. Judith stayed with him throughout the night, holding the horse's head, handing Gavin cloths and ointments before he knew he needed them. Never had he felt so close to anyone as he had then. At dawn, with a feeling of triumph, they stood together and watched the little colt take its first shaky steps.

Yet for all their closeness in spirit, their bodies were as far apart as ever. Gavin felt that at any moment he might go insane with wanting her. He wiped the sweat from his eyes as he stared across the yard and saw Judith walking toward him. Or did he imagine it? She seemed to be everywhere before his eyes, even when she was not.

"I brought you something cool to drink," she said, holding out a mug to him.

He stared at her intently.

She put the mug beside him on the bench. "Gavin, are you well?" she asked as she put a cool hand on his brow.

He grabbed her violently and pulled her down. His lips sought hers hungrily, forcing them open. He didn't think that she might deny him; he was past caring.

Her arms went about his neck and her response to his kiss was as eager as his. Neither cared that half the castlefolk watched. There was no one but the two of them. Gavin moved his lips to her neck. He wasn't gentle. He acted as if he would devour her if at all possible.

"My lord!" someone said impatiently.

Judith opened her eyes to see a boy standing nearby, a rolled paper in his hand. She suddenly remembered who and where she was. "Gavin, there is a message for you."

He didn't move his lips from her neck, and Judith had to concentrate very hard to keep her mind on the waiting boy.

"My lord," the boy said. "It's an urgent message." He was very young—before his first beard—and he looked on Gavin's kissing of a woman as a waste of time.

"Here!" Gavin said as he snatched the parchment from the boy. "Now go and don't bother me anymore."

He threw the paper on the ground before turning once again to his wife's lips.

But Judith was now very aware of their public place. "Gavin," she said sternly, struggling to get off his lap. "You must read it."

He looked up at her as she stood over him, his breath coming hard and fast. "You read it," he said as he grabbed the mug of liquid Judith had brought. Maybe it would cool his hot blood.

Judith unrolled the paper with a worried frown, her face draining of color as she read.

Instantly Gavin was concerned. "Is it bad news?" When she looked up, his breath stopped, for there again he saw the coldness in her eyes. Her beautiful, warm, passionate eyes flashed daggers of hate at him.

"I am three times a fool!" she said through clenched teeth as she threw the parchment in his face. She turned on her heel and stalked toward the manor house.

Gavin took the parchment from his lap.

My dearest, I send this in private so I may tell you of my love freely. Tomorrow I wed Edmund Chatworth. Pray for me, think of me, as I will think of you. Remember always that my life is yours. Without your

*love I am nothing. I count the moments until I am
yours again.*

> *All my love,*
> *Alice*

"Trouble, my lord?" John Bassett asked.

Gavin put the missive down. "More than I have ever known. Tell me, John, you are an older man. Perhaps you know something about women."

John chuckled. "No man does, my lord."

"Is it possible to give your love to one woman, yet desire another until you are nearly mad?"

John shook his head as he watched his master staring after his wife's retreating form. "Does this man also desire the woman he loves?"

"Surely!" Gavin answered. "But perhaps not . . . not in the same manner."

"Ah, I see. A holy love, as for the Virgin. I am a simple man. If it were me, I'd take the earthly one. I think love would come if the woman were a joy in bed."

Gavin propped his elbows on his knees, his head in his hands. "Women were created to tempt men. They are the devil's own."

John smiled. "I think that if I were to meet old Scratch, I might thank him for that bit of evil work."

For Gavin, the next three days were hell. Judith would neither look at him nor speak to him. If at all possible, she would not be anywhere near him. And the more haughtily she treated him the more furious he became.

"Stay!" he ordered her on one night as she started to leave the room when he entered.

"Of course, my lord," she said as she curtsied. Judith kept her head bowed, her eyes never meeting his.

Once Gavin thought her eyes were red, as if she'd been crying. But that was nonsense, of course. What reason did she have to cry? *He* was the one being punished, not her. He'd shown he wanted to be kind, yet she chose to despise him.

Well, she'd gotten over it once, and she would get over it
again. Yet the days passed, and still Judith was cold to him.
He heard her laughter, but when he appeared, the smile died
on her face. He felt he should slap her, force her to respond
to him; even anger was better than the way she looked
through him. But Gavin couldn't hurt her. He wanted to hold
her and even apologize. For what? He spent his days riding
hard, training hard, yet at night he didn't sleep. He found
himself making excuses to be near her, just to see if he could
touch her.

Judith had cried until she was nearly ill. How could she
have forgotten so soon that he was such a vile man? Yet for
all the anguish the letter caused, she had to steel herself from
running to his arms. Judith hated Gavin yet her body burned
for him every moment of every hour of every day.

"My lady," Joan said quietly. Many of the servants had
learned to tiptoe about their master and mistress lately. "Lord
Gavin asks you to come to him in the great hall."

"I will not!" Judith replied without hesitation.

"He said it was urgent, to do with your parents."

"My mother?" she asked, immediately concerned.

"I don't know. He said only that he must speak with you
at once."

As soon as Judith saw her husband, she knew something
was very wrong. His eyes were like black coals, his lips so
tightly drawn that they appeared to be only a slash across his
face.

He turned his wrath on her. "Why didn't you tell me you
were pledged to somone else before me?"

Judith was bewildered. "I told you I was pledged to the
church."

"You know I don't mean the church. What about that
man you laughed and flirted with at the tournament? I should
have known then."

Judith could feel the blood beginning to pound through
her veins. "You should have known what? That any man
would be a more suitable husband than you?"

Gavin took a step forward, his manner threatening, but

Judith did not retreat. "Walter Demari has lain claim to you and your lands. To prove his claim, he has killed your father and taken your mother captive."

Immediately, all the anger left Judith. She felt deflated and weak. She grabbed a chair back to steady herself. "Killed? Captive?" she managed to whisper.

Gavin calmed somewhat and put a hand on her arm. "I didn't mean to tell you like that. It's just that the man lays claim to what is *mine!*"

"Yours?" Judith stared at him. "My father killed, my mother captured, my lands seized—and you dare talk to me of what you have lost?"

He drew away from her. "Let's talk reasonably. Were you pledged to Walter Demari?"

"I was not."

"Are you sure?"

She only glared at him in answer.

"He says that he will return your mother to safety if you will go to him."

She turned instantly. "Then I will go."

"No!" Gavin said and pulled her back to the seat. "You cannot! You are mine!"

She stared up at him, her mind concentrating on business. "If I am yours and my lands are yours, how does this man plan to get them? Even if he fights you, he cannot fight all your kin."

"Demari doesn't plan to do so." Gavin's eyes bored into hers. "He has been told we don't sleep together. He asks for an annulment, that you declare before the king your distaste for me and your desire for him."

"And if I do this, he will release my mother, unharmed?"

"That is what he says."

"And what if I don't make this declaration before the king? What will happen to my mother?"

Gavin paused before answering. "I don't know. I cannot say what will become of her."

Judith was silent for a moment. "Then I am to choose

between my husband and my mother? I am to choose whether I give in to the greedy demands of a man I hardly know?"

Gavin's voice was different from anything she'd ever heard before. It was cold as hardened steel. "No, you do not choose."

Her head came up sharply.

"We may quarrel often within our own estates, even within our own chambers, and I may concede to you often. You may change the falconer's lures and I may be angry at you, but now you will not interfere. I don't care if you were pledged to him before we married, or even if you spent your childhood in bed with him. This is a matter of war now, and I will not argue with you."

"But my mother—"

"I will try to get her out safely, but I don't know whether I can."

"Then let me go to him. Let *me* try to persuade him."

Gavin was unyielding. "I cannot allow that. Now I must go and gather my men. We will leave early tomorrow morning." He turned and left the room.

Judith stood at the window of her bedchamber for a very long time. Her maid came and undressed her, putting her mistress's arms into a green velvet mink-lined robe. Judith was hardly aware of anyone else's presence. Her mother, who had sheltered her and protected her all her life, was threatened because of a man Judith hardly knew. She remembered Walter Demari only vaguely as a pleasant young man who talked to her of the tournament rules. She remembered clearly the way Gavin had said she had enticed the man.

Gavin. Gavin. Gavin. Always back to him. All roads led to her husband. He demanded, he commanded what she was to do. She was given no choice. Her mother was to be sacrificed to Gavin's fierce possessiveness.

But what would she do if she had a choice?

Suddenly her eyes glinted gold. What right did that odious little man have to interfere in her life? He played God when he made others choose between what was not his to own.

Fight! her mind cried out. Her mother had taught her pride. Would Helen want her only child to stand meek and quiet before the king and give in to some strutting popinjay merely because the man said she must?

No, she would not! And Helen would not want it so. Judith turned toward the door, not sure of her destination, but an idea, sparked by her new anger gave her courage. "So! Demari's spies say we don't sleep together, that our marriage could be annulled," she murmured as she walked down the deserted hall.

Her convictions were firm until she came to the open doorway of the room Gavin used. He stood before the window, lost in thought, one leg propped on the window seat. It was one thing to make noble boasts of pride, but another to confront a man who every night found reasons for avoiding his wife's bed. Alice Valence's icily beautiful face floated before her. Judith bit her tongue, the pain keeping the tears from her eyes. She had made her decision and now she must live with it; tomorrow her husband would go to war. Her bare feet were soundless on the rush-covered floor as she went to stand just a few feet behind him.

Gavin felt, more than saw, her presence. He turned slowly, his breath held. Her hair looked darker in the candlelight, its rich color gleaming against the green velvet. The dark mink emphasized the rich creaminess of her skin. He could not speak. The nearness of her, the quiet room, the candlelight were even more than his dreams. She stared at him then slowly untied the belt of her robe and it glided languidly over her smooth skin, falling to her feet.

His gaze roamed over her as though he were unable to fully comprehend her beauty. Only when he looked back at her eyes did he see she was troubled. Was that expression fear? As if . . . he would reject her? The possibility struck him as so humorous he nearly laughed aloud.

"Gavin," she whispered.

She had barely finished the syllable when she was in his arms, being carried to his bed, his lips already fastened to hers.

Judith was afraid of herself as well as of him. He could

sense it as he kissed her. He'd waited a long time for her to come to him. He'd stayed away from her for weeks, hoping she could learn to trust him. Yet now, as he held her, he felt no great sense of triumph.

"What is it, sweet? What troubles you?"

His concern for her made her want to cry. How could she tell him of her pain?

When he carried her to the bed and the candlelight danced over her body, her breasts rising with each breath, he forgot all thoughts of anything but the nearness of her. His clothes were hastily thrown aside and he gently eased himself down beside her. He wanted to savor his skin touching hers, inch by slow inch.

When the torture was more than he could bear, he grabbed her to him fiercely. "Judith, I have missed you."

She lifted her face to his to be kissed.

They had been apart too long to proceed slowly. Their need of each other was urgent. Judith grabbed a handful of flesh and muscle on Gavin's back. He gasped and laughed throatily. When her hands clawed at him again, he grasped both hands in one of his and held them over her head. She struggled to free herself, but he was too strong. When he entered her, she gasped, then thrust her hips up to meet his. He released her hands and she pulled him closer and closer to her. They made love quickly, almost harshly, before they obtained the release they sought. Then Gavin collapsed on her, their bodies still joined.

They must have dozed, but sometime later Judith was wakened by Gavin's slow rhythmic movement. Half-sleep, only half-aroused, she began to answer him with lazy sensual movements of her own. Minute by minute, her mind became more deeply lost to the feelings of her body. She didn't know what she wanted, but she was not content with her position. She was not aware of Gavin's consternation as she pushed him to the side, her hips never leaving his. Once he was on his back, she was astride him.

Gavin lost no time in wonder. His hands slid up her stomach to her breasts. Judith's head arched back and her throat, so smooth and white in the darkness, further inflamed him. He clutched at her hips, both of them lost to their rising passion. They exploded together in a flash of blue and white stars.

Judith collapsed above Gavin and he held her close to him, her hair wrapping itself around their sweat soaked bodies, encasing them in a silk cocoon. Neither one mentioned what ran through their minds: Tomorrow Gavin would leave to do battle.

Chapter 13

THE CHATWORTH manor was a two-story brick house with carved stone windows set with imported glass. It was long and narrow, and on either end was a stained-glass bay window. Behind the house was a lovely walled courtyard. Stretching for two acres before the house was lush lawn, at the end of which was the earl's private hunting forest.

Three people were emerging from these woods, walking across the lawn toward the manor. Jocelin Laing, his lute slung across his shoulder had an arm around two kitchen maids, Gladys and Blanche. Jocelin's hot, dark eyes were made even smokier by the afternoon he'd spent satisfying the greedy women. But Jocelin did not think of them as greedy. To him, all women were jewels, each one to be enjoyed for its own special brilliance. There was no jealousy or possessiveness in him.

Unfortunately, that was not the case with the women. At the moment, both were dreading leaving Jocelin.

"You were brought here for *her?*" Gladys demanded.

Jocelin turned his head and looked at her until she looked away and blushed. Blanche was not so easily awed. "It's a wonder Lord Edmund allowed you to come. He keeps Lady Alice like a prisoner. He doesn't even allow her to go riding unless he is with her."

"And Lord Edmund does not care for a horse hitting his soft backside," Gladys chimed in.

Jocelin looked puzzled. "I thought this was a love match—a poor woman marrying an earl."

"Love! Bah!" Blanche laughed. "That woman loves no one but herself. She thought Lord Edmund was a simpleton she could use as she wished, but he is far from simple. We know—don't we, Gladys—since we've lived here for years?"

"Oh yes," Gladys agreed. "She thought she could run the castle. I know her kind. But Lord Edmund would rather burn the place to the ground than give her free rein."

Jocelin frowned. "Then why did he marry her? He could have had his choice of women. Lady Alice had no lands to offer."

"She is beautiful," Blanche answered shrugging. "He loves beautiful women."

Jocelin smiled. "I am beginning to like this man. I agree with him most heartily." He gave Blanche and Gladys lascivious looks which made their cheeks flush and their eyes lower.

"Jocelin," Blanche continued, "he's not like you."

"No, he's not," Gladys said as she ran her hand along Jocelin's thigh.

Blanche gave her a strong look of reprimand. "Lord Edmund likes only her beauty. He cares nothing for the woman herself."

"Such as poor Constance," Gladys added.

"Constance?" Jocelin asked. "I don't know her."

Blanche laughed. "Look at him, Gladys. He has two women with him now—yet he worries that he doesn't know a third."

"Or is it that he worries whenever there is any woman he doesn't know?" Gladys asked.

Jocelin put his hand to his forehead in mock despair. "I am found out! I am undone!"

"That you are," Blanche laughed as she began to kiss his neck. "Tell me, sweet, are you ever faithful to any woman?"

He began to nibble her ear. "I am faithful to all women . . . for a time."

They arrived at the manor house, giggling.

"Where have you been?" Alice hissed at him as soon as he entered the great hall.

Blanche and Gladys hurried off to their duties in far parts of the house.

Jocelin was unperturbed. "You missed me, my lady?" he smiled, taking her hand and kissing it after making sure no one was about.

"No, I did not," Alice said honestly. "Not as you mean. Were you out with those hussies this afternoon while I sat here alone?"

Jocelin was immediately concerned. "You have been lonely?"

"Oh, yes, I have been lonely!" Alice said as she sank into a cushioned window seat. She was as gently lovely as when he'd first seen her at the Montgomery wedding; but now she had a finer-drawn look to her, as if she'd lost weight, and her eyes moved nervously from one point to another. "Yes," she said quietly. "I am lonely. I have no one here who is my friend."

"How can that be? Surely your husband must love one as beautiful as you."

"Love!" she laughed. "Edmund loves nobody. He keeps me as if I were a bird in a cage. I see no one, talk to no one." She turned to look at a shadow in the room, her beautiful face twisted with hatred. "Except her!" she snarled.

Jocelin looked toward the shadow, unaware anyone was near them.

"Come out, you little slut," Alice sneered. "Let him see you. Don't hide away like some eater of carrion. Be proud of what you do."

Jocelin strained his eyes until he saw a young woman step forward, her figure slight, her shoulders bowed forward, her head lowered.

"Look up, you whore!" Alice commanded.

Jocelin's breath stopped when he looked into the young woman's eyes. She was pretty—not of the beauty of Alice or the woman he'd seen as a bride, Judith Revedoune, but lovely nonetheless. It was her eyes that made him stare. They were violet pools filled with all the troubles of the world. He had never seen such agony and despair.

"He sets her on me like a dog," Alice said, regaining Jocelin's attention. "I cannot move without her following me. I tried to kill her once, but Edmund revived her. If I hurt her again, he threatened to lock me away for a month. I—" Just then Alice noticed her husband coming toward her.

He was a short, fat man with large jowls and a sleepy heavy-eyed look. No one would guess that any mind except the simplest existed behind that face. But Alice had learned too well of his cunning intelligence.

"Come to me," she whispered to Jocelin before he nodded briefly to Edmund and left the hall.

"Your taste has changed," Edmund observed. "That one doesn't look at all like Gavin Montgomery."

Alice only stared at him. She knew there was no use talking to him. She'd been married only a month, and every time she looked at her husband, she remembered the morning after her wedding. She had spent her wedding night alone.

In the morning, Edmund had called her to him. He was a changed man from the one Alice had first met.

"I trust you slept well," Edmund had said quietly, his little eyes in his too-fleshy face watching her.

Alice lowered her lashes prettily. "I was . . . lonely, my lord."

"You can stop your acting now!" Edmund ordered as he rose from his chair. "So! You think you can rule me and my estates, do you?"

"I . . . I have no idea what you mean," Alice stammered, her blue eyes meeting his.

"You—all of you, all of England—think I am a fool. Those muscled knights you thrash about with call me a coward because I refuse to risk my life fighting the king's battles. What do I care for anyone's battles except my own?"

Alice was stunned speechless.

"Ah, my dear, where is that simpering little look you wear for the men, those who drool over your beauty?"

"I don't understand."

Edmund walked across the room to a tall cabinet and poured himself some wine. It was a large, airy room set on the top floor of the lovely manor house of the Chatworth estate. All the furniture was of oak or walnut, finely carved, with wolf and squirrel pelts flung over the backs of the chairs. The glass he now drank from was made of rock crystal with little gold feet.

He held the crystal up to the sunlight. There were Latin words at the base of the vessel promising good fortune to the owner. "Do you have any idea why I married you?" He didn't give Alice a chance to answer. "I'm sure you must be the most vain woman in England. You probably thought I was as blind as that love-sick Gavin Montgomery. I know at least that you never even asked yourself why an earl would want to marry a penniless chit who slept with any man who had the equipment to please her."

Alice stood up. "I won't listen to this!"

Roughly, Edmund shoved her back into the chair. "Who do you think you are that you can tell me what you will do? I want you to understand one thing. I did not marry you for any love of you or because I was in awe of your so-called beauty."

He turned away from her and poured himself another glass of wine. "Your beauty!" he sneered. "I can't see what that Montgomery would want with a boy like you when he has that Revedoune woman. Now, there's a woman to stir a man's blood."

Alice tried to attack Edmund with her hands made into claws, but he easily knocked her aside.

"I'm tired of these games. Your father owns two hundred acres in the middle of my estates. The filthy old man was about to sell it to the Earl of Weston, who has been my enemy and my father's enemy for years. Do you know what would have happened to my estates if Weston owned land in the middle of them? A stream runs through there. If he dammed it, I'd lose hundreds of acres of crops as well as my serfs dying of thirst. Your father was too stupid to realize I only wanted you to get the land."

Alice could only stare. Why hadn't he spoken to her about the land Weston wanted? "But, Edmund. . . ." she said in her softest voice.

"Don't speak to me! For the last months I have had you watched. I know every man you've taken to your bed. And that Montgomery! Even at his wedding you threw yourself at him. I know about the time in the garden with him. Suicide! You? Ha! Did you know his wife saw your little play? No, I thought not. I drank myself into a stupor so that I wouldn't hear the laughter aimed at me."

"But, Edmund—"

"I told you not to speak to me. I went ahead with the marriage because I couldn't bear the land going to Weston. Your father has promised the deed to me when you produce a grandchild for him."

Alice leaned back against the chair. A grandchild! She almost smiled. When she'd been fourteen, she'd found herself pregnant and had gone to a filthy old woman in the village. The hag had removed the fetus. Alice had nearly died from the bleeding, but she'd been glad to get rid of the brat. She'd never destroy her slim figure for some man's bastard. In the years since, through all the men, she had never gotten pregnant again. She had always been glad that the operation had damaged her so she couldn't have children. Now, Alice knew her life had become hell.

It was an hour later, after Jocelin had finished playing for a group of kitchen wenches, that he walked along the wall of the great hall. The tension in the Chatworth castle was nearly unbearable. The servants were disorderly and dishonest. They seemed to be terrified of both the master and the mistress and did not waste time in telling Jocelin of the horrors of life in the castle. The first weeks after their marriage, Edmund and Alice had fought violently. Until, one of the servants laughed, the master discovered the Lady Alice liked a hand taken to her. Then Lord Edmund locked her away from everyone, kept her from all amusements and, most of all, kept her from enjoying any of his wealth.

Whenever Jocelin asked the reason for Edmund's punishments, the servants shrugged. It had something to do with the wedding of the Revedoune heiress and Gavin Montgomery. It started then, and they often heard Lord Edmund screaming that he would not be made a fool of. Already Edmund had had three men killed who were supposedly Alice's lovers.

Everyone laughed when Jocelin's face turned parchment-white. Now, as he walked away from the servants, he vowed to leave the Chatworth castle tomorrow. It was too dangerous here.

The very slightest of sounds, coming from a dark corner of the hall made him jump. He calmed his racing heart, then laughed at his nervousness. His senses told him there was a woman in the shadows and she was crying. As he moved toward her, she drew back, like a cornered wild animal.

It was Constance, the woman Alice hated so much. "Be still," he said quietly, his rich voice purring. "I won't harm you." Cautiously, he moved his hand to touch her hair. She looked up at him in fear, and he felt his heart go out to her. Who could have treated a woman so to make her so frightened?

She cradled her arm against her side as if in pain. "Let me see," he said gently and touched her wrist. It was some moments before she released her arm enough so he could touch it. The skin was not broken nor were any bones, as he at first suspected. In the dim light he could see it was reddened, as if someone had viciously twisted the skin.

He wanted to hold her, to comfort her, but her terror of him was almost tangible. She was shaking with fear. He knew it would be kinder to let her go than to force himself on her any longer. He stepped back and she fled quickly. Jocelin stood looking after her for a long while.

It was very late at night when he slipped into Alice's bedchamber. She was waiting for him, her arms open and eager. For all his experience, Jocelin was surprised at the violence of her actions. She grabbed him, her nails clawing into the skin of his back, her mouth seeking his, biting his lips. He drew away with a frown and she growled with keen irritation.

"You plan to leave me?" she demanded, her eyes narrow. "There were others who tried to leave me." Alice smiled when she saw his face. "I see you've heard about them," she laughed. "If you please me, you will find no cause to join them."

Jocelin did not like her threats. His first impulse was to leave. Then the candle by the bed flickered and he became acutely aware of how lovely she was, like cool marble. He smiled, his dark eyes glowing. "I would be a fool to go," he said as he ran his teeth along the cord of her neck.

Alice leaned her head back and smiled, her nails again digging into his skin. She wanted him quickly and with as much force as possible. Jocelin knew he hurt her and he also knew she enjoyed it. He did not receive any pleasure from their lovemaking; it was a selfish demonstration of Alice's demands. Yet he obeyed her, his mind never far from the idea of leaving her and her household on the morrow.

Finally she groaned and pushed him from her. "Go now," she commanded and moved away.

Jocelin felt sorry for her. What was life without love? Alice would never have love, for she never gave any.

"You did please me," she said quietly as he started to open the door. He could see the marks his hand had made on her neck, and he could feel the rawness of his back. "I will see you tomorrow," she said before he left.

Not if there is any chance of escape, Jocelin said to himself as he walked down the dark corridor.

"Here you, boy!" Edmund Chatworth said as he threw open his chamber door, flooding the corridor with candlelight. "What are you doing here, skulking about the hall at night?"

Jocelin shrugged idly and refastened his hose, as if he'd just answered a call of nature.

Edmund stared at Jocelin, then at the closed door of his wife's chamber. He started to speak, then shrugged his shoulders as if to say that it wouldn't be worth pursuing the matter. "Can you hold your tongue, boy?"

"Yes, my lord," Jocelin answered warily.

"I don't mean about a small matter—but one larger, more

important. There is a sack of gold in it for you if you don't speak." He narrowed his eyes. "And death to you if you do."

"Over there," Edmund said as he stepped aside and poured himself a flagon of wine. "Who would have thought a few taps would have killed her?"

Immediately, Jocelin went to the far side of the bed. Constance lay there, her face battered almost beyond recognition, her clothes torn off her body, hanging by a seam about her waist. Her skin was covered by scratches and small cuts; great lumps formed on her arms and shoulders. "So young," Jocelin whispered as he sank heavily to his knees. Her eyes were closed, her hair a mass of tangles and dried blood. As he bent and pulled her body gently into his arms, he felt her cold skin. Tenderly, he smoothed the hair away from her lifeless face.

"The damned bitch defied me," Edmund said as he stood behind Jocelin and looked at the woman who'd been his mistress. "Said she'd rather die than bed with me again." He snorted in derision. "In a sense, I only gave her what she wanted." He drained the last of the wine and turned to get more.

Jocelin did not dare to look up at him again. His hands were fists beneath the girl's body.

"Here!" Edmund said as he tossed a leather bag next to Jocelin. "I want you to get rid of her. Tie some stones to her and throw her in the river. Only don't let it be known what happened here this night. The news might cause problems. I will say she went back to her family." He drank more wine. "Damned little slut. She wasn't worth the money it took to clothe her. Only way I could get any movement from her was to hit her. Otherwise she lay like a log under me."

"Why did you keep her then?" Jocelin asked quietly as he removed his mantle to wrap the dead girl in it.

"Those damned eyes of hers. Prettiest things I ever saw. I could see them in my sleep. I set her on that wife of mine to report what went on, but the girl was a poor spy. Would never tell me a thing." He chuckled. "I think Alice hit her to make sure she said nothing. Well," Edmund noted as he turned away from Jocelin and the girl, "you have been paid. Take her away and do what you want with the body."

"A priest—"

"That old bag of wind?" Edmund laughed. "The Angel Gabriel couldn't waken the man after he has had his usual nightly flask of wine. Say some words over her yourself if you like, but no one else! You understand?" He had to content himself with Jocelin's nod. "Now get out of here. I'm tired of looking at her ugly face."

Jocelin neither spoke nor looked at Edmund as he swung Constance into his arms.

"Here, boy," Edmund said, surprised. "You left the gold." He dropped the bag onto the stomach of the corpse.

Jocelin used every bit of strength he had to keep his eyes lowered. If the earl saw the hate that burned there, Jocelin would not live to escape in the morning. Silently, he carried the body from the chamber, down the stairs and out into the starry night.

The stableman's wife, a fat, toothless old crone whom Jocelin had treated with respect and even affection, had given him a room atop the stables to use as his own. It was a warm place set in the midst of bales of hay. It was quiet and private; few people even knew of its existence. He would take the girl there, wash her and prepare her body for burial. Tomorrow he would take her outside the castle walls and give her a proper burial. Perhaps not in hallowed ground, blessed by the church, but at least in someplace free and clean of the stench of the Chatworth castle.

The only way to reach his room was by climbing a ladder set against the outside of the stables. Carefully, he settled Constance across his shoulders and carried her aloft. Once inside, he placed her tenderly on a soft bed of hay then lit a candle beside her. The sight of her in Edmund's room had been a shock, now it was a horror. Jocelin dipped a cloth in a bucket of water and began to wash the caked blood from her face. He did not realize there were tears in his eyes as he touched the battered form. Taking a knife from his hip, he cut away what was left of her dress and continued bathing her bruises.

"So young," he whispered. "And so beautiful." She was pretty—or had been—and even now, in death, her body was so lovely, slim and firm, though a little too much of her ribs showed.

"Please."

The word was whispered, so low that Jocelin almost did not hear her. He turned his head and saw her eyes were open, or one of them since the other was swollen shut.

"Water," she gasped through a parched and burning mouth.

At first he could only stare in disbelief then he grinned in sheer joy. "Alive," he whispered. "Alive!" He quickly got some watered wine, then carefully cradled her head in the crook of his arm while he held a cup to her swollen lips.

"Slowly," he said, still smiling. "Very slowly."

Constance leaned back against him, frowning as she tried to swallow, revealing deep bruises about her throat.

He ran his hand over her shoulder, and realized it was still cold to touch. What a fool he was to take Edmund's word of her death! She was freezing. That's what made her seem so cold. She lay on his one blanket, and since Jocelin knew of no other way to warm a woman, he lay beside her, holding her close to the warmth of him as he drew the blanket across both of them with great concern. Never had he lain with a woman and felt this way.

It was late when Jocelin woke, the girl cradled close to him. She stirred in his arms, grimacing because of her aching body. He moved from her side and placed a cool cloth on her brow, which had grown too warm with the beginnings of a fever.

Now, in the light of day, Jocelin began to see the situation realistically. What was he to do with the girl? He couldn't very well announce that she was alive. Edmund would take Constance as his again as soon as she was well. There was little likelihood that she could survive a second beating. If Edmund did not kill her, Jocelin was sure Alice would. With new eyes, Jocelin looked about the little room. It was private, well sealed against outside noises and difficult to reach. With luck and a great deal of care, he might be able to keep her hidden there until she was well. If he kept her alive and safe, then he would worry about what came next.

He lifted her and gave her more of the watered wine, but her swollen throat could take little of it.

"Joss!" a woman called from the foot of the ladder.

"Damn!" he said under his breath, cursing for the first time in his life his lack of freedom from women.

"Joss, we know you're there. If you don't come down, we'll come up."

He walked through a maze of baled hay to the open doorway and smiled down at Blanche and Gladys. "A beautiful morning, isn't it? And what might you two charming ladies want of me?"

Gladys giggled. "Are we to shout it for all the castle to hear?"

He grinned again and after one last glance over his shoulder, descended the ladder. He put an arm around each woman's shoulders. "Perhaps we could talk to the cook this morning. I find I'm famished."

The following four days were hell for Jocelin. Never in his life had he had to keep a secret, and his constant acts of subterfuge were exhausting. Had it not been for the stableman's wife, he would not have been successful.

"I don't know what you have hidden up there," the old woman said, "but I've lived long enough not to be surprised by anything." She cocked her head at Jocelin, admiring his looks. "It would be my guess it's a woman." She laughed at the expression on his face. "Oh, yes, it's a woman, all right. Now I must set my mind to figuring out why she must be kept hidden."

Jocelin started to speak but she held up her hand. "No need to explain. No one loves a mystery more than I do. Let me have my puzzle and I'll help you keep the other women from your room, though that won't be easy with the numbers that plague you. Someone ought to put you in a jar and pickle you, boy. You ought to be preserved—that's for certain. No other three men alive could pleasure as many girls as you do."

Jocelin turned away in exasperation. He was worried about Constance, and almost everyone had begun to notice his distraction. All except Alice. She demanded more and more of Jocelin, calling him constantly to play for her and every night to her bed, where the violence she desired drained him more each night. And constantly he had to listen to Alice's hatred of Judith Revedoune, and of how Alice was going to visit King Henry VII and get Gavin Montgomery back.

He looked to see if anyone watched him as he climbed the ladder to the little loft room. For the first time, Constance was awake to greet him. She sat up, clutching the blanket about her nude body. For days, while she'd been dazed with fever, Jocelin had cared for her, becoming as familiar with her body as his own. It did not occur to him that he was a stranger to her.

"Constance!" he said joyfully, not completely aware of her fear. He knelt beside her. "How good it is to see your eyes again." He took her face in his hands to examine the bruises which were healing quickly, thanks to her youth and Jocelin's care. He started to move the mantle from her bare shoulders to attend to her other wounds.

"No," she whispered, closing the mantle.

He looked down at her in surprise.

"Who are you?"

"Ah, sweet, don't be afraid of me. I'm Jocelin Laing. You met me before with the Lady Alice. Don't you remember?"

At the mention of Alice's name, Constance's eyes darted from one side of the room to the other. Jocelin pulled her into his arms—a place where she'd spent much time though did not know it. She tried to pull away from him, but she was too weak.

"It's all over now. You're safe. You are here with me and I won't let anyone harm you."

"Lord Edmund—" she whispered against his shoulder.

"No, he doesn't know you're here. No one does, only me. I've kept them all from knowing about you. He thinks you're dead."

"Dead? But—"

"Quiet." He smoothed her hair. "There will be time for talk later. First you must heal. I have brought you a soup of carrots and lentils. Can you chew?"

She nodded against him, not relaxed but not stiff either. He moved her to arm's length. "You can sit?" She nodded again, and he smiled as if she had accomplished a great feat of strength.

Jocelin had become adept at sneaking warm pots of food into the loft. No one seemed to think it odd that he carried his lute over his shoulder and the lute case in his arms. But each night he filled the case with food he hoped would nourish the feverish Constance.

He held the bowl and began to feed her as if she were a child. She moved her hand to take the spoon from him, but she shook too much to hold it. When she could eat no more, her eyes dropped in exhaustion. She would have fallen if Jocelin hadn't caught her. Too weak to protest, he cradled her in his lap and she drifted off to sleep easily, indeed feeling protected.

When Constance woke, she was alone. It took a few moments to remember where she was. The young man with thick black lashes who hummed in her ear couldn't have been real. What was real was Edmund Chatworth's hands about her throat, Alice's twisting of her arms, pulling her hair, any method to give pain that would not show.

Hours later, Jocelin returned and he held Constance in his arms, both snuggled deep under his mantle. He was not aware of time passing. For the first time in his life, the desires of women did not rule him. Constance's complete dependency on him brought an emotion he'd never known before—the beginning of love. All the love he'd ever felt for all the women was being concentrated into one fierce and burning passion.

But Jocelin was not a free man. There were others who watched him.

Chapter 14

THE LONG, thin black leather of the whip snaked angrily across the man's back. His back was already crisscrossed with many oozing stripes. He screamed loudly each time the whip struck him and twisted his hands frantically away from the braided rawhide thongs that held him to the post.

John Bassett looked toward Gavin, who nodded curtly. Gavin had no stomach for the punishment, and he had even less respect for the man's womanly screams.

John Bassett cut the bindings and the man fell into the grass. No one made any move to help him. "Shall I leave him?" John asked.

Gavin looked toward the castle across the narrow valley. It had taken two weeks to find Walter Demari. The wily little man seemed more interested in a cat-and-mouse chase than in getting what he wanted. For the last week, Gavin had camped outside the walls and worked on his attack. He had gone to the walls and called up challenges to the guards at the gate, but his words were ignored. Yet, even while the challenges were made, four of Gavin's men quietly dug beneath the ancient walls. But the walls were deep, the foundations broad. It was going to take much too long to break through. He feared that Demari would grow tired of waiting for Gavin's surrender and kill Helen.

As if he didn't have enough problems, one of his men, this mewling creature at his feet, had decided that since he was a knight of one of the Montgomeries, he was close to God. During the night, Humphrey Bohun had ridden into the nearest town and raped a merchant's fourteen-year-old daughter, then ridden back to camp triumphant. He was bewildered by Lord Gavin's rage when the girl's father told of his daughter.

"I don't care what you do with him. Just make sure he's out of my sight within the next hour." Gavin pulled his heavy leather gloves from where they hung over his belt. "Call Odo to me."

"Odo?" John's face took on a hard look. "My lord, you can't be thinking again of traveling to Scotland."

"I must. We've discussed this before. I don't have enough men to declare a full attack on the castle. Look at it! It looks as if a good wind would crumble the rest of the stones away but I swear the Normans knew how to build a fortress. I think it's made of poured rock. If we're to get inside before the end of the year, I'll need Stephen's help."

"Then let me go for him."

"And when were you last in Scotland? I have an idea where Stephen is, and tomorrow morning I'll take four men and find him."

"You'll need more protection than just four men."

"I can ride faster with fewer," Gavin said. "I can't afford to split up my men. Half of them are with Judith. Now, if I ride away with half again, it will leave you too unprotected. Let's just hope Demari doesn't realize I've gone."

John knew Lord Gavin was right, but he didn't like his master riding away without a good guard. But he'd learned long ago that it was no use trying to argue with a man as stubborn as Gavin.

The man at their feet groaned, recalling their attention to him. "Get him out of here!" Gavin said and stalked toward where his men were building a catapult.

Without thinking, John put a strong arm under the knight's shoulder and lifted him.

"All this because of a little slut!" the man hissed, spittle forming at the corners of his mouth.

"Shut up!" John ordered. "You had no right to treat the

girl like a heathen. If it'd been me, I would have had you hanged." He half-dragged the bleeding man to the edge of the camp, where John gave him a shove that sent him sprawling. "Now get out of here and don't come back."

Humphrey Bohun pulled the grass out of his mouth and looked after John's retreating form. "Oh, I'll be back. And it'll be me who's holding the whip next time."

The four men were very quiet as they made their way to waiting horses. Gavin had not told anyone except John Bassett of his journey to find Stephen. The three men who rode with him had all fought with Gavin in Scotland and they knew the rough, wild countryside. The group would travel as lightly as possible, without a herald carrying the Montgomery banner before them. All the men wore brown and green in an attempt to draw as little attention to themselves as possible.

They slipped silently into their saddles and walked their horses away from the sleeping camp.

They were barely ten miles from the camp when they were surrounded by twenty-five men wearing Demari's colors.

Gavin drew his sword and leaned over to Odo. "I will attack and cut a path through. You escape and get to Stephen."

"But my lord! You will be killed!"

"Do as I say," Gavin commanded.

Demari's men encircled the little group very slowly. Gavin looked about to find their weakest spot. They looked at him smugly, as if they knew the battle was already won. Then Gavin saw Humphrey Bohun. The rapist grinned in delight to see his former master so cornered.

Immediately, Gavin knew where he'd made his mistake. He'd spoken to John about his journey in front of this piece of filth. Gavin nodded to Odo, lifted his long steel broad sword with both hands on the hilt and charged. Demari's men were stunned. They had orders to take Lord Gavin prisoner. They'd assumed that when he was outnumbered more than six to one, he would surrender docilely.

That moment of hesitation cost Humphrey Bohun his life

and allowed Odo to escape. Gavin hacked at the traitor, and he died before he could even grab his sword. Another and another fell under Gavin's sword as it flashed brilliantly against the rays of the rising sun. Odo's well-trained animal leaped over the dead bodies and the screaming horses, and galloped for the safety of the woods. He had no time to see if anyone followed him. He kept his head low and molded himself to his horse.

Gavin had chosen his men well. The two who were now beside him backed their horses together, the animals trained to follow the commands given by their masters' knees. The three men fought valiantly and when one of them fell, Gavin felt part of himself fall. They were his men and he was close to them.

"Cease!" a voice commanded over the clash of steel against steel, the cries of anguish.

The men drew back quickly and when their eyes cleared, they began to assess the damage. At least fifteen of Demari's men lay dead or wounded, unable to stay on their mounts.

The horses of the men in the middle still stood their ground, rump to rump in pinwheel fashion. The man on Gavin's left had a deep slash across the top of his arm. Gavin, heaving with exertion, was covered with blood, but very little of it was his own.

The remaining of Demari's men looked on in silent tribute to the unarmored fighters.

"Take them!" said the man who seemed to be the leader of the attackers. "But see that Montgomery comes to no harm. He is needed alive."

Gavin lifted his sword again but suddenly there was a sharp sting and his hands were immobilized. A thin whip had been thrown, and his arms were pinned to his sides.

"Tie him."

Even as Gavin was dragged from his horse, his foot caught one man in the throat.

"Are you afraid of him?" the leader demanded. "You'll die anyway if you don't obey me. Tie him to that tree. I'd like him to watch how we treat captives."

Chapter 15

JUDITH WAS kneeling in the rose garden, her lap full of blossoms. Gavin had been gone a month now, with no word for the last ten days. There wasn't a moment that she didn't glance out a window or through a doorway to see if a messenger had arrived. She swayed between wanting to see him and dreading his return. He had too much hold over her, as he'd proven when she'd gone to his room the night before he left to fight for her lands. Yet she knew well enough that he had no such ambiguous feelings toward her. For him only the blonde Alice existed; his wife was only a toy to be used when he needed amusement.

She heard the clatter of arms as the men rode through the double gate that separated the inner bailey from the outer. She stood quickly, the roses falling to her feet as she picked up her skirts and began to run. None of them was Gavin. Judith released her pent-up breath, lowered her skirts and walked more sedately.

John Bassett sat atop his war-horse looking many years older than he had when he left some weeks before. His hair, graying at the temples, was even whiter now. His eyes were sunken, dark circles under them. The side of his chain mail had been torn and the edges of the cut were rusted from blood. The other men were no better; their faces haggard, their clothes torn and filthy.

Judith stood silently while John dismounted. "Take the horses," she said to a stableboy. "See that they are cared for."

John looked down at her a moment; then, with resignation, started to kneel to kiss her hand.

"No!" Judith said quickly. She was too practical to allow him to waste more energy in what, to her, was a useless gesture. She put her arm about his waist, guided his arm about her shoulders.

John stiffened, taken aback by the familiarity of his little mistress. Then he smiled fondly at the top of her head.

"Come and sit by the fountain," she said as she led him to the tiled pool just inside the garden wall. "Joan!" she commanded, "bring some of the other maids and send someone from the kitchen with food and wine."

"Yes, my lady."

She turned back to John. "I'll help you remove your armor," she said before he could protest.

Women came from inside the castle and soon the four men were bared from the waist up, their armor sent for repair. Each man ate ravenously of hot bowls of thick stew.

"You don't ask me the news," John said between bites, his elbow raised so Judith could clean and bandage the wound in his side.

"You will tell me," she said. "If it were good, my husband would have returned also. I can wait a long time for bad news."

John set the bowl down and looked at her.

"Is he dead?" she asked, not looking up at him.

"I don't know," he said quietly. "We were betrayed."

"Betrayed!" she cried, apologizing when she realized she'd hurt John's wound.

"One of the garrison knights, a new man named Bohun, slipped through the night to tell Demari that Lord Gavin planned to ride to his brother for help at dawn. Lord Gavin hadn't gone far when he was overtaken."

"But he was not killed?" Judith whispered.

"I don't believe so. We found no body," John said harshly, returning to his food. "Two of the men who rode with my lord were killed . . . killed in such a way that it lies

163

heavy on me. This is no ordinary man we deal with, but a devil!"

"Was there no ransom message or any word that they held him prisoner?"

"No. Nothing. The four of us must have gotten there moments after the battle. There were some of Demari's men still there. We fought them."

She tied the last knot on the bandage then looked up at him. "Where are the other men? There couldn't be only four left."

"They still camp outside Demari's walls. We go to fetch Lord Miles and his men. Lord Raine's leg wouldn't have had time to heal."

"And do you think Miles will be able to free Gavin?"

John didn't answer but concentrated on the stew.

"Come, you can tell me the truth."

He looked at her. "It's a strong castle. It can be taken without reinforcements only if we lay siege."

"But that would take months!"

"Yes, my lady."

"And what of Gavin and my mother who are held prisoner there? Wouldn't they be the first to starve if the food were gone?"

John stared at his bowl.

Judith stood, her fists clenched, her nails digging into her palms. "There is another way," she said evenly. "I will go to Walter Demari."

John's head shot up, one eyebrow raised. "And what can you do that men cannot?" he asked cynically.

"Anything that is required of me," Judith answered quietly.

John nearly threw his bowl. Instead, he grabbed her arm, his strong hand hurting her. "No! You don't know what you're saying. Do you think we deal with a sane man? Do you think he will free Lord Gavin and your mother if you were to give him what he wants? If you saw the men—what were once men," he added, "who rode with Lord Gavin, you wouldn't consider giving yourself to this Demari. There was no need for such torture, yet he seemed to do it for joy alone. If he were a man, I would consider your idea, but he isn't."

She shook her arm until John released it. "What else is there to do? A siege would most certainly cause their deaths, but you say a siege is the only way to attack. If I were to get inside the castle, perhaps I could find Gavin and my mother and arrange an escape for them."

"An escape!" he snorted. John had forgotten that she was the Lady Judith and had the authority to order him about; she was just a young and inexperienced girl now. "And how would you get out? There are only two entrances; both guarded well."

Judith squared her shoulders, her chin held high. "What choice do you have? If Miles were to lead an attack, Demari would surely put Gavin to death, as well as my mother. Do you love Gavin so little that you don't care whether he dies or not?"

Suddenly John knew she was right. And he knew that he would be the one to turn her over to Walter Demari's bloody hands. She had struck John's heart when she mentioned love for Lord Gavin. John couldn't love the young man more if he were his own son. She was right that there was a chance to save Lord Gavin if she surrendered herself. Lord Gavin might have him hanged for endangering Judith, but he knew he was going to obey her. "You are trying for martyrdom," John said quietly. "What is to keep Demari from killing you also?"

Judith smiled at him, put her hands on his shoulder, for she also knew she'd won. "If he killed me, he would lose the Revedoune lands. If I have learned nothing else, I know how much men will do for my property." Her eyes glinted for a moment. "Now, come inside where we may talk more freely. You and I have a great deal of planning to do."

He followed her dumbly. She acted as if they prepared the menu for a woodland picnic rather than gave herself, as a lamb to slaughter, to a butcher.

Judith wanted to leave immediately, but John persuaded her to wait and give him and his men some rest. Truthfully, he hoped to talk her out of her madness and to find an alternate plan, but her logic bewildered him.

For every reason he gave that she should not go, Judith gave ten more sensible ones why she should. And he agreed with her; he could see no other way of any chance of saving the prisoners . . . if they were prisoners.

But oh, how he dreaded Lord Gavin's wrath! He said as much to Lady Judith. She laughed. "If he is safe enough to indulge his anger, I will kiss his hand in thanksgiving."

John shook his head in wonder. The woman was too clever by half again. He didn't envy Lord Gavin the taming of her.

They couldn't take many men as a guard—they could not leave the estate unprotected—and already many of Gavin's knights waited for him. They were thankful it was only two days' travel to Demari's property.

Judith worked hard while John rested and ate. She ordered the loading of several wagons of grain and preserved meats to be prepared at the campsite. Another cart was given over to her clothes; the most beautiful of silks, velvets, brocades, cashmeres, along with a large ironbound chest filled with jewels.

When John mumbled something about women being ostentatious, Judith took him to task.

"Walter Demari hungers for some woman he believes to be beautiful. Would you like me to appear before him in homespun? He would say he'd changed his mind and have me thrown to the bottom of a well. He must be a vain man, or he wouldn't demand that a woman he hardly knows repudiate her husband and claim him as her true love. Therefore, I will play to his vanity and wear my most exquisite clothes for him."

John stared at her a moment, then turned away. He didn't know whether to praise her or be angry at himself for not thinking of what she said first.

For all the facade she showed to the world, Judith was scared. But for the life of her, she couldn't think of any alternative plan.

She lay awake all night thinking. Demari had sent no message of exchange. Perhaps he had already killed Gavin and Helen, and Judith was turning herself over to him for no reason.

She ran her hands over her stomach, knew it was still hard and flat. She was sure now that she carried Gavin's child. Was the baby part of the reason she worked to save her husband?

When the sun rose, Judith dressed slowly in a practical wool gown. She was strangely sedate, almost as if she walked to certain death. She went below to the little chapel for mass. She would pray for all of them—her husband, her mother and her unborn child.

Walter Demari sat before a wooden table in the great hall of his father's estate. Once the table had been a finely carved piece, but over time most of the heads of the beasts had been broken away, the necks rubbed smooth. Absently, Walter kicked at a chicken that pecked at the hose on his short, thin legs. He studied the parchment in front of him and refused to look at his surroundings. His father refused to give him anything but this run-down, neglected old tower. Walter buried his resentment deeply and concentrated on the task before him. When he was wed to the heiress to the Revedoune lands, then his father wouldn't dismiss him as if he didn't exist.

Behind Walter stood Arthur Smiton, a man Walter considered his friend. Arthur had helped Walter at every turn, agreeing that Walter should have had the lovely heiress instead of Gavin Montgomery. To repay Arthur for his loyalty, Walter had made the man his chief vassal. It was Arthur who had succeeded in capturing Lord Gavin.

"Arthur," Demari complained, "I don't know how to word the message. What if she won't come? If she *does* hate her husband, why should she risk so much for him?"

Arthur didn't let his emotions show. "Do you forget the old woman we hold? Isn't she the girl's mother?"

"Yes," Walter said and returned his attention to the parchment before him. It wasn't easy asking what he did. He wanted marriage to the Lady Judith in exchange for the free-dom of her husband and mother.

Arthur stood behind Walter for a moment, then moved away to pour himself a cup of wine. He needed a firm stomach to be able to withstand Walter's mewling. The love-sick young man made Arthur ill. Walter had come back from the Montgomery-Revedoune wedding so enthralled with the bride that he'd hardly been able to do anything except talk of her. Arthur looked on him with disgust. Walter had everything—lands, wealth, a family, hope for the future. He was not like Arthur, who had pulled himself up from the muck that had been his family. Anything he had he'd acquired through in-telligence, physical strength and, quite often, treachery and lying. There was nothing that he wouldn't do to get what he wanted. When he'd seen the spineless Walter mooning about a bit of a girl, Arthur developed a plan.

It hadn't taken long to learn of the quarrels the new bride had with her husband. Arthur, only a knight in Walter's gar-rison, had found a ready ear when he spoke of an annulment and a second marriage to Walter. Arthur couldn't have cared less about the girl, but the Revedoune lands were worth any amount of fighting. Walter hadn't wanted to attack Robert Revedoune, but Arthur knew Revedoune would stop at noth-ing to keep his daughter wed to the Montgomery family. It had been easy to kill the old man once he allowed them, as friends, inside his castle walls. His wife Helen had followed docilely and Arthur laughed, recognizing a well-trained woman when he saw one. He admired Revedoune for that.

"My lord," a nervous servant announced, "there are vis-itors outside."

"Visitors?" Walter asked, his eyes hazy.

"Yes, my lord. It is the Lady Judith Montgomery, sur-rounded by her men-at-arms."

Walter jumped up, the writing table upset, as he started after the servant.

Arthur grabbed his arm. "I pray you, my lord, take care. Perhaps it's a trap."

Walter's eyes burned. "What trap could there be? The men won't fight and endanger their lady."

"Perhaps the lady herself . . ."

Walter jerked away from him. "You go too far. Be careful you don't find yourself in the cellar with Lord Gavin." Stormily, he left the old tower, kicking sawdust-dry rushes out of his way. Arthur's word of caution had penetrated his brain, and now he ran up the narrow stone stairs to the top of the wall in order to be sure it was indeed the Lady Judith who waited below.

There was no mistaking her. The auburn hair that flowed down her back was not to be confused with anyone else's. "It is she," he whispered excitedly, then seemingly flew down the stairs, across the bailey to the front gate.

"Open it, man!" he bellowed to the gatekeeper. "And be quick about it!" The heavy iron-tipped portcullis was drawn upward slowly, Walter waiting impatiently.

"My lord," Arthur said at his side. "You can't let her bring her men inside. There are over a hundred of them. We could be attacked from within."

Walter turned his eyes away from the gate that creaked in protest as it rose. He knew Arthur was right, yet he wasn't sure what else to do.

Arthur fixed the weak blue eyes with his own dark ones. "I will ride out to meet her. You can't be risked. I will ride no farther than the range of the crossbowmen. When I'm sure it is the Lady Judith, my men and I will escort her through the gate."

"Alone?" Walter asked eagerly.

"She may have a personal guard if she so insists, but none other. We cannot allow her whole garrison to enter," he repeated.

The portcullis was up, the drawbridge down as Arthur mounted his horse and rode out, followed by five other knights.

Judith sat very still on her mount as she watched the raising of the gate. It took every ounce of her courage not to turn away. The old castle might be crumbling in places, but it looked very formidable when she was so close to it. She felt as if it was about to swallow her.

"There is time yet to leave, my lady," John Bassett observed as he leaned forward.

Six men were riding toward her, and she very much wanted to turn away. Then her stomach turned over and she had to swallow a sudden attack of nausea. Her child was reminding her of its presence. The baby's father and grandmother were inside those old walls and, if she could, she was going to get them out.

"No," she said to John with more strength than she actually felt. "I must attempt the task."

When the leader of the approaching men was close to Judith, she knew at once that he was the instigator of the whole plot. She remembered Walter as mild and meek but this man's mocking dark eyes showed no weakness. His clothes flashed with jewels; every color, every variety and size. His dark hair was covered by a small velvet cap, whose wide band on it held at least a hundred jewels. It looked almost like a crown.

"My lady," he said, bowing as he sat atop his horse. His smile was mocking, almost insulting.

Judith stared at him, her heart beating quickly. There was a coldness in his eyes that frightened her. He would not be one to easily overrule.

"I am Sir Arthur Smiton, chief vassal to Lord Walter Demari. He bids you welcome."

Welcome! Judith thought, controlling herself not to spit the word at him, thinking of her father butchered, her husband and mother held captive, several lives already lost. She inclined her head toward him. "You hold my mother captive?"

He looked at her speculatively, as if he tried to take her measure. She'd been sent no message, yet she knew what was needed.

"Yes, my lady."

"Then I will go to her." Judith urged her horse forward, but Arthur grabbed the bridle.

To a man, the one hundred knights who surrounded Judith drew their swords.

Arthur didn't lose his smile. "You can't think to enter our gates with so many men."

"You would have me go alone?" she asked, aghast. It was what she'd expected, but perhaps she could persuade Smiton to allow some of her men to accompany her. "You would perhaps have me leave my maid behind? Or my personal guard?"

He watched her intently. "One man. One woman. No more."

She nodded, knowing it was no use to argue. At least John Bassett would be with her. "Joan," she called as she turned and saw the girl eyeing Arthur speculatively. "Prepare the cart with my goods and follow me. John—" She turned and saw that he was already giving orders for the establishment of a camp outside the castle walls.

Judith rode across the drawbridge, under the arched stone gate, with her back straight. She wondered if she would ever leave the walls alive. Walter Demari stood waiting to help her dismount. She remembered him as a gentle young man, neither handsome nor ugly; but now his blue eyes showed weakness, his nose was too big, and his thin lips looked cruel.

He stared at her. "You are even more beautiful than I remembered."

She had dressed carefully that morning. A band of pearls encircled her head. Close to her body she wore a red silk petticoat with a wide border of white fur. Her gown was of maroon velvet, the hem embroidered with gold scrollwork. The sleeves were tight except at the shoulder, where the velvet was slit and the red silk pulled through. The neck was cut deep, her breasts swelling above the fabric. When she walked, she lifted the velvet overskirt and exposed the fur-trimmed silk beneath.

Judith managed to smile at this man of treachery, even as she twisted away from the hands about her waist. "You flatter me, my lord," she said, while looking at him through her lashes.

Walter was enchanted. "You must be tired and in need of refreshment. We would have had food prepared, but you weren't expected."

Judith didn't want him to think about why she came without a request. As she watched Walter's adoring look, she knew she would do well in establishing herself to be a shy young woman, the bashful bride. "Please," she said, her head bowed, "I would like to see my mother."

Walter didn't answer, but continued staring at her, her thick lashes touching her soft cheek, the pearls on her forehead echoing the creaminess of her skin.

John Bassett stepped forward, his jaw rigid. He was a big man, as tall as Gavin, but heavier with age. The steel-gray of his hair only emphasized the hardness of his body. "The lady wishes to see her mother," he said sternly. His voice was even, but it radiated power.

Walter hardly noticed John, he was too enraptured with Judith. But Arthur was very aware of him and recognized danger. John Bassett would need to be disposed immediately. Given the freedom of the castle, such a man could cause much trouble.

"Of course, my lady," Walter said, holding his arm out to her. One would have thought her visit was one of pleasure.

They made their way to the second-floor entrance of the tower; for in time of battle, the wooden steps were cut away to make the entrance several feet from the ground. Judith studied the interior as they walked across the great hall toward the stone steps. It was a filthy place, littered with bits of bone among the dry rushes on the floor. Dogs lazily nosed about the refuse. The deeply recessed windows had no wooden shutters, and in places the stones had fallen away, because the chinking was crumbling. She wondered if such a poor structure was indicative of the guardianship of the place. She meant to find out.

Helen sat in a chair in a little room cut into the thick stone walls on the third floor. Charcoal burned in a brass brazier; the tower had been built before fireplaces were known.

"Mother!" Judith whispered and ran forward to place her head against her mother's knees.

"My daughter," Helen gasped, then pulled Judith into her arms. It was a while before their tears quieted enough so they could speak. "You are well?"

Judith nodded, then looked past her mother to the men who stood there. "Are we to have no privacy?"

"Of course," Walter said then turned toward the door. "You will leave also," he said to John Bassett.

"No. I will not leave my lady alone."

Walter frowned, but he didn't want to upset Judith in any way.

"You should have left with them," Judith said sternly when Walter and Arthur were gone.

John sat heavily in a chair by the charcoal brazier. "I will not leave you alone."

"But I wish for some privacy with my mother!"

John neither spoke nor looked at her.

"He is a stubborn man," Judith said disgustedly to Helen.

"Is it stubborn when I don't let you have your way at all times?" he asked. "You are stubborn enough to rival a bull."

Judith opened her mouth to speak, but Helen's laugh stopped her.

"You are indeed well, my daughter." She turned to John. "Judith is all I have ever wanted her to be, and more," she said fondly, stroking her daughter's hair. "Now tell me why you are here."

"I . . . Oh, Mother," she began, tears starting in her eyes again.

"What is it? You can speak freely."

"No, I cannot!" she said passionately as she looked over at John so close by.

John gave her a look of such blackness that she was almost afraid of him. "Do not doubt my honesty. Talk to your mother. No word of what I hear will be repeated."

Knowing she could trust him, Judith relaxed as she sat on a cushion at her mother's feet. She wanted to talk, desperately needed to talk. "I have broken a vow to God," she said softly.

Helen's hand paused for a moment on her daughter's head. "Tell me of it," she whispered.

The words tumbled over themselves trying to escape. Judith told how she had tried again and again for some degree of love in her marriage, yet she had been thwarted at every effort. Nothing she did could loosen the hold Alice Chatworth had over Gavin.

"And your vow?" Helen asked.

"I vowed I would give nothing to him that he did not take. But I freely went to him the night before he came here." She blushed, thinking of that night of love, Gavin's hands and lips on her body.

"Judith, do you love him?"

"I don't know. I hate him, I love him, I despise him, I adore him. I don't know. He is so big—there is so much of him—that he devours me. I am always aware of him. When he enters a room, he fills it. Even when I hate him the most, when I see him holding another woman or reading a letter from her, I cannot rid myself of him. Is this love?" she asked as she gazed beseechingly up at her mother. "Is it love or merely possession by the devil? He is not kind to me. I'm sure he has no love for me. He has even told me so. The only place he is good to me is—"

"In bed?" Helen smiled.

"Yes," Judith said and looked away, her cheeks red.

It was several moments before Helen replied. "You ask me of love. Who knows less of it than I? Your father also had such a hold on me. Did you know that one time I saved his life? The night before he had beaten me, and the next morning, as I rode out with him, my eye was black and swollen. We rode alone, away from the escort, and Robert's horse bolted and threw him. He fell into the swamp along the north edge of one of the estates. The more he moved, the deeper he sank. My whole body ached from his beating, and my first thought was to ride away and let him die. But I couldn't. Do you know, he laughed at me, called me a fool when I'd saved him?"

She paused a moment. "I tell you this to show you that I

understand the way he has a hold on you. So did my husband. I know the power Gavin has over you, for my own marriage was the same. I can't say it was love, and I can't say yours is."

They sat quietly for a moment, both staring at the glowing charcoal.

"And now I rescue my husband as you rescued yours," Judith said. "Even though yours lived to beat you again, and mine will return to another woman."

"Yes," Helen said sadly.

"Did having a child matter?"

Helen considered. "Perhaps if the first ones had lived, but there were three dead, all boys. Then when you came, and you were a girl. . . ." She didn't finish the sentence.

"Do you think it would have mattered had the first one lived and been a son?" Judith persisted.

"I don't know. I don't believe he beat his first wife, who gave him sons. But he was younger then." She stopped abruptly. "Judith! Are you with child?"

"Yes. Two months gone."

John jumped to his feet in a clatter of armor and steel sword against stone. "You have ridden all this way and you are with child!" he demanded. He had been so quiet the two women had forgotten his presence. He put his hand to his forehead. "Hanging will be too good for me. Lord Gavin will torture me, as well I deserve, when he hears of this."

Judith was on her feet instantly, gold eyes blazing. "And who will tell him? You are sworn to secrecy!"

"How do you plan to keep this a secret?" he asked with heavy sarcasm.

"When it must be known, I plan to be far away from this place." Her eyes softened. "You wouldn't tell, would you, John?"

His expression didn't change. "Don't try such cajolery on me. Save it for that fish of a man, Walter Demari."

Helen's laugh interrupted them. It was good to hear her laugh, a sound too seldom heard in her unhappy life. "It does me good to see you like this, my daughter. I was afraid marriage might tame you and break your spirit."

Judith wasn't listening. John had heard too much. She had said too many intimate things in his hearing; now her cheeks were beginning to stain red.

"No," John said, with a sigh. "It would take more than a mere man to tame this one. Don't plead more, child. I will say nothing of what I have heard unless you ask me to."

"Not even to Gavin?"

He gave her a worried look. "I haven't seen him yet. I would give a great deal to know where he is being held, if he is well."

"Judith," Helen said, bringing their attention back to her. "You have yet to tell me why you are here. Did Walter Demari send for you?"

John sat down heavily in the chair. "We are here because the Lady Judith said we must come. She does not listen to reason."

"There was no other way," Judith said as she too sat down again. "What have they told you?" she asked her mother.

"Nothing. I was . . . brought here after Robert's death. I have spoken to no one for a week. Even the maid who empties the chamber pot doesn't speak to me."

"Then you don't know where Gavin is kept?"

"No, I gathered from your words only just now that he too was held. What does Lord Demari hope to gain?"

"Me," Judith said simply, then lowered her eyes before briefly explaining Walter's plan of annulment.

"But there can be no annulment if you carry Gavin's child."

"Yes," Judith said as she looked across her mother to John. "That is one reason it must be kept secret."

"Judith, what will you do? How do you expect to save yourself, Gavin, Joan and your husband's man from this place? You are no foil for stone walls."

John grunted in agreement.

"I don't know," Judith answered exasperatedly. "I could

see no alternative. At least now I have a chance of getting you out. But first I must find Gavin. Only then—"

"Did you bring Joan?" Helen interrupted.

"Yes," Judith said, knowing her mother had some idea.

"Tell Joan to find Gavin. If there is a man to find, she can do it. She is little more than a bitch in heat."

Judith nodded.

"And now, what of Walter Demari?" Helen continued.

"I have seen him only a few times."

"Is he to be trusted?"

"No!" John said. "Neither he nor that henchman of his can be trusted."

Judith ignored him. "Demari thinks I am beautiful, and I plan to be beautiful as long as it takes to find Gavin and make an escape."

Helen looked down at her daughter, so lovely in the glow of the coals. "You know so little of men," she observed. "Men are not like account books, where you add the figures and they give you a manageable sum. They are all different . . . and much more powerful than you or I."

Suddenly John rose and looked toward the door. "They return."

"Judith, listen to me," Helen said quickly, "Ask Joan how to deal with Walter. She knows a great deal about men. Promise me you will follow her advice, and don't let your own thoughts sway you."

"I—"

"Promise me!" Helen demanded, her hands holding her daughter's head.

"I will do my best. It is all I can promise."

"Then that must do."

The door burst open and no more words were spoken. Joan and one of the castle maids came to fetch Judith so that she might prepare for supper with his lordship. She hastily bid her mother good-bye, then followed the women, John close behind them.

The fourth floor contained the ladies' solar, a large, airy room, freshly cleaned with new rushes on the floor, new whitewash on the stones, almost as if a guest had been expected. Judith was left alone with her maid, John outside, guarding the door. At least Walter trusted her enough not to assign a spy to her. Joan brought a basin of heated water to her mistress.

As Judith washed her face and hands, she looked at Joan. "Do you know where Lord Gavin is kept?"

"No, my lady," Joan said suspiciously. She was not used to being asked questions by her mistress.

"Could you find out where he is?"

Joan smiled. "I am sure I could. This is a place full of gossipmongers."

"Will you need silver to get this information?"

Joan was shocked. "No, my lady. I will but ask the men."

"And they will tell you just because you asked?"

Joan was gaining confidence. Her lovely mistress knew little beyond running estates and keeping accounts. "It matters much *how* a man is asked."

Judith wore a dress of silver tissue. The skirt parted in front to reveal a wide expanse of deep green satin. The sleeves were large and bell-shaped, draping gracefully from wrist to halfway down the skirt. The sleeves were lined with more green satin. Her hair was covered with a matching French hood embroidered with silver fleurs-de-lis.

Judith sat down on a stool while Joan arranged the hood. "What if a woman wanted to ask something of Lord Walter?"

"Him!" Joan said heatedly. "I would not trust him, though that Sir Arthur who dogs him is not ill-favored."

Judith whirled to face her maid. "How can you say that? Arthur has such hard eyes. Anyone can see he is a greedy man."

"Lord Walter is not the same?" Joan pushed her mistress's head back around. She was feeling rather superior at the moment. "He is just as greedy, treacherous, brutal, and selfish. He is all of those and more."

"Then why—?"

"Because he is always the same. A woman would know

what to expect from him, and that would be whatever suited his needs best. You could deal with that."

"Then Lord Walter is not the same?"

"No, my lady. Lord Walter is a child, yet a man. He changes with the wind. He will want a thing—then, when he has it, he won't want it anymore."

"And this would pertain to women also?"

Joan dropped to her knees before her mistress. "You must hear me and listen well. I know men as I know nothing else in this world. Lord Walter burns for you now. He is mad with desire, and as long as he keeps that rage inside him, you will be safe."

"Safe? I don't understand."

"He has killed your father and taken your mother and your husband as prisoners only because of this passion of his. What do you think would become of all of you were this fire to be doused?"

Judith still didn't understand. When she and Gavin made love, no fires were quenched for longer than a few moments. In truth, the more time she spent in his bed, the more she wanted him.

Joan began to talk with exaggerated patience. "All men are not as Lord Gavin," she said, reading Judith's mind. "If you were to give yourself to Lord Walter, you would have no more hold over him. To men such as him, the game is everything."

Judith was beginning to understand. "How can I keep him from me?" She was fully prepared to give herself to a hundred men if it would save the lives of those she cared for.

"He will not force you. He must believe that he has wooed you and won. You may ask a lot of him and he will give it gladly, but you must be clever about it. He will be jealous. Do not hint that you care for Lord Gavin. Let him think you despise the man. Hold the carrot before his nose, but don't allow him to nibble."

Joan rose from her knees and gave a final critical look to her mistress's gown.

"And what of Sir Arthur?" Judith asked.

"Lord Walter will rule him—and if worse comes to worst, he can be bought."

Judith rose and stared at her maid. "Do you think I will ever learn so much about men?"

"Only when I learn to read," Joan said, then laughed at the impossibility of such a statement. "Why do you need to know of many men when you have Lord Gavin? He is worth all my men together."

As they left the chamber to descend the stairs to the great hall, Judith thought, Do I have Gavin? Do I want him?

Chapter 16

"MY LADY," Walter said as he took Judith's hand and kissed it. She kept her eyes lowered, as if in shyness. "It has been a long time since I saw you last, and you seem to have grown more lovely. Come and sit at the high table with me. We have prepared a late supper for you."

He led her to the long table set on a platform. The tablecloth was old and spotted, and the dishes were of battered pewter. When they were seated, he turned to her. "Your chamber is comfortable?"

"Yes," she answered quietly.

He smiled, puffing his chest out a little. "Come, my lady, you need not fear me."

Fear you! she thought furiously, her eyes meeting his. Then she recovered herself. "It is not fear I feel, but wonder. I am unused to the company of men, and those I have known . . . they have not been kind to me."

He took her hand in his. "I would amend that if I could. I know a lot about you, though you know little of me. Did you know I was a friend of your brothers?"

"No," she said in astonishment, "I didn't. Was it then my father pledged me in marriage to you?" she asked in wide-eyed innocence.

"Yes-no—" Walter stuttered.

"Ah, I understand, my lord. It was after my dear brothers' untimely death."

"Yes! It was then," Walter grinned.

"My poor brothers had so few friends. It was good they had you for a while. And my father! I would not speak ill of the man, but he was forever misplacing things. Perhaps he misplaced the betrothal agreement between us."

"There was no—" Walter began, then took a drink of wine to stop his words. He couldn't admit there had been no such document.

Judith put a tremulous hand on his forearm. "I have said something wrong? You will beat me?"

He quickly turned back to her and saw there were tears in her eyes. "Sweet Judith," he said as he kissed her hand passionately. "What is wrong with the world that a lovely innocent such as you is so terrified of men?"

Ostentatiously, Judith wiped a tear from her eye. "Forgive me. I have known so few and . . ." She lowered her eyes.

"Come, give me a smile. Ask some task or gift from me, and I will give it."

Judith looked up immediately. "I would like to have better quarters for my mother," she said firmly. "Perhaps on the floor with me."

"My lord!" Sir Arthur interrupted from Judith's other side. He had been listening to every word of their conversation. "There is too much freedom on the fourth floor."

Walter frowned. He wanted very much to please his sweet, shy captive, and being reprimanded before her by his man was not a means to that end.

Instantly, Arthur saw his mistake. "I meant, my lord, only that she should have a trustworthy guard near her, for her own sake." He looked at Judith. "Tell me, my lady, if you had only one man to guard you, whom would you choose?"

"Why, John Bassett," she said quickly. She could have bitten her tongue as soon as the words were out.

Arthur gave her a smug look before returning his gaze to Walter. "There. From the lady's own mouth. She has chosen the guard for Lady Helen."

And leave me without help should I try to escape, Judith

thought. Sir Arthur looked at her as if he could read her thoughts.

"An excellent idea!" Walter said. "That pleases you, my lady?"

She could think of no reason to give for keeping John to herself, and perhaps his absence would give her more freedom. "That would please me greatly, my lord," she said sweetly. "I know John will care for my mother well."

"And now we may turn to more pleasant matters. What do you say we ride out and hunt tomorrow?"

"Hunt, my lord? I . . ."

"Yes? You may speak freely to me."

"It is a silly wish."

"Come, tell me," Walter smiled tolerantly.

"I have only recently left my home, and I was always confined to one part of the estates. I have never seen one of these older castles. You will laugh at me!"

"No, I will not," Walter laughed.

"I'd like to see all of it, the mews, the stables, even the buttery."

"Then I shall take you on a full tour tomorrow," he smiled. "It's a simple request, and I would do anything to give you pleasure, my lady." His eyes burned into hers and Judith lowered her lashes, mostly to keep him from seeing the anger that glinted in hers.

"My lord," she said softly, "I find I am very tired. May I be excused?"

"Of course. Your wish is my command." He stood and held her hand as she rose from her chair.

John stood close behind her, his arms folded across his chest. "I would like to speak to my man for a moment," she said, going to him before Walter could answer. "Sir Arthur has made you a guard to my mother," she said without preamble.

"I will not. Lord Gavin—"

"Hush!" she said as she put her hand on his arm. "I don't wish to be heard. What reason would you give that you cannot leave my side? That silly man thinks I am his already."

"He makes advances to you?"

"No, not yet, but he will. You must stay with my mother. I don't believe Sir Arthur will let her out of that damp place if you refuse. She won't be able to stand that much longer."

"You think too much of your mother and too little of yourself."

"No, you are wrong. I am safe, but she could get a bone chill. If I were in the damp, I would demand equal treatment."

"You lie," John said flatly. "You could be safe at home now if you were not so stubborn."

"Do you lecture me *now?*" Judith asked, exasperated.

"It won't do any good. I will go to Lady Helen only if you promise you will do nothing that is foolish."

"Of course. I will even swear it if you wish."

"You are too glib, but there is no time to argue. They come. I will expect messages often. Perhaps it will keep my mind from the tortures Lord Gavin will apply to me."

When Judith and her maid were alone, Joan burst out laughing. "I have never seen such mummery to equal yours tonight!" she laughed. "You would do well in London. Where did you learn the trick of touching your nail to your eye to produce tears?"

Judith drew in her breath sharply. Joan's words brought back a vivid picture of Alice in Gavin's arms. "I learned the trick from a woman who lives by false words," she said grimly.

"Whoever she was, she must have been the best. I was half-convinced by you myself. I hope you got what you wanted."

"You were sure I wanted something?"

"Why else would a woman show tears to a man?"

Judith thought of Alice again. "Why else?" she muttered.

"And did you get what you wanted?" Joan persisted.

"Mostly. But that Arthur tricked me. John has been sent to guard my mother. Guard! Bah! How can two prisoners, locked away, guard each other? My man-at-arms has changed to a lady's maid, put under lock and key, and I am again alone with one more person to try to take from this place."

Joan undid the lacings at Judith's side. "I am sure it was to his best interests to take John from you."

"You are right. But Lord Walter is a fool. The man's tongue runs away with him. I must be more careful that I talk to him only away from Sir Arthur."

"That, my lady, may be the most difficult of all tasks." Joan pulled aside the down-filled covers for her mistress.

"What are you going to do, Joan?" Judith asked as she watched her maid run a comb through her brown hair.

"I will find Lord Gavin," she smiled. Maid and mistress were taking on a more equal role. "I will see you tomorrow, and I'll have news of him then."

Judith hardly heard the door close behind her maid. She thought she was too worried to sleep, but it was not so. She fell asleep almost instantly.

Walter and Arthur stood at one side of the great hall. The tables had been cleared and the men-at-arms spread straw-filled mattresses on the floor for the night.

"I don't trust her," Sir Arthur said under his breath.

"Trust her!" Walter exploded. "How can you say such a thing after you've seen her? She is a delicate flower of a girl. She has been beaten and so mistreated that she fears the slightest frown."

"She didn't seem so frightened when she demanded better quarters for her mother."

"Demanded! She could never demand anything. It isn't in her nature to do so. She was merely concerned for Lady Helen. And that is another example of her sweet nature."

"Such sweet nature obtained a great deal from you to-night. Look at how she had you nearly admit there was no written agreement of marriage from her father."

"What does that matter?" Walter demanded. "She doesn't want her marriage to Gavin Montgomery."

"And what makes you so sure of that?"

"I have heard—"

"Heard! Bah! Then why did she come here? She cannot be so simple that she believes there is no danger for her."

"Do you imply that I would harm her?" Walter demanded.

Arthur stared at him. "Not while she is new to you." He knew Walter well. "You must wed her before you bed her. Only then will you truly own her. If you take her now without the church, she may hate you as you say she hates her husband."

"I don't need advice about women from you! I am the master here. Have you no duties?"

"Yes, my lord," Arthur smirked. "Tomorrow I must help my master show our defenses to our prisoner." He walked away just as Walter threw a wine goblet at his head.

Judith woke very early, while the room was still dark. Immediately she remembered Joan saying that the morning would bring word of Gavin. She threw back the cover hastily, and put her arms through the sleeves of a bedgown of cinnamon brocade from Byzantium. The brocade was woven with lighter flowers in the fabric and was lined with cream cashmere. The straw pallet where Joan was to sleep was empty. Judith clamped her teeth together in anger and suddenly began to worry. Had Joan left her, too? Had Arthur discovered Joan in some act of spying?

The door opened almost silently, and a heavy-lidded Joan tiptoed through the shadows. "Where have you been!" Judith demanded in a tight whisper.

Joan's hand flew to cover her mouth to still the shriek gathering there. "My lady! You gave me a fright. Why aren't you in bed?"

"You dare to ask *me* why I'm not in bed?" Judith hissed before recovering herself. "Come, tell me of your news. Have you learned anything of Gavin?" Judith took her maid's arm and pulled her to the bed. They both sat cross-legged on the thick feather mattress.

But Joan's eyes didn't look directly into her mistress's intense golden stare. "Yes, my lady, I found him."

"Is he well?" Judith pressed.

Joan took a deep breath and rushed into her description.

"It was hard to find him. He is well guarded at all times and the entryway is . . . difficult. But," she smiled, "as luck would have it, one of the guards seemed to like me quite well, and we spent a lot of time together. He is such a man! All night he—"

"Joan!" Judith said sharply. "You are hiding something from me, aren't you? What about my husband? How is he?"

Joan looked at her mistress, started to speak, then dropped her face into her hands. "It is too horrible, my lady. That they could do such a thing to him is beyond belief. He is a nobleman! Even the worst serfs are not treated as he is."

"Tell me," Judith said in a deadly voice. "Tell me everything."

Joan lifted her head, fighting tears and the turning of her stomach. "Few of the castlefolk know he is here. He was brought alone, during the night and . . . thrown below."

"Below?"

"Yes, my lady. There is a space below the cellar—little more than a hole dug out amid the foundations of the tower. The moat water seeps across the floor and things . . . slimy things . . . breed there."

"And this is where Gavin is kept?"

"Yes, my lady," Joan said quietly. "The ceiling of that hole is the cellar floor, and it is high above the hole's floor. The only descent is down a ladder."

"You have seen this place?"

"Yes, my lady." She bowed her head again. "And I have seen Lord Gavin."

Judith grabbed the girl's arms fiercely. "You have seen him and you waited this long to tell me?"

"I didn't believe that . . . that man was Lord Gavin." She looked up, agony etching her face. "He has always been so handsome, so strong, but now there is little more than skin on his bones. His eyes are black circles that burn through you. The guard, the man I spent the night with, opened the trap-door and held a candle. The stench! I could barely look into the blackness. Lord Gavin—I wasn't at first sure it was he— covered his face from the brightness of just one candle. The floor, my lady—it crawled! There was no dry place on it. How does he sleep? There could be no place to lie down."

"You are sure this man was Lord Gavin?"

"Yes. The guard's whip licked at him, and he drew his hand away and stared up at us in hatred."

"Did he know you?"

"I don't think so. I feared that at first, but now I believe him to be beyond recognizing anyone."

Judith looked away in thought.

Joan touched her arm. "My lady, it is too late. He's not long for this world. He can't last for more than a few days, at most. Forget him. He is worse than dead."

Judith gave her a hard look. "Didn't you just say he is alive?"

"Only barely. Even if he were taken out today, the sunlight would kill him in moments."

Judith left the bed. "I must dress."

Joan looked at her mistress's straight back. She was glad she'd given up any idea of rescue. The shrunken, emaciated face still haunted her. Still, Joan was suspicious. She'd lived with Judith too long, and she knew her little mistress rarely let a problem go unsolved. There were times when Joan had been completely exhausted from arranging and rearranging some matter so that Judith could see it from all angles. Yet Judith never gave up. If she set her mind to the harvesting of a field before a certain date, it was harvested by then, even if Judith herself had to help in the threshing.

"Joan, I will need a garment of russet, very dark, like the serfs wear. And some boots—tall ones. It won't matter if they're too large—for I can lace them tight. And a bench. Make sure it is a long one, but narrow enough to fit through the trapdoor. Also, I will need an ironbound box. Not too big, but one I can strap to my stomach."

"Stomach?" Joan managed to get out. "You can't think— Haven't I explained to you that he is nearly dead, that he can't be rescued? You can't take a bench to him and think no one will notice. Food, perhaps, but—" Judith's look stopped her. She was a small woman, but when those gold eyes turned as hard as that, there was no disobeying her. "Yes, my lady," Joan said meekly. "A bench, boots, a servant's garments and . . . an iron box to fit your stomach," she said sarcastically.

"Yes, to fit my stomach," Judith said without humor. "Now help me dress." She lifted a yellow silk underdress from the large chest by the bed. There were twenty pearl buttons running from wrist to elbow. Over it she slipped a gown of tawny gold velvet with wide, hanging sleeves. A belt of brown silk cords threaded with pearls hung from her waist to the ground.

Joan took an ivory comb and began to arrange her mistress's hair. "Don't let him know you care anything for Lord Gavin."

"I don't need to be told that. Go now and find the things I want. And don't let anyone see you with them."

"I can't carry a bench about in secrecy."

"Joan!"

"Yes, my lady, I will do as I am told."

Hours later after he'd spent the morning escorting her through stables and dairies Walter said, "My lady, you must be tired; surely all this must have little interest for you."

"Oh, but it does!" Judith smiled. "The walls are so thick," she said with wide-eyed innocence. The castle was of the simplest form. It contained one large four-story stone tower set inside a single twelve-foot-thick wall. There were a few men atop the walls, but they looked sleepy and not very alert.

"Perhaps my lady would like to inspect the armor of the knights and look for flaws," Arthur said as he watched her.

Judith managed to keep her face blank. "I don't understand what you mean, sir," she said in confusion.

"Nor do I, Arthur!" Walter added.

Arthur didn't answer, but merely stared at Judith. She knew she had an enemy. He had easily seen through her interest in the fortifications. She turned to Walter, "I believe I'm more tired than I thought. It was indeed a long journey here. Perhaps I should rest."

"Of course, my lady."

Judith wanted to get away from him, be rid of his hand,

so often on her arm or her waist. Gratefully, she left him at her chamber door. She fell upon the bed fully dressed. All morning her mind had been full of what Joan had told her of Gavin. She could imagine him half-dead from the filth of the hideous place where he was kept.

The door opened, but she paid it no attention. A noble-woman was rarely allowed privacy. Maids always slipped in and out of her room. She gasped when a male hand touched her neck.

"My lord Walter!" she cried, looking quickly about the room.

"Have no fear," he said quietly. "We are alone. I've seen to that. The servants know my punishments are harsh if I'm disobeyed."

Judith was flustered.

"Do you fear me?" he asked, his eyes dancing. "You have no need to. Don't you know I love you? I have loved you since I first saw you. I waited in the procession that followed you to church. Shall I tell you how you looked to me?" He picked up a curl of her hair and wound it around his arm. "You stepped into the sunlight, and it was as if that light darkened when presented with your greater radiance. Your gold dress, your gold eyes."

He held up the strand of hair, rubbing it with the fingers of his other hand against his palm. "How I wanted to touch this fine stuff then. It was then that I knew you were meant to be mine. Yet you married another!" he accused.

Judith was frightened, not of him or what he could do to her, but of what she'd lose if he took her now. She buried her face in her hands as if she were weeping.

"My lady! My sweet Judith. Forgive me. What have I done?" Walter asked in bewilderment.

She made an effort to recover herself. "I am the one to ask forgiveness. It is just that men . . ."

"Men what? You can tell me. I am your friend."

"Are you?" she asked, her eyes pleading and excessively innocent.

"Yes," Walter whispered, devouring her as best he could.

"I have never had a man friend before. First my father and my brother's—No! I won't speak ill of them."

"There is no need," Walter said as he touched the back of her hand with his fingertips. "I knew them well."

"And then my husband!" Judith said fiercely.

Walter blinked at her. "Do you dislike him then? Is it true?"

Her eyes flashed as she looked at him with such hatred he was taken aback. It was almost as if it were meant for him instead of her husband.

"All men are the same!" she said angrily. "They want only one thing from a woman, and if she doesn't give it, she is forced. Do you know how vile rape is to a woman?"

"No, I—" Walter was confused.

"Men know little of the finer things of life—music and art. I wish I could believe there was a man somewhere on earth who didn't paw at me and make demands."

Walter gave her a shrewd look. "And if you found such a man how would you reward him?"

She smiled sweetly. "I would love him with all my heart," she said simply.

He raised her hand to his lips and kissed it tenderly. Judith lowered her eyes. "Then I will hold you to that," he said quietly. "For I would do a lot to have your heart."

"It has belonged to no one else," Judith whispered.

He released her hand and stood. "Then I will leave you to your rest. Remember, I'm your friend and I will be near if you need me."

As he left the room, Joan slipped inside. "Lady Judith! He hasn't . . . ?"

"No, nothing happened," she said as she leaned back against the headboard. "I talked him out of what he wanted."

"Talked! You must tell me—. No, do not. I would never need to know how to talk a man from making love to me. Whatever you did was good. Can you keep him from you, though?"

"I don't know. He thinks I'm a cowering simpleton, and I don't know how long I can keep up the deception. I hate myself when I lie like that!" Judith turned to her maid. "Is everything prepared for tonight?"

"Yes, though it wasn't easy."

"You will be well rewarded when we leave here, if we do. Now find some other women and prepare me a bath. I must scrub wherever that man has touched me."

John Bassett paced the floor of the room, his footsteps heavy. The toe of his soft slippers caught at something buried in the rushes, and he kicked at it in wrath. A beef bone, old and dry, went flying against the far wall. "A lady's maid." he cursed. Locked inside a room, allowed no freedom, his only company a woman who cowered from him.

Truthfully, it wasn't her fault that he was there. He turned and looked at her, huddled under a coverlet before the brazier. He knew her long skirts hid a badly sprained ankle which she had not allowed her daughter to see.

Suddenly his anger left him. It did him no good to let it eat at him. "I am poor company," he said as he moved a stool to the far side of the brazier and sat down. Helen looked at him with frightened eyes. He knew of her husband, and he was ashamed that he also had scared her. "It's not you who angers me, but that daughter of yours. How could a quiet and sensible woman such as yourself breed such a stubborn wench? She sought to rescue two prisoners, but now she has three to save—and with no more help than that hot-blooded maid of hers."

He turned and saw Helen was smiling, a smile of pure pride. "You take pride in such a daughter?" he asked, astonished.

"Yes, I do. She is afraid of nothing. And she always thinks of others first."

"She should have been taught to fear," John said fiercely. "Fear is good at times."

"If she were yours, how would you have taught her?"

"I would have—" John began. Obviously, beating was not the answer; he was sure Robert Revedoune had caused her a great deal of pain. He turned to Helen and smiled. "I don't believe she could have been taught. But if she were mine . . ." He smiled more broadly. "I would be proud of her, if she were mine. Though I doubt such beauty could have come from something as ugly as me."

"Oh, but you are not the least ugly," Helen said, her cheeks turning pink.

John stared at her, not having really looked at her before. The first time he'd seen her, at the wedding, he'd dismissed her as being haggard and plain, but now he could see she was neither. A month away from Robert Revedoune had done her much good. She didn't seem so nervous as before, and her hollow cheeks were filling out. Except for the widow's peak, her hair was covered, but he could see it was auburn, darker than her daughter's. And her eyes seemed to have tiny gold flecks in them.

"You stare at me, sir?"

With his usual bluntness, John said what he thought. "You are not old."

"I will be thirty-three years old this year," she answered. "That is an old woman."

"Bah! I remember a forty-year-old woman who—" He stopped and smiled. "Perhaps I shouldn't tell a lady that story. But thirty-three years is far from being old." He had an idea. "Do you know you are a rich woman now? You are a widow with great estates. Soon you will have men pounding at your door."

"No," she laughed, her cheeks flaming. "You jest."

"A rich as well as a beautiful widow," he teased. "Lord Gavin will have to cut through them to find you a husband."

"Husband?" Helen suddenly sobered.

"Here!" John commanded. "Don't look like that. Few are like that villain you married."

She blinked at what she should have considered rudeness; but coming from John, it was a statement of fact.

"Lord Gavin will find a good man for you."

She stared at him as if in speculation. "Were you ever married, John?"

He waited a moment before answering. "Yes, once when I was very young. She died of the plague."

"No children?"

"No. None."

"Did you . . . love her?" Helen asked timidly.

"No," he responded honestly. "She was a simpleminded child. It has long been a fault of mine that I cannot bear stupidity—in a man or a horse or a woman." He chuckled at some private thought. "Once I made a boast that I would lay my heart before a woman who could play a good game of chess. Do you know, I even once played a game with Queen Elizabeth?"

"And did she win?"

"No," he said in disgust. "She couldn't keep her mind on the game. I tried to teach Gavin and his brothers the game, but they are worse than some women. Only their father gave me a challenge."

Helen looked at him seriously. "I know the game. At least I know the moves."

"You?"

"Yes. I taught Judith to play, though she could never beat me. She was as the queen, always worrying about another problem. She couldn't give the proper concentration the game deserved."

John hesitated.

"If we are to spend some time here, perhaps you can give me lessons. I would appreciate any help."

John sighed. Maybe it was a good idea at that. At least it would help pass the time.

Chapter 17

JUDITH'S CHAMBER was as quiet as the rest of the Demari castle when she began her preparations to go to Gavin in the pit.

"Give the guard this," Judith said as she handed Joan a skin of wine, "and he will sleep through the night. We could set barrels of oil on fire next to him, and he won't wake."

"Which is what will happen when Lord Gavin sees you," Joan muttered.

"I thought you believed him to be nearly dead. Now don't talk any more, but do as I say. Is everything ready?"

"It is. Are you feeling better?" Joan asked concerned.

Judith nodded, swallowing hard in memory of her recent nausea.

"If you have kept anything down, you will lose it when you step into that vile pit."

Judith ignored her comment. "Go now and give the man his wine. I will wait a short time, then follow you."

Joan slipped silently from the room, an art she'd learned through long years of practice. Judith waited nervously for nearly an hour. She strapped the iron box about her stomach, then slipped the rough wool garment over her head. Had anyone noticed the serf walking quietly amid the sleeping knights, they would have seen a heavily pregnant woman, her hands at her lower back, supporting the burdensome weight of her belly. Judith had some difficulty managing the railless stone stairs that led to the cellar.

"My lady?" Joan called in a loud whisper.

"Yes." Judith made her way toward the single candle flame that Joan held. "Is he asleep?"

"Yes. Can't you hear him snoring?"

"I can hear nothing over my pounding heart. Set the candle down and help me unstrap this box."

Joan sank to her knees as Judith lifted her skirts to her waist. "Why did you need the box?" Joan asked.

"To store the food. To keep the . . . rats from it."

Joan shivered as her cold hands worked at the knots of rawhide. "There are more than rats down there. My lady, please—it isn't too late to change your mind."

"Are you saying you will go in my place?"

Joan's gasp of horror was her answer.

"Quiet, then. Think of Gavin who has to live there."

As the two women pulled the trapdoor back from the pit, the foul air made them turn their heads away. "Gavin!" Judith called. "Are you there?"

No answer came.

"Give me the candle."

Joan handed her mistress the taper and looked away. She didn't wish to look in the pit again.

Judith searched the black hole with the light. She had steeled herself for the worst, and she wasn't disappointed. Yet Joan had been wrong about the floor. It was not totally devoid of dry area—or at least comparatively dry. The dirt floor sloped away from the stone walls so that one corner was mere mud rather than the slime-infested water. In this corner Judith saw a hunched figure. Only the eyes that glared at her told her the heap was alive.

"Give me the ladder, Joan. When I'm on the bottom, send the bench down, then the food and wine. You understand?"

"I don't like this place."

"Neither do I." It wasn't easy for Judith to descend that ladder into hell. She dared not look down. There was no need to see what was on the floor; she could smell and hear the slithering movements. She set the candle on a jutting stone of the wall but didn't look at Gavin. She knew he worked to push himself upward.

"The bench now," Judith called up. It wasn't easy to maneuver the heavy piece down the ladder, and she knew Joan's arms were nearly pulled from their sockets. It was easier to lift it and set it against the wall next to Gavin. The box of food came next, followed by a large skin of wine.

"There," she said as she set the items on the edge of the bench then took a step toward her husband. She knew why Joan said he was near death. He was emaciated, his high cheekbones razor-sharp.

"Gavin," she said quietly and held her hand out to him, palm up.

He moved his thin and filthy hand slowly to touch her, as if he expected her to disappear. When he felt her warm flesh against his, he looked back at her in surprise. "Judith." The word was harsh, his voice hoarse from long disuse and a parched throat.

She took his hand firmly to hers then pulled him to sit on the bench. She held the skin of wine to his lips. It was a while before he understood he was to drink. "Slowly," Judith said as he began to gulp the heavy, sweet liquid. She put the wineskin down, then took a stoppered jar from the box and began to feed him rich, filling stew. The meat and vegetables had been cooked to a pulp easy for him to chew.

He ate little before he leaned back against the wall, his eyes closed in weariness. "It has been a long time since I have had food. A man doesn't appreciate what he has until it is taken from him." He rested a moment, then sat up again and stared at his wife. "Why are you here?"

"To bring you food."

"No, I don't mean that. Why are you in Demari's holdings?"

"Gavin, you should eat and not talk. I'll tell you everything if you will only eat more." She gave him a chunk of dark bread dipped in the stew.

Once again he turned his attention to eating. "Are my men above?" he asked, his mouth full. "I think I may have forgotten how to walk, but when I have eaten more, I will be stronger. They shouldn't have sent you down here."

Judith hadn't realized that her presence would make Gavin believe he was free. "No," she said as she blinked back tears. "I can't take you from here . . . yet."

"Yet?" He looked up at her. "What are you saying?"

"I am alone, Gavin. There are no men above. You are still a captive of Walter Demari, as is my mother, and now John Bassett."

He stopped eating, his hand paused above the jar. Abruptly, as if she had said nothing, he resumed. "Tell me all," he said flatly.

"John Bassett told me Demari had captured you and my mother. John saw no way to win you back except through siege." She stopped, as if finished with the story.

"So you came here and thought to save me?" He looked at her, his sunken eyes hot.

"Gavin, I—"

"And, pray, what good did you hope to do? To draw a sword and run them through and order my release?"

She clamped her jaw shut.

"I will have John's head for this."

"That is what he said," she muttered.

"What?"

"I said John knew you would be angry."

"Angry?" Gavin said. "My estates are left unguarded, my men are left leaderless, my wife is held prisoner by an insane man, and you say I am angry? No, wife, I am far more than angry."

Judith straightened her back, clenched her jaw. "There was no other way. A siege would have killed you."

"A siege, yes," he said fiercely, "but there are other ways to take this place than by siege."

"But John said—"

"John! He is a knight, not a leader. His father followed mine, as he follows me. He should have gone for Miles or even Raine, with his broken leg. I will kill John the next time I see him!"

"No, Gavin. He is not at fault. I told him I would go alone if he didn't bring me."

The candle made her eyes glow. The woolen hood had fallen away from her hair.

"I had forgotten how beautiful you are," he said quietly. "Let's not quarrel anymore. We can't change what has been done. Tell me what is happening above."

She told him of how she'd gotten better quarters for her mother, yet had also succeeded in getting John made prisoner. "But it is as well," she continued. "He wouldn't have allowed me down here."

"I wish he hadn't. Judith, you shouldn't have set foot in this place."

"But I had to bring you food!" she protested.

He stared at her, then sighed. He began to smile at her. "I pity John's having to deal with you."

She looked at him in surprise. "He said the same of you. Have I done so very wrong?"

"Yes," Gavin answered honestly. "You have put more people in danger, and any rescue now will be much more difficult."

She looked down at her hands.

"Come, look at me. It has been a long time since I saw anything that is even clean." He handed her the empty jar.

"I brought more food and a metal box to keep it in."

"And a bench," he said as he shook his head. "Judith, do you realize Demari's men will know who has sent these things when they see them? You must take them back."

"No! You need them."

He stared at her. All he'd done was complain about her. "Judith," he whispered, "thank you." He put his hand up, as if to touch her cheek, but stopped.

"You are annoyed with me," she said flatly, thinking that was why he wouldn't touch her.

"I don't want to soil you. I am more than filthy. I feel things crawl on my skin even now as you sit so close to me."

She took his hand and guided it to her cheek. "Joan said you were little more than alive, but she also said you looked up at the guard with defiance. If you still hated, you couldn't be so near death." She leaned toward him and he touched his mouth to hers. She had to content herself with that; he would not contaminate her further with his touch.

"Listen to me, Judith. You must obey me. I will brook no disobedience, do you understand? I'm not John Bassett you can twist about your fingers. And if you disobey me, it will no doubt cost many lives. Do you understand?"

"Yes," she nodded. She wanted guidance.

"Before I was taken, Odo was able to reach Stephen in Scotland."

"Your brother?"

"Yes, you don't know him. He will be told all of what Demari has done. Stephen will come soon. He is an experienced fighter, and these old walls won't stand long before him. But it will take days for him to travel from Scotland—even if the messenger can find him quickly."

"So what am I to do?"

"You should have stayed at home and waited with your embroidery frame," he said in disgust. "Then we would have had time. Now you must buy us time. Agree to nothing Demari says. Talk to him of women's things, but don't talk to him of annulment or your estates."

"He thinks I'm a simpleton."

"Deliver all men from such simple women! Now you must go."

She stood. "I will bring more food tomorrow."

"No! Send Joan. No one will notice that cat slipping from one bed to the next."

"But I will come in disguise."

"Judith, who else has hair the color of yours? If one strand were to escape, you would be recognized. And if you were found out, there would be no reason to keep the rest of us alive. Demari must think you will comply with his plans. Now go and obey me for once."

She stood and nodded as she turned toward the ladder.

"Judith," he whispered. "Would you kiss me again?"

She smiled happily and before he could stop her, her arms

were about his waist, holding him close to her. She could feel the change in his body, the weight he'd lost. "I have been frightened, Gavin," she confessed.

He lifted her chin in his hand. "You are braver than ten men." He kissed her longingly. "Now go and don't come again."

She nearly ran up the ladder and out of the dark cellar.

Chapter 18

THE CASTLE was quiet when Arthur finally allowed his anger to explode. He knew he should have kept his temper under control, but he'd seen too much in one day.

"You are a fool!" Arthur said with a sneer. "Don't you see how the woman plays you like a master harper plays a psaltery?"

"You overstep yourself," Walter warned.

"Someone must! You're so besotted by her that she could slip a knife between your ribs and you would murmur, 'Thank you.' "

Walter suddenly looked into his cup of ale. "She is a sweet and lovely woman," he murmured.

"Sweet! Bah! She is as sweet as verjuice. She has been here three days, and look at how far you have gotten with negotiations for an annulment. What does she say when you ask her?" He didn't give Walter time to reply. "That woman has a convenient hearing loss. At times she just looks at you and smiles when you ask her a question. You would think she is both deaf and dumb. You never press her, but only return her smile with a mindless one of your own."

"She is a beautiful woman," Walter said in defense.

"Yes, she is enticing," Arthur acknowledged and smiled to himself. Judith Montgomery was beginning to stir his blood also, though not in the holy way she affected Walter. "But what has her beauty accomplished? You are no nearer your goal than when she arrived."

Walter slammed down his goblet. "She is a woman, damn you, not a man you can reason with! She must be wooed and won. Women must be loved. And there is her father and that vile husband of hers. They have frightened her."

"Frightened!" Arthur snorted. "I have never seen a woman less frightened in my life. A frightened woman would have stayed home in her bed behind her castle walls. This one comes riding to our gate and—"

"And asks for nothing!" Walter said triumphantly. "She has asked for nothing but better quarters for her mother, a simple request. She spends her days with me and is pleasant company. Judith has not so much as asked about the fate of her husband. Surely that shows she doesn't care about him."

"I'm not so sure," Arthur said thoughtfully. "It seems unnatural for her to care so little about him."

"She hates him, I tell you! I don't see why you don't kill him and be done with it. I would wed her atop the dead man's corpse if the priest would allow it."

"Then you would have the king upon your head! She is a rich woman. Her father had the right to give her to a man, but now he is dead. No one else has the right except the king. The moment her husband is dead, she becomes the king's ward, the revenues from her estates his. Do you think King Henry would give a rich widow to the man who tortured and killed her husband? And if you took her without his permission, he would be even more angry. I've told you time and again: the only way is if she stands before the king and asks publicly for a release from her marriage and declares for you. King Henry loves the queen and is greatly moved by such sentimentality."

"Then I am proceeding properly," Walter said. "I'm making the woman love me. I can see it in her eyes when she looks at me."

"I say again, you are a fool. You see what you wish. I am not so certain that she doesn't scheme something. A plan of escape, perhaps."

"Escape from me? I don't hold her captive. She is free to go when she wants."

Arthur looked at the man with revulsion. He was not only a fool, but stupid as well. If Arthur were not cautious, all his carefully laid plans would be destroyed by a golden-eyed goddess. "You say she hates her husband?"

"Yes. I know she does."

"Do you have proof other than servants' gossip?"

"She never speaks of him."

"Perhaps the love she bears him hurts her too much to speak of him," Arthur said snidely. "Perhaps we should put her hatred to a test."

Walter hesitated.

"You're not so sure of her now?"

"I am! What do you plan?"

"We will bring her husband up from the pit, bring him before her and see her reaction. Will she cry in horror to see him as he must be now? Or will she be glad to see him so tortured?"

"She will be glad," Walter said firmly.

"Let us hope you are right. But I believe you are not."

The new quarters Judith had gotten for Lady Helen were large, airy and cleaner. A stout wooden partition had been nailed into the walls of the fourth-floor solar, creating the room. It was secluded from the rest of the castle, protected by a door of four-inch-thick seasoned oak.

There was little furniture. A large bed draped with heavy linen occupied one corner. A straw pallet was on the other side of the chamber. Two people sat across from the glowing brazier, their heads nearly touching over a chessboard set on a low table.

"You have won again!" John Bassett said in astonishment.

Helen smiled at him. "You seem pleased."

"Yes, I am. At least these days haven't been dull." During the time they had been together he'd seen many changes in her. She had gained weight; her cheeks were losing their hollows. And she had begun to relax in his presence. Her eyes no longer darted from side to side. In truth, they rarely left John.

"Do you think my daughter is well?" Helen asked as she set the chess pieces back in their original positions.

"I can only guess. If she had been harmed, I think we would know. I don't think Demari will lose much time in seeing that we suffer the same fate."

Helen nodded. She found John's harsh truthfulness refreshing after having lived with lies for so long. She hadn't seen Judith since that first night, and had it not been for John's steadiness, she would have worried herself into illness. "Another game?"

"No. I must have a rest from your attacks."

"It is late. Perhaps . . ." she began, not wanting to go to bed and leave his company.

"Will you sit by me a moment?" he asked as he rose and stirred the coals in the brazier.

"Yes," she smiled. This was the part of the day she loved the best—being carried from one place to another in John's strong arms. She was quite sure her ankle was well, but he didn't ask after it, and she did not mention it.

He looked down at her head cradled against his shoulder. "You look more like your daughter each day," he said as he carried her to a chair closer to the fire. "It's easy to see where she gets her beauty."

Helen didn't speak, but smiled against his shoulder, delighting in the strength of him. He had no more than deposited her in the chair when the door burst open.

"Mother!" Judith said as she rushed to Helen's open arms.

"I have been worried about you," Helen said anxiously. "Where have they kept you? They haven't harmed you?"

"What news?" John's deep voice interrupted.

Judith pulled away from her mother. "No, I am unharmed. I couldn't come because I've had no time. Walter Demari keeps me at something every moment. If I mention a visit to you, he finds someplace I must go." She sat down on a stool John placed behind her. "As for the news, I have seen Gavin."

Neither John nor Helen spoke.

"They keep him in a hole below the cellar. It is a slimy

place, and he cannot live much longer in it. I went to him and—"

"You went into the pit?" Helen asked, astonished. "Not while you carry a child! You endangered the baby!"

"Quiet!" John commanded. "Let her tell of Lord Gavin."

Judith looked at her mother, who usually cowered away from a man's sharp tones, but Helen only obeyed and showed no fear. "He was very angry at me for being here and said that he had already arranged for our rescue. His brother Stephen has been sent for."

"Lord Stephen?" John asked, then smiled. "Ah yes. If we can hold out until he comes, we will be saved. He is a good fighter."

"That is what Gavin said. I am to keep Demari from me as long as I can, to give Stephen time to bring his men."

"What else did Lord Gavin say?"

"Very little. He spent most of the time listing all that is wrong with me," Judith said in disgust.

"And are you able to keep Demari from you?" Helen wondered.

Judith sighed. "It's not easy. If he touches my wrist, his hand slides to my elbow. A hand on my waist rides up my ribs. I don't respect the man. If he were to sit down and talk reasonably to me, I would sign half the Revedoune lands over to him for a copper if he would only free us all. Instead he offers me daisy chains and love poems. There are times when I want to scream in frustration."

"What of Sir Arthur?" John asked. "I cannot see that man making daisy chains."

"No, he just watches me. I am never away from his eyes staring at me. I feel there is something he plans, but I don't know what."

"It will be the worst, I'm sure," John said. "I wish I could help you!"

"No, there is nothing I need help with now. I can only wait for Lord Stephen to arrive and negotiate or fight—whichever must be done. I will talk with him then."

"Talk?" John raised one eyebrow. "Stephen is little given to talking over his battle plans with women."

A knock sounded on the door. "I must go. Joan waits for me. I'm not sure I want Demari to know I'm here."

"Judith." Helen grabbed her daughter's arm. "You are caring for yourself?"

"As well as I can. I am tired—that's all." She kissed her mother's cheek. "I must go."

When they were alone, John turned to Helen. "Here, don't cry," he said sternly. "It will help nothing."

"I know," Helen agreed. "She is just so alone. She has always been alone."

"And what of you—have you not also always been alone?"

"I don't matter. I am an old woman."

He grabbed her harshly under her arms and pulled her to him. "You are not old!" John said fiercely before his mouth came down on hers.

Helen had been kissed by no man except her husband—and him only at the beginning of their marriage. She was startled by the chill that ran up her spine. She returned his kiss, her arms going about his neck, drawing him closer to her.

He kissed her cheek, her neck, his heart pounding in his ears. "It is late," he whispered, then swung her into his arms and carried her toward the bed. Each night he helped her unbutton her simple gown since she had no other maid. He was always respectful and kept his eyes turned away when she climbed into bed. Now he set her on her feet by the bed, then turned to walk away.

"John," she called, "you will not help me with the buttons?"

He looked back at her, his eyes dark with passion. "Not tonight. If I were to help you undress, you wouldn't climb into that bed alone."

Helen stared at him, the blood pounding through her body. Her experiences with a man in bed had been brutal times. But now she gazed at John and knew he would be different. What would it be like to lie happily in a man's arms?

She could hardly hear her own voice when she spoke. "I will still need help."

He walked to stand before her. "Are you sure? You are a lady. I am only your son-in-law's vassal."

"You have come to mean a lot to me, John Bassett, and now I would have you be all."

He touched the hood at her forehead, then pushed it away completely. "Come, then," he smiled. "Let me see those fastenings."

In spite of Helen's brave words, she was afraid of John. She had grown to love him over the last few days, and she wanted to give him something. She had nothing except her body. She gave herself as a martyr. She knew men received great pleasure from the joining in bed, but for her it had only been a quick, rather messy affair. She had no idea it could be any different.

She was surprised when he took his time undressing her. She thought a man would have thrown her skirts over her face and been done with it. John seemed to enjoy touching her. His fingers along her ribs sent little shivers through her skin. He lifted her dress over her head, then her underdress. He stepped away from her and looked at her as she stood wearing only the thin cotton chemise and her hose. He smiled warmly at her as if her body pleased him. He put his hands on her waist, then lifted the chemise away. His hands were on her breasts instantly, and Helen gasped in pleasure at his touch. He brought his lips to hers. She kept her eyes open as she stared in wonder. His gentleness sent waves of delight through her body. Her breasts ached against the rough wool of his doublet. She closed her eyes and leaned against him, her arms tightening. Never had she experienced this feeling before.

John pulled away from her and began to remove his clothing. Helen's heart was pounding. "Let me," she heard herself say, then drew back at her own boldness. John smiled at her with just the expression she was feeling—rising passion.

She'd never undressed a man before, except to help a visitor who she was helping to bathe. John's body was stout and muscular, and she touched his skin as each garment fell to the floor. Her breasts touched his arm, sending little sparks through her body.

When John was nude, he lifted Helen in his arms and carefully placed her in bed. She had a moment's regret that now the pain would begin and the pleasure end. John lifted her foot and set it in his lap. As Helen watched breathlessly, he untied her garter and rolled the cotton stockings off, kissing her leg every inch of the way. By the time he reached her toes, Helen could no longer hold herself up. Her body was strangely weak, her heart was now hammering in her throat. She reached her arms out for him to come to her, but he would not.

He reached for her other leg. Helen knew she could bear no more. Her body was beginning to ache for him. John laughed throatily and pushed away her clutching hands. It was an eternity before he'd kissed the other stocking off.

Helen lay back against the pillows, weakly. John came to her, kissed her, and her hands buried themselves into his shoulders. He ran his hand firmly down her side and pulled away her underpants. She pressed against him, could feel that he was ready for her. But John was not through with his torture of her. His head bent to her breasts, his tongue and teeth making little nibbles on the hard pink crests. Helen moaned, her head moving from side to side on the pillow.

John slowly moved a leg on top of her, then his whole weight. How good he felt! He was so strong and heavy. When he entered her, she cried out. She felt that she may as well be a virgin for all the experience she'd had in pleasure. Her husband had used her body, but John made love to her.

Her passion was as fierce as John's, and they came together in a fiery explosion. He pulled her close to him, his arm and one leg thrown across her as if he thought she'd try to escape. Helen burrowed herself even closer to him. If possible, she would have liked to slip inside his skin. Her body began to relax in the delicious pleasure of the aftermath of a night of love. She fell asleep with John's soft breath in her ear and on her neck.

* * *

Judith sat at the high table between Walter and Arthur. She picked at her food, unable to choke down the poorly cooked meal. But had it been the best food, it would not have mattered. She wore a cream silk undertunic and over it a gown of royal blue velvet. The large, hanging sleeves of the gown were lined with blue satin which was embroidered with tiny gold halfmoons. A gold filigree belt with a buckle set with a single large cabochon sapphire was about her waist.

Walter's hands constantly touched her. They were on her wrists, her arm, her neck. He didn't seem to realize they were in a public place. But Judith was very aware of the twenty-five knights who unabashedly stared at her. She could feel the speculation in their eyes. As she jabbed her fork into a piece of beef, she wished it were Walter's heart. It was a difficult thing to swallow one's pride.

"Judith," Walter whispered hoarsely into her ear. "I could devour you." He pressed his lips to her neck, and she could feel shudders of revulsion shaking her. "Why do we wait? Can't you feel my love for you? Don't you know of my desire for you?"

Judith kept herself stiff, refusing to allow herself to pull her body away. He nibbled at her neck, nuzzled her shoulder and she couldn't show how she felt. "My lord," she managed to say after several hard swallows, "don't you remember your own words? You said we must wait."

"I cannot," he choked. "I cannot wait for you."

"But you must!" Judith said with more anger than she had intended and jerked her hand from his violently. "Listen to me. What if I give in to my passions for you and go to your bed? Don't you think a child would be made? What will the king say when we appear before him with my belly swollen? Do you think anyone would believe the child is not my husband's? No annulment can be had if I carry his child. And you know a divorce must come from the pope. I have heard that one takes years."

"Judith—" Walter began, then stopped. Her words made sense. They also appealed to his vanity. How well he remembered Robert Revedoune saying that he gave his daughter to the Montgomery men to get sons. He knew he—Walter— could give her sons! She was right. If they were to come together, they would create a son in the first mating. He took a deep drink of wine, his mind mixed with pride and frustration.

"When do we go to the king, my lord?" Judith asked bluntly. Perhaps she could arrange an escape on their journey.

They sat at the dinner table, but Walter paid little attention to his audience. Now Arthur spoke. "Are you anxious to declare your desire for an annulment to the king?"

She didn't answer him.

"Come, my lady, we are your friends. You can speak freely. Is your passion for Lord Walter so deep that you cannot wait to declare it to the world?"

"I don't like your tone," Walter interjected. "She has nothing to prove. She is a guest, not a prisoner. She was not forced to come here."

Arthur smiled, his eyes narrowed. "Yes, she came freely," he said in a loud voice. Then, as he reached past Judith for a cut of meat, he lowered his voice. "But why did my lady come? I have yet to have an answer."

The meal seemed horribly long to Judith and she couldn't wait to leave. When Walter turned his back to her to speak to his steward, Judith seized the opportunity to get up from the table. She ran up the stairs, her heart pounding wildly. How much longer could she hold out against Walter Demari? Each minute his advances became more forward. She stopped running and leaned against the cold stone wall, trying to recover herself. Why did she always believe she could handle everything by herself?

"There you are!"

Judith looked up to see Arthur standing near her. They were alone in a deep recess of the thick walls.

"Are you looking for an escape route?" he smirked. "There is none. We are quite alone." His strong arm reached out and encircled her waist, pulling her close to him. "Where is that ready tongue of yours? Are you going to try to talk me out of touching you?" His hand ran over her arm, caressing it. "You are lovely enough to cause a man to lose his mind. I almost understand Walter's reluctance to bed you." He looked back at her face. "I see no fear in those gold eyes, but I would like to see them blaze with the heat of passion. Do you think I could make them do so?"

His hard lips swooped down on hers, but Judith felt nothing. She remained rigid against him.

He broke away from her. "You are an icy bitch," he growled, then crushed her closer to him. She gasped as the air was forced from her lungs. He took advantage of her open mouth and seized it again, thrusting his tongue inside until Judith gagged. His embrace hurt her; his mouth disgusted her.

Arthur pulled away from her again, loosening his hold, but he didn't release her. His eyes showed anger at first, then changed to mockery. "No, you are not cold. No woman with such hair and eyes could be. But who is it that melts that ice? Is it Walter with his hand-kissing, or perhaps it is that husband of yours?"

"No!" Judith said then closed her lips.

Arthur smiled. "For all Walter thinks otherwise, you are a poor actress." Arthur's face turned hard. "Walter is a stupid man, but I'm not. He thinks you came to this place out of love for him, but I don't believe it. If I were a woman, I would hope to use my beauty to free those I loved. Is it your plan to bargain yourself in exchange for your mother's and husband's release?"

"Let me go!" Judith demanded, twisting in his arms.

He held her more firmly. "You cannot escape me. Don't even try."

"What of Walter?" she challenged.

He laughed. "You play the game well, but beware that you play with fire and will get burned. Do you think I fear a bit of slime like Demari? I can handle him. Who do you think thought of this idea of annulment?"

Judith stopped struggling.

"Ah! So I have your attention. Listen to me. Walter will have you first, but you will be mine later. When he has grown tired of you and begins to take other women, you will be mine."

"I would sooner bed a viper," she hissed as his hand bit into her arm.

"Even to save that mother of yours?" he said in a deadly voice. "You have done a lot for her already. What more would you do?"

"You shall never know!"

He pulled her against him again. "Won't I? You think yourself a lady of some power while you hold that fool Demari in your hands, but I will show you who has the power here."

"What . . . what do you mean?"

He smiled. "You will know soon enough."

She tried to recover from the awful feeling his words gave her. "What are you going to do? You wouldn't hurt my mother?"

"No, I'm not so unsubtle as that. Only a bit of fun. It will do me good to see you squirm. When you have had enough, come to my bed some night and we will talk."

"Never!"

"Don't be so hasty." Suddenly Arthur released her. "I must go. You have my words to think about."

When she was alone, Judith stood very still, breathing deeply to calm herself. She turned toward her room, but was startled to see a man standing quietly in the shadows. He leaned lazily against the opposite wall of the hall. A lute was slung across his broad shoulders, and he idly used a knife to trim his nails. Judith did not know what made her look at him, except that he could have heard some of Arthur's threats. Yet her eyes were drawn to him though he did not raise his head to look at her. As she stared at him, he lifted his face to look at her. His dark blue eyes looked at her with such hate that she gasped. Her hand flew to her mouth, and she bit the back of it.

She turned and ran down the hall to her room where she threw herself onto her bed. The tears came slowly, fighting their way up from the pit of her stomach before they found release.

"My lady," Joan whispered as she stroked Judith's hair. They had grown closer in the last few days as the difference in their stations was lessened. "Has he hurt you?"

"No, I have hurt myself. Gavin said I should have stayed home with my sewing. I'm afraid he was right."

"Sewing," the maid questioned, smiling. "You would have snarled the threads worse than you snarl things here."

Judith looked up, aghast. Then, through her tears, she said, "You are good for me. I felt sorry for myself for a moment. You took Gavin food last night?"

"Yes."

"And how did he look?"

Joan frowned. "Weaker."

"How can I help them?" Judith demanded of herself. "Gavin said I was to wait for his brother Stephen, but how long? I must get Gavin out of that hole!"

"Yes, my lady, you must."

"But how?"

Joan was serious. "Only God can answer that."

That night, Arthur answered Judith's question. They sat at supper, a meal of soup and stews. Walter was quiet, not touching Judith as he usually did, but looking at her from the corner of his eye, as if he were judging her.

"Do you like the food, Lady Judith?" Arthur asked.

She nodded.

"Let us hope the entertainment pleases you also."

She started to ask what he meant, but did not. She wouldn't give the man such satisfaction.

Arthur leaned forward to look at Walter. "Don't you think it's time?"

Walter started to protest, but then seemed to think better of it. It was obviously something he and Arthur had discussed thoroughly. Walter waved his hand to two men-at-arms waiting by the doorway, and the men left.

Judith could not even swallow the food in her mouth and had to wash it down with wine. She knew Arthur planned some trick, and she wanted to be ready for it. She glanced about the hall nervously. Again she saw the man she'd seen in the hallway that afternoon. He was tall and slim with dark blond hair with a few lighter streaks. His jaw was strong and set in a firm line above a cleft chin. But his eyes were what held her. They were a deep, dark blue that blazed with the fire of hatred—hatred that was directed toward her. He mesmerized her.

The sudden, abnormal silence of the hall and the sound of dragging chains drew her eyes away. In the bright light of the great hall, Judith didn't at first recognize the form being dragged between the two knights as human. It was more an odorous pile of rags than a man. It was these few seconds of nonrecognition that saved her. She became aware of Arthur and Walter staring at her, watching her. She looked in puzzlement to them, and as soon as she turned away, she realized that the figure being carried into the hall was Gavin. She didn't look at him again, but kept her eyes fastened on Walter. That would give her time to think. Why did they present him to her like this? Didn't they know she wanted to run to him and help him?

The answer came to her instantly as she realized that was just what Arthur wanted her to do. He wanted to show Walter that she did not hate her husband.

"You don't know him?" Walter asked.

Judith looked up, as if in surprise, at the filthy man being led into the hall. Then she began to smile, very slowly. "It is as I have always wanted to see him."

Walter gave a shout of triumph. "Bring him here! My lovely lady sees him as she hoped he would be," he declared to everyone in the hall. "Let her enjoy this moment—she has earned it."

The two guards brought Gavin to the table. Her heart was beating wildly. Judith could risk making no errors now. If she showed how her heart went out to her husband, that display would no doubt cause many deaths. She stood, her hand trembling, and raised her wine goblet. She threw the contents in his face.

The liquid seemed to revive Gavin, and he looked up at her. His face, lean and sharp, showed surprise. Then wonder. Slowly he looked at Walter and Arthur, who stood beside his wife.

Demari put his arm possessively about Judith's shoulders. "Look now at who holds her," he boasted.

Before anyone could react, Gavin threw himself across the table at Walter. The guards who held his chains were pulled forward, stumbling, falling into the dishes of food. Walter could not get away fast enough, and Gavin's filthy hands closed around the smaller, gaudily-dressed man across the table.

"Seize him!" Walter gasped weakly, using his fingernails to claw at Gavin's hands around his throat.

Judith was stunned as were the retainers. Gavin must be half-dead by now, but his strength was still enough to pull two men off balance and nearly kill his captor.

The guards recovered themselves and yanked on the chains around Gavin's wrists. It took three mighty tugs before they succeeded in freeing Walter. The end of a chain was laid heavily across Gavin's ribs. He grunted and crumpled on one leg for a moment before righting himself. "I will kill you for this," he said, his eyes boring into Walter's before another chain was put to his ribs.

"Take him away!" Walter ordered as he rubbed his nearly crushed throat. He shivered as he still stared at Gavin.

When Gavin had been removed, Walter collapsed into his chair.

Judith knew he would be most vulnerable now. "That was pleasant," she smiled, then turned quickly to the trembling Walter. "Not, of course what he did to you—I don't mean that. But it was good to know he saw me with someone I could . . . care for."

Walter gazed back at her, his spine straightening a bit.

"But of course I should be angry with you." She lowered her eyes seductively.

"Why? What have I done?"

"You really should not have brought such dirt into the

presence of a lady. He looked so starved, I wonder he did not really want the food. How can he see what I now have when all he thinks of is nourishment and the things crawling on his skin?"

Walter considered this. "You are right." He turned to some men by the door. "Tell the guards to clean and feed him." He was ecstatic. Arthur had said Judith would cry when she saw her husband in such a state, but she had smiled!

Only Joan knew what that smile cost her mistress.

Judith turned away from Walter, wanting to leave the room and especially to leave his presence. She held her head high as she walked through the retainers.

"The woman deserves what she gets!" Said some men close to her.

"True. No wife has a right to treat a husband like that."

Each and every one of them despised her. And she too was beginning to hate herself. Judith walked slowly up the stairs to the fourth floor, wanting only privacy. At the top of the steps, an arm flew about her waist, and she was slammed against a man's chest that felt like iron. A knife went to her throat, the sharp edge nearly piercing her delicate skin. Her hands flew to his forearm, but they had no effect.

Chapter 19

"SAY ONE word, and I'll take that viperous head of yours off your body," said the deep voice, one she had never heard before. "Where is John Bassett?"

Judith could hardly speak but this was not a man to be disobeyed.

"Answer me!" he said as his arm tightened and the knife pressed harder against her throat.

"With my mother," she whispered.

"Mother!" he spat into her ear. "May that woman curse the day she gave birth to such as you!"

Judith couldn't see him, and she could hardly breathe from his arm cutting into her ribs and lungs. "Who are you?" she gasped.

"Yes, you should ask that. I am your enemy, and I would delight in ending your vile existence here if I didn't need you. How is John guarded?"

"I . . . cannot breathe."

He hesitated then loosened his grip, the knife easing away from her throat. "Answer me!"

"There are two men outside the door of the room he shares with my mother."

"Which floor? Come, answer me," he commanded as he tightened his hold once again. "Don't think someone will come to save you."

Suddenly it was all too much for Judith and she began to

laugh. Quietly at first, but growing more hysterical with each word. "Save me? And pray, who would save me? My mother is held prisoner. My only guard is also held. My husband is kept in a sewer. A man I detest has the right to paw me before my husband while another whispers threats into my ear. Now I am attacked by a stranger in the dark of the hall!"

Her hands on his forearm pulled the knife closer to her throat. "I pray you, sir, whoever you are—finish what you have started. End my life, I beg you. For what use is it to me? Must I stand and watch my every friend and relative slaughtered before me? I do not wish to live to see that end."

The man's arm relaxed. Then he pulled away from her hands that tugged at the knife. He resheathed the blade, then grabbed her shoulders. Judith was not surprised to recognize the jongleur from the great hall.

"I want to hear more," he said, his voice less harsh.

"Why?" she asked as she stared up into his deadly blue eyes. "Are you a spy set upon me by Walter or Arthur? I have said too much already."

"Yes, you have," he agreed bluntly. "If I were a spy, I would have a lot to report to my master."

"Tell him then! Get it over!"

"I'm not a spy. I am Stephen, Gavin's brother."

Judith stared, her eyes wide. She knew it was true. That was why she had been drawn to him. There was something in Stephen's manner, if not his looks, that reminded her of Gavin. She was not aware that tears were running down her cheeks. "Gavin said you would come. He said I had made a mess of everything, but that you would set it all to right again."

Stephen blinked at her. "When did you see him that he said this?"

"On the second night here. I went to him in the pit."

"In the—?" He'd heard tales of the way Gavin was kept— that much he'd been able to learn—but he could not get near his brother. "Come and sit here," he said, leading Judith to a window seat. "We have much to discuss. Tell me everything, from the start."

Stephen listened quietly while she told of Walter's murdering her father and claiming her lands, of how Gavin went to counter Walter's attack.

"And Gavin and your mother were taken?"

"Yes."

"Then why are you here? Didn't Demari ask for some ransom? You should be raising it from the serfs."

"I didn't wait for him to ask. I came with John Bassett, and we were welcomed into the castle."

"Yes, I imagine you were," Stephen said sarcastically. "Now Walter Demari has everyone—you, Gavin, your mother, Gavin's head man."

"I didn't know what else to do."

"You could have sent for one of us!" Stephen said angrily. "Raine, with his broken leg, would have done better than you, a woman, could have. John Bassett should have known—"

Judith put her hand on Stephen's arm. "Don't blame him. I threatened to go alone if he didn't lead me."

Stephen looked down at her small hand, then back at her eyes. "What of that I saw below? The castlefolk say you hate Gavin and would do anything to be free of him. Perhaps you want your marriage ended."

Judith quickly drew her hand away. He was beginning to remind her very much of Gavin. Her temper flared. "What I feel for Gavin is between him and me, and not for others to know."

Stephen's eyes blazed. He grabbed her wrist until she clenched her teeth in pain. "Then it is true. You care for this Walter Demari?"

"No, I don't!"

He tightened his grip. "Don't lie to me!"

Men's violence had always made Judith furious. "You are just like Gavin!" she spat. "You see only what you wish to see. No, I am not as dishonest as your brother. It is he who grovels at an evil woman's feet. But I will not so lower myself."

Stephen looked puzzled and loosened his hold. "What evil woman? What is this talk of dishonesty?"

Judith jerked her wrist away and rubbed it. "I came to save my husband because he was given to me before God and because I now carry his child. I have an obligation to try to help him, but I don't do so for love for him. No!" she said passionately. "He gives his love to that blonde!" She stopped and looked at her wrist.

Stephen's laughter made her look up. "Alice," he smiled. "Then that is what this is about? It's not a serious war for estates, but a lover's quarrel, some woman's problem."

"*Woman's—*"

"Quiet! We will be heard."

"It is more than a woman's problem, I assure you!" she hissed.

Stephen sobered. "You may deal with Alice later, but I must be sure you won't go to the king and ask for an annulment. We cannot afford to lose the Revedoune estates."

So that was why he cared whether she wanted Walter or not. It didn't matter that Gavin betrayed her with another woman, but heaven help her if she should feel anything for another man. "I cannot have the marriage annulled while I carry his child."

"Who else knows of this child? Surely not Demari?"

"Only my mother and John Bassett . . . and my maid."

"Not Gavin?"

"No. I had no time to tell him."

"Good. He will have enough on his mind. Who knows this castle best?"

"The steward. He has been here twelve years."

"You have a ready answer," Stephen said suspiciously.

"For all that you and your brother think otherwise, I have a brain to think with and eyes to see."

He studied her in the dim light. "You were brave to come here, though misguided."

"Should I take that as a compliment?"

"As you wish."

Judith narrowed her eyes. "Your mother must have been glad her second sons were not as her first two."

Stephen stared at her, then began to smile. "You must lead

my brother a merry chase. Now stop baiting me and let me see a way out of this mess you have made."

"I—!" she began then stopped. He was right, of course.

He ignored her outburst. "You succeeded in getting Gavin cleaned and fed, though your methods were disagreeable to my belly."

"Should I have run and embraced him?" she asked sarcastically.

"No, you did right. I don't believe he is well enough to travel yet, and he would be a hindrance to us as he is. But he is strong. In two days, with care, he will recover enough that we can escape. I must leave the castle and get help."

"My men are outside."

"Yes, I know. But my men are not here. I came nearly alone when I heard Gavin needed me. My men follow, but it will take at least two more days for them to reach us. I must go and lead them here."

She touched his arm again. "I will be alone again."

He smiled at her and traced the line of her jaw. "Yes, you will. But you will manage. See that Gavin is cared for and regains his strength. When I return, I will get all of you out of here."

She nodded, then looked down at her hands.

He lifted her chin and looked into her eyes. "Don't be angry with me. I thought you wanted Gavin dead. Now I see it isn't so."

She smiled tentatively. "I'm not angry. Only I am sick of this place, that man pawing me, the other—"

He put his finger to her lips. "Keep him from you a little longer. Can you do that?"

"I will try. I was beginning to give up hope."

He bent and kissed her forehead. "Gavin is fortunate," he whispered. Then he rose and left her.

Chapter 20

"HAVE YOU seen him?" Judith asked as she rose from her bed. It was the morning after she'd seen Stephen, and now she asked Joan what she'd discovered about Gavin.

"Yes," Joan answered. "And he is handsome once again. I feared the filth of that place had taken his looks from him."

"You think too much of looks."

"And perhaps you think too little of them!" Joan retorted.

"But Gavin is well? He hasn't been harmed by that foul place?"

"I am sure the food you sent kept him alive."

Judith paused. And what of his mind? How had he reacted to her throwing wine in his face? "Fetch me the serf's garment I wore. It has been washed?"

"You cannot go to him," Joan stated flatly. "If you were caught—"

"Bring me the dress and give me no more orders."

Gavin was being kept inside a room carved out of the base of the tower. It was a dreary place; no light reached it. Its only entrance was an ironbound oak door.

Joan seemed to be well acquainted with the guards who stood on either side of the door. The discipline was lax in the Demari estate, and Joan used this to her advantage. She winked suggestively at one of the men.

"Open up!" Joan bellowed outside the door. "We bring foodstuffs and medicines sent from Lord Walter."

Cautiously, an old and dirty woman opened the massive door. "How do I know you come from Lord Walter?"

"Because I tell you I am," Joan answered and pushed past the crone. Judith kept her head lowered, the rough woolen hood drawn carefully over her hair.

"You can see him," the woman said angrily. "He sleeps now and has done little else since he came here. He's in my care and I do a good job."

"Surely!" Joan said sarcastically. "The bed looks filthy!"

"Cleaner than where he's been."

Judith gave her maid a slight nudge to stop her from baiting the old woman.

"Leave us then and we will tend to him," Joan said.

The woman, her hair gray and greasy, her mouth full of rotted teeth, appeared to be stupid, but she was not. She saw the small, hidden woman nudge the other, and she was aware that the nasty-tempered one quieted instantly.

"Well, what are you waiting for?" Joan demanded.

The old woman wanted to see the face beneath the hood. "I must get some medicines," she said. "There are others who are sick and need me, even if this one doesn't." When she had a jar in her hand, she walked past the woman who intrigued her. When she was near the candle, she dropped the jar. The woman, startled, looked up, giving the crone a brief glimpse of her eyes. The candlelight danced in the lovely golden orbs. The old woman worked hard at not smiling outright. She'd seen those eyes on only one person.

"You are clumsy as well as stupid," Joan hissed. "Get out before I set those rags you wear to flame."

The woman gave Joan a malevolent look before she noisily left the room.

"Joan!" Judith said as soon as they were alone. "It is I who will set you alight if you ever treat anyone like that again."

Joan was shocked. "What does she mean to anyone?"

"She is one of God's children, the same as you or I." Judith would have gone on, but she knew it was useless. Joan was an incurable snob. She belittled anyone she didn't think better than she was. Judith went to her husband, preferring to use her time tending to him rather than lecturing her maid.

"Gavin," she said quietly as she sat on the edge of the bed. The candlelight flickered over him, playing with the shadows of his cheekbones and his jaw line. She touched his cheek. It was good to see him clean again.

He opened his eyes, the deep gray of them made even darker by the candlelight. "Judith," he whispered.

"Yes, it is I," she smiled as she pushed the hood of the mantle back and revealed her hair. "You look better now that you are washed."

His expression was cold and hard. "I don't have you to thank for that. Or perhaps you think the wine in my face cleansed me."

"Gavin! You accuse me wrongly. Had I gone to you with any greeting, Walter would have put an end to your life."

"Wouldn't that have suited you well?"

She drew back. "I won't quarrel with you. We may pursue the matter at leisure once we are free. I have seen Stephen."

"Here?" Gavin said as he started to sit up, the covers falling off his bare chest.

It had been a long time since the night Judith had been held against that chest. His sun-bronzed skin held her attention completely.

"Judith!" Gavin demanded. "Stephen is here?"

"He *was* here." She brought her eyes back to his. "He has returned to get his men."

"And what of my men? What are they doing? Or do they loll about outside the walls?"

"I don't know. I didn't ask."

"No, you wouldn't," he said with irritation. "When does he return?"

"Hopefully, tomorrow."

"Less than one day's time. Why are you here now? You have only one day to wait. If you were found here, you could cause great trouble."

Judith gritted her teeth. "Do you ever do anything except curse me? I came to this hell because you were held prisoner.

I have risked much to see that you are cared for. Yet you curse me at every opportunity. Tell me, sir, what *would* please you?"

He stared at her. "You have much freedom here, don't you? You seem to go wherever you wish with no hindrance. How do I know that Demari isn't waiting outside for you?" Gavin grabbed her wrist. "Are you lying to me?"

She twisted loose. "I am amazed at your vileness. What reason do you have to call me a liar? You are the one who has lied to me from the first. You may believe whatever you want. I should not have helped you. Perhaps then I would have gotten some peace. Or even more, I should have gone to Walter Demari when he first offered marriage. That surely would have been preferable to life with you."

"It is as I thought," Gavin said viciously.

"Yes! It is just as you thought!" Judith answered in kind. Her rage at his insinuations and accusations made her just as blind as he.

"My lady!" Joan interrupted the argument. "We must go. We've spent too much time here already."

"Yes," Judith agreed. "I must go."

"Who waits to escort my wife back to her room?"

Judith just looked at him, too angry to speak.

"Lady Judith," Joan said urgently. Judith turned away from her husband.

When they were beside the door, Joan whispered to her mistress. "It does no good to try to talk to a man when he is eaten with jealousy."

"Jealous!" Judith said. "One must care for another to be jealous. Obviously he doesn't care for me." She straightened the concealing hood over her hair.

Joan started to reply as they opened the door and left the cell. She stopped abruptly, her body rigid. Judith, behind her, looked up to see what caused her maid's concern.

Arthur stood there, his hands on his hips, his legs spread wide, his face a hideous scowl. Judith ducked her head and turned away, hoping he hadn't seen her.

Arthur walked toward her, his arm extended. "Lady Judith, I would like to speak to you."

Judith knew that the walk up the three flights of stairs to Arthur's room was the longest she'd ever taken. Her knees shook with fear and what was worse, the sickness she often felt in the morning was rising in her throat. Her impetuousness had probably ruined Stephen's plans and . . . and . . . She couldn't let herself think of what the result would be if Stephen did not get to them in time.

"You are a fool," Arthur commented when they were alone in his chamber.

"I have been called that before," Judith said, her heart pounding.

"In daylight, you go to him! You couldn't even wait until night."

Judith kept her head lowered, concentrating on her hands.

"Tell me, what plans did you concoct?" He stopped suddenly. "I was a fool to think this could have worked. I am more stupid than that man I serve. Tell me, how did you plan to extricate yourself from this web of lies?"

Her chin came up. "I will tell you nothing."

Arthur narrowed his eyes. "He will suffer. And do you forget that mother of yours? I was right not to trust you. I knew it well but I was half-blinded by you also. Now I find I am in this as deeply as you. Do you know who Lord Walter will blame when his plans are destroyed? When he sees he is not to have the hand of the Revedoune beauty? Not you, my lady, but me. He is a child who has been given power."

"Am I to feel compassion for you? It was you who tore my life apart so that now my family and I live on the brink of death."

"We understand each other then. We care nothing for the other. I wanted your lands and Walter your person." He stopped and looked steadily at her. "Though your person has intrigued me much of late."

"And how do you expect to remove yourself from this tangle you have created?" Judith asked, changing the subject and turning the tables on him.

"Well you should ask. There is only one way open to me. I must see this annulment through to its finish. You won't appear before the king, but you will sign a paper saying that you wish an annulment. It will be worded so that he cannot refuse the request."

Judith came half out of her chair, another, stronger attack of nausea invading her. She ran to the corner of the room to the earthenware chamber pot and relieved her stomach of its meager contents. When she'd recovered herself, she turned back to Arthur. "Forgive me. The fish last night must have been tainted."

Arthur poured a goblet of watered wine. She took it with trembling hands. "You carry his child," he stated flatly.

"No! I do not!" Judith lied.

Arthur's face hardened. "Shall I call a midwife to examine you?"

Judith looked into her goblet and shook her head.

"You cannot ask for an annulment," he continued. "I'd not thought of a child being conceived so soon. It seems we sink deeper and deeper into the muck pile."

"Are you going to tell Walter?"

Arthur snorted. "That idiot thinks you to be pure and virginal. He talks of love and life with you. He doesn't know you are twice as clever as he is."

"You talk too much," Judith said, her stomach once again settling. "What do you want?"

Arthur looked at her with admiration. "You are a woman of intelligence as well as beauty. I would like to own you." He smiled, then turned serious. "Walter will find out about your loyalties and the child. It's only a matter of time. Would you give a fourth of the Revedoune lands if I were to take you out of here?"

Judith thought quickly. The estates meant little to her. Was Arthur a surer chance than waiting for Stephen? If she refused Arthur, he could tell Walter and all their lives would be forfeit—after Walter finished his use of Judith. "Yes, you have my word. There are five of us. If you see all of us safe, one quarter of the lands are yours."

"I cannot guarantee all—"

"All of us or no bargain."

"Yes," he said. "I know you mean it. I must have time to arrange matters. And you must go to the dinner table. Lord Walter will be angry if you're not there to simper by his side."

Judith wouldn't take his arm as they left the room. He knew she liked him even less for turning against his master, and this made him laugh. The idea of loyalty to anyone other than oneself amused him.

When the door to Arthur's room closed behind them, the chamber appeared to be empty. For several moments it was shrouded in silence. Then the slightest of slithering noises could be heard from under the bed. The old woman inched from her hiding place with great caution. She grinned as she looked again at the coin clasped tightly in her hand.

"Silver!" she whispered. But what would the master give to hear what she had just heard? Gold! She didn't understand all of it, but she'd heard Sir Arthur call Lord Walter stupid, and she knew he meant to betray his lord for some land the Montgomery woman owned. There was also something about a baby that the lady would have. That seemed very important.

Judith sat quietly by a window in the great hall, wearing a light gray undertunic and a dress of dark rose Flemish wool. The sleeves were lined with gray squirrel fur. The sun was setting, making the hall darker with each moment. She was beginning to lose some of the fear that had invaded her that morning after her talk with Arthur. She glanced at the sun with gratitude. Only one more day, and Stephen would return and everything would be all right.

She had not seen Walter since dinner. He had invited her to go riding with him, but hadn't appeared to take her with him. Judith assumed that some castle business kept him away.

She began to worry when the sun set and the tables were laid for supper. Neither Arthur nor Walter appeared. She sent Joan to find out what she could, but that was little enough.

"Lord Walter's door is sealed and guarded. The men would answer no questions, though I tried every persuasion."

Something was wrong! Judith knew it when she and Joan retired to their chamber that night and heard a bolt thrown across the door from the outside. Neither woman slept much.

In the morning, Judith stood dressed in a severe gown of dark brown wool. She wore no ornament or jewels. She waited silently. The bolt was released and a man, dressed in chain mail for battle, boldly entered her room.

"Follow me," he said.

When Joan tried to come with her mistress, she was pushed back and the door rebolted. The guard led Judith to Walter's chamber.

The first sight she saw when the door was opened was what was left of Arthur chained to the wall. She turned her face away, her stomach heaving.

"Not a pretty sight is it, my lady?"

She looked up to see Walter lounging on a cushioned chair. His red eyes and his manner showed he was very drunk. His words were slightly slurred.

"But then, I have found you are no lady." He rose, stood still a moment as he tried to focus, then went to a table and poured himself more wine. "Ladies are true and good—but you, sweet beauty, are a whore." He walked toward her and Judith stood very still. There was nowhere to run. He grabbed her hair, pulling her head back. "I know everything now." He turned Judith's head so she had to look at the bloody figure. "Take a long look at him. He told me a lot before he died. I know you think I'm stupid, but I'm not so stupid that I can't control a woman." He pulled her back to look at him. "You did all this for your husband, didn't you? You came here to find him. Tell me: How much would you have done to save him?"

"I would have done anything," she said calmly.

He looked at her then smiled, pushing her away from him. "Do you love him so much?"

"It's not a question of love. He is my husband."

"But I offered you more love than he could ever have," Walter said, tears in his eyes. "All England knows that Gavin Montgomery hungers for that Alice Chatworth."

Judith had no answer to give him.

Walter's thin lips turned to a snarl. "I will not try to reason with you anymore. It's far past that time now."

He went to the door and opened it. "Take that thing away and throw it to the pigs. When you have finished with him, bring Lord Gavin and chain him in the same way."

"No!" Judith screamed as she ran to Walter and put both hands on his forearm. "Please don't harm him anymore. I will do what you say."

He slammed the door. "Yes, you will do as I say, and you will do it before that husband you prostitute yourself for."

"No!" Judith whispered.

Walter smiled at her whitened face. He turned and opened the door again and watched as the guards dragged Arthur's body away. "Come here!" Walter commanded when they were again alone. "Come and kiss me as you do that husband of yours."

She shook her head numbly. "You will kill us anyway. Why must I obey you? Perhaps I will bring our torture to a quicker end if I disobey you."

"You are indeed shrewd," Walter smiled. "But I would have it the opposite way. For every act you refuse me, I will slice a bit from Lord Gavin's flesh."

She looked at him in horror.

"Yes, you understand me."

Judith could hardly think. Stephen, she pleaded silently, don't take longer than you said. Perhaps she could prolong Walter's hurting of Gavin until Stephen and his men began their attack. The door opened again. Four burly guards entered, Gavin chained between them. This time Walter was taking no chances.

Gavin looked from Walter to his wife. "She is mine," he said under his breath and took a step forward. One of the guards brought the flat of a sword across Gavin's head and he slumped forward, unconscious.

"Chain him!" Walter commanded.

Tears came quickly to Judith's eyes. Tears at Gavin's bravery. Even though he was chained, he still attempted to fight.

Gavin's body was bruised and battered, weak from near starvation yet he still fought. Could she do any less? Her only chance was to stall for time until Stephen arrived. She would do whatever Walter asked.

He saw the resignation in her eyes. "A wise decision," Walter laughed when Gavin's arms were spread out, the iron rings about his wrists. Walter dismissed the guards. Laughingly he threw a cup of wine in Gavin's face. "Come now, my friend, you must not sleep through this. You have occupied my cellar a long time, and I know you couldn't have enjoyed your wife much there. Look at her. Isn't she lovely? I was ready to fight a battle for her. Now I find I don't have to." He held out his hand. "Come here, my lady. Come to your master."

Gavin's booted foot lashed out at Walter. The little man barely had time to step back.

A small whip hung over a side table. The leather was still bloody from use on Arthur's body. Walter flicked it, cutting Gavin across the face. A long gash appeared immediately, but Gavin didn't seem to notice. He lifted his foot again, but Walter was far out of range.

As Walter lifted the whip a second time, Judith ran in front of her husband, throwing her arms out to protect him.

"Get away!" Gavin growled at her. "I will fight my own battles."

Judith could only hiss at the absurdity of his words. Both of his arms were chained to a wall that was already covered with another man's blood, yet he thought he could fight a madman. She stepped away. "What do you want?" she asked Walter in a dead voice. She could feel Gavin's eyes boring into her back.

"Come here," he said slowly, careful not to get within reach of Gavin's feet.

Judith hesitated, but she knew she must obey. She took his hand, although his clammy flesh made her skin crawl.

"Such a lovely hand," Walter said as he held it up before Gavin's eyes. "Come, have you nothing to say?"

Gavin turned his eyes to Judith's, and a chill ran up her spine.

"My dear, I believe we wish to see more of your exquisite body." Walter turned to Gavin. "I have seen it often, have enjoyed it often. She was made for a man. Or should I say for many men?" Walter looked at Judith, his eyes hard. "I said you were to let us see what lies beneath those clothes. Do you think so little of your husband as to refuse him one last look?"

With trembling hands, Judith worked at the ties of the brown wool. She wanted to take as much time as possible.

"Here! You are too slow!" Walter slurred as he threw his goblet aside and drew his sword. He slashed the tunic and surcoat away, then dug his fingers into the neck of the bodice of her chemise. His nails slashed at the soft skin of her neck. Her underclothing was torn from her in a like manner.

She bent as if to cover herself, but the point of Walter's sword on her belly made her stand straight.

Her creamy shoulders gave way to her full breasts which, in spite of misery, stood high and proud. Her waist was still small, not yet distended by the child. Her legs were long and slim.

Walter stared at her in wonder. She was more than he had imagined her to be.

"Beautiful enough to kill for," Walter whispered.

"As I will kill you for this!" Gavin shouted. He strained violently against the chain.

"You!" Walter laughed. "What can you do?" He grabbed Judith, his arm about her waist. He turned her so she faced her husband, fondling her breast. "Do you think to rip the chains out of the wall? Look at her well, for it will be the last thing you see."

His hand slid to Judith's belly. "And look at this. It is flat now, but soon it will grow with my child."

"No!" Judith cried.

He tightened his grip about her waist until she couldn't breathe. "I have planted my seed there and it grows. Think of that while you rot in hell!"

"I would think of no woman you had touched," Gavin said, his eyes on his wife. "I would sooner mate with an animal."

Walter pushed Judith away. "You will regret those words."

"No! Do not!" Judith said as Walter advanced on Gavin with a drawn sword.

Walter was very drunk and the blade fell far wide of Gavin's ribs—especially as Gavin agilely sidestepped it. "You will hold still!" Walter shouted and aimed again, this time at his prisoner's head. The weapon, so inaccurately handled, did not slash but more slapped. The wide blade caught Gavin's ear and his head fell forward.

"Do you fall asleep?" Walter screamed as he tossed the sword aside and went for Gavin's throat with his bare hands.

Judith didn't waste a moment. She ran for the sword. Before she could think what she was doing, she took the handle in two hands and brought it down with all her might between Walter's shoulder blades. He stood suspended for a moment. Then, very slowly, Walter turned and looked at Judith before he fell. She swallowed hard as she began to realize she had killed a man.

Without warning, an enormous crash rocked the tower to its very foundations. She had no time to waste. The key to the rings about Gavin's wrists hung on the wall. Just as she unlocked the rings he began to stir.

Gavin caught himself as he started to collapse. He opened his eyes to see his wife standing near him, her nude body flecked with blood. Walter, a sword protruding from his back, lay at his feet. "Cover yourself!" he said angrily.

Judith had forgotten her unclothed state during the turmoil. Her garments lay in a heap, cut beyond repair. She opened a chest at the foot of the bed. It was filled with Walter's clothing. She hesitated. She didn't want to touch anything of his.

"Here!" Gavin said and flung a woolen tunic at her. "It's fitting you should wear his attire." He went to the window, giving her no time to speak.

Truthfully, she couldn't. The enormity of having slain a man was weighing on her.

"Stephen is here," Gavin announced. "He has tunneled under the wall and the stones have collapsed." He went to Walter, put his foot on the dead man's back and withdrew the sword. "You severed his spine," Gavin noted calmly. "I will know to watch my back. You are skillful."

"Gavin!" a familiar voice called from outside the door.

"Raine!" Judith whispered, tears beginning to form in her eyes. Gavin threw back the bolt.

"You are well?" Raine asked as he grabbed his brother's shoulders.

"Yes, as well as can be expected. Where is Stephen?"

"Below, with the others. The castle was easily captured once the wall was down. The maid and your mother-in-law wait below with John Bassett, but we cannot find Judith."

"She is there," Gavin said coldly. "See to her while I find Stephen." He pushed past Raine and left the room.

Raine stepped inside. At first he didn't see Judith. She sat on a chest at the foot of the bed wearing a man's tunic. Her bare legs hung below the hem. She looked up at him with tearful eyes. She was a forlorn-looking creature, and his heart went out to her. Raine clumped across the room to her, his leg still heavily bandaged. "Judith," he whispered and held out his arms to her.

Judith didn't hesitate to seek the comfort of his strength. Sobs tore through her. "I killed him," she cried.

"Who?"

"Walter."

Raine held her tighter, her feet nowhere near the floor. "Did he deserve killing?"

Judith buried her face in his shoulder. "I had no right! God—"

"Quiet!" Raine commanded. "You did what must be done. Tell me, whose blood is on the wall?"

"Arthur's. He was Walter's vassal."

"Come now, don't cry so much. All will be well. Come

below, and your maid will help you dress." He didn't want to know why her own clothes lay slashed on the floor.

"My mother is well?"

"Yes, more than well. She looks at John Bassett as if he were the Messiah come again."

She drew away from him. "You blaspheme!"

"Not I, but your mother. What will you say when she lights candles at his feet?"

She started to reprimand Raine, then smiled, the tears drying on her cheeks. She hugged him fiercely. "It is so good to see you again."

"Always, you give more to my brother than to me," came a solemn voice from the doorway.

She looked up to see Miles, his eyes as much on her bare legs as anything. She had been through too much to blush. Raine let her down and she ran to hug Miles.

"Has it been bad?" he asked as he held her close.

"More than bad."

"Well, I have news to cheer you," Raine offered. "The king summons you to court. It seems he has heard so many reports of you from your wedding that he wishes to see our little golden-eyed sister."

"To court?" Judith asked.

"Let her down!" Raine said to Miles with false annoyance. "You hold her too long for brotherly affection."

"It's just this new fashion she wears. I hope it will set a trend," Miles said as he set her on the floor.

Judith looked up at them and smiled. Then her tears began again. "It's good to see you both. I will go and dress," she said as she turned.

Raine swept his mantle from his shoulders and enveloped her in it. "Go then. We will wait downstairs for you. We leave today. I don't want to see this place again."

"Nor do I," Judith whispered, not looking back but carrying a vivid image of the room in her mind.

Chapter 21

"YOU KNOW of the child?" Stephen asked Gavin as they walked side by side in the Demari castleyard.

"I have been told," he said coldly. "Here, let's sit in the shade. I'm not used to the sunlight yet."

"They kept you in a pit?"

"Yes, for nearly a week."

"You don't look too starved. Did they feed you then?"

"No, Jud—my wife had her maid send food."

Stephen glanced up at what remained of the old tower. "She risked a great deal to come here."

"She risked nothing. She wanted Demari as much as he wanted her."

"That didn't seem to be true when I talked to her."

"Then you are wrong!" Gavin said with force.

Stephen shrugged. "She is your concern. Raine says you are summoned to court. We may travel together. I am also to appear before the king."

Gavin was tired and wanted nothing more than to sleep. "What does the king want with us?"

"He wants to see *your* wife and he wants to present me with one."

"You are to marry?"

"Yes, a rich Scottish heiress who hates all Englishmen."

"I know what it is to be hated by your wife."

Stephen grinned. "But the difference is that you care. I do

237

not. If she doesn't behave, I will lock her up and never see her again. I'll say she is barren and adopt a son who will inherit her lands. Why don't you do the same with this wife of yours if she displeases you?"

"Never see her again!" Gavin said, then caught himself when Stephen began to laugh.

"She stirs your blood? You don't need to tell me. I've seen her. Did you know I threatened her life after I saw her throw the wine in your face? She grabbed my blade and begged me to end it for her."

"You were fooled," Gavin said disgustedly, "as Raine and Miles are. They sit at her feet and gaze at her with cow eyes."

"Speaking of cow eyes, what do you plan to do about John Bassett?"

"I should marry him to her. If Lady Helen is anything like her daughter, his life will be hell. It is little enough punishment for his stupidity."

Stephen bellowed with laughter. "You are changing, brother. Judith obsesses you."

"Yes, as a boil on my backside. Come, let's hurry these people and leave this place."

Outside the Demari estate was the camp Gavin had left. John Bassett had not known about Gavin's tunneling under the walls, for Gavin never told any of his men all his plans. When Gavin had been taken captive and John had returned to the Montgomery estate, the men Gavin had chosen kept on with their digging. It had taken days, with no man getting more than a few hours' sleep at a time. As the men dug, they braced the earth over their heads with timbers. When they were nearly through to the other side, they built a hot fire inside the tunnel. Once the timber burned away, a section of the wall collapsed with a deafening crash.

In the ensuing confusion of setting up camp, Judith was able to escape for a few moments alone. A river ran through the trees beyond the open ground of the camp. She walked through the woods and found a secluded spot where she was hidden, yet able to enjoy the sound and sight of the water.

She had not realized how tense she'd been during the last week. The incessant conniving, the lying she'd done while Walter's captive had taken a toll on her. It was good to feel peaceful and free again. Now, in just a few brief moments, she wouldn't think of her husband or of any other of her many problems.

"You too seek solace," came a quiet voice.

She had heard no one approach. She looked up to see Raine smiling at her.

"I will go if you wish. I don't want to intrude."

"You aren't. Come and sit with me. I only wanted to put myself far away from noise and people for a while."

He sat beside her, his long legs stretched before him, his back against a rock. "I'd hoped to find things better between you and my brother, but they don't look as though they are," he said without preamble. "Why did you kill Demari?"

"Because there was no other way," Judith said, her head bowed. She looked up, her eyes full of tears. "It is an awful thing to have taken someone's life."

Raine shrugged. "It is necessary at times. What of Gavin? Didn't he explain such to you? Didn't he offer you comfort for what you did?"

"He has said very little to me," she said bluntly. "Let's talk of other things. Your leg is better?"

Raine started to speak, then they both looked toward the river when they heard a woman laugh. Helen and John Bassett walked along the edge of the water. Judith started to call to her mother, but Raine stopped her. He didn't think the lovers should be disturbed.

"John," Helen said, gazing at him with love. "I don't think I can bear it."

John tenderly pushed a bit of hair from her cheek. She looked like a radiant young girl. "We must. It will be no easier for me to have you taken from me, to see you wed to another."

"Please," she whispered, "I cannot bear the thought. Is there not some way—?"

John put his fingertips on her lips. "No, don't say it again. We cannot be wed. We have these few hours now—that's all."

Helen flung her arms about his chest, holding him as tightly as she could. John embraced her until he nearly crushed her. "I would leave everything for you," she whispered.

"And I would give anything if I could have you." He buried his cheek against the top of her head. "Come, let's go. Someone may see us here."

She nodded and the two of them walked away, slowly, their arms locked about each other.

"I didn't know," Judith said at last.

Raine smiled at her. "It happens at times. They will get over the pain. Gavin will find a new husband for your mother, and he will fill her bed."

Judith turned to him, her eyes a blaze of gold. "A new husband!" she hissed. "One who will fill her bed! Do men ever think of anything else?"

Raine looked at her in fascination. She'd never turned her wrath toward him. It was not just her beauty that fascinated him, but her spirit. He again felt the stirrings of love for her. He smiled. "There is little else to think of about women," he teased, only half-serious.

Judith started to speak until she saw the laughter in Raine's eyes, the dimples in his cheeks. "Is there no way for them?"

"No, none. John's parents are not even of noble birth, and your mother was married to an earl." He put his hand on her forearm. "Gavin will find a good man for her, one who will manage her property well and who will be kind to her."

Judith didn't answer him.

"I must go," Raine said abruptly as he awkwardly rose. "Curse this thing!" he said vehemently. "I had an ax blade in my leg that didn't cause me as much pain as this break."

She looked up at him. "At least it's set properly," she said, her eyes twinkling.

Raine winced at the memory of the pain when Judith had reset his leg. "I will remember not to come to you should anything else need doctoring. I'm not man enough to take any more of your healing. Will you return now to the tents?"

"No, I will sit alone awhile."

He looked about the place. It seemed safe enough, but he couldn't be sure. "Don't stay past sundown. If I don't see you before then, I will come for you."

She nodded and looked back at the water as he walked away. Raine's concern had always made her feel warm and protected. She remembered how glad she'd been when she saw him at the castle. His arms about her made her feel safe and secure. Then why didn't she look at him with passion? It was odd that she felt only the most sisterly affection for a man who treated her so kindly, while her husband—

She wouldn't think of Gavin while in this quiet spot. Any thoughts of him made her too angry. He'd believed Walter's words that she was carrying that man's child. Her hands went to her stomach protectively. Her child! Whatever happened, the baby would always be hers.

"What do you plan for her?" Raine asked as he made a great show of easing himself into a chair in Gavin's tent. Stephen sat to one side, running a knife along a whetstone.

Gavin was on the other side, eating, as he had been doing ever since he left the castle. "I assume you mean my wife," Gavin said as he speared a piece of roast pork. "You seem overconcerned with her," he challenged.

"And you seem to ignore her!" Raine spat. "She killed a man for you. That's not easy for a woman—yet you don't even speak to her of it."

"What comfort could I give her after my brothers have given her so much?"

"She gets little enough elsewhere."

"Shall I have my squire fetch swords?" Stephen asked sarcastically. "Or perhaps you would like full armor?"

Raine relaxed immediately. "You are right, brother. I just wish that this other brother of mine were as sensible."

Gavin glared at Raine, before looking back at his food.

Stephen watched Gavin's eating for a moment. "Raine, are you trying to interfere between Gavin and his wife?"

Raine shrugged and adjusted his leg. "He doesn't treat her well."

Stephen smiled in understanding. Raine had always been a fighter for the underdog. He would champion any cause that he felt needed him. The silence between the brothers grew heavy until Raine rose and left the tent.

Gavin looked after him then pushed the food away, full at last. He stood and walked toward his cot.

"She carries the man's child," Gavin said after a time.

"Demari's?" Stephen asked then gave a low whistle at Gavin's nod. "What will you do with her?"

Gavin sank onto a chair. "I don't know," he said quietly. "Raine says I didn't comfort her, but how could I? She killed her lover."

"Was she forced?"

Gavin hung his head. "I don't believe so. No, she couldn't have been. She had the freedom of the castle. She came to me in the pit and again when I was brought from there and taken to a tower cell. Had she been forced, she wouldn't have had such freedom."

"That's true, but doesn't her visiting you mean that she desired to help you?"

Gavin's eyes blazed. "I don't know what she desires. She seems to be on the side of whoever holds her. When she came to me, she said she did everything for me; yet when she was near Demari, she was wholly his. She is a clever woman."

Stephen ran his thumb along the edge of his knife, testing it. "Raine seems to think a great deal of her, and Miles also."

Gavin snorted. "Miles is too young to know yet that women have anything besides a body. And Raine he has championed her cause for long."

"You could declare the child to be another's and set her aside."

"No!" Gavin said almost violently, then looked away.

Stephen laughed. "You are still hot for her? She is beautiful but there are other beautiful women. What of Alice, whom you declared you loved?"

Stephen was the only person Gavin had ever confided in about Alice. "She was married not long ago to Edmund Chatworth."

"Edmund! That bit of slime! Didn't you offer her marriage?"

Gavin's silence was his answer.

Stephen put his knife back in the case at his side. "Women aren't worth the worry you spend on them. Take that wife of yours and bed her, and don't give her another thought." He dismissed the subject and rose. "I think I'll go to sleep. It's been a long day. I'll see you tomorrow."

Gavin sat alone in his tent, the darkness rapidly gathering. Set her aside, he thought. He could do that since she carried another man's child. But he couldn't imagine not seeing her.

"Gavin," Raine interrupted his thoughts. "Has Judith returned? I told her she mustn't stay out past sunset."

Gavin rose, his jaw clenched. "You think too much of my wife. Where was she? I'll find her."

Raine smiled at his brother. "By the stream, through there," he pointed.

Judith knelt by the side of the river, her hand playing in the cool, clear water.

"It's late. You must return to the camp."

She looked up, startled. Gavin towered over her, his gray eyes dark in the fading daylight. His expression was closed.

"I don't know these woods," he continued. "There may be danger."

She stood, her shoulders back. "That would suit you, wouldn't it? A dead wife is surely better than a dishonored one." She lifted her skirts and strode past him.

He grabbed her forearm "We must talk, seriously and without anger."

"Has there been anything else between us except anger? Say what you must—I grow weary."

His face softened. "Does the burden of the child tire you?"

Her hands flew to her stomach. Then she straightened, her chin up. "This baby will never be a burden to me."

Gavin looked across the water, as if he struggled with some great problem. "For all that has happened since, I believe you meant well when you gave yourself into Demari's hands. I know you have no love for me, but your mother was held also. For her alone, you would have risked what you did."

Judith nodded, frowning slightly.

"I don't know what happened after you came to the castle. Perhaps Demari was kind to you and you needed kindness. Perhaps even at the wedding, he offered you kindness."

Judith couldn't speak as her bile rose.

"As for the child, you may keep it and I won't set you aside, as perhaps I should. For if the truth were known, maybe some of the blame is mine. I will care for the child as if he were my own, and he shall be given some of your lands to inherit." Gavin paused and stared at her. "Do you say nothing? I have tried to be honest . . . and fair. I don't believe you could ask for more."

It took Judith a moment to recover herself. Her teeth were clamped together when she spoke. "Fair! Honest! You don't know the meaning of those words! Just look at what you're saying. You are willing to concede that I came to the castle for honorable purposes, but after that, you insult me horribly."

"Insult you?" Gavin asked, bewildered.

"Yes! Insult me! Do you believe me to be so baseborn, that I would give myself freely to a man who threatened my mother and my husband—for before God, you are that! You say I needed kindness! Yes, I do, as I have never had kindness from you. But I'm not so shallow as to break my vows to God for a little thoughtfulness. Once I broke such a vow, but I won't do so again." She looked away, her face warm with memory.

"I have no idea what you mean," Gavin began, his own temper flaring. "You talk in riddles."

"You hint that I am an adulteress. Is that a riddle?"

"You bear the man's child. How else can I say it? I have offered to care for the baby. You should be grateful that I don't cast you aside."

Judith stared at him. He didn't ask if the child was his. He assumed that Walter's words were the true ones. At her wedding, Judith's mother had said that a man would believe the lowest-born serf before he believed a woman. It was true. And if Judith denied sleeping with Walter? Would he believe her? There would be no way to prove her words.

"You have no more to say?" Gavin demanded, tight-lipped.

Judith glared at him, speechless.

"Then you agree to my terms?"

Well, she would play the game his way. "You say you give my child my lands. You sacrifice little."

"I keep you! I could set you aside."

She laughed. "You could always have done so. Men have that right. You keep me while you desire me. I'm no fool. I would have something more than just an inheritance for my child."

"You ask payment?"

"Yes, for coming to you at the castle." The words hurt. She was crying inside, but refused to show it.

"What do you want?"

"I would have my mother given in marriage to John Bassett."

Gavin's eyes opened wide.

"You are her nearest male relative now," Judith pointed out. "You have the right."

"John Bassett is—"

"Don't tell me. I know too well. But can't you see how she loves him?"

"What has love to do with it? There are estates to be considered, properties to be joined."

Judith put her hands on his arms, her eyes pleading. "You don't know what it is to live without love. You have given yours, and I have no chance for it. But my mother has never loved a man as she loves John. It's in your power to give her what she most needs. I beg you, don't let your animosity toward me keep you from letting her have some happiness."

He stared down at her. She was so beautiful but he saw also a lonely young woman. Had he really been so harsh to her that she needed Walter Demari, if even for a few moments? She said he'd given his love, yet at that moment he couldn't remember Alice's face.

He pulled Judith into his arms. He remembered how frightened she was when she'd been treed by the boar. So little courage—yet she'd confronted an enemy, as if she alone could slay dragons.

"I don't hate you," he whispered, holding her close, his face buried in her hair. Raine once asked what was wrong with her, and now Gavin asked himself that question. If she did carry another man's infant, wasn't it his fault for leaving her unprotected? In all their marriage, Gavin could remember being kind to her only once. The day they had spent together in the woods. Now his conscience hurt him. He'd planned that day only to woo her back to his bed. He thought only of himself and not of her. He bent and put his hand under her knees. He sat down on the sweet-smelling grass, his back against a tree and held her curled in his arms. "Tell me what happened at the castle," he said gently.

She didn't trust him. Always, when she trusted him, he flung her words back in her face. But his body felt good to her. This feeling is all we share, Judith thought. Only lust exists between us. Not love or understanding—or, least of all, trust.

Judith shrugged, refusing to reveal anything to him. Her lips were so close to his neck. "It's over now. It is better forgotten."

Gavin frowned, wanting to press her to talk to him but her nearness was more than he could bear. "Judith," he whispered as his mouth came down on hers.

Her arms went about his neck and drew him closer, her mind going blank at the touch of him. Forgotten were any ideas of understanding and trust.

"I have missed you," Gavin whispered against her neck.

"Do you know that when I first saw you at Demari's, I thought I was dead?"

She leaned her head away, giving Gavin the arch of her slender throat.

"You were like an angel bringing light and air and your beauty into that . . . place. I was afraid to touch you for fear that you weren't real—or that you were real, and I would be destroyed if I dared touch you." He fumbled with the laces at her side.

"I am most real," Judith smiled.

He was so enchanted by her look that he pulled her to face him and kissed her deeply. "Your smiles are rarer and more precious than diamonds. I have seen so few of them." His face blackened suddenly with memory. "I could have killed you both when I saw Demari touch you."

She stared at Gavin in horror, then tried to push away.

"No!" he said and held her close. "Do you give him more than me, your husband?"

Judith was in an awkward position, but she managed to draw her hand back and slap him across the cheek.

His eyes blazed as he caught her hand in his, crushing her small fingers together. Then suddenly he pulled her hand to his mouth and kissed it. "You are right. I am a fool. It's done. It's behind us. Let's look to the future and to tonight only." His mouth captured hers and Judith fought any rage. In truth, she thought of nothing at all as his hands roamed beneath her clothes.

They were hungry for each other, more than hungry. The starvation Gavin had experienced in the tent was nothing compared to what he felt at having to do without his wife.

The indigo-blue wool dress was torn away, as was the linen undertunic. The tearing fabric added to the passion, and Judith's hands struggled with Gavin's clothes. But his hands were faster than hers. Instantly, his clothes lay in a heap on top of hers.

Frantically, Judith pulled him to her and Gavin more than met her ardor. Within moments they came together in a fiery starburst that left them both exhausted.

Chapter 22

"HE THINKS he's better than us," Blanche said spitefully. She and Gladys were in the Chatworth buttery, filling jugs with wine for the eleven o'clock meal.

"Yes," Gladys said but with less venom. She missed Jocelin very much, but she was not angry about it as Blanche was.

"What business do you think keeps him away from us?" Blanche asked. "He spends little enough time with her," she jerked her head upward to indicate Alice Chatworth's room. "And he is seldom in the hall."

Gladys sighed. "He seems to spend most of his time alone in the hayloft."

Blanche suddenly stopped her task. "Alone! Is he alone, though? We haven't thought of that. Could he keep a woman up there?"

Gladys laughed. "Why would Jocelin want just one woman when he can have many? And what woman is missing? Unless he has one of the serfs, I know of no one who could have been missing so long."

"Then what else could hold a man like Jocelin? Here, you!" Blanche called to a passing serf girl. "Finish filling these mugs."

"But I—," the girl began but Blanche gave her arm a vicious pinch. "I will," she said sullenly.

"Come, Gladys," Blanche called. "While Jocelin is busy somewhere else, let's put an end to this mystery."

The two women left the little buttery and walked the short distance to the stables.

"See, he removes the ladder each time he leaves," Blanche observed. She walked quietly into the stables, Gladys close behind her. Blanche put a finger to her lips and pointed to the fat stableman's wife. "The old dragon keeps watch over him," she whispered.

The girls took the ladder, being careful not to make any noise. They placed it against the outside wall, the end braced against the opening to Jocelin's room. Blanche lifted her skirts and climbed up. When they were once inside, their view of the little room blocked by the stacks of hay, a woman's voice reached them.

"Jocelin? Is that you?"

Blanche smiled in malicious triumph at Gladys and led the way into the open area. "Constance!"

The woman's lovely face was still battered, but it was beginning to heal. Constance retreated, her back against a pile of hay.

"So! You are the reason Jocelin neglects us. I thought you left the castle," Gladys said.

Constance could only shake her head.

"No! She didn't," Blanche spat. "She saw Jocelin and decided he was to be hers. She couldn't bear to share him."

"That isn't so," Constance said, her lower lip trembling. "I nearly died. He cared for me."

"Yes, and you care for him, don't you? What sorcery did you use to charm him?"

"Please . . . I meant no harm."

Blanche was not listening to the woman's pleas. She knew Jocelin had not put the marks Constance now bore on her face and body. Only Edmund Chatworth could have done that. "Tell me, does Lord Edmund know where you are?"

Constance's eyes widened in horror.

Blanche laughed. "See, Gladys, she is the lord's mistress— yet she betrays him with another. What do you say we return her to her master?"

Gladys looked at the terrified young woman with sympathy.

Blanche grabbed her friend's upper arms, her fingers digging into the soft flesh. "She has betrayed us, yet you hesitate before giving some of her own in return? This conniving little bitch has taken Joss from us. She had Lord Edmund, but she wanted more. She wasn't content with one man, but she must have all of them at her feet."

Gladys turned to Constance with a look of hate.

"If you do not go with us, we will tell Lord Edmund that Jocelin has been hiding you," Blanche smiled.

Constance silently followed them down the ladder. She would not allow herself to think, only to know that she protected Jocelin. In all her life, no one had offered her tenderness. Her world was filled with people like Edmund and Blanche and Alice. Yet, for nearly two weeks, she had lived in a dream in Jocelin's arms. He had talked to her, sung to her, held her close and made love to her. He whispered that he loved her and she believed him.

Now, following Blanche and Gladys was like waking from a dream. Unlike Jocelin, Constance did not make plans for when they would leave the Chatworth castle, when she was fully healed. She knew that the time they had in that loft was all the time they would ever know. Docilely, she followed the women, accepting her fate; the idea of escape or struggling never entered her mind. She knew where they led and when she entered Edmund's chamber, her chest tightened as if iron bands were drawn about it.

"Stay here and I will fetch Lord Edmund," Blanche ordered.

"Will he come?" Gladys asked.

"Oh, aye, when he hears what I will say to him. Do not let her leave the room."

Blanche was back in moments, a furious Edmund on her heels. He did not like having his dinner interrupted, but the mention of Constance had made him follow the presumptuous servant girl. Once in the room, he slammed and bolted the door behind him, his eyes on Constance, ignoring the nervous looks of the two maids.

"So, my sweet Constance, you did not die after all." Edmund put his hand under her chin and lifted her face to meet his. He saw only resignation there. Her bruises marred her beauty, but she would heal. "Those eyes," he whispered. "They have haunted me for a long time."

He heard a noise behind him and turned to see the two maids trying to sneak the bolt from the door. "Here!" he commanded and grabbed the arm of the nearest one, Gladys. "Where do you think you're going?"

"To our duties, my lord," Blanche said, her voice unsteady. "We are your most loyal servants."

Gladys had tears in her eyes as Edmund's fingers bit into her skin. She tried to pry his fingers loose.

Edmund flung the girl to the floor. "Did you think you could bring her here and leave her like so much baggage? Where has she been?"

Blanche and Gladys exchanged glances. They hadn't thought of this. All they wanted to do was get Constance away from Jocelin. They wanted things the way they once were, with Jocelin teasing them, making love to them.

"I—I don't know, my lord," Blanche stuttered.

"You think I'm a fool?" Edmund said and advanced on her. "The girl has been well hidden, or I would have known of her. Her presence has not been part of the castle gossip."

"No, my lord, she . . ." Blanche could not think fast enough to create a story. Her tongue tripped her.

Edmund stopped, then looked at Gladys cringing on the floor. "There is something to this story that you hide. Whom do you protect?" He grabbed Blanche's arm and twisted it painfully behind her back.

"My lord! You hurt me!"

"I will do more than that if you lie to me."

"It was Baines of the kitchen," Gladys said loudly, wanting to protect her friend.

Edmund released Blanche's arm as he considered this. Baines was a thoroughly disliked man, foul, evil-tempered, he knew that. But Edmund also knew Baines slept in the kitchen. He had no privacy, certainly not enough to hide a battered girl until she was healed. It would have caused talk throughout the castle.

"You lie," Edmund said in a deadly voice, then advanced slowly on her.

Gladys cringed away from him, half-crawling across the rushes. "My lord," she said, every fiber of her body trembling.

"It is your last lie," he said as he grabbed her about the waist. She started struggling when she saw him carrying her toward the open window.

Blanche stared in horror as Edmund carried the fighting Gladys. When they reached the window, Gladys held her arms out against the framework but she was no match for Edmund's strength. He gave one push at the small of her back and she fell forward, clutching at the air. Her scream, as she fell three stories to the courtyard below, seemed to make the walls tremble.

Blanche could only stare, her knees turning to water, her stomach heaving.

"Now," Edmund said as he turned back to Blanche. "I wish to know the truth. Who kept her?" he nodded toward Constance who stood silently against the wall. Edmund's murder of Gladys had not shocked Constance; it was what she had expected.

"Jocelin," Blanche whispered.

At the name, Constance's head came up. "No!" She could not bear for Jocelin to be betrayed.

Edmund smiled. "That pretty singer?" He was the one who took her that night—a fact Edmund had forgotten. "Where does he sleep that he could keep her unnoticed?"

"Above the stables in the loft." Blanche could hardly speak. She kept looking at the window. Only a moment before, Gladys had been alive. Now her body lay broken and crushed on the pavement.

Edmund nodded at Blanche's answer; he knew the truth when he heard it. He took a step toward her and she cringed away from him, her back to the door.

"No, my lord, I told you what you wanted to know." He kept coming toward her, a slight smile on his face. "And I brought you Constance. I am a true servant to you."

Edmund liked her terror; it proved that he was strong. He stood close to her, reached a fat hand to caress the line of her jaw. There were tears in her eyes, tears of fear. Even as he struck her, he smiled.

Blanche fell to the floor, her hand on the side of her face, her eye already turning purple.

"Go," he said, half-laughing as he threw open the door. "You have learned your lesson well."

Blanche was out of the room before the door closed. She ran down the stairs and out the manor house. She kept running through the castle yard, through the open gate. She did not answer the calls of the men from atop the walls. She only knew that she wanted to be away from anything to do with the Chatworth estate. Only when the pains in her side forced her, did she stop. Then she walked, never once looking back.

Jocelin slipped four plums inside his doublet; he knew how much Constance loved fresh fruit. In the last weeks, his life had begun to revolve around what Constance did and did not like. Watching her unfold, petal by soft petal, had been the most delightful thing that had ever happened to him. Her gratitude for every pleasure, no matter how small, was warming, though his heart ached at the thought of her life before— that a bouquet of flowers could make her cry.

And in bed, he smiled wickedly. He was not such a martyr as to forgo all selfish pleasures. Constance wanted to repay him for his kindness and wanted to show him her love. At first her anticipation of pain had made her rigid, but the feel of Jocelin's hands on her body, knowing they would not hurt her, made her wild with passion. It was as if she wanted to crowd all the love she would ever know into a few short weeks.

Jocelin smiled as he thought of their future together. He would stop traveling and settle down, would make a home for Constance and himself. Then they would have several violet-eyed children. Never in his life had he wanted more than freedom and a comfortable bed and a warm woman. But never had he been in love before. Constance had changed his whole life. Just a few more days—as soon as Constance was well enough to stand the long journey, they would leave.

Jocelin was whistling as he left the manor house and walked past the kitchen toward the stables. He froze when he saw the ladder leaning against the wall. Of late he had been careful to remove the ladder. The stableman's wife kept a sharp eye on it for him, and Jocelin rewarded her with numerous smiles and a few genuinely affectionate hugs. He did not think of any danger to himself, but only to Constance.

He ran the last few feet and sped up the ladder. His heart was beating wildly as he searched the tiny room, as if he'd find her beneath the hay. He knew without a doubt that Constance would not leave on her own. No, she was like a fawn, timid and fearful.

Tears blurred his eyes as he made his way down the ladder. Where would he find her? Perhaps some of the women played a joke on him and he would find her safe in some corner, munching on a raisin bun. Jocelin did not believe it, even as he pictured the dream.

He was not surprised when he saw Chatworth at the foot of the ladder, flanked by two armored guards. "What have you done with her?" Jocelin demanded as he jumped from the second rung of the ladder, his hands going for Edmund's throat.

Edmund's face was beginning to turn blue before his men could disengage Jocelin. They held him securely by the arms.

Edmund pulled himself from the dust and looked with disgust at his ruined clothing. The velvet would never be the same again. He rubbed his bruised throat. "You will pay for this with your life."

"What have you done with her, you piece of pig's offal?" Jocelin sneered.

Edmund gasped. No one had ever dared talk to him like that before. He drew back his hand and slapped Jocelin across the face, cutting the corner of his mouth. "Indeed, you will pay for this."

He stepped out of range of Jocelin's feet, more wary of the jongleur than he had been. Behind that face lurked a man he had not guessed existed, thinking Jocelin only to be another pretty boy. "I will enjoy this," he sneered. "Tonight you will spend in the oubliette, and tomorrow you will see your last sunrise. All day you will suffer. But tonight perhaps you will suffer more. While you sweat in that jar, I will take the woman."

"No!" Jocelin yelled. "She has done nothing. Let her go, I will pay for taking her."

"Yes, you will. As for your noble gesture, it is hollow. You have nothing to bargain with. I have you both. Her for my bed, and you for any other pleasures I choose. Take him and let him think on what it means to defy an earl."

Constance sat at the window of Edmund's room. Spirit was gone from her. No more would she see Jocelin again, no more would he hold her in his arms and tell her he loved her more than the moon loved the stars. The only hope was that he had managed to escape. She had seen the way that Blanche ran from the room. Constance prayed that the woman had gone to warn Jocelin. She knew that Blanche cared for him, had heard her call for him. Surely, Blanche had warned Jocelin, and together they were safe.

Constance felt no jealousy. In truth, she wanted only Jocelin's happiness. If he'd asked her to die for him, she would gladly have done so. What did her poor life matter?

A commotion and the sunlight on a familiar head drew her attention. Two burly guards half-dragged a struggling Jocelin across the yard. As she watched, one of the men cuffed Jocelin hard on the collarbone, causing Joss to slump to one side. With difficulty, he kept on his feet. Constance held her breath, wanting to call to him, but she knew it would endanger him more. As if he sensed her, he twisted and looked up at the window. Constance lifted her hand. Through her tears, she could see the blood on his chin.

As the guards jerked Jocelin around, Constance suddenly realized where they were taking him, and her heart stopped. The oubliette was a horrible device; a jug-shaped chamber cut into the bowels of solid rock. A prisoner must be lowered through its narrow neck by a pulley. Once inside, he could neither sit nor stand, but must half-squat, his back and neck continually bent. There was little air and quite often no food or water. Nobody could last more than a few days, and only the strongest that long.

Constance watched the guards strap Jocelin to the pulley and lower him into that hellhole. She stared for a few moments longer as the cover was fastened, then looked away. There was no hope now. Tomorrow Jocelin would be dead, if he lived through the night, for Edmund would surely devise some additional torture.

On a table a large wine beaker and three glasses were set. These glasses were for Edmund's private use, as he saved all the most beautiful objects for himself. She did not think of what she did, for her life was over and only one last act was needed to complete the deed. Smashing a glass against the table, she took the jagged base in her hand and went to the cushioned window.

It was a lovely day, summer in full bloom. Constance hardly felt the sharp edge as she slashed it across one wrist. She looked at the blood flowing from her body with a sense of relief. "Soon," she whispered. "Soon I will be with you, my Jocelin."

Constance cut her other wrist and leaned back against the wall, one wrist in her lap, the other on the windowsill, her blood seeping into the mortar of the stones. A soft summer breeze blew at her hair and she smiled. One evening she and Jocelin had gone to the river, spending the night alone in the soft grasses. They had returned very early the next morning before the castle was fully awake. It had been a night of rapture and whispered love words. She remembered every word Jocelin had ever spoken to her.

Gradually, her thoughts became lazier. It was almost as if she went to sleep. Constance closed her eyes and smiled slightly, the sun on her face, the breeze in her hair, and thought no more.

"Boy! Are you all right?" a voice called down to Jocelin in a hoarse whisper.

He was dazed and had trouble understanding the words. "Oubliette" meant chamber of forgetfulness, and it earned its name.

"Boy!" the voice demanded again. "Answer me!"

"Yes," Jocelin managed.

A heavy sigh answered him. "He is well," a woman's voice said. "Put this around you and I will pull you up."

Jocelin was too dazed to fully realize what was happening to him. The woman's hands guided his body through the neck and up to the cool night air. The air—the first real breath he'd had in many hours—began to clear his mind. His body was cramped and stiff. When his feet touched the ground, he unbuckled the pulley strap.

The stableman and his fat wife stared at him. "Love," she said. "you must leave at once." She led the way through the darkness to the stable.

With each step, Jocelin's head cleared more. As he had never before in his life experienced love until recently, neither had he known hate. Now, walking across the courtyard, he looked up at Edmund's dark window. He hated Edmund Chatworth, who now lay with Constance.

When they were in the stables, the woman spoke again. "You must go quickly. My husband can get you over the wall. Here—I have packed a bundle of food for you. It will last you a few days if you are careful."

Jocelin frowned. "No, I cannot go. I cannot leave Constance with him."

"I know you won't go until you know," the old woman said. She turned and motioned for Jocelin to follow her. She lit a candle from another one on the wall and led Jocelin to an empty stall. A cloth was draped over several bundles of hay. Slowly she pulled the cloth away.

At first Jocelin did not believe what he saw. He had seen

Constance once before when he thought her to be dead. He knelt beside her and took the frigid body in his arms. "She is cold," he said with authority. "Fetch blankets so I can warm her."

The old woman put a hand on Jocelin's shoulder. "All the blankets in the world won't help. She is dead."

"No, she is not! She was like this before and—"

"Don't torture yourself. The girl's blood is gone. She has none left."

"Blood?"

The woman moved the cloth back and held up Constance's lifeless wrist, the vein exposed, severed.

Jocelin stared at it silently. "Who?" he finally whispered.

"She took her own life. No one else did it."

Jocelin looked back at Constance's face, finally realizing that she was gone. He bent and kissed her forehead. "She is at peace now."

"Yes," the woman said, relieved. "And you must go."

Joss pulled away from the woman's clutching hand and walked purposefully toward the manor house. The great hall was covered with sleeping men on straw pallets. Jocelin was silent as he slipped a sword from the wall where it hung amid a mixture of many weapons. His soft shoes made no noise as he went up the stairs to the fourth floor.

A guard slept in front of Edmund's door. Jocelin knew he would have no chance if the guard was to waken, for Jocelin's wiry strength was no match for a seasoned knight's. The man never uttered a sound as Jocelin rammed the sword through his belly.

Jocelin had never killed a man before and this one gave him no pleasure.

Edmund's door was not locked. He felt safe in his own castle in his own room. Jocelin pushed the door open. He didn't enjoy what he did, nor did he wish to linger over it as some would have done. He grabbed Edmund's hair in his hands. Chatworth's eyes flew open—and then widened as he saw Jocelin.

"No!"

It was the last word Edmund Chatworth spoke. Jocelin pulled the sword across the man's throat. In death, the earl disgusted Joss as much as when alive. Jocelin tossed the sword to the side of the bed and walked to the door.

Alice could not sleep. She had not been able to sleep properly for weeks—not since the jongleur had stopped coming to her bed. She had threatened him repeatedly, but to no avail. He had just looked at her through those long lashes of his and said nothing. Truthfully, she was a bit intrigued by a man who treated her so badly.

She threw the curtains of her bed back and pulled on a bedrobe. Her feet were soundless on the rushcovered floor. Once in the hall, Alice sensed something was wrong. Edmund's door was open, the guard before it sat in an odd position. Curious, she walked toward him. Her eyes were accustomed to the dark, and the hall was lit only patchily by the torches along the wall.

A man left Edmund's room, looking neither right nor left but walked straight toward her. She saw the blood on his doublet before she saw his face. Alice gasped and put her hand to her throat. When he stopped before her, she hardly recognized him. Here was no laughing boy, but a man who looked at her with boldness. A small chill of fear went up her spine. "Jocelin."

He walked past her as if he had not seen her or did not care that he had. Alice stared after him, then slowly walked to Edmund's room. She stepped over the dead guard, her heart pounding. When she saw Edmund's body, the blood still running from the slashed throat, she smiled.

Alice went to the window, her hand on the sill, covering a stain made by another's innocent blood on the day before. "A widow," she whispered. A widow! Now she had it all—wealth, beauty and freedom.

For a month she had been writing letters, begging for an invitation to King Henry's court. When it had come, Edmund had laughed at her, saying he refused to spend the money on such frivolities. In truth, he would not be free at court to toss serving girls from windows as he was in his own castle. Now, Alice thought, she could go unencumbered to the king's court. And there would be Gavin! Ah yes, she had arranged that also. That red-headed whore had had him too long. Gavin was hers and he would remain so. If she could get rid of that wife of his, then he would be hers entirely. He would not deny her gowns of gold cloth. No, Gavin would deny her nothing. Had she not always gotten what she wanted? Now she wanted Gavin Montgomery again, and she would get him.

Someone walking across the courtyard caught her attention. Jocelin made his way to the stairs leading to the top of the wall, a leather sachel over his shoulder.

"You have done me a great favor," she whispered. "And now I will repay you." She did not call the guards. Instead, she stood silently, planning what she would do now that she was free of Edmund. Jocelin had given her much—access to great wealth—but most of all; he had given her Gavin.

Chapter 23

IT WAS hot in the tent. Gavin couldn't sleep. He stood and looked down at Judith, sleeping peacefully, one bare shoulder exposed above the linen sheet. Quietly, he drew on his clothes, smiling at his wife's still form. They'd spent a good part of the evening making love, and now she was exhausted. But he was not. No, far from it. Loving Judith seemed to set a spark to him and light a fire that was unquenchable.

He took a velvet mantle from a chest, then pulled the sheet from her and wrapped her in the cloak. She snuggled against him like a child—never waking, sleeping the sleep of the innocent. He carried her out of the tent, nodded to the guards on duty and walked toward the forest. He bent his head and kissed her sleep-softened mouth.

"Gavin," she murmured.

"Yes, it's Gavin."

She smiled against his shoulder, her eyes never opening. "Where are you taking me?"

He chuckled and held her closer. "Do you care?"

She smiled broader, her eyes still closed. "No, I do not," she whispered.

He laughed, deep in his chest. At the side of the river he sat her down and she gradually began to wake. The coolness of the air, the sound of the water and the sweetness of the grasses added to the dreamlike quality of the situation.

Gavin sat beside her, not touching her. "You once said

you broke a vow to God. What vow was it?" He tensed for her answer. They had not spoken again of the time at Demari's, yet Gavin wanted to know what befell her there. He wanted her to deny what he knew to be true. If she loved Demari, why had she killed him? And if she did go to another man, wasn't it Gavin's own fault? He knew the vow she broke was the one she made before a priest and hundreds of witnesses.

The darkness covered Judith's blushes. She was unaware of Gavin's train of thought. She remembered only that she had gone to him before he left for battle.

"Am I such an ogre that you cannot tell me?" he asked quietly. "Tell me this one thing, and I'll ask nothing more of you."

It was a private thing to her, but it was true; he had asked her little. There was a full moon and the night was bright. She kept her eyes turned away from his. "I made a vow to you at our wedding and . . . I broke it."

He nodded; it was as he feared.

"I knew I broke it when I came to you that night," she continued. "But that man had no right to say we didn't sleep together. What was between us was ours to deal with."

"Judith, I don't understand you."

She looked at him, startled. "I speak of the vow. Didn't you ask me of it?" She saw he still didn't understand. "In the garden, when I saw you and—" She broke off and looked away. The memory of Alice in his arms was still vivid to her, and much more painful now than it was then.

Gavin stared at her, trying to remember. When it finally came to him, he began to chuckle.

Judith turned on him, her eyes blazing. "You laugh at me?"

"Yes, I do. Such a vow of ignorance! You were a virgin when you made it. How were you to know what pleasures were to be had in my bed, and that you couldn't keep yourself away from me?"

She glared at him, then stood. "You are a vain and insufferable man. I give you my confidence, and you laugh at me!"

She threw her shoulders back, the mantle wrapped tightly about her, and arrogantly started to walk away from him.

Gavin, with a lecherous grin on his face, gave one powerful tug to the cloak and pulled it off her. Judith gasped and tried to cover herself. "Will you go back to camp now?" he taunted, rolling the velvet mantle and placing it behind his head.

Judith looked at him, stretched out on the grass, not even looking at her. So! he thought he had won, did he?

Gavin lay quietly, expecting any moment that she would return and beg him for her clothes. He heard a great deal of rustling in the bushes and smiled confidently. She was too modest to return to camp without her clothes. There was silence for a moment, then he heard a rhythmic movement of leaves, as if . . .

He was on his feet in an instant, following the sound. "Why you little minx!" he laughed as he stood before his wife. She wore a very concealing gown of tree leaves and the branches of several shrubs. She smiled up at him in triumph.

Gavin put his hands on his hips. "Will I ever win an argument with you?"

"Probably not," Judith said smugly.

Gavin chuckled devilishly. Then his hand swept out and tore away the fragile garment. "You don't think so?" he asked as he grabbed her by the waist and picked her up. The nude curves of her body were made silver by the moonlight. He swung her high in his arms, laughing at her gasp of fright. "Don't you know a good wife does not argue with her husband?" he teased.

He sat her on the branch of a tree, her knees at eye level. "I find you particularly interesting this way." He looked at her face, his own smiling, then he froze when he saw the sheer terror in her eyes.

"Judith," he whispered. "I forgot your fear. Forgive me." He had to pry her hands loose from the tree limb, the knuckles white. Even when she was loose, he still had to drag her across the limb, scraping her bare bottom on the rough bark. "Judith, forgive me," he whispered as she clung to him.

He carried her back to the edge of the river and wrapped the mantle about her, holding her in his lap and cuddling her close. His stupidity infuriated him. How could he have forgotten something so important as her terrifying fear of heights? He lifted her chin and kissed her sweetly on the mouth.

Suddenly her kiss turned to passion. "Hold me," she whispered desperately. "Don't leave me."

He was struck by the urgency in her voice. "No, sweet, I won't."

Always she had been a woman of passion but now she was in a frenzy. Her mouth clung to his; then her lips ran along his neck. Never had she been so aggressive.

"Judith," he murmured. "Sweet, sweet Judith." The mantle fell away and her bare breasts pushed against him, insolently and demanding. Gavin's head began to swim.

"Do you leave these garments on?" she asked in a harsh whisper as her hands ran under the loose tabard. Gavin could hardly bear leaving the nearness of her body for even a few moments to remove his clothing. His doublet was quickly tossed over his head, then his shirt. He hadn't bothered with underwear when he left the tent.

Judith pushed him to the ground and leaned over him. He lay very still, scarcely able to breathe. "It is you who looks to be frightened," she laughed.

"I am." His eyes twinkled. "Will you have your way with me?"

Her hand moved over his body, delighting in his smooth skin, the thick mat of hair on his chest. Then it moved lower and lower.

He gasped, his eyes turning black. "Do what you wish," he said hoarsely. "Only do not take your hand away."

She laughed throatily, feeling a surge of power course through her. She had control of him. But the next moment, feeling his hardness in her hand, she knew he had as much power over her. She was insensible with desire. She climbed on top of him, leaned over and hungrily sought his mouth.

Gavin lay still as she moved on him but soon he could lay

still no longer. He grabbed her hips and guided her—faster, harder, his fierceness beginning to match her own.

And then they exploded together.

"Wake up, you hussy," Gavin laughed and slapped Judith's bare buttocks. "The camp wakes and will search for us."

"Let them," Judith murmured and pulled the mantle closer to her.

Gavin towered over her, her body between his feet. Never had he experienced such a night as the one just past. Who was this wife of his? An adulteress? A woman who went from one loyalty to the next, as the wind carried her? Or was she good and kind, as his brothers thought? Whatever she was, she was a demon when it came to lovemaking. "Shall I call your maid to dress you here? Joan will have a few words to say, no doubt."

When Judith sleepily thought of Joan's smirks, it took little time for her to come fully awake. She sat up and looked at the river, then took a deep breath of cool, morning air. She yawned and stretched, the mantle falling away, exposing one full, impudent breast.

"God's teeth!" Gavin swore. "Cover yourself, or we will never reach London and the king."

She smiled at him enticingly. "Maybe I would rather stay here. Court couldn't be half as pleasant."

"Yes," Gavin laughed, then bent and wrapped her in his mantle and swooped her into his arms. "Come, let's return. Miles and Raine leave us today, and I wish to speak with them."

They were silent as they returned to the tent. Judith snuggled against Gavin's shoulder. Would that it could always be like this, she thought. He could be kind and tender when he wanted. Please God, she prayed, let this last between us. Don't let us quarrel again.

An hour later, Judith walked between Raine and Miles, each man holding her hand. They looked to be an incongruous group: two large men dressed in heavy wool traveling clothes, Judith between them, barely reaching to their shoulders.

"I will miss you both," Judith said, squeezing their hands. "It's good having all my family near, though my mother rarely leaves John Bassett's side."

Raine laughed. "Do I hear jealousy in that?"

"Yes," Miles said. "Aren't we enough for you?"

"Gavin seems to be enough," Raine teased.

Judith laughed, her cheeks turning pink. "Is there ever anything that one brother does that the others don't know about?"

"Not much," Raine said then looked over her head to Miles. "There is the question of course of where our little brother spent last night."

"With Joan," Judith said before she thought.

Raine's eyes danced in laughter while Miles's were, as usual, unreadable.

"I . . . know because Joan had a lot to say about him," said Judith, stammering.

Raine's dimples deepened. "Don't let Miles scare you. He is very curious as to what the woman said."

Judith smiled. "I will tell you the next time I see you. Perhaps I can encourage you to visit sooner than you planned."

"Well said!" Raine laughed. "Now, in truth, we must go. We wouldn't be welcome at court unless we paid our own way, and I cannot afford the extra expense."

"He is rich," Miles said. "Don't let him fool you."

"Neither of you fool me. Thank you both for all your time and concern. Thank you for listening to my problems."

"Shall we all cry, when we could be kissing this delicious woman?" Miles asked.

"You are right for once, little brother," Raine said as he lifted Judith from the ground and planted a hearty kiss on her cheek.

Miles took her next and laughed at his brother. "You don't know how to treat a woman," he said as he gathered Judith in his arms and gave her mouth a very unbrotherly kiss.

"You forget yourself, Miles," came a deadly voice. Judith broke away from her brother-in-law to see Gavin staring at them, his eyes dark.

Raine and Miles exchanged looks. It was the first time that Gavin had ever shown any real jealousy. "Put her down before he draws a sword on you," Raine said.

Miles held Judith for a moment longer and looked down at her. "She might be worth it." He set her gently on the ground.

"We will see you again soon," Raine told Gavin. "Perhaps at Christmas we can get together. I should like to see that Scottish lady Stephen is to marry."

Gavin placed a possessive hand on Judith's shoulder and drew her close to him. "At Christmas," he said. His brothers mounted their horses and rode away.

"You aren't really angry?" Judith asked.

"No," Gavin sighed. "But I didn't like seeing a man touch you—even my own brother."

Judith took a deep breath. "If they come at Christmas, the baby will be born then."

The baby, Gavin thought. Not "my baby" or "our baby," but "the baby." He didn't like to think of the child. "Come we must break camp. We have stayed here too long."

Judith followed him, blinking back tears. They didn't mention the time at Demari's castle nor did they talk of the baby. Should she tell him that the child could only be his? Should she plead with him to listen to her, to believe her? She could count days and tell him how far along she was, but once Gavin had hinted that she might have slept with Demari at her wedding. She returned to the tent to direct the maids in the packing.

They made camp early that night. There was no hurrying to reach London, and Gavin enjoyed the time on the journey. He had begun to feel close to his wife. They often talked as if they were friends. Gavin found himself sharing childhood secrets with her, telling her of the fears he'd had when his father died and left him with so much land to manage.

He sat now at a table, a ledger open before him. Every

penny spent must be recorded and accounted for. It was a tedious job, but his steward had fallen ill with some fever, and Gavin could not trust one of his knights' ciphering.

He took a drink from a mug of cider and looked across the room to his wife. She sat on a stool by the open tent flap, a ball of blue yarn in her lap. Her hands struggled with a long pair of knitting needles. As he watched, she made more and more of a mess. Her lovely face was contorted with the effort, the tiny tip of her tongue showing between her lips. He looked again at the books and realized that her attempt at knitting was an effort to please him. He had told her often enough of his displeasure when she interfered in the castle business.

Gavin smothered a laugh as she snarled at the yarn and muttered something beneath her breath. He calmed himself. "Judith," he said, "perhaps you can help me. You don't mind setting that aside?" he asked with all the seriousness he could muster. He tried not to smile as she eagerly tossed the yarn and needles against the tent wall.

Gavin pointed to the ledger. "We've spent too much on this journey, but I don't know why."

Judith pulled the ledger around. Here at least was something she understood. She ran her fingers down the columns, her eyes moving from one side to another. She stopped suddenly. "Five marks for bread! Who has been charging so much?"

"I don't know," Gavin said honestly. "I only eat the stuff, I don't bake it."

"You have been eating gold! I shall tend to this straightaway. Why didn't you show me this before?"

"Because, dear wife, I thought I could run my life on my own. Pity any man who thinks so."

She stared at him. "I will find this baker!" she said as she started to leave the tent.

"Shouldn't you take your knitting? Perhaps you won't find enough to occupy you."

Judith looked over her shoulder at Gavin and saw he was teasing her. She returned his smile, then picked up the ball of yarn and tossed it to him. "Perhaps *you* are the one who needs occupation." She glared pointedly at the ledgers, then left the tent.

Gavin sat and held the yarn for a moment, turning it around in his hands. The tent was too empty when she was gone. He went to the open flap and leaned against the pole, watching her. She never screamed at a servant, but somehow she got more work out of them than he ever had. She took care of the food, the laundry, the setting up of camp, everything, with ease. Yet she never showed any strain and one would never guess she managed six things at once.

She finished talking to the man whose cart was loaded with bread. The short, fat man went away, shaking his head, and Gavin smiled in amusement. He knew just how the baker felt. How many times had Gavin been right yet felt he'd lost the argument? Judith could twist words around until a person couldn't remember his own thoughts.

Gavin watched her walk about the camp. She stopped to taste the stew in a pot, spoke to Gavin's squire where the boy sat on a stool polishing his master's armor. The boy nodded and smiled at her, and Gavin knew there would be some small change made in the simple procedure. And the change would be for the better. Never had he lived or traveled in such comfort—and with such little effort made on his part. He remembered the times he left his tent in the morning and stepped into a pile of horse manure. Now he doubted if Judith allowed the muck to hit the ground. His camp was the cleanest he had ever seen.

Judith felt him staring at her and turned and smiled, looking away from the chickens she inspected. Gavin felt his chest tighten. What did he feel for her? Did it matter that even now she carried another man's child? All he knew was that he wanted her.

He walked across the grass and took her arm. "Come inside with me."

"But I must—"

"You would rather stay outside?" he asked, one eyebrow raised.

She smiled delightedly. "No, I don't think so."

They made love leisurely, savoring each other's bodies until their passion mounted. This was what Gavin loved about making love to Judith. The variety. She never seemed to be the same twice. One time she would be quiet and sensual, the next aggressive and demanding. At other times she would be laughing and teasing, another acrobatic, experimental. But no matter how she was, he loved loving her. Even the thought of touching her excited him.

Now he held her close, his nose buried in her hair. She moved against him as if she could get closer to him; it was not possible. He kissed the top of her head drowsily and fell asleep.

"You are falling in love with him," Joan said the next morning as she combed her mistress's hair. The light through the tent walls was soft and dappled. Judith wore a dress of soft green wool, a braided leather belt about her waist. Even in the simple, unadorned traveling garment, her skin glowed and her eyes were all the jewels she needed.

"I assume you refer to my husband."

"Oh, no," Joan said nonchalantly. "I meant the pie man."

"And how . . . can you tell?"

Joan didn't answer.

"Isn't it right for a woman to love her husband?"

"It is if the love is returned. But be careful and don't fall so hard for him that you are torn apart if he is untrue."

"He has hardly been out of my sight," Judith said in his defense.

"True, but what of when you are at the king's court? You won't be alone with Lord Gavin then. There will be the most beautiful women in England. Any man's eyes would stray."

"Be quiet!" Judith commanded. "And tend to my hair."

"Yes, my lady," Joan said mockingly.

All day, as they traveled, Judith thought of Joan's words. Was she beginning to fall in love with her husband? She had seen him once in another woman's arms. She had been angry then but angry at the fact that he paid her so little respect. But now the idea of seeing him with another woman made her feel as if little slivers of ice were being driven through her heart.

"Judith, are you well?" Gavin asked from the horse beside her.

"Yes . . . no."

"Which is it?"

"I am worried about King Henry's court. Are there many . . . pretty women there?"

Gavin looked across her to Stephen. "What do you say, brother? Are the women at court lovely?"

Stephen looked at his sister-in-law, unsmiling. "I believe you will hold your own," he said calmly, then reined his horse away, going back to his men.

Judith turned to Gavin. "I didn't mean to offend him."

"You didn't. Stephen keeps his worries to himself but I know he dreads his coming marriage. And I don't blame him. The girl hates the English and is sure to make his life hell."

Judith nodded and looked back at the road.

It was when they stopped for dinner that she was able to escape for a few moments. She found a wild raspberry bush outside the camp and set to filling the skirt of her tunic.

"You shouldn't be here alone."

Judith gasped. "Stephen, you startled me."

"If I were an enemy, you could be dead now—or else taken and held for ransom."

Judith stared up at him. "Are you always so full of gloom, Stephen, or is it just this Scottish heiress who worries you so?"

Stephen let out his breath. "Am I so transparent?"

"Not to me, but to Gavin. Come and let's sit awhile. Do you think we could be thoroughly selfish and eat all these berries ourselves? Have you seen your Scottish lady?"

"No," Stephen said, plopping a sun-warmed berry in his mouth. "And she is not mine yet. Did you know that her father made her laird of the MacArran clan before he died?"

"A woman who inherits on her own?" Judith's eyes had a faraway look.

"Yes," Stephen said in disgust.

Judith recovered herself. "Then you don't know what she looks like?"

"Oh yes, I know that. I'm sure she is as small and dark and shriveled as a pine cone."

"Is she old?"

"Maybe she is a young, fat pine cone."

Judith laughed at his air of doom. "All four of you brothers are so different. Gavin is so quick-tempered—icy one moment, fire the next. Raine is laughter and teasing, and Miles is . . ."

Stephen smiled at her. "Don't attempt to explain Miles to me. That boy tries to populate all of England with his children."

"And what of you? Where do you fit? You are a middle son, and you seem to me the least easy to know."

Stephen looked away. "It wasn't easy when I was a boy. Miles and Raine had each other. Gavin had the worry of the estates. And I . . ."

"You were left alone."

Stephen looked at Judith in astonishment. "You have bewitched me! In only moments I have told you more than I have ever told anyone else."

Judith's eyes sparkled. "If this heiress of yours is not kind to you, let me know and I will scratch her eyes out."

"Let's just hope she has both of them to begin with."

They burst into laughter.

"Let's hurry and eat these or we'll have to share them. If I'm not mistaken, Elder Brother approaches."

"Do I ever find you except in the company of men?" Gavin frowned down at them.

"Do you ever greet me with anything except criticism?" Judith retorted.

Stephen snorted with laughter. "I think I should return to camp." He leaned over and kissed Judith's forehead. "If you need help, little sister, I too can find another's eyes."

Gavin grabbed his brother's arm. "Has she enticed you, too?"

Stephen looked back at his sister-in-law, her lips stained dark pink with berry juice. "Yes. If you do not want her . . ."

Gavin gave him a look of disgust. "Raine has already asked."

Stephen laughed and walked away.

"Why did you leave the camp?" Gavin asked as he sat beside her and took a handful of berries from her lap.

"We reach London tomorrow, don't we?"

"Yes. The king and queen don't frighten you, do they?"

"No, not them."

"What then?"

"The . . . women of the court."

"Are you jealous?" he laughed.

"I don't know."

"How could I have time for other women when you're near? You keep me so tired, I do well to stay on my horse."

She did not laugh with him. "There is only one woman I fear. She has separated us before. Don't let her—"

Gavin's face was hard. "Don't speak of her. I have treated you well. I don't pry into what happened at Demari's; yet you seek my soul."

"And she is your soul?" Judith asked quietly.

Gavin looked at her, her eyes warm, her skin soft and fragrant. The past nights of passion flooded his memory. "Don't ask me," he whispered. "I'm sure of one thing only, and that is that my soul is not my own."

The first thing Judith noticed about London was the stench. She thought she knew all the smells humans could create having spent summers in castles overrun with heat and humanity. But nothing prepared her for London. Open gutters ran on each side of the cobbled streets, overflowing with all manner of waste. From the heads of fish and rotting vegetables to the contents of the chamber pots, it all lay in the streets. Pigs and rats ran freely, eating the refuse, spreading it everywhere.

The houses, half-timbered and stone structures were three and four stories high, and so close together that little air and no sun reached between them. The horror Judith felt must have showed on her face, for both Gavin and Stephen laughed at her.

"Welcome to the city of kings," Stephen said.

Once inside the walls of Winchester, the noise and stench were less. A man came to take their horses, and as soon as Gavin helped Judith from hers, she turned to see to the ordering of the carts of baggage and furniture.

"No," Gavin said. "I am sure the king has heard of our arrival. He won't appreciate waiting while you set his castle to rights."

"My clothes are clean? They aren't too mussed?" Judith had dressed carefully that morning in a tawny silk undertunic and a bright yellow velvet dress. The long, hanging sleeves were lined with the finest Russian sable. There was also a wide border of sable along the hem of the gown.

"You are perfect. Now come and let the king look at you."

Judith tried to still her beating heart at the idea of meeting the king of England. She didn't know what she expected, but the rather ordinary great hall was not it. Men and women sat about, playing chess and other games. Three women sat on stools at the feet of a handsome man who played a psaltery. Nowhere did she see any man who could be King Henry.

Judith was astonished when Gavin stopped before a plain middle-aged man with small blue eyes and thin white hair. He looked very tired.

Judith recovered herself and quickly curtsied.

King Henry took her hand.

"Come to the light and let me look at you. I have heard much of your beauty." He led her away, towering over her, for he was six feet tall. "You are as pretty as I have heard. Come here, Bess," King Henry said, "and see the Lady Judith, Gavin's new bride."

Judith turned and saw a pretty middle-aged woman behind her. She had been surprised that Henry was the king, but there was no doubt that this woman was queen. She was a regal woman, so sure of herself, that she could be kind and generous. Her eyes held welcome for Judith. "Your Majesty," Judith said and curtsied.

Elizabeth held out her hand. "Countess," the queen said. "I'm so glad you could come to stay with us for a while. Have I said something amiss?"

Judith smiled at the woman's sensitivity. "I haven't been called 'countess' before. It has been such a short time since my father's death."

"Yes, that was tragic, wasn't it? And the man who did the deed?"

"He is dead," Judith said firmly, remembering too well the feel of the sword sinking into Walter's spine.

"Come, you must be tired after your journey."

"No. I'm not."

Elizabeth smiled fondly. "Then perhaps you would like to come to my chambers for some wine."

"Yes, Your Majesty, I would."

"You will excuse me, Henry?"

Judith suddenly realized she had turned her back on the king. She turned, her cheeks flushed pink.

"Don't mind me, child," Henry said in a distracted manner. "I am sure Bess will put you to work on the wedding plans for our oldest son, Arthur."

Judith smiled and curtsied to him before she followed the queen up the wide stairs to the solar above.

Chapter 24

ALICE SAT on a stool before a mirror in a large room on the top floor of the palace. All around her were a profusion of bright colors. There were purple and green satins, scarlet taffetas, orange brocades. Each cloth, each garment had been chosen as an instrument to call attention to herself. She had seen Judith Revedoune's gowns at her wedding and Alice knew that the heiress's taste ran to simple colors of lush, finely woven fabrics. Alice meant to draw attention away from Gavin's wife with her brilliant clothes.

She wore an undertunic of pale rose, the arms embroidered with black braid swirling round and round. Her crimson velvet dress was cut in deep scallops at the hem and the skirt was appliquéd with enormous wildflowers of every known color. The capelet about her shoulders was her pride. It was of Italian brocade, and in the fabric were colored animals, each one as large as a man's hand, woven in green, purple, orange and black. She was sure no one would outshine her today.

And it was very important that Alice draw attention to herself today because she was to see Gavin again. She smiled at herself in the mirror. She knew she needed Gavin's love after that awful time she'd spent with Edmund. Now that she was a widow, she could look back on Edmund almost fondly. Of course, the poor man was only jealous.

"Look at this circlet!" Alice suddenly commanded her

maid, Ela. "Do you think that blue stone matches my eyes? Or is it too light?" Angrily, she snatched the golden circle from her head. "Damn that goldsmith! He must have used his feet to do such clumsy work."

Ela took the headdress from her angry mistress. "The goldsmith is the king's own, the best in all of England, and the circlet is the most beautiful one he has ever created," Ela soothed. "Of course the stone looks light—no stone could match the rich color of your eyes."

Alice looked back at the mirror and began to quiet. "Do you truly think so?"

"Yes," Ela answered honestly. "No woman could rival your beauty."

"Not even that Revedoune bitch?" Alice demanded, refusing to use Judith's married name.

"Most assuredly. My lady, you don't plan something . . . that goes against the church, do you?"

"How could what I do to her be against the church? Gavin was mine before she took him, and he will be mine again!"

Ela knew from experience that it was impossible to reason with Alice once her mind was set on something. "Do you remember that you mourn your husband as she mourns her father?"

Alice laughed. "I imagine we feel the same about those two men. I have heard that her father was even more despicable than my late beloved husband."

"Don't speak so of the dead."

"And don't you reprimand me, or I will see you go to someone else." It was a familiar threat—one Ela no longer paid any attention to. The worst punishment Alice could imagine was to deny a person her company.

Alice stood and smoothed her gown. All the colors and textures flashed and competed with one another. "Do you think he will notice me?" she asked breathlessly.

"Who could not?"

"Yes," Alice agreed. "Who could not?"

* * *

Judith stood silently by her husband's side, overawed by the king's many guests. Gavin seemed at ease with them all, a man respected, his word valued. It was good to see him in another setting besides a highly personal one. For all their quarrels and disputes, he took care of her, protected her. He knew she was not used to crowds, so he kept her close to him, not forcing her to go to the women, where she would be among strangers. He took much ribbing about this but he smiled good-naturedly with no embarrassment, as most men would have shown.

The long trestle tables were being set for supper, the troubadors organizing their musicians, the jongleurs, the acrobats rehearsing their stunts.

"Are you enjoying yourself?" Gavin asked, smiling down at her.

"Yes. It's all so noisy and active, though."

He laughed. "It will get worse. Let me know if you get tired, and we'll leave."

"You don't mind that I stay so near you?"

"I would mind if you didn't. I wouldn't like you to be free amid these people. Too many young men—and old men, for that matter—look at you."

"They do?" Judith asked innocently. "I hadn't noticed."

"Judith, don't tease these men. The morals at court are very loose, and I wouldn't like for you to be trapped in some web of your own innocent making. Stay by me or Stephen. Don't venture too far away alone. Unless"—his eyes hardened in memory of Walter Demari—"you wish to encourage someone."

She started to speak, to tell him what she thought of his insinuations, but an earl of somewhere—she could never keep them straight—came to talk to Gavin. "I will go to Stephen," she said and walked along the edge of the enormous room to where her brother-in-law leaned against the tapestried wall.

He, like Gavin, was dressed in a rich garment of dark wool, Stephen's brown, Gavin's gray. The form-fitting doublets were also of finely woven dark wool. Judith couldn't help but feel a shiver of pride at being associated with such magnificent men.

Judith noticed a pretty, freckle-faced young woman with a turned-up nose who kept looking at Stephen from around her father's back. "She seems to like you," Judith said.

Stephen didn't look up. "Yes," he said dejectedly. "But my days are numbered, aren't they? A few weeks from now, and I'll have a bit of brown woman on my arm, screeching at my every movement."

"Stephen!" Judith laughed. "She surely couldn't be as bad as you think she is. No woman could be. Look at me. Gavin hadn't seen me before our marriage. Do you think he also worried that I was ugly?"

He looked down at her. "You don't know how much I envy my brother. You are not only beautiful, but wise and kind as well. Gavin is the most fortunate of men."

Judith felt her cheeks turning pink. "You flatter me, but I like to hear it."

"I am no flatterer," Stephen said bluntly.

Suddenly the congenial atmosphere in the hall changed, and both Stephen and Judith looked toward the people around them, feeling that some of the tension was directed toward them. Many people looked at Judith—some in apprehension, some smiling snidely, others in bewilderment—not understanding what the current carried.

"Judith," Stephen said, "have you seen the garden? Queen Elizabeth has some beautiful lilies, and her roses are magnificent."

Judith frowned at him, knowing he wanted her out of the hall for some reason. Several people moved aside and she saw the reason for the tension. Alice Chatworth walked regally into the hall, her head high, a smile of great warmth on her face. And the smile was for one person alone—Gavin.

Judith stared at Alice, her gown seeming gaudy and ill-matched. Alice's pale skin, her obviously artificially darkened eyes did not seem at all beautiful to Judith.

The crowd grew quieter as the "secret" of Alice and Gavin was whispered from one person to the next. Judith turned from the woman to look at her husband. Gavin regarded Alice with an intensity that was almost tangible. His eyes were mesmerized by hers, and nothing seemed likely to break the contact. He watched her make her way slowly toward him and when she was close, she held out her hand. He took it and kissed it lingeringly.

The king's laughter was heard above the small sounds of the hall. "You two seem to know each other."

"We do," Gavin answered, smiling slowly.

"Most assuredly," Alice answered, giving him a demure, closed-lip smile.

"I think I should like to see the garden now," Judith said quickly and took Stephen's extended arm.

"Judith," Stephen began when they were alone in the lovely garden.

"Don't speak to me of her. There is nothing you can say that will give me comfort. I have always known of her. Since the day of our wedding." She looked down at a rose bush, the air heavy with fragrance. "He has never been false to me on her account. He hasn't hidden from me that he loves her or tried to pretend he cares for me in any way."

"Judith, stop this! You can't accept the woman."

Judith turned to Stephen. "And what else can I do? Pray tell me what. He believes me wicked at every turn. If I go to him when he is held captive, he believes I go to my lover. If I carry his child, he believes it belongs to another."

"The child is Gavin's?"

"I see he has told you that he thinks that my baby is Demari's."

"Why don't you tell him the truth?"

"And have him call me a liar? No, thank you. This child is mine, regardless of the father."

"Judith, it would mean a lot to Gavin to know the child was his."

"Will you run and tell him?" she asked heatedly. "Will you knock his mistress down to get close to him? The news will make him quite happy, I'm sure. He has the Revedoune lands, an heir on the way, and his blonde Alice to love. Forgive me if I am selfish enough to want to keep some small thing for myself for a while."

Stephen sat on a stone bench and stared at her. He knew better than to confront his elder brother at this moment when he was so angry. A woman like Judith didn't deserve such neglect and ill treatment as Gavin heaped upon her.

"My lady," a woman called.

"Here, Joan," Judith answered. "What is it?"

"The tables are set for supper and you must come."

"No, I will not. Please say that I am indisposed. Plead my condition as the cause."

"And let that whore have him!" Joan screeched "You *must* attend."

"I agree, Judith."

Joan whirled, not previously aware of Stephen's presence. She flushed becomingly. She never quite got over the striking handsomeness of the men in her mistress's new family. Even the way they moved set her to trembling with desire.

"Do you plan to attack him here?" Judith demanded. "You forget yourself at times, Joan."

"It's the man who makes me do so," the maid murmured. "Lord Gavin has asked for you."

"I'm pleased he remembers me," she said sarcastically.

"Yes, I remembered you," Gavin said from the gateway. "Go," he said to the maid. "I would like to speak to my wife alone."

Stephen stood. "I too will go." He gave his brother one hard look, then left.

"I don't feel well," Judith said. "I must go to my room."

Gavin caught her arm and drew her close to him. Her eyes looked at him coldly. How long had it been since she'd looked at him like that! "Judith, don't hate me again."

She tried to twist away from him. "You humiliate me, and I'm not to show anger? I didn't know you thought I was a saint. Perhaps I should make an application for canonization."

He chuckled at her sharp wit. "I did nothing but look at her and kiss her hand. I haven't seen her for a while."

Judith sneered at him. "*Look* at her!" she spat. "The rushes were nearly set on fire."

He looked down at his wife in wonder. "Are you jealous?" he asked quietly.

"Of that blonde who lusts for my husband? No! I would find a worthier candidate if I were to feel jealousy."

Gavin's eyes flared for a moment. He had never before allowed anyone to say anything against Alice. "Your anger says you lie."

"Anger!" she said, then quieted. "Yes, I am angry because you display your passion for everyone to see. You have embarrassed me before the king. Didn't you see how the people stared and whispered?" She wanted to hurt him. "As for jealousy, one must love another for that emotion to occur."

"And you bear me no love?" he asked coldly.

"I have never said so, have I?" She couldn't read his expression. She didn't know whether she hurt Gavin or not; but even if she had, her cruel words gave her no pleasure.

"Come, then," he said, taking her arm. "The king waits supper for us, and you will not insult him with your absence. If it is indeed your wish to stop the gossip, you must play the loving wife."

Judith followed him docilely, her rage strangely gone.

As newly arrived guests and ones to be especially honored, Gavin and Judith were seated by the king and queen; Judith to the king's right, Gavin to the queen's left and beside Gavin, Alice.

"You seem distraught," King Henry said to Judith.

She smiled. "No, it's only the journey and the child that weary me."

"A child, so soon? I'm sure Lord Gavin is especially pleased with that."

She smiled but could give no answer.

"Gavin," Alice said softly so no other ears would hear her words, "it has been so long since I've seen you." She was cautious with him, for she sensed things had changed between them. He had obviously not forgotten his love for her or he couldn't have looked at her as he had earlier. But he had only just finished kissing her hand when his eyes drew away from her and searched the hall. They settled when he saw his wife's retreating back. Moments later, he had deserted Alice and followed Judith.

"My condolences on your husband's early demise," Gavin said coldly.

"You will think I'm heartless, but I grieve very little for the man," Alice murmured sadly. "He was . . . unkind to me."

Gavin looked at her sharply. "But wasn't he your choice?"

"How can you say that? I was forced into the marriage. Oh Gavin, if you had only waited, we could have been together now. But I'm sure the king would allow us to marry." She put her hand on his arm.

He looked at her hand, so thin and pale, then back at her eyes. "Do you forget that I'm married? That I have a wife?"

"The king is a sympathetic man. He would listen. Your marriage could be annulled."

Gavin turned back to his food. "Don't speak to me of annulment. I have heard the word enough to last me a lifetime. She carries a child. Even the king wouldn't dissolve such a marriage." Gavin gave his attention to the queen and began asking questions about the forthcoming marriage of Prince Arthur to the Spanish Catherine.

Alice sat quietly, thinking of Gavin's words. She meant to find out why he was sick of the word "annulment" and why he referred to his wife's baby as "a child"—almost as if he hadn't fathered it.

An hour later, the tables were cleared and stacked against the wall, making room for any who cared to dance. "Would you dance with me?" Gavin asked his wife.

"Should I ask permission?" she asked, looking at Alice where she sat amid several young male admirers.

Gavin's fingers bit into Judith's arm. "You are unfair to me. I didn't arrange the seating for supper. I'm doing all in my power to pacify you, but there are some things I cannot control."

Maybe I am unreasonable, she thought. "Yes, I will dance with you."

"Or perhaps a walk in the garden," he smiled. "It's a warm night."

She hesitated.

"Come with me, Judith." They had no more stepped through the gate when he pulled her into his arms and kissed her hungrily. She clung to him desperately. "My sweet Judith," he whispered. "I don't know that I can bear any more of your anger. It hurts me deeply when you look at me with hatred."

She melted against him. It was the closest he'd ever come to saying he cared for her. Could she trust him, believe in him?

"Come upstairs with me. Let's go to bed, and don't let us quarrel again."

"Are you saying soft words to me in hopes that I won't be cold in bed?" she asked suspiciously.

"I say soft words because I feel them. I don't wish them thrown back at me."

"I . . . apologize. It was unkind of me."

He kissed her again. "I will think of some way for you to apologize for your hasty temper."

Judith giggled and he smiled warmly at her, his hand caressing her temple. "Come with me—or I'll take you in the king's garden."

She looked about the dark place, as if considering.

"No," he laughed. "Don't tempt me." He took her hand and led her up the stairs to the top floor of the manor house. The enormous room had been divided into small bedrooms for the night by folding oak screens.

"My lady," Joan said sleepily when she heard them approach.

"You won't be needed tonight," Gavin said in dismissal.

Joan rolled her eyes and slipped away through the maze of screens.

"She has her eye on your brother," Judith said.

Gavin raised one eyebrow. "Why should you care what Stephen does with his nights?"

Judith smiled up at him. "You waste ours in needless talk. I'll need help with these buttons."

Gavin was becoming quite efficient at undressing his wife. When he started to fling his own clothes away, Judith whispered, "Let me. I will be your squire tonight." She unbuckled the belt that held the doublet over his hard, flat stomach and slipped it over his head. The long-sleeved tunic came next, baring his chest and the upper part of his thighs between the hose and the brief undergarments.

A fat candle burned by the bed and she pushed Gavin toward it, looking at his body with interest. Judith had explored him with her hands but never so thoroughly with her eyes. Her fingertips ran over the muscles of his arm, and his rippling stomach.

"Do I please you?" he asked, his eyes dark.

She smiled at him. At times he could be a little boy, worried whether he pleased her or not. She didn't answer but moved down on the bed and untied the hose, pulling them away from his heavily muscled legs. He lay very still, as if afraid to break the spell. She ran her hands from his feet to the sides of his hips, and deftly untied the linen braies. Her hands roamed over his body.

"You please me," she said as she kissed him. "Do I please you?"

He couldn't answer but pushed her to the bed and moved on top of her. His passion was such that he could not wait for her long, but Judith also needed him as fiercely as he needed her.

Later, Gavin held her closely in his arms as he heard her quiet, even breathing of sleep. When had he fallen in love with her? he wondered. Perhaps he was in love with her when he'd first taken her home and left her on the doorstep. He smiled in memory of how angry he'd been because she'd dared defy him. He kissed her sleeping forehead. Judith would defy him when she was ninety, he thought, looking forward to the idea.

And what of Alice? When had he ceased to love her? Had he ever loved her? Or had it been a young man's passion for a beautiful woman? She was beautiful, it was true, and tonight he'd been startled when he saw her again, somewhat over-whelmed by her radiance. Alice was a kind and gentle woman, as sweet as Judith was acid, but in the last few months he'd grown to love a bit of vinegar with his food.

Judith moved in his arms and he pulled her closer. He accused her of dishonesty but he didn't really believe his own words. If she carried another man's child, then she had con-ceived it while trying to protect her husband. Misguided, surely, but her heart was always good. She would give up her own life to save her mother, and even a husband who abused her.

He held her so tightly that she woke, fighting for breath.

"You are strangling me!" she gasped.

He kissed her nose. "Have I ever told you that I like vin-egar?"

She gave him a blank look.

"What sort of wife are you?" Gavin demanded. "Don't you know how to help a husband sleep?" He rubbed his hips against hers and her eyes widened. "To sleep so would cause me much pain. You wouldn't want that, would you?"

"No," she whispered, her eyes half-closed. "You shouldn't have to bear such pain."

Gavin was the one who was aroused and Judith lay still in a coma of red and silver light as he ran his hands over her body. It was as if he'd never touched her before, and her body was completely new to her. After his hands became familiar with her soft, smooth skin, he started exploring again with his eyes.

Judith cried out in desperate longing for him, but he only laughed at her and pushed her hands away from his shoulders. When she was trembling with desire, he entered her and they came together almost instantly. They fell asleep, joined, Gavin still on top of her.

When Judith woke the next morning, Gavin was gone and the bed felt cold and empty. Joan helped her dress in a gown of maroon velvet, the neckline square and cut very low. Her sleeves were lined with fox. Across her breast and around her waist were gold cords, fastened at the shoulder with a diamond brooch. At supper there'd been talk of a day's hawking, and she wished to join the hunt.

Gavin met her at the foot of the stairs, his eyes dancing in delight. "You're a sleepy one. I'd hoped to find you still in bed, and perhaps join you there."

She smiled teasingly. "Shall I return?"

"No, not now. I have some news for you. I have spoken to the king, and he agrees to allow John Bassett to marry your mother." King Henry was a Welshman, a descendant of commoners.

She stared at him.

"Doesn't that please you?"

"Oh, Gavin!" she said and launched herself from the steps into his arms. Her arms were so tight about his neck, that he nearly choked. "Thank you. Many thousands of times, thank you."

He laughed and hugged her closer to him. "If I'd thought your reaction would have been like this, I would have talked to the king last night."

"You couldn't have handled more last night," Judith said flatly.

He laughed and squeezed her until she cried for release, her ribs nearly breaking. "You don't think so?" Gavin challenged. "Goad me some more and I'll take you upstairs and keep you there until you are too sore to walk."

"Gavin!" she gasped, her face red. She looked around to see if anyone was listening.

He chuckled and kissed her lightly.

"My mother knows of her marriage?"

"No, I thought maybe you'd like to tell her."

"I'm ashamed to say I don't even know where she is."

"I sent John to look after the lodging of my men. I would imagine your mother to be somewhere near him."

"True, she doesn't often leave his side. Gavin, thank you. It was very kind of you to grant me this favor."

"I wish I could grant you everything that you wanted," he said softly.

She looked at him in wonder.

"Go then," he smiled. "Tell your mother, then join me in the courtyard for the hunt." He set her down, then gazed at her with concern. "You are well enough to ride?"

It was the first time that he had mentioned the child in any way but anger. "Yes," she smiled. "I'm quite well. Queen Elizabeth says the exercise will do me good."

"Just be sure you don't overdo," Gavin cautioned.

She smiled and turned away, her mind warm from his concern. She felt light with happiness.

Judith walked down the stairs and out of the great hall. The enormous castleyard that stood inside the guarded walls was filled with people. The noise was nearly deafening as men and women shouted to servants and servants yelled at each other. Everything seemed so disorganized that Judith wondered how anything got done. A long building stood at the end of the courtyard. Horses pranced about outside, held by their grooms. It was obviously the stables.

"Ah, if it isn't little Miss Red-Hair," came a purring voice that halted Judith instantly. "Are you on your way to some tryst with a lover, perhaps?"

Judith stopped and stared at Alice Chatworth. Her enemy—face to face.

"I'm sure you must remember me," Alice said sweetly. "We met at your wedding."

"I'm sorry I was not able to attend yours, although Gavin and I shared your message of undying love," Judith returned in kind.

Alice's eyes shot blue fire, her body stiffened. "Yes, it is too bad it all ended so soon."

"Ended?"

Alice smiled. "Haven't you heard? My husband, poor dear, was murdered in his sleep. I'm a widow now, and free. Oh yes, very free. I assumed Gavin told you. He was most interested in my . . . ah . . . new status."

Judith turned on her heel and stalked away. No, she hadn't known Alice was no longer married. Now all that stood between Alice and Gavin was herself. No Edmund Chatworth hindered them.

Chapter 25

JUDITH CONTINUED to walk toward the stables, but she had no idea where she was going. Her mind was only aware of the fact that Alice Chatworth was a widow.

"Judith."

She looked up and managed to smile at her mother.

"Will you ride in the hunt today?"

"Yes," she said, the joy gone from her day.

"What's wrong?"

Judith tried to smile. "I lose my mother—that's all. Did you know that Gavin has given permission for your marriage to John Bassett?"

Helen stared at her daughter. She neither spoke nor smiled. Slowly, the color drained from her face. She fell forward into her daughter's arms.

"Help!" Judith managed to gasp.

A tall young man who was nearby ran to her and quickly lifted Helen.

"To the stables," directed Judith, "out of the sun."

Once in the shade, Helen began to recover almost instantly.

"Mother, you are well?"

Helen looked meaningfully at the young man.

He understood the look. "I'll leave you alone," he said and walked away before Judith could even thank him.

"I . . . didn't know," Helen began. "I mean I didn't know Lord Gavin even knew of my love for John."

Judith stopped herself from laughing aloud. "I asked him some time ago for permission, but he wanted to consult the king. Yours will be an unusual wedding."

"And soon enough," Helen murmured.

"Soon—? Mother!"

Helen smiled like a child caught in some mischief. "It's true—I bear his child."

Judith sank into a pile of hay. "Shall we deliver together?" she asked in wonder.

"Close."

Judith laughed. "Arrangements must be made quickly, so the baby will be able to claim a name."

"Judith!" She looked up to see Gavin coming toward them. "A man said your mother took ill."

She rose and took his arm. "Come, we must talk."

Moments later, Gavin shook his head in disbelief. "And to think I believed John Bassett to be a sensible man!"

"He's in love. Men and women do unusual things when they're in love."

Gavin looked at her eyes, the gold especially brilliant in the sunlight. "I'm well aware of that."

"Why didn't you tell me she was a widow?" Judith asked quietly.

"Who?" he asked, honestly puzzled.

"Alice! Who else?"

He shrugged. "I didn't think to tell you." He smiled. "I find I have other thoughts when you are near me."

"Are you trying to change the subject?"

He grabbed Judith by the shoulders, lifting her from the ground. "Damn you! It's not I who am obsessed with the woman, but you. If I cannot reason with you, I'll try to shake some sense into you. Would you like to be shaken in public?"

He shook his head in wonder when she smiled at him sweetly. "I would rather attend the hunt. Perhaps you could help me mount my horse?"

He stared at her a moment, then set her down. He would *never* understand women.

* * *

The hunt was exhilarating to Judith, the little tiercel hawk on a perch on her saddle. Her hawk brought down three cranes, and she was well pleased with the day's hunting.

Gavin wasn't as lucky. He was barely in his saddle when he received a whispered message from a maid. Stephen wished to meet with him on some private matter when they were two miles outside the castle walls. His brother asked that he tell no one about the meeting—even his wife. Gavin was puzzled by the message as it didn't sound like Stephen. He left the hunting party while Judith was engrossed in the flight of her tiercel, cursing his brother under his breath for taking him away from such a lovely sight.

Gavin didn't ride directly to the place indicated but tied his horse some distance away and approached cautiously, sword drawn.

"Gavin!" Alice said, her hand to her breast. "You gave me a terrible fright."

"Where is Stephen?" Gavin asked, still looking about the place warily.

"Gavin, please put your sword away. You frighten me!" Alice smiled, but her eyes didn't look fearful.

"You have called me, and not Stephen?"

"Yes, it was the only way I knew to get you here." She lowered her eyes. "I thought you wouldn't come for me alone."

Gavin sheathed his sword. It was a quiet and secluded place, much like the one where she used to meet him.

"Ah, so you think of that time also. Come, sit by me. We have a lot to talk about."

He stared at her and without wanting to he began to compare her to Judith. Alice was pretty, yes, but her little mouth with its closed-lip smile seemed ungenerous—stingy, almost. Her blue eyes rather reminded him of ice rather than sapphires. And the red, orange and green she wore seemed gaudy instead of brilliant, as he used to think of her clothes.

"Have things changed so much that you sit so far away from me?"

"Yes, they have." Gavin didn't see the brief frown that crossed her pale brow.

"Are you still angry with me? I've told you over and over that I was married against my will to Edmund. But now that I am a widow we—"

"Alice," he interrupted, "please don't talk of that again." He had to tell her, and he dreaded hurting her. She was so soft and delicate, so unable to take the pain of life. "I will not leave Judith, neither through annulment nor divorce nor any other unnatural means."

"I . . . don't understand. There is a chance for us now."

He put his hand over hers in her lap. "No, there is not."

"Gavin! What are you saying?"

"I have grown to love her," he said simply.

Alice's eyes blazed at him a moment before she recovered her temper. "You said you would not. On your wedding day you *promised* me that you wouldn't love her."

Gavin almost smiled in memory. Two vows had been made that day. Judith had vowed to give him only what he took. How deliciously she had broken that vow! And he, too, had broken his. "Don't you remember that you threatened to take your own life? I would have done or said most anything to keep you from doing that."

"But now you no longer care what I do with my life?"

"No! It's not that. You know you will always have a place in my heart. You were my first love, and I will never forget you."

Alice looked up at him, wide-eyed. "You talk as if I were already dead. Tell me, has she taken all your heart that I can have none?"

"I told you that you had a part, Alice, don't do this to us. You must accept what has happened."

Alice smiled, her eyes beginning to fill with tears. "Should I accept it with the fortitude of a man? But Gavin, I'm a woman—a frail and fragile woman. Your heart may be cold to me, but mine is only warmer at seeing you again. Do you know what it was like being married to Edmund? He treated me like a servant, locked me in my room continually."

"Alice—"

"And can you guess why? Because at your wedding he had me watched. Yes, he knew when we went alone to the garden. He knew the times when I was alone with you in your tent. Remember the time you kissed me with such feeling, the morning after your wedding?"

Gavin nodded, not wanting to hear her confession.

"During our marriage, he never lost a moment to remind me of the time I had spent with you. Yet I bore it all, willingly—gladly almost—for I knew you loved me. Each and every lonely night I lay awake and thought of you, of your love for me."

"Alice, you must stop."

"Tell me," she said quietly, "didn't you once think of me?"

"Yes," he answered honestly. "I did at first. But Judith is a good woman, kind and loving. I never thought I would love her. It was a marriage for estates, as you know."

Alice sighed. "What am I to do now? My heart is yours—has always been, will always be."

"Alice, this won't help. It's over between us. I'm married and I love my wife. You and I must part ways."

"You are so cold to me." Alice touched his arm, then moved her hand up to his shoulder. "Once you were not so cold."

Gavin clearly remembered making love to Alice. Then he had been blinded by his love for her, and he believed anything she did was the way it should be done. But now, after months of passion with Judith, the idea of bedding Alice almost repulsed him. The way she could not stand to be touched before or after lovemaking. No, with Alice it was sex—a pure animal drive, nothing else.

Alice saw the expression on his face but didn't understand it. She continued with her hand until she touched his neck. He stood immediately. Alice stood also, but she took his reluctance at her touch as a sign of his growing desire for her. She stood boldly against him, her arms going around his neck.

"I see you do remember," she whispered, raising her face to be kissed.

He gently pulled her arms from his neck. "No, Alice."

She glared at him, her hands clenched into fists at her sides. "You are so unmanned by her that you are afraid of her?"

"No," Gavin said, surprised, both at Alice's reasoning and her outburst. Anger was unnatural to Alice, who was always so sweet-tempered.

Alice quickly realized she'd made an error in revealing her true emotions. She blinked her eyes until great jewellike tears formed. "This is good-bye," she whispered. "May I not have even one last kiss? You would deny me that, after all we've meant to each other?"

She was so delicate and he'd loved her so much once. He wiped a tear from her cheek with his fingertip. "No," he whispered. "I wouldn't deny myself one last kiss." He took her gently in his arms and kissed her sweetly.

But Alice wanted no sweetness. He had forgotten her violence by half. She thrust her tongue in his mouth, grinding her teeth against his lips. He felt no building ardor as he once would have, but only a faint sense of distaste. He wanted to get away from her. "I must go," he said, concealing his revulsion.

But Alice could feel that something was very wrong. She thought to bring him under control through that kiss but she knew she hadn't. If anything, he was more remote than before. She bit her tongue over her sharp words and managed to look properly sad as he made his way through the trees to his waiting horse. "Damn that bitch!" Alice said through clenched teeth. That red-haired she-devil had taken her man!

Or at least she thought she had. Alice began to smile. Maybe that Revedoune woman thought she had Gavin, that she could crook her little finger and he would come to her. But she was mistaken! Alice would not allow someone to take what was hers. No, she would fight for her property and Gavin was hers . . . or he would be again.

She had done so much to get where she was now, at the

king's court near Gavin; she had even allowed her husband's murderer to escape. She would watch the woman and find her weakness. Then Alice would regain what was hers. Even if she decided to cast Gavin aside, it was to be her decision and not his!

Gavin rode back to the hunting party quickly. He had been gone a long time, but he hoped no one had missed him. He sent up a silent prayer of thanks that Judith hadn't seen him kissing Alice. No amount of explaining in the world would have pacified her. But all that was over. As difficult as it had been, he had told Alice, and now he was forever free of her.

Gavin saw his wife ahead, swinging her lure to bring her tiercel back to the perch. Suddenly his desire for her was boundless. He urged his mount forward until he was almost galloping by the time he reached her horse. He bent forward and jerked the reins.

"Gavin!" Judith called as she grabbed the pommel of the saddle, her tiercel flapping its wings in fright.

The people around them hooted in laughter. "They have been married how long?"

"Not long enough," came the reply.

Gavin stopped both horses when they were some distance away in a secluded glade.

"Gavin! Have you lost your mind?" Judith demanded.

He slid from his horse then lifted her from hers. He didn't speak to her but began kissing her hungrily. "I was thinking of you," he whispered. "And the more I thought of you, the more my need . . . arose."

"I can feel your need." She looked about her. "This is a pretty place isn't it?"

"It could be prettier."

"Yes, it could," she answered as he kissed her again.

The sweet outdoor summer air added a great deal to their passion as did the slightly naughty idea that they were doing something somewhere they shouldn't. Judith giggled when Gavin made a comment on King Henry's numerous children. He stopped her laughter with his lips.

They fumbled with each other's clothing hurriedly and made love as if they'd not seen each other for years. Later, they cuddled close together, wrapped in warm sunlight and the delicate scent of wildflowers.

Chapter 26

ALICE LOOKED over the heads of the many men around her to the slim, blond, handsome man leaning against the wall. He had a pensive expression on his face that she recognized as that of someone in love. She smiled sweetly at a man nearby but Alice didn't really hear him. Her mind was completely on that afternoon, when Gavin said he was in love with his wife. She watched as Gavin held his wife's hand and led her through the intricate steps of a dance. It didn't matter that Alice had several young men at her feet. Being scorned by Gavin only made her want him more. Had he sworn he loved her still, perhaps she would have considered one of the many marriage proposals offered to her. But Gavin had rejected her, and now she knew she must have him. Only one thing stood in her way, and that she planned to remove.

The young blond man stared at Judith with fascination, his eyes never leaving her. Alice had noticed him at dinner when he looked up at the high table, not even blinking as he stared at Judith. Alice realized that the woman was too stupid to even be aware of an admirer, for Judith's eyes never left Gavin.

"Will you excuse me?" Alice murmured demurely and dismissed the men around her as she walked toward the man against the wall.

"She is lovely, isn't she?" Alice asked, gritting her teeth against the words.

"Yes," he whispered, the word coming from his soul.

"It's sad to see a woman such as that so unhappy."

The man turned and looked at Alice. "She doesn't look to be unhappy."

"No, she makes a good show, but the unhappiness is there."

"You are Lady Alice Chatworth?"

"Yes. And you?"

"Alan Fairfax, my beautiful countess," he said as he bowed and kissed her hand. "At your service."

Alice laughed gaily. "It is not I who need your service, but the Lady Judith."

Alan looked back at the dancers. "She is the most beautiful woman I have ever seen," he whispered.

Alice's eyes glittered like blue glass. "Have you told her of your love?"

"No!" he said, frowning. "I am a knight, sworn to honor, and she is a married woman."

"Yes, she is, though most unhappily."

"She doesn't look to be unhappy," he repeated as he watched the object of his affections look up at her husband with great warmth.

"I have known her a long time and she is indeed miserable. Only yesterday she was crying to me that she desperately needed someone to love, someone who would be sweet and gentle with her."

"Her husband is not?" Alan was concerned.

"It's not common knowledge"—Alice lowered her voice— "but he beats her often."

Alan looked back at Judith. "I don't believe you."

Alice shrugged. "I didn't mean to spread gossip. She is my friend and I would like to help her. They won't stay at court for long, and I'd hoped that before they left dear Judith could find just a few moments of pleasure."

It was true that Lady Judith was lovely; her radiant coloring saw to that. Her auburn hair was visible beneath a veil of transparent gauze. The silver tissue of her dress hugged lush curves. But what Alan thought was even more striking than her beauty was the vitality she seemed to emanate. She looked at everyone, from king to serf, with a calm level look that said she cared. She never giggled or flirted or played the coy maiden. Alan was truly fascinated by her. He would give a lot to have her once turn those warm golden eyes on him.

"Would you like to see her alone?"

Alan's eyes sparkled. "Yes, I would."

"Then I will arrange it. Go to the garden and I'll send her to you. We're great friends and she knows she can trust me." Alice stopped and put a hand on Alan's arm. "She'll worry that she is safe from her husband's finding her. Tell her he is with me—then she'll know that she has no fear of being discovered."

Alan nodded. It wouldn't hurt to spend some time with the lady, and since her husband rarely let her out of his sight, Alan would use this opportunity.

Judith stood close to Gavin, drinking a mug of cool cider. She was warm from the dancing, and it was pleasant to lean against the cool stone and watch the others. A man came with a message for Gavin, which he repeated quietly, for Gavin's ears alone. Gavin frowned.

"Have you had bad news?" she asked.

"I don't know. Someone says I must meet them."

"No name?"

"No. I asked a horse merchant about a mare—perhaps it's only that." He turned and caressed her cheek. "There is Stephen. Go and stay by him. This won't take long."

"If I can find a way through the women around Stephen!" she laughed.

"You will do as I say."

"Yes, my lord," she said mockingly.

He shook his head at Judith, but smiled, then turned and left.

She went to stand by Stephen who strummed on a lute and sang for a group of pretty and adoring young women. Stephen had told her that he meant to use his last days of freedom to advantage.

"Lady Judith?"

"Yes." She turned to a maid, one she did not recognize.
"There is a man waiting for you in the garden."

"A man? My husband?"

"I don't know, my lady."

Judith began to smile. No doubt Gavin planned some
moonlight tryst. "Thank you," she said, leaving the hall to go
to the garden. The garden was dark and cool, with many secret shadows that told of several couples locked together in
each other's arms.

"Lady Judith?"

"Yes." It wasn't possible to see clearly but she saw a tall,
slim young man with bright eyes, a prominent nose and lips
a little too full.

"Allow me to introduce myself. I am Alan Fairfax of Lin-
colnshire."

She smiled at him as he took her hand and kissed it.

"Are you looking for someone?"

"I thought my husband would be here."

"I haven't seen him."

"You know him then?"

He smiled, showing even white teeth. "I have seen you. It
is more that I know you and am aware of who is near you."

She looked at him in wonder. "A very pretty speech, sir."

Alan held his arm out for her. "Shall we sit here a moment
while we wait for your husband?"

She hesitated.

"As you see, the bench is in plain view. I ask nothing of
you but that you sit and talk to a lonely knight."

The bench was directly under a bright torch held in the
garden wall. Judith could see him more clearly. His lips were
sensual, his nose thin and aristocratic. His eyes were almost
black in the darkness. Judith was wary of him. The last man
she had sat and talked with was Walter Demari, and that had
led to disaster.

"You seem ill at ease, my lady."

"I'm not used to courtly ways. I've spent very little time
with men who aren't related to me."

"But you wish to spend more?" he encouraged.

"I hadn't thought about it. I have my husband and his brothers. They seem to be enough."

"But here at court a lady may be freer. It's acceptable to have many friends, both men and women." Alan took her hand from her lap. "I should very much like to be your friend."

She jerked away from him, frowning, then rose. "I must return to the hall and my husband."

He stood beside her. "There's no need to fear him. He is safely away. He is with your friend Alice Chatworth."

"No! You insult me!"

"No," Alan said, bewildered. "I didn't mean to. What have I said?"

So! Gavin was with Alice. Perhaps he arranged that she should spend this time with another man in the hope that she would be occupied. But she had no desire to stay with a stranger. "I must go," she said quickly, turning on her heel.

"Where have you been?" Gavin demanded, meeting her before she reached the hall.

"With my lover," she said calmly. "And you?"

His hands tightened on her arms. "Are you teasing me?"

"Perhaps."

"Judith!"

She glared at him. "Wasn't the Lady Alice especially lovely tonight? Gold cloth goes well with her hair and eyes, don't you think?"

Gavin loosened his hold somewhat, smiling slightly. "I didn't notice. Are you jealous of her?"

"Do I have cause?"

"No, Judith, you do not. I have told you she is gone from my life."

She sneered at him. "Next you will be telling me your love is now mine."

"And if I did?" Gavin whispered with such an intensity she was almost frightened.

Her heart fluttered. "I don't know if I would believe you," she said quietly. Or was she afraid that if he said he loved her that she would return the words? Would he laugh at her?

Would he and his Alice lay in each other's arms and make light of what to Judith was life and death?

"Come inside, then. It grows late."

What was there in his voice that made her want to comfort him?

"You leave tomorrow?" Gavin asked as he wiped sweat from his brow. He had been training since sunup on the king's long sand-covered field. There were many knights and squires present from all over England.

"Yes," Stephen said with an air of gloom. "I feel as though I'm going to my death."

Gavin laughed. "It won't be so bad. Look at my marriage. It has turned out quite well."

"Yes, but there is only one Judith."

Gavin smiled and scratched at the heavy armor he wore. "Yes, and she is mine."

Stephen returned his smile. "All is well between you then?"

"It's coming along. She is jealous of Alice and forever accuses me of all manner of happenings with her, but Judith will come round."

"And what of your Alice?"

"I'm no longer interested. I told her so yesterday."

Stephen gave a low whistle. "You told Alice, whom you once loved, that you now prefer another? I would fear for my life if I were you."

"Perhaps from Judith, but not from one as sweet as Alice."

"Alice Chatworth? Sweet? You are truly blind, my brother."

As always, Gavin was angered when someone spoke ill of Alice. "You don't know her as I do. She was very hurt when I told her, but she accepted it regally, as I knew she would. If Judith hadn't captured me so completely, I would still think of Alice as a choice for my wife."

Stephen thought it was better not to comment further. "Tonight I plan a splendid drunk. I will drink the castle dry.

Then, when I see this bride of mine, I'll be better able to stomach her. Would you care to join me? We shall celebrate my last moments of freedom."

Gavin smiled in anticipation. "Yes, we haven't celebrated our escape from Demari's. Stephen, I didn't tell you my thanks."

Stephen hit his brother on the back. "You must return the favor when I need you."

Gavin frowned. "Maybe you can find me a man to replace John Bassett."

"Ask Judith," Stephen said, his eyes twinkling. "Perhaps she can run your men also."

"Don't even hint such an idea to her. She complains now that she has too little to do here."

"That's your fault, brother. Don't you keep her busy?"

"Have a care! I may begin to hope that your Scottish heiress is as ugly as you think she is."

Judith sat in the great hall amid a group of women. All of them, including the queen, sat behind beautiful rosewood and brass embroidery frames. Their hands flew deftly and swiftly over the fabric, beautiful colors of silk streaming from their needles. Judith sat quietly in a chair, a piece of embroidery before her, too; but she merely stared at it, feeling awkward, not knowing what else to do with herself. At least Gavin could do his work even when he was away from home. But he had threatened her against cleaning the king's fishpond . . . or his pantry or anything else, for that matter.

"I think that sewing is the most feminine of arts. Don't you agree, Your Majesty?" Alice said quietly.

Queen Elizabeth didn't even look up. "I believe it would depend upon the woman. I have seen some women use a crossbow, yet retain their femininity, while another who looked sweet and performed all the female arts to perfection, could underneath be cruel."

Judith looked up in surprise as a giggle escaped from a pretty young woman next to her.

"You don't agree, Lady Isabel?" Queen Elizabeth asked.

"Oh yes, Your Majesty, I most certainly do." The two women exchanged understanding glances.

Alice, furious at being set down, continued. "But would a true woman wish to use a crossbow? I cannot see that there would be a need. Women are always protected by men."

"May a woman not help her husband? I once took an arrow meant for John," Lady Isabel said.

Several of the women gasped in horror.

Alice looked at the green-eyed woman with disgust. "But a true woman could not do violence. Could they, Lady Judith? I mean, a woman couldn't kill a man, could she?"

Judith looked down at the empty canvas on the stretcher.

Alice leaned forward. "Lady Judith, you couldn't kill a man, could you?"

"Lady Alice!" Queen Elizabeth said sharply. "I believe you pry into matters that are not your concern."

"Oh!" Alice feigned surprise. "I didn't know the Lady Judith's handiness with a sword was a secret. I won't speak of it again."

"No, you won't," Lady Isabel lashed out, "now that you have told everything."

"My lady!" Joan announced loudly, "Lord Gavin requests you immediately."

"Is anything wrong?" Judith asked, rising quickly.

"I don't know," Joan said, an odd, blank expression on her face. "You know how he cannot bear for you to be out of his sight for very long."

Judith gave her a look of astonishment.

"Come quickly. He won't wait long."

Judith refrained from reprimanding her maid before the queen. She turned and excused herself from the women, glad to see that Alice's eyes smoldered in anger. When they were away, Judith turned back to her maid. "You forget yourself."

"No! I only helped you. That cat would tear you to shreds. You're no match for her."

"She doesn't frighten me."

"Then perhaps she should. She is an evil woman."

"Yes," Judith agreed. "I am aware of that. I am grateful

though that you took me from that place. I almost prefer Alice's company to sewing, but the two together are more than I can bear!" She sighed. "I suppose Gavin didn't send for me."

"Why must he send for you? Don't you think he will be pleased to see you?"

Judith frowned.

"You are a foolish woman," Joan said, risking harsh words from her mistress. "The man wants you, yet you don't see it."

Once outside in the bright sunlight, Judith forgot all thoughts of Alice. Gavin leaned over a large trough of water, bare from the waist up as he washed himself. Judith crept silently behind him then leaned over and gave him a nipping kiss on his neck. The next moment she found herself gasping for breath as Gavin swung round and knocked her into the trough. Both of them were very surprised.

"Judith! Are you hurt?" Gavin asked as he put his hand out to her.

She knocked it away, wiping water from her eyes, looking at her soaked and ruined gown, the crimson velvet plastered to her body. "I am not, you clumsy oaf. Do you think I'm your war-horse, that I may be treated as an animal? Or perhaps you think I'm your squire?" She put her hand to the side of the trough to lift herself, but her feet slipped and she went under again. She gasped as she looked up at Gavin. His arms were folded across his chest and he wore a broad smile.

"You are laughing at me!" she hissed, enraged. "How dare—"

He grabbed her shoulders and lifted her dripping body. "May I offer my apologies? I'm not exactly calm since Demari's. I was too late in recognizing your kiss as a kiss. You shouldn't sneak upon me, but give me some warning."

"You needn't fear such happening again," Judith said grimly.

"Only you, my little wife, would be so saucy while being held over a body of water. I could drop you in again."

"You wouldn't dare!"

He grinned then lowered her slowly until her toes came near the water again.

"Gavin!" she cried, half-pleading.

He drew her to him, then gasped as her cold body touched his skin.

"You are well repaid," she laughed. "I hope you freeze."

"Not with you near." He swung her into his arms. "Let's go to our room and remove these wet clothes."

"Gavin, you can't think—"

"Thinking, while you are in my arms, is a waste of time. If you don't want to cause more attention drawn to yourself, be quiet and let me have my way."

"And if I don't?"

He rubbed his cheek against her wet one. "You will find those pretty cheeks will turn very red."

"Then I am a captive?"

"Yes," he answered firmly and carried her up the stairs.

Queen Elizabeth walked beside her husband. They stopped when they saw Gavin knock Judith into the water. Elizabeth would have gone to help Judith, but Henry stopped her.

"Look at their love play. It pleases me when I see a couple so in love. It isn't often that a marriage of estates turns to happiness."

Elizabeth sighed. "I'm glad to see them each loving the other. I wasn't sure there was love there. Lady Alice seems to think the Lady Judith isn't a fit match for Lord Gavin."

"Lady Alice?" King Henry asked. "She is that blonde woman?"

"Yes. Edmund Chatworth's widow."

Henry nodded. "I would like to see her married soon. I have watched her. She plays with men, rather like a cat with a mouse. She seems to care for one, then the other. The men are in love with her beauty and will take much from her. I wouldn't like to see them come to blows. But what has the woman to do with Lord Gavin and that lovely wife of his?"

"I'm not sure," Elizabeth said. "There is some gossip that Gavin was once in love with Lady Alice."

Henry nodded toward Gavin as he lifted his wife into his arms. "He is not so now, as everyone can see."

"Maybe not everyone. Lady Alice baits Lady Judith constantly."

"We must stop this," Henry said.

"No," Elizabeth put a hand on her husband's arm. "We can give no orders. I fear it will only make Alice more angry, and she is the kind of woman who would find a way to say what she wanted no matter what orders were given her. I think your idea of marriage to be the best. Can't you find a husband for her?"

Henry watched Gavin carrying his wife toward the manor house, teasing and tickling her, causing Judith's laughter to ring through the yard. "Yes, I will find Lady Alice a husband, and quickly. I wouldn't like to see anything come between those two."

"You are a good man," Elizabeth said and smiled up at her tall husband.

Henry chuckled. "Only to a few, my dear. You should ask the French who is a good king or not."

Elizabeth waved her hand. "You are too soft on them, too good to them."

He bent and kissed her forehead. "And if I were a French king, I'm sure you'd say the same of the English."

She smiled lovingly up at him and he laughed and squeezed her arm.

There was someone else who took a special interest in the play of the Montgomeries. Alan Fairfax had started forward, his hands on his sword when he saw Gavin knock Judith into the trough. Then he looked about guiltily. A man could treat his wife in any manner he wished, and Alan had no right to interfere.

As Alan watched, he saw Gavin's concern for Judith, how he took her from the water, held her and kissed her. This was no man who beat his wife! Alan frowned as he began to realize that he had been played for a fool.

He went back into the manor house where he found Alice

Chatworth crossing the great hall. "I would like a word with you, my lady," he said, his fingers tightening on her arm.

She gasped at the pain, then smiled. "Of course, Sir Alan. My time is yours to command."

He drew her to the side of the room, into the shadows. "You have used me, and I don't like that."

"Used you? Pray, how so, sir?"

"Don't play the coy virgin with me. I know of the men who frequent your bed. You are a woman of some intelligence, I am sure, and you have manipulated me for your own purpose."

"Release me or I will scream!"

His hand dug deeper into her arm. "Don't I please you? My friends tell me you're not averse to pain."

Alice glared at him. "What is it you wish to say to me?"

"I don't care to be used. Your lies could have given Lady Judith great trouble, and I would have been the cause."

"Didn't you say you wished a few moments alone with her? I gave you that time—that's all."

"By trickery! She is a good woman and happily wed, and I'm no villain to resort to rape."

"Then you do desire her?" Alice smiled.

He released her quickly. "What man wouldn't? She is beautiful."

"No!" Alice hissed. "She's not as beautiful—" She stopped herself.

Alan smiled. "As you, Lady Alice? No, you are wrong. I have watched Lady Judith for days, and I have come to know her. She is not only beautiful on the outside, but inwards as well. When she is old and not so lovely, she will be well loved. But you! Your beauty is on the outside alone. If it were taken away from you, only a querulous, evil-minded, vicious woman would remain."

"I shall hate you for this!" Alice said in a deadly voice.

"Someday every second you have spent hating will show on your face," Alan noted calmly. "Whatever your feelings for me, don't think I can be used again." He turned his back on her and left her alone.

Alice watched his retreating back but her vengeance was for Judith rather than for Alan. The woman had been the cause of all her problems. Nothing had been the same since Gavin had decided to marry the bitch. Now Alice was insulted by a young man because of the deviousness of that Revedoune woman. Alice was even more determined to put an end to a marriage that she considered wrong.

"Judith, sweet. Stay in bed," Gavin murmured against her sleepy cheek. "You need rest, and the water may have given you a chill."

Judith didn't answer. She was sated with their lovemaking and feeling drowsy and languid.

He nuzzled his face against her neck once more and slipped from the bed. He dressed quickly, watching her all the while. When he was dressed, he smiled at her, kissed her cheeks and left the room.

Stephen met him at the foot of the stairs. "I can't walk through a room that I don't hear more gossip of you!"

"What now?" Gavin asked suspiciously.

"Only that you beat your wife and throw her in troughs of water, then flaunt her before everyone."

Gavin smiled. "It's all true."

Stephen returned his brother's grin. "Now we understand each other. I thought you didn't know how to treat a woman. Is she asleep?"

"Yes. She will stay there the night." Gavin lifted one brow. "I thought you would have a hogshead of wine ready."

"I do," Stephen grinned. "I didn't want you to feel the lesser man by my drinking twice as much as you."

"You!" Gavin snorted. "My younger brother? Didn't you know I got drunk the first time before you were born?"

"I don't believe you!"

"It's true. I'll tell you the story though it is a very long one."

Stephen slapped his brother on the back. "We have all night. The morning is when we'll repent what we've done."

Gavin chuckled. "You shall repent with your ugly Scottish

bride, but I will wearily lay my head in my beautiful wife's lap and kindly allow her to cosset me."

Stephen groaned. "You are a cruel man!"

For both brothers, the night was a special time of closeness. They celebrated their release from Demari. They celebrated Gavin's good fortune in his marriage, and they commiserated together on the prospect of Stephen's forthcoming one.

"I'll give her back to her people if she disobeys me," Stephen said. The wine they drank was so bad that they had to strain it through their teeth, but neither of them noticed.

"Two disobedient wives!" Gavin said in a slur as he raised his mug. "If Judith were to obey me, I would think a devil had stolen her mind."

"And left only her body?" Stephen leered.

"I will call you out for that," Gavin said as he fumbled for his sword.

"She wouldn't have me," Stephen responded as he refilled his cup.

"You don't think so? She certainly seemed pleased with Demari." Gavin changed from happiness to sadness in moments, as only a drunk could.

"No, she hated the man."

"But she bears his child!" Gavin said, sounding like a little boy about to cry.

"You have no sense, brother! The child is yours, not Demari's."

"I don't believe you."

"It's true. She told me."

Gavin sat at the thick table silently for a moment then started to rise, but his head swam. "You're sure? Why didn't she tell me?"

"She said she wanted to keep some small thing to herself."

Gavin sat down heavily. "She considers my son a small thing?"

"No. You don't understand women."

"And you do?" Gavin asked archly.

Stephen refilled his brother's mug. "No more than you do,

I'm sure. Perhaps even less, if that is possible. Raine could explain what she said better than I. She said you already had the Revedoune lands and Alice, and she would give you no more."

Gavin's face blackened as he rose. Then suddenly he calmed and sat down again, a slight smile on his face. "She is a witch, isn't she? She swings her hips before me until I am blind with desire. She curses me when I merely talk to another woman."

"One you have freely admitted you loved."

Gavin waved his hand as if that didn't matter. "And yet she holds the key that would unlock all secrets and free us both from the strain that is between us."

"I don't see any reluctance on your part," Stephen said.

Gavin chuckled. "No, none on mine, but I have been reluctant to . . . force myself on her. I thought that Demari meant something to her."

"Only a means to save your unappreciative neck."

Gavin smiled. "Pass me that wine. We have more to celebrate tonight than a mere Scots princess."

Stephen grabbed the jug before Gavin could touch it. "You are a cruel brother."

"I learned it from my wife," Gavin smiled and filled his own mug.

Chapter 27

"I CANNOT allow this!" Ela said, her backbone held rigid. She stood beside Alice in a little partitioned chamber in the castle.

"Since when do you allow or disallow what I want?" Alice sneered. "My life is my own and all you do is help me dress."

"It isn't right that you throw yourself at this man. There isn't a day that some man doesn't ask to marry you. Can't you content yourself with one of them?"

Alice turned on her maid. "And let *her* have him? I would die first."

"Do you really want him for your own?" Ela persisted.

"What does that matter?" Alice demanded as she adjusted her veil and circlet. "He is mine and will stay mine."

The stairway was dark when she left the room. Alice had soon discovered that the court of King Henry was an easy place to find out what she wanted to know. There were many who were willing, for a price, to do anything that she asked. Her spies had told her that Gavin sat below with his brother, away from his wife. Alice knew how befuddled a man could get with drink, and she planned to use the opportunity to the best advantage. He wouldn't be able to resist her when his mind swam from drink.

She cursed when she reached the great hall and neither Gavin nor his brother were in sight. "Where is Lord Gavin?" Alice asked harshly of a yawning servant girl. The floor was cluttered with sleeping retainers on straw pallets.

"He left—that's all I know."

Alice grabbed the girl's arm. "Where?"

"I have no idea."

Alice pulled a gold coin from her pocket and watched the girl's eyes gleam. "What would you do for this?"

The girl came fully awake. "I would do anything."

"Good," Alice smiled. "Then listen to me carefully."

Judith woke from a sound sleep to a faint scraping at the door. She stretched out her arm before she opened her eyes, only to find Gavin's side of the bed empty. She sat up, knitting her brows, then remembered he'd said something about saying good-bye to Stephen.

The scratching at the door continued. Joan, who often stayed with her mistress when Gavin was away, wasn't in the room. Reluctantly, Judith threw the covers back and slipped her arms into the emerald-green velvet of her bedrobe. "What is it?" she asked as she opened the door to a servant girl.

"I don't know, my lady," the girl said with a smirk. "I was told that you were needed and must come straightaway."

"Who said this? My husband?"

The girl shrugged in reply.

Judith frowned. The court crawled with anonymous messages, and all of them seemed to lead to places she did not care to be. Yet perhaps her mother needed her. More likely Gavin was too drunk to mount the stairs and she must help him. She smiled at the thought of the tongue-lashing she would give him.

She followed the girl down the dark stone stairs to the floor below. It seemed darker than usual; some of the torches on the walls hadn't been lit. Cut within the twelve-foot-thick walls were dreary rooms, not favored by the nobler guests. The servant girl stopped before one of these rooms that lay near the steep circular stairwell.

The girl gave Judith a look that she didn't understand, then disappeared into the darkness. Judith was aggravated at this skulking about and meant to say so when a woman's voice caught her attention.

"Gavin," the woman whispered loudly.

It was a whisper of passion. Judith could only remain frozen in place. Tinder was struck and a candle lit. Judith could see clearly then. Alice, her thin, bony body nude from the waist up, lay half under Gavin. The candlelight revealed his bronze skin to advantage—there was none of it hidden. He lay on his stomach, his bare legs covering Alice's.

"No!" Judith whispered, her hand to her mouth, her eyes blurring with tears. She wanted it to be a nightmare, but it was not. He had lied to her, over and over again. And she had come so close to believing him!

She backed away from them, Gavin not moving, Alice holding the candle, watching Judith, smiling at her from her position under Gavin. "No!" was all Judith could say. She moved farther and farther back, unaware of the staircase with no railing.

Her feet unsteady, Judith was not even conscious at first that she stepped into midair. She screamed as she fell down one step, then two, then five. Frantically, she clawed at the air, screaming again as her body fell sideways and missed the stairs altogether. Judith hit the floor below with a horrible thud, her fall finally cushioned by the pallet of one of King Henry's knights.

"What was that?" Gavin asked in a slurred voice as he raised his head.

"It was nothing," Alice murmured, her heart beating quickly with pure joy. Perhaps the woman had killed herself and Gavin would truly be Alice's once again.

Gavin raised himself on one elbow. "My God! Alice! What are you doing here?" His eyes roamed over her nude body. The only thought that occurred to him was that he had not realized she was so scrawny. There was no desire for that body he had once loved.

Alice's joy was killed by the look in Gavin's eyes. "You do . . . not remember?" Her words were halting. She was truly stunned by Gavin's reaction. She had been so certain that once she held him again, he would be hers.

Gavin frowned at her. He had been drunk, true—but not

so drunk that he didn't remember the night. He knew full well that he hadn't gone to Alice's bed, nor had he asked her to his.

His accusations were ready, but suddenly the great hall on the floor below them was alive with light and noise. Men shouted to each other. Then a bellow that fair shook the rafters rose: "Montgomery!"

Gavin was out of the bed in one swift movement, hastily throwing his tunic over his head. He took the steps two at a time, but he stopped at the last turn of the spiral staircase. Judith lay just below him on a pallet, her auburn hair in a tangled mass about her head, one leg bent under her. For a moment, his heart stopped.

"Don't touch her!" he said with a low growl as he leaped the last steps and knelt beside her. "How?" he murmured as he touched her hand, then felt for the pulse at her neck.

"She seems to have fallen down the stairs," Stephen said as he knelt next to his sister-in-law.

Gavin looked up and saw Alice on the landing, her robe clutched about her, smiling slightly. Gavin felt there was something missing in the puzzle but he had no time to search for it.

"The physician has been sent for," Stephen said as he held Judith's hand. She didn't open her eyes.

The physician came slowly, dressed in a rich fur-collared robe. "Give me room," he demanded. "I must look for broken bones."

Gavin moved back and watched the man run his hands over Judith's limp body. Why? How? Gavin kept wondering. What was she doing on the stairs in the middle of the night? His eyes went back to Alice. The woman stood quietly, avid interest on her face, as the doctor examined Judith. The room where Gavin awakened to find himself in bed with Alice was at the head of the stairs. He felt the blood drain from his face as he glanced again at his wife. Judith had seen him in bed with Alice! She had backed away, probably too upset to look where she was going, and had fallen. But how had she known where he was? Only if someone had told her where to look.

"No bones seem to be broken," the physician said. "Take her to her bed and let her rest."

Gavin murmured a prayer of thanksgiving, then bent and lifted his wife's limp form. The crowd of people around them gasped when he held her. The pallet and her gown were soaked with blood.

"She miscarries the child," Queen Elizabeth said at Gavin's elbow. "Carry her above. I will have my own midwife look at her."

Gavin could feel the warmth of Judith's blood on his arm through the sleeves of his tunic. A strong hand was placed on his shoulder, and he knew without looking that Stephen was there.

"My lady!" Joan gasped when Gavin entered the room carrying Judith. "I just now returned and she was gone. She has been hurt!" Joan's voice showed the love she had for her mistress. "Will she be all right?"

"We don't know," Stephen answered.

Gavin gently put his wife on the bed.

"Joan," Queen Elizabeth said. "Fetch warm water from the kitchen and clean linen."

"Linen, Your Majesty?"

"For absorbing the blood. She miscarries the baby. When you have the linen, fetch Lady Helen. She will want to be with her daughter."

"My poor lady," Joan whispered. "She wanted this child so much." There were tears in her voice as she left the room.

"Go now," Elizabeth urged as she turned back to the two men. "You must leave her. You are of no use. We will see to her."

Stephen put his arm around his brother's shoulders but Gavin shrugged it away. "No, Your Majesty, I won't go. Had I been with her tonight, she wouldn't have been hurt."

Stephen started to speak but Elizabeth stopped him. She knew it would be no use. "You may stay." She nodded to Stephen and he departed.

Gavin stroked Judith's forehead as he looked up at the queen. "Tell me what to do."

"Take her robe off."

Gavin carefully untied the garment, then gently lifted Judith and took her arms from the sleeves. He was horrified to see the blood on her thighs. He stared at it for a moment, not moving.

Elizabeth watched him. "Birthing is not a pleasant sight."

"This is not a birth, but a . . ." He could not finish.

"She must have been far along to show so much blood. This will indeed be a birth, though with less pleasant results."

They both looked up as the midwife, a fat, red-faced woman burst into the chamber. "Do you intend to freeze the poor girl?" she demanded. "Here! We need no men," she said to Gavin.

"He will stay," Queen Elizabeth said firmly.

The midwife looked at Gavin for a moment. "Go then and fetch the water from the maid. She takes too long to carry it up the stairs."

Gavin reacted immediately.

"Her husband, Your Majesty?" the midwife asked when Gavin was gone.

"Yes, and their first child."

The fat woman snorted. "He should have taken better care of her, Your Majesty, and not let her roam about the halls at night."

As soon as Gavin set the water down inside the room, the woman snapped more orders at him. "Find her some clothes and keep her warm."

Joan, who had entered behind Gavin, rummaged in a chest and handed him a warm woolen gown. Gavin carefully dressed Judith, all the while watching the blood slowly seep from her. Perspiration appeared on her forehead and he wiped it away with a cool cloth. "Will she be all right?" he whispered.

"I can't answer that. It depends on whether we can get all the birth out of her and if we can get the bleeding to stop." Judith moaned and moved her head. "Keep her quiet or she'll make our work harder."

"Judith," Gavin said quietly. "Be still." He took her hands in his when she began to move them about.

She opened her eyes. "Gavin?" she whispered.

"Yes. Don't talk now. Be still and rest. You will be well soon."

"Well?" She did not seem fully aware of her state. Then a violent cramp shot through her. Her hands clutched at his. Judith looked up at him, bewildered. "What happened?" she gasped then her eyes began to focus clearly. The queen, her maid and another woman knelt over her, looking at her with concern. Another spasm rocked her.

"Come," the midwife said. "We must knead her stomach and help her."

"Gavin!" Judith said in fright, panting after the last pain.

"Quiet, my love. You will soon be well. There will be other children."

Her eyes opened in horror. "Child? My baby? Am I losing my baby?" Her voice rose almost hysterically.

"Judith, please," Gavin said, soothing her. "There will be others."

Another pain shot through Judith as she stared at Gavin, her memory returning. "I fell off the stairs," she said quietly. "I saw you in bed with your whore and I fell from the stairs."

"Judith, this is not the time—"

"Don't touch me!"

"Judith," Gavin said, half-pleading.

"Do I disappoint you that I'm not dead? As my child is now dead?" Her eyes blinked back tears. "Go to her. You wanted her so badly, and you are welcome to her!"

"Judith—" Gavin began, but Queen Elizabeth took his arm.

"Perhaps you should go."

"Yes," he agreed as Judith refused to look at him. Stephen waited outside the door for him, his brows raised in question. "The child is lost and I don't know yet if Judith will live."

"Come below," Stephen said. "They won't allow you to stay with her?"

"Judith wouldn't allow it," Gavin said flatly.

Stephen didn't speak again until they were outside the manor house. The sun was just beginning to rise, the sky gray. The commotion caused by Judith's fall made the castlefolk rise earlier than usual. The brothers sat on a bench by the castle wall. "Why was she walking about the hall at night?" Stephen asked.

"I don't know. When you and I parted, I fell into a bed—the nearest one at the top of the stairs."

"Perhaps she woke and found you were gone and came to search for you."

Gavin didn't answer.

"There is more to this that you aren't telling me."

"Yes. When Judith saw me, I was in bed with Alice."

Never before had Stephen offered a judgment of his brother. Now his face blackened. "You may have killed Judith! And for what? That bitch—" He broke off when he saw Gavin's bleak profile. "You were too drunk to want a woman. Or if you wanted one, Judith waited above for you."

Gavin stared across the courtyard. "I didn't take her to bed," he said quietly. "I was asleep and I heard a noise which woke me. Alice lay beside me. I wasn't so drunk last night that I would have taken her to my bed and not remembered."

"Then how?"

"I don't know."

"I do!" Stephen said through clenched teeth. "You are a sensible man except when it comes to that witch!"

For the first time, Gavin didn't defend Alice.

Stephen continued. "You have never been able to see her for what she is. Don't you know she sleeps with half the men at the court?"

Gavin turned and stared at him.

"You may look at me in disbelief, but she is the jest of all the men—and I'm sure most of the women. From stableboy to earl, she doesn't care, so long as they have the equipment to pleasure her."

"If she's like that, then I have made her that way. She was a virgin when I first took her."

"Virgin, hah! The Earl of Lancashire swears he had her when she was only twelve years old."

Gavin's expression was one of disbelief.

"Look at what she has done to you. She has controlled you and used you—and you have allowed it. No, you have begged for more. Tell me, what method did she use to keep you from loving Judith straightaway?"

Gavin stared with sightless eyes. He was reliving the scene in the garden on his wedding day. "She vowed to kill herself if I loved my wife."

Stephen leaned his head back against the stone wall. "God's wounds! And you believed her? That woman would willingly kill thousands before she would endanger one hair on her own head."

"But I asked her to marry me," Gavin persisted. "Before I ever heard of Judith, I asked her to marry me."

"Yet she chose a rich earl instead."

"But her father—"

"Gavin! Can't you look at her with clear eyes? Do you think that drunkard of a father of hers ever gave anyone an order? Even his servants don't obey him! Were he a strong man, would she have had such freedom to slip about the countryside with you at night?"

It was hard for Gavin to believe all this of Alice. She was so pink and blonde, so delicate, so shy. She looked up at him with great tears in her eyes and his heart melted. He remembered how he felt when she threatened to take her own life. He would have done anything for her. Yet even then his attraction to Judith had been enormous.

"You aren't convinced," Stephen said.

"I'm not sure. Old dreams die hard. She is a beautiful woman."

"Yes, and you fell in love with that beauty. You never questioned what else was there. You say you didn't take her to your bed. How did she get there then?"

When Gavin didn't answer, Stephen continued. "The slut stripped her own clothes off and planted herself there. Then she sent someone to summon Judith."

Gavin rose. He didn't want to hear any more. "I must go and see if Judith is well," he murmured and walked back to the manor house. All his life, since he was sixteen, Gavin had been responsible for property and men. He had never had the carefree time of his brothers to court women and learn of their natures. True, there had been many women in his bed, but always they were gone quickly. No woman had spent time close to him, laughing and talking with him. He had grown up believing all women were like he remembered his mother— pretty, sweet-tempered, gentle. Alice had always seemed to be the epitome of those traits, and as a result, he had become infatuated with her almost immediately.

Judith had been the first woman he had really known. At first she had infuriated him. She was not obedient, as a woman should be. She would rather concern herself with his household account books than the colors used in a piece of embroidery. She was breathtakingly beautiful, but she seemed unaware of her beauty. She did not spend hours on her clothes. In truth, Joan often chose her mistress's attire. Judith seemed to be everything undesirable, unfeminine. Yet Gavin had fallen in love with her. She was honest, brave, generous— and she made him laugh. Never once had Alice shown even a touch of humor.

Gavin stood outside the door of Judith's chamber. He knew he no longer loved Alice, but could she be as treacherous as Stephen said? As Raine and Miles also said? How did she come to be in his bed except for the reason Stephen gave?

The door opened and the midwife stepped into the hall. Gavin grabbed her arm. "How is she?"

"Sleeping now. The child was born dead."

Gavin took a deep, calming breath. "Will my wife recover?"

"I don't know. She has lost much blood. I don't know if it was from the infant, or perhaps something inside was damaged in the fall."

Gavin's face drained of color. "Didn't you say she lost blood from the child?" He didn't want to believe that something else could be wrong.

"How long have you been wed to her?"

"Nearly four months," he answered, surprised.

"And she was a virgin when you took her?"

"Yes," he said, remembering the pain he had caused her.

"She was quite far along. The child was well formed. I would say she conceived that first night or the next. No later. Perhaps there is so much blood because the child was so well advanced. It's too early to tell."

She turned to go, but Gavin grabbed her arm. "How will you know?"

"When the bleeding stops and she is still alive."

He released her arm. "You say she sleeps. May I go to her?"

The old woman chuckled. "Young men! They never seem to deny themselves. You bed one woman while another waits for you. Now you hover over the first one. You should choose one or the other."

Gavin swallowed his reply, but his scowl made the smile leave her face.

"Yes, you may go to her," the woman said quietly, then turned and went down to the stairs.

The rain came down in slashing sheets. The wind bent the trees almost in half. Lightning flashed and far away a tree split and crashed. But the four people who stood around the tiny coffin that the workers had just lowered into the ground, were unaware of the cold torrent. Their bodies swayed with the gale, but they did not notice it.

Helen stood by John, her body limp, leaning heavily against the strength of him for support. Her eyes were dry and hot. Stephen stood close to Gavin, ready if his brother should need him.

It was John and Stephen who exchanged looks, the rain running down their faces, dripping into their clothes. John gently led Helen away from the little gravesite and Stephen guided Gavin. The storm had started suddenly, after the priest had begun to read the words over the tiny coffin.

Stephen and John looked as if they were leading two blind

and helpless people across the graveyard. They led Helen and Gavin into a mausoleum and left them there while they went to get the horses.

Gavin sank heavily onto an iron bench. The child had been a son. His first son, he thought. Every word he'd said to Judith about the child not being his rang in his ears. And the baby was dead because of him. He dropped his head into his hands.

"Gavin," Helen said as she sat beside him and put her arm about his shoulders. They'd had so little to do with each other since Helen screamed she wished she'd killed her daughter before allowing her to marry him. But over the months many things had changed. Helen had found out what it was like to love someone, and now she recognized love in Gavin's eyes. She saw the pain he suffered over his lost child, the fear he had of losing Judith.

Gavin turned to his mother-in-law. He never thought of any hostility between them. He saw and remembered only that Helen was close to the woman he loved. He put his arms about her, but he did not hold her. No, it was Helen who held her son-in-law, and Helen who felt the hotness of his tears through her rain-soaked gown. And finally Helen found release for her own tears.

Joan sat by her sleeping mistress. Judith's color was gone, her hair damp with perspiration. "She will soon be well," Joan said to Gavin's unasked question.

"I'm not so sure." He touched his wife's hot cheek.

"It was a nasty fall she took," Joan said, staring intently at Gavin.

Gavin only nodded, more concerned with Judith than with any talk.

"What do you plan to do to her?" Joan continued.

"Do to her?" Gavin demanded. "I hope only to see her well once again."

Joan waved her hand. "No, I mean to Lady Alice. What punishment do you plan for the trick she played? Trick!" Joan snorted. "A trick that may cost my lady her life!"

"Don't say that," Gavin growled.

"I ask you again: what punishment do you plan?"

"Hold your tongue, woman! I know nothing of a trick."

"No? Then I will speak my piece. There is a woman below, in the kitchen, who cries her eyes from her head. She has a gold coin which she says Lady Alice gave her to lead my lady to you while you were in bed with that whore. The girl says she thought she would have done anything for the coin, but she didn't mean murder. She says Lady Judith's baby's death and maybe the lady's own death are her fault and that she will go to hell for their murders."

Gavin realized it was time to face the truth. "I would like to see this woman and speak with her," he said quietly.

Joan rose. "I will fetch the girl if I can find her."

Gavin sat with Judith, watching, noting that her natural color was returning.

It was some time later when Joan came back, pulling a frightened and cowering girl behind her. "This is the slut!" Joan said and gave the servant a vicious push. "Look at my mistress as she lies there. You have killed a baby, and now you may kill my lady. And she never hurt a soul. Do you know she often lectured me for mistreating scum like you?"

"Quiet!" Gavin commanded. The girl was obviously very frightened. "Tell me what you know of my wife's accident."

"Accident, ha!" Joan snorted, then quieted at Gavin's look.

The girl, her eyes darting from one corner of the room to the other, told her story in disjointed, hesitant sentences. At the end, she threw herself at Gavin's feet. "Please, my lord, save me. Lady Alice will murder me!"

Gavin's face showed no pity. "You ask me for help? What help did you give my wife? Or our child? Shall I take you to where they have buried the child?"

"No," the girl cried desperately, her head touching the floor.

"Get up!" Joan commanded. "You dirty our floor!"

"Take her away," Gavin said. "I cannot bear the sight of her."

Joan grabbed the girl's hair and viciously pulled her up, then gave her a hard kick toward the door.

"Joan," Gavin said. "Take her to John Bassett and tell him to see that she is safe."

"Safe!" Joan exploded then her eyes hardened. "Yes, my lord," she said in a falsely submissive voice. She closed the door, twisting the girl's arm behind her back. "She kills my lady's baby, and I am to see her safe!" she muttered. "No, I will see that she gets what she deserves."

At the top of the spiral stairs, Joan's hand bit into the terrified girl.

"Here! stop that!" John Bassett growled. He had never been far from Judith's room over the last several days. "Is this the one Lady Alice paid?" There wasn't a person in the castle who wasn't aware of the story of Alice's treachery.

"Oh please, sir," the girl begged, falling to her knees. "Don't let her kill me. I won't do anything like that again."

John started to speak. Then he gave Joan a look of disgust and lifted the maid. Joan stood for several minutes, watching their retreating backs.

"Too bad he took her. You could have saved me some work," said a quiet voice behind her.

Joan whirled to face Alice Chatworth. "I would rather see you at the bottom of the stairs," Joan sneered.

Alice's blue eyes blazed. "I will have your life for that!"

"Here? Now?" Joan taunted. "No, that's not your way. You hire people to do your work for you—then you simper as if you were an innocent maid."

No one had ever dared say such things to Alice!

"Come," Joan taunted. "Why do you hesitate? I stand on the brink of the stairs."

Alice was tempted to try to give the maid one hard push, but Joan looked to be strong, and Alice couldn't risk losing such a struggle. "You will look to your life for this," Alice sneered.

"No, I will look to my back, where such as you would strike." Joan stared at the woman, then began to laugh. She laughed all the way up the stairs until she reached her mistress's room.

The midwife and Gavin hovered over Judith. "The fever has begun," the old woman said quietly. "Now prayers will help as much as anything else."

Chapter 28

JUDITH WAS dreaming. Her body was hot and sore, and she had trouble concentrating on what was happening. Gavin was there, smiling at her, but his smile was false. Behind him stood Alice Chatworth, her eyes glowing in triumph. "I have won," the woman whispered. "I have won!"

Judith woke slowly, coming fretfully from the dream that seemed real as she felt the ache of her body, as if she'd slept for days on a board. She moved her head to one side. Gavin sat sleeping in a chair by the bed. Even asleep he looked tense, as if he were ready to spring to his feet. His face was haggard, his cheekbones prominent under his skin. He wore several days' growth of beard, and there were dark circles under his eyes.

Judith was puzzled for a few moments, wondering why Gavin should look so tired and she should ache so badly. Her hand moved under the covers and touched her stomach. It had once been hard and slightly rounded, but now it was sunken and soft. And oh so horribly empty!

She remembered everything then, remembered Gavin in bed with Alice. He had said he no longer cared for her and Judith had begun to believe him. She had started to think of a good life together, of when their child would be born and they would be happy. What a fool she had been!

"Judith!" Gavin said in a strangely harsh voice. He quickly sat beside her on the bed, his hand feeling her forehead. "The fever is broken," he said with relief. "How do you feel?"

"Don't touch me," she whispered. "Get away from me!"

Gavin nodded, his lips set in a firm line.

Before either of them could speak again the door opened and Stephen entered. The worried expression on his face gave way to a broad smile when he saw she was awake. He quickly went to the side of the bed opposite Gavin. "Sweet little sister," he murmured. "We thought we might lose you." He touched her neck gently.

At the sight of a familiar and loved face, Judith felt tears come to her eyes.

Stephen frowned and looked to his brother but Gavin shook his head. "Here, sweet," Stephen said, gathering Judith in his arms. "Don't cry," he whispered as he stroked her hair.

"Was it a boy?" she whispered.

Stephen could only nod.

"I lost him!" she cried desperately. "He didn't even have a chance of life before I lost him. Oh, Stephen, I wanted the baby so much. He would have been good and kind and so very beautiful!"

"Yes," Stephen agreed. "Tall and dark like his father."

Judith's sobs tore through her. "Yes! At least my father was right about getting a grandson. But he is dead!"

Stephen looked over her head to his brother. He didn't know who was the most grief-stricken, Gavin or the woman he comforted.

Gavin had never seen Judith cry. She showed him hostility, passion, humor, but never this horrible racking grief. He felt a deep sadness that she did not share her grief with him.

"Judith," Stephen said. "You must rest. You have been very ill."

"How long have I been ill?"

"Three days. The fever nearly took you from us."

She sniffed, then abruptly drew away from him. "Stephen! You were to leave. You will be late for your own wedding."

He nodded grimly. "I was to wed her this morning."

"Then you have left her at the altar."

"I would hope she heard that I didn't arrive and would not go so far."

"Did you send a message?"

He shook his head. "If the truth were told, I forgot. We have all worried greatly about you. You don't know how close you came to death."

She did feel weak and extremely tired.

"Now you must sleep again."

"And you will go to your bride?" Judith asked as he helped her lie down.

"I can go now that I know the fever is broken."

"Promise me," she said tiredly. "I wouldn't wish you to start your marriage as mine was. I want better for you."

Stephen glanced quickly at his brother. "Yes, I promise. I will leave within the hour."

She nodded, her eyes closing. "Thank you," she whispered and fell asleep.

Gavin rose from the bed as his brother did. "I too forgot your marriage."

"You had other things on your mind," Stephen answered. "Is she still angry with you?"

Gavin gave his brother a cynical look. "More than angry, I would say."

"Talk to her. Tell her how you feel. Tell her the truth about Alice. She will believe you."

Gavin looked across the room at his sleeping wife. "You must pack now. That Scots bride will have your hide."

"If that were all she wished, I would give it to her gladly."

Both men left the room, closing the door behind. Gavin clasped his brother to him. "Christmas," he said smiling. "Bring that wife of yours to us at Christmas."

"Yes, I will. And you will speak to Judith?"

Gavin nodded. "When she is better rested and I am bathed."

Stephen smiled. Gavin had not left his wife's side for the three days of her fever. Stephen cuffed his brother affectionately and turned and left the hallway.

*   *   *

When Judith woke again, it was dark in the room. Joan was sleeping on a pallet near the door. Judith's head was clearer and she felt stronger and very hungry. "Joan," she whispered.

The maid was on her feet instantly. "My lady," she said and grinned happily. "Lord Gavin said you were well again, but I didn't believe him."

"I would like some water," Judith said through parched lips.

"Yes," Joan laughed merrily. "Not so fast," she said as Judith greedily drank from the cup.

The door opened and they both turned to see Gavin entering with a tray of food.

"I don't want to see him," Judith said firmly.

"Go!" Gavin commanded Joan.

The maid put down the cup and left hastily.

Gavin set the tray down on a small table by the bed. "You are feeling better."

She stared at him but wouldn't answer.

"I brought you some broth and a bit of bread. You must be very hungry."

"I don't want anything from you. Neither food nor company."

"Judith," he said with great patience, "you are acting like a child. We'll speak of this again when you're well."

"Do you think time will change my mind? Will time give me back my baby? Will time let me hold him, love him, even let me see the color of his eyes?"

Gavin took his hands away from the tray. "He was my child, too, and I have lost him also."

"So, you have learned that much! Should I feel pity for your sorrow? You didn't even believe him to be yours. Or did you lie about that also?"

"I haven't lied to you, Judith. If you will only listen, I'll tell you everything."

"Listen?" she said calmly. "When have you ever listened to me? I have tried from the moment we married to please you, yet there was little I could do that didn't make you angry. Always, I felt I was compared to someone else."

"Judith," he said and took her hand from her lap.

"Don't touch me! I am fouled by your touch."

His eyes turned from gray to black. "I have something to say, and I will say it even though you try hard to prevent me. Much of what you say is true. I did love Alice, or I thought I did. I fell in love with her before I even heard her speak. I created a woman for her to be, and she became that woman. We never spent much time together, only swift moments here and there. I never knew what she was really like, only what I wished her to be."

Judith didn't answer. Gavin couldn't read her thoughts.

"I fought against loving you," he continued. "I thought my heart belonged to Alice. But now I know that was not so. Judith," he said quietly, "I have loved you for a long time. Perhaps I have loved you from the first. I do know that now I love you with all my heart and soul."

He stopped and watched her, but her expression didn't change.

"Shall I fall into your arms now and declare my great love for you also? Is that what is expected of me?"

Gavin was stunned. Perhaps he had expected her to say she loved him.

"Your lust killed my child!"

"It was not my lust!" Gavin said passionately. "I was tricked. Stephen and I drank too much together. A leopard could have climbed into bed with me and I wouldn't have known it!"

Judith smiled icily. "And did you enjoy the leopard's claws? You have before."

Gavin gave her a cold look. "I have tried to explain my actions to you, but you won't listen. I have told you of my love—what more can I do?"

"You don't seem to understand. I don't *care* that you love me. Your love is worthless, given freely to whoever requests it. Once I might have done much to hear those words, but they are no longer sweet to me. It has taken the death of my child to clear my mind of such fairy tales as love."

Gavin sat back, staring at her. He didn't know what else to say. "I have been wrong on all counts. You are right to be angry."

"No," she smiled "I'm not angry. Neither do I hate you. I merely find life with you intolerable."

"What do you mean?"

"I shall beg the king to ask the pope for a divorce. I don't believe that even the pope would wish me to live with you after this. You shall keep half my land and—" She broke off as Gavin stood.

"I will send Joan to you. You must eat," Gavin said, then left the room.

Judith lay back against the pillow. She felt drained. How could she believe he loved her when all she could see was Alice rising from under his nude body?

For three more days, Judith didn't leave her bed. She slept a great deal and ate dutifully. Her spirits were so low that food meant little to her. She refused to see anyone, most especially her husband. Preferring to keep her opinions to herself, Joan hardly spoke to her mistress.

On the morning of the fourth day, Joan pulled the covers from Judith. "You will not lie in bed today. There is work to be done and you must exercise." Joan took a new robe from the foot of the bed—a robe to replace the bloodstained one of green velvet. The robe was of a deep gray velvet with a wide mink collar, a mink edge along the front and around the hem. Intricate gold embroidery ran around the shoulders.

"I don't want to get up," Judith said and turned over.

"You will!"

Judith was still too weak to resist. Joan easily pulled her mistress from the bed and helped her into the velvet robe. She led Judith to a deep window seat. "Now you will stay there while I get clean linen."

The summer breeze did feel good on Judith's face. She had

a wonderful view of the garden. She leaned back against the embrasure and watched the people below.

"Gavin?" someone said quietly at his side. He sat alone in the garden, a place where he'd spent a lot of time lately. He whirled quickly at the familiar voice. It was Alice, her skin radiant in the early morning light. He had purposely put off dealing with her; he didn't trust his own reactions. "Do you dare show yourself to me?"

"Please, allow me to explain—"

"No. You cannot explain."

Alice looked away, her hand at her eye and when she looked back, there were great, glittering tears present. Gavin looked at her and wondered how her tears had once had the power to move him. How different Judith's were! Great wrenching sobs that tore through her. She cried from grief, not to enhance her beauty.

"I did it only for you," Alice said. "My love for you is so strong that—"

"Don't speak to me of love! I wonder if you know what it is. Do you know that I talked to the girl you paid to bring Judith to you? You planned well, didn't you?"

"Gavin, I—"

He grabbed her arms and shook her. "You killed my child! Does that mean nothing to you? And you nearly killed my wife—a woman I love." He pushed Alice away from him. "I could have you before a court for this, but I blame myself as much as you. I was a fool not to have seen through you."

Alice drew her hand back and slapped him across the cheek. He allowed it for he felt he deserved it.

"Get out of my sight and don't tempt me to wring that pretty neck of yours."

Alice turned on her heel and fled from the garden.

Ela crept from the shadows. "I told you not to go to him. I told you to wait. He is very angry with you and well you deserve it." Ela was puzzled when her mistress walked behind the kitchen, into an alley.

Alice leaned against the wall. Her shoulders shook.

Ela went to her mistress and pulled her head to her ample bosom.

This time, Alice cried genuinely. "He loved me," she said through painful sobs. "He did love me once and now he doesn't anymore. I have no one else left."

"Hush, sweetheart," Ela soothed. "You have me. You have always had me." Ela held her as she had when Alice was a child and the lovely little girl had cried at the neglect of her mother. "Lord Gavin is only one man. There are others. You are so very beautiful. There will be many men to love you."

"No!" Alice said with such violence that it shook her body. "I want him—I want Gavin! Another man will not do!"

Ela tried to calm her mistress, but couldn't. "You shall have him then," she said finally.

Alice raised her head, her eyes and nose red and swollen. "Do you promise?"

Ela nodded. "Haven't I always given you what you want?"

"Yes," Alice agreed. "You have. And you will get Gavin for me?"

"I swear it."

Alice gave a small smile. Then, in a rare burst of affection, she gave Ela a swift kiss on the cheek.

The maid's old eyes misted. Of course she would do any-thing for this sweet girl who was so misunderstood by the people around her. "Come upstairs," she said sweetly. "We will plan a new gown."

"Yes," Alice smiled, sniffing loudly. "A merchant brought some Frankish wools this morning."

"Let's go and see them."

Judith had watched from the window only long enough to see her husband speak to his mistress. "Joan, I would like to see the king," she said, turning away from the sight.

"My lady, you cannot ask King Henry to come here."

"I don't intend to do so. You must help me dress, and I will go below to see him."

"But—"

"Don't argue with me!"

"Yes, my lady," Joan said in a hard voice.

An hour later, Judith appeared in the great hall, leaning heavily on her maid's arm.

A young man came to her side. "Alan Fairfax, my lady, if you don't remember."

"Of course I do." She managed a small smile. "You are kind to help me."

"It is a pleasure. You wish to see the king?"

She nodded gravely. She took Alan's arm and he led her to the king's chamber. It was an elegant room with a hammer-beam ceiling, linenfold paneling, and oak floors covered with Persian carpets.

"Countess!" the king said when he saw her. He had an illuminated manuscript in his lap. "You should not have left your bed so soon." He put the book aside and took her other arm.

"You are very kind, both of you," she said as Alan and Henry helped her into a chair. "I would like to speak to you, Your Majesty, on a private matter."

Henry nodded toward Alan and the knight left them. "Now, what matter is so important that you must weary yourself to seek me?"

Judith looked down at her hands. "I would like a divorce."

King Henry was silent for a moment. "Divorce is a grave undertaking. Do you have cause?"

There were two types of divorce and three reasons for each. The best Judith could hope for was a separation, allowing her to live apart from her husband for the rest of her life. "Adultery," she said quietly.

Henry considered this. "If such grounds were allowed, neither of you could remarry."

"I do not wish to. I will enter a convent, as I was trained for."

"And what of Gavin? Would you deny him the right of a new wife and of sons to follow him?"

"No," she whispered. "He has his rights."

Henry was watching her intently. "Then we must look to

a divorce which declares your marriage null and void. You are not related?"

Again she shook her head, thinking of Walter Demari.

"What then of Gavin? Was he pledged to another?"

Judith lifted her chin. "He did ask another woman to marry him."

"And this woman is?"

"Lady Alice Chatworth."

"Ah," Henry sighed and leaned back in his chair. "And now the lady is a widow and he wishes to marry her?"

"Yes, he does."

King Henry frowned. "I don't like divorce, but I also don't like my earls and countesses so unhappy. This will cost you a great deal. I am sure the pope will require that you endow a chapel or a nunnery."

"I will do that."

"Lady Judith, you must let me think about this. I must speak to the others involved before I make a decision. Alan," he called, "take the countess to her room and see that she is made to rest."

Alan smiled broadly as he helped Judith to her feet.

"The Lady Judith looked to be very sad," Queen Elizabeth commented as she entered the room just as Judith was leaving and took a seat next to her husband. "I know how she feels after having lost a child."

"It's not that, or at least the child is not all that weighs upon her. She asks for a divorce from Gavin."

"No!" Elizabeth said, dropping her knitting to her lap. "I have never seen two people more in love. They argue, true, but I have seen Lord Gavin lift her in his arms and kiss her."

"It seems that Lady Judith is not the only woman Gavin kisses."

Elizabeth was silent. Not many men were faithful to their wives. She knew that even her husband at times . . . "Lady Judith asks for a divorce for this reason?"

"Yes. Gavin seems to have asked Lady Alice Chatworth to marry him before he married Judith. It is a verbal contract and grounds for divorce. That is, if the woman will accept Gavin."

"She will!" Elizabeth said angrily. "She will be glad to take Gavin—she has done so much to obtain him."

"What are you talking about?"

Elizabeth quickly told her husband of the castle gossip how Lady Judith had fallen and miscarried her child.

Henry frowned. "I do not like such happenings between my subjects. Gavin should have been more discreet."

"There is some doubt whether he asked the woman to his bed, or whether she placed herself there."

Henry chuckled. "Poor Gavin. I wouldn't want to be in such a state as he."

"Have you talked to him? I do not think he wants this divorce," Elizabeth stated.

"But if he were pledged to the Lady Alice before his marriage . . ."

"Then why did she marry Edmund Chatworth?"

"I see," Henry said seriously. "I think I will investigate this further. There is more here than appears on the surface. I will talk to both Gavin and Lady Alice."

"I hope your talks take a long while."

"I don't understand."

"If Judith is allowed to separate from her husband, their marriage will indeed end; but if they were forced to stay near one another, they might realize they do care for each other."

Henry smiled fondly at his wife. She was a wise woman. "I will indeed take a long time before I send a message to the pope. Where are you going?" he asked as she stood.

"I would like to talk to Sir Alan Fairfax. I wonder if he would be willing to help a lady in distress."

Henry gave her a puzzled look, then picked up his manuscript. "Yes, my dear. I am sure you will handle all of this without me."

Two hours later the door to Judith's chamber was thrown open. Gavin stalked into the room, his face blackened with fury.

Judith glanced up from the book in her lap.

"You asked the king for a divorce!" he bellowed.

"Yes, I have," she replied firmly.

"Do you plan to tell the world of our differences?"

"If that is what it takes to rid myself of you."

He glared at her. "You are a stubborn woman! Do you ever see anything but one side? Do you ever listen to reason?"

"Your idea of reason is not the same as mine. You want me to forgive you for adultery time and again. I have done so many times, yet now I can no more. I plan to rid myself of you and enter a convent, as I should have done long ago."

"A convent!" he said in disbelief, then smiled mockingly. He took one swift step toward her and threw an arm around her shoulders. He lifted her from the bed and his mouth covered hers. He was not gentle, but even his harshness set Judith afire. Her arms went around his neck, pulling him to her violently. Abruptly, he released her, letting her fall onto the feather mattress. The sides of the soft mattress rose around her.

"Make up your mind that you'll never be rid of me. When you are ready to admit that I'm the man you need, come to me. Perhaps I'll take you back." He turned and stalked from the room before Judith could say a word.

Joan stood in the open doorway, a look of adoration on her face.

"How dare he—" Judith began then stopped at Joan's look. "Why do you look at me so?" she demanded.

"Because you are wrong. That man loves you, has told you so, yet you won't listen to him. I have been on your side throughout your marriage, but now I'm not."

"But that woman—" Judith said in a strange, pleading voice.

"Can't you forgive him? He thought he loved her once. He would be less of a man if he were willing to forget her when he first saw his beautiful wife. You make great demands of him."

"But my baby!" Judith said, tears in her voice.

"I told you of Alice's treachery. How can you hold him responsible?"

Judith was silent for a while. The loss of the child hurt her so badly. Perhaps she wanted someone to blame and Gavin was a convenient person to inflict it on. She knew what Joan said of Alice was true. That night, things had happened so quickly; but now, days later, she knew that Gavin's body on Alice's had been too inert.

"He says he loves you," Joan continued in a quieter voice.

"Do you do anything besides listen at doors?" Judith snapped.

Joan smiled. "I like to know what happens to those I care for. He loves you. What do you feel for him?"

"I . . . I don't know."

Joan uttered an oath that made Judith's eyes widen. "Your mother should have taught you something besides accounts. I don't believe I have seen a woman love a man as you love Lord Gavin. Your eyes have not left him since he lifted you from that white horse at your wedding. Yet you have fought him on every count . . . as he has you," she added before Judith could interrupt. "Why don't the two of you stop fighting and make some more babies? I should like one near me."

Judith smiled even as her eyes filled with tears. "But he doesn't love me, not truly. Even if he did, he is furious with me. Should I go to him and tell him that I don't want a divorce, that I . . . I . . . ?"

Joan laughed. "You can't even say it. You love him, don't you?"

Judith was very serious before she answered. "Yes, I do."

"Now, we must plan. You cannot go to him. He would gloat over it for years to come, and besides you would make a poor job of it. You would no doubt be cold and logical when you should weep and sigh."

"Weep and—!" Judith was offended.

"See you what I mean? Once you said I make too much of a person's appearances, and I said you make too little of them. For once you are going to use your beauty to its best advantage."

"But how? Gavin has seen me in every way. My appearance will have no affect on him."

"You think not?" Joan laughed. "Listen to me and in a few days I will have Lord Gavin groveling at your feet."

"It would be nice for a change," Judith smiled. "Yes, I would like that."

"Then leave it to me. There is an Italian cloth merchant downstairs and—"

"I need no more clothes!" Judith said, glancing at the four large trunks in the room.

Joan smiled in a secret way. "Let me handle the men. You just rest. You're going to need your strength."

The news of Judith's desire for a divorce spread throughout the court like a fire. Divorce was not uncommon, but Judith and Gavin had been married only a short while. The reaction of the people of the court was unusual. The women— orphaned heiresses, young widows—flocked to Gavin. They sensed that his long love affair with Alice Chatworth was over. Obviously his lovely wife had no hold on him. They saw Gavin as an unattached man who would soon need to choose one of them for a wife.

But the men did not run to Judith. They were not given to acting first and thinking later. The queen kept Judith at her side, giving her preferential treatment, or, as the men saw it, guarding her as a bear with her cubs. The men also knew that it was unusual for King Henry to keep the warring couple at court. The king didn't like divorce and usually sent the couple away. True, the Lady Judith was lovely and very rich, but too often a man felt Gavin's eyes on him when he stayed too long at the golden-eyed beauty's side. More than one man voiced the opinion that a good beating would have kept Judith from making their differences public.

"My lady?"

Judith looked up from her book and smiled at Alan Fair-fax. The new gown she wore was extremely simple. It had a plain square neck and long, tight sleeves. It hung past her feet so it made a small pool of fabric when she stood. She had to throw part of it over her arm in order to walk. The sides were laced tightly. But what was truly unusual about the gown was its color. It was black—solid, midnight black. There was no belt, no mantle. About her neck was a collar of gold filigree set with large cabochon rubies. Her hair was uncovered, left loose to hang down her back. She'd objected when Joan showed her the black dress and she wondered at how appropriate it was. She had no idea that the black made her skin glow like a pearl. The gold of the collar reflected her eyes and the rubies took second place to the blaze of her deep, rich auburn hair.

It was all Alan could do to keep from staring with his mouth agape. Judith obviously had no idea she was driving the men of the court wild, as well as her husband. "You sit inside on such a lovely day?" he finally managed.

"It would seem so," she smiled. "If the truth were known, I haven't been very far outside these walls in several days."

He held his arm out. "Then perhaps you would like to walk with me?"

She rose and took his arm. "I would indeed enjoy that, kind sir." Judith held his arm firmly. She was glad to talk to a man again. For days they had all seemed to shy away from her. The thought made her laugh aloud.

"Something amuses you?" Alan asked.

"I was thinking that you are a brave man. For the last week, I had begun to fear that I had the plague—or perhaps even worse. If I only look at a man, he scurries away as if in mortal fear."

It was Alan's turn to laugh. "It's not you but your husband who sends them into the shadows."

"But he may . . . soon be my husband no longer."

"May?" Alan asked, one eyebrow raised. "Do I hear a note of uncertainty?"

Judith was quiet a moment. "I fear I am transparent."

He covered her hand with his. "You were very angry and rightly so. The Lady Alice—" He stopped when he felt her stiffen. "It was unkind of me to mention her. You have forgiven your husband then?"

Judith smiled. "Can one love another without forgiveness? If it's possible, then that is my fate."

"Why don't you go to him and end this estrangement?"

"You don't know Gavin! He would gloat and lecture me on my waywardness."

Alan chuckled. "Then you must make him come to you."

"That is what my maid says, though she gives me no lessons on how to return my husband to my side."

"There is only one way. He is a jealous man. You must spend some of your time with another, and Lord Gavin will soon see his mistake."

"But what man?" Judith asked, thinking that she knew so few people at court.

"You wound me sorely," Alan laughed, raising his hand to his breast in mock despair.

"You? But you have no interest in my cause."

"Then I must force myself to spend time with you. Surely, it will be a most difficult task. But truthfully, I owe you a favor."

"You owe me nothing."

"No, I do. I was used to play a trick on you, and I would like to repay you."

"Trick? I don't know what you mean."

"It's my secret alone. Now, let's talk no more of serious matters. This is a day for pleasure."

"Yes," she agreed. "We know little of each other. Tell me about yourself."

Alan smiled teasingly. "I have had a long and interesting life. I'm sure my story will take the entire day."

"Then we should start," Judith laughed.

Chapter 29

ALAN AND Judith left the noise and confusion of the king's manor and strolled toward the wooded park outside the castle walls. It was a long walk, but one they both enjoyed.

It was an interesting afternoon for Judith. She realized how few men she had known in her life. Alan was entertaining and the day passed quickly. He was fascinated that she was so well educated. They laughed together over Judith's confession of how her maids sneaked romantic tales to her and how she read to them aloud. Alan was certain Judith was not fully aware of how unorthodox her childhood had been. Only late in the afternoon did she speak of her married life. She told of her reorganizing of Gavin's castle, briefly mentioned her talks with the armorer. Alan began to see the cause of Gavin's outbursts of temper. It would take great strength in a man to be able to stand aside and let his wife's word take precedence over his.

They talked and laughed until the sun was low in the sky. "We must return," Alan said. "But I hate to end this day's enjoyment."

"I agree," Judith smiled. "It has indeed been enjoyable. I'm pleased to get away from court. There's too much gossip and backbiting there for me."

"It's not a bad place—unless you're the object of the abuse."

"As I am now?" Judith winced.

"Yes. No one has had so much to talk of for years."

"Sir Alan," she laughed. "You are cruel to me." She tucked her hand around his arm and smiled up at him.

"So!" a voice hissed close to them. "This is where you hide?"

Judith whirled to see Alice standing close to them.

"He will be mine soon!" Alice sneered and moved closer to Judith. "When he rids himself of you, he will come to me."

Judith stepped back. The light in Alice's blue eyes was unnatural. Her lips curled and showed her uneven teeth, which she usually was so careful to hide.

Alan put himself between Alice and Judith. "Get away from here!" he said in a low, threatening voice.

"Are you hiding behind your lover?" Alice screeched, ignoring Alan. "Can't you wait for the divorce before you take other men?"

Alan's hand clamped onto Alice's shoulder. "Go and don't return. If I see you near Lady Judith again, you'll answer to me."

Alice started to speak but Alan's hand digging into her shoulder prevented her. She turned on one heel and stalked away.

Alan turned back to Judith, to see her staring after the woman. "You look almost frightened."

"I am," she said and rubbed her arms. "The woman gives me chills. Once I thought her to be my enemy, but now I almost pity her."

"You are kindhearted. Most women would hate her for what she has done to you."

"I did once. Maybe I still should. But I can't blame her for all of my problems. Many have been caused by myself and—" She stopped and looked down at the ground.

"And your husband?"

"Yes," she whispered. "Gavin."

Alan stood very close to her. The darkness was rapidly gathering, and he had spent the whole day with her. Maybe it was the delicate light on her hair and eyes, but he knew he couldn't keep himself from kissing her. He took her chin in his hand and lifted her face. Her lips met his. "Sweet, lovely Judith," he whispered. "You are too often concerned with others and yourself not enough." He bent and pressed his lips to hers.

Judith was startled, but she didn't find Alan's caress offensive. Nor did she find it particularly exciting. Her eyes stayed open, and she noticed Alan's lashes on his cheek. His lips were soft and pleasant, but they set no fire in her.

The next moment, the world had opened up and emitted hell. Judith was violently pushed away from Alan, her back slamming into a tree, her senses leaving her briefly. She looked about her dazedly. Alan was on the ground, blood trickling from the corner of his mouth. He rubbed his jaw, flexing it. Gavin stood over him, then bent as he went for the man again. "Gavin!" Judith screamed and flung herself at her husband.

Gavin carelessly tossed her aside. "Do you dare touch what is mine?" he growled at the knight. "I will take your life for this!"

Alan was on his feet instantly, his hand going for his sword. They glared at each other, not speaking, their nostrils flared in anger.

Judith placed herself between the two men, facing Gavin. "You want to fight for me after you have willingly turned me aside?"

At first Gavin didn't seem to hear her or even be aware of her presence. Slowly, he pulled his eyes away from Alan to look at his wife. "It wasn't I who set you aside," he said calmly. "It was you."

"It was you who gave me just cause!" she stormed. "It was you who throughout our marriage fought me when I tried to offer you love."

"You never offered me love," he said quietly.

Judith stared at him, the anger leaving her. "Gavin, I have done nothing else since we were married. I have tried to do and be what you wanted of me, but you wanted me to be . . . her! I could be no one but myself." Judith bent her head to hide her tears.

Gavin took a step toward her, then looked back at Alan with hatred.

Judith felt the tension and glanced up. "If you touch one hair on his head, you will regret it," she warned.

Gavin frowned and started to speak, then gradually began to smile. "I had begun to think that my Judith was gone," he whispered. "She was only hidden under a cloak of sweetness."

Alan coughed to cover the laughter that threatened to escape.

Judith straightened her spine and held her shoulders back as she started to walk away from both men. It disgusted her that both of them were laughing at her.

Gavin watched her for a moment, torn between his fight with Alan Fairfax and his desire for his wife. Judith easily won the tug-of-war. Gavin took three long strides, then pulled her into his arms, sweeping her from the ground. Alan quickly left the two of them alone.

"If you're not still, I will set you in a tree until you can no longer move." The horrible threat quieted her. Gavin sat down on the ground with her and pinned her arms between their bodies. "That is better," he said when she was calmer. "Now I will talk and you will listen. You have humiliated me publicly. No!" he interrupted himself. "Don't speak until I'm finished. I can withstand your fun of me in my own castle, but I've had enough of this in front of the king. By now all of England laughs at me."

"At least I have some pleasure in that," Judith said smugly.

"Do you, Judith? Has any of this given you pleasure?"

She blinked rapidly. "No, it hasn't. But it wasn't my fault."

"That's true. You have been innocent of most of it, but I've told you I loved you and I have asked for your forgiveness."

"And I told you—"

He put two fingers over her lips and smothered her words. "I'm tired of fighting you. You are my wife and my property, and I plan to treat you as such. There will be no divorce."

His eyes blackened. "Neither will there be more afternoons spent with young knights. Tomorrow we'll leave this gossip-ridden place and return home. There, if need be, I will lock you in a tower room and only I will have a key. It will take a long time to still the laughter throughout England, but it can be done." He paused but she didn't speak. "I'm sorry about the trick Alice played, and I shed my own tears over our lost son. But a divorce now won't change the past. I can only hope that soon I will get you with another child and that will heal your wound. But if you think it won't, it will not matter, for I am to have my own way."

Gavin had said all of this in a deliberate manner. Judith didn't answer, but lay quietly in his arms. "Don't you have anything to say?" he asked.

"And what would I say? I don't believe I'm allowed an opinion."

He didn't look at her but stared across the green country-side. "Is the idea so repulsive to you?"

Judith could contain herself no longer. She started laughing and he stared at her in wonder. "You say you love me, that you will keep me apart from everyone but you, locking me in a tower room where we spend nights of passion. You admit the woman you swore you loved has played you false. You say all these things to me and ask if I am repulsed. You have given me what I have most wanted since I first saw you at the church."

He continued staring at her. "Judith . . ." he began, hesitating.

"I love you, Gavin," she smiled. "Is that so difficult to understand?"

"But three days ago—the divorce—"

This time she put her fingers to his lips. "You ask for forgiveness from me. Can't you forgive me?"

"Yes," he whispered as he bent and kissed her. He drew away abruptly. "And what of that man who kissed you? I will kill him!"

"No! It was but a token of friendship."

"It didn't look—!"

"Are you getting angry again?" she demanded, her eyes shooting sparks. "I have stood by for several days and watched woman after woman paw you."

He chuckled. "I should have enjoyed it, but I didn't. You have ruined me for all time."

"I don't understand you."

"The women talked of nothing but clothing and"—Gavin's eyes twinkled—"face creams. I had more trouble with the ledgers, and not one woman could I find who could help me!"

Judith was instantly concerned. "Do you again allow some baker to rob us?" She started to push away from him. "Come on, let's go. I must see to this straightaway."

Gavin tightened his arms about her. "You will not leave me now! Damn the ledgers! Can't you think of anything else to do with that sweet mouth of yours but talk?"

She smiled at him innocently. "I had thought I was but your property and you the master."

He ignored her jibe. "Come then, slave, and let's find a secret den in this dark wood."

"Aye, my master. Most willingly." They walked hand in hand into the forest.

But Judith and Gavin were not alone. Their words of love, their play, had been witnessed by Alice. She watched them with feverish blue eyes.

"Come, love," Ela said as she forcibly steered her mistress away. She looked with hate at the couple who walked through the trees, their arms and bodies intertwined. Those devils played with Alice! she thought. They teased and laughed at her until the sweet and lovely child nearly lost her mind. But they would pay, she vowed.

"Good morning," Judith whispered and snuggled closer to her husband. He kissed the top of her head but didn't speak. "Are we really going today?"

"If you wish."

"Oh yes, I do. I've had enough of gossip and sly looks and men asking me improper questions."

"What men?" Gavin frowned.

"Do not bait me," she answered, then suddenly sat up in the bed, the covers falling away. "I must speak to the king! Now! He cannot keep believing that I want the divorce when I don't. Perhaps the messenger can be overtaken."

Gavin pulled her down in the bed beside him. He ran his teeth along the cord of her neck. He'd made love to her in the forest yesterday and most of last night, but he wasn't anywhere near satiated. "There's no need for such haste. No message will reach the pope."

"No message?" Judith asked as she moved away from Gavin. "What are you saying? It's been days since I talked to the king about a divorce."

"No message was ever sent."

Judith pushed forcibly away from him. "Gavin! I demand an answer. You speak in riddles."

He sat up in the bed. "King Henry told me first of your request and asked if I wanted a divorce. I told him it was an absurdity you had dreamed of while you were so angry with me. I told him you would repent it in a short while."

Judith's mouth opened to speak, her eyes wide. "How dare you!" she finally gasped. "I had every right—!"

"Judith," he interrupted. "A divorce cannot be granted to every wife who is angry at her husband. Soon there would be no marriages left."

"But you had no right—"

"I have every right! I'm your husband and I love you. Who else has rights if I don't? Now come back here and let's stop talking."

"Don't touch me! How can I face the king after what you have said."

"You have been facing him for days, and you seem to have come to no harm." Gavin leered at her bare breasts.

She snatched the covers under her arms. "You have laughed at me!"

"Judith!" Gavin said in a low, threatening voice. "I have taken a great deal from you over this. I have been laughed at, ridiculed, all in an attempt to appease you. But all that is at an end. If you don't behave now, I will turn that pretty bottom of yours over my knee and spank you. Now come here!"

Judith started to defy him, but then she smiled and snuggled against his chest. "What made you so sure I wouldn't divorce you?"

"I guess I knew I loved you enough to forbid it. I would truly have locked you in a tower before I let another man have you."

"Yet you bore the laughter about the divorce."

Gavin gave a derisive snort. "I had no intentions of doing that. I didn't know your tantrum would leak into public knowledge. But then I had forgotten what gossip there was at court. No one does anything that everyone else doesn't know of it."

"How did the news spread?"

Gavin shrugged. "A maid, I guess. How did the knowledge of Alice's trick spread?"

Judith's head came up. "Don't speak that woman's name to me!"

He pulled Judith back to his chest. "Have you no forgiveness in your heart? The woman loves me, as I once believed I loved her. She has done everything for that love."

Judith gave a sigh of exasperation. "You still don't believe any wrong of her, do you?"

"You are still jealous?" he asked, smiling.

She looked up at him, her eyes very serious. "In a way, I am. She will always be a perfect woman to you. What she did, you believe she did out of love for you. She is a pure, perfect woman to you and will always be. While I am . . ."

"You are what?" he teased.

"I am earthy. I am the woman you have and can have, while Alice represents an ethereal love to you."

He frowned. "You say I'm wrong, yet why else would she have done what she did?"

Judith shook her head at him. "Greed. She believes you are hers and I have taken you. She loves you no more than she loves me—except that you have the wherewithal to give her body some pleasure . . . however brief."

He raised one eyebrow. "Do you insult me?"

"No, but I listen to gossip. The men complain of her penchant for violence."

Gavin drew his breath in sharply. "Let's not speak of this again," he said coldly. "You are my wife and I love you, but even so I'll not listen to you malign such an unhappy woman. You have won and she has lost. That should be enough for you."

Judith blinked back tears. "I love you, Gavin. I love you so much, but I fear that all your love will not be mine as long as the disease of Alice Chatworth eats at your heart."

Gavin frowned, tightening his hold on her. "You have no reason to be jealous of her."

Judith started to speak but of what use would her words be? She knew she would always share a tiny bit of her husband's love with an icy blonde beauty. And no words would ever change those feelings.

Saying good-bye to the people Judith liked at court was not easy. The queen especially had become her friend. As Judith curtsied before the king, she felt her face grow hot. She regretted the publicity of her seeking a divorce, but if she had not realized her mistake, she and Gavin would not be together now. As she lifted her head to the king, she smiled. Knowing that Gavin loved her and that she loved him was worth all the embarrassment and teasing.

"We will miss your lovely face," King Henry smiled. "I hope you come to see us again soon."

Gavin put an arm possessively about his wife's shoulders. "Is it her face or the amusement she provides?"

"Gavin!" Judith gasped in horror.

The king threw back his head and roared with laughter. "It's true, Gavin," he said after a while. "I vow I've not been so entertained in years. I'm sure no other marriages will be half so fascinating."

Gavin returned his king's smile. "Then you might watch Stephen. I've just heard that that Scots bride of his took a knife to him on his wedding night."

"Was he harmed?" Henry asked, concerned.

"No," Gavin grinned. "Though I imagine his temper wasn't so well controlled. But then perhaps the woman had some reason for her anger—Stephen was three days late for his own wedding."

King Henry shook his head in disbelief. "I don't envy the man." He smiled again. "At least all is well with one of the Montgomery brothers."

"Yes," Gavin said as he stroked Judith's upper arm. "All is indeed well."

They finished their last good-byes and left the great hall. It had taken most of the day to complete the packing for the journey home. Truthfully, they should have waited until the next day, but everyone seemed as ready to leave as Judith and Gavin. What with the time at Demari's and at court, they had been away a long while.

As they mounted their horses and waved good-bye to the several people who gathered to see them off, only one watched with concern. Alan Fairfax hadn't been able to find a moment alone with Judith as he had hoped. Early that morning Alice Chatworth had left the castle with her servants and household goods. All of the castlefolk seemed to believe that the woman accepted defeat when Judith and Gavin were reconciled. But not Alan. He felt he knew Alice better than that. Alice had been humiliated. He knew that she would seek revenge.

When the bailey was cleared and the Montgomery group well outside the castle walls, Alan mounted his horse and followed at a discreet distance. It wouldn't hurt to be cautious—at least until the Lady Judith was safe inside her own castle walls. Alan smiled and flexed his sore jaw where Gavin had struck him the day before. He hadn't openly voiced his fears of Alice; he knew Lord Gavin believed him to have an un-chivalrous concern for his wife. Perhaps it was true, Alan thought. Perhaps at first; then he had come to know her and began to look on her as a little sister. He sighed and then nearly laughed aloud. At least he could tell himself that. With the way she looked at Lord Gavin, there was no hope for anything else.

Chapter 30

THE WARM water felt heavenly against Judith's bare skin. But better than the water was the freedom. There were no court gossips watching them, commenting on their improper behavior. For their behavior now was very improper for an earl and his countess, the rulers of vast estates. They'd traveled for three days when they saw the lovely blue lake, a corner of it hidden and secluded by overhanging willow trees. Now Gavin and Judith frolicked about like children.

"Oh, Gavin," Judith said in a voice that was half giggle and half whisper.

Gavin's laugh rumbled deep in his throat as he lifted her out of the lake then threw her back in again. They had been playing in the water for an hour, chasing each other, kissing and touching. Their clothes lay in a heap on the bank as they moved through the water unencumbered.

"Judith," Gavin whispered as he drew her close, "you make me forget my duties. My men aren't used to such neglect."

"Nor am I used to so much attention," she said, nipping at his shoulders.

"No, don't start again. I must return to camp."

She sighed but knew he was right. They walked ashore where Gavin quickly dressed, then stood and waited impatiently for his wife.

"Gavin," she smiled, "how can I dress when you glower so? Go back to camp and I will follow in a few moments."

He frowned. "I don't want to leave you alone."

"I am within sound of the camp. I won't come to any harm."

He bent and gave her a fierce hug. "You must forgive me if I'm too protective. I came too close to losing you after the child."

"It wasn't that that nearly caused you to lose me," she retorted.

He laughed and smacked her on her bare wet bottom. "Get dressed, you saucy wench, and return to camp quickly."

"Yes, my lord," she smiled.

When Judith was by herself, she dressed slowly, feeling that it was good to have some solitude for a moment of reflection. The last few days had been bliss. Gavin was at last hers. No more did they hide their love from each other. When she was dressed, she didn't return to the camp, but sat quietly under a tree, enjoying the peaceful place.

But Judith wasn't alone. Not far away stood a man who had hardly left her side since they left court; yet she had not seen him and had no idea he stayed so nearby. Alan Fairfax remained a discreet distance away, where he could see the emerald-green of Judith's gown, yet far enough away that he didn't interfere in her privacy. After these days of following her, he'd begun to relax. Several times he'd wondered just what he was doing when she had her husband who had hardly left her side.

Alan was cursing himself for his stupidity and didn't hear the footsteps so close behind him. A sword came down on the side of his head with brutal force. He slumped forward, his head on his chest and then fell heavily into the leaves of the forest floor.

Without warning, a hood was thrown over Judith's head and her arms pinned behind her when she started to struggle. The suffocating fabric muffled her screams. She was thrown across a man's shoulder, the air nearly forced from her lungs.

The man walked past Alan's inert body, and looked up in question to the woman on the horse.

"Leave him. He will tell Gavin that she's gone. Gavin will come to me then, and we'll see which of us he chooses."

The man's face gave no betrayal of his thoughts. He merely collected his money and performed the tasks. He slung his bundle across the saddle and followed Alice Chatworth through the forest.

Alan awoke some time later, his thoughts confused, his head splitting. He put his hand against a tree to steady himself as he stood. As his eyes began to focus again, he remembered Judith and knew that he must find Gavin so they could search for her. He stumbled awkwardly toward the camp.

Gavin met him halfway. "What are you doing here?" he demanded. "Isn't it enough that you touch my wife at court? Do you think I'll allow you your life again?"

"Judith has been taken!" Alan said, his hand to his pounding head.

Gavin grabbed the smaller man by the neck of his clothes, lifting him from the ground. "If you so much as harm her, I—!"

Alan gasped, forgetting his head and jerking from Gavin's grasp. "It's you who may have hurt her. You wouldn't believe Lady Alice capable of any wrongdoing, so you left Judith unprotected."

"What are you saying!"

"You are a dense man! Alice Chatworth has taken your wife prisoner—and you stand here talking."

Gavin stared at him. "Alice . . . my wife . . . I don't believe you!"

Alan turned away. "Believe me or not, but I'll not waste any more time talking. I'll ride after her alone."

Gavin didn't speak again but turned and went back to the camp. Within moments, he and several of his men were saddled and quickly reached Alan's side. "The Chatworth manor?"

"Yes," Alan answered gravely.

Those were the only words exchanged as the noblemen rode side by side following Judith's captors.

*   *   *

"Welcome to my home," Alice said when the hood was taken from Judith's face. Alice watched the younger woman gasp for breath. "You didn't like the ride? I'm very sorry. A woman such as yourself is used to only the best, I'm sure."

"What do you want of me?" Judith asked, trying to ease the soreness of her shoulders as the ropes on her wrists nearly pulled her arms from their sockets.

"Of you I want nothing," Alice stated. "You have what is mine and I wish its return."

Judith's chin came up. "Do you mean Gavin?"

"Yes," Alice sneered. "I mean Gavin. My Gavin. Always my Gavin."

"Then why didn't you marry him when he asked you?" Judith asked calmly.

Alice's eyes widened, her lips curled into a snarl, exposing her teeth, and her hands formed claws as she lunged for Judith's face.

Judith turned away and the claws didn't reach her.

Ela forcibly grabbed her mistress's arm. "Now, sweet, don't upset yourself. She's not worth it."

Alice seemed to relax.

"Why don't you go and rest?" Ela soothed. "I'll stay with her. You must look your best when Lord Gavin arrives."

"Yes," Alice said quietly. "I must look my best." She left without looking at Judith.

Ela placed her large, soft form in a chair close to the one Judith was tied to and took out some knitting.

"Whose house is this?" Judith asked.

Ela didn't look up. "The Chatworth estate, one of them that my Lady Alice owns," she responded proudly.

"Why am I here?"

Ela paused briefly in her knitting, then resumed. "My lady wishes to see Lord Gavin again."

"Do you believe that?" Judith demanded, her composure leaving her. "Do you believe that crazy woman wants only to see my husband?"

Ela threw down the knitting to her lap. "Don't you call my lady crazy! You don't know her as I do. She's not led an easy life. There are reasons . . ." She stomped across the room toward the window.

"You know, don't you?" Judith asked quietly. "She's insane. Gavin's rejection of her has driven her to madness."

"No!" Ela began, then calmed. "Lord Gavin wouldn't reject my Alice. How could any man deny her? She is beautiful, has always been beautiful. Even as a baby, she was the loveliest anyone had ever seen."

"And you have been with her since she was a child?"

"Yes. I've been with her always. I was past the age for children of my own when she was born. She was given into my care, and she has been a gift of heaven to me."

"Is there nothing you wouldn't do for her?"

"No," Ela said firmly. "I would do anything for her."

"Even killing me so she can take my husband."

Ela looked back at Judith, her old eyes worried. "You won't be killed. It's just that my Lady Alice needs time again with Lord Gavin and you won't allow her that. You are a selfish woman. You have taken what was hers, yet you have no pity or sympathy for my lady's pain."

Judith could feel her temper rising. "She has lied to me, tricked me, done everything she could to take my husband. One of her pieces of treachery cost me the life of my child."

"A child!" Ela hissed. "My lovely lady can have no children. Don't you know how much she has wanted one? Lord Gavin's child! The one you stole from her. It's only fitting that you should lose what should have been my Lady Alice's."

Judith started to speak, then stopped. The maid was as mad as her mistress. No matter what anyone said, Ela would defend Alice. "What are your plans for me?"

Ela realized Judith was calmer and she resumed knitting. "You will be our . . . guest for a few days. Lord Gavin will come, and he will be allowed to spend some time with Lady Alice. Once they are together again, he'll see how much he loves her. It will only take a few days—perhaps only hours— for him to forget you. For in truth he loved her long before he even met you. Theirs is a *true* love match—not one of estates, as is your marriage. Now my Lady Alice is a wealthy widow. She too can bring vast lands to the Montgomery family."

Judith sat quietly and watched Ela knitting. The old woman had a contented look on her face. There were many questions Judith would like to have asked—such as how Alice planned to free Gavin so they could marry. But Judith wisely didn't put any more questions to the maid. It would have been useless.

All through the hard and fast ride to the Chatworth manor, Gavin was silent. He couldn't believe he would find Judith held prisoner by Alice. He knew of Alice's deception at court and what others said of her, but he truthfully could find little wrong with her. He still considered her a sweet-natured woman driven to great lengths through her adoration of him.

The front gate was standing open. Gavin gave Alan a glance of triumph. This was no place that held an heiress captive.

"Gavin," Alice said as she rushed into the inner bailey to meet him. "I hoped you would come to see me." She was exceptionally pale in a blue silk gown that matched her eyes.

Gavin dismounted and held himself stiffly away from her. "Is my wife here?" he asked coldly.

Alice's eyes widened. "Your wife?" she asked innocently.

Alan's hand swept out and grabbed the woman's upper arm. "Where is she, you bitch? I haven't time to play your games!"

Gavin gave Alan a vicious shove and knocked the young man against his horse. "Don't you touch her again!" he warned. He turned back to Alice. "I want an answer to my question."

"Come inside," Alice began, then stopped when she saw Gavin's face. "She is not given to visiting me."

"Then we must leave. She is taken captive and we must find her." He turned to mount his horse again.

"No! Gavin, don't leave me," she cried as she flung herself at him. "Please don't leave me!"

Gavin turned to set her aside.

"Your wife is here."

He turned to see Ela standing in the doorway.

"The woman is kept here, safe now, but she won't be so safe if you spurn my Lady Alice."

Gavin was next to the fat woman in seconds. "Do you threaten me, old hag?" He turned back to Alice. "Where is she?" he demanded.

Alice's eyes spilled over with great, lovely tears. She didn't speak.

"You waste time!" Alan said. "We'll tear this place apart to find her."

Gavin took a step toward the manor house.

"You won't find her!"

Gavin whirled. The voice was a distorted version of Alice's—high and screeching. Her little mouth was pulled back in a snarl, and he saw that her teeth were badly crooked. Why hadn't he seen that before?

"She is where you nor any man will find her," Alice continued, for the first time dropping her facade of sweetness before Gavin. "Do you think I would give that whore my best room? She deserves only the bottom of the moat!"

Gavin took a step toward her, disbelieving the drastic change in Alice. She didn't seem even remotely kin to the woman he once loved.

"You didn't know she gave herself to many men, did you? Did you know the child she lost was not even yours, but Demari's?" Alice put her hand on his arm. "I could give you sons," she leered, her face and voice a caricature of the woman he thought he knew.

"This is what you have neglected Judith for," Alan said quietly. "Can you see now what everyone else does?"

"Yes, I see it," Gavin said in disgust.

Alice backed away from the men, her eyes wild. She picked up her skirts and turned and ran, Ela following her.

When Alan started in pursuit, Gavin said, "Leave her. I would rather have my wife back than punish Alice."

Alice ran from one building to the next, hiding, skulking,

furtively looking about. Gavin had looked at her as if she repulsed him. Somewhere in her mind she knew Ela followed her, but her mind didn't seem to be able to think of more than one thing at a time. Right now all she could think of was the fact that another woman had taken her lover from her. Quickly, she climbed the tower steps making sure no one was after her.

Judith looked up at Alice as she stood in the doorway. The woman's hair was disarranged, her veil askew.

"So!" Alice said, her eyes glinting wildly. "You think you will get him back?"

Judith cringed against the ropes, her throat raw from calling out. But the walls were too thick for her to be heard.

Alice swept across the room grabbing a pot of hot oil from the brazier. A wick floated on top of the oil, ready to be lit. Alice held the oil carefully as she walked toward her prisoner. "He won't think you are lovely once this eats away half of your face."

"No!" Judith whispered and drew back as far as she could.

"Do I frighten you? Do I make your life hell as you have made mine? I was a happy woman before I knew of you. My life hasn't been the same since I first heard your name. I had a father who loved me. Gavin worshiped me. A rich earl asked to marry me. Yet you have taken them all away from me. My father hardly recognizes me now. Gavin hates me. My rich husband is dead. And all because of you."

She moved away from Judith and buried the pot of oil deeper into the coals. "It must be hot, very hot. What do you think will happen when your beauty is gone?"

Judith knew it was impossible to reason with the woman, but she still tried. "What you do to me won't bring back your husband, and I don't even know your father."

"My husband!" Alice sneered. "Do you think I want him back? He was a swine of a man. Yet he once loved me. He changed after he went to your wedding. You made him believe I wasn't worthy of him."

Judith couldn't speak. Her eyes stared at the heating oil.

*   *   *

"My lord," Ela said nervously. "You must come. I'm afraid."

"What is it, you old hag?" Gavin demanded.

"My lady. I fear for her."

Gavin would have gone to great lengths to keep from hurting a woman. Even seeing Alice as she truly was, he couldn't demand that she tell him where Judith was. Now he grabbed Ela's arm. "What are you saying? I grow tired of this game of hide-and-seek. Where is my wife?"

"I meant no harm," Ela whispered. "I only tried to get you back for my lady. It was what she wanted so much. I always try to get her what she wants. But now I'm afraid. I wish the Lady Judith no harm."

"Where is she?" Gavin demanded, tightening his grip.

"She has locked the door and—"

"Go!" Gavin said and pushed the woman. He and Alan followed her across the courtyard to the tower. Please, God! Gavin prayed, let nothing happen to Judith.

At the first pounding on the door, Alice jumped. She knew the bolt wouldn't hold long. She took a long, sharp knife from her side and held it to Judith's throat as she untied the binding ropes. "Come," she said as she grabbed the oil in the other hand.

Judith felt the blade at her throat and the heat from the pot of oil near her cheek. She knew that the slightest movement could startle the nervous Alice and release the oil or push the knife into her throat.

"Up here!" Alice commanded Judith as they slowly made their way up a narrow wooden stairway to the rooftop. Alice stood back, away from the edges, her arm around Judith, holding the knife closely to her neck.

Gavin, Ela and Alan burst through the doorway seconds later. When they saw the empty chamber, they followed Ela up the stairs. They all froze at the sight of the wild-eyed Alice holding Judith.

"My sweet Lady Alice—" Ela began.

"Don't you talk to me!" Alice said, tightening her grip.

"You said you'd get him back for me. But he hates me—I know he does!"

"No!" Ela said, taking a step forward. "Lord Gavin doesn't hate you. He protects his wife because she's his property. No other reason. Now come and let's talk. I'm sure Lord Gavin will understand why this has happened."

"No!" Alice sneered. "Look at him. He despises me! He snarls at me and looks as if I were the lowest form of life. And all for this red-haired slut!"

"Do not harm her!" Gavin warned.

Alice cackled. "Harm her! I will more than harm her. See this?" She held the pot of oil aloft. "It is very, very hot. It will scar her face. What will you say when she's no longer so lovely?"

Gavin took a step forward.

"No!" Alice screeched. "Get up there!" she commanded Judith, pushing her closer to the edge near a chimney pot.

"No!" Judith whispered. She was very frightened but her terror of heights was even greater.

"Do as she says," Gavin said in a low voice, realizing finally that Alice was not sane.

Judith nodded and stepped up on the edge of the roof. In front of her was the upward thrust of the chimney. She grabbed it, her arms tightly rigid.

Alice began to laugh. "She fears this place! She is a child, and you wanted this bitch over me. I am a true woman."

Ela put her hand on Gavin's arm as he started forward. The two women were in a precarious position. Judith's eyes were glazed with fright, her knuckles white as she held onto the bit of brick in front of her. Alice waved the knife and the pot of boiling oil about wildly. "Yes," Ela said. "You are truly a woman. If you will come down, Lord Gavin will soon be sure of that."

"Are you trying to trick me?" Alice asked.

"Have I ever tricked you?"

"No," Alice said and smiled down at the old woman for a moment. "You are the only one who has always been good to me."

The momentary lapse of concentration caused Alice to stumble. Ela grabbed frantically at her beloved mistress, catapulting her body from the slate roof of the manor. Alice grabbed at her maid at the same time as Ela pushed her mistress to safety. Ela fell over the side of the house, taking several seconds before she hit the stones below. Alice fell backward, away from the edge, thanks to the sacrifice of her maid. But the pot of oil in her hand fell with her, spilling across her forehead and cheek. She began to scream horribly.

Gavin made one leap across the roof to where Judith still clung. Her extreme fear of heights and her resulting iron grip on the chimney had saved her life.

Alice's screams filled the air as Gavin pried Judith's fingers loose from the brick. He held her close, feeling her body tighten, her heart pounding.

"Look what you've done to me!" Alice screamed through her pain. "And Ela—you have killed my Ela! She was the only one who ever truly loved me."

"No," Gavin answered, looking at Alice's mutilated face with great pity. "It was not I nor Judith who has harmed you, but only yourself." He turned to Alan as he picked Judith up in his arms. "See to her. Don't let her die. Perhaps that scar will be a fitting reward for her lies."

Alan looked with distaste at the cringing woman, then walked toward her.

Gavin took Judith down the stairs to the room below. It was some moments before she was able to relax. "It's over now, my love," Gavin whispered. "You are safe now. She will harm you no more." He held her very tightly.

Alice's screams, now little more than hoarse groans, came closer. Gavin and Judith watched as Alan led her below. She stopped and gave Judith one last vicious look, then turned away when she saw the sorrow in Judith's eyes. Alan led her from the room.

"What will happen to her now?" Judith asked quietly.

"I don't know. I could give her to the courts, but I think perhaps she's been punished enough. No longer will her beauty ensnare men."

Judith looked up at him in surprise and studied his face.

"You look at me as if you're seeing me for the first time," he said.

"Maybe I am. You're free of her."

"I have told you before that I no longer loved her."

"Yes, but there was always a part of you that was hers, a part I couldn't touch. But now she no longer possesses you. You are mine—totally and completely mine."

"And that pleases you?"

"Yes," she whispered. "It pleases me greatly."

Highland Velvet

To Mia
(the gorgeous one in Louisville)
with love

Author's Note

WHENEVER ANYONE has read this book before publication, she has asked me the same questions: Why isn't a kilt mentioned, and what were the tartan colors of Clan MacArran?

The early Highlanders wore a simple garment (*plaide* is Gaelic for *blanket*) that they spread on the ground, then lay upon and pulled the edges to their sides and belted. This formed a skirt at the bottom, and the upper part of the plaid, or blanket, was pinned at one shoulder.

There are several stories of how the kilt came into being. One story is about an Englishman who abridged the costume for the convenience of his Highland iron-workers. Of course, the Scots deny that this story is true. Whichever story is true, the modern kilt was not in existence before 1700.

As for the tartan colors, the clan members wore whatever color appealed to them or could be made from dyes from plants in their area. The clans were identified by colored cockades in their hats.

Again, there are several stories about the origin of the clan tartans. One is that the export merchants gave clan names to the yards of plaid they manufactured so they could be more easily identified. Another is that the British Army, with its love of uniformity, insisted that each Scots company wear a tartan of the same color and design. Either way, there were no clan tartans before 1700.

Jude Deveraux, 1981
Santa Fe, New Mexico

Prologue

STEPHEN MONTGOMERY still sat very straight on his horse even after the long night's ride. He didn't like to think of the bride who waited for him at the end of his journey—who had been waiting for him for three days. His sister-in-law, Judith, had had a few choice things to say about a man not bothering to show up for his own wedding, nor making the effort to send a message of regret at his lateness.

But despite Judith's words and the realization of the insult he'd paid his future wife, he'd been reluctant to depart King Henry's estate. Stephen had been hesitant to leave his sister-in-law's side. Judith, his brother Gavin's beautiful golden-eyed wife, had fallen down a flight of stairs and lost the badly wanted child she carried. For days Judith hovered between life and death. When she woke and learned her baby was gone, one of her first thoughts was typically about someone other than herself. Stephen had not remembered his own wedding date nor given a thought to his bride. Judith, even in her grief and pain, had reminded Stephen of his duties and the Scotswoman he was to marry.

Now, three days later, Stephen ran his hand through his thick, dark blond hair. He wanted to stay with his brother, Gavin. Judith was more than angry with him. Her fall had not been an accident but had been caused by Gavin's mistress, Alice Chatworth.

"My lord."

Stephen slowed his pace and turned to his squire.

"The wagons are far behind us. They cannot keep pace."

He nodded without speaking and reined his horse toward the narrow stream that ran by the rough road. He dismounted, knelt on one knee, and splashed his face with cold water.

There was another reason Stephen didn't want to travel to meet this bride he'd never seen. King Henry meant to reward the Montgomerys for their faithful service over the years, so he gave the second brother a rich Scots bride. Stephen knew he should be grateful, but not after the things he'd heard of her.

She was, in her own right, the laird of a powerful Scots clan.

He looked across the green meadow on the far side of the stream. Damn the Scots anyway for their absurd belief that a mere woman was intelligent and strong enough to lead men. Her father should have chosen a young man for his heir instead of a woman.

He grimaced as he imagined what kind of woman could inspire her father to name her chief. She had to be at least forty years old, hair the color of steel, a body thicker than his own. On their wedding night no doubt they'd arm wrestle to see who would get on top . . . and he'd lose.

"My lord," the boy said. "You do not look well. Perhaps the long ride has made you ill."

"It's not the ride that's turned my stomach." Stephen stood up slowly, easily, his powerful muscles moving under his clothes. He was tall, towering over his squire, and his body was lean and hard from many years of strenuous training. His hair was thick with sweaty curls along his neck, his jaw strong, his lips finely chiseled. Yet now there were sunken shadows under the eyes of brilliant blue. "Let's return to our horses. The wagons can follow us later. I don't want to put off my execution any longer."

"Execution, my lord?"

Stephen did not answer. There were still many hours before he'd reach the horror that awaited him in the solid, bulky shape of Bronwyn MacArran.

Chapter 1

1501

BRONWYN MACARRAN stood at the window of the English manor house, looking down at the courtyard below. The mullioned window was open against the warm summer sun. She leaned forward slightly forward slightly to catch a whiff of fresh air. As she did so, one of the soldiers below grinned up at her suggestively.

She stepped back quickly, grabbed the window, and slammed it shut. She turned away angrily.

"The English pigs!" Bronwyn cursed under her breath. Her voice was soft, full of the heather and mist of the Highlands.

Heavy footsteps sounded outside her door, and she caught her breath, then released it when they went past. She was a prisoner, held captive on England's northernmost border by men she'd always hated, men who now smiled and winked at her as if they were intimate with her most private thoughts.

She walked to a small table in the center of the oak-paneled room. She clutched the edge of it, letting the wood cut into her palms. She'd do anything to keep those men from seeing how she felt inside. The English were her enemies. She'd seen them kill her father, his three chieftains. She'd seen her brother driven nearly insane with his futile attempts to repay the English in their own kind. And all her life she'd helped feed and clothe the members of her clan after the English had destroyed their crops and burned their houses.

A month ago the English had taken her prisoner. Bronwyn smiled in memory of the wounds she and her men had inflicted upon the English soldiers. Later four of them had died.

But in the end she was taken, by the order of the English Henry VII. The man said he wanted peace and therefore would name an Englishman as chief of Clan MacArran. He thought he could do this by marrying one of his knights to Bronwyn.

She smiled at the ignorance of the English king. She was chief of Clan MacArran, and no man would take her power away. The stupid king thought her men would follow a foreigner, an Englishman, rather than their own chief because she was a woman. How little Henry knew of the Scots!

She turned suddenly as Rab growled. He was an Irish wolfhound, the largest dog in the world, rangy, strong, hair like soft steel. Her father had given her the dog four years ago when Jamie'd returned from a trip to Ireland. Jamie had meant to have the dog trained as his daughter's guardian, but there was no need. Rab and Bronwyn took to each other immediately, and Rab had often shown that he'd give his life for his beloved mistress.

Bronwyn's muscles relaxed when Rab's growl stopped— only a friend produced such a reaction. She looked up expectantly.

It was Morag who entered. Morag was a short, gnarled old woman, looking more like a dark burl of wood than a human being. Her eyes were like black glass, sparkling, penetrating, seeing more of a person than what was on the surface. She used her lithe little body to advantage, often slipping unnoticed amid people, her eyes and ears open.

Morag moved silently across the room and opened the window.

"Well?" Bronwyn demanded impatiently.

"I saw ye slam the window. They laughed and said they'd take over the weddin' night ye'd be missin'."

Bronwyn turned away from the old woman.

"Ye give them too much to speak of. Ye should hold yer

head high and ignore them. They're only Englishmen, while ye're a MacArran."

Bronwyn whirled. "I don't need anyone to tell me how to act," she snapped. Rab, aware of his mistress's distress, came to stand beside her. She buried her fingers in his fur.

Morag smiled at her, then watched as the girl moved toward the window seat. She had been placed in Morag's arms when Bronwyn was still wet from her birth. Morag had held the tiny bairn as she watched the mother die. It'd been Morag who'd found a wet nurse for the girl, who'd given her the name of her Welsh grandmother, and who'd cared for her until she was six and her father'd taken over.

It was with pride that Morag looked at her charge now nearly twenty years old. Bronwyn was tall, taller than most men and as straight and supple as a reed. She didn't cover her hair like the Englishwoman, but let it flow down her back in a rich cascade. It was raven-black and so thick and heavy it was a wonder her slender neck could support the weight. She wore a satin dress in the English style. It was the color of the cream from the Highland cattle. The square neck was low and tight, showing Bronwyn's firm young breasts to advantage. It fit like skin to her small waist, then belled out in rich folds. Embroidery entwined with thin gold strands edged both the neck and the waist and fell in an intricate waterfall down the skirt.

"Do I meet your approval?" Bronwyn asked sharply, still irritated over their quarrel about the English attire. She had preferred Highland clothes, but Morag persuaded her to wear English garb, telling her to give the enemy no reason to laugh at her in what they referred to as "barbaric dress."

Morag chuckled dryly. "I was thinkin' it was a shame no man would be takin' that gown from ye tonight."

"An Englishman!" Bronwyn hissed. "Do you forget that so soon? Has the red of my father's blood faded before your eyes?"

"Ye know it hasn't," Morag said quietly.

Bronwyn sat down heavily on the window seat, the satin of the dress flowing about her. She ran her finger along the heavy embroidery. The dress had cost her a great deal, money that could have been spent on her clan. But she knew they would not have wanted to be shamed before the Englishmen, so she bought dresses that would have been the pride of any queen.

Only this gown was to have been her wedding dress.

She plucked violently at a piece of gold thread.

"Here!" Morag commanded. "Don't destroy the dress because ye're mad at one Englishman. Perhaps the man had a reason to be late and miss his own weddin'."

Bronwyn stood up quickly, causing Rab to move protectively to her side. "What do I care if the man never appears? I hope he had his throat cut and lies rotting in some ditch."

Morag shrugged. "They'll only find ye a new husband, so what does it matter if this one dies or not? The sooner ye have yer English husband, the sooner we can go back to the Highlands."

"It's easy for you to say!" Bronwyn snapped. "It's not you who must wed him and . . . and . . ."

Morag's little black eyes danced. "And bed him? Is that what's worryin' ye? I'd gladly trade with ye if I could. Think this Stephen Montgomery would notice 'twere I to slip into his bed?"

"What do I know of Stephen Montgomery except that he has no more respect for me than to leave me waiting in my wedding dress? You say the men laugh at me. The man who is to be my husband holds me up for their ridicule." She squinted at the door. "Were he to come through there now, I'd gladly take a knife to him."

Morag smiled. Jamie MacArran would have been proud of his daughter. Even when she was still held prisoner she kept her pride and her spirit. Now she held her chin high, her eyes flashing with daggers of crystal-blue ice.

Bronwyn was startlingly beautiful. Her hair was as black as a moonless midnight in the Scots mountains, her eyes as deep blue as the water of a sunlit loch. The contrast was arresting. It wasn't unusual for people, especially men, to be struck speechless the first time they saw her. Her lashes were thick and dark, her skin fine and creamy. Her lips of dark red were set above her father's chin, strong, square on the tip, and slightly cleft.

"They'll think ye're a coward if ye hide in this room. What Scot is afraid of the smirks of an Englishman?"

Bronwyn stiffened her back and looked down at the cream-colored gown. When she'd dressed that morning, she thought to be wed in the dress. Now it was hours past time for the marriage ceremony, and her bridegroom had not shown himself, nor had he sent any message of excuse or apology.

"Help me unfasten this thing," Bronwyn said. The gown would have to be kept fresh until she did marry. If not today, then at another time. And perhaps to another man. The thought made her smile.

"What are ye plannin'?" Morag asked, her hands at the back of Bronwyn's dress. "Ye've a look of the cat that got the cream."

"You ask too many questions. Fetch me that green brocade gown. The Englishmen may think I'm a bride in tears at being snubbed, but they'll soon find the Scots are made of sterner stuff."

Even though she was a prisoner and had been for over a month, Bronwyn was allowed the freedom of Sir Thomas Crichton's manor. She could walk about the house and, with an escort, on the grounds. The estate was heavily guarded, watched constantly. King Henry had told Bronwyn's clan that if a rescue attempt were made, she would be executed. No harm would come to her, but he meant to put an Englishman in the chiefship. The clan had recently seen the death of Jamie MacArran as well as of his three chieftains. The Scots retreated to watch their new laird held captive and planned what they'd do when the king's men dared to try to command them.

Bronwyn slowly descended the stairs to the hall below. She knew her clansmen waited patiently just outside the grounds, hiding in the forest on the constantly turbulent border between England and Scotland.

For herself she did not care if she died rather than accept the English dog she was to marry, but her death would cause strife within the clan. Jamie MacArran had designated his daughter as his successor, and she was to have married one of the chieftains who had died with her father. If Bronwyn were to die without issue, there would no doubt be a bloody battle over who would be the next laird.

"I always knew the Montgomerys were smart men," laughed a man standing a few feet from Bronwyn. A thick tapestry hid her from his view. "Look at the way the eldest married that Revedoune heiress. He'd hardly got out of his marriage bed when her father was killed and he inherited the earldom."

"And now Stephen is following in his brother's footsteps. Not only is this Bronwyn beautiful, but she owns hundreds of acres of land."

"You can say what you like," said a third man. His sleeve was empty, his left arm missing. "But I don't envy Stephen. The woman is magnificent, but how long will he be able to enjoy her? I lost this fighting those devils in Scotland. They're only half human, I tell you. They grow up learning nothing but plunder and robbery. And they fight more like animals than men. They're a crude, savage lot."

"And I heard their women stink to high heaven," the first man said.

"For that black-haired Bronwyn I'd learn to hold my nose."

Bronwyn took a step forward, a feral snarl on her lips. When a hand caught her arm, she looked up into a young man's face. He was handsome, with dark eyes, a firm mouth. Her eyes were on a level with his.

"Allow me, my lady," he said quietly.

He stepped forward to the group of men. His strong legs were encased in tight hose, his velvet jacket emphasizing the width of his shoulders. "Have you nothing better to do than gossip like old women? You talk of things you know nothing about." His voice was commanding.

The three men looked startled. "Why, Roger, what's

wrong with you?" one asked, then stared over Roger's shoulder and saw Bronwyn, her eyes glittering in stormy anger.

"I think Stephen had better come soon and guard his property," one of the other men laughed.

"Get out of here!" Roger ordered. "Or shall I draw my sword to get your attention?"

"Deliver me from the hot blood of youth," one man said wearily. "Go to her. Come, the outside is cooler. The passions have more room to expand in the out-of-doors."

When the men were gone, Roger turned back to Bronwyn. "May I apologize for my countrymen? Their rudeness is based on ignorance. They meant no harm."

Bronwyn glared at him. "I fear it is you who are ignorant. They meant great harm, or do you consider murdering Scots no sin?"

"I protest! You're unfair to me. I have killed few men in my life and no Scots." He paused. "May I introduce myself? I am Roger Chatworth." He swept his velvet cap from his head and bowed low before her.

"And I, sir, am Bronwyn MacArran, prisoner to the English and, of late, discarded bride."

"Lady Bronwyn, will you walk with me in the garden? Perhaps the sunshine will take away some of the misery Stephen has foisted upon you."

She turned and walked beside him. At least he might keep the guards from tossing rude jests at her. Once they were outside, she spoke again. "You speak Montgomery's name as if you know him."

"Have you not met him yourself?"

Bronwyn whirled on him. "Since when have I been afforded any courtesy by your English king? My father thought enough of me to name me laird of Clan MacArran, but your king thinks I have too little sense to even choose my own husband. No, I have not seen this Stephen Montgomery, nor do I know anything about him. I was told one morning I was to marry him. Since then he has not so much as acknowledged my presence."

Roger lifted a handsome eyebrow at her. Her hostility

made her eyes sparkle like blue diamonds. "I'm sure there must be an excuse for his tardiness."

"Perhaps his excuse is that he means to assert his authority over all the Scots. He will show us who is master."

Roger was silent for a moment as if he were considering her words. "There are those who consider the Montgomerys arrogant."

"You say you know this Stephen Montgomery. What is he like? I don't know if he's short or tall, old or young."

Roger shrugged as if his mind were elsewhere. "He is an ordinary man." He seemed reluctant to continue. "Lady Bronwyn, tomorrow would you do me the honor of riding into the park with me? There's a stream running across Sir Thomas's land, and perhaps we could carry a meal there."

"Aren't you afraid that I'll make an attempt on your life? I have not been allowed off these grounds for over a month."

He smiled at her. "I would like you to know there are Englishmen with more manners than to, as you say, discard a woman on her wedding day."

Bronwyn stiffened as she was reminded of the humiliation Stephen Montgomery had caused her. "I would very much like to ride out with you."

Roger Chatworth smiled and nodded to a man passing them on the narrow garden path. His mind was working quickly.

Three hours later Roger returned to his apartments in the east wing of Sir Thomas Crichton's house. He'd come there two weeks ago to talk to Sir Thomas about recruiting young men from the area. Sir Thomas had been too busy with the problems of the Scots heiress to talk of anything else. Now Roger was beginning to think fate had brought him here.

He kicked the stool out from under his sleeping squire's feet. "I have something for you to do," he commanded as he removed his velvet jacket and slung it across the bed. "There's an old Scotsman named Angus lying about somewhere. Look for him and bring him to me. You'll probably find him wherever the drink is flowing freely. And then bring me half a hogshead of ale. Do you understand me?"

"Yes, my lord," the boy said, backing out of the doorway, rubbing his drowsy eyes.

When Angus appeared in the doorway, he was already half drunk. He worked for Sir Thomas in some sort of capacity, but generally he did little except drink. His hair was dirty and tangled, hanging well past his shoulders in the Scots manner. He wore a long linen shirt, belted at the waist, his knees and legs bare.

Roger glanced at the man and his heathen attire with a brief look of disgust.

"You wanted me, my lord?" Angus said, his voice a soft burr. His eyes followed the small cask of ale that Roger's squire was carrying into the room.

Chatworth dismissed the boy, poured himself an ale, sat down, and motioned Angus to do likewise. When the filthy man was seated, Roger began. "I'd like to know about Scotland."

Angus raised his shaggy brows. "You mean where the gold is hidden? We're a poor country, my lord, and—"

"I want none of your sermons! Save your lies for someone else. I want to know what a man who is to marry the chief of a clan should know."

Angus stared hard for a moment, then he closed his mouth with his mug of ale. "An *eponymus*, eh?" he mumbled in Gaelic. " 'Tisn't easy to be accepted by the clan members."

Roger took one long step across the room and grabbed the mug of ale from the man. "I didn't ask for your judgments. Will you answer my questions, or do I kick you down the stairs?"

Angus looked at the cold mug with desperate eyes. "Ye must become a MacArran." He looked up at Roger. "Takin' that you mean that particular clan."

Roger gave a brief, curt nod.

"Ye must take the name of the laird of the clan, or the men can't accept ye. Ye must dress as the Scots or they'll laugh at ye. Ye must love the land and the Scots."

Roger lowered the ale. "What about the woman? What must I do to own her?"

"Bronwyn cares about little else except her people. She would have killed herself before she married an Englishman, but she knew her death would cause war within her clan. If ye make the woman know ye mean well for her people, ye'll have her."

Roger gave the man the ale. "I want to know more. What is a clan? Why was a woman made chief? Who are the enemies of Clan MacArran?"

"Talking is thirsty work."

"You'll have all you can hold, just as long as you tell me what I want to know."

Bronwyn met Roger Chatworth early the next morning. In spite of her good intentions, she'd been so excited about the prospect of a ride in the woods that she'd hardly been able to sleep. Morag had helped her dress in a soft brown velvet gown, all the while issuing dire warnings about Englishmen bearing gifts.

"I merely want the ride," Bronwyn said stubbornly.

"Aye, and what mere trifle does this Chatworth want? He knows ye're to marry another."

"Am I?" Bronwyn snapped. "Then where is my bridegroom? Should I sit in my wedding gown for another full day and wait for him?"

"It might be better than chasing after some hot-blooded young earl."

"An earl? Roger Chatworth is an English earl?"

Morag refused to answer, but gave the gown a final straightening before pushing her from the room.

Now, as Bronwyn sat atop the horse, Rab running beside her, she felt alive for the first time in many weeks.

"The roses have returned to your cheeks," Roger said, laughing.

She smiled in return, and the smile softened her chin and lit her eyes. She spurred the horse to a faster pace. Rab with his long, loping strides kept pace with the horse.

Roger turned for a moment to glance at the men following them. There were three of his personal guards, two squires, and a packhorse loaded with food and plate. He turned and looked ahead at Bronwyn. He frowned when she glanced over her shoulder and spurred her mount even faster. She was an excellent horsewoman, and no doubt the woods were full of men from her clan, all eager and willing to help her escape.

He threw up his hand and motioned his men forward as he set spurs to his own mount.

Bronwyn made her horse come close to flying. The wind in her hair, the sense of freedom, were exhilarating. When she came to the stream, she was going full speed. She had no idea if the horse had ever taken a jump before, but she urged it on regardless of the risk. It sailed over the water as if it had wings. On the far side she pulled the animal to a halt and turned to look back.

Roger and his men were just approaching the stream.

"Lady Bronwyn!" Roger shouted. "Are you all right?"

"Of course," she laughed, then led her horse through the water to where Roger waited for her. She bent forward and patted the horse's neck. "He's a good animal. He took the jump well."

Roger dismounted and walked to her side. "You gave me a terrible fright. You could have been injured."

She laughed happily. "A Scotswoman is not likely to be injured while atop a horse."

Roger put his arms up to help her dismount.

Suddenly Rab jumped between them, his lips drawn back showing long, sharp teeth. He growled deeply, menacingly. Roger instinctively retreated.

"Rab!" The dog obeyed Bronwyn immediately. He moved away but his eyes, with a warning gleam, never left Roger. "He means to protect me," she said. "He doesn't like anyone touching me."

"I'll remember that in future," Roger said warily as he aided Bronwyn off her horse. "Perhaps you'd like to rest after your ride," he suggested. He snapped his fingers, and his squires brought two chairs upholstered in red velvet. "My lady," Roger offered.

She smiled in wonder at the chairs set in the woods. The

grass under their feet was like a velvet carpet. The stream played its music, and even as she thought that, one of Roger's men began to strum a lute. She closed her eyes for a moment.

"Are you homesick, my lady?" Roger asked.

She sighed. "You could not know. No one not of the Highlands could know what it means to a Scot."

"My grandmother was a Scot, so perhaps that qualifies me to have some understanding of your ways."

Her head came up abruptly. "Your grandmother! What was her name?"

"A MacPherson of MacAlpin."

Bronwyn smiled. It was good to even hear the familiar names once again. "MacAlpin. 'Tis a good clan."

"Yes. I spent many evenings listening to stories at my grandmother's knee."

"And what sort of stories did she tell you?" Bronwyn asked cautiously.

"She was married to an Englishman, and she often compared the cultures of the two countries. She said the Scots were more hospitable, that the men didn't shove the women into a room and pretend they had no sense as the English do. She said the Scots treated women as equals."

"Yes," Bronwyn agreed quietly. "My father named me laird." She paused. "How did your English grandfather treat his Scots wife?"

Roger chuckled as if at some private joke. "My grandfather lived in Scotland for a while, and he knew my grandmother to be a woman of intelligence. He valued her all his life. There was never a decision made that was not made by both of them."

"And you spent some time with your grandparents?"

"Most of my life. My parents died when I was very young."

"And what did you think of this non-English way of treating women? Surely, now that you are older, you've learned that women are only of use in the bed, in creating and delivering children."

Roger laughed out loud. "If I even had such a thought,

my grandmother's ghost would box my ears. No," he said more seriously, "she meant for me to marry the daughter of a cousin of hers, but the child died before our marriage. I grew up calling myself MacAlpin."

"What?" She was startled.

Roger looked surprised. "It was in the marriage contract that I'd become a MacAlpin to please her clan."

"And you'd do that? I mentioned to Sir Thomas that my husband must become a MacArran, but he said that was impossible, that no Englishman would give up his fine old name for a heathen Scots name."

Roger's eyes flashed angrily. "They don't understand! Damn the English! They think only their ways are right. Why, even the French—"

"The French are our friends," Bronwyn interrupted. "They visit our country as we do theirs. They don't destroy our crops or steal our cattle as the English do."

"Cattle." Roger smiled. "Now there's an interesting subject. Tell me, do the MacGregors still raise such fat beasts?"

Bronwyn drew her breath in sharply. "Clan MacGregor is our enemy."

"True," he smiled, "but don't you find that a roast of MacGregor beef is more succulent than any other?"

She could only stare at him. The MacGregors had been the enemies of the MacArrans for centuries.

"Of course, things may have changed since my grandmother was a Highland lass," Roger continued. "Then the favorite sport of the young men was a swift moonlight cattle raid."

Bronwyn smiled at him. "Nothing's changed."

Roger turned and snapped his fingers. "Would you like something to eat, my lady? Sir Thomas has a French chef, and he has prepared us a feast. Tell me, have you ever eaten a pomegranate?"

She could only shake her head and look at him in wonder as the baskets were unloaded and Roger's squire served the meal on silver plates. For the first time in her life she had the thought that an Englishman could be human, that he could learn, and desired to learn, the Scots' ways. She picked up a piece of pâté, molded into the shape of a rose and placed on a cracker. The events of the day were a revelation to her.

"Tell me, Lord Roger, what do you think of our clan system?"

Roger brushed crumbs from his doublet of gold brocade and smiled to himself. He was well prepared for all her questions.

Bronwyn stood in the room where she'd spent too much time in the last month. Her cheeks were still flushed and her eyes still bright from the morning's fast ride.

"He's not like other men," she said to Morag. "I tell you, we spent hours together and we never once stopped talking. He even knows some Gaelic words."

" 'Tisn't hard to pick up a few hereabouts. Even some of the Lowlanders know Gaelic." It was Morag's worst insult. To her the Lowlanders were traitorous Scots, more English than Scot.

"Then how do you explain the other things he said? His grandmother was a Scot. You should have heard his ideas! He said he'd petition King Henry to stop the English from raiding us, that that would bring more peace than this practice of capturing Scotswomen and forcing them to marry against their will."

Morag screwed her dark, wrinkled face into walnut-shell ugliness. "Ye leave here this mornin' hatin' all English and come back bowin' at one's feet. All ye've heard from him are words. Ye've seen no action. What has the man done to make ye trust him?"

Bronwyn sat down heavily on the window seat. "Can't you see that I want only what is best for my people? I am forced to marry an Englishman, so why not one who is part Scot, in mind as well as in blood?"

"Ye have no choice of husbands!" Morag said fiercely. "Can't ye see that ye are a great prize? Young men will say anything to get under a pretty woman's skirts. And if those skirts are covered with pearls, they'll kill themselves to have them."

"Are you saying he's lying?"

"How would I know? I've only just seen the man. But I have *not* seen Stephen Montgomery. For all ye know, his mother could have been a Scot. Perhaps he'll appear with a tartan across his shoulder and a dirk in his belt."

"I could not hope for so much," Bronwyn sighed. "If I met a thousand Englishmen, not one of them would understand my clan as Roger Chatworth does." She stood. "But you are right. I will be patient. Perhaps this man Montgomery is unique, an understanding man who believes in the Scots."

"I hope ye do not expect too much," Morag said. "I hope Chatworth has not made ye expect too much."

Chapter 2

STEPHEN HAD ridden fast and hard all day and well into the night before he reached Sir Thomas's house on the border. Stephen had long since left the wagons and his retainers behind. Only his personal guard managed to stay with him. A few hours ago they'd encountered a storm and a river about to burst its banks. Stephen slogged through the muck. Now, as he reined into the courtyard, he and his men were covered with lumps of mud. A tree branch had struck Stephen over the eye, and the blood had dried, giving him a swollen, grotesque appearance.

He dismounted quickly and threw the reins to his exhausted squire. The big manor house was lit by a myriad of candles, and music floated on the air.

Stephen stood inside the door for a moment to allow his eyes to adjust to the light.

"Stephen!" Sir Thomas called as he hobbled forward. "We've been worried about you! I was going to send men out to search for you in the morning."

A man came to stand behind the aged and gout-crippled knight. "So this is the lost bridegroom," he smiled, looking Stephen up and down, noting his filthy, torn clothing. "Not everyone has been worried, Sir Thomas."

"Aye," someone else laughed. "Young Chatworth seems to have done quite well without the belated bridegroom."

Sir Thomas put his hand on Stephen's shoulder and guided

him toward a room off the hall. "Come in here, my boy. We need time to talk."

It was a large room, paneled in oak carved in the linenfold pattern. Against one wall was a row of books above a long trestle table. Completing the sparse furnishings were four chairs set before a large fireplace, where low flames burned cheerfully.

"What is this about Chatworth?" Stephen asked immediately.

"Sit down first. You look exhausted. Would you like some food? Wine?"

Stephen tossed a cushion out of a walnut chair and sat down gratefully. He took the wine Sir Thomas offered. "I'm sorry I'm late. My sister-in-law fell and lost the baby she carried. She nearly died. I'm afraid I didn't notice the date and only realized it after I was already three days late. I rode as hard as I could to get here." He picked a piece of caked dirt from his neck and threw it into the fireplace.

Sir Thomas nodded. "That's obvious from the look of you. If someone hadn't told me you approached bearing a banner of the Montgomery leopards, I'd never have recognized you. Is that cut above your eye as bad as it looks?"

Absently, Stephen felt the place. "It's mostly dried blood. I was traveling too fast for it to run down my face," he joked.

Sir Thomas laughed and sat down. "It's good to see you. How are your brothers?"

"Gavin married Robert Revedoune's daughter."

"Revedoune? There's money in that match."

Stephen smiled and thought that the last thing Gavin cared about was his wife's money. "Raine is still talking about his absurd ideas about the treatment of serfs."

"And Miles?"

Stephen finished the wine in his cup. "Miles presented us with another of his bastard children last week. That makes three, or four, I lost count. If he were a stallion, we'd be rich."

Sir Thomas laughed and refilled both metal goblets.

Stephen looked up at the older man as he lifted his drink again. Sir Thomas had been a friend of his father's, an honorary uncle who brought the boys gifts from his many trips abroad, had been at Stephen's christening twenty-six years ago. "Now that we're through with that," Stephen said slowly, "perhaps you'll tell me what you're hiding."

Sir Thomas chuckled, a soft sound deep within his throat. "You know me too well. It's nothing really, an unpleasantness, nothing serious. Roger Chatworth has spent a great deal of time with your bride, 'tis all."

Standing up slowly, Stephen walked toward the fireplace. Bits of mud fell from his clothes as he moved. Sir Thomas could not know what the name Chatworth meant to Stephen. Alice Valence had been his brother's mistress for years. Repeatedly, Gavin had asked her to marry him. She refused, preferring to marry the rich Edmund Chatworth. Soon after her marriage, Edmund was murdered and Alice reappeared in Gavin's life. She was a treacherous woman, and she had climbed into bed with a drunken, sleepy Gavin, then arranged for Judith to see them together. In her agony Judith fell down the stairs and lost her child and nearly lost her own life.

Roger Chatworth was Alice's brother-in-law, and even the mention of the name made Stephen grit his teeth.

"There must be more to this," Stephen said finally.

"Bronwyn hinted last evening that perhaps she'd be more pleased with Roger for a husband than one who is so . . . discourteous."

Stephen smiled and went back to the chair. "And how does Roger take all this?"

"He seems amenable. He rides with her each morning, escorts her to supper in the evening, spends time in the garden with her."

Stephen drank the last of the wine and began to relax. "It's well known that the Chatworths are a greedy bunch, but I didn't know to what degree. He must be very hungry to endure the woman's company."

"Endure?" Sir Thomas asked, surprised.

"There's no need to be dishonest with me. I heard how she fought like a man when she was surrounded, and worse how even her own father considered her enough of a man to name her his successor. I almost feel sorry for Roger. It would serve him right if I let him have the hideous woman."

Sir Thomas stood with his mouth agape, then slowly his eyes began to twinkle. "Hideous, is she?" he chuckled.

"What else could she be? Don't forget I've spent some time in Scotland. A wilder, more savage group of people I've never run across. But what could I say to King Henry? He thought he was rewarding me. If I stepped aside and let Roger have her he'd forever be in my debt. Then I could marry some sweet, pretty little woman who wouldn't try to borrow my armor. Yes," he smiled, "that's just what I think I'll do."

"I agree with you," Sir Thomas said firmly. "Bronwyn is truly a hideous woman. I'm sure Roger is only interested in her land. But just so you can tell King Henry you were fair, why don't you meet her? I'm sure she'll take one look at you, filthy as you are, and refuse to marry you."

"Yes." Stephen grinned, his white teeth only making him seem dirtier by contrast. "Then tomorrow both the woman and I can tell Roger of our decision. Then I can go home. Yes, Sir Thomas, it's a splendid idea."

Sir Thomas's eyes shone like a boy's; they fairly danced. "You show an uncommon wisdom for a man so young. Just wait here, and I'll have her brought down the back stairs to this room."

Stephen gave a low whistle. "Back stairs, is it? She must be worse than I imagine."

"You'll see, my boy. You'll see," Sir Thomas said as he left the room.

Bronwyn sat buried to her chin in a tub of hot, steamy water. Her eyes were closed, and she was thinking about going home. Roger would be with her, and together they'd lead her clan. It was a picture she was beginning to conjure more and more often in the last few days. Roger was one Englishman she could understand. Every day he seemed to know more about the Scots.

As Morag burst into the room she opened her eyes. "He's here," the old woman announced.

"Who is here?" Bronwyn asked stubbornly, knowing exactly whom Morag meant.

Morag ignored her question. "He's talking to Sir Thomas but I'm sure ye'll be called for in a few minutes, so get out of that water and get dressed. Ye kin wear the blue dress."

Bronwyn leaned her head back. "I'm not finished with my bath, and I have no intention of meeting him merely because he's bothered to appear. He kept me waiting for four days, so maybe I'll make him wait for five."

"Ye're bein' childish, as ye well know. The stable boy said the man's horses had been run near to death. Ye can see he tried to get here in a hurry."

"Or perhaps he always mistreats his horses."

"Ye're not too big to take a switch to! Now get out of that tub or I'll throw a bucket of cold water over yer head."

Before Morag could act, the door was suddenly thrust open again, revealing a pair of guards.

"How dare you!" Bronwyn yelled as she sank lower into the water.

Instantly Rab rose from his place at the foot of the tub, ready to attack.

The men had barely a glimpse of Bronwyn before they were knocked off balance by a hundred and twenty pounds of snarling, sharp-toothed dog.

Morag grabbed Bronwyn's thin linen chemise and tossed it to her. She stood in the tub and hastily pulled it over her wet body, the hem of it falling into the water. She grabbed a woolen tartan from Morag as she stepped out of the tub.

"Quiet, Rab!" Bronwyn ordered. The hound obeyed immediately, coming to her side.

The guards stood up slowly, rubbing their wrists and shoulders where Rab had toyed with them. They did not know that the dog killed only on direct command from Bronwyn; otherwise he protected her without doing permanent damage. The men had seen the tub taken to Bronwyn's room, had heard her splashing. They used Sir Thomas's orders as an invitation to see her in her bath. Now she was wrapped from head to toe in a Scots plaid. There was no outline of her body showing, only her face, her eyes shining with humor.

"What do you want?" Bronwyn asked, laughter in her voice.

"You are to come to Sir Thomas's study," one of the guards said sullenly. "And if that dog ever again—"

She cut him off. "If you ever again enter my room without my permission, I will allow Rab to have your throat. Now lead the way."

They looked from Bronwyn to the big wolfhound, then turned away. Bronwyn held her head high as she followed them down the stairs. She would let no one see her anger at the way she was being treated by this Stephen Montgomery. Four days late for his wedding, then, the moment he arrives, she is dragged before him like an errant serving wench.

When Bronwyn was inside the study, she looked from Sir Thomas to the man standing by the fireplace. He was tall, but he was filthy beyond belief. Of his face she could tell nothing. It seemed to be swollen on one side, and she wondered if it was a permanent affliction.

Suddenly one of the guards saw a way to repay her for her sport of him. Grabbing the trailing end of the long tartan, he gave Bronwyn a sharp shove. She fell forward, and the guard yanked back on the plaid.

"You!" Sir Thomas bellowed. "Out of my sight! How dare you treat a lady like that! If you're within fifty miles of here in the morning, I'll have you hanged!"

Both guards turned and quickly left the room as Sir Thomas bent to retrieve the garment.

Only momentarily stunned, Bronwyn quickly got off her knees and stood. The thin chemise clung to her still-wet body as if she were nude. She started to cover herself with her hands until she glanced up at Stephen. He was no longer nonchalantly leaning against the fireplace but had come to attention, staring at her in open-mouthed disbelief. His eyes were wide, showing white all around them, his mouth so agape that his tongue fairly fell out.

She curled her lip at him, but he didn't even notice. All he could see was what was below her neck. She put her arms straight to her sides and glared at him.

It seemed an extraordinarily long time before Sir Thomas placed Bronwyn's plaid gently about her shoulders. She wrapped it tightly about her body.

"Well, Stephen, shouldn't you greet your bride?"

Stephen blinked several times before he could recover himself. Slowly he walked to her.

Bronwyn was a tall woman, but she had to look up to meet his eyes. He looked worse in the dim light. The candlelight seemed to make eerie shadows of the mud and dried blood on his face.

Lifting a curl from her breast, he felt it between his fingers. "You've made no mistake, Sir Thomas?" he asked quietly, his eyes never leaving hers. "This is the laird of Clan MacArran?"

Bronwyn stepped back. "I have a tongue and a brain of my own. You need not speak as if I weren't here. I am the MacArran of MacArran, and I am sworn to hate all Englishmen, especially ones who insult my clan and me by appearing late and unwashed before me." She turned to Sir Thomas. "I find I am greatly fatigued. I would like to be excused, if you can grant this poor prisoner so great a request."

Sir Thomas frowned. "Stephen is your master now."

She whirled to face him, gave him one scathing look, then left the room without his permission.

Sir Thomas turned to Stephen. "I'm afraid she lacks some in manners. These Scotsmen should take a firm hand to their womenfolk more often. But in spite of her sharp tongue, do you still think she is hideous?"

Stephen could only stare at the doorway where Bronwyn had just left. Visions of her danced before him—a body he thought existed only in dreams, black hair and sapphire eyes. Her chin had jutted out at him so that he ached to kiss it. Her breasts were full, hard against the wet, clinging fabric; her waist small and firm; her hips and thighs round, impudent, tantalizing.

"Stephen?"

Stephen nearly fell into the chair. "Had I known," he

whispered, "had I any idea, I would have come weeks ago when King Henry promised her to me."

"Then she meets with your approval?"

He ran his hand across his eyes. "I think I'm dreaming. Surely no woman could look like that and be alive. You must be playing a trick on me. You don't plan to substitute the real Bronwyn MacArran on my wedding day, do you?"

"I assure you she is real. Why do you think I keep her guarded so heavily? My men are like dogs ready to fight over her at any moment. They stand around and repeat stories of the treacherous Scots to each other, but the truth is, individually each of them has generously offered to take your place in the girl's bed."

Stephen curled his lip at this. "But you have kept them from her."

"It hasn't been easy."

"And what of Chatworth? Has he taken my place with my wife?"

Sir Thomas chuckled. "You sound as if you're jealous, and a moment ago you were willing to give her to Roger. No, Roger has never spent an unchaperoned moment with her. She is an excellent horsewoman, and he would not ride out alone with her for fear she'd run to her Scots."

Stephen snorted in derision. "It's more like the Chatworth name has too many enemies to ride out alone." He stood up. "You should have locked her in her room and not let her ride with any man."

"I'm not so old that I can resist a face like Lady Bronwyn's. She has merely to ask me for something, and I'll give it to her."

"She is my responsibility now. Do I have the southeast room again? Could you send a bath and some food? Tomorrow she won't be insulted by my appearance."

Sir Thomas smiled at Stephen's calm self-assurance. Tomorrow should prove to be an exciting day.

As the early-morning sunlight fell across the room, Bronwyn stood by the table, a note in her hand, a frown creasing her brow. She wore a velvet gown of peacock blue. The puffed sleeves were slashed, and tiffany silk of pale green was drawn through the openings. The front of the skirt was cut to show more of the green tiffany.

She turned to Morag. "He asks me to meet with him in the garden."

"Ye look presentable enough."

Bronwyn crumbled the note in her hand. She was still angry over the way he'd commanded her presence last night. This morning he offered no apology nor explanation for his behavior or his lateness. He merely requested that she do exactly what he wanted when he wanted.

She looked at the serving girl who waited for the answer. "Tell Lord Stephen I will not meet with him."

"Will not, my lady? You are unwell?"

"I am quite well. Give my message as I said, then go to Roger Chatworth and tell him I will meet him in the garden in ten minutes."

The girl's eyes widened, then she left the room.

"Ye'd do well to make peace with yer husband," Morag said. "Ye'll gain nothing by making him angry."

"My husband! My husband! That's all I hear. He is not my husband yet. Am I to jump at his call after he has ignored me these past days? I'm laughed at by everyone in the manor because of him, yet I am to fall at his feet like an obedient wife the moment he bothers to appear. I don't want him to get the idea I'm a pliable, cowardly woman. I want him to know I hate him and all his kind."

"And what of young Chatworth? He's an Englishman."

Bronwyn smiled. "At least he is part Scot. Perhaps I can take him to the Highlands and we can make a whole Scot of him. Come, Rab, we have an appointment."

"Good morning, Stephen," Sir Thomas called. It was a lovely morning, the sunlight bright, the air fresh from a quick shower the previous night. The scent of roses was in the air. "You certainly look better than you did yesterday."

Stephen wore a short jacket of deep brown worsted. It

emphasized the breadth of his shoulders, the thickness of his chest. His legs were encased in hose that hugged every muscular curve of his powerful thighs. His dark blond hair curled along his collar, his eyes sparkled above his strong jaw. He was extraordinarily handsome.

"She refused to see me," he said without small talk.

"I told you her ways were sharp."

Stephen suddenly jerked his head up. Bronwyn was coming toward them. At first he did not see Roger beside her. His eyes were for her alone. Her heavy, thick hair flowed down her back, unhampered, uncovered. The sunlight flashed off it, making it glitter like specks of gold dust. The blue of her dress repeated the blue of her eyes. Her chin was as stubborn in the daylight as it had been at night.

"Good morning," Roger said quietly as they paused for a moment.

Bronwyn nodded to Sir Thomas, then her eyes lingered on Stephen. She did not recognize him. She only thought that she'd never seen a man with such eyes. They seemed to see through her. It was with difficulty that she looked away and continued down the path.

When Stephen recovered enough to finally realize that Roger Chatworth walked beside the woman he was to marry, he growled low in his throat and took a step forward.

Sir Thomas caught his arm. "Don't go after him like that. I'm sure Roger would like nothing better than a fight. And for that matter, so would Bronwyn."

"I may give it to them both!"

"Stephen! Listen to me. You've hurt the girl. You were late, you sent no message. She is a proud woman, more proud than a woman has a right to be. Her father did that when he made her his heir. Give her time. Take her riding tomorrow and talk to her. She's an intelligent woman."

Stephen relaxed and took his hand off his sword hilt. "Talk to her? How could I speak to a woman who looks like that? Last night I could hardly sleep because she haunted me so. Yes, I'll take her riding, though perhaps it's not the kind of riding you mean."

"Your wedding is set for the day after tomorrow. Leave the girl virgin until then."

Stephen shrugged. "She's mine. I'll do as I will with her."

Sir Thomas shook his head at the arrogance of the young man. "Come, look at my new hawks."

"My sister-in-law, Judith, showed Gavin a new lure. Perhaps you'd like to see it."

They left the garden and walked toward the mews.

As she walked with Roger, Bronwyn kept looking about the garden for the man she'd met the night before. The only stranger she saw was the man with Sir Thomas. The rest of the men were the same, staring at her, laughing in the same derogatory way when she passed.

But none of them resembled the ugly, filthy man she'd been dragged before. Once she glanced over her shoulder to where Sir Thomas had been. Both he and the stranger were gone. The man's eyes haunted her. They made her want to run away from him yet at the same time kept her from moving. She blinked to clear her vision and turned to someone safer—Roger. His eyes were smiling and kind and not disturbing in any way.

"Tell me, Lord Roger, what else is there to know about Stephen Montgomery besides that he is an ugly man?"

Roger was startled by her question. He wouldn't have thought a woman introduced to Stephen would think him ugly. Chatworth smiled. "Once the Montgomerys were rich, but their arrogance displeased a king and he took their wealth."

She frowned. "So now they must marry wealth."

"The wealthiest women they can find," he emphasized.

Bronwyn thought of the men who'd died with her father. She would have chosen one of them for her husband, and she would have wed a man who loved her, one who wanted something besides her lands.

As Morag pulled a bucket of water from the well, her eyes never left the quiet young man who leaned against the garden wall. For the last several days Morag had never been too far from Bronwyn's side, though the girl was often unaware of Morag's presence. She didn't like the way Bronwyn was flaunting herself with this Roger Chatworth. Nor did Morag like Chatworth, a man who'd court a woman a few days before she was to marry another.

Morag had heard Bronwyn's ravings the night she'd returned from meeting Stephen Montgomery. She'd heard what a leering, drooling idiot Montgomery was. Bronwyn screamed that she'd never marry him, that he was vile, repulsive.

Morag set the water bucket on the ground. For nearly an hour she'd been watching the blue-eyed man stare at Bronwyn as she sang to a tune Roger was playing on a lute. The stranger had hardly even blinked. Just stood and watched her.

"So ye're the one she's to marry," Morag said loudly.

Stephen had difficulty looking away. He peered down at the gnarled woman and smiled. "How did you know?"

"It's the way ye're lookin' at her, like ye already own her."

Stephen laughed.

"She said ye were the ugliest man created."

Stephen's eyes sparkled. "And what do you think?"

Morag grunted. "Ye'll do. And don't try to get compliments out of me."

"Now that I've been put in my place, perhaps you'll tell me who you are. I take it by your accent that you're a Scot like my Bronwyn."

"I'm Morag of MacArran."

"Bronwyn's maid?"

Morag's back stiffened. "Ye'll do well to learn that we're freemen in Scotland. I do what I can to earn my bread. Why were ye late for yer own weddin'?"

Stephen looked back at Bronwyn. "My sister-in-law was very ill. I couldn't leave until I knew she was going to live."

"And ye couldna' send a message?"

Stephen gave her a sheepish look. "I forgot. I was worried about Judith and I forgot."

Morag gave her little cackle of a laugh. She could feel herself being charmed by this tall knight. "Ye're a good man that ye could care enough about someone else to forget yer own interests."

Stephen's eyes sparkled. "Of course, I had no idea then what your mistress looked like."

The woman laughed again. "Ye're a good, honest boy . . . for an Englishman. Come inside and have some whiskey with me. Ye're not afraid of a little whiskey so early in the day?"

He held out his arm to her. "Maybe I can get you drunk and ply you with questions about Bronwyn."

Morag's cackle rang out across the garden. "There was a time, young man, when men wanted me drunk for other reasons." They walked together into the house.

Bronwyn frowned at the laugh. She'd been all too aware of the man staring at her, and she'd found it oddly unsettling. She glanced at him occasionally, and she had an impression of easy grace, power, and a strength held lightly under control. Morag's too-intimate conversation with the man disturbed her. The old woman didn't usually take to men, especially Englishmen, and Bronwyn wondered how this man could charm her so easily.

"Who is that man with Morag?"

Roger frowned. "I thought you'd met him. That's Stephen."

She stared at Stephen's retreating form, watched how he offered his arm to the wrinkled woman. Morag's head barely reached above Stephen's elbow.

Suddenly Bronwyn felt even further insulted. What kind of man was he that would stand by while another courted the woman he was to wed? He'd been only a few feet away, yet he hadn't even bothered to speak to her.

"Lady Bronwyn, has something upset you?" Roger asked, watching her closely.

"No," she smiled. "Absolutely nothing. Please continue to play."

It was nearly evening when Bronwyn saw Morag again. The setting sun made the room dim. Rab stood close by his mistress's side while she combed her long hair. "I see you had a visitor this afternoon," she said as if it were of no importance.

Morag shrugged.

"Did you speak of anything interesting?"

Again Morag merely shrugged.

Bronwyn put down her comb and went to the window seat where Morag sat. "Will you answer me!"

"Ye're a nosy one. Since when do I have to make an answer about my private conversations?"

"You've been drinking in the afternoon again. I can smell it."

Morag grinned. "That boy can certainly hold his whiskey. I bet he could drink a Scot under the table."

"Who?" Bronwyn demanded.

Morag gave her a sly look. "Why, yer husband of course. Who else would ye be houndin' me for answers about?"

"I am not . . . !" Bronwyn calmed herself. "He is not my husband. He doesn't even bother to speak to me much less appear for his wedding."

"So that's what's still botherin' ye. I figured ye'd see us together. Were ye plannin' to snub him while you had the arm of young Chatworth?"

Bronwyn didn't answer.

"I thought so! Let me tell ye that Stephen Montgomery isn't used to being snubbed by any woman, and if he does decide to marry ye after the way ye've carried on with Chatworth, ye should consider yerself fortunate."

"Fortunate!" Bronwyn managed to gasp. It was all she could say. Another word from Morag and she just might wring that scrawny little neck. "Come, Rab," she commanded and left the room.

She hurried down the stairs to the garden below. It had already grown dark, and the moon shone brightly over the trees and hedges. She walked along the paths for quite some time before she finally sat down on a stone bench in front of a low wall. How she wanted to go home! She wanted to get away from these foreigners, out of these foreign clothes, away from foreign men who looked at her only as a prize of war.

Suddenly Rab stood and gave a low growl of warning.

"Who's there?" she asked.

The man stepped forward. "Stephen Montgomery," he said quietly. He looked larger in the moonlight, towering over her. "May I sit with you?"

"Why not? What say do I have in any matter concerning the English?"

Stephen sat beside her and watched as she controlled Rab with a single hand gesture. He leaned back against the wall, his long legs stretched before him. Bronwyn moved closer to the edge of the bench, away from him. "You'll fall if you move any farther."

She stiffened. "Say what you want and have done with it."

"I have nothing to say," he said easily.

"You certainly seemed to have 'nothing' to say to Morag."

He smiled, the moonlight showing his even, white teeth. "The woman tried to get me drunk."

"And did she succeed?"

"You don't grow up with three brothers and not learn how to drink."

"You merely drank and had no conversation?"

Stephen was silent for a moment. "Why are you so hostile to me?"

She stood quickly. "Did you expect me to welcome you with open arms? I stood in my wedding gown for six hours waiting for you to come. I have seen my entire family slaughtered by the English yet I am told I must marry one. Then I am disregarded as if I did not exist. And now you make no apology to me but ask why I am hostile."

She turned away and started back toward the house.

He grabbed her arm and pulled her around to look at him. She wasn't used to a man so much taller than her. "If I offered you an apology, would you accept it?" His voice was quiet, deep, as liquid silver as the moonlight. It was the first time he'd ever touched her or even been so close. He took her wrists, ran his hands up her arms, gripping her flesh beneath the silk and velvet.

"King Henry only wants peace," he said. "He thinks that if he puts an Englishman in the midst of the Scots, they'll see we aren't so bad."

Bronwyn looked up at him. Her heart was pounding quite hard. She wanted to get away from him, but her body wouldn't obey her. "Your vanity is alarming. Judging from your lack of manners, my Scots would see the English as worse than they feared."

Stephen laughed softly, but it was obvious his mind was not on her words. He moved his left hand to touch her throat.

Bronwyn tried to jerk from his grip. "Unhand me! You have no right to paw me . . . or to laugh at me."

Stephen made no effort to release her. "You're a delicious thing. I can only think that had I not missed our wedding, I could take you upstairs to my chamber this very moment. Perhaps you'd like to forget the day of waiting for our wedding and go with me now?"

She gasped in horror, causing Rab to growl menacingly at Stephen. She twisted sharply away from the hands that held her. Rab stepped between his mistress and the man who touched her. "How dare you?" she said between clenched teeth. "Be grateful I do not turn Rab onto you for that insult."

Stephen laughed in astonishment. "The dog values its life." He took a step closer and Rab growled louder.

"Don't come any closer," Bronwyn warned.

Stephen looked at her in puzzlement. He put his hands up in a pleading gesture. "Bronwyn, I didn't mean to insult you. I—"

"Lady Bronwyn, may I help you?" Roger Chatworth asked, stepping from the shadows of the hedges.

"Have you lately taken to skulking in shadows, Chatworth?" Stephen snapped.

Roger was calm, smiling. "I prefer to think of myself as rescuing ladies in distress." He turned to Bronwyn, his arm extended. "Would you like an escort to your chambers?"

"Chatworth, I'm warning you!"

"Stop it! Both of you!" Bronwyn said, disgusted at their childish quarrel. "Roger, thank you for your kindness, but Rab will be all the escort I need." She turned to Stephen and gave him an icy glare. "As for you, sir, I am grateful for an excuse to leave your vile company." She turned away from the men, and Rab followed her closely as she went back to the house.

Roger and Stephen stared after her for a long while, then, without looking at each other, they turned away.

Bronwyn had difficulty sleeping. Stephen Montgomery disturbed her a great deal. His nearness was unsettling, and tonight she hadn't been able to think properly while he was touching her. Was this the man she was to present to her clan as a leader? He didn't seem to have a serious bone in his body.

When she did sleep, she had bloody dreams. She saw the men of her clan following an English flag, and one by one they were slaughtered. Stephen Montgomery stood holding the banner, ignoring the Scots' death as he kept trying to thrust his hand down Bronwyn's dress.

In the morning her mood wasn't lightened by an invitation from Stephen asking her to go riding with him. She'd crumbled the note and told Morag she wouldn't go. But Morag had a way of nagging that always made anyone do what she wanted. The old woman had already gotten Bronwyn to tell her why she was so angry at Stephen.

Morag snorted. "He's a healthy young man, and he asked ye to spend the night with him. I remember some other men asking, and ye certainly weren't insulted then."

Bronwyn was silent, thinking that the English had ended her days of freedom and laughter.

Morag didn't allow Bronwyn's silence to disturb her. She wanted something, and she wouldn't stop until she got it. "He asks ye to spend the day with him. After all, yer wedding is set for tomorrow."

"How do you know so much? I haven't heard of the new date."

"Stephen told me this morning," Morag said impatiently.

"So! You've seen him again! What is it about him that interests you? There are other men, even Englishmen, who are better."

Morag sniffed. "Not any I've met."

"Roger Chatworth is a kind, intelligent man, and he has a strong strain of Scots blood."

"Did he tell ye that?" Morag snapped. "Perhaps he meant he liked the Scots' land. I think Roger Chatworth would love to have the land ye possess."

Bronwyn's eyes flashed angrily. "Isn't that what all these Englishmen want? If I were fat and old, they'd still want me."

Morag shook her head in disgust. "One moment ye decry Stephen for his hotness, the next ye complain that the men want only yer wealth and not yer person. Give him a chance to redeem himself. Talk to him, spend the day with him, ask him why he was late."

Bronwyn frowned. She didn't want to see Stephen again, ever, if that were possible. She could imagine Roger riding beside her, but she couldn't imagine Stephen doing anything but what he wanted, regardless of her wants. She looked up at Morag. "I'll try to talk to him . . . if he can keep his hands still long enough to talk."

Morag cackled. "I think there's hope in yer voice."

Chapter 3

IN SPITE of her reluctance to spend the day with her betrothed, Bronwyn dressed carefully. She wore a simple wool dress the color of dark wine. It was trimmed with a border of seed pearls around the deep, square neckline. The sleeves were tight, showing the curve of her arm.

As she walked down the stairs, Rab close at her heels, she held her head high. She planned to give Stephen Montgomery a chance to show that he meant well toward her and her people. Perhaps she had hastily judged him and he wanted what was best for her clan. She could forgive him for being late for their wedding. After all, what did her personal inconvenience matter? What was important was Stephen's attitude toward her clan, whether they could accept him or not. She wanted peace between the Scots and the English as much as King Henry did—more, since it was her family members who had been slaughtered.

She stopped at the foot of the stairs and stared out into the sunlit garden. Stephen was leaning against a low stone wall, waiting for her. She had to admit he was a handsome man, and her attraction to him was extraordinary, but she couldn't let her personal feelings—either love or hate—stand before the needs of her clan.

"Good morning," she said quietly as she walked up to him. He stared down at her with a burning intensity. He familiarly took a curl of hair from her shoulder.

"Is this the Scots' custom, to not cover the hair?" He wrapped the silken stuff about his fingers.

"Until a woman has a child, she usually leaves her hair uncovered. Except when wearing a tartan," she added, watching him to see if he'd make any comment or show any sign of recognition.

"A child." Stephen smiled. "We'll see what we can do about that." He nodded toward the far end of the garden. "I have a couple of horses waiting. Are you ready?"

She twisted her head so that he dropped her hair. "A Scotswoman is always ready to ride." She lifted her long skirts and strode ahead of him, ignoring his amused chuckle.

A pretty black mare waited beside Stephen's roan stallion. The mare pranced, lifting her feet high in excitement to be away. Before Stephen could help her, Bronwyn vaulted into the saddle. The heavy, full skirts were awkward, and she cursed the English manner of dress for the hundredth time. She was glad Stephen had not given her one of those absurd sidesaddles like Roger had.

Before Stephen had even mounted his horse, she urged the mare forward. It was a spirited animal, as anxious to run as Bronwyn was. She guided the horse, full speed, toward the path Roger had shown her. She leaned forward in the saddle, delighting in the wind on her face and throat.

Suddenly she saw a movement out of the corner of her eye. Twisting around, she saw that Stephen was close behind her, gaining on her. She laughed aloud. No Englishman born could beat a Scotswoman on a horse! She talked to the mare and applied the crop to her flank. The horse sprang forward as if it had wings. A feeling of power and exultation coursed through Bronwyn.

Glancing over her shoulder, she frowned at seeing Stephen still gaining on her. Ahead the path narrowed, too narrow for two horses side by side. If he wanted to pass her, he'd have to leave the path, go into the forest, and risk running his horse's legs into a rabbit hole or hitting a tree. She guided the mare to the middle of the path. She knew what a Scotsman would do if she blocked his path, but these Englishmen were soft things, lacking guts and stamina.

The mare ran at a hard run. Stephen was nearly on her now, and Bronwyn smiled in triumph at his confusion. It was when her mare reared slightly and screamed that Bronwyn had her hands full keeping her seat. Stephen's war-trained stallion had nipped the mare's rump as it crowded the smaller horse.

Bronwyn worked hard at controlling the mare and cursed the English for taking her own horse from her. This animal was a stranger to her and not as receptive to her commands.

The mare screamed again as the stallion bit it a second time, then, against Bronwyn's commands, it pulled aside and Stephen went thundering by. The look he threw Bronwyn made her utter a horrendous Gaelic oath. She jerked the reins and led the mare back to the center of the path.

Through all of the race Bronwyn had never allowed the mare to slow down. It was only through her extraordinary affinity with horses that she was able to control the animal as it jumped into the forest, away from the charging stallion.

When she came to the stream and jumped it, Stephen was there, waiting for her. He'd dismounted and was standing calmly by his horse as it drank. "Not bad." He grinned up at her. "You have a tendency to pull the right rein harder than the left, but you could be quite good with a little training."

Bronwyn's eyes shot blue fire at him. Training! She'd had her own pony when she was four, had ridden with her father in cattle raids since she was eight. She'd ridden at night across the moors, up the rocks by the sea coast . . . and he said she needed training!

Stephen laughed. "Don't look so stricken. If it'll make you feel any better, you're the best woman rider I've ever seen. You could give most Englishwomen lessons."

"Women!" she managed to gasp. "I could give all Englishmen lessons!"

"From where I stand, you just lost a race to an Englishman. Now get off that horse and rub it down. You can't let a horse stand in its own sweat."

Now he dared tell her how to tend to her horse. She sneered at him, raised her riding whip, and bent forward to strike him. Stephen easily sidestepped the lash, then gave her wrist one sharp, painful turn, and the crop fell to the ground. Bronwyn was caught off balance by the unexpected movement. The heavy English dress had wrapped around her leg in such a way that she lost her footing in the stirrup and pitched forward.

She grabbed the pommel and would have recovered herself but Stephen's hands were already on her waist. He pulled her toward him and she pulled away from him. For a moment it was a struggle of strength, but what infuriated Bronwyn was that Stephen seemed to be thoroughly enjoying her humiliation. He was playing with her, letting her seem to win before he pulled her down again.

He laughed and gave one powerful tug and lifted her from the saddle, lifting her high above his head. "Did you know that that hole in your chin gets deeper when you're angry?"

"Hole!" she gasped and drew her foot back to strike him.

Considering that her feet were a yard above the ground and her sole support was Stephen's hands on her waist, it was not a wise move. He laughed at her again, tossed her in the air, then, as she struggled for balance, he caught her in his arms. He hugged her to him and kissed her ear loudly. "Are you always so entertaining?" he laughed.

She refused to look at him even though he held her aloft. Her arms were pinned to her sides or she would have struck him. "Are you always so flippant?" she retorted. "Do you never have a thought besides that of pawing women?"

He rubbed his face on her soft cheek. "You smell good." He looked back at her. "I'll admit you're the first woman who's affected me like this. But then you're the first wife I've had, a woman who was completely and totally mine."

She stiffened even more in his arms, if that were physically possible. "Is that all a woman is to you? Something to own?"

He smiled, shook his head, and set her down, his hands on her shoulders. "Of course. What else are women good for? Now pull some grass and get that sweat off your horse."

She turned away from him gratefully. They didn't speak while they unsaddled their horses and began rubbing them down. Stephen made no attempt to help her with the heavy saddle, pleasing Bronwyn because she would have refused him. She might be a woman, but she was far from helpless as he seemed to think.

When the animals were tethered, she looked back at him.

"At least you know something about horses," he said. He laughed at her expression, then went to stand beside her. He ran his hand down her arm, and his face became serious.

"Please don't start that again," she snapped and jerked away from him. "Do you never think of anything else?"

His eyes sparkled. "Not when you're around. I think you've bewitched me. I'd make you another proposition, but the last one made you too angry."

Mentioning the scene in the garden made Bronwyn look about her. Rab lay quietly by the stream. It was odd that he'd not threatened Stephen when he'd touched her. The dog still growled whenever Roger got too near. "Where are your men?"

"With Sir Thomas, I assume."

"You don't need them for protection? What about my Scots? Didn't you know they wait in the forest, ready to rescue me?"

Stephen took her hand and pulled her toward some rocks. She tried to free herself but he wouldn't allow it. He pulled her down to sit beside him, then stretched out beside her, his head cradled in his hands. Apparently he didn't seem to think her questions deserved an answer. Instead, he stared up through the trees at the brilliant blue sky. "Why did your father name you chief of his clan?"

Bronwyn stared at him for a moment, then smiled. This was what she wanted, to talk to him about what was most important in the world—her people. "I was to marry one of three men, any one of whom would have made an excellent laird. But none of the young men was within the nine degrees of kinship from which a chief can be chosen. My father named me the next MacArran, understanding that I'd marry one of those men."

"And the men?"

Bronwyn's mouth twisted angrily. "They were killed with my father. By the English!"

Stephen didn't seem to respond except for a slight knitting of his brows. "So now whoever marries you must become the laird?"

"*I* am the laird of MacArran," she stated firmly and started to rise.

He grabbed her hand and pulled her back to the ground. "I wish you'd stop being angry with me for longer than a breath. How am I supposed to understand you if you run away?"

"I don't run away from you!" She snatched her hand away because he'd begun to kiss her fingertips. Bronwyn made herself ignore the sensations running along her arm all the way to her earlobe.

Stephen sighed and lay back down. "I'm afraid I can't look at you and talk at the same time." He paused. "Surely your father must have had another relative who could inherit."

Bronwyn calmed herself. She knew exactly what this stupid Englishman was saying. He meant that surely *any* man would have been better than a female. She did not mention her older brother, Davey. "The Scots believe women have intelligence and strength of character. They do not expect us to be only bearers of children and nothing else."

Stephen grunted in reply, and Bronwyn had a delicious vision of smashing his head with a large rock. She smiled at the thought. As if understanding her, Rab lifted his big head and looked at her in question.

Stephen seemed unaware of the exchange near him. "What would be my duties as laird?"

She gritted her teeth and tried to be patient. "I am the MacArran, and my men answer to me. They would have to accept you before they obeyed you."

"Accept me?" he asked and turned toward her, but her

breasts above the pearl-bordered neckline distracted him so badly that he had to look away in order to keep his composure. "I would think it would be more whether I accepted them."

"Spoken like a true Englishman!" she sneered. "You think that the circumstances of your birth place you above everyone else. You think your ways and ideas make you better than the poor Scots. No doubt you think us cruel and savage compared to you. But we do not capture your women and force them to marry our Scotsmen, though they'd make better husbands than any Englishman."

Stephen didn't take offense at her outburst. He merely shrugged. "I'm sure every man thinks his homeland is the best. Truthfully, I know very little about Scotland or the people there. I spent some time in the Lowlands, but I don't believe that's like the Highlands."

"The Lowlanders are more English than Scots!"

He was quiet for a moment. "It seems that being the chief of a clan—pardon me," he said with an amused little chuckle, "being the husband of a chief entails some responsibility. What must I do to be accepted?"

Bronwyn relaxed her shoulders. Since he looked away from her, she had leisure to look at him. He was so tall, taller than most of the men she'd met. His long body stretched out before her, and she was well aware of his nearness. In spite of his words she wanted to sit beside him, enjoyed gazing at him, at his strong legs, at the thickness of his chest, at the dark blond curls along his collar. She liked that his dress was subdued, not gaudy like so many of the Englishmen's. She wondered how he'd look in a Scots tartan, his legs bare from mid-thigh to just below his knees.

"You must dress as a Scot," she said quietly. "The men will always be aware that you're one of the enemy if you do not wear a plaid."

Stephen frowned. "You mean run around barelegged? I heard the Highlands get quite cold."

"Of course, if you aren't man enough—" His arrogant look stopped her.

"What else?"

"You must become a MacArran, be a MacArran. The MacGregors will be your enemies, your name will become MacArran. You will—"

"What!" Stephen said as he jumped to his feet and towered over her. "Change my name! You mean to say *I*, a man, am to take my wife's name?" He turned away from her. "That's the most absurd thing I've ever heard. Do you know who I am? I am a Montgomery! The Montgomerys have lasted through hundreds of wars, through many kings. Other families have risen and fallen, but the Montgomerys have survived. My family has owned the same land for over four hundred years."

He turned back to her and ran his hand through his hair. "And now you expect me to give up the Montgomery name for that of my wife?" He paused, then chuckled. "My brothers would laugh me to hell and back if I were to consider such a thing."

Bronwyn rose slowly, letting his words sink in. "You have brothers to carry on your family name. Do you know what would happen if I were to take an Englishman home who does not even attempt to understand our ways? First my men would kill him, then I would need to choose a new husband. Do you know what conflict that would cause? There are several young men who'd like to become my husband. They would fight."

"So! I'm to give up my name so you can control your men? And what if they still didn't accept me? Perhaps I should dye my hair or cut off an arm to please them. No! They'll obey me or they'll feel this!" He quickly drew his long sword from the sheath at his side.

Bronwyn stared at him. He was speaking of murdering her people, her friends, her relatives, the people whose lives she held in her hands. She could *not* return to Scotland with this madman.

"I cannot marry you," she said quietly, her eyes hard and deadly serious.

"I don't believe you have a choice," Stephen said as he

resheathed his weapon. He hadn't meant to get so angry, but the woman needed to know from the start who was in control . . . as did the Scots she called "her" men. "I am an Englishman," he said quietly, "and I will remain English wherever I go. You should understand that, as I don't believe you're willing to change your Scots ways."

Her body was feeling quite cold in spite of the warm autumn day. "It is not the same. You'd be living with my people, day in and day out, year after year. Can't you see that they could *not* accept you if you strut about in your fine English clothes with your old English name? Every time they saw you, they'd remember their children the English had killed, they'd see my father, slain while he was a young man."

Her plea reached Stephen. "I will wear the Scots' garb. I'll agree to that."

Sudden, red-hot anger replaced the coldness in Bronwyn's body. "So you'll agree to wear the plaid and saffron shirt! No doubt you like the image of showing your fine, strong legs to my women."

Stephen's mouth dropped open slightly, then he grinned so broadly he threatened to split his face in half. "I hadn't thought of that, no, but it's nice to know you have." He stuck his leg out, flexed the big muscle running from the top of his knee. "Do you think your women will agree with you?" His eyes sparkled. "Will you be jealous?"

Bronwyn could only stare in astonishment. This man could not be serious for a moment. He teased her and laughed at her when she talked of life and death. She grabbed her skirts and started toward the stream.

"Bronwyn!" Stephen called. "Wait! I didn't mean to make light of what you said." He'd instantly understood his mistake. He grabbed her wrist, whirled her to face him. "Please," he begged, his heart in his eyes. "I didn't mean to offend you. It's just that you're so beautiful that I can't think. I look at your hair and I want to touch it. I want to kiss your eyes. That damned dress is so low you're about to fall out of it, and it's driving me insane. How do you expect me to talk seriously about the disputes between the Scots and the Englishmen?"

"Disputes!" she spat. " 'Tis more like war!"

"War, whatever," he said, his focus on her breasts, his hands running up her arms. "God! I can't stand so near you and not have you. I've been in this condition so long I'm in pain."

Involuntarily she looked down, then her face turned red.

Stephen smiled at her with hooded eyes, a knowing smile.

She curled her lip back and snarled at him. He was a low-minded man, and he obviously thought she shared his lack of character. She twisted away from his searching hands, and when he refused to release her, she gave him a sharp shove. Stephen didn't budge, but the impact against his hard chest made Bronwyn lose her balance. She had no idea she was so near the edge of the stream.

She fell backward as she frantically tried to grab hold of something. Stephen put out his hand to catch her, but even as it touched her wrist, she slapped at it. He gave a slight shrug and stepped back, since he had no desire to wet his own clothes from the splash she was going to make.

The water from the stream must have come from the mountains of the Highlands. There was no other way it could have been so cold. Bronwyn sat down hard in the water, and the heavy wool dress soaked up the liquid ice as if it'd been waiting for such a chance.

She sat still for a moment, slightly dazed, and looked up at Stephen. He was grinning at her as a cold drop of water clung to the tip of her nose. Rab stood beside Stephen and began to bark at her, his tail wagging in delight at her game.

"Could I offer you assistance?" Stephen asked cheerfully.

Bronwyn brushed a wet black curl off her cheek. Any moment her teeth would begin chattering, but she would yank them from her mouth before she'd let him see. "No, thank you," she said as loftily as she could manage.

She looked around her for something to use as balance, but there was nothing unless she crawled to a rock some feet away. She would never crawl before him! "Come, Rab!" she commanded, and the large dog quickly splashed into the water after his mistress.

Bronwyn wiped more water from her face, studiously avoiding Stephen's grinning face. Placing her hands on the dog's back, she started to lift herself up. The wool dress was extremely heavy to begin with, but thoroughly soaked with water, it was impossible. This in addition to the slippery stones under her feet were too much.

She was in a half-crouch, a position that had taken her minutes to achieve, when her feet flew out from under her. Rab jumped away as Bronwyn fell again, this time flat on her back, her face going under the water. She came up gasping.

The first sound she heard was Stephen's laughter, then with a sense of betrayal she heard Rab's bark—a bark that sounded suspiciously like a canine laugh.

"Damn both of you!" she hissed and grabbed the cold, clinging, offending skirt.

Stephen shook his head at her, then entered the water. Before she could speak he'd bent and picked her up in his arms. She would have given a lot then to be able to pull him into the water with her, but his footing was too sure. When he bent to lift her, he kept his legs straight, using only his back and avoiding most of the contact with the water.

"I would like you to release me," she said as primly as possible.

Stephen gave a one-shoulder shrug, then dropped his arms. In a reflex motion, to keep from falling back into the icy water, she gasped and threw her arms about his neck.

"Much better!" he laughed and hugged her to him so tightly she couldn't remove her arms.

He waded ashore with her and then stopped, still holding her. "I don't believe I've ever seen blue eyes with black hair before," he whispered, his eyes devouring her face. "I'm more than sorry I missed our wedding."

She knew exactly why he was sorry, and his reasons didn't help her mood any. "I am cold. Please release me," she said flatly.

"I could warm you," he said as he drew her earlobe between his teeth.

Bronwyn felt a chill run along her arm, a chill that had nothing to do with the wet dress she wore. The sensation frightened her; she didn't want it. "Please let me go," she said softly.

Stephen's head came up quickly, and he looked at her with concern. "You are cold. Take that dress off and you can wear my jacket. Should I build a fire?"

"I'd prefer that you released me and we rode back to the house."

Reluctantly, Stephen stood her in front of him. "You're shivering," he said as he moved his hands along her arms. "You'll be ill if you don't get out of that dress."

She backed away from him. The sodden gown slapped about her legs, the sleeves dragged her arms down.

Stephen gave her a look of disgust. "That damned thing is so heavy you can scarcely walk. Why in the world you women wear such fashions is beyond me. It's so heavy now I doubt if your horse could carry you."

Bronwyn straightened her shoulders even though the dress threatened to drag them down again. "Women! It's you Englishmen who impose these fashions on your women. It is an attempt to keep them immobile since you aren't men enough to deal with free women. I had this dress made so I wouldn't shame my clan. The English too often judge a person by her clothes."

She held the fabric out. "Do you know how much this cost me? I could have purchased a hundred head of cattle for what this one garment cost me. Yet you have ruined it."

"I? It was your stubbornness that ruined it. Just as now. You stand there shivering because you'd rather freeze than do what I say."

She gave him a mocking smile. "At least you are not completely stupid. You do understand some things."

Stephen chuckled. "I understand much more than you imagine." He removed his jacket and held it out to her. "If you're so afraid of me, go into the woods and change."

"Afraid!" Bronwyn snorted and ignored the offered clothing. She walked slowly, kicking the skirt as she moved, to the saddle on the ground. She withdrew a Highland tartan from the attached bag. She didn't bother looking back at Stephen as she went into the woods, Rab following her.

She had a great deal of difficulty with the catches that ran down the back of the dress. By the time she got to the last one, her skin was nearly blue. She grabbed the dress and pulled it from her shoulders, the last hooks snapping apart. She let the dress fall in a heap at her feet.

The thin linen of her undertunic and the once-stiff petticoat were dyed pink from the burgundy wool. She longed to remove her underwear but didn't dare with someone like Stephen Montgomery near. At the thought, she looked around her to make sure he wasn't spying on her, then lifted the petticoat and removed her silk stockings. When she'd removed as much clothing as she dared, she wrapped herself in her plaid and walked back to the stream.

Stephen was nowhere in sight.

"Looking for me?" he asked from behind her.

When she turned, he was grinning at her, her wet dress thrown over his arm. It was obvious he'd hidden and watched her undress.

Her eyes were cold as she stared at him. "You think you've won, don't you? You're so confident that soon I will be at your feet that you treat me like a toy of yours. I'm not a toy, and most especially, I am not yours. For all your English vanity, I am a Scotswoman and I have some power."

She turned to where the black mare was tied; then stopped and looked back at him. "What power I have, I will use." Ignoring his presence, she pulled the tartan up to her knees, grabbed the horse's mane, and swung onto its back. She kicked it forward, already in a gallop by the time she reached Stephen.

He didn't try to stop her but mounted his stallion bareback and followed her. He would send someone later for the saddles.

It seemed a long way back to the manor house, and the

horse's sharp backbone hitting him seemed just punishment for his behavior. She was a proud woman, and he had treated her badly. It was just that she did things to him. He looked at her, and he had difficulty thinking. She tried to talk to him, and all he could think about was getting her in bed. Later, he thought, after they were married and he'd bedded her a few times, he'd be able to look at her without his blood boiling.

Bronwyn stood before the mirror in her room. She felt much better now that she'd had a hot bath and some time to think. Stephen Montgomery was not the man to become her husband. If he antagonized her people as he did her, he would be killed instantly, and then the English would come down upon their heads. She'd not marry a man who would surely cause war as well as strife within her clan.

She adjusted her hair again. She'd pulled the top of it back from her forehead, allowing the rest of it to hang freely down her back. A servant girl had brought her freshly cut autumn daisies, and Bronwyn had made a band of these across the back of her head.

Her gown was of emerald-green silk. The trailing sleeves were lined with gray squirrel fur, accenting the gray silk revealed by the part in the front of the bell-shaped skirt.

"I want to look my best," Bronwyn said, catching a glimpse of Morag in the mirror.

Morag snorted. "I'd like to think ye were dressin' to please Sir Stephen, but I don't think so."

"I will *never* dress for him!"

"As far as I can tell, the man only wants ye undressed," Morag mumbled.

Bronwyn didn't bother to answer, nor would she allow herself to become upset. What she needed to do would affect the lives of hundreds of people, and she couldn't enter upon it when she was angry.

Sir Thomas was waiting for her in the library. His smile of greeting was cordial but reserved. He heartily wished he could get rid of the beautiful woman so his men would stop snapping over her.

When Bronwyn was seated, a glass of wine refused, she began. She knew the real reason that she couldn't accept Stephen: because he refused to accept the Scots' ways. But she'd planned a more English reason to give Sir Thomas.

"But my dear," he said in exasperation, "Stephen was chosen for you by King Henry."

Bronwyn lowered her head in shy submission. "And I'm willing to accept a husband chosen for me by the English king, but I am chief of Clan MacArran, and Stephen Montgomery is merely a knight. I would have trouble with my men if I were to marry him."

"But you think they'd accept Lord Roger?"

"Since his brother's recent death, he is an earl, more nearly my rank as chief."

Sir Thomas grimaced. He was getting too old for this sort of thing. Damn those Scots anyway for allowing a woman to think for herself. None of this would be happening if Jamie MacArran hadn't named his daughter his successor.

He walked to the door and asked for Stephen and Roger to be brought to him.

When the young men were seated, one on each side of Lady Bronwyn, Sir Thomas told them of her plan. He watched the men's faces carefully. He saw the light come into Roger's eyes, and Sir Thomas turned away from him. Stephen sat quietly; the only sign he gave that he heard was a slight darkening of his eyes. Bronwyn never moved, the green of her dress giving her eyes a new depth, the daisies in her hair making her appear sweet and innocent.

Roger was the first to speak when Sir Thomas finished. "The Lady Bronwyn is right. Her title should be honored."

Stephen's eyes flashed. "Of course you'd think that, since you plan to gain a great deal by such a decision." He turned to Sir Thomas. "The king spent a year choosing a bride for me. He wanted to reward my family for helping patrol the Lowlands borders."

Bronwyn whirled on him. "Kill and rape, you mean!"

"I meant what I said: patrol. We did very little killing."

His eyes went to her breasts and his voice lowered. "And almost no raping."

Bronwyn stood. "Sir Thomas, you've been to the Highlands." She ignored his shudder of unpleasant memory. "My people would be dishonored if I were to bring back a lowly knight who was to be their laird. King Henry wants peace. This man," she pointed at Stephen, "would only cause more trouble if he entered the Highlands."

Stephen laughed as he stepped behind Bronwyn and put a strong arm around her waist. He held her tightly against him. "This isn't a matter of diplomacy but a girl's anger. I asked her to come early to my bed, before the wedding, and she thought I'd insulted her."

Sir Thomas smiled, relieved. He started to speak.

Roger stepped forward. "I protest! Lady Bronwyn is not a woman to be put aside so easily. What she says makes sense." He turned to Stephen. "Are you afraid to put the winning of her to a test?"

Stephen raised one eyebrow. "I don't believe the Montgomery name has 'coward' attached to it. What did you have in mind?"

"Gentlemen! Please!" Sir Thomas fairly shouted. "King Henry sent Lady Bronwyn here for a wedding, a happy occasion."

Bronwyn jerked from Stephen's grasp. "Happy! How can you say the word when I am to be married to this greedy, insufferable lowling? I swear I'll murder him in his sleep the first opportunity I get."

Stephen smiled at her. "So long as it's after the wedding night, I might be content."

Bronwyn sneered.

"Lady Bronwyn!" Sir Thomas commanded. "Would you leave us?"

She took a deep breath. She'd said what she wanted, and now she could no longer bear being near Stephen. With great grace Bronwyn lifted her skirts and stepped from the room.

"Stephen," Sir Thomas began. "I wouldn't like to be the cause of your murder."

"I'm not threatened by the words of a woman."

Sir Thomas frowned. "You say that from innocence. You've never been north to the Highlands. There is no government there, not like we have. The lairds rule their clans, and no one rules the lairds. All Lady Bronwyn has to do is murmur discontent, and every man, or woman for that matter, in her clan would be ready to end your life."

"I am willing to take that chance."

Sir Thomas stepped forward and put a hand on Stephen's shoulder. "I knew your father, and I feel he wouldn't want me to send his son into sure death."

Stephen stepped back from the friendly hand. His face changed into one of furor. "I want that woman! You have no right to take her from me." He whirled on Roger, who had begun to smile. "I'll meet you on a battlefield, and then we'll see who is most worthy to claim chiefship."

"Accepted!" Roger snapped. "Tomorrow morning. The winner will wed her in the afternoon, bed her at night."

"Done!"

"No," Sir Thomas murmured, but he knew he'd lost. They were two hot-blooded young men. He sighed heavily. "Leave me, both of you. Prepare your own battlefield. I want nothing to do with it."

Chapter 4

STEPHEN STOOD beside his stallion, covered in steel from head to foot, the sun beating down on his armor. It was weighing him down, but he'd long ago learned to handle its weight.

"My lord," his squire said, "the sun will be in your eyes." Stephen nodded curtly. He was well aware of the fact. "Let Chatworth have what advantage he can. He'll need it."

The boy smiled in pride at his master. It had taken a long while to dress Sir Stephen in the layers of padded cotton and leather that went under the steel plates.

Stephen mounted his horse with ease, then reached to take his lance and shield from the boy. He didn't bother to look to his right. He knew Bronwyn stood there with a face as white as the gold-trimmed ivory dress she wore. It didn't help his spirit any to know the woman would like to see him lose or perhaps even be killed.

He adjusted the long wooden lance against his armor. He and Roger had not spoken since last night, and Sir Thomas had been true to his word; he was ignoring the fight. Thus no rules had been established. It was a joust, a fight to see who could stay on his horse longest.

Stephen's war-horse, a massive black stallion with heavy feathering on its feet, pranced once in impatience. The animals were bred for power and stamina rather than swiftness.

Stephen's men surrounded him, then pulled back as Roger appeared at the far end of the sand-covered field. A low wooden fence ran down the center.

Stephen lowered his helmet plate, leaving only a slit for his eyes, his head completely covered. A young man raised a banner, and when he lowered it, the two noble men charged at each other, lances raised. It was not a test of speed, but of strength. Only a man in the peak of condition could withstand the lance shattering against his shield.

Stephen gripped his horse hard with his powerful thighs when Roger's lance squarely hit his shield. The lance shattered, as did Stephen's. Stephen reined his horse back to his end of the field.

"He's good, my lord," one of Stephen's men said as he handed his master a new lance. "Watch the tip this time. I think he means to run it under your shield."

Stephen nodded curtly and shut his helmet again.

The banner was lowered to begin the second charge. All Stephen had to do was knock his opponent from his horse, and by all rules of jousting, he'd win. When Roger charged again, Stephen dipped his shield lower and effectively kept Roger from hitting him. Taken aback, Roger didn't see Stephen's lance as it struck his side. He reeled in the saddle and nearly fell from the mighty blow, but he managed to keep his seat.

"He's dazed," the man at Stephen's side said. "Hit him this time and he'll go down."

Again Stephen nodded and slammed his helmet shut.

Roger concentrated on his attack and didn't take care of defending himself. As he dipped his lance Stephen hit him again, this time much harder than before. Roger fell backward then toward the side, landing hard in the dirt at the feet of Stephen's horse.

Stephen glanced briefly at his opponent lying in the dust and then looked away toward Bronwyn.

But Roger Chatworth was not a man to turn one's back on. He grabbed a spike-headed club from his horse's saddle and ran with it aloft.

"Stephen!" someone screamed.

Stephen reacted instantly but not quite quickly enough. Roger's club came down hard on Stephen's left thigh. The steel armor bent and jammed into his flesh. The unexpected impact sent him reeling, and he fell from his stallion, clutching at the pommel.

Stephen righted himself and saw that Roger was again advancing on him, prepared to attack again. He rolled away, steel hinges creaking in protest.

Stephen was thrown a club just as Roger's club hit his shoulder. Stephen grunted and slammed his club into Roger's side. As Roger staggered sideways Stephen pursued him. Stephen meant to win this battle.

His second blow, on Roger's right shoulder blade, sent Roger sprawling. The armor protected the men from cut flesh, but the immense force of each blow was stunning.

Roger lay still, obviously dazed. Stephen withdrew his sword, straddled Roger's shoulders, and kicked open his face plate. Then Stephen, with both hands on the hilt, held the sword over him.

Roger glared up at the victor. "Kill me and be done with it! I would've killed you."

Stephen stared down at him. "I've won. It's enough for me." He stepped to one side of Roger's inert form and removed his gauntlet. He held out his bare hand, palm up to his prostrate opponent.

"You insult me!" Roger hissed, lifting his head and spitting on Stephen's offered hand. "I'll remember this."

Stephen raked his hand across his armor. "I'm not likely to forget it." He resheathed his sword and turned away.

He walked straight to Bronwyn, who was standing beside Morag. Bronwyn was rigid as Stephen approached. He stopped before her and slowly removed his helmet, tossing it to Morag, who caught it with a grin.

Bronwyn retreated a step.

"You cannot escape me again," Stephen said as he grasped her upper arm with his uncovered hand. He pulled her to him, his one arm stronger than her whole body.

He pulled her soft body against the steel of his armor. The coldness of it, the hardness of it, made Bronwyn gasp. More steel struck her back as his arms encircled her.

"You're mine now," Stephen murmured as his lips touched hers.

It was not the first time Bronwyn had kissed a man. There had been several stolen moments during fast cattle raids across the heather.

But it was the first time she'd experienced anything like this kiss. It was soft and sweet, but at the same time it was taking from her things she'd never given before. His mouth played with hers, touching it, caressing it, yet plundering it. She stood on tiptoe to reach him better, turned her head to more of a slant. He seemed to want her to part her lips, and she did so. The cold-hot touch of the tip of his tongue on hers sent little shivers down her spine. Her body seemed to go limp, and when her head moved back, his followed hers, holding her captive more than any chains could.

Abruptly Stephen pulled away, and when Bronwyn opened her eyes, he was grinning insolently at her. She realized that she was held entirely by his grip, that his kiss had made her surrender her entire body weight to him. She straightened, letting her own feet support her again.

Stephen chuckled. "You are mine more than you know." He released her and pushed her toward Morag. "Go and ready yourself for our wedding . . . if you can wait that long."

Bronwyn turned away quickly. She did not want him or anyone else to see her brilliantly red face or the tears that were forming. What none of his insults could do, his kiss was accomplishing in making her cry.

"What are ye greeting about?" Morag snapped as soon as they were alone in the room. "He's a fine, handsome man ye're to marry. Ye got your way, and he had to fight for ye. He proved himself to be a strong, aggressive fighter. What more do ye want?"

"He treats me like a tavern wench!"

"He treats ye like a *woman*. That other one, that Roger, can't see ye for yer lands. I doubt he even knows ye're a woman."

"That's not true! He's like . . . Ian!"

Morag frowned as she thought of the young man, killed

when he was only twenty-five. "Ian was like a brother to ye. Ye grew up with him. Had he lived to marry ye he'd probably have felt guilty about bedding ye, felt like he was taking his sister to bed."

Bronwyn grimaced. "There's certainly no guilt in this Stephen Montgomery. He wouldn't know the meaning of the word."

"What's upsetting ye?" Morag demanded so loudly that Rab gave a little bark of concern. She stopped, and the wrinkles in her face rearranged themselves. Her voice became quieter. "Is it tonight?"

Bronwyn looked at Morag with such a bleak expression that Morag gave a snort of laughter.

"So ye are a virgin! I was never sure what with the way the laird let ye run wild with the young men."

"I was always protected. You know that."

"Sometimes a young man isn't the best protector of a young woman's virtue." She smiled. "Now stop yer frettin'. 'Tis an enjoyable experience ahead of ye; and unless I miss my guess, this Stephen knows how to make a woman's first time easier."

Bronwyn walked to the window. "I imagine he does. If I believed the way he acts, I'd think he's bedded half of England."

Morag looked at Bronwyn's back. "Are ye afraid yer inexperience will displease him?"

Bronwyn whirled about. "No pale Englishwoman can compete with a Scotswoman!"

Morag chuckled. "Yer color's comin' back. Now out of that dress, and let's get ye in yer weddin' dress. It's only a few more hours before ye go to the kirk."

Bronwyn's face lost its color again, and with resignation she set about the long process of changing.

Stephen sat buried up to his neck in a tub of very hot water. His leg and shoulder burned from the blows Roger had given him. His eyes were closed as he heard the door open and shut. "Go away!" he growled. "I'll call when I need you."

"And what will you call?" came an amused, familiar voice.

Stephen's eyes flew open, and the next minute he was bounding across the room, nude, dripping water. "Chris!" he laughed as he clasped his friend to him.

Christopher Audley returned the greeting briefly, then pushed Stephen away. "You're soaking me, and I don't want to have to change again for your wedding. I haven't missed it, have I?"

Stephen stepped back into the tub. "Sit over there so I can see you. You've lost weight again. Didn't France agree with you?"

"It agreed too well. The women nearly wore me away with their demands." He set a chair by the tub. He was a short, thin, dark man with a small nose and chin and a short, well-trimmed beard. His eyes were brown and large, rather like a doe's. He used his soft, expressive eyes to their best advantage in bringing women to him.

He nodded toward Stephen's shoulder and the bruise. "Is that a new wound? I didn't know you'd been fighting lately."

Stephen dipped a handful of water over the injury. "I had to fight Roger Chatworth for the woman I'm to wed."

"Fight?" Chris said in astonishment. "I spoke to Gavin before I left, and he said you were almost sick at the prospect of the marriage." He smiled. "I saw that wife of Gavin's. She's a beauty, but from what I hear she's a hellion. She had the whole court agog with her escapades."

Stephen waved his hand in dismissal. "Judith's calm compared to Bronwyn."

"Is Bronwyn the heiress you're to marry? Gavin said she was fat and ugly."

Stephen chuckled as he soaped his legs. "You won't believe Bronwyn when you see her. She has hair so black that it almost makes a mirror. The sun flashes off of it. She has blue eyes and a chin that juts out in defiance every time I speak to her."

"And the rest of her?"

Stephen sighed. "Magnificent!"

Chris laughed at Stephen's tone. "Two brothers couldn't be as fortunate as you and Gavin. But why did you have to fight for her? I thought King Henry gave her to you."

Stephen stood up and caught the towel Chris tossed him. "I was four days late to the wedding, and I'm afraid Bronwyn has taken a . . . disliking to me. She has some absurd idea that if I marry her I must become a Scot, even change my name. I don't know for sure, but I think Chatworth may have hinted that he'd do anything she wanted if she married him."

Chris snorted. "And no doubt she believed him. Roger always could charm the women, but I've never trusted him."

"We jousted for her, but when I tossed him in the dirt, he came at my back with a war club."

"The bastard! I always wondered how much of his brother was in him. Edmund was a vile man. I guess you won the fight."

"I was so damn mad that he'd attack me that I was close to killing him. Actually he begged me to do so, said I'd insult him if I didn't."

Chris was thoughtful for a moment. "You've made an enemy of him. That could be bad."

Stephen walked to the bed, where his wedding clothes lay. "I don't blame the man for trying for Bronwyn. She'd make any man fight for her."

Chris grinned. "I've never seen you act this way toward a woman before."

"I've never seen a woman like Bronwyn before." He stopped, then yelled "Come in" to a knock on the door.

A young maidservant stood there, her arms outstretched, a shimmering gown of silver cloth across them. She stared at the bare-chested Stephen.

"What is it?" he demanded. "Why didn't you give the dress to the Lady Bronwyn?"

The girl's lower lip trembled.

Stephen pulled his shirt on, then took the dress from the girl. "You can tell me," he said quietly. "I know the Lady Bronwyn has a sharp tongue. I won't beat you for repeating what she said."

The girl looked up. "She was in the hall, my lord, when I found her, and there were several people about. I gave her the dress, and she seemed to like it."

"Yes! Go on!"

The girl finished in a rush. "But when I said it was from you, to be worn for the wedding, she threw it back at me. She said she had a wedding dress, and she'd never wear yours. Oh, my lord, it was awful. She was very loud, and all the people laughed."

Stephen took the gown from the girl and gave her a copper penny.

As soon as the girl was gone, Chris began to laugh. "A sharp tongue did you say? It sounds to me like it's more like a knife blade."

Angrily Stephen thrust his arms through his doublet. "I've had about enough of this. It's time someone taught that young lady some manners."

He tossed the dress over his shoulder and left the room, taking long strides toward the Great Hall. He'd gone to a lot of trouble to get the exquisite garment. Bronwyn had complained about her ruined dress after she'd fallen in the stream, and so Stephen had made an attempt to repay her—not that he'd done anything to cause her to fall in the water, of course. He'd ridden into town and found the silver fabric, then paid four women to sit up all night sewing it. The material was a soft, fine wool with every other weft-thread a hair-thin piece of silver wire. It was heavy and luxurious. It shimmered and glowed even in the darkness of the hallways. In all likelihood it had cost more than all the gowns Bronwyn owned.

Yet she refused to wear it.

He saw her as soon as he entered the Great Hall. She sat on a cushioned chair wearing a dress of ivory satin. A young man sat close to her strumming a psaltery.

Stephen planted himself between them.

She gave one startled glance at him, then turned away.

"I would like you to wear this dress," he said quietly.

She didn't look up at him. "I have a wedding dress."

Someone near Stephen gave a low chuckle. "Having women problems again, Stephen?"

Stephen stood still a moment, then jerked Bronwyn to her feet. He didn't say a word, but the black look on his face was more than enough to keep her quiet. He locked his fingers about her wrist and pulled her after him. Her feet tangled in her skirts, and once she nearly fell before she could lift the fabric with her free hand. She knew Stephen would drag her if she fell behind.

He fairly tossed her inside her empty chamber, then slammed the door shut. He threw the dress on the bed. "Put it on!" he ordered.

Bronwyn held her ground. "I am not now, nor will I ever be, yours to command."

His eyes were hard and dark. "I've done everything humanly possible to make up for being late."

"Late!" she snarled. "Do you think that's why I hate you? Do you really know so little about me that you think I'm so vain as to hate you just because you have the manners of a boor? I wanted you to lose today because Roger Chatworth would have been better for my clan. They'll hate you as I do because of your arrogance, because of the way you think you own everything. You even believe you can dictate the dress I wear to be married in."

Stephen took one step forward, then grabbed her jaw in his hand, his thumb and fingers digging into her cheeks. "I'm sick of hearing of your clan, and I'm even more sick of hearing Chatworth's name from your lips. I had the dress made for you as a gift, but you're too stubborn, too hot-headed to take it as such."

She tried to free her head but couldn't. He tightened his grasp, causing tears to come to her eyes.

"You are my wife," he said, "and as such you will obey me. I know nothing about your people, and I can only deal with them when I meet them. But I do know how wives should act. I went to a great deal of trouble to have this dress made for you, and you are going to wear it."

"No! I will not obey you! I am the MacArran!"

"Damn you!" he said, grabbing her shoulders and beginning to shake her. "This is not between England and Scotland nor between a laird and a clansman. This is between *us*—a man and a woman! You are going to wear that dress because I am your husband and I say you will!"

He stopped shaking her and saw that his words had made no impression on her. He bent and flung her over his shoulder.

"Release me!"

He didn't bother to answer her as he tossed her on the bed, face down.

"Stop it! You're hurting me!"

"You've done more than hurt me," he retorted as his big fingers fumbled at the tiny buttons down the back of her dress. His legs straddled her. "Tonight I'll show you the wounds Roger made on me. Hold still or I'll tear this damn dress to pieces."

Instantly Bronwyn lay still.

Stephen gave the back of her a look of disgust. "It seems that I get the most response out of you when I threaten to cost you some money."

"We're a poor country and can't afford the waste that I see here in England." She was quiet while Stephen worked on the buttons. "You . . . fought well this morning."

He paused for a moment before he started again on the buttons. "That must have been hard for you to say, considering that you were hoping I was killed."

"I wanted no one killed! All I wanted was—"

"Don't tell me! I already know what you wanted! Roger Chatworth."

It was an odd moment. Bronwyn felt strangely intimate with Stephen, as if they'd known each other for many years. She knew she couldn't explain to him why she wanted Roger. She'd certainly tried often enough! Now it was almost pleasant to hear the note of jealousy in his voice. Let him think that she burned for Roger. It might do him good.

"There! Now get up and let's get that dress off."

When she didn't move, he leaned over her and ran his lips along her neck. "Let's not wait until tonight."

His words as well as his actions made Bronwyn come alive. She quickly rolled out from under him. She grabbed the front of her dress as it fell forward. "I'll put the dress on, but first you must leave."

Stephen lay back on his elbow. "I have no intention of leaving."

Bronwyn started to argue, but she knew it was no use. Besides, he'd seen her in wet underclothes twice before. At least this time she'd be hidden more completely by their dryness. She stepped out of the gown and carefully laid it across a wooden chest.

Stephen's eyes watched her hungrily, and when she went to get the silver dress, he held it away from her so that she had to step very close to him to get it. He had time to plant one quick kiss on her shoulder before she moved away.

The heavy silver fabric was beautiful, and she ran her hand admiringly over the skirt before she slipped it over her head. It fit perfectly, hugging her small waist, flaring gracefully over her hips. As it settled about her body she looked up at Stephen in astonishment. The neckline was not the deep square that was fashionable but was high, all the way to the base of her throat, where a tiny collar of lace rested.

Stephen shrugged at her puzzlement. "I'd prefer that not so much of what's mine be shown to the other men."

"Yours!" she gasped. "Do you plan to always choose all in my life? Am I no longer to even select my own clothes?"

He groaned. "I knew your sweetness wouldn't last for long. Now come over here so I may fasten it."

"I can do it myself."

He watched her struggle for a few moments before he pulled her to him. "Do you think you will ever learn that I am not your enemy?"

"But you are my enemy. All Englishmen are enemies to my clan and me."

He pulled her between his legs and began to fasten the tiny buttons. When they were done, he turned her around, holding her fast between his knees. "I hope to someday teach you that I am more than an Englishman." He ran his hands up her arms. "I am looking forward to tonight."

Bronwyn tried to twist away from him. Stephen sighed and released her. He stood beside her, then took her hand in his. "The priest and our guests are waiting below."

Bronwyn reluctantly took his hand. His palm was warm and dry, callused from years of training. Stephen's squire waited outside the door, holding out a heavy velvet jacket to his master. Bronwyn watched as Stephen thanked the boy, who looked up proudly at his master and wished him luck and happiness.

Stephen smiled and raised Bronwyn's hand to his lips. "Happiness," he said. "Do you think that for us happiness is possible?"

She looked away and didn't answer as they started down the stairs together, hand in hand. The silver dress weighed on her, and with each step she was reminded of this stranger's domination of her.

Many people waited at the foot of the stairs, all men, all friends of Sir Thomas's, men who'd fought against the Highlanders. They made no effort to conceal their animosity toward the Scots. They laughingly talked of Stephen's "conquering" of the enemy that night. They laughed at the way Bronwyn had fought them after they killed her father. They said that if Bronwyn were half as wild in bed, Stephen was in for a treat.

She lifted her head high, telling herself that she was the MacArran and she must make her clan proud of her. The English were a crude, bragging lot of men, and she wouldn't lower herself to their level by replying to their disgusting comments.

Stephen's hand tightened on hers, and she looked up at him in surprise. His face was solemn, his mouth set in a grim line; a muscle worked in his jaw. She would have thought he would enjoy the comments of his countrymen since they were proof that he'd won a prize of war. He turned and looked down at her, and his eyes were almost sad, as if he meant to apologize to her.

The wedding was over very quickly. Truthfully, it didn't seem much like a wedding at all. Bronwyn stood before the priest, and in that moment she realized how alone she was. When she'd imagined her marriage, it had been in the Highlands, in the spring, when the earth was just beginning to come alive. She would be surrounded by her family and all the members of her clan. Her husband would have been someone she knew.

She turned and looked at Stephen. They knelt side by side inside the little chapel in Sir Thomas's house. Stephen's head was reverently bowed. How far away he seemed, how remote. And how very little she knew of him. They had grown up in two different worlds, in completely separate ways of life. All her life she'd been taught that she had rights and powers, that her people would turn to her for help. Yet this Englishman had known only a society where women were taught to sew and to be extensions of their husbands.

Yet Bronwyn was condemned to sharing her life with this man. He'd already made it clear that he believed her to be his property, something he owned and could command at will.

And tonight . . . Her thoughts stopped because she could not bear to think of tonight. This man was a stranger to her—a total stranger. She knew nothing about him. She didn't know what he liked to eat, if he could read or sing, what sort of family he had. Nothing! Yet she was to climb into bed with him and share the most intimate experience of life, and everyone seemed to think she should enjoy it!

Stephen turned and looked at her. He'd been aware of her staring at him, and it pleased him. There was puzzlement and perplexity on her lovely brow. He gave her a slight smile that he meant to be reassuring, but she looked away from him and again closed her eyes over her clasped hands.

For Bronwyn the day seemed to wear on endlessly. The men who were the wedding guests made no attempt to hide the fact that their only interest was in the wedding night. They sat about the great trestle tables and ate and drank for hours. And the more they drank, the cruder their jests became. With each statement, each drunken jibe, Bronwyn's hatred for the

English increased. They cared nothing for the fact that she was a woman; to them she was only a trophy to be enjoyed.

When Stephen reached for her hand, she drew back from him, and this action caused a new round of raucous laughter. She didn't look at Stephen, but she saw that he drank deeply of the strong red wine.

The rays of sun lengthened across the room, and a couple of the men, drunk, began a quarrel and proceeded to wrestle with each other. No one tried to stop them, as they were too drunk to do much harm.

Bronwyn ate very little and drank even less. As the night approached she could feel her insides tightening. Morag had been right: what bothered her was the thought of tonight. She tried to reason with herself that she was a woman of courage. Several times she'd led cattle raids on the MacGregors. She'd rolled up in a plaid and slept through a snowstorm. She'd even fought the English beside her father. But nothing had ever frightened her like the idea of tonight. She knew about the physical act of mating, but what accompanied it? Would she change? Would this Stephen Montgomery own her after mating, as he seemed to believe? Morag said the bedding was a pleasant experience, but Bronwyn had seen young men turned to jelly because they believed they were in love. She'd seen happy, exciting women become plump, complaisant housewives after a man slipped a ring on their finger. Something more than just mating happened in a marriage bed, and she was afraid of that unknown thing.

When Morag came from behind and told Bronwyn it was time to ready herself for bed, Bronwyn's face turned white and her hands gripped the carved lions' heads of the chair.

Stephen held her arm for a moment. "They are jealous. Please ignore them. Soon we'll be able to close the door and shut them out."

"I'd rather stay here," Bronwyn snarled at him, then followed Morag out of the Great Hall.

Morag didn't speak as she unfastened the silver dress. Bronwyn was like an obedient doll as she slipped nude beneath the covers of the bed. Rab lay down on the floor, close to his mistress.

"Come, Rab," Morag called. The dog didn't budge. "Bronwyn! Send Rab out. He won't like being with you tonight."

Bronwyn glared at her. "You fear for the dog but not for me? Has everyone left me? Stay, Rab!"

"Ye're feelin' sorry for yerself, 'tis all. Once it's over and done with ye won't feel so sad." She stopped as the door suddenly burst open.

Stephen rushed in and slammed the door behind him. "Here, Morag," he said. "Go quickly. They'll be angry when they see I've escaped them. But I can't stand another moment of them, and I'll not subject Bronwyn to any more of their crudities. Damn them!"

Morag grinned and put her hand on his arm. "Ye are a good lad." She leaned forward. "Beware of the dog." She gave his arm a final pat. He opened the door for her and then closed it behind her.

Stephen turned to Bronwyn and smiled at her. She sat up in the bed, her black hair cascading over the sheets. Her face was white, her eyes large and frightened in her face. Her knuckles, which clutched the sheet to her chin, were white from her hard clasp.

Stephen sat down heavily on the edge of the bed and pulled off his shoes, then removed his jacket and doublet. As he was unbuttoning his shirt he spoke. "I'm sorry there wasn't a more festive atmosphere for our wedding. What with Sir Thomas's house so near the border, many of the men's wives are afraid to visit."

He stopped as he heard the men pounding on the door.

"No fair, Stephen!" they yelled. "We want to see the bride. You have her all your life."

Stephen stood up and turned to face his wife as he unbuckled his sword and small knife. "They'll go away. They're too drunk to do much harm."

When he was nude, he slipped beneath the sheet beside her. He smiled at her glassy, straightforward stare. He put his hand out to touch her cheek. "Am I so formidable that you can't look at me?"

Suddenly Bronwyn came alive. She jumped out of the bed and pulled the sheet with her. She backed against the wall, and a startled Rab came to stand before her. She stared at Stephen as he lay in the bed. His nude body, his muscular legs covered with pale blond hair, looked strangely vulnerable. His chest was even thicker than it seemed when clothed. She pressed her body closer to the wall. "Do not touch me," she said under her breath.

Slowly, and with great patience, Stephen threw his legs over the side of the bed. She kept her eyes on his face and could see that he considered her outburst little more than a nuisance. He walked past her to the table where a goblet and glasses sat beside a bowl of fruit. He poured her some wine. "Here, drink this and calm down."

She knocked the glass from his hand, sending it flying across the room where it fell into pieces. "I will not allow you to touch me," she repeated.

"Bronwyn, you're only nervous. Every bride is scared her first time."

"First time!" she said in a high pitch. "Do you think this is my first time? I have lain with half the men of my clan. I just don't want any filthy Englishman touching me, that's all."

Stephen did not lose his patient smile. "I know as well as you do that that's a lie. You wouldn't be so frightened if you'd been with a man before. Now please relax. You're only making things worse. Besides, what can you do?"

She hated his smug self-assurance that she was helpless against him. She hated everything about him. He stood there so confident. Even nude he emanated a feeling of power. Bronwyn returned his smile, for she had something that would take that smile from his face.

"Rab!" she commanded. "Attack!"

The huge dog hesitated only a moment, then it sprang off its feet and headed directly for Stephen's head.

Stephen moved to one side, his reactions even faster than

the dog's. As Rab flew toward him, a mass of snarls and long, pointed teeth, Stephen doubled his fist and slammed it into the side of the dog's great square head. Rab's flight immediately changed direction, and he hit the wall with force, then slid to a heap on the floor.

"Rab!" Bronwyn screamed and dropped her sheet as she ran to him.

The dog tried to stand but weaved about in a stunned way.

"You've hurt him," Bronwyn cried as she looked up at Stephen standing over them.

Stephen had given the dog only a brief glimpse to see that it was unhurt, then his eyes were on Bronwyn alone. He stared, open-mouthed, at her rosy-tipped breasts, her round hips covered with skin like ivory satin.

"I'll kill you for this!" Bronwyn screamed.

Stephen was too dazed with the beauty of her to see that she was reaching for the knife that lay by the fruit on the table. It was a dull knife, but the little point was sharp. He saw the flash of it only an instant before it would have sunk into his shoulder. He moved to one side, and it cut his skin.

"Damn!" he said as he put his hand over the wound. Suddenly he was very tired. Blood oozed between his fingers. He sat down on the bed, moved his hand, and looked at his shoulder. "Tear off a piece of that sheet so I can tie this."

Bronwyn stood still, the knife still in her hand.

Stephen looked back at her, his eyes raking her body. "Do it!" he commanded, then watched as she knelt and tore a long strip of linen from the sheet. She wrapped the rest of the sheet around her.

Stephen didn't ask for her help in bandaging his arm. When he'd tied it, using one hand and his teeth, he turned to the dog. "Rab, come here," he said quietly. The dog obeyed instantly. Stephen carefully examined the dog's head but saw nothing hurt. He patted the animal, and Rab rubbed his head on Stephen's hand. "Good boy. Now go over there and sleep." Rab went to where Stephen pointed and lay down.

"Now, Bronwyn," he said in the same tone, "come to bed."

"I'm not Rab to change loyalties so quickly."

"Damn you!" Stephen said, then took one long stride toward her and grabbed her wrist. He pulled the sheet away from her and tossed it to the floor. "You're going to obey me if I have to beat you." He threw her over his bare thighs, bottom end up, and applied several hard, painful smacks to her firm, round buttocks.

When he finished, when each cheek bore the prints of his fingers, he threw her to the far side of the bed. He ignored the tears of pain in her eyes. He stretched out beside her, threw one arm around her waist, one heavy thigh over hers.

Stephen lay still for a moment, feeling Bronwyn's delicious skin next to his, and he wanted very much to make love to her. But he was also very, very tired. He'd fought Roger that morning, and Bronwyn, as well as her dog, the rest of the day. A sudden feeling of contentment washed over him. He had her and she was his to enjoy for the rest of his life. His muscles began to relax.

Bronwyn lay under Stephen in a rigid position, braced for what was to come. Her backside burned from his spanking, and she sniffed once through her tears. When she felt him relax, then heard the even breathing that unmistakably said he was asleep, she felt relieved—then she was insulted. She started to move away from him, but he held her in a grip that threatened to break her ribs. When she saw there was nothing else she could do, she began to relax. And when she did, she found she rather liked his skin next to hers. His shoulder was hard and firm, and she rested her cheek against it. The candles in the room guttered, and she smiled dreamily as Stephen buried his face deeper in her hair.

Chapter 5

STEPHEN WOKE very early the next morning. At first he was only aware of the pain and stiffness of his bruised shoulder and his gashed upper arm. The room was dark and quiet, with only the faintest pink light coming through the tall window.

Stephen first became aware of the smell of Bronwyn. Her thick black hair was wrapped around his arm. Her thigh rested between his. He forgot any feelings of discomfort in an instant. He took a deep, slow breath and looked at her. Asleep and relaxed, her eyes didn't shout hatred at him; her chin was lowered and defenseless, soft and womanly.

Cautiously he moved his hand to touch the side of her face. Her cheek was as smooth as a baby's, softly rounded, sleep-pinked. He buried his fingers in her hair, watched the curls grab at his forearm like a rose bush climbing a trellis. It seemed as though he'd wanted her all his life. She was the woman he'd dreamed about. He had no desire to rush his pleasure of her. He'd waited so long, and now he wanted to take his time and savor her.

He was aware when she first opened her eyes. He made no quick movements, did nothing that would startle her. Her eyes, large and blue, swallowing her face, reminded him of the deer in the Montgomery parkland. As a boy Stephen had been able to creep up on them; then he'd just sit and watch, and after a while the animals would lose their fear of him.

He touched her arm, ran his hand down it to catch her

hand. Slowly he raised it to his lips, and as he put one finger in his mouth he looked into her eyes and smiled. She looked at him with a worried expression, as if she were afraid he'd take something more from her than her virginity. He wanted to reassure her but he knew no words could, that the only way to make her understand was to awaken her response to him.

He shifted so that both of his arms were free, and he felt her stiffen beside him. With one hand he held her fingertips to his mouth, touching the soft pads with his teeth and tongue. He ran his other hand across her ribs, hugging her waist, caressing her hip. Her body was firm, the muscles under her soft skin shapely and hard from use. He felt her draw in her breath sharply when he touched her breast. Very gently he let his thumb touch the pink tip. Even as he felt the crest grow firm under his touch, she did not relax. Stephen frowned slightly, realizing he was getting nowhere. All his gentleness had only made her more rigid.

His hand moved from her breast to her thigh. He bent his head and touched his mouth to her neck, then moved his lips down her shoulder to her breast while his hand played with the delicate shape of her knee. He felt her give a tiny shudder of pleasure, and he smiled as he moved to her left breast, his hands on her waist. He frowned as he felt her tense again.

He moved away from her. She lay on her back, staring up at him in wonder. He ran his fingertips along the line of her hair by her temple. Her hair was spread about her like a waterfall of liquid black pearls.

She's different, he thought, different from other women. Special, unique.

He grinned at her, and with a quick jerk he tossed aside the sheet that covered her legs from the knee down.

"No," Bronwyn whispered. "Please."

Her legs were magnificent: long, slim, curvaceous. She'd ridden all her life, learned to run long distances up hills and through valleys. Her legs were sensitive. Stephen realized it wasn't his touch on her breast that had caused that little tremor of pleasure but his hand on her knee.

He moved to the foot of the bed, looking at her, enjoying the beauty of her. He bent forward and put his hands on her ankles, then slowly ran them upward over her knees and thighs. Bronwyn jumped like someone had just touched her with a hot coal.

Stephen laughed deep within his throat and moved his hands down again. He took one of her feet in his hand, then his lips moved to her legs. He kissed them, ran his tongue over the sculpture of her knee.

Bronwyn moved restlessly under him. Little chills of pleasure shot through her body, running down her arms, across her shoulders. She'd never felt like this before. Her body was trembling, and her breath was rapid and uneven.

Stephen roughly turned her over on her stomach and put his mouth to the back of her knee. Bronwyn nearly went off the bed, but Stephen's hand on the small of her back kept her in place. She put her face in the pillow and moaned like someone in pain. Stephen kept torturing her. His hands and mouth explored every inch of her sensitive legs.

He wanted her so badly he couldn't resist her any longer. He turned her over again, and this time his mouth sought hers. He wasn't prepared for the force of her passion. She clung to him, her arms holding him in a viselike grip. Her mouth seemed to want to take the essence out of him. He knew what she wanted, but he also knew that she did not know.

When she started to push him down in the bed, her hands frantically running along his back and arms, he pushed her back. He mounted her, her legs opening naturally for him. She was ready for him. Her eyes opened wide, and she gasped when he first entered her. Then she closed her eyes, tilted her head back, and smiled. "Yes," she whispered. "Oh, yes."

Stephen thought his heart would stop. The look of her, her words uttered in a guttural tone, were more enticing than any love poem. Here was a woman! A woman unafraid of a man, one who could match him in passion.

He began to move atop her, and she didn't hesitate to follow his lead. Her hands caressed his body, rubbed his inner thighs until Stephen thought he might be blinded by the force of the mounting desire within him. Yet Bronwyn met him thrust for thrust, giving and receiving. When he finally did explode within her, he shuddered violently, the force threatening to tear him apart.

He collapsed on Bronwyn, sweaty, limp, and held her so tightly he nearly crushed her.

Bronwyn didn't mind not breathing. For a moment she thought she must be dead. No one could go through what she'd just experienced and live. Her whole body throbbed, and she felt as if she couldn't have walked if her life depended on it. She drifted to sleep with her arms and legs still wrapped around Stephen.

When she awoke, she stared up into his amused blue eyes. Sunlight poured into the room, and in a flash she remembered everything that had happened between them. She could feel her face filling with hot blood. It was odd that now she couldn't seem to remember the feelings that had made her act in such an embarrassing way.

He touched her cheek, his eyes full of laughter. "I knew you'd be worth a fight," he said.

She moved away from him. She felt good. Actually she felt the best that she had in a long time. Of course! she thought. It was because she knew she was the same. She'd spent the night with a man and she hadn't changed. She still hated him; he was still the enemy. He was still an insufferable, arrogant braggart. "That's all I am to you, isn't it? To you I'm a wench to warm your bed."

Stephen smiled lazily. "You near set it on fire." He ran his hand over her arm.

"Release me!" she said firmly, then jumped from the bed and grabbed her green velvet chamber robe.

One quick knock sounded on the door, and Morag entered, carrying a ewer of hot water. "I heard yer quarrels all the way down the stairs," she snapped.

"There must have been other sounds you heard," Stephen said as he propped his hands behind his head.

Morag turned and grinned at him, her old face folding

into so many wrinkles that her eyes disappeared. "Ye look well pleased with yerself." She gave an appreciative look at the sight of him, his sun-bronzed skin against the sheet, the heavy muscles of his chest and arms hard even when they were relaxed.

"More than pleased, I should say. No wonder you Highlanders never come south." His eyes roamed to Bronwyn, who was glaring at him with hatred.

Chris Audley appeared at the door.

"Are we allowed no privacy?" Bronwyn snapped as she turned toward the window, Rab at her side. She didn't touch the dog, as she felt betrayed by him, too both last night and this morning when he'd allowed Stephen to . . . to . . . Her face began to feel warm again.

Stephen smiled at Chris. "She likes being alone with me."

"What happened to your arm?" Chris asked, nodding toward the bandage crusted with dried blood.

Stephen shrugged. "A mishap. Now if the two of you are satisfied that we didn't kill each other, perhaps you'd leave my wife and me alone so she could tend to my wound."

Morag and Chris smiled at him, gave one brief glance to Bronwyn's rigid back, and left.

Bronwyn whirled to face Stephen. "I hope you bleed to death," she spat at him.

"Come here," he said patiently, sweetly, and held out his hands to her.

In spite of her thoughts she obeyed him. He caught her hand and pulled her down to sit on the edge of the bed beside him. He rolled toward her, and the sheet slipped down, exposing more of his hip and waist. Bronwyn looked away, back to his face. She had to control an urge to touch his skin.

He held both her hands in one of his, then touched her cheek with his free hand. "Perhaps I tease you too much. You pleased me greatly this morning."

He watched the slow flush stain her cheeks. "Now what may I do to please you, short of throwing myself from the window?"

"I would like to go home," she said quietly, all of her

longing sounding in her soft voice. "I want to go home to the Highlands, to my clan."

He bent forward and kissed her lips as softly and as sweetly as a spring rain. "Then we shall go today."

She smiled at him and then started to move away, but he held her hands firmly. Her face turned to coldness in an instant.

"You certainly distrust me, don't you?" He looked at the bloody bandage on his arm. "This needs to be cleaned and dressed properly."

She twisted away from him. "Morag can do it, and I'm sure it'd give her great pleasure, as she seems to lust after you as it is."

Stephen tossed the sheet aside and stood before her. He pulled her into his arms. "I wish that were jealousy in your voice. I don't want Morag to change the bandage. You made the wound, you must dress it."

Bronwyn couldn't move, could hardly think when he held her so close. She was remembering the feel of his lips on the back of her knees. She pushed him away from her. "All right, I'll do it. I'm sure it will be faster if I get it done with than argue with you. Then we can go home."

He sat down on the window seat, leaned back against the cushions, seemingly oblivious to the fact that he was nude. He held his arm out to her, smiling as she avoided looking at him.

Bronwyn didn't like his smugness, his easy self-assurance that his nearness had any effect on her. And worse, she hated the way his beautiful body kept drawing her eyes to it. She smiled wickedly as she ripped the bandage from his arm. Bits of raw skin and newly formed scab came away from the cut.

"Damn you!" Stephen yelled as he came up off the seat. He thrust his hand behind her neck and drew her to him. "You'll regret that! Someday you'll know that one drop of my blood is more precious than any angry feelings you carry."

"Is that your fondest wish? I tell you now that you'll not get it. I married you because it saved warfare within my clan.

I do not kill you now because your old king would cause my clan grief."

Stephen pushed her away so violently that she slammed against the bed. "You do not kill me!" he sneered. Blood was running down his arm from the reopened wound. He stood and grabbed his clothes from the floor. "You think too much of yourself," he said as he thrust his legs into hose and breeches. He tossed his shirt and doublet over his arm. "Be ready in an hour," he said flatly as he slammed from the room.

The room seemed unnaturally silent when Stephen was gone, and somehow it seemed too big and too empty. She was glad, of course, that he was gone. For one brief moment she wondered who he'd get to dress the wound on his arm, then she shrugged. What did she care? She went to the door and called Morag. There was a great deal to be done in an hour.

They rode hard all that day and into the night. Bronwyn felt her heart and mind lighten the farther north they rode. She hated the noise and the many baggage wagons that followed them. To her Scots' sense of economy, the wagonloads of goods were needless. A Scotsman would take what he wore on his back, what food he could carry in a pack. The Englishmen stopped at midday for a cooked meal. Bronwyn had been too impatient to eat much.

"Sit down!" Stephen commanded. "You'll make my men nervous with your constant jumping about."

"Your men! What of my men who wait for me?"

"I can only take care of one group of men at a time."

"You can—!" she began, then stopped. Several of Stephen's men were watching them with interest. Christopher Audley smiled at her, his eyes twinkling. Bronwyn knew he was a pleasant young man, but now no one pleased her. She wanted to get out of these cursed Lowlands as soon as possible.

They crossed the Grampians at night. They were low mountains interspersed with wide valleys. As soon as they crossed, the air seemed to grow cooler, the landscape wilder, and Bronwyn began to breathe easier. Her shoulders relaxed, the muscles in her face untightened.

"Bronwyn!" Stephen said from beside her. "We must stop for the night."

"Stop! But—" She knew it was no use to go on. Only Morag felt as she did; the others needed their rest before they could continue. She took a deep breath and knew that being this close to home would help her sleep tonight. She dismounted her horse and unfastened her saddlebag. At least she could get out of the confining English clothes.

"What's this?" Stephen asked, touching the plaid over her arm. "Is this what you wore the first night I met you?" he asked, his eyes bright with memory.

She snatched it from his grasp and walked into the darkness of the trees. It wasn't easy to unfasten the English dress by herself, but she was determined to be rid of it. Once the heavy velvet dress was carefully placed on a rock, she stripped down to her skin. The Scots' way of dress was simple and gave the people freedom. She slipped a soft cotton chemise over her head, then a saffron-colored, long-sleeved shirt. The sleeves were gathered at the shoulder, tight at the cuffs. The skirt was cut of wide gores, small at the hips but free-flowing enough to allow her run or ride a horse. It was of a soft blue heather plaid. A wide belt with a big silver belt buckle went around her small waist. Another plaid, a six-yard cloak, she deftly threw about her shoulders, then pinned it with a big, hinged brooch. The heavy silver brooch had been handed from daughter to daughter for generations.

"Here, let me see," came a voice from behind her.

She whirled about to face Stephen. "Were you spying on me again?" she asked coldly.

"I prefer to think of it as protecting you. There's no telling what could happen to a pretty lady alone in the woods."

She backed away from him. "I think the worst has already happened." She didn't want him near her, didn't want a repeat of the power he'd had over her last night. She turned and ran back to camp.

"Didn't you forget these?" Stephen called after her, holding up her shoes. He laughed when she didn't look back.

Bronwyn limped into the tent that she'd been told was Stephen's. His men were efficient at making a camp that resembled a small town. She winced even as her foot touched the edge of the carpet spread over the good Scots soil. She'd forgotten that it'd been months since she'd run barefoot across the open ground. Her feet had grown soft, and after her short run she'd cut and bruised them.

She sat down on the edge of the wide cot and bent to inspect them. When the tent flap opened and Stephen entered, she stood up quickly even though her hurt feet brought tears of pain to her eyes.

Stephen tossed her shoes into a corner. He sat down on the cot. "Let me see them."

"I have no idea what you're talking about," she said haughtily, walking away from him.

"Bronwyn, why must you always be so stubborn? You hurt your feet, I know you did, so come over here and let me look at them."

She knew that sooner or later they'd have to be tended. Reluctantly she sat down on the cot beside him.

With a sigh of exasperation, he bent and pulled her feet into his lap. Bronwyn fell back onto her arms. Stephen frowned as he inspected the cuts, one of them quite deep. He bellowed for his squire to bring him a basin of hot water and clean bandages.

"Now put your feet in here," he said when he'd set the water on the floor.

She watched as he tenderly washed and rinsed her feet and then put them into his lap to dry and bandage them. "Why do you do this for me?" she asked quietly. "I am your enemy."

"No you're not. You're the one who fights me, not the other way around. I'd be only too willing to live in peace with you."

"How can there be peace when my father's blood is a wall between us?"

"Bronwyn—" he began, then stopped. It was no use arguing with her. Only his actions would be able to persuade her that he meant only good for her and her clan. He patted the bandage on her left foot. "That should hold you for a while." When she started to move away, he held her feet in his lap. His eyes turned darker as he ran a hand up her calf. "You have beautiful legs," he whispered.

Bronwyn wanted to pull away from him because she recognized the look in his eyes, but he hypnotized her, kept her still even though he held her lightly. Both of his hands went under her long skirt, and she lay back against the pillows, still as he caressed her legs and buttocks.

He lay beside her, pulled her into his arms, and began to kiss her face, her ears, her mouth. His hands expertly unfastened her brooch, her belt buckle. Her clothes slipped from her body before she knew they were even unfastened. Stephen moved away from her for only seconds while he discarded his own clothes. He laughed low in his throat as Bronwyn's hands sought his body and pulled him back close to her.

He fastened his mouth onto hers, tasting the sweetness of her tongue. "Who am I?" he whispered as he ran his teeth along her neck.

She didn't answer him but rubbed her thighs along his. Her heart was racing, and in spite of the cool night a slight sheen of sweat was beginning to form on her skin.

He grabbed her hair, the thickness of it swallowing his hand. "Who am I? I want to hear you say my name."

"Stephen," she whispered. "And I am the MacArran."

He laughed, his eyes brilliant. Even in her passion she didn't lose any of that incredible pride of hers. "And I am the conqueror of the MacArran," he laughed.

"Never!" she said in a throaty whisper as she grabbed his hair and pulled back hard. His head jerked backward, and she put her teeth to his throat. "Who is the conqueror now?"

Stephen pulled her on top of him, ran his hands up and down her firmly. "We English would lose all our wars 'twere such as you the enemy." Suddenly he lifted her, then slowly lowered her so that she sat on his shaft.

Bronwyn gasped in surprise, then gave a deep moan of pleasure as she bent over him and began to move up and down. Stephen stayed very still, allowing her to control their pleasure. When he felt her excitement begin to peak, he rolled her to her back, and she clasped at him with her strong arms and legs. They exploded together in a blinding flash.

Exhausted, they fell asleep as they were, wrapped together, their skin glued together by sweat and passion.

An owl woke Bronwyn. She awoke with her eyes wide and her senses alert. Stephen was sprawled half on top of her, pinning her beneath him. She frowned as she remembered their previous passion. It was gone now, and her head ruled her disobedient body.

The sound of the owl was very familiar. She'd heard that signal all her life. "Tam!" she half whispered. Slowly and with more gentleness than she felt, she pushed Stephen's sleep-heavy limbs off her body.

She dressed quickly in the dark, making almost no noise. She found her shoes where Stephen had tossed them and made her way outside the tent. She stood still for a few moments and listened as Rab stood beside her. Stephen had planted guards, and they walked about the edge of the camp. Bronwyn gave them a look of disgust as she slipped past them and into the forest. The heathery blend of her plaid and her dark hair made her nearly invisible.

She walked quickly and surely through the forest, her passage making little noise. Suddenly she stood very still. She sensed that someone was near.

"Jamie taught ye well," came a deep voice from behind her.

She turned, a brilliant smile on her face. "Tam!" she gasped an instant before she flew into his arms.

He held her very close, her feet off the ground as she gave over her whole weight to him. "Did they treat ye well? Are ye unhurt?"

She moved away from him. "Let me look at ye." The moonlight made Tam's hair even more silver than it actually was. He was a man of average height, no taller than Bronwyn, but he was powerfully built with arms and a chest an oak would envy. Tam was her father's cousin, and he'd been her friend all her life. One of Tam's sons had been one of the three men she would have chosen to be her husband.

Tam gave a deep laugh. "Yer eyes are better than my old ones. I can't tell if ye're well or not. We wanted to come for ye, but we were afraid for yer safety."

"Let's sit down."

"Ye have time? I hear ye have a husband now."

She could see the concern in his face, could even see that there were more lines about his eyes. "Aye, I have a husband," she said when they were seated side by side on a boulder. "He's an Englishman."

"What is he like? Does he plan to stay in Scotland with ye or go back to his England?"

"What do I know? He's an arrogant man. I've tried to speak to him of my clan, but he never listens. He is sure that there is no way of anything except the English way."

Tam touched her cheek. For so many years he'd thought of this girl as his daughter. "Has he hurt ye?" he asked quietly.

Bronwyn was glad for the darkness and the cover of her blushes. Stephen hurt her pride by making her writhe under him and above him. She could keep her head as long as he did not touch her. But that wasn't something you could say to a man who was like a second father. "No, he hasn't hurt me. Tell me, how is my clan? Have you had much trouble with the MacGregors?"

"Nay. It's been quiet while ye were gone. We've all been greatly worried. The English king promised ye wouldna' be harmed." He put out his hand as Rab came to his side. He patted the big head absently. "There are things ye aren't telling me. What of this husband of yers?"

Bronwyn stood. "I hate him! He will cause more problems than I need. He laughed at me when I told him he must try to be accepted by my clan. He travels with an army of men and baggage."

"We heard ye days ago."

"I worry that his ignorance and his stupidity will harm my men. He will no doubt try to force my men to conform to his ways. Someone will slip a dirk between his ribs, and the English king will bring his soldiers down upon my clan's heads."

Tam stood and put his hands on Bronwyn's shoulders. They were small shoulders to bear the weight of the responsibility she carried. "Perhaps not. Perhaps some small pieces of his skin can be removed, and that will help him to learn our ways."

Bronwyn turned and smiled up at him. "You are good for me. The English say we are a savage, crude lot. They'd believe so for sure if they could hear you."

"Savage, are we?" Tam asked, teasing her.

"Aye, and they say the women are as bad as the men."

"Hmph!" Tam grunted. "Here, let's see if ye remember any of what I taught you."

Before she could blink, he'd drawn his dirk and had it aimed at her throat. He'd spent years teaching her ways to protect herself from strong men. She moved to one side in a quick, fluid movement, but it wasn't quick enough. The knife pressed against her throat.

Suddenly, from out of the trees, a man flew, literally off his feet, as he sailed through the air and slammed against the side of Tam. Bronwyn leaped to one side, and Tam struggled to keep his balance. He was a massive, thick man, and his strength was in his ability to stand firm against all comers. Bronwyn had seen four strong, grown men leap at him, and Tam had remained standing.

Tam shrugged, and the man fell off him as Tam blinked at him in curiosity.

Bronwyn smiled when she saw Stephen lying on his back. It would be a pleasure to see him laid low. He'd beaten Roger Chatworth, but Roger was an Englishman, trained in rules of chivalry and sportsmanship. Tam was a real fighter.

Stephen lost no time contemplating his assailant. All he knew was that he'd seen this man hold a knife to his wife's throat. To him, it was their lives to Tam's. He grabbed a piece of a log from the ground, and as Tam turned in puzzlement to Bronwyn, Stephen slammed the wood into the back of the big man's knee.

Tam gave a deep grunt and fell forward. Stephen, on his knees, plowed his fist into Tam's face and felt the man's nose crunch.

Tam knew that Stephen was not an unknown or Rab would have given warning, but when he felt his nose break, he no longer cared who his attacker was. He opened his big hands and went for Stephen's throat. Stephen knew he had no chance against the man's strength, but his youth and agility were more than a match. He sidestepped Tam's hands, then ducked and pummeled both fists into the rock-hard stomach. Tam didn't seem to notice Stephen's blows. He grabbed Stephen by the shoulders, picked him up, and bashed him against a tree—once, twice. Stephen was dazed as his body hit the tree, but he lifted his legs and used all his strength to push against Tam's chest. The strength in Stephen's legs was enough to make Tam pause in his squashing of Stephen.

Stephen brought his arms up under Tam's wrists, and the suddenness of his action made Tam release him. Instantly Tam was after Stephen again, his giant hands going after the younger man's throat. Stephen had only seconds to escape. He threw his legs into the air and did a perfect backward flip.

Tam stood in a crouch for a moment. One second his enemy was there and the next he was gone. Before he could blink he felt a cold, steel blade at his throat.

"Don't move," Stephen said, panting, "or I'll cut your throat."

"Stop it!" Bronwyn screamed. "Stephen! Release him this instant!"

"Release him?" Stephen asked. "He tried to kill you." He frowned when he felt Tam's deep laughter.

"Kill me!" Bronwyn said. "You are the stupidest man I ever met. Rab would have been after him if there'd been any danger. Now put down that knife before you hurt someone."

Slowly Stephen resheathed his knife. "The damn dog was

so still he could have been dead for all I knew." He rubbed the back of his head. His spine felt like it'd been broken.

"He's right, Bronwyn," Tam said. "He did what he should have done. My name's Tam MacArran," he said as he held out his hand to Stephen. "Where did ye learn to fight like that?"

Stephen hesitated for a moment before he took the man's hand. What he really wanted to do was turn Bronwyn over his knee for calling him stupid when he'd been trying to protect her. "Stephen Montgomery," he said, shaking Tam's hand. "I have a brother built like you. I found the only way to beat him was to be faster. An acrobat taught me a few tricks, and they've come in handy."

"I should say so!" Tam said, rubbing his nose. "I think it may be broken."

"Oh, Tam!" Bronwyn cried, giving Stephen a look of hate. "Come back to camp and let me look at it."

Tam didn't move. "I think ye should ask yer husband's permission. I take it ye are her husband?"

Stephen felt himself warming to the man. "I already have scars to prove it."

Tam chuckled.

"Let's go and see if we can find some beer. And I'd like to talk to those guards of mine. How in the world they didn't hear Bronwyn leaving camp I'll never know. A man in full armor could have made less noise."

"Less noise!" Bronwyn said. "You Englishmen are—"

Tam put his hand on her shoulder and stopped her. "Even if the others didn't hear you, your husband did. Now go ahead and get me some warm water for washing. I think there's dried blood all over me." He looked at Stephen fondly. "You have some strength in your fists."

Stephen grinned. "Another blow on that tree and my back would have broken."

"Aye," Tam said. "Ye have no meat on ye for padding."

"Ha!" Stephen snorted. "If I got as heavy as you I wouldn't be able to move."

The men grinned at each other and followed Bronwyn and Rab back to camp.

"Stephen!" Chris said when they reached camp. "We heard the noise, but it took us a while to see that you were gone. God's teeth! What happened to you, and who's this?"

Torches were being lit as the men began to wake, disturbed by the commotion. "Go back to sleep, Chris," Stephen said. "Just get someone to send us some hot water and open a keg of beer, will you? Come inside, Tam."

Tam looked about the inside of the tent. The walls were lined with pale blue silk, the ground covered with carpets from the Orient. He sat down in a carved oak chair. "Fine place ye have here," he said.

"It's a waste of money!" Bronwyn snapped. "There are people going hungry and—"

"I paid people to make this tent, and I assume they bought food with the money," Stephen retorted.

Tam looked from one to the other. He saw anger and hostility coming from Bronwyn, but from Stephen he saw tolerance and maybe even affection. And Stephen had attacked him when he thought Tam was threatening Bronwyn.

The hot water was brought, and the two men stripped to the waist and began to wash. Bronwyn felt Tam's nose and assured him it wasn't broken. Stephen's back was a mass of bloody places where the tree bark had pierced his skin.

"I think your husband's back needs attention," Tam said quietly.

Bronwyn gave Stephen a look of disdain and left the tent, Rab behind her.

Tam picked up a cloth. "Sit down, boy, and I'll see to yer back."

Stephen was obedient. As Tam gently washed the young man's back, Stephen began to speak. "Perhaps I should apologize for my wife's manners."

"No need to. I think I should apologize to ye, since I was one of the ones who helped make her the way she is."

Stephen laughed. "I had more reason to fight you than I

knew. Tell me, do you think she'll ever get over being angry at me?"

Tam wrung out the bloody cloth. "It's hard to say. She and Davey have a lot of reasons to hate the English."

"Davey?"

"Bronwyn's older brother."

Stephen whirled about. "Brother! Bronwyn has a brother, yet her father named her his successor?"

Tam chuckled and pushed Stephen back around so he could finish cleaning his back. "The Scots' ways must seem strange to ye."

Stephen snorted. "Strange is a mild word for your actions. What kind of man was Bronwyn's father?"

"It's better that ye ask about her brother. Davey was a wild boy, never quite right from the day of his birth. He's a handsome lad and has some winning ways about him, and he could always get people to do what he wanted. The problem was that he never seemed to do what was best for the clan."

"But Bronwyn did? All she cares about is her clan—and that damned dog of hers."

Tam smiled at the back of Stephen's head. "Her father, Jamie, never had any illusions about his daughter. She has a hot temper, and sometimes she's a wee bit unforgiving." He ignored the look Stephen gave him. "But, as ye say, she loves the clan. She puts them first, above all else."

"So she was named laird over her brother."

"Aye, she was, but it wasn't as simple as all that. She had an agreement with her father that she was to marry a man he chose. He gave her a choice of three young men, all of them strong and stable, what Bronwyn needed to counteract her quick temper." Tam tossed the cloth in the basin and sat down again in the chair.

"And the men?" Stephen asked as he put his shirt back on.

"They were killed, all of them, along with Jamie."

Stephen was quiet for a moment. He knew the four men had been killed by the English. "And was Bronwyn in love with one of them? Had she made her choice?" He looked up when Tam took so long to answer. The man seemed to have aged in the last few minutes.

Tam lifted his head. He tried to move his strong features into a smile. "I like to think she had chosen, that there was one man she loved best." He took a deep breath and met Stephen's eyes squarely. "One of the young men killed was my eldest son."

Stephen stared at the man. They'd only met a few hours ago and now his body ached from Tam's beating, but he felt he'd known the man for years. The strong jaw, the wide nose, the dark eyes and long gray hair, seemed familiar. He felt Tam's sorrow at the loss of his son.

"And what of David?" Stephen asked. "Did he step aside gracefully for his little sister?"

Tam snorted, his eyes clearing. "No Scot ever did anything without passion. Davey threatened to divide the clan against his father when Jamie first declared Bronwyn his heir."

"Did he? What did Bronwyn say?"

Tam put his hand up and laughed. "She told me ye were a stupid man. Ye don't seem so to me."

Stephen gave him a look that said what he thought of Bronwyn's opinion of him.

Tam continued. "Davey did raise some men to follow him, but they wouldn't fight their own clan members, so they retreated to the hills, where they live in exile."

"And Bronwyn?"

"The poor darlin'. She adored Davey. I told ye he was a persuasive young man. She told her father she refused to take what was Davey's by right. But Jamie only laughed at her and asked if she wanted to stand aside and see war within her own clan."

Stephen stood. "And of course Bronwyn would do what was best for her clan," he said with a hint of sarcasm.

"Aye, that she would. The girl'd kill herself if she thought the clan could benefit by her death."

"Or she'd keep herself alive and suffer a fate worse than death."

Tam gave him a shrewd look. "Aye, she'd do that too."

Stephen smiled. "You'll ride with us to Bronwyn's home?"

Tam stood, moving his great bulk slowly. "I would be honored."

"Then could I offer you a space in my tent?"

Tam raised one eyebrow. "This is too fancy for me. I need no spoilin' at this stage in my life. I have my plaid but I thank ye just the same."

For the first time Stephen became aware of Tam's dress. He wore a shirt with big, gathered sleeves, and a long, quilted doublet that hung to mid-thigh. On his feet he wore crude, thick shoes over heavy wool hose that reached only to below his knee. His muscular knees were bare. About his shoulders was thrown a long, wide piece of tartan cloth. A thick, wide belt was around the doublet, a dirk at his side.

Tam stood quietly during Stephen's examination, waiting for the usual English comments.

"You might get cold," Stephen said.

Tam grinned. "We're no weak men, we Scots. I'll be seein' ye in the mornin'." He left the tent.

Stephen stood still for a moment, then went to the flap. He gave a low, quiet whistle, and after a moment Rab came to him. "Bronwyn," he commanded in a quiet voice.

The dog gave a quick lick to Stephen's hand, then walked toward the dark woods with Stephen following.

Bronwyn was asleep, wrapped tightly and snugly in her plaid. He smiled down at her, pleased with her ability to sleep on the cold, hard, damp ground. He bent and picked her up. Her eyes opened briefly, but he kissed the corner of her mouth and this seemed to reassure her. She snuggled against him as he carried her back to his tent and his bed.

Chapter 6

IT WAS late afternoon the next day when they reached Larenston Castle. Bronwyn, too impatient to wait any longer, spurred her horse forward.

"Go with her," Tam urged Stephen. "I'll wager ye've never seen anything like Larenston."

Curious to see the place that was to become his home, Stephen urged his horse up the grassy hill.

Tam was right: nothing could have prepared him for Larenston. The hill he was on fell away sharply to a wide, deep valley where shaggy cattle grazed and crofters' cottages rested. A narrow road led through the valley and up the wall on the far side. At the top of the valley wall was a high, flat, red-stone peninsula that jutted out into the sea like a huge armored fist. The peninsula was connected to the mainland by a piece of rock only the width of the narrow road. The sides fell away in sheer drops to the sea. Guarding the entrance to the peninsula were two massive gatehouses, each three stories high.

The castle complex itself consisted of several stone buildings and one enormous hall in the center. There was no surrounding wall. There was no need for one. The sheer cliffs rising out of the sea could be guarded by a few men with bows and arrows.

Bronwyn turned to him, a light in her eyes that he'd never seen before. "It has never been taken," she said flatly before she started down to the valley below.

Stephen had no idea how they knew she was arriving, but suddenly every door to every cottage opened and people came running toward her, their arms open.

Stephen put his horse to a gallop to keep up with her, then he stood back as she hastily dismounted and began hugging people—men, women, children, even a child's fat pet goose. He was touched by the scene. He'd seen her only as an angry young woman. She'd told him her clan meant her life to her, but he hadn't visualized the individuals of the clan. She seemed to know them all personally, called each person's name, asked after their children, their illnesses, if they had everything they needed.

He lifted himself in the saddle and looked around. The ground was poor. His horse pawed it and turned up little more than peat moss. Yet he saw fields. The barley growing was stunted but it was making an effort. The cottages were small, very poor looking.

It came to Stephen that these people were akin to the serfs on his brother's estates. Bronwyn owned the land and they farmed it. The very same as the serfs.

He looked back at her as she accepted a piece of cheese from a woman. These people were her serfs, yet she treated them as part of her family. He couldn't imagine any lady he knew touching a serf much less hugging one. They were calling her Bronwyn, not Lady Bronwyn as was her right.

"Ye are frownin', lad," Tam said from beside him. "What of our ways displeases ye?"

Stephen removed his hat and ran his hand through his thick hair. "I think I have some things to learn. I don't think I understand what a clan is. I thought her clan members were like my men. They're all from noble houses."

Tam watched him for a moment. "Clan is a Gaelic word which means children." His eyes twinkled. "And as for nobility, ye can ask any Scot and he can trace his ancestry back to a Scots king."

"But the poverty . . ." Stephen began, then stopped, afraid he'd offended Tam.

Tam's jaw hardened. "The English and the soil God gave

us have made us poor. But ye'd best learn that in Scotland a man's worth is based on what he is inside and not the gold he has in his pocket."

"Thank you for the advice. I'll remember it." He urged his horse forward until he was beside Bronwyn. She gave only a brief look up at him, then turned away to continue listening to an old woman's talk of some new cloth dyes.

One by one the people began to quieten as they stared up at him. His clothes were very different. Most of the Scotsmen wore nothing on their legs, neither shoes nor hose, while some wore the short hose like Tam's.

But Stephen's eyes were on the women. They didn't have the pale, protected complexions of an English lady but a golden tan from their days out-of-doors. Their eyes sparkled, and their glorious hair hung free to their small, belted waists.

Stephen swung down from his horse, took Bronwyn's hand tightly in his left one, and extended his right. "Allow me to introduce myself. I'm Stephen Montgomery."

"An Englishman!" a man near Stephen said, his voice virulent with hatred.

"Aye, an Englishman!" Stephen said with emphasis, his blue eyes hard as he held the Scotsman's.

"Here!" Tam said. "Leave him be. He attacked me when he thought I meant to harm Bronwyn."

Several people smiled at the absurdity of this statement. It was obvious who'd won, since Tam weighed at least sixty pounds more than the slim Stephen.

"He won," Tam said slowly. "He near broke my nose, then took a knife to my throat."

The people were silent for a moment, as if they didn't believe Tam.

"Welcome, Stephen," one of the pretty young women said as she shook his outstretched hand.

Stephen blinked several times at being called by his first name, then he smiled and began shaking more hands.

"It won't be so easy with my men," Bronwyn was saying as they rode side by side down the road that connected the peninsula to the mainland. The road was so narrow that only two could ride together. Stephen gave a nervous look at the sheer wall to his left. One wrong move and he could be over the side. Bronwyn didn't seem to notice their danger, since she'd traveled the narrow road all her life.

"My men are not so easily won as my women," she said haughtily. She looked at him, saw the way he kept glancing down toward the sea. She smiled and reined her horse sharply toward his.

Stephen's horse shied away from Bronwyn's; then when it felt one foot step into the nothing beside the road, it panicked and reared. Stephen fought desperately for a moment to bring the horse under control and keep it from falling off the road and into the nothingness to the side.

"Damn you!" Stephen yelled when he once again had control of the horse.

Bronwyn laughed at him as she looked back over her shoulder. "Are our Scots' ways too fierce for you?" she taunted.

Stephen dug his spurs into his horse's side. Bronwyn saw him coming at her but didn't react fast enough. Stephen grabbed her about the waist and pulled her into the saddle before him.

"Release me!" she demanded. "My men are watching!"

"Good! Then they saw you try to make a fool of me. Or were you hoping I'd fall over the side?"

"And have King Henry's troops down on us? No, I don't wish your death on Scots' soil."

Stephen gasped at her honesty. "Perhaps I asked for that." He put a finger to her lips when she started to speak. "But I didn't ask to be made to look like a fool, so you'll pay for it. How many other men have ridden into Larenston with the MacArran across their saddle?"

"We have brought back many dead, usually killed by—"

He stopped her words with a kiss.

In spite of herself Bronwyn clung to him, her arms going about his neck, her lips fastening hungrily on his. He pulled her close to him, his hands caressing her back. He could feel her skin, warm through the linen of her shirt. He decided he liked the Scots fashion. The heavy English fabrics hid the feel of a woman's skin.

Stephen was the first to come out of the trance. He felt they were being watched. He opened his eyes, lifted his head slightly, his lips still on Bronwyn's. He hadn't realized that his horse had kept moving up the trail toward the gatehouses. Several men surrounded them, all solemn, serious men, their faces closed, showing no emotion.

"Bronwyn, love," Stephen said quietly.

Bronwyn reacted immediately. She jerked away from him and looked down at her men. "Douglas," she whispered and slid down into the man's waiting arms. One by one she greeted the men.

Stephen dismounted slowly and led his horse as he followed her through the gate. The spiked, iron portcullis was drawn up. The men did not speak to him or look at him, but Stephen was very aware of the way they surrounded him, solemnly, distrustfully. Bronwyn walked ahead of him, laughing with her men, asking questions and receiving answers.

Stephen felt very much the alien, the outsider. The men who walked beside him were wary of him, and he felt their hostility. These men were dressed differently from the men in the valley. Some wore short hose and shoes like Tam, others wore tall boots reaching to their knees. Yet all of them were bare-legged from knee to thigh.

Once through the gate the land was open, and they went past several small buildings to the great house. Stephen recognized the outbuildings as a dairy, a blacksmith's, stables. There was even a small kitchen garden in one area. A place such as this could withstand a long siege.

The inside of the house was simple and unadorned. The stone walls were damp, unpainted, unpaneled. The small windows let in little light. It was cold inside the castle, colder even than the outside autumn chill, but there was no fire burning.

Bronwyn sat down in an uncushioned chair. "Now, Douglas, tell me of what has been happening."

Stephen stood to one side, watching. No one asked after her comfort or suggested she should rest.

"The MacGregors have been raiding again. They took six head of cattle two nights ago."

Bronwyn frowned. She'd deal with the MacGregors later. "What problems inside the clan?"

The man called Douglas tugged absently at a long lock of hair. "The land by the loch is in dispute again. Robert says the salmon are his while Desmond demands he be paid for them."

"Have they drawn swords yet?" Bronwyn asked.

"No, but they are close. Shall I send some men in to settle this thing? A little blood shed in the right places will stop their quarrels."

Stephen started to rise. He was used to making decisions of this sort. Tam's hand on his arm stopped him.

"Can you think of nothing else but your sword arm, Douglas?" she asked angrily. "Did it never occur to you that the men have a reason for their quarrels? Robert has seven children to feed, and Desmond has an ailing wife and no children. Surely there must be a way to solve their problems."

The men gave her blank looks.

She sighed. "Tell Robert to send his oldest and youngest children to Desmond to foster. Robert will not demand fish that are going to feed his own children, and Desmond's wife will stop feeling sorry for herself for having no children of her own. Now, what else has happened?"

Stephen smiled at her wisdom. It had come from her love and knowledge of her clan. It was a wonder to see her in her home surroundings. With each passing moment she seemed to come more alive. Her chin no longer jutted forward in anger as she looked at the people around her. Her shoulders were still straight but not as if she meant to ward off blows and angry words.

He watched the faces of the men around her. They respected her, listened to her, and each decision she made was wise and in the best interests of her clan.

"Jamie taught her well," Tam said quietly.

Stephen nodded. This was a completely different side of her, one he'd never imagined existed. He knew her to be angry, impulsive, filled with hatred, given to using a knife and making impossible demands. He remembered laughing at her when she fell into the stream.

Suddenly he felt a swift wave of jealousy. He'd never seen this woman who sat so calmly before these men and made decisions that affected their lives. They knew a side of her that he'd never even guessed at.

Bronwyn rose and walked toward the stairway at the far end of the hall. Stephen followed her. It suddenly occurred to him that the men knew nothing about the backs of her knees. He smiled to himself and felt somewhat reassured.

"Look at him," Bronwyn said in disgust. It was early morning, the late-autumn air nippy. She looked down at Stephen from the window of their third-story chamber. He was in the courtyard below, he and Chris wearing full armor. The Scotsmen around them stood and stared in sullen silence.

They had been married for two weeks, and during that time Stephen had made a strong effort to train her men in the English way of fighting. She'd stood by while he lectured the men on the importance of protecting themselves. He'd offered to purchase armor for the men who trained the longest and hardest. But the Scotsmen had said little and didn't seem the least interested in the valuable prize of a suit of hot, heavy armor. They seemed to prefer their own wild costumes, which left half their bodies bare. The only concession toward war Stephen could get them to make was to wear a shirt of chain mail beneath their plaids.

Bronwyn turned away from the window, smiling to herself.

"Ye needn't be so pleased with yerself," Morag snapped. "Those men of yers could do with a little work. They sit about too much. Stephen makes them work."

Bronwyn kept smiling. "He's an obstinate man. Yesterday he dared to lecture my men that Scotland is a land of unrest, that he is trying to teach them to protect themselves. As if we didn't know! It's because of the English that—"

Morag put up her hand in defense. "Ye can try to drive him insane with yer constant lectures, but not me. What is it that upsets ye about him? Is it the way he makes ye cry out at night? Are ye ashamed of yer passion for the enemy?"

"I have no—" Bronwyn began but stopped when she heard the soft click of the door behind Morag. She turned and looked back at Stephen. She had to admit to herself that it upset her the way her body reacted to his touch. Quite often she found herself trembling as soon as the sun began to set. She was careful never to allow Stephen to see the way she felt. She never made an advance toward him or gave a word of affection to him; after all, he was her enemy, he was of the race that killed her father. It was easy to remember that he was her enemy during the day. He dressed as an Englishman, talked as one, thought as one. His difference screamed at her and her men. It was only at night when he touched her that she forgot who he was and who she was.

"Stephen!" Chris said as they walked across the sand-covered field. They stopped by the edge of the peninsula, gazing out at the sea. "You've got to stop working like this. Can't you see that they're not interested in what you're trying to do for them?"

Stephen removed his helmet. The cool wind rushed at his sweat-dampened hair. Each day he was increasingly frustrated at his attempts to work with Bronwyn's men. His own men trained each day, learning to handle their heavy armor and weapons. But Bronwyn's men stood on the outskirts and watched the Englishmen as if they were animals in King Henry's menagerie.

"There must be a way to reach them!" he said under his breath.

Suddenly he heard a man running toward them.

"My lord," one of Stephen's men said. "There's been an attack on some of the MacArran cattle in the north. The men are already saddling."

Stephen nodded once. Now he'd have a chance to show these Scotsmen what fighters his English knights were. He was used to protecting lands from poachers and thieves.

The heavy steel armor made quick movement impossible. His squire waited with his horse, it too wearing armor. The horse was a heavy one, bred through hundreds of years to be able to bear the weight of a man in full armor. The horse would never be called upon for speed but must stand steady through the thickest of battles, obeying its master's knee commands.

By the time Stephen and his armored men mounted, the Scotsmen were gone. Stephen grimaced and thought of the necessary discipline he'd have to enforce for punishment.

It wasn't until years later that Stephen could remember the events of that night on the Scots moors without once again experiencing a sense of shame and bewilderment.

It was dark when he and his men reached the place where the MacGregors had stolen the cattle. The noise they made as they rode echoed through the countryside. Their armor clanked; their heavy horses' hoofs thundered.

Stephen thought he must have expected the MacGregors to meet him like Englishmen in hand-to-hand combat. It was with consternation that he and his men sat atop their horses and watched the ensuing battle. It was like nothing Stephen had ever seen or imagined.

The Scots left their horses and melted into the woods. They discarded their plaids from their shoulders, leaving them free to run in their loose shirts. There were great shouts from the trees, then the sounds of the Scots' Claymores striking steel.

Stephen motioned for his men to dismount, and they followed the sound of the Scots into the trees. But the Scots had already moved elsewhere. The heavy armor made the Englishmen too slow, too unsteady.

Stephen was looking about in a confused manner when one of Bronwyn's men stepped from the shadows.

"We routed them," the Scotsman said, his mouth in a slight smirk.

"How many were hurt?"

"Three injured, none killed," he said flatly, then smiled. "The MacArrans are too fast for any MacGregor." The man was flushed from the excitement of the battle. "Shall I get some men together to lift you onto your horse?" he said as he smiled openly at Stephen in his armor.

"Why you—!" Chris began. "I'll take a sword to you here and now."

"Come on, English dog," the Scotsman taunted. "I can have your throat cut before you can move the hinges on that steel coffin."

"Cease!" Stephen commanded. "Chris, put your sword away. And you, Douglas, see to the wounded." Stephen's voice was heavy.

"You can't let him get away with such insolence," Chris said. "How do you plan to teach them to respect you?"

"Teach them!" Stephen snapped. "A man cannot teach another to respect him. He must earn respect. Come, let's go back to Larenston. I have some thinking to do."

Bronwyn tossed in the bed, slamming her fist into the pillow. She kept telling herself that she didn't care that Stephen preferred to spend the night somewhere else. She didn't care if he chose someone else to spend it with. She thought of her clan members. Margaret's daughter was a pretty thing, and she'd heard a couple of the men laughing about what a good time they'd had with her. She must speak to Margaret in the morning! It wasn't good to have a girl like that around.

"Damn!" she said aloud, and Rab growled. She sat up in bed, the covers falling away from her lovely breasts. It was cold in the bed alone. Morag had told her of the cattle raid. She had a few choice words to say about the MacGregors. Morag hissed when Bronwyn said she hoped Stephen wasn't killed because his death would bring the English king down on their heads.

Now she kept looking at the door, frowning once in a while.

When the door began to open, she held her breath. It

could be Morag with news. Her breath escaped when she saw Stephen enter, his hair as well as his shirt-front wet from dousing himself at the well.

Stephen barely looked at her. His blue eyes were dark, a crease between his brows. He sat down heavily on the edge of the bed and began to remove his clothes. He couldn't seem to put his mind on the task but kept pausing for long periods of time.

Bronwyn searched for something to say. "Are you hungry?" He didn't answer, so she moved across the bed to sit closer to him. The sheet was wrapped about her lower body, the upper bare. "I asked if you were hungry," she said loudly.

"Oh?" Stephen mumbled as he removed a boot. "I don't know. I don't think so."

Bronwyn had an urge to ask him what was wrong, but of course she'd never do anything like that. She didn't care what was wrong with the Englishman. "Were any of my men hurt in the cattle raid?"

When Stephen again didn't answer, she pushed his shoulder. "Are you deaf? I asked you a question."

Stephen turned to her as if he'd just realized she was there. His eyes raked her nude body, but he showed no interest as he stood and unfastened his belt. "No one was seriously hurt. A few stitches in one man's arm, but nothing else."

"Who? Whose arm needed stitches?"

Stephen waved his hand and stepped nude into the bed. He put his arms behind his head and stared at the ceiling. He didn't attempt to touch her. "Francis, I think," he said finally.

Bronwyn was still sitting, frowning at him. What was wrong with him? "Did our Scots' ways frighten you, Englishman? Were my men too strong for you or too fast?"

To her amazement Stephen did not take the bait.

"Too fast," he said quite seriously, still watching the ceiling. "They moved quickly and freely. Of course, they'd never last in England, because a few armed knights could cut fifty of them apart. But here—"

"Fifty!" Bronwyn breathed. The next instant she brought both her fists down against Stephen's broad, bare chest.

"You'll never see the day when one Englishman can harm fifty Scots," she fairly yelled as she beat her fists against his hard chest.

"Here! Stop that!" Stephen said, grabbing her fists in his hands. "I have enough bruises without your adding to them."

"I'll give you more than bruises," she said as she struggled against his grip.

Stephen's eyes lightened. He pulled on her hands and drew her forward; her breasts pressed against him. "I'd like more than bruises," he said huskily, his full attention at last on her. He released one of her hands and touched her hair. "Will you always bring me back to reality?" he asked as he touched her temple. "I think I could be worried about the greatest problem in the universe, and you would contrive to turn my thoughts to your lovely skin, your eyes," he said, moving his fingers, "your lips."

Bronwyn felt her heart begin to pound. His breath was so soft and warm. His hair was still damp, and a curl stuck by his ear. She had an urge to touch that curl, but she was always careful to make no advances toward him. "And were you worried about some great problem?" she asked nonchalantly, as if it didn't matter.

He stilled his fingers and his eyes captured hers. "Do I hear concern in your voice?" he asked quietly.

"Never!" she spat and rolled away from him. She expected to hear his amused laughter, but when he was silent, she had an urge to turn and look at him, keeping her back to him. He was very still, and after a while she heard the quiet, even tone of his breathing that meant he was asleep. She lay very, very still, and after a while she felt tears forming in the corners of her eyes. There were times when she felt so alone that she didn't know what to do. Her idea of marriage was of two people who shared their lives and their love. But she was married to an Englishman!

Stephen turned suddenly and threw a heavy arm around her, then drew her close to him. She tried to remain stiff and aloof from him, but in spite of herself she wiggled her bottom against him, snuggling closer.

"That's not the way to help a man sleep," Stephen whispered, then raised his head and kissed her temple. "What's this?" he said. "Tears?"

"Of course not. I merely had something in my eye, 'tis all."

He turned her about in his arms so that she faced him. "You are lying," he said flatly. He searched her face with his eyes, touched the cleft in her chin. "You and I are strangers," he whispered. "When will we become friends? When will you share yourself with me? When will you tell me the cause of your tears?"

"When you become a Scotsman!" she said as fiercely as she could. But Stephen's nearness made the words come out oddly, as if they were a plea instead of an impossible demand.

"Done!" he said with great confidence, almost as if he could actually change into a Scotsman.

She wanted to laugh at him, to tell him that he could never become a Scotsman—or her friend. But he pulled her even closer and began to kiss her. He kissed her as if he had all the time in the world, lazily, slowly. Bronwyn felt the blood pounding through her veins. She wanted to pull Stephen to her, but he held her off. He held her slightly away from his body so he could touch her breasts, stroke her ribs and stomach.

She arched away from him, her legs entwined with his, her thighs clasping one of his. Stephen's hand strayed downward to her legs, and he smiled when he felt her sharply indrawn breath.

"My beautiful, beautiful wife," he whispered as he ran his nails lightly along the tendon in the back of her knee. "I wish I knew how to please you out of bed."

She moved back to him, sought his lips, then ran her mouth down his neck. His skin tasted good, slightly salty with sweat, firm yet soft. She touched her tongue to his ear, and she felt a shiver run through him. A low rumble of laughter ran through her.

Stephen grabbed her shoulders fiercely. "Come here, laird of Clan MacArran." He pushed her down in the bed and lowered himself on top of her.

She arched up to meet him, lifting her hips high. She was a Scotswoman, and she was equal to him. Now she did not wait for his advances but met him evenly, with as much passion as his.

Later they lay together, so close they were as one. Bronwyn sleepily opened her eyes and saw the curl by Stephen's ear. It was the one she'd wanted to touch earlier. She moved her head and kissed that curl, feeling the soft hair between her lips. Then she pulled away, her face flushing. Somehow that kiss seemed more intimate than their lovemaking.

Stephen smiled slightly, his eyes closed, more asleep than awake, and pulled her even closer, more under him than beside him. Bronwyn could hardly breathe but it didn't matter. No, breathing was the last of her thoughts.

Stephen stood in the little crofter's cottage, warming his hands before the peat fire. A raw wind was blowing outside, and the fire was needed. Tam was visiting his sister, leaving Bronwyn's house for a few days. The thick older man sat on the far side of the stone-walled room, a fisherman's net spread across his bare knees. He was working the knots, his big hands pulling at the coarse ropes.

"So you want me to help ye to look less like a fool," Tam said seriously.

Stephen turned. He still wasn't quite used to the way the Scotsmen sat or stood, according to their own wishes, in his presence. He was perhaps too used to being "my lorded." "I wouldn't quite put it that way," he said. Thinking back over the events of the cattle raid, he shook his head. "I did look like a fool, both to my own men and to the Scots. I did feel as if I were standing in a steel coffin as Douglas said."

Tam paused for a moment as he tightened a knot. "Douglas always thought he should have been one of the men chosen by Jamie to be Bronwyn's husband." He chuckled at the expression on Stephen's face. "Don't worry, boy, Jamie knew what he was doing. Douglas is a follower, not a leader. He's too awed of Bronwyn to ever be her master."

Stephen laughed. "No man is strong enough to be her master."

Tam didn't comment on that statement, but he smiled to himself. Morag kept a close watch on the couple and reported to Tam. Tam wanted to make sure Bronwyn was in no danger of being harmed by the Englishman. From what Morag said, Stephen was the one in danger—of exhaustion.

Tam looked up. "The first thing ye must do is rid yerself of those English clothes."

Stephen nodded; he'd expected this.

"And then ye must learn to run, both for distance and speed."

"Run! But a soldier must stand and fight."

Tam snorted. "Our ways are different. I thought ye knew that already. Unless ye're willin' to learn, I'll be no use to ye."

With an air of resignation Stephen agreed.

An hour later he began to wish he hadn't agreed. He and Tam stood outside in the cold autumn wind, and Stephen had never felt so bare in his life. Instead of the heavy, padded, warm English clothes, he wore only a thin shirt, a belted plaid over it. He wore wool socks and high boots, but he still felt as if he were bare from the waist down.

Tam slapped him on the shoulder. "Come on, boy, ye'll get used to it. A little more hair and ye'll be nearer a Scot than ever."

"This is a damned cold country to be running about bare-assed," Stephen muttered as he flipped up the plaid and shirt to show one bare cheek.

Tam laughed. "Now you know what a Scotsman wears under his plaid." His face turned serious. "There's a reason for our dress. The plaid makes a man disappear in the heather. The dress is easy to remove, easy and fast to put on. Scotland's a wet country, and a man can't afford to have wet, clinging garments on his skin; he'd die of lung sickness if he did. The plaid is cool in summer, and the constant chafing of yer knees'll make ye warm in winter." His eyes twinkled. "And it allows free air circulation to all yer most vital parts."

"That it does," Stephen said.

"Ah! now ye look to be a man!" Morag said from behind him. She openly stared at his legs. "Wearin' all that armor has put some muscle on ye."

Stephen grinned at her. "If I weren't already married, I think I might consider asking you."

"And I might consider acceptin'. Though I wouldn't like to fight Bronwyn for ye."

Stephen gave her a bleak look. "She'd give me away to anyone if she could."

"As long as she could have ye in bed, is that it?" Morag cackled before turning away.

Stephen blinked once. The familiarity within a clan always startled him. Everyone seemed to know everyone else's business.

"We're wastin' time," Tam said. "Try runnin' to that pole down there," he pointed.

Stephen thought that running would be easy. After all, even children ran, and he was in good condition. But he felt his lungs were about to burst after his first short sprint. It took several minutes to calm his racing heart and regain his breath. His heart sounded as if it were about to break his eardrums.

"Here, drink some water," Tam said as he held out a dipper. "Now that ye have yer breath, run it again."

Stephen raised one eyebrow in disbelief.

"Come on, boy," Tam said. "I'll run it with ye. You wouldn't let an old man beat ye, would ye?"

Stephen gasped for air. "The last thing I'd call you is old." He tossed the dipper aside. "Come on, let's go."

Chapter 7

BRONWYN WAS standing alone at the foot of the stairs leading to the top of the old tower. Her eyes were dry and burning, almost swollen from the tears she hadn't shed. Clutched tightly in her hand was a heavy silver belt buckle. On the back was engraved: "To Ennis from James MacArran."

An hour ago one of the crofters had brought the buckle to her. Bronwyn remembered when her father had given the buckles to the three young men he'd chosen to succeed him. It had almost been a ceremony. There'd been food and wine, dancing, and much, much laughter. Everyone was teasing Bronwyn about which man she'd choose for her husband. Bronwyn had flirted and laughed and pretended that all of them were worthless compared to her father.

There'd been Ian, Tam's son. Ian was only as tall as she was but thick like his father. Ramsey was blond, broad-shouldered, with a mouth that sometimes made Bronwyn nervous. Ennis had freckles and green eyes, and he could sing so sweetly he could make you cry.

She squeezed the belt buckle until it cut into her palm. Now they were all dead. Strong Ian, handsome Ramsey, sweet Ennis—all dead and buried. Killed by the English!

She turned and hurried up the stairs to the top floor. From the bunch of keys at her side, she took one and unlocked an oak door. The heavy door creaked in protest as it swung on its unoiled hinges.

She thought she was braced for the sight of the room, but she wasn't. She almost expected her father to look up at her and smile. She hadn't been in the room since his death; she'd been afraid to see it again.

She stepped inside the room and looked about her. There was a plaid thrown across a chair, the bottom of it worn and ragged. Weapons hung on the stone walls, axes, Claymores, bows. She touched the worn place on her father's favorite bow. Slowly she walked to the chair near the one window in the room. The leather held the imprint of Jamie's body.

Bronwyn sat down in the chair, the dust whirling about her. Her father came often to this room to think and be alone. He allowed no one to enter it except himself and his two children. Bronwyn had teethed on an arrow from her father's pack.

She looked from one familiar, loved object to another and felt her head begin to ache. It was all gone now. Her father was dead, her brother had turned away from her with hatred in his heart, and the beautiful young men she would have chosen were rotting in a grave somewhere.

Now there was no laughter or love at Larenston. The English king had married her to one of his killers, and all happiness was gone.

The English! she thought. They thought they owned the world. She hated the way Stephen's men stood off from him, the way they bowed and scraped and called him "my lord." The English were a cold lot. She'd tried hundreds of times to tell him about the ways of the Scots, but he was too vain to listen.

She smiled to herself. At least her men knew who was laird. They laughed at Stephen behind his back. All morning she'd heard stories of the aborted cattle raid the night before. How ridiculous Stephen must have looked standing there in his foolish armor.

A noise in the courtyard below drew her attention. She went to the window to look down.

At first she didn't recognize Stephen. She thought only that he was a well-built man with an exceptional look of self-confidence. His belted plaid swung about his legs with a jaunty air. She gasped in indignation when she realized it was Stephen who walked so arrogantly and wore the Scots' dress as if he had a right to wear it.

Several of her men stood about the courtyard, and she was glad to see that they made no effort to greet him. They certainly knew an impostor when they saw one.

The smile left her face as first one man then another walked toward Stephen. She saw him smile and say something, then flip the tail of his plaid up. She heard laughter echoing.

Douglas—*her* Douglas!—stepped forward and put out an arm to Stephen. Stephen grabbed it, and the two of them hooked ankles and forearms and began a standing wrestle. It wasn't a minute later that Douglas went sprawling in the dirt.

She watched in disgust while Stephen challenged the men, one after another. She drew her breath in sharply when Margaret's daughter stepped forward, her hips swaying provocatively. She lifted her skirt to expose trim ankles and proceeded to show Stephen a few Highlands dance steps.

Bronwyn turned away from the window and left the room, locking the door behind her. There was anger in every step she took down the stairs.

Stephen was standing there. His hair was tousled, his cheeks pink from his day's exercise in the cold air. His eyes were flashing and bright. Behind him stood several of his men as well as Bronwyn's, and several pretty young women.

He looked at her like a boy trying to please. He held out his leg to her. "Will I pass?" he teased.

She glared at him for a moment, ignoring his muscular leg. "You may fool some of them, but you're an Englishman to me and will always be. Because you've changed your clothes doesn't mean you've changed inside." She turned and walked away from all of them.

Stephen stood still for a moment, frowning. Perhaps he did want them to forget he was an Englishman. Perhaps . . .

Tam slapped him on the shoulder. "Don't look so grieved."

Stephen turned to see that the Scotsmen behind him were smiling.

"For all she's a good laird, she's still a woman," Tam continued. "No doubt she was upset because ye were dancin' with the women."

Stephen tried to smile. "I wish you were right."

"Why don't ye go to her and soothe her?"

Stephen started to reply, then stopped. There was no use telling Tam that Bronwyn wouldn't welcome anything about him. He followed her up the stairs. She was standing over a weaver, directing the arrangement of the weft threads of a new plaid.

"Stephen," called one of the women, "but don't you look good." The pretty young woman almost leered at him in his short clothes.

Stephen turned to smile at the woman, but he caught sight of Bronwyn as she fairly snarled at him before she left the room. He caught her at the head of the stairs. "What's wrong with you? I thought you'd be pleased with my clothes. You said I must become a Scot."

"Dressing as one doesn't make you a Scot." She turned away from him.

Stephen caught her arm. "What's wrong? Are you angry because of something else?"

"Why should I be angry?" she asked, her voice heavy with sarcasm. "I'm married to my enemy. I'm—"

Stephen put his fingers to her lips. "Something is bothering you," he said quietly. He watched her face, but she lowered her eyes so he couldn't see the pain registering there. He took both her arms then ran his hands downward until they touched hers. Her left hand was clutched tightly over something. "What's this?" he asked softly.

She tried to pull away from him, but he forced her hand open. He stared at the buckle, read the inscription. "Did someone give this to you today?"

She nodded silently.

"Did it belong to your father?"

She kept her eyes lowered, and again she could only nod.

"Bronwyn," he said, his voice rich and deep. "Look at me." He put his hand gently under her chin and lifted her face. "I'm sorry, truly sorry."

"How can you know?" she snapped, jerking away from him. She silently cursed herself for almost believing in him, for letting his voice and his nearness affect her.

"I know what it's like to lose a father as well as a mother," he said patiently. "I'm sure it hurt me as badly as you've been hurt."

"But I did not kill your father!"

"Nor did I, personally, kill yours!" he said fiercely. "Listen to me, just once, listen to me as a man, not as a political pawn. We're married. It's done. There's no more stopping it. We could be happy, I know we could, if only you'd be willing to give us a chance."

Her face hardened, her eyes turning cold. "And will you brag to your men that you have a Scotswoman eating from your hand? Will you try to win my men, as well as my women, to your side as you did today?"

"Win!" Stephen began. "Damn you! I've spent all day running, literally, in this cold climate bare-legged and bare-assed too, if the truth be known, all to please you and those men you care about so much." He pushed her away from him. "Go and wallow in your hatred. It will keep you cold company at night." He turned away and left her.

Bronwyn stood very still for a moment before slowly going down the stairs. She wanted to trust him. She needed a husband to trust. But how could she? What would happen if her lands were attacked by raiding Englishmen? Could Stephen be expected to fight against his own people?

She knew how she reacted to him. It would be easy to forget their differences and succumb to his sweet touches, his rich voice. But when she needed to be wary and alert, her senses would be dulled. She couldn't afford that. She wouldn't risk her people's lives merely because she enjoyed a lusty time in bed with a man who could be a spy.

She sat in the little garden behind the tall stone house. She couldn't trust him. For all she knew, his entreaties for her to believe in him were a means to use her. She knew he had brothers. Perhaps he'd call them to his side once he made an opening in Bronwyn's defenses. Would he boast to his brothers that she would do what he wanted, that to make her pliable, he had only to kiss the back of her knees?

She stood and began to walk quickly to the edge of the peninsula. The sea beat against the rocks, and she could see for miles. It was a great responsibility to be laird of a clan. Many, many people looked to her for protection and, if need be, even for food. She worked hard at knowing her people and understanding them. She could not let her defenses down for even a moment. So when Stephen caressed her, held her, she had to protect herself against him, against allowing her emotions to rule her head. If ever she knew she could trust him, then she could ask what was in her heart.

"Bronwyn."

She turned. "What is it, Douglas?" She looked into the young man's brown eyes. She could see the unasked question in his eyes, as it was in all her men's eyes. They didn't know whether or not to trust Stephen and were waiting for her judgment. And she was to be judged also. If she was in error about him, they would no longer trust her.

"I have received word that the MacGregors plan another cattle raid tonight."

Bronwyn nodded. She knew Douglas had access to an informer. "Have you told anyone else of this?"

Douglas paused, reading her thoughts correctly, knowing she meant Stephen. "No one."

She looked back at the sea. "I will lead my men tonight, and we will show the MacGregors who is the MacArran. I'll not be laughed at again."

Douglas smiled. "It will be good to ride with you again."

She looked back at him. "Tell no one of our plans. No one! Do you understand?"

"Aye, I understand." He turned and left her.

The long dinner table was spread heavily with food. Stephen was at first suspicious of the abundance because Bronwyn's Scots sense of thrift made her set a more modest table. At dinner she'd smiled at him. This had surprised him, since he'd assumed she'd be angry after what had happened that afternoon. But perhaps she'd listened to his words, perhaps she was willing to give him a chance.

He sat back in his chair and ran his hand along her thigh. He smiled when he felt her jump.

She turned to him, her eyes soft and warm, her lips parted, and Stephen felt his body grow hot. He leaned toward her.

"This is not the time or place," she said, a note of sadness in her voice.

"Come above stairs with me then."

She smiled seductively. "In a moment. Perhaps you'd like to try a new drink I had made. It is of wine and fruit juices with a little spice." She handed him a silver goblet.

Stephen hardly noticed what he drank. Bronwyn had never looked at him as she was doing now, and his blood was beginning to boil. Her thick lashes lowered over her eyes, which had turned to a luster like a blue pearl. The tip of her pink tongue touched her lower lip, and Stephen felt chills run up his spine. So this is what she looked like when she was willing!

He put his hand over hers and had to control himself from squeezing it hard enough to break her fingers. "Come with me," he whispered huskily.

Before he'd finished climbing the stairs, he began to feel sleepy. By the time he reached the door to their bedroom, he could hardly keep his eyes open.

"Something's wrong with me," he whispered, the words an effort to get out.

"You're tired, that's all," Bronwyn said sympathetically. "You spent most of the day in training with Tam, and he can wear a man out. Here, let me help you." She put her arm around his waist and led him to the bed.

Stephen collapsed onto the bed's softness. His limbs felt heavy and useless. "I'm sorry, I . . ."

"Quiet," Bronwyn said softly. "Just rest. You'll feel better after a little sleep."

Stephen had no choice but to obey her as he easily slipped off into sleep.

Bronwyn stood over him for a moment, frowning. She hoped she hadn't put too much of the sleeping drug in his drink. She had a sudden pang of conscience as he lay there so quietly. But she had to make sure he didn't interfere tonight. She had to show the MacGregors they couldn't steal her cattle and get away with it.

She turned to leave the room, then looked back. With a sigh she pulled Stephen's boots off. He didn't move but lay still, so still, not watching her, not asking anything of her. She bent and touched his hair, then on impulse she gently kissed his forehead. She backed away from him, her face pink, cursing herself for being so foolish. What did she care about the Englishman?

Her men were already saddled and waiting for her. She pulled her long skirt up and slung her legs into the saddle. The men needed no verbal command as they followed her down the narrow path onto the mainland.

Douglas's informer had been right about the proposed cattle raid. Bronwyn and her men rode hard for two hours, then abandoned their horses and walked stealthily into the dark woods.

Bronwyn was the first to hear a man's footsteps. She put up her hand to halt her men, then signaled them to spread out, Douglas to stay with her. The men of Clan MacArran were silent as they slipped through the trees and surrounded the cattle thieves.

When she was satisfied that her men had had time to get to their places, she opened her mouth and gave a high-pitched cry that set the cattle to nervous prancing. The MacGregors dropped the ropes they held and grabbed their Claymores. But it was too late, for Bronwyn's men were upon them. They'd discarded their plaids so they were free to fight in their loose shirts. Their savage war cries echoed through the countryside. Bronwyn threw off her skirt and wore only her shirt and plaid, which reached just to her knees. She stayed in the background to direct the men and not hamper them with her frail strength. At times like this she cursed her lack of strength.

"Jarl!" she screamed in time to save one of her men from a Claymore across his head. She rushed across the grass just in time to thwart a MacGregor from jumping onto another man.

The moonlight caught the flash of a dirk as it poised above Douglas's head. She saw that Douglas had lost his weapon. "Douglas!" she called, then tossed him her weapon. The MacGregor behind him turned to look at her, and in that instant Douglas caught him under the ribs with the dirk. The man fell slowly.

The fighting seemed to come to a halt instantly. Bronwyn, sensing a change in the men, looked down at the man at her feet. "The MacGregor," she whispered. "Is he dead?"

"No," Douglas answered, "only wounded. He'll come to in a minute."

She looked about her. The other MacGregors had faded into the trees now that their leader was down. She knelt beside the fallen man. "Give me my dirk," she said.

Douglas obeyed her without hesitation.

"I'd like the MacGregor to remember me after tonight. How do you think he'd like my initial carved into his flesh?"

"Perhaps in his cheek?" Douglas said avidly.

Bronwyn gave him a cold look, her eyes made silver by the moonlight. "I don't want to cause more war, only a memory. Besides, I've heard the MacGregor is a handsome man." She pulled his shirt open.

"You seem taken with handsome men lately," Douglas said bitterly.

"Perhaps it is you who are worried about my men. Is it your jealousy or your greed that eats at you? See to my men and stop your childish tantrums."

Douglas turned away from her.

Bronwyn had heard tales of the MacGregor and knew he'd prize a scar made by a woman who had beaten him. She used the tip of her dirk and barely broke the skin as she carved a small B in his shoulder. She'd make sure he remembered her the next time he tried to steal her cattle.

When she'd finished, she ran back to her men, and together they ran to their horses. It was a heady experience: her first victory as laird of her clan.

"To Tam!" she cried when she was on her horse. "Let's rouse him from his bed. He'll want to hear how the Mac-Gregor wears the brand of the MacArran." She laughed as she thought of the rage of the man when he saw the present she'd given him.

But they weren't destined to get home so easily. Suddenly the skies opened, and a deluge of very cold rain poured down on them. All of them wrapped their plaids over their heads, and Bronwyn thought with longing of the warm skirt she'd left on the ground. Lightning flashed and the horses jumped about, skittish at the light and sound.

They rode back to Larenston along the cliff edge of the sea. It was not the safest way but the quickest, and they knew the MacGregors would not pursue them on unknown, dangerous pathways.

Suddenly a stupendous bolt of lightning tore through the skies and hit the ground directly in front of Alexander. The horse reared, pawing the ground frantically with its forefeet. The next instant a roar of thunder threatened to bring the rocks down about their heads. Alexander's horse changed direction, and its feet came down in midair, hanging over the edge of the cliff. For an instant horse and rider hung suspended, half on land, half in the air. Then suddenly they fell, Alex coming out of the horse's saddle.

Bronwyn was the first one to dismount. The cold rain pelted against her face. Her legs were blue with cold.

"He's gone!" Douglas shouted. "The sea has him now."

Bronwyn strained to see through the darkness and rain to look at the sea below. A flash of lightning showed her the horse's body below, still as it lay against the rocks. But there was no sign of Alex.

"Let's go!" Douglas shouted. "You can't help him."

Bronwyn stood. She was as tall as Douglas, on an equal

level with him. "Do you give me orders?" she demanded, then looked back toward the water. "Hold my ankles so I can see farther over the edge."

Bronwyn stretched out on her stomach as Douglas grabbed her ankles. Immediately two men came to her side to steady her arms. Another man put his hands on Douglas's shoulders.

Inch by inch Bronwyn eased herself over the side until she could see down the side of the sheer rock wall. It was frightening hanging over the edge, trusting her life to the strong hands about her ankles. Her first impulse was to say she saw nothing but she couldn't leave Alex if there was a chance he was still alive. She had to wait patiently for the next burst of lightning, then scan the area. Slowly she moved her head to see another part of the cliff. Her half upside-down position was making her dizzy, and the fear was making a knot in her stomach.

It was when she turned her head the third time that she thought she saw something. It seemed like an eternity before lightning illuminated the wall again. Her neck felt as if it would break from holding her head up.

The lightning flashed, and suddenly all her pain left her. There, to her left, about halfway down, was a familiar flash of the red plaid Alex favored.

She waved her hand, and the men pulled her up. "Alex! Down there!" she gasped, her mouth filling with rainwater. She impatiently wiped her forearm across her eyes. "He's on a narrow ledge. We'll tie a rope around me. I think I can get to him."

"Let me go!" Francis said.

"You're too big. There's not enough room on the ledge. Get me some rope and I'll put it over my shoulder. Understand?" Her shouts were accompanied by hand gestures.

The men nodded, and almost immediately she was coiling a rope to put around her shoulder. She gave one end to Douglas. "When I jerk twice, pull him up." Next she tied another rope about her waist. "When Alex is safe, get me."

She walked to the edge of the cliff. She wouldn't look

down at the hard nothingness below her. She paused for a moment. "Tam is my successor," she said, without adding that he would be only if she died.

The heavy rope cut into her waist, and although the men eased her down as slowly and gently as they could, she slammed against the rock wall several times. Her knees and shoulders ached painfully, and she could feel the skin coming off her hands as she clutched the rope. Think of Alex, she thought, think of Alex.

It was a long time before she reached the narrow ledge. There was barely room for her to put her feet beside Alex's big body. After some careful maneuvering, she managed to straddle his hips.

"Alex!" she shouted above the lashing rain.

The young man slowly opened his eyes, then looked at Bronwyn as if she were an angel on earth. "Chief," he whispered while closing his eyes, the sound of his words lost in the storm.

"Damn you, Alex, wake up!" Bronwyn screamed.

Alex opened his eyes again.

"Are you hurt? Can you help me with the rope?"

Alex suddenly became aware of his surroundings. "My leg's broken, but I think I can still move. How did you get here?"

"Don't talk! Just tie knots!"

She was standing in a precarious position, and there was very little room for moving about. She bent forward, keeping her legs straight, not changing the placement of her feet, as she and Alex fastened the rope around his body. They made a crude sort of sling, the rope going between his legs and around his back.

"Are you ready?" she shouted.

"You go first. I'll wait."

"Don't argue with me, Alex. This is an order." She gave two hard tugs on the rope, then felt it tighten as the men above pulled it up. She frowned as Alex slammed against the wall, further injuring his leg.

When he was just above her head, she plastered herself

against the rock. The rain slashed at her; the sheer wall of the cliff was hard and menacing against her back. Suddenly she felt very alone—and very frightened. Her concern for Alex had motivated her early courage, but now she had nothing. Alex was safe, and she was so alone and so frightened. It flashed through her mind that where she wanted to be right now was in Stephen's lap, sitting before a fire, his arms around her.

The rope about her waist tightened, and she had no more time for thought. Yet even as she held on to the rope, her hands tight, her feet wrapped about the cord to relieve the pressure on her waist, the image of Stephen stayed with her.

Somehow it was no surprise at all when she reached the top of the cliff to find Tam and Stephen pulling her up. Stephen put out his hands and caught her under the arms, then lifted her onto the land. He caught her close to him in an embrace that nearly crushed her, but she enjoyed the pressure, was glad she was no longer alone. He held her away from him, her face between his hands, and studied her. His eyes were dark and shadowed. She wanted to say something, that she was glad to see him, glad she was safe again, but his expression didn't allow for words.

Abruptly he moved his hands to her arms, then began an impersonal inspection of her. He tossed her back against his arm and ran his hand over her legs, frowning at the bloody places on her knees. All her soft feelings left her. How dare he inspect her in such a way in front of her men!

"Release me!" she commanded.

Stephen ignored her as he looked up at Tam, who hovered over them. "Several cuts and a few bruises, but it looks like nothing serious."

Tam stood up from his half-crouch and nodded. About ten years seemed to leave him.

Bronwyn kicked once and struggled against Stephen. "If you are quite finished with me," she said haughtily, "I'd like to go home."

Stephen turned to look at her, and she understood the expression on his face. He was angry—very, very angry. The rain was beginning to lessen somewhat and dawn was lighting the sky. She sat up and attempted to pull away from him. "I need to see to Alex."

"Alex is being cared for," Stephen said flatly, his teeth clenched. His hand firmly clasped her wrist, and as he stood he pulled her with him. He started toward his horse, dragging her behind him.

"I demand that you release me," she said as quietly as possible, since all her men were standing near them.

He whirled on her, jerked her close to him. "If you say one more word, I just may throw that bit of shirttail over your head and beat your backside black and blue. Alex is safe—safer than you are at the moment, so don't tempt me further. Is that clear?"

She put her chin in the air and glared at him. But she gave him no cause to carry out his threat. He turned and pulled her toward a waiting horse. He gave her no time to mount but picked her up and slammed her into the saddle so hard her teeth jarred together. Instantly he was on his own horse.

He held the reins to her horse. "Will you follow me, or must I lead your horse?"

She couldn't bear being led away like some naughty child. "I'll follow," she said, her back straight, her chin high.

They rode away from the men on the narrow cliff path, and Bronwyn didn't look back. Her humiliation was too complete. Her men respected her, obeyed her, but Stephen tried to reduce her to a child. Rab ran along beside the horses, following his mistress as he always did.

They rode for over three hours, and Bronwyn knew they were headed for her northernmost estates. The country was hilly, wild, with many streams to cross. Stephen kept a slow, steady pace, never looking at her but sensing when he needed to slow down to wait for her.

Bronwyn was very tired. She hadn't eaten since before the cattle raid during the night, and now that seemed like days ago. She was so hungry her stomach felt as if it were eating itself. The rain had slowed to a cold, wet drizzle, and she was chilled to the bone. She shivered often and sneezed a few times. Her legs were cut and bruised, and no matter which way she turned, the saddle rubbed on a sore place.

But she would have died before she asked Stephen to stop and rest.

Toward midday he halted, and Bronwyn couldn't help but breathe a sigh of relief. Before she could dismount, he was beside her, pulling her down from her horse. She was too weary, too cold, too hungry, to even remember the happenings of the night.

He stood her on the ground, then walked away from her. When he looked back, she saw that none of his anger had gone away. "Why?" he asked, and the word showed how much control he was using to keep from lashing out at her. "Why did you drug me?"

She tried to hold her shoulders straight. "The MacGregors were planning another raid, and I had to protect my people's property."

His eyes were cold and hard. "Has no one ever told you that it is a *man's* duty to lead a war party?"

She shrugged. "That is how you're taught in England. We're different in Scotland. I was fostered when I was seven, just as my brother was. I was taught how to ride and, if need be, how to use a sword."

"And you thought I wasn't capable of leading the men, so you threw off your clothes"—he sneered at the short skirt she wore—"and led them yourself. Do you consider me so little a man that you believe yourself to be a better one?"

"Being a man!" she said in disgust. "That's all you concern yourself with. On the last raid you went in your armor. Do you know the MacGregors *laughed* at me! They said the MacArrans had a woman for a laird and a steel pillar for a leader. Well, last night I made them stop laughing. I carved a B on the MacGregor's shoulder."

"You what!" Stephen spluttered.

"You heard what I said," she said arrogantly.

"Oh, God!" Stephen said, running his hand through his wet hair. "Don't you understand anything about a man's pride? All his life he'll bear the mark a woman put on him. He'll hate you—and your clan."

"You're wrong! Besides, the MacGregors and the Mac-Arrans already hate each other."

"Not as far as I can see. You seem to tease each other. It's more a game than a true war."

"You know nothing about it. You're an Englishman," she said as she turned back to her horse and began to unbuckle the saddle.

He put his hand across hers. "I want your word that you'll never drug me again."

She jerked away from his touch. "There are times when—"

He grabbed her shoulders and turned her to face him. "There is never a time when you can control my life as well as my reason. What would have happened if there'd been trouble and I was needed? I was asleep so hard someone could have torn down the castle and I wouldn't have known. I cannot live with someone I cannot trust. I want your promise."

She gave him a little smile. "I cannot give it."

He pushed her away from him. "I'll not endanger my men because of the whims of a foolish girl," he said quietly.

"Girl!" she said. "I am the MacArran. I have hundreds of men and women who obey me and respect me."

"And let you have your own way too often. You're an intelligent woman and your judgment is good. But you don't have the experience to lead fighting men. That I will do."

"My men won't follow you."

"They will as long as I am awake enough to lead them." He stared at her when she didn't answer. "I have asked you for your promise, now I will take it. If you ever drug me again I will take that dog away from you."

Bronwyn opened her mouth in astonishment. "Rab would always return to me."

"Not if he's several feet under the ground, he wouldn't."

She was slow in understanding his words. "You'd kill him? You'd kill a dog to get what you want?"

"I'd kill a hundred dogs, or horses, to save one man, either mine or yours. Their lives are in danger if I'm not there to protect them, and I can't spend my life worrying that my own wife will decide whether or not she wants me conscious on any given night. Do I make myself clear?"

"Very clear. You would no doubt enjoy killing my dog. After all, you've taken nearly everything else away from me."

Stephen gave her a look of exasperation. "It's obvious that you're going to see only what you want to. Just remember that if you love that animal, you'll think twice before tampering with my food again."

Suddenly it was all too much for Bronwyn. The long, wet night, the horror of being lowered down a cliff, and now the thought of losing Rab were all too much for her. She sank to her knees in the soggy ground, and Rab came to her. She put her arms around the big dog and buried her face in his rough, damp coat. "Yes, I love him," she whispered. "You English have taken away everything else, you might as well take Rab too. You killed my father and his three favorite men. You killed all my chances for happiness with a husband I could love." She lifted her head, her eyes bright with unshed tears. "Why don't you take Rab? And Tam too? And burn my house down while you're at it?"

Stephen shook his head at her, then offered her his hand. "You're tired and hungry and don't know what you're saying."

She ignored his hand and stood up.

Stephen suddenly grabbed her and pulled her into his arms. He didn't seem to notice her struggles to push him away. "Has it ever occurred to you that you could love me? If you did, it would save the both of us an awful lot of quarreling."

"How could I ever love a man I couldn't trust?" she asked simply.

Stephen didn't say a word but kept holding her to him, his cheek against her wet hair. "Come on," he said after a while. "It's about to rain again. We have several more miles before we reach shelter." He didn't look at her after he released her, and Bronwyn had a passing thought that he was sad. She dismissed it immediately and mounted her horse.

Chapter 8

IT WAS late afternoon before Stephen stopped in front of an old stone house. The back of the cottage was buried into the side of a little hill, the roof covered with grassy sod. Rain was beginning again, just when Bronwyn's clothes had begun to dry.

She stopped her horse but didn't dismount. She was too tired and weary to move.

Stephen put his hands to her waist and half dragged her to the ground. "Hungry?" he murmured just before he tossed her into his arms and carried her into the cottage.

The dirt-floored room was warm from a peat fire. There was a stool against the wall. He put her on it. "Stay here while I see to the horses."

She hardly noticed when he returned, she was so tired.

"I thought you Scots were a stout bunch," he teased, then laughed when she wearily sat upright, no longer leaning against the wall. "Come here and look what I have." He opened a chest along one wall and began withdrawing food. There was a warm pot of a heavenly smelling stew. Thick dark bread came next. There was fish and soup, fruit and vegetables.

Bronwyn felt as if she were in a dream. Slowly she left the stool and went to Stephen's side. Her eyes hungrily looked at each dish, then followed it to where he set it on the far side of him.

When she reached for a succulent piece of roast pork, Stephen pulled the dish away from her.

"There's a price for all this," he said quietly.

She moved away from him, her eyes glassy-hard. She started to rise.

Stephen set the dish down. "Here!" he said, grabbing her shoulders. "Is there no humor about you?"

"Not when it concerns a murdering Englishman," she said stiffly.

He suddenly pulled her close to him. "At least you are consistent." He held her away from him, caressed her cheek with the back of his knuckles. "And what do you think I would charge for the food?"

"That I and my men swear allegiance to you, that we would fight for you even if you bade us fight against our own people," she said flatly.

"Good God!" Stephen half yelled. "What a monster you must think I am." He stared at her, frowning for a moment, then he smiled. "The payment I want will cost you much more. I want a kiss from you. One kiss, freely given. One kiss that I don't have to fight you for."

Bronwyn's first reaction was to tell him what he could do with his food and his kisses, in Gaelic of course, but she was sure he'd understand. Then she paused. If nothing else, a Scotsman was practical. She couldn't very well let all that food go to waste.

"Aye," she whispered. "I'll kiss you."

She leaned forward, on her knees, and touched her lips to his. He started to grab her to him but she pushed his arms away. "Mine!" she said possessively. Stephen smiled and leaned back on his elbows, allowing her to take charge of him.

Her lips played with his ever so gently, touching them, moving on them. She used the very edge of her teeth, the tip of her tongue, to explore and search his mouth.

She moved away just enough to look at him. It was raining outside, and the soft sound made them feel isolated and especially alone. The soft gold of the flickering fire cast gentle shadows on his handsome face. With his eyes closed, his lips slightly parted, Bronwyn could feel her heart begin to pound. Was it her imagination or had he grown better-looking since she'd first met him? He suddenly seemed perfection in a male.

Yet he lay still, waiting quietly. There was no sign of the excitement that she was feeling. No sense of humor! she thought and smiled. Let's see how much humor you have, Englishman!

Stephen briefly opened his eyes before Bronwyn's lips descended on his again. This time she wasn't sweet or gentle but hungry. She bit at his lips, sucked at them.

Stephen lost his easy position of relaxation and fell against the hard floor. His hands closed about Bronwyn's waist, pulling her closer to him. She laughed deep within her throat and again pushed his hands away. Obediently he let them fall to his side.

She pulled her head away, her lips still fastened to his, and his head followed her. With one hand behind his head, her fingers twisted in his hair, she moved her other hand to his knee. As she began to move it slowly upward, she felt his body tremble. He wore the Scots' dress, and he was bare under the shirt and plaid. Inch by slow inch she caressed his inner thigh, higher and higher. When she touched him between his legs, Stephen's eyes flew open, and the next minute he'd thrown Bronwyn to her back and had one leg across her.

"No!" she said, pushing against him. "One kiss, that was your price." She was breathing so hard she could hardly talk, as if she'd been running for miles.

Stephen did not come to his senses quickly. He stared at her quite stupidly.

Both of her hands were against his chest. "You promised I could eat if I gave you one kiss. I believe I did that," she said in all seriousness.

"Bronwyn," Stephen said as if he were a dying man.

She smiled quite merrily and gave him a sharp push, then scrambled away from him. "Never let it be said that a Scotsman doesn't keep his word."

Stephen groaned and closed his eyes for a moment. "I must have aged twenty years since I met you. Drugs this morning, then you climbing a rock wall, and now you try to finish me. What more can I expect? The rack, or do you prefer the water torture?"

She laughed at him, then handed him a juicy piece of roast pork. She was already eating, her lips red from the kiss, glossy from the meat. She grabbed a piece of meat pie when Stephen took the pork. "How did you come to this place? Who brought the food? How did you hear about the cliff?"

It was Stephen's turn to laugh as he began to eat, but without Bronwyn's gusto. He still hadn't recovered from Bronwyn's hand between his legs. Tam had been more than right about the convenience of the Scots' dress.

"Douglas went to Tam," he said after a while, then frowned. "I wish I could teach your men to come to me," he said in disgust. "I seem to hear everything second-hand."

Bronwyn had her mouth and both hands full of food. "Douglas was merely being an obedient son."

"Son? What are you talking about?"

She blinked at him. "Douglas is Tam's son."

"But I thought Tam's son was killed."

She gave him a look of disgust as she buttered a piece of black bread. "A man may have more than one son. My father said Tam was trying to make his own clan. He has an even dozen sons, or did have until you English killed one."

Stephen put his hand up in defense. "Who are they?"

"Douglas, Alex, Jarl, Francis, are the oldest. Then he has some boys who are too young to fight, and his new wife is about to bear him a new one any day."

Stephen chuckled. It was always the quiet ones you needed to watch.

"You haven't answered my questions," Bronwyn said, not anywhere near to slowing down her eating. "And why did you bring me here?"

"I thought the ride might cool my temper, and I didn't want your men interfering," he said before answering her other questions.

"Tam tried to wake me but he couldn't." He gave Bronwyn a chastising look, but she ignored him. "Morag made me drink some disgusting concoction that nearly killed me. Before I could recover, I was on a horse and we were running along the cliff path. We got there just as Alex was being pulled up."

He put down the chicken leg he was eating and gave her a searching look. "Why did you have to go over the side? Why the hell did those men of yours *allow* you to do that?"

She set down the scone she was eating. "Can't you ever understand? *I* am the MacArran. It is I who allows or disallows. My men follow my orders, not the other way around."

Stephen rose to put more peat on the fire. His English upbringing warred within him. "But you're not strong. What if Alex had been unconscious and couldn't have helped you? You haven't the muscle to lift the dead weight of a man."

She was patient with him, realizing that he was trying to understand. "I went myself because I'm small. There was very little room on the ledge, and I felt I could move about more easily than a large man. As for lifting Alex, I can't lift his entire body but I knew I could get a rope under enough parts of him so that he could be pulled up. If I thought there'd been a better chance for Alex by sending someone else, I wouldn't have hesitated. I always try to do what is best for my people."

"Damn!" Stephen said fiercely, then jerked her to her feet. "I don't like hearing words of wisdom from a woman."

She blinked, then smiled at his honesty. "Don't you know some good leaders who use their heads instead of their muscles?"

He stared at her, then pulled her into his arms, his hand buried in her hair. "I was so angry," he whispered, "I didn't at first believe the men when they told me where you were. I don't think I breathed until I saw that you were all right."

She lifted her head and looked at him, her eyes searching his face. "If I had been killed, I'm sure Tam would have given some of my estates to you."

"Estates!" he gasped, then pushed her head back to his shoulder. "Sometimes you are a stupid woman. I should punish you for that insult." He wouldn't let her move when she tried to. "I think maybe I will delay your eating," he said huskily. He lifted her face and kissed her greedily, laughing

497

at the grease on her lips. "You're an earthy thing," he said, then said no more as she slipped her arms around his neck.

It took only moments to renew his passion. Recalling the events of the morning, his fear for her while she'd been suspended against a sheer rock wall, made him kiss her almost in desperation. He held her face in his hands, his tongue sweetly drawing on her nectar.

He put his arms beneath her knees and carefully laid her by the fire. He took his time undressing her, unbuckling her belt, then kissing her stomach. He slid her plaid away from her hips, then kissed her legs, the whole golden length of them.

"Come to me," she whispered.

But it was his turn to be the torturer. He pushed her pleading hands away, then began unbuttoning her blouse. He kissed each patch of skin as it was bared and smiled when she arched toward him.

He only laughed when she pulled on his hair, demanding that he come to her. He shook his head vigorously, his face buried in her breasts, and her hands fell away. He sat back on his heels and looked at her. Her body was so beautiful.

She opened her eyes to stare up at him and wondered what he was thinking. She watched as he threw off his clothes and came to lay beside her. She gasped as his skin touched hers.

It was warm in the room, but their hot skin touching made it an inferno. "Stephen," she whispered, the word sounding almost like an endearment.

"Yes," he murmured before pulling her under him.

In spite of their passion their lovemaking was slow. They took their time with each other. Bronwyn pushed Stephen to his back once and controlled their movements. Then, as their desire rose, faster and higher, Stephen shoved Bronwyn to the floor for the last few deep, hard thrusts.

Weak, he collapsed on top of her, his lips against her neck. Within minutes they both fell asleep.

Two weeks later Stephen's prediction that the MacGregor would hate Bronwyn came true.

Stephen had spent that two weeks learning from Bronwyn's men. That one disastrous cattle raid had shown him the need for learning to fight in the Scots manner. He learned to run, to use the heavy Claymore. He could slip in and out of his plaid in seconds. His legs grew brown and weathered, and he didn't even mind the cold when the first snows arrived.

As for Bronwyn, she watched him suspiciously, only relaxing her guard at night when she was in his arms.

Stephen had changed so much in the last few weeks that it seemed a long time since that cattle raid when Bronwyn had scratched her initial on her enemy's shoulder. The first sign Lachlan MacGregor gave of his anger was when he burned three crofters' houses on the northern estates.

"Was anyone hurt?" Bronwyn asked weakly when she heard the news.

Tam pointed to a young man standing amid the ruins. He turned, and on his cheek was branded an *L*.

Bronwyn put her hand to her mouth in horror.

"The MacGregor said he'd brand all the clan before he's finished. He said he nearly died from blood poisoning from the wound ye gave him," Tam continued.

She turned away and walked back to her horse. Stephen stopped her.

"You needn't worry that I'll lecture you," he said flatly when he saw her face. "Perhaps you've learned something from this. Now it's my turn to settle the matter."

"What are you planning to do?" she asked.

"I'm going to try to meet with the MacGregor and settle this once and for all."

"Meet with him!" she gasped. "He'll kill you! He hates the English more than I do."

"That's impossible," he said sarcastically as he mounted his horse and rode away from the smoldering ruins of the houses.

An hour later Chris was agreeing with Bronwyn. The two men, who had come to Scotland looking so much alike, were now very different in appearance. Chris still wore the English dress—a heavy velvet jacket lined in mink, satin breeches, and tight, fine woolen hose. But Stephen had changed completely;

even his skin had darkened. His hair hung past his ears, curling around them in a becoming manner. If anything, his legs were even more muscular from his daily sprints with the Scotsmen.

"She's right," Chris said. "You can't go knocking on the door and ask to see the MacGregor. I've heard some of the tales of what he's done. You'd be lucky if he killed you right away."

"What am I supposed to do then? Sit back and watch my people branded, burned out?"

Chris stared at his friend. "Your people?" he asked quietly. "When did you become a Scotsman?"

Stephen grinned and ran his hand through his hair. "They're good people, and I'd be proud to be one of them. It was just Bronwyn's temper that caused this mess. I'm sure it can be straightened out."

"Did you know this feud has been going on for hundreds of years? Every one of these clans is at war with one of the others. It's a barbaric place!"

Stephen merely smiled at his friend. A few months ago he'd have said the same thing. "Come on inside and let's have a drink. I got a letter from Gavin yesterday, and he wants me to bring Bronwyn home for Christmas."

"Will she go?"

Stephen laughed. "She'll go whether she wants to or not. What about you? Will you come with us?"

"I'd *love* to. I've had about all I can take of this cold country. I don't understand how you can move about when half of you is bare."

"Chris, you should try it. It gives a man a great deal of freedom."

Chris snorted. "The freedom to freeze off my finer parts isn't exactly what I want. Maybe you can tell me where to do some hunting. I thought I'd take some of your men and mine and see if I could get a deer."

"Only if you promise to take some of Bronwyn's men too."

Chris gave a little snort of derision. "I don't know

whether I should be insulted by that or not." He stopped at Stephen's expression. "All right, I'll do as you say. If there is any trouble, I guess it would be better if I had a few of your bare-legged men near me." He smiled and put his hand on Stephen's shoulder. "I'll see you tomorrow, and we'll have fresh venison."

Stephen never saw Chris alive again.

The winter sun was just setting when four of Bronwyn's men rode through the gates at the mouth of the peninsula. Their clothes were torn and bloody. One man bore a long, jagged gash across his cheek.

Stephen was on the training field, listening to Tam instruct him in the use of the lochaber axe. Bronwyn stood close by, watching the men.

Tam was the first one to see the disheveled and wounded men. He dropped the axe and ran forward, Stephen and Bronwyn close behind him. "What is it, Francis?" he gasped, pulling the young man from his horse.

"MacGregor," he said. "The hunting party was attacked."

Stephen was on his horse before Francis had dismounted. The boy looked up at Stephen. "Two miles past the loch on the East Road." Stephen nodded once before he rode away. He didn't seem to be aware that both Bronwyn and Tam were trying to keep up with him.

The fading sunlight flashed off Chris's armor as he lay so still on the cold Scots ground. Stephen leaped from his horse and knelt beside his friend. He tenderly pushed back the face plate.

He didn't look up when he heard the voice of one of Chris's men over his shoulder. "Lord Chris wanted to show the Scots how the English could fight," the man said. "He put on his armor and planned to meet the MacGregor face to face."

Stephen glanced down at Chris's quiet form. He knew the heavy armor had made his friend immobile, and the MacGregor had been free to hack at Chris at will. There were places unprotected by the armor, and now there were dents and mutilations in the steel.

"They tried to save him."

Stephen noticed for the first time the three Scotsmen who lay beside Chris. Their strong young bodies were bloody and ugly.

Stephen felt rage well up inside him. His friend! His friend was dead. He stood, then grabbed Bronwyn, turned her so she faced the four dead men.

"This is what has happened because of your escapade. Look at them! Do you know them?"

"Yes," she managed to whisper as she stared at them. She'd known the young men all her life, for all their short lives. She looked away.

Stephen buried his hands in her hair, pulling her head painfully back. "Do you remember the sound of their voices? Can you hear their laughter? Do they have any family?" He moved her head so she looked at Chris. "Chris and I were fostered together. We spent our childhoods together."

"Let me go!" she said desperately.

Abruptly Stephen released her. "You drugged me and led your men in a cattle raid, and you carved your initial on the MacGregor. Stupid, childish actions! And now we have paid for your actions, haven't we?"

She tried to hold her head high. She wouldn't believe he was right.

Douglas held his Claymore aloft. He'd ridden to the scene behind Bronwyn and his father. "We must revenge this act," he said loudly. "We must ride now and fight the MacGregor."

"Yes!" Bronwyn shouted. "We must repay him *now!*"

Stephen took one step forward and sank his fist into Douglas's face. He grabbed the Claymore just before Douglas fell.

"Hear me and hear me well," Stephen said in a quiet voice that carried to all the men. "This will be settled, but not by more blood being shed. This is a useless feud, and I'll not retaliate by drawing more blood. More deaths will not bring these men back." He gestured to the four bloody corpses at his feet.

"You're a coward," Douglas said in a low voice as he stood, rubbing his bruised jaw.

Before Stephen could speak, Tam stood next to his son. In his hand was his dirk. He held it low, aimed at his son's ribs. "Ye may disagree with the man, but ye'll not call him a coward," he said in his deep, rumbling voice.

Douglas locked eyes with his father, then he nodded once before he turned to Stephen. "We'll be willin' to follow ye," he said after a while.

"Follow *him!*" Bronwyn fairly shouted. "*I* am the MacArran. Are you forgetting that he's an Englishman?"

Tam spoke for his son. "I don't think we've forgotten so much as we've learned," he said quietly.

Bronwyn didn't ask what he'd learned. She looked at the faces of one man after another, and she could see they were changing toward her. Had it been a gradual thing, or did they too blame her for the men's deaths? She took a step backward from them, feeling as if she should put her hands up in protection. "No," she whispered before she turned and ran for her horse.

She didn't care where she went or how far. Tears blurred her vision so badly she could barely see. She rode for miles, across the hills and lochs. She never even noticed when she left the MacArran land.

"Bronwyn!" someone from behind her screamed.

At first she only spurred her horse faster, urging it away from the familiar voice. It wasn't until he was beside her that she realized it was her brother who called to her.

"Davey," she whispered and reined in her horse sharply.

Davey grinned at her. He was tall like Bronwyn, with their father's black hair, but he had inherited their mother's brown eyes. He was thinner than Bronwyn remembered, and his eyes seemed to have a wild inner glow. "You've been crying," he said. "Because of the men the MacGregor killed?"

"You knew?" she said, wiping her tears away with the back of her hand.

"It's still my clan, in spite of what Father said." For an instant his eyes were hard and cold, then they changed. "I haven't seen you in a long time. Sit with me and let your horse rest."

Suddenly her brother seemed like an old friend, and she pushed from her mind the last time she'd seen him—the night Jamie MacArran had named her laird. It had been an unexpected announcement and therefore more painful. All the clan had gathered and was waiting for the proclamation that Davey would be the next laird. James MacArran was always honest about himself and especially about his children. He told the clan about his children. He said Davey liked war too much, that he cared more for battle than for protecting his clan. He said Bronwyn had too much temper and too often acted before she thought. Both of his children felt deeply humiliated at their father's complaints. Jamie went on to say that Bronwyn could be controlled if she had a level-headed husband such as Ian, Ramsey or Ennis. Even after that statement no one guessed what Jamie had in mind. When he announced Bronwyn as his successor, provided she marry one of the young men, the hall was silent. Then, one by one, the clan raised cups to salute her. It took Davey a few moments to realize what was happening. When he did, he rose and cursed his father, called him a traitor, and declared himself no longer his son. He asked for men to follow him, to forever leave the clan. Twelve young men walked out of the hall behind Davey that night.

Bronwyn had not seen her brother since that night. Since then several men had been killed, her father included; she had been married to an Englishman. Suddenly all that Davey'd said so long ago seemed unimportant.

She dismounted her horse and put her arms around him. "Oh, Davey, everything has turned out so badly," she cried.

"The Englishman?"

She nodded against his bony shoulder. "He's changed everything. Today my men looked at me as if I were the intruder. I saw it in their eyes that they thought he was right and I was wrong."

"Do you mean he's turning the men against you?" Davey snapped, moving away from her. "How could they be so blind? He must be a good actor to overcome the horror of our father's death. How can the men forget that it was the English who killed the MacArran? And what of Ian? Has even Tam forgotten his son's death?"

"I don't know," Bronwyn said as she sat down on a fallen log. "They all seem to trust him. He dresses as a Scotsman. He trains with my men. He even spends time with the crofters. I see them together, laughing, and I know they like him."

"But has he ever done anything to gain their trust? I mean something besides kissing babies?"

She put her hands to her temples. All she could see was the four dead men on the ground. Had she caused their deaths? "He hasn't done anything to make them distrust him either."

Davey snorted. "He would be careful not to. He will wait until he gets their confidence before he brings his Englishmen here."

"Englishmen? What are you talking about?"

"Don't you see?" Davey said with great patience. "Tell me, is he planning to return to England soon?"

"Yes," she said, surprised. "I believe he plans us to leave in a few weeks."

"That's when he'll bring his Englishmen back here. He'll teach them all he's learned about fighting like a Scotsman, and we'll have very little defense against them."

"No!" she said as she rose. "Davey, you can't mean this. He's not like this. He can be kind, and I know he's concerned about my men."

He gave her a look of disgust. "I've heard how he makes you howl in bed. You're afraid of losing him. You'd sacrifice your clan for an Englishman's hands on your body."

"That's not true! The clan always comes first with me." She stopped abruptly. "I had forgotten how much we quarrel. I must go back now."

"No," Davey said quietly, his hand on her arm. "Forgive me for upsetting you. Sit here with me for a while. I've missed you. Tell me how Larenston is. Did you get the leak in the roof fixed? How many sons does Tam have now?"

She smiled as she sat down again. They talked for several minutes as the night closed about them, about the everyday happenings within the clan. She found out that Davey was living somewhere in the hills, but he was evasive about his life and so she respected his privacy.

"And do you enjoy being laird?" he asked amiably. "Do the men obey you?"

She smiled. "Yes. They treat me with great respect."

"Until this morning when they turned to your husband."

"Don't start again."

Davey leaned back against a tree. "It just seems a shame that centuries of MacArrans are now ruled by an Englishman. If you'd had time, you could have established your own authority, but you can't expect the men to follow a woman when a man is there pushing her behind him."

"I don't know what you mean."

"I was just daydreaming. What if this Stephen is a spy sent by King Henry? When he has the trust of your men, he could do a great deal of damage to Scotland. Of course, you'd be there and you'd try to get your men to follow you, but by then they would be so used to disobeying your orders that you'd never even get their attention."

She couldn't answer him. She was remembering all the times lately that her men had gone to Stephen, whereas when they'd first returned from England, her clan had asked only her opinion.

Davey continued. "Too bad you haven't had time alone with your clan. If you had, they'd see you had sense enough to lead them. When—or if—Montgomery betrayed you, you could lead the clan to safety."

She didn't like to think about his words. She had caused her men's deaths today. Her stupidity and arrogance had caused four deaths, and Stephen was right to blame her. Her men were right to turn to him. But what if Stephen were a spy? What if he did decide to use her men's trust against them? For generations the Scots had hated the English. Surely there was a reason for that hatred. For all she knew there could be a hundred tragedies in Stephen's life that would cause him to hate the Scots. Perhaps Davey was right and Stephen wanted to lead them all into slaughter.

She put her hands to her head. "I can't think," she whispered. "I don't know what he is or whether he can be trusted."

"Bronwyn," Davey said as he took her hands. "You may not believe this, but I want what is best for the clan. I've had months to come to terms with myself—and with you. I know you're the one who should be laird, not me." He put a finger to her lips. "No, let me finish. I want to help. I want to be sure he isn't a spy, that he won't turn on our clan."

"Sure? What do you mean?"

"I'll take him to my camp, that's all. He won't be harmed, and while he's gone you can reestablish yourself as the true head of Clan MacArran."

"Take him!" She rose, her eyes flashing even in the darkness of the night.

"He wouldn't be harmed. I'd be foolish to harm him. King Henry would declare war on Clan MacArran. All I want to do is buy you a little time."

She pulled away from him. "And what do you get out of it?" she asked coldly.

"I want to come home," he said heavily. "If I do this good deed for you, then I hope to come home with honor. My men and I are starving, Bronwyn. We aren't farmers, and we have no crofters to farm for us."

"You're welcome at home, you should know that," she said quietly.

He jumped up. "And have the men laugh at me, saying I came home with my tail between my legs? No!" He calmed somewhat. "It would save our dignity if we could return in triumph. We'll ride back into Larenston with your English husband, and everyone, from King Henry down, would be grateful to us."

"I . . . no, it's not possible. Stephen is—"

"Think about it. You'd have control of your people. I

could return home in honor. Or maybe you care more about this Englishman than your own brother," he sneered.

"No! Of course not! But if he were harmed—"

"You insult me! Do you think I have no brain? If I were to harm him, think what King Henry would do to us! Oh, Bronwyn, please consider it. It would be so good for the clan. Don't confuse them any more than they already are. Don't wait until you see them standing on a battlefield trying to choose between England and Scotland. Let them know they're Scotsmen. Don't make them divide their loyalties."

"Davey, I must go, please."

"You should go. Think about it. In three days I'll meet you along the cliff wall. Where Alex fell."

She looked up, startled.

"I know a lot about my clan," he said as he threw a leg into his saddle and rode away.

Bronwyn stared after him for a few minutes until the darkness swallowed him. She dreaded returning to Larenston, dreaded facing the deaths of her men, as well as Stephen's anger. But the MacArran couldn't afford to be a coward. She straightened her shoulders and mounted her horse.

Chapter 9

BRONWYN WALKED slowly across the courtyard. She'd had three days since her men were killed to think. Davey's words haunted her. Every minute she became more aware of the way her men were turning to Stephen. It was natural that they'd look to a man for leadership, since it'd been only months ago that they'd followed Jamie MacArran. But Bronwyn didn't trust any Englishman. She knew what foul, crude, greedy people they were. Hadn't she met several Englishmen when she was held captive at Sir Thomas Crichton's?

As for Stephen, the death of his friend affected him greatly. He didn't talk much, and Bronwyn often caught him staring into space. Immediately after the killings he ordered the packing for the trip to England to begin. He said that he wanted to take Chris's body back to his family.

At night, when they were alone, they lay side by side without touching, without speaking. Bronwyn was haunted by the sight of the three dead men. She wondered how her father came to terms with himself when he made a mistake that cost the lives of men he loved. She felt the knot forming in her throat. The laird of a clan shouldn't cry. She must be strong and not be afraid of being alone.

Besides the heaviness of her guilt, she had Davey's pleas to consider. She knew of the pride of her brother, knew that it had been difficult for him to ask anything of her. Yet how could she turn Stephen over to him?

She put her hands to her ears. She wanted to do what was right for everyone, but she felt so alone and so powerless. What *was* right?

She saddled her horse herself and left the peninsula to meet Davey.

Davey stared at her for some moments, his eyes hot and piercing. When Bronwyn looked down at her hands, trying to put her thoughts into words, he knew her decision.

"So!" he said, his eyes changing to an unforgiving look. "You're going to put your lover before the clan."

She looked at him without blinking. "You know that isn't true."

He snorted. "Then I can assume that it's me you don't believe in. I hoped you'd let me prove myself, prove that I've matured over that horrible boy who cursed his father."

"I want to, Davey," she said quietly. "I want to do what is right for everyone."

"Like hell you do!" he exploded. "You only care for yourself. You're *afraid* for me to return. You're afraid the men will follow me, the true MacArran." He turned toward his horse.

"Davey, please, I don't want us to part like this. Come home, at least for a while."

"And stand by and see my sister," he sneered the word, "take my rightful place in the clan? No thank you. I'd rather be king of my own poor kingdom than a servant in another." He nearly jumped into his saddle and thundered away.

Bronwyn had no idea how long she stood there alone, staring at the ground, feeling stupid and helpless.

"Who was that?" Stephen asked quietly.

She looked up at him, not surprised to see him there. So often he seemed to be near her even though she wasn't aware of his presence. "My brother," she said quietly.

"David?" he asked with interest as he looked in the direction of the galloping horse.

She didn't answer him.

"Did you ask him to come to Larenston?" he continued. "Did you tell him the gates are always open?"

"I don't need you to tell me what to say to my own brother." She turned away, tears in her eyes.

He grabbed her arm. "I'm sorry. I didn't mean it like it sounded."

She jerked away from him, but he drew her back, pulled her into his arms.

"I was wrong to curse you when I found Chris dead," he said quietly. "I was just so angry I wanted to lash out at someone. I was wrong."

She kept her face pressed to his chest. She longed for him to hold her in his arms. "No! You were right! I did kill my men and your friend."

He pulled her closer, felt the trembling in her body. Her shoulders were so small and delicate. "No, that's too much responsibility for you to assume." He lifted her chin. "Here, look at me. Whether you believe this or not, we're in this together, and I share the burden of the men's deaths."

"But I was the one," she said desperately.

He put his finger to her lips, then his eyes searched her face. "You're so young, not even twenty, but you're trying to take care of hundreds of people, even to protect them from me, a man who you think could be a spy."

He laughed at the expression on her face. "I'm beginning to understand you. Right now you're thinking that I have an ulterior motive for talking this way. You're thinking that I'm planning some treacherous act, and I want you quietly dazed by my honeyed words."

She pulled away from him. "Let me go!" His words were so close to what she'd been thinking that she was almost frightened.

He gave a low laugh. "Am I too close to home? You want me to remain a stranger, don't you? Someone you can easily hate. But I don't plan to leave you alone long enough to forget that I'm a man before I'm an Englishman."

"You—you're not making sense. I need to get back to Larenston."

He ignored her as he sat down on the grass and pulled

her down beside him. "Tomorrow we start for England. How do you feel about meeting my family?"

She stared at him. "I haven't thought of it." Her eyes flashed blue fire as she remembered her time at Sir Thomas Crichton's house. "I don't like the English people."

"You don't know them!" Stephen retorted. "You've met only the scum. I was embarrassed by my own people at the way they treated you at Sir Thomas's."

"None of them left me standing at the altar in my wedding dress."

He chuckled. "You're not about to forget that, are you? When you meet my sister-in-law Judith, perhaps you'll forgive me."

"What . . . what's she like?" Bronwyn asked tentatively.

"Beautiful! Kind and sweet-tempered and smart. She runs Gavin's estates with one eye closed. King Henry was quite taken with her and more than once asked her opinion."

Bronwyn sighed heavily, her breath catching in her throat. "It's good to hear of someone who is competent and doesn't mishandle her responsibilities. I wish my father had a daughter who was worthy of the title of laird."

He laughed and pulled her back against him, stretched out on the cold, damp ground. "For a woman, you're quite capable as a laird."

She blinked. "For a woman? Does that mean you think no woman is capable of being chief of a clan?"

He shrugged. "At least not one so young and pretty or so ill-trained."

"Ill-trained! I have trained all my life. You know I can read better than you as well as add a column of figures."

He laughed. "There's more to ruling men than adding numbers." He looked at her for a moment. "You're so beautiful," he said quietly as he bent forward to kiss her.

"Let me go! You are an insufferable, narrow-minded, ignorant—" She stopped because his hands were on her legs, caressing them.

"Yes," he whispered against her mouth. "What am I?"

"I do not know and I do not care," she said as if from a

long way away. She arched her neck backward as he touched it with his lips.

In spite of the seeming privacy Bronwyn and Stephen were not alone. David MacArran stood on the hill above them, watching them. "The whore!" he whispered. She put her own lust before the needs of her brother. And to think Jamie MacArran thought she was more worthy to be laird.

He raised his fist toward the couple below him. He'd show them! He'd show all of Scotland who was the most powerful man, the true laird of Clan MacArran.

He sharply reined his horse away and headed back toward his secret camp in the hills.

The sun was barely up as the wagons rolled down the steep path to the mainland. Stephen's men, now so brown, hardly distinguishable from Bronwyn's Scots, rode beside him. They were a quiet group, apprehensive about the outcome of the journey. The wagons were loaded with English clothes, and Bronwyn's men wondered if they'd be able to function in English society.

Bronwyn had her own worries. Morag had lectured her for a long time when the old woman heard about Davey's plan. "Don't ye be atrustin' him," she said, pointing a short bony finger at Bronwyn. "He always was a sly one, even as a boy. He wants Larenston, and he'll stop at nothin' to get it."

Bronwyn had defended her brother, but now she remembered Morag's warnings. She looked about her for the hundredth time.

"Nervous?" Stephen said from beside her. "You needn't be. I'm sure my family will like you."

It took her a full minute to understand what he was talking about. She put her nose haughtily in the air. "You should worry whether the MacArran will like them," she said as she spurred her horse forward.

It was sundown when the first arrow whizzed past Bronwyn's left ear. She'd just begun to relax and forget her apprehensions. At first she didn't realize what was happening.

"Attack!" Stephen yelled, and within seconds his men had

formed a circle of defense, their weapons ready. Bronwyn's men slipped off their horses, out of their plaids, and into the woods.

She sat stupidly on her horse as she saw one man after another go down.

"Bronwyn!" Stephen yelled. "Ride!"

She obeyed him instinctively. The arrows flew about her. One grazed her thigh, and her horse screamed as the shaft burned the animal's skin. It suddenly came to her why she was so stunned. The arrows were all directed at her! And one of the archers she'd seen in a tree was one of the men who'd left the clan to join Davey. Her brother was trying to kill her!

She put her head down and urged her horse forward. There was no need to turn around; she could feel the pounding of the horses' hoofs behind her. She followed Stephen's horse as he led her away from the flying arrows. For once there was no thought of whether she trusted him or not.

She screamed once when her horse was shot from under her. Before the animal could even go to its knees, Stephen had circled back, and his arm was about her waist as he pulled her to the front of his saddle. She twisted until she was astraddle, then bent low over the animal's neck.

They rode hard across unknown, wild country. Bronwyn could feel Stephen's big stallion beginning to tire.

Suddenly Stephen slumped forward onto Bronwyn's back. She didn't have time to think before she grabbed the reins and jerked sharply. The horse left the bit of a road and plunged into the woods. She knew she had to get Stephen off the horse before he fell. They couldn't move quickly in the woods, but perhaps she could find a few moments of cover.

She stopped the horse suddenly, the bit tearing its mouth. Stephen's inert body fell to the ground before Bronwyn could dismount. She gasped as she jumped beside him. There was a bloody place along the back of his head where an arrow had creased the skin. She didn't have much time to think, as she could already hear the other riders approaching. The forest floor was covered with dried leaves, and an idea came to her.

Quietly, so she wouldn't be heard, she led the horse away

from Stephen. She couldn't risk the sound of a slap, so she unfastened her brooch and jammed the sharp end into the horse's rump. It began running almost instantly. She ran back to Stephen, fell to her hands and knees, and pushed him against a fallen log. She covered him with armfuls of leaves. The heathery plaids he wore blended with the leaves. She lay beside him and dug herself in.

Seconds later they were surrounded by angry, stomping men. She held Stephen close to her, her hand over his mouth in case he should waken and make a sound.

"Damn her."

She held her breath; she'd recognize Davey's voice anywhere.

"She always did have seven lives! All of which I mean to take," he added viciously. "And that English husband of hers! I'll show King Henry the Scots rule Scotland."

"There goes her horse!" said another voice.

"Let's go!" Davey said. "She can't have gone too far."

It was a long time before Bronwyn moved. She was too stunned, too upset at first, to move. When her brain cleared a bit, she turned cautious. She wanted to be sure that Davey left no one behind in the area. She hoped to hear the sound of approaching horses, her own men, but when they did not appear in an hour, she stopped hoping.

It was full dark when Stephen groaned and made his first movement.

"Quiet!" she said, running her fingers along his cheek. Her right arm was dead from his weight on it for so long.

Slowly, listening for each sound of the forest around her, she moved the leaves away. Her eyes were keen in the dark, and she'd had some time to listen to her surroundings. There was a stream not far from them at the bottom of a steep ridge. She ran down to it, then knelt and tore away a large square of linen from her underskirt and wet it.

She knelt by Stephen, placed a few drops of water on his lips, then wiped the gash on the back of his head. The gash was not bad on his forehead, but she knew that sometimes such wounds had more serious consequences. It was quite possible that his brain could be addled.

He opened his eyes and stared up at her. The moonlight made his eyes silver. She leaned over him with concern. "Who am I?" she asked quietly.

His face was very serious, as if he puzzled over her question. "A blue-eyed angel who makes my life heaven and hell at the same time."

She groaned in disgust, then dropped the bloody cloth in his face. "You are, unfortunately, the same."

Stephen made a sorry attempt at a grin, then tried to sit up. He raised one eyebrow when Bronwyn quite naturally slipped her arm around him and helped him. "Is the news that bad?" he asked, his fingers rubbing his temple.

"What do you mean?" she asked suspiciously.

"If you're helping me, the news must be worse than I thought."

She stiffened. "I shouldn't have covered you but left you exposed for them to find."

"My head is killing me, and I don't feel like arguing. And what the hell did you do to my back? Drive steel pins into it?"

"You fell off your horse," she said with a certain amount of satisfaction. Even in the darkness she could see his look of warning. "I guess I should start at the beginning."

"It would please me greatly if you did," he said, one hand on his head, the other rubbing his back.

She told him as succinctly as possible about Davey's plan to kidnap Stephen.

"And no doubt you agreed," he said flatly.

"Of course not!"

"But getting rid of me would have solved many of your problems. Why didn't you agree to his plan?"

"I don't know," she said quietly.

"His arguments were quite logical, and it was a perfect way to get rid of me."

"I don't know!" she repeated. "I guess that I really didn't

trust him. Here, while we were under the leaves, I heard him say . . . that he meant to kill both of us."

"I guessed as much."

"How could you?"

He touched a curl of her black hair. "Just a guess based upon the number of arrows aimed directly at you. And the way they tried to separate us from the men. It's upset you, hasn't it?"

Her head snapped up. "What if you heard one of your brothers say he'd just tried to kill you?"

Even in the darkness she could see Stephen's face turn white. He looked at her in horror. "It is an impossible idea," he said flatly, finishing the subject. He looked around. "Where are we?"

"I have no idea."

"What about the men? Are they around here?"

"I'm only a woman, remember? How would I know about war strategy?"

"Bronwyn!" he warned.

"I don't know where we are. If the men don't find us soon, they'll return to Larenston, where we must go as soon as possible." She put her head to one side. "Quiet!" she whispered fiercely. "Someone's coming. We must hide!"

Stephen's first impulse was to meet whoever it was head on, but he had no weapon besides the little dirk at his side, and he had no idea how many people there were.

Bronwyn took his hand and pulled him forward. She led him to the crest of the steep ridge, then over the side. They quietly snuggled down into the thick bed of leaves and watched the two men who approached. They were obviously hunters, looking for game instead of the missing laird and her husband.

Stephen made a gesture as if he meant to say something to the men, but Bronwyn stopped him. He looked at her in surprise, but he didn't make a sound.

When the men were out of hearing distance, he turned to her. "They weren't David's men."

"Worse," she said. "They were MacGregors."

"Don't tell me you know each of the MacGregors personally."

She shook her head at his stupidity. "The cockades on their hats bore the MacGregor colors and insignia."

He gave her a brief look of admiration for her extraordinary night vision.

"I think I know where we are now."

He turned over, leaned back against the bank, and sighed. "Don't tell me," he said sarcastically. "Let me guess. We're in the middle of the MacGregor's land. We're weaponless, horseless, no food or gold. We're hunted by your brother, and the MacGregor would just love our heads on a platter."

Bronwyn turned to look at his profile, and suddenly a little giggle escaped her.

Stephen looked at her in astonishment, then he too smiled. "Hopeless, isn't it?"

"Yes," she agreed, her eyes dancing.

"Of course, this is no time to laugh."

"None whatever."

"But it is almost funny, isn't it?" he laughed.

She joined his laughter. "We'll probably be dead tomorrow, one way or another."

"So what do you want to do on your last night on earth?" he asked, his blue eyes picking up rays of moonlight.

"Someone could stumble on us at any moment," she said quite seriously.

"Hmmm. Shall we give them something to see?"

"Such as?"

"A couple of sublimely happy, totally nude woodspirits."

She pulled her plaid close about her. "It's awfully cold, don't you think?" she said coyly.

"I'll wager we can find a way to get warm. In fact, it makes a great deal of sense to combine our warmth."

"In that case—" She launched herself from the ground and jumped on him.

Stephen gave a gasp of surprise, then laughed. "I think I should have brought you to the MacGregor's land before."

"Quiet, Englishman!" she commanded as she lowered her head and began to kiss him.

Neither of them seemed to remember that they were perched on the side of a very steep ridge. Their passion, intensified by the danger of their predicament, made them oblivious to even more immediate dangers.

Bronwyn was the first one to lose her footing. She'd just moved to Stephen's side, slipped her skirt off while he removed his clothing, when the next instant she was rolling down the side of the hill.

Stephen made a grab for her, but his senses were dulled by his passion and he missed her. But he'd extended himself too far and tumbled down just after her.

They landed together in a tangle of nude, moonlit skin and a flurry of leaves.

"Are you all right?" Stephen asked.

"I will be as soon as you get off me. You're breaking my leg."

Instead of moving off her, he moved his body more fully onto her. "You never complained before that I was too heavy for you," he said as he began to nibble her ear.

She smiled as she closed her eyes. "There are times when you don't weigh much at all."

He moved his lips to her throat.

Suddenly something enormous and heavy landed smack on Stephen's back. He collapsed onto Bronwyn for a moment, then quickly lifted himself with his arms, protecting her. "What the hell!"

"Rab!" Bronwyn said, then squirmed out from under Stephen. "Oh, Rab," she said with great, deep joy. "Rab, sweet Rab." She buried her face in the dog's coarse fur.

Stephen sat back on his heels. "That's all I needed," he said sarcastically. "As if my back weren't sore enough already."

Rab moved away from Bronwyn to leap at Stephen. In spite of his words Stephen hugged the big dog while it licked his face and tried to smother him with affection.

"Now, aren't you ashamed," Bronwyn laughed. "He loves you and is quite glad to see you."

"I wish he'd paid more attention to *my* loving. Down, Rab! You're going to drown me. Here, boy, fetch." Stephen threw an imaginary stick, and the dog happily ran after it.

"That was terrible! You know he'll spend hours looking for it. He so wants to please."

Stephen reached out and grabbed her wrist. "I hope he spends the rest of the night. Do you know how delicious you look in the moonlight?"

She looked at him, his broad chest, his shoulders. "You're not exactly an unpleasant sight yourself."

He pulled her to him. "You keep this up and I may never return you to Larenston. Now where were we?"

"Your back was killing you and—"

His mouth on hers made her stop talking.

"Come here, wench," he whispered as he pulled her down into the leaves.

It was quite cold, but neither of them felt it. The leaves came up around them and sheltered them, hid them, warmed them. Bronwyn felt Stephen's thighs against hers, and she pulled him closer and closer to her.

They wrestled together, laughing. There were sticks and rocks poking their skin, but neither of them minded. Once Stephen began tickling Bronwyn, and the sound of her laughter, so unusual a sound to him, fired his passion to white-hot.

"Bronwyn," he whispered before pulling her under him and becoming serious.

When they came together, it was somehow different from the other times. In spite of their differences, their impossible situation, they made love as if they were free for the first time. There was not only passion but a sense of joy and fun too.

"I had no idea you were ticklish," Stephen whispered sleepily as he held Bronwyn close to him.

Rab snuggled on her other side. "Neither did I. Shouldn't we get our clothes?"

"In a minute," Stephen whispered. "In a min—"

* * *

They were awakened very early by Rab's growling. Stephen's reflexes were instant. He sat up and pushed Bronwyn behind him. He stared at a man who was some twenty feet away. He was a short, wiry man with brown hair and eyes. And he wore the MacGregor cockade.

"Good mornin'," he called heartily. "I didna' mean to disturb you. I came to get some water, but your dog wouldn't let me pass."

Stephen heard Bronwyn take in breath to speak. He turned and gave her a look of warning. She was half buried in the leaves, only her head and bare shoulders visible.

"Mornin'," Stephen called just as heartily, his voice heavy with the Scots burr. "Rab, come away, let the fine gentleman pass."

"I thank ye, sir," the man said as he walked the few feet to the stream.

"Rab, fetch our clothes," Stephen said, then watched as the dog obeyed. He looked back at the man at the edge of the stream, who was looking at the nude pair with curiosity. "A bit of Adam and Eve, aren't we?" Stephen laughed.

The man laughed also. "Just what I was thinkin'." He stood. "I didn't see your wagon or horses, so I had no idea anyone was here."

Stephen put on his shirt, then deftly threw his plaid about him and buckled his wide belt. Both men discreetly turned away as Bronwyn dressed. She didn't speak but was fascinated by Stephen's newly acquired accent.

"To tell the truth," Stephen said, "we have only what we have on our backs."

Bronwyn watched as he put his cap behind his back and tore the MacArran cockade from it.

"We were set upon by thieves."

"Thieves!" the man said. "In the MacGregor's land? He won't like that."

"Aye, that he won't," Stephen agreed. "Especially since it was some of those thievin' MacArrans. Oh! I'm sorry, my dear, I didn't mean to pull your hair," he said when Bronwyn gave a little gasp of horror.

"Ah, the MacArrans," the man said. "There's never been a more dishonest, treacherous, cowardly lot ever put on the face of the earth. Did you know that not long ago they nearly killed the MacGregor, merely because the man was riding across the woman's land? The hag took her knife to him and nearly mutilated him. I heard she tried to cut his manhood off. Probably jealous."

Stephen whirled Bronwyn to face him so the man couldn't see her face. "Let me help you with the brooch," he said pleasantly in his heavy burr.

"I barely scratched him," she said in disgust.

"What?" the man asked.

Stephen smiled. "My wife is warning me that I scratched her last time I fastened her brooch."

The man chuckled. "I'm Donald Farquhar of Clan MacGregor."

Stephen smiled happily. "I'm Stephen Graham, and this is my wife, Bronwyn." He smiled at the face she pulled at him.

"Bronwyn!" Donald said. " 'Tis an ill-favored name that one. Did ye know it was that witch the MacArran's name?"

Stephen held Bronwyn's shoulders firmly. "One can't help the name one was born with."

"No, ye canna." He looked at Bronwyn's long thick hair falling down her back, a few leaves stuck in it. "Anyone can see your Bronwyn isn't like that other one."

Bronwyn bent her head and acted as if she were kissing Stephen's hand, but in truth she applied her teeth sharply to the back of it. He released her, and she turned to smile at Donald. "And of course you've seen the MacArran many times," she said sweetly.

"No, not close, but I've seen her from a distance."

"And ugly is she?"

"Oh, aye. Great shoulders like a man and taller than most of her men. And a face so ugly she must keep it covered."

Stephen's fingers bit into her shoulders in warning. She nodded. "That's what I've always heard. It's nice to meet someone who knows her, so to speak," she said seriously.

Stephen bent forward to kiss her ear. "Behave yourself or you'll get us killed," he whispered.

Donald beamed at the two of them. "Ye must be newly-weds," he said happily. "I can't miss the way ye can't keep from touchin' one another."

"You miss little, do you, Donald?" Bronwyn said.

"I like to think I'm an observant man. Our wagon is on the ridge above. Perhaps you'd like to take a meal with us and meet my wife, Kirsty."

"No—" Bronwyn began, but Stephen stepped in front of her.

"We'd like that very much," he said. "We haven't eaten since yesterday noon. Perhaps you can give us directions. I'm afraid that after we were robbed, we wandered for quite some time and lost our way."

"But ye made good use of the time," Donald laughed, looking at the leaves with meaning.

"That we did!" Stephen said jovially, his arm firmly around Bronwyn's shoulders.

"Well, come on then. A MacGregor always welcomes a MacGregor." He turned and started up the hill.

"Don't do anything to endanger us," Stephen warned as they followed him.

"A MacGregor!" she muttered angrily.

"And an Englishman!" he added in the same tone.

"I don't know which is the lesser evil."

Stephen grinned. "Hate me but not him. He has the food."

At the top of the ridge all three of the people stopped and stared at the little woman bending over the fire. She was a delicate thing, no larger than a child, and her profile showed a little nose, a fragile mouth. But what was so unusual was that she was heavily, heavily pregnant. Her big belly stuck out in front of her like some massive monument. It was against all forces to reason that she was able to stand up and not let the weight of her burden pull her forward.

She did stand, quite easily, and turned to look at the three people watching her. For a moment she looked only at Donald, and a smile of pure adoration lit her face. When she turned and saw Bronwyn, her face changed. It seemed to go through several emotions: bewilderment, fear, disbelief, until finally she smiled.

Stephen and Bronwyn stood still, not breathing, expecting any moment that she'd announce who they were.

"Kirsty!" Donald said as he ran to his wife's side. "Are you all right?"

She put her hand on the side of her big belly and looked up in apology. "I'm sorry to greet ye like that, but I had a very strong kick."

Donald looked up and smiled. "He's a strong lad," he laughed. "Come and sit by the fire."

Stephen was the first to relax his muscles and walk toward the fire. Bronwyn followed him slowly. She still wasn't sure there hadn't been recognition on Kirsty's face. Perhaps she planned to tell Donald later and the MacGregors would attack them at night.

Donald introduced them to his wife, and even when the name Bronwyn was said, she only smiled. It wasn't a Scots name but a Welsh one, and it should have caused comment.

"Do you think we have enough food?" Donald asked.

Kirsty smiled. She had dark blonde hair and innocent brown eyes. It was difficult for anyone to mistrust her. "We always have enough to share," she said quietly.

They sat down to a meal of oatcakes baked on a griddle, and a savory rabbit stew. A cold wind blew around them. Donald's wagon stood at the edge of the road. It was small, with a wooden shelter built on top of it; a comfortable place but not meant for long-distance travel.

After breakfast Stephen proposed that he and Donald do some hunting.

Bronwyn immediately stood, brushed the crumbs off her skirt, and obviously meant to go with them.

Stephen turned to her. "Perhaps you should stay with Kirsty," he said quietly, with meaning. "A woman's place is by the fire."

Bronwyn felt anger flush through her. What did she know of cooking? She could help on the hunt. It was when she saw approval in Donald's face that she understood Stephen. Donald might begin to be suspicious of a woman who could hunt but couldn't cook. She sighed in resignation. "At least we'll have Rab for protection."

"No," Stephen said. "I think we'll need him on the hunt."

"Rab!" she commanded. "Stay with me."

"Come, Rab," Stephen said patiently. "Let's go hunting."

The big dog didn't even seem to consider moving from Bronwyn's side.

Donald chuckled. "That's a well-trained dog you have there."

"My father gave him to me," she said proudly.

"Your father?" Donald began.

"We'd better go," Stephen said quickly as he gave Bronwyn a look of warning.

She turned away from them and went to sit by the fire, close to Kirsty—her enemy.

Chapter 10

BRONWYN TWISTED a piece of grass about in her hands. Stephen's warning had made her realize how easily she could give herself away. She knew very little about being a wife and how the ordinary wife acted. All her life had been spent with men. She could ride and shoot, but cooking was a mystery to her. The everyday talk between women was also unknown to her.

"Have you been married long?" Kirsty asked.

"No," Bronwyn answered. "And you?"

"About nine months," Kirsty smiled as she rubbed her big stomach.

Bronwyn suddenly realized that someday her stomach could look like that. It had never occurred to her that she'd have to bear pregnancy. "Does the child hurt very much?" she asked quietly.

"Only now and then." Suddenly a look of pain crossed her face. "Tonight seems to be worse than usual," she said breathlessly.

"Could I get you something? Water? A pillow? Anything?"

Kirsty stared at her, her eyes blinking rapidly. "No, just talk to me. I haven't had a woman to talk to in a long time. Tell me, what's your husband like?"

"Stephen?" Bronwyn asked blankly.

Kirsty laughed. "Don't mind me. I'm just curious. You never seem to know a man until you live with him."

Bronwyn was cautious. "Were you disappointed in Donald?"

"Not at all. He was quite shy before we married, and now he's very kind, considerate. Your Stephen seems like a good man."

Bronwyn realized she'd never thought of Stephen as anything except an Englishman before. "He . . . he makes me laugh," she said after a while. "He makes me laugh at myself when I tend to be too serious."

Kirsty smiled, then she put her hand to her stomach and bent forward.

"What is it?" Bronwyn cried and went to her.

Kirsty sat up slowly, her breathing deep and difficult.

"Please let me help you," Bronwyn pleaded, her hands on Kirsty's arm.

Kirsty looked into Bronwyn's eyes. "You're very kind, aren't you?"

Bronwyn smiled. "I'm not a kind person in the least. I'm—" She broke off as she started to say she was the MacArran. But what was she away from her clan?

Kirsty put her hand over Bronwyn's. "I think you try to hide it. Tell me more about yourself. It keeps my mind off my own problems."

"I think I should call someone. I think you're about to have the baby."

"Please," Kirsty said desperately. "Don't frighten Donald. My baby isn't due yet. I can't have it now. Donald and I are going home to my parents'. My mother will deliver my child. It's just something I ate. I've had these pains before."

Bronwyn frowned as she sat back down on the ground.

"Tell me about yourself," Kirsty urged again. Her eyes were glazed. "What's it like to be married to an—"

Bronwyn's head came up sharply, but Kirsty didn't finish the sentence. She doubled over in pain, and the next minute Bronwyn caught the little woman in her arms.

"It's the baby," Kirsty whispered. "The baby is coming. You're the only one who can help me."

Bronwyn could only stare in horror. They were in the middle of nowhere, so who was going to be the midwife? She hugged Kirsty as another pain swept her. "Rab," she called quietly. "Go get Stephen. Get Stephen and bring him back here immediately."

Rab was away before Bronwyn finished speaking.

"Come inside the wagon, Kirsty," she said gently. Bronwyn was strong, and it was easy for her to get the small woman into the wagon. Kirsty lay down, and another pain made her double over.

Bronwyn looked out into the woods. No sign of the men. She went back to Kirsty, gave her a drink of water. Stephen would know what to do, she kept thinking. She didn't realize that for the first time she was depending on him.

She smiled when she heard Stephen's angry bellow.

"Bronwyn!"

She stepped down from the wagon.

"What the hell is this Satan-spawned dog of yours trying to do?" he demanded. "He jumped on me just as I was aiming at a deer. Then he nearly tore my leg off dragging me here."

She just smiled at him. "Kirsty is going to have her baby."

"Oh my God!" Donald breathed, then ran to the wagon.

"How soon?" Stephen asked.

"I think right away."

"Think!" Stephen said angrily. "Don't you know?"

"How would I know?"

He sputtered. "Women are supposed to know these things."

"And are they told them during reading lessons or sword play?" she asked sarcastically.

"Damned inadequate education for a girl if you ask me. There must have been some time when your family wasn't leading cattle raids."

"Damn you!" she began, then stopped when Donald stepped down from the wagon.

He was obviously worried. "She wants you," he said, his brow creased into a frown. There was a white line on each side of his lips. He reached for a piece of wood for the fire, but his hand shook so badly he dropped it.

"Me?" Bronwyn began, but Stephen gave her a sharp push forward.

"There's no one else," he said.

Her face lost all its color. "Stephen, I don't know the first thing about birthing a baby."

He put his hand to her cheek. "You're frightened, aren't you?"

She looked down at her hands.

"It couldn't be much different from a mare or a cow," he said helpfully.

"A cow!" Her eyes flashed at him, then she relaxed. "Stay with me," she said quietly. "Help me."

Stephen had never seen her look so soft, so in need of help. "How can I? A man can't attend a birth. Maybe if she were a relative of mine . . ."

"Look at him!" Bronwyn said, nodding toward Donald. "He only cares that his wife gets well. He doesn't care about anything else."

"Bronwyn!" Kirsty suddenly screamed from inside the wagon.

"Please," she said, her hand on Stephen's chest. "I've never asked you for anything before."

"Except to change my name, my nationality, my—"

She turned away from him, but he caught her arm. "Together," he whispered. "For once, let's do something together."

It wasn't an easy birth. Kirsty was very small, and the baby was large. None of the three of them knew much about having a baby, and they all agreed it was a wonderful experience. Bronwyn and Stephen sweated as much as Kirsty. When the head appeared, they looked at each other with pride. Stephen held Kirsty up so she could see while Bronwyn held the little head and gently guided the shoulders out.

The last part of the baby seemed to pop out, and Bronwyn held him in her arms.

"We did it!" she whispered.

Stephen grinned at her, then gave Kirsty a smacking kiss.

"Thank you," Kirsty smiled as she lay back against Stephen's arm, thoroughly exhausted but very happy.

It took them some minutes to clean the baby and Kirsty. Stephen and Bronwyn looked down at the mother and child, the baby already nosing around Kirsty's breast.

"Let's tell Donald he has a son," Stephen whispered.

Donald stood just outside the wagon, waiting, his face full of fear.

"Cheer up!" Stephen said, laughing. "Go have a look at the boy."

"A boy," Donald said in a very shaky voice before he climbed into the wagon.

It had grown dark while they were inside with Kirsty. The bright, cold day had turned to dark, even colder night.

Bronwyn stretched and drank deeply of the fresh, clear air. For some reason she had a feeling of freedom. She suddenly threw back her head, extended her arms, and twirled round and round.

Stephen laughed and grabbed her in his arms, lifting her feet off the ground. "You were wonderful," he said enthusiastically. "You were so strong and calm, and you helped make things easier for Kirsty." He braced himself as he realized he'd made an opening for Bronwyn to tell him of her training to become the MacArran.

Bronwyn smiled up at him, put her arms around his neck, and snuggled her face into his shoulder. "Thank you. But it was your knowing what to do that was the most help. If it'd been me alone, I think I would have just stopped and stared when the baby's head came."

Stephen didn't believe her for a moment, but it helped his pride to hear her say he was of some use to her. "Are you tired?" he asked quietly as he held her close and ran his hand over her hair.

"Very," she said, feeling quite comfortable and relaxed.

He bent and put his arm under her knees. "Let's go find some place to sleep." He carried her over the side of the ridge, then put her down as he deftly unfastened his plaid and spread it on the ground. Within minutes they were snuggled together, close for warmth, Rab against Bronwyn's back.

"Stephen?" Bronwyn asked quietly. "What are we going to do now? We still have no way to get to England, and alone we'll be recognized."

Stephen lay very still while his thoughts raced. Bronwyn had never asked his opinion before, nor had she lain beside him in just such a way before, with trust. He smiled, kissed the top of her head, and pulled her closer, and he knew his chest swelled several inches. "I haven't given it much thought, but I think that if we can, we should stay with Kirsty and Donald." He paused a moment. "What do you think?" As soon as the words were out, he realized how he'd changed. A few months ago he would have ordered his wife about what to do. Now he was asking her opinion.

Bronwyn nodded against him. "They're heading south to her parents. If we could travel there with them, maybe we could buy some horses."

"Buy? With our good looks?" Stephen asked. "We don't have anything worth a pence. We can't even repay Donald for his hospitality."

"A Scot won't need to be repaid."

"Even a MacGregor?" Stephen teased.

She gave a soft laugh. "As long as he believes we're not MacArrans. As for food, you're a good hunter, a better one than Donald, I'm sure. Now we just need a way to pay for some horses." She sighed. "Too bad Davey didn't attack us closer to the border."

"Why?"

"I would have had on one of those English dresses. The damned things are covered with jewels, and we could have sold them."

"If you'd been dressed as an Englishwoman we probably wouldn't be alive, and besides, we wouldn't have a warm plaid to roll about us."

She looked up at him. "I thought you hated our Scots dress. You said, if I remember correctly, that it left the whole bottom half of you bare."

"Don't be impertinent," he said in mock seriousness. "There's something to be said for quick access. A man can get out of a plaid in the time it takes an Englishman to think about undressing."

She smiled up at him. "Do I hear pride in your voice?" she teased. "And where in the world did you get that accent?"

"I have no idea what ye mean," he teased. "And if the truth were known, I think I put it on with the plaid."

"I like it," she said softly as she moved her knee up his bare leg and under the shirt he still wore. "How would you like to make love to a midwife? Or do you insist upon having the laird of a clan?"

He put his hand in her hair. "Right now I'll take you whatever you are. You're Bronwyn, a sweet, delicious bit of a thing who can ride like a demon, save her husband's life, and deliver a baby all in a few hours."

"I had a bit of help," she whispered before she lifted her mouth to his for his kiss.

Bronwyn too felt the strangeness of the place and time. She should be worried about her clan, but she knew Tam was there to guide them, and maybe her men would be better off if they didn't have to deal with the war that constantly raged between her and Stephen. Right now she didn't feel at all like being at war with him. She felt like she'd never felt before: soft and feminine. There were no decisions to make, no anger, no worry that Stephen was on the other side. Right now they were hunted equally.

"You have a faraway look," he said. "Will you share your thoughts with me?"

"I was thinking that right now I'm happy. I haven't had a happy or even a quiet thought since before my father died."

Stephen smiled because for the first time, she didn't accuse him of murder. "Come here, sweet, and see if I can't make you happier."

He took his time in undressing her. They twisted together under the swaddling plaid and laughed when an elbow punctured any delicate spot. It was an intimate wrestle, rolling, laughing, enjoying each other and their freedom.

Stephen's hands on Bronwyn's skin made her quieten. She was learning about the pleasures of his lovemaking. She kissed his face, his neck, watched the play of moonlight on his skin. He ran his lips across her shoulder, then down to her breast. She felt chills run through her. "Stephen," she whispered. He ran his hands over her waist and ribs. The strength of him excited her, made her feel small and in his power.

"You are so beautiful," he whispered.

She smiled and knew that he made her feel beautiful. He ran his hands down the inside of her thighs, and when he felt her tremble, the same emotion ran through him.

He moved on top of her slowly. She gave herself to him freely and eagerly, pulling his mouth down to hers. When she groaned aloud in her pleasure, Stephen kissed her deeply. The sounds she made, her abandonment to his lovemaking, were exciting to him.

They made love slowly, until Bronwyn clawed at Stephen, demanding more of him. She arched up to meet him, and he exploded in one massive thrust. She clasped him to her, not letting him go, wanting all of him.

They fell asleep that way, joined together, wrapped in each other's arms.

It was Bronwyn who woke first. Stephen held her so close to him that she could scarcely breathe. She watched him for a moment. There was a curl along his ear. She noticed how much he'd changed over the last few months. Gone was the pale English skin and the short, neat English hair. Yes, she thought, hardly anyone would recognize him as an Englishman now. She moved so she could kiss the curl of hair. She remembered that once she'd been afraid to make advances of such a nature toward him. This morning it seemed right that she'd kiss him awake.

He smiled before he opened his eyes.

"Good morning," she whispered.

"I'm afraid to look," he said dreamily. "Has someone changed my Bronwyn for a woodsprite?"

She bit his earlobe.

"Ow!" His eyes flew open, then he chuckled. "I don't

think I'll trade you for a sprite of any kind," he said as he moved toward her.

"Oh no you don't!" She pushed him away. "I want to see our baby."

"Our baby? I'd rather stay here and make one of our own."

She rolled away from him. "I'm not sure I want to go through what Kirsty did yesterday. Come on, I'll race you up the hill."

Stephen hurriedly dressed, and it wasn't until Bronwyn was already on the top of the ridge that her laughter caused him to turn. She held his boots aloft. He yelled to Rab to fetch his boots, and the tussle between dog and mistress gave him time to get up the hill. He wrestled the boots away from Bronwyn, then ran in his short wool hose to the wagon. He was sitting there calmly when she returned. "Good morning," he called as if he'd not seen her for days. "Did you sleep well?"

She laughed at him and went inside the wagon to see to Kirsty.

During the rest of the day there was little time for laughter or play. The men went hunting, and Bronwyn was left to care for Kirsty and the camp. She was appalled at the small amount of food the couple had. There were two small bags of oatmeal and little else. She didn't want to insult Kirsty by asking for more supplies, but she hoped there were more somewhere.

The men returned at sundown with only two small rabbits in their hands, hardly enough for one meal.

"Stephen," Bronwyn said as she drew him aside, "we can't keep taking from them. They have little enough as it is."

He leaned back against a tree. "I know, but at the same time I hate to leave them alone. Donald hardly knows which end of a bow to use. And the game in this area is wary of all hunters. I hate to leave them and I hate to stay."

"I wish we could help them some way. Here, drink this." She held out a mug.

"What is it?"

"Kirsty had me make it. It's made from some lichens with a little ale. She says it cures everything. All day she worried about you and Donald working in the cold."

Stephen sipped the hot liquid. "And did you worry about us?"

She smiled. "Maybe about Donald, but I knew you could take care of the both of you."

He started to answer, but the drink drew his attention. "This is really good. I think it's making my head stop hurting."

She frowned. "I didn't know your head was hurting."

"It hasn't stopped since your brother's arrow creased it." He dismissed the subject. "I just had an idea. Were these lichens hard to find?"

"Not at all," she said, curious.

Stephen's eyes began to glow. "Today Donald told me about a town near here. He wants to take his son to be baptized. If you and I could make up a tub of this stuff, maybe we could sell it."

"What a clever idea!" she agreed, already making plans.

They spent the evening hunting lichens. Donald took what money there was and used one of the wagon horses to go into town and buy more ale.

It was late when they rolled their plaids on the ground near the dying fire and went to sleep. Bronwyn stayed close to Stephen, happy enough to be near him without needing to make love. This feeling of closeness was new to her and made her feel warm and content.

Very early the next morning they hitched the wagon and rolled into the little walled town. There seemed to be hundreds of shops as well as tiny houses inside the walls, and the air was heavy and hardly worth breathing. The whole place made Bronwyn long for the out-of-doors.

She'd been to few towns in her life. Instead the merchants had traveled to Larenston to sell their goods.

Donald pulled the wagon off the narrow main street, just in front of an alleyway, and unhitched the horses. They set up a pot of the drink they'd made, then started to call to people to buy. Kirsty and Bronwyn sat inside the wagon and listened. Stephen's deep voice boomed out over all the noise of the town. He made some rather extraordinary promises for the drink, talking about his own slight experience with it as if it'd cured him from leprosy.

But no one bought from them.

People paused and listened, but they offered no pennies to buy the miracle liquid.

"Perhaps you should do some of those body flips like you did for Tam," Bronwyn teased.

Stephen ignored her taunts as he tried to coax a young man to buy by telling him the drink would improve his love life.

"Maybe you need some help, but I don't," the young man replied. The crowd laughed and began to move away.

"I think it's time I gave this a try," Bronwyn said as she began unbuttoning her shirt.

"Bronwyn!" Kirsty protested. "Are you planning to do something that'll make Stephen angry?"

She smiled. "Probably. Is this low enough?" She glanced down at the generous curve of her breasts exposed by the unbuttoned shirt.

"More than enough. Donald would have my hair if I walked about like that."

"The Englishwomen wear dresses cut as low as decently possible," Bronwyn replied.

"But you're not English!"

Bronwyn only smiled in answer as she climbed down the front of the wagon, on the far side of where Stephen stood.

Stephen smiled in surprise when he first heard Bronwyn call out. "This will cure anything from boils to the sweating sickness," she was saying. He watched as the crowd began to move to the side of the wagon.

"Is your wife unhappy?" Bronwyn called. "Maybe it's your fault. This drink will make you the most powerful of men. And as a love potion it's unsurpassed."

"Do you think it'll get me something like you?" a man shouted.

"Only if you were to drink a whole hogshead of it," Bronwyn replied instantly.

The crowd laughed.

"I think I'll try it," another man shouted.

"I'm going to buy some for my husband," a woman cried before she hurried to the end of the wagon, where Donald and Stephen waited.

For a while Stephen was too busy filling the townspeople's containers and taking pennies to really listen to Bronwyn. He was proud of the way she was selling and pleased that the people liked her. He chuckled once at the idea of an English lady acting as a barker with so much success.

It was when he began to hear the low, suggestive laughter of the men that she really got his attention.

One of the men holding out a cup turned to his companion. "She half as much promised to meet me by the town well."

Stephen's face turned cold. "Did she tell you that I'd be there too?" he asked in a deadly voice.

The man looked up at Stephen, at the challenge in the handsome face. The man backed away. "Don't blame me, 'twas her that gave me the idea."

"Damn her!" Stephen said viciously and threw the ladle into the drink. Just what the hell did she think she was doing?

He stopped when he rounded the corner of the wagon. Her shirt was unbuttoned, exposing a great deal of her high, firm breasts. She'd removed her concealing plaid, and her skirt clung to her hips. She walked back and forth in front of the ever increasing crowd of people. And the way she walked! Her hands were on her hips, and her hips swayed seductively.

For a moment he was shocked, too stunned to move; then he took two long strides toward her. He grabbed her arm, pulled her into the alleyway behind the wagon. "Just what the hell do you think you're doing?" he said between clenched teeth.

"Selling the tonic," she said quite calmly. "You and Donald didn't seem to be doing such a good job, so I thought I'd help."

He released her arm, then angrily began to button her blouse. "You were certainly enjoying yourself, weren't you? Parading yourself like a joywoman!"

She looked up at him and smiled happily. "You're jealous, aren't you?"

"Of course not!" he snapped, then stopped. "You're damn right I'm jealous. Those dirty old men have no right to see what's mine."

"Oh, Stephen, that's . . . that's, I don't know, but I find I'm quite pleased by your jealousy."

"Pleased?" he asked in bewilderment. "Next time I hope you depend on your memory and don't try to provoke the feeling afresh." He grabbed her in his arms and kissed her fiercely, hungrily, possessively.

Bronwyn responded, pushing her body against his, letting herself go to his possession of her.

Suddenly a bellowing voice that fairly shook the houses around them interrupted their kiss. "Where's the wench selling the tonic?"

Bronwyn reluctantly broke away, looking in puzzlement at Stephen.

"Where is she?" the voice boomed again.

"That's the MacGregor," she whispered. "I heard him once before."

She turned toward the voice, but Stephen caught her arm. "You can't go out there to meet the MacGregor."

"Why not? He's never seen me. He won't know who I am, and besides, how can I refuse? This is the MacGregor's land."

Stephen frowned but he released her. A refusal would make them seem suspicious.

"Here I am," she called as she left the alleyway, Stephen close behind her. The MacGregor sat on his horse, looking down at her in an amused way. He was a big, thick man, his hair gray at the temples, his jaw especially strong. His eyes were green and alive above a prominent nose. "And who wants me?" she asked arrogantly.

The MacGregor threw back his head and bellowed laughter. "As if you didn't know your own laird," he said, his eyes deepening to a shade of emerald.

She smiled up at him sweetly. "Is that the same laird who doesn't know his own clan members?"

He didn't lose his smile. "You're a saucy wench. What's your name?"

"Bronwyn," she said proudly as if the name were a challenge. "The same as the laird of Clan MacArran."

Stephen's hand clamped on her shoulder in warning.

The MacGregor's eyes turned hard. "Don't mention that woman to me."

Bronwyn put her hands on her hips. "Is that because you still bear her mark on your person?"

Suddenly there was dead silence around them. The crowd stilled, its breath held.

"Bronwyn," Stephen began, aghast at what she'd said.

The MacGregor put his hand up. "You're not only saucy but you have courage. No one else has dared mention that night to me."

"Tell me, what made you so angry about such a small mark?"

The MacGregor was quiet as he seemed to consider both her and her question. "You seem to know a lot about it." The tension seemed to suddenly leave him, and he smiled. "I think it was a matter of the woman herself. Had she looked a bit like you, I think I'd have born the mark proudly, but no witch-ugly woman is about to mark the MacGregor."

Bronwyn started to speak, but Stephen put both hands on her waist until she couldn't breathe. "Forgive my wife," he said. "She tends to be a bit outspoken."

"That she is," the MacGregor agreed enthusiastically. "I hope you keep her firmly in hand."

"All that I can reach," Stephen laughed.

"I like a woman with spirit," the MacGregor said. "This one's beautiful and has a head on her too."

"It's just that I'd like her to keep her thoughts to herself once in a while."

"Not many women can do that. Good day to you both," he said as he reined his horse away.

"Damn you!" Bronwyn said fiercely as she whirled to face Stephen.

Before she could speak, he gave her a teeth-jarring shake. "You could have gotten us in trouble!" he began, then looked up at the crowd that still stared at them. He grabbed her arm and pulled her to the side of the wagon. "Bronwyn," he said patiently, "don't you know what you could have done? I could see you announcing yourself as laird of Clan Mac-Arran."

"And if I did?" she asked stubbornly. "You heard him say—"

He cut her off. "What a man boasts of to a pretty girl and what he must do when faced with a crowd are two different things. Did you consider Kirsty and Donald? They've been giving us shelter."

To his astonishment Bronwyn relaxed, or rather deflated. The spirit seemed to leave her. She leaned forward into his arms. "You're so right, Stephen. Will I ever learn?"

He held her tightly to him, stroking her hair. He liked having her lean on him, mentally as well as physically.

"Will I ever be smart enough to deserve being the MacArran?"

"You will, love," he whispered. "The desire's within you, and you'll make it soon."

"Bronwyn?"

They both looked up to see Donald standing close to them. "Kirsty wanted me to ask if you were ready to see the priest. We thought we'd have the baby christened before nightfall. Neither of us likes being inside walls all night."

Stephen smiled. "Of course we're ready." He watched Donald, noticing that something was bothering the quiet young man. And why had he addressed Bronwyn first? It occurred to Stephen that if Donald had been inside the wagon, he could have heard them talk of Bronwyn being the Mac-Arran. If he did know, Stephen could see that Donald didn't mean to turn them over to the MacGregor.

*   *   *

The church was the largest building in the town, tall, awe-inspiring. Inside they were quiet, the baby asleep in Kirsty's arms.

"Could I speak to you?" she asked quietly before they reached the altar. "Will you be godparents to our son?"

Bronwyn stared for a moment. "You know so little of us," she whispered.

"I know more than enough. I know you'll take the responsibility of being godparents seriously."

Stephen took Bronwyn's hand. "Yes, we'll be godparents, and we'll abide by all that it means. The boy will never want for anything as long as we're alive," he said.

Kirsty smiled at both of them and went forward to the waiting priest. The baby was christened Rory Stephen. Stephen, after a startled look, grinned broadly. There was no protest from Bronwyn when he gave the surname of Montgomery to the priest.

As they left the church, he carried the child back to the wagon. He looked at Bronwyn. "Why don't we make one of these? I'd like a little boy with black hair and blue eyes and a hole in his chin."

"Are you saying my looks are more suited to a male?" she teased.

He laughed. "You know, I'm beginning to like you now that you're not always screaming that I'm an Englishman."

She looked at his long hair, the way he wore a plaid so easily. "You don't look much like an Englishman. What are your brothers going to say when they see their brother's become half Scots?"

He snorted. "They'll accept me as I am, and if they have any brains they'll learn a few things from us Scots."

"Us?" she asked sharply as she stopped walking.

"Come on and quit looking at me as if I'd grown two heads," he said.

She followed, watching him, and suddenly realized that he now used the Scots burr all the time, even when they were alone. His plaid hit his knees at just the right angle, and he walked as if he'd always been a Scotsman. She smiled and hastened her step. He looked good, carrying the baby easily in one arm, and she liked the way he slipped his other arm around her shoulders.

They walked back to the wagon together, laughing, happy.

Chapter 11

THEY TRAVELED very slowly for two days. Bronwyn tried to get Kirsty to stay in the wagon, but she only laughed. Stephen said Kirsty came out in self-defense after trying some of Bronwyn's cooking.

"This is the worst rabbit stew I ever tasted," Stephen said in disgust one evening. "It has no flavor at all."

"Rabbit?" Bronwyn said absently. She was holding the baby, watching its eyes follow the movement of the dying sunlight on her brooch. "Oh, no!" she said as she finally realized what Stephen had said. Her face turned a becoming shade of pink. "The rabbits are still hanging on the side of the wagon. I—"

Stephen's laughter cut her off. "What happened to that smart woman I married?"

Bronwyn smiled at him with great confidence. "She's still here. Anyone can cook. I can—" She stopped and looked up in bewilderment.

"We're waiting," Stephen said.

"Stop teasing her," Kirsty said quietly. "Bronwyn, as beautiful as you are, you don't need to cook. And besides, you are courageous, fearless, have great practical sense and—"

Bronwyn laughed. "See!" she said to Stephen. "I'm glad someone appreciates me."

"Oh, Stephen appreciates you," Kirsty smiled. "In fact, I

don't believe I've ever seen two people more in love than you two."

Bronwyn looked up from the baby, startled. Stephen was staring at her in an idiotic way, rather like the first time she'd seen him.

"She is pretty, isn't she?" he said. "If only she could cook."

He said it so wistfully that Bronwyn grimaced and threw a clump of dirt at his head.

He laughed and seemed to come back to the present. "Let me hold my godson, will you? He spends too much time with women." He laughed again at the reply Bronwyn made.

Late the next evening they rolled into sight of Kirsty's parents' home. It was a typical crofter's cottage, whitewashed stone with a thatched roof. There were a few fields of barley near it and some sheep as well as cattle. A steep rock formation ran along the back of the land not far from the cottage.

Kirsty's parents came out to meet them. Her father, Harben, was a short, gnarled little man, his right arm gone from his shoulder. His face was obscured by gray hair and a voluminous beard. But what could be seen looked to be forever angry.

Nesta, Kirsty's mother, was a tiny little thing, her gray hair pulled back tightly. She was as warm as Harben was cold. She hugged the baby, Kirsty, and Bronwyn all at once. She thanked Stephen and Bronwyn repeatedly for delivering her only grandchild. She kissed Stephen as enthusiastically as she did Donald.

Stephen asked if they could stay the night and be on their way in the morning.

Harben's face looked as if he'd just been insulted. "Stay only one night?" he growled. "What kind of man are ye? That wife of yers is too skinny, and where are yer children?" He didn't wait for Stephen to answer. "My home brew will put a baby in that flat belly of hers."

Stephen nodded his head as if he'd just heard a great piece

of wisdom. "And here I always thought that it was what I did that'd make her pregnant, and all along it was the home brew."

Harben made a sound that could have been a laugh. "Come inside and welcome."

It was after a simple supper of milk, butter, cheese, and oatcakes that they all sat around a peat fire inside the single room. Stephen sat on a stool whittling a toy for Rory Stephen. Bronwyn sat on the dirt floor, leaning against his knee. Kirsty and her mother were on the other side, Donald and Harben facing the fire.

Donald, who'd already shown he was a good storyteller, had just given a hilarious account of Bronwyn selling the drink and Stephen's reaction to her enticing movements. He finished with the story of Bronwyn meeting the MacGregor.

Bronwyn laughed at herself along with the others.

Suddenly Harben jumped up, overturning his stool.

"Father," Kirsty said quietly, looking worried, "is your arm hurting you?"

"Oh, aye," he said with great bitterness. "It never stops, not since the MacArrans took it off."

Stephen immediately put his hand on Bronwyn in warning.

"Now's not the time," Nesta began.

"Not the time!" Harben shouted. "When isn't it time to hate the MacArrans?" He turned to Bronwyn and Stephen. "See this?" he asked, indicating his empty sleeve. "What can a man do without a right arm? The MacArran himself took it off of me. Six years ago he raided my cattle and took my arm with him."

"Six years," Bronwyn whispered. "Didn't the MacGregor do some raiding too, and didn't he kill four men then?"

Harben waved his hand. "Served them right for stealin' from us."

"Should the MacArran have sat still while you killed his men? He shouldn't have revenged himself?"

"Bronwyn—" Stephen warned.

"Leave her alone," Harben snapped. "Ye got yerself a good one there. What do ye know of the MacArran?"

"He—"

Kirsty cut her off. "Bronwyn lives next to the border of MacArran land."

"Ah, you must have a lot of trouble with them," Harben said with sympathy.

"Actually, none at all," Bronwyn smiled.

"Ye must tell me how—" Harben began.

Kirsty stood. "I think it's time we all went to bed. We have to see to the milking in the morning."

"Aye," Harben said. "Mornings come earlier with every year."

It was later, when Bronwyn and Stephen were snuggled together under their plaids on a straw pallet, that she spoke. "Don't give me any lecture," she whispered with resignation in her voice.

He pulled her closer to him. "I wasn't planning to. I like to see you and old Harben argue. I think that for once you've met your match. Neither of you can believe anything good about the other's clan."

He kissed her when she started to reply, then they settled peacefully into sleep.

A rider brought news the next morning that changed Stephen's plans to leave Harben's cottage. It was known that the MacArran was missing as well as her English husband. The MacGregor had offered a generous reward for their capture.

Stephen grinned when Harben said he'd like to turn the ugly witch-woman over to the MacGregor. He stopped grinning when Harben referred to the Englishman as a worthless peacock who wasn't worth the dirt to bury him in. Stephen scowled as Bronwyn began to agree heartily with Harben's opinion of the English. She egged him on until Kirsty made her father stop his tirade.

"I'll repay you for that," Stephen whispered as they went to the leanto, where the milk cows waited.

"By subjecting me to your greedy English ways?" she teased, then walked ahead of him, her hips swaying seductively.

Stephen started to reply but he suddenly felt very greedy. He smiled at her and went to a cow.

Bronwyn had spent her life around the MacArran crofters, and she was at least familiar with farm work. Stephen knew only how to direct fighting men. He sat on a stool beside the cow and stared in bewilderment.

"Here," Kirsty said quietly and showed him how to squeeze milk from the cow. She ignored his cursing when he managed to get more milk on himself than in the bucket.

Later they pooled their milk so that Stephen's pail was as full as theirs. Nesta looked puzzled at the unusually low milk production, but she smiled fondly at all of them and sent them to the fields.

There were winter vegetables to be gathered and fences to be repaired. Donald and Bronwyn had a good laugh when they saw Stephen's face at the sight of the stone fence. He was as pleased as a child that here at last was something he could do. He carried more rocks than the rest of them put together. He was putting his back to what was more a boulder when Kirsty nudged Bronwyn. Harben was looking at Stephen with adoration in his eyes. "I think you have a home as long as you want," Kirsty said quietly.

"Thank you," Bronwyn said, and again she had the feeling that Kirsty knew a great deal about her.

That night it was a very tired group who returned to the warm little cottage. But they were a happy group. Harben watched them as they teased each other and laughed, recounting the day's events. He lit a pipe, put his elbow on his knee, and for the first time in years he didn't think of the day he'd lost his arm.

It was two days later when Kirsty and Bronwyn went to look for lichens on the other side of the rock ridge behind the cottage. Rory Stephen was snuggled warmly in a plaid, sleeping in a basket beside the stream. It had snowed lightly during the night, and the women were taking their time with their foraging. They were laughing, talking about the farm, their husbands. Bronwyn had never felt freer in her life. She had no responsibilities, no worries.

Suddenly she froze where she was. She hadn't really heard a sound, but something in the air made her know that danger was near. She'd had too many years of training to forget them for an instant.

"Kirsty," she said quietly—it was the voice of command. Kirsty's head came up sharply.

"Be very still. Do you understand me?" She was no longer a laughing woman but the MacArran.

"Rory," Kirsty whispered, her eyes wide.

"Listen to me and obey me." Bronwyn spoke clearly and deliberately. "I want you to go through those high weeds and hide."

"Rory," Kirsty repeated.

"You must trust me!" Bronwyn said firmly.

Their eyes locked. "Yes," Kirsty said. She knew she could trust this woman who'd become her friend. Bronwyn was stronger, faster than she, and Rory meant more to her than to risk him to a mother's vanity. She turned and walked away through the weeds, then crouched where she could see Rory's basket. She knew Bronwyn would have a better chance of escaping with the baby—the men could catch the weaker Kirsty in seconds.

Bronwyn stood quietly, waiting for she knew not what.

The rushing water was loud, and it covered the sound of the horses' hoofs. Four riders came into sight around the rock ridge almost before Kirsty could hide. They were English, dressed in the heavy padded clothes. Their doublets were frayed, their hose patched, and their eyes had a hungry look.

They saw Bronwyn immediately, and she recognized the light that came into their eyes. Rory began to cry, and Bronwyn ran to the baby, clasped it against her breast.

"What do we have here?" said a blond-haired man as he led his horse directly in front of her.

"A beauty on the Scots moor," laughed a second man as he led his horse behind her.

"Look at that hair!" said the first man.

"The women of Scotland are all whores," said a third man. He and the fourth one closed the circle around Bronwyn.

The man in front urged his horse forward until she had to step backward. "She doesn't look too frightened to me," he said. "In fact, she looks like she's just begging us to wipe that look off her face. Women should not have cleft chins," he laughed. "It isn't fitting."

"Black hair and blue eyes," said the second man. "Where have I seen that before?"

"I think I'd remember her if I'd seen her before," said the third man. He drew his sword and held it out toward Bronwyn, put the tip of it under her chin.

She looked up at him, her eyes glassy and hard, steady as she assessed the situation.

"God in Heaven!" said the second man. "I just remembered who she is."

"Who cares who she is," said the first man, dismounting. "She's something I plan to taste, and that's all I care about."

"Wait!" the second man cried. "She's the MacArran. I saw her at Sir Thomas Crichton's. Remember that she was wed to one of the Montgomerys?"

The man standing by Bronwyn stepped away. "Is that true?" he asked quietly in a voice of awe.

She only stared at him, her hands trying to soothe the child she held.

One of the men on horseback laughed. "Just look at her! She's the MacArran all right. Did you ever see a woman with such a proud look? I heard she made Montgomery fight for her even after King Henry promised her to him."

"She did," the second man confirmed. "But you can see why Montgomery was willing to draw his sword for her."

"Lady Bronwyn," said the first man, for her name was known in the higher circles of England, "where is Lord Stephen?"

Bronwyn didn't answer him. Her eyes flickered once in the direction of the rocks that separated her from Harben's cottage. The baby whimpered, and she put her cheek against its head.

"What a prize!" said the fourth man, who'd been very quiet. He said the words under his breath, wistfully. "What should we do with her?"

"Turn her over to the Montgomerys. I'm sure Stephen must be looking for her," said the first man.

"And no doubt will pay handsomely for her return," laughed another.

The fourth man moved his horse closer, forcing Bronwyn to step backward. "What of her clan?" he asked seriously. "Did you know the MacArrans are at war with the Mac-Gregors? This is MacGregor land, you know."

"Charles," said the first man slowly, "I think you're beginning to have some good ideas. She's obviously hiding. Whose child is that?" he asked, directing the question at Bronwyn.

"It's too old to be Montgomery's. Maybe she ran away from him to have another man's child."

The second man laughed. "He'd probably pay a lot to have her back then, maybe just so he can boil her in oil."

"What about asking ransom from all three: her clan, the MacGregor, and Montgomery?"

"And enjoying her ourselves while we wait," laughed the third man.

Kirsty watched from the weeds beside the stream. There were tears in her eyes and blood on her lower lip where she'd bitten it. She knew that Bronwyn could have gotten away. The rocks behind her were too steep for the men's horses, and Bronwyn could possibly have escaped from them. But not with the child. It would take the use of both hands to climb those rocks. Bronwyn couldn't get away as long as she held the child.

"I like the idea," said the first man. He stepped closer to Bronwyn. "You won't be harmed if you cooperate. Now give me that child." He talked to her as if she were dull-witted. When Bronwyn stepped backward, he frowned. "We know the babe isn't Montgomery's, so wouldn't it be better if we got rid of it now?"

Bronwyn stood firmly. "You harm me or my child, and all my clan, as well as the Montgomerys, will be down on your head," she said quietly.

The man looked at her in surprise for a moment, then he recovered himself. "Are you trying to frighten us?" He took a step nearer. "Give me the child!"

"Do not come any nearer," Bronwyn said flatly.

One of the men laughed. "I think you should watch out for her. She looks dangerous to me."

The man behind her slid to the ground. "Need some help?" he asked quietly.

The other two men stayed on their horses and moved closer.

Bronwyn did not panic. She could not put the child down and could not get to her knife. Her only chance was to be able to outrun the Englishmen, who were used to life on a horse. She easily sidestepped the man in front of her, nestled Rory against her, and began to run.

But even a Scotswoman was no match for a horse.

One of the men on horseback cut her off. His insidious laughter rang through the air. Rory began to cry as Bronwyn held him closer to her. She knew the men would kill the child if she put him down.

The men circled her once again. One of them grabbed her shoulder, then pushed her back toward the other man.

Suddenly an arrow appeared out of nowhere and sank into the breast of the first man just as he reached out to touch Bronwyn again.

The other three men were stunned. They stood and stared at their companion, silent, lifeless, at their feet.

Bronwyn lost no time wondering who shot the arrow. She used the few seconds of time to run for the rocks.

The men looked around them to find the source of the arrow. Before they could think, a lone Scotsman stood from the rocks and fired another arrow. The third man, also on foot, fell.

The two men on horses turned sharply and started back the way they came.

Stephen came over the rocks agilely and quickly, Rab behind him. The dog had given him the alarm. He ran after the men on horseback, loading his bow as he ran. One of the men went down as his horse kept running, his dead master's foot caught in the stirrup, the body dragging across the rough ground. Stephen kept running after the fourth man.

Slowly Kirsty came out of her hiding place. She was too frightened to move quickly. Bronwyn met her more than halfway. Kirsty took her child, held him tenderly, then looked up to see Donald coming toward her. She handed the baby to his father, then she clasped Bronwyn. Her body was trembling. "You saved him," she whispered shakily. "You could have gotten away but you didn't. You risked your life to save my baby."

But Bronwyn was hardly listening. She was looking at the space where Stephen had been. "He killed Englishmen!" she whispered again and again, feeling both happy and astonished. Stephen killed Englishmen to protect her and a Scots baby.

Donald put his hand on Bronwyn's shoulder. "You and Stephen will have to leave," he said sadly.

"Oh, Donald, please—" Kirsty began.

"No, it must be. The men—" He stopped when he saw Stephen appear.

Bronwyn walked toward him as if she were in a daze. She looked at him carefully, but she saw no sign of blood. He was sweaty from his run, and she wanted to wipe his brow. "Did they harm you?" she asked quietly.

He stared at her, then grabbed her to him. "That was a brave thing you did, the way you protected the baby."

Before she could speak, Donald was there. "Stephen? What of the other man?"

"He got away," Stephen said as he held Bronwyn close to him, running his hands over her back as if to assure himself she was safe.

Kirsty and Donald exchanged looks. "He'll go to the MacGregor, I'm sure," Donald said.

Bronwyn pushed away from Stephen's embrace. "How long have you known that I'm the MacArran?" she asked.

"Since I first saw you," Kirsty answered. "I saw you a year ago, one day when you were riding with your father. My mother and I were picking berries."

"So your mother knows too," Bronwyn said. She still held Stephen's hand and was glad for his reassurance. "And your father?"

Kirsty frowned. "He's too angry to be forgiving. I wanted more time. I wanted him to get to know both of you, then after you'd gone we would tell him. We knew he'd have trouble hating you."

"But there's been too little time," Donald added. "That Englishman will tell people."

"Stephen," Bronwyn said. "We must go. We can't endanger Kirsty and her family."

He nodded. "Donald, Kirsty—" he began.

"No," Kirsty said, interrupting him. "You don't need to say a word. You're my son's godparents, and I plan to hold you to it."

Stephen smiled at her. "He can foster with one of my brothers."

"An Englishman!" Bronwyn snapped. "No, Kirsty, he can come to the MacArrans."

Donald grinned. "Stop it, both of you. We'll make more boys for you. Now take the English horses and go home. There's time before Christmas for you to get to Stephen's brother's."

"Kirsty," Bronwyn began, and Kirsty hugged her fiercely. "What will people say when I tell them my best friend is a MacGregor?" Bronwyn laughed.

Kirsty was serious. "You must return to us and talk to the MacGregor. He's a good man, and he has an eye for a pretty woman. You must try to settle this feud. I wouldn't want our sons to have to fight each other."

"Nor would I," Bronwyn said, breaking away. "I give you my word that I'll return to you."

Stephen put his arm around her. "We have to come back so I can get more of Harben's home brew."

Donald laughed. "And Bronwyn, I believe I owe you something for laughing at me when we first met. When I think of all the things I said about the MacArran!"

"They're all true," Stephen laughed. "She is the most headstrong, disobedient—"

"Magnificent woman ever," Donald finished, then grabbed Bronwyn and hugged her. "I can never repay you for my son's life. Thank you." He set her aside, then hugged Stephen. "Go now, both of you. Take the Englishmen's horses and go." He pulled away from Stephen. "When Kirsty told me you were an Englishman, I didn't believe her. I still don't."

Stephen laughed. "I'm sure that was meant as a compliment. Kirsty, it's been an honor to meet you. I wish we could have stayed longer so my wife could learn more of your gentle ways."

Before Bronwyn could make a retort, Donald burst out laughing.

"That's just the way she appears, friend. She gets her way just as much as Bronwyn does, she just goes about it differently."

Bronwyn narrowed her eyes at Stephen. "Think before you reply," she warned.

Stephen pulled her to him. "I'm thinking we must go." He touched Rory's hand, felt the little fingers wrap around his for a moment, then grabbed Bronwyn's hand and walked toward the horses.

Neither of them could look back as they rode away. The short time in the crofter's cottage had been a time of peace, and it was too painful to think of leaving it.

They rode at a steady pace for several hours. They did not want to attract attention to themselves by proceeding at a quick run. Stephen stopped once and removed some of the more English trappings on the horses and threw them into the gorse. Bronwyn persuaded a crofter's wife to give her a pot of dark dye, and she dyed the white markings of the horses. If one looked closely, it could be seen that the forelegs were slightly purple instead of the deep chestnut of the rest of the horse.

Stephen was worried about food and wanted to spend the few coins they found in the saddlebags. But Bronwyn only laughed at him and reminded him that they were still in Scotland. Everywhere they went, they were received with hospitality and generosity. Sometimes a crofter had little enough for his own family, but he was always willing to share what he had with another Scot—or anyone who wasn't English. Bronwyn laughed at the way Stephen quite often joined the abuse against the English. One Scot after another showed Stephen fields burned by the English. One man introduced his grandchild, the product of an English rape on his young daughter. Stephen listened and replied in his soft, rolling burr that was now as natural to him as breathing.

At night they rolled together in their plaids and made love. Sometimes, during the day, they'd look at each other from atop their horses, and the next moment they'd be on the ground, their clothes scattered and abandoned.

Stephen had merely to look at Bronwyn and she knew what he was thinking. Her eyes would catch fire and her body would grow warm. She smiled at him as his arm slid around her waist and pulled her into the saddle in front of him.

"I don't think I can get enough of you," Stephen whispered as he nibbled on her earlobe.

"It's not for lack of trying," she said impudently, but she closed her eyes and moved her head so he had access to her neck. "Stephen!" she said suddenly and sat upright because several people were staring at them from the roadside.

"Mornin'," Stephen said, then returned to Bronwyn's neck.

She pulled away from him. "Have you no modesty? We should at least—" She stopped as she saw the light in his eyes. "There're a few trees over there," she whispered.

Rab kept guard as Stephen and Bronwyn lay side by side

in the little copse of trees. It seemed to Bronwyn that the more often they made love, the more Stephen's body fascinated her. The dappled light through the trees played on the dark skin over his muscles. She was fascinated by the strength and power of him, his ability to move her body with one hand. She teased him, rolled away from him, yet he had only to put one hand to her waist and pull her back to him.

They made love in every position imaginable. They had been away from her clan long enough to remove her sense of heavy responsibility, and she felt free and happy. She sought Stephen as eagerly as he sought her. She experimented, her body taking over her mind. She lay on her back, her legs thrown over Stephen as he lay on his side. She clutched at him, pulled him closer, groaned as his hands caressed her legs. Her whole body shuddered when they exploded together.

They lay still for a long while, wrapped about each other, neither of them noticing the cold winter air or the damp, nearly frozen ground.

"What's your family like?" Bronwyn asked huskily.

Stephen smiled and looked at her body, perpendicular to his. He was pleased that she looked weak and exhausted, exactly how he felt. He gave a little shiver as a gust of wind sent little needles through his body. "Get dressed and we'll make some oatcakes."

After they were dressed, Stephen went to his horse, took a broad metal plate from under the saddle flap, and got a bag of oatmeal. The disk had been their only purchase. Bronwyn had a fire going by the time he returned. They mixed the meal with water while the plate heated, then spread the paste thinly over the hot griddle. Stephen turned the cake with his fingers.

"You haven't answered me," Bronwyn said as she ate the first oatcake.

Stephen knew what she meant, but he didn't want her to see how pleased he was that she asked him about his family. He had a sudden feeling that he didn't ever want to reach the Montgomery estates, that he always wanted her to himself. The firelight flickered on her hair and flashed off the brooch at her shoulder. He didn't want to share her with anyone.

"Stephen? You're looking at me strangely."

He smiled and looked back at the oatcake on the griddle. "Just thinking. Let's see. You wanted to know about my family." He rolled a hotcake and began to eat it. "Gavin is the oldest, then me, then Raine and Miles."

"What are they like? Are they like you?"

"It's difficult to judge one's self. Gavin is tall and extremely stubborn. He's dedicated to the Montgomery lands and spends most of his time there."

"And he's the only one who's married."

"Are you forgetting me?" he laughed. "Gavin and Judith were married nearly a year ago."

"What's she like?"

"Beautiful! Kind, sweet, forgiving." He chuckled. "She'd have to be to live with Gavin. He doesn't know much about women, and as a result he gets in a lot of trouble with them."

"I'm glad he's the only one of you four who knows little about women."

Stephen missed the sarcasm in her words. He was beginning to remember his family with longing. "Then there's Raine. He's the one who's like Tam, heavy and thick, like our father. Raine is the . . . I don't know how to explain him. He is good, deep-down good inside. He can't stand any injustice. He'll put his own life in danger before he'd ever harm a serf or let anyone else harm one."

"And Miles?"

"Miles," Stephen said and smiled. "Miles is quiet and no one knows much about him. He keeps to himself, but every once in a while he explodes with the most horrible temper imaginable. Once when we were children he got angry at one of my father's squires, and it took all three of us to hold him back."

"What was the squire doing?" she asked curiously, accepting another oatcake.

Stephen's eyes danced with memory. "The boy was teasing a little girl. Miles loves women."

"All women?"

"All!" Stephen said. "And they follow him around as if

he had the key to all happiness. I never met a female who didn't like Miles."

"He sounds quite interesting," she said, licking her fingers.

"If you ever!" he began, then stopped because Bronwyn was looking at him with such interest. He turned his attention to the oatcakes. "And then there's Mary."

"Mary?"

"Our sister."

Something about the way he said the words made her stare at him. "I've never heard you mention a sister. What's she like? Will she be there at Christmas?"

"Mary is like the Madonna," he said reverently. "Even as children we knew she was different. She's the oldest child, and she always knew how to keep her younger brothers out of trouble. Sometimes Gavin and Raine were at each other's throats. Gavin was always aware that the land would be his someday, and he was always angry when Raine forgave a serf for causing any destruction to the land, even when it was clearly caused by an accident. Mary would come between them and in her soft voice soothe them."

"How?" Bronwyn asked, thinking of her own responsibilities with her clan.

"I never understood how she did it. That time when Miles tried to kill the squire, it was Mary who was able to calm him."

"And what of her now? Is her husband kind to her?"

"She has no husband. She asked to be allowed never to marry, and since we'd never met a man who we thought would ever be kind enough to her, we granted her wish. She lives in a convent not far from the Montgomery estates."

"It was kind of you to grant her wish. I've heard that Englishwomen usually have little choice about their futures."

Stephen didn't take offense at her words. "I think you're right. Perhaps they should learn from the Scots."

"They?" she said smoothly.

He laughed at her meaning. "Do you know, I am almost beginning to feel that I *am* a Scot." He stood up, stuck his bare leg out. "Do you think my own brothers will recognize me?"

"Probably," she said. "But I doubt if anyone else would." There was pride in her voice.

"I'd like to see if you were right."

"Are you planning something?" she asked suspiciously, because at that moment he looked like a mischievous little boy. "Stephen, we already have the MacGregors searching for us, my brother and his men, and no doubt some Englishmen since you did kill three of them. I would like to get to your brother's in one piece."

"We will," Stephen said, a faraway look in his eyes. "We might just pay a visit on the way though."

Bronwyn sighed, then stood and dusted her skirt. As she walked back to her horse, her mind was full of thoughts about little boys who never grew up.

Chapter 12

AS THEY entered England, Stephen could feel a difference in the air. Even on the border of Scotland, the people were not used to seeing the Highlanders. Some people stared openly at their dress; some shouted angry words because their land and property had been attacked by the Scots. Bronwyn rode with her back rigid and her head held high. She refused to answer anything the Englishmen said. Only once did she show any emotion. Stephen stopped at a farmer's well to replenish their water jugs, and the farmer ran after them with a haying fork. Stephen, the blood flushing his body, started after the little man who was cursing the Scots so vividly. Bronwyn grabbed her husband's arm and pulled him back to the horses. For hours afterward Stephen muttered about the stupidity of the English. Bronwyn only smiled at his words; there wasn't one she hadn't already thought or said.

Now they were arguing about something else. Two nights ago Stephen had told Bronwyn of a plan he had to fool a boyhood friend.

"No, I do not understand!" Bronwyn said for, she was sure, the hundredth time.

"It's a feud," Stephen said patiently. "You, above anyone else, should understand what a feud is."

"What is between the MacGregors and the MacArrans is real, based upon many years of anger and hostility. They've killed my men as well as stolen my cattle. Some of my women

560

care for MacGregor bastards." She gave him a pleading look. "Please, Stephen, this is a child's game, and it will only cause trouble. What does it matter whether this man recognizes you or not?"

Stephen refused to answer her, especially since she'd already asked the question several times. He couldn't explain to her about Hugh. He couldn't even remember the time with Hugh without embarrassment and no little pain.

They'd been together, patroling the Lowlands borders for King Henry, when word reached them that King Henry had chosen Stephen as a husband for the laird of Clan MacArran. Hugh had exploded with laughter. For days he did little else but conjure hideous pictures of Stephen's new bride. Before long the entire camp was talking of the ugly creature Lord Stephen would have to marry.

The decree was especially unpleasant because at the time Stephen thought he was in love. Her name was Margaret, Meg for short. She was a plump, pink-and-white blonde, the daughter of a Lowlands merchant. She had great blue eyes and a tiny little mouth that always seemed to be puckered for kissing. She was shy and quiet and she adored Stephen—or so he thought. At night Stephen would hold her in his arms, feel her soft white body, and imagine the hideous life ahead of him with a woman who was chief of a clan.

After several nights with no sleep, he began to think of refusing the king's offer. He thought of marrying the merchant's daughter. She wasn't rich but her father was comfortable, and Stephen had an income from a small estate of his own. The more he thought of the idea, the more he liked it. He tried to forget the wrath of the king when Stephen refused him.

But it was Hugh who shattered Stephen's dreams. Hugh told Meg of Stephen's forthcoming marriage, and the poor girl, distraught and helpless, had flung herself into Hugh's willing arms. Hugh didn't think twice about helping her into his bed, or so Meg had told Stephen.

Stephen was bewildered when he found his friend and the woman he loved together in bed. But oddly enough his be-

wilderment never turned to anger, and because of this he realized he hadn't really loved Meg or she him if she could so
easily turn to another. His only thought had been how to
repay Hugh with some of his own medicine. Before he could
make a plan, a messenger arrived saying Gavin needed help,
and Stephen went to his brother without another thought of
Hugh.

Now Stephen saw a way to repay his friend, and Hugh
was still his friend. If he, Stephen, could get inside Hugh's
estate and out again, undetected, yet leave a message that he'd
been there, then he felt he'd have accomplished something.
Hugh didn't like to feel there were strangers around him; he
rarely went anywhere without a full guard. Yes, Stephen
smiled, there were ways to repay Hugh Lasco.

They arrived at the Lasco estate just before sundown. It
was a tall, stone house, the windows covered with ironwork
shutters. The entrance courtyard was filled with people who
walked about in an orderly manner, as if they had a task and
were hurrying to do it. There were no groups of servants
standing about and gossiping.

Stephen and Bronwyn were challenged by guards as soon
as they were within sight of the house. Stephen, in a heavy
Scots burr, asked if he could sing for his supper. They waited
patiently while one of the guards returned to the house and
got permission from Sir Hugh.

Stephen knew Hugh considered himself an exceptional
lute player and wouldn't miss an opportunity to judge someone else's playing. He smiled when the guard told them to
take their horses to the stable, then go to the kitchen.

It was later, when they sat before a hearty meal at the
enormous oak table in the kitchen, that Bronwyn began to
resign herself to Stephen's plans. Not that he'd even told her
much about them! All she'd been able to find out was that
Stephen planned some boyish prank on his friend.

"What is Sir Hugh like?" she asked, her mouth full of
freshly baked bread.

Stephen snorted in derision. "He's handsome enough, I
guess, if that's what you mean, but he's short and thick, very

dark. And he is damned infuriating to be around. He moves slower than anyone else alive. In the Lowlands I was always worried that we'd be attacked and Hugh would be killed before he could even open his eyes, much less put his armor on."

"Married?"

He gave her a sharp look. He studied her for a moment in speculation. He could never see it himself, but for some reason women found Hugh quite attractive. To Stephen, Hugh's plodding, overly cautious ways were infuriating. But the women . . .

"I want you to keep your head down at all times," he said firmly. "Just this once I want you to try and act like an obedient, respectful wife."

She raised one eyebrow at him. "When have I ever been anything else?"

"Bronwyn, I'm warning you! This is between Hugh and me, and I don't want you involved."

"You sound almost as if you were afraid of him," she teased. "Is there something about him that makes women throw themselves at his feet?"

She meant her words lightly, but the look on Stephen's face told her she was closer to the mark than she realized. Suddenly she wanted to reassure him that it was highly unlikely that she'd ever throw herself at any man's feet. Of course, there had been a few times, a few positions, where she'd found her head against Stephen's feet. She smiled warmly in memory.

"I see nothing to laugh about!" Stephen said stiffly. "If you don't obey me, I'll—" He stopped as one of Hugh's guards approached and said Stephen was to come and entertain now.

The trestle tables had already been set in the Great Hall and the meal begun. Stephen half pushed Bronwyn onto a low stool against a far wall. She smiled impishly at his behavior and even smothered a giggle when he gave her such a black look of warning. She hoped she made him regret this whole childish scheme.

Stephen took the lute that was handed him, then sat several feet from the head table. He played quite well; his voice was rich and deep, and he carried the melody beautifully.

For a while Bronwyn looked about the room. The dark man at the head of the table never looked up at the singer. She watched without interest as he ate, as Stephen had said, very slowly. Each movement seemed to be planned and thought out.

She quickly lost interest in watching Hugh Lasco and leaned her head against the stone wall, closed her eyes, and gave her mind over to Stephen's music. She felt as if he played for her alone; once she opened her eyes and saw that he was watching her, and his look was as startling as a touch. She felt chills race across her body as she saw the expression in his eyes. She smiled in answer, then closed her eyes again. He sang a Gaelic song, and she was pleased that he'd taken the time to learn the words, probably from Tam. The sweet music, the words of love sung in her own language, made her forget she was in England, surrounded by Englishmen, married to an Englishman. Instead she was at home in Larenston, and she was with the man she loved.

She smiled dreamily at the thought, but even as she smiled she was aware of a change in Stephen's song. She opened her eyes quickly. He wasn't looking at her but across the room at Hugh. Slowly she turned her head. She knew before she looked that Hugh was watching her.

He was quite handsome in an earthy sort of way. He was dark-haired, dark-eyed. His mouth had lips a little too large for a man, but they only drew Bronwyn's attention. As she watched, Hugh blotted his lips in his slow manner, and it flashed across her mind to wonder if he moved that slowly and lingeringly in bed.

She smiled at her own thoughts. So that was Hugh's attraction! Of course, Stephen wouldn't be able to see it, but as a woman, she found his ways quite interesting. She smiled again as she thought of telling Stephen of her discovery.

She turned to her husband and saw him scowling at her, his brows drawn together, his blue eyes turned a dark sapphire. For a moment she wondered what she'd done to anger him, then she nearly laughed aloud. He's jealous, she thought with a sense of wonder, and that thought gave her more of a thrill than any of Hugh's hot looks.

She looked down at her skirt, traced her finger along the plaid. She shouldn't be, of course, but she was extraordinarily pleased that Stephen was jealous. She wouldn't dare tell him that Hugh had no more interest for her than . . . than the gardener, because it made her feel warm all over to think Stephen cared enough to be jealous.

Hugh said something to one of the two guards behind him, and the guard went to Stephen. Stephen listened to the man, handed him the lute, then strode angrily across the room, grabbed Bronwyn's arm, and half dragged her with him.

He spun her around once they were outside in the moonlit courtyard. "You certainly enjoyed yourself!" he hissed, his teeth clenched.

"You are hurting me," she said quite calmly, trying to pry his fingers from her upper arms.

"I ought to beat you!"

She glared at him. He was really going too far! "That is truly a man's logic! You were the one who wanted to come here. You were the one who insisted upon acting like a child. And now, to cover your own stupidity and childishness, you wish to beat *me!*"

He dug his fingers deeper into her arms. "I told you to sit quietly, out of sight, but there you were giving Hugh those enticing little smiles. You were telling him that anything he wanted from you he could have."

Her mouth dropped open in surprise. "That may be the most absurd thing I ever heard."

"You're lying! I saw you!"

Her eyes opened even wider, and she was very calm when she spoke. "Stephen, what in the world is wrong with you? I looked at the man as I would any man. I was curious because you talked of how slow he was, yet you seemed to think he had a lot of women."

"Were you trying to add yourself to his stable?"

"You are being crude and insulting," she said flatly. "And you are still hurting me."

He didn't release her. "Perhaps you wish the king had given you him for a husband, along with Roger Chatworth. If I can beat one, I can certainly beat the other."

The statement was so childish that Bronwyn could do nothing except laugh. "That is an irrational statement. I did nothing but look at the man. If I smiled it was because I was thinking of something else. I will remind you again that I never wanted to come here in the first place."

Suddenly all of Stephen's anger left him, and he grabbed her to him in a bone-crushing embrace. "Don't do that again," he said fiercely.

She started to reply that she hadn't done anything, but the way Stephen held her was almost comforting. Her arms hurt and she could feel the imprint of each of his fingers, but somehow she rather liked the idea that he was jealous of another man looking at her.

He held her away. "I almost wish you weren't so damned pretty," he whispered, then put his arm around her shoulders. "I'm hungry again. Let's see if there's anything left in the kitchen."

Bronwyn felt especially close to Stephen as they went back to the kitchen. It was almost as if they were in love and not just physical lovers. The kitchen people grumbled that they were back again, but Stephen winked at the cook, and Bronwyn saw the fat old woman melt under his warm blue eyes. She had her own pang of jealousy and realized she wanted all of Stephen's looks for her own.

They stood to one side for a moment, eating juicy apple-filled fried pies. "There's too much waste in here," Bronwyn said.

Stephen started to retort in defense of the English kitchen, but he'd been in Scotland too long. He'd lived with Kirsty's parents, seen their poverty. Even in Larenston the people were frugal, always aware of the value of food and that tomorrow it might all be gone. "Aye, it is," he said firmly. "We could use some of this food at home."

Bronwyn looked up at him with great warmth. She reached up and moved a curl from off his neck. The long hair and deep tan suited him. She glanced across the room and saw a buxom young cook's helper staring with interest at Stephen's bare, muscular thigh, which was exposed as he put one leg on the seat of a chair. She grabbed his hand. "I've had enough of this place. Shall we go outside?"

Stephen agreed with her and left before he noticed the kitchen maid.

It was the storm that kept them from leaving Hugh's estate. It came suddenly, raining violently. One minute the skies seemed to be clear, and the next there threatened to be a repeat of Noah's flood.

Bronwyn begged Stephen not to stay. She told him a little rain never hurt a Scotswoman, but he wouldn't listen. He didn't want to risk her to lung fever, not when he could possibly prevent it. So they prepared to spend the night at Hugh's house.

The Great Hall floor was covered with straw pallets, ready for the many retainers and guests. Stephen tried to find a private corner but there was no such thing. When he was settled beside Bronwyn, he slipped his hand under her skirt and touched her knee. She hissed at him and told him in no uncertain terms that she'd not perform in such a public place. He sighed and eventually agreed with her. She snuggled next to him and was asleep in minutes.

But Stephen couldn't sleep. He'd been in the open too long, and now all the walls seemed to be closing in on him. He shifted his position again and again, but the straw still felt too soft. Rab even growled at him once because he was so restless. He put his hands behind his head and stared up at the beamed ceiling. He kept remembering the way Hugh had looked at Bronwyn. Damn the man! Hugh thought he could get any woman he wanted. No doubt he was encouraged by the way Meg had gone to him.

The more he thought about the trick Hugh had played on

him, the angrier he became. In spite of Bronwyn's warnings he knew he wanted to let Hugh know he'd been there.

He quietly slipped off the pallet, commanded Rab to stay with Bronwyn, and silently went toward the eastern door to the Great Hall.

As children he and his brothers had often visited the Lasco estate. One day, when they were very young, he and Hugh had discovered a secret passage leading upstairs. They were trembling with excitement when they reached the door at the top of the stairs. They were surprised to find the door well oiled and silent as they slipped into the room behind a heavy tapestry. They weren't even sure where they were until they heard sounds coming from the bed. But it was too late then. Hugh's grandfather was in bed with a very young housemaid, and both of them seemed to be having a marvelous time. The old man found no humor in looking up and seeing two seven-year-old boys watching him with wide-eyed interest. Stephen still winced when he remembered the beating Hugh's grandfather gave them and the one he promised if they revealed their knowledge of the secret passage. Four years ago, when the old man died, Stephen cried at his funeral. He hoped he could pleasure young girls at the same age. Stephen laughed and was glad Bronwyn hadn't heard that thought.

He slipped behind a screen in the anteroom off the Great Hall. He went to the window seat and took his knife and pried off the linen-fold paneling behind the cushions. It had been a particularly violent pillow fight that had knocked the panel away the first time so long ago. He had to stick his arm through an inch of cobwebs before he could even see the outline of the stone staircase. Once inside, he pulled the panel back into place.

It was black inside the stairwell, and tiny feet scurried back and forth. More cobwebs hit his face, and he wished he had his sword to clear them away. The passage had been in constant use and had been kept clean when Hugh's grandfather was alive. Since Hugh lived alone, Stephen guessed he had no reason to hide his trysts from anyone.

The door at the top of the stairs opened with only a slight

creak, but Stephen had no time to wonder at this. His eyes were used to the black stairwell, and so the room, lit by a single fat night candle, seemed to blaze with light. Stephen smiled at his extraordinary luck, for Hugh lay asleep on the bed. Stephen smiled at the quiet, unsuspecting man, then removed his knife from its sheath at his side.

Even as a child Hugh had a fear of being unguarded. There had been a kidnap attempt on him when he was only five. He'd said very little about it then or since, but he never went anywhere without a guard. To wake in the morning and find a knife beside his head would more than repay him for the girl he'd taken from Stephen.

Stephen wrapped a bit of plaid around the hilt, then attached the MacArran cockade. Silently he placed the knife beside his friend. Grinning broadly, he turned toward the tapestry and the secret door.

"Seize him!" Hugh's deep voice rang out.

Four men jumped from the dark corners of the room and ran at Stephen. He ducked the first one, and his fist slammed into the face of the second. The man staggered backward. Stephen's reactions were faster than those of the other two men. He was at the door before he felt the tip of Hugh's sword on the back of his neck.

"Well done!" Hugh said with admiration. "I can see you didn't neglect your training in Scotland." He drew back his sword so Stephen could turn around.

Hugh was fully dressed. He held the sword at Stephen's throat, motioned his guards to surround his friend, then picked up the knife on his pillow. "MacArran, isn't it?" He tossed the knife in his left hand. "It's good to see you again, Stephen."

Stephen grinned broadly. "Damn you! How did you know?"

"Gavin came by a couple of days ago and said he was expecting you. He'd heard some tale of your getting into trouble in Scotland, and he was beginning to worry. He thought perhaps you'd stop here first."

Stephen shook his head. "Betrayed by my own brother."

He looked up in surprise. "But even expecting me, how . . . ?" He knew he looked quite different from the English Stephen he had been.

Hugh smiled, his eyes lighting warmly. "One of the songs you sang was one we learned together in the Lowlands, remember? How could you forget the time it took us to learn that chord?"

"Of course!" Stephen said, realizing he'd been over-confident in his disguise. "Bronwyn said it'd never work, that I'd give myself away."

"I must say that that accent of yours is well done, but you can drop it now."

"Accent?" Stephen asked, genuinely bewildered. "I stopped using the accent when we left the MacGregor's land."

Hugh laughed deeply. "Stephen, you really have become a Scot. Tell me what happened in Scotland. Did you marry that awful woman? What was she, the laird of some clan? And who was that delicious creature who kept staring at you with such lust while you played?"

Stephen frowned. "She is Bronwyn," he said flatly.

"Bronwyn? A Welsh name, isn't it? Did you find her in Scotland? And how did you escape your wife?"

"Bronwyn is the laird of Clan MacArran, and she is my wife." Stephen was very stiff, his lips hardly moving as he spoke.

Hugh's mouth dropped open. "You mean that blue-eyed angel is the chief of some clan, and you have the good fortune to be married to her?"

Stephen didn't answer but glared at Hugh. Why was he still standing surrounded by guards? "What's going on here?" he asked quietly.

Hugh smiled, his dark eyes sparkling. "Nothing at all. Just a little game, like the one you wanted to play on me." He rubbed the knife between his fingers. "Bronwyn, is it?" he asked quietly. He had lowered his sword point but it was still at the ready. "Remember when we first heard the news? You kept groaning and saying you wouldn't marry such an ugly woman. You wanted . . . what was her name? Elizabeth?"

"Margaret," Stephen snapped. "Hugh, I don't know what you have in mind, but—"

"I have in mind exactly what I had before."

Stephen stared at him, remembering all too well seeing Meg and him in bed together. The idea that he'd even touch Bronwyn . . . "You touch her and I'll kill you," he said in deadly earnest.

Hugh blinked in surprise. "You almost sound serious."

"I am more than serious."

Hugh smiled. "But we're friends. We've shared women before."

"Bronwyn is my wife!" Stephen shouted before he lunged at Hugh.

All four of the guards were on him at once, but even they couldn't hold him. Hugh moved away as quickly as he could, but Stephen still came for him. The chamber door suddenly flew open, and three more guards entered and seized Stephen.

"Take him to the tower room," Hugh said, looking at his friend in admiration, the seven guards holding him.

"Don't do it!" Stephen warned even as he was being dragged from the room.

"I won't force her if that's what you mean," Hugh laughed. "All I want is one full day, and if I haven't gotten her by then you'll know you have a faithful wife."

"Damn you!" Stephen cursed and made another lunge before he was forcibly pulled from the room.

Bronwyn stood before the long mirror and studied herself critically. It had taken over an hour to dress in the English gown. The skirt and sleeves were of a shimmering, muted orange brocade. Tied with ribbons at the shoulders, then drawn over her arms, was a small cloak of ermine. The skirt parted in front to show cinnamon velvet. The square neck was very low.

Her hair hung down her back in thick, fat curls with elf locks before her ears.

"You look lovely, my lady," said the timid little maid behind her. "Sir Hugh has never had a lady here who was so pretty."

Bronwyn looked at the woman and started to speak, but then she stopped. It hadn't taken her long to learn how useless questions were in the Lasco household. This morning she'd had to restrain Rab from attacking Hugh as he came to her pallet in the Great Hall. For some reason Rab took an extraordinary dislike to the man.

Hugh embarked on a long explanation of Stephen's absence before Bronwyn could ask a single question. When he'd finished his tale—that Stephen had gone to see to one of Hugh's estates as a favor to his old friend—he stood back and smiled at Bronwyn with great confidence.

She began firing questions at him. Why had Stephen left without speaking to her? What business couldn't Hugh handle on his own? How was Stephen more suited? If Hugh needed help, why didn't he ask Stephen's brothers earlier?

She watched as Hugh sputtered and seemed to trip over his words. He was looking at her oddly, sometimes not able to meet her forthright stare. After a moment he smiled, and she had the impression that an idea had just come to him. He began another story about how Stephen had wanted to prepare a surprise for her and he wanted Hugh to entertain her for the day.

Bronwyn closed her mouth on her questions. For now it would be better to act as if she believed Hugh's obviously false words. She smiled sweetly at the man who was an inch or two shorter than she was. "A surprise!" she said in what she hoped was a girlish and innocent voice. "Oh, what do you think it could be?"

Hugh smiled at her in a benevolent way. "We'll just have to wait and see, won't we? But in the meantime I have some entertainment planned. Pavilions are being erected and bonfires lit."

"Oh! How nice!" she said, clapping her hands together in childish glee and at the same time ordering Rab to keep away from the man's throat.

Hugh led her upstairs to a clean, warm room where the

brocade dress had been readied for her. The hem had been let down to accommodate her height. Bronwyn realized someone had worked on the dress all night. Hugh gave her one of his slow, seductive smiles just as he left the room, and Bronwyn had to work hard to give him the simpering little smile he seemed to expect in return.

Once alone, she ran to the window. On the grounds below carpenters worked quickly on a platform. There were six fires already lit and an enormous charcoal brazier set under an open canopy. She frowned in consternation. Why in the world would an Englishman plan an outdoor entertainment in December? Last night's rain had turned to snow, and the ground was lightly powdered. From what she'd seen of the English, they were weak creatures who liked to stay indoors.

The maid came and helped her dress, but Bronwyn could get little information from her. She said Sir Hugh had been up all night ordering the day's festivities. Bronwyn wondered if she was making too much of everything. Perhaps Stephen had been called away and Hugh merely wanted to honor his friend's bride. But would Stephen leave her to prepare some sort of surprise for her? Stephen was too much of a realist. More likely, he'd make her help him with her own gift.

Before she could sort out her thoughts, Hugh came to the door. He looked at her in awe, his eyes slowly running the length of her. "You are magnificent," he whispered. "Stephen is a very lucky man."

She thanked him and took the arm he offered her as they descended the stairs.

"You must tell me all about this clan of yours," he said, his eyes on her lips. "I imagine you were glad to get an English husband. Perhaps you can meet King Henry and thank him someday."

Bronwyn nearly exploded with the force of her reaction. She thought Stephen's vanity was the limit, but this man surpassed anything she'd ever imagined. "Oh, yes," she said in a gentle voice. "Stephen has been very good to me, and we've learned so much from him." She nearly choked as she thought how Stephen had changed but not her men.

"Of course," Hugh smiled. "We English are superior fighters, and you Scots could learn a great deal." He stopped. "I must apologize. I hadn't meant to say such things. After all, you are, what is it? The laird of a clan."

He said the words as if they were a token thrown to a beggar. She didn't dare reply because if he said one more word, she would probably let Rab have the worthless peacock. "Oh, look!" she exclaimed happily. "Isn't that pretty?" she cried, referring to the gaily colored pavilion.

Hugh stopped, glanced briefly up at the walls of his house, then took her hand and kissed it. "Nothing is too good for you, nothing is too beautiful for you."

She watched him with detached interest. When she'd first seen him, she thought his slow movements, his unusual mouth, were interesting, but now she found him rather tedious. For some reason he seemed to think, to assume, that she would like having her hand kissed by him.

She used all the control she could muster to keep from drawing away from him. Did all men consider themselves so appealing to women? She suddenly realized how little experience she'd had. The men of her clan never tried to touch her, probably out of fear of her father's wrath. In England she'd only spent time with Roger Chatworth, who wanted to talk of his plans for her people. Stephen was the only man who'd ever touched her and, it would seem, the only man to whom she could respond. At least it felt that way, since Hugh Lasco's touch made her want to pull away from him.

He seemed satisfied with her response, or lack of it, and led her to a gilded chair under the pavilion. Hugh clapped his hands once, and three jugglers appeared on the wooden platform before them. She gave a little smile to Hugh and pretended to watch the performers. But the truth was she was more interested in her surroundings. With each passing moment she grew more suspicious. Something was not quite right. Why were they being entertained outside?

Some dancing girls joined the jugglers, and Bronwyn could see that their shoulders were blue with cold. A raw wind began to blow in their faces. One of Hugh's retainers suggested the pavilion be turned to block the wind. Hugh's response was almost violent, refusing to turn the canvas another direction.

"You must pardon me, Sir Hugh," Bronwyn said in her sweetest voice. She had to have time to look about his house. Perhaps she could find a clue to the mystery. Perhaps Stephen hadn't really gone away.

"Oh, but you can't leave yet. Here. I'll have the fire made hotter. Or another brazier brought."

"I'm not cold," she said honestly as she kept herself from smiling at Hugh's blue nose. "I merely wish to . . ." She looked down at her hands in confusion.

"Of course!" he said in embarrassment. "I will send a guard—"

"No! I have Rab, and I'm sure I can find my way."

"Your wish is my command," he smiled, then kissed her hand again.

Bronwyn had to control herself from running inside the house. She wanted to do nothing to make Hugh suspicious. Once inside, though, she knew the need to hurry. "Rab," she commanded, "find Stephen."

Rab raced up the stairs in a spurt of joy. All morning he'd been straining against Bronwyn's commands. The dog stopped before a door she suspected was Hugh's. He sniffed and danced about until he took off up some stairs, Bronwyn lifting her heavy skirts and running after him.

At the top of the third flight of stairs was a heavy oak door, its window set with iron bars. Rab jumped up, his forefeet at the window. He barked twice in recognition.

"Rab!" came Stephen's voice.

"Get down!" Bronwyn commanded. "Stephen, are you all right? Why are you being held prisoner?" She held her hand out to him, grabbed his through the bars.

He took her hand in both of his, stared at her. "Is this the hand you've let Hugh kiss so often?" he asked coldly.

"This is no time for one of your jealousy attacks. Why are you being held prisoner? And what is that absurd celebration about?"

"Absurd?" Stephen sputtered, tossing her hand back

through the bars. "You didn't look like you weren't enjoying yourself. Tell me, do you find Hugh attractive? A lot of women do."

She stared at him, patted Rab who was nervous because his master was being held captive. Her mind was racing. "This isn't serious at all, is it?" she asked quietly. "This is some sort of game between you and your friend."

"It's not a game when my wife is involved," he said fiercely.

"Damn you, Stephen Montgomery!" she hissed. "I told you not to come here. No, you think you're so superior. Now I want to know what's going on and how to get you out of here, though I have no idea why I want you out."

Stephen narrowed his eyes at her. "If you give in to Hugh and let him win, I'll break your neck."

She was beginning to understand. "Do you mean that I am being used in some sort of wager? What is he supposed to win?"

When Stephen didn't speak, she answered for him. "I think I can guess. Hugh thinks he can woo me to his bed, and you believe him. Did it ever enter that swollen, vain, pea brain of yours that *I* might have some say in this? Do you think I am so mindless that any man who smiles at me and kisses my hand can have me in his bed? You should know I'd take a knife to him at the least. Rab growls every time Hugh touches me."

"Which seems to be often from what I can see."

Bronwyn noticed the window in the far side of the cell. So that's why Hugh refused to turn the pavilion. He wanted Stephen to be able to see them together. She looked at Stephen's cold, angry face, and she began to get angry too. Those two men were using her in some childish prank that was more suited to ten-year-olds. Hugh had said he could win Bronwyn to his bed, and Stephen obviously thought so little of her morals and integrity that he believed she could be won by any man who set himself to the task. And Hugh! He insulted her, treated her as if she were stupid, yet had every confidence that she'd succumb to his charms.

"Damn both of you!" she whispered before turning away.

"Bronwyn! Come back here!" Stephen commanded. "Tell Hugh you know of the plot and get the key from him."

She looked back at him and gave him her sweetest smile. "And miss the entertainment Sir Hugh has planned for me?" she asked, wiggling her eyebrows. She started down the stairs, her mouth set against the string of curses Stephen yelled after her. "Damn the both of them," she repeated to herself.

Chapter 13

BRONWYN WAS still fuming when she reached the foot of the stairs. Sir Hugh waited for her, an impatient look on his face. He looked as if he might chastise her for tarrying too long. Her first impulse was to lecture him about what he was trying to do, but the thought vanished as quickly as it came. Englishmen! she thought. When she'd first met Stephen, he knew there was no way but the English way. He laughed at her when she asked him to wear the Scots dress instead of the heavy English armor. Now she doubted if she could get him into one of Sir Hugh's heavy, padded jackets. But Stephen had had to go through a battle before he was willing to change.

Perhaps she could wage her own battle, and both of these Englishmen could learn something that every Scotsman knew—that women were quite capable of thinking on their own.

"I was beginning to worry about you," Sir Hugh said, extending his hand.

Bronwyn widened her eyes innocently. "I hope you don't mind but I was looking about your house. It is magnificent! Tell me, is all this yours?"

Sir Hugh took her arm and tucked it under his. His chest expanded visibly. "All of it and about seven hundred acres. Of course, I have another estate in the south."

She sighed heavily. "Stephen," she began shyly, "Stephen doesn't have a place such as this, does he?"

Hugh frowned. "Why, no. He does own some land some-where, I believe, and it has an old tower on it but not a house. But surely your own estates . . ."

Again she sighed. "But they're in Scotland."

"Oh, yes, of course. I understand. It's a cold, wet country, isn't it? No wonder you want to live here. Well, perhaps Stephen—" He broke off.

She smiled to herself. It was just as she thought. Hugh wasn't really interested in her, or at least he wouldn't actually dishonor his friend; he was merely bored and wanted to see Stephen fume. He mentioned his friend too often to be a true enemy. Stephen thought she could be enticed into any attractive man's bed, and Hugh merely used her as a means to antagonize his friend. Neither man considered her wants or thoughts.

She smiled more broadly as she began to wonder what would happen if she upset their plans somewhat. What would Sir Hugh say if she told him she was discontent with Stephen and that she would love to stay in England with a fine, handsome man like Hugh?

As they approached the pavilion she looked skyward. "I think the sun is about to shine. Perhaps we could move our chairs from under the canopy."

Sir Hugh smiled at her suggestion, then ordered the chairs brought forth.

Bronwyn ordered them set closer together, then smiled at Hugh's frown. She wasted no time once they were seated. Musicians played a sweet love song, but she never looked at them; she had eyes only for Hugh. "You have no wife, my lord?" she asked quietly.

"No . . . not as yet. I have not been as fortunate as my friend Stephen."

"Is he really your friend? Could you possibly be my friend also?"

Hugh looked deeply into her eyes, fearing that he'd lose himself in them. Stephen was indeed fortunate. "Of course, you are my friend," he said in a fatherly manner.

She sighed, moistened her lips and parted them. "I can tell

you are a sensitive, intelligent man. I wish I had a husband such as you." She smiled becomingly at the way his jaw dropped. "You must know about my marriage. I had no choice in the matter. I tried to choose someone else but . . . Lord Stephen . . ."

Hugh stiffened his back. "I heard that Stephen had to fight for you, and he did a damn good job of it too. I heard that Chatworth came at his back."

"Oh, yes, Stephen is a good fighter, but he isn't . . . how can I say it? He doesn't content me."

Hugh's eyes widened. "Are you saying that Stephen Montgomery is lacking in some way? Let me tell you that we've been friends all our lives. And as for his women!" He was starting to get angry now. "When we were in Scotland together, Stephen was half in love with a little whore, and he was blind to the fact that she was sleeping with half the troops. I paid her to go to bed with me at a time when I knew he'd see us together."

"Is that why he is so angry with you?" she asked, forgetting for a moment to use her honey-coated voice.

"He never would have believed me if I'd told him what she was. He couldn't see past her dimples."

Bronwyn drew back as she digested this news. So! Stephen was using her in a scheme to repay a man for taking one of his women. A woman he was half in love with! She felt a sharp pain through her breast, and burning tears gathered behind her eyes. He hadn't wanted to marry her because he'd been in love with a dimpled whore.

"Lady Bronwyn, are you all right?"

She touched her eye with her knuckle. "Something in my eye, I think."

"Here, let me see." He took her face in his large, strong hands, and Bronwyn looked up at him.

She knew Stephen was watching, and it crossed her mind to wonder if he was thinking of the woman he had wanted.

"I see nothing," Sir Hugh said, his hands never leaving her face. "You are an incredibly beautiful woman," he whispered. "Stephen is—"

She twisted away from him. "I don't want to hear that name again," she said angrily. "Today I'm free of him, and I want to remain so. Perhaps the musicians could spare some room for us and we could dance. I could show you some Scottish dances."

He gave a nervous look upward toward his house, then allowed himself to be pulled toward the wooden platform.

Sir Hugh didn't know when he'd been so entertained. He wasn't used to seeing a woman's hair flowing freely about her lithe body. Bronwyn's eyes flashed and laughed as he awkwardly tried to copy her intricate steps. The cold day seemed to grow warmer, and he forgot about her husband watching from above.

"Bronwyn," he laughed, having dropped the formal "Lady" an hour before, "I have to stop! I fear I have a stitch in my side."

She laughed at him. "You'd no' make a good Scotsman if you can stand so little exercise."

He took her arm. "I haven't worked so hard since I spent a week in training with the Montgomery brothers."

"Yes," she said as she sat down. "Stephen does train hard." Her expression became serious.

"He's a good man," Hugh said as he took a piece of cheese from a tray a servant held for him.

"Perhaps," she said, drinking deeply of warm, spiced wine.

"I envy him."

"Do you?" she asked, her eyes searching his. "Mayhaps you could replace him . . . in some ways." She watched with interest as Hugh began to take her meaning. The vain peacock! she thought. It never occurred to him—to any man— that he wasn't God's gift to women.

"Lady Bronwyn," he said formally. "I must talk seriously with you. About Stephen—"

"What was he like as a child?" she asked, cutting him off.

Hugh was obviously startled. "Serious, like Gavin. All the brothers grew up in a world of men. Perhaps if Stephen is awkward, it's because he knows very little about women."

"So unlike you," she purred.

Hugh smiled in a confident way. "I have had some experience, and I'm sure that's why you're . . . attracted to me. You've been married to Stephen so short a time. I'm sure that in years to come you'll grow . . . fond of one another."

"Is that what you want from life? Fondness?"

"I am a different man than Stephen," he said smugly.

Bronwyn smiled at him as a plan began to form in her mind. "Not long ago, while we were in Scotland, Stephen and I stayed with some farmers. One of the women made a delicious drink from some lichens. When we rode into your estate, I saw some growing near the rocks. I thought perhaps we could take a walk and collect them. I'd like to make the drink for you."

Hugh looked worried for a moment, then nodded in agreement. He didn't like the way the events were happening. It almost looked as if Stephen's wife wanted to betray her husband. Hugh wanted to report that Bronwyn could not be won by another man, but she seemed to be showing a preference for Hugh.

As they walked Hugh began to talk of Stephen, what an honorable man he was, how worthy he was of a woman of Bronwyn's standing. He spoke of how generous Stephen was in wearing that ridiculous Scots dress.

Bronwyn said very little as she gathered lichens and the dried heads of flowers in the little basket Hugh had given her. She listened carefully and said nothing.

It began to rain again when they returned to the house. Sir Hugh was very formal as he led her upstairs to a private solar. A servant brought hot wine and mugs so Bronwyn could prepare the drinks. As she carefully mixed and stirred the ingredients she watched Hugh, his thick chest puffed out, his mouth smug in his belief that he was being noble in refusing Bronwyn's advances.

"My lord," she said quietly, handing him the warm mug. Her hand touched his caressingly for a moment. She smiled as he declared the drink delicious and drained his cup then asked for more.

"I need to talk to you," he said seriously, sipping from the second mug of the hot liquid. "I mustn't let you leave here believing as you do."

"And what do I believe?" she asked sweetly.

"Stephen is my friend, has always been my friend. I just hope he will be my friend after this."

"And why should he not?"

"I guess that depends upon you. You must never mention your . . . your attraction to me."

"My attraction to you?" she asked innocently. She took a chair across from him. "Whatever do you mean?"

"Oh, come now, my lady. You and I both know what's been happening between us today. All women know about affairs of the heart."

She raised her eyebrows. "All women? Pray tell me what else all women know?"

"Don't turn coy on me!" he snapped. "I'm not so innocent about women as Stephen Montgomery is. Perhaps you'll be able to persuade him that you don't look at other men, and since he is my friend I will back your story, but don't try to play innocent with me."

"I am caught!" she said, smiling. "You know so much about women and about your friend that I have no means of escape."

Hugh started to speak, but a sudden pain shot through his gut and he closed his mouth.

"Here, let me refill your cup. You look pale."

Hugh grabbed the cup, drained it. He was out of breath when he recovered. "The fish must have been bad," he said, then dismissed the subject. "Where was I?"

"You were telling me how I was ready to leave my husband for you."

"You stretch my words," he said. "I—"

Bronwyn slammed the empty pitcher down on a table, and the glaze on the pottery crackled. "No! Let me tell you!" She stood over him, hands on her hips. "You say you are Stephen's friend, yet you play a childish trick on him and lock him where he can see you play the fool over his wife."

"Fool! You did not think I was a fool today."

"You think you can read my thoughts? Are you so vain that you think I can spend months in Stephen Montgomery's bed and yet be unsatisfied?"

"You said—"

"You were certainly ripe for believing anything you wanted. You act as if you did something noble in paying that whore to go to bed with you. You think you did Stephen a favor, but I wonder if you were just jealous. Every man in camp had to pay for her—all except one: my Stephen!"

"Your Stephen!" Hugh began, starting to rise, but another pain cut through him. He looked up in horror. "You poisoned me."

She smiled. "Not poison really, but you'll be quite ill for several days. I want you to remember today for a long time."

"Why?" he whispered, grabbing his stomach. "What have I done to you?"

"Nothing," she said seriously. "Absolutely nothing. I have been used to Englishmen too long to stand it another time. You used me to play a game with Stephen. It never occurred to you that I might have some thought in the matter. I could see it last night while Stephen played the lute. You were so sure of yourself, that any woman would want you."

Hugh doubled in pain. "You bitch!" he gasped. "Stephen is welcome to you."

"I'm a bitch because I decided to be more than a pawn in your little games? Remember, Sir Hugh, there's only one female on the chessboard, and she is the most versatile, most powerful piece." She bent and slipped the key from his doublet pocket before she turned away.

"Stephen saw you. He will never believe you weren't hot for me."

Her back stiffened. "Contrary to your thoughts of him, Stephen Montgomery is the most sane, intelligent man I have ever met." She paused at the door. "Oh, yes, and Sir Hugh, the next time you need help with your women, I'd advise you to ask for Stephen's advice. As far as I can tell, there's very little he doesn't know." She left the room.

Rab was waiting for her outside Hugh's door, and together they ran up the stairs to the room where Stephen was held. She looked through the barred door and saw Stephen glowering at her. The anger and hatred in his eyes made a chill run along her spine. She thrust the key into the lock and opened the door.

"You are free now," she said quietly. "It is still daylight, and we can ride toward your brother's estate."

Stephen sat silently, his eyebrows drawn together.

She walked close to him, put out her hand, and touched a curl of hair along his collar. "It would be better if you spoke about your anger."

He pushed her hand away. "Do you dare come to me directly from him? You wear a gown he gave you, the one you flaunted yourself in in front of him. Did he enjoy it? Did he enjoy the sight of the upper half of you bare?"

She sighed and sat down on the window seat. "Hugh said you'd not believe me innocent after what you'd seen."

"Hugh, is it?" Stephen growled and raised both his fists toward her, but then he dropped then helplessly at his side. "You have repaid me in full for marrying you. You waited long enough to have your revenge." He sat down heavily on a stool, ignoring Rab who nuzzled against him. "On our wedding night that knife of yours should have found my heart."

Bronwyn moved so quickly that even Rab didn't see her. She slapped Stephen across the face so hard his neck snapped backward. "Damn you to hell, Stephen Montgomery!" she gasped. "I am sick of being insulted. First that so-called friend of yours treats me as a piece of property to make a claim on, then when I refuse him and repay him for his vanity, he calls me a bitch. Now I must stand by and listen to you accuse me of being a whore. I am not your dimpled camp woman!"

Stephen paused in rubbing his bruised jaw. "What are you talking about? What woman?"

"She means nothing," she said angrily. "What have I done to cause you to believe I am a whore? When have my actions shown me to be dishonest or that I don't keep my vows?"

"You're not making sense. What vows?"

She gave a sigh of exasperation. "Our marriage vows, you dunce! I agreed to them. I would not betray them."

"You agreed to obey me too," he said sullenly.

She turned away from him. "Come, Rab. Let's go home."

Stephen was on his feet instantly. He grabbed her arm. "What do you think you're doing? Are you returning to Hugh?"

She pulled her foot back to kick him, but he whirled her about and pulled her to him, her back to his front.

"I nearly went insane," he whispered. "How could you have done that to me? You knew I was watching."

His words made her skin glow. It seemed like an eternity since he'd held her. She put her cheek against his arm. "You made me angry. The two of you were using me as if I had no rights of my own."

He turned her to face him, his hands on her shoulders. "We forgot that you're the MacArran, didn't we? Bronwyn, I—"

"Hold me," she whispered, "just hold me."

He nearly crushed her in his embrace. "I couldn't stand for him to touch you. Every time he touched your hand . . . and when he held your face in his hands!"

"Stop it!" she commanded. "Stop it this minute." She pulled away from him. "Nothing happened between Hugh Lasco and me. He thought he could win any woman in the world, and I wanted to show him he couldn't."

Stephen's anger returned. "You certainly did a good job of it. From here you looked as if you'd been lovers for years."

"Is that what you think? Do you believe I'd let a man paw me as he did if it weren't for a reason?"

Stephen's eyes darkened to almost black. "There was a reason! I know what you're like in bed. Maybe you wanted to find out if other men could make you cry. Tell me, did he find your knees the first time?"

She glared at him. "Do you honestly believe I spent the afternoon in bed with him?"

"No," he said, defeated. "There wasn't enough time, and Hugh . . ."

"Let me finish for you," she said flatly. "Hugh is your friend and you know he's an honorable man and wouldn't, in truth, do something so dishonorable. On the other hand, I am only a woman and therefore without honor. I am a piece of plant fluff and will go where the wind blows me, is that right?"

"You're twisting my words!"

"I don't believe I am. This morning, when I first saw you in here, you assumed that Hugh could have me if he wanted. All he had to do was ask or speak sweetly to me. If you knew anything about me, you would have sat in this cell and calmly waited for me. Then we could have laughed together over the jest I played on your Sir Hugh."

"What jest?" Stephen asked sharply.

Bronwyn felt that all the breath had been knocked from her. She'd learned so much about Stephen in the last few months, had come to trust him, believe in him, even think she loved him. But he'd learned nothing about her! He thought she was an empty-headed, weak plaything.

Her voice was expressionless. "I gave him a drink with some herbs in it that Kirsty said causes severe stomach cramps. He will be ill for days."

Stephen stared at her for a moment. How much he wanted to trust her! It seemed as if half his life had passed as he watched her leaning toward Hugh, talking to him. He'd torn at the bars on the windows when they'd danced together. Bronwyn's ankles showed beneath her skirt; the sunlight flashed off her dress. How could she ask him to be reasonable when she'd nearly turned him into an animal? If he could have gotten free, he would have killed Hugh, torn his friend apart with his bare hands.

He wiped his hand across his eyes. How could she ask him to think rationally when he couldn't think at all? He stared at her in wonder. What had she done to him? He hadn't had a clear thought since he'd first seen her, tossed on the floor in a wet chemise. He'd fought for her, nearly died when she risked her life over the side of a cliff for one of her men, nearly killed her when her childishness had cost Chris his life.

How could she talk to him of reason? Being near her took away all semblance of sanity.

"We should go," she said coldly, then turned away.

He watched her leave the room, Rab following her. He wanted to go to her, tell her he believed in her, knew she was honorable, but he couldn't. Hugh had proved once that he could take a woman from Stephen. Sweet Meg had loved Stephen, yet Hugh had been able to take her. Bronwyn made no secret of the fact that she considered Stephen her enemy. To her, one Englishman was as good as another. Perhaps Hugh had made promises concerning her clan. If her clan was involved . . .

He looked up as Rab gave a sharp bark at him. He came back to the present and ran down the stairs to Hugh's room.

Hugh lay on his bed, his knees drawn into his chest, four servants and three guards surrounding him. "Get out of here," he gasped through a well of pain. "I never want to see you or that bitch you married again."

Stephen backed away, but not before he began to smile. She'd been telling the truth!

"Get out, I say!" Hugh commanded. He grabbed at his stomach and fell back on the bed.

"Bested by a woman," Stephen laughed as he left the room. He hurried down the stairs to the Great Hall. Bronwyn waited for him, wearing her plaid skirt and white blouse. She was once more his Highlands lassie. He went to her, touched her arm, smiled at her.

She turned away coldly.

"Bronwyn," he began.

"If you're through here, I think we should ride. You are, of course, the master, and we will stay if that is your command."

He stared for a moment at the icy blueness of her eyes. "No, I don't want to stay," he said after a while. He turned away from her and walked toward the front door of the house.

Bronwyn followed him slowly. The whole episode had started as a game, a childish game of one-upmanship, but through it she'd learned something startling about her husband. For some reason she thought she was the one who had to learn to trust him. She'd watched him over the last few months, dispassionately observed the changes in him. She'd seen him go from being an arrogant Englishman to becoming almost a Scot. She'd seen a lot of the coldness toward his men leave him, and the men, who were Englishmen, changed almost as much as their master. One by one they began wearing a plaid and stopped spending hours a day polishing their armor. Then, just a few days ago, Stephen had killed three Englishmen in an effort to save Bronwyn and Kirsty's baby. To Bronwyn that act had been the final gesture she needed to make her believe in him.

But what had Stephen learned about her? He disapproved of everything she did. He cursed her if she led her men. He was angry if she risked her life to save someone else. What could she do to please him? Should she try to become someone else? Would he like her better if she were like . . . like his beautiful sister-in-law? She had a clear idea of what Judith was like: gentle, never raising her voice, always smiling sweetly at her husband, never arguing with him, always agreeable.

"That's what men really want!" she said under her breath. Stephen expected her to sit still and be quiet, to never contradict his words. Just like the Englishwomen! Damn him! she cursed. She was no milk-and-water Englishwoman! She was the MacArran, and the sooner Stephen Montgomery learned that the better for all of them.

She held her chin high as she walked toward the stables.

By a silent, mutual agreement they did not stop for the night. They rode at a steady pace, neither speaking, each with his own thoughts of the last two days. Stephen could think of little but the sight of Hugh's hands on Bronwyn. He knew she'd repaid Hugh, but he couldn't help wishing she'd not been so subtle and had taken a knife to the man.

As for Bronwyn, she had almost forgotten Hugh. What

mattered to her was that Stephen hadn't trusted her, had accused her of being a liar.

In the early dawn the walls of the old Montgomery castle rose before them. She had not expected this dark, massive fortress but a house more on the order of Hugh Lasco's. She glanced at Stephen and saw his face was alight, much as she must look each time she saw Larenston.

"We'll enter by the river gate," he said as he spurred his horse forward.

The front of the tall walls were set with two massive gate towers protecting the closed gates. She followed Stephen to low walls that made a roofless tunnel leading to the smaller gate at the far side of the castle walls.

Stephen slowed and cautiously entered the mouth of the narrow, walled alley. Immediately an arrow flew though the air to land at the feet of Stephen's horse.

"Who goes there?" demanded a faceless voice from the top of the wall above them.

"Stephen Montgomery!" he declared loudly.

Bronwyn smiled because Stephen's voice held the burr of the Highlands.

"You're not Lord Stephen, for I know him well! Now turn those nags about and leave. No one enters these walls but friends. Return in an hour to the front gate and beg entrance from the gatekeeper."

"Matthew Greene!" Stephen shouted up. "Have you forgotten your own master?"

The man leaned over the wall and stared downward. "It is you!" he said after a moment. "Open the gate!" he shouted, his voice full of joy. "Lord Stephen is safe! Welcome home, my lord."

Stephen waved his hand at the man and proceeded. All along the way men called in greeting from the top of the wall. At the end of the passageway a gate opened, and they rode inside to a private courtyard, the house looming over them.

"My lord, it's good to see you," said an old man as he took Stephen's reins. "I wouldn't have known you if the men hadn't told me it was you."

"It's good to be home, James. Are my brothers here?"

"Lord Gavin returned no more than an hour ago."

"Returned?"

"Aye, my lord, all your brothers have been searching for you. We heard you'd been killed by that heathen wife of yours."

"Watch yourself, James!" Stephen commanded. He absently stepped backward and took Bronwyn's hand. "This is my wife, the lady Bronwyn."

"Oh, my lady," the old man gasped. "Forgive me. I thought you were one of Lord Stephen's . . . I mean, he's often brought home . . ."

"You've said quite enough. Come, Bronwyn," Stephen said.

He gave her no chance to prepare herself. She was to be presented to his family looking like a serving wench. Even his servant thought so. She knew how the English set such store by a person's clothes, and she thought wistfully of the beautiful gowns she'd worn at Sir Thomas Crichton's. The best she could do was hold her head high and endure the English snubs. Except for the perfect Judith. No doubt she'd be kind and considerate, a soft-spoken pillow.

"You look scared to death," Stephen snapped, staring at her. "I assure you that Gavin rarely beats women, and Judith—"

She put up her hand. "Spare me. I've heard enough of this Judith." She straightened her back. "And the Scots will give up their plaids before you'll see the MacArran afraid of mere Englishmen."

He smiled at her, then pushed open the door to a room brilliant with early sunlight. Bronwyn only glanced at the beautifully paneled room before her attention was drawn to the two people standing in the middle of it.

"Goddamn you, Judith!" a tall man shouted. He had dark hair, gray eyes, and sharp cheekbones. An extraordinarily handsome man, and now his face was ablaze with anger. "I left exact orders as to how I wanted the dairy rebuilt. I even left drawings. As if I didn't have enough to worry about with

Stephen and his new wife missing, I return to find the foundations laid and they have no resemblance to my plans."

Judith looked up at him quite calmly. She had rich auburn hair only partially concealed by a French hood. Her eyes flashed gold. "Because your plans were completely inefficient. Have you ever made butter or cheese? Even milked a cow for that matter?"

The man towered over her, but the small woman didn't flinch. "What the hell does it matter that I've never milked a goddamn cow?" He was so angry that his cheekbones seemed ready to cut through his skin. "The point is that you countermanded my orders. How does that make me look to my dairymen?"

Judith narrowed her eyes at him. "They'll only be grateful they don't have to work in that rabbit warren you designed."

"Judith!" he growled. "If I thought it'd do any good, I'd beat you black and blue for your insolence."

"It's remarkable how angry you get when I'm right."

The man ground his teeth together and took a step forward.

"Gavin!" Stephen shouted from beside Bronwyn as he grabbed an axe from an arrangement of weapons on the wall.

Gavin, war trained, his senses always alert, recognized the call. He turned quickly, then grabbed the war axe that Stephen tossed to him. For a moment Gavin looked in puzzlement from his brother, who wore such odd clothing, to the axe he held.

"To protect you from Judith," Stephen laughed.

Before Gavin could react, Judith ran across the room and threw herself into Stephen's arms. "Where have you been? We've been looking for you for days. We were so worried about you."

Stephen buried his face in his sister-in-law's neck. "You're well now? The fever . . . ?"

Gavin's snort interrupted him. "She's well enough to put her nose into all my affairs."

"Affairs?" Stephen laughed. "Haven't you learned your lesson yet?"

"Hush, both of you," Judith said as she disengaged herself from Stephen.

Gavin clasped his brother to him. "Where have you been? We heard you'd been killed and then that you'd been killed a second time. It was . . ." He couldn't finish or tell Stephen of the agony they'd gone through while searching for him.

"I'm all right now, as you can see," Stephen laughed and stepped back from his brother.

"I can see that you've grown even more handsome," Judith said, frankly appraising her brother-in-law's brown, muscular legs.

Gavin threw his arm around Judith in a possessive way. "Stop flirting with my brother, and I'll tell you right now that I'm not going to wear one of those things."

Judith laughed quietly and fitted herself against her husband.

Bronwyn stood in the shadow of a tall chair, an outsider watching the family. So this was the gentle Judith! She was shorter than Bronwyn, a tiny bit of a thing, as lovely as a jewel. Yet she stood up to her tall husband without fear. This was no woman who spent her days sewing!

Judith was the first to notice Bronwyn watching them. Her first impression was that Stephen had done what he once threatened: locked his wife in a tower and found a beautiful commoner to make him happy. But as she watched Bronwyn she realized that no commoner could carry herself as Bronwyn did. It wasn't just the pride of being startlingly lovely, but some inner pride that made her stand that way. This was a woman who knew that she was worth something.

Judith pushed away from her husband and walked toward Bronwyn. "Lady Bronwyn?" she asked quietly, her hand extended.

Bronwyn's eyes met Judith's, and there passed between them an understanding. They recognized each other as equals.

"How did you know?" Stephen laughed. "James thought she was one of my . . . well, certainly not my wife."

"James is a fool," Judith said flatly. She stepped away from Bronwyn, studied the taller woman's clothes. "That skirt would give you much freedom, wouldn't it? And it wouldn't be as heavy as this gown, would it?"

Bronwyn smiled warmly. "It's wonderfully light, but then yours is so beautiful."

"Come to my solar and let's talk," Judith said.

The men stared at their departing wives in open-mouthed astonishment.

"I've never seen Judith take to anyone like that," Gavin said. "And how did she know she was your wife? From the way she was dressed, I would have agreed with James."

"And Bronwyn!" Stephen said. "She hates the English clothes. You can't imagine how many sermons I've heard about the confining way the English dress their women."

Gavin began to smile. "Black hair and blue eyes! Did I really see her or was it my imagination? I thought you said she was ugly and fat. She couldn't really be the laird of a clan, could she?"

Stephen chuckled. "Let's sit down, and do you think I could have something to eat?" His eyes twinkled. "Or do the servants only obey Judith now?"

"If I weren't so glad you were safe, I'd repay you for that remark," Gavin said as he left the room to order food and send men to find Raine and Miles.

"How is Judith, really?" Stephen asked when the food was brought. "I know you said in your letters that she was fully recovered from the miscarriage, but . . ."

Gavin picked up a hard-boiled egg from Stephen's plate. "You saw her," he said heavily. "I have to fight for every inch of control I have over my own people."

Stephen looked up sharply. "And you love it," he said slowly.

Gavin grinned. "She certainly makes life interesting. Every time I see one of those prim, pink-and-white wives of other men, I'm thankful I have Judith. I think I'd go crazy if I couldn't have a good, rousing fight once a week. Enough about me! What's your Bronwyn like? Is she always so sweet and docile as a few minutes ago?"

Stephen didn't know whether to laugh or cry. "Docile?

Bronwyn! She has no idea what the word means. She was standing to one side probably to judge whether to use a knife or that hell-hound dog of hers."

"Why should she do that?"

"She's a Scot, man! The Scots hate the English for burning their crops, raping their women, because the English are a damned, insufferable, arrogant lot of bastards who think they're better than the honest, generous Scots, and—"

"Wait a minute!" Gavin laughed. "The last I heard, you were an Englishman."

Stephen returned to his food, forcing himself to calm. "I guess I forgot for a moment."

Gavin leaned back in his chair and studied his brother. "From the length of your hair, I'd say you forgot some months ago."

"I wouldn't criticize the Scots' dress until you've tried it, if I were you," Stephen snapped.

Gavin put his hand on his brother's arm. "What's wrong? What is worrying you?"

Stephen rose and walked toward the fireplace. "Sometimes I don't know who I am anymore. When I went to Scotland, I knew I was a Montgomery, and I felt quite noble about my mission there. I was to teach the ignorant Scots our more civilized ways."

He ran his hand through his hair. "They aren't ignorant, Gavin. Far from it. Lord, but what we could learn from them! We don't even know the meaning of loyalty. That clan of Bronwyn's would die for her, and damned if she won't—and hasn't—jeopardized her life for them. Their women sit in on their decision-making councils, and I've heard the women make damn good decisions."

"Like Judith," Gavin said quietly.

"Yes!" Stephen said loudly. "But she has to fight you for every inch."

"Of course," Gavin answered firmly. "Women should—"

Stephen's laugh stopped him. "Somewhere along the way I stopped thinking 'women should.' "

"Tell me more about Scotland," Gavin said, wanting to change the subject.

Stephen sat down again, returned to the food. His voice sounded far away. "It's a beautiful place."

"I heard it does little but rain."

Stephen waved his hand. "What's a little rain to a Scot?"

Gavin was thoughtful, watching his brother, hearing beyond his words. "Christopher Audley came by some time ago. Did he find you before your wedding?"

Stephen pushed his food away. "Chris was killed in Scotland."

"How?"

Stephen wondered how he could explain that Chris was killed in what, to a knight like Gavin, would be a dishonorable fight. "A cattle raid. Some of Bronwyn's men were killed trying to protect him."

"Protect Chris? But he was an excellent fighter. His armor—"

"Damn his armor!" Stephen snapped. "The man couldn't run. He was, as Douglas said, trapped inside a steel coffin."

"I don't understand. How?"

Stephen was saved from answering by the door bursting open.

Raine and Miles exploded into the room. Raine bounded across the floor, his footsteps jarring the windows. He lifted his older, but lighter, brother into a crushing embrace. "Stephen! We heard you were dead."

"He will be if you don't release him," Miles said calmly.

Raine let up on some of the pressure he was exerting. "You're still a skinny little thing," he said smugly.

Stephen grinned at his brother, then proceeded to push his arms out against Raine's. He grinned more broadly as he felt Raine's arms move. Stephen pushed harder and Raine applied more pressure. Raine lost.

Stephen smiled at his brother in pure pleasure. There weren't many men who could overpower Raine's massive strength without resorting to a weapon. He offered silent thanks to Tam.

Raine stepped away and grinned at his brother with pride. "Scotland seems to agree with you."

"Or else you've neglected your training," Stephen said smugly.

Raine's dimples deepened. "Perhaps you'd like to test that."

"Here!" Miles said, stepping between his brothers. "Don't let Raine kill you before I can welcome you home." He embraced Stephen.

"You've grown, Miles," Stephen said, "and you've put on weight."

Gavin snorted. "It's the women. Two of the cook's helpers are trying to see which one can outcook the other."

"I see," Stephen laughed. "And the prize is our baby brother?"

Raine laughed. "What there is left of him after the other women have finished with him."

Miles ignored all of his brothers. He rarely smiled broadly, as his brothers did. He was a solemn man, and the emotion that he felt showed in his piercing gray eyes. Now he looked about the room. "James said your wife returned with you."

"Leave it to Miles," Gavin laughed. "At least now I can have Judith to myself once in a while. Every time I look up, she's with one of my worthless brothers."

"Gavin works her like a serf," Raine said half seriously.

Stephen smiled. It was good to be home again, to see Gavin and Raine arguing, to hear them teasing Miles. His brothers had changed little in the last few months. Raine, if anything, looked stronger and healthier, his love for the world carried openly. Miles still stood to one side, a part of the group yet separate. And Gavin drew them all together. Gavin was the solid one, the one who loved the earth. Where Gavin was, was home for the Montgomerys.

"I'm not sure I'm ready for you to meet Bronwyn," Stephen began.

"Shy, is she?" Raine asked, concerned. "I hope you didn't drag her all across England with you. Why didn't we see your baggage wagons? Where are your men?"

Stephen took a deep breath and laughed. They'd never believe him if he told the truth. "No, I wouldn't exactly call Bronwyn shy," he chuckled.

Chapter 14

BRONWYN SAT up to her neck in a tub of hot, soapy water. A fire burned brightly in the big fireplace, making the room warm and fragrant. She relaxed in the tub and looked about her. The bedchamber was beautiful, from the beamed ceiling to the Spanish-tile floor. The walls were of white-painted wood with tiny rosebuds twining about the joints. The enormous canopied bed was hung with deep rose velvet. The chairs, benches, and cabinets in the room were all handsomely carved with tall, pointed arches.

Bronwyn smiled and leaned back in the tub. It was pleasant to be in such luxury, even if at the same time she felt the money could have been spent for something else. She and Stephen had seen great poverty as they rode toward the Montgomery estate. For herself, she would have used the money on her people, but she knew the English were different.

She closed her eyes and thought of the last few minutes. She smiled as she thought of the Judith she'd expected and the Judith she met. She'd expected a soft, sweet woman, but there was nothing soft about Judith. There wasn't a servant who didn't jump to do her bidding. Before Bronwyn was fully aware of what was happening, she had found herself undressed and in a tub. She hadn't known it but the hot water was exactly what she needed.

The door opened softly, and Judith entered. "Feeling better?" she asked.

"Much. I had forgotten what it was like to be so pampered."

Judith grimaced and held out a large, warm towel for Bronwyn. "I'm afraid the Montgomery men are not ones for pampering their women. Gavin thinks nothing of asking me to ride with him through the worst of storms."

Bronwyn wrapped the towel around her body and looked at Judith carefully. "And what would you do if he bade you stay at home?" she asked quietly.

Judith laughed warmly. "I would not stay at home. Gavin too often overlooks what he considers unimportant details, such as a steward stealing grain from the storehouses."

Bronwyn sat down before the fire and sighed. "I wish you could look at my account books. I'm afraid I too often neglect them."

Judith picked up an ivory comb and began to untangle her sister-in-law's freshly washed hair. "But you have more to consider than just the beans in a storehouse. Tell me, what's it like to be the laird of a clan, to have all those handsome young men obey your every wish?"

Bronwyn exploded with laughter, both at Judith's wistful tone and at the absurdity of the idea. She stood, slipped on a robe of Judith's, and began to pull at the tangles in her hair. "It is a great responsibility," she said seriously. "And as for my men obeying me . . ." She sighed and pulled some hair from the comb.

"In Scotland we're not like you are in England. Here women are treated as if they were different."

"As if we have no minds!" Judith said.

"Yes, that's true, but when men believe women are intelligent, they expect more from them."

"I don't understand," Judith answered.

"My men do not obey me blindly. They question me every step of the way. In Scotland every man believes he is every other man's equal. Stephen tells his men to saddle their horses and be ready to ride in an hour. His men don't even question him."

"I'm beginning to understand," Judith said. "Would your

men want to know where they are going and why? If so, that could be quite . . ."

"Infuriating at times," Bronwyn finished for her. "There is a man, an older man, Tam, who watches my every move and comments on every decision I make. Then there are all of Tam's sons, who contradict me at every opportunity. In truth, I make only the minor decisions. All the major ones are a joint effort."

"But what if you want something and they are against it? What do you do?"

Bronwyn smiled slowly. "There are ways of getting around men, even ones who hover like eagles."

It was Judith's turn to laugh. "Like the dairy! I couldn't let Gavin build that awful one he'd drawn. I had the men work all night to get the foundations dug before he returned. I knew he was too frugal to have them torn out and too proud to admit I was right."

Bronwyn sat down on the bench beside her sister-in-law. "And to think that I dreaded meeting you. Stephen said . . . well, the way he described you made me think you were nothing more than a pretty, but lifeless, idiot."

"Stephen!" Judith laughed, then took Bronwyn's hand. "I was the one who caused him to be late for your wedding. I was appalled when I found out he hadn't even sent you a message to explain himself." She hesitated a moment. "I heard it caused you some problems."

"Stephen Montgomery caused his own problems," Bronwyn said flatly. "There are times when he can be the most arrogant, insufferable, infuriating—"

"Fascinating man alive," Judith said heavily. "Don't tell me. I know all too well, since I'm married to one. But I wouldn't trade Gavin for all the sweet-smelling, chivalrous men in the world. You must feel the same way about Stephen."

Bronwyn knew she needed to reply, but she had no idea what she meant to say.

Suddenly Rab was on his feet, his tail wagging as he barked excitedly at the chamber door.

Stephen entered and knelt as he scratched Rab's ears. "You two look happy about something," he said.

"A moment's peace and quiet has been a joy," Bronwyn retorted.

Stephen smiled at Judith. "While we're here, perhaps you can sweeten her tongue. By the way, there's a man downstairs raving something about some dresses."

"Wonderful!" Judith declared and practically ran from the room.

"What was that all about?" Stephen asked, rising and walking toward his wife. He lifted a damp curl from her breast. "You look as enticing as a fresh spring morning."

She pulled away from him and looked back at the fire.

"Bronwyn, you still aren't angry about what happened at Hugh's, are you?"

She turned to face him. "Angry?" she asked coldly. "No, I'm not angry. I was merely foolish, that's all."

"Foolish?" he asked, putting his hand on her shoulder. He didn't mind her rages or even when she took a knife to him nearly as much as he was distressed by this coldness of hers. "How were you foolish?"

She turned to face him. "I had begun to believe that there could be something between us."

"Love?" he asked, his eyes bright, a smile beginning to curve his lips. "It's not wrong to admit you love me."

She curled her lip at him and pushed his hand away. "Love!" she said angrily. "I'm talking about more important things than love between a man and a woman. I'm talking of trust and loyalty and the faith one person must have in another."

He frowned at her. "I have no idea what you're talking about. I thought love was what most women wanted."

She sighed in exasperation, and her voice was quiet when she spoke. "When are you going to learn that I am not 'most women'? I am Bronwyn, the MacArran, and I am unique. Perhaps most women do think love is the major goal of their lives, but I have love. My men love me, Tam loves me. I have friendships with the women of my clan and now even Kirsty, a MacGregor."

"And where do I fit into this?" Stephen asked, his jaw set.

"I'm sure we do love each other, in our own way. I cared for you when Davey's arrow wounded you, and you often exhibit that you care for me."

"Thank you for small favors," he said grimly. "And here I thought you'd be pleased to hear that I love you."

She looked at him sharply and felt her heart jump at his words, but she wouldn't tell him so. "I want more than love. I want something that will last past my smooth skin and my narrow waist." She paused for a moment. "I want respect. I want honor and trust. I do not want to be accused of being a liar, nor do I want your jealousy. As the MacArran, I must live in a world of men, and I do not want a husband who accuses me of all manner of dishonorable things when I am out of his sight."

A muscle in Stephen's jaw worked. "So! I am to stand by and watch man after man touch you and say nothing?"

"I do not believe there has been more than one man. You should have reasoned that there was a purpose behind my actions."

"Reasoned! Damn you, Bronwyn! How can I think when someone else touches you?"

Rab's bark kept her from replying.

The door opened a crack. "Is it safe?" Judith asked, watching Rab.

"Come, Rab," Bronwyn commanded as Judith entered. "He won't hurt you unless you come at me with a weapon."

"I'll remember that," Judith laughed and held out her arms. Across them lay a gown of deep, rich dark brown velvet, embroidered all over with heavy gold thread. "For you," she said. "Let's see if it fits."

"How . . . ?" Bronwyn began as she held the luscious gown up to her.

Judith smiled secretly. "There's an awful little man who works for Gavin; Gavin was always locking him in the cellar for all manner of . . . indiscretions. I decided to use the man's talents. I gave him a bag of silver, told him how tall you were, and told him to get me a gown worthy of a lady."

"It's beautiful," Bronwyn whispered, running her hands over the velvet. "You've been so kind to me, made me feel so welcome."

Judith was staring at Stephen, who had his back to them. She put her hand on his shoulder. "Stephen, are you all right? You look tired."

He tried to smile at her and absently kissed her hand. "Perhaps I am." He turned to Bronwyn. "My brothers would like to meet you," he said formally. "I would be honored if you'd visit with us." He turned and left the room.

Judith didn't ask about what had happened between the newlyweds. She only wanted to make their visit as free of strife as possible. "Come and I'll help you dress. Tomorrow you should be able to try on the new clothes I've ordered for you."

"New . . . ? You shouldn't have done that."

"But I did, so the least you can do is enjoy them. Now let's see if this fits."

It was hours later when Bronwyn was dressed and groomed to Judith's satisfaction. Judith said she'd learned many tricks while she was at court, a place she never cared to visit again. She liked Bronwyn's Scots way of leaving her hair free so much that she discarded her own hood and let her rich auburn hair flow down her back. Judith wore a gown of violet satin, the sleeves and hem trimmed in dark brown mink. A gold belt set with purple amethysts was about her waist.

Bronwyn smoothed the velvet over her hips. The dress was heavy and confining, but today she liked it. The low, square neckline showed her full breasts to advantage. The puffed sleeves were slashed to pull through tissue-thin cloth of gold. She straightened her shoulders and went down the stairs to meet her brothers-in-law.

The four men stood side by side in front of the stone fireplace in the winter parlor, and both Bronwyn and Judith paused for a moment to look at them with pride.

Stephen had trimmed his long hair and discarded his Scots clothes, and Bronwyn felt a sudden pang of loss for the Highlander he'd been. He wore a coat of dark blue velvet, collared with rich sable. His heavy, muscular legs were encased in dark blue wool hose.

Gavin dressed in gray, his coat lined with gray squirrel fur. Raine wore black velvet, the collar embroidered with silver thread worked in an intricate Spanish design. Miles's coat was of emerald-green velvet, the sleeves cut and slashed to reveal silver tissue beneath. There were pearls sewn onto his shirt sleeves.

Miles was the first to turn and see the women. He set his silver wine chalice on the mantelpiece and went forward. He stopped in front of Bronwyn, his eyes darkening almost to black—a hot black fire. He dropped to one knee before her. "I am honored," he whispered in great reverence, his head bowed.

Bronwyn looked at the others in consternation.

Judith smiled with pride at her sister-in-law. "May I introduce Miles?"

Bronwyn held out her hand, and Miles took it, and kissed it lingeringly.

"You've made your point, Miles," Stephen said sarcastically.

Gavin laughed and slapped Stephen on the shoulder so hard his wine sloshed onto his hand. "Now I have someone to help me with our baby brother," Gavin said. "Lady Bronwyn, may I introduce myself more formally? I am Gavin Montgomery."

Bronwyn took her hand from Miles's grasp, and only reluctantly did her eyes leave him. There was something extraordinarily intriguing about the young man. She gave her hand to Gavin, then turned toward the other brother. "And you must be Raine. I've heard quite a bit about you."

"Any of it good?" Raine asked, taking her hand, smiling so his dimples were quite deep.

"Very little of it," she answered honestly. "One of my men, Tam, a great oak of a man, was Stephen's trainer in Scotland. For weeks on end I heard your name used as a cry to goad Stephen whenever he tried to get away from Tam's rather strenuous demands."

Raine laughed loudly. "It must have worked, for he beat me in a short wrestle this morning." He eyed Stephen. "Though of course he has yet to accept my challenge to a longer match."

Bronwyn widened her eyes and studied the massiveness of Raine's wide shoulders and thick chest. "It seems to me that the first time would be the only necessary time to beat a man."

Raine grabbed her by the shoulders and exuberantly kissed her cheek. "Stephen, you should keep this one," he laughed.

"I am trying," he said as he took her hand just before Miles reached for it again. "Dinner is laid, shall we go?" he asked, his eyes searching hers.

She smiled at him sweetly, as if they'd never had a quarrel. "Yes, please," she said demurely.

It was while they sat at dinner, as course after course of food was brought, that Bronwyn realized how different these people were from the English people she'd met before. This laughing, happy family bore no resemblance to the men she'd met at Sir Thomas Crichton's. Judith had gone to great expense and trouble to make her welcome. Stephen's brothers accepted her, did not make sneering remarks because she was the laird of a clan.

Suddenly everything seemed to be spinning around and around. She'd grown up hating the MacGregors and the English. Now she was godmother to a MacGregor, and she found herself loving this warm, close English family. Yet the MacGregors had killed the MacArrans for centuries. The English had killed her father. How could she love people she should hate?

"Lady Bronwyn?" Gavin asked. "Is the wine too strong for you?"

"No," she smiled. "Everything is very nearly perfect. And that, I'm afraid, is my problem."

He studied her for a moment. "I want you to know that we're your family too. If you need any of us at any time, we'll be here."

"Thank you," she answered seriously. She knew he meant his words.

After dinner Judith took Bronwyn on a tour of the area inside the castle walls. There were two sections to the castle, the outer one where the castle retainers lived and worked, and the more protected inner circle for the family. Bronwyn listened and asked hundreds of questions about the incredibly efficient and well-organized castle complex. The acres of land inside the tall, thick walls were almost self-sustaining.

Stephen stopped them as they were speaking to the blacksmith and Judith was showing her a new forging technique.

"Bronwyn," Stephen said, "may I speak to you?"

She knew he had something serious to say, so she followed him outside where they could be private.

"Gavin and I are returning to Larenston to get Chris's body."

"Tam will have buried him by now."

He nodded. "I know, but I feel we owe it to Chris's family. They don't even know yet that he's dead. It will help some if he can be buried in his own land."

She nodded in agreement. "Chris didn't like Scotland," she said solemnly.

He ran his knuckles along her cheek. "It's the first time we've been apart since we were married. I'd like to think—" He stopped and dropped his hand.

"Stephen—" she began.

Suddenly he took her into his arms and held her close to him. "I wish we could go back to the time we spent with Kirsty and Donald. You seemed happy there."

She clung to him. In spite of the danger they'd been in, she too remembered the time as happy.

"You've come to mean so much to me," he whispered. "I hate to leave when you're so . . . cold to me."

When she laughed, he pushed her away, frowning. "Do I amuse you?" he asked angrily.

"I was thinking that I feel far from cold right now. Tell me, how long do you have before you leave?"

"Minutes," he said in such a tone of regret that she laughed again.

"And how long before you return?"

He put his fingers under her chin. "Three long, long days, at least. Knowing Gavin, we'll ride hard." He smiled. "We won't stop every few hours as you and I did."

She slipped her arms up around his neck. "You will not forget me while you are gone?" she whispered, her lips against his.

"As easily as I could forget a thunderstorm," he said evenly, chuckling when she tried to move away. "Come here, wench," he commanded.

His mouth took possession of hers in such a way that she forgot all thoughts of honor and respect. She remembered only their romps on the Highlands moors. His hand moved her head to slant against his mouth, and she opened her lips under his, drinking in the sweetness of the tip of his tongue. She pressed her body closer to his and tightened her arms.

"Stephen—" she began.

He put two fingers on her lips. "We have much to talk of when I return. Are you willing?"

She smiled happily. "Yes, I am very willing."

He kissed her once again, with longing and promises of what was to come. When he turned away, it was with obvious reluctance.

It was at night that Bronwyn realized how much she missed Stephen. The big bed in the lovely tiled bedchamber seemed cold and unbearable. She thought of Stephen riding back into Scotland without so much as a night's rest. She cursed herself for not insisting she'd return with him.

The more she thought, the more restless she became. She tossed the covers aside and walked quickly across the cold floor to a chest in the corner. She withdrew her Highlands clothes, and within minutes she was fastening her plaid to her shoulder. She thought perhaps a walk in the cold courtyard below would help her sleep.

As soon as she was outside, the clatter of horses' hoofs on the bricked yard echoed against the buildings. "Stephen!" she gasped and began to run forward. She knew that only family would be allowed to enter at night.

"Lady Mary," someone said quietly. "It's good to see you again. Was your trip pleasant?"

"As good as I could wish, James," came a gentle, soft voice.

"Shall I fetch Lady Judith?"

"No, don't bother her. She needs her rest. I can find my own way."

Bronwyn stood in the shadows and watched as one of the castle retainers helped Lady Mary dismount. She remembered how Stephen had compared his sister to the Madonna, said she was the peacemaker and that she lived in a convent near the Montgomery estates.

"We expected you earlier," James said. "I hope nothing was wrong."

"One of the children was sick. I stayed to tend the child."

"You're too kind-hearted, Lady Mary. You shouldn't take in them beggars' children. Some of them have murderers for fathers. And mothers too if the truth be known."

Mary started to speak, then stopped and whirled to face Bronwyn. She smiled. "I had the oddest feeling I was being watched." She stepped forward. "You must be Stephen's Bronwyn."

The courtyard was very dim with only the moonlight and one lantern for light. Mary was short and plump with a perfectly oval face. It was a face anyone would trust.

"How did you know?" Bronwyn smiled. "I haven't been able to fool any of the Montgomerys."

"I've heard of the heartiness of the Scots. And to withstand this wind when there is no need, it would take a great deal of stamina."

Bronwyn laughed. "Come inside to the winter parlor, and I'll have a roaring-hot fire for you in minutes."

"It sounds heavenly," Mary said, keeping her hands under her plain dark wool mantle.

Mary followed her sister-in-law into the large, paneled room, then stood quietly by as Bronwyn did indeed stoke and load the fire herself. She smiled, pleased that a lady of Bronwyn's rank felt secure enough to do humble work.

Bronwyn turned. "You must be tired. Perhaps you'd rather have the fire lit in your room."

Mary sat down in a cushioned chair and put her hands toward the fire. "I am tired, too tired to go to sleep. I'd just like to sit here a moment and get warm."

Bronwyn paused a moment before returning the iron fire tool to its holder. Mary did indeed look like the Madonna. Her oval face had a high, clear forehead above soft, expressive brown eyes. Her mouth was small, tender, delicate, and there was a dimple in one cheek. Raine's dimples, Bronwyn thought.

"It's good to be home again," Mary sighed, then looked back at Bronwyn. "Why are you awake?" she asked sharply. "Has Stephen . . . ?"

Bronwyn laughed and took a chair beside Mary. "He and Gavin have returned to Scotland to . . . bring home the body of a friend."

"Christopher," Mary said and sighed as she leaned back in the chair.

"You know about him?" Bronwyn asked almost fearfully.

"Yes. Stephen wrote me about his death."

Bronwyn was very quiet. "Did he say how I was the one who caused Chris's death?"

"No! And you shouldn't even think that. He said that Chris's own arrogance caused his death. He said that all Englishmen were committing suicide when they entered the Highlands."

"The English have killed many Highlanders!" Bronwyn said fiercely, then turned and looked quickly at Mary. "I apologize. I forget—"

"That we are English? That's a compliment, I'm sure." She studied Bronwyn in the soft glow of the firelight. "Stephen wrote me of your beauty, but he didn't tell me half of it."

Bronwyn grimaced. "He sets too much store by a woman's looks."

Mary laughed. "You've discovered what Judith has also. My brothers think all women are like me, without spirit or passion."

Bronwyn looked at her. "But surely—"

Mary put her hand up. "But surely a woman with brothers as passionate as mine must have some of her own? Is that what you meant to say?" She didn't wait for an answer. "No, I'm afraid I tend to run away from life. Women like Judith—and you if I guess correctly from Stephen's letters—grab life with both hands."

Bronwyn didn't know what to say. She thought about what an odd conversation they were having. They were talking as if they'd known each other for years instead of a few minutes. But somehow the quietness of the room, and the way the light of the fire seemed to isolate them from the dark corners, made everything seem quite ordinary.

"Tell me, are you lonely?" Mary asked. "Do you miss your Scots ways? What of your family and friends?"

It was a while before Bronwyn spoke. "Aye, I miss my friends." She thought of Tam and Douglas and all her people. "Yes, I miss them very much."

"And now it seems that Stephen is gone also. Perhaps tomorrow we could ride together. I'd like to hear some about Scotland."

Bronwyn smiled and leaned back in the chair. She'd very much like to spend the day with this woman. There was something quiet and peaceful about her, something Bronwyn felt she needed right now.

Bronwyn spent the next two days with Lady Mary, and it didn't take long to grow to love the woman. While Judith was busy with the account books and the worries of managing her own vast estates, as well as Gavin's, Mary and Bronwyn discovered their mutual love of people. Bronwyn had never been able to interest herself in numbers on paper, but she could tell more about the prosperity of a place by talking with the people than any other way. She and Mary rode across the acres and acres of land and talked with everyone. The serfs were timid at first, but they soon responded to Bronwyn's openness. She was used to speaking to underlings as equals, and one by one Mary saw the men and women straighten their shoulders in pride. Bronwyn sent people who were ill to bed. She asked for, and was happily given, extra supplies for some families' children.

But she wasn't always generous with her bounty. She considered the serfs people and so did not look at them with pity. She found several men who were stealing from their masters, and she saw that they were punished. Some quiet, hardworking, loyal families were put in places of responsibility and position.

On the evening of the first day Judith and Bronwyn spent hours together, Judith listening with admiration to all Bronwyn had to say. Judith realized her sister-in-law's wisdom immediately and took all her advice.

On the other hand Bronwyn learned a great deal about organization and efficiency, all of which knowledge she planned to take back to Larenston. She studied Judith's designs for buildings, her garden plans. Judith promised to send a wagonload of bedding plants to Larenston in the spring.

And Judith was a wonder with the breeding of animals. Bronwyn was fascinated by the way Judith had bred and cross-bred her sheep and cattle until she produced more meat, milk, and wool.

When Bronwyn retired for the night, she was too tired to stay awake. Charts and numbers swam before her eyes. A hundred faces and names floated through her dreams.

In the morning she was up early and in the stables before most of the castlefolk were awake. She wore her Highlands dress again, since she found the people responded enthusiastically to the simple clothes.

She swung a light saddle onto the back of a strawberry mare.

"My lady," came a strong young voice from beside her. "Allow me."

She turned to see a short, handsome blond man, one of Miles's men, who'd accompanied her and Mary the day before. "Thank you, Richard."

His eyes, a dark green, warmed as he looked at her. "I had no idea you knew my name. It is an honor for me."

She laughed. "Nonsense! In Scotland I know all my men's names, and they call me by mine."

He bent to fasten the cinch. "I've been talking to some of Lord Stephen's men who were with him in Scotland. They said you often traveled at night, alone, with your men."

"True," she said slowly. "I am the MacArran, and I am the leader of my men."

He smiled in a slow, provocative way. "May I say that I envy your Highlanders? In England we are seldom led by a woman and never one so beautiful."

She frowned and reached for the reins of her horse. "Thank you," she said stiffly and led the animal from the stables.

"What do you think you're doing?" snapped a man behind Richard.

Richard glanced at the door Bronwyn had used before turning to the man behind him. "Nothing that would interest you, George," he said, shoving his way past the knight.

George grabbed Richard's arm. "I saw you talking to her, and I want to know what you said."

"Why?" Richard snapped. "So you can have her all to yourself? I heard what you and the rest of Stephen's men said about her."

"*Lord* Stephen to you!"

"You're a hypocrite! You call her Bronwyn and talk to her as if she were your little sister, yet let someone else speak to her and you want to draw a sword. Let me tell you that I for one don't mean to treat her like anything but the Scots whore she is. No lady would talk to the men and the serfs like she does unless she was after what they carry between their legs. And I—"

George's fist smashed into Richard's mouth before he could say another word. "I'll kill you for that!" George yelled as he went for Richard's throat.

Richard was able to sidestep the second blow. He clasped his hands together and brought them down across the back of George's neck. George went sprawling forward, face first into the straw.

"What's going on here?" Bronwyn demanded from the doorway.

George sat up and rubbed his neck. Richard's nose was bleeding, and he wiped the blood away with the back of his hand.

"I asked a question," Bronwyn said quietly, watching the two men. "I will not ask the cause of your quarrel, as that is personal, but I want to know who struck the first blow."

Richard looked at George pointedly.

"I did, my lady," George said as he started to rise.

"You, George? But—" Bronwyn stopped herself. There must have been a good reason from someone of George's quiet, steady nature to strike a first blow. She didn't like Richard and she didn't trust him. Yesterday he'd too often leered at the young serf girls. But she couldn't leave George and Richard alone together, and she couldn't take George with her because he was the one who started the quarrel. It was better to keep Richard with her and protect Stephen's man.

"Richard," she said quietly, "you may go with Lady Mary and me today." She gave one look of regret to George and left the stables.

"Hot for me, the woman is," Richard laughed as he left the stables before George could attack him again.

Chapter 15

MARY SWUNG into the saddle and gave her sister-in-law a sleepy look. She wondered if cold or exhaustion were words Bronwyn knew. They'd ridden all day yesterday until even the guards who followed them were tired. Then Bronwyn had sat with Judith, eagerly talking and asking questions until after midnight.

Mary stretched and yawned, then smiled. No wonder Stephen wrote that he had to work hard to keep up with his wife. She suddenly wondered if Stephen ever told Bronwyn how much he admired her. Stephen's letters were full of praise for his new people and his new life, and especially his courageous wife.

Mary urged her horse forward to catch Bronwyn. Already the Scotswoman was stopping at a serf's hut.

It was late morning when they finally stopped on the side of a hill for a moment's rest. The men stretched out on the grass, breathing deeply, eating hungrily of bread, wine, and cheese.

Mary and Bronwyn sat on the crest of the hill at a place where Bronwyn could see across the countryside. It had taken all of Mary's strength to follow.

"What was that?" Bronwyn asked suddenly.

Mary listened for a moment, but all she heard was the soft sigh of the wind and the guards' voices.

"There it is again!" Bronwyn looked over her shoulder,

and Rab came to nudge her. "Yes, boy," she whispered. She stood quickly. "Someone's hurt," she said to Mary as she began to run to the top of the hill, Rab beside her.

The guards looked up, but they gave the women privacy, thinking a call of nature took them over the crest of the hill.

Mary strained her eyes but saw nothing. Below them lay a pond, the edges half frozen, great thin sheets of ice floating in the water.

Bronwyn strained her eyes until suddenly Rab gave a sharp bark. "There!" Bronwyn yelled as she began to run.

Mary didn't see a thing but lifted her heavy skirts and followed. It was only when she was halfway to the pond that she saw the child's head and shoulders. The child was trapped in the icy water.

Mary felt a shiver run along her spine, and she began to run faster and faster. She didn't notice when she passed Bronwyn. She ran straight into the water and grabbed the child.

The little boy looked up at her with great, blank eyes. Only minutes were left if they were to keep the child from freezing.

"He's stuck!" Mary called to Bronwyn. "His foot seems to be caught on something. Can you throw me your knife?"

Bronwyn's mind worked quickly. She knew the child could stand little more of the icy water so time was of the essence. If she tossed Mary the knife and Mary didn't catch it, they'd probably lose the child. There was only one way to make sure Mary got the knife.

"Rab!" Bronwyn said, and the dog recognized the sound of urgency in her voice. "Go to the men and get help. Bring someone here. We need help, Rab."

The dog shot away like an arrow from a bow. But he did not head toward the guards who waited just over the hill.

"Damn!" Bronwyn cursed, but it was already too late to call the dog back to her.

She took her knife from her side and plunged into the cold water. She moved as quickly as she could, hindered by the growth under the water. Mary was blue with cold, but she held on to the boy, whose face was turning gray.

Bronwyn knelt, the water smacking against her chest like a brick wall. She felt for the child's legs, felt the undergrowth that held him. Her teeth were beginning to chatter as she sawed away at the tough growth.

"He's free!" she whispered after a moment. She saw that Mary's face was beginning to lose its blueness, turning to the more dangerous gray. Bronwyn knelt and lifted the child. "Can you follow?" she called over her shoulder to Mary.

Mary didn't have the excess strength to reply. She concentrated all her energies on moving her legs and following Bronwyn's quickly moving form.

Bronwyn barely reached the edge of the pond before the child was taken from her arms. She looked into Raine's serious face.

"How . . . ?" Bronwyn began.

"Miles and I were riding to meet you when your dog came to us. Rab was bounding like a demon." As Raine spoke he was constantly moving. He put the child into one of his men's arms, then wrapped his cloak around Bronwyn's cold, wet shoulders.

"Mary?" Bronwyn asked as she began to shiver.

"Miles has her," Raine said as he tossed his sister-in-law into his saddle and mounted behind her.

They went quickly back to the Montgomery castle. Raine held his horse under control with one hand while his other hand rubbed Bronwyn's shoulders and arms. She realized she was freezing, and she tried to make herself into a ball and snuggle against Raine's solid warmth.

Once inside the gates Raine carried Bronwyn upstairs to her bedchamber. He stood her in the middle of the floor while he opened a chest and pulled a heavy robe of golden wool from it. "Here, put this on," he commanded as he turned his back on her and began to stoke the fire.

Bronwyn's fingers trembled as she tried to unfasten her shirt. The wet, clammy fabric clung to her. She peeled it away from her skin, then took the robe Raine had tossed on the bed beside her. The wool was heavy and thick, but she couldn't yet feel any of its warmth.

Raine turned back to her, took one look at her colorless face, and swept her into his arms. He sat down in a large chair before the fireplace with her in his lap. He tucked the big robe, one of Stephen's, around her, held her closely as she drew her legs in to her chest and tucked her head into Raine's broad chest.

It took several minutes before she was able to stop shivering. "Mary?" she whispered after a moment.

"Miles is taking care of her, and by now Judith has her in a hot tub of water."

"And the child?"

Raine looked down at her, his eyes turning dark blue. "Did you know it was only a serf's child?" he asked quietly.

She pulled away from him. "What does it matter? The child needed help."

Raine smiled at her and pulled her back to his chest. "I didn't think it would matter to you. I know it wouldn't to Mary. You'll have trouble with Gavin, though. He wouldn't risk a hair on one of his family's heads for all the serfs in the world."

"I've dealt with Stephen for months, so I guess I can deal with Gavin." She gave a great sigh of resignation.

Raine gave a laugh that started in his flat belly. She felt it before she heard it. "Well said! I see you understand my elder brothers."

She smiled against his chest. "Raine, why haven't you ever married?"

"The universal question from women," he chuckled. "Did you consider that no one would have me?"

The question was so absurd she didn't even reply.

"Actually I've turned down six women in eight months."

"Why?" she asked. "Were they too ugly, too thin, too fat? Or didn't you meet them?"

"I met them," he said quietly. "I'm not like my brothers, who are willing to meet their brides on their wedding days. The fathers made the offers, and I spent three days with each woman."

"Yet you turned them all down."

"Aye, that I did."

She sighed. "What do you expect of a woman? Surely one of them must have been pretty enough."

"Pretty!" Raine snorted. "Three of them were beautiful! But I want more than a pretty woman. I want a woman who has a thought in her head besides the latest embroidery pattern." His eyes twinkled merrily. "I want a woman who'll walk into an icy pond and risk her life to save a serf child."

"But surely, had any woman seen the child—"

Raine looked away from her to the fire. "You and Mary are special, as is Judith. Did you know Judith once led Gavin's men when Gavin was held captive by some madman? She risked her own life to save his." He smiled down at her. "I'm waiting until I get someone like you or Judith."

Bronwyn considered this for a moment. "No, I can't see that we're what you want. Gavin is attached to the land, and so is Judith. They fit together. And Scotland is for me. Stephen is free to live there with me. But you . . . I feel you never stay in one place too long. You need someone as free as you are, someone who isn't tied to a piece of stone and earth somewhere."

Raine looked at her with his mouth agape, then closed it and smiled. "I won't ask how you know all that. I'm sure the answer would be that you're a witch. Now, since you seem to know so much about me, I'd like to ask you some personal questions."

He paused and looked into her eyes. "What is wrong between you and Stephen?" he asked quietly. "Why are you angry at him all the time?"

Bronwyn was slow to speak. She knew of the closeness between the brothers, and she wasn't sure how Raine would take to any criticism of his elder brother. But how could she lie?

She took a deep breath and spoke the truth. "Stephen thinks I have no honor or pride. He believes anyone before he believes me. In Scotland he thought everything I did was wrong, and in truth some of it was, but he had no right to treat me as if everything I did was wrong."

Raine nodded in understanding. It had taken Gavin a while to realize Judith was more than just a pretty body.

But before he could say a word, the door burst open and a tired, dirty Stephen stormed into the room.

"Miles said Bronwyn jumped into an icy lake!" he thundered. "Where is she?" Even as he said the words, he saw her in Raine's lap. He took two long steps across the room and snatched her from him.

"Damn you!" he bellowed. "I can't leave you for more than an hour without your getting into trouble."

"Release me!" she said coldly. He'd been away for days, the first time they'd ever been separated, and now all he did was curse her.

Stephen must have felt some of her thoughts. He set her on the floor before him. "Bronwyn," he said quietly, touching her cheek.

She gathered the bottom of the wool robe off the floor and walked toward the door. She was one of the few women in the world who could manage to look dignified while barefoot and wearing a robe hanging several inches past her hands.

She put her hand on the door latch and, without turning, said, "Someday you'll learn that I am neither a child nor an idiot." She opened the door and left the room.

Stephen took a step toward the closed door, but Raine's voice stopped him.

"Sit down and let her alone," Raine said with resignation.

Stephen looked toward the door for a moment longer, then turned and took a chair across from Raine's. He ran his hand wearily through his dirty hair. "Is she unhurt? Will she be all right?"

"Of course," Raine answered confidently. "She's strong and healthy, and from what you say of the Scots she's lived out-of-doors most of her life."

Stephen stared at the fire. "I know," he said heavily.

"What's eating you?" Raine demanded. "You're not the Stephen I know."

"Bronwyn," he whispered. "She's going to be the death

of me. In Scotland one night she decided to lead her men on a raid against her clan's enemy. In order to assure herself that I'd be out of the way, she drugged me."

"She did what?" Raine exploded, realizing the full danger of Bronwyn's act.

Stephen grimaced. "One of her men found what she'd done and helped wake me. When I found her, she was down the side of a cliff, dangling by a rope about her waist."

"Good God!" Raine gasped.

"I didn't know whether to beat her or lock her away to protect her against herself."

"And which did you do?"

Stephen leaned back in the chair. His voice was full of disgust. "What I always end up doing: I made love to her."

Raine chuckled deeply. "It seems to me your problem would be if she were selfish and cared only about herself."

Stephen stood and walked to the fireplace. "She cares too little for herself. Sometimes she makes me ashamed of myself. When it comes to that clan of hers, she does whatever she thinks is best without regard to her own safety."

"And you worry about her?" Raine asked.

"Damned right! Why can't she stay at home and have babies and care for them—and me—as a wife should? Why does she have to lead cattle raids, carve her initials on a man's chest, roll in her plaid and sleep on the ground in perfect comfort? Why can't she be . . . be . . ."

"A simpering little mealy-mouthed wench who'd look at you with adoring eyes and embroider all your shirt collars?" Raine suggested.

Stephen sat down heavily. "I don't want that, but there has to be some compromise."

"Do you really want to change her?" Raine asked. "What is it about her that made you love her in the first place? And don't tell me it was her beauty. You've been to bed with several beautiful women, but you've not fallen in love with them."

"Is it so obvious?"

"To me and probably to Gavin and Miles, but I don't

think it is to Bronwyn. She doesn't believe you care for her at all."

Stephen sighed. "I've never met anyone like her, male or female. She's so strong, so noble, almost like a man. You should see the way her clan treats her. The Scots aren't like us. The serf children run to her and hug her, and she kisses all the babies. She knows the name of every person on her land, and they all call her by her first name. She goes without food and clothes so her clan can have more. One night, about a month after we were married, I noticed her wrapping bread and cheese in her plaid. She ignored me but kept looking toward Tam. He's a man who often acts as her father. I realized she was doing something she didn't want Tam to see, so after supper I followed her off the peninsula. She was taking the food to one of her crofter's children, a sulking little boy who'd run away from home."

"And what did you say to her?" Raine asked.

Stephen shook his head in memory. "Me, the great wise one, I told her she had to send the boy back to his parents instead of encouraging him to run away from home."

"And what did Brownyn say?"

"She said the boy was as important to her as the parents, and she had no right to betray him just because he was a boy. She said he'd go home in a few days and accept his punishment as he should."

Raine gave a low whistle of admiration. "Sounds like you could learn something from her."

"You think I haven't? She's changed my whole life. When I went to Scotland, I was an Englishman, and now look at me. I can't abide these English clothes. I feel like Samson with my hair cut short. I find myself looking at the English countryside and thinking it's dry and hot compared to home. Home! I swear I'm homesick for a place that I never saw before a few months ago."

"Tell me," Raine said, "have you told Bronwyn how you feel? Have you told her you love her and are only concerned with her safety?"

"I've tried to. Once I tried to tell her that I loved her, and she said it didn't matter, that honor and respect were more important to her."

"But from what you say, you do have those feelings for her."

Stephen started to grin. "It's not easy telling Bronwyn anything. We had . . . I guess you could call it an argument before we arrived here." He told Raine briefly about the trick of Hugh Lasco's.

"Hugh!" Raine snorted. "I never much liked the man with his slow ways."

"Bronwyn didn't seem to mind them," Stephen said in disgust.

Raine laughed. "Don't tell me you are touched by Gavin's jealousy!"

Stephen whirled on his brother. "Just wait until you are obsessed by some woman! I'll wager you aren't so cool-headed then."

Raine put up his hand. "I hope I look on love as a joy and not as the disease you seem to be eaten with."

Stephen turned away and stared into the fire. Sometimes his love for Bronwyn did seem like a disease. He felt she'd taken his soul along with his heart.

When Bronwyn left her own bedchamber, she went to Mary's. Mary was in bed, Judith hovering over her, placing hot bricks throughout the bed.

"Judith," Mary said quietly. "I am not about to die of a little cold water." She looked across the room and smiled at Bronwyn. "Come and help me persuade Judith that our escapade was not of the killing sort."

Bronwyn smiled at the women and studied Mary. Her pale skin was even paler, and there were bright pink patches on her cheeks. "It was nothing," Bronwyn said. "But I envy you with the control of spirit so you can rest." Her eyes twinkled. "I'm so excited about the new dress Judith promised me that I cannot rest. Perhaps we could see it now," she said suggestively to Judith.

Judith understood immediately, and the two women quietly left the room. "Do you think she will be all right?" Judith asked as soon as they were in the hall.

"Yes, she needs rest, I can tell. I don't believe our Mary is completely in this world. I think Heaven owns part of her. Perhaps that's why she's so weak."

"Yes," Judith agreed. "Now, about that gown—"

Bronwyn waved her hand. "It was only an excuse to give Mary a chance to rest."

Judith laughed. "As becoming as Stephen's robe is, it doesn't substitute for the gown you need. Now come with me, and I want no excuses."

An hour later Bronwyn stood arrayed in a gown of lush, deep green velvet. The color was of a forest just at sunset. The undersleeves were of brilliant green silk, and the loose, hanging oversleeves were banded with a wide border of red fox. Heavy gold cords were attached to the shoulders and hung below the deep, square neckline.

"It's beautiful, Judith," Bronwyn whispered. "I don't know how to thank you. All of you have been so generous."

Judith kissed her friend's cheek. "I must go now and do the day's work. Perhaps Stephen would like to see the new gown," she suggested.

Bronwyn turned away. Stephen would only complain that the neck was too low or some other such accusation.

After Judith was gone, Bronwyn went to the cold courtyard below. She threw a fox-lined mantle about her shoulders and walked toward the stables.

"Bronwyn," an unfamiliar voice said once she was inside the dark place.

She looked into the shadows and saw the man who'd fought Stephen's George that morning. "Yes," she said curtly. "What is it?"

The man's eyes sparkled even in the dimness. "The English gown becomes you." Before she could speak, his manner changed to a more formal one. "I've heard your Scotsmen are quite good with a bow. Perhaps you"—this seemed to amuse him—"could teach me a better way to handle a bow."

She ignored the undercurrent of laughter in the man's

voice. Perhaps his laughter was meant as a defense in case she refused his request. But Bronwyn had spent many hours learning how to handle a bow, and she was used to training men. It was good that this Englishman wanted to learn the Scots' ways. "I would be happy to give you instruction," she said, then walked past the man—and straight into Stephen's hard chest. The man quickly left the stables.

"What were you saying to the man?" Stephen asked flatly.

She twisted out of his grip. "Do you never say anything to me except in anger? Why can't you be like other husbands and greet your wife in a friendly manner? I have not seen you in days, and all you have done is curse me."

He grabbed her into his arms. "Bronwyn," he whispered. "You will be the death of me. Why did you have to jump into an icy pond in the dead of winter?"

She pushed away from him. "I refuse to answer such questions."

He grabbed her again, pulled her mouth to his, bruising her, his teeth hard against her lips. He seemed as if he wanted more than just a kiss from her. "I missed you," he whispered. "Every minute I thought of you."

Her heart was pounding in her breast. She felt like she could melt against him. But his next words broke the spell.

"Was that one of Miles's men you were talking to when I entered?"

She tried to pull away from him. "Is this your jealousy again? I can hear it in your voice."

"Bronwyn, no. Listen to me. I only want to warn you. The Englishmen are not like your Highlanders. You can't talk to them as if they were your brothers as you do your own men. In England too often the ladies sleep with their husbands' men-at-arms."

Bronwyn's eyes widened. "Are you accusing me of sleeping with your men?" she gasped.

"No, of course not, but—"

"But you accused me of doing just that with Hugh Lasco."

"Hugh Lasco is a gentleman!" Stephen snapped.

Bronwyn nearly jumped away from him. "So!" she blazed.

"At least you think I am a discriminating whore!" She whirled about and started toward the door.

Stephen grabbed her arm. "I am not accusing you of anything. I am trying to explain that things are different in England than in Scotland."

"Oh! So now I'm too stupid to be able to learn the difference between one country and another. You can adjust but I can't!"

He stared at her. "What's wrong with you? You aren't acting like yourself at all."

She turned away from him. "And what would you know of me? You've never done anything but curse at me since I met you. Nothing I do outside the bedroom pleases you. If I lead my men, that makes you angry. If I try to save one of your brother's serfs, that angers you. If I'm kind to your men, you accuse me of sleeping with them. Tell me, what can I do to please you?"

Stephen glared at her with cold eyes. "I had no idea you found me so unpleasant. I will leave you to your own company." He turned away stiffly and left her.

Bronwyn stared after him, tears beginning to form in her eyes. What *was* wrong with her? Stephen hadn't really accused her of sleeping with the man, and he had every right to warn her about what his men would think. Why couldn't she welcome him home like she wanted to? All she wanted was to be held by him, loved by him. Yet for some reason she started a quarrel every time he approached her.

Suddenly she felt as if her whole body ached. She put her hand to her forehead. She wasn't used to not feeling well, and now she realized she'd been ignoring the feeling for days. Of course, her late nights with Judith and this morning spent in a half-frozen pond hadn't helped her any. She cursed the disease-ridden English countryside and left the stables.

"Bronwyn," Judith called. "Would you like some fresh bread?"

Bronwyn leaned back against the stone wall of the stables. The quarrel was upsetting her stomach. The thought of food nauseated her. "No," she whispered, her hand to her stomach.

"Bronwyn, what is it?" Judith asked, setting the basket down. "Aren't you feeling well?" She put her hand on her sister-in-law's forehead. "Here, sit down." She urged her to a barrel set by the wall. "Breathe deeply and it will pass."

"What will?" Bronwyn asked sharply.

"The nausea."

"The what?" Bronwyn gasped. "What are you talking about?"

Judith paused. "Unless I miss my guess, you're going to have a baby." She smiled broadly at Bronwyn's look. "It is rather startling when you first realize it." She caressed her own stomach. "We'll deliver close together," she said proudly.

"You! You're going to have a baby too?"

Judith had a faraway smile on her face. "Yes. I . . . lost my first one, a miscarriage, so for this one I'm being so careful I'm not even telling anyone. Except Gavin, of course."

"Of course," Bronwyn said and looked away, then back again. "When is your baby due?"

"In seven months." She chuckled.

"What are you laughing at?" Bronwyn asked. "I need some humor right now."

"I was just thinking that my mother will be able to come to my lying-in." She paused, then began to explain. "I thought she would not be able to come, as she was to deliver at the same time."

"Your mother! How fortunate you are to have your parents alive."

"No," Judith smiled. "My father died several months ago."

"And the child is not his?" Bronwyn asked quietly.

"Oh, no, and I am pleased by that. My father often beat my mother. She was held captive by a young man, and her guard was Gavin's best man, John Bassett. I'm afraid my mother and he found an extraordinary means of entertainment."

Bronwyn laughed.

"Yes," Judith continued. "When Gavin found out there was to be a child, he allowed John and my mother to marry."

"And she's had her own babe now?"

"It's due in a couple of months, so she should be well enough to travel to me when I am due. I must get back to work now. Why don't you just sit there and rest?"

"Judith, you said your mother was being held captive. How did she escape?"

Judith's golden eyes darkened with memory. "I killed her captor, and Stephen's men brought down the wall of the old keep."

Bronwyn could see the pain in Judith's eyes. She asked no more questions before Judith turned away toward the gate that separated the two parts of the castle complex.

Bronwyn sat still for quite some time. A baby! she thought. A soft, sweet thing like Kirsty's baby. Her mind seemed to leave her, and she hardly noticed when she stood and began to walk. She thought of Tam and how proud he'd be of her. She smiled dreamily when she thought of Stephen's reaction to the news. He'd be so happy! He'd grab her and toss her above his head and laugh with pleasure. Then they'd argue over whether the child would be named MacArran or Montgomery. There was no doubt, of course, that he'd be a MacArran.

She kept walking in a dreamlike trance, never noticing when she reached the open gate. The men on the wall guarding the entrance didn't challenge her or hinder her movements in any way.

What would she name her child? she thought. James for her father, and perhaps another name for Stephen's family. What if the babe was a girl? she thought and smiled warmly. Clan MacArran would have two female lairds in a row. She must teach her daughter all the things she'd need to know to be laird.

"My lady," someone said.

Bronwyn hardly heard the voice. She was in a trance, and very little penetrated it. In fact, she was hardly aware that she'd walked for quite some time and was now out of sight of the castle guards.

"My lady," the voice repeated. "Are you well?"

Bronwyn looked up at the man with an angelic smile of great warmth. "I am well," she said in a vague manner. "I am more than well."

The man dismounted and went to her side. "I can see that," he said in a low voice, his lips close to her ear.

Bronwyn still paid little attention to the man. All she could think of was her child. Morag would love another baby to care for, she was thinking as the man's lips touched her ear. The touch brought her out of her reverie.

She jumped away from him. "How dare you," she gasped. No man except Stephen had ever touched her unless she allowed him. She gave a quick look about her and realized how far she was from the castle.

Richard misinterpreted her look. "There's no need to worry. We're quite alone, and Lord Gavin has just returned from Scotland, so everyone is busy at the moment. We have time."

She backed away from him. A thousand thoughts flew through her mind. Stephen's warnings screamed at her. And worry for her baby occupied most of her mind. Please don't let my child be hurt!

"There's no reason to fear me," Richard said in a honey-coated voice. "We could have fun, you and I."

Bronwyn straightened her shoulders. "I am Bronwyn MacArran, and you will return to the castle."

"MacArran!" he laughed. "The men said you were an independent woman, but they didn't say you'd go so far as to disown your husband."

"You are insulting. Now go and leave me alone."

Richard's smile left his face. "You think I'm going to leave you after the way you've been teasing me? You chose me to accompany you this morning. I'll wager you were sorry when we had no time to be alone."

She was aghast. "Is that what you thought? That I wanted to be alone with you?"

He touched her hair, his little finger grazing her breast.

Her eyes opened wide, then she looked for Rab. The dog was always with her.

"I took the precaution of locking your dog in a granary," Richard smiled. "Now, come and stop playing these games. You know you want me as much as I want you." He grabbed Bronwyn, his hand twisting in her hair. He ground his lips against hers.

Bronwyn felt waves of anger shoot through her. She relaxed in his arms, leaned backward, and as he bent forward to press against her, she brought her knee up.

Richard groaned and released her abruptly.

Bronwyn struggled to keep from falling, then tripped on the heavy velvet skirt. She cursed as she gathered handfuls of the fabric and began to run. But no matter how much she held, more fabric swirled about her legs and hindered her. She tripped once again, then slung the velvet over her arm. The third time she tripped, Richard was upon her. He grabbed her ankle, and she fell forward, face down into the cold, hard earth. She gasped for air.

Richard ran his hand up her legs. "Now, my fiery Scotswoman, we'll see if that fire can be put to use."

Bronwyn tried to kick out at him, but he held her to the ground. He grabbed her dress and tore it, exposing the skin of her back to the cold winter air.

"Now," he said as he placed his lips to the nape of her neck.

The next moment Richard screamed as a mass of gray fur and sharp teeth attacked him. Bronwyn rolled away as Richard tried to stand and fight Rab.

An arm pulled her up. Miles drew her to him, held her with one arm, his drawn sword in the other. "Call your dog off him," Miles said quietly.

Bronwyn's voice was shaking. "Rab!" she commanded.

The dog reluctantly left off his attack and went to her side.

Richard tried to stand. There was blood on his arm and his thigh. His clothes were torn in several places. "The damned dog attacked me for no reason!" he began. "Lady Bronwyn fell, and I stopped to help her."

Miles stepped away from his sister-in-law. His eyes were

as hard as steel. "You do not touch the Montgomery women," he said in a deadly voice.

"She came at me!" the man said. "She asked—"

They were the last words he ever spoke. Miles's sword went straight through Richard's heart. Miles barely glanced at the dead man, one of his own men. He turned to Bronwyn and seemed to sense what she felt—helpless and violated.

He put his arms around her gently and drew her to him. "You're safe now," he said quietly. "No one else will try to harm you."

Suddenly her body began to tremble, and Miles drew her closer. "He said I had encouraged him," she whispered.

"Hush," Miles said. "I've been watching him. He didn't understand your Scots ways."

Bronwyn pulled away to look at him. "That's what Stephen said. He warned me of talking to the men. He said the Englishmen didn't understand when I talked to them."

Miles smoothed the hair from her forehead. "There's a formality between an English lady and her husband's men that is not in your culture. Now let's return. I'm sure someone will have seen me leave following your dog."

She glanced at the dead man beside them. "He locked Rab away and I didn't even notice. I was—" She couldn't tell anyone about the baby before she told Stephen.

"I heard the dog yelping, and when I released him, he went crazy, barking at me, sniffing the earth." He looked with admiration at the big dog. "He knew you were in trouble."

She knelt and rubbed her face in Rab's rough coat.

They both turned at the sound of horses. Gavin and Stephen rode toward them quickly. Stephen slid from the saddle before the horse came to a full stop. "What happened here?" he demanded.

"The man tried to attack Bronwyn," Miles said.

Stephen glared at his wife, his eyes taking in the scraped place on her cheek, her torn gown. "I told you," he said through clenched teeth. "You wouldn't listen to me."

"Stephen," Gavin said, his hand on his brother's arm. "Now's not the time."

"Not the time!" Stephen exploded at his wife. "Not an hour ago you listed all my faults. Did you find someone else with fewer faults? Did you encourage him on purpose?"

Before anyone else could speak, Stephen turned away and mounted his horse. Bronwyn, Miles, and Gavin watched helplessly.

"He should be whipped for that!" Miles sneered.

"Quiet!" Gavin commanded. He turned to Bronwyn. "He's upset and confused. You have to forgive him."

"He's jealous!" Bronwyn whispered fiercely. "That empty jealousy of his changes him into a madman." She felt weak and defeated. He cared nothing for her but only for his own jealousy.

Gavin put his arm around her protectively. "Come home and let Judith get you something to drink. She makes a delicious apple drink."

Bronwyn nodded numbly and allowed herself to be put onto Miles's horse.

Chapter 16

THE DRINK Judith gave Bronwyn put her to sleep almost instantly. She'd had too much in one day—the rescue of the child and the near rape. She dreamed of being lost and of searching for Stephen, but he wasn't there.

She woke suddenly, her body coated in sweat, and reached for him. The bed was empty. She sat up and looked about the dimly lit room, searching for him.

She felt unbearably lonely. Why did she quarrel with Stephen all the time? When Miles had told her the Scots' ways were different, she didn't get angry. It was only when Stephen said the same thing that she flew into a rage.

She threw the covers back and grabbed a robe Judith had lent her. She must find Stephen and tell him that she'd been wrong. She must tell him about the child and ask that he forgive her for her foul mood.

Rab followed her as she went to a chest and withdrew her plaid. The dog was afraid to let her out of his sight.

She dressed quickly and left her room. The house was silent and dark as she made her way downstairs. A single fat candle shown from the half-open winter parlor door. The fire was nearly dead.

She pushed the door open as she heard a woman giggle. Bronwyn halted as she realized she'd probably interrupted Raine or Miles with one of the housemaids. She turned to go as the woman's words stopped her.

"Oh, Stephen," the woman giggled. "I've missed you so much. No man has hands like yours."

Bronwyn heard the deep rumble of a familiar laugh.

She was not a timid woman to run crying from the room. She'd had one insult too many for the day. She pushed the heavy door open with a vicious shove and marched to the fireplace.

Stephen sat in a large chair, fully clothed, a plump young girl, bared from the waist up, sprawled across his lap. He disinterestedly had one hand on her breast; the other held a flagon of wine.

Rab bared his teeth at the girl, and she gave one look from Bronwyn to the dog, screamed, then fled the room.

Stephen only glanced at his wife. "Welcome," he slurred and held up his cup to her.

Bronwyn felt her heart pounding. To see Stephen touching another woman! Her skin felt as if it were on fire and her head throbbed.

Stephen looked up at her. "How does it feel, my dear wife?" His eyes were red, his movements slow. He was obviously drunk. "I've had to stand aside and watch you play with man after man. Do you know how I felt when you let Hugh touch you?"

"You did this on purpose," she whispered. "You did this to punish me." She held her shoulders back. She wanted to hurt him, to make him ache as she did. "I was right when I told Sir Thomas Crichton I couldn't marry you. You aren't fit to be married to a Scotswoman. I've stood by for months and watched you ape our ways. And I've seen you fail at everything."

In spite of his drunkenness he reacted swiftly. He threw his flagon to the floor, sprang to his feet, and grabbed her by the neckline of her dress. "And what have you given me?" he rasped. "I have made every effort to learn from you, but when have you listened to me? You've fought me at every moment. You've laughed at me before your men, even scorned my advice in front of my own brothers. Yet I've taken everything because I am fool enough to believe I loved you. How can anyone love someone as selfish as you? When are you going to grow up and stop hiding behind your clan? You aren't concerned with your clan; your only concern is what you want and what you need."

He pushed her away as if he were suddenly very tired of her. "I'm tired of trying to please some cold woman. I'm going to find one who can give me what I need."

He turned away and drunkenly left the room.

Bronwyn stood where she was for a long time. She had no idea he despised her so much. How many times had he been close to saying he loved her yet she'd ignored him? Oh, but she'd been fiery and proud when she told him that of course they cared for each other but that what she wanted was more important than love.

What meant more to her than Stephen's love? She could see now that there was nothing nearly as important. She'd had that love in the palm of her hand, and she'd thrown it right back in his face. In Scotland he'd worked hard to be fair and to learn how to live in her country. Yet what had she done to conform to his way of life? Her biggest concession was to dress in the luscious English fashions, and she'd even complained about that.

She clenched her hand. Stephen was right! She was selfish. She demanded he become a Scot, change every fiber of his being, yet she'd never done a thing for him. From the moment they'd met, she'd made him pay for the privilege of marrying her.

"Privilege!" she gasped aloud. She'd made him fight for her on their wedding day. She'd taken a knife to him on their wedding night. What was it Stephen had said? "Someday you'll know that one drop of my blood is more precious than any angry feelings you carry."

How could she have hurt that beautiful body she knew so well? How could she have drawn blood from him?

Tears began to run down her face. He loved her no longer. He'd said that. She'd had his love and discarded it like so much rubbish.

She blinked at the tears and looked around her. Stephen

Bronwyn backed away from her. "I'd rather not," she said flatly.

The old woman shrugged and invited them to spend the night with her.

In the morning she grabbed Bronwyn's palm and her face clouded. "Beware of a blond-haired man," she warned.

Bronwyn snatched her hand away. "I'm afraid your warnings are too late," she said, thinking of Stephen's sun-kissed hair, and left the little house.

They rode all day and stopped that evening in the roofless shelter of a destroyed castle.

Miles was the one who realized it was Christmas Eve. They made a celebration of sorts, but Miles recognized Bronwyn's sadness and left her to her own thoughts. It occurred to Bronwyn that part of Miles's fascination lay in the way he seemed to understand what a woman was feeling. He didn't demand anything of her as Stephen did or try to talk to her as Raine did. Miles quietly understood and left her alone. She had no doubt that if she wished to speak, Miles would make an excellent listener.

She smiled at him and took the oatcake he offered. "I'm afraid I've caused you to miss Christmas with your family."

"You're my family," he said pointedly. He looked at the black sky over the ruined walls around them. "I just hope that for once it doesn't rain."

Bronwyn laughed. "You're too used to your dry country." She smiled in memory. "Stephen never seemed to mind the rain. He—" She broke off and looked away.

"I think Stephen would live underwater to be with you."

She looked up, startled, and remembered the kitchen maid sprawled across her husband's lap. She blinked several times to clear her vision. "I think I'll go to sleep."

Miles watched in amazement as she curled up in her thin plaid and immediately relaxed. He sighed and wrapped his fur-lined mantle closer about his body. He didn't think he'd make a good Scot.

It was still morning when they reached the hill overlooking Larenston. Miles sat still in astonishment as he gaped at the fortress on the peninsula. Bronwyn spurred her horse forward, then leaped into a big man's arms.

"Tam!" she cried, burying her face in the familiar neck.

Tam held her away. "Ye put new gray hair on my head," he whispered. "How can someone so little get into so much trouble?" he asked, ignoring the fact that she was a bit taller than he. Indeed, she was small next to his great mass.

"Did ye know the MacGregor has asked to meet with ye? He sent a message about some drink and a saucy wench who'd laughed at him. Bronwyn, what have ye done?"

Bronwyn stared at him in astonishment for a moment. The MacGregor asked to meet with her! Perhaps now there would be a way to prove to Stephen she wasn't so selfish.

She hugged Tam again. "There's time to tell you all of it. I want to go home now. I'm afraid this trip has made me tired."

"Tired?" Tam asked, alarmed. He'd never heard her use the word before.

"Don't look at me like I was daft," she smiled. "It's not easy carrying another person all the time."

Tam understood instantly, and his face nearly split with his grin. "I knew that Englishman could do something right without any training. Where is he, anyway? And who is he?"

Bronwyn answered questions all the way across the narrow strip of land and up the trail to Larenston. Her men joined her and fired hundreds of questions at her. Miles stood back, staring in awe at the sight. Bronwyn's servants and retainers acted more like an enormous family than the classes of society that they were. The men greeted Miles affectionately, talking constantly of Stephen this and Stephen that.

Bronwyn left the men and went upstairs to her room. Morag greeted her.

"Did ye trade one brother for another?" she accused.

"No greeting?" Bronwyn said tiredly as she headed for the bed. "I bring you a new child and you can give me no fond greeting?"

Morag's wrinkled face grinned. "That's my sweet Stephen. I knew he was a man."

Bronwyn lay down on the bed and didn't bother to argue with Morag. "Go and meet the other Englishman I brought you. You'll like him." She pulled a quilt over her. All she wanted to do was sleep.

The weeks came and went and all Bronwyn did was sleep. Her body was exhausted from the turmoil and the changes that the baby was making. Miles came one morning to tell her he was returning to England. He thanked her for her hospitality and promised to make her apologies to Judith and Gavin. Neither mentioned Stephen.

Bronwyn tried not to think of her husband, but it wasn't easy. Everyone asked questions about him. Tam demanded to know why the hell she left England so suddenly. Why didn't she stay and fight for him? His mouth dropped open when Bronwyn suddenly burst into tears and ran from the room. After that fewer people asked questions that she couldn't answer.

Three weeks after she returned home, one of her men told her a guard of Englishmen was approaching Larenston.

"Gavin!" she cried and ran upstairs to change her clothes. She donned the cloth-of-silver dress Stephen had given her and stood ready to greet her brother-in-law. She was sure it was Gavin approaching. He'd been to Scotland before, and he would be the one to give her news of Stephen. Perhaps Stephen had forgiven her and was coming to her. No, it was too much to ask.

Her smile faded when Roger Chatworth walked into the Great Hall. She was appalled at what she'd done. She'd ordered the visitor to be allowed entrance to Larenston without actually knowing who he was. And her men had obeyed her with no questions. She looked at the faces of her men and saw their concern for her. They would do anything to make her return to herself again.

She tried to cover her disappointment and held out her hand. "Lord Roger, how nice to see you again."

Roger dropped to one knee and took her hand, held it to his lips. His blond hair was darker than she remembered, the scar by his eye even more prominent. He brought back memories of the time at Sir Thomas Crichton's house. She'd been so lonely then, and Roger had been so kind, so understanding. He'd even been willing to risk his life to do what she wanted.

"You are more beautiful than I remembered," he said quietly.

"Come now, Lord Roger, I don't remember you as a flatterer."

He stood, his eyes on hers. "And what do you remember about me?"

"Only that you were willing to help me at a time when I needed help. Douglas," she called, "make Lord Roger and his men welcome."

Roger watched as the man obeyed her instantly. He looked around at the bare, unadorned walls of Larenston. The road into the peninsula had been lined with very poor little houses. Was this all the wealth there was to the MacArrans?

"Lord Roger, come to my solar and talk with me. What brings you to Scotland? Oh, but I forgot that you have relatives here, don't you?"

Roger lifted one eyebrow. "Yes, I do." He followed her upstairs to another bare room, where a small fire blazed cheerfully in the fireplace.

"Won't you sit down?" Bronwyn gave a curt look at Morag, then asked the disapproving little woman to bring them wine and refreshments.

When they were seated and alone, Roger leaned toward her. "I will be honest with you. I came to see if you needed any assistance. When I saw Stephen at King Henry's court and—"

"You saw Stephen at court!" she gasped.

He watched her face. "I thought perhaps you didn't know. There were too many women near him and—"

Bronwyn rose and went toward the fire. "I'd prefer not to hear the rest of what you have to say," she said coldly. She was beginning to remember all about Roger Chatworth. He'd stabbed at Stephen's back once before.

"Lady Bronwyn," he said desperately. "I meant no harm. I thought you knew."

She whirled on him. "I've matured a great deal since I last saw you. Once I was easy prey for your handsome ways, and I was childishly angry because my husband was late for our wedding. But now I am older and much, much wiser. As you have guessed, I'm sure, my husband and I have quarreled. Whether we will settle our differences or not I don't know, but the quarrel will remain between us."

Roger's dark eyes narrowed. He had a way of tilting his head back so he seemed to be looking down his narrow, aquiline nose. "Do you think I've come here to carry gossip like some fisherman's wife?"

"It would sound so. You've already mentioned the women around Stephen."

Roger began to smile slowly. "Perhaps I did. Forgive me. I was only surprised to see him away from your side."

"So you hurried to tell me of his . . . escapades?"

He stared at her, his handsome face warm and alive. "Come and sit down, please. You weren't always so hostile to me. Once you even asked that we be married."

She took the chair beside him. "That was a long time ago. At least it was long enough for lives and feelings to change drastically." She watched the fire and was silent.

"Aren't you curious as to the real purpose of my journey here?" When she didn't answer, he continued. "I have a message from a woman named Kirsty."

Bronwyn's head shot up sharply, but before she could speak, Morag came in with a tray of food. It seemed hours before she left. The old woman insisted on adding wood to the fire and asking Roger questions.

Bronwyn wanted to ask questions too. How did he know Kirsty? What message could he have? Did it have something to do with the message the MacGregor had sent Tam saying he wanted to meet Bronwyn?

"If that's all, Morag!" Bronwyn said impatiently, then ignored the old woman's look as she left the room. "Now! What have you heard from Kirsty?"

Roger leaned back in his chair. This Bronwyn wasn't what he'd expected. Perhaps it was being in her own country or maybe it was Montgomery's influence, but she wasn't the easily manipulated young woman he'd first met. He'd heard part of the story of Bronwyn and Stephen in the MacGregor's land by chance. A man, poor and hungry, had asked to join his garrison. One night Roger'd overheard the man telling of his adventures in Scotland with the ravishing MacArran laird. Roger'd taken the man upstairs with him and gotten the whole story. Of course, it was only a part of the story, and Roger had spent considerable money finding out the rest of it.

When all the pieces were together, he knew he could somehow use it. He laughed at Stephen for foolishly parading himself before these crude Scots in a manner and dress as crude as their own. He sipped his wine and thought again with hatred of the time Stephen had dishonored him on a battlefield. Too many people had heard of that fight, and often he heard whispers of "the back attacker." He'd repay Stephen for that new nickname he now had.

His plan had been to seduce Stephen's wife, take what he'd fought for. But Bronwyn had fouled his plans. She was obviously not a woman who followed a man easily. Perhaps if he had time. . . . But no, he had no idea how long Stephen would be away.

Then a new plan began to come to him. Oh, yes, he thought, he'd repay Montgomery in full.

"Well!" Bronwyn said. "What was the message? Does she need me?"

"Yes, she does," Roger smiled. And I need you even more, he thought.

Chapter 17

BRONWYN LAY in bed, staring at the underside of the canopy. Her entire body was tense with excitement. For the first time in weeks she felt like she was alive. Her sleepiness was gone, her nausea had passed, and now she was pleased that something was about to happen.

When she'd come home and Tam had told her of the MacGregor's message, she'd ignored it. She'd been too wrapped up in her own problems, her own misery, to even consider anyone but herself. Stephen said she was selfish, that she never listened to him or learned from him. Now she had a chance to do something that would please him. He'd always wanted her to settle her differences with the MacGregor, and now Kirsty had opened the way.

When Tam had first told her of the MacGregor's message, she'd half-heartedly talked of meeting him. The protest from her men shook the walls. Bronwyn had easily dismissed the matter and settled back into her mood of feeling sorry for herself.

Now that was all over. She saw a way to win Stephen back. She must prove to him that she had learned something from him, that she wasn't a selfish person.

Roger Chatworth had told her an incredible story about meeting Kirsty and Kirsty asking him to tell Bronwyn that a meeting had been arranged. The MacGregor and the Mac-Arran were to meet alone, just the two of them, tomorrow night. Kirsty said the MacGregors were very much against the meeting, just as she was sure the MacArrans were. Therefore she'd made every effort to arrange a private meeting. She sent Bronwyn and Stephen her love and begged her to do this for the sake of peace for them all.

Bronwyn threw back the covers and went to the window. The moon hadn't set yet so there was still plenty of time. She was to meet Roger Chatworth outside Larenston Hall, by the mews, and she would lead him off the peninsula. There were horses waiting for them, and together they'd ride to meet Kirsty and Donald.

It wasn't easy to wait. She was dressed long before it was time. For a moment she stood over the bed, caressed the pillow where Stephen usually slept. "Soon, my love, soon," she whispered. Once there was peace between the clans, she could hold her head up before Stephen again. Maybe then he'd think her love was worthy of having.

It was easy to slip out of her room. She and David had often, as children, sneaked out to the stables, sometimes to meet Tam or one of Tam's sons. Rab followed her down the worn stone steps, sensing from his mistress the need for quiet.

Roger Chatworth stepped from the shadows as quietly as a Scotsman.

Bronwyn nodded to him curtly, then gestured Rab to be quiet. The dog had never liked Roger and made no secret of it. Roger followed her along the steep, dark path. She could feel the tension in his body, and more than once he grabbed her hand to steady himself. He clung to her and stood still until he got his breath.

Bronwyn tried to conceal her disgust. She was glad she now knew that not all Englishmen were like this one. Now she knew there were brave, courageous men like her husband and his brothers. They were men a woman could cling to and not the other way around.

Roger began to breathe easily once they reached the mainland and the horses. But they couldn't speak until they were out of the valley of MacArrans. Bronwyn led them around the valley by the sea wall. She went slowly so Roger could steady his horse. The night was black, and she led by instinct and memory rather than sight.

It was close to morning when they halted on the ridge that overlooked her land. She stopped in order to allow Roger to rest a moment.

"Are you tired, Lady Bronwyn?" he asked, his voice shaky. He had just been through what, to him, was obviously an ordeal. He dismounted his horse.

"Shouldn't we go on?" she urged. "We aren't very far from Larenston. When my men—"

She stopped because she didn't believe what she saw. Roger Chatworth, in one swift, fluid motion, took a heavy war axe from his saddle and struck Rab with it. The dog was looking at its mistress, concerned more with her than Roger, and so reacted too slowly to miss the lethal blow.

Instantly Bronwyn was out of her saddle. She fell to her knees at Rab's side. Even in the dark she could see a great gaping hole open in Rab's side. "Rab?" she managed to gasp through a thickened throat. The dog moved its head only slightly.

"It's dead," Roger said flatly. "Now get up!"

Bronwyn turned on him. "You!" She wasted no more energy on words. One instant she was on the ground, and the next she was flying through the air, her knife drawn and aimed for Roger's throat.

He was unprepared for her action and staggered backward under the weight of her. Her knife blade cut into his shoulder, barely missing his neck. He grabbed her hair and pulled her head backward just as she brought her knee up between his legs. Roger staggered again, but he held on to her, and when he fell to the ground, he took her with him. She jerked her head to one side and bit him until he released her hair. When she was free, she charged him again with her knife.

But the knife never made contact because four pairs of hands grabbed her and pulled her away.

"You took long enough!" Roger snapped at the men holding Bronwyn. "Another minute and it might have been too late."

Bronwyn looked at Rab, silent on the ground, then back at Roger. "There was no message from Kirsty, was there?"

Roger ran his hand across the cut she'd made in his shoulder. "What do I care about some damned Scot? Do you think I'd deliver messages like some serf? Have you forgotten that I am an earl?"

"I had forgotten," Bronwyn said slowly, "what you are. I had forgotten the way you attack a person from behind."

They were the last words she spoke for quite some time, for Roger's fist came flying toward her jaw. She was able to move to one side quickly enough that he clipped her cheek instead of smashing her nose as was his aim. She crumpled forward in an unconscious heap.

When Bronwyn woke, she had trouble knowing where she was. Her head pounded with a black fury that she'd never experienced before, and her thoughts were disorganized. Her body ached and her mouth was immobile. She gave no more than a few attempts at thought and went back to sleep.

When she woke again, she felt better. She lay still and realized that half of her pain came from a gag around her mouth. Her hands and feet were also tightly tied. She listened and felt and knew she was in a wagon thrown onto a heap of straw. It was night, and she knew she must have slept through the day.

There were times when she wanted to cry from the pain of not moving. The ropes cut into her, and her mouth was dry and swollen from the gag.

"She's awake," she heard a man say.

The wagon stopped, and Roger Chatworth bent over her. "I'll give you some water if you swear you won't scream. We're in a forest and no one could hear you anyway, but I want your word."

Her neck was so stiff she could barely move it. She gave him her word.

He lifted her and untied the gag.

Bronwyn knew she'd never felt anything so heavenly in

her life. She massaged her jaws, wincing at the bruised place Roger's fist had made.

"Here," he said impatiently, thrusting a cup of water at her. "We don't have all night."

She drank deeply of the water. "Where are you taking me?" she gasped.

Roger snatched the cup from her. "Montgomery may tolerate your insolence, but I won't. If I wanted you to know anything, I'd tell you." Before she could stop looking with longing at the cup he'd taken, he grabbed her hair, tossed the half-full cup aside, and replaced the gag. He shoved her back into the straw.

Through the next day Bronwyn dozed. Roger threw burlap bags over her to hide her. The lack of air and movement made her lightheaded. Her senses drifted about, and she was in a state of half awareness, half sleep.

Twice she was taken from the wagon, given food and water, and allowed some privacy.

On the third night the wagon stopped. The bags were taken off her, and she was roughly lifted from the wagon bed. The cold night air hit her as if she'd been thrown into icy water.

"Take her upstairs," Roger commanded. "Lock her in the east room."

The man held Bronwyn's limp form almost gently. "Should I untie her?"

"Go ahead. She can scream all she wants. No one will hear her."

Bronwyn kept her eyes closed and her body limp, but she worked on regaining consciousness. She began to count, then she named all of Tam's children and worked at remembering their ages. By the time the man placed her on a bed, her mind was functioning quickly. She had to escape! And now, before the castle could settle into a routine, was her best time.

It was difficult to remain still and lifeless as the man gently untied her feet. She willed blood into them, using her mind instead of moving her ankles. She concentrated on her feet and tried to ignore the thousands of painful needles that seemed to be shooting through her wrists.

The gag came last as she closed her mouth and moved her tongue over the dryness in her mouth. She lay still, her mind beginning to race as the man touched her hair and her cheek. She cursed his touch but it at least gave her body time to adjust to the blood that was once again beginning to flow.

"Some men get everything," the man said with a wistful sigh as he heaved himself off the bed.

Bronwyn waited until she heard a footstep and hoped the man was walking away. She opened her eyes only slightly and saw him lingering by the door. She turned quickly and saw a pitcher on a table by the bed. She rolled toward it, grabbed it, and slung it across the room. The pewter clattered noisily against the wall.

She lay still again, her eyes open only a slit, as the man rushed toward the noise. Bronwyn was off the bed in seconds and running toward the door. Her ankle gave way under her once but she kept going, never looking at the man. She grabbed the handle on the heavy door and slammed it shut, then slipped the bolt into place. Already she could hear the man pounding, but the sound was muffled and weak through the heavy oak.

She heard footsteps and just had time to slip into a dark window alcove before Roger Chatworth came into sight. He stopped before the door, listening to the man's pounding and the indistinct voice for a moment. Bronwyn held her breath. Roger smiled in satisfaction, then passed her as he went toward the stairs.

Bronwyn allowed herself only seconds to calm her racing heart, and for the first time rub her aching wrists and ankles. She flexed her bruised jaw repeatedly as she slipped silently from the shadows and followed Roger down the stairs.

He turned left at the bottom of the stairs and entered a room. Bronwyn slipped into a shadow just beside the half-open door. She could see inside the small room quite well. There was a table and four chairs, a single fat candle in the center of the table.

A beautiful woman sat with her profile to Bronwyn. She wore a brilliant, flashing gown of purple-and-green striped satin. The delicate features of her face were perfect, from her little mouth to her blue, almond-shaped eyes.

"Why did you have to bring her here? I thought you could have her any time you wanted," the woman said angrily in a sneering voice, so unlike her lovely face.

Roger had his back to Bronwyn as he sat in a chair facing the woman. "There was nothing else I could do. She wouldn't listen to what I meant to tell her about Stephen."

"Wouldn't listen to you?" the woman taunted. "Damn the Montgomery men! What was Stephen doing at King Henry's court anyway?"

Roger waved his hand. "Something about petitioning the king to stop the raids in Scotland. You should have seen him! He practically had the whole court weeping with his tales of the noble Scots and what was being done to them."

Bronwyn closed her eyes for a moment and smiled. Stephen! she thought. Her dear, sweet Stephen. She came back to the present and realized she was wasting time listening to these two. She must escape!

But Roger's next words halted her. "How the hell was I to know you'd choose this time to kidnap Mary Montgomery?"

Bronwyn stopped dead still, her whole body listening.

The woman kept her face turned as she smiled broadly, showing crooked teeth. "I meant to have his wife," she said dreamily.

"By that I take it you mean Gavin's wife, Judith."

"Aye! that whore who stole my Gavin!"

"I'm not sure he was ever yours, and if he was, you were the one who discarded him when you agreed to marry my dear, departed older brother."

The woman ignored him.

"Why did you take Mary instead?" Roger continued. They may have been discussing the weather for all the interest he showed.

"She was returning to that convent where she lives, and

she was conveniently at hand. I'd like to kill all the Montgomerys one by one. It doesn't matter which I begin with. Now! tell me of this one you captured. She is Stephen's wife?" Still the woman did not turn. She kept her profile to both Roger and Bronwyn.

"The woman has changed. In England, before she married, she was easy to manipulate. I told her an outrageous story about some cousins in Scotland." He paused to give a derisive laugh. "How could she believe that *I* am related to a filthy Scot?"

"You got her to ask for a fight between you," the beautiful woman said.

"It was easy enough to put ideas in her empty head," Roger said. "And Montgomery was willing enough to fight for her. He was so hot for her his eyes were burning out of his head."

"I've heard she's beautiful," the woman said with great bitterness.

"No woman is more beautiful than all that land she owns. Had she married me, I would have sent English farmers in there and gotten some good out of the land. Those Scots think they should share the land with the serfs."

"But you lost her and the fight," the woman said quietly.

Roger stood, nearly upsetting the heavy chair. "The bastard!" he cursed. "He ridiculed me. He laughed at me—and he's made all of England laugh at me."

"Would you rather he killed you?" she demanded.

Roger stood in front of her. "Wouldn't you rather have been killed?" he asked quietly.

The woman bent her head. "Yes, oh, yes," she whispered, then her head came up. "But we will make them pay, won't we? We have Stephen's wife and Gavin's sister. Tell me, what do you plan for the two of them?"

Roger smiled. "Bronwyn is mine. If I can't have the lands, I must make do with the woman herself. Mary is of course yours."

The woman put up her hand. "She is poor sport for anyone. She's terrified of everyone and everything. Perhaps I

651

tears. Stephen would never love her again if another man took her. He was already so jealous that he mistrusted her every action. How would he be after Roger Chatworth got through with her?

She stood, unfastened her belt and her skirt, and let them slide to the floor. And how would she react to Roger's touch? Stephen had only to look at her and she fairly attacked him. His merest touch would set her to trembling with passion. Would Roger be able to do the same?

"Hurry up!" Roger commanded. "I've been waiting months for this."

Bronwyn closed her eyes for a moment and took a deep breath as she let the shirt fall to the floor. She kept her chin high and her shoulders back as Roger took a candle and came toward her.

He stared at her, his eyes roaming over her satin skin, her high, proud breasts. He touched her hip gently, ran his finger along the soft pad of flesh around her navel. "Beautiful," he whispered. "Montgomery was right to fight for you."

A sudden knock on the door made them both jump. "Quiet!" Roger commanded as he glanced at the door.

"Roger," came the voice through the door, a young man's voice. "Are you awake?"

"Get in the bed!" Roger said under his breath. "Stay under the covers and don't make a sound. Do I need to threaten you?"

Bronwyn obeyed him quickly, glad for any excuse to hide her nude body from his sight. She buried herself under the furs and coverlets while Roger hastily drew the curtains around the bed.

"Brian, what is it?" Roger asked in a completely different, gentle voice as he opened the door. "Did you have another bad dream?"

Bronwyn moved silently so she could see through the curtains. Roger lit several candles on a table by the bed. He stepped aside, and she could see the young man who entered.

Brian was probably twenty years old, but his slight build made him appear to be little more than a boy. He walked with a hesitant step, as if one leg were stiff but he'd learned to walk with only a slight limp. He was obviously Roger's brother, a younger, weaker, more delicate version of his strong, healthy older brother.

"You should be in bed," Roger said in a kind voice, a voice Bronwyn had never heard from him before. Roger's love for this boy was apparent in every word he spoke.

Brian eased himself into a chair. "I was waiting for you to return. I couldn't even find out where you went. Alice said . . ." He stopped.

"Did she upset you?" Roger asked earnestly. "If she did—"

"No, of course not," Brian said. "Alice is an unhappy woman. She is miserable over Edmund's death."

"Yes, I'm sure she is," Roger said sarcastically. He changed the subject. "I visited my other estates to see that the serfs were not robbing us blind."

"Roger, who is the woman who keeps crying?"

Roger's head shot up. "I . . . I don't know what you mean. There isn't any woman crying."

"For three nights now I've heard someone crying. Even during the day I catch just a bit of the sound."

Roger smiled. "Perhaps the house has a ghost. Or maybe Edmund—" He stopped abruptly.

"I know what you mean," Brian said flatly. "I know more about our elder brother than you think. You were going to say that perhaps the crying is the ghost of one of Edmund's women. Maybe it was the one who killed herself on the night Edmund was murdered."

"Brian! How do you hear of these things? It's late and you ought to be in bed."

Brian sighed, then allowed Roger to help him out of the chair. "I think I will go to bed. Will I see you in the morning? Alice is so much better when you're here, and I miss Elizabeth already. Christmas is much too short."

"Yes, of course, I'll be here. Good night, little brother. Sleep well." He stood for a moment after the door closed.

Bronwyn didn't move as she watched Roger. Roger may

be a liar, he might attack a man's back, but he loved his younger brother.

Roger turned and threw the bed curtains aside. "Did you hope I'd forgotten you?" His voice was cold again.

She held the bedclothes to her neck and backed toward the far edge of the bed. "Who is Elizabeth?"

Roger gave her a smirking look. "Elizabeth is my sister. Now come here."

"Is she older or younger than Brian?" She was talking rapidly.

"Would you like to see my family tree?" He grabbed her arm, pulled her to him. "Elizabeth is three years younger than Brian."

"Is she—" Her words stopped as Roger pulled her into his arms and began to kiss her hungrily.

She was quite still as he kissed her. His lips were firm and pleasant, his breath sweet even, but there was no fire. He ran his mouth down her neck as his hands caressed her back. His fingers played down her spine, then gripped her buttocks and pressed her to him. He was fully dressed, and the padded velvet of his clothes felt good against her cool, bare skin.

But aside from a pleasant sensation, there was no fire. She felt like an outsider, as if she observed what was happening rather than experienced it.

"You do not fight me?" Roger asked in a throaty whisper, a hint of humor in his voice.

"No," she said honestly. "I—"

Again he stopped her words with a kiss. Gently he lay her down in the bed and began to kiss her neck as his hands freely caressed her breasts. His lips followed his hands.

"No, Roger, I don't fight you," she said, her voice full of honesty. "Truthfully, I find there is nothing to fight. I must admit I was curious about how I'd react to another man touching me. Stephen says I am after him so often he hasn't enough time to recover."

She gave a little laugh, stared at the canopy, and put her hands behind her head. "Not that Stephen *always* told the truth," she chuckled. "But I find it's just not the same. You touch me in the same places Stephen touches me, but with you I feel nothing. Isn't that odd?"

She looked with innocent eyes at Roger, who was bending over her, his hands still, his eyes wide. "I'm really sorry. I don't mean to offend you. I'm sure some women like you. I guess I just happen to belong to one man alone."

Roger raised his hand to strike her, and Bronwyn's eyes turned cold. "I'll not fight you nor will I react to your love-making. Does it anger you that you aren't half the man Stephen Montgomery is? Either in bed or out of it?"

"I'll kill you for that!" Roger growled as he lunged for her.

Bronwyn rolled away from him, and he landed on his face in the soft mattress. She jumped from the bed and looked about for a weapon but could find none.

Roger stopped as he started after her. Damn, but she made a startling sight. Her black hair swirled about her like a demon cloud. Her proud, strong body taunted him. She was breathtaking, like an ancient primitive queen, arrogant, defiant, threatening him with her small strength.

Every word she'd said about her husband screamed at him. She knew men well, didn't she? With each word he'd felt his passion shrink. What man could take her when he knew she laughed at him? If she feared him he would rape her, but this laughter of hers was too much.

"Guards!" he bellowed.

Bronwyn knew he planned to release her from the duty of his bed. She grabbed her clothes and by the time the door opened, she was wrapped in her plaid, the rest of her clothes under her arm.

"Take her to the east room," Roger said tiredly. "And I will have the man's head who lets her escape."

Bronwyn did not breathe easily until she heard the bolt shoot home and she was alone in the room. The guards had released the man she'd locked in the room hours before.

She sank down on the bed and instantly began to tremble. Her body ached from having been tied in a wagon for three days. Her fear for Mary tormented her, and now the episode with Roger further weakened her.

Once when she was just a girl she'd gone riding with one of her father's men. They'd stopped to rest the horses, and the man had tossed her to the ground and began to undress her. Bronwyn had been extremely innocent and very frightened. The man undressed himself, and when he stood over her he thrust his manhood out at her as if he were massively proud of the thing. Bronwyn, who'd only seen horses and bulls, began to laugh at the man, and before her very eyes he'd deflated. She'd learned several lessons that day. One, to never ride alone with just one man, and two, whereas fear seemed to excite the man, her laughter only crushed him.

She never told her father about the encounter, and three months later the man was killed in a cattle raid.

It should have been good to see Roger hurt as she'd hurt him, but it wasn't. She fell down onto the covers of the bed, hiding her face, burying her head. She wanted Stephen so badly, needed him so much. He was the foundation of her being. He kept her from doing stupid, impulsive things. If he'd been with her, she would never have left Larenston. Rab would be alive and she wouldn't be held prisoner by Roger Chatworth.

Stephen was with his king, pleading with the man to stop the raids on her country. Her country! Hadn't Stephen proved he was a Scot? He deserved the title more than anyone else.

Bronwyn had no idea when she began to cry. The tears just began to flow silently at first, then with deep, wrenching sobs. She swore that if she ever managed to get herself out of this mess, she'd be honest with Stephen. She'd tell him how much she loved him and needed him. Oh, yes! How very, very much she needed him.

She cried for Mary, for Rab, for Stephen, and most of all for herself. She'd had something so beautiful and she'd thrown it away. "Stephen," she whispered and cried some more.

When her body was dry and she could cry no more, she slept.

Chapter 18

BRIAN CHATWORTH was very quiet as he made his way down the stairs to the cellar. The Chatworth house had been built over an old castle, a place his grandfather had conquered and destroyed. Some people said it was bad to have built over the home of an enemy.

Brian thought of his brother's words about a ghost and smiled. Roger was so protective of his little brother and sister. When they were children, they needed protection from their older brother. But now, since Edmund's death, there was no need of hiding and lying. There was a woman crying, and Brian meant to find out about her. It was probably a kitchen maid who'd fallen in love with Roger and now cried because Roger didn't return her love. Brian realized that Roger thought his little brother knew nothing that went on between men and women. To Roger, Brian was still a frightened, hiding little boy.

He paused at the bottom of the stairs. The cellars were dark, full of wine barrels and casks of salted fish. As he listened he heard a roll of ivory dice and a couple of guards laughing and cursing. He slipped between the barrels and went toward the back where he knew a locked cell was. He had no idea why he sneaked about except that he'd learned to be good at it when Edmund was alive. Besides, he'd rather Roger didn't think Brian had no faith in his brother.

The crying became louder as he neared the cell door. It

then she looked like an angel. One of the woodcarvers used her for a model for all the cherubs in the chapel. I was eight. We were playing in the sand in the jousting field. Our brother Edmund was already grown then, twenty-one years old."

Brian paused a moment. "I don't remember everything. Later, they said Edmund was drunk. He didn't see Elizabeth and me as he charged onto the field."

Mary gasped in horror.

"We would have been killed if it weren't for Roger. He was fourteen and big and strong. He ran right in front of Edmund's horse and grabbed both of us. But the horse's hoof hit his left arm and he dropped me." Brian looked away for a moment. "The horse crushed my leg from the knee down." He gave a weak smile. "I'm lucky I didn't lose it. Elizabeth said it was Roger's care that saved the leg. He stayed beside me for months afterward."

"You love him very much, don't you?"

"Yes," Brian answered simply. "He . . . protected both Elizabeth and me all our childhoods. He put Elizabeth in a convent when she was six."

"And she's there now."

Brian smiled. "Roger says he's looking for a man fit for her but he's not found one yet. How can you find a husband for an angel?" He laughed in memory at something Elizabeth had said. She'd suggested Roger find her a devil. Roger had not found Elizabeth's statement humorous. Too often, Roger didn't laugh at Elizabeth's sharp remarks. Sometimes her tongue was at odds with her sweet looks.

"We can't let our families fight," Mary was saying. "You've shown me that your brother is a kind, loving man. He's just angry at Stephen. And no doubt your sister-in-law is angry too."

Brian almost laughed at that. Alice's half-crazy rages were more than anger. Sometimes she was totally insane and sleeping herbs had to be given her. She screamed about Judith and Gavin Montgomery constantly.

"You've said so little about yourself," Brian said quietly. "Here you are held prisoner, you've been crying for days, yet you ask about me. Tell me, why have you been crying? For yourself or for your brothers?"

Mary looked at her hands. "I am a weak, cowardly thing. I wish I could pray as I should, but my brothers have taught me realism. When they find I am gone, they will be so angry. Gavin and Stephen will calmly prepare for war, but there will be nothing calm about either Raine or Miles."

"What will they do?"

"No one can tell. They do whatever seems good at the moment. Raine is usually so gentle, a great bear of a man, but he can stand no injustice. And Miles has a horrible temper! No one can guess what he will do."

"This must be stopped," Brian said, rising. "I will go to Roger and demand that he release you."

Mary stood beside him, shorter than he. "Do you think demands will make him angry? Shouldn't you ask?"

Brian looked at her, her soft roundness, her great liquid eyes. She made him feel as strong as a mountain. He'd never asked Roger for anything—except his very life. She was right. How could he make demands of someone he loved so much?

He touched Mary's face. "I will take you from this place. I promise you that."

"And I believe you," Mary said with great trust. "You must go now."

Brian looked about the small, damp cell. There was straw on the floor and it was none too clean. The only furniture was a hard cot and a bucket in a corner. "This is a foul place. You must leave with me now."

"No!" She backed away from him. "We must be careful. We cannot anger your brother. If he is like mine, he may say things he will regret later, but then he will be forced to hold to them. You must wait until morning when he is rested and then talk to him."

"How can you concern yourself with my brother when it means another night for you in this hell-hole?"

She answered him only with the look in her eyes. "Go in peace now. You needn't worry about me."

Brian stared at her a moment, then grabbed her hand and

kissed it. "You are a good woman, Mary Montgomery." He turned and left her.

Mary looked away as she heard the door locked once again. She hoped she hadn't let Brian see how very frightened she really was. Something scurried across the floor and she jumped. She shouldn't cry, she knew, but she was such an awful coward.

Roger looked at his little brother with shock.

"I want her out of that cell," Brian said quietly. He'd done as Mary'd said and waited until morning to confront Roger. Not that Brian had slept any, nor had Roger from the look of the dark circles under his eyes.

"Brian, please . . ." Roger began in that voice he used only for his younger brother and sister.

Brian didn't relent. "I still haven't heard why you have her prisoner, but whatever the reason, I want her out of that cell."

Roger turned away from Brian so the pain in Roger's eyes couldn't be seen. How could he explain his humiliation at the hands of the Montgomerys? It had hurt him when his sister-in-law threw herself at Gavin and was rejected by him. Later Bronwyn had chosen him and he'd felt redeemed. But Stephen had gotten in a lucky blow that had sent Roger sprawling. He'd been so angry, he hadn't thought but had attacked Stephen's back. Now he wanted to let the Montgomerys know he couldn't always be beaten.

"She won't be harmed," Roger said. "I promise you I won't harm her."

"Then why hold her? Release her now before there is a full-scale war."

"It's too late for that now."

"What do you mean?"

Roger looked back at his little brother. "Raine Montgomery was leading several hundred of the king's soldiers to Wales when he heard I had Mary. He turned the men and led them toward here to attack us."

"What! We are about to be attacked? We have no defenses. Doesn't he know he can't lead men like that in these days? We have courts and laws to protect us from attack."

"The king met Raine before he could get to us. The king was so angry at Raine's use of his men in a personal fight that King Henry declared Raine an outlaw. He has retreated to the forest to live."

"Good God!" Brian breathed, easing himself into a chair. "We have no defenses such as that massive fortress of the Montgomerys'. If we release Mary—"

Roger looked at his brother in admiration. "I had not meant to include you in this feud. You must leave here. Go and stay at one of my other estates. I will come to you soon."

"No!" Brian said firmly. "We must settle this quarrel. We will send messages to the king and to the Montgomerys. Until then I will personally look out for Mary." He stood and limped from the room.

Roger glared at the door after Brian closed it. He ground his teeth in anger, then grabbed a war axe from the wall. He slung the weapon across the room, where it sank into the oak door. "Damn all the Montgomerys," he cursed. He was glad the king was angry at them. They did nothing but take. They'd taken his sister-in-law's beauty and half her mind as well. They'd taken all those lands in Scotland that should have been his. And now they worked to take away his brother's admiration. Brian had never before defied Roger, had never done anything to contradict him. Now Brian thought he could make decisions and tell Roger what to do.

The door opened and Alice entered. Her gown was of emerald-green satin trimmed with rabbit fur that had been dyed yellow. A veil of tissue-thin silk covered her face. "I just saw Brian," she said in a quarrelsome voice. "He was helping that Montgomery woman up the stairs. How can you order her from the cellar? A woman like that should be thrown to the dogs."

"Brian found her on his own. It was his decision to care for her."

"Care for her!" Alice screeched. "You mean you're going to treat her like a guest like that one upstairs?" She smirked in laughter. "Or are you no longer giving the orders in this house? It looks like Brian is the man of this household now."

"You should know all the men, shouldn't you? From all reports, you've had all of them."

Alice smiled at him. "Are you jealous? I heard you sent Stephen's wife from your room last night. Couldn't you 'perform' with her?" she taunted. "Perhaps you should send Brian to do that for you too."

"Get out!" Roger said in a low voice that left no doubt of his meaning.

Bronwyn stared out the window at the snow in the court-yard below. She had been Roger Chatworth's prisoner for a month, and in that time she saw no one except a maid or two. They brought her food, firewood, clean linen. Her room was cleaned, the chamberpot emptied, but she spoke to no one. She tried to ask the maids questions, but they looked at her with great fear and tiptoed from the room.

There hadn't been a method she hadn't used in attempting to escape. She'd tied sheets together and let herself down the side of the house. But Roger's guards had caught her when she reached the ground. The next day a man had come and put bars over the window.

She'd even started a fire to create a diversion, but the guards held her as they put the fire out. She'd made a weapon from the handle of a pewter pitcher and wounded one guard. The two guards were replaced with three, and Roger came and said he'd tie her if she caused him any more problems. She begged Roger for news of Mary. Did the Montgomery brothers know the women were being held captive?

Roger answered none of her questions.

Bronwyn sank back into her loneliness. The only thing she had to occupy herself was her memory of Stephen. She had time to go over every moment of their life together, and she knew where she'd make changes. She should have realized a whole race of people couldn't be as bad as the men who ogled her at Sir Thomas's house. She shouldn't have been so angry because Stephen was so interested in her person and not in her clan. She shouldn't have trusted Roger's stories so completely.

No wonder Stephen had said she was selfish. She always seemed to see just one side of a problem. She thought of Stephen with his king, and she knew that when—if—she left Roger Chatworth's alive, she would go to Kirsty and try to arrange peace with the MacGregor. She owed that to Stephen.

"Brian, they're lovely," Mary smiled, accepting the little leather shoes from him. "You spoil me."

Brian looked at her, and the love poured from his eyes. They'd spent most of the last month together. He'd never again asked Roger to release Mary, because Brian didn't want to see her go. For Mary took away the loneliness in his life. Too often Roger was off to some tournament, and Elizabeth was always locked away in her convent. As for the other women, Brian had long ago learned that women made him feel shy and awkward. Mary was ten years older than he and as unworldly as he. Mary never giggled or asked him to dance or expected him to chase her around the rose-bushes. Mary was quiet and simple, demanding nothing from him. They spent the days playing a lute, and sometimes Brian told stories, stories that had always been in his head but he'd never told anyone. Mary always listened and always made him feel strong and protective, something more than just a younger brother.

It was this new feeling of protectiveness that kept him from telling her that Bronwyn had also been taken as a prisoner. He wasn't as blindly trustful of his brother as he once was, and he asked the servants questions, wanting to know what went on in his own house. He'd immediately demanded Bronwyn's release, and Roger had quickly obliged. Now only Mary was held captive.

"No one could spoil you enough," he smiled.

Mary blushed prettily and lowered her lashes. "Come and sit by me. Have you heard any news?"

"No, nothing," Brian lied. He knew Raine was still outlawed, still living in a forest somewhere, the head of a gang of ruffians if Alice was to be believed. But Brian never told Mary of Raine's plight. "It turned colder last night," he said, warming his hands at the fire in her room. By mutual agreement they never mentioned Roger or Alice. They were two lonely people who came together out of mutual need. Their world consisted of one large, pleasant room on the top of floor of the Chatworth house. They had music and art and joy in each other, and neither of them had ever been happier.

Brian lay back against the cushions of a chair before the fire and thought for the thousandth time how he'd like this to go on always. He never wanted Mary to return to her "other" family.

It was that evening that Brian spoke of his dreams to Roger.

"You what?" Roger gasped, his eyes wide.

"I want to marry Mary Montgomery."

"Marry!" Roger staggered back against a chair. To be allied with a family he considered his enemy! "The woman is of the church, you can't—"

Brian smiled. "She's taken no vows. She lives with the nuns as one of them, that's all. Mary is so gentle. She only wants to help the world."

The two men were interrupted by Alice's high laugh. "Well, Roger, you have certainly done well. Your baby brother wants to marry the older sister of the Montgomerys. Tell me, Brian, how old is she? Old enough to be the mother you've always wanted?"

Brian had never had any reason to experience rage before. He'd always been protected by Roger from most of the unpleasantries of the world, but now he snarled as he went after Alice.

Roger caught his slight young brother. "There's no need for that."

Brian looked into Roger's eyes. For the first time in his life Brian didn't think his brother was perfect. "You're going to let her say those things?" he asked quietly.

Roger frowned. He didn't like the way Brian was looking at him, so coldly, as if they weren't the closest of friends. "Of course, she's wrong. I just think you haven't thought about this thoroughly. I know you're young and you need a wife and—"

Brian jerked away from Roger. "Are you saying I'm too stupid to know what I want?"

Alice screamed with laughter. "Answer him, Roger! Are you going to let your brother marry a Montgomery? I can hear all of England now. They'll say you couldn't get Stephen in the back one way so you got him another. They'll say the Chatworths take only the leavings of the Montgomerys. I couldn't get Gavin. You couldn't get Bronwyn, so you sent your crippled brother after their old-maid sister."

"Shut up!" Roger roared.

"The truth hurts, doesn't it?" Alice taunted.

Roger clenched his jaw. "My brother will not marry a Montgomery."

Brian pulled himself up to his full height. He was half the size of Roger. "I *will* marry Mary," he said firmly.

Alice laughed again. "You should have put him in charge of the other one. He might have spent his lust on her but at least he wouldn't be talking of marriage."

"What are you talking about, you hag?" Brian demanded. "What other one?"

Alice glared at him through her veil. "How dare you?" she gasped. "How dare you call me a hag? My beauty was so great that once I wouldn't have looked at a crippled weakling like you."

Roger took a step forward. "Get out of here before I scar your other cheek."

Alice snarled at him before she turned to leave. "Ask him about Bronwyn upstairs," she laughed before she hurried from the room.

Roger turned to meet Brian's cold eyes. He didn't like the way Brian was looking at him. It was almost as if Brian no longer worshipped his big brother.

"You said you released her," Brian said flatly. "How many other lies have you told me?"

"Now, Brian," Roger began in that special tone he always used for his little brother and sister.

Brian moved away from him. "I am not a child and I will not be treated as one! What a fool I've been! No wonder the Montgomerys don't attack us. You hold two of their women, don't you? How could I have listened to you? I never even questioned that whatever you did was right. I was too happy with Mary to even think for myself. But then I've always been too busy to think for myself, haven't I?"

"Brian, please . . ."

"No!" Brian shouted. "For once you're going to listen to me. Tomorrow morning I'm going to take Mary and Bronwyn back to their family."

Roger could feel the hair rising on the back of his neck. "They are my prisoners and you will do no such thing."

"Why are they your prisoners?" Brian asked. "Because you attacked Stephen Montgomery's back? Because you were beaten by him?"

Roger staggered backward. "Brian, how can you talk to me like this? After all I've done for you?"

"I'm sick of hearing how you saved my life and Elizabeth's! I'm sick of being grateful to you every moment of my life. I've served my time of being your little brother. I'm a grown man now, and I can make my own decisions."

"Brian," Roger whispered. "I never meant to ask gratitude from you. You and Elizabeth have been my whole life. I have no one else. I never wanted anyone else."

Brian sighed and his anger left him. "I know you didn't. You've always been good to us, but it's time now to leave you and get out on my own. I want to marry Mary, and I mean to do it." He turned away. "Tomorrow I will take the women home."

Roger began shaking as soon as Brian left the room. No battle or tournament had ever left him as weak as this confrontation with Brian had. Moment by moment he'd seen his dear, sweet little brother change. He'd seen Brian's blind adoration of his big brother leave him.

Roger collapsed in a chair and stared at the tiled floor.

Brian and Elizabeth were all he had. The three of them had stayed together, a strong force against Edmund's evilness. Elizabeth had always been independent. Her angelic face hid a strong nature, and she'd often stood up to Edmund. But Brian had always looked to Roger for love and protection. Brian was content to allow Roger to make all his decisions for him. And Roger loved the role. He loved Brian's worship of him.

But tonight he'd seen that adoration drain away. Brian had changed from a sweet, loving young boy into a hostile, demanding, arrogant man.

And all because of the Montgomerys!

Roger didn't know when he started drinking. The wine seemed available, and he took it without a thought for what he did. All he could remember were Brian's cold eyes and that the Montgomerys had even cost him his brother's love.

The more he drank, the more he thought of all the troubles the Montgomerys had caused him. Alice's lost beauty seemed to be a direct insult to him. After all, she was his relative. Judith and Gavin had toyed with Alice; worst of all, they'd laughed at her—just as they laughed at Roger. He could hear the taunts of the men at court, where he'd gone after his battle with Stephen. "I hear you made a play for that little chieftess of Montgomery's. Not that I blame you from what I heard, but were you so hot for her you sought her at the cost of Stephen's back?"

Over and over the words came back to him. King Henry's son had just married a Spanish princess, and the king did not want his good mood spoiled by Roger's unchivalrous activities.

Roger slammed down his pewter tankard on the chair arm, and a piece of the carving fell away. "Damn them all!" he cursed. Brian was ready to throw away years of love and loyalty for a woman he hardly knew. He thought of Bronwyn's trick of laughing at him when he'd tried to make love to her. A whore's trick! Just like Mary's trick of telling Brian she wasn't of the church. Brian seemed to think Mary was pure, worthy of marriage, but she was clever enough to be able to seduce an innocent boy ten years her junior. Did she hope to use him to gain her freedom, or was she trying for the Chatworth wealth? The Montgomerys were making a habit of marrying great fortunes.

Roger rose unsteadily to his feet. It was his duty, as Brian's guardian, to show his little brother what lying bitches all women were. They were like Alice or Bronwyn. None of them were sweet and gentle, and certainly none were worthy of his brother Brian.

He staggered out of the room and up the stairs. He had no idea where he was going, and it was only when he reached Bronwyn's room that he paused. A vision of her black hair and blue eyes floated before him. He remembered every curve of her lush body. He put his hand on the door bolt before he remembered the way her cleft chin jutted up at him in defiance. He moved away from the door. No, he wasn't drunk enough to be able to withstand her ridicule of him. It wasn't possible to get that drunk!

He went up another flight of stairs to the top floor of his house. His problems were caused by that slut who dressed as a nun and enticed his little brother. Her evil ways were causing the break-up of his family. Brian said that tomorrow he was leaving the Chatworth estate. He was going to marry a Montgomery and leave Roger. As if the Montgomerys didn't have enough family already, they were going to take Roger's!

Roger lifted the bolt from the door of Mary's room. The moonlight was streaming through the window, and a night candle burned by the bed.

"Who is it?" Mary whispered, sitting up in bed. There was fear in her voice.

Roger tripped over a chair, then sent it crashing against a wall.

"Who is it?" Mary said louder, her voice beginning to shake.

"A Chatworth," Roger growled. "One of your jailors." He towered over the bed, looking down at her. Her long brown hair was twisted into a braid. Her eyes were wide with fear.

"Lord Roger, I . . ."

"You what?" he demanded. "Aren't you going to welcome me to your bed? Isn't one Chatworth as good as another? I can release you as well as Brian. Come, let's see what you have that has enticed my brother so much."

Roger grabbed the cover Mary held clutched to her neck and tore it from her. He stared in a glazed way at the prim cotton gown she wore. Most women wore nothing to bed, yet this woman, a harlot supreme, wore a gown. For some reason this only angered Roger more. He grabbed the collar of the gown and tore it off of her. He didn't notice her body or listen to her when her terrified screams began. All he could hear was Brian saying he was leaving his home for this woman. He'd show Brian what a whore the woman was and that she wasn't worth his dear little brother's affection.

He fell on Mary's plump, innocent body in a mindless state. He removed only enough of his clothes to perform the deed. Her legs were held rigidly together and he had to pry them open. Her screams had subsided into a whimper of terror. Her body was as rigid as a piece of steel.

It was no pleasure to rape her. She was dry and tense, and Roger had to pound against her to gain admittance. It was over in seconds. The drink and the emotion he'd spent worked together to exhaust him. He rolled off of her and collapsed on the bed beside her. Now Brian wouldn't leave him, he thought as he closed his eyes. Next Christmas, Brian, Elizabeth, and he would be together, just as they always had.

Mary lay quite still as Roger rolled away from her. Her body felt violated, unclean. Her first thought was of her brothers. How could she face them again when she was what Roger had called her over and over, a whore? Brian could never again sit with her, talk to her.

Very calmly, she rose from the bed. She ignored the pain in her body and the blood on her thighs. With great care she pulled her only gown over her head. It was a simple thing of dark blue wool, a gown the sisters had made for her. She looked about the room for one last time, then walked to the window.

The cold night air blew into her face, and she breathed deeply of it. She lifted her eyes toward Heaven. She knew the Lord could not forgive her for what she did, but then neither could she forgive herself for what had happened. "Good-bye, my brothers," she whispered to the wind. "Good-bye, my Brian."

She crossed herself, put her hands across her breasts, and jumped to the stones below.

The animals of the Chatworth estate sensed something wrong before the people did. The dogs began to bark; the horses became restless in their stalls.

Brian, upset and unable to sleep, threw on a robe and made his way outside. "What is it?" he asked a stableboy who was running past him.

"A woman threw herself from a top-floor window," he called over his shoulder. "I've got to find Lord Roger."

Brian's heart stopped at the boy's words. It had to be one of the women who was held captive. Please let it be the woman he didn't know, Bronwyn, he prayed. But even as he thought the words, he knew who lay dead.

He walked calmly toward the side of the house that contained the window to Mary's room. He pushed through the crowd of servants peering down at the body.

"She's been raped," a woman said quietly. "Look at the blood on her!"

"It's just like when Lord Edmund was alive. And here I thought the younger one was going to be better."

"Get out of here!" Brian shouted. It made him sick that they felt free to look at his beloved Mary. "Did you hear me? Get out of here!"

The servants weren't used to taking orders from Brian, but they recognized the tone of authority when they heard it. They turned quickly and left to hide in the dark corners and stare at Brian and this woman they'd never seen before.

Brian gently smoothed Mary's clothes. He straightened her neck from its unnatural angle. He wanted to carry her into the house and even made a few attempts, but he wasn't strong enough. Even his weakness seemed to feed the anger rising in him. The servants assumed Roger had raped her, but Brian didn't believe them. One of the guards! he thought.

As he stood he began to imagine tortures for the man, as if it would help bring his Mary back.

As if in a trance, he walked up the stairs to Mary's room. The guards started to hinder him, but they stepped back when they saw Brian's face. He pushed open the door to Mary's room.

He stared for some moments at Roger's form, dead asleep, snoring, as he lay in Mary's bed. He didn't seem to have any thoughts, only a feeling that ran through him. He seemed to grow and strengthen with each passing moment.

With great calmness he turned and took a pitcher of cold water from a table. He poured it over Roger's head.

Roger groaned and looked up. "Brian," he said groggily with a faint smile. "I was dreaming of you."

"Get up!" Brian said in a deadly voice.

Roger became alert. He was war-trained and knew how to control his senses when he felt there was danger. "What has happened? Is Elizabeth—" He broke off as he sat up and realized where he was. "Where is the Montgomery woman?"

Brian's face didn't change from its look of steel. "She lies dead on the stones below."

A flicker went across Roger's face. "I wanted to prove what kind of woman she was. I wanted to show you—"

Brian's low voice cut him off. "Where is Stephen Montgomery's wife?"

"Brian, you must listen to me," Roger pleaded.

"Listen!" Brian gasped. "Did you listen to Mary's screams? I know she was a timid woman and I'll wager she screamed a lot. Did you enjoy it?"

"Brian . . ."

"Cease! You have said your last words to me. I am going to find this other woman you hold, and we are leaving here." His eyes narrowed. "If I ever see you again, I will kill you!"

Roger fell backward as if he'd been struck. He watched numbly as Brian left the room. He looked at the blood on the sheet beside him and thought of the woman lying dead below. What had he done?

It didn't take Brian long to find Bronwyn. He knew she'd be in the room where Edmund once kept his women. Again the guards outside the door didn't challenge him. The undercurrent of the night's tragedy was being felt even through the walls.

Bronwyn was awake and standing ready when Brian entered her room. "What has happened?" she asked quietly of the hard-looking young man before her.

"I am Brian Chatworth," he said, "and I am taking you to your family. Are you ready?"

"My sister-in-law is also being held prisoner. I won't go without her."

Brian clenched his jaw. "My brother has raped your sister, and she has killed herself."

He said the words flatly, as if they meant nothing to him, but Bronwyn sensed something deeper. Mary, she thought, sweet, dear, gentle Mary! "We cannot leave her here. I must take her back to her brothers."

"You need not worry about Mary. I will take care of her."

Something about the way he said "Mary" told Bronwyn a lot. "I am ready," she said quietly and followed as he left the room.

Once they were outside in the cold night air, Brian turned to her. "I will arrange for a guard to accompany you. They will take you wherever you want. Or you may return with me to the Montgomery castle."

It didn't take Bronwyn long to make a decision. She'd had a month to think about it while she was confined in the room alone. She had to make peace with the MacGregors before she could see Stephen again. She had to prove that her love was worthy of him. "I must return to Scotland, and I want no English guards. I will travel more easily alone."

Brian didn't argue with her. His own misery and hate occupied all of his thoughts. He nodded curtly. "You may have a horse and whatever provisions you need." He turned to leave but she caught his arm.

"You will care for Mary?"

"With my life," he said from deep within him, "and I will revenge her death also." He walked away.

Bronwyn frowned as she thought how Mary would hate any talk of revenge. Suddenly she looked about her and realized her freedom for the first time. She must go as quickly as possible, before more violence erupted in this place. She had much work to do. Perhaps the saving of lives, even Scots' lives, would please Mary's ghost. She turned toward the stables.

Chapter 19

BRONWYN LEANED her head against the warm side of the cow as she milked it. She was glad she'd come to Kirsty's parents' cottage instead of returning to Larenston. Kirsty and Donald had taken little Rory Stephen and returned north to their home. Bronwyn turned back to her horse and started to mount when Harben caught her arm.

"Ye'll stay with us, lass, until ye've met with the Mac-Gregor. That is, if ye still want to."

She looked from Harben to Nesta and back again. "How long have you known?"

"Donald told me after ye left. I always suspected something, though. Ye don't talk like an ordinary woman. Ye have more . . ."

"Self-confidence?" Bronwyn asked hopefully.

Harben snorted. "More like as it's more insolence." He stared at her. "The MacGregor will like ye." His eyes went to her expanding stomach. "I see that man of yers enjoyed my home brew."

She laughed at him.

Harben led the way into his little cottage. "One thing I don't understand. I can see that you're the MacArran, but I can't see that that man of yours is an Englishman. I'd rather believe in a MacArran than an Englishman."

They went into the cottage, laughing, Nesta smiling at both of them. It was Nesta who kept the farm going and saw that Bronwyn and Harben worked while they argued.

It had taken a few days to arrange a meeting with the MacGregor. He agreed to tell no one and to bring no men with him, just as Bronwyn did. The next morning, at dawn, in the mist of the moors, they would meet.

She pulled harder on the cow and brushed at a stray strand of hair that bothered her. She finished the milking, swatted absently at her hair, and carried the pail to the far end of the barn, noticing that it was already growing dark outside. Just as the last drops of milk splashed into the pail, she heard a noise that made her stop instantly.

There was a little bark, just a small sound, but something about it reminded her of Rab, and tears instantly came to her eyes. She remembered all too clearly seeing Rab on the ground, the gaping wound in his side.

The sound came again, and she turned, the bucket still in her hand. There, standing quietly, his eyes alight, his tail wagging, was Rab.

She just had time to drop the bucket because the next moment all one hundred and fifty pounds of the dog were upon her. The dog knocked her back against a manger and nearly broke her in half.

"Rab!" she whispered, hugging the dog in return. "Rab!" She laughed as he threatened to drown her in his exuberance. "Oh, sweet dog," she cried. "Where did you come from? I thought you were dead!" She buried her face in his fur.

Suddenly a low piercing whistle came, and Rab went rigid. The next instant he stood on the ground in front of her. "What is it, boy?"

She looked up, and there stood Stephen. His hair was shorter but he wore the Scots dress. She looked him up and down slowly. It seemed she had forgotten how large he was, how strong and muscular he was. His blue eyes looked at her in an intense way.

"Do I get the same welcome as Rab?" he asked quietly.

She didn't think but leaped at him, her arms going about his neck, her feet off the floor.

Stephen didn't say a word but began kissing her with all the hunger he felt. It had been so very long since he'd touched her. He stepped backward, carrying her, and fell into a thick pile of hay. Even as they fell, his hands were on the buttons of her shirt.

"We can't . . ." Bronwyn murmured against his lips. "Harben . . ."

Stephen bit her earlobe. "I told him we planned an orgy for the rest of the day."

"You didn't!"

"I did!" he mocked, laughter in his eyes. Then the expression on his face changed. His eyes widened and he looked at her in astonishment. The next moment he was tearing her clothes off her and gaping at the hard mound of her stomach.

He looked up at her in question.

She smiled and nodded at him.

Stephen's shout of happiness scared the chickens from the barn rafters. "A baby!" he laughed. "Harben was damn right about his home brew."

"I was carrying the child before we met Kirsty, so Morag says."

He lay beside her and pulled her nude body close to him. "Then maybe it was me and not Harben," he said from some deep, inner joy.

Bronwyn nuzzled against him and rubbed her thigh between his. "It may as well have been the home brew," she said sadly. "I don't remember anything else that could have given me a baby."

He chuckled, then moved quickly as he pushed her face-down in the hay. In an instant he was out of his plaid. He kept his knee on the small of her back. When he was nude, he bent and kissed the back of her knees. "I haven't forgotten you completely," he murmured as he ran his teeth along her tendons. His hands caressed her legs as his mouth tormented her. She moaned under him and tried to turn over, but he held her fast as he continued his sweet torture of her.

His skin against hers sent shivers all through her body. His mouth traveled up to her spine, his legs against hers. The hardness and the hairiness of his thighs worked to excite her.

His big hands caressed her back, played with the soft shape of her.

Just after she knew she could stand no more, he turned her over. He kissed her while his hand rubbed her stomach then inched up to her breasts. She arched toward him as his mouth touched her breasts.

He moved upward again, his teeth running along her neck. She grabbed at him, pulled him down on top of her. "Hungry, my laird?" he growled in her ear.

She bit at him, almost too hard, and the next moment he was on her. It had been so long since they'd been together, and Stephen's mouth on her knees had excited her to a fever pitch. It took only a few thrusts before both of them were shuddering in the throes of their love.

"Oh, Stephen," she whispered, clutching him to her. It was so good to feel safe again, to not be alone. She didn't realize when the tears started.

Stephen moved from atop her and pulled her into the haven of his strong arms. He covered them with his plaid, and Rab snuggled against his mistress's back.

The safety and security she felt made her cry even harder.

"Was it horrible?" he asked quietly. "We felt so helpless, but there was so little we could do."

She wiped her tears away and looked at him. "Mary?"

He pushed her head down. "Brian Chatworth brought her back to us." He was silent for a moment. Now was not the time to talk of his grief—and rage—at the death of his sister. Sweet, gentle Mary, who only did good in her life, did not deserve death in such a vile manner. Miles had been the one to nearly kill Brian before Gavin and Stephen could prevent him. When Brian's story was told, it rang true that even held captive, Mary gave love. Brian's grief was obvious as he held the lifeless body of the woman he loved.

"Brian went to find Raine, wherever he is now," Stephen continued. "We heard he was hiding in the forest. Why didn't you return to Larenston? Tam has aged twenty years in the last month. He knew so little about what had happened. They found Rab in the morning, and Tam was sure you were dead."

"I wanted to do something for Mary."

"For Mary? You came to Harben's because of Mary?"

Bronwyn began to cry harder. "You were right. I had so long to think about it. I'm so selfish and I don't deserve your love."

"What the hell are you talking about?" he demanded.

"What you said. When you were holding that woman," she sniffed disjointedly.

Stephen frowned as he tried to remember what she was talking about. Since they'd been married, he'd not touched another woman. Every woman he saw paled in comparison to Bronwyn's beauty and spirit. He smiled as he remembered the night at Gavin's castle. "Aggie!" he laughed. "She's the castle whore. I was sitting there feeling miserable and sorry for myself when she came in the room, opened her blouse, and threw herself across my lap."

"You certainly didn't push her off! You were enjoying her when I came in."

"Enjoying her?" he questioned, then shrugged. "I'm a man and I may be angry and upset, but I'm not dead."

Bronwyn grabbed a clump of hay and threw it at his head.

He pinned her arms to her side. "Tell me what I said that night," he insisted.

"You don't remember!" How could he forget something that meant so much to her?

"All I remember is us screaming at each other, then I got on my horse. I don't even remember where I was going. Somewhere along the way I fell on the ground and slept. In the morning I realized I'd probably lost you through my idiocy, and so I decided to do something to try to win you back."

"Is that why you went to King Henry? To win me back?"

"I didn't do it for any other reason," he said. "I hate court. All that waste!"

She stared at him, then laughed. "You sound like a Scot."

"King Henry also said I was no longer English, that I sounded like a Scot."

She laughed and began to kiss him.

He pushed her away. "I still haven't had an answer from you. All the time I was at court I thought you were with my brothers. Gavin was so angry he refused to write me. I think he assumed I knew you'd walked out of his house that night I left. You and Miles scared them half to death, you know."

"But not you?" she asked. "What did you think when you found out I'd returned to Scotland?"

"I didn't have time to think!" he said in disgust. "Gavin, Raine, Miles, and Judith lectured me for days. When they got through, they stopped speaking to me."

"And all the time I was in Scotland, you didn't even send a message to me!"

"But *you* left *me!*" he half shouted. "You should have sent a message to me!"

"Stephen Montgomery!" she gasped. "I did not leave you. You've just said you rode to King Henry. Was I supposed to sit and wait for your return? What should I have told your family, that you preferred a fat trollop to me? And after the things you said!" She looked away from him.

He put his fingers on her chin and drew her face back so she looked at him. "I want to know what I said. What made you leave me? I know you, and if it'd been only the wench you wouldn't have left. You'd probably have taken a hot poker to her."

"She deserved torturing!" Bronwyn said hotly.

Stephen's tone was firm, almost cold. "I want to hear what you have to say."

Although he was above her, she looked away. The tears came to her eyes easily. She'd never cried so much in her life, she thought with disgust. "You said I was selfish, that I was too selfish to love. You said I hid behind my clan because I was afraid to grow up. You said . . . you were going to find a woman who wasn't cold and who could give you what you need."

Stephen's mouth dropped open in astonishment, then he started to laugh.

She looked up at him in shock. "I see nothing humorous in my faults," she said coldly.

"Faults!" he gasped amid his laughter. "Lord! I must have been very drunk! I didn't know anyone could get that drunk."

She tried to roll away from him. "I will not be laughed at! Perhaps it's my selfish nature that causes me to be unable to see the humor in your words."

Stephen pulled her back to him. She pushed him, and for a moment he let her win the struggle, then, still laughing, he pulled her back under him. "Bronwyn," he said seriously. "Listen to me. You are the most unselfish person I ever met. I have never seen anyone care so little for herself and so much for others the way you do. Didn't you realize that that's why I was so angry when you went over the side of the cliff? You had the power to order anyone else to go, or you could have done as Douglas advised and regarded Alex as dead. But not you! Not my dear, sweet laird. You thought only of the life of one of your clan members, not of yourself."

"But I was so afraid," she confessed.

"Of course you were! That just emphasizes your courage—and your unselfishness."

"But why . . . ?" she began.

"Why did I call you selfish? I guess because I was so hurt, because I love you so much and you didn't love me. And to tell the truth you sometimes make me feel very mortal. I'm afraid I don't have half your courage."

"Oh, Stephen, that's not true. You're very courageous. You took on four Englishmen with only a bow when we were at Kirsty's the first time. And it took great courage to give up your English clothes and become a Scot."

"Become a Scot?" he asked, one eyebrow raised. He was very serious. "Once you said you'd only love me if I became a Scot."

He waited but she made no answer. "Bronwyn, I love you, and the closest wish to my heart is that you love me also." He put his finger to her lips and gave her a threatening look. "And if you repeat all that about 'of course we're fond of each other,' I may break your pretty little neck."

"Of course I love you, you fool! Why do you think my stomach aches and my head swims when you're near? And it grows worse when you're far away. The only reason I went with Roger Chatworth was to prove to you that I wasn't selfish. I would have done anything to make you love me."

"Running off with my enemy is not likely to prove you love me," he said coldly, then he began to smile. "Are you saying you love me or that I make you ill?"

"Oh, Stephen," she laughed, realizing he believed in her. He didn't accuse her of sleeping with Roger Chatworth. He was beginning to master his jealousy!

Suddenly they both stopped and stared. A sharp movement in her stomach had been felt by both of them.

"What was that?" he asked.

"It felt like a kick," she said in wonder. "I think your child just kicked us."

Stephen rolled off her and reverently caressed her stomach. "Did you know about the baby when you left me?"

"I didn't leave you," she pointed out, "but yes, I knew about it."

He was quiet as he held his hand warmly against her bare stomach.

"Are you happy about our child?" she whispered.

"A little frightened perhaps. Judith lost her first child. I wouldn't want anything to happen to you."

She smiled at him. "How could anything happen with you around to protect me?"

"Protect you!" he exploded. "You never listen to me, never do anything I say. You drug me. You leave my family's protection in the middle of the night. You—"

She put her fingers to his lips. "But I love you. I love you very, very much and I need you. I need your strength, your level-headedness, your loyalty, and your peacemaking ways. You keep me and my clan from declaring war on our enemies. And you make us see that the English aren't all ignorant, greedy, lying—"

He gave her a soft kiss to quiet her. "Don't ruin it," he said sarcastically. "I love you too. I've loved you from the moment I saw you with your clan. I'd never seen a pretty woman, except Judith, who was any more than an ornament. It was a shock to see your men listen to you and see the way they respected you. It was the first time I saw you as something besides . . ."

Her eyes sparkled. "A good romp in bed?"

He laughed. "Oh, yes, most definitely that." He began to kiss her more seriously, his hands on her body.

"Stephen," she whispered as he kissed just behind her ear. "Tomorrow I meet with the MacGregor."

"That's nice," he murmured, moving down to her neck. "Very nice."

She moved her head so he could kiss her mouth.

Suddenly he jerked away from her. Rab gave a little bark of alarm. Stephen stared at his wife in horror. "You jest!"

She smiled sweetly. "I meet with the MacGregor at dawn tomorrow." She lifted her head and began kissing him again.

He rolled away, then jerked her upright. "Damn you!" he said through clenched teeth. "Are you starting again? No doubt the meeting is alone in some secret place."

"Of course it's alone. I can't very well ask my clan to accompany me. I intend to settle this war before I enter into it more fully."

Stephen closed his eyes for a moment and tried to calm himself. "You cannot meet this man alone. I forbid it."

Disbelief registered immediately on Bronwyn's face. "You what? You forbid it! How dare you! Do you forget that *I* am the MacArran? Just because I love you doesn't give you rights over my duties as chief."

"Will you shut up a minute?" he demanded. "You always believe I'm against you. Now listen to me. Who else knows of this meeting?"

"Harben is the only one. He arranged it. We were afraid to even tell Nesta that the time was set, for fear it'd get her hopes up."

"Get her hopes up!" he gasped. "Is that all you think of? Consideration for others?"

"You make it sound like something evil."

"In your case it sometimes is." He again tried to calm himself. "Bronwyn, don't you realize that you must, at times, think of yourself?"

"But I am! I want peace for my clan."

Stephen looked at her with great love. "All right, listen to me. Picture this if you will. You and the MacGregor meet in some lonely spot, no doubt in the fog, and the only person who knows about the meeting is Harben. What if the MacGregor decided to end his feud with the MacArrans by killing their laird?"

"That's insulting!" she gasped. "This is a peace meeting. The MacGregor wouldn't do that."

He held his hands heavenward as if for help. "I can't get you to see any middle ground, can I? Six months ago you hated everything about the MacGregor, and now you plan to turn your life over to the man."

"But what else can I do? If the MacGregor and I reach some sort of peaceful agreement, we can stop the killing. Isn't that what you wanted? Haven't you always said you wanted the feud ended? Our private war caused the death of your friend."

He grabbed her and hugged her to him. "Yes, I agree with you. I want all those things—but when I think of what it could cost! How could I let you go out there alone and meet with a man twice your size? He could kill you with one blow."

She lifted her head, but he pushed her down again.

"You won't go alone. I'm going with you."

"But you can't!" she exploded. "The message was for me to be alone."

"You already carry another person, so what does one more matter?"

"Stephen . . ." she pleaded.

"No!" He glared at her. "For once you're going to obey me, do you understand?"

She started to argue, but she knew it was no use. Truthfully, she was glad he was going with her. She lifted her face for his kiss.

He just touched his lips to hers then pulled away.

She looked up in surprise.

He nodded toward the window. "Unless I'm wrong, it's about an hour before sunrise now. I think we should leave."

"We couldn't spare even a few minutes?" she asked wistfully.

"You're a naughty child," he teased. "Now let's get dressed and go conquer the MacGregor as you've conquered me."

She lay back in the hay and watched him as he dressed quickly. Too soon was his strong body covered. And to think she once thought of him as her enemy! "You, my lord, are my conqueror," she sighed, then reluctantly began to dress.

They sobered as they saddled their horses and prepared for the short journey to the meeting place. Stephen considered locking Bronwyn in the barn and going alone, but she, seeming to sense his thoughts, refused to tell him where she was to meet the MacGregor.

The meeting place was as Stephen had thought—secluded, enclosed by rock, lonely-feeling with its heavy shroud of fog.

As soon as he dismounted, Stephen felt the point of a sword at the base of his neck. "And who are you?" the MacGregor growled.

"I came to protect her," Stephen answered. "Laird though she is, she doesn't meet men alone."

The MacGregor looked at Bronwyn, tall, slim, beautiful. She held the enormous dog in check as he threatened to attack the big man. The MacGregor laughed and sheathed his sword. "I don't blame you, boy. Though she might need protection for some reason other than the one you mean."

Stephen turned to meet the man eye to eye. "I'll protect her in all ways," he said with meaning.

The MacGregor laughed again. "Come over here and sit down. I've given this idea of peace some thought, and the only way I can see is to unite the clans in some way." He looked at Bronwyn as she sat down on a rock. "I'm not married any longer. Had I seen the MacArran earlier I would have offered for her."

Stephen stood behind his wife and put his hand possessively on her shoulder. "She's taken and I'll fight—"

"Stop it, both of you!" Bronwyn demanded, shrugging Stephen's hand away. "You're like two rutting stags clashing. Stephen, if you do not behave you'll have to return to Harben's."

The MacGregor laughed.

"And you, Lachlan! I'll have you know there's more to the MacArran than a face! If you can't deal with me on an intelligent level, perhaps you can send one of your chieftains."

It was Stephen's turn to laugh.

Lachlan MacGregor raised one eyebrow. "Perhaps I don't envy you after all, boy."

"She has compensations," Stephen added smugly.

Bronwyn wasn't listening to him. "Davey," she whispered.

Stephen stared at her as he began to understand what she meant. "He tried to kill us," he said quietly, but Bronwyn's look stopped him. He understood what she felt: blood was thicker than water.

He turned to the MacGregor. "She has an older brother, about twenty. The boy is going crazy with jealousy. Rather than stay in a clan where his younger sister is laird, he's hiding in the hills somewhere. Recently he made an attempt on our lives."

The MacGregor frowned, nodded his head. "I can understand the boy. I would have done the same thing."

"Understand him!" Bronwyn said. "I'm his laird. He should have accepted what our father said. I would have accepted him."

"Of course," Lachlan waved his hand. "But you're a woman." He ignored her sputters.

Stephen smiled warmly at the MacGregor.

"I have a daughter," Lachlan continued. "She's sixteen and a pretty little thing and as sweet and pliable as a woman can be." He gave one look at Bronwyn. "Perhaps we could arrange a marriage."

"What else do you offer him besides your insipid daughter?" Bronwyn asked levelly.

Lachlan winced before he answered. "He can't be laird, but he can be chieftain. It's more than he has now, and he'd be the laird's son-in-law."

"He's a hot-tempered lad," Stephen said. "That's why Jamie MacArran didn't name him as chief."

"You've never even met him!" Bronwyn said. "How do you know what he's like?"

"I listen," Stephen said in dismissal.

"I can handle him," Lachlan asserted. "I'll not die as early as Jamie did and leave the boy alone. I'll keep him with me always and teach him the right ways. I'd rather have an angry young man than a placid one. I can't abide a man, or woman," he smiled at Bronwyn, "with no spirit."

"I can vouch for the spirit of the MacArrans," Stephen laughed.

"I'll wager you can," the MacGregor chuckled. "This Davey should make my daughter happy if he's anything like his sister."

Stephen grew serious. "What will your clan say when you bring in a MacArran?"

"They'll not say anything to me, but they'll have a lot to say to young Davey. Let's hope he can handle it."

Bronwyn stiffened. "My brother can handle any Mac-Gregor."

Lachlan laughed, then put out his hand to Stephen. "It's settled then."

The MacGregor turned to her. "Now you, young woman, I owe you for a B I still carry on my shoulder." He grabbed her and kissed her on the mouth heartily.

Bronwyn looked quickly at her husband, worried about his jealousy, but Stephen was looking at them fondly. They stood together as Lachlan rode away. Bronwyn turned to him. "In the future I wish you'd remember that *I* am the MacArran, as I have shown you tonight."

Stephen smiled lazily. "I plan to change that."

"What is that supposed to mean?"

"Didn't I tell you I petitioned the king to change my name?"

Bronwyn stared at him stupidly.

"My name is now Stephen MacArran. Aren't you pleased?"

She threw her arms around his neck and began covering his face with kisses. "I love you, love you, love you! You are a MacArran! This will prove to my clan that you can be trusted."

Stephen hugged her and laughed. "They never doubted me. It was only you." He pulled her closer. "Bronwyn, we're not enemies any longer. Let's try to be on the same side."

"You're a MacArran," she whispered in awe.

He stroked her hair. "Everything will be all right now. I'll go find Davey and—"

"You!" She pulled away from him. "He's my brother!"

"The last time you saw him he tried to kill you!"

Bronwyn dismissed this. "He was angry then. All my family has a temper. He won't be angry when he hears my plan."

"Yours! I believe it was a joint effort."

"Possibly, but Davey will still only listen to me."

Stephen started to speak but then kissed her instead. "Could we continue this later? I suddenly feel something's come between us."

She looked up at him innocently. "My stomach?"

He grabbed her hair and pulled her head back. "How does it feel to kiss the MacArran?"

"*I* am the MacArran!" she said. "I . . ."

She couldn't say any more because Stephen's hand had slipped down to the back of her knees.

Velvet Song

PART I

The South of England

January 1502

Chapter 1

THE LITTLE village of Moreton was surrounded by a high stone wall, the gray of the stones casting a long, early-morning shadow over the many houses packed inside. Well-worn pathways connected the buildings, radiating out from the central position of the towering church and the tall white town hall. Now, in the dim light of the morning, a few dogs began to stretch, sleepy-eyed women lazily walked toward the town well and four men waited, with axes over their shoulders, while the gatekeepers opened the heavy oak gates in the stone wall.

Inside one house, a plain, narrow, two-story, white-washed house, Alyxandria Blackett listened with every pore of her body for the creak of the gates. When she heard it, she grabbed her soft leather shoes and began tiptoeing toward the stairs, which were, unfortunately, on the other side of her father's bedroom. She'd been dressed for hours, waking long before the sun rose, slipping a plain, rather coarse woolen dress over her slight figure. And today, for once, she didn't look down in disgust at her body. It seemed that all her life she'd been waiting to grow up, to gain some height and, most of all, to gain some curves. But at twenty she knew she was always going to be flat-chested and hipless. At least, she thought with a sigh, she had no need for corsets. In her father's room, she tossed him a quick glance to make sure that he was sleeping, flipped the wool of her skirt over her arm and started down, skipping the fourth step, as she knew it creaked badly.

Once downstairs she didn't dare open a window shutter. The sound might wake her father, and he very much needed his rest now. Skirting a table covered with papers and ink and a half-finished will her father was drafting, she went to the far wall, gazing up with love at the two musical instruments hanging there. All thoughts of self-pity for what God had forgotten in her physically disappeared when she thought of her music. Already a new tune was beginning to form in her head, a gentle, rolling melody. It was obviously a love song.

"Can't make up your mind?" came her father's voice from the foot of the stairs.

Instantly, she ran to him, put her arm around his waist and helped him sit at the table. Even in the dark room she could see the bluish circles under his eyes. "You should have stayed in bed. There's time enough to do a day's work without starting before daylight."

Catching her hand for a moment, he smiled up into her pretty eyes. He well knew what his daughter thought of her little elfin face with its tip-tilted violet eyes, tiny nose and curvy little mouth—he'd certainly heard her wail about it enough—but to him everything about her was dear. "Go on," he said, pushing her gently. "Go and see if you can choose which instrument to take and leave before someone comes and complains they must have a song for their latest love."

"Perhaps this morning I should stay with you," she whispered, her face showing her concern for him. Three times in the last year he'd had horrible pains in his heart.

"Alyx!" he warned. "Don't disobey me. Now gather your things and leave!"

"Yes, my lord," she laughed, giving what, to him, was a heart-melting smile, her eyes turning up at the corners, her mouth forming a perfect cupid's bow. With a swift, practiced gesture she pulled the long, steel-stringed cittern from the wall, leaving the psaltery where it was. Turning, she looked back at her father. "Are you sure you'll be all right? I don't have to leave this morning."

Ignoring her, he handed her her scholar's box, a lap desk containing pen, ink and paper. "I'd rather have you creating music than staying home with a sick old man. Alyx," he cautioned. "Come here." With a familiar gesture he began to plait her long hair into a fat braid down her back. Her hair was heavy and thick, perfectly straight without a hint of curl and the color was, even to her father, very odd. It was almost as if a child had thrown together every hair color possible on one very small young woman's head. There were streaks of gold, bright yellow, deep red, a golden red, mouse brown and, Alyx swore, even some gray.

When her hair was braided, he pulled her cloak from the wall, put it about her shoulders and tied the hood over her head. "Don't get so engrossed you forget to stay warm," he said with mock fierceness, turning her about. "Now go, and when you return I want to hear something beautiful."

"I'll do my best," she said, laughing as she left the house, closing the door behind her.

From their house at the very back of the town wall, directly across from the big gates, Alyx could see nearly all of the town as the people were beginning to stir and get ready to greet the day. There was a matter of inches between the houses and in the tiny alleyway that ran along the wall. Half-timbered and stone, brick and stucco houses sat side by side, ranging in size from the mayor's house down to the tiny houses of the craftsmen and, like her father's, the lawyers'. A bit of breeze stirred the air and the shop signs rattled.

"Good morning," a woman sweeping the gravel before her house called to Alyx. "Are you working on something for the church today?"

Slinging the cittern by its strap onto her back, she waved back at her neighbor. "Yes . . . and no. Everything!" She laughed, waving and hurrying toward the gate.

Abruptly, she stopped as she nearly ran into a cart horse. One look up showed her that John Thorpe had purposefully tried to trip her.

"Hoa, now, little Alyx, not a kind word for me?" He grinned as she sidestepped the old horse.

"Alyx!" called a voice from the back of the wagon. Mistress Burbage was emptying chamber pots into the honey wagon John drove. "Could you come inside for a moment? My youngest daughter is heartbroken, and I thought perhaps a new love song might make her well."

"Aye, and for me," John laughed from atop the wagon. "I have need of a love song, too," he said, ostentatiously rubbing his side where two nights before Alyx had given him a fierce pinch when he'd tried to kiss her.

"For you, John," she said very sweetly, "I'll write a song as sweet as the honey in your wagon." The sound of his laughter almost hid her answer to Mistress Burbage that she'd see her after evening mass.

With a gasp, Alyx began to run toward the gate. In another few moments she'd get caught and would never get her time alone, outside the walls, to work on her music.

"Ye're late, Alyx," the gatekeeper said, "and don't forget the sweet music for my sick babe," he called after her as she ran toward the orchards outside the walls.

Finally, she reached her favorite apple tree and, with a laugh of sheer happiness, opened the little desk and set about preparing to make a record of the music she heard in her head. Sitting down, leaning back against, the tree, she pulled her cittern across her lap and began to strum the tune she'd heard this morning. Totally absorbed, working with melody and lyrics, recording on paper the notes, she was unaware of the hours passing. When she came up for air, her shoulders stiff, fingers sore, she had written two songs and started on a new psalm for the church.

With a long, exuberant stretch, she set aside her cittern, rose and, one hand on a low, bare branch of the apple tree, gazed out across the fields of crops, past them to the earl's enclosed sheep pastures.

No! she would not let herself think of the earl, who'd pushed so many farmers from the land by raising their rents and then fencing it and filling the space with his profitable sheep. Think of something pleasant, she commanded herself, turning to look the other way. And, of course, what else was there really beautiful in life besides music?

As a child she'd always heard music in her head. While the priest droned on in Latin at Mass, she'd occupied her mind with creating a song for the boys' choir. At the Harvest Festival she wandered away, preoccupied with songs only she could hear. Her father, a widower for years, had been nearly insane trying to find his lost child.

One day when she was ten, she'd gone to the well to draw water. A troubadour visiting the town had been sitting with a young woman on a bench, and beside the well, unattended, was his lute. Alyx had never touched any musical instrument before, but she'd heard enough and seen enough to know basically how to make a lute play. Within minutes, she'd plucked out one of the hundreds of tunes chorusing through her head. She was on her fourth song before she realized the troubadour was beside her, his courting forgotten. Silently, without a word between them, needing only the language of music, he had shown her how to place her fingers for the chords. The pain of the sharp strings cutting into her small, tender fingertips was nothing compared to her joy at being able to hear her music outside her mind.

Three hours later, when her father, with a resigned air, went to look for his daughter, he found her surrounded by half the townspeople, all of them whispering that they were seeing a miracle. The priest, seeing a wonderful possibility, took her to the church and set her before the virginals. After a few minutes of experimenting, Alyx began to play, badly at first, a magnificat, a song of praise to the church, softly speaking the words as she played.

Alyx's father was thoroughly relieved that his only child wasn't light in the head after all, that it was just so filled with music that sometimes she didn't respond to everything said to her. After that momentous day, the priest took over Alyx's training, saying her gift was from God and as God's spokesman, he would take charge of her. He didn't need to add that as a lawyer, her father was far away from God's holiness and the less she associated with such as him, the better.

There followed four years of rigorous training in which the priest managed the loan of every instrument created for Alyx to learn to play. She played the keyboard instruments, horns, strings with and without a bow, drums, bells and the huge pipe organ the priest shamed the town into buying for the Lord (and for him and Alyx, some said).

When the priest was sure she could play, he sent for a Franciscan monk who taught her how to write music, to record the songs, ballads, masses, litanies, whatever she could set to music.

Because she was so busy playing instruments and writing down notes, it wasn't until she was fifteen that anyone realized she could sing. The monk, who was nearly ready to return to his abbey, since Alyx had learned all he could teach her, walked into the church very early one morning and was surrounded by a voice so powerful he could feel the buttons on his cloak trembling. When he was able to convince himself that this magnificent sound came from his very small pupil, he fell to his knees and began to give thanks to God for letting him have contact with such a blessed child.

Alyx, when she saw the old monk on his knees at the back of the church, holding his cross tightly, tears running down his face, stopped singing immediately and ran to him, hoping he wasn't ill, or, as she suspected, offended at her singing, which she knew was dreadfully loud.

After that, as much attention was paid to her voice as to her playing and she began to arrange choral groups, using every voice in the little walled-off town.

Suddenly, she was twenty years old, expecting any day to grow up and, she desperately hoped, out. But she stayed little, and flat, while the other girls her age married and had babies, and Alyx had to be content to sing the lullabies she'd written to teething infants.

What right did she have to be discontent, she thought now, hanging onto the apple tree? Just because the young men all treated her with great respect—except, of course, John Thorpe, who too often smelled like what he hauled—was no reason to be discontent. When she was sixteen and of marriageable age and not so old as now, four men had offered her marriage, but the priest said her music was a sign that she was meant for God's work and not some man's lust and therefore refused to allow any marriage. Alyx, at the time, was relieved, but the older she got, the more she was aware of her loneliness. She loved her music and especially loved what she did for the church, but sometimes . . . like two summers ago when she'd had four glasses of very strong wine at the mayor's daughter's wedding, she grabbed her cittern, stood on a table and sang a very, very bawdy song, which she made up as she went along. Of course, the priest would have stopped her, but since he'd had more wine than anyone else and was rolling in the grass, holding his stomach with laughter at Alyx's song, he certainly wasn't capable of stopping anyone. That had been a wonderful evening, when she'd been a part of the people she'd known all her life, not something set aside by the priest's command, rather like a holy bit of St. Peter's skull in the church, awe inspiring but far from touchable.

Now as she always did, she began to turn her thoughts to song. Breathing deeply, spacing her breath as she'd been taught, she began a ballad of life's loneliness, of a young woman seeking her own true love.

"And here I am, little songbird," came a man's voice from behind her.

So intent on singing—and, indeed, her voice would have covered the sound—she had not heard the young men on horseback approaching. There were three of them, all big, strong, healthy, lusty as only the nobility could be, their faces flushed from what she guessed to be a night of revelry. Their clothes, the fine velvets and fur linings with a jewel winking here and there, were things she'd seen only on the church altar. Dazed, she looked up at them, didn't even move when the largest blond man dismounted.

"Come, serf," he said, and his breath was foul. "Don't you even know your own lord? Allow me to introduce myself. Pagnell, soon to be Earl of Waldenham."

The name brought Alyx alive. The great, greedy, ugly

Waldenham family drained the village farmers of every cent they had. When they had no more, the farmers were thrown off the land, left to die wandering the country, begging for their bread.

Alyx was just about to open her mouth to tell this foul young man what she thought of him when he grabbed her, his hideous mouth descending on hers, his tongue thrusting, making her gag.

"Bitch!" he gasped when she clamped her teeth down on his tongue. "I'll teach you who is the master." With one grasp, he tore her cloak away and instantly his hand was at the collar of her dress, tearing easily, exposing one small, vulnerable shoulder and the top of her breast.

"Shall we throw such a small fish back?" he taunted over his shoulder to his friends, who were dismounting.

The reference to her lack of physical endowment above the waist was what changed Alyx's fear to anger. Although she may have been born this man's social inferior, her talent had caused her to be treated as no one's inferior. In a gesture none of the men expected, Alyx pulled up her skirt, raised her leg and viciously kicked Pagnell directly between the legs. The next instant pandemonium broke loose. Pagnell bent double in pain while his companions desperately tried to hear what he was saying as they were still much too drunk to fully comprehend what was going on.

Not sure where she was going or in which direction, Alyx began to run. Her lung power from her many years of breathing exercises held her in good stead. Across cold, barren fields she ran, stumbling twice, trying to hold her torn gown together, the skirt away from her feet.

At the second fence, the hated sheep enclosure, she stopped, slumped against the post, tears running down her face. But even through tears she could see the three horsemen as they combed the area looking for her.

"This way!" came a voice to her left. "This way!"

Looking up, she saw an older man on horseback, his clothes as rich and fine as Pagnell's. With the look of a trapped animal, she began to run again, away from this new man who pursued her.

Easily, he caught up with her, pacing beside her on his horse. "The boys mean no harm," he said. "They're just high-spirited and had a little too much to drink last night. If you'll come with me I'll get you away from them, hide you somewhere."

Alyx wasn't sure if she should trust him. What if he handed her over to those lecherous, drunken noblemen?

"Come on, girl," the man said. "I don't want to see you hurt."

Without another thought, she took the hand offered to her. He hauled her into the saddle before him and kicked the horse into a gallop, heading toward the faraway line of trees.

"The King's forest," Alyx gasped, holding onto the saddle for dear life. No commoner was allowed to enter the King's forest, and she'd seen several men hanged for taking rabbits from it.

"I doubt Henry will mind just this once," the man said.

As soon as they were inside the forest, he lowered her from his horse. "Now go and hide and do not leave this place until the sun is high. Wait until you see other serfs out about their business, then return to your walls."

Wincing once at his calling her, a freewoman, a serf, she nodded and ran deeper into the forest.

Noon took a very long time in coming, and while she waited in the dark, cold forest in a torn dress without her cloak, she became fully aware of her terror at what could have happened at the hands of the nobles. Perhaps it was her training by the priest and the monk that made her believe the nobles had no right to use her people as they wished. She had a right to peace and happiness, had a right to sit under a tree and play her music, and God gave no one the power to take such a thing away from another person.

After only an hour her anger kept her warm. Of course, she knew her anger came partly from a happening last summer. The priest had arranged for the boys' chorus and Alyx to sing in the earl's—Pagnell's father's—private chapel. For weeks they'd worked, Alyx always trying to perfect the music, driving herself to exhaustion rehearsing. When at last they had performed, the earl, a fat man ridden with gout, had said loudly he liked his women with more meat on them and for the priest to bring her back when she could entertain him somewhere besides church. He left before the service was finished.

When the sun was directly overhead, Alyx crept to the edge of the forest and spent a long time studying the countryside, seeing if she saw anyone who resembled a nobleman. Tentatively, she slowly made her way back to her apple tree— hers no longer, as now it would carry too many ugly memories.

There Alyx suffered her greatest shock, for broken into shreds and splinters lay her cittern, obviously trampled and retrampled by horses' hoofs. Quick, hot tears of anger, hate, frustration, helplessness welled up through her body, spilling down her cheeks unheeded. How could they? she raged, kneeling, picking up a piece of wood. When her lap was full of splinters she saw the uselessness of what she was doing and with all her might began to fling the pieces against the tree.

Dry eyed, shoulders back, she started for the safety of her town, her anger capped for the moment but still very close to the surface.

Chapter 2

THE BIG room of the manor house was hung with brilliant tapestries, the empty spaces covered with weapons of every kind. The heavy, massive furniture was scarred, gouged from ax blades and sword cuts. At the big table sat three young men, their eyes heavily circled from a short life of little sleep and much wine.

"She bested you, Pagnell," laughed one of the men, filling his wine cup, sloshing it on his dirty sleeve. "She beat you, then disappeared like the witch she is. You heard her sing. That wasn't a human voice but one meant to entice you to her and when you went—" He stopped, slammed his fist into his palm and laughed loudly.

Pagnell put his foot on the man's chair and pushed, sending man and chair sprawling. "She's human," he growled, "and not worth my time."

"Pretty eyes," one of the other men said. "And that voice. You think when you stuck it in her, she'd cry out in some note that'd curl the hairs on your legs?"

The first man laughed, righting his chair. "Romantic! I'd make her sing me a song about what she'd like me to do to her."

"Quiet, both of you," Pagnell growled, draining his wine. "I tell you she was human, nothing more."

The other men said nothing and sat silently for a moment, but when a servant girl passed through the room, Pagnell grabbed her. "In the village, there's a girl who can sing. Who is she?"

The servant girl tried to twist away from his painful grip. "That's Alyx," she whispered.

"Stop twisting or I'll break it," Pagnell commanded. "Now tell me exactly where this Alyx lives inside your beastly little town."

An hour later, in the dark night, Pagnell and his three cohorts were outside the walled village of Moreton, tossing pronged, steel hooks to the top of the wall. After three tries, two hooks held, their attached ropes hanging down the wall to the ground. With much less expertise than if they'd been sober, the three men pulled themselves up the ropes to the top of the wall, pausing for a moment before retrieving the hooks and ropes and lowering themselves down to the ground in the narrow alleyway behind the closely packed houses.

Pagnell raised his arm, motioning for the men to follow him as he quietly went to the front of the houses, his eyes searching the street signs hanging over the silent houses. "A witch!" he muttered angrily. "I'll show them how mortal she is. The daughter of a lawyer, the scum of the earth."

At Alyx's house he paused, slipping quickly to the side of it and a latched shutter. One strong blow, one quick sound and the shutter was open and he was inside.

Upstairs, Alyx's father lay quietly, his hands clutching at his breast, at the pains starting there once again. At the sound of the shutter giving, he gasped, not at first believing what he heard. There had been no robberies in town for years.

Quickly striking flint and tinder, he lit a candle and started down the stairs. "What do you ruffians think you're doing?" he demanded loudly as Pagnell helped his friend through the window.

They were the last words he uttered for in a second, Pagnell was across the room, his hand on the old man's hair, a dagger digging deeply as he slashed the man's throat. Without even a second glance to the body as it thudded lifelessly to the floor, he went back to his friends at the window. When they were through, he started up the stairs.

Alyx had not been able to sleep after the day's ordeal. Every time she closed her eyes she saw Pagnell, smelled his horrible breath, felt his tongue in her mouth. She'd somehow been able to keep what had happened from her father, not wanting to worry him, but for the first time in her life something besides music occupied her thoughts.

So upset was she that at first she did not hear the sounds below stairs, only becoming aware of her surroundings when she heard her father's angry voice and the odd thud that followed.

"Robbers!" she gasped, flinging back the woolen covers to stand nude in the room. Quickly, she grabbed her dress, pulling it over her head. Why would anyone want to rob them? They were too poor to be worth robbing. The Lyon belt! she thought, perhaps they've heard of that. Opening a small wall cupboard, she expertly lifted the false bottom and removed the only thing of value she owned, a gold belt, and fastened it about her waist.

A noise in her father's room startled her as footsteps came toward her room. Grabbing a stool and a heavy iron candlestick, she positioned herself behind the door, waiting breathlessly.

The door on its leather hinges opened very slowly, and when Alyx had a good clear shot at the foreign head, she brought down the candlestick with all her might.

Crumpling at her feet was Pagnell, his eyes open for just an instant, seeing her before falling unconscious.

The sight of him, this nobleman, in her little house, renewed her terror of the afternoon. This was no ordinary robbery, and where was her father? More footsteps, heavy ones, pounding up the stairs, brought her to her senses. After one desperate glance, she knew the window was her only means of escape. Running to it, she didn't give a thought to how high she was when she lowered herself and jumped.

The fall slammed her into the ground, where she rolled back against the wall, stunned, breathless for a full terrifying minute. There was no time to lie in the dirt and try to collect herself. Limping, a pain in her side and left leg, she hobbled toward the side of her house where a shutter gaped open.

The moonlight was not a good source of light, but lying beside her father in a tilted candlestick holder was a glowing candle—all she needed to see clearly the great gaping hole in her father's throat, his head lying in a pool of his own blood.

Dazed, Alyx left the window and began to walk away from her house. She didn't notice the cold air on her arms, the chill piercing through her crudely woven wool gown. No longer did she care about Pagnell or what he intended to do to her, what he took from her house, because he had already taken all he could. Her father, the one person who had loved her not because she was a musician but just because he liked her, was dead. What more could the nobleman take than that?

Walking, not seeing where she was going, she finally half fell, half collapsed in front of the church, on her knees, her hands clasped, and began praying for her father's soul, that he be received in Heaven with all the welcome he deserved.

Perhaps it was the years of training Alyx had received that made her able to concentrate so single-mindedly, or perhaps it was her grief, but she heard nothing of the turmoil that went on about her, neither, saw nor heard the crackling flames that consumed her house and cremated her father's lifeless body. The constant fear of fire within the walls brought most of the citizens from their houses, and in their terror they did not see Alyx's slight form huddled in the recessed door of the church.

At first light, the gates were opened, and waiting outside were six armored knights bearing the emblem of the Earl of Waldenham. The great stallions' hoofs cut into the narrow paths between the houses, the knights slashing with two-handed swords at any sign or roof projection that got in their way as they moved slowly, possessively, through the town. Women grabbed their children away from the dangerous horses, holding them, paralyzed, as they watched these massive, formidable, helmeted men make their way through the peaceful town.

The knights paused at the smoldering ruins of the Blackett

house and the leader pulled a parchment from his saddle, nailing it to one standing, charred post. Without lifting his helmet, he looked down from atop his tall horse to the wide-eyed, frightened townspeople. With one swift gesture he took the lance he carried and deftly speared a dog, tossing the instantly killed body into the ashes.

"Read this and beware!" he said in a growl that reverberated off the stone walls of the town.

Without heed for the townspeople, the men kicked their horses forward and thundered out of the town, taking the opposite side, destroying yet another road before they vanished through the gates, leaving a stunned populace behind them.

It was some moments before anyone recovered enough to look toward the paper nailed to the post and the priest, who was able to read, stepped forward. He took his time in the reading of the parchment, and the townspeople were silent while they waited. When at last the priest turned, his face was white, drawn.

"Alyx," he began slowly. "Alyxandria Blackett has been accused of heresy, witchcraft and thievery. The Earl of Waldenham says the girl used her devil-given voice to entice his son, and when he tried to resist her, she profaned the church. At his further resistance, she smote him with her evil powers and robbed him."

For a moment, no one could even breathe. Alyx's voice given by the devil? Perhaps she was astonishingly gifted, but surely God had given her her ability. Didn't she use her voice in praise of the Lord? Of course, there were some songs she created that were far removed from church music, perhaps . . .

As one, they looked up as they saw Alyx walk across the ground that separated her house from the back of the church, saw her stumble slightly over a torn piece of earth cut by the knights' horses. With puzzled expressions, some with doubt on their faces, they parted to let her pass. She stood still and silent, gazing at what had been her house.

"Come, my child," the priest said quickly, his arm about her shoulders, as he half pulled her to the parish house. Once inside, he began to work quickly, tossing bread and cheese into a canvas bag. "Alyx, you must leave this place."

"My father," she said quietly.

"I know, we saw his body inside the flames. Hush, now, he was already dead, and I will say twenty-five Masses for his soul. We must worry about you now."

When he saw she wasn't really listening, he gave her a sharp shake, making her head snap back. "Alyx! You must listen to me." As a light began to come back into her eyes, he told her about the notice for her arrest. "There is a reward for you, either dead or alive."

"Reward?" she whispered. "Of what value am I?"

"Alyx, you are of great value, but you have angered an earl for some reason. I have not told anyone of the reward, but they will soon find out and they will not all protect you. Some greedy cur will be only too willing to give you away for the reward."

"Then let them! I am innocent and the king—"

The priest's laugh cut her off as he wrapped her in a heavy, too long cloak. "You would be found guilty and the best you could hope for is a hanging. I want you to go now and wait for me at the edge of the King's forest. Tonight I will come for you, and I hope I will have a plan that we can use. Go now, Alyx, and quickly. Let as few people see you as possible. I will come tonight and bring you an instrument and more food. Perhaps we can find a way for a young girl to earn her keep."

Before Alyx could reply to what was happening, she was pushed out the door, the bag of food about her shoulder, her hands holding the long cloak up. She hurried toward the gate, making no attempt to hide, but since nearly all the townspeople were still gathered at the ruins of Alyx's house, no one saw her.

Once in the forest, she sat down, exhausted, grief-ridden, her mind unable to comprehend or believe the events of the last few hours. An hour passed in which the image of her dead father stayed fixed before her eyes and she remembered their life together, the way he'd cared for her. At last, after a night of prayer and a hideous morning, she began to cry, and cry, and cry, and wrapping the cloak over her head, huddling down into a tight little ball, she gave vent to her grief. After a long while, her tired muscles began to relax and she fell asleep, still shaking, buried under the folds of the cloak.

It was close to sunset when she woke, her muscles aching, her left leg hurt from her jump from the window, her head throbbing. Carefully, she pushed back the wool from her face only to see a man sitting on a log not far from her. With a frightened gasp, she looked about for a way to escape.

"There's no need to run from me," the man said gently, and his voice made her recognize him. He was the servant of Pagnell, the one who'd helped her escape the nobleman yesterday.

"Did you come for the reward?" she asked with a half sneer. "Perhaps I will tell how you helped me before. I don't think your master will like that."

To her surprise the man chuckled. "Have no fear of me, child," he said. "Your priest and I have had a good long talk while you slept and we have a plan for you. If you are willing to listen I think we can hide you well enough that no one will find you."

Nodding curtly, she looked at him, waiting for him to continue. As his plan unfolded, her eyes widened in a mixture of horror, fear and some feeling of anticipation at the prospect of adventure.

The servant had a brother who had once been a soldier for the king, but since the man had had the misfortune to live through all his battles to an old age, he'd been discharged from service with no means to support himself. For two years he had wandered alone, nearly starving until he happened on one of a band of outlaws, misfits and out-of-works who made their life in a vast forest just north of the town of Moreton.

For a moment, Alyx sat quietly. "Are you proposing I join this band?" she asked in disbelief. "As an . . . an outlaw?"

The servant understood her outrage. The priest had been full of praise for the girl's good qualities. "Yes and no," he answered. "A young girl such as yourself would not be safe with the band. For all they have a leader now and there is a measure of Christian goodness among them and some discipline, still a little thing like you would not last long."

With a sigh of relief, Alyx gave a little smile.

"And, too," he continued, "no one would hesitate to take you to the earl for the reward."

"I can sing. Perhaps someone would hire—"

Putting up his hand, he cut her off. "Only the nobles can afford their own musicians, or perhaps some rich merchant, but there again, a lone girl, unprotected . . ."

Dejected, Alyx's shoulders slumped. Was there anywhere safe for her?

When the servant saw that she was aware of the problem of hiding her, he went on with his plan quickly. "If you became a boy, you could hide with the outlaws. With your hair cut and boy's clothes, perhaps a binding about your chest, you might pass. The priest says you can change your voice at will, and your looks might well suit a boy as well as a girl."

Alyx wasn't sure she should laugh or cry at his last remark. It was true that she was no classic beauty with full lips and big blue eyes, but she liked to think . . .

"Come now," the servant chuckled, "there's no need to look like that. I'm sure when you reach an age, you'll fill out and look almost as lovely as a lady."

"I'm twenty years old," she said, eyes narrowed.

The servant cleared his throat in embarrassment. "Then you should be grateful for your looks. Now, come on, for it grows dark. I brought some boy's clothes, and when you're ready, we'll travel. I want to be back before I'm missed. The earl likes to know where his servants are."

This idea that she might be endangering him made her move quickly, taking the folded clothes he offered. At the touch of the cloth, she paused for just a moment before fleeing to the trees to change. It took only seconds to rid herself of the dress she wore, but the boy's garments were unfamiliar. Tightly woven cotton knit hose covered her legs up to her waist, where she tied them snugly. A cloth came next, and she tried not to give a sigh of disgust when she realized she needed very little binding to flatten her breasts. A cotton shirt, fine and soft, went on, a heavier wool shirt with wide sleeves over that and, on top, a long doublet of sturdy, closely woven wool. The doublet came to the bottom curve of her buttocks and was beautifully trimmed with gold scrollwork. Never had she had such rich clothing next to her skin, and she could feel the raw places, rubbed by her woolen dress, beginning to heal. And the freedom of the boy's clothes! she thought as she kicked high with first one leg and then the other.

Slipping on knee-high boots, lacing them at the sides of her ankles, she lifted her gold belt from the heap of her dress and hid the belt about her waist, under doublet and wool shirt. Ready at last, tying an embroidered sash about her waist, she went out to where the earl's servant waited for her.

"Good!" he said, turning her about, inspecting her, frowning at her legs, which were just a little too fine looking for a boy's. "Now for your hair." He took a pair of shears from a pouch at her side.

Alyx took a step backwards, her hand on her long, straight hair. It had never been cut in her life.

"Come on," the man urged. "It's getting late. It's only hair, girl. It will grow again. Better to cut your hair than have it burned, with your head, in a witch's fire."

With fortitude, Alyx turned her back to the man and let him have access to her hair. Surprisingly, as it fell away, her head felt strangely light and not at all unpleasant.

"Look at it curl," the man said, trying to please her, to make light of her horrible situation. When he'd finished, he turned her around, nodding in approval at the curls and waves that clouded about her puckish little face. He thought to himself that the short hair and the boy's clothes suited her better than the ugly dress she'd worn.

"Why?" she asked, looking at him. "You work for the man who killed my father, so why are you helping me?"

"I've been with the lad"—she knew he meant Pagnell—"since he was a babe. He's always had all he wanted, and his father's taught him to take what he should not have. I have tried at times to make amends for the boy's misdeeds. Are you ready?" He obviously didn't want to discuss the subject anymore.

Alyx rode behind the man on the gentle horse and they set off, staying at the edge of the forest, toward the north. All through the ride the servant lectured her on how she must act to keep her secret. She must walk as a boy, shoulders back, taking long strides. She mustn't cry or laugh in a silly way, must swear, mustn't bathe overmuch, must scratch and spit and not be afraid to work, to lift and tote, or turn up her nose at dirt and spiders. On and on he went until Alyx nearly fell asleep, which cost her another lecture on the softness of girls.

When they arrived at the edge of the forest where the outlaws hid, he gave her a dagger to wear at her side to protect herself and told her to practice the use of it.

Once they entered the dark, forbidding forest, he stopped talking and Alyx could feel the tension run through his body. She found that her hands, gripping the edge of the saddle, were white knuckled.

The call of a night bird came softly to them and the servant answered it. Farther into the forest another call and answer were exchanged, and the servant stopped, setting Alyx down and dismounting. "We will wait here until morning," he said in a voice that was almost a whisper. "They will want to find out who we are before they let us enter their camp. Come, boy," he said louder. "Let's sleep."

Alyx found she could not sleep but instead lay still under the blanket the servant gave her and went over in her mind all that had happened, that because of some nobleman's whim she was here alone in this cold, frightful forest while her dear father's life had been cut short. As she thought, anger began to replace her fear as well as her grief. She would overcome this problem and someday, somehow, she'd revenge herself on Pagnell and all of his kind.

At first light, they were back on the horse and slowly made their way deeper and deeper into the maze of the forest.

Chapter 3

AFTER A very long time of tiptoeing through the tangle of trees and undergrowth, following no path that Alyx could see, she began to hear voices, quiet voices, mostly male. "I hear the men talking," she whispered.

The servant gave her a look of disbelief over his shoulder, for he heard nothing but the wind. It was quite some time before he, too, heard the voices.

Suddenly, surprisingly, a deep tangle of growth parted and before them was a small village of tents and crude shelters. A gray-haired man, a deep, old scar running from his temple, down his cheek, his neck and disappearing into his collar, caught the reins of the horse.

"You had no trouble, brother?" the scarred man asked, and when his brother nodded, he looked at Alyx. "This the lad?"

She held her breath under his scrutiny, fearing he'd see her for female, but he dismissed her as not of importance.

"Raine is waiting for you," the scarred man said to his brother. "Leave the boy with him and I'll ride out with you and you can give me the news."

With a nod, the servant reined his horse toward the direction in which his brother pointed.

"He didn't think I wasn't a boy," Alyx whispered, half pleased, half insulted. "And who is Raine?"

"He's the leader of this motley group. He's only been here

a couple of weeks, but he's been able to whip some order into the men. If you plan to stay here you must obey him at all times or he'll have you out on your ear."

"The king of the outlaws," she said somewhat dreamily. "He must be very fierce. He isn't a . . . a murderer, is he?" she gasped.

The servant looked back at her, laughing at her girlish changes in mood, but when he saw her face, he stopped and followed her mesmerized gaze straight ahead of them.

Sitting on a low stool, his shirt off, sharpening his sword, was the man who was unmistakably the leader of any group of men in his presence. He was a big man, very large, with great bulging muscles, a deep thick chest, thighs straining against the black knit hose he wore. That he should be shirtless in January in the cold, sunless forest was astonishing, but even this far away Alyx could see that he was covered with a fine sheen of sweat.

His profile was handsome: a fine nose, black, black hair, sweat dampened into curls along his neck, deep set serious eyes under heavy black brows, a mouth set into a firm line as he concentrated on the whetstone before him and the sharpening of the sword.

Alyx's first impression was that her heart might stop beating. She'd never seen a man like this one, from whom power came as if it were the sweat glistening on his body. People often said she had power in her voice, and she wondered if it was like the power of this man, an aura surrounding all of his enormous, magnificent body.

"Close your mouth, girl," the servant chuckled, "or you'll give yourself away. His lordship won't take to a lad drooling on his knees."

"Lordship?" Alyx asked, coming up for air. "Lordship!" she gasped and reason came back to her. It wasn't power she saw coming from this man, it was his sense that all the world belonged to him. Generations of men like Pagnell had reproduced themselves to create men like the one before her—arrogant, prideful, sure that everyone was destined to be their personal servant, taking what they wanted, even an old, ailing lawyer who got in their way. Alyx was in this cold forest and not at home practicing her music where she belonged because of men like this one who sat on a stool and waited for others to come to him.

The man turned, looking up at them with blue eyes, serious eyes that missed little of what he saw. As if he were a king on a throne, Alyx thought, and indeed he made the rough stool look like a throne, waiting for his lowly subjects to approach. So this was why she had to dress as a boy! This man with his lordly, superior ways, demanding that everyone bow and scrape before him, bend down so he could place his jeweled shoes on their behinds. He was the leader of this group of outlaws and murderers, and how had he gotten that dubious honor? No doubt from all of them believing in the natural superiority of the nobility; that this man, because of his birth, had the *right* to command them and they, as stupid as criminals must be, did not question his authority, merely asked how low they should grovel before his lordship.

"That's Raine Montgomery," the servant said, not seeing the way Alyx's eyes hardened, a great change from her original softness. "The king has declared him a traitor."

"And no doubt he well deserves the title," she spat, still watching Raine as they drew nearer to the man, his strength seeming to pull them toward him.

The servant glanced at her in surprise. "He was once a favorite of King Henry's and was leading men to the king's own Wales when Lord Raine heard that his sister had been taken prisoner by Lord Roger Chatworth and—"

"A feud among themselves!" she snapped. "And no doubt many innocent men were killed to feed these nobles' taste for blood."

"No one was killed," the man said, bewildered by her attitude. "Lord Roger threatened to kill Lord Raine's sister, so Lord Raine retreated; but King Henry declared him a traitor for using the king's own men in a personal war."

"Lords!" Alyx snarled. "There is only one Lord and King Henry was right to declare the man a traitor, since he well deserved the title for using our good king's men for his own personal fight. So now he hides in the forest using the ruffians as his subjects. Tell me, does he kill them at will or is he content with having them serve his dinner to him on silver platters?"

At that the servant laughed, at last understanding her hostility toward Lord Raine. No doubt the only noblemen she'd met were Pagnell and his father. Using them as criteria, she had reason to despise Lord Raine.

"Come sit down," Raine said, taking the reins and looking up at the weary man on the horse.

Alyx's first thought was: He can sing! Any man with such a deep, rich voice had to be able to sing. But the next instant her kind thoughts were gone.

"Step down here, boy, and let's have a look at you," Raine said. "You look a bit thin to me. Can you do a day's work?"

Alyx had never ridden astride a horse before, and the new exercise had made the inside of her legs stiff and sore. When she tried to swing off the top of the horse with at least a bit of bravado, her hateful legs refused to obey, and the left one, still hurt from her fall, collapsed under her.

Raine placed a steadying hand on her upper arm, and to Alyx's chagrin her body reacted instantly to this man who represented everything she hated. "Get your hand off me!" she snarled at him, seeing the surprised look on his handsome face before she had to grab the saddle of the horse to keep from falling. The stupid horse shied away, causing Alyx to stumble again before she could right herself.

"Now, if you are quite finished," Raine said, his blue eyes alight, that delicious voice of his running across her like melted honey, "perhaps we can find out something about you."

"This is all you need to know about me, nobleman!" she hissed, drawing the knife at her side, pointing it at him, despising his easy assurance that she meant nothing while he was God's gift to the earth.

Completely startled by the boy's hostility, Raine was unprepared for the sharp little dagger lunging at him and barely had time to move away before it cut, not where it aimed, his heart, but the top of his arm.

Stunned at what she'd done, Alyx stood still, her eyes fastened to the slow trickle of blood coming from the man's bare arm. Never in her life had she hurt anyone before.

But she didn't have long to think on her rash act because before she could begin to apologize, or before she could even blink an eye, Raine Montgomery had grabbed the seat of her pants and her collar and sent her sliding, face down, across about half an acre of forest floor. She should have closed her gaping mouth because her lower teeth acted as a shovel and collected bushels of leaves, dirt and whatever other filth made the spongy floor.

"Now, you young devil!" Raine said from his place behind her.

Sitting up, using both hands and furiously gouging handfuls of Heaven-knows-what from her mouth, wincing at her sore leg, she looked up to see him standing at what seemed to be quite a distance from her. Between them was a deep, scoured path that had been made by Alyx's body. And what she saw renewed her anger. Raine Montgomery, that vile nobleman, was surrounded by a disreputable looking crew of men and women, all laughing, showing black, rotten teeth, choking on their tongues, generally enjoying her agony. Raine himself was laughing harder than anyone, and the sight of deep, long dimples in his cheeks emphasizing his mirth did nothing for her temperament.

"Come on," said a voice beside her, the man who'd brought her, as he helped her stand. "Hold your tongue or he may toss you out altogether."

Alyx started to speak but paused to remove a piece of stick from its hiding place between her gum and cheek and missed her chance.

The man used this opportunity to speak to Raine, his fingers biting warningly into Alyx's arm, fairly shouting to be heard over the raucous laughter. "My lord, please forgive the lad. Yesterday a nobleman killed his father and burned his house. He has reason to hate and I fear it extends to all men of your class."

Instantly, Raine sobered and looked at Alyx with sympathy, which made her stiffen and look away. She did not want his pity.

"What nobleman did this?" Raine asked, his voice full of concern.

"The Earl of Waldenham's son."

Spitting in pure disgust, Raine's face twisted for a moment, his fine lips curling into a snarl. "Pagnell," he said, his voice full of contempt. "The man doesn't deserve the title of man or nobleman. Come with me, boy, and I will teach you we're not all cut of the same cloth. I need a squire and you will do nicely."

In two steps he was beside her, his arm companionably about her shoulders.

"Do not touch me," she gasped, jumping away from him. "I do not need your pity or the soft job of serving your sweet cakes. I am . . . a man and I can hold my own. I will work and earn my keep."

"Sweet cakes, is it?" Raine asked as a dimple flashed in his left cheek. "I have a feeling, boy," he said, looking her up and down, "you have no idea what work is. You have legs and arms more suited for a girl."

"How dare you insult me so!" she gasped, scared that she was going to be revealed at any moment, grabbing for her dagger but finding only an empty sheath.

"Another of your mistakes," Raine said. "You dropped it to the ground." Slowly, with great show, he removed her little knife from the waist of his hose, those tight, tight hose that clung to his body, a triangular patch loosely tied over his maleness. "I'll teach you to keep your weapons about you and not discard them so lightly." Idly, he ran his thumb along the blade. "It needs sharpening."

"It was sharp enough to cut your thick hide," she said confidently, smiling back at him, glad she could repay him for some of his self-assurance.

As if just remembering the bloody cut, he glanced at it

before looking back at her. "Come with me, squire, and tend to my wound," he said flatly, turning his back on her as if he expected her to follow him.

Alyx instantly decided that she did not want to stay in this camp at the mercy and whim of this man Raine, who attracted her so yet made her so angry. And she did not like these dirty, greedily staring people who surrounded her, watching as if she were part of a play put on for their entertainment.

She turned to the servant who'd brought her. "I don't wish to stay here. I will take my chances elsewhere," she said, turning toward the saddled horse.

"Neither do you know how to obey an order," came Raine's voice from behind her, an instant before his big hand clamped on her neck. "I'll not let a little thing like your terror of me keep me from acquiring a good squire."

"Get away from me!" she yelled as he pushed her ahead of him. "I don't want to stay here. I won't stay here."

"As I see it you owe me for spilling some of my blood. Now get in there!" he said as he pushed her inside a large canvas tent.

Trying not to cry at the pain in her leg, at the battering her already bruised body was taking, she clutched at a tent pole and tried to stay upright.

"Blanche!" Raine bellowed out of the tent flap. "Bring me some hot water and some linen and make sure it's clean!"

"Now, boy," he said, turning back to her and, for a moment, studying her. "You've hurt your leg. Take off those hose and let me look at it."

"No!" she gasped, backing away from him.

He looked truly puzzled. "Is it me you fear or"—he gave a bit of a smile—"that you're modest? Oh, well," he said, sitting down on the cot at the edge of the tent, "perhaps you should be shy. If I had legs like yours I'd be ashamed of them, too. But don't worry, lad, we'll put some muscle on your scrawny body. Ah, yes, Blanche, put it there and go."

"But don't you want me to dress your wound?"

Alyx looked from her scrutiny of her legs, thinking that they weren't so bad at all, to see the woman who spoke. Her sensitivity to sound and especially to voices made her look up sharply. The hint of a whine, the begging quality, somehow overridden by a touch of insolence, grated along her spine. She saw a plump woman with stringy, dirty blonde hair, looking at Raine as if she might devour him at any moment.

With pure disgust, Alyx looked away.

"The boy will dress the wound."

"I most certainly will not!" Alyx said vehemently. "Let the woman do it, 'tis woman's work and she looks as if she'd like the job." Smiling, Alyx thought perhaps she might like being a male and not having to do all the thankless drudgery tasks of a woman.

Raine, in one unseen, swift gesture, leaned forward, grabbed Alyx's thigh in one of his big hands and pulled. As her leg went flying out from under her she landed very hard on her already bruised rump.

"You need some manners as well as muscles. Go now, Blanche," he said pointedly to the staring woman. When they were alone he turned back to Alyx. "I'll be forgiving for a few days since you've not had a noble background, but if your manners don't soon improve, I'll take a switch to that puny body of yours and see if you can learn to behave. The water grows cold, so come and clean this wound and bind it."

Reluctantly, Alyx stood, rubbing her buttocks, limping a bit on her leg. When she reached Raine, he extended his arm, that large brown muscular arm, blood from shoulder to forearm, for her to clean. As she touched him with the warm cloth she realized how cold her hands were, how warm his skin— and how deep the cut. It did not set well with her that she had hurt anyone like this.

"The first time you've drawn blood?" Raine asked gently, his face near hers, his voice soft as he watched her.

She barely nodded, not wanting to meet his eyes as tears choked her throat and she remembered her life before two days ago.

"How did you hurt your leg?" he asked.

Blinking rapidly, refusing to cry, she glared at him. "By running from one of your kind," she spat at him.

"Good lad." He smiled and again those dimples appeared. "Don't let anyone scare you. Keep your head high no matter what happens."

She rinsed out the bloody cloth and started washing all of his arm.

"Should I tell you the duties of a squire?" he asked.

"Having never had your advantages of personal servants I am afraid I am at a loss as to what one should do for h—"—she had almost said "her"—"his master."

A snort from Raine was his reply to her answer. "You are to clean my armor, care for my horses, help me personally in any way you can, and"—his eyes twinkled—"serve me my sweet cakes. Do you think you can do all that?"

"There's no more?" she taunted.

"A true squire would learn the rudiments of training to be a knight, using a sword, a lance, that sort of thing, as well as write his lord's letters and at times deliver important messages. I do not expect so much from you though since—"

Alyx cut him off. "Since I am not of your class and you do not think I have the brain to learn? My father was a lawyer and I can read and write better than most of your nobles, I'll wager, and I can do it in Latin and French as well as English."

Raine tested his arm for a moment, curling his hand into a fist, making his bicep bulge, all the while smiling slightly, not at all offended by her accusations. Finally, he looked back at her. "You're still too small to do much heavy training," he said, "and it has little to do with your birth status. As for reading and writing, you must be better than I am, for I do not read more than the names of my family. Good!" he said as he stood. "You have a delicate hand with a wound. Perhaps Rosamund can use your help."

"Another of your women?" Alyx sneered, motioning her head toward the tent flap where Blanche had been.

"Are you jealous?" he asked, and before Alyx could sputter that she was jealous of no women, he added, "You'll have your share of women yet, when you get your first beard and we put a little meat on you." Cocking his head, looking at her, he said, "You're pretty enough if you don't get scarred on the battlefield. Women like pretty faces on their men."

"Such as yours?" she snapped and could have bitten out her tongue.

"I do well enough," he said, obviously highly amused. "Now I have some work for you to do. This armor needs cleaning and after that it must be polished to keep the rust off." Quickly, he piled pieces of steel armor together, back and front together forming a large shell which held arm and leg coverings. The helmet went on top.

Confidently, arrogantly, Alyx held out her arms and in the next moment she staggered backward and would have fallen had not Raine caught her at the small of her back.

"It's a mite heavy for a lad your size."

"My size!" she gasped, trying to steady herself. "If you weren't as large as a pair of oxen the armor need not be so big."

"Your insolence is going to earn you some bruises, and I would advise you to show some proper respect for your leige lord." Before she could make a reply, he fairly pushed her from the tent. "There's a stream to the north," he said, piling several cloths on her burden of mud-encrusted armor. "Wash it well then bring it back. And if I find one new dent in it I will add five dents to your hide. Is that clear, boy?"

Alyx could barely nod, as she was more concerned with staying upright under her burden, wondering how in the world she was going to walk, than making any smart retorts to Raine. Slowly, one step at a time, she started forward, her arms already aching, her neck craned sideways to see around the high pile of steel she carried. When her body hurt so badly there were tears in her eyes, she finally saw the stream. At its side she started to drop the armor to her feet, but remembering Raine's threat, she braced her legs apart, squatted and carefully lowered all seventy pounds of it to the ground.

For a moment she sat there, her arms extended, wondering if they'd ever feel the same again. When feeling came back to them, and all the feeling was pain, she plunged her arms, shirt and all, into the cold clear water of the stream.

Several minutes later she glanced back at the pile of armor with a great sigh. So much for women's drudgery. What was the difference between washing dishes and washing armor? With another sigh she picked up the cloths and began removing the crust of mud, sweat, rust and whatever else held the filth together.

An hour later she'd succeeded in taking the dirt off the armor and placing it on herself. Never had she sweat so much in her life, and every drop made the dirt cling to her skin. Removing her tunic, she used a clean cloth to wash most of the dirt from it and left it to dry on a rock while she washed her face and arms.

As she came up from washing and reached for a dry cloth, someone handed it to her. Quickly drying her face, she opened her eyes to see an astonishingly handsome man. Dark wavy hair framed a perfectly formed, high-cheekboned face. Hot, dark eyes blazed under long thick lashes. Alyx blinked twice to make sure this dark angel was real and, in her stunned silence, she did not see the sword pointed at her belly.

Chapter 4

"WHO ARE you?" this man who was too perfect-looking to be real asked.

Alyx, unused to danger in her life, did not fully react to the sword, but what she did react to was the music in this man's voice. She'd felt that Raine, with his deep voice, could sing if he tried, but she was sure this man *did* sing. "I am Raine's new squire," she said quietly, using her voice and all her many years of training to bring the voice from deep within her chest.

For a moment he stared at her, puzzled, speechless, and very slowly he resheathed his sword, his eyes never leaving hers. "There's something about your voice. Have you ever done any singing?"

"A bit," she said, her eyes dancing, every ounce of her confidence making itself known in that simple statement.

Without another word he reached to his back and the quiver of arrows he carried there and pulled out a flute. He started to play a simple, common song that Alyx knew well. For a moment she closed her eyes, letting the music float about her. The last few days had been the longest she'd ever gone without music since that day ten years ago when she'd picked up the troubadour's lute. As the music filled her, her lungs filled with air and she opened her mouth to sing.

After only four notes, the young man stopped playing, his mouth dropping open in disbelief, his eyes wide. Alyx grinned, kept singing and motioned for him to continue.

With one quick glance of thankfulness raised toward Heaven and a laugh of pure joy, the man again put the flute to his lips.

Alyx followed the tune for quite some time, but her need to create was too strong to let it rest. Here was someone who could play, and she wondered what else he could do. Looking about for something to give her more sound, she saw a hollow log quite near. Still singing, never losing a beat, she grabbed the back, breastplate and thigh covering of Raine's armor and set them near the log. Sticks quickly made drumsticks and for a moment she stopped singing, tapping out sounds on the pieces of armor and the log. When she had the sounds down she began to hum some of the music in her head.

Fascinated, the young man watched her, and when she began to sing, a new song this time, he followed her on his flute, slowly at first until he caught the tune and rhythm. When he added a variation of his own she laughed, still singing, and followed him easily. It became a bit of competition after that, with Alyx going one way and the man another, yet both following each other, testing one another's skill.

And when the man tossed the flute to the ground and added his strong, clear voice to hers, it was Alyx's turn to be stunned for a moment, at least enough to make her miss a beat which, from the look on his face, gave the man great joy. Grabbing her hands, both on their knees, facing each other, they blended their voices together, sending them upward toward Heaven.

At last they stopped and all around them was utter and complete silence, as if the wind and birds had stopped to listen to their magnificent music. Hands still clasped, they were still, looking at each other with a mixture of love, awe, surprise, delight and kinship.

"Jocelin Laing," the beautiful young man finally said, breaking the silence.

"Alyx . . . ander Blackett," she answered, stumbling over the male name.

One of Jocelin's perfect brows lifted and he started to say something but Raine's voice stopped him.

"Joss, I see you've met my new squire."

Almost with guilt, Alyx dropped Jocelin's hands and stood, only to find her sore leg going under her.

Roughly, Raine grabbed her arm. "If the two of you are through entertaining each other, you can bring my armor back and scrape the rust off of it. Joss, did you get any game?"

With what were surely spots of color on his cheeks, Jocelin faced Raine, his slim, broad-shouldered body appearing miniature next to Raine's massive form. "I have four rabbits by the stream."

"Rabbits!" Raine grunted. "I'll go and look for a deer or two later, but now, boy, come back to camp and let's have a look at that leg. You'll be no use to me if you're crippled."

With resignation, Alyx collected the pieces of armor and Jocelin loaded them into her arms, along with her damp tunic. She followed Raine back to the camp, wondering just how much of the singing he'd heard.

If he'd heard any of it, he didn't comment as he entered the tent and pointed for Alyx to set his armor down.

"Now pull off those hose and let's look at that leg."

"My leg is healing nicely," she said, standing firmly where she was.

Narrowing his eyes at her, he took a step closer. "You might as well understand now that everyone in this camp pulls his weight. We can't afford the time to deal with sick people. Get undressed while I get Rosamund," he said, slipping on a shirt and doublet over his hose before leaving the tent.

As soon as he was gone, Alyx quickly removed the tight hose, grabbed a cloth and tied it about her waist, bringing the end up and over the Lyon belt secreted beneath her clothes so that she formed a loincloth. A great deal of her thigh and hip were exposed, and as she looked down at them, thinking that they weren't bad-looking at all, she knew that now she'd be exposed as a female. Oh, well, she sighed, it was nice to think that some part of her, if not her face, was so pretty it could only belong to a woman.

A sound at the tent opening made her look up and there, in profile, was surely one of the most beautiful women ever made on earth. Lashes so long they looked unreal, curled over pretty green eyes, a perfect nose and mouth that curved back, its lips finely shaped, chiseled, a classic beauty, how every woman dreams of looking. And behind her was Raine. No wonder he never noticed his squire! she thought. With women like this one around, why would he look at something plain and ordinary like her?

"This is Rosamund, a healer," Raine said, and his voice held a sweet softness that made Alyx look at him in wonder. It would be nice to hear him use that voice when he spoke to her.

The next moment Rosamund turned and an involuntary gasp escaped Alyx, for the entire left side of Rosamund's face was covered with a deep pink strawberry mark—the sign of the devil. Instantly, her hand raised to cross herself in hopes of warding off the evil power, but her eyes were drawn to Raine's and those blue orbs were fastened on hers in warning and threat.

"If you'd rather I didn't touch you . . ." Rosamund began in a voice that showed she was perfectly used to being repulsed.

"No, of course not," Alyx said hesitantly, then gained strength. "There's nothing wrong with my leg, only what this great horse of a man thinks is wrong."

With surprised eyes, Rosamund looked up at Raine, but he only snorted. "The boy has no manners—yet," he added, his words carrying a threat. He seemed satisfied that Alyx was going to treat Rosamund with respect and turned away from them, never once glancing at Alyx's legs, she noticed with chagrin.

Gently, Rosamund took Alyx's leg, lifted it, turned it this way and that, seeing no external signs of injury.

"My name is Raine Montgomery," he said, his back to them. "I prefer my name to being referred to as . . . whatever animal you choose."

"And should I preface it with 'your majesty' or will 'your lordship' do?" She knew she was greatly daring and had no

at Alyx. When she stood, he took a long sword from a passing man and handed it to her. "Take the hilt in both hands and come for me."

"I don't want to hurt anyone," she said instantly. "I didn't even want to hurt Pagnell when—"

"What if I were Pagnell?" he said archly. "Come for me or I will go for you."

The pain, so recent, so deep, made her raise the heavy sword from where its tip dangled in the dust and she thrust at him. When the blade was a hairsbreadth from his belly, he sidestepped, evading her. Again she lunged and again, again, and still she couldn't touch him. She started for one side, changed in midthrust and made for his other side, but no matter what she did she could not hit him.

Panting from her exertions, she stopped, resting the sword tip in the dirt, her arms aching, quivering from the exertion, while Raine, smiling and confident, grinned at her until she longed to ram him with the steel she held.

"Now I will give you another chance. I will stand perfectly still while you swing at me."

"There's a trick," she said with such fatalism that he laughed aloud.

"No trick, but you must lift the sword above your head and come straight down. If you can do that you will strike me."

"I could not hurt someone. To draw blood—"

His face showed his belief in her swordsmanship. "Think of all my sheep, all the farmers I have caused to starve because of my greedy ways. Think of—"

Alyx happily lifted the sword straight up, planning to bring it down on his head, but at the moment she reached up the blasted, uncooperative sword started pulling her arms backward. Already tired and weakened, her arms could not hold it and for a few seconds it was a struggle—and the damned piece of steel won. The smirk on Raine's face as she stood there holding the long sword, its tip planted between her heels, made her furious.

"You're as weak a boy as I ever saw. What have you done with your life?"

She absolutely refused to answer that question as she twisted the sword around to the front of her.

"Lift it to the top of your head, lower it and do it again and again until I return. If I see you slacking, I'll double your practice time," he said as he left her.

Up and down, over and over she lifted the sword, her arms screaming with the exercise.

"You'll learn," said a voice behind her and she turned to see the scarred soldier, the brother of the man who'd brought her here.

"Has your brother left? I wanted to thank him, although right now I'm not sure this is any better than what could have happened to me."

"He needed no thanks," the man said gruffly, "and you'd better not stop because Lord Raine, is looking this way."

With trembling arms, Alyx resumed her exercise, and it was several moments before Raine returned to show her how to hold the sword at arm's length, one arm at a time, lifting and lowering it repeatedly.

After what seemed like an eternity, he took the sword from her and started walking back toward the camp. Her arms and shoulders feeling as if they'd been put to the rack, Alyx followed him silently.

"Food, Blanche," he said over his shoulder on the way to his tent.

Gratefully, Alyx sat down on a stool while Raine took another and began to sharpen the point of a long lance. With her head leaning against a tent pole, she was almost asleep when Blanche came in bearing crockery bowls full of stew and curds and whey mixed with soft cooked lentils and more of the heavy black bread, with hot spiced wine in mugs.

As Alyx lifted her wooden spoon, her arms started to jerk spasmodically, protesting what she'd just done to them.

"You're too soft," Raine grunted, his mouth full. "It'll take months to harden you up."

Silently, Alyx knew she'd die if she had to take even a

week of today's torture. She ate as best she could, too weary to pay much attention to the food, and she was falling asleep when Raine grabbed her upper arm and pulled her up.

"The day's young yet," he said, obviously laughing at her exhaustion. "The camp needs food and we must get it."

"Food?" she groaned. "Let them starve and let me sleep."

"Starve!" he snorted. "They'd kill each other for what food there is and only the strongest would survive. And you," he said, his fingers meeting as they encircled her upper arm, "you wouldn't last an hour. So we go to hunt to keep you alive as well as them."

With one jerk, she moved away from his touch. Stupid man, she thought, couldn't he see that she was female? Without another word, he was out of the tent and she ran after him, following him to the edge of camp where the horses were kept. All along the way she saw the people of the camp, resting, digesting their food, no one continuing to work except Raine.

"Could it be possible that you could ride?" he asked, his voice showing he had no hope.

"No," she whispered.

"What have you done with your life?" he demanded again. "I have never known a boy who couldn't ride."

"And I have never known a man who knew so little about the people outside his own world. Have you spent your life on a jeweled throne doing nothing but fighting with swords and riding great horses?"

Flinging a heavy wood-based saddle on his horse, he said, "You have a sharp tongue on you, and if it were not for us training to fight, who would protect you when there is war?"

"The King, of course," she answered smugly.

"Henry!" Raine gasped, one foot in the stirrup. "And who do you think protects Henry? Who does he call when he is attacked if not his nobles? Give me your arm," he said and easily pulled her up to sit on the hard rump of the horse behind his saddle. Before she could say a word, they were off at a teeth-jarring pace.

Chapter 5

AFTER WHAT seemed to be hours of banging up and down on the bony backside of the horse, her knuckles white from gripping the edge of the saddle, Raine abruptly halted the animal and Alyx came close to flying backward over the tail.

"Hold on," he growled as he grabbed the nearest part of her, which was her sore thigh, making her gasp in pain. "Quiet!" he commanded. "There, through the trees, see them?"

Dashing away tears of pain with her sleeve, she was finally able to see a family of wild pigs scrounging in the undergrowth. The pigs halted, looked up with their mean little eyes glaring out of their lean, tough bodies and snorted over the long sharp tusks protruding from their mouths.

"Hold onto me," Raine bellowed seconds before he spurred his horse forward and went after the largest pig, lance held point down. "Grip the horse with your knees," he said when Alyx, openmouthed, held her breath as the pig began to charge them. The animal was so big compared to the horse's thin legs.

Suddenly, Raine dipped sideways, his body parallel to the ground. Since Alyx was holding onto him, she went down with him. Unbalanced, falling, she held onto Raine with all her might as he thrust his lance into the backbone of the furious animal. The hideous scream was the voice of death, and Alyx buried her face in Raine's broad back.

"Let me go!" he growled, shaking the pig off his lance, then prying Alyx's fingers from his chest. "You nearly toppled us. Now hold the saddle with all your strength." With that command he was off again, tearing through the forest, dodging tree branches overhead, trees to both sides, as he ran after another pig. Two more were brought down as cleanly as the first before he stopped and again had to pry Alyx's fingers from his stomach. She had no idea when she'd grabbed him and was glad he made no further comment on her cowardice.

When he was free of her grip, he dismounted, took several leather thongs from his saddle and, after a cautious approach to the animals, trussed their feet. "Get down," he said and waited patiently for her to obey.

Her legs, unaccustomed to the exercise, buckled under her and she clutched at the saddle to keep from falling.

Ignoring her, Raine slung the dead pigs over the back of his horse, then went immediately to the horse's head to calm him as he pranced, not liking the smell of blood so close to him.

"Lead the horse and follow me," he said to her, turning his back to her and walking ahead.

After one fearful look at the stallion, its ears back, eyes wild, sweaty from its run, Alyx gave a deep swallow of sheer terror and reached for the reins. The stallion danced away once and Alyx jumped, glancing quickly toward Raine where she could just see him through the trees.

"Come on, horse," she whispered, approaching the animal slowly but again it moved away from her.

Frustrated, she stood still, eyes locked with the horse's and softly, she began to hum, trying different notes, different tempos until she sensed the horse rather liked a very old, simple round. As the horse seemed to calm, she reached for the reins and her voice gained strength as she gained confidence.

Several minutes later, swaggering with pride at her accomplishment, she reached the small clearing where Raine waited impatiently with the third pig.

"It's a good thing I have guards posted," he said, flinging

the trussed pig on the stallion's back, "otherwise with all your noise anyone within a mile could have heard you."

Absolute shock nearly flattened Alyx. Since she was ten years old all she'd ever heard was the most profuse praise for her music and now it was being referred to as "noise." Without another word from her she allowed Raine to pull her into the saddle in front of him and together they rode back to camp, her back slamming into his chest.

Once back in the camp, Raine dismounted, ignoring Alyx, still in the saddle, as he untied the pigs and slung them in the general direction of a campfire. As Jocelin came forward, Raine tossed him the reins. "Show the boy how to clean a horse," he said before striding toward his tent.

After a reassuring smile for Alyx, Joss led the horse toward the clearing where the other horses were kept.

"Boy!" Alyx muttered as she dismounted, holding onto the saddle for support. "Boy, do this; boy, do that. That's all he ever says." When Joss had unfastened the saddle cinch, Alyx stood on tiptoe, grabbed the saddle and pulled and promptly fell backward, landing in a heap with the heavy saddle on top of her.

Obviously trying not to laugh, Jocelin removed the saddle while Alyx rubbed her bruised chin where it had struck her. "Is Raine making your life miserable?"

"He's trying to," she said as she took the saddle from him and, after three tries, managed to set it atop a wooden construction. "Oh, Joss," she gasped. "I'm so very tired. This morning he had me scour his armor, then I spent hours with that heavy sword. Now it's hunting and looking after that great beast."

At that comment the stallion rolled its eyes and began to prance. Without a thought, Alyx sang six notes and the animal calmed.

Jocelin had to control his look of amazement at her unconscious use of her voice before he could speak. "Raine has a lot of people to care for."

"A lot of people to play the lord with, you mean," she snapped, following Joss's lead in wiping down the horse.

"Perhaps. Perhaps a man like Raine is so used to taking responsibility he takes it without thinking."

"For me, I'd like fewer orders," she said. "Why does he command everyone? Why does he believe he rules everyone? Why doesn't he just let the people rest?"

"Rest!" Joss said from the other side of the horse. "You should have seen this place a few weeks before he arrived. It was like the worst sections of London, people slitting one another's throats for a few pennies, stealing so much you had to stay up all night to guard your possessions. Displaced farmers were at the mercy of murderers and—"

"And so this righteous Raine Montgomery set everything to rights, correct?"

"Yes, he did."

"Did anyone ever consider he did it because he felt it was his God-given right over his underlings?"

"You're awfully young to be so bitter, aren't you?" Joss asked.

Alyx stopped brushing the horse. "Why are you here?" she asked him. "How do you fit into this group? You're not a murderer and you don't look like someone too lazy to work. The only thing I can imagine is that some jealous husband is after you," she teased.

Instantly, Jocelin tossed the brush down. "I have to go back to work," he said in a hard, flat voice and walked away from her.

For a full, stunned minute Alyx could not continue. Never in her life would she have insulted Jocelin. He was the only one she could talk to, sing with and—

"When you finish that you can fetch me some water from the stream," came a whiny voice from behind her, cutting off Alyx's thoughts.

Slowly, with deliberation, she turned toward Blanche. For all Alyx's words on Raine's arrogance, Alyx also had a great deal of class pride. This woman with her slovenly dress, her coarse voice, her uneducated accents, was certainly not of the same class as Alyx. Ignoring her, Alyx turned back to the horse.

"Boy!" Blanche demanded. "Did you hear what I said?"

"I heard you," Alyx said, dropping her voice to a low tremor. "And I'm sure half the camp did, too."

"You think you're too good for me, don't you, you in your pretty clothes with your fine manners. Just because you've spent today with him doesn't mean you'll spend every day with him."

With a sneer, Alyx kept working on the horse. "Go about your business, woman. I have none with you."

Blanche grabbed Alyx's arm, pulled her about. "Until this morning I waited on Raine, brought his food to him and now he orders me to prepare a bed in his tent for you. What kind of boy are you?"

It took Alyx a moment to understand Blanche's insinuations and when she did, her eyes blazed purple fire. "If you knew anything about the nobility you'd know that all the lords have squires. I merely perform the duties of any good squire."

Blanche, obviously attempting to appear as part of the nobility, tried to stand erect. "Of course," she snapped. "I know about squires. But just you remember," she said threateningly, "Raine Montgomery is mine. I care for him as his lady would—in every way." With that, she turned on her heel and left through the trees.

"Lady!" Alyx muttered, going after the horse with a vengeance. "What would a slut like that know of being a lady?" Angry, she was unaware of time passing until she heard Raine's voice close to her.

"Boy," he said, making her jump. "You've got to be faster than that with a horse. There's plenty more work to be done."

"More?" she whispered and looked so sad that Raine smiled, eyes twinkling, and Alyx straightened. She'd give him no reason to laugh at her again.

After setting aside the brush, whispering one last tune to the stallion, Alyx followed Raine back to the camp, where he went directly to a group of disreputable-looking men huddled about a fire. Raine, with his proud stance, his noble bearing, made these men seem even filthier than they were.

"Here, you three," Raine said in a low growl. "You take the first watch."

"I ain't stayin' out in them woods," one man said as he turned to walk away.

Grabbing him with one hand, Raine pulled the man back and administered a swift kick to his backside that sent him sprawling. "If you eat, you work," he said in a deadly voice. "Now get to your posts. I will come later, and if any of you are asleep, it will be the man's last sleep."

With his features set in a grim line, Raine watched the men as they left the camp, sulking like little children. "Those are your fine friends," he said in an undertone to Alyx as he turned away.

"They are no friends of mine!" she snapped.

"Nor is Pagnell a friend of mine!" he retorted.

Halting, she stared after his broad back. It was true, she knew. She had no right to hate him because of what another man had done.

"Blanche!" Raine grunted. "Food!"

With that, Alyx went tearing after him because she was very hungry. Inside the tent, Blanche placed roast boar, bread, cheese and hot wine before them, and Alyx tore into the food with gusto.

"That's the way, boy!" Raine laughed, slapping her on the back, making her choke. "Keep eating like that and you'll put some size on yet."

"Keep working me like today and I'll die in a week!" she gasped, trying to dislodge a piece of pork from her throat, ignoring Raine's laughter.

The meal finished, Alyx looked with longing toward the pallet along one wall of the tent. To rest, she thought, just to lie down and be still for a few hours would be heaven on earth.

"Not yet, boy," Raine said, grabbing her arm and pulling her upright. "There's still work before we can sleep. The guards need to be checked, I have animal traps set and we both need a bath."

That startled her awake. "Bath!" she gasped. "No, not me."

"When I was your age I had to be forced to bathe, too. Once my older brother scoured me with a horse brush."

"Someone forced you to do something?" she asked, incredulous.

Raine's pride seemed to be at stake. "Actually, it took both my older brothers, and Gavin came away with a blacked eye. Now, come on. We have work to do."

Reluctantly, Alyx followed him, but no matter how hard she tried, she could put no energy in her steps. Like someone dead, she followed Raine through the forest, occasionally bumping into trees, stumbling over rocks, as he went around the perimeter of the camp making sure the guards were on duty and awake and removing rabbits and hares from his traps. At first he tried to talk to her, explain what he was doing, how to toss a rock and see if the guards responded, but after a while he studied her in the moonlight, noting her exhaustion, and stopped talking.

At the stream outside the camp he told her to sit still and wait for him while he bathed. Half asleep, reclining on the bank, her head propped on her arm, Alyx watched with languid interest as Raine removed his clothing and stepped into the icy water. Moonlight silvered his body, caressed the muscles, played along his thighs, made love to those magnificent arms. Lifting herself on her elbows, Alyx unabashedly watched him. All her life had been given to music. While other girls were flirting with the boys at the town well, Alyx was composing a Latin lamentation for four voices. When her friends were getting married, she was inside the church organizing a boys' chorus. She'd never had time to talk to boys, to get to know them—actually, had never been interested in them, had always been too busy to even notice them.

Now, for the first time in her life, watching this nude man bathing she felt the first stirrings of . . . of what? She certainly knew about mating, had even listened to some of the gossip from the recently married women, but she'd never felt any interest in the process. This man standing before her, rising out of the water like some heavenly centaur, made her feel things she'd never thought possible.

Lust, she thought, sitting up farther. Pure and simple lust was what she was feeling. She'd like for him to touch her, to kiss her, to lie beside her, and she would very much like to touch that skin of his. Remembering how it felt when she'd straddled his back, she began to tingle, her legs seeming more alive, even her feet growing warm.

When he left the water and came toward her, she almost lifted her arms toward him.

"You look lazy," Raine commented, drying himself off. "Sure you won't take a bath?"

All Alyx could do was watch the course of the cloth he used for drying as it ran over his body and vaguely shake her head.

"I warn you though, boy, you start smelling so bad you drive me from the tent and I'll bathe you myself and it won't be a gentle bath."

Eyes wide, Alyx looked up at him, her breathing changing just slightly. To be bathed by this great god of a man, she thought.

"Are you all right, boy?" Raine asked, concerned, kneeling beside her as he frowned at her odd expression.

Boy! she grimaced. He thought she was a boy, and what if she were revealed as a girl? He was of the nobility and she was only a poor lawyer's daughter. "Aren't you going to get cold?" she asked flatly, rolling away from him to stand apart, not watching as he dressed.

When he was finished, she silently followed him back to camp, where she collapsed on her pallet but did not sleep until Raine had settled himself on his narrow cot. Content at last, she fell asleep.

Chapter 6

LEANING OVER the edge of the water, Alyx studied her own reflection. She did look like a boy, she thought with disgust. Why couldn't she have been born beautiful, with lovely features that could never be mistaken for a male's no matter what she wore? Her hair, all a mass of curls, its color not sure of which way to go, changing with each strand, eyes turned up, lips like a pixie's, were not what a woman's should be.

Just as tears were beginning to blur her vision, Jocelin's voice startled her. "Cleaning more armor?" he asked.

With a sniff, she turned back to her task. "Raine is too hard on it. Today I had to hammer out a dent."

"You seem to care much for his things. Are you perhaps beginning to believe that a nobleman could be worth something?"

"Raine would be worth much no matter what his birth," she said much too hastily, then looked away, embarrassed.

She'd been in Raine's camp for a week now, had spent nearly every second in his company and her opinions of him had completely reversed in that week. Once she'd believed he took over the camp, but now she knew it was that the outcasts forced him to take care of them. They were like children demanding that he provide for them, then acting rebellious when he did. He left his bed before anyone else and saw to the security of the people and always, late at night, he made sure the guard was alert and ready. He forced the people away from idleness and made them work for their own keep or else they'd sit and wait for him to provide for them, as if it were their due.

"Yes," she said quietly. "Raine is worth something, although he gets little reward for what he does. Why doesn't he leave this scurvy lot and leave England altogether? Surely a man with his wealth could make a decent home for himself."

"Perhaps you should ask him that. You are closest to him."

Close to him, she thought. That's where she wanted to be, even closer to him. Only now was she beginning to be able to function through her blinding fatigue, to live through the strenuous training sessions each morning, but as her muscles hardened and she began to feel better, she became more involved in the camp life.

Blanche occupied an exalted position in the camp, making everyone believe she shared Raine's bed and had his ear for anything they wanted. Alyx tried not to consider if Blanche ever had spent the night with Raine, but she liked to believe he had more taste than to use a slut like Blanche. And something else Alyx was able to find out about Blanche: she was terrified of Jocelin.

Jocelin, so incredibly handsome, so polite, so considerate, had every woman in camp panting after him. Alyx had seen women use every manner of enticement to lure him to their sides, but as far as she knew, Joss had never accepted an invitation. He preferred his duties and the company of Alyx to anyone else. And although he never mentioned her, he stayed well away from Blanche. When the woman happened to meet him she'd always turn tail and run.

Besides Joss, the only other decent outcast was Rosamund, with her beauty and the devil's mark on her cheek. Rosamund kept her head down, expecting people's hatred and fear. Once Raine had found a couple of men wagering on whether or not they'd be selling their souls if they took her by force. Twenty lashes each was his punishment for the men, followed by banishment, and Alyx felt a surge of jealousy that Raine so violently protected the flawed, beautiful healer.

"Alyx!" came a bellow through the trees that could only belong to Raine. At least now he called her by her name.

Using every ounce of power her voice contained, she yelled back at him, "I am working." The man was obsessed with work.

Coming through the trees, he grinned at her. "That voice of yours gives me hope that you'll grow, although it looks to me as if you're getting smaller." Critically, he eyed her legs stretched before her.

With a little smile, Alyx was glad to see that at least one part of her was unmistakably female. Her long legs and curvy little bottom had only been enhanced by the hard exercise of the last week. Perhaps now, at last, she would be revealed as a girl and then . . . what? She'd be tossed from Raine's tent and he'd once again only have that whore Blanche to care for him. Reluctantly, she slapped a steel leg sheath over her own legs.

"I'll grow," she snapped, "and when I do I'll pin you to the ground with your own sword." An upward glance at Raine saw that he seemed to be puzzled by something.

"You wanted Alyx for something?" Joss asked, his voice full of amusement as he interrupted the silence.

"Yes," Raine said quietly. "I need some letters written and some read to me. A messenger has come from my family. You can read, can't you?"

Curiosity made Alyx jump. She very much wanted to know about Raine's family. "Yes, of course," she said, gathering the armor and following Raine.

A man, dressed finely, his doublet embroidered with gold leopards, sat outside the tent, waiting patiently for Raine's command. With the wave of one hand, the young man was dismissed and Alyx wondered if all Raine's men obeyed so well and what a far cry from the outcasts they were.

There were two letters for Raine, one from his brother Gavin and one from his brother's wife, Judith.

The news from Gavin was bad. Bronwyn, Raine's other

sister-in-law, had been taken prisoner by the same man who held Raine's sister, Mary. Bronwyn's husband was waiting, sitting and waiting, afraid to make a move for fear Roger Chatworth would kill his wife.

"Your brother Stephen," Alyx asked tentatively, "he loves his wife?"

Raine only nodded, his lips drawn into a tight line, his eyes focused on nothing.

"But it says here that she was in Scotland when she was taken. Why was she in Scotland? The Scots are coarse, vicious people and—"

"Hold your tongue!" he commanded. "Bronwyn is the laird of a clan in Scotland and there is no finer woman. Read me the other letter."

Chastised, Alyx opened the letter from Judith Montgomery, fully aware of the way Raine's eyes softened as she began to read. The letter was full of prayers for Raine's safety and entreaties for him to leave England until it was safe for him to return. She asked after his comfort, whether he had food and warm clothing, which made Raine chuckle and Alyx bristle at her wifely tones.

"Does her husband know she concerns herself so for her brother-in-law?" she asked primly.

"I'll not have you speak of my family so," he reprimanded and Alyx hung her head, embarrassed at her jealousy. It wasn't fair that she had to pose as a boy and never have a chance of gaining his attention. If she could wear a pretty dress perhaps he'd notice her, but then again she certainly was no beauty.

"Take your head from the clouds, boy, and listen to me." His voice brought her to the present.

"Can you write what I say? I want to send letters back with my brother's man."

When she had pen, ink and paper, Raine began to dictate. The letter she was to write to his brother was one of anger and determination. He swore to stay as near as possible to his two sisters and he would wait as long as he could before bringing his fist to Chatworth's head. As for the King, he had no fear, since Henry's main source of income was from men he declared to be traitors. He told Gavin that Henry would pardon him as soon as he agreed to forfeit a goodly portion of his land.

Raine ignored Alyx's startled gasps at the insolent way in which he referred to their sovereign.

The letter to Judith was as warm and loving as hers had been, even once referring to his new squire, who thought he had no sense, not even enough to keep warm, and often covered him at night. With her head lowered, Alyx wrote, not allowing Raine to see her flushed cheeks. She'd had no idea he was aware of the many times she'd tiptoed about the tent, pulling the fur-lined coverlet about his bare shoulders.

The rest of the letter Alyx merely wrote, too embarrassed to even read what she wrote, and when she finished them she held them open, ready for Raine's signature. As he bent toward her, his face close to hers, she inhaled the smell of his hair, that thick, dark, curling mass and wanted to bury her face in it. Instead, she reached out and touched a lock of it, watched it curl about her fingertip.

Raine's head came up as if he'd been burned, his face inches from hers, his eyes wide as he looked at her. Alyx knew her breath had stopped and her heart had leaped to her throat. Now he'll know, she thought. Now he'll say that I am a girl, a woman.

Frowning, Raine stepped away from her, looking at her as if he couldn't quite decide what was happening. "Seal the letters," he said quietly, "and give them to the messenger." With that he left the tent.

Alyx gave a sigh that made one of the letters flutter to the floor and quick tears came to her eyes. Ugly, she thought. That's what I am—very, very ugly. No wonder no man ever even tried to contradict the priest and take me for his wife. Why fight for a prize not worth winning? Who wanted a flat-chested, boyish girl with a noisy voice for a wife? And no wonder Raine didn't see through her disguise.

With a sharp backhand swipe, she wiped her eyes and

returned to the letters before her. No doubt his sisters-in-law and his sister were beautiful, beautiful women with chests . . .

With another sigh she finished the letters, sealed them and took them outside to the messenger, walking with him to his horse.

"Have you seen this Lady Judith or the Lady Bronwyn?" she asked the messenger.

"Aye, many times."

"And are they, perhaps, handsome women?"

"Handsome?" he laughed, mounting his horse. "God must have been happy the day he created those women. Lord Raine will not leave England nor would I if I had either of those women in my family. Go on, boy, try and find someone to console him," he said, motioning toward the tent. "The loss of such beauty even for a moment must make him a miserable man."

Console him! Alyx muttered as she went back to the tent, only to be greeted by some commotion, Raine standing at the heart of it.

"It is well for your life that you did not kill her," he was saying to two men, one a pickpocket, the other a beggar. Both had been on guard duty all morning. "Alyx," he said over their heads. "Saddle my horse. We ride."

Taking off at a run, Alyx had the big horse saddled and ready by the time Raine reemerged from the tent, a battle ax and a mace in his hand. He had mounted and pulled her up behind him before she could ask a question, and in seconds they were galloping through the forest at a breakneck speed.

After a good run, as fast as the trees permitted, Raine drew to a halt and jumped from his horse. Catching the reins, Alyx slid forward into the saddle and got her first glimpse of what was going on. A pretty woman with big brown eyes, wearing a beautiful dress such as Alyx had never seen before, was flattened against a tree, looking with terror at three men from the camp as they brandished knives and swords at her.

"Get out of here, you scum," Raine growled, tossing first one man, then the other aside.

The woman, shaking in fear, looked up at Raine in total

disbelief. "Raine," she whispered before closing her eyes and starting to slide down the tree.

Raine caught her in his arms, lifted her, cradling her to him. "Anne," he whispered. "You are safe now. Alyx, fetch some wine. There's a pouch on my saddle."

Somewhat in awe of the scene before her, Alyx dismounted and took the hard leather container to him as he sat down on a fallen tree, holding this woman close to him.

"Anne, drink this," he said in a sweet, gentle voice, and the woman fluttered her lashes and began to drink. "Now, Anne," he said when she was fully awake. "Tell me what you were doing this deep in the forest."

The woman certainly didn't seem to be in any hurry to remove herself from Raine's lap, Alyx thought, as she looked with absolute wonder at the woman's dress. It was of deep, deep red silk, a fabric she'd only seen in church, and it was embroidered all over with tiny hares, rabbits, deer, fish, all sorts of animals. The square neckline was very low, exposing a great deal of the woman's ample breasts, and about the neckline and waist were trims of gold and red, sparkling jewels.

"Alyx!" Raine said impatiently, handing her the bag of wine. "Anne," he said with great tenderness, holding the full-grown woman as if she were a child.

"What are you doing here, Raine?" she asked in a soft voice.

Can't sing, Alyx immediately thought. No strength in her voice and just a hint of a whine.

"King Henry has declared me traitor," Raine said, one dimple flashing.

Anne smiled at him. "After your money, is he? But what have you done to give him reason to take your lands?"

"Roger Chatworth has taken my sister Mary and Stephen's new wife."

"Chatworth!" she exclaimed. "Didn't that woman Gavin was so in love with marry a Chatworth?"

"My discreet brother," Raine said in disgust. "The woman is a whore and one of the worst sort, but Gavin could never see it. If nothing else, my brother is loyal. Even after he married Judith he still loved Alice Chatworth for a while."

"But what has this to do with why you are here?"

Why doesn't she stand on her own feet, Alyx thought. Why does she so calmly sit on his lap and talk as elegantly as if she were in some nobleman's hall?

"It's a long story," Raine said. "Through an accident, Alice Chatworth was badly scarred, and what little there was of her mind went with her beauty. Her brother-in-law cared for her since she was a widow, and perhaps the woman poisoned his mind, because later Roger challenged my brother to a fight, the winner to get the wife King Henry promised Stephen."

"Yes," Anne said. "I remember now. There was a great deal of property involved."

"Stephen's Bronwyn is a wealthy woman, yes, but Stephen wanted the woman as much as the land," he smiled. "But Chatworth could not stand losing and he has taken prisoner my sisters."

"Raine, how dreadful. But how did King Henry—"

"I was taking some of the king's men to Wales when I heard of Mary's being taken and I turned and went after Chatworth."

"Leading the King's army?" she asked, and when he nodded, she grimaced. "So Henry has some reason to declare you a traitor. Is that why you are dressed like a farmer and roaming about these dreary woods?"

"Aye," he said, looking at her. "You look well, Anne. It's been a long time since—"

With that she jumped off his lap, standing before him, smoothing her dress, a gown Alyx longed to touch. "You'll not seduce me again, Raine Montgomery. My father has promised to find me a husband soon and I'd like to go to him as pure as possible so I'll stand for no more of your lovely words." Turning, she looked at Alyx for the first time. "And who is this lad who stares at us with his mouth agape?"

Immediately, Alyx closed her mouth and looked away from the both of them.

"This is my squire," Raine said, his voice full of laughter from Anne's words. "I may have to live in this forest, but I do have some amenities. He works hard and can read and write."

"I take it no one was able to drive that knowledge into your thick skull," she snapped. "Raine! Stop looking at me like that. You'll get nowhere with me. Now you, boy, do you have a name?"

"Alexander Blackett."

"Blackett?" she said. "Where have I heard that name before?"

From the issue for my arrest, Alyx thought in a panic. Why hadn't she changed her last name? Now this odious woman would reveal her disguise to Raine.

"It's a common enough name," Raine said in dismissal. "Alyx, go back to the camp and wait for me."

"No, boy!" Anne said. "Raine, I'm serious. I'll not be used by you again, and I will not stay alone with you. You must lead me back to the other hunters. When they see that I am lost they'll try to find me."

"I have guards," he said, catching her about the waist, pulling her between his thighs. "We'll have all the time we need alone. Alyx, leave us."

"I want that pretty little squire of yours to stay," Anne said, her hands on his shoulders, pushing him away. "You've been so long in this woods perhaps you've come to prefer pretty boys over—"

She never finished her sentence as Raine drew her close to him, pulling her mouth down to his.

Unabashedly, Alyx watched them. Never had she seen anyone kiss someone like this, with bodies together, heads moving. More than anything in the world, Alyx wished it were she Raine was holding in his arms.

So engrossed was she in the scene before her that when the first arrow came sailing through the air, landing inches from Raine's leg, she stood still, not sure what was happening. Raine reacted instantly, in one motion flinging both Alyx and Anne to the forest floor.

All the way back to camp, she held onto the saddle and watched Raine's blood seep down his thigh. The horse, smelling blood, began to prance, and, as a reflex, Raine clutched with his knees to control the animal. Alyx felt him stiffen at the pain that caused.

"Perhaps you could calm him with your songs," he said quietly.

"With my noise, don't you mean?" she answered, still hurt by his words.

"As you wish," he said stiffly.

Alyx had never heard this tone before, but she recognized it as a voice covering pain. He said his wound wasn't bad, but it showed no sign of ceasing to bleed. Now was no time to be angry. She began to sing and the horse calmed.

"I will have to show you to my brothers," he murmured. "They won't believe this unless they see it."

As they approached the camp, several people, sensing something was wrong, came out to greet them.

"It would be better if they did not see that I was wounded," Raine said to her. "They're hard enough to control and I need no new problems now."

Quickly, she slipped off the horse and went to stand at Raine's side, her body blocking the people's view of his leg.

"We heard there was a fight," a black-toothed man said, his eyes greedy.

"Only in your mind, old man," Alyx yelled, startling everyone with the power of her voice. Visibly, the crowd jumped, and so did Raine's horse. "Stand back," she ordered. "The animal's gone wild. We had to take a whip to him to control him."

While the people were looking with fear at the great horse, its eyes rolling, smelling Raine's blood, Raine swung a mace from the saddle. "Have you no work to do?" he growled. "Joss, come to my tent. I have work for you."

Grumbling, the people began to go back to their fires and hovels.

When the horse was in front of the tent, they stopped and Alyx braced herself to help Raine dismount.

"For God's sake don't help me," he said through clenched teeth. "They will see you. Go and hold the horse's head. Sing good and loud and draw attention to yourself."

Alyx did as she was bid and did indeed draw much attention to herself, so much that she was nearly half an hour getting away from the people who wanted her to sing song after song. At last, feeling she'd covered Raine's awkward dismounting, she went into his tent.

He was propped on his cot, wearing his shirt and loincloth, Rosamund kneeling by his thigh, a basin of bloody water by her knees.

"There you are!" Raine growled. "Can't you do more than display that voice of yours? Heaven help us if you should go to war. Your enemy would ask you to sing and you would drop all weapons in order to perform like some mummer. Go now, Rosamund, and see to the man I hurt. Jocelin, show her the way. And you, my worthless songbird, see if you can bind this leg or mayhaps sing the wound closed."

Alyx opened her mouth to speak, but Joss put his hand on her shoulder, his back to Raine. "He is in pain, remember that," he whispered before leaving the tent.

One look at Raine's pale face made her realize the truth of Jocelin's statement.

"Do not stare at me! Make yourself useful," Raine spat at her.

She wasn't going to stand for this treatment. His anger and hostility could only hurt him. "Be quiet, Raine Montgomery!" she ordered. "I'll not take more of your insults. Lie still and I will tend to your wound, but there is nothing you can do to change the fact that you have been wounded. Growling at me will only make you feel worse."

He started to rise, but one look from Alyx made him lie back. "They'll kill each other," he said hopelessly, meaning the outlaws outside his tent.

"It doesn't matter if they do," she said callously, moving to the far side of the cot and Raine's wounded leg. "There aren't five of them worth their space on earth."

Kneeling, she went down beside Raine's thigh and lifted

the cloth Rosamund had placed there. It was her first sight of such a wound, the skin cut, angrily inflamed from the puncture wound, blood still seeping out, and her stomach tightened.

"Are you planning to lose your dinner?" Raine taunted as he saw her pale. "I've had much worse wounds, only this one seems to be so deep."

His legs, with the heavy, muscular thighs stretched in front of her, had several thick ridges of scars. Tentatively, she touched one.

"An ax blade," he murmured, lying back, at last the loss of blood beginning to drain his strength.

As gently as she could, she cleaned the wound, frowned when she saw how dirty it was, as if the arrow had been filthy and had cleaned itself in Raine's flesh. When she was finished, she drew a stool near his bed and watched him, his eyes closed, his breathing shallow but even, and she hoped he was sleeping.

After a very long time, he spoke, his eyes staying closed. "Alyx," he whispered, and immediately she knelt by him. "Under the cot is a case. Would you get it?"

Instantly, she pulled the leather case out, smiled when she recognized it as containing a lute.

"Can you play it?" he asked.

Smiling confidently, she opened the case and withdrew the lute, her fingers already dancing in her anxiety to touch the strings. Softly she began to play and sing one of her own compositions.

It was hours later when she felt sure Raine was asleep, lying still and pale on the cot, and she put the lute aside. In the silence, with only his ragged breathing in the tent, she wished Rosamund would return. Raine seemed worse than he had been and she needed someone to tell her he was going to recover.

A glance about the tent showed her they needed water, and the side of her doublet was soaked with Raine's blood and needed to be washed. In the morning there would be questions from the outcasts as to where the blood came from.

Silently, buckets in both hands, she left the tent and headed for the river, avoiding all contact with the camp people. With a sigh of relief she saw Blanche engaged in a game of dice with several men and knew the woman would not leave to see to Raine.

It was almost dark by the time she reached the water, filled the buckets and began to wash the doublet. To her chagrin, her shirt was also soaked. After a moment's hesitation, she removed it and the binding on her breasts and began to wash everything, including her own dirty skin and hair. Nearly freezing, she dried herself with the binding cloth and gritted her teeth as she slipped into the very cold, very wet shirt and hose, tossing the doublet over her arm, grabbing the buckets and nearly running back to camp.

Inside the tent, she held her breath, listening, glad Raine was still sleeping. When she'd rid herself of the buckets, she quickly discarded her wet clothes and pulled on one of Raine's shirts, which covered her to her knees. She knew she was taking a chance, but, truthfully, she wasn't sure if she didn't hope he woke and found out she was a girl.

She'd no more put the shirt on than a groan from Raine made her turn.

"Mary," he said. "Mary, I'll find you."

With one leap she was beside him. He must stay quiet and not let the people in the camp know he was unwell. The idiots had some idea that Raine secreted jewels and gold inside his tent, and Alyx had no doubt they would love the opportunity to search.

"Mary," Raine called louder, one big arm waving, just missing Alyx's head.

"Raine, wake up," she whispered loudly. "You are having a bad dream." As she caught his arm and touched his skin, she realized immediately that he was feverish. His skin was hot to her touch.

"No," she gasped and cursed Rosamund for leaving the camp when Raine needed her. A fever! What could she do? Feeling totally useless, she dipped a cloth in one of the buckets of water and went to place it on his forehead, but one of

body trembled and quaked, shivered until her strength turned to jelly.

Sticky, horribly weak, unsure of what her body had just done and she had done to it, she clung to Raine, letting herself feel all of his hot skin, his breath, uneven, in her ear. Moving one arm, and feeling as if she'd just rolled down a steep hill covered with stones, Alyx touched the damp hair along his neck. In a quick, fierce movement, Raine grabbed her hand as he rolled to his side, pulling her with him and clutched her hand in his, so tight he threatened to break her fingers.

"Mine," he whispered, bringing her hand to his mouth and kissing two fingers before sleep overtook him.

For several minutes Alyx dozed, half in sleep, half out. Her body was exhausted, yet somehow she was more alive than she'd ever been. She felt no shame for mating with a man who was not her husband, and perhaps she should, but at this moment there was nothing in life she needed other than this dear man's leg across her, this wet stickiness holding more than their bodies together.

"I love you," she whispered to the man sleeping in her arms. "I know you can never be mine, but for this moment you are. I love you," she said again as she kissed one damp curl and fell asleep again, more happy than she'd ever been in her life.

Chapter 8

ALYX AWOKE to a tent bright with early morning light, and Raine's skin touching hers was hotter than the night before. Asleep, he moved restlessly, rolling about, ignoring Alyx's presence as he rolled across her, threatening to break her bones. Pushing with all her might, she managed to get him off her and quickly began to don her clothes, which were wet in places, dry in others since they'd lain crumpled in a heap all night. She dearly wished she could put on a dress and give up the pretense of being a boy. Men's clothes and men's ways gave one a great deal of freedom, but if she were a boy she'd have missed a night such as she had had last night.

She had barely fastened her doublet when the tent flap opened and Jocelin, Rosamund behind him, entered.

"How is he?" Joss asked, watching Alyx intently.

Before she could answer, Rosamund interrupted them. "He has a fever and we must bring it down. Fetch some cold water while I get my herbs."

Immediately, Alyx grabbed the buckets and went to the river.

The next three days were torture for Alyx. She and Rosamund worked continuously to bring Raine's fever down. His big body was plastered with poultices and the women had to force noxious concoctions down his throat. This forcing was always accompanied by terrible commands from Alyx in which she called Raine everything from a worthless beggar to an overgrown strutting peacock, making Rosamund giggle and, at times, blush. Alyx sang to him constantly, played the lute often, anything to soothe him, to keep him from thrashing about so.

And while Raine was raging with fever, Jocelin tried to keep command of the outlaw camp, enforcing the daily training Raine had begun, trying to keep the cutthroats from murdering each other.

"I don't believe they're worth it," Joss said, sitting on the floor at the foot of Raine's cot. "Why does he," motioning to the sleeping man to his left, "feel he has to take on their problems?" He accepted a bowl of stew from Rosamund.

"Raine adopts everyone," Rosamund said quietly, her head lowered, as it always was. "He truly believes we are worth saving."

"We?" Alyx questioned as she looked up from Raine. She never left his side, slept sitting on a stool, her head propped on the edge of his cot. "I do not consider myself the same as a murderer."

"And you, Rose?" Jocelin asked. "What crime have you committed?"

Rosamund did not answer, but when Joss turned his head she looked up at him in such a way that Alyx gasped aloud, quickly covering the sound with a little cough. Rosamund was in love with Jocelin. As Alyx looked from one to the other, each with their extraordinary beauty, she saw how suited they were for each other. She knew why Rosamund was in this horrid camp, because people believed she was marked with the devil, but why was Joss here?

Early the next morning, Raine's fever broke. Alyx was sleeping, her head next to his bare arm when she sensed he was different. Looking up at him, she saw his eyes were open, looking about the tent and finally resting on her face.

Immediately, Alyx's heart began to pound and her betraying skin began to blush. How would he react to their having made love?

After a moment he turned away from her, his eyes telling her nothing. "How long have I been ill?"

"Three days," she answered, her voice catching in her throat.

"And you have held order in the camp? Or have they murdered each other?"

"They . . . they are well. Jocelin has held a sword over their heads and has kept the peace." When he didn't reply, she drew in her breath. Now he would speak of them, their passion.

Instead, he struggled to sit up, and when Alyx started to help him, he pushed her away as if she were of no consequence. Tossing the wool blanket aside, he tore the bandages off his thigh and impersonally inspected the wound on his leg, pushed at it.

"It's healing," she ventured. "Rosamund said the wound was not bad, only the fever: We feared for your life."

Turning to her, he gave her a cold, hard look, and she could almost swear there was anger in his eyes. "Fetch me some food and a lot of it. I need to regain my strength."

Alyx didn't move.

"Damn you!" Raine bellowed, his voice shaking the walls of the tent. The explosion obviously depleted what little strength he had, and for a moment his hand went to his forehead. "Obey me," he said quietly, lying back. "And boy," he added as she reached the tent flap, water buckets in her hands. "Bring me hot wine."

"Boy!" Alyx gasped once she was outside the tent. "Boy!"

"Alyx?" Joss asked. "Was that Raine I just heard?"

Glumly, she nodded.

"Are you all right? What was he shouting about?"

"How should I know what that great ox was bellowing about?" she snapped. "How can a low being like myself know what a friend of the king thinks?"

To her consternation, Jocelin laughed aloud and left her, whistling what Alyx knew was a ribald little song.

"Men!" she cursed, tossing the buckets into the river, hauling up sand and rocks with the water and then having to repeat the process. The second time she paused, tears in her eyes. "Boy," she whispered to the cold, rushing water. Did she mean so little to him that he couldn't even remember their night together?

Perhaps he needed a few hours to remember, she thought as she went back to the tent, stopping to tell Blanche Raine wanted food.

"I should know," Blanche said, her voice sweet, insinuating. "He's already called me to him, and I must say that Raine Montgomery has lost none of his strength," she said loudly for the benefit of the people around her, ostentatiously fastening the top of the dirty shirt she wore. "I've taken him his food."

With her chin up, Alyx entered the tent, her shoulders dragged down by the heavy buckets.

"What took you so long?" Raine asked, his mouth full.

She whirled to face him. "I have more duties than fetching your food," she said angrily. "And it looks like that whore of yours can well provide for you."

"Fair enough," he said evenly, tearing into a leg of pork. "Perhaps we should work on your prudery. A woman is a woman, a fragile, helpless thing, someone to be protected and loved, no matter what her station in life. If you treat a whore like a lady, she'll be one, and a lady can become a whore. It all depends on the man. Remember that. You're a long way from reaching manhood yet, but when you do—"

"When I do I won't need any advice from you," she fairly shouted before turning toward the exit, where she slammed into Jocelin. With one angry glance at him, she pushed past him and left the tent.

Joss glanced at Raine, took a seat on a stool and idly began to strum the lute while Raine silently ate. After a moment, Joss stopped playing.

"How long have you known about Alyx?" Joss asked.

Only a hesitation in his eating showed that Raine had heard. "For a matter of hours, really," he said calmly. "And how long have you known?"

"Always." He laughed at Raine's expression. "I was surprised no one else did. To me she was like a little girl dressed in her brother's clothes. When you called her a boy I couldn't believe you meant it."

"I wish the hell you'd told me," Raine said with feeling, a dimple appearing in his cheek. "A few days ago she was writing a letter for me and I nearly kissed her. I was sick for hours afterward."

"You've worked her harder than anyone else, you know."

"Perhaps I was trying to change her shape," Raine laughed. "I've been fascinated by her legs for some time."

"And now what do you plan to do with her?"

Pushing the tray away, Raine leaned back on the cot, feeling very weak, very weary. "Do you know how much of her story is true? What has Pagnell done to her?"

"Accused her of robbing him, declared her a witch, put a fat reward on her head."

Raine lifted one eyebrow at Joss, feeling foolish that he knew so little about what went on under his nose. "How do you think the filth of this camp would react to a young girl in their midst? One whose capture would bring them a reward?"

A snort from Joss was the only answer.

"I think it's best she stay a boy," Raine said thoughtfully, "and under my protection. The fewer people who know of her true identity the better."

"But you will tell Alyx you know she's a girl, won't you?"

"Ha!" Raine grunted. "Let the baggage suffer as I have. She's flipped that pretty little tail of hers at me at every opportunity, and this morning when I realized how she'd played me for a fool, I could have wrung her neck. No, let her stew awhile. She thinks I don't remember—" He glanced quickly at Joss. "She thinks I don't know she's female, let her stay that way."

Jocelin stood. "You won't be too hard on her, will you? Unless I'm mistaken, I think she believes herself to be in love with you."

Raine's grin was face splitting. "Good. No, I'll not harm her, but I will make her taste a bit of her own medicine."

An hour later, when Alyx returned to the tent, her chin

pointed toward the sky, Raine and Jocelin were leisurely playing a game of dice, neither of them seeming to be much interested in the game.

"Alyx," Raine said, not bothering to look up. "Did you practice on the field today? You're scrawny enough without losing the little muscle you have."

"Practice," she gasped, then calmed herself. "For some reason I don't understand now, I was concerned about whether you lived or died and gave no thought to embellishing my puny body."

With an expression of astonishment and hurt, Raine looked up at her. "Alyx, how can you speak to me so? Are you truly angry that I lived? Go away, Joss, I'm too tired to play anymore. Perhaps I'll fetch myself some wine—as soon as I'm strong enough," he added, lying back on the cot with a great show of weariness.

Joss gave a choking cough before slipping the dice into his pocket, rolling his eyes at Raine and leaving the tent.

Alyx tried to remain aloof, but when she saw Raine collapsed on the cot, looking so pale, so helpless, she relented. "I will bring you wine," she sighed, and when she handed it to him his hand was trembling so that she had to put her arm around his shoulders, support him and hold the cup to his lips—those lips that even now made her breath come quick.

"You are tired," Raine said sympathetically. "And how long has it been since you've had a bath? No one in the world can get as dirty as a boy your age. Ah, well," he said, smiling, leaning back. "Someday when you've found the right woman you'll want to please her. Did I ever tell you of the time I was in a tournament outside Paris? There were three women who—"

"No!" she yelled, making him blink innocently at her. "I do not want to hear your dirty stories."

"A squire should have more of an education than just weapons. For instance, when you play the lute, the tunes you choose and the words you sing are more suited for a female. A woman likes a man who is strong, sure of himself, she'd never like a wailing youth who sounds more like a female."

"A wailing—!" she began, thoroughly insulted. She may not be beautiful, but she was sure of her music. "And what do you know of women?" she snarled. "If you know as little of women as music, you are as ignorant as you are—"

"As I am what?" he said with interest, propping himself on one elbow to face her. "As handsome? As strong? As lusty?" he asked, practically leering at her.

"As vain!" she shouted.

"Ah, would that the size of you matched the strength of your voice. Have you ever tried pulling down castle walls by screeching at them? Perhaps you could strike a note and an enemy's army of horses would follow you off into the wilderness."

"Stop it! Stop it!" she screamed. "I hate you, you great, stupid, cowering *nobleman!*" With that she turned toward the tent flap, but Raine, his voice low, commanding, called her back.

"Fetch Rosamund, would you? I don't feel well at all."

She turned one step toward him but recalled herself and left the tent. Outside many people stood, obviously having heard the argument inside the tent. Trying her best to ignore the people as they laughed and punched each other, Alyx went to the training ground and spent three hard hours practicing with a bow and arrow.

Finally, exhausted, she went to the river, bathed, washed her hair and ate before returning to the tent.

It was dark in the tent, and since no sound came from Raine she assumed he was asleep. Now, she thought, if she had the courage, she'd walk away from this camp and never return. Why did she think that what was special to her was anything at all to this lord of the realm? No doubt he was used to women slipping in and out of his bed and paid little attention to them. What did one more matter? If she revealed herself as his last conquest, would he laugh or perhaps try to establish her as one of his many women? Would she and Blanche take turns entertaining him?

"Alyx?" Raine asked sleepily. "You were gone a long time. Did you eat something?"

"A bucket full," she said nastily, "so I can grow to be the size of your horse."

"Alyx, don't be angry with me. Come and sit by me and sing me a song."

"I know no songs like the ones you like."

"I will manage," he said, and his voice was so tired she relented, taking up the lute and playing quietly, humming with the tune.

"Judith will like you," he murmured.

"Judith? Your brother's beautiful wife? Why should a lady like her bother with a baseborn lawyer's . . . son?" She'd almost said "daughter."

"She will like your music," he said, his voice heavy with sleep, and Alyx resumed her playing.

When she was sure he was asleep she went to him, knelt by his bed and for a moment watched him, doing little more than assuring herself that he was alive. Finally, she went to her own hard bed and used all her strength to keep from crying.

In the morning Raine insisted on going to the training ground. No protest from Alyx or Jocelin could persuade him to rest for another day. As he walked, Alyx could see the sweat on his forehead, the dull look in his eyes as he forced himself to move.

"If you die, what use will you be to us?" Alyx tossed at him.

"If I die will you go personally and notify my family?" he said in such seriousness that her breath caught. Then a dimple flashed and she knew he was teasing her.

"I will throw your great carcass over a horse and go to meet your perfect family, but I will not kneel with your sisters to mourn you."

"There will be other women besides my sisters to cry at my passing. Did I ever tell you about Judith's maid Joan? I have never met a more enthusiastic woman in my life."

At that Alyx turned away, her back rigid against the sound of Raine's rumbling laugh.

After an hour's training, Alyx ran back to the tent to fetch some of Rosamund's herb drink for Raine, and there she found Blanche sorting through his clothes.

"What do you think you're doing?" Alyx demanded, making Blanche jump guiltily.

"For . . . for laundry," she said, her eyes darting.

Alyx laughed at that. "Since when do you know what soap is?" With a quick movement she grabbed Blanche's arms. "You'd better tell me the truth. You know what the punishment for stealing is—banishment."

"I should leave here," Blanche whined, trying to twist away from Alyx. "There's nothing here for me anymore. Let me go!"

As Blanche pulled Alyx pushed, and Blanche went sailing across the room, her back hitting a tent pole.

"I'll repay you for this," Blanche sneered. "I'll make you sorry you ever took Lord Raine away from me."

"I?" Alyx asked, trying to keep the pleasure from her voice. "And how have I taken Raine?"

"You know he doesn't take me to his bed anymore," she said, rising. "Now that he has a boy—"

"Careful," Alyx warned. "It seems to me that you should worry about my anger toward you. What were you searching for when I came in?"

Blanche refused to speak.

"Then I guess I'll have to talk to Raine," Alyx said, turning to leave.

"No!" Blanche said, tears in her voice. "I have nowhere else to go. Please don't tell him. I'll not steal. I never have before."

"I have a price for not telling Raine."

"What?" Blanche asked, frightened.

"Tell me about Jocelin."

"Jocelin?" Blanche asked, as if she'd never heard the name before.

Alyx only glared at her. "I will be missed soon, and if I don't have the story by the time someone comes for me, Raine will hear of your stealing."

Immediately, Blanche began the tale. "Jocelin was a jongleur and all the highest-born ladies wanted him, not only for his music but for his . . ." She hesitated. "The man never grew tired," she said wistfully, making Alyx believe she had first-hand knowledge.

"He went to the Chatworth castle at the command of Lady Alice."

The name Chatworth made Alyx's head come up. Chatworth was the man who held Raine's sister and sister-in-law.

"Lady Alice is an evil woman," Blanche continued, "but her husband, Lord Edmund, was worse. He liked to beat women, watch their struggles as he took them. There was a woman, Constance, and he beat her until she died—or at least he thought she was dead. He gave the body to Joss to dispose of."

"And?" Alyx encouraged. "I haven't much time left."

"The woman was not dead and Joss hid her, nursed her back to health and he fell in love with her."

"Was this unusual for a man of Joss's . . . talents?"

Blanche suddenly began to look very nervous, her hands pulling on each other, standing on first one foot, then the other. "I don't believe he'd ever loved anyone before. When Lord Edmund found out the girl was still alive, he took her for his own again and threw Jocelin in an *oubliette*. And the girl . . . this Constance . . ."

"Yes?" Alyx said impatiently.

"She thought Joss was as good as dead and so she killed herself."

At that, Alyx crossed herself at such a sin. "But Joss did get out, and he came here," she finished.

"But first he killed Lord Edmund," Blanche said quietly, and with that she pushed past Alyx and ran from the tent.

"Killed a lord," Alyx whispered to no one. No doubt there was a huge reward for his head, and no wonder he wanted nothing to do with the women of the camp. Alyx knew very well what it was to love a man and to lose him.

"What are you doing in here?" Raine asked angrily from behind her. "You have been gone for at least an hour, and here I find you standing alone doing nothing."

"I'll work," she muttered, turning away.

He caught her arm but released her as quickly as he touched her. "Have you had some bad news?"

"None that would interest you," she snapped before leaving the tent.

Alyx's thoughts for the rest of the day were taken up with Jocelin. Joss was a sweet, kind, sensitive man, and he deserved someone to love him. She wished she could have fallen in love with Joss; how much easier everything would be. Someday, probably soon, Raine would leave the forest and go back to his rich family and she would be alone.

As she absently lifted a sword, trying to bring it straight down over her head, her eye caught a movement at the corner of the field. In the shadows, standing still, watching, was Rosamund. Following her glance, Alyx saw that the woman looked only at Jocelin, that in her eyes blazed passion and fire and, as Alyx recognized it, lust. Her head wasn't bowed, and for the first time there was no subservience about her, no apology for having been born.

"Alyx! You slacken!" Raine yelled at her, and with a grimace she put her mind back on her training.

That night, Raine, exhausted, still very weak, went to his cot to rest, while Alyx sat outside in the cold night air and ate a bowl of beans. Beside her sat Jocelin.

"You tore your shirt," she commented. "Someone should sew it for you."

Before Alyx could breathe, three women cheerfully said they'd sew it.

"No," Joss muttered, looking at his bowl. "It does well enough as it is."

"Give one of them your shirt," Alyx said impatiently. "I will fetch one of Raine's to warm you. He has more than enough of them."

Reluctantly, Joss took off his shirt as Alyx hurried to the tent, cast one look at Raine's sleeping form and hurried out again, a shirt over her arm. Outside, she paused. Jocelin sat before the fire, his body bare from the waist up, women all around him, their eyes greedy as they looked at Joss, at his handsomeness, his obvious melancholy, and far to one side stood Rosamund. But Jocelin never looked at any of the women.

At the fire, Alyx handed Joss the shirt and dipped herself a mug of boiling cider, blowing on the liquid to cool it.

Suddenly, a noise just outside the circle of light made everyone's head turn in that direction.

Later, Alyx didn't really remember consciously planning what she did. No one was looking, she was standing next to Jocelin's bare body and holding the hot cider. All she thought of was that if Joss were hurt, he'd have to go to Rosamund, and the next moment she poured half the cider on Joss's arm.

Instantly, she was sorry. Jocelin jumped away from her, the shirt falling from his lap.

"Joss, I . . ." she began, looking in horror at the skin on his arm turning red.

"Rosamund," someone whispered. "Get Rosamund."

Within seconds Rosamund was there, her cool fingers on Joss's arm, and she was leading him away into the shadows.

Alyx wasn't aware of it, but there were tears in her eyes and her body was trembling from what she'd just done. It had all happened so fast and she'd had no time to think.

A great hand clamped on the back of her neck, paralyzing her.

"You will follow me to the river, and if you do not I will take a whip to your back now," Raine growled in her ear, his voice barely concealing his rage.

Her guilt over what she'd done to Joss was replaced by sheer terror. A whip to her back? Swallowing, she followed Raine into the dark forest. She deserved punishment, for she had no right whatever to hurt her friend.

Chapter 9

AT THE river, Raine turned to her, his fine lips curled into a snarl. "I should beat you," he said fiercely as he pushed her once, lightly, sending her sprawling onto the cold earth.

"And what slight did you imagine Jocelin had done you?" he asked, teeth clenched. "Were you jealous of the cut of his doublet? Had he said something you disliked? Perhaps he played a better song than you."

That got her attention. "No one is better than I," she said firmly, her jaw jutted forward as she stared up at him.

"Damn you!" he said, grabbing the front of her shirt and pulling her upward. "I trusted you. I thought you were one of the few of your class who had a sense of honor. But you're like all the others—allowing your petty differences to override your honor."

The two of them were an odd couple, Raine twice Alyx's size, towering, looming over her, but Alyx's voice was second to no one's. "Honor," she yelled back at him. "You don't know the meaning of the word. And Jocelin is my friend. He and I have no differences." She made it clear who she had the differences with.

"So! Your low little mind poured boiling cider on him for the fun of it. You are like Alice Chatworth. That woman loves to give and receive pain. Had I known you were like her—"

With that Alyx doubled her fist and hit Raine in the stomach. While he was blinking at her, she grabbed his knife from the sheath at his side.

"Spare me the history of your stupid family," she shouted, pressing the point to his stomach. "I will explain to Jocelin what I did and why I did it, but for you, you vain, arrogant braggart, you deserve nothing. You judge and condemn without one word of facts."

Impatiently, Raine brushed at her arm to knock the knife away, but Alyx's reflexes had quickened in the last weeks and Raine's were dulled from his fever. The blade cut the back and side of his hand and caused both of them to halt as they watched the blood well from the cut.

"You thirst for blood, do you?" Raine said. "Either mine or my friend's. I will show you how to receive pain." He reached for her, but she sidestepped him.

It took two tries to catch her, and when he did his hands clamped down on her shoulders as he shook her very hard. "How could you do that?" he demanded. "I trusted you. How could you betray me?"

It was difficult for the words to register when her head was about to fly off, but she finally began to understand what he was saying. Jocelin was Raine's responsibility, and he took his duties seriously. "Rosamund, Rosamund, Rosamund," she began to chant.

When at last he heard her, he stopped shaking her. "Tell me," he yelled in her face.

Her body was weak from the force of his shaking of her. "Rosamund is in love with Jocelin, and I thought she could replace Constance, but not if they were apart."

This made no sense to Raine. His fingers tightened on her shoulders, and she wondered if soon they'd come through. Quickly, she explained Joss's story about Constance, omitting the name of Chatworth.

Stunned silence from Raine filled the air. "You are matchmaking?" he croaked. "You wounded Jocelin because of some idiotic ideas of love?"

"What would you know of love?" she tossed at him. "You know so little of women that you don't know one when you see one."

"True," he countered quickly. "I am an innocent when it comes to the lying, deceiving ways of women."

"Not all women are liars."

"Name one who is not."

She was dying to mention herself but could not. "Rosamund," she blurted. "She is a good, kind person."

"Not when she uses such methods to snare a man."

"Snare! Who would want to catch such a loathsome specimen as a man?" She stopped her tirade when she saw Raine's eyes sparkling. "You know," she gasped. "You know."

She did not waste much time in speculating on the truth of her assumptions but lifted herself from the ground and flew at him, her fists clenched. "You—!" she began in anger, but Raine stopped her. He caught her, clasping the slight body against him and drawing her mouth to his. Hungrily, he kissed her, his hand on the back of her head, his other hand about her waist, holding her off the ground.

"Remember that I am a weak man," he whispered. "And a long day on the training field has—"

Alyx bit him on the shoulder. "How long have you known?"

"Not as long as I would have liked. Why didn't you tell me from the start? I understand why you had to dress as a boy, but I would have kept the secret."

She nuzzled her face in his neck, such soft, sweet-tasting skin. "I did not know you. Oh, Raine, are you really, truly *very* weak?"

Raine's laugh rumbled through her body as he pulled her away from him, tossed her in the air. "Got your first taste of love and can't stop, is that it?"

"It is like music," she said dreamily, "the very best music."

"I'm sure I should take that as a compliment," he said, beginning to unbutton her doublet.

For a moment it flashed across Alyx's mind that he wouldn't like her flat-chested body now when no fever blurred his senses. "Raine," she said, her hand on his. "I look like a boy."

It took a while before he understood her words. "You drive me to distraction with those legs of yours, and now you say you look like a boy? I have done everything in my power to make a man out of you and failed. But I *have* made a woman out of you."

With her breath held, Alyx allowed him to undress her, and when he looked at her slight body with hot, wanting eyes, she forgot any feelings of being unworthy.

With a laugh, she tore at his clothes, pulling whatever she could reach away from his skin.

Raine lowered her to the ground, kept his hands on her bare back while she had her way with him. Never had he encountered such enthusiasm.

"I do not hurt you?" he murmured as he held her small body.

"Only a little and only in the right places. Oh, Raine, I thought you would never recover from your fever." With that she jumped atop him, and after a look of astonishment, he put his hands on her slim hips.

"Sing for me, my little songbird," he whispered as he lifted her and lowered her onto his shaft.

Alyx's gasp was indeed musical, and it took her only minutes to catch the rhythm of Raine's movement as his big hands traveled upward to her breasts, warming her, exciting her. His hands traveled all over her body, halting just briefly at the gold Lyon belt, then down to her thighs that worked as she raised and lowered herself.

Raine's fingertips explored, caressed, until his urgency increased and his hands dug into her hips, holding her, manipulating her as he desired. With one violent upward thrust, he spent himself as Alyx shivered, shuddered and fell forward onto him.

"How could so much woman have disguised herself as a boy?" he murmured, his hands tangled in her hair, kissing her temple. "No wonder you threatened to drive me insane."

"Oh?" she asked, trying to hide her interest in his answer. "When was that? I would never have guessed you knew I was alive except as someone to fetch for you."

"Perhaps when you bent over or tossed a leg before my face or other such unmanly things."

"Toss—! I did no such thing. And what about you? Having me climb on your back, to straddle you! Is that how you treat all boys?"

He laughed at her. "Boys would have been interested in my strength. Are you cold?"

She snuggled on top of him, her body touching only his. "No."

"Alyx!" His head came up. "How old are you?" There was fear in his face.

She gave him a haughty look. "I am twenty, and if you hope I will grow—"

Chuckling, he pushed her head back down. "God has given you the gift of music, what more could you want? I was afraid you were a child. You don't look more than twelve."

"Do you like my music?" she asked innocently, making her voice soft and seductive.

"You'll get no more compliments from me. It seems you've had too many already. Who has trained you?"

Briefly she told him of the priest and the monk.

"So that is how you come to be a virgin at twenty and Pagnell—Hush," he said when she started to speak. "He is a coward, and he will not harm you while you are near me."

"Oh, Raine! I knew you'd say that. I knew it! There are many advantages to being a nobleman. Now you can go to the king and beg his forgiveness, then you and I will go to your home. I will sing for you and play for you and we will be so very happy."

Raine, in one motion, pushed her off him and began to dress. "Beg the king's forgiveness," he said under his breath. "And what have I done to be forgiven? Do you forget that two of my family are being held prisoner? Do you forget *why* I am here? And what of those in that camp? One moment you preach about the Enclosure Acts and the next you demand the farmers leave this new home they have found."

"Raine," she pleaded, holding her shirt to her neck, "I didn't mean—Surely if King Henry heard your side of the story he'd help you. This man Chatworth should not be allowed to hold your family."

"Henry!" he snarled. "You talk of him as if he were a god. He is a greedy man. Do you know why he's outlawed me? For my lands! He wants to take all the power from the nobles and keep it for himself. Of course, your class wants him to do this since he does good things for you, but what happens when a bad king has the power? With the nobles, at least, a bad one controls only a small area. What if Pagnell were king? Would you wish to follow a man like him?"

Hastily she pulled on her shirt. She'd never seen Raine so angry. "I wasn't talking about all of England," she soothed. "I meant us. Surely you could do more good for your family if you were with them."

"And for that you wish me to go on bended knee to the king?" he whispered. "Is that what you want? You wish to see me groveling, forsaking my vows of honor?"

"Honor!" she said loudly. "What has honor to do with this? You were wrong to use the king's men."

For a moment she was sure he was going to strike her, but he took a step backward, away from her, his eyes blazing. "Honor is all to me," he whispered before turning back to the camp.

As quickly as she could, she dressed and ran after him.

Standing before Raine's tent was one of his brother's men, a message in his hand. She was glad to see the man. Perhaps some good news from home would make Raine forget his anger.

Hurrying forward, she took the message and without a glance from Raine, slipped inside the tent. Smiling, she opened the message, and the next moment, her shoulders fell.

"What is it?" Raine growled. "Is someone ill?"

There were tears in Alyx's eyes when she looked up at Raine. As they locked gazes, his eyes hardened.

"What is it?" he demanded of her.

"Your . . . sister Mary is . . . dead," she whispered.

Raine's face betrayed no emotion except for a bit of white appearing at the corners of his mouth. "And Bronwyn?"

"Escaped from Roger Chatworth, but she has not been found yet. Your brothers are looking for her."

"Is there more?"

"No. Nothing. Raine—" she began.

He brushed her aside. "Go! Leave me to myself."

Alyx started to obey him, but as she looked back and saw his rigid back, she knew she couldn't leave him. "Sit!" she commanded, and when he turned to her his eyes were like black coals from hell.

"Sit," she said, quieter, "and we will talk."

"Leave me!" he growled, but he sat on a stool and dropped his head into his hands.

Immediately, Alyx sat at his feet, not touching him. "What was she like?" she whispered. "Was Mary short or fat? Did she laugh often? Did she rail at you and your brothers? What did she do when you were so obstinate she wanted to take a club to your head?"

He looked up at that, his eyes dark, angry. "Mary was good, kind. She had no flaws."

"It's a good thing," Alyx said. "She would have to be a saint to stand your mule-headedness, and no doubt your brothers are as bad."

Raine's hand fastened about her throat as he went for her, the stool flying. "Mary was an angel," he said into her face, pinning her body, his hands tightening.

"You will kill me," she said in a resigned voice, gasping. "And still Mary will not come back."

After a moment, his hands dropped and he pulled her close to him, twisting her body in impossible directions as his arms wrapped about her. Slowly, he began to rock her as he stroked her hair.

"Tell me about your angel. Tell me about your brothers. What is Judith like? And Bronwyn?"

It wasn't easy to get him to talk, but as the words began to come, she saw a close, loving family. Mary was the oldest of the five and adored by her younger brothers. Raine talked of her selflessness and, recently, how she and Bronwyn had risked their lives to save a serf's child. He spoke of Judith, how his brother had treated her badly yet Judith had loved him enough to forgive him.

Alyx, living in her small, walled village, had never thought about the family life of the nobles, had assumed they lived untroubled lives. Listening to Raine, she had a glimpse of heartache and sorrow, of life as well as death. She was glad that she had not read aloud Gavin's message to Raine. Roger Chatworth had raped the virginal Mary and, in horror, she'd thrown herself from a tower window.

"Alyx," Raine murmured. "Now can you see why I cannot go to the King? Chatworth is mine. I will have his head before we are finished."

"What!" she gasped, pulling away from him. "You're talking of revenge."

"He has killed Mary."

"No! He did not!" She looked away, damning herself for saying that.

Forcibly, he turned her face back. "You have not told me everything in Gavin's message. How did Mary die?"

"She . . ."

His fingers tightened on her jaw, the pain causing her tears. "Tell me!" he commanded.

"She took her own life," Alyx whispered.

Raine's eyes bored into hers. "She was of the Church, and she would not have done that if she had no reason. What was done to her?"

She could see that he had guessed, but he was pleading to be told he was wrong. She could not lie to him. "Roger Chatworth . . . took her to his bed."

Violently, Raine shoved Alyx across the room. As he stood, he threw back his head and let out a cry of such despair, such rage, such hate, that Alyx cringed at the foot of the cot.

Outside, everything was unnaturally quiet, even the wind having stopped.

Glancing up at him, Alyx saw that he was beginning to tremble, then shake, and as he lowered his head, she saw that pure hate was causing the convulsions. Instantly, she left the floor to throw her arms around him.

"No, Raine, no!" she pleaded. "You cannot go after Chatworth. The King—"

He pushed her off him. "The man would be glad to have fewer nobles. He will take Chatworth's land as well as mine."

"Raine, please." She pressed herself against him again. "You cannot go alone, and your brothers are searching for Bronwyn. And what of the people out there? You cannot leave them to murder each other."

"Since when has your concern been for them?"

"Since I am in a terror of your being killed," she answered honestly. "How can you fight Chatworth? Your men are not here. You do have soldiers, don't you? Does Chatworth have knights?"

"Hundreds," Raine said through clenched teeth. "He is always surrounded by men, always protected."

"And if you went to him would he meet you fairly, one to one, or would you have to plow through his men first?"

Raine looked away from her, but she could see her words were making sense. How she wished she knew more about the nobility! Honor, think of honor and whatever you do, don't mention money, she warned herself.

"Chatworth is not honorable," she continued. "You cannot deal with him in the way of a knight. You must work together with your brothers." Silently she prayed they were not so hotheaded as Raine. "Please, wait until you are calmer. We'll write to your brothers and work out a plan together."

"I am not sure—"

"Raine," she said quietly, "Mary has been dead for days. Perhaps Chatworth has already been brought to justice. Perhaps he has escaped to France. Perhaps—"

"You try to coax me. Why?"

She took a deep breath. "I have grown to love you," she whispered. "I would die before I stood by and watched you be killed, and that is what would happen if you attacked Chatworth alone."

"I do not fear death."

She looked up at him in disgust. "Go, then!" she yelled. "Go and give your life to Chatworth. No doubt he'd like that. One by one he can destroy your family. And you will make it easy for him. Come, I will help arm you. You will wear your finest armor. We'll strap on every weapon you own, and when you are invincible, you can ride out to face this Chatworth's army of men. Yes, come on," she said, grabbing his armor's breastplate. "Mary will be pleased to look down from heaven and see her brother hacked to bits. It will give her soul great peace."

Raine's look was so cold she felt it piercing her skin.

"Leave me," he said at last, and she did.

Alyx had never known such fear as she felt at this moment. Even in the cold air outside the tent, she was sweating profusely.

"Alyx," came a whispered voice that belonged to Jocelin. In seconds she was in his arms, her tears flowing. "Raine's sister," she sobbed. "Mary is dead and Raine wants to face the murderer's army alone."

"Ssh," Joss calmed her. "He is not like us. We were taught to be cowards, to turn tail and run, to live to fight another day. There are not many men like Raine. He'd rather die than face dishonor."

"I do not want him to die. He cannot die! I have lost everyone—my mother, my father. I know I have no right, but I love him."

"You have every right. Now be quiet and think what you can do to prevent his suicide. Surely his brothers know how hotheaded he is. Can you persuade Raine to write his brother and you can add a note?"

"Oh, Joss," she said, grasping his arms. At his wince, she stopped. "Your shoulder where I poured the cider. I am sorry, I—"

"Quiet," he said, placing his fingertips on her lips. "Rosamund is caring for me. It is a small wound. Now go to Raine and talk to him and do not lose your temper."

Silently, Alyx reentered the tent. Raine sat on the edge of

the cot, head in his hands. "Raine," she whispered, touching his hair.

Fiercely, he grabbed her hand, kissed the palm. "I am useless," he said. "A man kills my sister and I can do nothing. Nothing!"

She sat by him, put her arms around him, her head on his arm. "Come to bed. It's late. Tomorrow we will write to Gavin. Perhaps he can do something."

Docilely, Raine allowed himself to be put to bed, but when Alyx started toward her own pallet, he caught her arm. "Stay with me."

There was no possibility that she was going to reject such an offer. With a smile, she glided into his arms. All night, as she dozed fitfully, she was aware that Raine lay awake beside her.

In the morning there were shadows under his eyes and his temper was black. "Wine, I told you!" he bellowed at Alyx. "Then fetch pen and paper."

The letter Raine dictated to be sent to his brother was one of anger and revenge. He vowed to take Roger Chatworth's life, and if Gavin did not help him, he would go alone.

Alyx added her own message to the bottom, pleading with Gavin to talk some sense into Raine, that he was ready to take on all of Chatworth's men alone. Sealing the letter, she wondered what this great Lord Gavin would think of her presumption.

It was two days before replies came. The messenger, nearly dead from the pace he'd set, practically fell on Alyx. With trembling hands, she broke the seal.

King Henry was furious with both the Montgomerys and the Chatworths. He was placing a heavy fine on Roger Chatworth and renewing his issue for Raine being a traitor. He wanted both noblemen out of England and he was doing what he could to bring it about. He was angered by Raine's hiding in England, and it was rumored that Raine was raising an army to fight against the King.

With eyes filled with fright, Alyx looked up at Raine. "You would not do such a thing, would you?" she whispered.

"The man worries more as he grows older," Raine said in dismissal. "Who can train such scum as those to fight?"

"This is proof that you must stay in hiding. Your brother says King Henry would love to use you as an example of what would be done to others who do not believe he is the man with the power."

"Gavin worries about losing his land," Raine said in disgust. "My brother cares more for soil than he does for honor. Already he has forgotten our sister's death."

"He has forgotten nothing!" Alyx shouted at him. "He remembers he has other people in his family. Would it make you happier if he sent you to your death? He lost his unborn babe not long ago, he has lost his only sister, his brother's wife is missing and now he is to encourage you to willingly give your life for something as stupid as revenge?"

"For my sister's life!" he yelled back at her. "Do you expect me to stand still after what has been done to me? Is there no way one of your class can understand the meaning of honor?"

"My class!" she yelled back at him. "Do you think because of your high birth you are the only one with feelings? In one night one of your kind slashed my father's throat and burned my house. If that were not enough, I was declared a thief and a witch. And all this because of some man's lust. Now you talk to me of revenge, ask me if I understand it. I cannot step out of this forest for fear of my life."

"Alyx," he began.

"Don't touch me!" she shouted. "You with your superior ways. You ridicule us because we concern ourselves with money, but what else do we have? We scrape all our lives and give a big piece of our income to support you in your fine houses so you can have the freedom to spout about honor and revenge. If you had to worry where your next meal came from, I wonder how much you would talk of honor."

"You do not understand," he said sullenly.

"I understand perfectly and you damn well know it," she said before leaving the tent.

Chapter 10

IT WAS many hours before Alyx could calm herself. She sat alone by the river. Perhaps she was right in hating Raine because he was part of the nobility. There were barriers between them that could never come down. Everything he believed was the opposite of what she knew to be true. All her life she'd had to contend with work, chores before her music, chores after. There was always the worry that they were not going to have enough food. If it hadn't been for the priest, they would have gone without many winters. Sometimes Raine complained about the food in the camp, but the truth was she'd had more variety and quantity than she'd ever had.

When Pagnell had killed her father, she'd done what she could to survive. Survival! That meant nothing to someone like Raine and his powerful brothers. War, revenge, honor, these childish games of kidnapping each other were things that had never entered into her life.

"May I join you?" Jocelin asked. "Like to share your thoughts with me?"

Her eyes glistened. "I was imagining Raine behind a plow. If he had to worry about his fields growing he wouldn't have time to think of murdering this Chatworth. And if Chatworth were driving a team of oxen he wouldn't have had the energy to kidnap Raine's sister."

"Ah, make everyone equal," he said. "Rather like King Henry wants. Give all the power to one man and none to anyone else."

"You sound like Raine," she accused. "I thought you'd be on my side."

Jocelin leaned against a rock and smiled. "I am on no one's side. I have seen both ways of life and the poverty of the lower class doesn't appeal to me nor the . . . the decadence of the upper class. Of course, there are people in the middle. I think I should like to be a rich merchant, a buyer and seller of silks, and grow a fat belly."

"There were rich merchants in Moreton, but they weren't happy either. They were always worried about losing their money."

"Rather like Raine is worried about losing his honor?"

Alyx smiled at him, realized he was leading toward something. "What are you trying to tell me?"

"That all of us are different, that nothing is all good or bad. If you want Raine to understand your ways, be patient. Screeching at him will do little."

She laughed at that. "Screeching, is it? Perhaps I am a bit loud."

Jocelin gave an exaggerated groan. "You do realize that you are as stubborn as he is, don't you? Both of you are so sure you're right, that your way is the only one."

For a quiet moment, Alyx considered this. "Why do you think I love him, Joss? I know he's lovely to look at, but then so are you. Why would I love Raine when I know nothing can ever come of that love? The best I can hope for is to be made his family musician, to serve his . . . his wife and children."

"Who knows what makes us love?" Joss said, a faraway look in his eyes.

"It was almost as if I'd known Raine before I met him. All the way into the forest I kept thinking how I hated all the nobility, but as soon as I saw Raine—" She laughed. "I really did try."

"Come on, let's go back. I'm sure Raine will have work for us to do. And try to remember that he needs comfort now as much as lectures on what a mule he is."

"I will try," she said, taking his hand as he helped her up.

In the shadows of the trees stood a woman everyone seemed to have forgotten—Blanche. Her face contorted into ugliness when she saw Jocelin take Alyx's hand. For the last few days Alyx and Raine had been tearing at each other as only lovers can. They seemed to think the inside of the tent gave them privacy, but their two voices were so loud that stone walls wouldn't have sheltered them. The people in the camp wagered on who was going to win the arguments, saying the boy could hold his own. They cheered when Alyx said her class of people had too much work to do to talk about honor.

But there were things the people didn't hear, things that only Blanche heard as she fastened her ear to the tent wall: that Alyx had been declared a witch because of some man's lust, that Alyx loved Raine, and at night were the unmistakable sounds of lovemaking.

Once she'd had a good position in a castle, Edmund Chatworth's castle, and she'd had Jocelin for a lover. Now, in the rare times when Joss did look at her, his lips curled into a snarl and his eyes glowed with hatred. All because of that disgusting whore Constance! Constance had taken Joss away from Blanche, away from women everywhere. Jocelin, who used to laugh and sing, who took three women to his bed at once and made them all happy, was like a celibate priest now. Yet recently, he'd been looking at that devil-marked Rosamund with more than a little interest.

And now she was losing Raine—great, handsome, powerful, rich Raine. And to what? A skinny, short-haired, flat-chested boy/girl. If I were to wear men's clothes, Blanche thought, no one would mistake me for a boy. But that Alyx had no curves and her face looked like an elf's. So why was Raine panting after her? She was no highborn lady but of the same class as Blanche. Before Alyx came, Blanche was Raine's personal attendant and once, oh lovely night! she'd shared his bed. Now it was never likely to happen again—unless she could get rid of Alyx.

With a new, determined look on her face, she turned back to the camp.

*   *   *

For weeks Alyx worked to keep Raine from declaring war on Roger Chatworth. The letters that went from Montgomery Castle and back again began to be exchanged weekly. More than once, Alyx thanked the Lord Raine couldn't read, because at the bottom of her letters to Gavin, she added a postscript of her version of the truth. She told Gavin how Raine's anger grew each day, how he was driving himself harder and harder on the training field, preparing himself for battle with Chatworth.

In return Gavin wrote of Bronwyn's having been found, of her baby due in August. He wrote of their youngest brother's rage at his sister's death and how Miles had been sent to relatives on the Isle of Wight, in hopes that their uncle could cool Miles' temper. In a lighter vein, Gavin said that their uncle was the one in a rage now since his ward had fallen in love with Miles and was vowing to follow him to the ends of the earth.

"What is this brother of yours like?" Alyx asked, curious.

"Women like Miles," was all Raine would say. There was no humor about him these days. Even his lovemaking had a desperate edge to it.

Another brother, Stephen, wrote from Scotland. The letter, to Alyx's mind, was odd, filled with anger against the English, talk of the year's poor crops.

"Is your brother a Scotsman?" she asked.

"He is married to the MacArran and has taken her name."

"He has given up a good English name for a Scot's?" She was incredulous.

"Bronwyn could make a man do anything for her," Raine said flatly.

Alyx bit her tongue to keep from making a snide comment about the idle, rich women Raine had always loved. Once she did say something of the sort and made Raine smile.

"Judith," he said with such longing that Alyx winced. "In my life I have never spent a day working as hard as she does each day."

"Chivalrous of you," Alyx had snorted, disbelieving what he said.

It was in April that things began to happen. The camp of outlaws seemed docile all through winter, but as the trees began to bud and there was a breath of fresh air about, they began to fight. Not fight each other head on, but sneak up quietly and club someone.

Raine's work increased a hundred fold. He was determined to keep order in the camp.

"Why do you bother?" Alyx snapped at him. "They aren't worth your time."

For the first time in a long while, she saw one of his dimples appear.

"Can't teach honor to one of their class, is that it? Only we are privy to those feelings."

"We?" she snorted. "Since when have I become one of your satin-clad ladies? I'll wager I can handle a sword as well as your Judith can handle a needle."

For some reason this seemed to highly amuse Raine. "You'd win that bet," he laughed. "Now come here and give me a kiss. I know you're the best at that."

Gladly, she clung to him. "Am I, Raine?" she asked seriously. She tried to live each day as it came, but sometimes she thought of the future, of seeing Raine with his lady-wife, of herself in the shadows.

"Now, what's that look for?" he asked, tipping her chin up. "Am I so difficult to be around?"

"I'm just afraid, that's all. We won't always be in the forest."

"That is something to be thankful for!" he said passionately. "No doubt decay has set into my house in these last months."

"If you went to the King—" she began tentatively.

"Let's not argue," he whispered against her lips. "Is it possible to love a woman and hate her mind?"

Before Alyx could reply, he began to kiss her, and after that there was no thought of anything but the feel of him against her body. They were never very discreet; they couldn't be. Although Alyx still kept up the pretense of working on the training field, she was never quite serious. Whenever she felt Raine's eyes on her, she did everything she could to entice him to her. She teased him mercilessly.

And oh, what freedom the boy's clothes gave her! Once when they'd gone hunting and were quite some distance from the camp, Alyx turned around in the saddle to face him and untied the triangle in front of her tight hose. Raine, at first astonished, soon began to react to her creativity. Within seconds, he, too, was unfastened and he pulled her on top of him.

They had not counted on Raine's stallion. The horse, nostrils flaring, went wild at the smell of their lovemaking. Raine was fighting the horse and trying to hold onto Alyx's ardent little body. But the point came when he could no longer control anything. As his body exploded in Alyx's, the great beast reared, making Alyx's eyes fly open in wonder.

Raine laughed so hard at her expression she was insulted. "No, I will not do it again," he said, grinning. "And to think you spent most of your life inside a church. Now you're"— he wiggled his brows—"riding horses."

She made an attempt to snub him, but as she tried to turn around, she realized the triangular patch on her hose was missing. For an hour she had to bear Raine's laughter while they scrounged in the leaves looking for the bit of fabric.

But Alyx had the last laugh. The sight of her so provocatively clad soon changed his words to honey. She, with all the pride she'd learned from him, made him fall to his knees and beg for her favors. Of course she hadn't realized at what level his mouth would be with him on his knees and her standing. In seconds, it was Alyx begging for mercy.

After a long, leisurely lovemaking, Raine extracted her hose patch from his pocket—where it had been all along. As she pummeled his chest with her fists in mock fury, he kissed her until she was breathless.

"Learn who is the master here, wench," he said, nuzzling her neck.

"Now we must return to camp. That is, if my horse will let me ride him. No doubt he is as in love with you as you are with him."

She tried not to, but she blushed furiously at his jest. Raine gave her taut buttocks a friendly slap and lifted her into the saddle. He shouted with laughter when the horse danced in protest as Raine mounted.

"He protests your weight, most likely," she said smugly.

"You do not protest my weight, so why should he?"

Alyx thought it was better to keep her mouth shut because she knew Raine was going to win.

Now, holding onto him, she tried not to think of the future, of the time when they would no longer be equals.

A shout outside the tent made them start apart.

"What is it this time?" Raine growled. "Another robbery or another beating?"

There was a mob of people approaching the tent, all of them angry.

"We demand you find the robber," said the leader. "No matter where we hide our things, they are taken."

Rage swept through Alyx. "And what right do you have to make demands, you stupid oaf?" she yelled. "Since when is Lord Raine your protector? You should have gone to the gallows long ago."

"Alyx," Raine warned, clamping his hand onto her shoulder so hard she nearly fell. "Have you kept watch?" he asked the leader of the mob. "Have you hidden your goods?"

"*Well!*" he said, glancing hostilely toward Alyx. "Some of us have buried them. John here had his knife under his pillow and in the mornin' it was gone."

"Yet no one has seen this thief?" Raine asked.

Blanche stepped forward. "It must be someone small, someone light enough to slip about so easy." Her eyes darted to Alyx.

The mob turned their malevolent glances toward the boy next to Raine.

"It would have to be someone fearless," Blanche continued. "Someone who thought he was protected."

Involuntarily, Alyx took a step backward, closer to Raine.

"Blanche," Raine said quietly, "do you have someone you suspect? Get it out in the open."

"No one for sure," she said, loving the way everyone listened to her. "But I have me ideas."

Alyx, regaining her courage, started to step forward, but Raine stopped her.

"We'll catch the thief," one of the men said, "and when we do, is he gonna be punished?"

Alyx was so stunned by the look of hate in the man's eye that she didn't really hear Raine's answer. Somehow he was able to promise them enough that, grumbling, they finally dispersed.

"They hate me," Alyx whispered as Raine pushed her into the tent. "Why would they hate me?"

"You hate them, Alyx," Raine said. "They feel it even if you never say so. They think you put yourself above them."

She thought she was used to Raine's blunt way of speaking, but she was not prepared for this. "I don't *hate* them."

"They are people the same as you and me. We had the advantage of a family. Do you know the woman without a right hand? Maude? Her father cut off her hand when she was three so she'd get more money when she begged. She was a prostitute by the time she was ten. They are thieves and murderers, but it's only what they've known."

Alyx sat down heavily on a stool. "In these last months you've never mentioned this. Why?"

"It is your opinion. Each of us must do what we must."

"Oh, Raine," she cried, throwing her arms about his neck. "You are so good and kind, so noble. You seem to love everyone while I love no one."

"A saint is what I am," he agreed solemnly. "And my first act of sainthood is to declare my armor filthy and to deputize one scrawny angel to clean it."

"Again? Raine, in the next letter could I ask your brother for a *real* squire?"

"Up, you lazy child," he commanded, grabbing the pieces of steel, but as she stood at the door, loaded down, he gave her a fervent kiss. "To remember me by," he whispered before pushing her outside.

At the stream, Jocelin met her, five rabbits on a string

across his shoulder. They spoke only briefly before Joss went back to the camp. He was spending more and more time with Rosamund.

Alyx tried her best to put the incident of the robberies out of her mind. Surely the people would not believe Blanche's insinuations.

Two seemingly uneventful days went by and then there was another robbery and again people looked at Alyx suspiciously. Blanche, Alyx thought. The woman had certainly been busy in the last few days.

Once, when she ladled herself a bowl of stew, someone jostled her and the hot broth burned her hand. It seemed to be an accident but she wasn't sure. Another time she heard two men loudly discussing people who thought they were better than others.

On the fourth day, as she was walking on the training field, a sword accidently cut her arm. At Raine's questioning, no one seemed to have had his hand on the sword, and when he made them all train an extra hour, they glowered at Alyx.

In the tent, Raine was quiet as he bound her wound.

"Say something!" she demanded.

"I don't like this. I don't like to see you hurt. Stay closer to me. Don't leave my sight."

She only nodded at him. Perhaps she had been too hostile to these people. Perhaps they did deserve some of her time. She didn't know much about people really, only music. In Moreton she'd been popular because she gave people her music, but here they seemed to want something else. She knew Blanche was turning the people against her, but if she'd been kind over the last months Blanche wouldn't have had such an easy job.

That evening she borrowed Raine's lute and sat by the campfire and began to play. One by one, the people got up and left. For some reason this frightened her more than anything else.

For two days Alyx stayed close to Raine. The camp people now had someone to turn their hatred on, and they showed their feelings at every opportunity.

It was on the evening of the second day, while Alyx was just a few feet from Raine's side, that a man suddenly grabbed her and began searching her. Before Alyx could even cry out, the man yelled in triumph and held aloft a knife Alyx had never seen before.

"The boy took it," the man yelled. "We have proof."

Instantly, Raine was beside Alyx, pulling her behind him. "What does this mean?" he demanded.

The men grinned at the crowd gathering around them. "Your high-nosed little boy can't deny this," he said, holding the knife out for examination. "I found this in his pocket. I've had me suspicions for some time, but now we're all sure." He pushed his face close to Alyx's and his breath was foul. "Now you won't be thumin' your nose at us."

In seconds, he was picking himself up from the ground where Raine had tossed him. "Get back to work!" Raine ordered.

The people, the crowd growing larger by the moment, refused to move. "He's a thief," someone said stubbornly. "Beat him."

"Tear the flesh off his back and then see how proud he is."

Alyx, eyes wide, moved behind Raine.

"The boy is no thief," Raine said stubbornly.

"You nobles talk about fair treatment," someone in the back yelled. "This boy steals from us and is allowed to go unpunished."

"No!" yelled at least five people.

Raine drew his sword, pointed it at them. "Get away, all of you. The boy is no thief. Now, who will be the first to lose his life over this lie?"

"We'll punish the boy," someone yelled before the crowd began to disperse.

Chapter 11

IT WAS a very long while before Alyx could move away from the protection of Raine's solid form. Her knees were trembling and she clung to his arm.

"I didn't steal the knife," she finally managed to whisper.

"Of course not," Raine snapped, but she could tell from his expression that he wasn't dismissing the incident.

"What will happen now?"

"They will work to get what they want."

"And what is that?"

"A trial and your banishment. Before you came I promised them justice. I swore that all wrongdoers would be punished."

"But I have done no wrong," she said, on the verge of crying.

"Would you like to put that before a group of them? They would find you guilty even if you were the Holy Mother."

"But why, Raine? I have done nothing to them. Last night I even tried to sing for them, but they turned away."

He was serious when he looked down at her. "Has your music always been enough for people? Has no one ever asked more of you than to sing prettily?"

She had no answer for him. For her there'd been no life except her music. To the people of her town all they'd expected of her was music, and it was enough for them as well as for herself.

"Come," Raine said. "We must make some plans."

Glumly, she followed him, her head down, not meeting an eye of anyone they passed. This anger directed toward her was something so new to her.

Once they were in the tent, Raine spoke quietly. "Tomorrow we will leave the forest."

"Leave? We? I don't understand."

"The people are poisoned against you, and it will no longer be safe for you to stay here. I cannot protect you every minute of the day and I cannot allow them to harm you. Tomorrow morning we'll leave."

Alyx so aware of the hate of the people just outside the thin walls, could barely listen to him. "You cannot leave," she murmured. "The King will find you."

"Damn the King!" Raine said angrily. "I cannot stay here and worry that each day one of them will turn on you. You cannot sing your way out of this, Alyx. For all their look of it they are smarter than the horses you charm. They will do what they can to hurt you."

Alyx was beginning to listen to him. "You would go with me?"

"Of course. I couldn't very well let you leave alone. You wouldn't last a day outside in the world."

Tears blurred her eyes. "Because other people would also find out what I am? That I am a vain, arrogant person who cares for no one but herself?"

"Alyx, you are a sweet child and you care for me."

"Who could not love you?" she asked simply. "You have more kindness in your little finger than I have in all my body. And now you risk capture and imprisonment to save me."

"I will take you to my brother and—"

"And Gavin will risk the King's wrath because he harbors a woman wanted for witchcraft. Would you jeopardize all your family for me, Raine? Do you love me that much?"

"Yes."

Alyx's eyes flew to his, saw the love there, and instead of giving her pleasure it gave her pain. "I must be alone," she whispered. "I must think."

He followed her to the tent flap and as she left, he called Jocelin to him.

As Alyx made her way through the dark forest to the stream, her thoughts jumbled about in her mind. She sat on a rock, staring at the dark, sparkling water.

"Come out, Joss," she called. "You are a poor follower," she said despondently when he sat beside her. "Did Raine order you to protect me?"

Joss remained silent.

"He has to protect me now," she said. "He can't leave me alone for even minutes for fear someone will punish me."

"You have done no wrong."

"I have not stolen, true, but what good have I done? Look at Raine. Now he could be in another country living in comfort, but he chooses to stay in this cold forest and help his countrymen. He protects them, sees that they are fed, works for them always. And yet there is a reward on his head and he must stay here while his family needs him. His sister is raped and commits suicide and in his grief he does not even stop work for an hour."

"Raine is a good man."

"He is a perfect man," she said.

"Alyx," Jocelin whispered, his hand on her arm, "Raine will protect you from the people, and what time he can't be near, I will be. Your love for him has helped him through his grief."

It came as no surprise to her that Joss knew she was a woman. "What good is my love? I am not worthy of him. Tomorrow he plans to leave this camp, to ride freely into the sunlight of a country where he is fair game for the King's wrath. He will leave the safety of the forest and risk prison or even death to protect me."

Again Jocelin was silent.

"Don't you have anything to say? No soothing words telling me Raine's life will be safe?"

"He will be in great danger if he leaves the forest. Raine is well-known and easily recognized."

A great sigh escaped Alyx. "How can I let him risk so much for me?"

"So what do you plan to do?" Joss asked sharply.

"I will leave by myself. I cannot stay and cause Raine worry, and he cannot leave with me. Therefore I will go alone."

Joss's laugh startled her. "I'm sure Raine Montgomery will be as obedient as a lap dog. You will inform him you plan to leave and he will meekly kiss you goodbye and wish you well."

"I am prepared for a fight."

"Alyx," Jocelin laughed. "Raine will toss you across his horse and carry you out of the forest. You can yell all you want, but when it comes to the point, muscle will win over words."

"You are right," Alyx gasped. "Oh, Joss, what can I do? He cannot risk his life for me."

"Love him," Joss said. "That's all he wants. Go with him, stay with him. See him through everything."

She jumped up from the rock, hands on hips, glaring at Jocelin. "What am I to do when he is killed because of me? Should I hold his cold hand and sing a sweet song to the Lord? No doubt I'll make magnificent music, and everyone will say how I must have loved him. No! I don't want cold hands. I want hot ones loving me—or loving anyone, for that matter. I'd rather give Raine back to Blanche than see him dead."

"Then how are you going to make him stay here?" Jocelin asked quietly.

She sat down again. "I don't know. Surely there must be something I could say. Perhaps if I insulted his family."

"Raine would laugh at you."

"True. Perhaps if I told him he were a . . ." She couldn't think of a single thing she hadn't already called him. Obviously names would not harm him. "Oh, Joss," she said desperately, "what can I do? Raine must be protected from himself. If he were to leave the forest no doubt he'd pursue Chatworth, and then the King would become involved in the quarrel and—I can't let it happen! What can I do?"

It was a long moment before Jocelin spoke and when he did, she barely heard him. "Go to bed with me."

"What!" She whirled on him. "I am talking to you of a man's safety, his possible death and you are trying to woo me to your bed? If you want a woman, get one of those hags who pant after you. Or take Rosamund to your bed. I'm sure she'd enjoy it more than I would."

"Alyx," he chuckled, hand on her arm. "Before you launch into me more fully, listen to me. If you are serious about Raine's staying here, there is nothing you can say to make him stay, but perhaps there is something you can do. He doesn't really know you very well, not enough to trust you, or perhaps no man ever trusts a woman. If Raine were to find you with another man there would be nothing you could say to make him take you back. He would let you go and he would stay here."

"He would hate me," she whispered. "He can have a violent temper."

"I thought you were serious about this. A moment ago you said you'd rather Blanche had him." He nearly choked on the woman's name. "Are you hoping that you can leave Raine now and later when he is again in the King's good graces, you can come back to him? That would only happen in a song you wrote yourself. The only way Raine Montgomery will let you leave this forest without him is if his feelings for you are totally reversed."

"To change his love to hate," she whispered.

"Do you dream of his standing and waving goodbye to you, tears in his eyes?" Joss asked sarcastically. "Alyx, you love him too much to hurt him. Tomorrow let him take you out of here. His brothers will protect him until the King pardons Raine."

"No! No! No!" she shouted. "No one could protect him from an arrow. Even in this forest surrounded by guards, he was shot. To leave would risk death. How could I hurt him more than to kill him?"

She buried her face in her hands. "But to have him hate

me! To change the way he looks at me from love to hate—
Oh, Joss, that is a great price to pay."

"Do you want his love or his life? Would you rather sing
over his grave or know he is alive but in another woman's
arms?"

"I'm new to this idea of love, but right now the idea of
another woman touching him makes me prefer his death."

Joss tried to keep from smiling. "Is that what you truly
want?"

"No," she said softly. "I want him alive, but I also want
him with me."

"You must choose one."

"And you believe the only way to get him to stay is to . . .
to bed someone else?"

"I can think of nothing else."

Her eyes widened. "But what of you, Joss? Raine would
be very angry with you."

"I daresay he will."

"What will you do? Your life here could be hell."

Joss cleared his throat. "If I want to keep my life, I think
I should leave also. I wouldn't like to indulge in a duel with
Raine after making love to his woman."

"Oh, Joss," she sighed. "I would be ruining your life as
well as mine. You're wanted for murder. What if someone
recognizes you?"

She didn't see Joss start at her words. He had no idea she
knew his history.

"I'll grow a beard and you, as a boy, will not be known.
We'll sing together, play, and we'll be able to earn our keep."

Pagnell was her first thought, but she brushed it away. For
the first time in her life she wasn't going to think of herself
first. "Raine has had so much tragedy in his life. His sister's
death was so recent, and now . . ."

"Make up your mind, Alyx, and get your clothes off. If
I'm right, Raine is coming this way now."

"Now?" she gasped. "I need time to think."

"Choose," he said, close to her. "Dead and yours or alive
and someone else's?"

The image of Raine quiet, forever silent, made her throw her arms about Jocelin's neck, her lips seeking his.

For many years, Jocelin had been an expert at removing women's clothes, and it was something he had not forgotten. Even if Alyx did wear boy's clothes, it was amazing how quickly Joss's skillful fingers rid her of them. Before she could come up for air, both of them were nude from the waist up, bare flesh against skin.

Jocelin entwined his hands in Alyx's hair and pulled her head back and kissed her hungrily as her eyes flew open in alarm.

She did not have a second to consider Joss's kiss because Raine's powerful hands pulled them apart, sending both of them flying across the stream bank.

"I will kill you," Raine said under his breath, his eyes boring into Jocelin's.

Alyx, dazed from the flight Raine's hands had sent her on, thrust her arms into her shirt as she saw Raine drawing his sword and bellowed, "No!" loud enough to make the trees drop their nighttime dew. Give me strength, she prayed as she stood.

She placed her body before Joss's. "I will give my life for this man," she said with feeling. As she saw the looks on Raine's face changing from bewilderment to hurt, to anger, to coldness, she felt them in her heart.

"Have I been a fool?" he asked quietly.

"Men are like music," she said as lightly as she could manage. "I cannot exist on a diet of love songs or alone on dirges. I need it all. I must have variety in men as well as in my songs. You, ah, you are a song of fury, of cymbals and drums, while Joss"—she fluttered her lashes—"Joss is a melody of flutes and harps."

For a moment, she thought perhaps Raine was going to tear her head from her body, and instead of feeling fear she was almost welcoming him. Her soul was praying that he wouldn't believe her. Could he truly believe that music meant more to her than he did?

"Go from my sight," he whispered from deep inside himself. "Let . . . your friend care for you from now on. Leave tonight. I do not want to see you again."

With that he turned to leave, and Alyx was several steps toward him before Joss grabbed her arm. "What can you say to him now except the truth?" he asked. "Leave him alone. Break the tie now. Wait here and I will return in a short while. Do you have any other clothes or other possessions?"

She shook her head and was barely aware that Jocelin left her alone.

There didn't seem to be any thoughts that went through her head as she waited for him to return. Raine believed her, believed that she thought her music was so very, very important. The people of the camp were willing to believe she was a thief and were eager to see her punished. Yet what had she ever done in her life to make anyone trust her, believe that she was a good person?

"Are you ready?" Jocelin asked from beside her, Rosamund a silent shadow behind him.

"I am sorry I have caused you—" she began.

"No more," Joss said firmly. "We must look to the future now."

"Rosamund, you will look after him? See that he eats? See that he doesn't train too hard?"

"Raine will not listen to me as he does to you," she said in her soft voice, her eyes devouring Jocelin.

"Kiss her," Alyx whispered. "Someone should give their love and not hide it." With that she turned away, and when she looked back she saw Rosamund clinging fiercely to Jocelin. When he returned to Alyx there was a look of surprise on his face.

"She loves you," Alyx said flatly before they started the long journey to reach the outer edges of the forest.

PART II

August 1502

Chapter 12

ALYX PUT her hand on the small of her back and eased herself down in a grassy patch just off the road, giving a grateful little smile to Joss when he handed her a cup of cool water.

"We'll rest here for tonight," he said, his eyes studying the tired lines on her face.

"No, we must play tonight—we need the money."

"You need rest more!" he snapped, then sat down beside her. "You win. You always do. Hungry?"

Alyx gave him a look that made him smile, and he glanced downward to her big belly as it pushed out the wool of her dress. The summer's heat and their constant walking made Alyx miserable.

It had been just over four months since they'd left Raine's camp, and in that time they'd barely stopped walking. At first it hadn't been difficult. They were both strong and healthy and they were popular musicians. But after a month on the road, Alyx became ill. She vomited so often people refused to travel with them, fearing the boy had some disease. And Alyx became so weak she could hardly walk.

They stayed for a week in a little village while Jocelin sat by the city gates and sang for pennies. Once Alyx came to him carrying bread and cheese, and as he watched her he thought how she'd changed since the time in the forest. Perhaps it was because he'd grown to care about her lately that she seemed to have grown lovelier, softer, prettier. Her boyish swagger had turned into a gentle, rolling, definitely female walk. And even though she'd been ill, she was gaining weight.

All of a sudden; it had hit Joss what was "wrong" with Alyx: she was carrying Raine's child. By the time she reached him he was laughing, and if they'd been alone, he'd have swirled her about in his arms.

"I will be a burden to you," Alyx said, but her eyes were alight. Before Joss could reply, she began chattering. "Do you think he will look like Raine? Would it be wrong to pray for a child to have dimples?"

"Let's save our prayers and wish for the means to dress you as a woman. If I travel with a pregnant boy I don't think I will live long."

"A dress," Alyx smiled, something soft and nice to make her feel like a woman again.

Once Jocelin was relieved of his feeling that Alyx was dying of some dread disease, he was more confident about allowing her to journey from castle to castle. And Alyx, after finding she had not lost all of Raine, was in much better spirits. She talked constantly about the baby, what it would look like, how Raine's features would look on a girl and if she did have a girl, she hoped the child would not grow to be quite as big as her father. Alyx also laughed over the fact that she never did anything properly. Instead of being ill the first three months, she was ill the second three.

Joss listened to everything over and over again. He was so pleased she was no longer silent and sullen as she'd been for months after they left the forest. At night, sleeping on pallets on the floor of whatever house they were performing at, he often heard her crying, but she did not mention her sorrow during the day.

Once they played and sang at a large manor house belonging to one of Raine's cousins. Alyx had again become very silent, but he could almost feel her straining to hear any bit of news.

Jocelin had dropped a few hints to Montgomery's wife and the woman had told him much. Raine was still in the forest and King Henry, in his grief over the death of his eldest son, had nearly forgotten the outlawed nobleman. The King was much more worried about what to do with his son's wife, the Princess Katherine of Aragon, than what to do about a private feud. He ignored the petitions of the Montgomery family to punish Roger Chatworth. After all, Chatworth had not killed Mary Montgomery, only raped her. He had harmed her in no way. It was on the girl's soul that she committed suicide.

There was news that in July Judith Montgomery had borne a son and later in August Bronwyn MacArran had also been delivered of a son. The Montgomery cousins were still incensed over Stephen's adopting the Scot's name and ways.

Alyx listened avidly to everything Jocelin reported to her.

"It's good that I'm no longer with him," she said quietly, strumming a lute. "His family is full of ladies while I am a lawyer's daughter. If I had stayed with him I don't believe I could have been docile or polite to his lady-wife and she wouldn't have wanted me near, though some of these ladies I see are cold-blooded wenches. Perhaps he could have used a little warmth."

Jocelin tried to show her that what was different between her and the ladies could be solved with a silk dress, but Alyx wouldn't see it. He knew she brooded not only over Raine but over the hatred of the people in the forest.

As Alyx's pregnancy advanced she grew quieter, more thoughtful, and she seemed much more aware of the world than she had been when he first met her. Once in a while, not often, really, she'd stop practicing to help someone do something. On the road they always traveled with a group rather than risk the highway robbers alone, and Alyx sometimes took a few children for a walk to give the mothers some peace, and once she shared her food with a toothless old beggar. Another time she prepared a meal for a man whose wife was lying under some trees giving birth to her eighth child.

The people smiled in gratitude and as a result they'd made friends wherever they traveled. A child once gave Alyx a little bouquet of wildflowers, and there'd been tears in Alyx's eyes.

"These mean a great deal to me," she'd said, clutching them tightly.

"She was repaying you for helping her yesterday. The people here like you." He motioned to the travelers beside them.

"And not music," she whispered.

"Pardon?"

"They like me for something besides my music. And I have given them something besides music."

"You have given of yourself."

"Oh, yes, Joss," she laughed. "I have tried to do things that were difficult for me. Singing is so very, very easy."

Jocelin laughed with her. That anyone could say that music such as Alyx produced was easy was amazing.

Now, in August, when the burden of the heavy child was dragging on her, her steps were slower and slower and Joss wished they could afford to stay in one place for a length of time.

"Are you ready to go?" she asked, trying to heave herself upward. "We'll make the castle by nightfall if we hurry."

"Stay here, Alyx," he urged. "We have food."

"And miss the lady's betrothal celebration? No, once we're there we'll have plenty to eat, and all we have to do is create a divine bit of music celebrating the heiress's slender charms. I do so hope this one is pretty! The last one was so ugly I confessed the severity of the lies I sang to the priest."

"Alyx!" Joss said in mock chastisement. "Perhaps the lady was beautiful inside."

"Only you would think such a thing. Then, of course, with your face you can afford to be generous. I saw the way the ugly girl's mother threatened to devour you. Did she make you an offer after the singing?"

"You ask too many questions."

"Joss, you can't keep cutting yourself off from people and life. Constance is dead."

It had taken Alyx a long time to get him to tell her about the woman he'd once loved.

Jocelin set his jaw in such a way that Alyx knew he was

refusing to speak of himself. Between them, her problems were common property while his were his own.

"Of course, none of the women have been as lovely as Rosamund. Except for her devil's mark, that is. That hideous thing makes it difficult to see any beauty at all. I wonder if it really is Satan's sign."

Jocelin whirled on her. "It is more likely a mark of God's favor because she is a good, kind, passionate woman."

"Passionate, is she?" Alyx teased as he turned away.

"You are cruel, Alyx," he whispered.

"No, I only want you to see that there is no reason for you to bury yourself with me. You cannot hold yourself inside. You have so much to give, yet you stay inside yourself."

When he looked at her, his eyes were cold. "Raine is not here, so why don't you find someone else to love? I've seen many men, from noblemen down to stable boy, give you looks. They'd take you even with your big belly. Why not marry some merchant who will give your child a home and who will make love to you every night?"

After his attack, she was quiet for a few moments. "Forgive me, Joss. I had hoped Rosamund could replace Constance, but I see she cannot."

Jocelin turned away because he didn't want Alyx to see his face. Too often in the last months the face he remembered at night was Rosamund's, not Constance's. Rosamund, so silent, almost apologizing for her existence, was quite often the woman he saw, not as the quiet, gentle woman he knew but as the woman who'd kissed him goodbye. For the first time since Constance's death, a spark had shot through him. Not that there hadn't been a few women here and there, but before he'd met Constance and since then he'd been detached, always apart from the women. Only that one brief time when he'd held Rosamund had he felt even a flicker of real desire, real interest in a woman.

Joss took Alyx's hand in his and together they started toward the castle that loomed ahead of them. It was an old place, one tower crumbling, and Alyx knew they'd have another drafty sleeping place. In the last months of traveling she'd learned a great deal about the nobility. Perhaps the most significant thing was that noble women had as little freedom as women anywhere. She'd seen great ladies with blackened eyes from their husband's beatings. She'd seen weak, cowardly noblemen who were treated with contempt by their wives. There were matches of great love, couples who hated each other, households of great decadence and some based on love and respect. She'd begun to realize that nobles had problems very similar to those of the people in her own small town.

"Daydreaming?"

"Thinking about my home, what a protected childhood I had. I almost wish my music hadn't set me apart from everyone else. It makes me feel as if I don't quite belong anywhere."

"You belong wherever you want."

"Joss," she said seriously, "I don't deserve either you or Raine. But someday I hope I can do something worthy."

"Did you know you talk more like Raine every day?"

"Good!" she laughed. "I hope I can rear his child to be even half as good as he is."

As they approached the old castle, they had to wait to be admitted, since there were hundreds of people entering before them. The betrothal was to join two powerful, rich households and the guests and entertainment were to be sumptuous.

Joss kept his arm around Alyx's shoulders as he led her through the crushing crowds.

"Are you the singers?" a tall woman shouted down at Alyx.

Alyx nodded up at her, awed by the dark, steel-banded hair, the richness of her gown.

"Follow me."

Gratefully, Alyx and Jocelin followed her up a narrow, winding stone stairway to a large round room at the top of the tower, where several women were pacing and showing signs of agitation. In the center of the room was a young woman wailing loudly.

"Here she is," a woman beside Alyx said.

Alyx looked up at an angelic face, blonde hair, blue eyes, an ethereal, delicate smile.

"I am Elizabeth Chatworth."

Alyx's eyes widened at the name, but she said nothing.

Elizabeth continued. "I'm afraid our little bride-to-be is terrified," she said in a tone of exasperation and disgust. "Do you think you could calm her enough so that we could get her downstairs?"

"I will try."

"If you can't, then I'll have to put my hand to her cheek and see if that music will quieten her."

Alyx had to smile at this sweet-looking woman's words. They did not fit her face at all. "What is she frightened of?" she asked, trying to decide what music to play.

"Life. Men. Who knows? We have both just come from the convent, and you'd think Isabella was going to her death."

"Perhaps her betrothed—"

"He's manageable," Elizabeth said with a wave of dismissal. Her eyes went to Jocelin, who was staring openly at Elizabeth. "You're pretty enough to not frighten the rabbit," she said. A loud wail from Isabella sent Elizabeth to her side.

"My goodness," Alyx said, feeling as if she'd just left a storm. "I don't believe I've ever met anyone quite like her before."

"And I pray we don't again," Joss said. "She calls us. Heaven help the man who dares disobey that one, although . . ."

Alyx looked up at him, saw the speculative gleam in his eye. "She'll have your hair if you disobey her."

"It's not my hair she'd remove, and damned if I'd mind letting her."

Before Alyx could reply, Joss pushed her toward the crying bride.

It took an hour to calm the woman, and all the while Elizabeth Chatworth paced behind the chair, now and again narrowing her eyes at the weeping Isabella. Once she opened her mouth to say something but Alyx, fearing the woman would ruin what she and Joss had accomplished, sang even louder to cover the beginning of Elizabeth's sentence.

When at last Isabella was ready to go downstairs, all of

her maids went with her, leaving Jocelin and Alyx alone with Elizabeth Chatworth.

"You did well," Elizabeth said. "You have a magnificent voice, and unless I miss my guess you are well trained."

"I have spent some time with a few teachers," Alyx said modestly.

Elizabeth's eyes fixed on Jocelin in a piercing gaze. "I have seen you before. Where?"

"I knew your sister-in-law, Alice," he answered softly.

Elizabeth's eyes turned hard. "Yes," she said, with a brief, insolent look up and down Joss's form. "You would be her type. Or perhaps any man with the proper equipment is pleasing to her."

Jocelin had an expression on his face Alyx had never seen before. She wished he'd say no more. After all, it was Joss who'd killed Edmund Chatworth, Elizabeth's brother.

"And how are your brothers?" Joss asked, and there was challenge in his voice.

For a long moment Elizabeth's eyes bored into his, and Alyx held her breath, praying Elizabeth would not know who Joss was.

"My brother Brian has left my home," she said quietly, "and we do not know where he is. There is rumor that he is held by one of the filthy Montgomerys."

Jocelin's hand clamped down on Alyx's shoulder brutally. "And Roger?" he asked.

"Roger . . . has changed. Now!" she said smartly. "If we are through discussing my family, I am sure you are wanted below." With that, she swept from the room.

"Filthy!" Alyx yelled before the door was closed. "Her brother kills my Raine's sister and she dares call us filthy!"

"Alyx, calm yourself. You cannot take on a woman like Elizabeth Chatworth. She'd eat you alive. You don't know what kind of brother she grew up around. Edmund was mean, vicious, and I've seen Elizabeth stand up to him at times when even Roger backed down. And she adores her brother Brian. If she thought the Montgomerys caused him to be taken from her home, she'd be full of hate."

"But she has no right! It was the Chatworths' fault."

"Quiet! and let's go downstairs." He eyed her sharply. "And none of your tricks of writing songs about feuds. Do you understand me?"

She nodded once, but she didn't like making such a promise.

It was late at night, and most of the guests were lying drunken on the floor or sprawled across the tables when a servant whispered to the man sitting in the corner. With a smile, the man rose and went outside to greet these newly arrived guests.

"You'll never believe who is here," the man said to the one dismounting.

"What! no greeting?" he asked sarcastically. "No concern for my safety? Come, John, you're letting your teeth show."

"I have remained sober to tell you this. That should be enough."

"True, that is a great sacrifice." He gave the reins of his horse to a waiting servant. "Now, what is so important that it can't wait until I've had some wine myself?"

"Ah, Pagnell, you're too impatient. Remember that little songbird this winter? The one who knocked you over the head?"

Pagnell stiffened, glaring at John. It was all he could do to keep from fingering the ugly scar on his forehead. He'd had headaches ever since that night, and although he'd tortured to death some of the people from her town, no one would tell him where she was. Every time a pain shot through his head, he vowed he'd see her burn for what she'd done to him. "Where is she?"

John laughed deep in his throat. "Inside and swelled out with a brat. She's traveling with a pretty lad and the two of them are singin' as pretty as you please."

"Now? I thought everyone would be asleep."

"They are, but I marked where the lad and the songbird stretched out."

Pagnell stood still for a moment, contemplating his next

move. When he and his friends had gone over the town wall looking for Alyx, he'd been drunk and so had bungled the job. Now he mustn't make that mistake again.

"If she cried out," Pagnell said, "would she receive help?"

"Most of them are dead drunk; the snoring's so loud a charge of gunpowder might not be heard."

Pagnell looked up at the old stone walls. "Does this place have a dungeon, some place for keeping prisoners before they're executed?"

"Why wait? We'll tie her to a stake and burn her as the sun rises."

"No, some people frown at that, and with the King in this melancholy mood, who knows how he'll react? We'll do this legal. A cousin of mine is conducting court not far from here. We'll toss the slut in the cellar, then I'll talk to my cousin and when I return, we'll have a trial. *Then* we'll watch her burn. Now show me where she is."

Alyx was lying in an uncomfortable sleep, trying her best to position her big stomach, when a hideous whisper sounded in her ear. The voice, one she had never forgotten, and never would, sent shivers down her spine, made her skin tighten.

"If you want your little play fellow to live, you'll be quiet," came the voice.

Pressed against her throat was the sharp steel of a knife. She didn't need to open her eyes to see Pagnell's face leering into hers. It was a face that had haunted her dreams for months.

"Have you thought about me, sweetheart?" he whispered, his face very, very close to hers. His hands went down to caress her hard stomach. "You gave to somebody else what you fought me for. You're going to die for that."

"No," Alyx whispered as the knife pressed forward.

"You going to go peacefully, or do I have to slip a knife into his heart?"

She knew well who he meant. Jocelin was asleep not a foot from her, his breath coming even and deep, not even aware that her life was in danger.

"I'll go," she managed to say.

Trembling, too frightened to cry, Alyx heaved herself upward, Pagnell's knife scraping, cutting the skin of her throat once. It wasn't easy to make her way through the bodies sprawled on the floor. Each time she stumbled, Pagnell twisted her arm behind her back, almost pulling it from the socket.

When they came to the dark, cold, stone stairs leading downward, he pushed Alyx so hard she slammed into the wall and tripped down four steps until she caught her balance. Pausing for a moment, her hands protectively on her belly, she tried to catch her breath.

"Go on," Pagnell sneered, pushing her again.

Alyx managed to get down to the bottom without falling again. The room they were in was cold and totally dark, the ceiling very low. Barrels and sacks of stores crowded the floor. She whirled when she heard the door creak open.

Pagnell stood in front of a heavy door, open to reveal a yawning black nothingness. "In here," he growled.

"No." She backed away, but the room was so crowded there was nowhere to go.

He grabbed a handful of her hair and with one shove, slammed her into the blackness.

Crouching in a corner, surrounded by the cold blackness, she saw the door shut, blocking off the last ray of light, and heard the heavy iron bolt shoot into place.

Chapter 13

THE HIDEOUS little room seemed to be the epitome of every nightmare, every bad thought, every horrible story she'd ever heard. There was no light, and even after an hour she still could not see her hand before her face. For a very long time she remained huddled in the corner where Pagnell had tossed her, afraid to move.

If she could not see, she could certainly hear the noises of insects on the walls and floor, sounding loud and treacherous. What made her finally move was something scampering across the soft leather of her shoes. With a little squeal, she came upright, her hands trying to clutch the stones of the wall behind her.

"Calm yourself, Alyx," she said aloud, and her voice echoed off the walls. It would be morning before long and Jocelin would be looking for her—if he were still alive. No, she couldn't depend on anyone getting her out of here. She had to try to find her own means of escape.

Cautiously, hands out like a blind person, she took a step forward and nearly fell across a low bench. Kneeling, she ran her hands over it and was glad to see that she could make out the shadow of it. When she'd finished her exploration of the bench, she moved to the walls, feeling her way to the door. For all the door gave when she pushed against it, she might have been trying to move the stone walls.

The room was about six feet square with stone walls and

a dirt floor, and the only furniture was the short bench. There was no window in the door and no light came in around the corners. The low ceiling allowed her to explore every inch of the room. There were no windows, no gratings, no weak places anywhere. When she finished, the upper half of her body was covered with spiderwebs, and there were tears on her face. Angrily, she tried to brush the sticky things from her face and clothes, all the while crying and cursing Pagnell and men of his kind.

After several hours she sat down on the bench, knees drawn up, and put her head down. Absently, she pushed the baby's foot down from where it was kicking her in the ribs, and as her child became more active, restless, she started to sing to him. Gradually, he quietened and so did Alyx.

Overhead, she heard people walking and knew the ceiling was the castle floor. Somewhere up there Jocelin was trying to find her. She began to imagine ways to escape and wished she could start a fire, thinking that perhaps she could burn her way out. But, of course, the smoke would probably kill her before the fire burned the door.

When the door opened, the sound, so loud in the quiet room, startled her so badly she nearly fell off the bench. Candlelight flooded the room and nearly blinded her.

"There you are," came a voice she knew was Elizabeth Chatworth's.

Alyx gave no thought to her class as she threw her arms about Elizabeth. "I am so very, very glad to see you. How did you find me?"

Elizabeth gave Alyx a one-arm hug. "Jocelin came to me. It's that idiot Pagnell, isn't it? That man is as vicious as any man created. Now, come on before the dunce returns."

"Too late," came a drawling, half-amused, half-angry voice from the doorway. "You haven't changed much, Elizabeth, you're still giving orders to everyone."

"And you, Pagnell, are still tearing wings off butterflies. What has this one done to you? Refused your advances as any woman with any sense would do?"

"Your tongue is too sharp, Elizabeth. If I had time I'd teach you softer ways."

"You and how many other men?" Elizabeth spat. "You're scared to death of me because what I say is true. Now get out of the way and let us pass. We've had enough of your nasty little games. Go find someone else to play with. This child is under my protection."

He planted himself in front of Elizabeth and Alyx, not letting them out of the little cell.

"You go too far!" Elizabeth hissed. "You're no longer threatening a helpless servant. My brother will have your head if you harm me."

"Roger is too busy plotting against the Montgomerys to give a thought to anyone else. I hear he stays drunk all the time now that dear, sweet, crippled Brian has gone off sulking somewhere."

Alyx didn't see the little eating dagger Elizabeth pulled from the sheath at her side, but Pagnell did. With a sidestep he dodged her, caught her arm and, twisting it, pulled her to him. "I'd like to feel you under me, Elizabeth. Do you bring as much fire to your bed as you do to everything else?"

Alyx saw that now was her chance. On the wall outside the cell, to her left, was a heavy ring of keys. In one swift motion she flung them at Pagnell's head, catching him on the temple.

He released Elizabeth, staggered back one step and put his hand to his head, stared at the blood on his hand. By the time he regained his senses, Elizabeth and Alyx were halfway up the stairs.

Pagnell caught Elizabeth's skirt and jerked so hard she came tumbling backward, slamming into his chest. "Ah, my dear Elizabeth," he drawled into her ear, his arm about her waist, the other hand going to her ample breast. "I've dreamed of this moment for a long time."

Alyx knew Pagnell's attention was on Elizabeth and she could have escaped, but she couldn't leave Elizabeth alone because it was obvious what he planned for the young noblewoman. She could think of nothing else but to throw her body weight onto both of them.

Pagnell stumbled backward, still clutching Elizabeth, while Alyx rolled away, her hands protecting her stomach. Elizabeth saw her opportunity and slammed her elbow into Pagnell's ribs, making him grunt in pain. With one swift motion she grabbed a small oaken cask and brought it down with considerable force on Pagnell's head.

Oak staves broke away and dark red wine ran down his face, over his clothes as, after one startled look, he lapsed into unconsciousness.

"Such a waste of good wine," Elizabeth said, looking across the inert man to Alyx. "You haven't harmed your baby, have you?"

"No, he's secure enough."

"Thank you," Elizabeth said. "You could have run away, but you stayed to help me. How can I reward you?"

"Excuse me," came a voice from the doorway.

They turned to see a tall dark man, sword drawn.

"I hate to interrupt this little meeting, but unless you revive my friend and quickly, I shall take pleasure in killing the both of you."

Elizabeth made the first move, jumping away from Pagnell's body to the dark man's right side. "Go to his other side, Alyx," she directed. "He cannot take both of us at once."

Immediately, Alyx obeyed, and the man moved his head back and forth like a baited bull, watching the two women. A groan from Pagnell made the man look at his friend. As he did, Alyx made a quick move toward him. He backed into the opening of the stairway, guarding the entrance.

"God's teeth!" Pagnell cursed, trying to clear his vision. "You'll be sorry for this, Elizabeth," he groaned. "Hold them there, John. Don't let them get nearer. Neither of them is human. Pity to man the day woman was created."

"You wouldn't know what a woman was," Elizabeth hissed. "No female worth her salt would let you near her."

Shakily, Pagnell stood, looking in disgust at his wine-stained doublet. Suddenly, his head came up and he began to smile at Elizabeth in a nasty way. "Last night when I rode in I saw the camp of Miles Montgomery." He grinned broader at the way Elizabeth stiffened at the name. "I wonder if Miles would like a guest? I heard he was so angry at the death of his sister that his brother sent him to the Isle of Wight to keep him from declaring open war on the Chatworth family."

"My brother would annihilate him," Elizabeth said. "No Montgomery—"

"Spare me, Elizabeth, especially since from the story I heard, Roger attacked Stephen Montgomery's back."

Elizabeth leaped for him, hands made into claws, and Pagnell caught her to him.

"I hear Miles is a great lover of women and has many bastards. Would you like to add yours to his stable, my virginal little princess?"

"I would die first," she said with feeling.

"Perhaps. I'll leave that up to Miles. I would take care of you myself, but first I have a debt owed me by that one." He motioned his head toward Alyx, who stood quietly, John's sword in her back.

"And how do you get me out of here?" Elizabeth asked, smiling. "Do you think there won't be a protest if you carry me through the hall?"

Pagnell seemed to consider this for a moment as he looked about the dark cellar. With a smile, he looked back at her. "How do you think Miles will like playing Caesar?"

Puzzled, Elizabeth had no reply.

Pagnell grabbed her arm behind her. "John, watch that one carefully while I take care of Elizabeth. My head hurts too much to tussle with both of them again."

"More than your head will hurt if you harm me," Elizabeth warned.

"I'll leave that worry to Miles. The Montgomerys are altogether too high above themselves. I'd like to see all of them brought down, their land dispersed."

"Never!" Alyx shouted. "No slime-infested carrion such as you will ever destroy a Montgomery."

The full power of Alyx's voice made all of them stop and

stare at her. Elizabeth stopped struggling against Pagnell and her gaze on Alyx turned speculative. Pagnell's look was calculating.

John gave Alyx a nudge with his sword tip. "Raine Montgomery is said to be hiding in the forests somewhere, king of a band of criminals."

"This bears investigation," Pagnell said, giving Elizabeth's arm a twist. "But first we must deal with this one." Pulling her with him, he grabbed a length of hemp rope from atop a pile of wine barrels and began to tie Elizabeth's hands behind her back.

"Think what you're doing," Elizabeth said. "I'm not some—"

"Shut up!" Pagnell commanded, clipping her on the shoulder with his fist. When her hands were bound, he pushed her onto grain sacks and bound her ankles. With his knife he cut a piece of red silk from her dress. "A kiss, Elizabeth?" he teased, holding the gag close to her lips. "Just one before Miles Montgomery takes them all?"

"I'll see you in hell first."

"I'm sure you'll be there with me if some man doesn't dull the edges of that tongue of yours."

Before she could speak again, he tied the cloth tightly over her mouth. "Now you look almost appealing."

"What do you do with her now?" John asked. "We can't very well carry her out like that."

From a far corner of the cellar Pagnell picked up a dirty, moth-eaten piece of canvas and, after a couple of shakes which sent dust flying, he spread it at Elizabeth's feet. "We shall roll her in this and carry her out sight unseen."

Alyx watched Elizabeth, her eyes widening with fear now, but all Alyx could think of was that Elizabeth would be much better off with Miles than anyone else. "You'll be safe with Miles," she said, trying to reassure Elizabeth.

Again, they all stared at Alyx, but she ignored them. Elizabeth needed her help now.

Not at all gently, Pagnell pushed Elizabeth onto the filthy canvas and rolled her in it, hiding her completely.

"Can she breathe?" Alyx asked.

"Who cares? If she dies she can tell no tales. As it is, after Miles finishes with her she won't even remember me."

"Miles won't harm her," Alyx said passionately. "He's good and kind like his brother."

Pagnell laughed at that. "No one has ever had a temper to match Miles's. As soon as he finds she's a Chatworth . . . oh, I almost envy him, but I'm not a fool like Miles. He won't care about Roger Chatworth, and when Roger hears what Miles has done to his beloved baby sister—The King will have all the Montgomery lands to award to him who does favors for the King. And I shall be there to collect."

"You are a vile pig of a creature."

The back of Pagnell's hand slammed into Alyx's jaw, sending her reeling. "I'll ask for the advice of an underling like you when I want it. Is it Raine Montgomery who's put ideas into your head? The man thinks he can reform all of England. He hides in the forest and sneers at anything material, spouting about the old ways of honor and nobility while the people of your class grow fat and rich."

Alyx wiped blood from the corner of her mouth. "Raine is worth a hundred of you," she said.

"Raine is it? No 'Lord Raine'? Do you carry his brat? Is that what makes you think you're so high and mighty? When the flames lick up your legs we shall see if the name of Montgomery is so gentle on your lips. John!" he said sharply. "Take Elizabeth away. Give her to Miles Montgomery and see what he wants to do with her. And John," he warned, "Elizabeth's virginity is a known fact, and I want her to arrive at Miles's feet intact. Let all of Roger Chatworth's wrath come onto the Montgomery heads and not mine. Do I make myself clear?"

John gave him an insolent look as he tossed the bundle containing Elizabeth across his shoulder. "Montgomery will receive her in the best possible condition."

"But make sure he is inclined to forget she is a high-born lady. See if you can rearrange her clothing to stir his blood."

With a parting grin, John left the cellar.

"What do you want from me?" Alyx asked, backing away from Pagnell as he came closer to her. "I have done you no wrong."

He glared at her big belly. "You have given to another man what should have been mine." He grabbed her arm and pushed a small, sharp dagger to her ribs. "Now, go up the stairs and out the door and then to the stables. If you make a single sound it will be your last."

Her breath held, Alyx had no choice but to obey him. Once in the great hall there were guests milling about, but no one paid the least attention to Pagnell and the cheaply clad girl. They were nursing swollen heads and bruised bodies from where they'd slept across stools and tables.

Alyx searched for Jocelin, but she saw no sign of him. Every time she attempted to move her head, Pagnell's knife pushed harder against her until she kept her head straight. Perhaps Jocelin didn't know she was in trouble. Perhaps he was with a woman and hadn't yet discovered she was missing from the hall. For all their closeness, they respected each other's privacy. There were whole days when they didn't see each other and no questions were asked later.

Outside, Pagnell pushed her toward the stables, where he bellowed to a servant to saddle his horse. Before Alyx could think, she was slammed into the saddle, Pagnell behind her, and they set off at a pace that made Alyx's teeth jar.

It was nightfall when they finally stopped before a tall stone house at the edge of a small village. Pagnell pulled her from the horse, grabbed her arm and dragged her to the door.

A short, fat, balding man greeted them. "You took longer than I thought. Now what is so important I must wait for you this late at night?"

"This," Pagnell said, pushing Alyx into the room before him. It was a large, dark room, a few candles on a table at one end.

"What do I care for a dirty, pregnant lowling like that? Surely you could have found a tastier bit than that for your sport."

"Get over there," Pagnell commanded, pushing her toward the table. "If you say one word I'll slit your throat."

Too tired to reply, Alyx moved, sank down to the floor before an empty fireplace in a shapeless heap.

"Explain," the fat man said to Pagnell.

"What, uncle, no welcome, no wine?"

"If your news is good enough, I will feed you."

Pagnell sat down in a chair before the table, studying the sputtering candles. It wasn't that his uncle was so poor that made him use such cheap tallow but that for the last three years the man had done little except wait for his own death.

"What are your feelings toward Raine Montgomery?" Pagnell asked softly, watching with interest as his uncle's face turned from white to red to purple.

"How can you say that man's name to me in my own house?" he gasped. Three years before, in a tournament, Raine had killed Robert Digges's only child. No matter that the son had been trying to kill Raine rather than just unhorse him or that his son had already killed one man and severely wounded another that day. It had been Raine's lance that had taken Robert's son's life.

"I thought you felt the same way," Pagnell smiled. "Now I have a way to repay the man."

"How can you? The man hides in the forest and not even the King can find him."

"But our good king doesn't have the bait that I do."

"No!" Alyx shouted, getting to her feet with what strength she had left.

"See," Pagnell said, amused, "with every breath she takes she defends the man. Whose child do you carry?"

Alyx gave him a stubborn look. If she hadn't tried to reassure Elizabeth about the Montgomery men, Pagnell wouldn't know about her relationship with Raine, but Elizabeth had helped her.

"Pagnell," Robert commanded, "tell me all of your story."

Briefly, Pagnell told his version of the story, that Alyx had used her voice to entice him. Then, when he'd gotten close, she'd disappeared into thin air. Later, he'd gone looking for her and she'd leapt on him with the force of demons. He showed his uncle the scar on his head. "Could a little thing like that have left such a scar unless she were helped by the Devil?"

Robert gave a weak laugh, a snort of derision. "It sounds to me like she outsmarted you."

"She's a witch, I tell you."

Robert waved his hand in dismissal. "All women are witches to some extent. What does the girl have to do with Raine Montgomery?"

"I believe she's spent the last few months in his camp and it's his child she carries. If we were to let it be known that we mean to burn her as a witch, he'd come after her. And when he does, we'd be ready for him. You could have him, and we could share the King's reward."

"Wait a minute, boy," Robert interrupted. "Look at her! You mean to use that as bait? Raine Montgomery can have his pick of women. No doubt there are lean pickings in the forest and she probably does carry his child, but why would he risk his life to come after *that*? And why would you spend so much time searching for a flat-chested, hipless, plain-faced child such as her?"

Pagnell gave his uncle a look of contempt before turning to Alyx. "Sing!" he commanded.

"I will not," she said firmly. "You plan to murder me anyway, so why should I obey you?"

"You will die," he said evenly, "but the question is whether you will burn before or after the child's birth. If you disobey me I will see that the child dies with you. Now sing for your child's life."

Alyx obeyed him instantly, her hands on her stomach as she lifted her voice in a plea to God for her child's life.

There was a long silence when she finished, both men watching her intently.

Robert, rubbing away the chills on his forearms, spoke first. "Montgomery will come after her," he said with conviction.

Pagnell smiled in satisfaction, glad his uncle could see why he'd spent so many months searching for the girl. "In the morning we begin the trial, and when she's found guilty we will tie her to a stake. Montgomery'll come for her and we'll be ready for him."

"How can you be sure he'll hear of this in time? And if he does come, are you sure you can take him?"

"I tossed the chit in a cellar for a few hours and let it be known to the pretty boy she was with what I planned to do with her. He rode away like a shot and I'm sure he was headed south toward the forest where Montgomery hides. And as for men, there won't be time for him to collect them. Now he's surrounded by criminals and out-of-works. None of them can ride a horse, much less wield a sword."

Alyx bit her lower lip to keep from defending Raine. It was much better that Pagnell thought Raine defenseless; perhaps then Pagnell would send only a few men to capture Raine.

What was she thinking about? Raine would never come after her after what she'd done to him. She doubted very much if he'd speak to Jocelin. The forest guards reported to Raine whenever someone approached, and all Raine had to do was refuse Joss entrance—which he'd surely do. If Jocelin tried to sneak into the forest, Raine could order the guards to kill him. No! Raine wouldn't do that, would he? And what if Jocelin did somehow get to Raine? Would Raine believe Joss? Would he care what happened to Alyx?

"He'll come," Pagnell repeated. "And when he does, we'll be ready for him."

Chapter 14

ALYX LOOKED out the window of the small stone-walled room and into the courtyard below, watching with horrified fascination as the carpenters built the gallows for her burning. It had been eight long, terrifying days since she'd been taken by Pagnell, and during that time she'd been subjected to a fiasco of a trial.

The men who ran the trial had been some of Pagnell's relatives, and he'd easily persuaded them to his views. Alyx listened to it all, for they talked about her as if she weren't there, and her head echoed with Raine's words.

Raine and she had argued so many times about the rising middle class. Alyx had always adored King Henry, loved the way he was taking away the power from the nobles, was forcing the nobles to pay wages and no longer own serfs. But Raine said the King was turning the nobles into fat merchants, that if the ruling class had to count pennies they would forget their knightly virtues, would no longer know the meaning of honor. She talked of people being more equal, but Raine asked who would do the fighting if England were attacked. If there weren't a class of people freed from money making to stay strong and practice warfare, who would protect England?

As Alyx sat through the "trial," she began to see more clearly what Raine meant. The judges didn't for a minute believe she was a witch, and Alyx marveled at this because the people in her town believed quite strongly in witches, and had a multitude of ways to protect themselves from evil curses.

All the judges cared about was winning the King's favor and reaping the rewards that came with the King's pleasure. Pagnell told them that she carried Raine Montgomery's child and, like vultures, they jumped on this fact. Raine had been declared a traitor, and with a little more pushing, he could have his lands given to someone else. King Henry loved to create his own nobles, to give out titles to anyone rich enough to buy one. The judges hoped he would give some of the Montgomery lands to them if they delivered Raine—or his head—to the King.

Alyx sat silently through the whole proceedings as they plotted and planned, laughed and argued. At the end, they pushed her into a cart and drove her through the little town— she didn't even know its name—a man walking before her declaring her to be a witch.

As if she were someone else, Alyx watched the people cross themselves, make crosses of their fingers, turn away lest she look on them with an evil eye, and the bolder ones threw food and offal at her. She wanted to cry out that what was being done to her had nothing to do with witchcraft but greed—the greed of men already rich. But as she looked at the fascinated/scared expressions of the dirty, diseased people, she knew she could not reason with them. She was not going to do away with centuries of ignorance in a few minutes.

When the cart ride was over she was dragged to the ruins of an old stone castle, one tower standing, and pushed up the stairs. Many hours later she was given a small bowl of water and Alyx washed the stench from her body as best she could.

They kept her there for days, guards on the floor below and more on the roof. At night the townspeople gathered to circle the tower and chant exorcisms to guard themselves against her evil. Alyx merely sat in the center of the cold little room and tried to listen to the music that ran through her head. She knew the judges delayed her execution to give Raine time to arrive to rescue her. She prayed with all her might for his safety, pleaded with God to let him realize he was walking into a trap. The judges and Pagnell had been so right when they said that Raine could not go for his own knights. In fact,

Pagnell had taken his own men north to Raine's home to guard that Raine did not ride there first.

Alyx sat and thought over the men in Raine's camp, what poor soldiers they were, how lazily they trained—and how much they hated her. "Please," she prayed, "do not let Raine come alone. If he comes, let him have a guard and let the men protect him."

Before daylight on the ninth day, a fat, stinking old woman came bearing a plain white linen sheath for Alyx to wear. Without a protest, calmly, Alyx slipped it on, leaving it loose over her stomach. At the proceedings she'd pleaded for her child's life, but the men had only given her a blank look, totally uninterested in her. One of the judges told Pagnell to silence her and one slap from him had made Alyx hold her tongue. There was nothing she could say to sway them anyway. They figured they had to burn her now while Raine was still hot for her and the child must also be endangered. Pagnell laughed and said he'd hold Raine and make him watch while Alyx burned.

With her chin high, using all her strength to control the shaking in her knees, Alyx descended the stairs before the old woman who carried Alyx's dress over her arm—pay for risking being in the same room with the witch.

A priest waited at the foot of the stairs, and quickly, Alyx made her confession, denying that she was a witch or that she carried the Devil's child. With an air of disbelief, he blessed and sent her on her way.

It must have looked strange, Alyx thought, for someone of her size to be escorted by so many large men: one in front, one in back, two on each side. The clanking of the full armor they wore was the only thing louder than the pounding of her heart as she fixed her eyes on the platform in front of her. A tall stake reached skyward and all around it was a pile of brush and dried grasses.

The crowd was joyous as they watched her approach, jubilant at the special treat that awaited them. Not many witches were burned nowadays.

As Alyx climbed the stairs, the guards kept her circled,

their backs to her as their eyes scanned the horizon. Involuntarily, Alyx also looked at the landscape. Hope and fear mixed together within her. She feared for Raine's life should he try to save her, yet she hoped she would not have to die.

A guard grabbed her arm, pulled her to the stake and tightly tied her wrists behind her.

Alyx lifted her eyes skyward, fully aware that this would be the last time she'd see the day. The early morning sunlight was just lightening the day and she looked across the high brush and into the crowd. It was bad, very bad, that these were the last faces she'd ever see, that she'd go to Heaven—or Hell—with these faces on her mind.

Closing her eyes, she tried to picture Raine.

"Get on with it," came a voice that made Alyx open her eyes. Voices were life to her; she'd more likely remember a voice than a face or a name. Scanning the crowd, she saw no one she knew. They all seemed to be an especially dirty, scarred lot.

"Let me light the fire," came the voice again, and this time Alyx looked into Rosamund's eyes. A chill went all over her skin, her scalp tightening and a tiny flame of hope surged through her.

The guards, all around her, were taking their time in lighting the fire as they studied the country around them, looking for some sign of a knight and his men.

Not sure whether to trust her eyes, she looked at the crowd again.

"What're ye waitin' for?" came a voice Alyx knew as well as her own. There, in the forefront, with blackened teeth and a dirty, bloody bandage over one eye was Jocelin. Beside him stood a man Alyx recognized from the forest camp, one of the men who'd accused her of stealing. They were changed, some looking dirtier than she remembered, but the whole forest camp was there, gazing up at her with half-smiles of conspiracy as they saw she recognized them.

In spite of all she could do, tears began coursing down her cheeks, but through her blurred vision she could see that

Joss was trying to say something to her. It took a long moment to understand what he was mouthing.

"This fire should make the witch sing loudly," he said, and Alyx recognized exasperation in his voice.

Surreptitiously, she glanced at the guards as they frowned at the bare distance, never even glancing at the crowd at the foot of the platform.

"We've waited long enough," said one of the black-robed judges from behind Alyx. "Let the witch burn."

One of the guards lowered a flaming torch toward the bracken and as he did so, Alyx filled her lungs to capacity with air. Desperation, fear, hope, joy, all combined in her voice and the note she emitted was so strong, so loud, that for a moment everyone was paralyzed.

Jocelin was the first to move. With a cry much like Alyx's, he leaped to the top of the platform and behind him came twenty men and women. One confessed murderer threw his weight onto the guard holding the torch, sending the flames backward, to land in the pile of branches behind Alyx, where they went up instantly.

There were six guards and four judges on the platform. The judges ran away at the first sign of trouble, their robes raised to their knees, flying out behind them.

Smoke curled around Alyx's body as she watched the men and women fight the steel-clad knights. With each blow that hit flesh she felt it in her own. These people she had treated so badly were risking their lives to save her.

The smoke grew thicker, making her cough and her eyes water. Heat, like the hottest sun, hurt the back of her. Trying to see, she looked at the people around her, fully aware how fragile they were compared to the knights in their heavy armor. Her only consolation was that Raine had been sensible enough not to risk his life in this fight. At least he'd stayed away somewhere safe.

It was some time before she became aware that one of the knights was not being attacked by the forest people. It was only when she heard his roar, hollow from inside the helmet, that she realized that one of her guards was Raine.

"Jocelin! Cut her loose!" Raine commanded as he brought a double-edged ax down on the shoulder of an armored knight, sending the man to his knees. A woman jumped on the fallen knight, pulled his helmet off, while a one-eyed man slammed a club into the head of the dazed knight.

The smoke was so thick Alyx could see no more and her throat was raw from coughing. More tears flowed as Joss cut the ropes about her wrists, grabbed her hand and pulled her away from the burning brush.

"Come with me," he said, pulling her by the hand.

She'd halted, looking back at the platform. Raine fought two men at once, swinging mightily at them with a steel-studded mace, sidestepping, moving with slow grace in the heavy armor. Behind blazed the fire, flashing off the men's armor, turning it to a frightening, bloody red.

"Alyx!" Jocelin shouted at her. "Raine gave me orders of where to take you. He's angry enough at both of us. For once, obey him."

"I can't leave him!" she tried to say, but her raw throat and the lump there made it come out as a croak.

One strong pull from Joss and they were running together. After a very long time she saw horses coming toward them.

"He's late," Joss yelled, panting from the run. "Come on, Alyx!"

At least the running kept her mind from the danger Raine was in. Carrying the extra weight of her unborn child made her awkward, and she needed every bit of her wind.

When they reached the horses, Jocelin mounted and pulled her up behind him and, to her chagrin, they headed away from where Raine and the others fought. Alyx tried to protest, but again her voice failed her. Her silence was so uncharacteristic that Joss turned to look at her, and his snort of laughter showed he understood her predicament.

They rode hard for two hours and when they stopped at last, it was at a monastery. Alyx, exhausted from her fear during the last several days, could hardly stand when Joss helped her down.

"Is your voice really gone?" Joss asked, half amused, half in sympathy.

She again tried to speak, but only a rasp that hurt her throat came out.

"Maybe it's better this way. Raine is angry enough to tear the tongues out of both of us. Are you all right, though? They didn't harm you while you were a captive?"

Alyx shook her head.

Before Joss could speak again, a tonsured, brown-robed monk opened the heavy wooden door.

"Won't you come in, my children? We are ready for you."

Alyx touched Jocelin's arm and frowned in question. What did the monk mean by "ready"?

"Come inside. You'll find out," Joss said, smiling.

Inside the wall was a large, lovely courtyard, green and shady in the early morning August sunlight. There were doors off three sides of the courtyard, a thick stone wall behind them.

"We have a few rooms for women visitors," the monk said, glancing down at Alyx's soot-covered coarse white gown. "Lord Raine has made arrangements for your comfort."

Moments later Alyx was in a spacious room off the courtyard and given a mug of thick buttermilk to drink. She was only halfway through it when the sound of clanging steel came through the door.

"Alyxandria!" came a bellow that could only be Raine's.

Out of habit, Alyx opened her mouth to answer him in kind, but only a painful yelp came out. With her hand at her throat, she opened the door.

Raine whirled to look at her and for a moment their eyes locked. There were shadows under his eyes and his hair was sweat-plastered to his head in black curls. Dents in his armor were numerous. But what was frightening was the fury in his eyes.

"Come out here," he growled, and his tone left no room for disobedience.

When she stood before him he clutched her shoulders,

stared for a moment at her stomach, then looked back into her eyes. "I should beat you soundly for this," he said.

Alyx tried to speak, but the rawness of her throat made tears in her eyes.

He looked puzzled for a moment, then one dimple flashed in his cheek. "The smoke take your voice away?"

She nodded.

"Good! That's the best news I've heard in months. When we get through with this I have a few things to say to you and for once you're going to listen." With that he grabbed her shoulder and pushed her toward a small gate in the wall. Outside was a tall, deeply recessed door that obviously belonged to a chapel. Not waiting for her to enter on her own, Raine opened the door and pushed her inside. Before the altar stood Jocelin and a tall, slim man whom Alyx had never seen before.

"In your armor?" the stranger asked, looking at Alyx curiously.

"If I took time to change no doubt she'd slip through my fingers again. You have the ring, Gavin?"

Alyx's eyes opened wide at the name. So this was Raine's older brother, the man she'd written to and begged to help control Raine's anger at Roger Chatworth. As she looked up at Gavin, thinking he wasn't at all like Raine physically and Raine was so much more handsome, she was barely aware of a priest before them, talking.

"Pay attention, Alyx," Raine commanded, and Gavin coughed to cover a laugh.

In consternation, Alyx looked at the men surrounding her. Jocelin's eyes danced with laughter, Raine's smouldered with barely controlled rage and Gavin seemed to be amusedly tolerant of everything. The priest was waiting patiently for something from her.

"Alyx!" Raine growled. "I know you can't speak, but you could at least nod your head—unless of course you'd rather not marry me. Perhaps you'd rather have Jocelin . . . again?"

"Marry?" she mouthed.

"For the Lord's sake, Raine! Sorry, Father," Gavin said.

"Have pity on her. She's had a shock. One minute she's about to be burned at the stake and the next she's getting married. She needs a moment to adjust."

"And since when have you known so much about women?" Raine asked hostilely. "You dumped Judith on your doorstep hardly minutes after you married her, and if I hadn't broken my leg, she'd have been alone."

"If you hadn't been there she might have come to me sooner. As it was—"

"Quiet!" Jocelin shouted, then stepped backward when the two Montgomery brothers turned their wrath on him. He took a deep breath. "Alyx was looking at Lord Gavin and I'm not sure she realized she was marrying Lord Raine. Perhaps if it were explained to her, she'd answer the questions properly, even without her voice."

The full realization of what was going on hit Alyx and, with her usual ladylike finesse, her eyes widened and her mouth dropped open.

"Is that horror at the idea?" Gavin laughed.

Raine looked away from Alyx, obviously not sure what her expression meant. "She carries my child. She will marry me," he said flatly.

Alyx couldn't speak, but she could hiss at him through her teeth, and when Raine still wouldn't look at her she looked about for other means of getting his attention. He didn't ask her to marry him, didn't allow her the sweet pleasure of throwing herself at him and telling him she loved him, but instead stood sullen and angry and announced she would marry him.

"Would you like to borrow my sword?" Gavin asked, and his voice was so full of laughter he could hardly speak. "Oh, Raine." He slapped his brother's shoulder, making the armor clank, but Raine didn't move. "I hope she leads you a merry chase. Judith's going to like a sister-in-law who looks daggers at her husband. It'll make her feel less alone in the world."

Raine didn't bother to look at Gavin and Alyx sensed there was some old argument involved. Never in her life had she wished more for the power of her voice than she did at this moment. She'd make Raine look at her if she could speak.

"My lady," the priest said, and it took Alyx a while to understand that he was speaking to her. "It is not the church's place to encourage unwanted marriages. Is it your desire to marry Lord Raine?"

She looked up at Raine's profile, furious that he wouldn't look at her. With two steps, she planted herself in front of him, his eyes focused somewhere over her head. Slowly, she reached out and took his hand, held it in hers. His hand was cut in several places, bloody, bruised, and as she looked down at it she knew he'd been hurt saving her. She raised it to her lips and kissed his palm, and when she looked up, his eyes were on her. For a moment they seemed to soften.

"She will marry me," he said as he glanced back at the priest.

Alyx wanted to curse at him for his self-assurance and for his refusal to weaken in his anger at her. Silently, she moved back beside him and the marriage was completed, a gold ring slipped onto her finger.

Raine gave no one time to congratulate her. "Come, Lady Alyx," he said, fingers digging into her upper arm. "We have a great deal to discuss."

"Leave her alone, Raine," Gavin said. "Can't you see she's tired? And besides, this is your wedding day. Rail at her some other time."

Raine didn't bother to even look at his brother as he ushered Alyx from the chapel back through the courtyard and into her room. The moment the door was closed, Raine leaned against it.

"How could you, Alyx?" he whispered. "How could you say you cared for me then put me through the last few months of hell?"

It was very frustrating not to be able to talk. She looked about for a pen and paper but remembered Raine couldn't read.

"Do you know what it's been like the last few months?" He tossed his helmet on the bed. "For years I've searched for a woman I could love. A woman with courage and honor. A woman who wasn't afraid of me or after money or land. A woman who made me think."

He began unbuckling the leather straps that held his armor in place, tossing piece after piece in a heap on the bed. "First you drive me nearly insane in those tight hose, flipping about in front of me, looking up at me with big eyes so full of hunger you frightened me."

With one movement, he pushed all the armor to the side, sat down on the edge of the bed and began unfastening his leg coverings. Alyx knelt before him and helped. Raine leaned back on his elbows, never stopping his tirade.

"When I found you were a female I had a fever and wasn't sure I wasn't dreaming, yet that night I found more joy than I ever had. There was no coyness about you, no holding back, just exuberance, pleasure given, pleasure received. Later I was furious at you for having played such an ugly trick on me, but I forgave you."

He said the last as if he were the most magnanimous person alive, ignoring Alyx's look of disgust as he raised his leg for her to unbuckle the second leg sheath.

A knock on the door made him pause. Several servants, dressed more costly than Alyx had ever been, entered the room bearing a large oak tub and several buckets of steamy hot water.

"Put it there," Raine said distractedly.

Standing, Alyx watched the procession with disbelief. A tub full of hot water, brought by servants and set before them as if they were royalty. Never in her life had she had a full hot bath. In Moreton she'd bathed from a basin and in the forest there'd been the icy stream.

"What is it, Alyx?" Raine asked when they were alone again. "You look as if you'd seen a ghost."

Silently, she pointed at the steaming tub.

"You want to bathe first? Go ahead."

Cautiously, she knelt by the tub, put her hands into the water and smiled up at Raine as he began to remove the leather padding he'd worn under his armor.

"Don't try to distract me," he said a little too sweetly. "I am still considering blistering your behind. Do you know how I felt after I found you with Jocelin?"

She looked away from him, remembering the hurt in his eyes that night.

"It took me years to find you, then to have you tell me your . . . your music meant more than I did. Close your mouth! You did in effect say that. You know, Alyx, I rather like your not being able to talk. My brother wouldn't believe that a little thing like you could outshout fifty grown men. I offered for him to put some money on his big mouth, but he declined.

"Alyx," he warned, "don't look so offended. You have no right to be offended. No! I am the one who's gone through hell these last months. I never knew where you were, how many men you were sleeping with."

At that, she sent him a look of blackness.

"You were the one who made me believe you lacked virtue—that is the kindest way I can say it. At camp I drove the people nearly insane. Some of them rebelled and refused to go near the training field."

He frowned for a moment at the way she was pointing at him. "I spent a great deal of time there, if that's what you mean. I was trying to wear myself out so I wouldn't remember you and Joss."

Alyx narrowed her eyes at him, used her hands to form a large curving mound over her chest.

"Oh, Blanche," he said, understanding so easily that Alyx hissed at him. "It would serve you right if I had invited her into my bed, but after you I wanted no other woman. Damn you, Alyx! Stop looking so pleased with yourself. I was miserable while you were gone."

She pointed at herself and all her love showed in her eyes.

He looked away and his voice was hoarse when he spoke again. "I nearly killed Joss when he came to me. I refused to see him and the guards wouldn't let him pass, but he knows his way about the forest too well. One night I'd had a little too much to drink and when I woke in the morning Joss was sitting on a stool by my bed. It took a while before I would listen to him."

Alyx heard the understatement in his words and rolled her eyes so exaggeratedly that Raine pointedly ignored her.

"I can tell you that it didn't help my sore head any to hear of Pagnell's capture of you, nor that the loathsome man planned to set a trap for me."

Alyx, sitting by the tub, reached up and grabbed Raine's hand. He wore only a loincloth now. To think that he had risked his life for her.

"Alyx," he said softly, kneeling before her. "Don't you realize yet that I love you? Of course I'd come for you."

She tried to show him, with her hands and expressions, how she'd worried about Pagnell harming him.

"What?" Raine said, standing. "You thought I didn't know about the trap?" He was obviously insulted. "You thought some mosquito like Pagnell could maneuver a Montgomery into his clutches?"

With a swift gesture, he tore off the loincloth and stepped into the tub. "The day a bit of filth like that—Alyx, you didn't *really* believe that Pagnell—?"

She threw up her hands, bowing before him with mock humility.

"Well, perhaps you should be forgiven: You don't know what the man is like. Maybe to you all noblemen are alike."

Now she was the one insulted. By "you" he meant people of her class, lowlings who believed in witches and the goodness of the King, who thought the trials were honest and fair and other stupid things. She slammed her fist into the water, splashing it into Raine's face.

He grabbed her wrist. "Now what was that for? Here I've forgiven you for leaving me, saved your skin from a fire and married you and you aren't even grateful."

Oh how very, very much she wished she could talk. She'd tell him in a voice that'd pin his ears back that she left him to keep him safe from the King's wrath and she was facing being burned because she carried *his* child. As for marrying her, he'd no doubt done it out of his stupid sense of honor.

"I don't like what you're thinking," he said, pulling her closer to him. "Gavin laughed at me when I said you'd be grateful for what I'd done. He said women never reacted the way they should, I mean with logic. Now what have I done?"

She'd doubled her fist and threatened to smack him in the nose.

"Alyx, you really are trying my patience. Don't you have even one kind thought for me? I've been through an awful couple of days. I had to scale that tower wall at night, kill the guard on the roof and put on his armor, all so quietly the other man wouldn't hear me."

As he held both her wrists, she could feel herself melting. No matter that it was his fault that she was facing being burned; he had risked a great deal to rescue her.

"Aren't you pleased with me just a little?" he murmured against her lips. "Aren't you just a little bit glad to be married to me?"

As Alyx felt her body dissolving, disappearing under his strong will, she wasn't aware of how he was pulling her across the tub. With a great loud splash, he pulled her onto his lap, water sloshing over the sides.

"Now I have you," he laughed as she tried to sit up. "Now I'll make you pay for your lack of gratitude." He laughed again as Alyx tried to protest, her voice croaking, but as he began to kiss her, she forgot about speaking.

Chapter 15

ALYX'S ARMS went about Raine's neck and all thoughts of anger were gone. It had been so long since she'd seen him, and her hunger for him was overwhelming. Eagerly, she pulled him closer to her, her mouth clinging to his, her tongue invading his mouth, seeking as much of him as she could reach.

"Alyx," he whispered into her hair, and there were tears in his voice. "I saw you as I went up the wall, sitting alone in that tower room, crying softly, so little, so sad. Right then I wanted to kill all the guards, but I knew I couldn't rely on the men from the forest to help me. If my brothers had been free, I would have tried it, but I wouldn't risk injuring you."

Her head came up at the mention of brothers. Elizabeth!

"What is it, Alyx? What's wrong?"

She tried to get out the word "Elizabeth," but it was unintelligible. After several more attempts she managed to say "Miles."

"Did you meet my little brother? No, you couldn't have. He's been on the Isle of Wight. After Mary . . . died, Miles nearly went crazy and Gavin persuaded him to go visit Uncle Simon. He left the Isle a few weeks ago."

Raine was puzzled at Alyx's vigorous shaking of her head. Miles, she kept mouthing. "Has something happened to Miles? Is he in danger?"

Alyx nodded yes, and before she had made one more nod,

Raine was out of the tub, Alyx under his arm. Hastily, he set her down, wrapped a cloak around her and pulled on his loincloth. "We'll go see Gavin and you can write what you have to say."

Alyx's face was red the instant they left their room. She wore only a wet sheath under the cloak while Raine wore practically nothing as he pulled her through the holy monastery. They found Gavin in the stables.

"You aren't ready to ride so soon, are you, brother?" he teased. "Surely your bride deserves some attention."

Raine ignored his jibe. "Alyx says Miles is in trouble. She'll write for you what's happened."

Gavin's face immediately turned serious. "Come to the monk's study."

He led the way with such long strides that Alyx would not have been able to keep up if Raine hadn't grabbed her arm and pulled her behind him. He'd better enjoy this time while she had no voice, she thought.

The monk in the study protested a woman's presence, but the men ignored him.

"Here!" Gavin said, thrusting paper, pen and ink before her.

It took her several minutes to write the story of Pagnell's tying of Elizabeth Chatworth and his plan to deliver her to Miles. Raine and Gavin hung over her shoulder until her palms began to sweat.

"Elizabeth Chatworth," Gavin said, "I thought she was still a child."

Alyx shook her head.

"What does she look like?" Raine asked seriously.

Alyx's expression was enough to make them understand.

"The King isn't going to like this," Gavin said. "He has placed a heavy fine on the Chatworth estates and ordered Roger away from all Montgomery land."

"Land!" Raine shouted. "Is that all you care about? Chatworth kidnapped Bronwyn and killed Mary. What does it take to make you consider people instead of land?"

"I care more for my brothers than *any* land. What will

happen if Miles rapes this Chatworth girl? It will look as if we are disobeying the King, and who will suffer then? You! He will never pardon you and you will have to spend your life in that forest with that army of cutthroats. And how will the King punish Miles? By outlawing him, too? I'm worried about losing two of my brothers because of Pagnell's nasty tricks."

Raine was still glaring at his brother while Alyx looked at Gavin with new respect.

"It's been days," Raine said finally. "I'd put my life on it that the girl is virgin no longer, and I'll wager that Miles raped no one. Perhaps if he knew who she was, he released her, and all we can do is pray she doesn't bear his child."

Gavin's snort said a great deal. "I'll take half my men and leave now and try to find Miles. Maybe I can talk some sense into him. Perhaps the girl's fallen in love with him and won't demand his head."

Alyx grabbed Gavin's arm and shook her head vigorously. Elizabeth Chatworth was never going to fall in love with a Montgomery in less than a fortnight.

"A hellion, is she?" Gavin asked, then paused and raised Alyx's hand to his lips. "Raine is going to take you home and you'll meet my Judith. I'm sorry your wedding has been such a hurried affair. When this is all settled we'll give a tournament in your honor."

Still holding her hand, he looked back at his brother. "You'll be safe at the Montgomery castle for a while. Take her there, let her rest. You haven't seen my son yet, either. And buy her some clothes!"

Alyx was sure Raine would take offense at Gavin's tone, but Raine was smiling. "It's good to see you again, brother," he said softly, his arms open. The brothers clasped each other fiercely for a long moment.

"Give Miles my best and try to keep him out of trouble," Raine smiled. "And when he returns he can meet my wife."

With one flashing grin, Gavin left them.

Raine turned back to Alyx. Her cloak had fallen open and the damp gown clung to her. "Now, if I remember correctly, we were just starting something when my little brother's problems interrupted us."

Alyx took a step away from him, gesturing toward the room they were in.

With a laugh, Raine swept her into his arms, carried her through the courtyard and back to their room. Heedless of the piles of dirty armor on the bed, he tossed her in the midst of it and in one gesture stretched out on top of her.

"Will I hurt the child?" he murmured, biting her earlobe. Her headshaking was so vigorous that he gave a warm, seductive laugh as his hand trailed downward and pulled at the linen gown. The coarse, poorly sewn garment came away from her body with one easy tear.

Alyx had never been very proud of her body, always wishing for more curves, but now, bloated with child as she was, she didn't want him to see her in daylight. Her attempts to cover herself were brushed away by Raine.

Moving off her, he kissed her stomach, caressed it. "It's my child who distorts you, and I love it as well as his mother."

"Daughter?" she managed to say, hurting her raw throat.

"I only ask for your safety and, if God wills, the life of the child. I would love to have a daughter. With you for a mother, Bronwyn and Judith for aunts, I will gladly leave her all my estates. I'm sure she'll run them better than I do."

She tried to speak again, but he didn't let her as he began kissing her neck again. When she felt him remove his loincloth, knew his skin was next to hers, she forgot her worries about how she looked.

She had no idea how much she'd missed him physically, how much she needed the caress of his hands. He touched her body all over, running his hard fingertips over her skin from toes to head, making her feel cherished, loved. Even now when she could feel the power of his hunger for her, he took his time, loved her, touched her.

She lay on her back, eyes closed, her arms lightly about his neck as he ran his hands over her. When he touched her inner thighs, she opened her eyes, met his and the deep, dark blue piercing through her made chills run along her spine. The power of this man, the strength, the size of him, all held in leash as he fondled her, excited her horribly.

With an upward thrust of her body, she pressed against him, kissed his mouth hungrily, making him laugh deeply as he rolled onto his back and pulled her on top of him. The armor surrounding them clanged and a couple of pieces fell to the floor.

Alyx ran her teeth down Raine's neck, her hands sinking into the mass of muscle of his upper arms. Glorious! she thought, such a magnificent, splendid man—and all hers!

The laughter that came from her burned throat wasn't pretty, but the deep, raspy quality of it was seductive. She ran her thumb down Raine's ribs so hard he pushed her arm away as he sought her mouth. But Alyx applied her thumb to his other side, laughed again when he twisted away from her.

"Hellion!" he murmured, grabbing her by the hair and pulling her head back as he lifted his head and bit into her stomach.

Gasping, Alyx brought her feet forward, attempted to get away from him. Raine caught her left foot and proceeded to bite each one of her toes. The sensation that ran up her made her stop all movement.

She lay on top of him, stretched out, her feet in his face, his in hers. Two can play this game, she thought as she raked her teeth across the soft underpad of Raine's toes. She was quite pleased to feel him jump beneath her, and another piece of armor went crashing to the floor.

Raine's arms, longer than hers, slid up the sides of her legs, caressing and kneading so provocatively that after a moment she could think of nothing else but his hands on her body.

She began to tremble, shiver, and her skin seemed as hot as when the fire had been licking at her back.

Raine grabbed her hips and as if she had no weight at all, picked her up and set her down on his manhood with such an accurate thrust that Alyx let out a raspy squeal.

"Swordplay," Raine laughed. "I'm very accurate with a sword."

Alyx leaned forward and with her strong thighs began a rhythm that left Raine too busy to speak again. He lay still, his face a mask of almost pain as he held back, all his senses given over to the enjoyment of what Alyx was doing.

When he could stand no more, he grabbed her to him, rolled her over and with two hard, almost violent thrusts, they ended together, shaking, quivering, clutching as if they might get even closer.

After several moments, Raine raised his head and gave Alyx a smile that said more than all the words in the world. With a grunt of satisfaction, he rolled off her, pulling her close to him, their sweaty skin glued together. And together they slept.

It was early evening when they woke and Raine made an awful sound as he pulled a sharp, hard knee up from under the small of his back. "How can anything so small be so dangerous?" he asked a sleepy Alyx.

With one sharp smack on her buttocks, he moved away from her to stand and stretch. "Up!" he commanded. "We've stayed here too long already. It'll take us two days to get home as it is."

Alyx didn't relish moving to ride on a horse and her expression said so. She'd much rather stay here—in bed—with Raine for a few more days.

"Alyx, don't tempt me. Get out of there this minute or I shall return to the forest and send some of Gavin's men to escort you to the Montgomery estates."

That made her jump. Within seconds she was out of bed and had pulled the torn white sheath over her head.

"Filthy thing," Raine said, fingering it. "Judith will find you dresses fit for a Montgomery. It will be nice to see you dressed as you should be, although I must say I like your hair like this." He rubbed her curls as if he still thought of her as his squire.

There was no time for anything else as he pushed her out the door and tossed her into the saddle of a horse. Except for messengers, Alyx had never seen knights as they were with their lord master. Raine had only to hint at a command and Gavin's men jumped to obey. Quickly, efficiently, they cleared the armor Raine had taken from Pagnell's man from the room while Raine dressed in the dark green wools he'd worn in the forest. One of the knights gave such a look of astonishment that Raine laughed.

"They itch, too," he said. "Ready, Alyx?"

Before she could answer, they were off, galloping at a pace that she should have been used to. It was no surprise to her when Raine rode through half the night. But what did surprise her was the way Gavin's men treated her. They asked after her health, if she were tired. When they stopped to eat and rest the horses, some of the men presented her with flowers. One man spread his cloak for her to sit on. No one seemed to notice that the fur-lined cloak was of far better quality than the sack she wore.

With surprise and disbelief in her eyes, she looked up at Raine but saw that he thought nothing of the way the men treated her. A knight asked permission to play the lute for her, and as three men sang together. Raine raised one eyebrow at her, for the men were not very good. Alyx looked away, because to her, the knights, so kind, so polite, were perfect.

When Raine lifted her back on her horse, he said, "They are practicing their chivalry on you. I hope you can bear with them."

Bear with them! she thought as they started riding again. She felt as if she'd just seen a glimpse of heaven and, indeed, she could withstand it.

At night they stayed at an inn and Alyx was embarrassed by the way she was dressed. There was no need to be. The innkeeper took one look at Raine and the twenty men in their rich green and gold and he practically lay down to be their carpet. Food such as Alyx had never seen before was set before them in a quantity that made her gasp.

"May they sit with you?" Raine asked.

It took her a moment to realize he was asking permission for these lovely men to sit at the same long oak table with her. With a large smile, she gestured to them and the chairs.

The men's table manners were so good that Alyx was overly cautious about her own. All through the meal they offered her prize tidbits of meat and fruit. One man peeled an apple, placed a sliver on a plate and asked if she'd accept it.

They expressed sympathy about her lost voice, which made Raine laugh and say they were missing more than they knew. Formally, they asked Lord Raine to explain this. He said they'd not believe what he said, which made Alyx blush.

In their room was a large, soft bed, sparkling clean, and Alyx immediately snuggled under the light blanket. In seconds, Raine joined her there, pulling her close to him, his hands caressing her stomach, smiling when the baby jumped.

"Strong," he murmured, falling asleep. "A good, strong child."

In the morning the landlord tapped on their door and delivered fresh baked bread and hot wine, along with twenty red roses from Gavin's knights.

"That's Judith's doing," Raine said, dressing. "They're all half in love with her, and it looks like you've won their hearts, too."

Alyx shook her head at this and indicated that they only cared for her because of her relationship to him.

He kissed her nose. "Perhaps all men fall in love with women who can't speak."

Alyx grabbed a pillow and threw it at him, catching him in the back of the head.

"Is that any way for a lady to act?" he teased.

In spite of his light manner, Alyx worried about his words all day. She wasn't a lady and she didn't know how one should behave. How could she possibly meet this paragon, Judith Montgomery, dressed in a sooty, scorched, shapeless sack?

"Alyx, what's wrong with you? Are those tears I see?" Raine asked from beside her.

She tried to smile and indicate that there was something in her eye and she would be fine in a moment. After that, she tried to control herself better, but by the time they rode into sight of the Montgomery castle, she was ready to turn tail and run.

The massive stone fortress, centuries old, was even more formidable than she had imagined. As they rode closer to it, the old stone walls seemed to be crushing down on her.

Raine led them to the back entrance, to announce their arrival to as few people as possible. The path to the gate was lined with high stone walls and as they rode, men called down in joyful greeting to Raine. He seemed so at home here that the man she knew began to seem far away. The men who obeyed him without question, the whole vast scope of this place, was closer to the real man than the artificial outlaw camp.

They rode into a courtyard and, to Alyx's astonishment, houses, looking comfortable, with many windows, were inside the walls. In the few castles where she and Jocelin had sung, the people still lived in the towers, which were so uncomfortable most castles had been abandoned.

They had barely stopped when out of a little walled garden came running a breathtakingly beautiful woman wearing a gown of flashing red satin.

"Raine," she called, running, arms open.

She can't sing, Alyx thought defensively, watching her husband leap from his horse and run toward the woman.

"Judith," he said, grabbing her, twirling her about, feet off the ground, kissing her mouth, in Alyx's opinion, much too exuberantly.

"My lady," came a voice to Alyx's left. "May I help you down?"

Her eyes never leaving Raine and the exquisite Judith, she let herself be lifted down.

"Where is she, Raine?" Judith was saying. "Your message was so garbled we could hardly understand it. We must have misheard because it seemed the messenger was saying your wife was about to be burned at the stake."

"True. I rescued her at the very last moment." His voice held a great deal of pride. With one arm around Judith, he led her to Alyx, whom he casually embraced. "This is Alyx and this vision is my unworthy brother's wife."

Alyx nodded once, openly staring at her sister-in-law. She'd never seen anyone who looked like this before: gold eyes, auburn hair barely visible under a pearl embroidered hood, a small voluptuous figure.

Judith pulled away from Raine. "You must be tired. Come with me and I'll have a bath brought for her." She took Alyx's hand in hers and started toward the house.

"Oh, Judith," Raine called from behind them. "Alyx lost her voice because of the smoke."

Beside her, Alyx felt Judith stiffen and knew it was because Raine dared to marry someone like her. Rapidly, she tried to blink back tears.

"You are tired," Judith said sympathetically, but there was an edge to her voice.

Alyx had no time to look at the house as Judith led her up the stairs and into a large paneled room. Alyx's house in Moreton could have been set in the room at least four times.

Heavy footsteps on the stairs made Judith turn. Raine stood just inside the doorway, grinning. "She's pretty, isn't she?" he said fondly, looking at Alyx. "Too bad her voice is gone, but I'm sure it's only temporary."

"No thanks to you," Judith said, leading Alyx to a chair.

"What does that mean?" Raine asked, bewildered. "I rescued her."

Judith whirled on him. "From what? From Pagnell's trap? She was used as bait to lure you to him. Raine," she calmed, "I think you should leave now. I don't think your sweet little wife wants to hear what I plan to say to you."

"Sweet!" Raine snorted. "And what reason do you have to be angry with me?" He was offended.

"You are trying my patience, Raine," she warned. "Alyx, are you hungry."

"Look, Judith, if you have something to say, say it."

"All right, then we'll leave this room. Your wife needs her rest."

Alyx was beginning to get an idea of what Judith had to

say. She grabbed her sister-in-law's hand and with her eyes urged her to continue. There were so many things she would like to say to Raine.

Judith blinked in understanding and whirled back to face Raine. "All right, I shall tell you what I have to say. You men, all of you, all four of you brothers, think nothing of dragging a woman all over England with no thought to her safety or comfort."

Raine's jaw jutted out. "We stayed in a very comfortable inn last night."

"You what! You took your lady wife into a public place dressed like that? How dare you, Raine? How dare you treat any woman like that?"

"What was I supposed to do, shop for clothes? Perhaps I should have ridden to London and asked the King for a bit of silk."

"Don't try to gain sympathy from me for being declared a traitor. It was your own Montgomery hotheadedness that caused all your problems."

At this Alyx began to clap her hands.

Judith flashed an understanding half-smile at her while Raine glared.

"I can see I'm not needed here," Raine said.

"You're not running away from this," Judith said. "I want you to run downstairs, pull Joan from whatever corner—or bed—she's lounging in, then order a bath sent up here. Oh, Raine, how could you do this to this poor child? The mother of your baby? It's been days since the fire and she's still covered with soot, and how you must have ridden to get here so fast! Now go along and get yourself cleaned up and dressed properly."

With his jaw still out, refusing to speak, Raine left the room, the door slamming behind him.

With a sigh, Judith looked back at Alyx. "You have to stand up for yourself or men will take advantage. Are you well? Raine didn't harm you in his haste, did he?"

Alyx only shook her head, looking at Judith with admiration and the beginnings of love.

"It's a good thing the three of us are all sturdy and strong or else we'd be dead by now."

Alyx held up three fingers, frowned in question.

"Bronwyn, Stephen's wife. You'll have to meet her. She is lovely, absolutely lovely, but Stephen drags her everywhere, makes her sleep on the ground rolled up in a wool blanket. It's really dreadful."

A knock on the door interrupted Judith, and seconds later servants arrived with a tub and pails of hot water. "I should send Raine more often," Judith said. "He certainly gets things done quickly."

Alyx gave a little giggle and Judith smiled back.

"They are good men. I wouldn't trade Gavin for anyone, but sometimes you have to raise your voice a bit. Someday you'll get over your awe of your husband and you'll find yourself shouting right back at him. You may not think so now, but you will."

Alyx merely smiled and allowed herself to be led to the tub.

Chapter 16

RAINE, UP to his neck in a tub of hot water, his eyes still blazing with anger, looked up hostilely as the door to his room opened. Gavin burst in.

"Miles has taken the Chatworth girl to Scotland, and from what I can gather he had to drag her there while she screamed curses at him. Damn him!" he said passionately. "Why do I have so much trouble with my younger brothers? Only Stephen—"

"You'd better stop," Raine warned. "I'm in a mood to drive a sword through someone's belly."

"And what has happened now?" Gavin asked tiredly, sitting down across from Raine. "I have more problems than I need. Has your wife said an unkind word to you?"

"Not *my* wife." He stopped. "What do you plan to do about Miles? Do you think he's taking her to Stephen?"

"I can only hope so. Sir Guy is with him, so perhaps he can talk some sense into Miles."

"Do you have a reason why Miles should keep the girl? Other than for his own pleasure, that is? I can't imagine our little brother forcing a woman to do anything, nor can I imagine one refusing him. I've never seen him have any trouble with women."

"One of Miles's men broke his arm right after Lady Elizabeth was delivered and so stayed behind when Miles went to Scotland. I caught him on the road."

"And what was his bad news? It couldn't be as bad as the look on your face."

"There were four men in Miles's tent at the time. Pagnell's man was allowed to enter, all the men holding swords on him. He was carrying a long carpet in his arms. He paused just inside the entrance, tossed it to the floor, gave it a push with his foot and unrolled it."

"Well?" Raine demanded.

"It unrolled at Miles's feet, uncovering Elizabeth Chatworth wearing nothing but several feet of blonde hair."

"And what did our little brother do?" Raine asked, torn between laughing and groaning at the picture he'd conjured.

"From what I found out, all the men stood and stared without moving until Lady Elizabeth jumped up, grabbed a cloth from a cot and an ax from a corner and took after Miles."

"Was he harmed?"

"He managed to dodge her blows and sent the other men from the tent. When the lady started cursing worse than what anyone had heard before, Sir Guy took the men out of hearing distance of the tent."

"And no doubt she was purring the next morning," Raine said, smiling. "Our little brother has a way with women."

"I don't know what happened after that. An hour later the man I spoke to broke his arm and was sent back to Miles's house."

"Then how did you know they went to Scotland?" Raine asked.

"I went to Miles's campsite and when no one was there, I asked some of the tradesmen in the area. Over a week ago Miles and his men left, and several people heard them say they were going to Scotland."

"No clue as to why?"

"Who can say what goes on in Miles's mind? I know for sure he wouldn't harm the girl, but I'm afraid he'll hold her to punish Chatworth."

"Miles would fight a man, many men, but he wouldn't take his grudges out on a woman. That's Chatworth's game,"

Raine said grimly. "I'm sure he had a reason to take her from England. What do you plan to do now?"

Gavin was quiet for a moment. "I'll leave him to Stephen and see what he can do with Miles. And Bronwyn has a level head on her. Perhaps she can do something with Miles."

Raine stood in the tub. "I doubt if anyone can reason with him where women are concerned. If the woman took more than ten minutes to fall in love with him, it would be the first time such a thing has happened. Maybe Miles saw it as a challenge."

Gavin snorted. "Whatever his reasons, he's tempting the King's wrath. King Henry's changed since his eldest son died."

Drying himself, Raine stepped from the tub, gave a kick to his clothes heaped at his feet. "It will be good to get out of these for a while."

"How long do you think you can stay?"

"Three, four days at most. I need to get back to the camp."

"Are your outlaws so important?"

Raine considered for a moment. "They aren't all outlaws, and perhaps if you'd lived their life you would have different ideas about right and wrong."

"Stealing is wrong no matter what," Gavin said firmly.

"Would you sit by quietly and let Judith and your new son starve to death? If they were hungry and a man pushing a cart of bread walked by, would you sit on your high morals and let it go?"

"I don't want to argue with you. Does Alyx know you plan to return?"

"No, not yet. I'm not sure I'll tell her, but just slip away. If I don't I'm sure she'll try to go with me. I want her here with you and Judith. I want her to live the way she never has before."

With one sweep he picked up his old clothes, flung them into a corner and reached for the silver embroidered, black velvet gown on the bed.

"What's this?" Gavin asked, moving to lift something from Raine's dirty clothes. He held up a gold belt.

"It's Alyx's Lyon belt, as she calls it, but for the life of me I can't make out anything like a lion on it. One of the guards at the trial took it from her, and I had a devil of a time getting it from him."

With a frown on his face, Gavin took the belt to the window and studied it in the sunlight. "It looks very old. Is it?"

"I guess. Alyx says it's been handed down from mother to daughter in her family for as long as anyone can remember."

"Lions," Gavin muttered. "There's something familiar about this belt. Come downstairs with me to the winter parlor."

When Raine was dressed, he followed his brother to the paneled room. On one wall hung an old and faded tapestry. It had been there for ages and was so familiar to Raine it was nearly invisible.

"Did Father ever tell you about this tapestry?" Gavin asked. When Raine shook his head, Gavin continued. "It was woven in the time of Edward the First, and the subject was a celebration of the greatest knight of the century, a man called the Black Lion. See, here he is atop the horse and this lovely lady was his wife. Look at her waist."

Raine looked, somewhat bored by Gavin's recitation of the family history, but saw nothing special. He was always a man concerned with today and now, not centuries ago.

Gavin gave his brother a look of exasperation. "I saw a drawing of this belt—" he pointed to the tapestry—"long ago. The Black Lion's wife's name was something to do with a lion, and for a wedding gift the Lion gave his wife a belt of a lion and his lioness."

"You don't think Alyx's belt could be that one. It would have to be a couple of hundred years old."

"Look at the way this thing is worn down," Gavin said, holding Alyx's belt aloft. "The links have been wired together with iron and the design is almost gone, but from what I can see of the clasp it could be lions."

"How would Alyx have gotten the belt?"

Gavin didn't need to be reminded of his new sister-in-law's origins. "The Black Lion was a fabulously wealthy man, but he had one son and eight daughters. He gave all his daughters enormous dowries, and to his eldest daughter went the lion belt to pass on to her eldest daughter."

"You don't think Alyx—" Raine began.

"The Black Lion's eldest son was named Montgomery, and it's through him that all our family has descended. Don't you remember Father saying you were like the Black Lion? The four of us were tall, slim and fair while you were always shorter, sturdier."

Raine remembered all the teasing he'd taken as a child and sometimes wondered if he was a full brother to his sister and three brothers. But he'd been twelve when his father had died, and there were many things he didn't remember.

"Father said you were like him." He pointed to the massive blackhaired man atop the rearing stallion in the tapestry.

"And you think this belt Alyx has could have belonged to the man's wife?" Raine took the belt from his brother. "She cherishes it, never lets it out of her sight. I knew it would be taken from her at the trial. She hasn't mentioned it to me, but last night she must have been dreaming and she cried out about this bit of gold."

"Did you know the Black Lion married a woman well beneath him? Not quite Alyx's status, but compared to him, the Montgomerys are as poor as gamekeepers."

Raine rubbed the worn belt between his fingers. "It's too farfetched to believe. But sometimes I feel as if I've known Alyx longer than just a few months. I've been with women more beautiful than her, and certainly women who treated me with more respect, but when I first looked at her—" He stopped and laughed. "When I first saw her I thought she was a boy and I thought that if I had a son he would look like Alyx. There was something about her . . . I don't know how to explain it. Was it the same with you and Judith?"

"No," Gavin said flatly, looking away. He hated any reminder of how he'd treated Judith when they were first married.

"Speaking of your wife," Raine said. "She gave me a tongue-lashing when I arrived."

Gavin laughed at that. "And what had you done? If I remember correctly, she usually fawns over you to no end."

"She said I was mistreating my wife by bringing her here."

"Because of the King?" Gavin asked. "We discussed it and she agreed that you would be safe for a few days. It will take that long for someone to recognize you and get word to the King."

"No, it wasn't that." Raine was truly puzzled. "It was something about not buying her enough dresses. Perhaps she thinks I carry dresses on my saddle."

"I'm certainly glad I arrived in time to defend myself," Judith said from the doorway, smiling. Immediately, she went to her husband and kissed him. "You are safe? Well?"

"As well as can be," he said, holding her close to him. "And what is this I hear about your berating my brother? I hope you did not hurt him. He's not as strong as I am."

"Delicate," Judith said sweetly. "All of your brothers are as delicate as spring flowers." She smiled up at Raine, both men overpowering her slight form. "I merely said that Raine should not have dragged his wife across the country when she is carrying his child and she is ill from the fire's smoke and all the while dressed worse than the lowest menial."

Judith started to say more but turned as in the doorway stood Alyx, but an Alyx no one had seen before. She wore a gown of deep, dark purple velvet, the low, square neckline hung with a heavy silver chain, a large purple amethyst in the center. The back of her head was covered with a simple hood of silver cloth embroidered with purple flowers. Her violet eyes sparkled brilliantly.

Raine moved toward her, lifted her hand and kissed it. "I am overwhelmed with such beauty," he said sincerely.

"You are different," she whispered.

"And you can talk. Can you sing yet?"

"Don't rush her, Raine," Judith said. "I've given her honey and herbs, but I think she'll heal much faster if she doesn't use her voice. Dinner is ready. Is anyone hungry?"

Alyx was glad she couldn't speak because she didn't believe she could have anyway. Raine had always seemed so much more than the people around him even when he dressed in his forestry clothes, but now, in his black and silver, he was awesome. He fit so well into this magnificent house, and he saw nothing unusual about so many people bowing toward him.

As Raine led her to the tables set in the Great Hall, she had to work to keep her mouth from dropping open. The meal she'd seen at the inn had seemed like a feast, but on these tables was food enough for a village.

"Who are these men?" she whispered to Raine beside her. There were over a hundred people eating with them.

Raine glanced up, noticing the people as if from her eyes. "They're Gavin's men, a few of mine, some of Stephen's. Those men are Montgomerys, cousins, I think. You'll have to ask Gavin for the exact relationship." He pointed toward the end of the table where they sat. "Some of them are castle retainers. You can ask Judith. I'm sure she knows who everyone is."

"Yours so big?" she rasped.

"No," he grinned. "My estates are small compared to this. Judith is the rich one. She brought great wealth when she married into our family, and she has to support many people. She's always buying and selling and counting grain in the storerooms."

"Me?" Alyx asked, scared.

Raine took a while to understand her. "You mean will you have to run my estates? I don't see why not. You can read and write. That's more than I can do." He looked away as one of his cousins spoke to him.

Alyx had difficulty eating more of the meal and after a while sat quietly as course after course was brought into the room. Most of the food she'd never seen before, and new names and flavors were beginning to run together.

After a long while, Raine stood and introduced her and the people shouted a welcome to her.

Judith asked Alyx if she'd like to rest, and together they went back to Alyx's room.

"Is it all a bit bewildering?" Judith asked. Alyx nodded her head.

"Tomorrow there's a fair in the village, and I'll see if Raine will take you to it. You'll have some fun and not have so many new people to deal with. But now, why don't you rest? Gavin and Raine are preparing a message to send to Miles, and you'll have hours to rest because I'm sure they'll argue for that long."

When Alyx had removed her dress and slipped beneath the covers, Judith took her hand. "You have nothing to fear from us. We are your family from now on and whatever you do will meet our approval. I know that all this"—she motioned to the elegant room—"is new to you, but you'll soon learn and we're here to help you."

"Thank you," Alyx whispered and was asleep before Judith was out of the door.

Nothing could have prepared Alyx for the fair set up in Montgomery pastureland. She'd slept soundly and long and when she woke, her voice was at least half restored. The sound was there and she was glad, even if the tones were gone.

"Do you think I'll be able to sing again?"

Raine laughed at the fear in her voice and helped her button the purple dress Judith had altered to fit Alyx. "I'm sure that in another few days the birds will fly into the room just to hear you."

Laughing, she whirled about the room, the bell-shaped skirt swirling around her. "Isn't it lovely? It is the most beautiful dress on the earth."

"No," Raine laughed, grabbing her. "It is you who makes it lovely. Now stop turning about before you make my child dizzy. Are you ready for the fair?"

The fair was like a city, a city composed of people from all over the world. There were stalls for animals, stalls of lead and tin from England, booths of Spanish wines, German commodities, Italian cloths, toy shops, wrestling matches, games of skill, butchers, fishmongers.

"Where do we begin?" Alyx asked, clinging to Raine's arm. They were surrounded by six of Gavin's knights.

"Perhaps my lady is hungry?" asked one knight.

"Or thirsty?"

"Would my lady like to see the jugglers or the acrobats?"

"I hear there's a fair singer just this way."

"The singer," Alyx said firmly, making Raine laugh.

"To see what you have to compete with?" he teased.

She smiled at him, too happy to let his teasing bother her. After a brief visit to the singer, who was no good at all in Alyx's opinion, they stopped at a gingerbread stall and Raine bought her a spicy fresh-baked lady.

Eating her treat, looking this way and that, she was hardly aware when Raine stopped before an Italian's booth.

"What do you think of this?" Raine asked, holding up a length of violet silk.

"Lovely," she said absently. "Oh, Raine, there is a bear doing tricks."

"Your bear of a husband is going to do tricks if you don't listen to him." When she looked up, he continued. "I have had enough of Judith's berating me. Choose the colors you want and I'll have them sent to the castle."

"Choose?" she asked dumbly, looking at the wealth before her.

"Give us everything you have in purple," Raine said quickly. "And those greens. You'll look good in those, Alyx." He turned back to the merchant. "Cut off enough of each one for a dress and send it to the castle. A steward will pay you." With that he took Alyx's arm and pulled her away.

Like a child, Alyx looked backward, her gingerbread in her mouth. There must have been three shades of purple, four of green in each type of fabric, and the types included silks, satins, velvets, brocades and others Alyx didn't recognize. Raine stopped before the performing bear, but when he saw Alyx wasn't watching, he pulled her to another booth—a furrier's.

This time he didn't wait for her to choose but ordered a cloak lined with lambskin and another with leopard from Asia. He told the furrier to see the cloth merchant and send some bits and pieces for trim for the dresses he'd ordered.

By now Alyx was recovering herself. She was being dressed without even so much as a consultation as to what she wanted. If she had any idea of what she did want, she'd protest Raine's highhandedness.

"Do you choose your own clothes like this?" she ventured. "Do you leave the choices up to the merchants?"

He shrugged. "I usually wear black, saves time that way. Miles is the one who knows clothes."

"And what about Stephen? What does he know?"

"He keeps Gavin and me apart and all he wears are the Scots' clothes, leaving most of him bare."

"Sounds interesting," Alyx murmured, making Raine give her a sharp look.

"Behave yourself. Look at this. Have you seen this before?"

What Alyx saw was a woman working with hundreds of wooden spools on a fat little pillow. "What is it?" The finished product looked to be white silk cobwebs.

"It's lace, my lady," the woman said and held up a collar for Alyx's inspection.

Gently, Alyx touched it, almost afraid it would fall apart.

"Here," Raine said, pulling a bag of gold from under his doublet. "Let me have three of those. Take your pick, Alyx, and we'll give one to Judith and send the other to Bronwyn."

"Oh, yes," she breathed, pleased at the idea of a gift to Judith.

The lace collars were carefully laid in a thin wooden box and given to one of the knights to carry.

The next few hours were the happiest Alyx had ever known. Seeing Raine in his natural environment, seeing him get the respect he deserved, was a joy to her. Yet this man who was so honored could sit down with the lowest beggar and listen to the man.

"You're looking at me oddly," Raine said.

"I am counting my blessings." She looked away from him. "What are all those people looking at?"

"Come on and we'll see."

The crowd in front of them parted to let the seven big men and the small woman through. Inside the circle were four half-dressed women, their flat bellies bare, their legs visible through transparent silks, undulating to some strange music. After her initial shock, Alyx glanced up at her husband, saw he was completely captivated by the women, as were the guards around them. And to think that moments before she'd been thinking Raine was close to the Lord's angels!

With an exclamation of disgust, which Raine didn't even hear, Alyx began backing out of the crowd, leaving the men to their obsession.

"My lady," said someone beside her. "Let me lead you out of this crush. You're so small that I fear for your safety."

She looked up into the dark eyes of a very handsome man. He had blond hair streaked by the sun, an aquiline nose over a firm mouth. There was a curved scar by his left eye and shadows under his eyes. "I'm not sure—" she began. "My husband . . ."

"Let me introduce myself. I am the Earl of Bayham and your husband's family and mine are well acquainted. I've traveled a long way to speak to Gavin, but when I saw the fair I hoped to find one of the family here."

A heavy-set man who'd had more than a little to drink lunged toward them, and the earl put out a hand, protecting Alyx.

"I feel it's my duty to protect you from this mob. Let me lead you out of here."

She took the arm he offered. There was something about him that seemed both sad and kind at the same time, and she instinctively trusted him.

"How did you hear of my marriage?" she asked. "It was so recent and I haven't come from the same people as my husband."

"I have a special interest in what the Montgomery family does."

He led her away from the noise of the fair, to a bench just inside a small grove of trees. "You must be very tired since you've not sat down all morning. And surely the child must be a heavy burden."

Gratefully, she sat down, rested her hands on her stomach, and looked up at him. "You have indeed been watching us. Now, what do you want to talk to me about that you needed me away from my husband?"

At that the earl smiled slightly. "The Montgomerys choose their women well, for brains as well as beauty. Perhaps I should reintroduce myself. I am Roger Chatworth."

Chapter 17

ALYX, FEELING so smug because she thought she'd guessed that this man wanted her to use her influence on her husband, suddenly felt very frightened. Clumsily, her fear showing on her face, she started to stand.

"Please," he said softly. "I don't mean to harm you. I only want to talk to you for a moment." He sat down on the end of the bench, feet away from her, his head down, hands clasped. "Leave. I won't stop you."

Alyx was already past him when she turned back. "If my husband sees you, he will kill you."

Roger didn't answer and Alyx, frowning, telling herself she was a fool, went back to the bench. "Why have you risked coming here?" she asked. "I would risk anything to find my sister."

"Elizabeth?"

Perhaps it was the way she said the name, but Roger's head came up sharply. "You know her? What do you know?" His hands made fists.

"Pagnell, the earl of Waldenham's son—"

"I know the piece of slime."

Quickly, Alyx told the story of how Elizabeth had helped her and how Pagnell had punished Elizabeth.

"Miles!" Roger said, standing. He was richly dressed in dark blue velvet, a satin brocade doublet, his long, muscular legs tightly encased in dark hose. This was not the man Alyx would have imagined as anyone's enemy.

"And what has Miles done with my innocent sister?" Roger demanded, his eyes flashing.

"Not what you did with the Lady Mary," Alyx shot back.

"The woman's death is on my soul, and I have paid for it with the loss of my brother. I do not plan to lose my sister as well."

Alyx had no idea what he was talking about. What did Roger's brother have to do with Mary's death? "I don't know where Miles and Elizabeth are. I have not been well. Perhaps while I was resting Raine found out about Miles, but I know nothing."

"What of the Lady Judith? I don't think much is done that she doesn't know about. Did she tell you something?"

"No, nothing. Why are you free when my husband has to hide, yet it was you who killed Mary?"

"I did not kill her!" he said vehemently. "I—no! I don't want to discuss it, and as for being free, the King has taken all my rents for the next three years. Most of my men have left me because I cannot pay them. I have only one small estate to house what is left of my family, which now consists of one vicious sister-in-law. My brother hates me and has vanished from the earth, and now my lovely, sweet sister is held prisoner by a boy who is notorious for his deflowering of women. I have not been punished? Your husband still retains his lands, his own steward runs them while a King's man runs mine. Do you know what will be left in three years' time? Your husband has all of his family. He even has the leisure to fall in love and marry while I have no one left—one brother killed, one turned against me, my sister a prisoner. And you say I am not punished? That I am free?"

He stopped after this speech and looked away, unseeing, into the distance.

"I don't know what has happened to Elizabeth. Gavin went after Miles, but he came back right away. I didn't speak to him when he returned."

"I will kill him if he harms her."

"And what will that gain?" Alyx shouted, hurting her sore throat, but at least her voice made him blink. "Will any of you rest until all of you are killed? Miles did not take Elizabeth; she was given to him. He is innocent. Pagnell is the one who should bear your wrath. But you are too used to hating the Montgomerys and blaming them for all your problems."

"What could I expect from a Montgomery?" he asked sullenly. "Already you believe them to be gods on this earth."

"Stupid man!" she spat. "I only want this war of yours to end. Raine has to live in a forest surrounded by criminals and all because of you."

"Gavin started this by playing with my sister-in-law. One woman wasn't enough for him. He also wanted Alice."

Alyx put her hands to her head. "I don't know any of this. You must go now. Raine will be looking for me."

"Do you mean to protect me?"

"I plan to protect my husband from a fight and me from his wrath."

"I cannot leave until I find out about Elizabeth."

Alyx gritted her teeth. "I don't know where Elizabeth is."

"Will you find out and tell me?"

"Absolutely not!" She was astonished that he'd ask this. "Miles is with her, and I'll not do anything to endanger him."

Roger's mouth made a grim line. "You are a fool to come out here with me. I could take you now and demand Elizabeth's release while I hold you."

Swallowing once, Alyx knew she must brave this out and not let him see her fear. "You have no guards near you. Will you strike a pregnant woman? How far will you get alone with me? Elizabeth still believes you are a good man. Would she still if you took yet another Montgomery prisoner?" Alyx could tell by his face that she was striking a nerve. "How did you explain Mary's death to her?"

Alyx paused a moment, watching him. "You must go."

Before either of them could react, through the trees burst Raine and his guards. Instantly, four swords were at Roger Chatworth's throat.

Raine grabbed Alyx, held her with one arm, his sword drawn in the other. "The bastard has not harmed you?" Raine growled. "Kill him," he said in the next breath.

"No!" Alyx screamed at the top of her lungs and successfully made the men halt. Instantly, she placed herself before Roger. "He has done me no harm. All he wants to know is where his sister is."

"In the grave beside mine," Raine said, eyes narrowed.

"She's not dead," Alyx said. "Raine, please, let's end this feud now. Swear that you'll see that Elizabeth is returned to Roger."

"Roger, is it?" Raine breathed in through his teeth, glaring at her until she took a step backward, closer to Roger. "How long have you known him?"

"How—?" she began, bewildered. "Raine, please you're not making sense. He's a man alone and I don't want to see him killed. He wants his sister. Do you know where she is?"

"Now you ask me to betray my brother for this filth. Has he told you of Mary's last moments alive?" He looked at Roger, a snarl curling his lip. "Did you enjoy the sound of her body breaking on the stones?"

Alyx could feel herself becoming ill at the images Raine conjured, and she almost wanted to turn Roger over to him. But the King would only have another excuse to keep Raine's lands. He'd never pardon Raine if an earl were killed by him.

"You have to release him," she said quietly. "You cannot kill him in cold blood. Come, Roger. I will walk with you to your horse."

Without a word, Roger Chatworth walked before her back into the fair where his horse waited. Neither Raine nor his guards followed.

"He will never forgive you," Roger said.

"I didn't do it for you. If Raine killed you, the King would never forgive him. Go now and remember that a Montgomery was good to you when you didn't deserve it. I want no harm to come to Miles or Elizabeth and I will do what I can to see that she is returned to you."

With a look of disbelief, awe and gratefulness, he turned his horse and rode away from the Montgomery estates.

Alyx stood still a moment, her heart beating wildly as she thought about facing Raine again. Of course he'd be angry, but when she explained why she'd helped his enemy, he'd understand. Slowly, dreading the coming argument, she walked back toward the trees where the guard stood.

It took only seconds to see that Raine wasn't there. "Where is he?" she asked, sure he had gone to some private place for their coming battle.

"My lady," one of the guards began. "Lord Raine has returned to the forest."

"Yes, I know," she said. "Where we can be alone. But which direction did he take?"

For a moment Alyx only looked at the man, and after a long while she came to realize what the man meant. "The forest? You mean the camp of the outlaws?"

"Yes, my lady."

"Fetch my horse! I'll go after him. We can catch him."

"No, my lady. We have orders to return you to Lord Gavin. You are not to follow Lord Raine."

"I must go," she said, looking up at the men pleadingly. "Don't you see that I had to keep Raine from killing Chatworth? The King would put Raine on the block if he killed an earl. I must explain this to my husband. Take me to him at once!"

"We cannot." The guard hardened his jaw against the look of sympathy in his eyes. "Our orders come from Lord Raine."

"Perhaps if my lady were to speak to Lord Gavin," another guard suggested.

"Yes," she said eagerly. "Let's return to the castle. Gavin will know what to do."

Once mounted, Alyx set a pace that the knights had difficulty keeping up with. As soon as the horse's hooves touched the pavement of the courtyard, Alyx was off and running into the house.

She slammed into one empty room and started for another, then stood still and bellowed, "Gavin!"

In seconds, running down the stairs came Gavin, his face a mask of incredulousness. Judith was close behind him.

"Was that you calling?" Gavin asked, awed. "Raine said you had a strong voice but—"

Alyx cut him off. "Raine has returned to the outlaw camp. I must go to him. He hates me. He doesn't understand why I did it. I must explain."

"Slow down," Gavin said. "Tell me what's happened from the beginning."

Alyx tried to breathe deeply. "Roger Chatworth—"

The name was enough to make Gavin explode. "Chatworth! Has he harmed you? Has Raine gone after him? Fetch my men," he said to one of his men standing behind Alyx. "Full armor."

"No!" Alyx shouted, then put her face in her hands. The tears were finally starting.

Judith put her arm around Alyx. "Gavin, talk to the men while I take care of Alyx." She led Alyx to a cushioned niche under a window, took her hands in her own. "Now tell me what has happened."

Alyx's tears and her sense of urgency made her nearly incoherent. It was only by careful questioning that Judith was able to piece the story together.

"I didn't understand," Alyx sobbed. "Roger kept talking about things I didn't understand. Who is Alice? Who was his brother? What did he have to do with Mary's death? Raine was so angry. He ordered Roger killed and I had to stop him. I had to!"

"It's a good thing you did. Now I want you to sit here quietly while I go find Gavin. I'll tell him your story and Gavin will be able to reason with Raine."

Judith found her husband and twenty knights in the courtyard, looking as if they were preparing for war. "Gavin! What are you doing?"

"We're going after Chatworth."

"Chatworth? But what about Raine? He believes Alyx sided with Chatworth. You have to go to Raine and make him understand. Alyx was protecting Raine—not Chatworth."

"Judith, I don't have time to solve a lovers' quarrel now.

I have to find Miles and warn him about Chatworth or else find Chatworth and see that he can't gather an army and go after my brother."

"Get Miles to release Elizabeth. That's what Chatworth wants," Judith said. "Give him back his sister."

"Like he returned mine? Across a horse, face down?"

"Gavin, please," Judith pleaded.

He stopped a moment and pulled her to him. "Raine is safer in the forest. No doubt Chatworth will let the King know of Raine's threats and that will renew the King's wrath. And Alyx was to stay here anyway, so it's worked out well. Now Miles is of more concern to me. I don't believe he's harmed the girl, but I'd hoped we'd have time before Chatworth found out where she was. I have to warn my brother and give him protection if he needs it."

"And what of Alyx? Raine believes she betrayed him."

"I don't know," Gavin said, dismissing the subject. "Write him and send a messenger. Raine is safe—angry perhaps, but anger won't harm him. Now I must go. Look after Alyx while I'm gone and feed my son."

She smiled up at him and he kissed her lingeringly. "Take care," she called after him as he and his men rode out.

Judith's smile didn't last long as she reentered the house and saw Alyx sitting alone on the window seat.

"Is Gavin going to Raine?" Alyx whispered, hope in her voice.

"Not now. Perhaps later he will go. Now he has to warn Miles that Roger Chatworth knows a Montgomery holds Elizabeth."

Alyx leaned back against the stone casing. "How could Raine believe I'd betray him? Chatworth asked me to find out where Elizabeth was, but I refused. I only wanted to help Raine, to help the whole family. Now I have worsened all of it."

"Alyx," Judith said, taking her sister-in-law's cold hands. "There are things you don't know, things that happened before you were part of our family."

"I know about Mary's death. I was with Raine when he found out."

"Before that there were events—"

"Having to do with this Alice Roger mentioned and his brother?"

"Yes. Alice Chatworth started it all."

Alyx was amazed at the coldness in Judith's eyes, at the way her lovely features changed. "Who is Alice?" Alyx whispered.

"Gavin was in love with Alice Valence," Judith said in a small voice. "But the woman would not marry him. Instead she caught herself a rich earl, Edmund Chatworth."

"Edmund Chatworth," she said. The man Jocelin had killed.

"Edmund was killed one night by a singer who was never caught," Judith continued, not knowing Alyx's knowledge.

"I always believed Alice Chatworth knew more about what happened than she told. As a widow she decided she could afford to marry Gavin, but Gavin refused to put me aside and marry her. Alice did not take losing very well." Judith's voice was heavy with sarcasm. "She took me prisoner and threatened to pour boiling oil on my face. There was a scuffle and the oil scarred Alice."

"Roger said his household consisted of one vicious sister-in-law. Surely he cannot have harmed Mary because of the scarring?"

"No, later Roger was in Scotland and met the woman King Henry had promised Stephen for a bride. Bronwyn is rich and well worth a fight. Roger claimed her for his and he and Stephen fought. Roger is a proud man and a renowned knight, but Stephen bested him and in a rage, Roger attacked Stephen's back."

"Stephen was not hurt, was he?"

"No, but Roger's reputation was destroyed. All over England people laughed at him and began calling a back stabbing a 'Chatworth.' "

"And so Roger retaliated by taking Mary. He must have

seen the Montgomerys as the cause of all his humiliations," Alyx said.

"He did. He begged Stephen to kill him on the battlefield, but Stephen wouldn't and Roger felt further insulted. So Roger held Mary and Bronwyn prisoners for a while. I don't believe he'd have harmed Mary if it weren't for Brian."

"And who is Brian?"

"Roger's young brother, a crippled, shy boy who fell in love with Mary. When Brian told Roger he planned to marry Mary, Roger got drunk and climbed in bed with Mary. You know what Mary did. Brian brought her body back to us."

"And now Miles has Elizabeth," Alyx said. "Raine is outlawed. Roger has lost his family and his wealth and now Miles's life may be in danger. Is there no way to stop this hatred? What if Roger kills Miles? What will happen then? Who will be next? Will any of us ever be safe again? Will our children grow up to hate Chatworths? Will my child fight Roger's?"

"Quiet, Alyx," Judith said softly, pulling Alyx into her arms. "Gavin has gone to warn Miles and he will be safe. Besides, Bronwyn is there with her men, and even if Chatworth were to raise an army, he won't be able to fight the MacArrans."

"I hope you're right. And Raine will be safe in the forest."

"Let's go and write letters to Raine now. We'll send a messenger tonight."

"Yes," Alyx said, sitting up, brushing tears away. "As soon as Raine knows the truth I'm sure he'll forgive me."

Chapter 18

RAINE RETURNED Alyx's letters unopened. Although he read Judith's explanation of what had happened, he made no comment in the verbal messages he sent back. He had no squire now, so Judith had to be careful to send only messengers who could read.

Alyx seemed to accept all that was happening stoically, yet each morning her eyes were red and her appetite was all but gone.

When Gavin returned from Scotland, he gasped at the sight of Alyx, nearly skin and bones except for her stomach sticking out in front.

"What is your news?" Judith asked before he could say anything about Alyx's appearance.

"We found Chatworth and detained him for a while, but he escaped."

"Did you harm him?" Judith asked.

"Not one hair!" Gavin snapped. "When he was gone we went to Scotland, but he hadn't appeared there. My guess is Chatworth went to King Henry."

"Did you see Miles?"

Gavin nodded his head in frustration. "He has always been stubborn, but now he goes too far. He refuses to release Elizabeth, and nothing anyone could say made him see reason."

"And what about Elizabeth?"

"She fights him constantly. They would argue over the color of the sky, but sometimes I see her looking at him with something besides hate. Now, how is Alyx?"

"Raine returns her letters unopened and I've had no mention of her, although my letters plead with him to listen. The messenger says Raine has him skip the passages dealing with Alyx."

Gavin's frown said a great deal. "My brother would forgive a triple murderer, but if he thinks his honor is besmirched he is remorseless. I'll write to him and tell him of Alyx's condition. When's the child due?"

"In a few weeks."

Raine did not answer Gavin's words about Alyx either.

In November, Alyx was delivered of a large, healthy baby girl who smiled seconds after her birth and showed that she had Raine's dimples. "Catherine," Alyx whispered before falling asleep.

But in the next weeks, the child was not so happy. Catherine cried constantly.

"She cries for her father," Alyx said bleakly, and Judith almost shook her.

"If I didn't know better," Judith said, "I'd think she was hungry."

Judith's words were prophetic because as soon as a wet nurse was found, Catherine quieted.

"What good am I?" Alyx wailed.

Judith did shake her. "Listen to me! You have to think of your child. Perhaps you can't feed her, but there are other things you can do. And if the child isn't enough, I can find work for you to do."

Alyx nodded numbly and before she knew what was happening, Judith gave her more work than she knew existed. Alyx was given ledgers to read, columns of figures to add, bushels of grain to count and record. There were storerooms to clean, meals to oversee and hundreds of people to care for.

Alyx was given the care of the hospital for two weeks and learned she was good at cheering the patients. Judith was pleased with Alyx's musical ability, but she saw no reason for

Alyx to spend the day alone working on music. She composed songs as she bandaged a wounded leg or as she was riding to the village below the Montgomery castle.

It was a bit of a shock to Alyx when neither Judith nor Gavin was awed by her talent but took it in stride. They, too, had talents, but they did not indulge them to the exclusion of work.

Alyx wasn't sure when she started to realize how selfish her life had been. She'd been set apart from the people of her village by her talent. Everyone had been reserved toward her, had treated her as if she were someone touched by Heaven. In her smug sureness she'd decided she hated the nobles because of what one man had done. But in truth she was jealous. She'd always felt she was the equal of anyone, but actually, what had she ever given to anyone? Her music? Or was her music really for herself?

She realized that Gavin's men and the servants were kind to her because of her relationship to Raine, but she wanted to give something that wasn't so easy for her.

She set up a school for the many children in the castle complex and began to teach them to read and write. There were many days when she wanted to quit, but she kept on and was rewarded once in a while when a child learned a new word.

In the afternoons she worked with the wounded and ill. Once a man's leg was crushed under a wine barrel and it had to be taken off. Alyx took his head in her hands and used all her training, and all her feeling, to hypnotize him with her voice. Afterward, she cried for hours.

"It hurts to become involved," she said to Judith. "One of my children, a lovely child, fell off the wall yesterday and she died in my arms. I don't want to love people. Music is safer."

Judith held her and soothed her and they talked for a long time. In the morning Alyx went back to her school. Later, the man who'd lost his leg asked for her and there were tears of gratitude on his face for Alyx's help.

Judith was behind Alyx. "Did God give you your talent

to help men who need you or should you save it for prettily dressed people in church?"

At Christmas, Judith's mother came to visit them. Helen Bassett didn't look old enough to be anyone's mother. At her side was her husband John, who looked as content as any man could. Together they smiled at their eleven-month-old daughter, who was just learning to walk.

Judith's son was six months old, Alyx's daughter two months. Everyone tried to make the festivities merry and no one mentioned how many of the family were missing.

"We were all together last year," Gavin muttered into his ale cup.

There was no word from Raine.

In January, everything seemed to happen at once. Roger Chatworth had indeed gone to King Henry—but not alone. Whether by chance or contrivance, Pagnell had appeared at the same time.

Roger said Miles was holding his sister prisoner in Scotland and Pagnell said he had proof, not just the vague rumors of before, that Raine was training non-nobles to fight as knights, that he was attempting to raise an army against the King.

King Henry said he was heartily sick of the feud between the Chatworths and the Montgomerys and he wanted Lady Elizabeth released. If Miles did not do so, he would be declared a traitor and his lands confiscated. As for Raine, if he put more weapons in those outlaws' hands, the King would burn the forest and all of them together.

Gavin sent a messenger to Scotland, pleading with Stephen to force Miles to obey the King. Before there was a reply, it was heard that Pagnell had been found dead and it was whispered that the Montgomerys were responsible. The King added this to a long list of grievances.

"He wants what we've held for centuries," Gavin said. "Other kings have tried to take it and have failed. This one will, too." He grabbed a mace from the wall. "If Stephen cannot reason with Miles, I can."

Within an hour he was off again for Scotland.

"And what about Raine?" Alyx asked quietly as she held Catherine. "Who is going to warn him about the King's threats?"

"King Henry won't burn the forest," Judith said practically. "There are too few of them left. Raine wouldn't really march on the King with his band of cutthroats, would he?"

"Perhaps. Raine would dare anything if he saw some injustice. If he thought his brother were in danger there is no predicting what he might do."

"Miles will listen to Gavin this time—I hope," Judith said. "Roger will get his sister back and everything will be settled."

They looked at each other for a long moment, neither of them believing Judith's words.

"I'm going to Raine," Alyx said softly, then opened her eyes in surprise.

"Will he allow you into the forest? Oh, Alyx, I'm not sure you should do that. The Montgomery men can get terribly angry."

"Has Gavin's anger ever kept you from doing what you had to do? If Gavin were in danger would you hesitate helping him in any way you could?"

Judith was quiet for a moment. "I once led Gavin's men against a man who held him captive."

"I merely ride into a forest. Would you care for Catherine? She's too young to take with me. It will be cold there."

"Alyx, are you sure?"

"I might be able to distract Raine. I'm sure he's brooding over all that has happened and no doubt contemplating all manner of horrors to commit against Roger Chatworth. Sometimes I can outshout him and force him to listen to me. He probably won't know what Gavin is doing to persuade Miles to release Elizabeth."

She stood, clutching her baby tightly. "I must prepare. I'll need a tent, for I can't see Raine willingly sharing his with me."

"He might forgive you the moment he sees you," Judith said, eyes dancing.

"Forgive me!" Alyx said, then saw she was teasing. "I'll

make him sorry he accused me of betraying him. And I'll need medicines. I owe something to those outlaws Raine leads. They helped me once, but I never helped them. I want to make up for some of my neglect and my arrogance."

"How soon do you want to leave?" Judith asked.

"Before Gavin returns or we may have trouble. How soon can we gather things together?"

"A day if we hurry."

"Judith," Alyx said. "You are an angel."

"Perhaps I just want to see my family safe. Come along now, we have work to do."

Silently, Alyx groaned. Raine had once said Judith did twice as much in a day as anyone else. Alyx guessed it was closer to three times as much. Quickly, she handed Catherine to a maid and hurried after her sister-in-law.

Chapter 19

"I DON'T like this place," Joan said from the horse beside Alyx's. "It's too dark. Are you sure Lord Raine lives in a place like this?"

Alyx didn't bother to answer. Judith had said her maid, Joan, would be an asset in this venture, that Joan could keep Alyx looking good enough to make Raine notice and Joan could ferret out all sorts of information. Judith had also warned that Joan was much too familiar and must be constantly reminded of her place.

"Hello," Alyx called up into a tree.

Joan looked at her as if she'd lost her mind. "Is the tree expected to answer you?" She added, "My lady" when Alyx gave her a sharp look.

From the tall branches of the tree dropped what Joan saw as a divine man.

"Joss!" Alyx laughed, and before she could dismount Jocelin had grabbed her about the waist and pulled her into his arms.

For a moment they just laughed and hugged until Alyx pulled away and looked at him. "You've changed," she said quietly. "There are roses in your cheeks."

Joan coughed loudly. "Perhaps the gentleman would like roses elsewhere than his cheeks."

"Joan!" Alyx warned. "I'll leave you overnight alone in this forest if you don't behave."

"Is that the voice of command I hear?" Joss asked, holding her hands at arms' length. "You have more than changed. I have never seen such a lovely lady. Walk with me and let's talk."

When they were away from Joan and the loaded horses, he asked, "You have a child?"

"A daughter with Raine's dimples and my eyes. She is sweet and perfect in every way. How is he?"

Jocelin knew who she meant. "Not well. Wait! He is physically well, but he is sad, never smiles and when a messenger comes from his brother he is angry for days." He paused. "What happened after your marriage?"

Briefly, she told him of Roger Chatworth.

"So, you have left your child and come back to Raine."

"No doubt he will welcome me with open arms." She grimaced. "There are several reasons why I've returned. I owe the people here something for saving me from the burning. How many . . . died?"

"Three, and a fourth one later."

Her hand tightened on Joss's arm. "The King's anger at the Montgomerys and the Chatworths is increasing daily. Gavin has gone to Scotland to reason with one brother while Raine is mine to deal with."

"Do you know that he won't let any messenger read anything concerning you in a letter?"

"I guessed as much. Damn Raine and his honor! If he'd just listen for ten sentences he'd find out I'm not a traitor. The best I can hope for is to distract him for a while. I'm afraid he may decide to go after Roger Chatworth on his own, and no doubt he will if he thinks his baby brother is in danger. If his 'little' brother weren't such a seducer of women perhaps none of this would be happening. But the Montgomery brothers stand up for each other no matter what."

"Distract him?" Joss asked, smiling. "I think you'll do that. Do you know how good you look? The violet of your dress makes your eyes glow."

"Speaking of seducers," she teased, looking him up and down. "I thought I'd wear simple clothes more suited for the forest, but Judith planned my wardrobe, saying beautiful gowns would make me more visible to Raine. Have I really changed?"

"Yes, you've filled out. Now, who is that greedy wench you brought with you?"

For a moment Alyx studied Joss. In all the time she'd known him, she'd never seen him so full of laughter or tease so much. "How is Rosamund?" she asked tentatively.

Jocelin tossed his head back and laughed. "You are too clever. She's magnificent and getting better. Now, let's go into camp. Raine will be glad to see you no matter what he says."

Although Alyx thought she was prepared for her first sight of Raine, she wasn't. He'd lost weight and the striations in his muscles were standing out. He was standing by a campfire looking down at two men who talked to him earnestly.

For a moment Alyx stood completely still, watching him, remembering every inch of him, wanting to run to him, launch herself into his arms, feel him welcoming her.

But when he turned, her breath caught in her throat. Hate she could have dealt with, but Raine's eyes did not show the warm fires of hate. Instead there was nothing there but a frigid wasteland of ice: blue so cold it sent slivers of ice through her body. There was no flicker of recognition and especially none of welcome.

Without moving, Alyx watched as Raine turned his back on her and walked toward the training field.

"A mite angry, isn't he?" Joan said from behind Alyx. "Those Montgomerys do have tempers. Did I ever tell you about the pit Lady Judith climbed into to save Lord Gavin? Of course, any woman in her right mind would risk all for such a man as Lord Gavin. And Miles, too. I've never been to bed with Lord Raine, though. Is he pleasing?"

"You go too far!" Alyx snapped, spinning around.

Joan gave a catlike grin. "At least I got you to quit feeling sorry for yourself. Now where do you want the tent? You decide while I fetch a few men to help us."

With that she was off, silently slipping into the group of

people who were slowly gathering about Alyx and the four loaded horses.

"We see you didn't get much of you burned," one man said, looking Alyx up and down insolently.

"Can't burn real witches," a woman said.

"Fancy dressin'," came another voice. "Who'd you sleep with to get that?"

Alyx put her chin up. "I want to thank all of you for coming to my rescue when I needed help. I'm sure I didn't deserve it, but thank you."

This seemed to take the crowd back for a moment.

"Nobody meant to help you," said a man with a scarred face. "'Twas for Lord Raine that we went. And now, from the looks of him, he wishes we'd let you burn."

This caused a great roar of laughter from everyone and, shaking their heads, slapping one another's backs, they went back to the camp, leaving Alyx alone.

"You plannin' to cry?" Joan asked nastily in Alyx's ear. "They'd like that. Here, come see what I found."

With one deep sniff, Alyx turned away from the forest camp. Had she expected them to see that she'd changed? She looked up at Joan, who was flanked by four large, good-looking young men.

"They'll help us set up the tent," Joan said, slipping her arms through two of the men's.

Alyx had to smile at Joan, who could be made happy so easily. Judith had said Joan was a cat slipping from bed to bed. With amazement, Alyx watched as Joan began to give the young men orders, all the while giving them a caress here and there. Once Joan looked up and winked at Alyx. Insolent girl! Alyx thought, turning away to hide a smile.

At the horses she began to unload the bundles she and Judith had packed.

"Need any help?" asked one of Joan's young men from behind her as he took the bundle from her.

"Thank you," she said, smiling up at him. "Are you new in the camp?"

At that he laughed and his brown eyes sparkled. "I was

here before Raine, was here when you were a boy. You've changed some," he teased, watching her.

"I don't . . ." she began before looking away.

"I don't guess you looked at any of us. It was always him you watched." He jerked his head toward Raine's tent. "I don't guess I blame you, seein' as how he's a rich nobleman and you are—were—a . . ." He stopped.

"Is that how it looked?" Alyx said, mostly to herself.

"It did explain a great deal when Lord Raine told us we were to rescue you."

"Told you, did he?" she asked. "No doubt everyone was quite cheerful at the prospect of saving *me*."

The young man cleared his throat and shifted his burden. "I'll take this to the camp for you."

"Wait!" she called. "What is your name?"

"Thomas Carter," he said, grinning.

Thoughtfully, Alyx finished unloading the horse. She'd spent months in this camp and to her knowledge she'd never even seen Thomas Carter, yet he'd been here all along and had even risked his life to rescue her.

Frowning, she went back to the camp and was very pleased when Thomas smiled at her.

Joan and the young men had the tent erected in a very short time and the goods stored inside. Outside blazed a warm campfire.

"Come up in the world, ain't ya?" asked a woman from across the fire, her eyes glaring at Alyx. There was an enormous goiter on her neck, making her hold her head to one side.

"Could we share what we have with you?" Alyx asked quietly, then turned to glare at Joan, who'd gasped in protest.

The woman shook her head, her eyes wide, and left them.

"You can't let that diseased scum near us!" Joan hissed. "Would you like to have one of those things on your neck? All she has to do is sit by us and—"

"Quiet!" Alyx said, seeing herself in Joan. "I'll not have you snubbing these people. They saved my life and for all their filth and disease they deserve more than I can repay. And as for you, you will treat them well—and not just the men."

Joan set her jaw firmly, muttering something about Alyx betraying her class, that she was becoming more like Lady Judith every day. Without a sound, she slipped off into the darkness.

Like Lady Judith, Alyx thought, and knew she'd never had such a compliment before. Smiling, she stood and went into her tent. Alone on the little cot, she was reminded of her nights with Raine. At least now she was close to him, and for the first time in months she was able to sleep well. Her last thoughts before falling asleep were of Catherine.

In the morning, Alyx awoke refreshed, smiling. The clean, cold, forest air felt good to her and even somewhat like home. Joan was not in sight, so Alyx dressed alone in a dress of emerald green wool trimmed with gold braid. A little cap on the back of her head did nothing to conceal the curls about her face. Her hair was longer now, and no longer did she hate the unusual color that made every strand seem to be an individual.

Outside the tent, she was greeted by an exhausted-looking Joan sitting lifelessly on a tree stump of a stool. Her hair was down her back, the shoulder of her dress torn. There was a bruise on her neck. She looked up at Alyx with bright eyes staring out of bluish eye sockets. "They are lusty men," she said wearily, yet so happily, that Alyx worked to keep from laughing.

"Go and rest," Alyx said sternly. "And when you awaken we'll talk of your disgusting conduct."

Heavily, Joan rose and walked toward the tent.

Alyx caught her maid's arm. "All four of them?" she asked curiously.

Joan only nodded, her eyelids drooping wearily, as she went inside the tent.

Alyx was contemplating this—four men at once?—when Raine presented himself before her, his eyes blazing angrily. She gulped twice. "Good morning," she managed to say.

"Damn your mornings!" he growled, glaring at her. "That

harlot you brought with you has worn out four of my men. They're no good to me at all this morning. Can't even lift a sword. I don't know why you came here, but I think it's time you returned."

She smiled at him sweetly. "What a charming welcome, my husband. I apologize for my maid, but as you may remember I haven't had much practice in handling underlings. We can't all be born to the nobility. As to why I came here, I have a debt to pay."

"You owe me nothing."

"You!" Alyx spat, then calmed herself, forcing a smile. "Perhaps I do owe you something, but I owe more to these people."

"Since when have you cared?" He narrowed his eyes at her.

"Since they risked their lives to save me," she said calmly. "Would you care to join me for a bit of food to break your fast? I can offer you a cold meat pie."

He seemed to want to say something but turned on his heel and left her.

Alyx kept smiling, her heart pounding as she watched his broad back retreat.

"Pleased with yourself?" Jocelin asked from behind her.

Alyx laughed aloud. "Am I so transparent? Raine Montgomery is an arrogant man, isn't he? He thinks I'm here only because of him."

"And aren't you?" Joss asked.

"I shall drive him insane," Alyx said happily. "Would you like something to eat? Do you have time to sit with me and answer some questions?"

The questions Alyx asked were about the camp people, questions she should have known the answers to, since she'd lived with them for months. But she felt like an outsider.

"They won't be easy to win," Jocelin said. "They have many grudges against you. Blanche has blamed many problems on you."

"Blanche!" Alyx said, sitting up straight. Pieces of the puzzle were falling into place.

"Blanche was the woman who caused Constance's death. How else would she have known about Edmund Chatworth? You must hate Blanche."

"I am through with hating." He stood. "Would you like to see Rosamund? If you want to help the people, she can tell you how to start."

Alyx wasn't prepared for the changes in Rosamund. Her eyes shone so brightly when she looked at Jocelin that the birthstain on her cheek almost disappeared. Joss's eyes were no less bright.

"Alyx would like to help you," he said in a soft, sweet voice, taking Rosamund's hand.

Rosamund gave Alyx a tolerant smile that made Alyx stiffen her back, and she thanked heaven for Judith's training.

"I'm sure we can find something for you to do," Rosamund said in her soft voice.

It took Alyx a week to make Rosamund realize she meant business. During that time Alyx worked early and late and no job was beneath her. She washed and bandaged running sores. She delivered a child to a woman eaten with the French pox and when the blind baby died, she buried it; no one else would touch the poor thing. She sang to an old woman who screamed incoherently at ghosts only she could see.

"Her ladyship's doin' us low ones a favor," a man said to her as she went through the dark to her tent. "Afraid to dirty her hands, she was, and now nothin's dirty enough for her. But I don't see Raine bowin' before her."

In her tent, Alyx put her hands to her temples. Her head ached from noises and ugly smells. The sick allowed her to touch them, but the healthy people ignored her except to taunt her. And as for Raine, she rarely even saw him.

"Did you come here to win Raine or these diseased scum?" Joan asked frequently.

"Raine," Alyx had whispered, rubbing her temples. Now the tent was empty, Joan obviously sleeping somewhere else. Alyx wasn't used to having servants and was a failure at controlling Joan. Seeing that the water buckets were empty, Alyx grabbed them and went to the river.

Kneeling at the bank she looked about her, at the sparkling surface of the water, broken diamonds in the moonlight. A sound made her turn and her heart leaped to her throat at the sight of Raine, his big body—a body she knew so well—blocking the moon.

"Have you proven what you wanted?" he asked quietly, his voice as smooth and hard as steel. "Did you expect to bandage one nasty wound and the people would fall at your feet in gratitude? They are better judges of people than I am."

"And pray tell me what that means," she said, aghast.

"You are a good actress. Once I believed you were . . . honest, but I learned the hard way. I hope they do not fall as far as I did."

She stood, hands into fists at her side. "Spare me your self-pity," she said through her teeth. "Poor Lord Raine lowered himself to fall in love with a commoner, and then when she did her best to save him from the King's wrath, he knew at once she'd overstepped her bounds."

Her voice rose. "I want to tell you something, Raine Montgomery. It doesn't matter if these people do hate me. I damn well deserve it. And as for their falling at my feet, I don't expect them to. At least they are the honest ones. You hold yourself up like some martyr and won't listen to anyone. Instead you'd rather believe yourself wronged and to think that only you has a sense of honor."

"And what do you, a woman, know of honor?" he sneered.

"Very little. In fact I know very little about anything except music. But at least I'm willing to admit I have faults. I have wronged these people, and I'm trying to right my wrong. You, my high lord, have wronged me—and your daughter whom you don't even ask about."

"I have heard of her," Raine said stiffly.

Alyx let out a sound that ran across Raine's skin like a steel rasp. "How big of you!" she spat. "The great, lordly Raine, lord of the forests, king of the outlaws, has heard of his own daughter."

She quietened. "I came here to win you back, but now

I'm not sure I want you. Stay away from me. Take your cold honor to bed with you."

"There are other women willing to share my bed," he said, eyes hard.

"My pity goes to them," Alyx forced out. "As for me, I prefer a different sort of man, one who is not so stiff and cold, one who is still alive."

She did not see his arm shoot out. He was always faster, stronger, than she remembered. His strong fingers bit into the back of her waist and as her eyes locked with his, he smiled slightly, humorously, as he pulled her close to him.

Bending his head, his lips hovered above hers. "Cold, am I?" he said, and his voice sent chills down her spine.

Some small part of Alyx's brain could still reason. He meant to teach her a lesson, did he? she thought, as she stood on tiptoe and slipped her arms about his neck.

When their lips touched, both of them drew in their breaths sharply and pulled away from each other, violet eyes staring into blue. Alyx blinked once, twice, before Raine's mouth descended on hers with the hunger of a dying man. He straightened, his arms about her, and her feet came off the ground as he grabbed the back of her head in his strong hand and turned her head sideways. His tongue thrust inside her mouth, sending sparks so hot through her body that they seemed to burn away her strength. Her body went limp against his, allowing him to support her full weight.

His lips began working against hers, pulling her closer, his hand massaging, kneading her head, his fingers playing with the muscles in the back of her neck.

Alyx began to tighten her grip in her attempt to get nearer. Her legs moved upward until they were about his waist. She turned her head, taking the initiative as her tongue tangled with his, her teeth hard against his lips.

The sound of approaching riders, many horses strong, came through to Raine's sense of danger. Slowly, groggily, he came out of the red fog and roughly, angrily, set Alyx away from him.

For a moment, his expression was soft; then it turned cold

again. "Did you hope to entice me back to you?" he whispered. "Did you use the same weapons on Chatworth?"

It took Alyx a moment to understand what he meant. "You are a fool, Raine Montgomery," she said softly. "Does your hate override your love?" With that, she lifted her skirts, forgetting the water buckets at her feet, and turned back to camp. Behind her she heard Raine talking to the riders, his voice unnecessarily angry.

Chapter 20

"FOR WHAT good it is," Joan was saying as she combed Alyx's curls, "the people are less angry with you." There was no congratulation in Joan's voice. "When are you going to stop wasting your time and go after Lord Raine? We've been here two whole weeks and still he only glares at you. You should strip off your clothes and climb into bed with him."

"He'd gloat too much," Alyx said, buttoning the purple wool of her sleeve. "I'll not give him the satisfaction of winning so easily. He's said some awful things to me."

At this, Joan laughed. "What does it matter what men *say?* They have brains only for killing each other. Put a sword in a man's hand and he's happy. A woman must work to teach him there are things in life besides war."

"Perhaps you're right. Raine worries more about whether I have betrayed him than he does about how his child fares alone without its mother. Perhaps I should return to my Catherine and leave Raine to his brooding."

"Brooding is correct," Joan said. "Did you know that he has slept with no woman since he returned from Lord Gavin's?"

Alyx's smile started small and stretched very wide.

"He loves you, Alyx," Joan said softly.

"Then why doesn't he show it! Why does he sneer and glower at me! When I am with Rosamund I'll look up and there he'll be, watching me with his cold looks. I feel as if I've had the icy river water tossed on my body."

Joan laughed delightedly. "He *is* showing you that he cares! What do you expect him to do—apologize?" Joan laughed even harder at this idea. "The Lord made women stronger so they could put up with men's weaknesses. You say you were wrong to treat the forest people as you did, so you admitted it and set about changing your error. Do you think any man could be so strong?"

"Raine has accused me of being a traitor," she said stubbornly.

"The King has said Lord Raine is a traitor. The King is wrong, but will he admit it? No more so than your husband will come to you and ask you to forgive him."

"I don't like this," Alyx said, her lower lip thrust out. "I have done no wrong to Raine. Roger Chatworth—"

"Damn Chatworth!" Joan said. "Raine's pride is hurt. You stayed beside some other man instead of your husband. Above all else, men expect blind loyalty."

"I am loyal, it is—"

She cut herself off when a breathless Jocelin burst into the tent unannounced.

"You should come," he said to Alyx. "Maybe you can prevent a death."

"Whose?" Alyx asked, standing immediately and following Joss before he could answer.

"Brian Chatworth has just begged entrance into the camp. Raine is donning armor to meet him."

"But Judith said Brian loved Mary, that Brian brought her body back to them."

"Maybe it's the name Chatworth. That alone would send Raine into a rage."

Jocelin pulled Alyx onto a horse and set out quickly, dodging tree branches as they rode. When at last they stopped, the sight ahead of them surprised Alyx. In a small clearing, lit by the early morning sun, stood a young man. He was small, slight, even delicate. Yet he had the facial features of Roger Chatworth. Had Alyx seen him elsewhere she would have guessed this near boy was Roger's son.

Alyx slid off the horse before Joss could dismount. "May

I welcome you?" she said, walking toward the boy. "I am Alyxandria Montgomery, Lord Raine's wife. I have met your brother."

Brian pulled himself to his full height. "I have no brother," he said in a surprisingly masculine voice. "I come to join Lord Raine in his fight to avenge his sister's death."

"Oh, my," Alyx said, astonished. "I had hoped you offered some solution to this feud."

"We're all wishing that," came a voice from above Alyx's head.

She looked up but could see no one. "Who are you? You're not one of Raine's guards."

"Oh, but I am, and are you truly Raine's wife?"

Alyx listened to the voice, sure she'd never heard it before, yet something about it was familiar. It was definitely a voice full of humor. She glanced at Brian and Jocelin. Brian's face was immobile, too hard for one so young, while Joss gave a shrug.

Her attention was suddenly given to the appearance of Raine riding his great heavy war horse, wearing full armor, covered from head to foot in steel.

Dismounting, he walked toward Brian Chatworth, and the young man did not flinch. One blow from Raine's hand would have been enough to send him sprawling. "Do you plan to hide behind my wife's skirts?" Raine said in a low voice. "She is known to protect Chatworths."

Alyx put herself between Brian and Raine. "And do you make war on children?" she yelled up at him. "Can't you listen to him? Or are you too pig-headed to give the boy a chance?"

Raine never said a word to Alyx because laughter coming from the trees made him halt.

Alyx watched, openmouthed, as a man dropped to the ground. He was wearing the most extraordinary clothes she had ever seen: a big-sleeved shirt, a soft yellow color, was covered by a bright blue tartan blanket wrapped about his waist in such a way that it formed a skirt and then was tossed over one shoulder, a heavy belt holding it in place. His knees were bare, his calves encased in heavy wool socks, thick shoes on his feet.

"Stephen," Raine breathed, his eyes softening.

"Aye, 'tis me," this oddly dressed man said. He was tall and slim with dark blond hair, a very handsome man. "I've brought this boy to you. He wants to share your exile and would like to learn from you."

"He's a Chatworth," Raine said, his eyes hardening again.

"Yes, he's a Chatworth," Alyx said. "And you'll not forgive him, will you? No doubt you'll hate this man for daring to bring him here. Go," she said to Stephen. "It's no use trying to reason with him. He has a piece of wood for a brain."

To her surprise, Stephen began to laugh, a great, deep, joyful laugh.

"Oh, Raine," he cried, slapping Raine on his armored shoulder, making the steel rattle. "How Gavin and I have prayed for this time. So you've fallen head over heels for a woman who fights you at every step? Gavin had written us what a sweet, helpful, congenial little thing our new sister was." He turned to Alyx. "Judith said you had a strong voice, but a moment ago you nearly knocked me from the tree."

"You are Stephen Montgomery," Alyx said in wonder. He did look a bit like Gavin, but besides his clothing, his accent was strange.

"MacArran," Stephen corrected, smiling at her. "I am married to the MacArran and my name is hers. Now do I get a kiss or would you rather fight with my brother?"

"Oh, a kiss!" Alyx said so enthusiastically that Stephen laughed again before drawing her into his arms. His kiss was less than brotherly. "Can you help me talk some sense into him?" she whispered. "He is obsessed with the Chatworths."

Stephen winked as he released her, turning back to Raine. "I've come a long way, brother. Will you offer me no refreshment?"

"And what about him?" Raine motioned toward Brian.

"He may come, too," Stephen laughed. "He can help me disarm you. And you, Alyx, will join us?"

"If I am invited," she said, looking directly at Raine.

"*I* invite you," Stephen said, as he threw an arm around Alyx's shoulders and started forward. "Follow us, Brian," he called over his shoulder.

"Are you always so courageous?" Alyx asked, looking up at Stephen.

Stephen's face was serious. "How long has he been like this?"

"I'm not sure I know what you mean."

"Unsmiling, angry, glaring at everyone. This isn't like Raine."

She thought a moment before she answered. "He has been this way since Mary's death."

Stephen nodded once. "Raine would take it hard. That's one reason why I brought Brian. They are very much alike. Brian is eaten with hatred for his brother. And what of you? My brother's black moods don't frighten you?"

"He thinks I've betrayed him."

"Yes, Gavin and Judith told me."

Her voice became louder. "He won't listen to me. I tried to explain, but he sent my letters back unopened. And he won't listen to Gavin, either."

Stephen squeezed her shoulders. "Gavin will always think of Raine and Miles as children. Raine and Gavin can't be in a room two minutes without arguing. Stay with me and I'll see if I can make him listen."

Alyx gave him such a radiant smile that Stephen laughed. "My Bronwyn will have your heart on a platter if you keep looking at me like that. Can you really sing as well as Judith says?"

"Better," Alyx said with such confidence that Stephen laughed again.

They stopped before Raine's tent and Stephen muttered something about wasting money that Alyx didn't understand. Rather like a sulky boy, Raine followed them inside and, after one malevolent look cast at Alyx, turned to Stephen. "What has caused you to travel so far south? Have those Scots tossed you out?"

"I came to meet my new sister-in-law, of course."

"She would prefer that you were a Chatworth."

Stephen paused, Raine's helmet in his hand. "I cannot allow you to say such things," he said quietly. "Don't cause a quarrel between us. Do you plan to disown me because I have brought a Chatworth to your camp?"

"You are my brother," Raine said flatly.

"Meaning that you trust me?" There was laughter under his voice. "Tell me, brother, what bothered you the most, that your wife talked to a Chatworth or that she dared to talk to any handsome man?"

"Chatworth!" Raine said loudly, with a glance at Alyx, who was studying her fingernails.

"Did I ever tell you the trick Hugh Lasco played on me?" Stephen knelt to unbuckle Raine's leg protectors.

As Stephen began to tell some long-winded, slightly unbelievable tale, Alyx watched Raine. After a while she began to understand Stephen's point. Stephen had believed all manner of low-minded things about his wife, and as a result of his mistrust, he'd almost lost her.

"Alyx," Stephen turned to her suddenly. "Are you in love with Roger Chatworth? Are you contemplating leaving Raine for him?"

The idea was so ridiculous that Alyx laughed—until she saw the smoldering light in Raine's eyes. "Roger Chatworth deserves to die for what he did to Mary but *not* at my husband's hands. He's not worth seeing Raine hanged for his murder."

For a moment Alyx thought Raine might be listening to her, but the moment passed as he sat down on the cot and began removing the cotton pads that protected his skin from the steel armor. "Women have glib tongues," he murmured.

Stephen glanced at Alyx, saw her eyes shoot fire. "You have my permission to take an ax to him," he said amiably. "Alyx, could you fetch us some food? I may die of hunger soon."

As soon as they were alone, Raine turned to his brother. "Why have you come? Surely you want more than to step between my wife and me."

"Someone should," Stephen snapped. "Her heart is in her eyes. Can't you forgive her? She doesn't know our ways, and women have such strange ideas about honor. I hear you haven't seen your daughter. She looks like you."

Raine refused to be swayed. "Why did you bring Chatworth?"

"For the reason I said: he wants to train with you. The King won't like your training one nobleman to fight another. And what is this I hear of your raising an army of criminals to overthrow the King?"

Raine guffawed at this idea. "What liar told you this?"

"Pagnell of Waldenham told King Henry this. Hadn't you heard? I thought Alyx came to warn you of this. The King's ears are being filled with lies against the Montgomerys."

"Alyx hasn't seen fit to warn me," Raine said.

"And I'm sure you sat down and asked her nicely why she deserted her child and the comfort of Gavin's house to come live near you in this cold forest."

"I neither need nor want your interference in my life."

Stephen shrugged. "I remember a few kicks I received when Bronwyn and I had problems."

"And now all is sweetness and light with you, is it?" Raine asked, one eyebrow raised.

Stephen cleared his throat. "We do have . . . ah, a few disagreements now and then, but generally she learns the true way."

"I'd like to hear Bronwyn's version of that," Raine said before changing the subject. "Have you seen Miles?"

Stephen was saved from answering by the appearance of Alyx bearing a tray, Joan behind her with a second tray. Stephen didn't want to tell Raine that his problem with women was mild compared to Miles's.

As soon as Alyx realized that Joan was going to make a fool of herself over Stephen, she sent the maid out. The meal was an awkward one, the first Raine and Alyx had shared since she returned to the forest. Stephen did nearly all the talking, entertaining them with stories of Scotland.

"And you should see my son," Stephen boasted. "Already

905

Tam has taken him riding and he can't really sit up yet. You and I weren't on a horse until we could walk. And how is your daughter, Alyx?"

For the first time in two weeks Alyx let herself think completely about her daughter. "She is strong," she said dreamily, "short and healthy with a lusty cry that made Judith's son cry too."

"Protective of his cousin, no doubt," Stephen said. "She has your eyes."

"You saw her?" Alyx came off her stool. "When? Was she healthy? Had she grown any?"

"I doubt if she's changed much since you've seen her, but I agree about her voice. Do you think she'll be able to sing?" He turned to Raine. "She has those dimples you got from Mother's family."

"I must see to the camp." Raine stood so suddenly he nearly upset the food Alyx had brought. Quickly, he left the tent.

"He'll come around," Stephen said confidently, smiling at Alyx's tearing eyes.

Alyx tried not to think of Raine's constant anger and instead turned her attentions to Brian Chatworth. He was a miserable young man, his eyes black with a deep, burning hatred, and he never smiled nor seemed to find pleasure in anything. Alyx could not persuade him to talk or to confide in her about any subject. Her questions about where he'd been for the last several months since Mary's death were met by silence.

Alyx gave up after a while and left him to the men on the training field. As for Raine, he neither looked at nor spoke to the boy and spent most of his time with Stephen.

After Stephen had been in camp for three days, Joan came to Alyx.

"I think they're fighting," Joan said excitedly.

"Who? Not Raine and Brian Chatworth?"

Joan's voice was impatient. "Of course not! Lord Raine and Lord Stephen have gone deeper into the forest, and one of the guards has reported loud voices coming from there. Everyone's planning to go and watch."

"You will not!" Alyx said, pushing past her maid and out into the cool air. "Jocelin," she shouted when she saw her friend. "Stop them. Leave Raine in private. And you," she turned to Joan. "Help keep the men in camp. Do what you must. But nothing lewd," she called over her shoulder as she hurried forward.

Jocelin enlisted the aid of some ex-soldiers to help him while some of the wounded helped Alyx, and Joan had her own methods of making men obey her. Together they managed to keep the camp people away from where Raine and Stephen were having their "discussion."

"They're just settin' now," said a guard as he was replaced by someone else.

Alyx walked away, not wanting to hear any more of the facts. Raine was so much heavier than his brother, obviously so much stronger. Stephen couldn't possibly win a fight between them, and Alyx prayed Raine would hold back and not truly hurt his slim brother.

At sundown, Alyx took the water buckets to the river, hoping to escape the gleeful voices of the people in the camp. They were all huddled about campfires, listening to the guards with rapt attention.

She stood beside the river, motionless, glad for the quiet, when a sound made her whirl. Coming toward her, walking heavily, wearily, was Raine. Perhaps she should have listened to the people's comments so she would have been prepared for her first sight of him. The left side of his face was swollen and turning purple. There were bruises on his jaw, his eye a flamboyant mixture of unnatural colors.

"Raine," she whispered, making him look up and away from her as he knelt by the water. She forgot any memories of anger between them but ran to him, knelt beside him. "Let me see," she said.

Docilely he turned his head to her and she placed cool fingers on his misshapen face. Without a word, she raised her skirt, tore away linen petticoat, dipped it in cold water and touched his face.

"Tell me all of it," she said in a half-command. "What sort of club did Stephen use on your face?"

It was a long moment before Raine spoke. "His fist."

Alyx paused in her washing of Raine's face. "But a knight—" she began. She'd heard Raine shout a hundred times about how unchivalrous, how unmanly it was to fight with one's hands. Many honorable men had died rather than lose their honor by using their fists.

"Stephen has learned some strange ways in Scotland," Raine said. "He says there is more than one way to fight."

"And no doubt you stood there like a great ox and let him beat you rather than do an unknightly thing such as hit his face in return?"

"I tried!" Raine said, then winced and calmed himself. "He danced about like a woman."

"Don't insult my sex. No woman did this to your face."

"Alyx." He grabbed her wrist. "Have you no feeling for me? Will you always side with others against me?"

She took his face gently in her hands, her eyes searching his. "I have loved you since the first moment I saw you. Even then, when I had planned to hate you, I was drawn to you. I fought against loving you, but it was as if some great power controlled me and I had no say in what I did. Don't you realize that I'm always on your side? That day at the fair if you'd killed Roger Chatworth you could have been hanged. I pretended to bed Jocelin to keep you from leaving the safety of the forest. What more can I do to prove my loyalty and love?"

He pulled away from her. "Perhaps it's your methods I don't like. Why can't you tell me what you're doing? Why must you fight me all the time?"

"Fighting is the only way you'll listen to me," she said in exasperation. "I told you you could not leave the forest when the people accused me of stealing, but you wouldn't listen. I told you not to kill Roger Chatworth, but you stood there like a bull with veins standing out on your neck." Her voice was rising.

"I don't know who unmans me most—my brother or you."

His tone was so little-boy, feel-sorry-for-himself that Alyx tried not to laugh. "What did you and Stephen quarrel about?"

Raine rubbed his jaw. "Stephen suggested I consider that perhaps you weren't disloyal when you saved Chatworth's miserable life."

Raine turned and looked at her. "Have I been wrong? Have I treated you very badly? Is there any love in your heart left for me?"

She touched his cheek. "I will always love you. I sometimes think I was born loving you."

A single dimple appeared in his cheek and she caught her breath as she thought he was going to pull her into his arms. Instead, he reached under his doublet and rummaged in his pocket. "Perhaps I can purchase a smile or two," he said as he dangled the Lyon belt before her eyes.

"My belt!" she gasped. "How did you find it? I thought it was lost forever. Oh, Raine!" She threw her arms around him and began kissing his face so enthusiastically that she caused him great pain, but he didn't mind.

"You are the best husband," she whispered, kissing his neck. "Oh, Raine, how I have missed you."

She didn't say anymore because his hands twisted in her hair and pulled her head backward as his lips came down on hers. Alyx was sure she would burst apart into little pieces. She catapulted all her weight against him, and as he was in a precarious position, he fell backward, caught himself, then changed positions on her mouth and let himself fall, pulling Alyx with him.

Mouths attached, they rolled sideways, then changed directions, and in one quick movement landed themselves in the icy river water, Alyx on bottom.

"Raine!" Alyx screeched in pain as his heavy body rolled

atop her arm, scraping it against a rock. "You're breaking me!" Already, her teeth were beginning to chatter.

"It would be small payment for what you've done to me," he said, lying in the water as if it were a feather bed. "Before I met you my life was peaceful and calm. Now my own brother beats me."

"Which you deserved!" she spat. "It's the only way to make you listen. Now let me up and let me get dry before I freeze to death."

"I know a way to keep you warm." He began to nuzzle her neck.

"You great stupid boar," she yelled into his ear, making him move away and shake his head to clear the ringing. "I'm cold and wet, and if you don't let me up I'll bring the whole camp to my rescue."

"You think they'd come to rescue you or would they side with me?"

She pushed at him. "They wouldn't recognize you with your great purple face."

He chuckled at that and easily moved off her. "You look good, Alyx," he said, his eyes alight, looking at her wet dress, which clung to her.

Alyx put her arms behind her and started to push herself up and found the wet dress to be very heavy. With another chuckle, Raine stood, lifted her and started toward the darkest part of the forest.

"The camp is that way," she pointed.

"Alyx, someone should teach you that you shouldn't always give orders. Perhaps you are right now and then, but sometimes you should listen and leave the commands to the men."

"I have to do what is right, and if you need to be saved from yourself, I will," she said arrogantly.

"You are leading up to a paddling such as you've never had before—if you've ever had one, which I doubt. That priest who trained you should have applied a lute to the bottom half of you now and again and perhaps you'd have a little humility."

"I have as much humility as you do," she said, watching him. "If you do foolish things, am I to stand aside and not raise my voice?"

"Alyx, you are going too far," he warned.

"And how will you punish me for speaking the truth?"

"Not in a way that you'll like."

"How can you threaten me after all I've done for you? I've saved you from Roger Chatworth. I was nearly burned at the stake because the judges wanted your lands. I left with Jocelin to keep you safe in the forest."

Raine grabbed her shoulders and held her at arms' length, her feet off the ground. One half of his face was swollen purple, but the other half was red with rage. "You've gone too far," he said through his teeth.

Before Alyx could take a breath, Raine had seated himself on a stump, pulled Alyx across his lap, bottom end up and tossed her skirts over her head. He gave her one strong, painful whack across her buttocks.

"You were not tried as a witch because of *me*," he said. "You had your quarrel with Pagnell before I ever met you."

Alyx didn't have a chance to answer as Raine smacked her bottom again. "True, I was angry and perhaps should not have ordered Chatworth to be killed, but as we were in a secluded place, who would have known to tell the King? I am not as stupid as you seem to think and would not have left the body near my brother's estate."

Again, his hand came down. "I don't like having my orders countermanded and especially not before my men. Is that clear?" Again he punctuated this with a blow.

Alyx, tears in her eyes, nodded silently.

"Good! Now, as for you and Jocelin, I don't like games and jests at which I'm the butt. It hurt too much to see you with another man, and later when I found out it'd all been a trick, as if I were a dunce to be made a fool of, I could have killed you. And you risked the life of my daughter with your stupid jests."

A very hard blow hit her. "You nearly lost my daughter to the fire as well as to the hazards of the road while you and

Jocelin wandered about the country. I want no more of it, Alyx." He struck her again. "Do you understand me? You are my wife and you damn well better start acting like it."

With one more painful spank, he pushed her off his lap.

Alyx sat up, wincing with pain when her bottom hit the forest floor.

There were so many tears in her eyes that she could hardly focus.

Raine stood, towering above her. "When you're through sulking," he said, "come back to the tent and I'll make love to you so passionately you'll forget who you are." With that, he walked away from her.

For a moment, Alyx sat staring after him, then she closed her mouth and stood. No sulking in the world was worth missing a bout of lovemaking. As quickly as her stiff legs could carry her, she ran after Raine.

Chapter 21

ALYX LAY on her back on Raine's cot, a bare leg dangling over the edge, one soft leather shoe hooked over two happy toes. All of her was immensely happy, from toes up to the roots of her hair. Raine had made good his promise. All last night he'd been insatiable, never letting her sleep, tossing her around like a rag doll. She'd be on top, then on bottom, then he'd stretch her sideways and pull her between his legs. One minute he was sweet and gentle, the next fierce, driving, and the next he'd be almost bored, as if he'd forgotten she was there. At those times Alyx would do something naughty to get his attention back to her. His sensuous laugh would make her aware that he was manipulating her and was far away from being bored.

The sun was coming up when she finally pleaded with him to halt. He'd merely kissed her nose, smiled lopsidedly with his battered face, rose, washed, dressed and left the tent. Alyx settled her sore, bruised, exhausted body to a few hours' sleep.

Now, awake at last, she lay still, humming to herself and remembering last night.

"Looks like you finally learned what to do with a man," Joan said, slipping inside the tent. "I wondered if all the brothers were as good as Lord Miles. It looks like you think so. Did you know you were smiling in your sleep?"

"Be quiet, you insolent woman," Alyx said in such a friendly way that Joan only laughed.

"You'd better get up. Lord Stephen has had some news from Scotland and he's leaving very soon."

"It's nothing bad, is it?" Alyx asked, reluctantly sitting up, wincing at a pain in her back. Sometimes Raine seemed to think she was a piece of cloth the way he wrapped her about his body, one leg here, another one there, an arm over there. There was a crick in her neck and the memory of what Raine had done to hurt *that* area made her grin.

Joan was looking at her with unconcealed interest. "My four men together could not have made me look as you do now. Is Lord Raine really such a lover?"

Alyx shot her a dangerous look. "I'll have your heart on a platter if you so much as look at him."

Joan only grinned. "I've been trying for years and he's not interested. What will you wear today?"

Alyx dressed carefully in a dress of palest lavender, trimmed in rabbit fur dyed a deep, luscious purple.

"Ah," Stephen said when he saw her, "such beauty in the midst of such a wilderness." He took her hand and kissed it.

Alyx caught his hand, examined his knuckles, which were raw, cut, not yet beginning to heal. "May you lose your hand if you strike my husband again," she whispered passionately.

Stephen blinked once before he laughed. "And my brother worries about your loyalty. You must come and meet my Bronwyn. She will like you."

"I've heard you have news."

Stephen's face darkened. "Roger Chatworth found Miles and Elizabeth alone and has run a sword through Miles's arm. Lady Elizabeth has returned to England with her brother."

"Then perhaps soon this feud can end. Roger has his sister safe. All that's left is to make the King forgive Raine."

"Perhaps," Stephen said. "Now I must go home and help my clan. My little brother is in a rage and wants to ride on Chatworth."

"Go!" she said. "Stop him."

He kissed her hand again. "I will do what I can, and now I know I leave Raine in good hands. He is a stubborn man."

Alyx laughed at that. "In your . . . talk yesterday, did you by chance mention Brian Chatworth? Now that Roger has harmed Miles, will Raine take it out on Brian?"

"No, I don't think so. This morning Raine and Brian talked for a long time and I believe Raine's heart has gone out to the boy. I don't believe there'll be more problems. In fact, they're on the training field now. I must go. My men wait for me."

"Your men?" Alyx asked, astonished. "I saw no one. I assumed you were alone."

Stephen seemed pleased by this. "There are six MacArrans with me, all stationed about the forest, keeping watch."

"But we have guards. They should have come into the camp near the fires and had some hot food. They'll freeze out there."

Stephen laughed hard at this. "The English are a soft lot. Our summers aren't as warm as your winters. You'll have to come to the Highlands someday. Douglas says your singing will make his brothers cry."

There were so many questions Alyx wanted to ask, but she had no idea where to start. Her emotions showed on her face.

"You'll have to come," Stephen smiled, kissed her cheek and disappeared into the trees, the short plaid swirling about his thighs.

What followed for Alyx were three days of relative peace. Raine seemed to grow an attachment for the crippled Brian and was impressed by Brian's eagerness to learn.

"The hate is eating him," Raine said as he and Alyx lay in bed. "He thinks that if he trains hard enough he'll be able to fight his brother, but Roger is formidable. He would slay Brian in one thrust."

"Brother against brother," Alyx whispered and shuddered.

Alyx felt sorry for Brian, who slept apart from the people of the camp.

"I don't trust him," Joan said. "He says too little and he has nothing to do with anyone."

"He's been hurt. He'll get over it," Alyx defended the boy.

edge of the cot. "Please don't go. If you aren't killed, you'll be hurt badly."

"Alyx." He nearly smiled at her as he touched her hair. "Perhaps you don't know, but the estates I have I purchased with money I'd won in years of tournaments. I've been through hundreds of these challenges."

"No," she said with feeling. "Not like this one. The hatred that you and Chatworth have for each other wasn't involved in those fights. Please, Raine."

He stood. "I'll listen to no more. Now, will you help me arm myself or must I get Jocelin?"

She also stood. "You ask me to help prepare you for your death? Should I be the dutiful wife and murmur soft words about honor? Or should I talk of Mary and how she died and add fuel to your hate? If Mary were alive would she want you to fight for her? Wasn't her whole life an attempt at peace-making?"

"I don't want us to part with angry words between us. This is something I must do."

She was so angry she was shaking. "If we part now as you walk off to answer a challenge that wasn't made by you, then it will be with angry words—and it will be final."

Their eyes held each other's for a long while.

"Think carefully on what you say," Raine said quietly. "We've quarrelled before over this matter."

"Raine, can't you see how this hatred is eating at you? Even Stephen saw how it had changed you. Forget Roger Chatworth. Go to the King, beg his forgiveness and let us live, not this constant talk of death and dying."

"I am a knight. I am sworn to avenge wrongs."

"Then do something about the Enclosure Acts!" she screamed. "They're wrong. But cease this hideous feud with Roger Chatworth. His sister will bear a Montgomery. A new life for Mary's. What more could you want?"

Outside, the trumpets sounded, and the noise went through Alyx.

"I must dress," Raine said. "Will you help me?"

"No," she said quietly. "I cannot."

"So be it," he whispered. With one last look at her, he turned toward his armor.

"You are choosing between me and Roger Chatworth today," she said.

He didn't answer her but kept at his armor. Alyx left the tent.

"Go to him, Jocelin," she said once she was outside. To Joan, she said, "Come, we must pack. I'm going home to my daughter."

Alyx had every intention of being out of the forest before any fighting began. Of course Raine could win, she thought, but could she stand by and watch bits and pieces hacked off him? She was sure Roger Chatworth would be as filled with hatred as Raine was.

It was two hours before she heard the first sounds of steel against steel as they echoed through the forest. Slowly, she dropped the gown she was folding and left her tent. Whatever he did, whoever he fought, for whatever reason, he was hers.

She was almost to the clearing where the men fought when Joan stopped her.

"Don't look," Joan said. "Chatworth is merciless."

Alyx stared at her maid a moment, then started forward.

"Joss," Joan called. "Stop her."

Jocelin grabbed Alyx's arms, held her in place. "It's a slaughter," he said, catching her eyes. "Perhaps Roger's hatred was greater and has given him more strength. But whatever the reason, Raine is losing badly."

Alyx pushed away from Joss. "Raine is mine in death as well as alive. Let me go!"

With one look at Joan, Jocelin released her.

Nothing could have prepared Alyx for the sight in front of her. The two men fought on foot, and Raine's armor was so covered with blood that the gold Montgomery leopards were nearly hidden. His left arm seemed to be hanging by a thread, but he kept fighting, swinging valiantly with his right. Roger Chatworth seemed to be toying with the weakened, bloody man as he circled him, teased him.

"He's dying," Alyx said. Raine always believed in honor

so much, but now, to die like this, as an animal in a cage, at the mercy of Chatworth's torments.

She started forward, but Joss caught her. "Raine!" she yelled.

Roger Chatworth turned toward her, looked at her, although his face couldn't be seen beneath the helmet. As if understanding her misery, he circled once more and plowed his ax into the small of Raine's back.

Raine hesitated for a moment then fell forward, face down, Roger standing silent over him.

Instantly, Alyx pulled away from Joss and ran forward. Slowly, she knelt beside Raine's torn body and pulled his head into her lap. There were no tears, only a deep numbness, a feeling that her blood was also pouring onto the ground.

With great reverence, she lifted his head and removed his helmet.

The gasp she let out at the sight under the helmet made Roger Chatworth turn back. After one long moment of disbelief, he threw back his head and let out a horrible cry—a cry very much like the one Raine had given when he heard of Mary's death.

"A life for a life," whispered Brian from Alyx's lap. "Now Mary can rest."

With a trembling hand, Alyx touched Brian's sweaty cheek, watched as he gave his last breath and died in her arms.

"Leave him," Roger said as he bent and picked up his brother's body in his arms. "He is mine now."

Alyx stood in her blood-soaked gown and watched as Roger carried Brian toward the waiting Chatworth men and horses.

"Alyx," Joss said from beside her. "I don't understand. Why is Chatworth taking Raine's body?"

Her body was shaking so much she could hardly speak. "Brian wore Raine's armor and Roger has killed his young brother."

"But how—?" Joss began.

Joan held up thistle down, the ends of it soaked in blood. "He must have planned this for a long while. No doubt he used the down to pad a hauberk so Lord Raine's armor would fit."

Alyx turned to them with wide eyes. "Where is Raine? He wouldn't have docilely allowed Brian to take his armor."

It took them some time to find Raine, his armor missing, lying in his leather padding, soundly asleep under a tree. Joan laughed when she saw him, but Alyx didn't. The unnatural position of Raine's body alarmed her.

"Poison!" Alyx screamed and ran to her husband. The warmth of him showed he wasn't dead, but he might have been for all the notice he paid her.

"Fetch Rosamund at once," Jocelin ordered Joan.

Alyx started to slap Raine's cheeks when her voice couldn't rouse him. "Help me stand him up."

It took all Joss's strength and Alyx's to lift Raine's inert form, but still he slept on.

Rosamund came running and after only a glance at Raine she looked at Joss with fear in her eyes. "I hoped I was wrong. My opium was stolen two days ago, and I hoped the thief knew how to use it."

"Opium?" Alyx demanded. "Isn't that a sleeping drug? My sister-in-law used it."

"It's common enough," Rosamund answered, "but what most people don't know is that if too much is taken, the victim could sleep until death."

Alyx's eyes widened. "You don't think Brian Chatworth gave Raine a great deal, do you?"

"A thimbleful is too much. We must assume Lord Raine has taken too much. Come, there is much, much work to be done."

It took a full day to clean out Raine's system. Rosamund gave him vile-tasting concoctions that made him vomit, that emptied his bowels. And constantly, men took turns walking him.

"Sleep, let me sleep," was all Raine would mumble, his eyes closed, his feet dragging.

Alyx allowed no one to stop walking him nor would she let him turn away from the liquids that were forced down his throat. After many hours, he began to regain control of his feet and started walking somewhat under his own power. His body was empty of all solid matter and Rosamund began to make him drink buckets full of water, hoping to flush him more. Raine was waking enough to protest more loudly.

"You didn't leave me," he said once to Alyx.

"I should have, but I didn't," she snapped. "Drink!"

At noon of the second day, Rosamund finally allowed Raine to sleep and gratefully, she and Jocelin also rested. Tired beyond belief, Alyx went to each of the people of the camp and thanked them personally for helping her with Raine.

"You ought to sleep yourself," came a gruff voice, and Alyx recognized one of the men who'd accused her of stealing. "We don't want to save one of you just to lose the other."

She smiled at him so gratefully that he turned red and looked away. Still smiling, she staggered into Raine's tent and fell asleep beside him.

Alyx stayed with Raine for another week—until he found her holding a woman's baby and crying silently.

"You must go back to Gavin," Raine told her.

"I can't leave you."

He raised one eyebrow. "You've seen that your presence here won't prevent what's going to happen. Chatworth will lay his brother to rest, then we shall see what will happen. Go home and see to our daughter."

"Perhaps a visit," she said, her eyes alight. "Maybe just for a week or so, then I'll return to you."

"I don't think I can live long without you. Go now and tell Joan to pack for you. You can see our Catherine in three days' time."

Alyx's thanks, her joy at the thought of seeing her daughter again, made her leap into Raine's arms. And her kisses soon led them elsewhere. Before either of them realized what was happening, they were rolling on the floor on top of a Saracen carpet, tossing pieces of clothing here and there.

Gleefully, they made love and Raine was pleased to see so

much happiness in his wife's eyes. Afterward, he held her close. "Alyx, it meant a great deal to me that you stayed during the fight with Chatworth. Whether you admit it or not you have a high sense of honor—not the honor I believe in but your own special sort. Yet you forgot it for love of me. I thank you for that."

He smiled when he felt her tears wet his shirt. "You are going to see our daughter, yet all I get are tears."

"Am I selfish for wanting everything? I want you to see our daughter, for the three of us to be together."

"I will soon. Now give me a smile. Do you want me to remember you in tears or with your own special impish smile?"

At that she smiled and Raine kissed her. "Come on, let's start getting you ready."

Alyx kept telling herself the parting was only for a month or so, but she had a sense of permanence, as if she'd never see the forest camp again. The people seemed to think the same thing.

"For your baby," said a man as he handed her a toy whittled out of a bit of green oak. There were more gifts, all homemade, all simple, and each one brought fresh tears to her eyes.

"You stayed up with my baby when she was sick," said one woman.

"And you buried mine," said another.

When it was time to leave, Raine stood quietly behind Alyx, his hand on her shoulder, and he was radiating his pride in her. "Don't stay away too long," he whispered, giving her one last kiss before setting her on her horse.

Alyx rode away, her head twisted back over her shoulder, watching all the people waving at her until the trees hid them.

Chapter 22

FOR TWO whole weeks, Alyx was content to play with her child, to create lullabies for Judith's son and Catherine. She sent long, glowing messages to Raine describing the perfections of their daughter and parcels of medicines to Rosamund. A messenger returned with the news of the camp saying that Blanche had been caught stealing and had been banished from the forest. Alyx felt no joy at the announcement.

After two weeks of bliss, she began to miss Raine, and she left the children's nursery in search of his family.

"I'd heard you were with us again," Gavin teased, "but I wasn't sure. Come and join us. Judith is with the falconer and I was about to join her."

"Do you think the King will like this hawk, Simon?" Judith was asking the grizzled old falconer.

"Aye, my lady. There's no finer in the land."

Judith held the big, hooded bird on the end of her gloved arm, studying the hawk, frowning.

"Are you planning a gift for the King?" Alyx asked.

"I'll try *anything*," Judith said vehemently. "Since Brian Chatworth's death and Elizabeth's pregnancy, the King despises the name of Montgomery."

"And now since the Queen's death—" Gavin began.

"Queen Elizabeth died!" Alyx said loudly, and the hawk fluttered its great wings until Judith soothed it. "I'm sorry," she said. She knew nothing of hawks and hawking. "I hadn't heard the Queen had died."

"He's lost his eldest son and his wife in under a year and his son's widow's family threatens to take her dowry back. The man does little but brood now. Once I could have gone to him and talked to him."

"And what would you ask him?" she asked, hope in her voice.

"I want this feud ended," Gavin said. "There has been a life taken from the Montgomerys and one from the Chatworths. Perhaps if I could speak to the King I could persuade him to pardon Raine?"

"And what about Miles?" Alyx asked. "He has heartily used Elizabeth Chatworth. I don't think her brother will forgive him that."

Gavin and Judith exchanged looks and Judith spoke. "We have corresponded with Miles, and if the King gives permission, he is willing to marry Elizabeth."

"No doubt Roger Chatworth will welcome a Montgomery into his family with open arms," Alyx smiled. "So! You'll use the gift of the hawk to persuade the King. Does he like to go hawking?"

Again, Gavin and Judith exchanged looks.

"Alyx," Gavin began, "we've been waiting to speak to you. We knew you wanted to spend some time with Catherine, but now there's no more time to lose."

For some reason, Alyx began to feel a sense of dread. Absurd, of course, but still, cold little fingers went up her spine. "What did you want to talk to me about?"

"Let's go inside," Judith said, handing the hawk to Simon.

Once the old man was inside the stone falconery, Alyx stood her ground. "Tell me what I should know," she said flatly.

"Gavin!" Judith said. "Let me tell her. Alyx, the King doesn't particularly care for hawking. Right now he cares for nothing or no one—except one thing." She paused a moment. "Music," Judith said quietly.

Alyx stood still a moment, staring. "You want me to go to the King of England, sing him a song and while I'm there casually beg him to forgive my husband and to give the hand of a wealthy heiress to her sworn enemy?" She smiled. "Never have I said I was a magician."

"Alyx, you could do it," Judith encouraged. "No one in the country has a voice or talent to match yours. He'll offer you half of his kingdom if you but make him forget for an hour or so."

"The King?" Alyx sputtered. "What do I care for the King? I would love to play and sing for him. My concern is Raine. He's spent a year trying to make me understand his sense of honor and now I do—at least to the extent that I know he wouldn't thank me for begging before the King."

"But if you could get a pardon for Raine . . ." Judith argued.

Alyx turned to Gavin. "Were you in Raine's place, would you want Judith to go to the King for you or would you expect to fight your own battles?"

Gavin's face was serious. "It would not be easy for me to swallow such a humiliation."

"Humiliation!" Judith said. "If Raine were free, he could come home and we could be a family again."

"And our strife would be internal," Gavin said. "I can see Alyx's point. I don't think she should go against her husband. We will all fight our own battles and keep the King out of this."

Judith seemed to want to reply, but as she looked from Gavin to Alyx, she remained quiet.

But what made Alyx change her mind was Roger Chatworth's growing anger. Gavin sent out spies and they came back with the news that Roger was vowing death to both Miles and Raine to revenge his young brother and the loss of his sister's virtue.

"Raine has no men to fight Chatworth," Alyx said. "And will Miles last against a seasoned warrior such as Roger?"

"He has the backing of all the Montgomery forces," Gavin said quietly.

"You are talking about war!" she yelled. "A private war which will cause you all to lose your lands and the King—" She stopped. Everything seemed to go back to the King.

With tears in her eyes, she fled the room. Was she the only one who could possibly prevent a private war? She'd once told Jocelin she'd do *anything* to keep Raine alive, that she'd rather see him with another woman than dead. Yet he'd been so very, very angry when she did what she felt she had to. He did not want her to interfere in his life and especially in what he considered his honor.

What if she kept quiet now, didn't try to win a pardon from the King and there was a war? Would she be happy knowing Raine died with his honor intact? Or would she curse herself for all eternity for not at least trying to prevent the battles?

With quiet dignity, she stood, smoothed her dress and went downstairs to the winter parlor where Judith and Gavin sat over a game of draughts.

"I will go to the King," Alyx said quietly. "I will sing with all my might and I will ask, plead, beg, whatever I have to do, to get him to pardon Raine and to arrange the marriage of Elizabeth and Miles."

Alyx stood outside the King's chamber, her body trembling so badly she feared her dress would fall off. What was she, a common lawyer's daughter, doing here?

A shout from inside the chamber and a sound of something breaking made her gasp. After a moment, a slim man tiptoed out of the room, a red mark on his cheek, a flute in his hand.

He gave Alyx an insolent look. "He's in a bad mood today. I hope there's more to you than appears."

Alyx pulled herself up to all of her small height and glared at him. "Perhaps it's the music he hasn't heard today that's put him in a bad temper."

The man grunted and left her alone.

Alyx adjusted her dress again, a wonderful concoction of deep green velvet with sleeves and skirt inset so heavily embroidered with gold thread that the fabric was stiff. The dress had been Judith's design and the embroidery was a fanciful arrangement of centaurs and fairies playing many musical instruments. "For luck," Judith had said.

"Come in and wait," said a dark-clad man, just his head sticking out of the door. "His Majesty will hear you in a moment."

Alyx picked up her cittern, a magnificent thing of rosewood and inlaid ivory, and followed the man.

The King's chamber was a large room paneled in oak, richly done, but certainly no better than the rooms at Montgomery Castle. This surprised Alyx. Perhaps she'd expected the King's rooms to be made of gold.

She took the seat the man pointed to and watched. The King sat on a red-cushioned chair and Alyx wouldn't have known he was the King except that occasionally someone would bow before him. He was a tall, somber, tired-looking man, and as he drank from a silver goblet, she saw he had few teeth and they were blackish. He frowned at the singer before him, and the young man's nervousness was apparent in every word he sang. The air was charged with tension as the musician tried to please him.

With the big room echoing as it did and everyone being so stiff, it was no wonder he was displeased, Alyx thought. None of the music made him forget for a moment his sadness. If I were in charge, I'd put the musicians together, challenge them with some new music. When they were enjoying themselves, the King would find pleasure.

Alyx sat still for a moment longer. There were eleven musicians auditioning for the King today. Lately, he'd been staying alone in his rooms, refusing even to attend the Queen's funeral. Alyx had had to wait a week to get this chance to play and sing for him. And would she shake and quiver before him as these others were doing?

Think of Raine, she told herself. Think of all the Montgomerys.

She took a deep breath and stood, offered a silent prayer of hope, then let her voice take over.

"Here!" she said loudly to the singer. "You'll have us all in tears. What we need is laughter and no more tears."

Someone put a cautioning hand on her arm, but Alyx looked straight at King Henry. "With your permission, Your Majesty." She curtsied, and the King gave her a nonchalant wave.

Alyx's heart was in her throat. Now if she could just get the musicians to cooperate. "Can you play a harpsichord?" she asked a man who gave her a hostile look.

"Wait your turn," he hissed.

"I have more to lose than you do. Perhaps together we can work some magic." She cocked her head. "Or is your talent too limited?"

The man, after one considering look, went to the harpsichord.

As if they were all the choirboys she'd taught at Moreton, she began ordering the men about, giving them different instruments that were abundant in the room.

Once they were seated or standing, she flew about, giving melody here, rhythm there. About halfway through she began to sing and two of the musicians were immediately won to her side. Grinning, they picked up the melody and stayed with her.

It seemed to Alyx everything was taking so long and she only felt encouragement when the man on the harpsichord added his voice to hers. The man on the harp caught the melody and showed his talent with those heavenly strings.

Alyx had chosen an old song, hoping they'd all know it, but perhaps it was her rendition of it that made them awkward. The man she'd given a tambourine moved to a kettledrum hidden in a shadowy corner and the sound began to make the floor vibrate.

Finally, finally, everyone seemed to have caught the song, and Alyx dared to turn and look at the King. His face was impassive, silent, but the men behind him looked astonished. At least she knew now that what she was doing wasn't an everyday occurrence.

They repeated three choruses of the song and Alyx started them on something new, church music this time, and when that was done she went to a folk song.

It had been an hour since she'd started and she quieted the musicians. This time, she'd sing alone, unaccompanied. Once, four years ago, a singer had come to Moreton and the villagers had said Alyx at last had some competition from someone. Alyx, frightened of looking bad, stayed up all night and composed a song that would be difficult for even her to sing, a song that covered the entire range of her abilities. The next day, she'd sung the song and the visitor, an older woman, had looked at Alyx with tears in her eyes and kissed Alyx on both cheeks, saying Alyx should give thanks daily for her gift from God.

Now, Alyx planned to sing that song. She'd hated it ever since she wrote it because the woman she'd meant to humble had actually humbled her. But now she needed to do what she could to win the King's favor.

The song showed the heights and depths of Alyx's voice, as well as the controlled softness and extraordinary volume. She built up to the total power of her voice slowly, liltingly, and just when it seemed she could go no further, she put everything into one note and held it—and held it until there were tears in her eyes and her lungs were dry.

When she finished, she dropped to a deep curtsy and there was total, absolute silence about her, the sound of Alyx's last note still reverberating off the walls, swirling about the people like blue and yellow lights.

"Come here, child." The King broke the silence.

Alyx went to him, kissed his hand, kept her head bowed.

He leaned forward, lifted her chin. "So you are the newest Montgomery wife." He smiled at her startled look. "I try to keep up with what happens in my realm. And I find the Montgomery men marry the most entertaining women. But this . . ."—he motioned to the musicians about the room— ". . . this is worth a king's ransom."

"I am pleased to give you pleasure, Your Majesty," Alyx whispered.

He gave the first indication of a smile. "You have more than pleased me. Now, what do you ask in return? Come, you didn't leave Gavin's home for no reason."

Alyx tried to gather her courage. "I would like to end the feud between the Montgomerys and the Chatworths. I propose a blood bond between them, Miles to marry Lady Elizabeth Chatworth."

King Henry frowned. "Miles is a felon by the Act of 1495. He abducted the Lady Elizabeth."

"He did not!" Alyx bellowed in her usual manner. "Forgive me, Your Majesty." She fell to her knees before him. "Miles did not abduct her, but it was because of me that Lady Elizabeth has suffered."

"You! Fetch a stool," King Henry commanded and when Alyx was seated, he said, "Now tell me all of the story."

Alyx told of Pagnell accusing her of using her voice to seduce him, of her hiding in the forest, of falling in love with Raine. She watched his eyes, saw that he was interested in her story and went on to tell of her capture by Pagnell and Elizabeth's abduction.

"You say he meant to roll her in a carpet and hand her to Lord Miles?" King Henry asked.

She leaned forward. "Please don't repeat this, but I heard she was delivered without a stitch of clothing on and that she attacked Lord Miles with an ax. Of course the story could be wrong."

The King gave a sound very like a laugh. "Go on with your story."

She told him of the witchcraft trial, how the men had used her to entice Raine to her rescue.

"And he saved you at the last moment?"

"A little after the last moment. The smoke was so bad I lost my voice for days."

He took her hand in his. "That," he said with great gravity, "was a tragedy. And what happened after this magnificent rescue?"

Her voice changed as she told of her child and her return to the forest and meeting Brian Chatworth. She told the way Brian had dressed in Raine's armor and how Raine had nearly died from the opium.

"So now you'd like Lord Miles to marry Lady Elizabeth."

Chapter 23

A MONTH passed and there was no word from Raine—and all correspondence sent to him was ignored. For the first weeks Alyx was sad but her sadness soon turned to anger. If his pride meant more than their love and their daughter, so be it.

Her anger fed itself for an entire summer. She watched Catherine grow, saw that the little girl had indeed inherited her father's sturdiness.

"There'll be no chance for a slim, elegant lady," Alyx sighed, looking at Catherine's chubby legs as she took her first steps.

"All babies are fat," Judith laughed, tossing her son into the air. "Catherine looks more like Raine every day. Too bad he can't see her. One look at those violet eyes and her dimples and he'd melt. Raine could never resist a child."

Judith's words haunted Alyx for days and at the end of the fourth day she made a decision. "I'm going to send Catherine to her father," Alyx announced one evening as Judith was weeding the roses.

"I beg your pardon?"

"He may not forgive me, but there's no reason Catherine should be punished. She's almost a year old now and he's never even seen her."

Judith stood, wiping her hands. "What if Raine doesn't return her? Could you bear losing both your husband and your daughter?"

"I'll say I'm sending her until Christmas, then Gavin will fetch her. Raine will honor the agreement."

"If he agrees."

Alyx didn't answer. She hoped with all her heart that Catherine would win her father's heart, melt it.

Days later, when Catherine was ready to leave, Alyx almost changed her mind, but Judith held her shoulders and Alyx waved goodbye to her daughter, who was escorted by twenty of Gavin's men and two nurses.

Alyx waited breathlessly for the next weeks. No message came from Raine, but one of the nurses wrote regularly, sending her letters via a complicated network arranged by Gavin through Jocelin.

The nurse wrote of the turmoil that had been caused by Lady Catherine's arrival and how brave the little girl had been. Raine's house, his men and Raine himself had frightened her badly. At first the nurse thought Lord Raine was going to ignore his daughter but once, while playing in the garden, Raine had retrieved Catherine's ball and he'd sat a few moments on a bench watching her. Catherine had begun rolling her ball toward her father and he had played with her for an hour.

The letters of the nurse began to describe more and more incidents. Lord Raine took Catherine for a ride. Lord Raine put his daughter to bed. Lord Raine swears his daughter can talk, that she is the smartest child in all of England.

Alyx was glad to hear the news but she was unhappy at being so alone. She wanted to share the pleasure of their daughter with her husband.

In the middle of November, the letters stopped and it wasn't until nearly Christmas that she heard any more news. Gavin came to her and said that Catherine had been returned and waited below in the winter parlor.

Alyx flew down the stairs, tears blurring her eyes as she saw her daughter in an elaborate dress of gold silk standing quietly before the fire. It had been months since they'd seen each other and Catherine took a step away from her mother.

"Don't you remember me, sweetheart?" Alyx whispered pleadingly.

The child took another step backward and as Alyx moved forward, Catherine turned and ran, grabbing her father's legs.

Alyx turned startled eyes up at Raine's intense blue ones. "I . . . I didn't see you," she stuttered. "I thought Catherine was alone."

Raine didn't say a word.

Alyx's heart jumped into her throat and threatened to choke her. "You look well," she said as calmly as she could.

He bent and picked up his daughter and, jealously, Alyx saw the way Catherine clung to him.

"I wanted you to meet your daughter," she whispered.

"Why?" he asked and his voice, that deep rich voice she knew so well, nearly made her cry.

But Alyx refused to cry. "Why?" she hissed. "You hadn't seen your daughter in her entire life and you ask me why I sent her to you?"

His voice, quiet, low, interrupted her. "Why would you send her to a man who deserted you, who left you alone to fight his battles?"

Alyx's eyes widened.

Raine stroked his daughter's hair. "She is a beautiful child, kind and giving like her mother."

"But I'm not—" Alyx began, then stopped as Raine started walking toward her. He passed her, opened the door and handed Catherine to the waiting nurse. "Could we talk?"

Silently, Alyx nodded her head.

Raine walked to the fireplace and studied the blaze for a moment. "I think I could have killed you when you went to the King," he said with feeling. "It was as if you were announcing to the world that Raine Montgomery couldn't handle his own problems."

"I never meant—"

He put up his hand to silence her. "This isn't easy for me, but it must be said. While we were in the forest it was easy for me to see why people disliked you. You put yourself so above them and they resented you so much. When you came to understand what you were doing you set about to do something about it. You changed, Alyx."

He paused for a long moment. "It's not so . . . comfortable to look at myself, to judge myself."

His broad back was to her, his head low, and her heart went out to him. "Raine," she whispered. "I understand. You don't have to say anymore."

"But I do!" He turned to face her. "Do you think it's easy for me—a man—to realize that a little bit of a child/woman such as you can do something I can't?"

"What have I done?" She was genuinely astonished.

At that he paused and smiled, and there was much love in his eyes. "Perhaps I thought I should have my way because I was sacrificing all I had for some filthy beggars. Maybe I liked being a king of criminals."

"Raine." She reached out her hand to touch his sleeve.

He caught her hand, raised her fingertips to his lips. "Why did you go to King Henry?"

"To ask him to pardon you. To persuade him to let Elizabeth and Miles marry."

"It hurt my pride, Alyx," he whispered. "I wanted to march into King Henry's chamber wearing silvered armor and talk to the King as an equal." A dimple appeared in his cheek. "But instead, my wife went and pleaded for me. It hurt very much."

"I didn't mean to . . . Oh, Raine, I would beg anyone to save you."

He didn't seem to notice that his hand was nearly crushing hers. "I have been distorted with pride. I want to . . . ask your forgiveness."

Alyx wanted to shout that she'd forgive him anything, but now was not the time for flippancy. "In the future I am sure I will do other things to wound your pride."

"I'm sure you will."

Her chin raised a fraction. "And what will you do when I offend you?"

"Rage at you. Get very, very angry. Threaten to murder you."

Velvet Angel

To Joan Schulhafer, who started as my publicist and became my friend. Thank you for all the love and laughter, and most of all, for all you taught me.

Chapter 1

THE SOUTH OF ENGLAND
August 1502

ELIZABETH CHATWORTH stood on the very edge of the steep cliff, gazing toward the sea of tall barley grasses. Below her, seemingly tiny men walked with scythes on their shoulders, a few rode horses and one drove a team of oxen.

But Elizabeth didn't really see the men because her chin was held too high and it was locked into place so rigidly that nothing was going to bring it down. A warm gust of wind tried to force her away from the edge but she braced her legs and refused to move. If what had already happened to her today and now what she faced did not sway her, no mere wind was going to break her stance.

Her green eyes were dry but her throat was swollen shut with a lump of anger and unshed tears. A muscle in her jaw flexed and unflexed as she breathed deeply, trying to control her pounding heart.

Another gust of wind blew her tangled mass of honey blonde hair away from her back and, unbeknownst to Elizabeth, one last pearl disentangled itself and slid down the torn, dirty red silk of her dress. The finery she'd worn to her friend's wedding was now shredded beyond repair, her hair loose and flowing, her cheek smudged—and her hands were crudely tied behind her back.

Elizabeth lifted her eyes toward heaven, unblinking at the bright daylight. All her life, she'd had her looks referred to as angelic and never had she looked so delicate, so serene, so brother Brian's disappearance. And indirectly, a Montgomery had caused her own capture.

Elizabeth had been an attendant at a friend's wedding and by accident she'd overheard an odious man she'd known all her life, Pagnell, planning to turn a pretty little singer over to his corrupt relatives to be tried as a witch. When Elizabeth tried to rescue the girl, Pagnell had caught them and, as a joke, had decided to have Elizabeth delivered to her enemy, a Montgomery. Perhaps things wouldn't have been so bad if the singer, in a generous but not wholly intelligent gesture, had not given the information that she was somehow connected with a Montgomery.

Pagnell had bound and gagged Elizabeth, rolled her in a filthy piece of canvas and ordered his man, John, to deliver her to the notoriously lecherous, satyric, hot-blooded Miles Montgomery. Of all the four Montgomery men, Elizabeth knew that the youngest, a boy of only twenty years, just two years older than Elizabeth, was the worst. Even in the convent where she'd spent the last several years, she'd heard stories of Miles Montgomery.

She'd been told that he'd sold his soul to the devil when he was sixteen and as a result he had an unholy power over women. Elizabeth had laughed at the story but she'd not told the reason for her laughter. She thought it much more likely that Miles Montgomery was like her dead brother Edmund and had ordered women to his bed. It was a pity that this Montgomery's seed seemed to be so fertile, for it was rumored that he had a hundred bastards.

Three years ago a young girl, Bridget, had left the convent where Elizabeth often lived to go and work at the ancient Montgomery fortress. She was a pretty girl with big dark eyes and swaying hips. To Elizabeth's disgust, the other residents alternately acted as if the girl were going to her wedding or to be a human sacrifice. The day before Bridget left, the prioress spent two hours with her and at vespers the girl's eyes were red from crying.

Eleven months later, a traveling musician brought them the news that Bridget had been delivered of a large, healthy boy who she named James Montgomery. It was freely admitted that Miles was the father.

Elizabeth joined in the many prayers offered for the girl's sins. Privately she cursed all men like her brother Edmund and Miles Montgomery—evil men who believed women had no souls, who thought nothing of beating and raping women, of forcing them to do all manner of hideous acts.

She had no time for more thoughts as John grabbed a handful of her hair and pulled her to her feet.

"Your time for prayers is over," he said into her face. "Montgomery has made camp and it's time he got a look at his next . . ."—he smiled—"mother of his next bastard."

He laughed aloud when Elizabeth struggled against him, and when she realized he enjoyed her struggles, she stopped and gave him her coldest look.

"Witch!" he flung at her. "We'll see if this devil Montgomery can capture the angel you look like—or will he find your heart as black as his own?"

Smiling, his hand twisted in her hair, he brought a sharp little dagger to rest against her throat. When she didn't flinch at the feel of the cold steel against her skin, his smile changed to a smirk.

"Sometimes the Montgomery men make the mistake of talking to women instead of using them as God meant them to be used. I plan to see that this Montgomery has no such ideas."

Slowly, he trailed the tip of the blade down her throat to the high square neck of what was left of her gown.

Her breath held, her eyes on his, her anger held under rigid control, she stood very still. She would not goad him to use the knife on her.

John did not cut her skin, but the blade easily parted the front of her dress and her tight corset under it. When he'd exposed the full curve of her breasts, he looked back into her face. "You've been hiding a great deal, Elizabeth," he whispered.

She stiffened and looked away from his face. It was true that she dressed conservatively, flattening her breasts, thickening her waist. Her face attracted more men than she wanted, but aside from covering her hair she could do nothing about her face.

John was no longer interested in her face as he concentrated on slicing away the rest of her gown. He'd seen very few women nude and never one of Elizabeth Chatworth's station—or her beauty.

Elizabeth's spine was so stiff it could have been made of steel and when her clothes fell away and her bare skin felt the warm August sun, she knew that this was more painful than what had heretofore been done to her.

An ugly expletive from John, uttered from deep within him, made her blink.

"Damn Pagnell!" he cursed and reached for her.

Elizabeth stepped backward and tried to muster her dignity as she glared at John, saw he was practically foaming at the mouth. "You touch me and you're a dead man," she said loudly. "If you kill me, Pagnell will have your head—and if you do not, I will see that he finds out what you have done. And have you forgotten my brother's rage? Is your life worth one coupling with *any* woman?"

It took a moment for John to sober and bring his eyes to her face. "I hope Montgomery causes you endless misery," he said with great feeling and stalked away to the carpet slung across his horse's rump. Without a glance at her, he unrolled it on the ground.

"Lie down," he commanded, his eyes on the carpet. "And let me warn you, woman, that if you disobey me I will forget Pagnell and Montgomery and your brother's wrath."

Obediently, Elizabeth lay down on the carpet, the short woolen nap pricking her skin, and when John knelt over her, she held her breath.

Roughly, he pushed her to her stomach, cut the bindings on her wrists, and before Elizabeth could even blink, he tossed the edge of the carpet over her and began rolling her in it. There were no more thoughts. Her only concern was a primitive instinct to continue breathing.

It seemed an eternity that she lay still, her head tilted back as she sought the air coming from the top of the carpet roll. When she was at last moved, lifted, she had to struggle to find air, and when she was tossed across the back of the horse, she thought her lungs would collapse.

John's muffled words came through the layers of carpet. "The next man you see will be Miles Montgomery. Think on that while we ride. He won't be as kind to you as I have been."

In a way, the words were good for Elizabeth because the idea of Miles Montgomery, of his evil ways, gave her some incentive to work hard at breathing. And when the horse jolted her, she cursed the Montgomery family, their house, their retainers—and she prayed for the innocent Montgomery children who were part of this immoral clan.

The tent of Miles Montgomery was a splendid affair: deep green sendal trimmed in gold, the gold Montgomery leopards painted along the scalloped roof border, pennants flying from the crown. Inside, the walls were lined with pale green silk. There were several collapsible stools, cushioned with blue and gold brocade, a large table carved with the Montgomery leopards and, against opposite walls, two cots, one abnormally long, both draped with pelts of long-haired red fox.

Four men stood around the table, two dressed in the rich uniform of the Montgomery knights. The attention of the other two men was given to one of the retainers.

"He says he has a gift for you, my lord," the knight was saying to the quiet man before him. "It could be a trick. What could Lord Pagnell have that you would want?"

Miles Montgomery raised one dark eyebrow and it was enough to make his man back down. Sometimes men newly in his service thought that since their master was so young, they could take liberties.

"Could there be a man rolled in the carpet?" asked the man beside Miles.

The subdued retainer craned his neck to look up at Sir Guy. "A very small one, perhaps."

Sir Guy looked down at Miles and there passed a silent

communication between them. "Send him and his gift in," Sir Guy said. "We will meet them with drawn swords."

The knight left and within seconds he returned, his sword pointed at the small of the back of the man carrying the carpet. Insolently, smirking, John half tossed his bundle to the carpeted ground and with his foot pushed it very hard, sending it, unrolling, toward Miles Montgomery's feet.

When at last the carpet stopped, there were four stunned faces as they gaped at what lay before them: a nude woman, her eyes closed, long thick lashes soft on delicately colored cheeks, great massive torrents of honey blond hair wrapped and twisted about her, curls tickling her waist and the tops of her thighs. She was outrageously curved with large firm breasts, a tiny waist, long, long legs. And her face was something men expected to see only in heaven—delicate, ethereal, not quite of this world.

Smiling triumphantly, John slipped out of the tent unnoticed.

Elizabeth, half dazed from the lack of air, opened her eyes slowly and looked up to see four men standing over her, their swords drawn but aimed toward the ground. Two of the men were obviously retainers and she dismissed them. The third man was a giant, several inches over six feet, steel gray hair, a scar running diagonally across his entire face. Although the man was indeed frightening, she somehow sensed he was not the leader of this group.

Beside the giant was another man dressed resplendently in deep blue satin. Elizabeth was accustomed to seeing strong, handsome men, but something about this one with his leashed power held in check so easily made her stare. The other men's eyes were fastened on Elizabeth's body, but this man turned and she looked for the first time into the face of Miles Montgomery, and their eyes locked.

He was a handsome man, very very handsome, with dark gray eyes under heavy, arched brows, a thin nose with slightly flaring nostrils and a full sensual mouth.

Danger! was Elizabeth's first thought. This man was dangerous to women as well as men.

She broke eye contact with him and in seconds she stood, grabbing a pelt from one of the cots near her and a war ax from the top of the table. "I will kill the first man who comes near me," she said, holding the ax with one hand while she tossed the pelt over one shoulder, leaving the other bare, one leg exposed from waist to bare foot.

The giant took a step toward her and she raised the ax, both hands on the handle.

"I know how to use this," she warned, looking up at the man with absolutely no fear.

The two knights took a step closer toward her and Elizabeth backed away, looking from one to the other. The back of her knees hit the edge of the cot and she could go no farther. One of the knights smiled at her and she snarled at him in return.

"Leave us."

The words were quiet, uttered in a low voice, but it held command and all of them looked at Montgomery.

The giant of a man gave Elizabeth one last look, then nodded at the two knights and the three of them left the tent.

Elizabeth tightened her grip on the ax, her knuckles already white, as she glared across the space toward Miles Montgomery. "I will kill you," she said through her teeth. "Do not think that because I'm a woman I won't enjoy hacking a man to pieces. I would love to see the blood of a Montgomery spilled upon the earth."

Miles didn't move from his place by the table, but kept watching. After a moment he lifted his sword and Elizabeth drew in her breath, preparing for the battle to come. Very slowly, he placed his sword on the table and turned away from her, presenting his profile. Again slowly, he removed the jeweled dagger he wore at his side and placed it on the table beside the sword.

He turned back to her, his face expressionless, his eyes giving nothing away, and took a step toward her.

Elizabeth lifted the heavy ax and held it in readiness. She would fight to the death, for death was preferable to the beating and rape she knew this devil-man planned.

Miles sat down on a stool, several feet in front of her; he did not speak, but only watched her.

So! he did not think a woman a worthy opponent, but disarmed himself and sat down while she held a weapon of death over his head. With one lunge, she leaped forward and swung the ax at his neck.

Effortlessly, he caught the handle in his right hand, easily held it and looked into her eyes as she stood close to him. For a moment she was paralyzed, hypnotized by his eyes. He seemed to be searching her face for something, as if he asked silent questions of her.

She jerked the ax away from his grip and nearly fell when she found he released it freely. She caught herself at the edge of the table. "Damn you!" she said under her breath. "May the Lord and all His angels curse the day a Montgomery was born. May you and all your descendants writhe in the fires of hell forever."

Her voice had risen almost to a shout and outside she could hear movement.

Miles still sat there, watching her silently, and Elizabeth could feel her blood beginning to boil. When she saw her hands starting to shake, she knew she must calm herself. Where was the cool detachment she'd cultivated over the years?

If this man could remain calm, so could she. She listened and if her guess were correct, the sounds she heard outside were the men moving away. Perhaps if she could get past this one man, she could escape and get home to her brother.

With her eyes on Miles, she began to walk backward, circling him as she made her way toward the tent flap. Slowly, he turned on the stool and watched her. Outside she heard the whinny of a horse and she prayed that if she could just make it outside she'd be free.

Even though her eyes never left Miles's, she still never saw him move. One moment he was sitting, relaxed, on the stool and the next, just as her hand touched the tent flap, he was beside her, his hand around her wrist. She brought the ax straight down toward his shoulder but he caught her other wrist and held her.

She stood still, imprisoned lightly, painlessly, by his grip, and glared up at him. He was so close she could feel his breath on her forehead. As he looked down at her, he seemed to be waiting for something and then he looked puzzled.

With eyes as hard as the emeralds they resembled, she glared up at him. "And now what comes next?" she asked, hatred in her voice. "Do you beat me first or rape me? Or perhaps you like them both at the same time. I am a virgin and I've heard it hurts most the first time. No doubt my added pain will give you much pleasure."

For just a second, his eyes widened as if in astonishment and it was the first unguarded expression Elizabeth had seen on his face. His gray eyes locked into hers so hard that she looked away.

"I can endure what you deal out," she said quietly, "and if your wish is to see me beg, you will fail."

His hand released her wrist holding the tent flap and he cupped the left side of her cheek, gently turning her back to look at him.

She stiffened at his touch, hating his hands on her.

"Who are you?" he half whispered.

She straightened her spine even more and hatred flamed in her eyes. "I am your enemy. I am Elizabeth Chatworth."

Something passed quickly across his face and then was gone. After a long moment, he removed his hand from her cheek and, after a backward step, he released her other wrist. "You may keep the ax if it makes you feel safer but I cannot let you leave."

As if dismissing her, he turned his back and walked toward the center of the tent.

Immediately, Elizabeth was through the tent flap and out of the tent and, just as quickly, Miles was beside her, his hand once again encircling her wrist.

"I cannot let you leave," he repeated, this time more firmly. His eyes traveled downward to her bare legs and up again. "You aren't dressed for running away. Come inside and I'll send my man to purchase clothes."

She jerked away from him. The sun was setting and in the twilight he looked even darker. "I want no clothes from you. I want nothing from any Montgomery. My brother will—"

She broke off at his look.

"Do not mention the name of your brother to me. He killed my sister."

Miles recaptured her wrist and gave a light tug. "Now I must insist that you come inside. My men will be returning soon and I don't think they should see you dressed like this."

She held her ground. "What does it matter? Isn't it the custom of men like you to throw female captives to their knights when they've finished with them?"

She wasn't sure but she thought she saw just a flicker of a smile on Miles's lips. "Elizabeth," he began, then paused. "Come inside and we'll talk there." He turned toward the dark trees near them. "Guy!" he bellowed, making Elizabeth jump.

Immediately, the giant stepped into the clearing. After only a cursory glance at Elizabeth, he looked at Miles.

"Send someone into the village and find some suitable women's clothes. Spend what you need." The voice Miles used to his man was quite different from the one he used with her.

"Send me with him," Elizabeth said quickly. "I will talk to my brother and he will be so grateful that you've released me unharmed that it will end this feud between the Chatworths and Montgomerys."

Miles turned back to her and his eyes were hard. "Don't beg, Elizabeth."

Without thought but with a cry of rage, she lifted the ax again and aimed for his head. In one seemingly practiced motion, he pulled the ax from her hand, flung it away and swung her into his arms.

She wasn't about to give him the pleasure of struggling against him and instead she stiffened, hating the feel of his clothes against her skin. The fox pelt hung to one side, baring the leg against his body.

He carried her inside the tent and gently laid her on one of the cots.

"Why do you bother with clothes for me?" she hissed. "Perhaps you should do your coupling in the fields like the animal you are."

He walked away, his back to her, and poured two goblets of wine from a silver vessel on the table. "Elizabeth," he said, "if you keep asking me to make love to you, I will eventually succumb to your temptations." He turned, walked toward her and sat on a stool a few feet away. "You've had a long day and you must be tired and hungry." He held out a full wine goblet to her.

Elizabeth swept it away, the wine spilling, staining one of the luxurious carpets that comprised the floor of the tent.

Miles glanced at it, unconcerned, and drank his wine. "And now, Elizabeth, what am I to do with you?"

Chapter 2

ELIZABETH SAT upon the cot, her legs well covered, only her head and one shoulder bare, and refused to look at Miles Montgomery. She would not lower herself to try and reason with him as he seemed to consider her ideas begging.

After a time of silence, Miles rose and stepped outside the tent, his hand holding the flap doorway open. She heard him order a basin of hot water.

Elizabeth didn't respond to his momentary absence but thought that he had to sleep sometime and when he did, she would escape. Perhaps it would be better to wait until she had some proper clothes.

Miles didn't let his man enter with the water, but carried it in himself and set it at the side of the cot. "The water is for you, Elizabeth. I thought perhaps you'd like to wash."

She kept her arms folded across her chest and her head turned away from him. "I want nothing from you."

"Elizabeth," he said and there was exasperation in his voice. He sat down beside her, took her hands in his. He waited patiently until she turned her angry glare toward him. "I am not going to hurt you," he said gently. "I have never beat a woman in my life and I don't plan to start now. I cannot allow you to jump on a horse wearing practically nothing and ride across the countryside. You wouldn't last an hour before you'd be attacked by hordes of highwaymen."

"Am I to believe you're any better?" Her hands clasped

his for a moment and her eyes softened. "Will you return me to my brother?"

Miles's eyes looked into hers with an almost frightening intensity. "I . . . will consider it."

She thrust his hands from hers and looked away. "What could I expect from a Montgomery? Get away from me!"

Miles rose. "The water grows cold."

She looked up at him with a slight smile. "Why should I wash? For you? Do you like your women clean and fresh smelling? If so, then I'll never wash! I will grow so dirty I will look like a Nubian slave and my hair will crawl with lice and other vermin that will soil your pretty clothes."

Miles looked at her a moment before speaking. "The tent is surrounded by men and I will be outside. If you try to leave, you will be returned to me." With that, he left her alone.

As Miles knew he would be, Sir Guy was waiting for him outside the tent. Miles nodded once and the giant followed him into the trees.

"I sent two men for the clothes," Sir Guy said. When Miles's father died, Miles was nine and the elder Montgomery's dying wish was that Sir Guy take care of the young boy who was sometimes like a stranger even in his own family. Miles talked as much to Sir Guy as he did to anyone.

"Who is she?" Sir Guy asked, his hand on the bark of an enormous old oak tree.

"Elizabeth Chatworth."

Sir Guy nodded once. The moonlight cast eerie shadows on the scar across his face. "I thought as much. Lord Pagnell's sense of humor would run to delivering a Chatworth to a Montgomery." He paused, watching Miles for a long moment. "Do we return her to her brother on the morrow?"

Miles walked away from his man. "What do you know of her brother, Edmund Chatworth?"

Sir Guy spit lustily before answering. "Compared to Chatworth, Pagnell is a saint. Chatworth loved to torture women. He used to tie them up and rape them. On the night he was killed—and bless the man who did the killing—a young woman cut her wrists in his chamber."

Sir Guy watched as Miles clenched and unclenched his fists, and Guy regretted his words. More than anything else in the world, Miles loved women. Hundreds of times Guy had had to pull Miles off a man who'd dared to wrong a woman. As a boy he'd attacked grown men and when his temper was aroused it was all Guy could do to hold him. Last year, Guy had not succeeded in keeping Miles from killing a man who'd slapped his sharp-tongued wife. The king'd almost refused to pardon Miles for that fracas.

"Her brother Roger isn't like Edmund," Sir Guy said.

Miles whirled on him, his eyes black. "Roger Chatworth raped my sister and caused her suicide! Do you forget that?"

Guy knew that the best way to handle Miles's temper was to remain silent on the subject that angered him. "What do you plan to do with the girl?"

Miles turned away, ran his hand down the trunk of a tree. "Do you know that she hates the Montgomery name? We have been innocent in all the hatred between the Montgomerys and Chatworths yet still she hates us." He turned to face Sir Guy. "And she seems to hate me in particular. When I touch her she is repulsed. She wipes where I have touched her with a cloth, as if I'd defiled her."

As soon as Sir Guy closed his open mouth, he almost laughed. If possible, women loved Miles more than he loved them. As a child, he'd spent most of his time surrounded by girls, which is one reason why Miles was put in Sir Guy's charge—to make sure he turned into a man. But Guy had known from the first that there was no doubt of young Miles's masculinity. He just liked women. It was a quirk, rather like the love of a good horse or a sharp sword. At times, Miles's absurdly gentle treatment of women was a bother, such as his lethally enforced rule of no raping after a battle, but on the whole, Sir Guy'd learned to live with the boy's affliction—he was all right otherwise.

But Sir Guy had never, *never* heard of a woman who wasn't willing to lay down her life for Miles. Young, old, in between, even newborn girls clung to him. And Elizabeth Chatworth wiped away his touch!

Sir Guy tried to put this information into perspective. Perhaps it was like losing your first battle. He reached out and put a big hand on Miles's shoulder. "We all lose now and then. It doesn't make you less of a man. Perhaps the girl hates all men. With her brother for an example—"

Miles shrugged the hand away. "She's been hurt! *Badly* hurt! Not just her body that's covered with bruises and scratches, but she's built a wall around her of anger and hatred."

Sir Guy felt that he was standing on the edge of a deep ravine. "This girl is a highborn lady," he said quietly. "You can't keep her prisoner. The king has already outlawed your brother. You don't need to provoke him anymore. You must return Lady Elizabeth to her brother."

"Return her to a place where women are tortured? That's where she learned to hate. And if I return her now, what will she think of the Montgomerys? Will she have learned that we aren't evil as her brother was?"

"You can't think to keep her!" Sir Guy was aghast.

Miles seemed to be considering this. "It will be days before anyone learns where she is. Perhaps in that time I can show her—"

"And what of your brothers?" Sir Guy demanded. "They're expecting you home. It won't take Gavin long to find that you hold Elizabeth Chatworth prisoner." He paused, lowering his voice. "The girl will have only good to say about the Montgomerys if you return her unharmed."

Miles's eyes sparkled. "I believe Elizabeth would say she used an ax to force me to return her." He gave a slight smile. "My mind is made up. I will keep her for just a little while, long enough to show her that a Montgomery isn't like her dead brother. Now! I must return and"—he smiled more broadly—"give my dirty little captive a bath. Come on, Guy, don't look like that. It's just for a few days."

Sir Guy kept quiet as he followed his young master back to camp, but he wondered if Elizabeth Chatworth could be conquered in just a few days.

* * *

but besides the disgusting ordeal of voluntarily touching him, she refused to beg to any man.

Miles combed her wet hair with a delicate ivory comb and when he was finished, he left the tent and returned in moments with a lovely gown of red samite, a mixture of silk and wool. There were also underclothes of fine lawn.

"You may finish bathing or not, as you like," he said, "but I would suggest you put the clothes on." With that he left her alone.

Elizabeth did wash, hurriedly, wincing a few times at bruises but hardly noticing them. She was glad for the clothes because they gave her more freedom to carry out her plans to escape.

Miles returned with a loaded tray of food, and he lit candles in the dark tent. "I brought a bit of everything as I have no idea what you like."

She didn't bother to answer him.

"Does the gown please you?" He was watching her closely but she looked away. The gown was an expensive one, trimmed with embroidery done in gold wire. Most women would have been pleased with it, but Elizabeth didn't seem to notice whether she wore silk or russet.

"The food grows cold. Come and eat here at the table with me."

She looked at him. "I have no intention whatsoever of eating anything at your table."

Miles started to speak but closed his mouth instead. "When you grow hungry enough, the food will be here."

Elizabeth sat on the cot, her legs stretched before her, her arms folded, and concentrated on the tall, ornate candlestand in front of her. Tomorrow she would find a way to escape.

Ignoring the smells of the food Miles was eating, she lay down and forced her body to relax. She would need strength for tomorrow. The long ordeal of the day made her exhausted body quick to fall asleep.

Elizabeth woke in the middle of the night and instantly she tensed, sensing some sort of danger but too sleep-befuddled to remember it. Within minutes, her mind cleared and quietly she moved her head to look at Miles, asleep in the cot on the other side of the tent.

As a child living in a household filled with horrors, she'd learned the art of moving about soundlessly. Stealthily, not allowing the noisy dress to make a sound, she tiptoed toward the back of the tent. No doubt guards were stationed all around, but at the back they'd be less alert.

It took her many minutes to lift the back of the tent enough to crawl under it. She compressed her body into a thin line and rolled, not in one movement, but inch by cautious inch. A guard walked past her but she clung to a bit of shrubbery and faded into its outline. When the guard had his back turned, she ran for the forest, seeking out and using every deep shadow. Only through years of practice, of dodging her brother Edmund and his "friends," was she able to slip away so silently. Roger had chided her, saying she would make an expert spy.

Once inside the forest, she allowed herself to breathe and used her will to calm her racing heart. Forests at night were no stranger to her and she began walking at a brisk, easy pace. It was amazing how little noise she made.

When the sun rose, Elizabeth had been walking for about two hours, and her pace was beginning to slow. She hadn't eaten in over twenty-four hours, and her energy was flagging. As her feet dragged, her skirt caught on shrubs, branches caught in her hair.

After another hour, she was trembling. She sat on a fallen log and tried to compose herself. Perhaps it was understandable that she didn't have a great deal of strength, since the combination of lack of food and the ordeal of the previous day had taken nearly all of it. The thought of rest made her eyes heavy and she knew that if she didn't, she'd never be able to continue.

Wearily, she lowered herself to the forest floor, ignoring the little crawly things on the underside of the log; it wasn't the first time she'd spent the night in a forest. She made a feeble attempt to cover herself with leaves but was only half finished when she fell back, asleep.

She woke to a sharp poke in the ribs. A big, burly man dressed in little more than rags grinned down at her, one of his front teeth missing. Two other men, filthy men, stood behind him.

"Told you she wasn't dead," the burly man said as he grabbed Elizabeth's arm and pulled her upright.

"Pretty lady," said one of the other men, putting his hand on Elizabeth's shoulder. She went one way and his hand stayed where it was; the dress tore, exposing her shoulder.

"Me first!" gasped the third man.

"A real lady," said the burly man, his hand on Elizabeth's bare shoulder.

"I am Elizabeth Chatworth and if you harm me the Earl of Bayham will have your heads."

" 'Twas a earl that tossed me off my farm," said one man. "Me wife and daughter died of the winter cold. Froze to death." His expression was ugly as he looked at Elizabeth. She would have backed away but the log behind her imprisoned her.

The burly man put his hand to Elizabeth's throat. "I like my women to beg."

"Most men do," she said coolly and the man blinked at her.

"She's a mean one, Bill," said another man. "Let me have her first."

Suddenly, the man's expression changed. He gave a strange gurgle and fell forward onto Elizabeth. Deftly, she sidestepped his falling form and barely gave a look to the arrow protruding from his back. As the two men were gaping at their dead companion, Elizabeth lifted her skirts and leaped over the log.

Out of the forest came Miles. He grabbed Elizabeth's arm and his face made her breath catch. It was contorted with rage, his lips a single line, his eyes black, his brows drawn together, his nostrils flared. "Remain here!" he ordered.

For a moment she obeyed him and because of her hesitation she saw why Miles Montgomery had been awarded his spurs on the field of battle before he was eighteen. The men he faced were not unarmed. One held a spiked ball on a chain and expertly swung it at Miles's head. Miles ducked while wielding his sword at the other man.

Within seconds, he had destroyed both men while barely quickening his own pulse. It did not seem possible that this killer could have washed her hair without so much as creating a single tangle.

Elizabeth didn't waste time contemplating the complexities of her enemy but started running away from the battle area. She knew she could not outrun Miles but she hoped she could outsmart him. At the first low hanging branch, she caught it and swung herself upward.

Within seconds, Miles appeared below her. There was blood on his velvet doublet, blood on his drawn sword. Like a baited bear, he swung his head from side to side, then stopped and listened.

Elizabeth held her breath and didn't make a sound.

After a moment, Miles suddenly turned on his heel and looked up at her. "Come down here, Elizabeth," he said in a deadly voice.

Once, when she was thirteen, this same thing had happened. Then she'd leaped from the tree, straight onto the hideous man pursuing her, knocked him down and before he'd recovered his wind, she escaped. Without another thought, she threw herself onto Miles.

But he did not fall. Instead, he stood steady and held her tightly to him.

"Those men could have killed you," he said, seemingly unaware of her attempt to knock him down. "How did you slip past my guards?"

"Release me!" she demanded, struggling against him, but he held her easily.

"Why didn't you obey me when I told you to wait for me?"

That idiot question stopped her struggles. "Should I have waited for one of those ruffians if he'd commanded me to do so? What's the difference between them and you?"

His eyes showed anger. "Damn you, Elizabeth! What do

you mean that I'm like those scum? Have I harmed you in any way?"

"So you found her," came Sir Guy's voice and there was a hint of amusement in it. "I am Sir Guy Linacre, my lady."

Elizabeth, her hands pushing hard against Miles's shoulders, nodded at Sir Guy. "Are you finished mauling me?" she snapped at Miles.

He released his grip on her so suddenly she almost fell. The quick change of motion was too much for Elizabeth's empty stomach. At once, she put her hand to her forehead and as things grew black, she put out her hand in search of something to steady herself.

It was Sir Guy who caught her and swung her into his arms.

"Do not touch me," she whispered from inside the fog she was experiencing.

As Miles took her from Sir Guy, he said, "At least it isn't *only* me she repulses." When Elizabeth opened her eyes, Miles was giving her a look of disgust. "How long has it been since you've eaten?"

"Not long enough to make me welcome you," she answered tartly.

At that Miles laughed, not one of his little half-smiles but a deep-down laugh, and before Elizabeth could react, he bent his head and kissed her lips soundly. "You are utterly unique, Elizabeth."

She wiped her mouth with the back of her hand so hard she threatened to remove her skin. "Put me down! I am perfectly capable of walking."

"And let you try and run again? No, I think I'll keep you chained to me from now on."

Miles put Elizabeth on his horse before him and together they rode back to the camp.

Chapter 3

SHE WAS surprised to see that the tents had been taken down and mules were packed and ready to leave. Elizabeth wanted to ask where he was taking her but she kept rigid in the saddle, touching Miles as little as she could, refusing to speak to him.

He led the horse away from the waiting men and into the woods, Sir Guy remaining behind. Inside the forest was set a table laden with several steaming dishes. A small, old man hovered over the array, but left when Miles gave a dismissing motion of his hand.

Dismounting, Miles held up his arms for Elizabeth, but she ignored him and slid to the ground without aid. She did this slowly so as not to repeat her ridiculous act of half fainting.

"My cook has prepared a meal for us," Miles said as he took her hand and led her forward.

She jerked from his touch and glanced at the food. Tiny roasted quails lay upon a bed of rice, surrounded by a cream sauce. A platter contained raw oysters. There were sliced hard-cooked eggs in a saffron sauce, sliced salted ham, fish eggs on twice-baked bread, flounder stuffed with onions and nuts, poached pears, cream tarts, a pie oozing blackberries.

After a look of astonishment, Elizabeth turned away. "You travel well."

Miles caught her arm and when he spun her around, Elizabeth again felt dizzy and clutched at a stool at her feet. "The food is for you," he said, helping her to sit down. "I will not allow you to starve yourself further."

"And what will you do?" she asked wearily. "Put hot coals to the bottoms of my feet? Or perhaps you have your own special ways of forcing women to do what you want."

A frown crossed Miles's face, drawing his brows together. He grabbed her upper arms and pulled her to stand before him. "Yes, I do have my own forms of punishment."

Elizabeth had never seen this look of his, with his eyes just this shade of gray, looking as if tiny blue fires burned behind the gray. Bending, he put his lips to her neck, ignoring her when she stiffened and tried to pull away from him.

"Do you have any idea how desirable you are, Elizabeth?" he murmured against her neck. His lips nibbled upward, barely touching her skin, just enough to impart warmth to her, while his right hand played with the shoulder exposed by her torn dress. His fingers moved inward slowly, caressing the top of her breast while his teeth gently touched her earlobe.

"I would like to make love to you, Elizabeth," he whispered, so low that she felt more than heard his words. "I would like to thaw your cool exterior. I'd like to touch and caress every morsel of you, to look at you, to have you look at me with all the desire I feel for you."

Elizabeth had stood quite still during Miles's touching of her and, as always, she felt nothing. He did not truly repulse her as his breath was not foul and he didn't hurt her, but she felt none of the blood-quickening rush the girls in the convent had giggled about.

"If I swear to eat will you stop this?" she asked coolly.

Miles pulled away from her, studied her face for a moment, and Elizabeth prepared herself for the coming abuse. All men, when they found she was not overwhelmed by their lovemaking, responded by calling her many ugly names.

Miles gave her a quiet smile, caressed her cheek one more time, and offered his arm to lead her to the table. Ignoring his arm, she went to the table alone, not allowing Miles to see her confusion.

He served her himself, placing choice tidbits upon an ornate silver plate, and smiled when she ate her first bite.

"And now you are congratulating yourself on having kept me from starving myself," she said. "My brother will thank you for returning me to him in good condition."

"I am not returning you yet," Miles said softly.

Elizabeth refused to allow him to see how he upset her, but continued eating. "Roger will pay you whatever ransom you ask."

"I will take no money from my sister's murderer," Miles said, the sound coming from a closed throat.

She threw the quail leg she was eating to her plate. "You have said this before. I know nothing of your sister!"

Miles turned toward her and his eyes were the color of steel. "Roger Chatworth tried to take the woman who was promised in marriage to my brother Stephen, and when Stephen fought for his bride, your brother attacked his back."

"No!" Elizabeth gasped, standing.

"Stephen bested Chatworth but refused to kill him, and in retaliation, Chatworth kidnapped my sister and, later, Stephen's bride. He raped my sister and, in horror, she cast herself from a window."

"No! No! No!" Elizabeth shouted, her hands over her ears.

Miles stood, grabbed her hands, held them. "Your brother Brian loved my sister and when she killed herself, he released my sister-in-law and brought the body of my sister to us."

"You are a liar! You are evil! Release me!"

Miles drew her closer, held her loosely in his arms. "It's not pleasant to hear that someone you love has done so much wrong."

Elizabeth'd had much experience in getting away from men and Miles'd had no experience in women struggling against his grasp. Quickly, she brought her knee up between his legs and instantly he released her.

"Damn you, Elizabeth," he gasped, leaning against the table, cupping himself.

"Damn you, Montgomery," she shot back as she grabbed

a pitcher of wine and flung it at his head just before she turned to flee.

He ducked the pitcher and caught her arm in the same motion. "You'll not escape me," he said, pulling her toward him. "I'm going to teach you that the Montgomerys are innocent in this feud, even if I have to die proving it."

"The idea of your death is the first pleasant notion I've heard in days."

For a moment Miles closed his eyes as if in a silent prayer for help. He seemed recovered when he looked back at her. "Now, if you have finished eating, we must ride. We are going to Scotland."

"To—!" she began, but he put a finger to her lips.

"Yes, my angel"—his voice was heavy with sarcasm— "we are going to spend time with my brother and his wife. I want you to get to know my family."

"I know more than enough about your family. They are—"

This time, Miles kissed her and, if she did not react to his touch, when she turned away she was silent.

They rode for many hours at a slow, steady pace. The many baggage mules behind them bearing furniture, clothing, food, armor, weapons, made their progress ponderous.

Elizabeth was given her own horse but a rope was tied to the saddle and attached to Miles's horse. Twice he tried to make conversation but she refused to speak to him. Her mind was too busy thinking about, and trying not to think about, what Miles had told her about her brother.

For the last two years the only contact she'd had with her family was through Roger's letters and snatches of gossip from traveling musicians. Of course the musicians were aware she was a Chatworth and so had said little either way about her family.

But the extensive Montgomery family was another matter. They were a favorite subject of songs and gossip. The oldest brother, Gavin, had jilted the beautiful Alice Valence and on the rebound she'd married Elizabeth's brother Edmund. Elizabeth had begged Roger to stop the marriage, saying that the poor woman didn't deserve to be shackled to the treacherous Edmund. Roger said there was nothing he could do to prevent the marriage. Only a few months later, Gavin Montgomery had married the magnificently wealthy Revedoune heiress, and after Edmund's murder, the jealous heiress had tossed boiling oil on poor Alice Chatworth's face. Elizabeth had written from the convent and begged Roger to care for her brother's widow and Roger had quickly agreed.

Less than a year later, Roger had written that the Scottish heiress, Bronwyn MacArran, had pleaded to be allowed to marry Roger but Stephen Montgomery was forcing the poor woman to become his bride. Roger had challenged Stephen in an attempt to protect the MacArran woman, and during the fight, Montgomery had cleverly made it appear that Roger attacked his back. As a result, Roger was disgraced.

She wasn't sure why Brian had left his home; Roger would never say. But she was sure it had to do with the Montgomerys. Brian was sensitive and gentle. Perhaps he could no longer stand all the horrors that had been done to his family because of the Montgomerys. But whatever made Brian leave had nothing to do with the lies she'd heard today. She doubted if Roger even knew the Montgomery men had a sister.

All during the long ride, she'd idly been tucking the torn shoulder of her dress inside the high neckline. When Miles called a halt to the procession, she was startled to see that it was growing dark. Her thoughts had kept her occupied for hours.

Before them was an inn, half timbered, old but prosperous-looking. The landlord stood outside, his big red face split by a welcoming grin.

Miles stood beside her. "Elizabeth"—he held up his arms for her—"do not embarrass yourself by refusing me," he said, a twinkle in his eye as he glanced at her raised foot.

Elizabeth considered for a moment, then allowed him to help her from her horse, but she stepped away from his touch as soon as she was on the ground. Two of his men entered the inn first while Miles caught Elizabeth's arm.

"I have something for you." Watching her closely, he held out a lovely, intricately wrought gold brooch of a pelican, its beak tucked under its outstretched wing, standing on a band of diamonds.

Elizabeth's eyes didn't flicker. "I don't want it."

With a look of exasperation, Miles pinned the shoulder of her gown together. "Come inside, Elizabeth," he said flatly.

Obviously, the innkeeper was expecting them, for the bustle of activity within was enormous. Elizabeth stood to one side as Miles conferred with Sir Guy while the landlord waited for their commands.

It was a large room set with tables and chairs, a big fireplace to one side. For the first time, Elizabeth really looked at Miles's men. There were an even dozen of them and it seemed they gave remarkably little trouble. Now they walked about, opening doors, quietly checking for any hidden danger. Did Miles Montgomery have so many enemies he must always be wary—or was he just cautious?

A pretty young maid curtsied before Miles and he gave her his little half-smile. Elizabeth watched curiously as the maid blushed and preened under Miles's gaze.

"Yes, my lord," she said, smiling, bobbing up and down. "I hope ye like the meal I've cooked."

"I will," Miles said so matter-of-factly that it made his enjoyment seem a sure fact.

With another blush, the girl turned back to the kitchen.

"Are you hungry, Elizabeth?" Miles asked, turning back to her.

"Not for what you seem to inspire." She nodded toward the maid's retreating back.

"How I wish there were jealousy in those words. But I have patience," he added with a smile and gave her a little push toward the table before she could answer.

Miles and she sat at a small table, apart from his men but in the same room. Dish after dish was brought to them but Elizabeth barely ate.

"You don't seem to have a big appetite at best."

"If you were held prisoner would you gorge yourself on your captor's food?"

"I would probably not lose a moment in planning my captor's death," he answered honestly.

Elizabeth glared at him in silence and Miles concentrated on his food.

Halfway through the long, silent meal, Miles caught the hand of one of the maids placing a dish of fresh salmon on the table. As Elizabeth looked up in surprise, she saw that the maid's hands were scratched and raw.

"How have you injured yourself?" Miles asked gently.

"The berry brambles, milord," she answered, half frightened, half fascinated by Miles's attention.

"Landlord!" Miles called. "See that the girl's hands are cared for and she's not to put them in water until they heal."

"But my lord!" the man protested. "She's only a scullery maid. She's serving tonight because my regular girl has the pox."

Sir Guy slowly rose from the head of the table of Miles's retainers, and all that was needed was the size of the giant and the landlord took a step backward.

"Come, girl," the landlord said angrily.

"Thank . . . thank you, my lord." She bobbed a curtsy before she fled the room.

Elizabeth cut herself a slice of French cheese. "Did Sir Guy come to your defense for the girl's sake or his own?"

Miles's expression went from amazement to amusement. He caught her hand and kissed the palm. "Guy doesn't like fights over scullery maids."

"And you do?"

Smiling, he shrugged. "I prefer to avoid fights about anything. I am a peaceful man."

"But you would have fought a fat, congenial landlord over the scratched hands of a worthless girl." It was a statement.

"I do not consider her worthless. Now"—he dismissed the subject—"you must be tired. Would you like to retire?"

Miles's men all bid her goodnight and she nodded toward

them, following Miles and the landlord up the stairs to the single room—and single bed—that awaited them.

"So! You have waited until now to force me to your bed," she said when they were alone. "Perhaps the tent walls were too thin to muffle my cries."

"Elizabeth," he said, taking her hand. "I will sleep on the windowseat and you may have the bed. I cannot allow you to have a room alone because you'd find some way to leave."

"Escape, you mean."

"All right, have it your way, escape. Now come here. I want to talk to you." He pulled her to the windowseat, sat down and pulled her to sit beside him. When he drew her back against his chest, she began to protest.

"Relax, Elizabeth. I will leave my hands here about your waist and not move them, but I'll not let you up until you relax and talk to me."

"I can talk sitting up, away from you."

"But I cannot keep from touching you," he said with feeling. "All the time I want to caress you, to soothe away your hurt."

"I am not hurt." She pushed at his arms holding her to him. He was a large man, tall and broad, and the outward curve of his chest just fit the arch of her back.

"But you are hurt, Elizabeth, probably more than you know."

"Ah yes, I see now. There is something wrong with me because I don't salivate with adoration whenever you are near me."

Miles kissed her neck, chuckling. "Perhaps I deserved that. Hold still or I'll kiss you more." Her abrupt stillness made him wince. "I want you to tell me what you like. Food does not interest you, nor pretty dresses. Gold and diamonds don't even make you blink. Men don't rate a glance from you. What is your weakness?"

"My weakness?" she asked, thinking about it. He was stroking her hair at her temple and in spite of herself, she was beginning to relax. The last two days of tension and anger were draining her strength. His long legs were stretched out on the windowseat and she was between them. "What is your weakness, Montgomery?"

"Women," he murmured, dismissing the question. "Tell me about you."

The muscles in her neck were relaxing and her weight was easing against him. It wasn't a bad feeling to be held so safely by such strong arms when the man wasn't pawing at her, tearing her clothes, hurting her. "I live with my two brothers, both of whom I love and who love me. I am far from being a pauper and I have but to hint at a jewel or gown I'd like and my brother Roger purchases it for me."

"And . . . Roger"—he tripped over the name—"is good to you?"

"He protects me." She smiled and closed her eyes. Miles was massaging the tight muscles in her neck. "Roger has always protected Brian and me."

"Protected you from what?"

From Edmund, she almost said but caught herself. Her eyes flew open and she sat up. "From men!" she spat. "Men have always liked my looks but Roger kept them away from me."

He kept her hands imprisoned. "You know many tricks for repulsing men and you have wrapped yourself in steel. You are obviously a naturally passionate woman, so what has killed your passion? Was it that perhaps Roger was not always near enough to protect you?"

Elizabeth refused to answer him and she cursed her momentary trustfulness. After a while, Miles gave an exaggerated sigh and released her. Immediately she sprang away from him.

"Go to bed," he said tiredly as he stood, turning his back on her.

Elizabeth didn't trust him to keep his word about not sleeping with her, but she would do nothing to entice him. Fully clothed except for her soft leather shoes, she slipped into the big bed.

Miles blew out the single candle and for a long moment stood silhouetted before the moonlit window.

When Elizabeth heard no sounds from him she quietly

"Hush, sweetheart," he whispered, standing, the child clinging to him.

To Sir Guy and the knights, this was a familiar sight, and they waited patiently, with a bored air, while Miles comforted the child. Elizabeth didn't concern herself with Miles. Her one and only thought was for the injured child. She stretched out her arm, put her hand on the back of the crying child's head.

The child pulled her face away from the hollow in Miles's shoulder, and through tear-blurred eyes she looked at Elizabeth. With a fresh burst of tears she lifted her arms and lunged forward into Elizabeth's grasp.

It was difficult to tell who was more astonished: Miles, Sir Guy or the Montgomery knights. Miles gaped at Elizabeth and for a moment his pride took a beating.

"Hush now," Elizabeth said in a gentle voice such as Miles had never heard before. "If you stop crying Sir Guy will give you a ride on his shoulders."

Miles coughed to cover the laugh that threatened to choke him. Between Sir Guy's size and the hideous scar on his face, most people, and especially women, were terrified of him. He'd never seen anyone dare to volunteer the giant to be a child's horse.

"You'll be so tall," Elizabeth continued, swaying with the child, "you'll be able to reach up and catch a star."

The child gave a sniff, pulled away from Elizabeth and looked at her. "A star?" she hiccuped.

Elizabeth caressed the child's wet cheek. "And when you get the star, you can give it to Sir Miles to repay him for the new dress he's going to purchase for you."

The eyes of Miles's men went to their lord to watch his reaction—and no one dared laugh at his look of indignation.

The child sniffed again and twisted to look at Lord Miles. She gave him a smile, but when she looked at Sir Guy she clung to Elizabeth.

"There's no reason to be afraid of him," Elizabeth said. "He likes children very much, don't you, Sir Guy?"

Sir Guy gave Lady Elizabeth a hard, assessing look. "In

truth, my lady, I like children a great deal but they have little use for me."

"We shall remedy that. Now, child, go with Sir Guy for your ride and bring back a star."

The child, a bit hesitant at first, went to Sir Guy and clung to his head when he set her on his shoulders. "I'm the tallest girl in the world," she squealed as Sir Guy walked away with her.

"I've never seen you smile before," Miles said.

Elizabeth's smile disappeared instantly. "I will reimburse you for the child's dress when I am home again." She turned away.

Miles caught her hand and led her away from his men's listening ears. "The child was only a beggar's."

"Oh?" she said offhandedly. "I thought perhaps she was one of yours."

"Mine?" he asked, bewildered. "Do you think I'd allow one of my children to run about in rags, with no supervision?"

She turned on him. "And how do you know where all your children are? Do you keep ledgers full of their names? Their whereabouts?"

Miles's face showed several emotions: disbelief, some anger, amusement. "Elizabeth, how many children do you think I have?"

She put her chin into the air. "I neither know nor care how many bastards you have."

He caught her arm, turning her to face him. "Even my own brothers exaggerate about my children so why should I expect more from outsiders? I have three sons: Christopher, Philip and James. And any day I expect to hear word of another child of mine. I am hoping for a daughter this time."

"You are hoping—" she gasped. "It doesn't bother you about their mothers? That you use the women, then discard them? And what of the children? They must grow up with the label of bastard! Outcasts because of some hideous man's one moment of pleasure."

His grip tightened on her arm and there was anger in his eyes. "I do not 'use' women," he said through clenched teeth.

"The women who have given me children came to me freely. And all my children live with me, are cared for by competent nurses."

"Nurses!" She tried to pull away from him, but couldn't. "Do you toss the children's mothers into the street? Or do you give them a little money like you did Bridget and send them on their ways?"

"Bridget?" Miles searched her face for a moment. His rising temper calmed. "I assume you mean the Bridget who is the mother of my James?" He didn't wait for her answer. "I will tell you the truth about Bridget. My brother Gavin sent a message to St. Catherine's convent to ask for some serving girls. He wanted girls of good reputation who wouldn't be tantalizing his men and causing fights. From the moment this Bridget entered our house she pursued me."

Elizabeth tried to pull away from him. "You are a liar."

Miles caught her other arm with his hand. "Once she told me that she'd heard so much about me that she felt like a child who'd been told not to play with fire. One night I found her in my bed."

"And you took her."

"I made love to her, yes, that night and several other nights. When she realized she was going to have my child, I took a lot of ribbing from my brothers."

"And you cast her out—after you took her child away, that is."

He gave her a small smile. "Actually, she cast me aside. I was away for four months and she fell in love with Gavin's second gardener. When I returned I talked with them, told them I'd like to have the child and would raise him to be a knight. Bridget agreed readily."

"And how much money did you give them? Surely you must have offered some consolation to a mother giving up her child."

Miles released her arms, glaring at her. "Did you know Bridget very well? If you did you'd know she was more interested in her pleasures than motherhood. The gardener she was marrying didn't want Bridget or the child and later he asked for money for 'what he was giving up.' I gave him nothing. James is mine."

She was silent for a moment. "And what of your other children's mothers?" she asked quietly.

He walked away from her. "I fell in love with the younger sister of one of Gavin's men when I was just a boy. Christopher was born when both Margaret and I were only sixteen. I would have married her but her brother sent her away. I didn't know about Kit until Margaret died of smallpox a month after Kit's birth."

He looked back at Elizabeth and grinned. "Philip's mother was a dancer, an exotic creature who shared my bed for two"—he sighed—"two very interesting weeks. Then nine months later she sent a messenger with Philip. I've never seen or heard from her since."

Elizabeth was fascinated with his stories. "And this new child?"

Miles ducked his head and if he'd been a woman she would have thought he blushed. "I'm afraid this child may cause some problems. The mother is a distant cousin of mine. I resisted her as long as I could but . . ." He shrugged. "Her father is very angry with me. He says he'll send the child to me but . . . I'm not sure he will."

Elizabeth could only shake her head at him in disbelief. "Surely there must be other children." Her voice was sarcastic.

He frowned slightly. "I don't think so. I try to keep track of my women now and watch for children."

"Rather like gathering eggs," she said, eyes wide.

Miles cocked his head to one side and gave her an intense look. "One moment you condemn me for leaving my children in rags, strewn about the country like so much refuse, and now you damn me for caring for them. I am not a celibate man nor do I intend to be, but I take my responsibilities seriously. I love my children and I provide for them. I should like to have fifty of them."

"You have a good start," she said, sweeping past him.

Miles stood still, watching her walk back toward his men

and the horses. She stood a little apart from the men, with that stiff-backed carriage of hers. She wasn't like either of his sisters-in-law, used to authority, at ease with the people who worked for them. Elizabeth Chatworth was rigid whenever she was near men. Yesterday, by accident, one of his men on horseback had brushed against her and Elizabeth had reacted so sharply, pulling her horse's reins so unexpectedly, that her horse had reared. She'd controlled the animal and held her seat but the experience had disgusted Miles. No woman—or man for that matter—should be so frightened of another human's touch.

Sir Guy returned, alone, to the men and at once he searched for Miles, walking toward him when he saw him. "It's getting late. We should ride." He paused. "Or perhaps you've reconsidered about returning the lady to her brother."

Miles was watching Elizabeth, who was now talking to the mother and the little girl who'd fallen earlier. He turned back to Guy. "I want you to send a couple of men to my northern estate. They are to bring Kit to me."

"Your son?" Sir Guy questioned.

"Yes, my son. Send his nurse with him. No! On second thought, bring him alone but with a heavy guard. Lady Elizabeth will be his nurse."

"Are you sure of what you're doing?" Sir Guy asked.

"The Lady Elizabeth likes children so I will share one of mine with her. If I can't reach her heart one way, I will use another."

"And what will you do with this woman once you've tamed her? Once, when I was a boy, there was a cat that had lived wild and it claimed the area around a certain shed as its own. Whenever anyone went near the shed, the cat scratched and bit. I set myself the job of taming it. It took many weeks of patience to gain the cat's trust but I felt triumphant when it began to eat from my hand. But later the cat began to follow me everywhere. I tripped over it constantly and it became a major nuisance. After several months I was kicking the cat, hating it because it was no longer the wild thing I'd loved at first, but only another cat, just like all the others."

Miles continued to study Elizabeth. "Perhaps it *is* the chase," he said quietly. "Or perhaps I'm like my brother Raine, who can't stand any injustice. All I know now is that Elizabeth Chatworth fascinates me. Maybe I do want to have her eat from my hand—but maybe when she does, it will be because I'm her slave."

He turned back to Sir Guy. "Elizabeth will like Kit and my son can only benefit from knowing her. And I'd like to see my son as well. Send the message."

Sir Guy nodded once in agreement before leaving Miles alone.

Minutes later they were mounted and ready to leave. Miles didn't try to talk to Elizabeth but silently rode beside her. She was beginning to look tired and by midday, he was of half a mind to return her to her brother.

A half-hour later, she suddenly sprang to life. While Miles had been feeling sorry for her, she'd worked loose the rope attaching their horses. She kicked her horse forward, used the loose end of her reins to slap the rumps of two horses in front of her, and with the rearing horses as a shield, she gained precious seconds to escape. She was half a mile down the rutted, weed-infested road before Miles could get around his men and follow her.

"I will bring her back," he shouted over his shoulder to Sir Guy.

Miles knew the horse Elizabeth rode had little speed in it but she got what she could out of it. He was close enough to catch her when the girth of his saddle slipped and he was sent sliding to one side. "Damn her," he gasped, knowing very well who'd loosened the saddle, but, at the same time, he smiled at her ingenuity.

But Elizabeth Chatworth wasn't prepared for a man who'd grown up with three older brothers. Miles was used to practical jokes such as loosened cinches and he knew how to handle them. Expertly, he shifted his weight to the front of the horse, in essence riding bareback but sitting on the horse's neck, the saddle behind him.

now and then and I've been drunk before, but I like willing women in my bed. Now, let's get you out of this dress."

She jerked away from him, her eyes hostile.

"I plan to sleep on that cold, hard, lonely cot but I think you must be sick of that gown. You'd be more comfortable sleeping without it."

"I am more comfortable *in* my clothes, thank you."

"All right, have your own way." He turned away and began to undress while Elizabeth fled to the protection of her bed.

The single candle was still burning and when Miles wore only his loincloth, he bent over her, pulling the blanket from over her face. She lay stiff, rigid, while he sat on the edge of the bed, his hand caressing the hair at her temple. Not speaking, he simply looked at her, enjoying the feel of her skin.

"Goodnight, Elizabeth," he whispered as he planted a soft kiss on her lips.

Her hand shot out to wipe it away but he caught her wrist. "What would it take to make you love a man?" he murmured.

"I don't think I could," she replied honestly. "At least not as you mean."

"I'm beginning to think I want to test that. Goodnight, my fragile angel."

He kissed her again before she could protest that she was far from fragile, but this time she was able to wipe the kiss away.

Miles continued to study Elizabeth. "Perhaps it *is* the chase," he said quietly. "Or perhaps I'm like my brother Raine, who can't stand any injustice. All I know now is that Elizabeth Chatworth fascinates me. Maybe I do want to have her eat from my hand—but maybe when she does, it will be because I'm her slave."

He turned back to Sir Guy. "Elizabeth will like Kit and my son can only benefit from knowing her. And I'd like to see my son as well. Send the message."

Sir Guy nodded once in agreement before leaving Miles alone.

Minutes later they were mounted and ready to leave. Miles didn't try to talk to Elizabeth but silently rode beside her. She was beginning to look tired and by midday, he was of half a mind to return her to her brother.

A half-hour later, she suddenly sprang to life. While Miles had been feeling sorry for her, she'd worked loose the rope attaching their horses. She kicked her horse forward, used the loose end of her reins to slap the rumps of two horses in front of her, and with the rearing horses as a shield, she gained precious seconds to escape. She was half a mile down the rutted, weed-infested road before Miles could get around his men and follow her.

"I will bring her back," he shouted over his shoulder to Sir Guy.

Miles knew the horse Elizabeth rode had little speed in it but she got what she could out of it. He was close enough to catch her when the girth of his saddle slipped and he was sent sliding to one side. "Damn her," he gasped, knowing very well who'd loosened the saddle, but, at the same time, he smiled at her ingenuity.

But Elizabeth Chatworth wasn't prepared for a man who'd grown up with three older brothers. Miles was used to practical jokes such as loosened cinches and he knew how to handle them. Expertly, he shifted his weight to the front of the horse, in essence riding bareback but sitting on the horse's neck, the saddle behind him.

He lost some speed when the horse threatened to revolt at this new position, but Miles controlled the animal.

Elizabeth turned her mount into a corn field when the primitive road disappeared and she was disconcerted to see Miles close on her heels.

He caught her in the corn field, grabbing her about the waist. She fought him wildly and Miles, with no stirrups to anchor himself, started falling. When he went down his arm was still fastened around Elizabeth's waist.

As they both fell, Miles twisted and took most of the jolt, cushioning Elizabeth, putting his arm up to protect her back from a flying hoof. The horses ran for a few more feet then stood, sides heaving.

"Release me," Elizabeth demanded when she caught her breath. She was sprawled on top of Miles.

His arms held her to him. "When did you loosen the cinch?" When she didn't answer he hugged her until her ribs threatened to break.

"At dinner," she gasped.

He moved his hand to the back of her head, forcing it to his shoulder. "Elizabeth, you are so clever. How did you manage to sneak past my men? When did you leave my sight?"

His neck was sweaty and his heart was pounding against her own. The exercise had done away with her tiredness and she was glad for it even if she hadn't succeeded in her escape.

"You gave me a good run," he said, amused. "If my brothers hadn't thought it a great joke to send me out with a loosened cinch, I wouldn't have known how to handle it. Of course *they* were careful that I was on a slow mount so if I fell I wouldn't kill myself." He moved to look at her face. "Would you have been terribly glad to see me break my neck?"

"Yes, very," she said, smiling, practically nose to nose with him.

Miles laughed at that, kissed her quickly, pushed her off him and stood, frowning as she wiped the back of her hand across her mouth. "Come on, there's an inn not far from here and we'll stop for the night." He didn't offer to help her up.

When they returned to the men, Sir Guy gave Elizabeth a quick look of admiration and she guessed that he'd be more vigilant from now on. She wouldn't have more chances to toy with the men's gear.

It wasn't until they were mounted again that Elizabeth saw that Miles's forearm was cut and bleeding. She knew it had happened when he'd put his arm between her and the horse's hoof. Sir Guy inspected the cut and bound it while Elizabeth sat on her horse and watched. It seemed odd that this man, a Montgomery, would protect a Chatworth from harm.

Miles saw her watching. "A smile from you, Elizabeth, would make it heal faster."

"I hope it poisons your blood and you lose your arm." She kicked her horse forward.

They didn't speak again until they arrived at the inn at which, as before, Miles had sent someone ahead to prepare for them. This time, Miles and Elizabeth were given a private dining room.

"Tell me more about your family," he said.

"No," she answered simply, reaching for a dish of snails in garlic sauce.

"Then I will tell you of mine. I have three older brothers and—"

"I know about them. You and your brothers are notorious."

He raised one eyebrow at her. "Tell me what you've heard."

"With pleasure." She cut into a beef and chicken pie. "Your brother Gavin is the eldest. He was to marry Alice Valence but he rejected her so he could marry the rich Judith Revedoune, who is a vicious-tempered woman. Between your brother and his wife they succeeded in driving Alice—now Chatworth—insane."

"Do you know your sister-in-law?"

Elizabeth studied the food on her plate. "She wasn't always as she is now."

"The bitch was born a whore. She rejected my brother. Now, tell me of Stephen."

"He forced a woman who wanted my brother to be his bride."

"And Raine?"

"I know little of the man, except that he's magnificent on a battlefield."

Miles's eyes burned into hers. "After your brother raped my sister and Mary killed herself, Raine led some of the king's men to attack your brother Roger. The king has declared Raine a traitor and my brother lives in a forest with a band of criminals." He paused. "And what of me?"

"You are a lecher, a seducer of young girls."

"I am flattered that my virility is so overrated. Now let me tell you the truth about my family. Gavin had to take over the raising of three brothers and the managing of estates when he was but sixteen. He barely had time to find out about women. He fell in love with Alice Valence, begged her to marry him, but she refused. He married Judith Revedoune and only after a long while did he realize he loved Judith. Alice tried to scar Judith with hot oil but Alice was the one scarred."

"You lie constantly," Elizabeth said.

"No, I do not lie. Stephen is the peacemaker in our family and he and Gavin are close. And Raine—" He paused and smiled. "Raine believes the world's burdens rest upon his big shoulders. He is a good man but unbelievably stubborn."

"And you?" Elizabeth asked softly.

He took his time answering. "I am alone. My brothers seem so sure of what they want. Gavin loves the land, Stephen is a crusader about his Scots, Raine wants to change the world, but I . . ."

She looked up at him and for a moment there was a silent exchange. She too had felt alone in her life. Edmund was evil, Roger was always angry and she'd spent her life escaping Edmund and his friends while trying to protect Brian.

Miles took her hand in his and she didn't pull away. "You

and I have had to grow up quickly. Do you remember being a child?"

"All too well," she said flatly, pulling her hand away.

For a while they ate in silence. "Was your home . . . happy?" she asked, as if it didn't matter.

"Yes." He smiled. "Each of us was fostered but we still spent a great deal of time together. It's not easy being the youngest son. You get knocked about a bit. And were you happy?"

"No. I was too busy running from Edmund to think of anything as silly as happiness. I would like to retire now."

Miles followed her to their room and she saw that tonight a cot had been set along one wall.

"No windowseat," he said cheerfully, but Elizabeth didn't laugh. He took both her hands in his. "When are you going to trust me? I am not like Edmund or Pagnell or any other of the disgusting men you know."

"You are holding me prisoner. Do men as good as you think you are hold innocent women captive?"

He kissed her hands. "But if I returned you to your brother, what would you do? Would you wait for Roger to find you a husband and then happily settle down to wedded bliss?"

She pulled away from him. "Roger has given me permission to never marry. I have considered taking vows of the church."

Miles gave her a look of horror. Before she could protest, he pulled her into his arms, stroked her back. "You have so much love to give. How could you think to hide it? Wouldn't you like to have children, to watch them grow? There's nothing like a child looking at you with complete adoration and trust."

She lifted her head from his shoulder. She was growing almost used to his touching and holding of her. "I've never before met a man who loved children. All the men I know care only for fighting, drinking, raping women."

"There's something to be said for a good rousing fight

now and then and I've been drunk before, but I like willing women in my bed. Now, let's get you out of this dress."

She jerked away from him, her eyes hostile.

"I plan to sleep on that cold, hard, lonely cot but I think you must be sick of that gown. You'd be more comfortable sleeping without it."

"I am more comfortable *in* my clothes, thank you."

"All right, have your own way." He turned away and began to undress while Elizabeth fled to the protection of her bed.

The single candle was still burning and when Miles wore only his loincloth, he bent over her, pulling the blanket from over her face. She lay stiff, rigid, while he sat on the edge of the bed, his hand caressing the hair at her temple. Not speaking, he simply looked at her, enjoying the feel of her skin.

"Goodnight, Elizabeth," he whispered as he planted a soft kiss on her lips.

Her hand shot out to wipe it away but he caught her wrist. "What would it take to make you love a man?" he murmured.

"I don't think I could," she replied honestly. "At least not as you mean."

"I'm beginning to think I want to test that. Goodnight, my fragile angel."

He kissed her again before she could protest that she was far from fragile, but this time she was able to wipe the kiss away.

Chapter 5

MILES, ELIZABETH, Sir Guy and the Montgomery knights traveled for two more days before reaching the southern border of Scotland. Elizabeth tried once more to escape—at night while Miles slept close to her—but she didn't reach the door before he caught her and led her back to bed.

Elizabeth lay awake a long time after that, thinking about how she was a prisoner and yet not a prisoner. She had never been treated with as much courtesy as Miles Montgomery treated her. He did insist upon touching her at every opportunity but she was growing used to that. It certainly was no pleasure but it was no longer as vile as it'd seemed at first. Once, at an inn where they'd stopped for dinner, a drunk had fallen toward Elizabeth and, as a reflex, she'd stepped nearer to Miles for protection. He had been inordinately pleased by that.

Today he'd told her that from now on they'd be using his tent as the inns were not as abundant in Scotland. He hinted that once they crossed the mountains, there could be trouble since the Highlanders didn't like the English.

All through supper, he'd seemed preoccupied and had conferred with Sir Guy several times.

"Are the Scots as bloodthirsty as all this?" she asked after he'd left the supper table the second time.

He didn't seem to understand what she was talking about. "I'm meeting someone here and he's late. He should have been here by now."

"One of your brothers—or is it a woman?"

"Neither," he said quickly.

Elizabeth asked no more questions. As she crawled into her bed, wearing the same dress Miles had given her, she turned to her side to watch him on his cot. He tossed and turned every moment.

When a loud knock came on the door, Elizabeth sprang out of bed almost as quickly as Miles. Sir Guy entered, a little boy behind him.

"Kit!" Miles cried, grabbing the child, hugging him fit to crush him. The boy didn't seem to mind as he also clung to Miles.

"What took them so long?" Miles asked Sir Guy.

"They were caught in a rainstorm and lost three horses."

"No men?"

"Everyone was saved but it took a while to replace the horses. Young master Kit held onto his saddle when two knights couldn't," Sir Guy said with pride.

"Is that true?" Miles asked, turning the boy around.

Elizabeth saw a small replica of Miles but with brown eyes instead of gray, a handsome boy, his face solemn.

"Yes, Papa," Kit answered. "Uncle Gavin said that a knight always stays with his horse. Afterward, I helped the men pull the baggage from the water."

"You're a good boy." Miles grinned, hugging Kit once again. "You may go, Guy, and see that the men are fed. We'll leave first thing in the morning."

Kit smiled goodbye to Sir Guy, then whispered loudly to his father. "Who is she?"

Miles stood Kit on the floor. "Lady Elizabeth," he said formally, "may I present Christopher Gavin Montgomery."

"How do you do?" she said, taking the child's extended hand. "I am Lady Elizabeth Chatworth."

"You are very pretty," he said. "My papa likes pretty women."

"Kit—" Miles began, but Elizabeth interrupted him.

"Do you like pretty women?" she asked.

"Oh yes. My nurse is very, very pretty."

"I'm sure she is if your father hired her. Are you hungry? Tired?"

"I ate a whole sackful of sugared plums," Kit said with pride. "Oh Papa! I have a message for you. It's from someone named Simon."

A frown crossed Miles's face, but as he read the message he broke into a grin.

"Good news?" Elizabeth asked, not able to hide her curiosity.

Miles sobered himself as he tossed the note to his rumpled cot. "Yes and no. My cousin has been delivered of my daughter but my Uncle Simon is threatening my life."

Elizabeth wasn't sure whether to laugh or be disgusted. "You have a little sister, Kit," she said at last.

"I have two brothers already. I don't want a sister."

"I believe your father makes those decisions. It's late and I think you should be in bed."

"Kit can take the cot and I'll . . ." Miles began, eyes twinkling.

"Kit will sleep with me," Elizabeth said loftily, offering her hand to the child.

Kit accepted readily and he yawned as she led him around the bed.

Miles watched, smiling a bit triumphantly, as Elizabeth undressed the sleepy little boy down to his underwear. He readily went into her arms as she lifted him into bed. Elizabeth crawled in beside him, pulled Kit to her.

For a moment Miles stood to one side, watching them. With a smile, he bent and kissed both foreheads. "Goodnight," he whispered before going to his cot.

During the next day, it didn't take Miles long to see that Elizabeth's interest extended only to Kit. And the child took to Elizabeth as if he'd known her forever. All Elizabeth would say was, "I have always liked children and they seem to know this." Whatever the reason, Kit seemed perfectly at ease with Elizabeth. In the afternoon, he rode with her, fell asleep against her. When Miles suggested he take the heavy child, Elizabeth practically snarled at him.

At night they curled up with each other on a single cot and slept peacefully. Miles looked down at them and felt like an outsider.

They traveled for three more days and Elizabeth knew they must be getting close to the MacArrans' land. Miles had been in deep thought all day and twice she'd seen him arguing with Sir Guy. From the frown on Sir Guy's face, Miles was obviously planning something the giant didn't like. But whenever Elizabeth got within hearing distance the men stopped talking.

At midday Miles stopped the entourage of men and mules and asked if she and Kit would like to dine with him. Usually they all ate together, within sight and protection of each other.

"You seem pleased with yourself about something," Elizabeth said, watching him.

"We're within a day's ride of my brother and his wife," Miles said happily, lifting Kit from Elizabeth's horse.

"Uncle Stephen wears a skirt and Lady Bronwyn can ride a horse as fast as the wind," Kit informed her.

"Stephen wears a plaid," Miles amended as he pulled Elizabeth from her horse, ignoring her attempts to brush his hands away. "My cook has laid a meal for us inside the forest."

Kit took Elizabeth's hand and Miles held the child on the other side and together they walked into the forest.

"What do you think of Scotland?" Miles asked as he held her arm as she stepped over a fallen log.

"It's as if the place has been untouched since the beginning of time. It's very rough and . . . untrimmed."

"Rather like its people." Miles laughed. "My brother has let his hair grow to his shoulders and his clothing . . . no, I'll let you see for yourself."

"Aren't we going a bit far from your men?" The primitive forest closed around them and the undergrowth was making it more difficult to walk.

Miles drew an ax from where it was slung across his back and began to hack away a wider path.

With a look of puzzlement, Elizabeth turned to him. He

was wearing somber clothes of dark green, a brown cloak about his shoulders—and he was heavily armed. There was a longbow with a quiver of arrows on his back, as well as the ax, his sword on his hip and a dagger at his waist. "Something is wrong, isn't it?"

"Yes," he said, looking about her. "The truth is, Elizabeth, I was given a message to meet someone here, but we've gone too far."

She raised one eyebrow. "You would risk your son's life in this secret meeting?"

He slipped his ax back into its sheath. "My men are all around us. I wanted you close to me rather than leave you and Kit with any of my men."

"Look, Papa!" Kit said excitedly. "There's a deer."

"Shall we go and see the deer?" she said calmly. "Run ahead of us and we'll catch you." Keeping Kit in her sight, she turned to Miles. "I will stay with Kit and you go look for your men. I feel there's been some trick to separate us."

Miles's eyes widened at her ordering of him, but within moments he disappeared into the forest while Elizabeth hurried after Kit. When Miles seemed to take forever before he returned, she looked about with anxious eyes.

"Are you unhappy, Elizabeth?" Kit asked, catching her hand.

She knelt to his level. "I was just wondering where your father is."

"He will return," Kit said confidently. "My papa will take care of us."

Elizabeth tried not to show her disbelief. "I am sure he will. I hear a stream in that direction. Shall we find it?"

They had some trouble breaking through the underbrush but they made it to the stream. It was a wild, rushing body of water, cascading angrily over rocks, tearing at the rocky shore.

"It's cold," Kit said, stepping back. "Do you think there are any fish in it?"

"Salmon, most likely," said Miles from behind Elizabeth,

and she jumped. Miles put his arm about her shoulders. "I didn't mean to frighten you."

She stepped away from him. "What about your men?"

He gave a look to Kit who was throwing forest debris into the water and watching it being swept away. He took her hands in his. "My men are gone. There's no sign of them. Elizabeth, you won't panic, will you?"

She looked into his eyes. She was frightened to be in a strange land with a child and this man she didn't trust. "No," she said firmly. "I don't want to frighten Kit."

"Good." He smiled, squeezing her hands. "We are on the southern boundaries of MacArran land now and if we walk due north we should reach some of the crofters' cottages by evening tomorrow."

"But if someone has spirited away your men—"

"My concern now is for you and Kit. If we stay in the forest perhaps we can escape notice. I don't mind a fight, but I don't want you or Kit harmed. Will you help me?"

She didn't pull away from his hands. "Yes," she said softly. "I'll help you."

He released one of her hands. "These mountains are cold even in the summer. Put this around you." He held up a large piece of woolen fabric woven in a deep blue and green tartan.

"Where did you get this?"

"This was all that was left of the meal my cook left. The food was gone but the cloth he spread it on, one of the plaids Bronwyn gave me, was left behind. We'll need this tonight." He kept her hand clasped tightly as she tossed the plaid over her arm and they walked toward Kit.

"Would you like to walk to Uncle Stephen's house?" Miles asked his son.

Kit gave his father a shrewd look. "Where is Sir Guy? A knight doesn't walk."

"A knight does what is necessary to protect his women."

Between the two males passed a long look. Kit might be only four years old but he'd known since birth that he was to be a knight. He'd been given a wooden sword at two and all the stories he'd heard were of chivalry and knighthood. Kit took Elizabeth's hand. "We will protect you, my lady," he said formally and kissed her hand.

Miles touched his son's shoulder in pride. "Now, Kit, run ahead and see what game you can find us. Even a rabbit or two will do."

"Yes, Papa." He grinned and scurried away along the side of the stream.

"Should you let him out of our sight?"

"He won't be. Kit has more sense than to stray too far."

"You seem little concerned about the loss of your men. Were there signs of a battle?"

"None." He seemed to dismiss the subject as he stooped, plucked a delicate yellow wildflower and slipped it behind her ear. "You look as if you belong in this wild place with your hair down, your torn dress held together with diamonds. I wouldn't mind giving you many diamonds, Elizabeth."

"I would prefer freedom."

He stepped away from her. "You are no longer my prisoner, Elizabeth Chatworth," he declared. "You may leave my presence forever."

She looked about the wild, rough forest. "You are very clever, Montgomery," she said with disgust.

"I take it that means you'll stay with me," he said, eyes twinkling, and before she could answer he lifted her, swirled her about in his arms, planting a kiss on her cheek.

"Release me," she said but there was a hint of a smile about her lips.

He nuzzled her earlobe. "I think you could have me at your feet if you so wished," he whispered.

"Bound and gagged, I'd hope," she retorted, pushing away from him. "Now, do you plan to feed us or do you carry that bow only because it looks good?"

"Papa!" Kit yelled before Miles could answer. "I saw a rabbit!"

"I'm sure it's waiting for me to come and slaughter it," Miles said under his breath as Kit came thrashing toward them.

A sound from Elizabeth that could only be described as a giggle made Miles turn an astonished face toward her.

Elizabeth refused to look at him. "Where is the rabbit, Kit? Your brave father will face the animal, and perhaps we'll get some supper, if not dinner."

After an hour of walking, with Miles seeming more concerned with toying with Elizabeth's fingers, they saw no more rabbits. It was later than she'd thought and it was growing dark—or perhaps the forest just seemed dark.

"We'll camp here for the night. Kit, gather firewood." When the child was gone, Miles turned to Elizabeth. "Don't let him out of your sight. I'll find us some game." With that he slipped away into the forest.

As soon as Miles was gone, Elizabeth began to feel the isolation of the forest. She followed Kit, loading her arms with dry branches. She hadn't noticed it before, but she felt as if eyes were watching her. In her brother's house she'd learned to develop a sixth sense about men who hid in corners, ready to pounce on her.

"Are you frightened, Elizabeth?" Kit asked, his eyes wide.

"Of course not." She forced a smile but she kept remembering all the stories she'd heard about the savagery of the Scots. They were wild people, torturers of little children.

"My papa will protect you," Kit said. "He was given his spurs when he was just a boy. My Uncle Raine says Papa is one of the greatest knights in England. He won't let anyone get you."

She pulled the boy into her arms. "Your papa is indeed a great fighter. Did you know that three men attacked me a few days ago? Your papa slew them in minutes and he wasn't even hurt." For all the child's bravado, Elizabeth could see that he was frightened. "I think your papa could fight off all the men of Scotland. There's no one anywhere who is as brave and strong as your papa."

A low chuckle made Elizabeth look around to see Miles holding two dead rabbits by their ears. "I thank you for the tribute, my lady."

"Elizabeth was scared," Kit explained.

"And you were right to comfort her. We must always protect our women. Would it be possible that you'd know how to skin rabbits, Elizabeth?"

She lowered Kit and took the rabbits with an air of confidence. "You'll find that a Chatworth is no Montgomery lady to sit about on satin cushions and wait for the servants to bring her food."

"You've described Stephen and Gavin's wives perfectly. Come, Kit, let's see if the Montgomery men can be useful."

In a very short time, Miles and Kit had a fire going and Elizabeth had the rabbits skinned and skewered. Miles used his ax to drive stakes into the ground and set up a turnspit for the rabbits. Leaning back on his elbows, Miles idly watched the fire while Kit turned the meat.

"You seem very relaxed," Elizabeth said, frowning, keeping her voice low. "We're unprotected in a strange land, yet you build a fire. We can be seen for miles."

He tugged on her skirt until she sat down, a few feet from him. "This land belongs to my brother and his wife, and if the MacArrans see us they'll recognize the Montgomery leopards on my cloak. The Scots rarely kill women and children outright. You'll be delivered to Stephen and all you'll have to do is explain who you are."

"But what has happened to your men?"

"Elizabeth, my men are gone with no trace of a fight. I would imagine they were escorted to Larenston, Bronwyn's castle. Right now my concern is for the safety of you and Kit. When we reach Larenston and my men aren't there, then I'll worry. Kit! You're allowing the meat to burn on one side."

He moved closer to her. "Elizabeth, you're as safe as you can be. I've scouted this area and seen no one. You're cold," he said when she shivered. He took the plaid from the ground behind her, pulled it around both their shoulders and drew her toward him.

"It's only for warmth," he said when she struggled against him, and refused to loosen his grip.

"I've heard that before!" she snapped. "The warmth is only the beginning. Do you enjoy forcing me?"

"I do not enjoy your hints that I'm like one of your brother's slimy friends," he snapped.

Elizabeth stopped struggling. "Perhaps life with Edmund *has* distorted my thinking a bit, but I don't like to be pawed."

"You've made that clear enough, but if we're to survive the night I think we need each other's warmth. Kit, break off a leg. It looks done to me."

The rabbits were barely cooked inside, charred outside, but the three of them were too hungry to care.

"I like it, Papa," Kit said. "I like it here in the forest."

"It's awfully cold," Elizabeth said, huddled in the plaid. "If this is summer, what is winter like in Scotland?"

"Bronwyn thinks England is hot. In the winter she wraps herself in one of those plaids and sleeps on the snow."

"No!" Elizabeth breathed. "Is she truly such a barbarian?"

Smiling, Miles turned to his son, saw his eyes drooping.

"Come lay down beside me," Elizabeth said and Kit went to her.

Miles spread his cloak, motioned for Elizabeth and Kit to lie on it, covered them with the plaid. After tossing more wood on the fire, he lifted the plaid and crawled in beside Kit.

"You can't—" she began but stopped. There was nowhere else for him to sleep. Between them, Kit's sleeping body kept them warm. Elizabeth was very aware of Miles so close to her, but instead of frightening her his presence was reassuring.

With her head propped on her arm, she watched the fire. "What was Kit's mother like?" she asked softly. "Did she fall in love with you the first time she saw you in your armor?"

Miles gave a snort of laughter. "Margaret Sidney turned up her pretty little nose at me and refused to speak to me. I did everything I could to try and impress her. Once, when she came to the training field to bring water to her father, I turned to look at her, lost my stirrup and Raine hit me in the side with his lance. I still have the scar."

"But I thought—"

"You thought that I'd sold my soul to the devil and as a result I could have any woman I wanted."

"I had heard that story," she said evenly, not looking at him.

He caught her free hand from Kit's side, kissed her fingertips. "The devil hasn't made an offer for my soul, but if he did, I might think about it."

"You blaspheme!" she said, pulling her hand away. She was quiet for a moment. "But your Margaret Sidney changed her mind."

"She was sixteen and so very beautiful and so in love with Gavin at the time. She wanted nothing to do with a boy like me."

"And what changed her mind?"

He grinned broadly. "I persisted."

Elizabeth stiffened. "And when you got her, how did you celebrate?"

"By asking her to marry me," Miles shot back. "I told you I loved her."

"You give your love lightly. Why didn't Bridget marry you or this cousin who just bore your daughter?"

He was quiet for several moments. "I have loved only one woman; I have made love to many women. I have asked only Kit's mother to marry me and when I ask again, it will be because I love the woman."

"I pity her." Elizabeth sighed. "She will have to put up with your bastards being presented, two and three a year."

"You don't seem to mind this child of mine, and you held the girl at the inn when you thought she was mine."

"But I, happily, am not married to you."

Miles's voice lowered. "If you were my wife, would you mind receiving new children every few months?"

"I wouldn't blame your four children for your past transgressions, but if I should marry any man, which I will not do, and if my husband humiliated me by impregnating every servant girl in England, I believe that I would arrange his death."

"Fair enough," Miles said, an undertone of amusement in his voice. He turned on his side, put his arm over Kit, around Elizabeth's shoulders, and drew both of them to him. "Goodnight, my angel," he whispered and was asleep.

Chapter 6

MILES WAS awakened by Kit's foot in his ribs as the boy painfully climbed over his father. "Be very quiet, Papa," Kit whispered loudly and juicily in the vicinity of Miles's ear. "Don't wake Elizabeth." With that he was over his father and running into the dim forest.

Miles watched his son and rubbed his bruised ribcage.

"Will you live?" Elizabeth asked laughingly from beside him.

He turned and their eyes met. Elizabeth's hair was spread about her and her face was sleep softened. He'd not realized how stern a control she kept on herself. Cautiously, smiling slightly, he moved his hand from her shoulder to her cheek, gently caressed the outline of her jaw.

His breath held when she didn't pull away. It was as if she were a wild animal he was trying to tame and he must move very slowly so as not to frighten her away.

Elizabeth watched Miles, felt his hand on her face with a sense of wonder. His eyes were liquid, his lips full and soft. She'd never allowed a man to touch her before and never wondered what it would be like to feel a man's caress. But now she lay stretched out, facing Miles Montgomery, only inches separating their bodies, and she wondered what it would feel like to touch him. There was a dark growth of beard on his cheeks, emphasizing the sharp cut of them. A curl of dark hair touched his ear.

As if reading her thoughts, Miles lifted Elizabeth's hand, placed it on his cheek. She let it rest there for a moment, her heart pounding. It was as if she were doing something forbidden. After a very long moment, she moved her hand to touch his hair. It was soft and clean and she wondered how it smelled.

Her eyes went back to Miles's and she sensed that he was going to kiss her. Pull away, she thought, but she didn't move.

Slowly, his eyes telling her she could refuse him, he drew near her and when his lips touched hers, she kept her eyes open. What a pleasant feeling, she thought.

He just touched her lips with his and held them there, not forcing her mouth open, not grabbing her and throwing his weight onto her as other men had done, but just the light, highly pleasant kiss.

He was the first to pull away and there was a light of such warmth in his eyes that she began to stiffen. Now would come the pouncing.

"Hush," he soothed, his hand on her cheek. "No one is going to hurt you ever again, my Elizabeth."

"Papa!" Kit yelled and the spell was broken.

"No doubt he's spotted a unicorn this time," Miles said under his breath as he reluctantly rose. His jest was rewarded by the hint of a smile from Elizabeth.

Rising, Elizabeth winced at an ache in her shoulder. She wasn't used to sleeping on the ground.

Acting as if it were the most natural thing in the world, Miles began to knead Elizabeth's shoulders. "What have you found now, Kit?" he called above her head.

"A path," Kit yelled back. "Can I follow it?"

"Not until we get there. Better?" he asked Elizabeth, and when she nodded he kissed her neck and quickly began to gather their few belongings.

"Are you always so free with women?" she asked and there was curiosity in her voice. "When you visit someone's house do you freely kiss all the women?"

Miles didn't pause in burying the dead coals of last night's fire. "I can be civilized, I assure you, and usually I limit my kissing to hands—at least in public." He looked back at her, smiling, eyes sparkling. "But with you, my lovely Elizabeth, from our first . . . ah, meeting, nothing has been done in the usual manner. I can't help but feel that you were a gift to me, a very precious gift, but, nonetheless, something that is mine to keep."

Before she could answer—and, in truth, she was too stunned to answer—he caught her hand and began pulling her to where Kit glared at them impatiently. "Let's go and see where this path takes us."

Miles held her hand as Kit led them down the narrow, long-disused path. "What do you think of my son?"

Elizabeth smiled at the boy who was poking at a mushroom on the ground. As she watched, he straightened and began running ahead of them. "He's very independent, intelligent and quite adult for his age. You must be very proud of him."

Miles's chest swelled visibly. "I have two more at home. Philip Stephen is as exotic-looking as his mother, with a temper that sets his nurse trembling, and he's only a year old."

"And your other boy? Bridget's son?"

"James Raine is exactly opposite of Philip and the two of them are together constantly. I have a feeling it may always be that way. James gives Philip his toys when Philip demands them." He chuckled. "The only thing James will share with no one is his nurse. He screams even if I touch her."

"He must do a great deal of screaming," Elizabeth said sarcastically.

"James is silent practically always," Miles said, laughing. He leaned closer to her. "But then he does go to bed quite early."

She pushed him away playfully.

"Papa," Kit yelled, running to them. "Come and look. It's part of a house but it burned down."

Around the bend was what was left of a burned crofter's cottage, most of the roof collapsed, only one corner standing.

"No, Kit," Miles said when his son started to enter the

ruin. Heavy, charred beams slanted from the one standing wall to the ground. "Let me test it first."

Elizabeth and Kit stood together while Miles grabbed one beam after another and swung his weight on it. A few bits of dirt came falling down but the beams held.

"It seems safe enough," Miles said as Kit ran inside the structure and began looking into crevices.

Miles took Elizabeth's arm. "Let's walk up the hill because, if I'm not mistaken, I think those are apple trees."

There was a small orchard on top of the hill and most of the trees were dead, but there were about a dozen scrawny, nearly ripe apples hanging from some of the branches. As Elizabeth reached for one of them, Miles's arm slid about her waist and lifted her. She caught the apple and he slowly lowered her, the front of her body sliding down his. His lips had just reached hers when Kit called out.

"Look what I found, Papa."

Elizabeth turned away to smile at Kit. "What is it?"

With a dramatic sigh, Miles set Elizabeth down.

"It's a swing!" Kit yelled.

"So it is," Miles said, holding Elizabeth's hand. He grabbed the ropes of the swing and gave them a couple of sharp jerks. "Let me see how high you can go," he said to his son.

Elizabeth and Miles stood back as Kit took over the swing, using it in an aggressive way to propel himself upward until his feet touched a tree branch.

"He'll hurt himself," Elizabeth said, but Miles caught her arm.

"Now show Elizabeth what you can do."

She gasped as Kit, still swinging very high, pulled his legs up and stood in the swing.

"Now!" Miles commanded, his arms open wide.

To Elizabeth's disbelief, Kit sent his small body flying through the air and into Miles's arms. As Kit screamed with delight, Elizabeth felt her knees weaken.

Miles put his son down and caught her arm. "Elizabeth, what's wrong? It was only a child's game. When I was Kit's age, I used to jump into my father's arms in just the same way."

"But if you stepped away . . ." she began.

"Stepped away!" He was aghast. "And let Kit fall?" He pulled her into his arms, soothing her. "Did no one play with you as a child?" he asked quietly.

"My parents died soon after I was born. Edmund was my guardian."

That simple statement said a great deal to Miles. He pulled her away to look at her. "Now we shall make up for your lack of a childhood. Get in the swing and I'll push you."

She was glad to put away her memories of Edmund and she went readily to the swing.

"I will, Papa," Kit said, pushing the wooden bottom of the swing and not making much progress. "She's too heavy," Kit whispered loudly.

"Not for me." Miles laughed, kissed Elizabeth's ear and took the ropes. "Wipe it away, Elizabeth," he said as he pulled her far back off the ground.

"I can't now, but I will," she tossed over her shoulder.

Miles released her and she went flying. Every time she returned, he gave her a push on her bottom instead of the swing's and all Elizabeth did was laugh. Her skirt went up to her knees, she kicked off her shoes and stretched her legs out.

"Jump, Elizabeth!" Kit commanded.

"I'm too heavy, remember?" she teased, laughing.

Miles stood to the side of her. The more time he spent with her, the more beautiful she grew. Her head was back and she was laughing as he'd never seen her laugh before.

"Papa can catch you," Kit persisted.

"Yes, Papa is more than willing to catch the Lady Elizabeth." Miles grinned, standing before her. He saw a look of doubt cross her face. "Trust me, Elizabeth." He was smiling but was deadly earnest at the same time. "I won't step aside; I'll catch you no matter how hard you fall."

Elizabeth didn't play Kit's trick of standing in the swing, but she did release the ropes and go flying headlong into

Miles's arms. When she hit him, the breath was almost knocked from her.

Miles clasped her tightly, then with a look of horror he said, "You *are* too heavy, Elizabeth."

His fall was the most ostentatious fake she'd ever encountered, and as he went down with great loud groans she giggled, clinging to him. With a loud, heartfelt, "Uh oh," from Miles, they began rolling down the steep hill. It was a terribly insincere roll. When Miles was on the bottom, he clutched at Elizabeth, his hands running down the length of her and when she was on the bottom, his arms and knees kept her off the ground so that not even a rock jabbed at her.

Elizabeth's giggle turned into a laugh which made her very weak and her hands were quite ineffectual at pushing him away. He'd pause with her on top just long enough for her to push at his arms, then he'd turn and she'd hang on for dear life.

At the bottom of the hill, he stopped, flung his arms outward, closed his eyes. "I'm crushed, Elizabeth," he said in a wounded tone.

Kit, wanting to join the fun, came tearing down the hill and jumped into the middle of his father's stomach, catching him unaware.

The groan Miles gave this time was genuine, and Elizabeth broke into new gales of laughter.

With great show, Miles set his son off his stomach and turned to Elizabeth. "Like to see me in pain, do you?" His voice was serious but his eyes were alive with teasing. "Come on, Kit, let's show Lady Elizabeth she can't laugh at two knights of the realm."

Eyes wide, Elizabeth stood and backed away, but Miles and Kit were too fast for her. Miles caught her shoulders while Kit threw his body weight onto her legs. Elizabeth tripped over her skirt, Miles tripped over his son and Kit just kept pushing. The three of them went down in a laughing heap as Miles began to tickle Elizabeth's ribs and Kit joined his father.

"Enough?" Miles asked, close to Elizabeth's face which

was streaming with tears. "Are you willing to admit to our being the best of knights?"

"I . . . never said you weren't," she gasped.

Miles's tickling became more severe. "Tell us what we are."

"The bravest, handsomest knights in all of England—in all the world."

His hands stilled, slipping about her waist, his thumbs just under her breasts. "And what is my name?" he whispered, completely sober.

"Miles," she whispered back, her eyes on his. "Miles Montgomery." Her arms were on his shoulders and now they slipped about his neck, lightly.

Miles bent and kissed her, softly, but there was for the first time a tiny spark between them.

Kit jumped on his father's back and Miles's face slid from Elizabeth's, and he just missed slamming into the dirt.

"Let's swing again, Papa."

"To think that I used to love my son," Miles whispered in Elizabeth's ear before he rose, his son attached to his back.

None of them had noticed that the sky had darkened in the last few minutes, and they each gasped when the first cold drops hit them. The sky opened up and nearly drowned them.

"To the cottage," Miles said, pulling Elizabeth up, his arm about her shoulders, and together they ran for shelter.

"Did you get wet?" he asked as he lowered Kit from his back.

"No, not much." She smiled up at him for just a moment before turning toward Kit.

Miles casually put his hand on Elizabeth's shoulder. "Why don't the two of you build a fire while I find us something to eat?"

Kit agreed enthusiastically while Elizabeth gave a dubious look to the torrential rain outside. "Perhaps you should wait until it slackens."

Miles gave her a smile of delight. "I'll be safe enough. Now, the two of you stay in here and I'll not be far away."

With that, he slipped between the charred beams and was gone.

Elizabeth went to the edge of the shelter and looked after him. She was certain Miles Montgomery had no idea how unusual today had been to her. She'd spent an entire morning with a man and not once had any violence occurred. And the laughter! She'd always loved to laugh but her brothers were so solemn—anyone living in the same house with Edmund Chatworth soon grew to be solemn. But today she'd laughed with a man and he'd not tried to tear her clothes off. Always before, if she even smiled at a man, he'd grabbed her, hurt her.

It wasn't that Elizabeth was so beautiful that she drove men to uncontrollable passion. She knew she was pretty, yes, but if she'd heard correctly she was no match for the Revedoune heiress. What had always made Elizabeth the victim of men's aggressions was her brother Edmund. His distorted sense of humor ran to wagering with his guests as to who could get Elizabeth in bed with him. Edmund hated that Elizabeth wasn't terrified of him. When she was a child he used to bring her home from the convent where she lived most of the time and he'd often hit her, knock her down stairs. But somehow Elizabeth had escaped uninjured.

When she was twelve, she began to stand up for herself. She'd successfully held off Edmund with a lighted torch. After that Edmund's game grew more serious, and Elizabeth grew more wary, more skillful at fending off her attackers. She'd learned how to hurt men who were trying to use her. She'd persuaded Roger to show her how to use an ax, a sword, a dagger. She knew how to defend herself with a razor-sharp tongue.

After weeks with Edmund and the men he surrounded himself with, Elizabeth would escape back to her convent, usually with Roger's help, and she'd be able to rest for a few weeks—until Edmund came for her again.

"I have the fire going, Lady Elizabeth," Kit said from behind her.

She turned a warm smile on him. Children had always

been her love. Children were what they seemed, never trying to take from her, always giving freely. "You've done all the work and I've just been standing here." She went to him. "Perhaps you'd like me to tell you a story while we wait for your father."

She sat down, leaning against the wall, her feet toward the fire, her arm around Kit. Tossing Miles's cloak over them, she began to tell Kit about Moses and his people of Israel. Before she was to the Red Sea opening, Kit was asleep, curled up against her.

The rain beat down on the bit of roof over their heads, leaking in three places. While she watched the fire, Miles came in out of the mist, gave her a smile and fed the fire. He was silent as he skinned and dressed a young pig, cut the meat into chunks and set them to roast on sticks.

As she watched, she couldn't help but think what an odd man he was. Or were most men like him? Roger'd always said that Elizabeth only saw the dregs of mankind, and from the way some of the young women at the convent rhapsodized over their lovers, Elizabeth'd often thought that perhaps some men weren't like the ones she fought off.

Miles knelt by the fire, his hands quickly working with the meat. Within reach was his bow, his arrows over his back, his sword never leaving his side. Even as they'd been tumbling down the hill, Miles's sword had been attached to his hip. What sort of man could laugh with a woman and at the same time be prepared for danger?

"What are you thinking?" Miles asked quietly, his eyes intense.

She recovered herself. "That you're so wet you're about to drown the fire."

He stood, stretched. "This is a cold country, isn't it?" With that he slowly began to remove his wet clothes, spreading each piece by the fire.

Elizabeth watched him with detached interest. Nude men weren't unfamiliar to her, and often her brother's men had trained wearing the small loincloths. But she doubted if she'd ever really *looked* at any of the men.

Miles was lean but muscular and when he turned toward her, wearing only the loincloth, she saw he had a great amount of dark hair on his chest, a thick, V-shaped, curling abundance of it. His thighs were large, heavy from training in armor, and his calves were well developed.

"Elizabeth," Miles whispered. "You will have me blushing."

It was Elizabeth who blushed and could not meet his eyes when she heard him chuckle.

"Papa," Kit said, rousing. "I'm hungry."

Reluctantly, Elizabeth released the child. As much as she loved children, there had been few of them in her life. There was nothing quite like a child in her arms, needing her, trusting her, touching her.

"There's pork and a few apples," Miles told his son.

"Are you cold, Papa?" Kit asked.

Miles didn't look at Elizabeth. "I have the warm glances of a lady to keep me warm. Come eat with us, Lady Elizabeth."

Still pink-cheeked, Elizabeth joined them and it wasn't long before she got over her embarrassment. At Kit's insistence, Miles told stories of when he and his brothers were growing up. In every story, he was the hero, saving his brothers, teaching them. Kit's eyes shone like stars.

"And when you took your vows," Elizabeth said innocently, "didn't you foreswear lying?"

Miles's eyes twinkled. "I don't think they extended to impressing one's son or one's . . ." He seemed to search for a word.

"Captive?" she supplied.

"Ah, Elizabeth," he said languidly. "What would a lady think of a man whose older brothers constantly tried to make his life miserable?"

"Did they?"

She was so earnest in her question that he knew she took him literally. "No, not really," he reassured her. "We were left alone at an early age and I guess some of our pranks were a bit hazardous, but we all lived."

"Happily ever after," she said heavily.

"And what was it like living with Edmund Chatworth?" he asked casually.

Elizabeth shifted her legs under her. "He also liked . . . pranks," was all she'd say.

"Did you have enough, Kit?" Miles asked, and as he reached for another piece of pork, she saw the long gash on the inside of his wrist. It had opened again and was bleeding.

Miles never seemed to miss even a glance of hers. "The bow string hit it. You may doctor it if you wish," he said so eagerly, with so much hope, that she laughed at him.

She raised her skirt, tore off a long piece of petticoat and wet it in the rain. Miles sat cross-legged before her, his arm extended as she began to wash away the blood.

"I can't tell you how good it is to see you smile," he said. "Kit! Don't climb on those beams. Take the cloth from inside the quiver and clean my sword. And watch that you don't damage the edge." He looked back at Elizabeth. "I take it as an honor that you smile at me. I'm not sure, but I feel that you don't smile at many men."

"Very few," was all she'd answer.

He lifted her hand from his wrist and kissed her palm. "I'm beginning to think you're as angelic as you look. Kit adores you."

"I have a feeling Kit has never met a stranger, that he adores everyone."

"I don't." He kissed her hand again.

"Stop it!" She pulled away from him. "You are entirely too free with your kisses."

"I am doing very well at limiting myself to kisses. What I'd like to do is make love to you. Kit!" he yelled at his son who was waving the sword above his head. "I'll have your hide if you even consider thrusting that at anything."

In spite of herself, Elizabeth had to laugh as she thrust Miles's cleanly bandaged arm back to him. "I think you should leave your son at home when you try courting."

"Oh no." He smiled. "Kit has accomplished more than I could have in months."

With that cryptic remark, he moved to take his cherished sword from his son's reckless hands.

Chapter 7

THAT NIGHT the three of them slept together again, Kit firmly wedged between them. Elizabeth lay awake for a long time listening to the breathing of Miles and Kit. The past two days had been so unusual, so unlike anything she'd ever experienced before. It was like a bit of sunshine after years of rain.

When she woke she was alone on the cloak, the plaid tucked about her. Sleepily she smiled, snuggled deeper under the covers, and for a second she wished she could always stay in this place, that each day could be filled with laughter.

Turning to her back, stretching, she looked about the little shelter, saw that it was empty. Her senses had dulled over the last few days. Usually, she slept with one ear open, but somehow, Miles and Kit had managed to leave without disturbing her. She listened now for any sounds of them, smiling when she heard slow, quiet footsteps not too far away.

Stealthily, soundlessly, she left the shelter and faded into the surrounding forest. Once inside, hidden, she heard the unmistakable sounds of Kit and Miles to her left. Then who was skulking about in the undergrowth ahead of her?

Using all her years of experience at escaping her brother's friends, she slipped through the forest effortlessly. It was some minutes before she saw who was trying so hard to sneak up on them.

Lying on his stomach, his long, long body held immovable, was Sir Guy, only his head turning from side to side as he scanned the horizon where Kit and Miles scampered.

With no more sound than a breath of air, Elizabeth crept behind Sir Guy. Stooping, she picked up a small, elongated rock and clutched it in her fist. Roger had taught her that even her small, weak fist could carry some power if she held a hard object. With the rock in one hand, she bent and grabbed Sir Guy's small dagger from its sheath at his side.

The giant stood in one fluid, quick movement. "Lady Elizabeth!" he gasped.

Elizabeth stood back, at arm's length from the man. "Why are you following us? Did you betray your master and now you come to kill him?"

The scar across Sir Guy's face whitened but he didn't answer her. Instead, he turned his head in the direction of Miles and gave a high, piercing whistle.

Elizabeth knew Miles would come at the call, that it was a signal between them. If Sir Guy felt free to call his master, then Miles must know something of the reason for the giant's hidden presence.

In a remarkably short time, Miles appeared, sword drawn, alone.

"The lady asks if I mean to kill you," Sir Guy said solemnly.

Miles looked from one to the other. "How did she find you?"

Sir Guy's eyes never left Elizabeth's face. He seemed to be embarrassed and admiring all at once. "I didn't hear her."

Miles's eyes twinkled. "Give him back the dagger, Elizabeth. There needn't be any concern for Guy's loyalty."

Elizabeth didn't move. Her hand clutched the rock, hidden in the folds of her skirt, and at the same time she made note of the flat rock Sir Guy's softly clad foot was resting upon. Feet were vulnerable in even the strongest men.

"Where are your men?" she asked Miles, her eyes on Sir Guy.

"Well . . . Elizabeth," he began. "I thought perhaps . . ."

From the slight changes in Sir Guy's face, Elizabeth knew that whatever had been done had been Miles Montgomery's idea.

"Speak up!" she commanded.

"We're on MacArran land and I knew we'd be safe so I decided to walk with you and Kit. There's never been any danger."

She whirled to face him but kept Sir Guy in her view. "This was all a trick," she said evenly. "You lied about your men disappearing. You lied about being in danger. You did this all in an attempt to get me alone."

"Elizabeth," he soothed. "We were surrounded by people. I thought perhaps that if we could be alone for a time you might come to know me. And Kit—"

"Don't profane that child's name! He was not in this ugly plot of yours."

"It wasn't a plot," he pleaded, his eyes soft.

"But what of danger? You risked my life and that of your son. These woods are full of savage men!"

Miles smiled patronizingly. "True, but these savages are related to me by marriage. I'm sure we're surrounded by MacArrans even now."

"I've heard no one except this great thrashing boar."

Sir Guy stiffened beside her.

"There was no harm done." Miles smiled at her. "Give me the dagger, Elizabeth."

"No harm except lies given to a woman," she spat at him.

After that, everything seemed to happen in a single flash. She lunged at Miles with the dagger. Sir Guy's hand knocked it from her grasp, and as the little knife went flying, Elizabeth's heel came down on the two smallest toes of Sir Guy's left foot. Miles, as he turned astonished eyes to Sir Guy's cry of pain, didn't see Elizabeth's fist, wrapped about the rock, as it plowed into his stomach. With a great whoosh of pain, Miles bent over.

Elizabeth stepped back, watching as Sir Guy sat on the ground and tried to remove his boot, his face showing his pain. Miles looked as if he might lose his dinner.

"Well done," came a voice from behind her. She whirled about to look into the face of a strikingly beautiful woman, with black hair and blue eyes, as tall as Elizabeth, which was rare. A big dog stood beside her.

"That should teach you, Miles," she continued, "that all women don't appreciate being used as a man sees fit."

Elizabeth's eyes widened as from the trees men began to drop and, coming from the direction of the cottage, an older man was leading Kit by the hand.

"Lady Elizabeth Chatworth," the woman said, "I am Bronwyn MacArran, laird of Clan MacArran and sister-in-law to this scheming young man."

Miles was recovering himself. "Bronwyn, it's good to see you again."

"Tam," Bronwyn said to the older man. "See to Sir Guy's foot. Did you break it?"

"Probably," Elizabeth answered. "When I've done it before I've found it usually breaks the man's smallest toe."

Bronwyn gave her an acknowledging look of appreciation. "These are my men. Douglas." As she called each man's name, he stepped forward, nodded at Lady Elizabeth. "Alex, Jarl and Francis."

Elizabeth gave each man a hard, appraising look. She didn't like being surrounded by men and she moved so Sir Guy was no longer behind her. The many men near her made her feel as if she were locked in a small stone cell.

Miles, rubbing his stomach, noticed the move and came to stand nearer to Elizabeth, and when Tam took a step closer, Miles touched the man's arm, his eyes giving warning. With a quick frown of puzzlement, Tam released Kit and stepped away from Elizabeth, noticing that her eyes were wary, watching.

"And where is my worthless brother?" Miles asked Bronwyn, who was quietly watching the scene before her.

"He is patrolling the northern borders but I expect him to meet us before we reach Larenston."

Miles took Elizabeth's arm, tightened his grip when she tried to move away from him. "Bronwyn has a baby," he said aloud. Under his breath, he whispered, "You're safe. Stay close to me."

Elizabeth gave him a withering look that said she didn't feel he was safer than any other man, but she didn't move from his side. The men who stood close to Bronwyn were wildly dressed, their knees bare, their hair down to their shoulders, great long wide swords at their belts.

Bronwyn felt there was more wrong than just Miles's childish trick played on Elizabeth, but she had no idea what it was. Perhaps when they returned to Larenston she could find out what this tension in the air meant. "Shall we ride?"

Elizabeth stood still, not moving until Bronwyn's men were in front of her. There was a long walk to where the horses were hidden and the men were a silent group. Sir Guy hobbled along slowly, leaning on a thick staff.

"I want to ride behind the men," Elizabeth said to Miles, her jaw set.

He started to protest but stopped, murmured something to Bronwyn and at her nod, the Scotsmen and Sir Guy rode ahead, Kit settled with Tam.

"Elizabeth," Miles began from atop the horse beside her. "Bronwyn's men mean you no harm. There's no reason to fear them."

She glared at him. "Am I to take your word for their trustworthiness? You who have lied to me? You who are of a family that is at war with my family?"

Miles glanced heavenward for a moment. "Perhaps I was wrong to play the trick on you, but if I'd asked you to spend a few days frolicking in the forest with Kit and me, what would have been your answer?"

She looked away from him.

"Elizabeth, you must admit you enjoyed yourself. There, for a few hours, you weren't afraid of men."

"I am *never* afraid of men," she snapped. "I have merely learned to be cautious."

"Your caution overtakes your entire life," he said sternly. "Look at us now, eating the dust of Bronwyn's men because you fear that one of them will attack you if you don't have him in your sight."

"I have learned—" she began.

"You have learned only the bad part of life! Most men are not like Edmund Chatworth or Pagnell. While we're here in Scotland you're going to learn that some men can be trusted. No!" he said, his eyes locking with hers. "You are going to learn that *I* can be trusted." With that he spurred his horse forward to ride beside Sir Guy, leaving Elizabeth alone.

Bronwyn glanced back at Elizabeth, then turned her horse to ride beside the blonde woman. They were a striking pair: Elizabeth with her delicate fair features; Bronwyn's strong, sculptured features.

"A lovers' quarrel?" Bronwyn asked, her eyes searching Elizabeth's face.

"We are not lovers," Elizabeth said coolly.

Bronwyn raised her eyebrows at that, thinking that it must be a first for Miles to spend any time with a woman and not possess her. "And how does a Chatworth come to ride with a Montgomery?" she asked in the same tone as Elizabeth had used with her.

Elizabeth gave Bronwyn a scathing look. "If you plan to pour out venom about my brother Roger, you should think twice."

Bronwyn and Elizabeth faced each other across the horses and after a moment—in which many signals passed between them—Bronwyn gave a curt nod. "Ask your brother about his Scots relatives," she said frigidly before reining her horse away, leaving Elizabeth to herself.

"And have you angered Bronwyn?" Miles asked when he once again rode beside her.

"Am I to listen to all manner of evilness against my own brother? That woman swore to marry Roger but went back on her word. And as a result—"

"As a result Roger Chatworth attacked my brother's back," Miles interrupted. He paused, leaned across her horse to take her hand in his. "Give us a chance, Elizabeth," he said softly, his eyes meltingly imploring. "All I ask is that you give all of us time to show you that we can be trusted."

Before Elizabeth could answer, the sound of thundering hooves came to them. With a glance up, she saw that every man had his claymore drawn, and before she could protest, Bronwyn's Scots had encircled the two women. Miles moved his horse closer to Elizabeth.

"It's that idiot husband of mine," Bronwyn said, and her pleased tone was completely at odds with her words.

Five men came to a halt before them, the leader a tall man with dark blond hair that came to his shoulders, a good-looking man who was obviously enjoying the sparks his wife was shooting at him.

"You're getting old, Tam," the blond man said lazily, leaning on the front of his saddle.

Tam merely gave a grunt and resheathed his claymore.

"Damn you, Stephen," Bronwyn hissed. "Why were you riding along the cliff like that? And why didn't you give any warning of your approach?"

Slowly, he dismounted his horse, tossed the reins to one of the men behind him and walked toward his wife. Casually, he put his hand on her ankle and started traveling upward.

Bronwyn kicked out at him. "Let me go!" she demanded. "I have more important duties than to play games with you."

With lightning quickness, Stephen caught her waist and hauled her out of the saddle. "Did you worry about me riding along the cliff?" he murmured, pulling her to him.

"Tam!" Bronwyn gasped, pushing at Stephen.

"The lad needs no help from me," Tam answered.

"But I would be willing to help," Miles said quietly.

Stephen released his wife abruptly. "Miles," he gasped, and hugged his brother when Miles was dismounted. "When did you arrive? Why are you in Scotland? I thought you were with Uncle Simon—and what's this I hear about Uncle Simon wanting your head on a platter?"

Miles gave a bit of a smile and a shrug to his brother.

Stephen grimaced as he knew he wasn't likely to get anything from his younger brother. Miles was so closemouthed it was infuriating.

"Miles brought Elizabeth Chatworth," Bronwyn said flatly.

Stephen turned to look through the men and upwards to

see Elizabeth. For all her soft features, she looked rigid, unbending, as she sat stiffly in the saddle. Stephen started toward her but Miles caught his arm.

"Do not touch her," Miles said conversationally as he moved toward Elizabeth.

After a second's astonishment, Stephen grinned. He well understood jealousy; he'd just never seen it in his brother before.

As Miles put his arms up to Elizabeth and she hesitated, he said, "Stephen will not harm you and he'll be expecting the same courtesy." There was a twinkle in Miles's eyes.

Elizabeth couldn't help a slight smile as she glanced at Sir Guy, who had shot a couple of glances toward her that said she was part monster, part witch. They had to wait to be introduced to Stephen because Kit, who'd fallen asleep against Tam, had wakened and launched himself onto his beloved uncle. Stephen had Kit settled on one arm as he extended his hand to Elizabeth.

Elizabeth stood rigid and did not take his hand.

Miles sent his brother a look of warning and Stephen, with a knowing smile, dropped his hand.

"You are welcome to our home," Stephen said.

"I am a Chatworth."

"And I am a Montgomery *and*"—he glanced at Bronwyn—"a MacArran. You *are* welcome. Shall we walk along the cliff? It's steep and can sometimes be frightening."

"I can ride a horse," Elizabeth said flatly.

Miles took her arm, raised her fingers to his lips. "Of course you can. My clumsy brother is only trying to make an excuse to talk to you."

"Uncle Stephen!" Kit said. He'd been trying so hard to wait until the adults were finished speaking. "Lady Elizabeth hit Papa and made Sir Guy limp and we slept in the forest without a tent or anything." He smiled at Elizabeth who winked back at him.

"Made Sir Guy limp?" Stephen laughed. "Somehow I doubt that."

"Lady Elizabeth Chatworth broke Sir Guy's toes," Bronwyn said coolly.

Stephen narrowed his eyes at his wife. "I'm not sure I like your tone."

Miles spoke quickly to get his brother's attention. "How are the MacGregors?"

What followed was half-description, half-argument as Bronwyn and Stephen talked of the clan that had been the enemy of Clan MacArran for centuries—until a few months ago when a truce had been made. Bronwyn's brother Davy had married the daughter of the MacGregor.

As they talked, they walked along the treacherous cliff road, one side high rock, the other a sheer drop. Elizabeth, caught close to Miles, beside Stephen, Bronwyn ahead of them, listened with no little fascination to the exchange between the married couple. They argued heatedly but with absolutely no animosity. The men behind them talked among themselves, so this bantering was obviously not new to them. Bronwyn taunted Stephen, called him several names and Stephen merely smiled at her and told her her ideas were ridiculous. Of all the marriages Elizabeth had seen, the husband would have blackened the wife's eye if she'd said half what Bronwyn was saying.

Elizabeth glanced at Miles, saw he was smiling benignly at Bronwyn and his brother. Kit began to enter the argument, taking Bronwyn's side, running ahead to grab her hand.

"He's your son." Stephen laughed, looking at his brother.

Because Stephen looked toward Miles, toward the rock wall, he saw the rocks tumbling from above—aiming for Elizabeth. With a knight's instincts, he acted as quickly as he thought, making a leaping grab for Elizabeth. The two of them slammed into the rock wall, Stephen's big body pinning Elizabeth, crushing her as the rock fell behind him.

Elizabeth also reacted without thinking. For a few moments, her guard had been down, but with men behind her, beside her, she'd remained nervous. Her senses did not register the reason for Stephen's abrupt attack but only knew that once again a man was threatening her.

She panicked. Not just a small uproar, but Elizabeth let out a scream that startled the already nervous horses. And she didn't stop with one scream, but she began clawing and kicking like a caged wild animal.

Stephen, stunned by her reaction, tried to catch her shoulders. "Elizabeth," he shouted into her terrified face.

Miles had been struck on the shoulder and back by falling stones, knocking him to his knees. The moment he heard Elizabeth's screams he went to her.

"Goddamn you!" he bellowed at his brother. "I told you not to touch her." With a hard push he shoved Stephen away, tried to catch Elizabeth.

"Quiet!" he commanded.

Elizabeth was still in a frenzy, scratching Miles, trying to tear away from him.

He caught her shoulders, gave her a sharp shake. "Elizabeth," he said patiently, loudly. "You are safe. Do you hear me? Safe." It took another shake before she turned eyes to his—eyes such as Miles had never seen before, frightened, terrified, helpless eyes. For a moment they looked at each other and Miles used all his strength of character to will her into peacefulness. "You are safe now, my love. You'll always be safe with me."

Her body began trembling and he pulled her into his arms, held her close to him, stroked her hair. When he glanced at Stephen standing near them, he said, "Leave a horse. We'll follow later."

Elizabeth was hardly aware of the funeral-quiet procession passing them. Her fear had made her weak and all she could do was lean against Miles for support, while he stroked her cheek, her neck, her arm. After many minutes, she pulled away from him.

"I have made an ass of myself," she said with such despair that Miles smiled at her.

"Stephen didn't understand when I told him not to touch you. I'm sure he thought it was mere jealousy."

"You are not jealous?" she asked, pulling away, trying to change the subject.

"Perhaps. But your fears are more important than my jealousy."

"My fears, as you call them, are none of your concern." She succeeded in pulling completely away from him.

"Elizabeth." His voice was pleading, very low. "Don't keep all this inside you. I've told you I'm a good listener. Talk to me. Tell me what has made you so afraid."

She caught the rock wall with her hands behind her. The solid mass felt good, gave her a feeling of reality. "Why have you sent the others away?"

A flicker of anger crossed his eyes. "So I'd have no witnesses when I ravished you. Why else?" When he saw that she wasn't sure he was being sarcastic, he threw up his hands in despair. "Come on, let's go to Larenston." He grabbed her arm much too hard. "You know what you need, Elizabeth? You need someone to make love to you, to show you that your fear is much worse than the reality."

"I've had many volunteers for the task," she hissed at him. "From what I've seen, you've known only rapists—not lovers."

With that, he practically tossed her into the saddle and mounted behind her.

Chapter 8

ELIZABETH PUT her hand to her forehead and opened her eyes slowly. The big room where she lay upon the bed was empty, dark. It had been many hours since she and Miles had ridden into the fortress of Clan MacArran. It was an ancient place, set on the edge of a cliff like some giant eagle using its talons to hold on. Some woman who looked as old as the castle handed Elizabeth a hot drink laced with herbs, and when the woman's back was turned, Elizabeth dumped the drink into the rushes behind a bench. Elizabeth had a knowledge of herbs and she had a good guess as to what the drink contained.

The gnarled little woman, whom Bronwyn called Morag, watched Elizabeth with sharp eyes and after a few moments Elizabeth feigned sleepiness and lay upon the bed.

"She needs the rest," Bronwyn said over her. "I've never seen anyone go insane quite as she did when Stephen pulled her from under the falling rocks. It was as if demons had suddenly entered her body."

Morag gave a little snort. "Ye fought Stephen long and hard when ye first met him."

"It wasn't the same," Bronwyn insisted. "Miles calmed her but only after a long time of shaking her. Did you know she broke Sir Guy's toes?"

"And I heard the two of ye quarreled," Morag snapped.

Bronwyn straightened defensively. "She dares to defend Roger Chatworth to me. After what he has done—"

"He's her brother!" Morag spat. "Ye would expect her to be loyal yet ye seem to think she should see your way at once. Bronwyn, there is more than one way of things in the world." She bent and spread a large blue and green plaid over Elizabeth's quiet form. "Let's leave her in peace. A messenger has come from Stephen's eldest brother."

"Why didn't you tell me?" Bronwyn said, angry at being treated as a child and more angry because she deserved the treatment.

Elizabeth lay perfectly still after the door had closed, listening for anyone's breathing. Sometimes men had pretended they'd left a room but in truth they were actually only hiding in dark corners. When she was sure she was alone, she turned over and cautiously opened her eyes. She was indeed alone.

She sprang from the bed and went to the window. It was just growing dark outside, the moonlight beginning to silver the steep walls of the gray stone castle. Now was the time to escape, now before a routine was set, before all the Mac-Arrans were informed she was a prisoner.

As she watched, on the ground below, four men walked past, their bodies sheathed in plaids. With a smile, Elizabeth began to form a plan. A quick, silent search of the room revealed a chest of men's clothes. She pulled up the silk skirt of her gown, tied it about her waist, then pulled on a voluminous men's shirt and slipped into heavy wool socks. For just a second, she looked down at her knees, blinked at the idea of appearing in public so very bare—nude almost. There were no shoes so she had to make do with her own soft shoes, her toes tightly jammed with the added bulk of the socks. Rolling the plaid about her so it formed a short skirt and could be tossed across a shoulder took several attempts, and she was sure she still didn't have it right when she tied a belt about her waist. It was much too long to buckle.

With her breath held, she cautiously opened the door, praying that as yet no guard had been posted outside her door. Her luck held and she slipped through a narrow opening and out into the dim hall. She'd memorized the way out of the castle when Miles had led her to the room and now, as she paused to get her bearings, she listened for sounds.

Far away, to her left and below, she could hear voices. Slowly, melting into the wall, she glided down the stairs toward the main exit. Just as she was moving past the room where people were gathered, she heard the name Chatworth. She glanced toward the door to the outside but at the same time she wanted information. With no more noise than a shadow, she moved to where she could hear.

Stephen was speaking. "Damn *both* of you, Miles!" Anger permeated his voice. "Gavin has no more sense than you do. The two of you are helping Chatworth accomplish what he wants. He's coming close to destroying our family."

Miles remained silent.

Bronwyn put her hand on Miles's arm. "Please release her. Lady Elizabeth can return to England with an armed guard and when Gavin hears she's released, he'll let Roger Chatworth go."

Still Miles did not speak.

"Goddamn you!" Stephen bellowed. "Answer us!"

Miles's eyes ignited. "I will not release Elizabeth. What Gavin does with Roger Chatworth is my brother's business. Elizabeth is mine."

"If you weren't my brother—" Stephen began.

"If I weren't your brother, what I did would have no effect on you." Miles was quite calm, only his eyes showing his anger.

Stephen threw up his hands in despair. "You talk to him," he said to Bronwyn. "None of my brothers has any sense at all."

Bronwyn planted herself before her husband. "Once you fought Roger Chatworth for what you believed to be yours. Now Miles is doing exactly the same thing and yet you rage at him."

"It was different then," Stephen said sullenly. "You were given to me by the king."

"And Elizabeth was given to me!" Miles interjected with

great passion. "Bronwyn, am I welcome here? If not I and my men will leave—with Lady Elizabeth."

"You know you are welcome," Bronwyn said softly. "Unless Chatworth is prepared for war, he'll not attack the MacArrans." She turned to Stephen. "And as for Gavin holding Chatworth prisoner, I'm glad for it. Do you forget what Chatworth did to your sister Mary or that he held me prisoner for a month?"

Elizabeth slipped away after hearing those words. They were going to find that she wasn't the docile captive they assumed she would be.

Outside, a fog was rolling in from the sea and she smiled in secret thanks for the Lord's help. Her first necessity was to get a horse because she could not walk out of Scotland. Standing still, she listened, stiffly intent, trying to ascertain where the stables were.

Elizabeth was quite good at stealing horses; she'd had a great deal of practice in her short lifetime. Horses were like children. They needed to be talked to quietly, simply, with no quick movements. There were two men at one end of the stables, laughing, talking in low tones about the latest women they'd bedded.

With great stealth, Elizabeth eased a bridled horse from the far end of the long stable. She pulled a saddle from the stall wall and waited until she was outside before saddling the animal. She thanked heaven for the relative noisiness of so many people living together on a few acres of land. A creaky cart went by; a man leading four horses tied the animals not far from the stables and two of the horses started nipping each other. As a consequence, three men began shouting and cracking whips. None of the people milling about even glanced at the slight figure in the shadows, a plaid covering the person's head.

When Elizabeth mounted, she lazily followed the cart out the open gates of Larenston and, like the cart driver, raised her hand in silent greeting to the guards above her. The guards were there to keep people from entering; people leaving were of little interest to them.

The only way to reach the MacArran fortress was across a frighteningly narrow bit of land. Elizabeth's already racing heart threatened to break her ribs. The cart in front of her was unusually narrow and, even so, its wheels rode just on the edges of the road—inches in either direction and the man, cart and horse would be over the side.

When she reached the end of the road, she breathed a sigh of relief for several reasons—the end of the treacherous path and, so far, no alarm had been sounded.

The cart driver looked over his shoulder and grinned at her. "Always glad when I come off that path. Are ye goin' this way?"

Straight ahead was the easy way, through the crofters' farms where people would see her and could give a search party directions. To the right was the cliff road, the one she and Miles had ridden on. To ride along the cliff at night . . .

"Nay!" she said in her huskiest voice to the cart driver. Obviously the man would want to talk if she rode with him. She pointed a plaid-covered arm toward the cliff.

"You young'uns!" The man chuckled. "Well, good luck to ye, lad. There's plenty of moonlight, but watch yer step." With that he clucked to his horse and drove away.

Elizabeth lost no time in contemplating her fear but urged her mare toward the black emptiness before her. At night the road looked worse than she remembered. Her horse fidgeted and after only a second's hesitation, she dismounted and began to lead her.

"Damn Miles Montgomery!" she muttered. Why did he have to come to a savage place like this? If he were going to hold someone captive, he should have done it in civilized surroundings.

The howl of a wolf directly overhead made her stop muttering. Silhouetted atop the cliff were three wolves, heads low, watching her. The horse danced about and Elizabeth wrapped the reins around her wrist. As she moved, the wolves moved with her. Another one joined the pack.

It seemed to Elizabeth that she had traveled for miles but she couldn't even see the end of the cliff road. For a moment, she leaned against the rock wall, tried to calm her racing heart.

The wolves, seeming to believe their victim was admitting defeat, growled collectively. The horse reared, tore the reins from Elizabeth's hands. She made a leap for the horse, lost her footing and fell half over the edge of the cliff. The freed horse went tearing down the path.

She lay still for a moment, trying to regain her composure and to figure out how to free herself. Precariously, she clung to the edge of the cliff, one leg dangling with no support, her other foot straining to hold on. Her arms were hugging rock, her chin pressing downward. She moved her left arm, and as she did, rock crumbled from under her. With a gasp of terror she began to move her right leg to search for a foothold—but found none. Another bit of rock crumbled and she knew she had to do something.

Using every bit of strength in her arms, she tried to push herself up, inching her hips to the left. When her left knee caught on the solid rock road, she had to blink away tears of relief. Inch by slow inch, she moved her aching, bruised body back onto the road.

On hands and knees she crawled to the safety of the rock wall and sat there, tears rolling down her cheeks, her chest heaving. Blood trickled down her arms and her raw knees burned.

Above her came a great cry of animals fighting. Pushing herself away from the wall, she saw an animal attacking the wolves. "That great dog of Bronwyn's," she gasped and closed her eyes in silent prayer for a moment.

She didn't sit there long. Soon her disappearance would be discovered and she needed to be well ahead of her Montgomery enemies.

When she stood, she realized she was hurt worse than she thought. Her left leg was stiff, her ankle painful. When she wiped away the tears from her cheeks, her hand showed bloody in the moonlight. With raw palms, she began to feel her way along the road, not trusting her sight to guide her but needing the solid rock for direction.

The moon had set by the time she reached the end of the road, but instead of being frightening, the black open space was welcome to her. She pulled the plaid closer about her, ignored her weak legs and began walking.

When two pinpoints of light shone at her, chest height, she gasped, stopped, looked about for some weapon. For several moments she locked eyes with the animal, whatever it was, before it moved. The animal was almost touching her before she realized it was Bronwyn's dog.

The dog cocked its head at her quizzically and Elizabeth wanted to cry with relief.

"You killed the wolves, didn't you?" she said. "Good boy. Are you friendly?" Tentatively, she put out her hand, palm up, and was rewarded with a lick of the dog's tongue. As she began stroking the animal's big head, it nudged her hand, pushing her back toward the cliff road.

"No, boy," she whispered. Her standing still was making her feel her cuts and bruises more. And it seemed like days since she'd slept. "I want to go this way, not back to Bronwyn."

The dog gave a sharp yip at his mistress's name.

"No!" she said firmly.

The dog watched her for a moment as if considering her words, then turned toward the forest ahead of them.

"Good boy." She smiled. "Maybe you can lead me out of this place. Lead me to another clan that will return me to my brother for the reward he'll pay."

She walked behind the dog, but as she began to stumble, it stopped, nudging under her arm until she began to lean on it. "What's your name, boy?" she whispered tiredly. "Is it George or Oliver or is it some Scots name I've never heard?"

The dog slowed its step even more for her.

"How about Charlie?" she said. "I rather like the name Charlie."

With that she collapsed in a heap beside the dog, asleep, or perhaps in a faint.

The dog nudged her, sniffed her, licked her bloody face,

and when nothing made her rise he settled beside her and slept.

The sun was high overhead when Elizabeth woke and looked up at the massive, shaggy head of the dog. The animal's eyes were questioning, as concerned about her as a human. There was an ugly cut covered with dried blood under one of the dog's eyes.

"Get that from fighting the wolves?" She smiled up at the dog, scratching its ears. As she started to rise, her legs gave way under her and she clutched the dog. "It's a good thing you're strong, Charlie," she said, using the dog's back to brace herself.

When she was at last on her feet, she looked down at herself and groaned. Her skirt was half tied up, half hanging down to her ankles. Her left knee was cut, scraped, still oozing blood, while her right knee was merely raw. With determination, she tossed the plaid over her arms, not wanting to see the damage done to them. When she touched her hair she felt dried bits of blood so she moved her hand away.

"Can you find some water, Charlie?" she asked the dog. "Water?"

The dog took off instantly across the rocky landscape, returning when Elizabeth could follow only at a snail's pace. The newly healed scabs had opened and there were warm trickles of blood on her body.

The dog led her to a small stream where she washed as best she could. When she met her liberators, she wanted to be as presentable as possible.

She and the dog walked for hours, staying close to the rocks and the few trees. Once they heard horses and instinctively Elizabeth hid, pulling the dog to her side. There was no way she could have held the big dog had it decided to leave her, but for the moment the animal seemed content to stay with her.

By sundown, what little strength she had left was gone, and it didn't seem to matter when the dog began barking at something she couldn't see. "No doubt it's Miles or your mistress," she said heavily and slid to the ground, closing her eyes.

When she opened them again a man she'd never seen before stood over her, legs wide, hands on hips. The dying sunlight haloed his gray hair, made shadows on his strong jaw.

"Well, Rab," he said in a deep voice, stroking the dog, "what have you brought me this time?"

"Don't touch me," Elizabeth whispered as the man bent toward her.

"If you're worried I'll harm you in any way, young woman, you needn't be. I'm the MacGregor and you're on my land. Why is Bronwyn's dog with *you?*" He eyed her English clothes.

Elizabeth was tired, weak, hungry, but she wasn't dead. The way this man said Bronwyn told her they were friends. Tears began falling down her cheeks. Now she'd never get home. No friend of the MacArrans would return her to England, and Roger's capture by a Montgomery could start a private war.

"Don't greet so, lass," the MacGregor said. "Soon you'll be in a nice safe place. Someone will tend to your cuts and we'll feed you and—What the hell!"

Elizabeth, as the man leaned closer, had pulled his dirk from its sheath and aimed for his stomach. Sheer weakness had made her miss.

Lachlan MacGregor sidestepped, took the dirk from her and flung her over his shoulder in one quick movement. "Give me no more trouble, lass," he commanded when she started to struggle. "In Scotland we don't repay kindness by stabbing someone."

He tossed Elizabeth on his horse, whistled for Rab to follow and the three of them set off at a furious pace.

Chapter 9

ELIZABETH SAT alone in a big room in the MacGregor castle, the oak door barred. The room was mostly bare except for an enormous bed, a chest and three chairs. A fireplace was along one wall, filled with logs, but no fire warmed the cold stones.

Elizabeth huddled in one of the chairs, the plaid from Bronwyn wrapped about her, her sore knees drawn in to her chest. It had been several hours since the MacGregor had tossed her in the room without so much as a backward glance. No food had been sent to her, no water for washing, and the dog, Rab, had bounded away at the first sight of the MacGregor fortress. Elizabeth was too tired to sleep, her mind in too much of a turmoil to allow her much rest.

When she first heard the familiar voice, muffled through the heavy door, her first reaction was one of relief. But she quickly recovered from that. Miles Montgomery was as much her enemy as anyone else.

When Miles opened the door and walked in boldly, she was ready for him. She sent a copper and silver goblet from the mantelpiece flying at his head.

Miles caught the object in his left hand and kept walking toward her.

She threw a small shield from the wall at him and he caught that in his right hand.

With a little smile of triumph, Elizabeth grabbed a battered helmet from the mantel and drew back her arm to throw it. He had no more hands with which to catch this object.

But before she could throw the helmet, Miles was before her, his arms drawing her close to him.

"I was very worried about you," he whispered, his face buried against her cheek. "Why did you run away like that? Scotland isn't like England. It's treacherous country."

He didn't hold her very tightly, at least not enough to cause her to want to struggle, but instead she almost wished he'd pull her closer. As it was, she had to stand very still or else his arms might drop away altogether. At his idiot words, though, she did move away. "I am attacked by wolves, nearly fall into the sea and some man throws me about like a sack of grain and *you* tell *me* this is treacherous country!"

Miles touched her temple and she did not move away from him. There was an unusual light in his eyes. "Elizabeth, you make your own problems."

"I did not ask to be delivered into my enemy's hands nor to be brought as a prisoner into this hostile country and as for that man—"

Miles interrupted her. "The MacGregor was quite angry at your taking a knife to him. A few months ago he nearly died from Bronwyn's using a knife on him."

"But they seemed to be friends."

Before she could speak another word, the chamber door opened and in walked two brawny Scotsmen carrying an oak tub. Behind them came a dozen women bearing buckets of hot water. The last woman held a tray with three decanters and two goblets.

"Knowing your propensity for not bathing, I have taken the liberty of ordering a bath." Miles smiled at her.

Elizabeth didn't answer him but put her nose into the air and turned toward the cold fireplace.

When the room was empty of people except for the two of them, Miles put his hand on her shoulder. "Come and bathe while the water is hot, Elizabeth."

She whirled on him. "Why should you think that I'd do for you what I haven't done for other men? I ran away from you at Larenston and now you seem to think I'll leap into your arms because you've shown up here. What difference does it make whether I'm held prisoner by the MacGregor or a Montgomery? If the truth be known, I prefer the Mac-Gregor."

Miles's jaw hardened and his eyes darkened. "I think it's time some things were made clear between us. I have been more than patient with you. I have stood by silently while you hurt Sir Guy. I have shared my son with you. I have watched as you put the entire Clan MacArran in turmoil and now you've come close to injuring the MacGregor. The peace be-tween the MacGregors and MacArrans is too new and fragile. You could have destroyed what it's taken Stephen a year to build. And look at you, Elizabeth! Have you seen yourself? There is dried blood all over you, you're obviously exhausted and you've lost much weight. I think it's time I stopped letting you have your own way."

"My . . . !" she sputtered. "I do not want to be held pris-oner! Do you understand me? Can I get anything through your thick head? I want to go home to my brothers and I will do whatever I can to get there."

"Home!" Miles said through clenched teeth. "Do you have any idea what the word means? Where did you learn how to break men's toes? How to use a knife so efficiently? What made you decide all men were evil creatures? Why can't you abide any man's touch?"

Elizabeth just looked at him sullenly. "Edmund is dead," she said after a while.

"Will you always live under a cloud, Elizabeth?" he whis-pered, his eyes soft. "Will you always see only what you want to see?" After a long sigh, he held out his hand to her. "Come and bathe before the water cools."

"No," she said slowly. "I don't want to bathe."

She should have been used to Miles's extraordinary quick-ness, but as usual she was unprepared for it.

"I've had enough of this, Elizabeth," he said before tossing the damp plaid from her. "I've been patient and kind but from now on you're going to learn a little obedience—and trust. I am not going to harm you; I have *never* harmed any woman but I cannot stand by and allow you to hurt yourself."

With that, he tore the front of her dress away, exposing her breasts.

Elizabeth gasped, crossed her arms in front of her and jumped back.

Easily, Miles caught her, and in two swift tears he had her nude. He didn't seem to pay any attention to her body as he picked her up and carried her to the tub where he gently set her into the water.

Without a word, he picked up a cloth, soaped it and began to gently wash her face. "Struggle and the soap will be in your eyes," he said, making her hold still.

She refused to speak to him while he washed the upper half of her body, glad for the soap that hid her red face as his hands glided lingeringly over her high, firm breasts.

"How did you hurt yourself?" he asked conversationally as he soaped her left leg, careful of the ugly cuts and scrapes on her knee.

The water was relaxing her and there was no reason not to tell him. She lay back in the tub, closed her eyes and told him of the night she'd spent along the cliff road. Halfway through the story, a glass of wine touched her hand and she drank of it thirstily. The intoxicant immediately went to her head and, dreamily, she kept talking.

"Rab stayed with me," she concluded, drinking more wine. "The dog understood that I didn't want to go to Bronwyn, but instead he led me to Bronwyn's friend." The wine was making her so relaxed she didn't even feel angry at the dog or the MacGregor or anyone else.

"Miles," she said conversationally, unaware of the pleasure she gave him in using his Christian name. "Why *don't* you strike women? I don't believe I've met a man who doesn't use force to get his way."

He was gently washing her toes. "Perhaps I use a different kind of force."

That was all he was going to say and for a while they were silent. Elizabeth didn't realize that he kept her glass full of wine and by now she had drunk nearly an entire decanter-ful.

"Why didn't you speak up to your brother this morning? Or was it yesterday morning?"

Miles's momentary pause in washing her was his only sign that he understood her question. She'd never really asked something so personal before, as if she were interested in him.

"My three elder brothers are very pig-headed men. Gavin's never heard anyone's opinion except his own and Raine likes to imagine himself as a martyr for all lost causes."

"And Stephen?" she asked, drinking more wine, watching him through lowered lashes. His hands on her felt so very, very good.

"Stephen fools people into believing he's a willing com-promiser, but when it comes to the point, he insists upon his own way. Only for Bronwyn was he willing to look at some-one else's view, and she had to fight him—and still fights—for everything. He makes jests about what to her is life and death."

Elizabeth considered this for a moment. "And you are their little brother. No doubt they will always consider you someone to be instructed, someone who must be taken care of."

"And is that the way you are treated also?" he half whis-pered.

The drink, the hot water, made her loosen her tongue. "Roger thinks I have only a quarter of a brain. Half is missing because I am a woman, half of that gone because he remem-bers me in swaddling clothes. When I told him some of what Edmund was doing to me, he wasn't sure whether to believe me or not. Or perhaps he didn't want to see the things his own brother did or allowed to happen.

"Damn!" she said, half rising from the tub. With a violent jerk she threw the goblet across the room, slamming it into the stone wall. "I *am* half a woman. Do you know what it feels like to watch Bronwyn and your brother, to see them laugh and love? The two of them sneak little touches when they think no one is looking. Whenever a man touches me, I—"

She broke off, her eyes wide, her head reeling from the drink. "Make love to me, Miles Montgomery," she whispered huskily. "Make me not afraid."

"I had planned to," he said throatily as he pulled her into his arms.

She still stood in the tub, and as Miles's mouth came down on hers, she kissed him back—kissed him with all the passion, all the anger she felt at having been cheated of a normal attitude toward love. While other women were learning how to flirt, Elizabeth's brother had been gambling, promising his little sister's virginity to the winner, and Elizabeth had learned to use a knife. She had preserved her precious virginity and for what? The convent? For a life where she grew harder and angrier every year until she turned to stone—an unloved, useless old woman?

Miles pulled back from her slightly, controlling the kiss, keeping her from hurting herself as she tried to grind her lips against his teeth. His hands were playing up and down her wet back, his fingertips caressing the indentation of her spine.

His lips moved to the corner of her mouth, his tongue touching the tip of hers before he trailed to her cheek, kissing her while his hands toyed with her skin.

Elizabeth tilted her head back and to one side as Miles's teeth ran along her neck and to her shoulder. Perhaps this was the true reason why she'd never allowed a man to touch her. Maybe she'd always known that unless she fought like a demon she'd succumb like this—wantonly, unashamedly.

"Miles," she whispered. "Miles."

"Always," he murmured, nibbling her ear.

With one swift motion he lifted her from the tub and carried her to the bed. Her body was wet, her hair cold and clinging to her, but Miles wrapped a towel about her and began rubbing. The briskness of his rubbing sent new warmth through her and everywhere, every time he touched her she wanted more. She had a whole lifetime of touching to make up for.

Suddenly Miles was beside her, nude, his glorious skin warm, dark, inviting.

"I am yours, Elizabeth, as you are mine," he whispered as he placed her hand on his chest.

"So much hair." She giggled. "So very much hair." She buried her fingers in the short black curling stuff and pulled. Obediently, Miles rolled closer to her, snuggled her golden body to the length of him.

"What does it feel like?" she asked anxiously.

"You'll not know for a long while." He smiled. "When we become one, there'll be no fear in your eyes."

"Become one," she whispered as Miles again began to kiss her neck. He kissed her neck for a very long time before he moved to her arm, his tongue making little swirling motions inside her elbow. It was odd how little vibrations seemed to be traveling from her fingertips, across her breasts to her other fingertips.

She lay still, eyes closed, arms open, legs open as Miles touched her. Those big hands that could wield a sword, could protect a child from harm, could control an unruly horse, were tenderly, slowly setting her body on fire.

When his hand moved from her throat to her cheek, she turned her head and kissed the palm, put both her hands on his and began to make love to that hard delicate hand, scraping it against her teeth, tasting his skin, running her tongue around and around the hairs on the back of his hand.

She was rewarded by a primitive sound from Miles that set her heart racing.

"Elizabeth," he groaned. "Elizabeth. How I have waited."

Elizabeth decided she wasn't really in the mood for more waiting. Instinctively she tried to wiggle further under Miles, but he refused to allow that. Instead, he brought his mouth to her breast and Elizabeth nearly came off the bed.

Miles chuckled at her reaction and she felt his laughter all along the length of her. Love and laughter, she thought. That's what Miles had added to her life.

Miles's lips on her breasts soon made her stop thinking. He straddled her hips, on his knees, his hands about her waist, squeezing, caressing, and gradually he began using his fingers to guide her hips into a slow, undulating rhythm.

She caught the rhythm easily. Her breathing deepened and her hands on Miles's arms tightened, her fingers digging into his muscles. His body surrounding her, warm, hard, sculptured, was all she was aware of as her whole body began to move sensuously.

"Miles," she whispered, her hands moving to his hair. She was not gentle as she pulled his face to hers, sought his lips in a kiss such as she'd never dreamed of before. There was sweat on both of them, salty, hot sweat.

Elizabeth drew her knees up, clutched Miles's hips and when she did, he entered her.

There was no pain as she was more than ready for him, but for a moment she trembled with the force of her reaction. Miles held still, also slightly trembling, until Elizabeth started the slow rhythm he'd taught her with his hands.

Slowly, together, they made love. After only moments, Elizabeth lost herself in a sea of passion she'd never known existed before. As Miles increased his speed, she locked her legs about him and gave herself up to her senses. With one blinding flash, Elizabeth's body convulsed and her legs began to shake violently.

"Hush," Miles soothed as he lifted onto one elbow and stroked her temple. "Hush, my angel. You're safe now."

He withdrew from her, pulled her into his arms. "My promised angel," he whispered. "My angel of rain and lightning."

Elizabeth didn't understand his words completely but she did, perhaps for the first time in her life, feel safe. She fell asleep instantly, her body so close to Miles's that she could scarcely breathe.

When Elizabeth awoke, she stretched luxuriously, feeling each and every muscle of her body, wincing when she pulled the torn skin of her knees. Her eyes opened and the first thing she saw was a long table covered with steaming food. She was sure she'd never been so hungry in her life. Grabbing Bronwyn's plaid from the floor, she tossed it about her body haphazardly and went to the table.

Her mouth was full of a bit of poached salmon when the door opened and Miles walked in. Elizabeth froze, her hand halfway to her mouth as she began to remember the previous night. There was such a disgustingly *knowing* look in Miles's dark eyes that Elizabeth began to grow angry. Before she could even sort her feelings, Miles casually began to discard the Scots clothes he wore.

What right did he—! Elizabeth thought, choking on the salmon as she tried to speak. But he did have a right. After the way she'd acted last night, he had every right to believe the very worst of her. But still she'd like to wipe that expression off his face.

Elizabeth didn't really consider what she did, but beside her were two heaping platters of warm, soft tarts, baked to a golden turn, heavy with summer fruit. With a smile, her eyes locked with Miles's, she slipped her hand under a tart and, still smiling, sent it flying toward him.

He wasn't expecting missiles sent at him and the pie hit his collar bone, splashing his cheek, running down his chest in a warm ooze of cherries and juice.

Elizabeth knew that whatever happened now it was worth it for the look on Miles's face. He was totally, completely, shocked. With her hand over her mouth to cover a giggle, Elizabeth sent two more pies flying at him, hitting his bare hip with the first one, the chair behind him with the other one.

Miles looked at Elizabeth with an odd expression, discarded the rest of his clothes and kept walking toward her.

The plaid Elizabeth had worn fell from her body and Elizabeth, eyes wide, began to throw pies in earnest, using both hands. She wasn't sure but she thought she saw murder in those gray eyes.

Miles kept coming, only moving when a tart came flying at his face. His entire body was covered in a mixture of peaches, cherries, apples, dates, plums, all running down his muscular body in a glorious riot of colors—and flavors, Elizabeth thought irrelevantly.

When he reached the table, his piercing eyes held hers and she didn't dare move. He bolted over the table to stand beside her and Elizabeth, breath held, looked up at him. But as she looked, a cherry, plump and juicy, ran down his forehead, his nose, and hung for just a second before plopping down onto the floor. Another giggle escaped Elizabeth.

Slowly, tenderly, Miles drew her into his arms. "Ah, Elizabeth," he said, "you are such a joy."

As his lips came near hers, she closed her eyes, remembering all too well the sensations of last night. He bent her backward in his arms and Elizabeth gave herself over to the strength of him. He had power over her. All he had to do was touch her and she began to tremble.

But lips did not touch hers. Instead, she received a face full of juicy, syrupy peach pie. As peaches ran into her ears, her eyes flew open. Gasping, she looked up into Miles's devilish face.

Before she could even protest, with a wicked little smile, he lifted her and set her on the table—smack in the middle of the second platter of tarts. Fruit juice oozed over her legs, somehow did the impossible and traveled up her spine. Her hands were covered, peaches dripped off her chin, her hair was glued to her body.

With utter disgust, she lifted her hands, brushed them against each other, saw that did no good whatever, and on second thought, she ate two apple slices from the back of her wrist.

"A little too sweet," she said seriously, looking at Miles. "Perhaps we should complain to the cook."

Miles, nude before her, showed that his mind was not on the cook. Elizabeth's eyes widened in mock dismay. It was difficult, if not impossible, to retain one's composure while sitting in a puddle of fruit pies. She opened her arms to her sticky lover and he came to her.

When Elizabeth kissed Miles's neck and came away choking on a cherry pit, their laughter began. Miles noisily began eating peaches from her forehead while Elizabeth nibbled plums from Miles's shoulder.

Miles grabbed her, rolled onto his back amid a great clatter of dishes and the squish of food, and set her down on his swollen manhood. There was no more laughter as their thoughts turned serious and they made love with vigor, twice changing positions, ending with Miles on the bottom.

Elizabeth lay quite still on top of him, weak, exhausted, thinking she might die before she had energy to rouse herself.

But Miles, with a grunt, lifted both of them and removed a small earthenware bowl that had once contained a sauce of some sort from the small of his back, and flung it to the floor.

Elizabeth raised herself and absently scratched her thigh. "You are a sight, Miles Montgomery," she said, smiling, brushing a poached egg from his hair. The yellow was working its way down toward his scalp.

"You are not exactly presentable at court." With another groan of pain, he removed a serving fork from under his buttocks.

"What do you think your MacGregor is going to think of this?" Elizabeth asked, moving off Miles. She sat up, cross-legged beside him and surveyed the room. The walls, floors, furniture were covered with smashed tarts, and the table was a disaster, everything overturned, dripping, running together—except for a couple of dishes at the very end of the table. On her hands and knees, Elizabeth crawled toward the undisturbed food, squealed once when Miles gave her buttocks a sweet caress, but came back with a bowl of chicken cooked with almonds and a small loaf of wheat bread.

Miles, still stretched on his back on the table, raised himself on his hand. "Still hungry?" he teased.

"Starved." She grabbed a spoon from under Miles's ankle and dug into the stew, and when Miles turned soulful, forlorn eyes up to her, she began to feed him also. "Don't get used to this," she commanded as she shoveled more food into his mouth.

Miles merely smiled at her and occasionally kissed her fingers.

All in all, they found quite a bit of undestroyed food on the table. Elizabeth hung over the side, with Miles holding an ankle and a wrist, and retrieved a whole roast partridge which had caught on the leg stretchers. Miles refused to feed himself and Elizabeth was "forced" to feed him, even to stripping the meat from the partridge bones.

"Worthless is what you are," Elizabeth said, scratching. The food on her body was beginning to dry and it *itched!*

"What you need," Miles murmured, running nibbling kisses up her arm, "is—"

"I don't want to hear any of your suggestions, Montgomery!" she warned. "Last night you got me drunk and pounced on me in a tub and now . . . this!" There were no words to describe the fragrant mess about them. "Damn!" she cursed, using both hands to scratch her thigh. "Is there nothing normal about you?"

"Nothing," he reassured her as he lazily stepped down from the table and began to dress. "There's a lake not far from here. How about a swim?"

"I have no idea how to swim."

He caught her waist and lifted her from the table. "I'll teach you," he said so lewdly that Elizabeth laughed and pushed against him.

"Underwater?" she said, and when Miles seemed to consider this seriously, she nearly ran from him, slipping once on an ooze of cod livers but catching herself on the table edge. In record time, she'd slipped into a tartan skirt, a saffron-colored shirt and tossed a plaid about her shoulders. The skirt had been in the line of fire of a cheese tart.

"Do I look as bad as you?" she asked as he pulled food from his hair.

"Worse. But no one will see us." With that cryptic sentence, he walked toward a tapestry on the far wall, pulled it aside and revealed a staircase built inside the thick stone walls. He took Elizabeth's hand and led her into the dark, cold passage.

Chapter 10

TWO HOURS later they were washed and Miles was drying Elizabeth with a plaid.

"Quite useful, aren't they?" she murmured, wrapping the tartan cloth about her cool body. The Scots summer was not conducive to lying about nude.

"Many things about the Scots are practical as well as pleasant—if you'd give them half a chance."

She stopped drying her hair. "What does it matter to you whether I like the Scots or not? I understand your wanting to get me into your bed but I don't understand this constant . . . interest, I guess, in my welfare."

"Elizabeth, if I'd merely wanted you in my bed I could have taken you that first day when you were delivered to me."

"And you would have lost part of yourself to my ax blade," she snapped.

After a moment's surprise, Miles began to laugh. "You and that ax! Oh Elizabeth, you were such a charming sight with your leg sticking out and surrounded by so much hair. You were—"

"You do not have to laugh *quite* so hard," she said stiffly. "It was not humorous to me. And I may yet escape you."

That sobered him. He pulled her down to the ground beside him. "I don't want to have to go through more nights like those. Rab was missing and we found dead wolves along the cliff and the mare you rode came back limping. We were really afraid you'd fallen over the cliff."

She pushed at him because he was holding her so tightly she couldn't breathe. As she looked up at him, she frowned. She'd always thought that if a man did take her virtue, she would hate him, but hate was far removed from what she felt for Miles. Between them now was a soft sense of sharing, as if they'd always been here and always would be.

"Is it always like this?" she whispered, looking up at the trees overhead.

There was a pause before Miles answered. "No," he said so softly it could have been the wind.

She knew he understood what she meant. Perhaps he was lying to her, perhaps tomorrow he'd again be her enemy, but right now he wasn't.

"There were never days like this when my brother was alive," she began, and when she started she couldn't stop. Although she'd fought Miles at every opportunity, she now knew that in truth she'd never been in any real danger—not the danger she'd experienced for most of her life. In the last few weeks she'd seen courtesy; she'd seen love between Bronwyn and Stephen, Miles and his son—and love that asked very little in return was something she'd not seen in her lifetime.

Instead of telling a horror tale of all the atrocities Edmund had committed, she talked of the way she and her two other brothers had bound themselves together. Roger had not been very old when his parents died and he'd been turned over to the rule of his treacherous brother. He'd done all he could to save his younger siblings but at the same time he wanted to live his own life. Every time that Roger slipped in his vigilance, Elizabeth was summoned from her convent and used in Edmund's nasty games. Roger, in remorse and guilt over his lapse, would strike out and renew his vows to protect Brian and Elizabeth, but always, Edmund's slimy ways would undermine Roger's good intentions.

"He's never had anyone but us," Elizabeth said. "Roger is twenty-seven but he's never been in love, never even had the time to while away a summer afternoon. He was old by the time he was twelve."

"And what of you?" Miles asked. "Didn't you consider that you deserved some time for laughter?"

"Laughter." She smiled, snuggling against him. "I don't think I remember any laughter in my life until a certain young man rolled down a hill with me."

"Kit is a delightful child," Miles said with pride.

"Kit, ha! It was someone larger who, even as he rolled, protected his fine sword."

"Noticed that, did you?" he said softly, tucking a strand of her hair behind her ear.

For a moment they were silent, with Elizabeth looking at him in puzzled silence. "You are not a kidnapper," she said at last. "I have seen you with men and with women and if you are nothing else in life, you are kind to women. So why do you not release me? Is it because, as you said, I have so many . . . problems?" She said the last stiffly.

He did not take her question lightly and it was a while before he answered. "All my life I've seemed to enjoy the company of women. I like nothing better than to lie about with a beautiful woman in my arms. My brothers seemed to think this made me less of a man but I don't guess one can change how one is. As for you, Elizabeth, I saw something I'd never seen before—a man's hatred and anger. My sister-in-law Judith could probably organize all of England, yet she needs my brother's strength and love. Bronwyn loves people and could make anyone do her bidding, but she's unsure of herself and needs Stephen's stubborn belief in himself to back her."

He paused. "But you, Elizabeth, are different. You could probably exist alone and you wouldn't even know there was more to life."

"Then why . . ." she began. "Why hold someone like me prisoner? Surely some soft, docile woman would be more to your liking."

He smiled at the insult in her tone. "Passion, Elizabeth. I think you are surely the most passionate human on earth. You hate violently and I am sure you will love just as violently."

She tried to move away but he pinned her to the ground, his face near hers. "You'll love only once in your life," he said. "You'll take your time in giving your love but once it is given, no power on earth—or hell—will break that love."

She lay still under him, gazing up into those deep gray orbs that burned into her.

"I want to be that man," he said softly. "I want more than your body, Elizabeth Chatworth. I want your love, your mind, your soul."

When he bent to kiss her, she turned her head away. "You don't ask much, do you, Montgomery? You've had more than I've given any other man—but I don't think I have more to give. My soul belongs to God, my mind to myself and my love goes to my family."

He rolled away from her and began to dress. "You asked me why I keep you prisoner and I've told you. Now we'll return to the MacGregor's and you will meet his men. The MacGregor is angered over your taking a knife to him and you will apologize."

She did not like his attitude. "He is a friend to the MacArrans who are related to my enemies, the Montgomerys"—she smiled sweetly—"therefore I had every right to try and protect myself."

"True," he agreed, handing her her clothes, "but if the MacGregor isn't appeased, it could cause problems between the clans."

She began to dress sullenly. "I don't like this," she muttered. "And I'll not enter a hall of strange men without a weapon."

"Elizabeth," Miles said patiently. "You cannot wield an ax at every gathering of men you enter. Besides, these Scots have some beautiful women of their own. Perhaps they won't be so enraptured with your charms that they're driven to insane acts of lust."

"I didn't mean that!" she snapped, turning away from him. "Must you laugh at . . . ?"

He put his hand on her shoulder. "I don't mean to laugh at you, but you have to begin to realize what is normal and what isn't. I'll be there to protect you."

"And who will protect me from you?"

At that, his eyes lit and he ran his hand down the side of her breast. "You will be pleased to know that no one will protect you from me."

She pulled away from him and finished dressing.

What Miles had planned for Elizabeth was, to her, sheer torture. He clamped his fingers down on her elbow until pain shot up her arm, and he forced her to shake hands with over a hundred of the MacGregor men. When she finished, she collapsed in a chair against the wall and shakily drank the wine Miles handed her. When he complimented her as if she were a dog that'd performed a trick correctly, she sneered at him, which made him kiss her fingers and laugh.

"It will get easier," he said confidently.

Indeed, it did get easier, but it took weeks. Miles never let up on her for a moment. He refused to let her walk behind the men and when she turned constantly to check the men's whereabouts, he made her be still. They rode on a hunt and once Elizabeth was separated from Miles. Three MacGregors found her, were quite cordial to her, but by the time she reached Miles, there was terror in her eyes. Instantly, he pulled her onto his horse, held her and soothed her and when that wasn't enough, he made love to her under a beech tree.

There was one man at the MacGregor's who Miles warned her against: Davy MacArran, Bronwyn's brother. Miles had a fierce dislike for the boy who was actually older than himself. Miles said, with great contempt, that Davy had tried to kill his own sister.

"For all the arrogance of my brothers," Miles said, "they would give their lives for me as I would for them. I have no use for men who go against their families."

"As you are asking me to do?" she retorted. "You are asking me to forsake my brothers and give myself body and soul to you."

There was a flicker of anger in Miles's eyes before he left her alone in the room they shared.

Elizabeth went to the window to look down at the men in the courtyard below. It was an odd feeling to know that if she wanted she could walk in that courtyard and not be molested. She need have no fear that she would have to fight for her life. There was no urge on her part to test her knowledge but it was pleasant to consider.

The MacGregor walked by and the powerful strut of the big man almost made her smile. His vanity had taken a beating at Bronwyn's hands and again at Elizabeth's, and when Miles had practically pushed Elizabeth before him, the MacGregor'd hardly looked at her. This had *never* happened to her before and before she knew what she was doing, she found herself practically coaxing him to talk to her. It had taken only minutes before she felt him twining about her fingers. He liked pretty women and he was old enough that he was beginning to wonder whether pretty women liked him. Elizabeth soon dispelled that idea.

Later Miles looked at her in disgust. "You changed quickly from the frightened rabbit to the temptress."

"Do you think I make a good temptress?" she taunted. "Lachlan MacGregor is a widower. Perhaps—"

She didn't finish because Miles kissed her so hard he nearly bruised her lips. With her fingertips on her lower lip, she watched his broad back as he moved away from her— and smiled. She was beginning to realize that she had some power over Miles, but as yet she didn't know the extent of her power.

Now, as she watched the courtyard, men, wearing the MacArran cockade, rode into the area. The MacGregors falsely acted with nonchalance, but Elizabeth saw that all the men's hands were very close to their sword belts. Miles came from inside the MacGregor's stone house and talked to the MacArrans.

Elizabeth watched for only a moment before turning back to the room with a sigh, and she began to gather Miles's belongings. She knew without a doubt that they would be leaving.

Miles opened the door, paused for a moment, saw what she was doing and began to help her. "My brother Gavin has come to Larenston."

"With Roger?" She paused with her hand on a velvet cape.

"No, your brother has escaped."

She whirled to face him. "Unharmed? With all his body parts?"

Miles's eyes widened for a moment. "As far as I know, everything is attached." He caught her hands. "Elizabeth . . ."

She pulled away. "Perhaps you should have one of the MacGregor's beautiful lasses to pack your fine belongings." With that she fled to the stairs behind the tapestry.

In spite of everything she could do, tears began to fall. She tripped in the black darkness, barely caught herself from falling and ended up sitting down hard on a stone stair as several rats squealed in protest at her disturbance.

Sitting there, crying as if her life were over, she knew she had no reason to cry. Her brother was no longer a prisoner as she was; he was unharmed. And now Gavin Montgomery had come, no doubt to force his younger brother to release her. By this time tomorrow she'd probably be on her way home. No more would she have to shake hands with strange men. No more would she be a captive, but she'd be free to go home to her own family.

A sound on the stairs above her made her turn and although she couldn't see him, she knew Miles was there. Instinctively, she held her arms out to him.

Miles grabbed her so hard she knew her ribs would crack, and all she did was cling to him all the more tightly. They were like two children hiding from their parents, frightened of tomorrow, making the most of now.

To them there was no dust or filth, no angry little eyes watching them as they fumbled with each other's clothes, their lips joined, never parting. The violence with which they came together was new to Elizabeth, as Miles had always been gentle with her, but when her nails dug into his back, he reacted. The stairs bit into the back of her as Miles lifted her hips and took her with a blinding, fierce passion, but with no more fierceness than Elizabeth sought him. She braced her feet against the stairs and pushed upward with all the force of her strong young body.

The flash of light that tore through them left them both weak, trembling, holding onto each other as if to let go meant they'd die.

Miles was the first to recover. "We must go," he whispered tiredly. "They wait below for us."

"Yes," she said. "Big brother calls." Even in the darkness, she could feel Miles's eyes on her.

"Don't be afraid of Gavin, Elizabeth."

"The day a Chatworth is afraid of a Montgomery—" she began but Miles kissed her to silence.

"That's what I like! Now if you can keep your hands off me long enough, we'll ride to Larenston."

"You!" She started to strike him but he bolted up the stairs before she could, and when Elizabeth tried to move, she winced at a hundred bruised places. She emerged from behind the tapestry bent over, her hand to her back. Miles's conceited chuckle made her straighten painfully. "If women didn't always have to be on the bottom—" she snapped, then stopped when she saw the MacGregor leaning against a chest.

"I was going to say I hoped you enjoyed your visit, Lady Elizabeth." The big man's eyes twinkled so merrily that Elizabeth busied herself in packing, pointedly ignoring him, so pointedly that she didn't hear him move behind her. When his hands touched her shoulder, she gasped, but Miles caught her arm, warned her with his eyes.

"We've enjoyed ye, Elizabeth," the MacGregor said as he removed the crude pin she wore at her shoulder and replaced it with a large round silver one, bearing the MacGregor standard.

"Thank you," she said quietly, and to the amazement of all three of them, she quickly kissed the MacGregor's cheek.

Miles's hand on her arm tightened and he looked at her with such pleasure that his whole body fairly glowed.

"Sweet lass, come and see me again."

"I will," she said and smiled genuinely because she meant her words.

Together the three of them walked down to the courtyard and the waiting horses. Elizabeth looked at all the MacGregor men with curiosity because she knew she was going to miss them. With a sense of wonder at what she was doing, she voluntarily shook hands with some of the men. Miles stayed close to her and she was well aware of his presence, and grateful for it, but her fear at touching the men and being touched by them was only just that—fear, not terror.

She was glad when she came to the end of the line and could mount her horse. Behind her were Bronwyn's men, strangers to her, and she could have cried out at the injustice of having to leave a place she was just beginning to trust.

Miles leaned across and squeezed her hand. "Remember that I am here," he said.

She nodded once, kicked her horse forward and they were off.

For how long will you be here? she wanted to ask. She knew much about Gavin Montgomery. He was a greedy, treacherous man whose jilting of Alice Chatworth had nearly driven her insane. And Gavin was the head of the Montgomery family. For all Miles's bravado, he was only twenty years old and Gavin had the guardianship of his young brother. Would Gavin take her away, use her in his own games against the Chatworth family? Miles believed Roger'd killed Mary Montgomery. Would this Gavin use Elizabeth to repay the Chatworths?

"Elizabeth," Miles said. "What are you planning?"

She didn't bother to answer him, but kept her head high as they entered Larenston.

Miles helped her from her horse. "No doubt my eldest brother is inside, waiting to get his hands on me," Miles said, eyes twinkling.

"How can you laugh about this?"

"The only way to deal with my brother is to laugh," he said seriously. "I'll come to you later."

"No!" she gasped. "I'll meet your brother with you."

Miles cocked his head, studied her. "I do believe you mean to protect me from my brother."

"You are a gentle man and—"

At that Miles laughed so loud, he startled the horses. He kissed her cheek heartily. "You are a dear, sweet child. Come along then and protect me if you want, but I'll keep an eye on Gavin's toes."

Gavin, Stephen and Sir Guy waited for them in the upstairs solar. Gavin was as tall as Miles but his face was more sculptured, hawklike, and his expression was of pure unadulterated rage.

"Is this Elizabeth Chatworth?" Gavin said through clenched teeth. He didn't wait for an answer. "Send her away. Guy, see to her."

"She stays," Miles said in a cool voice, not bothering to look at either of his brothers. "Sit, Elizabeth."

She obeyed him, sinking into a chair that dwarfed her.

After one angry glance at Elizabeth, Gavin turned to Miles who was pouring himself a glass of wine. "Goddamn you to hell and back, Miles!" Gavin bellowed. "You walk in here as if you hadn't nearly caused a private war between our families and you bring this . . . this . . . ."

"Lady," Miles said, his eyes growing dark.

"If she were a lady, I'd swear she isn't now after having spent weeks with you."

Miles's eyes turned black. His hand went to his sword but Sir Guy's hand made him pause.

"Gavin," Stephen warned, "you have no right to make insults. Say what you have to."

Gavin moved closer to Miles. "Do you know what your little escapade is costing our family? Raine can't even show his face but must hide in a forest, and I have spent the last month in the company of that bastard Chatworth—all in an attempt to save your worthless japing hide."

Elizabeth waited for Miles to retort that Raine's outlawing was not Miles's fault, but Miles remained silent, his eyes still dark, locked on his eldest brother.

A muscle in Gavin's jaw worked frantically. "You will release her to me and I will return her to her brother. I'd hoped that by now you'd come to your senses and let her go.

I'm sure you've taken her virginity and that will no doubt cost me much, but . . ."

"Will it cost you or Judith?" Miles asked calmly, turning his back on his brother.

A silence fell on the room and even Elizabeth held her breath.

"Stop it, both of you," Stephen interceded. "And for God's sake, Gavin, calm down! You know how Miles is when you insult his woman-of-the-moment. And you, Miles, you're pushing Gavin too far. Miles, Gavin has held Chatworth in order to give you some time to release Lady Elizabeth, and you can imagine that he was, ah, disappointed when Chatworth escaped and still you held Elizabeth. All you have to do is send her back with Gavin and all will be well."

Elizabeth again held her breath as she watched Miles's back and after a moment she felt Gavin watching her. It was then she decided she didn't like the man. She returned his arrogant look with one of her own. She looked away to see Miles watching them.

"I will not release her," Miles said softly.

"No!" Gavin bellowed. "Does the family mean nothing to you? Would you rather risk our name, the name of generations of Montgomerys, merely for the spread of a woman's thighs?"

Gavin wasn't expecting the fist that plowed into his face, but it didn't take him but seconds to recover and leap at Miles.

Chapter 11

STEPHEN AND Sir Guy used all their strength to restrain the two men.

It was Gavin who calmed first. He shook Stephen's arms away, walked toward the window and when he looked back, he had control over himself. "Send Lady Elizabeth away," he said quietly.

Sir Guy released Miles and Miles nodded to Elizabeth. She started to protest but knew that now was not the time. Miles was not going to turn her over to his brother, of that she was sure.

When the men were alone, Gavin sank into a chair. "Brother against brother," he said heavily. "Chatworth would love to know what he's doing to us. Stephen, pour me some wine."

When he held the cup, he continued. "King Henry has ordered this feud between the Montgomerys and Chatworths to cease. I have pleaded that our family is innocent in everything. Raine attacked Chatworth because of what had been done to Mary and I know you are innocent in the kidnapping of this Elizabeth."

Gavin drank deeply. He was used to these one-sided conversations with his young brother. Getting words from Miles was much worse than teeth pulling. "Has your Elizabeth told you of the young singer who was with her when Pagnell rolled her in a carpet? You should ask her because that singer has recently married Raine."

Miles's eyes widened slightly.

"Ah! At last I get some response from my brother."

"Gavin," Stephen warned. "How is Raine's wife involved in all this?"

Gavin waved his hand. "Pagnell was after her for some reason, tossed her in a dungeon and Elizabeth Chatworth tried to save her. In so doing, the Chatworth woman got caught and in jest was delivered to our lecherous little brother. God's teeth, why didn't you return her to Chatworth as soon as you found out who she was?"

"As he returned my sister?" Miles asked quietly. "When did you start being such a peacemaker?"

"Since I have seen my family torn apart by this hatred. Hasn't it occurred to you that the king will have some say in all this? He's punished Raine by outlawing him and Chatworth has been heavily fined. What will he do to you when he hears that you hold the Chatworth woman?"

"Miles," Stephen said. "Gavin's concern is for you. I know you've grown to care for the girl but there's more here than you think."

"Elizabeth deserves more than to be sent back to that hellhole of Chatworth's," Miles said.

At that, Gavin groaned, closed his eyes for a moment. "You've been around Raine too long. Whatever you think of Chatworth, no matter what he's done, he's done it with the belief that he was in the right. I've spent weeks with him and—"

"You are well known to side with the Chatworths," Miles said evenly, referring to Gavin's long affair with Alice Chatworth. "I'll not release her and no words from anyone will make me do so. The woman is mine. Now, if you will excuse me, I'd like to see Bronwyn."

In spite of her surety that she would be allowed to stay with Miles, Elizabeth still paced the floor. She cursed herself because she knew that she wanted to stay in Scotland, wanted to stay in a place where she could learn to be unafraid. Roger, she thought, dear, protective, angry Roger was in England somewhere, looking for her, frantic to find her, yet she hoped with all her heart that he'd not succeed.

"Just a little more time," she whispered. "If I can but have one more month I'll leave readily. And I shall have memories to last me a lifetime."

She was so absorbed in her own thoughts that she didn't hear the door open behind her, and when she heard the light footsteps, she whirled about, ready to do battle.

"Did . . . did you enjoy the MacGregors?" Kit stammered, unsure of what the fury on her face meant.

Instantly, Elizabeth's face changed. She knelt, opened her arms to the child and held him very, very close.

"I missed you so much, Kit," she whispered. When her eyes cleared, she held him away from her. "I stayed in a big room with a secret staircase behind a tapestry and your papa and I had a pie fight and we went swimming in a very cold lake."

"Bronwyn gave me a pony," Kit answered, "and Uncle Stephen took me riding and what kind of pies?" He leaned forward and whispered loudly, "Did you make Papa angry?"

"No." She smiled. "Not even when I hit him square in the face with a cherry tart. Come and sit down by me and I'll tell you about how Bronwyn's dog saved me from wolves."

It was some time later that Miles found them together, asleep, both looking perfectly content. For a long time Miles stood over them, quietly watching. When he heard the muffled sounds of horses in the courtyard below and knew it was Gavin leaving, he bent and kissed Elizabeth's forehead. "I'll give you more children, Elizabeth," he murmured, touching Kit's cheek. "See if I don't."

"I most certainly will not!" Elizabeth said to Miles, her face set grimly. "I have nearly killed myself doing what you want but I will not remain here alone while you chase about the countryside having a good time."

"Elizabeth," Miles said patiently, "I am going hunting and you will not be here alone. All the MacArrans—"

"MacArrans!" she shot at him. "All those men near me

for three days! No, I will not stay here. I'll go on the hunt with you."

"You know I'd love to have you but I think you need to stay here. There will be times when I can't be with you and you need to learn . . ." He stopped when she turned away.

"I don't need you or any other man, Montgomery," she said, shoulders stiff.

Miles touched her but she moved away. "Elizabeth, we've been through too much together to let this come between us. I think you should stay here with Kit and the men and try to conquer some of your fear. If you don't think you can do that, tell me and of course you can go with me. I'll be downstairs."

Elizabeth didn't look at him before he left the room. Nearly two months had passed since that day Gavin had first arrived, and during that time Elizabeth had found out what happiness was. She and Miles and Kit had spent lovely, long days together, playing in the newly fallen snow, laughing together. And Christmas had been such as she'd never experienced before—a family together.

Bronwyn had taught her a great deal, not by lectures but by example. Elizabeth rode with Bronwyn a few times and visited some of the crofters. There were a few instances of panic and once when Elizabeth drew a knife on a man who was following her too closely, Bronwyn had interceded and calmed Elizabeth. After that there was no more of the initial hostility between the women. Bronwyn seemed to adopt Elizabeth as a young sister rather than look on her as a potential rival. When Bronwyn started ordering Elizabeth about just as she did everyone else, Miles and Stephen relaxed. Three times Elizabeth told Bronwyn she could drop herself off the cliff road and Bronwyn had laughed heartily.

Rab also seemed to have adopted Elizabeth and quite often he'd refuse to obey either woman, skulking off into the shadows instead. When Stephen called the dog a coward, both women turned on him.

And daily, Miles and Elizabeth drew closer. Sometimes, while she watched Miles training, the upper part of his body bare, glistening with sweat, she felt her knees go weak. *Al-*

ways, Miles sensed her presence during those times and the hot looks he turned on her would make her tremble. Once, Stephen's lance had just missed Miles's head because Miles was concentrating on Elizabeth's lustful looks. Stephen had been so angry he'd started choking Miles.

"Another inch and I could have killed you," Stephen screeched in rage.

Both Bronwyn and Elizabeth, as well as Rab and Sir Guy, entered into that fracas. Stephen, his entire body red with fury, had demanded that Miles take Elizabeth away from the training ground. Miles, completely unruffled by his brother's anger, had agreed readily. And what a memorable afternoon that had been! In spite of Miles's outward calm, Stephen's unusual anger had upset him and he alternately attacked Elizabeth and clung to her. They made love in the bed, across a chair, the arm nearly breaking her back, and against a wall. Unfortunately, Miles slammed Elizabeth against a tapestry and she grabbed it. The heavy, dusty rug fell on them, knocked them to the floor—but they kept on until they started coughing. Locked together, they crawled from under the tapestry and continued on the cold stone floor. When they appeared for supper that night, flushed and exhausted, the entire Clan MacArran set up a howl of laughter. Stephen was still angry and all he'd say was to issue an order for Elizabeth to stay away from the training ground.

Two whole months and one week together, almost five months since her "capture," she thought.

But now she knew that time was running out.

Gavin sent a messenger to Miles. Roger Chatworth and Pagnell had gone to the king together and Roger'd told King Henry that Raine Montgomery was trying to raise an army against the king, and that Miles was holding Elizabeth in bondage. The king declared that if Miles did not release Elizabeth, he'd be declared a traitor and all his lands confiscated. As for Raine, the king threatened to burn the forest.

Gavin had pleaded with Miles to release Elizabeth. Miles spent days hardly speaking, but sometimes looking at her with great longing, and Elizabeth began to realize that their days together were numbered. Miles began to push her to spend time with the MacArrans, almost as if he were trying to prepare her for the future—a future without him.

Elizabeth was torn both ways. She did want to learn how to cope with her terror of men, but at the same time she wanted to spend every moment with Kit and Miles.

"Damn!" she muttered, alone in the room. How had she come so far from independence to utter dependence?

Gavin had come to Scotland again, this time in a rage that made his first one seem mild, and for the first time Elizabeth felt some guilt at wanting to stay in the peaceful MacArran household. When Miles came to their room, she asked him to allow her to leave with Gavin. She'd planned to say she wanted to save both his family as well as hers but Miles never gave her a chance. Both Stephen and Gavin's rages together were nothing compared to Miles's. He cursed in three languages, he threw things, tore a chair apart with his bare hands, took an ax to a table. It took both Tam and Sir Guy to hold him.

Gavin and Stephen had obviously seen their little brother like this before. Even Gavin gave up and went home after Miles's display. And Elizabeth was left weakened, looking down at the drugged Miles with tears in her eyes. Roger and Miles, she thought over and over, Roger and Miles. She had a home with two brothers, one of whom was tearing the Isles upside down to find her, yet she sat and cried over her enemy, a man who'd also protected her, who'd shown her patience and kindness and taught her that life could be good.

Drowsily, Miles opened his eyes. "Did I frighten you?" he asked huskily.

She could only nod.

"I frighten myself. They don't happen too often." He caught her hand, held it to his cheek like a child's toy. "Don't leave me again, Elizabeth. You were given to me; you are mine." With that often repeated refrain, he slipped away into sleep.

That had been four days ago, a mere short four days ago, but now he was planning to leave her alone for three days while he and Stephen went boar hunting. Perhaps Miles didn't sense her feeling of dread. Perhaps he was just sure enough of himself that he thought he could always keep her at his side. But Roger was on his way to Scotland and when he arrived with his army, what would she do? Could she stand by and see the MacArrans fight her brother? Could she watch a personal fight between Roger and Miles? Would she hold Kit in her arms and watch Miles die or would she hold Miles at night and taste the blood of her brother?

"Elizabeth?" Bronwyn asked from the doorway. "Miles said you're not going on the hunt."

"No," she said with some bitterness. "I'm to stay here and surround myself with men. Men behind me, men beside me, men watching my every move."

Bronwyn was silent for a moment, watching the blond woman. "Are you worried about Miles or your brother?"

"Both," Elizabeth replied honestly. "And were you ever worried about bringing an English husband into the midst of your Scotsmen? Did you wonder if you could trust him?"

Bronwyn's eyes danced with mirth. "The thought crossed my mind. All Stephen wanted was for me to admit that I loved him. But I was sure there was more to love than just some undefinable feeling."

"And is there?"

"Yes," Bronwyn said. "For some women I think they love a man in spite of what he is, but for me I had to know Stephen was what my clan needed as well as what I wanted."

"What if you'd loved him, loved him deeply, but your clan hated him? What if your staying with Stephen meant you would have alienated your clan?"

"I would have chosen my clan," Bronwyn answered, watching Elizabeth intently. "I would give up many things, even my own life, to keep from starting a war within my family."

"And that's what you think I should do!" she spat. "You think I should return to my brother. Now, while Miles is gone, is a perfect time. If I could have a few of your men I could . . ." She stopped as she locked eyes with Bronwyn.

At last Bronwyn spoke. "I honor my husband's brother. I will not help you to escape."

Elizabeth put her arms around Bronwyn. "What am I to do? You saw how Miles acted when I said I should return to Roger. Should I try to escape again? Oh Lord!" She pushed away. "You are my enemy as well."

"No." Bronwyn smiled. "I'm not your enemy, nor are any of the Montgomerys. We've all grown to love you. Kit would follow you to the ends of the earth. But the time will come when you'll have to choose. Until that moment arrives, no one can help you. Now come downstairs and kiss Miles goodbye before he starts wrecking more of my furniture. We have little enough as it is. And, by the way, how did that tapestry get on the floor?"

Elizabeth's red face made Bronwyn laugh loudly as they descended the stairs.

"Elizabeth." Miles laughed, pulling her into a darkened corner where she kissed him enthusiastically. "I'll only be gone for three days. Will you miss me so much?"

"You are the lesser of evils. If you come back and half-a-dozen men have their toes broken, it will be your fault."

He caressed her cheek. "After Sir Guy's experience, I don't think they would mind."

"What do you mean?"

"Bronwyn put that ugly giant in the care of some little flirt and now the two are inseparable. She has him fetching water for her and no doubt if he could hold a needle, he'd embroider her shirt collars."

Elizabeth almost kicked Miles at that because the shirt he wore under the Scots plaid was one she'd embroidered for him.

"Here, my little captive, behave yourself or I'll send you home."

Her eyes hardened at that, but Miles only laughed and nuzzled her neck. "What you feel is in your eyes. Now kiss me again and I'll be back very soon."

Minutes later she stood with empty arms and a heavy heart. Something was going to happen and she knew it. Her first impulse was to hide in her room, to remain there for three days, but she knew Miles was right. Now was a good time to try and overcome some of her fears.

By early afternoon she'd arranged an expedition of her own. She and Kit would ride out with ten MacArran men, Tam included, to a ruin Bronwyn had told her about. Kit could go exploring and she could work on swallowing her fear.

By the time they reached the ruin, Elizabeth's heart was pounding but she was able to smile at Tam as he helped her from her horse. When she heard a man behind her, she didn't turn quickly but tried to act in a normal manner. As she turned to face Jarl, she was rewarded with a smile of great pride from the young man, and Elizabeth let out a small laugh.

"Does everyone know about me?" she asked Tam.

"My clan has a great respect for you because you can slip about the woods as well as any Scotswoman, and we like people who are fighters."

"Fighters! But I have submitted to my enemies."

"Nay, lass." Tam laughed. "Ye've only come to your senses and seen what fine people we Scots are—and to a lesser degree, the Montgomerys."

Elizabeth joined in the laughter with him, as did the men around them.

Later, as Elizabeth sat on a stone of the ancient fallen-down castle, she watched the men below her, realized that she wasn't really afraid of them and thought how good that felt. She owed much to Miles Montgomery.

Because she was so intent upon the sight before her and perhaps because her wariness had dulled in the last few months, she didn't at first hear the whistle coming from the trees behind her. When it did penetrate her peace-drugged brain, every cell of her body came alert. First she looked to see if any of the MacArrans had heard the sound. Kit was playing with young Alex and making a great deal of noise while the others looked on fondly.

Slowly, as if she were going nowhere really, Elizabeth left

the boulders and disappeared into the trees with all the noise of a puff of smoke. Once inside, she stood still and waited and her mind was taken back to the days of her childhood.

Brian had always been the one to be protected. Older than Elizabeth but seeming younger, he'd never been able to develop the protective techniques that Elizabeth had. If a man attacked Elizabeth, she had no qualms about drawing a knife on him, but Brian couldn't. Time after time Elizabeth had rescued Brian from some gaggle of men Edmund had brought to their home. While Edmund roared with laughter, shouting insults at his weakling of a brother, Roger and Elizabeth had soothed the young, crippled Brian.

There had been so many days that Brian had spent in hiding, without food or drink, that they'd devised a way of signaling. Roger and Elizabeth were the only ones who knew the high-pitched whistle and they'd always come when Brian called.

Now, Elizabeth stood still, waiting for Brian to appear. Was he alone or with Roger?

The young man who stepped into the clearing was a stranger to Elizabeth and for a moment she could only gape at him. He'd always been handsome in a delicate way, but now he looked wraithlike and his face was that of some terrible specter.

"Brian?" she whispered.

He gave her a curt nod. "You look healthy. Does captivity agree with you?"

Elizabeth was nearly knocked speechless by this. She'd never heard her young brother say such a thing to anyone, much less to her. "Is . . . is Roger with you?"

Brian's sunken features darkened even more. "Do not say that vile name in my presence."

"What?" she gasped, moving toward him. "What are you talking about?"

For a moment, his eyes softened and he lifted a hand to caress Elizabeth's temple, but fell away before he touched her. "Many things have happened since we last saw each other."

"Tell me," she whispered.

Brian moved away from her. "Roger kidnapped Mary Montgomery."

"I had heard that but I can't imagine Roger . . ."

Brian turned on her with eyes like hot coals. "Do you think he's related to Edmund with no taint of blood? Do you think any of us escaped the evil that controlled our eldest brother?"

"But Roger . . ." she began.

"Do not even speak the name to me. I loved the woman Mary, loved her such as I could never love again. She was good and kind without a single wish to harm, but he—your brother—raped her and she cast herself from a window in horror."

"No," Elizabeth said calmly. "I cannot believe it. Roger is good. He doesn't harm people. He never wanted this war between the Montgomerys and Chatworths. He took in Alice when her own family wouldn't have her. And he—"

"He attacked Stephen Montgomery's back. He lied to Bronwyn MacArran and held her prisoner for a while. When Mary died, I released Bronwyn and took Mary back to Gavin. Did they tell you of the rage of Miles Montgomery when he saw his sister? It lasted for days?"

"No," Elizabeth whispered, vividly imagining Miles's fury. "They have said little about any of the war." After the first few days, it seemed to be a silent mutual agreement that she and Miles would not speak of their families' problems.

"Brian," she said softly. "You look tired and worn. Come back to Larenston with me and rest. Bronwyn will—"

"I'll not rest as long as my brother is alive."

Elizabeth gaped at him. "Brian, you cannot mean what you say. We'll contact Roger, then we'll sit down and talk about this."

"You don't understand, do you? I mean to kill Roger Chatworth."

"Brian! You can't forget a lifetime of good in one day. Remember how Roger always protected us? Remember how he risked his life to save you the day Edmund ran you down and crushed your leg?"

Brian's face didn't lose any of its hardness. "I loved Mary and Roger killed her. Someday you'll understand what that means."

"I may love a hundred people but that will not make me stop loving Roger, who has done so much for me. Even now he searches for me."

Brian looked at her in question. "You slipped away easily enough from your guard. If you're held so loosely, why don't you escape and go to Roger?"

Elizabeth moved away from him but Brian caught her arm. "Do the Montgomery men hold such attraction for you? Which is it? The married one or the boy?"

"Miles is far from being a boy!" she snorted. "Sometimes age is deceptive." She ceased when she saw Brian's expression.

"Do you forget that I was there at the Montgomery estate? So it's Miles you've come to love. A good choice. He's a man with enough fire to match your own."

"What I feel for any Montgomery doesn't change what I feel for Roger."

"And that is? What keeps you from going to him? These Scots can't be too difficult to escape. You deceived Edmund for years."

She was silent for a moment. "It isn't just Miles. There's a peacefulness here that I've never known before. No one puts knives to my throat. There are no distant screams at Larenston. I can walk down a corridor and not have to slide from shadow to shadow."

"I saw a glimpse of that once," Brian whispered, "but Roger killed it and now I mean to kill him."

"Brian! You must rest and think what you're saying."

He ignored her. "Do you know where Raine Montgomery is?"

"No," she said, startled. "He's in a forest somewhere. I met a singer who'd been with him."

"Do you know where I can find her?"

"Why do you care where this Raine is? Has he done something to you?"

"I plan to beg him to teach me how to fight."

"Not to fight Roger?" she gasped, then smiled. "Brian, Roger will never fight you, and look at you. You aren't half the size of Roger and you look as if you've lost weight. Stay here and rest a few days and we'll—"

"Don't patronize me, Elizabeth. I know what I'm doing. Raine Montgomery is strong and knows how to train. He'll teach me what I need to know."

"Do you really expect me to help you?" she asked angrily. "Do you honestly think I'd tell you where this Montgomery was even if I knew? I'll not aid you in your madness."

"Elizabeth," he said softly. "I came to say goodbye. I have waited in these woods for weeks, waiting for a time to see you, but you're always heavily guarded. Now that I have seen you I can leave. I will fight Roger and one of us will die."

"Brian, please, you have to reconsider."

As if he were an old man, he kissed her forehead. "Live in peace, my little sister, and remember me kindly."

Elizabeth was too stunned to reply, but as Brian turned away, Scotsmen began to drop from the trees. Stephen Montgomery, sword drawn, planted himself before Brian Chatworth.

Chapter 12

"DO NOT hurt him," Elizabeth said heavily, without the least fear that Stephen would harm her young brother.

Stephen caught her tone and resheathed his sword. "Go with my men and they'll feed you," he said to Brian.

With one last look at Elizabeth, Brian left the clearing, surrounded by MacArrans.

Elizabeth stood glaring at Stephen for a moment and in that time she understood a great deal.

Stephen had the courtesy to look somewhat embarrassed. With a sheepish grin, he leaned against a tree, took the dirk from the sheath on his calf and began to whittle on a stick. "Miles knows nothing about this," he began.

"You used me as bait to capture my brother, didn't you?" she blurted.

"I guess you could say that. He's been in the woods for days, skulking about, living on bare sustenance, and we were curious as to who he was and what he wanted. Twice while you were with Miles he came near but my men frightened him away. We decided to let you go to him. You were never alone; my men and I were directly overhead, swords and arrows drawn."

Elizabeth sat down on a large rock. "I don't much like being used like this."

"Would you rather we killed him on sight? A few years ago a lone Englishman couldn't have ridden onto MacArran land and lived to tell of it. But the boy seemed so . . . frantic that we wanted to find out about him."

She considered this a moment. She didn't like what he'd done but she knew he was right. "And now that you have him, what do you plan to do with him?" Her head came up. "Does Bronwyn know of this cat-and-mouse game of yours?"

She wasn't sure, but she believed Stephen's mouth whitened a bit. "As I love life, I am thankful she does not," he said with great feeling. "Bronwyn does not do things in secret—at least not too many anyway. She would have hauled the boy into Larenston and Miles . . ." He broke off.

"Miles's hatred of the Chatworths runs deep," she finished.

"Only of the men." He smiled. "Roger Chatworth caused our sister's death and Miles isn't likely to forgive that. You've only seen the side of him he shows to women. When confronted with a man who's hurt a woman, he is unreasonable."

"You were sure Brian was a Chatworth then?"

"He has that look about him."

Elizabeth was quiet for a moment. Brian *had* had some of Roger's look just now, a look of defiance and anger, covered by an expression of I-don't-care. "You heard what Brian said. Can we hold him here and keep him away from Roger?"

"I think he might go mad. He doesn't look too far from that now."

"No," she said heavily. "He doesn't." She looked up at Stephen expectantly.

"I believe I'll do just what Brian asks: I'll take him to my brother Raine."

"No!" Elizabeth said, standing up. "Raine Montgomery will kill him. Didn't he attack Roger?"

"Elizabeth," Stephen soothed. "Raine will take to the boy because Brian helped Mary. If Raine is nothing else, he's fair. And besides that," Stephen said with a little smile, "my brother will work Brian so hard the young man won't have time to hate. Within three days Brian will be so tired, all he'll think of is sleeping."

She studied him a moment. "Why should you help a Chatworth? Mary was your sister also."

"I thought you believed we Montgomerys lied about your brother's involvement in her death."

"If Miles killed a stranger's sister, would you hate your brother without so much as asking Miles why? Perhaps Roger was involved, but perhaps there were reasons for his actions. I do not and will not hate either of my brothers without just cause."

"Well said." Stephen nodded. "I do not bear any love for your brother Roger for what he's done, but my quarrel is with him, not with his family. My brothers don't feel the same way, which is why Gavin was so rude to you. To him family is everything."

"And is Raine the same way? Will he hate Brian on sight?"

"Perhaps, which is why I'm going with Brian. I'll be able to talk to Raine, and if I know my brother, he'll end by adopting your young Brian." He tossed the stick away and resheathed his knife. "And now I must be off. It will take us days to find my brother."

"Now?" she asked. "You'll leave before Bronwyn and Miles return from the hunt?"

"Oh yes." He grimaced. "I don't relish being around when my lovely wife finds out I tricked her into leaving Larenston so I could tend to this English trespasser alone."

"Or Miles," she said, eyes sparkling. "I don't believe he'll take this calmly."

Stephen groaned, making her laugh. "You, Montgomery, are a coward," she pointed out.

"Of the worst sort," he agreed readily, then turned serious. "Will you pray for me while I'm gone? Perhaps if Raine and Brian get along, we can make some progress in ending this war."

"I would like that," she answered. "Brian is a sweet, gentle man and Roger loves him very much. Stephen," she said in a low voice, "if I ask you a question, will you answer me honestly?"

"I owe you that much."

"Has anyone seen Roger?"

"No," Stephen answered. "He's disappeared. The Mac-Gregors are looking for him and my men are always alert. We nearly lost you once and it won't happen again. But no, so far there is no sign of Roger Chatworth."

For a moment they stood quietly, looking at each other. A few months ago this man was her enemy, as were all men. With one step forward, she came close to him, reached up and put her hand to his cheek.

Stephen seemed to understand the full impact of the honor she was bestowing upon him. He caught her hand, kissed the palm. "We Montgomerys are heartbreakers," he said with dancing eyes. "We'll end this feud with love words instead of swords."

She pulled away from him as if she were insulted, but her laughter escaped. "I will indeed pray for you. Now go before my Miles finds you and gives you a good thrashing."

He lifted one eyebrow at that. "Poor little brother, when some woman decides she owns him." With that he left her alone in the clearing.

Elizabeth sat alone for quite some time and now that she was listening carefully to the sounds around her, she could hear the MacArrans. There were still two men in the trees above her. Far off she could hear Kit's laughter and Tam's deep rumbling answer.

In the last months her senses had dulled greatly. Before her swam the angry face of Brian and she knew that once she, too, had felt such hatred. She hoped with all her being that Stephen would be able to take some of Brian's hate away, or perhaps this Raine Montgomery could do it.

With a heavy heart, she returned to the ruins and the laughter of Kit. In a few days, she'd have Miles's anger to deal with and that would take her mind off her problems.

Bronwyn returned to Larenston the next day and went first to her five-month-old son, Alexander. The child had a wet nurse as Bronwyn was too often away to feed him, but she made sure the boy knew who his mother was. As she was contentedly cuddling her son, Rab at her feet, Elizabeth told her about Brian and how Stephen had taken him to Raine. For a moment, Bronwyn's eyes flashed. "Damn him!" she muttered but calmed when Alex let out a yowl. "Hush, love," she cooed. When Alexander was quiet, she looked back at Elizabeth. "I don't like that he used you. He should have brought your brother here. Stephen forgets that Brian Chatworth released me from your brother's clutches. I wouldn't have harmed the boy."

"I think Stephen was more concerned about Miles—that *he* might harm Brian." Elizabeth leaned forward and caressed Alex's silky head.

Bronwyn's keen eyes missed nothing. "And when is your child due?" she asked evenly.

Elizabeth met Bronwyn's eyes.

Bronwyn stood, carried her son to his cradle. "Morag told me you've had no flow since you've been here. You've not been ill?"

"Not at all. I wasn't sure what was wrong with me at first, but it didn't take long to understand. Who have you told?"

"No one. Not even Stephen. Especially not Stephen. No doubt he'd want to celebrate. Are you planning to marry Miles?"

Elizabeth tucked the soft plaid around Alex's feet. "He hasn't asked me, but even if he did, there is more between us than marrying and having babies. Roger won't give up merely because I become a Montgomery. He'd have to know I go of my own free will and that I wasn't forced."

"And would Miles have to force you?" Bronwyn asked quietly.

Elizabeth smiled. "You know as well as I that he's forced me in nothing. But I don't think Miles would like marriage to me. I'd demand fidelity from my husband and Miles Montgomery doesn't know the meaning of the word."

"I wouldn't underestimate any of the Montgomery men," Bronwyn answered. "They may seem to be an arrogant, inflexible lot but there's more to them than pretty faces and virile bodies."

"They are indeed that." Elizabeth laughed as they left the room.

The next day Bronwyn returned to the hunt and it was while Elizabeth was being a helpless maiden in distress and Kit was saving her from a three-headed, fire-breathing dragon that Elizabeth suddenly stopped.

"Elizabeth!" Kit said impatiently, wooden sword brandished over his head.

She couldn't explain what was wrong with her but chills were covering her body. "Miles," she whispered. "Here!" she said to the woman holding Alex. "Take care of Kit."

With that she tore toward the stairs, down and out into the courtyard. When she reached the stables, she had her hand on a saddle before Douglas was beside her.

"I can't let you leave," Douglas said, regret in his voice.

"Out of my way, you fool," she spat at him. "Miles is in trouble and I'm going to him."

Douglas didn't waste time asking her how she knew this since no messenger had come from the hunting party, but he stepped out of the stables, gave three low whistles and in seconds two of his brothers were there.

Elizabeth wasn't used to saddling her own horse and it was a slow process, but the men didn't help her. Douglas checked the tightness of her cinch before catching her foot and practically tossing her into the saddle. Elizabeth didn't even flinch when he touched her.

As they started off, Elizabeth gave no thought as to where she was going but cleared her mind, visualized Miles and set off at a frightening pace, Douglas, Jarl and Francis behind her. The four horses thundered down the narrow, steep-sided road out of Larenston, turned right and headed along the cliff.

Elizabeth had no fear of the road nor did she worry about the men behind her. Once she was again on flat land, she paused only seconds. To the left was the MacGregors, and to the right was unknown territory. She kicked her horse to the right, somehow knowing this was the way.

One of the men yelled at her in warning once and she flattened herself against the horse's sweaty neck as she barely missed being hit by a tree branch. Other than that, the men were silent as they rode hard to keep up with her.

After a long time of riding, Rab came bounding from the underbrush, barking hard. He seemed to expect Elizabeth and had come to guide her the last part of the way.

Elizabeth was forced to slow her horse to a brisk walk as the four of them and Rab made their way through thick undergrowth into a clump of trees so dense the sunlight was hidden.

Rab began to bark again before the people came into view. Bronwyn and her men were standing in a group, looking down at something on the ground. Sir Guy was kneeling.

Bronwyn turned at her dog's bark and lifted surprised eyes to Elizabeth.

Her horse was still moving as Elizabeth slid to the ground and ran forward, pushing through the people.

Miles lay on the ground, eyes closed, his entire body covered in blood. His clothes were torn and she could see great gashes in his flesh, in his left thigh, in his right side.

She pushed Sir Guy away, knelt, pulled Miles's head into her lap and began to wipe the blood from his face with the hem of her skirt.

"Wake up, Montgomery," she said firmly with no sympathy or pity in her voice. "Wake up and look at me."

It seemed an eternity before Miles's lashes fluttered. When he did look at her he gave a little smile, let his eyes shut again. "Angel," he whispered and was silent.

"Water," Elizabeth said to the stunned faces over her. "I'll need water to wash his wounds, and is there a crofter's house near here?" Bronwyn only had time to nod before Elizabeth continued. "Go and clear the place out. Take the crofters to Larenston but leave me alone with him. Send Morag and her herbs and I'll need sharp steel needles and thread. Guy! Fetch a big plaid and we'll carry him to the hut. Well!" she snapped. "Get busy, all of you."

Instantly, men went off in all directions.

Bronwyn flashed Elizabeth a quick grin. "Are you sure you aren't a Scot?" With that she was off toward Larenston. Elizabeth, alone for a few moments, held Miles. "You'll be all right, Montgomery," she whispered. "I'll see to it."

She wasted no more time on sentimentality but took the dagger that lay on the ground beside him and began cutting away his clothes in order to examine his wounds. There seemed to be more blood on him than a man's body could hold.

Rab came up to her as she was slicing away Miles's shirt. "Where's the blood from, Rab?" she asked. "Go and find what did this to Miles."

With two great barks, the dog left them alone.

To Elizabeth's relief there was only the one gash on Miles's upper body, and that wasn't deep but would have to be sewn. There were several long bloody cuts on his left arm but nothing serious. His legs were another matter. The wound on his thigh was deep and ugly and there were more cuts on one ankle.

She shifted him once to try to see his underside to look for wounds.

With a groan of pain, Miles opened his eyes, looked at her. "You'll have to get on top, Elizabeth, or else I'll bleed all over you," he said with a glance down at his bare body.

"Quiet!" she commanded. "Save your strength to get well."

As she spoke, Rab began pulling the carcass of an enormous, long-tusked boar into the clearing. The dead animal's face was covered in blood and there were several knife wounds in its side.

"So you won a fight with a boar," she said in disgust, tenderly wrapping him in the plaid she wore about her shoulders. "I don't guess it occurred to you not to ride out alone."

Before she could say another word, Rab dragged another boar carcass to lie beside the first one, this one also slashed.

Elizabeth began to wipe Miles's dirty face. "We're going to take you not far from here where it's warm and where it'll be quiet. Now I want you to rest."

Sir Guy with a man and woman came thrashing through the undergrowth, their arms slung with great heavy plaids.

"There's a strong barley broth on the fire," the woman said, "and oatcakes on the hearth. Bronwyn'll send more plaids if ye need them."

Sir Guy, kneeling, pulled the plaid off Miles's body and studied the wounds, looking up in surprise when Rab pulled a third boar carcass into the clearing.

"How many of them are there?" Elizabeth asked.

"Five," Sir Guy said. "His horse must have thrown him into a family of them. He had only his sword and the little dagger but he killed all five of them and managed to drag himself here. Rab led us to the boars but ran off before we found Lord Miles."

"He came to get me," Elizabeth said. "Can you carry Miles?"

Without much show of effort, Sir Guy carefully picked up his young master as if he were a child. Instantly, his wounds began to renew their vigor in bleeding.

"Careful!" Elizabeth half screeched, and the look Guy gave her made her quiet.

Sir Guy led the way as he carried Miles through the trees toward the crofter's cottage, and laid him gently on a cot against one wall. It was a tiny, dark, one-room hut, the open hearth the only source of light. There was a crude table and two chairs and no other furniture besides the cot. A pot of water simmered over the fire. Immediately, Elizabeth dipped clean cloths that had been left for her in the water and started washing Miles. Sir Guy lifted him, helped her remove the shreds of his clothes from under him. To Elizabeth's relief, there were no more wounds on the back of him other than minor cuts and bruises.

She had him almost washed when Morag and Bronwyn arrived together, Morag carrying a big basket of medicines.

"I can't see as well as I used to," Morag said, looking down at Miles, nude, the two wounds gaping redly. "One of ye will have to tend to him."

"I will," Elizabeth said quickly. "Tell me what to do and I can do it."

Sewing a man's flesh was far different from sewing on cloth, Elizabeth soon discovered. The muscles of her body tightened each time she slid the needle inside Miles's skin.

Miles lay still, not moving, barely breathing, his body pale from the loss of blood as Elizabeth stitched. Bronwyn threaded the needles, cut and helped to knot.

When Elizabeth finished at last, she was trembling.

"Drink this," Bronwyn ordered.

"What is it?" Elizabeth asked.

"Lord only knows. I learned long ago not to ask what Morag puts into her concoctions. Whatever it is, it'll taste vile but it will make you feel better."

Elizabeth drank the brew, leaning against the wall, her eyes on Miles. When Morag started to hold a cup to Miles's pale lips, she thrust her mug at Bronwyn and went to him.

"Drink this," she whispered, holding his head. "You must get your strength back."

His eyes moved, his lashes barely parted as he looked up at her. "Worth it," he whispered as he drank Morag's brew.

Morag gave a derisive snort. "He'll stay on his back for a year if ye pamper him."

"Well, let him!" Elizabeth snapped back.

Bronwyn laughed. "Come sit down, Elizabeth, and rest. I want to know how you knew Miles had been wounded. We'd only just found him when you rode up."

Elizabeth sat on the floor by Miles's head, leaned back and shrugged. She had no idea how she'd known he was injured—but she had.

Her moments of rest were short-lived. Seemingly seconds later, Morag had something else for Elizabeth to feed Miles.

Night came and Bronwyn went back to Larenston. Elizabeth sat beside Miles, watching him, knowing that he didn't sleep, while Morag nodded in a chair.

"What . . ." Miles whispered. "What is Raine's wife like?"

Elizabeth thought he was delirious since she'd never met Raine or his wife.

"Singer," Miles said. "Pagnell."

Those words were enough of a key to make her understand. She was surprised that one of the Montgomery lords would marry a lowly little singer. Elizabeth told Miles the story of meeting Alyxandria Blackett, of hearing her extraordinary voice and later her attempt to rescue the singer from Pagnell's clutches—which led to Elizabeth's own capture.

Miles smiled at that and searched for her hand. Still touching her, he fell asleep just as the sun began to rise.

Morag woke and began to mix another batch of herbs, dried mushrooms and several things Elizabeth didn't recognize.

Together they changed the bloody bandages on Miles's wounds and Morag applied warm, wet, herb-filled poultices over the sewn cuts.

Miles slept again in the afternoon and Elizabeth left the little cottage for the first time. Sir Guy sat outside under a tree and only looked up in question when he saw her.

"He's resting," she said.

Sir Guy nodded and stared off into space. "Not many boys could fall into a pack of five boars and come out alive," he said with pride.

There were tears in Elizabeth's eyes as she placed a trembling hand on the giant's shoulder. "I will do all in my power to see that he gets well."

Sir Guy nodded, not looking at her. "You have no reason to help him. We've treated you badly."

"No," she answered. "I have been given more than courtesy; I have been given love." With that she turned away toward the stream that ran through the MacArran land. She washed, tidied her hair, sat down for a moment's rest, wrapped in her plaid, and when she woke it was night. Sir Guy sat not far away from her.

Sleep-dazed, she hurried back to the cottage.

Miles was awake and the frown he wore disappeared when he saw her.

"There she is," Morag scolded. "Now maybe you'll drink some of this."

"Elizabeth," Miles said.

She went to him, held his head while he drank nearly a cup of the brew and continued to hold him until he fell asleep.

Chapter 13

"YOU WILL not walk," Elizabeth said to Miles with steely firmness.

"I have lost too many nights' sleep in trying to heal your wounds without watching you break them open."

He looked up at her with meltingly soft eyes. "Please, Elizabeth."

For a moment she almost relented, but stopped herself with a laugh. "You are a treacherous man. Now be still or I'll tie you to the bed."

"Oh?" he said, eyebrows raised.

Elizabeth blushed at what he was obviously thinking. "Behave yourself! I want you to eat more. You'll never get well if you don't eat."

He caught her hand and, with surprising strength, pulled her down beside him. Or perhaps it was that Elizabeth had no will to resist him. He was half sitting up, propped on pillows against the corner of the room, his legs on the cot before him. Carefully, she stretched beside him. It had been four days since Miles had been gored but his youth and natural resistance had made him recover quickly. He was still weak, still in pain, but he was starting to heal.

"Why have you stayed with me?" he asked. "One of Bronwyn's women could have tended me."

"And have her jump in bed with you and tear your stitches?" she asked indignantly.

"I'll tear my stitches if you make me laugh. How could I have touched another woman when you're so close?"

"When I'm gone, I'm sure you'll manage to gather your courage."

His hand tangled in her hair, pulled her head back and his mouth took hers possessively. "Haven't you learned yet that you're mine?" he half growled. "When are you going to admit that?"

He didn't give her a chance to answer as he kissed her again, and much of the worry Elizabeth'd felt in the last days went into that kiss to make it one of desperation.

The touch of cold steel against Miles's throat made them break apart. Instinctively, he reached for his own sword but met only bare flesh under the plaid he wore.

Over them stood Roger Chatworth, his eyes full of hate, his sword pressing against the vein in Miles's neck.

"Do not," Elizabeth said, moving away from Miles. "Do not harm him."

"I would like to kill all the Montgomerys," Roger Chatworth said.

Miles, in one quick motion, moved sideways, caught Chatworth's wrist.

"No!" Elizabeth screamed and clung to her brother's arm. Miles's bandages began to redden.

"He's hurt," Elizabeth said. "Would you kill a man who can't fight back?"

Roger turned his full attention to her. "Have you become one of them? Have the Montgomerys poisoned you against your own blood relations?"

"No, Roger, of course not." She tried to remain calm. There was such a wild look in Roger's eyes that she feared to anger him. Miles lay against the wall, panting, but she knew that at any moment he'd leap again and tear his wounds further. "Have you come for me?"

There was a sudden hush in the little room as both men watched her. She had to leave with Roger. If she did not, he'd kill Miles. She knew that very well. Roger was tired, angry, beyond all rational thinking.

"It will be good to go home," she said, forcing a smile.

"Elizabeth!" Miles warned.

She ignored him. "Come, Roger, what are you waiting for?" Her heart was pounding so hard she could barely hear her own voice.

"Elizabeth!" Miles shouted at her, his hand clutching at the hole in his chest.

For a moment Roger looked from one to the other, hesitating.

"I'm growing impatient, Roger! Haven't I been away long enough?" She turned on her heel to leave, paused at the door. Her eyes stayed on Roger's, not daring to look at Miles. She couldn't risk even one look at him or she'd lose her resolve.

Slowly, puzzled, Roger began to follow her. A horse waited obediently not far from the cottage. Elizabeth kept her eyes on the animal, not daring to look around because she knew she'd see the body of Sir Guy. Only his death would have kept the giant from protecting his master.

Another shout, stone-shaking, came from the cottage. "ELIZABETH!!"

Swallowing the lump in her throat, Elizabeth allowed Roger to help her on his horse.

"We must have food," Roger said and turned away from her.

"Roger!" she yelled after him. "If you harm him I—" she began and saw that he was ignoring her. She dismounted in a flash and was after him—but not in time.

Roger Chatworth ran his sword through Miles's arm and as Miles lay there bleeding, Roger said, "Raine's wife spared my life and it's to her that you owe your filthy life now." He turned to Elizabeth in the doorway. "Get on the horse or I'll finish the job, if he doesn't bleed to death as it is."

Trembling, feeling very ill, Elizabeth left the cottage and mounted the horse. Within seconds, Roger was behind her and they set off at a grueling pace.

Elizabeth sat before her embroidery frame, working on an altar cover of St. George slaying the dragon. In one corner was a boy who looked remarkably like Kit and St. George . . . the saint had some of the look of Miles Montgomery. Elizabeth stopped for a moment as the child in her womb kicked her.

Alice Chatworth sat across from her, a mirror held to reflect the unscarred half of her face. "I was so beautiful then," Alice was saying. "Absolutely no man could resist me. All of them were ready to lay down their lives for me. All I had to do was hint at something I wanted and it was given to me."

She switched the mirror to the misshapen side of her face. "Until the Montgomerys did this!" she hissed. "Judith Revedoune was jealous of my beauty. She is such an ugly, freckled, red-haired thing that she was worried over my dear Gavin's love. And well she should have been."

Elizabeth gave an exaggerated yawn, ignored Alice's look of hate and turned to Roger, who was standing by the fireplace, mug of wine in hand, his face brooding. "Roger, would you like to go for a walk with me in the gardens?"

As usual, Roger looked at her stomach before he looked back at her face.

"No, I have to talk to my steward," he half mumbled, his eyes searching her face.

She could feel what he wanted to say, what he'd said many, many times: You've changed.

She'd been back with her brother and her "family" for two weeks and it brought home to her how much she *had* changed in her five months with the Montgomerys. The time had not been enough to make any changes in the Chatworth household, but it was enough for Elizabeth to have started the makings of a new person.

For all her insistence that Roger was different from Edmund, she saw that Roger had actually not enforced his own beliefs within his household. In many ways, the Chatworth house was the same as when Edmund was alive. The reason Roger could easily have Alice live with him was that he was oblivious to her. Roger lived with such inner turmoil, with all his love and care given to Elizabeth and Brian, that he was truly unaware of a great deal that went on around him.

Elizabeth had no more than dismounted her horse, tired after days of travel, when two of Roger's men, who had once been with Edmund, began to make snide comments to her. They hinted that they could hardly wait to catch her alone.

Elizabeth's first reaction had been fear. It had been as if she'd never left the Chatworth estates. Her mind raced over her repertoire of debilitating tricks to use on the men. But her thoughts went back to Sir Guy and how she'd broken his toes, how he'd hobbled for weeks—and later she'd sat with him, saw tears of worry gathering in his eyes over a man they both loved.

She would not return to her skulking, fearful ways. She'd come a long way in conquering her fear of men and she wasn't going to throw all she'd learned away.

She'd turned to Roger and demanded that he send the men away immediately.

Roger'd been very surprised and had quickly hustled her out of the stables. He'd tried to patronize her but Elizabeth wouldn't listen to him. The idea that his dear little sister would talk back to him shocked as well as hurt him. To his mind, he'd just rescued her from a hellhole and she was ungratefully complaining.

For the first time in her life, Elizabeth told her brother the whole truth about Edmund. Roger's face had drained of blood, he'd staggered backward into a chair and looked as if someone had beaten him. All these years he'd thought he'd protected his dear little sister but, in truth, she'd lived in hell. He had no idea Edmund had summoned her from her convent whenever Roger left the estates. He didn't know that she'd had to defend herself from his men.

By the time Elizabeth finished, Roger was ready to kill the men in the stables.

Roger Chatworth's fury was something to be reckoned with. Within three days, he'd put fear in the hearts of his household. Many men were dismissed and if a man so much as looked at Elizabeth with slanted eyes, she went to Roger. No more was she going to stand for such insolence. Before, she'd not known how a lady should be treated, as her only experience was with Edmund, but now she'd had five months in a place where she didn't have to be afraid of walking in a garden alone.

Roger had been taken aback by her demands and she realized how she and Brian had always protected him. Roger could be so kind and at the same time so cruel. She tried only once to talk to him about the Montgomerys, but Roger'd exploded with such hatred, she feared for his life.

Since it had been months since he'd seen her, he quickly noticed the changes in her body, remarked that she'd put on weight. Elizabeth had put her chin in the air and, with no regret, stated that she carried Miles Montgomery's child.

She had expected rage—she was prepared for rage but the deep, deep hurt in Roger's eyes threw her off balance.

"Go. Leave me," he'd whispered and she obeyed.

Alone in her room, Elizabeth'd cried herself to sleep as she had every night since leaving Miles. Would Miles realize she'd gone with Roger to save her lover? Or would Miles hate her? What would they tell Kit about where Elizabeth had gone? She lay on her bed and thought of all the people she'd come to care about in Scotland.

She longed to send a message to someone in Scotland but there was no one she could trust to deliver it. But yesterday, as she took her afternoon walk, an old woman she'd never seen before offered her a basket of bread. She started to refuse it until the woman lifted the cloth and showed a MacArran cockade. Elizabeth grabbed the basket quickly and the old woman was gone before Elizabeth could thank her. Greedily, she tore into the basket.

There was a message from Bronwyn saying she well understood why Elizabeth'd returned with Roger—but Miles didn't. Sir Guy had been hit with three arrows but they thought he'd live. While Miles was untended, he'd gone into a rage, torn all his stitches apart. When Morag found him he was in a fever and for three days they didn't believe he'd live. Stephen had returned from Raine's outlaw camp as soon as he heard Miles had been injured. He bore the news that Raine was taking young Brian under his wing and Stephen had every hope of there soon being peace between the two families. Bronwyn added that Miles was recovering slowly and he refused to mention Elizabeth's name.

Today, as Elizabeth thought of that last sentence, her skin grew cold, making her shiver.

"You should have a cloak," Roger said from behind her.

"No," she murmured, "my plaid is enough."

"Why do you flaunt that thing in front of me?" Roger exploded. "Isn't it enough that you carry a Montgomery within you? Do you have to slap me in the face every time I see you?"

"Roger, I want this hatred to end. I want—"

"You want to be my enemy's whore!" he snarled.

With one quick angry look she turned away from him.

He caught her arm, his eyes soft as he looked at her. "Can you see this from my side? I spent months in hell looking for you. I went to Raine Montgomery to ask where you were, yet he drew a sword on me. If his new wife hadn't stepped between us I'd be dead now. I went to the king on my knees and do you think that was easy? I bear no love for the man since he's fined me so heavily for what happened to Mary Montgomery, but for you I'd have gone on my knees before the devil."

He paused, put his hands on both her arms. "And getting in and out of Scotland was no easy task either, yet when I found you you were cuddled beside Montgomery as if you wanted to become a part of him. And the playacting you did! I felt as if I were the enemy because I was rescuing my own sister from a man who'd held her captive and taken her virtue. Explain all this to me, Elizabeth," he whispered.

She leaned her head forward to touch his chest. "How can I? How can I tell you what has happened to me in the last few months? I've seen love and—"

"Love!" he said. "Do you think that if a man takes you to his bed, he loves you? Has Montgomery sworn undying love to you? Has he asked to make a Chatworth his wife?"

"No, but—" she began.

"Elizabeth, you know so little of men. You were a pawn

in this feud. Don't you know that the Montgomerys are laughing because a Chatworth bears a Montgomery child? They'll think they've won."

"Won!" she spat at him, pulling away. "I hate this all being thought of as a game. What should I tell my child, that he was a chess piece, used by two families in their silly war?"

"Silly? How can you say that when Brian is out there somewhere, possibly hating me because of the Montgomerys?"

She hadn't told him of seeing Brian in Scotland. "Did it ever occur to you, Roger, that perhaps *you* caused Brian to leave? I would like to hear your side of what happened to Mary Montgomery."

He turned away from her. "I was drunk. It was a hideous . . . accident." He turned back, his eyes pleading. "I can't bring the woman back and the king has punished me more than enough with his fines. Brian has left me and you return from my enemy bloated with his child, and instead of the love you once gave me, now all you do is question me, doubt me. What more punishment do you intend for me?"

"I'm sorry, Roger," she said softly. "Perhaps I have changed. I don't know if Miles loves me. I don't know if he'd want to marry me to give our child a name, but I do know that I love him and if he asked me, I'm sure I'd follow him wherever he led."

Only Roger's eyes showed the pain he felt at her words. "How could you turn against me so completely? Is this man so good in bed that your screams of pleasure make you forget the love I bear you and have always had for you? Does five months with him wipe out eighteen years with me?"

"No, Roger. I love you. I will always love you, but I want you both."

He smiled at that. "How very young you are, Elizabeth. You want a man who, I hear, is also wanted by half the women of England. You want a man who takes you to his bed, gets you with child and never speaks of marriage. And what kind of marriage would it be? Will you care for all his bastards as you have for his eldest son?"

"What do you know of Kit?"

"I know a great deal about my enemies. Miles Montgomery likes women. You are one of many to him and I respect the man for at least not lying to you and saying you were going to be his one and only love."

He touched her arm. "Elizabeth, if you want a husband, I can find someone for you. I know several men who'd take you bearing another man's child, and they'd be good to you. With this youngest Montgomery you'd be miserable inside a year."

"Perhaps," she said, trying to think rationally. Maybe Miles's hands on her had made her lose reason. He'd always been kind to her, but then he'd been kind to serving girls. If she did desert her brother for a Montgomery, Roger would hate her, and what would she feel for Miles years from now? What if, as a practical joke, someone else "gave" him a pretty young girl? Would he decide she belonged to him also? Would he bring her home to Elizabeth, smiling, expecting her to care for the girl as she did for his bastard children?

"Let me find someone for you. I'll bring many men for your approval and you can choose who you want. At least look at them. If you want to remain unmarried, you can."

She looked at him with love. He'd be laughed at for allowing his sister to bear a child out of wedlock. Some would say she should be killed if she refused to wed. Roger had suffered much disgrace over the last few years, yet he was willing to risk more for her sake.

At her smile, he grinned, and for the first time he looked as if he had a reason for living.

"Yes, I'll look at your men," she said from her heart. She would try with all her might to fall in love with one of them. She'd have a kind, loving husband, children to love and her brothers, because somehow she'd reunite Brian and Roger.

Elizabeth learned a great deal about love in the next few days. Never, before she met Miles, had she had any idea what love was. She'd never even considered loving a man, but then Miles came along and changed that. Within five months of his patience and humor he'd made her love him. She knew she'd always have a soft spot for Miles but there were many men who were good and kind in the world. All she had to do was fall in love with one of them and it would solve everything.

But Elizabeth underestimated herself.

Roger began parading men before her like so many studs ready to service her. There were tall men, short men, thin men, fat men, ugly men, men so handsome you merely gaped at them, swaggering men, bold men, men who made her laugh, one who sang beautifully. On and on they came.

At first Elizabeth was flattered by their attentions, but after just a few days, her old fears began to return. A man touched her shoulder and she jumped high, put her hand on her eating dagger at her side. After a week, she was finding excuses to remain in her room, or else she was always in Roger's company.

Then suddenly, Roger left the estates. He said nothing to her but rode out with eight men at a furious pace. A servant said Roger'd received a message from a dirty, black-toothed man and within seconds Roger'd left. The message was tossed into the fire.

Elizabeth was close to tears knowing that there were eleven male guests below and she was their hostess. She couldn't talk to one man with any coherence because she was always concerned with where the other men were. All Miles's months of patient training were disappearing. Once she brought a brass vase down on the head of a man who'd dared to walk up behind her.

With her skirts flying about her, she fled to her room and refused to return to the hall.

She lay on her bed a long time and all she could remember was Miles. Every time she met a man, she compared him to Miles. Some utterly splendid man would be introduced to her and all she'd think was, he moves his hands too quickly or some other such nonsense. And one night, she'd allowed a man to kiss her in the garden. She'd caught herself just before she brought her heel down on his little toes, but she couldn't keep herself from wiping her mouth with the back of her hand. The poor man'd been terribly insulted.

Elizabeth tried very hard, but not a single man even interested her. As the days passed, she wished she could see Bronwyn and ask advice. She was considering writing a letter when the bottom dropped out of her world.

A haggard, wasted Roger returned bearing the mutilated body of Brian.

Elizabeth greeted him but Roger merely looked through her as he tenderly carried Brian's body upstairs and locked himself in a room. For two days he stayed locked inside with Brian's body and when he emerged, his eyes were sunken and black.

"Your Montgomerys did that," he said hoarsely as he strode past Elizabeth and Alice.

They buried Brian that afternoon but Roger didn't reappear. Elizabeth planted roses on the grave and shed tears for both her brothers.

Alice hounded Elizabeth mercilessly, screeching that the Montgomerys should die for all they'd done. She was fascinated by lamps full of hot oil and waved them around maniacally. She said Elizabeth's child would be born with the mark of Satan and would be cursed for all eternity.

One by one, the male guests left the bereaved and somewhat insane household and Elizabeth was left alone with her sister-in-law.

In early March a messenger wearing full regalia came from the king.

It was a day before the men Elizabeth sent out could find Roger where he'd been—alone in a shepherd's stone hut. He looked to be a skeleton of himself, his cheeks gaunt under a beard, his hair long and dirty, his eyes wild and frightening.

He silently read the message in Elizabeth's presence, then tossed it into the fireplace.

"Tell the king no," he said calmly before leaving the room.

Elizabeth could only gasp, and wonder what message the king had sent. With as much calmness as she could muster, she dismissed the king's men and sat down to wait. Whatever Roger had refused to do would no doubt soon be known to them when the king heard of the refusal. She put her hand on her growing belly and wondered if her child would live to worry about being called a bastard.

Chapter 14

SIX DAYS after the king's messenger had come and gone, Elizabeth was alone in the garden. She had not seen or heard from Roger in days and Brian's death was making Alice lose what sanity she had. It wasn't that the woman cared for Brian but it was the fact that a Montgomery had killed him. Elizabeth thought of this Raine with hatred.

A shadow moved across her path and involuntarily she gasped before looking up—into the dark, intense eyes of Miles Montgomery. His eyes contemptuously swept her up and down, made note of the ivory satin of her gown, the double rows of pearls, the blood-red ruby at her breast.

Elizabeth felt she wanted to drink in all of him, that she couldn't get enough of him. There were dark, faintly yellow shadows under his eyes and he was thinner. Obviously he wasn't fully recovered from his fever.

"Come," he said hoarsely.

Elizabeth didn't hesitate as she followed him through the garden and into the forest park of the Chatworth estates. Supposedly these boundaries were guarded, but somehow Miles had entered undetected.

He didn't speak to her, didn't look at her and it wasn't until they reached the two waiting horses that she realized what was wrong: He hated her. His rigid body, his cold eyes all screamed it.

She became rigid herself when they reached the horses. "Where are you taking me?"

He turned toward her. "The king has ordered us to marry. Your brother has refused the order. If we disobey, both your brother and I will be declared traitors and our lands confiscated." His eyes touched on the ruby. "You need have no fear. After the marriage I will return you to your precious brother, but even you would not like to have all the things that mean so much to you taken away."

He turned away from her. Elizabeth tried to mount her horse but her long skirt and trembling body made that impossible. Miles came up behind her and, touching her as little as possible, flung her into the saddle.

Elizabeth was too stunned, too much in a state of shock, to even think as they set off quickly to the north. Her eyes were so dry they burned and all she thought of was the way the horse's mane whipped in the wind.

They halted less than an hour later on the outskirts of a small village, before a pleasant little house beside a church. Miles dismounted, didn't look at her as she struggled to get down from her horse.

A priest opened the door to them. "So this is the lovely bride, Miles," he said. "Come along, I know how impatient you are."

As Miles strode ahead, ignoring Elizabeth, she ran after him, caught his arm. The look he gave her as he glanced from her hand to her face made her breath catch. She dropped her hand. "After this is over, could we talk?" she whispered.

"If it doesn't take too long," he said coolly. "My brother is waiting for me."

"No," she said, trying to regain her dignity. "I'll not keep you long." With that, she gathered her skirts and walked ahead of him.

The marriage was over in minutes. There were no witnesses from either family, only a few strangers who the priest knew. For all the feeling either participant put into the words, they could have been negotiating a grain contract.

When they were pronounced man and wife, Miles turned toward her and Elizabeth held her breath. "I believe we can talk in the vestry," was all he said. Chin up, Elizabeth led the way.

When they were alone in the room, he lazily leaned against the wall. "Now you have your chance to say what you want."

Her first impulse was to tell him where he could spend the rest of his life but she calmed herself. "I didn't know of the king's order that we marry. If I had I would not have refused. I would do a great deal to settle this feud."

"Even to sleeping with your enemy?" he taunted.

She gritted her teeth. "Roger has been very upset at Brian's death." For a moment her eyes flashed fire.

Miles's nostrils flared. "Perhaps you hadn't heard that Raine survived your brother's poison."

"Poison!" she gasped. "Now what do you accuse Roger of?"

"Not Roger," Miles said. "Your brother Brian poisoned Raine."

"Well, Brian certainly paid for the attempt! I hear Raine is a large man. Did he enjoy tearing my slight brother apart? Did he enjoy hearing Brian's frail bones snap?"

Miles's eyes hardened. "I see that once again you have heard only one side. Did Roger say Raine killed Brian?"

"Not in so many words, but . . ."

Miles came away from the wall. "Ask him then. Have your perfect brother tell you the truth about who killed Brian Chatworth. Now, if you have nothing else to accuse me of, I must go."

"Wait!" she called. "Please, tell me the news. How is Sir Guy?"

Miles's eyes turned black. "What the hell do you care? Since when have you cared about anyone except your treacherous brother? Guy nearly died from your brother's arrows. Perhaps he should practice his marksmanship. Another inch and he'd have reached Guy's heart."

"And Kit?" she whispered.

"Kit!" Miles said through clenched teeth. "Kit cried for

three days after you left but now he won't even allow Philip's nurse in the same room. The nurse's name is Elizabeth."

"I never meant . . ." she began. "I love Kit."

"No, Elizabeth, you don't. We were nothing to you. You repaid us all for holding you against your will. You are, after all, a Chatworth."

Her anger exploded in her. "I'll not stand for more of your insinuations! What was I supposed to do when my brother held a sword at your throat? Should I have stayed with you? He would have killed you! Can't you understand that I left with him in order to save your ungrateful life?"

"Am I supposed to believe that?" he said, low. "You stand before me dripping pearls, wearing a ruby that costs more than all I own and tell me you followed your brother in order to save me? What has made you think I'm stupid?"

"Tell me then," she shot back, "what should I have done?"

His eyes narrowed. "You claim your brother loves you so much, you should have told him you wanted to stay with me."

She threw up her hands at that. "Oh yes, that would have worked so well. Roger no doubt would have resheathed his sword and gone home docilely. Roger's temper is second only to yours. And, Montgomery, how was I to know you *wanted* me to remain with you?"

He was silent for a moment. "My wants have always been clear. I hear you have been sleeping with many men lately. I'm sure your marital status won't interfere with your activities, although my child will curb you for a while at least."

Very calmly, very slowly, Elizabeth stepped close to him and slapped him across the face.

Miles's head snapped to one side and when he looked back at her, his eyes were ablaze. With one quick, violent gesture he caught both her hands in one of his, pushed her back against the stone wall. His lips came down on hers hard, plundering.

Elizabeth reacted with all her pent-up desires and pushed her body into his hungrily.

His lips made a hot trail down her neck. "You love me, don't you, Elizabeth?"

"Yes," she murmured.

"How much?" he whispered, touching her earlobe with the tip of his tongue.

"Miles," she murmured, "please." Her hands were held against the wall, above her head, and she desperately wanted to put her arms around him. "Please," she repeated.

Abruptly, he pulled away from her, dropped her hands. "How does it feel to be turned down?" he said coldly, but a vein in his neck pounded. "How does it feel to love someone and be rejected? I pleaded with you to stay with me but you chose your brother. Now see if he can give you what you need. Goodbye, Elizabeth . . . Montgomery." With that he left the room, closing the door behind him.

For a long while Elizabeth was too weak to move, but she finally managed to make her way to a chair and sit on it. She was there, in a daze, when the priest entered, obviously agitated.

"Lord Miles had to leave but an escort awaits you outside. And this was left for you." When Elizabeth didn't react, the priest took her hand and closed it around something cold and heavy. "Take your time, dear, the men will wait."

It was several minutes before Elizabeth gathered her strength enough to stand. The object in her hand fell and clanged against the stone floor. Kneeling, she picked it up. It was a heavy gold ring, sized small enough to fit her hand, set with a large emerald that was incised with three Montgomery leopards.

Her first impulse was to toss the ring across the room, but with a grimace of resignation, she slipped it on her left hand and left the room to go to the guard waiting for her.

Roger met her a half-mile from the estate with an armed guard, swords drawn. She kicked her horse ahead to meet him.

"Death to all Montgomerys!" he cried.

Elizabeth grabbed his horse's bridle, succeeding in nearly

pulling her arm from its socket and making Roger's horse rear. Both of them fought their horses for a moment.

"Why do you come riding with Montgomerys?" Roger bellowed.

"Because *I* am a Montgomery," she shouted back.

That statement successfully made Roger pause.

"How dare you not tell me of the king's order that I marry Miles!" she yelled at him. "What else have you lied to me about? Who killed my brother Brian?"

Roger's anger made his face turn red. "A Montgomery—" he began.

"No! I want the truth!"

Roger looked at the guard of men behind her as if he were planning their deaths.

"You tell me the truth here and now or I ride with them back to Scotland. I have just been married to a Montgomery and my child has every right to be raised as one."

Roger was breathing so hard, his chest was swelling to barrel size. "*I* killed Brian," he shouted, then quietened. "I killed my own brother. Is that what you wanted to hear?"

Elizabeth had expected any answer but that one and she felt deflated. "Come back to the house, Roger, and we'll talk."

When they were alone in the solar, Elizabeth demanded that Roger tell her everything about the wars between the Chatworths and the Montgomerys. It wasn't an easy story to listen to and it was even harder to get Roger to tell the unbiased truth. Roger's view of the events was colored by his emotions.

In Scotland he'd seen a chance to marry Bronwyn MacArran, which would have been an excellent match for him. He did tell the woman a few falsehoods in order to make him appear more favorable to her—but what were a few lies in courtship? He'd even maneuvered Stephen Montgomery into fighting for her, but when Stephen won so easily Roger'd been enraged and attacked Stephen's back. Roger's humiliation at that had been too much to bear. He'd kidnapped Bronwyn and Mary merely to show the Montgomerys he was a power to be reckoned with. He never meant the women any harm.

"But you did harm Mary," Elizabeth said angrily.

"Brian wanted to marry her!" Roger defended himself. "After all I'd suffered at the hands of the Montgomerys and then Brian wanted to marry their old, plain, spiritless daughter. No one else in England would have her. Can you imagine how the Chatworths would have been laughed at?"

"Your pride sickens me. Brian lies dead rather than married. Did you get what you wanted?"

"No," he whispered.

"Neither have I." She sat down. "Roger, I want you to listen to me and listen well. The anger between the Montgomerys and Chatworths is over. My name is now Montgomery and my child will be a Montgomery. There will be no more fighting."

"If he tries again to take you—" Roger began.

"Take me!" She stood so fast the chair fell over. "This morning I begged Miles Montgomery to take me with him, but he refused. And I don't blame him! His family has lost someone they loved because of you, yet they have not killed you as probably they should have."

"Brian—"

"*You* killed Brian!" she shouted. "You have caused all of this and so help me God, if you so much as look at a Montgomery wrong, I'll take a sword to you myself." With that she left the room, nearly tripping over Alice who, as usual, was eavesdropping.

It was three days before Elizabeth could control her anger enough to think. When she did think, she decided to look at what she had and do something with it. She was not going to have her child growing up as she had. She would probably never live with Miles so the closest thing to a father her child would have was going to be Roger.

She found Roger brooding before the fireplace and if she'd been a man, she would have pulled him out of his chair and given his backside a good swift kick.

"Roger," she said in a voice filled with honey, "I never noticed before, but you're getting a roll about your middle."

He put his hand to his flat stomach in surprise.

Elizabeth had to repress her smile. Roger was a very good-looking man and he was used to women noticing him. "Perhaps at your age," she continued, "a man should grow stout and his muscles weak."

"I'm not so old," he said, standing, sucking in his stomach.

"That was one thing I liked about Scotland. The men were so trim and fit."

He cocked his head at her. "What are you trying to do, Elizabeth?"

"I'm trying to keep you from living in a world of self-pity. Brian is dead and even if you fall in bed drunk every night for the rest of your life, you won't be able to bring him back. Now go get those lazy knights of yours and put them to work."

There was just a hint of a smile in his eyes. "Perhaps I do need some exercise," he said before leaving the room.

Six weeks later, Elizabeth was delivered of a very large, healthy baby boy whom she named Nicholas Roger. The child showed right away that he had inherited Gavin Montgomery's high cheekbones. Roger took to the child as if he were his own.

When she was up from her childbed, she began to work on making a home for little Nicholas. The first thing she did was order a guard near the baby at all times because Alice seemed to think the child was Judith and Gavin's and Elizabeth didn't trust the crazy woman's actions.

Nicholas was barely a month old when the first letter arrived from Judith Montgomery. It was a reserved letter inquiring after the child, saying Judith regretted not meeting Elizabeth but Bronwyn sang her praises. There was no mention of Miles.

Instantly, Elizabeth wrote back, raving about little Nick, saying he looked like Gavin and did Judith have any advice for a new mother?

Judith responded with a trunkful of exquisite baby clothes that her son, now ten months old, had outgrown.

Elizabeth, with a bit of defiance, showed the clothes to Roger and told him she'd started a correspondence with Judith Montgomery. Roger, sweat-drenched from the training field, said nothing—but Alice had a great deal to say, all of which was ignored by everyone.

It wasn't until Judith's fifth letter that she mentioned Miles and then seemingly only in passing. She said Miles was living with Raine, both men were without their wives and both men were miserable. That news made Elizabeth's whole week seem wonderful. She laughed at Nick and told him all about his father and his stepbrother Kit.

In September, Elizabeth sent Judith bulbs for her garden, and tucked away inside was a doublet, very adult-looking, that Elizabeth had made for Kit. Judith wrote back that Kit loved the doublet but both he and Miles were under the impression Judith had made it, which made Gavin laugh because Judith was always too busy to have the patience to sew.

Just after Christmas, Judith sent a long, serious letter. Raine and his wife had reunited and Miles had come to visit them before returning to his own estates. Judith was appalled at the change in Miles. He'd always been a loner but now he rarely spoke at all. And worst of all, his love of women seemed to have disappeared. The women were still drawn to him but he looked at them suspiciously and without the least concern. Judith had tried to talk to him but all he'd said was, "I'm a married man, remember? Husbands and wives should remain faithful to each other." With that, he laughed and walked away. Judith pleaded with Elizabeth to forgive Miles and she also warned Elizabeth that all the Montgomery men were insanely jealous.

Elizabeth replied with a long, long letter of anger. Miles was the only man who'd ever touched her; she'd begged him to take her with him when they were married but he refused. She told how she'd gone with Roger only to save Miles's life. She ranted for pages about what a fool she'd been to believe in her brother so blindly, but it was Miles who was keeping them apart, not her.

As soon as Elizabeth sent the letter off with the messenger, she wanted it back. In truth, she'd never met Judith Montgomery. If just a small portion of what Alice thought was wrong with the woman was right, Judith was a monster. She could hurt Elizabeth's chances with Miles.

The month before an answer came nearly drove Elizabeth mad. Roger kept asking her what was wrong. Alice did more than that—she sneaked into Elizabeth's room, found Judith's letters and read them, giving a detailed account to Roger afterward. When Roger merely turned away, Alice threw herself into a fit of rage which lasted nearly a whole day.

Judith's answer to Elizabeth was short: Miles would be camping twenty miles from the Chatworth estate on 16 February, just outside the village of Westermore. Sir Guy was willing to help Elizabeth in any way he could.

This letter Elizabeth slept with, carried about with her and finally hid behind a stone in the fireplace. She walked about on a cloud for a few days, then came down. Why should she think Miles would want her again? What could she do to make him want her?

"You are mine, Elizabeth," he'd said. "You were given to me."

A plan began to form in her mind. No, she couldn't, she thought. A giggle escaped her. She just really wouldn't have the nerve. What if she "gave" herself to Miles again?

As Elizabeth was in the solar conjuring delightful, naughty visions, Alice was in Elizabeth's room, slipping about and searching. When she found Judith's latest letter, she took it to Roger, but this time he didn't turn away. For the next few days there were three people in the Chatworth house who were making plans—all in direct opposition to each other's.

Chapter 15

"I MOST certainly will not!" Sir Guy said as he looked down at Elizabeth. His voice was low but it seemed louder than a shout.

"But Judith said you were willing to help me."

Sir Guy drew himself up to every inch of his extraordinary height. The scar across his face was a brilliant purplish red. "*Lady* Judith"—he emphasized the word—"had no idea you'd ask something so preposterous of me. How can you think of such a thing?" he said in a shaming voice.

Elizabeth turned away from him, gave a swift kick to the carpet on the ground. It had seemed such a good idea at the time: She'd get Sir Guy to deliver her to Miles, nude, rolled in a carpet. Perhaps the repeat of the scene would make him laugh and he'd forgive her. But Sir Guy refused to cooperate.

"Then what am I going to do?" she asked heavily. "I know he won't see me if I ask him straightforward."

"Lady Alyx sent her daughter to Lord Raine and the child acted as an emissary."

"Oh no! I'll not let Miles get his hands on Nick. Miles would hire another nurse and add the boy to his collection. I'd never see Miles *or* Nick again." She leaned against a tree and tried to think. If she did arrange a meeting with Miles she doubted if he'd listen to her. Her only real chance was to make his eyes darken with passion and then he wouldn't be able to help himself. Perhaps she could talk to him, after they'd made love.

As she was thinking, she toyed with her long black cloak, a lovely thing of velvet lined with black mink. It covered her from neck to feet. A new light came into her eyes as she looked back up at Sir Guy. "Can you arrange to give me some time alone with Miles? Not in his tent but in the woods? And I mean really alone! No doubt he'll call for his guard, but I want no one to come."

"I don't like that idea," Sir Guy said stubbornly. "What if there were some real danger?"

"True," she said sarcastically, "I might wrestle him to the ground and take a knife to his throat."

Sir Guy lifted one eyebrow and ostentatiously shifted off the foot Elizabeth'd injured.

Elizabeth gave him a small smile. "Please, Guy, I haven't hurt a man in a long time. Miles is my husband and I love him and I want to try to make him love me again."

"I believe Lord Miles more than loves you—he's obsessed with you, but you've hurt his pride. No woman anywhere has ever given him any trouble."

"I'll not apologize for leaving Scotland with Roger. At that time it's what I had to do. Now, will you give me time alone with my husband?"

Sir Guy took his time before he nodded once. "I will no doubt come to regret this."

Elizabeth shot him a dazzling smile, her whole face lighting up. "I will make you godfather to our next child."

Sir Guy snorted. "In one hour Lord Miles will be standing here. I will give you an hour with him."

"Then you'll find us in an embarrassing situation," she said frankly. "I mean to seduce my husband. Give us at least three hours alone."

"You are no lady, Elizabeth Montgomery," he said, but there was a twinkle in his eye.

"Nor do I have any pride," she agreed. "Now go while I ready myself."

When she was alone, Elizabeth lost some of her bravado. This was perhaps her only chance to win her husband back and she prayed that everything would go well. With trembling hands, she began to unbutton her gown. She hoped she knew Miles well enough to know that he might be able to resist her logically, but could he resist her physically?

She hid her clothes under leaves and, nude, she wrapped the concealing cloak about her body. To the world she'd appear to be a lady of decorum. When she was ready, she sat down on a stump and began to wait.

When she first heard someone walking toward her, she stiffened, recognizing Miles's step, quick, light, purposeful. She rose to meet him.

At his first sight of her there was a look of welcome, of eagerness, but then his vision clouded and he looked at her coldly. "And have you misplaced your brother?" he asked.

"Miles, I have arranged this meeting in order to ask if we might live together as man and wife."

"All three of us?"

"Yes." She smiled. "The two of us with our son Nicholas."

"I see. And what, pray tell, will your brother do without the sister he has so often killed for?"

She stepped closer to him. "A great deal of time has passed since we last saw each other, and I'd hoped that by now you'd conquered some of your jealousy."

"I am not jealous!" he snapped. "You had a decision to make and you made it. Now I will have someone escort you back to your brother. Guards!"

A look of puzzlement crossed Miles's face when no men appeared at his call, but before he could say a word, Elizabeth opened her cloak, revealing her nude body. Miles, gaping, could only gasp.

Elizabeth let the cloak fall closed but held it open to reveal the length of her from her waist to her toes, rather like when she'd first met him and was draped in the fur pelts. Stealthily, like a huntress, she walked toward him, put her hand to the back of his neck.

Involuntarily, his hand went to touch the satin skin of her hip.

"Do I have to beg, Miles?" she whispered, her eyes on his

lips. "I have been wrong in so many things. I have no more pride. I love you and I want to live with you. I want more children."

Slowly, Miles's lips moved closer to hers. He appeared to be using all his willpower to resist her. "Elizabeth," he murmured, his lips touching hers lightly.

Long-repressed and banked fires ignited between them. Miles's arms slid under the cloak, pulled her off the ground as he clutched her to him, his kiss deepening. His mouth moved over her face as if he meant to devour her. "I've missed you. Oh God, there were times when I thought I'd go insane."

"I'm sure I did," she answered, half laughing, half crying. "Why couldn't you realize I loved only you? I could allow no other man to touch me."

He kissed away her tears. "I hear John Bascum had four stitches taken in his head from where you struck him."

She kissed his mouth and stopped him from talking. Without either of their realizing it, they were starting toward the ground. Elizabeth's fingers were buried in the fastenings of Miles's clothes, while his hands roamed eagerly over her body.

"Unhand her!" came a deadly voice from above them.

It took both Elizabeth and Miles a moment to understand who was speaking.

Roger Chatworth held his sword on Miles.

Miles gave Elizabeth a hard look and began to stand. "She is yours," he said to Roger, his chest heaving.

"Damn you to hell, Roger!" Elizabeth shouted up at her brother, grabbing a handful of stones and throwing them at his head. "Just once, can't you stay out of my life? Put that sword away before someone gets hurt!"

"I will hurt a Montgomery if he—"

"You may try," Miles sneered, drawing his sword.

"No!" Elizabeth screamed, jumping up to stand between the two men, facing her brother. "Roger, let me make this clear. Miles is my husband and I am going to return to his home with him, that is if he'll have me after the fools you've made of both of us."

"Some husband he is," Roger sneered. "He doesn't come

near you for months, hasn't even seen his own son. Is this what you want, Elizabeth? You'd give up the home I've provided for a man who cares nothing for you? How many women have you impregnated since Elizabeth, Montgomery?"

"More than you could in a lifetime," Miles replied calmly. Elizabeth stepped closer to Miles as Roger lunged. "If I had any sense I'd tell both of you to go to the devil."

"Let me rid you of him," Roger said, but when his sword tip touched Elizabeth's cloak, he halted. "Have you no shame? Have you greeted this man like . . . like this?"

"Roger, you are a pigheaded fool who understands only what is pounded into your head." With a swirl of velvet and mink she turned, stood on tiptoe and planted her mouth on Miles's. Miles was beginning to understand that this time Elizabeth was choosing him over her brother. He caught her to him in a rib-crushing embrace and kissed her with promises of tomorrow.

Roger, fuming, so angry he was trembling, was unaware of the man sneaking up behind him. Nor did he hear the swoosh of air as the club came down on the side of his head. Silently, he crumpled to the ground.

Miles and Elizabeth would have been oblivious to the crashing of a tree but something made Elizabeth's eyes flicker open. A club was coming down on Miles's head. She pushed him to the left just enough so that the club struck her and not him.

Miles did not at first realize what had made Elizabeth go so completely limp. With one hand supporting her, he turned, but too late to avoid the blow that felled him.

The three men, dirty, burly men, stood over the two men and a woman on the ground.

"Which one is Montgomery?" one man asked.

"How would I know!"

"So which do we take?"

"Both!" said the third one.

"And the doxy?" a man asked, using his club to part Elizabeth's cloak.

"Throw her in with them. The Chatworth woman said

there might be a woman and to get rid of her, too. I'm plannin' to make her pay for each body. Now, get that man's clothes off while I tend to this one." The third man cut a long strand of Elizabeth's blonde hair and tucked it into his pocket. "Come on, hurry up. The wagon won't wait all day."

When Elizabeth woke, the pounding, galloping pain in her head was so bad she wasn't sure she ever wanted to wake up. Even the ground under her seemed to be moving. As she started to sit up, she fell backward, banging her head not on the ground but on wood.

"Quiet, sweetheart," came Miles's voice from behind her. She turned to meet Miles's intense stare. He wore nothing but his loincloth, his arms behind him at an unnatural angle, his ankles tied. Beside him, snoring, was Roger, also bound.

As Elizabeth's head cleared, she realized her own wrists and ankles were also bound. "Where are we?" she whispered, trying not to let her fear show.

Miles's voice was deep, strong, comforting. "We're in the hold of a ship and I would imagine we're bound for France."

"But who? Why?" she stammered.

"Maybe your brother will know," Miles said flatly. "Right now we must free ourselves. I'll roll over to you and use my teeth to untie your hands, then you can free me."

Elizabeth nodded, willing herself to calmness. If Roger'd had anything to do with their capture, he wouldn't also be here, she told herself. When her hands were free, she gave a great sigh of relief, turned to Miles and instead of freeing his hands, she opened her cloak, pressed her bare body against his and kissed him. "Have you thought about me?" she whispered against his lips.

"Every moment." Eagerly he leaned forward to kiss her again.

Laughing, she pushed him away. "Shouldn't I untie you?"

"The parts of me that need freedom have it," he said as he moved his hips closer to hers.

Elizabeth buried her fingers in his shoulders and invaded his mouth with her own.

Only the loud, wakening groans of Roger made her pull away.

"If I didn't hate your brother before, I would now," Miles said with feeling as Elizabeth sat up, leaned over him, and began to untie the ropes on his wrists.

"What is this?" Roger demanded. He sat up, fell down again and finally managed to sit. "What have you done now, Montgomery?"

Miles did not answer the challenge but rubbed his wrists as Elizabeth worked on the ropes on her own ankles. As Miles began to untie his ankles, Roger exploded again.

"Do the two of you plan to free yourselves and leave me here? Elizabeth, how can you forget . . ."

"Do be quiet, Roger," Elizabeth said. "You've done more than enough harm already. Do you have any idea where this ship is taking us?"

"Ask your lover. I'm sure he's the one who planned this."

Miles didn't bother to answer Roger as he turned to Elizabeth. "I want to know whether I have your loyalty for the moment. If someone opens the hatch I'll jump him while you use the ropes to tie him. Can I depend on you?"

"Whether you believe it or not, you have always had my loyalty," Elizabeth said in a cold voice.

"Have you tried demanding our release?" Roger asked. "Offer them money."

"And will you empty your pockets for them?" Miles asked, glancing at the small strip of cloth that Roger wore.

No one said any more as the hatch began to open and a foot appeared on the ladder.

"Down!" Miles commanded and both Roger and Elizabeth feigned sleep as they sprawled on the wooden floor. Miles silently slipped to the far side of the ladder.

The sailor stuck his head down, seemed satisfied with the two prisoners' silence and took another step. At the same moment he realized one prisoner was missing, Miles grabbed both the man's feet and sent him sprawling. There was no sound except a heavy thud, lost in the creaking and groaning of the ship.

Roger lost no time in springing into action as he lifted the sailor's head by his hair. "He'll be out for a while."

Miles was unbuttoning the man's clothes.

"And do you expect me to remain here while you take his clothes and escape?" Roger demanded. "I'll not leave myself at the mercy of a Montgomery."

"You will!" Elizabeth hissed. "Roger, I am sick of your distrust. *You* are the one who has caused most of the problems between the Montgomerys and Chatworths, and now if we're to get out of this, you must learn to cooperate. What can we do, Miles?"

Miles was watching her as he struggled into the too-small clothes. Sailors were often chosen because of their diminutive size since small men could maneuver more easily inside the confines of a ship. "I will return as soon as I've found out anything." With that he was up the ladder and out.

Elizabeth and Roger tied and gagged the unconscious sailor and left him in a corner.

"Will you always side with him?" Roger asked sulkily.

Elizabeth leaned back against the wall of the ship. Her head hurt and her empty stomach was growing queasy from the motion. "I have a great deal to make up to my husband. Perhaps Miles was right and there was something I could have done the day you came to us in the crofter's hut. You've never been one to listen to reason, but perhaps I could have at least tried."

"You insult me! I have always been good to you."

"No! You've always taken advantage of what good you've done for me. Now listen to me. However we got into this mess, we must get out. You must cooperate."

"With a Montgomery?"

"With *two* Montgomerys!" she snapped.

For a few moments Roger was quiet. "Alice," he muttered. "She brought me the letter from Gavin Montgomery's wife. She knew where you were meeting your . . ."

"Husband," Elizabeth supplied. "Oh Roger!" she gasped.

"Nicholas. He's with Alice, alone. We must get back to my son."

Roger put his hand on her arm. "The child has a guard and they have orders not to let Alice near the boy. They won't disobey me."

"But what will happen to him if we don't return?"

"No doubt the Montgomerys will take over his care."

Their eyes met and it was a moment before Roger realized what he'd said. He was very close to admitting that, just perhaps, he'd been wrong in his accusations of the Montgomerys. Maybe all Elizabeth's thousands of words had begun to sink in.

They turned, breath held, as the hatch door opened, and expelled it when Miles entered.

Elizabeth flew to him, clasped his neck, nearly knocking the bundles from his hands. "We think it was Alice who arranged everything. Oh my Miles, you weren't hurt?"

Miles looked at her suspiciously. "You blow quickly from hot to cold and back again. No, I had no trouble. I brought food and clothes." He tossed Roger a loaf of hard bread and handed a bundle of clothing to Elizabeth. After one glance at the bound and gagged sailor, silent, eyes wide open in fear, Miles sat down with Roger and Elizabeth.

Besides the bread, there was dried meat and a vile-tasting grog which Elizabeth gagged over.

"What did you see?" Roger asked.

Miles realized that Roger was swallowing a great deal of pride to ask such a question. "It's an old ship, falling apart, and it's run by a crew that's mostly drunk or dying. If they know we're prisoners, they're not interested."

"They sound like the type of men Alice would know," Elizabeth said in disgust. "Are we headed toward France like you thought?"

"Yes. I recognize the coastline. When it's dark we'll slip out, take one of the rowboats and row ashore. I don't want to risk a welcoming party when the ship docks." He looked to Roger and Roger gave a nod of his head.

"And how do we get back to England?" Elizabeth asked, chewing.

"I have relatives about four days' ride from where we'll land. If we can get to them we should be safe enough."

"Of course we have no horses or food to last us the journey," Roger said, drinking deeply of the awful brew.

"Perhaps we can manage," Miles said quietly, taking the jug. There was a slight emphasis on the word "we."

"Yes, maybe we can," Roger answered just as quietly.

They ate in silence and when they'd finished, Roger and Elizabeth dressed in the sailors' clothes. The striped cotton shirt stretched taut across Elizabeth's breasts and she was pleased to see a flicker of interest in Miles's eyes. She'd already proved that though he might still be angry with her, he still desired her—and hadn't he said he'd thought of her "every moment"?

When it grew even darker in the smelly little room, Miles again slipped up the ladder and this time he was gone a frighteningly long time. He returned emptyhanded.

"I stocked the rowboat with all the food I could find." He looked at Roger. "I must trust you to protect my back. Elizabeth will be between us."

Roger, like Miles, was too tall to stand in the hold. Miles could pass as a sailor in his ill-fitting clothes, a day's growth of black beard on his cheeks, his eyes wild and fierce, but Roger couldn't. Roger's heavier form had split the seams of the shirt and his aristocratic blondness could not be mistaken for that of a dirty seaman. And Elizabeth in the form-fitting clothes was hopeless. Her features were too delicate to ever look like a man's.

Under the watchful eyes of the bound sailor who was trying to disappear into the woodwork, they made their way up the ladder. Miles stayed several paces ahead, a small knife in his hand. It was the only weapon he'd returned with and he'd offered no explanation as to how he'd obtained it.

The cool night air made Elizabeth realize how hideous the hold had been and her head began to clear as a breeze rushed over her. Miles caught her arm, giving a slight impatient jerk, and she gave her attention back to the moment.

There were three men on deck—one at the helm, two sauntering about on opposite sides of the ship.

Miles ducked, to disappear in a tangle of enormous ropes, and instantly Roger and Elizabeth followed his example. Crouching until her legs ached, they inched along the ship wall, slowly, carefully so as to make no sound.

When Miles stopped, he waved an arm and Roger seemed to understand. He slipped over the side of the ship, and Elizabeth held her breath, expecting to hear a splash as Roger fell, but none came. The next moment Miles motioned her over, too. Without another thought, she threw a leg over the side of the ship and the rest of her followed. Roger caught her and silently lowered her to a seat in the rowboat.

Her heart was pounding as she watched Roger, Miles helping from above, begin to lower the little boat down the side of the ship. Muscles in Roger's arms strained as he took the weight, not letting it drop and hit the water loudly. Elizabeth made a move to help but Roger impatiently motioned her away. As she moved back to her seat, her foot caught on something. It was all she could do to stifle a scream as she saw a hand near her foot—the hand of a dead sailor.

Suddenly, the rowboat lurched and she heard Roger's intake of breath as he fought to control their plunge. For some reason Miles had abruptly released the ropes overhead. Roger managed to set the boat into the water with only a whisper. Pulling back, he looked up toward the ship.

Miles was nowhere to be seen and for a moment Elizabeth felt panic. How deep did Roger's hatred run? Could she fight Roger if he decided to leave Miles behind?

But Roger merely stood in the boat, looking up expectantly, his legs wide apart and braced against the rolling boat.

When Elizabeth was near tears of worry, Miles looked over the side, saw where Roger was and the next minute he tossed a body into Roger's arms. Roger seemed to be waiting for just this and he didn't fall when the body hit him. The next moment Miles was traveling down the rope with lightning speed and he was only half-in when Roger pushed off and began to row. Miles kicked the second dead sailor's body beside the other one, grabbed the second oars and started rowing.

Elizabeth couldn't say a word as she watched the two of them working together, the boat gliding away into the night.

Chapter 16

"LET'S GET rid of them," were the first words spoken after an hour of silence.

Miles nodded in agreement and kept rowing as Roger slipped the two bodies into the water.

Roger resumed rowing. "We'll have to have other clothes. Something plain that won't arouse suspicion."

"Suspicion of what?" Elizabeth asked. "Do you think the sailors will try to find us?"

Roger and Miles exchanged looks that made Elizabeth feel like an outsider.

"If we let it be known that we're of the Montgomerys or Chatworths," Roger began patiently, "we'd be held for ransom within minutes. Since we travel without a guard we must travel incognito."

"As musicians perhaps," Elizabeth added. "We should have Alyx with us."

The mention of Miles's new sister-in-law made Roger reminisce about the time Alyx saved his life. The telling took until dawn, when the men finally reached shore.

"Keep your cloak about you and stay close to me," Miles ordered under his breath. "They'll be setting up a market soon and we'll see if we can find some clothes."

Even though light was just breaking, the town square was alive with people bringing in goods to sell. Roger, in his clothes with burst seams, his arrogant stance, caused many looks, as did Elizabeth, her hair dirty and tangled but her body covered in an expensive cape. But it was Miles who received the most looks—all from females.

A pretty young woman, surrounded by young men, looked up from her wares and met Miles's dark eyes.

Elizabeth stepped forward, hands made into claws. With a chuckle, Miles caught her arm. "How'd you like to have the lady's dress?"

"I'd like to have her hide nailed to my door."

Miles gave Elizabeth such a hot look that she felt her heart begin to beat faster. "Behave yourself and obey me," he said, walking toward the woman who was giving him such heated looks.

"And what can I do for you?" the woman fairly purred, her language a gutter French.

"Could I persuade you out of your clothes?" Miles half whispered, his fingers caressing a large cabbage as he spoke a perfect, classical French.

Elizabeth could have been part of the roadway for all the attention the woman paid her.

"Aye, you could," she whispered, her hand closing over Miles's. "And what would you like to offer in return?"

Miles drew back, his eyes alight, that half-smile of his that Elizabeth knew so well on his lips. "We'll barter a cloak, fur lined, for three suits of clothes and provisions."

The woman looked Elizabeth up and down. "*Her* cloak?" she spat.

By now two of the men had walked toward the group and from the look of them, they were the woman's brothers. Elizabeth, angry at Miles's flirting, even if it were for a good cause, looked up through her lashes at the men. "We have had a most unfortunate accident," she said in French, not quite as good as Miles's, but adequate. "We were hoping to trade this unworthy cloak for a few garments, although perhaps your sister's would be a bit small." At that she casually let the cloak fall to her hips, revealing a skin-tight shirt and pants even tighter. Miles angrily pulled the cloak back to her shoulders but not before the young men gasped in appreciation.

"Will there be a trade?" Miles said through clenched teeth, not looking at Elizabeth.

The brothers agreed readily, the sister having been pushed into the background.

A few minutes later, Elizabeth stepped into a doorway and changed clothes under the cover of her cloak. The dress she wore was plain homespun, loose, comfortable, concealing.

When Miles and Roger were also dressed plainly but with tight hose displaying their muscular thighs, they filled packs with food and set off toward the south.

They were well out of town before Miles spoke to Elizabeth. "And did you learn that trick while at your brother's house? You seem to have recovered quickly from your fear of men."

"And what was I supposed to do? Stand by and let that slut maul you? No doubt you would have taken her against the wall if she'd asked that price."

"Perhaps," was all Miles said and lapsed into one of his infuriating silences.

"Why is it that you accuse me of all manner of bad doings? I have never done anything to deserve your mistrust. I stayed with you in Scotland and—"

"You ran away and nearly killed the MacGregor. You left with your brother," Miles said flatly.

"But I had to!" Elizabeth insisted.

Roger had been walking on the other side of Elizabeth, silent until now. "I would have killed you, Montgomery, if she hadn't gone with me. And I wouldn't have believed whatever she said about wanting to stay with you."

"Why are you telling me this?" Miles asked Roger after a pause.

"Because Elizabeth's ranted at me for a long time about how . . . wrong I've been. Perhaps there's some truth in her words."

They walked in silence for some time, no one speaking his or her thoughts.

As the sun rose higher, they stopped and ate, drinking water from a roadside stream. Elizabeth caught Miles watching her several times and she wondered what he was thinking.

They passed many travelers on the road, rich merchants with donkeys laden with gold, many wandering peasants, musicians, blacksmiths and once a nobleman escorted by twenty armed knights. For an hour afterward Roger and Miles made derogatory remarks about the knights, ranging from their colors to their old-fashioned armor.

As the sun started its descent, the men looked about for a place to spend the night. Although they risked being arrested as poachers, Roger and Miles chose to stay in the king's forest, away from the campers along the roadside.

As they ate, Miles and Roger talked about training, mentioned a few people they both knew and generally acted as if they were old friends. Elizabeth walked away into the shadows and neither man even noticed. Several minutes later she was near tears as she leaned against a tree and listened to the night sounds.

When Miles's hand touched her shoulder, she jumped away.

"Is something wrong?" he asked.

"Wrong!" she hissed at him, her eyes filling with tears. "How could anything be wrong! You held me prisoner for months, made me fall in love with you, yet when I sacrificed everything to save your worthless life, you hated me. I have borne your child, I have conspired with your relatives and your own man to win you back, yet all I get from you is coolness. I've kissed you and you've responded but you've offered me nothing on your own. What must I do to make you understand that I didn't betray you? That I didn't choose my brother over you? You heard Roger say he would have killed you if I hadn't gone with him." She couldn't continue as the tears were choking her.

Miles leaned against a tree, several feet away from her. The moonlight silvered his hair and eyes. "I thought only my brothers were subject to the old demon of pride. I thought Raine was a fool when he refused to forgive his wife for going to the king to beg for a pardon. I could have forgiven you a king but you chose one man over me, someone else's home over mine. And when I heard the stories of all the men you'd bedded I knew I could have killed you."

When she started to protest, he put up his hand. "Perhaps it's because I've dealt with so many unfaithful wives, women who've risen from my bed and put on their wedding clothes. Maybe that distorted my view of all women. And finally, you were my prisoner but you came to me so easily."

"I fought you!" she said hotly, insulted.

Miles merely smiled at her. "Raine said I was jealous, and the irony of it was that I was jealous of the same man as he was. Raine believed his wife Alyx had a great affection for Roger Chatworth."

"Roger, I'm sure, knew nothing of this."

"So I gathered when he told the story of Alyx saving his life. Alyx did it to save Raine because my brother is a hot-headed, stubborn man who never listens to reason."

"Raine!" Elizabeth sputtered. "Did he rage so that he tore his stitches? Did he have to be drugged to make him sleep?"

Miles gave her a quick smile, teeth flashing. "Raine wears out lances when he's angry. I have my own way."

He was silent for a long moment. "How is our son?" he asked quietly.

"He has high cheekbones like your brother Gavin. There is no doubt of the family resemblance."

"I never doubted it, not truly. Elizabeth . . . ?"

"Yes," she whispered.

"Why did you leave me? Why didn't you return to me within a week or so? I waited every day; I prayed for your return. Kit cried himself to sleep. So many mothers have left him."

Tears were rolling down Elizabeth's cheeks. "I was afraid of Roger. He wasn't sane. Brian had vowed to kill Roger and I was afraid that if I weren't there to stop him, Roger'd declare war on all the Montgomerys. I hoped to make him see the truth; I hoped to learn the truth about the hatred of the two families."

"And the men?" Miles said. "Pagnell told everyone of how you were delivered to me and every man who courted you made sure I heard all the details."

Elizabeth put her hand up. "You were not only the first man to make love to me, you were the first man to speak to me without a leer on his face, the first man to make me laugh, the first man to show me kindness. Even you have said I know nothing about men."

"So you found out," Miles said bitterly.

"In a way, I did. I thought about it dispassionately and I knew that it would be better if I loved any man but a Montgomery. If I were married to someone else perhaps Roger would forget that I carried a Montgomery's child and maybe some of his hatred would leave him. So I decided to meet some men and see if maybe I loved you merely because you were the first."

Miles was silent, his eyes burning into her.

"Some of the men made me laugh, some were kind, some made me feel beautiful, but none of them did all things. As the weeks went by, instead of fading, everything about you became clearer. I remembered your every gesture and I began comparing the men to you."

"Even to the size of—"

"Damn you!" Elizabeth cut him off. "I did not bed any of the men and I have a feeling you know that, yet you want to hear me say it."

"Why didn't you take them to your bed? Some of the men you met are very successful with women."

"As you are?" she spat at him. "Here you stand demanding celibacy from me, yet what about you? When I tell you there have been no other men will you allow me to come to your pure bed? This morning I had to drag you from a woman. How do you think I've felt while holding your son and knowing that at that moment you could be in bed with one or two—or more—women?"

"More?" he mocked, then lowered his voice seductively. "There have been no women since you."

Elizabeth didn't believe she'd heard correctly. "No—" she began, eyes wide.

"My brother Raine and I moved into one of his keeps and in a rage we dismissed every woman, even the laundresses. We trained all day, drank all night and cursed women constantly. Raine came to his senses first when his wife sent their daughter to him. Little Catherine made me miss my own children so I went back to Gavin's for Christmas and Judith—" He ran his hand through his hair.

"I used to think Gavin was hard on his sweet little wife but I'd never been on the sharp side of her tongue. The woman never left me alone. She was merciless. She talked constantly about our son, sighed over the fact that her son would never know his cousin and she even hired a man to paint a picture of an angel with long blond hair holding a little boy inside my shield. Inside my shield, mind you! I told Gavin I was going to wring his wife's neck if he didn't do something but Gavin laughed so hard I never mentioned it again. When she received your letter about how you were willing to forgive me, Judith launched into me with renewed force."

Miles closed his eyes a moment in memory. "She enlisted Alyx's help and Alyx came up with a dozen songs about two lovers who were held apart by a stupid, vain man who just happened to look exactly like me. One evening at dinner Alyx led twenty-two musicians in a song that made everyone laugh so hard two men fell off their stools and broke ribs. Alyx was at her best."

Elizabeth was so astonished at his story she could barely speak. "And what did you do?"

He winced in memory. "I very calmly bounded over the table and took Alyx's throat in my hands."

"No!" she gasped. "Alyx is so tiny, so—"

"Both Raine and Gavin drew swords on me and as I stood there, about to kill this pretty little songbird, my brothers' swords at my neck, I realized I wasn't myself. The next day Judith arranged the meeting between us." His eyes twinkled.

"The meeting where you wanted Sir Guy to deliver you to me in a carpet."

Elizabeth wouldn't look at him. She thought Sir Guy had been on her side, yet all along he'd been reporting—and laughing—to Miles. How the two of them must have slapped each other's backs at her wanting to seduce her own husband. What had happened to that prideful woman who'd once stood on a cliff edge and vowed never to submit to any man?

"Excuse me," she whispered as she swept past Miles on her way back to Roger.

Miles caught her in his arms, pulling her close to him.

When Elizabeth saw that he was smiling at her with such a *knowing* little grin, she brought her elbow down hard into his ribs and was rewarded with his whoosh of pain. "I hate you, Montgomery!" she yelled into his face. "You've made me beg and cry and taken all my pride." She tried to hit him again but he pinned her arms to her side and she couldn't move.

"No, Montgomery," he said, moving his lips near hers. "You love me. You love me so much you're willing to beggar yourself for me. I've made you cry in passion and I've made you cry tears of love."

"You've humiliated me."

"As you've done to me." He held her as she struggled against him. "Every woman has come to me easily but only you have made me work. Only with you have I been angry, jealous, possessive. You were given to me and you are mine, Elizabeth, and never again will you be allowed to forget it."

"I never did—" she began but he cut her off by kissing her. Once his lips touched hers, she was lost. She could no more argue with him than she could have run away.

His arms loosened their grip on her just long enough for her to slide her arms about his neck and pull him even closer.

"Never, *never* forget it again, Montgomery," he whispered by her ear. "You will belong to me always—in this century and in the next. Forever!"

Elizabeth barely heard him as she stood on tiptoe and raised her mouth to his.

She had no idea how much she had missed him physically. He was the only man on earth she could be with so trustingly, the only man she wasn't wary of. All the years of holding herself in reserve were showing themselves in her eagerness, her ferocity. She put her hands in his hair, feeling it curl about her fingers, and pulled his head closer.

A low, throaty laugh came from Miles. "A tree you said? Take the woman against a tree?" he said.

Miles knew what she wanted—not a sweet, gentle love-making but one of all the fury she felt. His hands began tearing at her clothes, one hand on the ties of her linen underwear, the other on his own trunk hose. Elizabeth kept kissing him, her mouth wrapped around his, tongues entangled.

When her back slammed into a tree, she merely blinked and applied her teeth to Miles's neck, tearing at his skin as if she meant to flay him.

Miles lifted her, put her legs about his waist, her skirt bunched between them. Neither of them cared for the niceties of removing their clothes. His hands on her bottom, he lifted her, set her down on his shaft with the force of a falling anchor.

Elizabeth gasped, buried her face in Miles's neck and held on for dear life as his strong arms lifted her up and down. Her head went back as she felt a scream building inside her. Sweat began to drip off Miles and he rubbed the salty stuff on her, plastering her hair to the both of them.

With one last, fierce thrust that sent Elizabeth into an ecstasy, Miles pulled her to him, shuddering, his hot body erupting again and again.

Elizabeth, her body tight, convulsing in waves of pleasure, felt quick tears in her eyes. Slowly she came back to earth, her legs feeling weak, aching from clasping Miles with every ounce of her strength.

He leaned away to look at her, caressed her wet hair, kissed her temple. "I love you," he said tenderly, then smiled roguishly. "And besides that you're the best . . ."

"I understand." She laughed. "Now are you going to let me down or are you going to kill me against this tree?"

With one more kiss, Miles set her feet on the ground and gave an ungentlemanly, prideful laugh when Elizabeth's legs collapsed under her and he had to hold her to keep her from falling.

"Braggart!" she hissed, clutching him, but she gave him a smile and kissed the hand holding her arm. "Am I really the best?" she asked as if it meant nothing to her. "You still find me attractive even after I've borne a child?"

"Tolerably so," Miles said seriously.

Elizabeth laughed, smoothed her skirts and tried to regain her composure as they walked back to where Roger waited.

Chapter 17

THE THREE of them walked together for two days and they were blissful ones for Elizabeth. There were nights of love-making and days of love. Miles gave her his complete attention. They held hands and talked softly or laughed uproariously at the silliest things. They made love beside a stream and later bathed in its icy water.

Roger watched them with an air of aloofness, and sometimes Elizabeth felt a pang of guilt for the pain she knew she was causing him. A few times he made remarks about Miles's unknightly behavior but Miles said that until he reached his relatives, he was a carefree peasant.

Their progress was slow and the four-day journey on horseback was stretching into several more days on foot.

On the fourth day, the trio left the roadside just before noon to rest and refresh themselves. Roger, after directing an unnoticed look of contempt toward his sister and Miles, walked away from them, deeper into the forest. When he'd first heard his sister had been taken prisoner, his pain had been great—but now he could see that he'd lost her much more completely than if she were a prisoner.

Reminiscing over his problems, he walked past the earth-torn edge of the little gully without paying the least attention. He was several feet past the obvious signs of a struggle before he recognized them. Turning back, he examined the earth.

He'd been walking along the edge of a steep-sided bank

that fell away to a stream of rushing water and, clearly, on the edge were the signs of someone falling. Often, after a battle, Roger'd had to search for his men who were wounded and lost, and now his knight's instincts rose like the hairs on his neck. Immediately, he started down the side, skidding in his haste.

What he saw at the bottom was not what he expected. Sitting on a rotten piece of log, her feet hidden under a jumble of large rocks, was a pretty young woman, richly dressed in burgundy velvet trimmed about the neckline with large golden amethysts. Her dark eyes, almost too big for her face, looked up at Roger with pleasure.

"I knew you'd come," she said in English that was pleasantly and softly accented.

Roger blinked once in confusion but ignored her remark. "Did you fall? Are you hurt?"

She smiled at him, making her eyes turn liquid. She looked to be quite young, a child really, wearing a dress much too old for her. Dark hair peeped from under a pearl-embroidered hood. More pearls draped down the front of her dress.

"My foot is caught and I cannot move it."

Women! Roger thought, moving to examine the rocks that pinned her feet. "You must have heard me above. Why didn't you call out to me?"

"Because I knew you'd come for me."

Insane, Roger thought. The poor girl was possessed by spirits. "When I lift this rock I want you to move your foot. Do you understand me?" he said as if talking to an idiot.

She merely smiled in answer and when the rock was moved, she pulled her foot from under it.

Her right foot was pinned differently and Roger saw that if he moved one stone, another would fall and perhaps break her ankle. She was a little thing and he doubted her fragile bones could stand much.

"Do not be afraid to tell me," she whispered. "I'm not a stranger to pain."

Roger turned to look at her, at her big eyes looking at

him with so much trust, and that trust both frightened him and made him feel powerful.

"What is your name?" he asked, studying and considering the rocks around her little foot.

"Christiana, my lord."

Roger's head came up sharply. His dirty peasant's clothes had not fooled her, so perhaps she wasn't stupid after all. "Chris then." He smiled. "May I borrow your eating dagger? I'll put together something to hold those rocks while I move these." He pointed.

She handed him the knife quickly and he bit his lips to keep from cautioning her about handing knives to strangers. The jewels on her dress were worth a fortune and the pearl necklace she wore was without equal.

He moved but a few feet from her to cut several tree branches. Removing his doublet, he pulled out his shirt and cut strips of cloth from the tail to use in building a platform to fit under the rocks.

"Why is no one searching for you?" he asked as he worked.

"Perhaps they are; I don't know. I dreamed of you last night."

He gave her a sharp look but said nothing. Girls everywhere seemed to be full of romantic ideas of being rescued. It was hard for a man to live up to.

"I dreamed," she continued, "of this forest and this place. I saw you in my dream and I knew you'd come."

"Perhaps the man in your dream was merely fair-skinned and resembled me," Roger said patronizingly.

"I saw many things. The scar by your eye—you received it from your brother when you were only a boy."

Involuntarily, Roger's hand went to the curved scar by his left eye. He'd come close to losing his eye that day and very few people who knew how he got the scar were still alive. He doubted if even Elizabeth knew.

Christiana merely smiled at his look of surprise. "I have waited all my life for you."

Roger shook his head to clear it. "That was a lucky

guess," he said. "About the scar I mean. Now hold very still while I prop these rocks up." There was no need to tell her to be still as she'd hardly moved since he'd arrived.

The rocks were not small and Roger had to sweat some before he could move the largest one. And even as it rolled away, more came crashing down onto the weak, makeshift platform he'd created. With lightning speed he jumped onto Christiana, knocking her backward and rolling her away from the crushing boulders. Even as he moved her, he heard her intake of breath as the rocks scraped away some of her skin.

The sound of the rocks filled the air and Roger covered Christiana's body with his own, protecting her from dust and fragments. When it was safe, he started to pull away from her but she put her hands on the sides of his head and pulled his lips to hers.

For a long time Roger'd been concerned only with bringing his brother and sister back to him and he'd had no time for women. He'd had no idea his desires were so pent-up inside him. Once, years ago, he'd been almost carefree, laughing with pretty young girls, tumbling about with them in clandestine meetings, but his anger at the Montgomerys had changed all that.

At the first touch of the girl's lips, Roger's first thought was: serious. She may look to be little more than a child, but she was a woman and her purpose was one of seriousness. She kissed him with such intensity that he drew back from her.

"Who are you?" he whispered.

"I love you and I have waited always to meet you."

Roger, lying on top of her, looked deeply into her dark eyes, eyes that seemed to be trying to pull his soul out of his body, and he was frightened. He moved off her. "We'd better get you back to your parents."

"I have no parents," she said, sitting up.

Roger looked away from her eyes that seemed to be accusing him of deserting her. Part of him wanted to run away from this strange woman and another part wanted to fight to the death to keep her near him.

"Let me see your ankle," he said at last.

Obediently, she turned and held out her foot to him.

He frowned when he saw it, cut and bruised, blood running freely. "Why didn't you show this to me?" he snapped. "Here"— he handed her back her knife—"cut off some of your underskirt. I can't afford to lose more of my shirt. It's the only one I have at the moment."

She smiled at that and began slicing away at a fine lawn petticoat. "Why are you here in France and dressed like that? Where are your men?"

"You tell me," he said nastily, taking the strips from her. "Perhaps tonight you'll dream the rest of my life."

As soon as he turned away toward the stream, he regretted his words, but damn! the woman gave him chills. He could still feel her kiss—an odd combination of a woman who wanted to jump into his bed and a witch who wanted his soul.

At that thought he smiled. He was getting fanciful. She was a young girl who needed his help, nothing more or less. The best thing he could do would be to dress her ankle and return her to her guardians.

When he returned to her with dampened cloths, he could see tears glistening on her lashes, and he was immediately contrite. "I'm sorry, Chris," he said as if he'd known her always. "Damn! Give me your ankle."

A small smile came through her tears and he couldn't help returning it, and she smiled broadly as she put her foot in his hand.

"Let me have your knife again and I'll cut away your hose," he said, after he'd gently removed her embroidered slipper.

Without a word, Christiana slowly raised her dress on one side to the top of her thigh and unfastened her hose. Her eyes on Roger, and his on her slim curvy leg, she inched the hose downward toward her bloody ankle. When she reached her calf she held up her leg. "You may remove the rest."

Roger suddenly felt sweat breaking out on his body and a flame of desire so hot shot through him that his veins seemed to be on fire. With shaking hands, he removed her stocking, one hand on fabric, the other on the back of her bare knee.

The sight of blood on her ankle soothed him somewhat and he began to calm. "You are toying with things you don't understand," he said tightly, wetting her ankle to get the torn stocking off.

"I do not play children's games," she said softly.

Roger tried to concentrate on the task before him as he carefully cleaned her ankle, then bound it. "Now we must return you," he said as if he were her father, but his left hand was still on her ankle and began to caress her leg as his hand moved upward. He replaced her dagger in the sheath at her side.

Her eyes locked with his. She didn't move away but seemed to welcome him.

Roger came to his senses abruptly. No matter how appealing this urchin was, she wasn't worth his life. Someone would be looking for her soon and if he, looking to be a peasant, were found making love to her, obviously a noblewoman, no one would ask questions before they put a sword through his heart. And besides, he wasn't sure he liked the idea of being intimate with this strange young woman. What if she were a witch and she did mean to take his soul?

"Why did you stop, my lord?" she whispered in a throaty voice.

Primly, he pulled her skirt down. "Because you're a child and I'm—Do you always offer yourself to strangers?"

She didn't respond to the question but the answer was in her eyes. "I have loved you always and will love you always. I am yours to command."

Roger felt himself getting angry. "Now see here, young woman! I don't know who you think I am nor who you are, but I think it's best that you get back to your people and I to mine. And I hope you pray to God—if you believe in Him—for forgiveness for your actions."

With that he bent, tossed her small body over his shoulder and began to climb the steep bank.

By the time he reached the top of the bank, both his anger

and his passion had calmed. He was too old and too sensible to allow a romantic bit of a girl to bother him.

He stood her before him, holding her shoulders to steady her, and smiled. "Now where may I take you? Do you remember which way you came from?"

She looked confused for a moment. "Of course I remember the way. Why are you sending me away? Would you kiss me again? Would you kiss me as if you loved me in return?"

Roger held her at arms' length. "You are too forward and no, I will not kiss you again. You must tell me where you belong."

"I belong with you but—" She stopped as a blast from a stag's horn sounded. Her eyes changed to wild, frightened. "I must go. My husband calls. He must not find you. Here!"

Before he could speak, she'd taken her little dagger from her side and crudely cut the largest amethyst from the front of her dress. An ugly, irreparable hole was left in the expensive velvet.

"Take this," she offered urgently.

Roger's back stiffened. "I do not take tribute from women."

The horn sounded again and Christiana's fright increased. "I must go!" She stood on tiptoe, quickly kissed his tightened lips. "I have a beautiful body," she said, "and lovely soft hair. I will show you sometime."

When the horn sounded a third time, she gathered her skirts and began to run awkwardly, her ankle bending every few steps. She'd not gone far when she turned and tossed the amethyst toward him. He made no move to catch it. "Give it to the woman who travels with you. Is she your sister or your mother?"

The last words were called over her shoulder as she disappeared from his sight.

Roger stood still, rooted into place for a very long time, his eyes staring sightlessly toward the place where she'd disappeared. His head felt strange, light, as if he'd just been through some experience that wasn't real. Had the girl really existed or had he fallen asleep and dreamed her?

"Roger!" came Elizabeth's voice from behind him. "We've been looking for you for an hour. Are you ready to travel? There are a few hours before nightfall."

Slowly, he turned toward her.

"Roger, are you all right?"

Miles had left his wife's side and was looking about the area. Sometimes men who'd been wounded had Roger's look—just before they fell down. Miles saw the amethyst on the ground, but before he could touch it, Roger swept it into his hand, fingers closing tightly around it.

"Yes, I'm ready to go," he said tersely. Before he left he gave one last look about the forest, his thumb rubbing the jewel in his hand. "Her husband!" he muttered angrily. "So much for love." He thought about throwing the amethyst away, but he couldn't do it.

It was Miles who was truly aware of Roger's distant moodiness that night. Miles had snared a rabbit—illegally—and it was turning over a spit as the three of them sat around the fire. He didn't want to worry Elizabeth, telling her there was no danger—and indeed the life of the French peasant seemed carefree compared to life at her brother's house—but Miles was always on guard, always aware of potential danger. At night he slept lightly and he gained respect for Roger as he saw that the knight was also wary.

Elizabeth lay sleeping, her head in her husband's lap. Roger sat apart, turning something over and over in his hand. Miles was not a person to directly ask after something that wasn't his concern, but Roger felt the younger man's interest.

"Women!" Roger finally said with great disgust and pocketed the amethyst. But as he stretched out on the cold forest floor, his hand sought the jewel and held it all night.

The morning dawned bright and clear and Elizabeth, as usual, was extraordinarily happy. Another day and they'd reach the French Montgomerys. Then they could go back to England and their son and, like a fairy tale, live happily ever after.

"You seem especially happy." Miles smiled down at her. "I think you like this peasant life."

"For a while," she said smugly, "but don't get the idea I'll always wear rags. I'm an expensive woman." She rolled her eyes at him flirtatiously.

"You will have to earn your keep," he said arrogantly, looking her up and down.

"I do that well enough. I—"

She stopped as the clatter of many horses and many men forced them to the side of the road. It was obviously a rich group of men, their horses draped in silks, their armor painted and well tended. There were about a hundred men and baggage wagons, and in the middle was a young girl, her hands tied behind her back, her face bruised, but she held her head high.

Elizabeth shivered as she remembered all too well how it felt to be a captive, but this girl looked as if she'd been beaten.

"Chris," Roger whispered from beside her and it was a heartfelt sound.

Miles was watching Roger intently and when Roger made a move forward, Miles caught his arm. "Not now," Miles said quietly.

Elizabeth turned back toward the passing procession. So many men for such a small girl, she thought sadly. Her head turned with a snap. "No!" she gasped up at Miles. "You can't possibly be considering rescuing the girl."

Miles looked back at the knights and didn't answer Elizabeth. When she spoke again he turned such hot eyes on her that she became silent.

The trio stood for some time after the knights went past. Elizabeth's mind kept screaming no, no, no! Miles couldn't risk his life for a woman he didn't know.

As they started walking again, Elizabeth began her plea as calmly and rationally as she could. "We'll be at your relatives' soon and they'll know who the girl is, who holds her prisoner—and why. Perhaps she killed a hundred people. Perhaps she deserves her punishment."

Both Miles and Roger looked straight ahead.

Elizabeth clutched Miles's arm. "I was held prisoner once and it hasn't worked out badly. Perhaps—"

"Be quiet, Elizabeth!" Miles commanded. "I can't think."

Elizabeth felt herself begin to shiver. How could he, weaponless, rescue a girl guarded by a hundred armored knights?

Miles turned to Roger. "Should we volunteer our services as wood gatherers? At least we'll gain entrance to their camp."

Roger gave Miles a calculating look. "This isn't your fight, Montgomery. The girl was beaten because of me and I'll get her out alone."

Miles kept looking at Roger, his eyes blazing, and after a moment, Roger gave in.

After one curt nod, Roger looked away. "I don't know who she is except that her name is Christiana. She gave me a jewel, cut it from her dress, and no doubt that's why she's been beaten. She has a husband and she is terrified of him."

"A husband!" Elizabeth gasped. "Roger, please, both of you, listen to reason. You can't risk your lives for a married woman. How long have you known her? What does she mean to you?"

"I never saw her before yesterday," Roger half whispered. "And she means nothing to me—or perhaps she does. But I cannot let her be beaten because of me."

Elizabeth began to realize there was no sense in arguing further. She'd never seen Roger do something so foolhardy but she was sure Miles would risk his life for a scullery maid. She took a deep breath. "Once, on the road, a peasant offered me a bouquet of flowers and she was allowed past the guard to give them to me."

"You will remain behind," Miles said in dismissal.

Elizabeth didn't answer but set her jaw. The odds were better if three people attacked a hundred than if there were just two.

Chapter 18

THEY FOLLOWED the guard until nearly sunset, when the men made camp, and quite easily Miles and Roger, forsaking their usual shoulders-back stance, slipped among the knights, their arms loaded with wood. In the shadows of the trees, Elizabeth watched. Her early offer of help seemed to be hollow, the words of a braggart. Now, watching all those men, it was as if she'd never left her brother's house. Even as she stood hidden, she glanced behind her to make sure none of the men was there, ready and waiting to touch her.

Both Miles and Roger had given her strict orders that under no circumstances was she to leave her hiding place. They'd made it clear that they had enough to do without worrying about her also. Roger'd given her the girl's amethyst and Miles'd told her how to get to his relatives—in case anything happened to either of them. Elizabeth'd felt a hint of panic at the pronouncement but she'd kept her fears to herself. The men wanted her to wait far away but she'd stubbornly insisted on a place where she could watch. They'd refused to tell her their plan and Elizabeth began to suspect they had no real plan at all. No doubt Miles intended to hold the men at swordpoint while Roger fled with the girl.

Watching, she saw a scuffling, awkward old man, who she couldn't quite believe was her proud brother, move slowly toward where the girl was tied. She sat, leaning against a tree, hands and feet bound, head lowered.

When Roger awkwardly dropped the entire load of wood on the girl's feet, Elizabeth held her breath. She didn't know how much contact Roger'd had with the girl and she looked too young to have much sense. Would she give Roger away?

There was a brief flicker across the girl's face—but that could have been from pain—and then her face calmed. Elizabeth almost smiled. The girl was certainly not stupid. There wasn't another movement or expression from her as Roger began to clear the fallen wood away. A knight, cursing Roger, kicked him in the leg, and as Roger rolled, kicked him again in the ribs. And even as Roger took the blows, Elizabeth saw the flash of a knife as he cut the bindings from the girl's feet under the cover of the wood.

But Elizabeth saw something Roger couldn't: Behind him an older man, richly dressed, hung with jewels, his garments interwoven with gold wire, had never taken his sunken little eyes off the bound girl. The dying sunlight caught just a bit of flash of Roger's knife.

On the far side of the camp, Miles kicked a burning log out of the fire, setting some grasses on fire. He slipped away before he could receive punishment for his actions and several knights began to fight the fire.

But the diversion wasn't enough. The men guarding the girl didn't glance at the fire—and the old man continued to glare at her with hatred.

The dark seemed to be coming quickly but there was enough light for Elizabeth to see a shadowy Miles slip a sword from a scabbard.

He did plan to fight! she thought. He planned to create some commotion so Roger could get the girl away. If fire had failed, perhaps a little clashing steel would work.

Elizabeth rose from her safe ditch, made a quick prayer for forgiveness for sinning and began unbuttoning her coarse woolen gown all the way to her waist. Perhaps she could get the men's attention—and especially the attention of the old man.

Her entrance was quick and dramatic. She ran into the clearing, leaped the last few feet, so close to one of the fires that she almost straddled it. Hands on her thighs, legs spread, she bent forward, the open bodice gaping, and practically touched the old man's head with her breasts. Slowly, seductively, she began to sway her shoulders, back and forth, from side to side, one raised, the next one higher, always working back until she was leaning backwards over the fire. With one hand she pulled the cotton cap from her head and let her hair cascade down to her knees. It hung over the fire, turning almost red in the light and looking as if it were part of the flames.

When she straightened, her hands insolently on her hips, she gave a laugh—a loud, arrogant, challenging laugh—and she had everyone's attention. The old man looked at her with interest and at last his eyes weren't on the girl not two feet from Elizabeth.

Elizabeth had never danced before but she'd seen enough lascivious entertainments at her brother's house to know what could be done. One of the knights began to play a lute and another a drum. Elizabeth began to undulate slowly—not just her hips, but her entire body moving every inch from fingertips to toes. And she used her magnificent hair to advantage, swirling it about, slapping men across the face with it. When one knight came too close, Elizabeth swept downward, grabbed a rock and plowed her fist into the man's stomach.

Everyone laughed uproariously at the knight's pain and from then on it was more a chase than a dance. For Elizabeth it was a nightmare come true. She was back in her brother's house and his men were pursuing her. She forgot about the last months of freedom but regressed to a time when she had to survive.

On her toes, she whirled about a knight and lifted his sword from his belt. With garments flying, hair tangling about her body, she dodged at the men trying to catch her. She didn't hurt any of them but she managed to draw blood now and again. Forcing herself to laugh and keep up the charade of dancing, she jumped atop a table set with food, kicking plates and goblets everywhere. When a knight's hand touched her ankle, she moved away, her heel "accidentally" coming down on his fingers. He went away with a cry of pain.

Elizabeth's nerves were at the breaking point as the men began to clap in rhythm. Bending, she turned her hair around and around in time to their applause. Hoping that by now Roger and Miles had had time to release their captive, she threw her skirts high, the men cheering at the sight of her legs, and leaped to the ground directly in front of the old man.

She landed in a low bow before him, head low, hair a curtain about her. Panting, sides heaving, she waited.

With great ceremony, the man rose and put one bony hand under Elizabeth's chin, lifting her face to meet his.

Out of the corner of her eye, Elizabeth could see that the girl was gone and now it would be only moments before someone noticed.

Elizabeth rose and, praying for more time, hoping to distract the men, shrugged her shoulders and let the top of her dress fall away to her waist.

There was a great hush among the people, almost all of whom were behind her. The old man's eyes greedily roamed over her exquisite, high, firm breasts. Then, with a smile showing blackened teeth, he removed his own heavy cloak and put it about Elizabeth's shoulders.

Holding onto the ties in a degrading manner, he began to pull Elizabeth into the darkness of the forest.

Concealed in her hand was a knife she'd taken from one of the knights. As the old man turned, he saw that the bound girl was gone, but before he could call out, Elizabeth moved forward, caught his earlobe between her teeth, pressed the knife to his ribs and growled, "Walk!"

They were enveloped in the darkness before the cry was given that the prisoner had escaped.

"Run!" Elizabeth commanded the old man, pushing on the knife.

Quickly, he turned and backhanded Elizabeth across the face.

But before he could move, Roger leaped from the trees, his big hands around the old man's throat. Perhaps it was the surprise or the excitement of Elizabeth's dance, but Roger barely touched him and the ugly old man fell dead at their feet.

Roger lost no time but caught Elizabeth's waist and shoved her up into a tree.

Knights swarmed across the ground under them, their drawn swords glinting in the moonlight. Roger put his arms around Elizabeth and held her close, her head buried in his shoulder. She was trembling over her entire body and even now, in the safety of her brother's arms, she could still feel the men's hands clutching at her.

"Miles," she whispered to Roger.

"Safe," was all Roger'd say as he pressed her even closer.

They waited for some time, through all the hue and cry of finding the old man dead. Finally, two knights carried the body back to the camp and the search for the girl seemed to be ended as the men saddled horses and began to ride out.

Roger held Elizabeth a while after the forest was quiet.

"Come," he commanded. "Montgomery waits for us."

Roger climbed down first, then caught Elizabeth, who still wore the old man's cloak. The velvet swirling about her, she ran after Roger through the cold, damp forest.

Elizabeth hadn't realized how worried she'd been about Miles's safety until she saw him again. He emerged from a stagnant pond, holding the hand of the girl. Both of them were wet, slimy, and the girl's teeth were chattering.

After one grateful look at Miles for his safety, Elizabeth removed the old man's cloak and put it around the girl's shoulders.

"It is his!" Christiana said, stepping away from the cloak as if it were evil.

Roger caught the cloak, tossed it back to Elizabeth and removed his own doublet, wrapping the girl in it. She melted into Roger's arms as if she were part of his skin.

"We must go," Miles said, taking Elizabeth's hand. "They'll be back for her soon."

They traveled all night. Elizabeth knew she was past exhaustion but she kept going, sometimes stealing looks at the girl who'd caused this flight. Wearing Roger's doublet, which dwarfed her, she looked even younger and more fragile than she first appeared. She was never more than an inch or two from Roger's side even though sometimes branches hit her face. As for Roger, he didn't seem to want her any farther away.

Elizabeth hardly looked at Miles because his eyes blazed with anger and a few times he threatened to crush her hand in his. Once, she tried to talk to him and explain why she'd had to disobey his orders and enter the rescue, but Miles looked at her with eyes blackened with rage, and Elizabeth practically crawled back inside the concealing cloak.

Toward morning, Miles said, "We'll join the travelers on the road and we must get her some clothes."

Christiana still wore her bejeweled dress, the pearls about her neck. It somehow emphasized her fallen status—she still wore her riches but now her fine dress was torn, her hair matted, her cheek bruised and the slime from the pond was dried and still clinging to her.

When at last they stopped beside the road, near a large group of travelers just waking, Elizabeth nearly fell in an exhausted heap. Miles caught her to him, pulled her across his lap. "If you ever do anything like that again, wife—" he began but stopped when he kissed her so hard her mouth was bruised.

Tears came to her eyes, tears of joy that he was safe. There'd been a time, when she saw Miles draw a sword, that she was sure she'd never see him alive again. "I would risk all for you," she whispered and fell asleep in his arms.

It seemed like only moments before Elizabeth was wakened again and they began walking just a short distance behind the other travelers. The girl, Christiana, now wore a coarse woolen dress with a large concealing hood.

At midday they stopped and the men left the women alone while they went to the travelers to negotiate for bread and cheese, using the hated cloak.

Elizabeth leaned against a tree, her body trying to relax,

but Christiana's nearness prevented rest. She couldn't help resenting the girl who'd nearly caused their deaths.

"Will you hate me for long, Elizabeth?" Christiana asked softly.

Elizabeth gave her one startled look before turning away. "I do not . . . hate you."

"You are not accustomed to lying," the girl said.

Elizabeth turned on her. "My husband could have been killed rescuing you!" she said fiercely. "As well as my brother! What hold do you have on Roger? Have you bewitched him?"

Christiana did not smile nor did she frown. Her big eyes blazed with intensity. "I have always dreamed of a man like Roger. I have always known he'd come for me. Last year my uncle gave me in marriage to a cruel man but still I knew Roger would come. Three nights ago I dreamed and I saw his face. He was traveling in coarse clothes and with a woman related to him. I knew that he'd finally come."

Elizabeth looked at the girl as if she were a witch.

Chris continued, "You curse me for putting the man you love in danger, but what would you risk to be with your man? Perhaps if I were braver I could have gone to the torture and death my husband planned for me, but instead I sat in camp tied to the tree and prayed with all my might for my Roger to come."

She looked away, down the road to where Miles and Roger were approaching, and an inner light appeared in her eyes. "God has given me Roger to repay me for what has happened to me before. Tonight I will lie with Roger and after that I am ready to forsake all life, if need be. I have risked his life, yours and your kind husband's for this one night with my beloved."

She put her hand over Elizabeth's and her eyes were pleading. "Forgive me if I have asked too much of all of you."

Elizabeth's anger evaporated. Her hand took Christiana's. "Don't talk of death. Roger needs love perhaps more than you do. Stay beside him."

For the first time, Chris gave a bit of a smile and a single dimple showed in her left cheek. "Only force will take me away from him."

Elizabeth glanced upward, saw Roger standing over them, his face showing puzzlement. He's bewildered by all this, Elizabeth thought. Chris confuses him as much as she does us.

They rested only minutes, ate hurriedly and were again on their way.

That night, as Elizabeth snuggled in Miles's arms, she had her first chance to talk to him. "What do you think of this young woman you risked your life for?" she asked.

"I know she's dangerous," he answered. "She was married to the Duke of Lorillard. As a child I used to hear of his cruelty. He's been through seven or eight rich, highborn young women. They all seem to die within a few years of marriage."

"Is Chris highborn?"

Miles gave a snort. "She's descended from generations of kings."

"How do you know all this?"

"From my French relatives. They've had a few dealings with the Lorillard family. Elizabeth," he said solemnly, "I want you to keep these." He closed her hand over the long strand of pearls Christiana'd worn yesterday. "Tomorrow, late, we should reach the home of my relatives but in case we don't . . . No!" He put a finger to her lips to quiet her. "I want to tell you the truth so you can be prepared. The Lorillard family is powerful and we've taken the life of one member and now harbor another. They'll tear the countryside apart looking for us. If anything happens, take the pearls and go back to England to my brothers. They will take care of you."

"But what about your French relatives? Couldn't I go to them?"

"I'll tell you the story someday, but for now let's just say that the Lorillards know me. If I'm captured, the way to my people here will be blocked. Go home to my brothers. Will you swear that? No more attempts to rescue me, but get home to safety."

She refused to answer him.

"Elizabeth!"

"I swear I will go home to your brothers." She sighed.

"And what about the rest?"

"I will make no more promises!" she hissed at him, turning her face up to his to be kissed.

They made love slowly and deliberately, as if tomorrow would never come. Miles's words of warning made Elizabeth feel desperate, as if they had only a few hours together. Twice, tears came to her eyes, tears of frustration that they'd been so close to safety and one woman's lust had put them in danger.

Miles kissed away her tears and whispered that she was to live for the moment and she could save her anger and hatred until later when they had the leisure.

She fell asleep holding Miles as tightly as she could and during the night she moved on top of him. He woke, smiled, kissed the top of her head, pulled a wad of her hair out of his mouth, hugged her and went back to sleep.

Roger woke them before daybreak and after one look, Elizabeth was sure he'd never been asleep. Christiana appeared from the trees, her eyes alive, her lips full and reddened, whisker burn on her neck and the side of her face. As they began to walk, Elizabeth saw Roger constantly cast looks toward Chris—looks of awe and pleasure. By noon, he had his arm around the girl, pulling her close to him. And once, to Elizabeth's surprise, he caught Chris in his arms and kissed her passionately. Roger'd always been decorous, aware of his place in life, his knightly vows, and he never made public displays of affection.

Miles caught Elizabeth, pulled her away from the spot where she stood gaping at her brother.

It was an hour before sunset when men burst from the trees, swords drawn and pointed at the throats of the four travelers.

A man, old, ugly, stepped from behind the knights. "Well, Montgomery, we meet again. Take them!" he commanded.

Chapter 19

ELIZABETH SAT still on the horse for just a moment as she saw, through tears, the ancient Montgomery fortress. So many things had changed in the last few weeks that she wasn't sure either England or the massive stronghold would still be there.

One of the horses of the three big men behind her stamped impatiently, bringing Elizabeth to her senses. With a great cry, she used the ends of her reins as a whip and spurred the horse forward. For all that she'd never visited the Montgomery estates, she knew the plan of it well. In Scotland, Miles had told her about the place, even drawn a sketch in the dirt.

She headed for the heavily guarded back gate, the family entrance. As she came to the walls that surrounded the narrow entrance, she barely slowed her horse.

Immediately, guards, arrows aimed, challenged her.

"The wife of Miles Montgomery," one of the men behind Elizabeth bellowed upward.

Six arrows landed in the ground before Elizabeth's horse, and the tired animal reared, one hoof breaking two shafts. Elizabeth used all her strength to control the frightened animal.

Three armed knights now stood between her and the closed entrance.

"I am Elizabeth Montgomery and these men are with me," she said impatiently but with some respect. Not many places were guarded like this any more.

As if they were statues, the knights held their ground as more men dropped from the walls and aimed swordpoints at the men behind Elizabeth.

When twenty Montgomery knights were assembled, one guard spoke to her. "You alone may enter. Your men stay here."

"Yes, of course. Take me to Gavin. He can identify me."

The reins of Elizabeth's horse were taken from her and she was led into a clean, spacious courtyard before a large house. More buildings were tucked inside the high surrounding walls.

One of the guards entered the house and moments later a pretty woman appeared, her face smudged with flour, sesame seeds dotting her hair.

"Take me to your master," Elizabeth ordered the woman. "I have news that concerns him."

"Are you Elizabeth?" the small woman asked. "Do you have news of Miles? We were told you'd both been killed. Henry! Help her from her horse and bring the men with her inside and feed them."

At that moment Bronwyn appeared in the doorway and behind her the little singer Elizabeth'd met years before, Alyx.

"Elizabeth!" Bronwyn cried, running forward.

Elizabeth nearly fell into her sister-in-law's arms. "I am so glad to see you! It's been such a long journey. Where's Stephen? We have to return and get Miles and Roger. They've been taken by a French duke and we have to ransom them or rescue them or—"

"Slow down," Bronwyn said. "Come inside and have something to eat and we'll make plans."

"Henry!" the woman behind Elizabeth commanded. "Fetch my stepfather and Sir Guy. Send them to me and prepare seven horses for a journey. Send a rider ahead immediately and have a ship prepared for travel to France. I want *no* delay. Is that understood?"

Elizabeth had stopped, gaping at the woman she'd first thought was a servant.

"May I present Lady Judith?" Bronwyn said with some amusement.

Judith brushed her hand at a stray strand of hair and a flurry of golden sesame seeds fell away. "Do you know where Miles is held?"

"Yes, I've just come from there."

"And ridden hard by the look of you," Bronwyn said.

"Hello, Alyx," Elizabeth said, extending her hand to the quiet woman who had moved to stand beside Bronwyn.

Alyx nodded in greeting and smiled shyly. She'd never felt so insignificant before as she did now, surrounded by her magnificent sisters-in-law.

At that moment Sir Guy came running. The giant looked as if he'd lost weight. Behind him came Tam, his sturdy form fairly making the ground shake.

"You have word of my Lord Miles?" Sir Guy called, his eyes roaming over Elizabeth. "We were told you were dead."

"And who told you this?" Elizabeth asked, voice rising. "Did no one search for us?"

"Come inside," Judith said, her hand on Elizabeth's arm. "Tell us what has happened."

Minutes later Elizabeth sat at a big table, eating energetically of the vast quantity of food set before her, while telling her story. Around her were her three sisters-in-law, a man she didn't know—John Bassett, Judith's mother's husband—Sir Guy and Tam.

With her mouth full, she told hurriedly of how the three of them were tossed into the hold of a ship, how they'd escaped and traveled south until Roger decided to risk their lives for a bit of a girl who was someone else's wife.

Bronwyn interrupted with a barrage of hatred directed toward Roger Chatworth but Tam ordered her to be quiet. Surprisingly, Bronwyn obeyed the older man.

Elizabeth briefly told of their rescue of the young Christiana.

Judith asked many questions, both about Elizabeth's participation in the rescue and about Christiana. "I know of her,"

Judith said. "And I know of her husband and his family. The younger brother, not the duke, hates Miles."

"Why?" Elizabeth blurted.

"There was a young woman who—"

Elizabeth put up her hand. "Tell me no more. I think it's the younger man who holds Miles and Roger. The duke died in Roger's hands."

"He enjoys killing!" Bronwyn said.

Elizabeth didn't waste time defending her brother but continued with her story, telling of the old duke's sudden death. She stopped eating when she told of their capture by the dead duke's brother. Miles had been wounded when he pulled a knight from his horse, tossed Elizabeth into the saddle and slapped the horse's rump. She'd gone tearing down the weed-infested, rutted road, working hard at trying to get the dangling reins. When she did have control of the horse, she glanced backward to see half-a-dozen men chasing her. She whipped her horse forward and spent the next hours trying to escape them.

Elizabeth skipped over the next ten days of her story hurriedly. She used the pearls of Christiana's necklace to purchase her way back to England. Praying she wasn't hastening her own death, she hired three men off the road, men who'd once been soldiers, but their master had died and the successor wanted younger men.

The four of them traveled night and day, changing horses often, sleeping for only a couple of hours at a time.

When they reached the coast, Elizabeth had paid ten pearls for a ship and crew to take them back to England and she'd slept for the whole three days of sailing. They arrived in the south of England, purchased horses and a few supplies and took off again, never pausing until they reached the Montgomery estates.

"So," Elizabeth concluded, "I have come to get Miles's brothers. We must set out at once for France."

A knight entered, whispered something to Judith and left. "Lady Elizabeth," Judith said, "there are things you don't know. Soon after you, Miles and your brother were cast into the ship, Alice Chatworth"—Judith nearly choked on the name—"couldn't resist bragging about what she'd done. She sent a messenger and a letter telling us everything."

Alyx spoke for the first time, her voice soft but easily heard. "Raine, Stephen and Gavin left for France immediately while we"—she nodded toward Judith and Bronwyn—"came here to wait for news."

"Then the men are already in France?" Elizabeth asked, rising. "I must leave now. If I may have some men I'll find Miles's brothers and lead them to the place where Miles is held."

"Do you know the Duke of Lorillard's castle? Do you know where his brother lives?" Judith asked, leaning forward.

"No, but surely—" Elizabeth began.

"We can't risk it. The duke was a 'friend' of my father." Judith sneered at this. "I know where all four of the Lorillard estates are and I doubt if any other Montgomery does. Raine might, since he's fought in tournaments in France, but if the men have separated . . . no, it's decided." She stood.

"Like hell it is!" roared the man at her side, John Bassett, as he rose to tower over her.

Judith merely blinked at his voice but remained calm. "The horses are ready and we will ride soon. Bronwyn, do you have enough of those tartan skirts of yours? They'll be comfortable on the long journey."

John grabbed her arm harshly. "You'll not go risking your life again," he said. "You nearly killed us all when you went after Gavin. This time, young lady, you'll remain here and let the men handle this."

Judith's eyes turned as hot as molten gold. "And where will you look for my husband?" she seethed. "Have you ever been to France? And if you by chance found him, where would you tell him to look for Miles? Use what sense you have, John! Leave the other women here but Elizabeth and I must go with you."

Alyx looked at Bronwyn and then let out a yell of "NO!" that made dust trickle down from the ceiling.

Alyx's face turned a becoming shade of pink and she

looked down at her hands. "I mean that Bronwyn and I would rather go with you. Perhaps we can help," she whispered.

"Bronwyn," Tam began while Sir Guy was looking down his nose in an intimidating way at Elizabeth. Instantly, the room erupted into argument. Alyx, having no man to tower over her, slipped away unnoticed, ran up the stairs to Bronwyn and Stephen's room and pulled several plaids from a trunk. Even upstairs she could hear the loud voices downstairs.

On impulse, she grabbed a bagpipe from the wall. Multicolored tartans over her shoulders, she set the pipes to wailing as she started downstairs. By the time she reached the Great Hall, where everyone stood looking up at her, they were silent.

She dropped the pipe from her mouth. "If you men ride without us," she said into the silence, "we will leave, alone, an hour later. Do you ride with us or before us?"

The men were quiet, jaws working, lips in tight lines.

"While we are wasting time," Alyx continued, "Miles is being held prisoner, or perhaps being tortured at this very moment. I suggest we ride—NOW!"

Judith walked forward, took Alyx's face in her hands, kissed both of her sister-in-law's cheeks. "We ride!" Judith declared, taking the plaids from Alyx's shoulders and tossing one to Elizabeth. "John, see to the supplies. Guy, go to my steward. We'll need gold for this journey. Tam, make sure we have arrows aplenty and check the strings on the bows. Bronwyn, make sure we have horses that can travel. Alyx, bring something to make music with. We may need it."

Elizabeth began smiling at the first order. "And me?" she asked as everyone started off in different directions to obey Judith.

"Come with me," Judith said, starting up the stairs.

Halfway up the stairs, Judith paused, her eyes boring into Elizabeth's. "Alice Chatworth contracted smallpox and although she lived, the unscarred side of her face was badly pocked." Judith paused. "She took her own life by casting herself from the battlements of one of her estates." She looked away, then under her breath said, "The same wall old Ela fell from."

Elizabeth didn't understand the last statement but as she followed Judith up the stairs, she was glad Alice was dead. At least now she could be sure of her son's safety.

Elizabeth had heard talk of what a worker Judith Montgomery was but she soon decided Judith was a demon. She allowed no one any weakness—nor any rest.

They made the trip to the south of England in just two days, changing horses often. No one spoke but merely rode as hard and fast as possible. In many places the roads were so bad they were nonexistent, and they tore through newly plowed fields while farmers raised fists in anger. Twice Tam and Guy jumped from their horses, used battle axes to chop down fences. Behind them sheep grazed.

"The owner will take Judith to court," Elizabeth said, for the huge sheep pens were obviously owned by someone rich.

"This land belongs to Judith," Bronwyn called over her shoulder as she kicked her horse forward.

Alyx and Elizabeth exchanged looks of awe before they, too, set their horses at the usual spine-jarring pace.

When they reached the southern tip of England at dawn the third morning, a ferry waited to take them to the island where more of the Montgomerys lived.

"My clan is small compared to this family," Bronwyn said tiredly before she sat down in the wet bottom of the ferry, pulled her plaid over her head and fell asleep.

An hour later they were awakened and, as sleepwalkers, they mounted fresh horses and rode to the Montgomery estates. Even as tired as she was, Elizabeth felt the age and serenity of the fortress, the stones laid over two hundred years before by the knight known as the Black Lion.

Inside the gates, Judith touched Elizabeth's arm and nodded toward a child peeping out from a doorway. She was about a year and a half old, with dirty hair, torn clothes and the wary look of a hungry dog.

"One of Miles's children," Judith said, watching Elizabeth's face.

A surge of anger shot through Elizabeth. "She shall be mine when I return." With one last look, Elizabeth swept past the others and into the house.

They stayed at the old castle only long enough to eat, then were off on the ship that waited for them. All seven of them immediately curled up on deck and went to sleep.

Many hours later, when they were refreshed, the women began to discuss their plans.

"We will have to gain access to the castle," Judith said. "Alyx's music will open any door to us. Can either of you play or sing?"

Bronwyn swore she had a voice of lead; Judith admitted to being tone deaf. Elizabeth whispered, her throat dry, "I can dance."

"Good!" Judith declared. "Once we're inside—"

"You will do nothing," John Bassett said from behind her. "You will point out the new duke's estate to us and we will find your husbands and bring them to it. They will rescue Lord Miles." With that he turned on his heel and left them.

Judith gave her sisters-in-law a little smile. "Years ago I had a little trouble when I attempted to rescue Gavin. John has never forgiven me, and since he married my mother he feels responsible for me." She leaned forward. "We'll have to be more discreet in our planning."

Elizabeth leaned against the side of the ship and suppressed a laugh. There Judith sat, so very pretty, so tiny, her hands in her lap, looking for all the world like a demure, helpless young lady. It was hard to believe her fierce spirit. Bronwyn stood by the rail, the sun flashing off the water and highlighting her strong-featured beauty. Elizabeth knew Bronwyn for the passionate, brave, loyal woman she was. And Alyx, so quiet and shy, looking as if she were afraid of all of them, yet Elizabeth had seen glimpses of her spirit through Alyx's magnificent voice.

And Elizabeth? Did she fit with these women? She wondered if she could stand up under Judith's scrutiny.

＊　　＊　　＊

They purchased horses as soon as they stepped ashore in France and Judith led them southwest. For the last day Judith had been agreeing with everything the men told her. Once Bronwyn punched Elizabeth so that she looked up at John Bassett when he swelled out his chest as he lectured Judith. Tam also gave Bronwyn curt orders. Sir Guy spoke only once to Elizabeth.

Glancing up at him through her lashes, looking demure and angelic, she asked him how his toes were. The giant's scar whitened and he walked away. Bronwyn held her ribs as she nearly split her sides laughing. Judith, when told the story of Sir Guy's toes, gave Elizabeth a look of admiration and speculation.

Alyx merely tuned her lute and that act seemed to show whom she thought was going to win the power battle.

John Bassett rented rooms in an inn not far from the duke's estates, the one the locals said he was residing in at present. The three men had to leave the women alone as they went to search for the husbands. John looked as if he were going to cry when he met with stubborn silence as he begged Judith to swear to God that she would wait for the return of the men.

"Must I put a guard on you?" John asked, exasperated.

Judith merely looked at him.

"I've a good mind to take you with me, but we'll have to split up and it takes more than one mere man to control a hellion like you. There should be a special saint to guard husbands like Gavin."

"You're wasting time, John," Judith said patiently.

"She's right," Guy said, not looking at any of the women.

John caught Judith to him, kissed her forehead. "May the Lord protect you." With that, the three men left.

Judith leaned against the door and let out a deep sigh. "He means well. Now, shall we get to work?"

Elizabeth soon came to realize what a magnificent planner Judith was—and she knew how to use her gold. She hired a total of twenty-five people to spread word of the world's greatest singer and the universe's most exotic dancer. She planned for the excitement of expectation to be feverish by the time Alyx and Elizabeth appeared, for she wanted all eyes on them while she and Bronwyn slipped away.

In the early afternoon, Judith dressed in rags, blackened one front tooth with a nasty mixture of gum and soot and delivered fresh-baked bread to the duke's castle. She came back with wonderful news.

"Miles is alive," she said, scratching and discarding the filthy clothes. "The duke always seems to have prisoners and he always keeps them in the top of the tower. This tastes awful!" she said, scrubbing at her teeth. "It seems the whole Lorillard family are masters of torture and right now they're working on the girl.

"I'm sorry, Elizabeth," Judith added quickly. "From the gossip, I don't know if she's still alive or not, but the two men are."

"What about Miles's wound?" Elizabeth asked.

Judith put out her hands, palms up. "I couldn't ask directly and all I could find out was that the prisoners are always kept in the top of the tower."

"That should be easy," Bronwyn said. "We merely attach wings to our horses and fly to the top."

"There's a staircase," Judith said.

"Unguarded?" Bronwyn asked.

"The door to the rooms where the prisoners are kept is guarded but another stair branches up to the roof." Judith slipped a clean shift over her head. "There are windows in the rooms and if we could go down from the roof . . ."

Only Bronwyn was aware of the tight white lines forming at the corners of Judith's mouth. At times Judith seemed fearless, but she had an absolute terror of high places. Bronwyn touched Judith's arm. "You stay and dance to Alyx's music. Elizabeth and I will lower ourselves and . . ."

Judith put up her hand. "I could as likely dance as I could make the horses fly. Alyx would be singing, I'd never be able to keep the rhythm and I'd start looking at the tables and thinking of how many storage bins were needed for that much food. I'd probably forget to dance and start ordering the servants about."

All three women unsuccessfully tried to suppress giggles, both at Judith's accuracy and her forlorn expression.

Judith rolled her eyes at them. "I'm strong and I'm small and I can most easily go down a rope and slip inside a window."

No amount of talking could persuade Judith of any other course and soon they sat down to rest, each with her own thoughts of the dangers to come. Elizabeth never spoke of her fear of the men touching her and Judith's terror of high places wasn't mentioned again.

As dusk approached, Judith sank to her knees and began to pray and soon the other three women joined her.

Chapter 20

ALYX WAS the one who surprised the women the most. For the last few days she'd had the least to say, had followed her outspoken, beautiful sisters-in-law without a suggestion or complaint. But as soon as Alyx had a musical instrument in her hands and was told to perform, she far outstripped her sisters in flamboyance.

Judith and Bronwyn, dressed in filthy, concealing rags, blended into the procession that followed Alyx and Elizabeth. Elizabeth, strutting, already drawing attention to her well-endowed body, wore cheap cloth of garish, outlandish colors that would have attracted attention on their own.

As soon as Alyx entered the Great Hall of the old castle, she let out a note that made everyone pause. Bronwyn and Judith had never heard the full volume of Alyx's voice and they halted for a moment, listening with some awe.

"I'll give you a rhythm," Alyx whispered to Elizabeth. "Follow it with your body."

Every eye was on Alyx and the beautiful woman beside her. Abruptly Alyx let her voice drop and once again the audience began to breathe, and with a mixture of laughter and applause, they began to move about. "Now!" Judith hissed at Bronwyn and the two women disappeared into a darkened hole in the wall.

With their very heavy skirts flung over their arms, they tore up the old stone stairs, up two flights, three flights, and as they neared the top, a noise made them flatten themselves against the wall. Listening with every pore, they waited for the guard to pass the opening.

Judith pointed to a crack of blackness on the left, away from the vigilant guard. They slipped into the opening with a whisper of sound. Rats squealed in protest and Bronwyn kicked one of the nasty things back down the stairs.

At the top of the stairs was an overhead door—a locked door.

"Damn!" Judith whispered. "We need a key."

But before she even spoke, Bronwyn went to the narrow trapdoor and began to run her hands along the edges. As she reached the far edge, she turned and gave Judith a triumphant smile, her teeth and eyes showing white in the darkness. Bronwyn threw an iron bolt and the door swung up easily. One loud squeak made them stop but they heard no sound of footsteps on the stairs. They squeezed through the opening and were on the roof.

For a moment they paused and breathed deeply of the clean night air. As Bronwyn turned to Judith, she saw the little woman was looking at the battlements with fear in her eyes.

"Let *me* go," Bronwyn said.

"No." Judith shook her head. "If something happened and I had to pull you up, I couldn't do it. But you can lift me."

Bronwyn nodded as she saw the sense in Judith's words. With no more sound, they removed their outer, coarse woolen skirts and began uncoiling heavy rope from the underside. Judith had paid four women to spend the afternoon sewing these skirts. Now the moonlight shone on their skirts of plaid, blue and green for Bronwyn, golds and browns for Judith.

As soon as Bronwyn's rope lay in a coiled heap, she went around the roof of the round tower to peer down from the crenelated battlements. "There are four windows," she informed Judith. "Which one holds Miles?"

"Let me think," Judith said, rope on her forearm. "That window is over the stairs, the opposite one facing the stairs, so the cell must be one of those two." She pointed to her right and left.

Neither of them had to mention that if Judith appeared in the wrong window it could mean her death.

"Come on, let's go," Judith said as if she were on her way to her own execution.

Bronwyn had used ropes all her life and, easily, she knotted a sort of seat for Judith. The full tartan skirt was pulled between her legs and fastened into the wide leather belt. Her heart already racing, Judith stepped into the rope sling, part around her waist, some between her legs.

As she stood on the battlement, Bronwyn smiled at her. "Concentrate on your job and don't think about where you are."

Judith only nodded since fear had already closed her throat.

Bronwyn wrapped one end of the rope around a stone crenelation and used that to lower Judith slowly.

Judith repeated psalms to herself, swearing her trust in God, as she looked for toe holds. Three times pieces of wall crumbled away under her feet and each time her heart jumped to her throat as she paused, expecting any moment to have a guard above her cut the rope that held her life.

After long, slow moments, she reached the window and as her foot caught the stone sill, a hand grabbed her ankle.

"Quiet!" a voice commanded as Judith gave a sharp gasp of terror.

Strong hands caught her calves, then her hips, and pulled her inside the window. Judith, so very glad to once again be on firm ground, clutched the inside of the sill so hard she threatened to break her fingers.

"Aren't you the one that's terrified of high places?"

Judith turned to look into Roger Chatworth's calm face. His shirt hung in rags on his strong body. "Where's Miles?" she said in a half-gasp, half-croak.

A sound from outside the cell made Roger grab her protectively.

"Talkin' to yourself, Chatworth?" the guard called out but didn't bother to walk toward the cell.

"No one better," Roger called back, holding Judith's trembling body.

"Who is above?" Roger said into her ear.

"Bronwyn."

Judith's answer was rewarded by an under-breath curse from Roger. She wanted to pull away from him but at the moment any comfort felt good. Roger drew her, still attached to the rope, to a far corner of the little room. "Miles is in the opposite cell," he whispered. "He's been wounded and I'm not sure he has the strength to climb your rope. The guard will sleep soon and we'll get out. I'll go first and then pull you up. But you cannot stay in this room alone. You must sit on the sill and if the guard looks in, you must jump off. Do you understand? As soon as I reach the top I'll pull you up," he repeated.

Judith let his words sink in. This was her family's enemy, had been the cause of Mary Montgomery's death. Perhaps he meant to kill Bronwyn and cut the rope holding her. "No . . ." she began.

"You have to trust me, Montgomery! Bronwyn can't pull you up and you couldn't possibly climb the rope. Damn women! Why didn't you send some men?"

That did it. Her eyes blazed. "You ungrateful—"

He put his hand over her mouth. "Good girl! Whatever I don't like about the Montgomerys, I like their women. Now let's waste no more time." With that, he led, half pulled, Judith to the window, picked her up and set her on the sill. "Put your hands here"—he indicated the ledge of the sill—"and hold on. When I start to pull you up, use your hands and feet to keep from hitting the wall." He gave her a little shake since Judith was staring glassily at the ground far, far below her. "Think about your husband's anger when he finds out you rescued a Chatworth before his brother."

Judith almost smiled at that—almost. She did lift her head and visualized Gavin and imagined being in his safe arms. She swore she'd never again do anything so stupid as try to rescue

a man again. Unless of course Gavin needed her. Or his brothers. Or one of her sisters-in-law. Or perhaps, too, her mother.
And her children by all means. And—

The tug on the rope as Roger grabbed it above her head
nearly sent her flying. "Mind on your work, woman!" he
commanded.

She ducked his feet as he swung above her and, her senses
once again alert, she tilted her head back and watched him
climb the rope, hand over hand.

Bronwyn greeted Roger at the top with a knife aimed at
his throat and held him there, suspended over the wall, hands
supporting his body weight.

"What have you done with Judith?" Bronwyn growled.

"She waits below for me to pull her up and every minute
you delay comes closer to costing her her life."

At that moment, several things happened. One, Judith,
either in fear or necessity, swung away from the windowsill
and the momentum almost made Roger lose his grip.

"Guards!" came a shout from below.

"The door!" Roger said, fighting to stay on the wall.
"Lock the door!"

Bronwyn reacted at once, but by the time she reached the
door, a guard was already through it. She didn't hesitate as
she slipped her knife between his ribs. He fell atop the door
and Bronwyn had to push him aside to shove the bolt home.

She ran back to where Roger was pulling on Judith's rope,
and leaned between the crenelations to help. "What happened?" Bronwyn asked before Judith was even over the roof.

"Alyx and Elizabeth were tossed in the cell with Miles. I
stayed and listened as long as I could but when the guard
looked for Chatworth, he called out. What happened to
him?"

Bronwyn assisted Judith onto the roof. "There," she nodded toward the dead man not far away.

"Who heard him call?" Roger demanded.

"I'm not sure anyone did," Judith said. "Hurry! We must
get them out of this place."

"There isn't time. Where are your husbands?" Roger asked.

"Here in France but—" Judith began but stopped as Roger took the second rope from the roof floor and tied it to a battlement. "They're on the other side."

Roger ignored her. "There isn't time. The old man will be up here in minutes. We've got to get down and get some help."

"You coward," Bronwyn hissed. "*You* escape. Judith and I will rescue our family."

Roger grabbed her arm harshly. "Shut up, you idiot! Do you forget that Elizabeth is my sister? I haven't time to argue but if we're all caught there'll be no one to lead a rescue. Now, can you get down that rope yourself?"

"Yes but—" Bronwyn began.

"Then do it!" He half tossed her over the wall, all the while securely holding her hands. "Go, Bronwyn!" he ordered, then gave her a quick smile. "Show us some of your Scots blood."

As soon as Bronwyn disappeared over the side, Roger grabbed Judith by the armpits and lifted her. "Good! You weigh no more than my armor." He half squatted. "Hang onto my back with all your strength."

Judith only nodded and obeyed, buried her face in Roger's shoulder and closed her eyes. She didn't look when he lowered himself over the side. Sweat broke out on his neck and she was aware of how he was straining.

"Are you going to let an Englishman beat you?" Roger spat across the void to Bronwyn.

Judith opened one eye and looked with admiration at her sister-in-law. Bronwyn had the rope wrapped around one ankle, the opposite foot on top, her hands easing herself down. At Roger's words, she speeded up her travel.

Judith didn't even consider leaving Roger's safe, broad back merely because they stepped onto land. As if it were something he did every day, he peeled her hands then her legs away from his body.

Trembling, Judith watched as he ran to the bottom of

Bronwyn's rope. She was still several feet from the ground. "Jump, Scot!" he ordered up at her.

There was a slight hesitation but Bronwyn obeyed, let go of the rope and landed heavily into Roger Chatworth's waiting arms. "You must weigh the same as my horse," he murmured while setting her down. "Is it too much to hope that you women have horses nearby?"

"Come, enemy," Bronwyn said, motioning with her arm.

Roger grabbed Judith's arm since she was standing still, looking straight up with horror to where she'd been. "Run!" he said and gave her a sharp slap on her rump. "Let's get my sister and Chris out of this!"

Miles was standing in the middle of the room as if waiting for them, when the door was thrown open and Elizabeth and Alyx were pushed inside.

"To keep you company, Montgomery." The guard laughed. "Enjoy tonight because it'll probably be your last one alive."

Miles caught Elizabeth before she fell, then reached for Alyx.

Without a word, expertly, he sat down on the floor, arms about both women's shoulders, as Elizabeth began kissing his face enthusiastically.

"They were told you were dead," Elizabeth said between kisses. "Oh Miles, I didn't know if I'd ever see you again."

Miles, smiling slightly, his eyes alight, kissed each woman's forehead. "I can die peacefully now."

"How can you joke—?" Elizabeth began, but Miles kissed her lips and calmed her.

The three of them came alert as the single guard called out as he ran up the stairs toward the roof. A heavy thud followed the guard's disappearance.

In the silence, eyes looking upward, Miles said, "Bronwyn?"

Both women nodded.

Miles took a deep breath, sighed. "Tell me what you've done."

Alyx was quiet as Elizabeth told of their rescue plan, how Judith was going down the wall and into Miles's cell. Alyx was watching Miles, leaning against his strong shoulder, happy for his comfort, and she saw his eyes darken. Raine would wring my neck if I told him of such a plan, Alyx thought and hot tears came to her eyes.

"Alyx?" Miles said, interrupting Elizabeth's story. "We'll get out of here. Right now my brothers . . ."

She wiped her eyes with the back of her hand. "I know. I was just thinking that Raine will have my hide for doing this."

Miles's eyes twinkled. "Yes, he will."

"You're hurt!" Elizabeth suddenly announced, her hand running over a dirty bandage about his ribs. There wasn't much of his shirt left but what there was, Elizabeth had been exploring under.

She leaned away from him. Only moonlight came into the little room but even in that light, as she parted his shirt, she could see all the scars. Running her fingertips along one, she spoke, "You had no scars when I first met you and you've received all of them through me."

He kissed her palm. "I'll put a few scars on you—scars you get from bearing twenty of my children. Now I want both of you to rest because I imagine morning will bring . . . new events."

Elizabeth's main concern in life had been seeing Miles safe again and now that she leaned against him, knew he was strong and well, she was content. She closed her tired eyes and slept instantly.

Not so Alyx. She had not been traveling as long as Elizabeth and wasn't as tired. She closed her eyes and was still but her mind raced.

After an hour, when the cell was barely growing light, Miles gently moved the women off him and went to stand before the window. With half-shuttered eyes, Alyx watched him, saw his awkward movements.

"Come join me, Alyx," he whispered, surprising her that he knew she was awake.

Alyx stepped over a sleeping Elizabeth and as she drew near Miles, he pulled her to him, his front to her back. "You've risked much to save me, Alyx, and I thank you."

She smiled, put her cheek against his wrist. "I'm the one who got us caught. The duke had seen me play in England somewhere, remembered me and also remembered that he'd heard I'd become a Montgomery. What do you think Bronwyn said when she saw Roger on the roof instead of you?" She turned in his arms. "You do think they got away, don't you? No guards were waiting for them at the bottom of the ropes, were they? Raine will come?"

With a smile he turned her back toward the window. "I *know* they got through. Look there, far to the west."

"I see nothing."

"In the haze, see the little sparkles?"

"Yes," she said excitedly. "What are they?"

"I could be wrong but I believe they're men in armor. And there, more to the north."

"More sparkles! Oh Miles." She turned, hugged his ribs tightly then suddenly let him go. "You're hurt worse than you told Elizabeth," she said accusingly.

He tried to smile but there was pain in his eyes. "Will you tell her and give her more to worry about? She was brave dancing for all those strange men, wasn't she?" he said proudly.

"Yes," Alyx said, turning back around. Together they stood there as the day began to dawn, watching the little pinpoints of light as they grew nearer and nearer.

"Who are they?" Alyx asked. "I know there are Montgomerys in France but there must be hundreds of knights approaching. Who are the others?"

"I doubt if there are any others," he answered. "There are Montgomerys all over France, and in Spain and Italy. When I was a boy and first earned my spurs it bothered me that I could go nowhere that I didn't have an uncle or a few cousins breathing down my neck, but now I believe every one of my relatives to be beautiful."

"I have to agree with that."

"There!" he said, pointing straight ahead. "Did you see it?"

"No, I saw nothing."

He grinned happily. "It's what I've been waiting to see. There it is again!"

Briefly, for less than a second, Alyx saw a different flash.

"It's my Uncle Etienne's banner. We've always joked about the Montgomery banner he carries. It's nearly as big as a house, but Etienne says just the sight of those three gold leopards will send most people running—and he wants to give them time to leave."

"I saw it!" Alyx gasped. On the horizon had appeared three flashes of gold, one above the other. "The leopards," she breathed. "Who do you think—?" she began.

"Raine will be leading Uncle Etienne. Stephen is coming with the men from the north and Gavin will arrive from the south."

"How can you know that?"

"I know my brothers." He smiled. "Gavin will wait a few miles away for his brothers and all three armies will attack at once."

"Attack?" she said through her teeth.

"Don't worry." He ran his hand along her temple. "I don't believe even the Duke of Lorillard will try to stand against the combined forces of the Montgomerys. He'll be given a chance to surrender to us peacefully. And besides, his fight is about Christiana, not with the Montgomerys."

"Christiana. The girl Roger Chatworth rescued? What has happened to her?"

"I don't know but I'll find out," Miles said with such feeling that Alyx was silenced. She knew better than to try to argue with one of the Montgomery men about something he planned to do. Together they watched the approaching armies of knights and when Elizabeth awoke, Miles held her also.

Trying to cheer them, he made a bawdy jest about Elizabeth's garish clothes.

"If Judith and Bronwyn liberated Roger Chatworth and

the three of them went for help, which brother do you think they reached first?" Alyx asked.

Neither Miles nor Elizabeth had an answer for her.

"I pray it wasn't Raine," Alyx whispered. "I think Raine would strike first and listen second."

In silence, they watched their rescuers approach.

Chapter 21

RIDING NEXT to Raine and Etienne Montgomery was Roger Chatworth, his mouth set in a grim line, his right arm—his sword arm—bound tightly but still bleeding, and next to him was Bronwyn sporting what promised to be an extraordinary example of a black eye. Roger's arm was the result of Raine's first sighting of his enemy and Bronwyn's eye came about when she placed herself between Raine and Roger. Judith would have joined the fracas but John Bassett leaped from his horse, knocked her to the ground and pinned her there.

It took four men to hold Raine and keep him from tearing Chatworth apart but he did finally calm somewhat and allowed Judith and Bronwyn, who was nursing her swollen eye, to tell him what had happened. All the Montgomerys were remounted halfway through the story. When Judith told of Alyx being thrown in the cell with Miles, Raine once again leaped for Roger. Roger held him off with a sword held in his left hand while Raine's relatives calmed them both.

They were all quiet now as they approached the old Lorillard castle.

Gavin Montgomery sat in steely silence atop his horse, three hundred armed men behind him, and watched the approaching Montgomerys. Beside him sat Sir Guy, the giant's scarred face immobile. Guy didn't like to remember Gavin's explosion when he found out Judith had come to France with the men.

"She has no sense in these matters!" Gavin'd roared. "She thinks waging war is like cleaning a fish pond. Oh Lord," he prayed fervently, "if she is still alive when I find her, I will kill her. Let's ride!"

Stephen ordered his men to the eastern side of the castle while he and Tam rode toward where Gavin waited on the south.

"Women?" he bellowed long before he reached Gavin.

"None!" Gavin answered so loudly his horse lifted both forefeet off the ground.

In a cloud of dirt, Stephen and Tam turned west and headed for Raine. When Stephen saw Bronwyn, he nearly cried with relief, then frowned at her swollen eye. "What happened?" he shouted over the sound of the horses, not touching her but eating her with his eyes.

"Raine—" was all Bronwyn got out before Stephen let go with a bellow of laughter. He looked fondly at Raine's big form held rigidly in the saddle.

Bronwyn didn't bother to look at her husband again but moved to the far side of Tam.

"Stephen," Judith called. "Is Gavin with them?" She pointed south.

Stephen nodded once and Judith, John behind her, was off like a shot of lightning toward the southern group of Montgomerys.

There was no fighting.

The new Duke of Lorillard, obviously just roused from his bed, his eyes red, his skin gray green from a night of excess, had not lived to his great age of fifty-eight by trying to fight the nearly one thousand angry men who now surrounded his house. Showing his faith in the honor of the name Montgomery, he walked into the armed knights and told Gavin that if he were given his freedom, the Montgomerys could have whatever, or whomever, they wanted from his castle without the loss of a single life.

Raine didn't want to accept the man's terms because the

duke was surrendering not only his land but two of his sons as well. Raine believed that a man who'd do that should die.

Both Bronwyn and Judith pleaded for the easiest way to rescue the people from the tower.

In the end, it was Gavin, as the oldest, who made the decision. The duke and five of his guard were allowed to ride away after all the gates had been ordered opened.

Amid protests, the women were ordered to stay behind while the three brothers, Roger and a dozen cousins rode into the duke's crumbling fortress.

Either the occupants didn't know—or didn't care—that they were under attack, or perhaps, as Stephen suggested, it was a common occurrence. They did not rouse themselves from their drunken stupors. Men and women sprawled about the floors and across benches.

Cautiously, swords drawn, the men stepped between the bodies and searched for the stairs Bronwyn and Judith had told them of.

At the top of the stairs the three brothers put their shoulders to a locked door that opened to the room containing the cells.

"Here!" Roger said, grabbing a key from the wall and unlocking the heavy wooden door.

They were greeted by Miles, looking calm and pleased with himself, an arm around each woman.

Alyx ran, leaped into Raine's arms where he held her very close, his eyes moist as he buried his face in her neck. "Every time you get near your sisters-in-law," he began, "you do something like this. From now on—"

With a laugh, Alyx kissed him to silence.

Elizabeth left Miles's arms and went to Roger, caressed his cheek, touched his bloody arm. "Thank you," she whispered. She turned to Gavin, their eyes meeting, and she nodded curtly to him. She couldn't forget the insults he'd paid her.

Gavin, with a grin that softened his sharp features, opened his arms to her. "Could you and I start again, Elizabeth?" he asked quietly.

Elizabeth went to him, hugged him and when Bronwyn and Judith arrived, more hugs and kisses were exchanged.

Miles's words broke the spell of happy reunion. With eyes locked with Roger's, he said, "Shall we go?"

At Roger's curt nod, Miles took a sword from the hand of a young cousin.

"Now's not the time for a fight," Stephen began but quieted at Miles's look.

"Chatworth has helped me. Now I go with him."

"With him?" Raine exploded. "Have you forgotten that he killed Mary?"

Miles didn't answer but left the room behind Roger.

"Raine," Alyx said in her softest voice. "Miles is wounded and so is Roger and I'm sure they're going after this woman Roger wants."

"Christiana!" Elizabeth said, coming out of her stunned state. She'd had no idea where her brother and husband were going. "Judith, Bronwyn." She turned.

Without hesitation, all four women started for the door.

Without a word, in unison, the men caught their wives about their waists, Raine catching both Alyx and Elizabeth, and carried them to the cell where they promptly locked them inside. For just a moment the men blinked at both the variety and the virility of the curses coming from the women. Judith intoned from the Bible, Bronwyn in Gaelic, Elizabeth used a soldier's language. And Alyx! Alyx used her magnificent voice to shake the stones.

The men grinned triumphantly at each other, motioned to their young cousins to follow and left the room.

"I never thought I'd see the day I'd help a Chatworth," Raine muttered, but stopped when he heard the clash of steel.

Six guards, awake, alert, were guarding the room that held Christiana, and they attacked Roger and Miles on sight.

Miles's side wound opened instantly as he ran a sword through one guard, stepped over the fallen body and went for two more men. Roger's sword was knocked from his left hand, he tripped over the body of the man Miles'd killed, fell, grabbed the sword in his right hand, came up and killed the man looming over him. His arm wound tore open.

As another man came at Roger, he raised his wounded arm helplessly. But as the guard's sword neared Roger's belly, the guard fell forward, dead. Roger rolled away in time to see Raine pull his sword out of the dead man's back.

The three brothers welded together to protect Roger and Miles and quickly dispatched the remaining guards. They wiped their swords on the nearby bedhangings.

It was Raine who offered his hand to Roger and for a moment Chatworth only looked at it as he would an offer of friendliness from a deadly serpent. With eyes wide in speculation, Roger accepted the offer and allowed Raine to help him stand amidst the fallen bodies. Their eyes locked for just seconds before Roger went to the bed and pulled back the hangings.

In the center was Christiana, curled into a ball, wearing only a thin bit of wool, her body black and blue. Her eyes were swollen shut, her lips cracked.

Slowly, Roger knelt by the bed and touched her temple.

"Roger?" she whispered and tried to smile, which caused her lower lip to start bleeding.

With a look of fury on his face, Roger bent and lifted her. Raine's hand came to rest on his shoulder. "We'll take her south to our family."

Roger only nodded and carried Chris out of the room.

Gavin assisted Miles in standing.

"Where are the women?" Miles asked.

His brothers were oddly silent and seemed to grow a little fearful.

"We, ah . . ." Stephen began.

Gavin's head came up. "I think I'll ride ahead. Here." He tossed a key to Miles. "Maybe you better look after the women."

"Yes," Stephen and Raine added hastily, all three stumbling over each other to get out of the room.

Miles looked at the key in his hand, realizing it was the

key to the cell where he'd been locked. "You didn't!" he said but his brothers were gone.

For a moment he stood there and, at last, he began to laugh, laugh as he'd never laughed before. A few years ago he and his brothers had been living alone in their safe little world of mere battles and wars. Then, one by one, they'd married four beautiful, charming women—and really learned what war was.

Just now he and his brothers had taken a castle and killed several men and they'd taken no notice of the danger, but when faced with four furious women locked in a cell, they turned cowards and ran.

Miles started for the door. Thank God he'd not been involved in locking the women up! He pitied his brothers when at last they saw their wives again.

Like hell he did! He thought of every time they'd treated him as their "little brother." Now they were going to pay for every trick they'd ever played on him.

He tossed the key up, caught it and, grinning, started toward the cell full of beautiful women. He just might lock himself *inside* for a few days.

What Happened to Everybody

CHRISTIANA RECOVERED completely, married Roger Chatworth and ten years later, after they'd almost given up hope, they had a daughter, who, to Roger's chagrin, married one of the Montgomerys from the south of England. The Chatworth name died out except, now and then, a child would be named Chatworth Montgomery.

Miles and Elizabeth either created or adopted a total of twenty-three children and one of their sons, Philip, was a great favorite of Henry VIII. Later, two of Miles's grandsons went to the new country of America and remained there.

Raine was hired by Henry VIII to train his young knights and Alyx became lady-in-waiting to Queen Catherine. The court was a happy place and the king listened to and put into action some of the reforms Raine wanted. Raine and Alyx had three daughters, the middle one inheriting Alyx's musical talent. There's a legend that some of our great singers of today are descended from Alyxandria Montgomery.

Bronwyn and Stephen had six children, five boys and a girl. Bronwyn's name became a legend in her clan and even today Clan MacArran children sing her praises. Bronwyn's daughter married Kirsty MacGregor's son. He took the name of MacArran and eventually became laird.

Lachlan MacGregor married one of Tam's daughters, became so enraptured with her that he turned clan business over to his men. Davy MacArran fought for power, won and became a MacGregor. But Lachlan's daughter, Davy's wife, wasn't the docile little thing everyone believed and in the end it was she who was actually the MacGregor.

Judith and Gavin held onto the Montgomery estates. They prospered and left the estate in such good shape financially that today it's one of the largest, richest private homes in the world. One of Judith's descendants runs the whole place. She's a small, pretty young woman with odd-colored eyes, unmarried because she's never met a man who's accomplished in his life half what she's done in hers. Next week she has an appointment to meet a thirty-year-old American, self-made millionaire, who says he's a descendant of a knight named Miles Montgomery.

I have great hopes for them.

Jude Deveraux
Santa Fe, New Mexico
June, 1982